THE EDINBURGH EDITION OF
THE WAVERLEY NOVELS

EDITOR-IN-CHIEF
Professor David Hewitt

VOLUME SIX

THE HEART OF MID-LOTHIAN

EDINBURGH EDITION OF THE WAVERLEY NOVELS

to be complete in thirty volumes

Each volume will be published separately but original conjoint publication of certain works is indicated in the EEWN volume numbering [4a, b; 7a, b, etc.]. Where EEWN editors have been appointed, their names are listed

WALTER SCOTT

THE
HEART OF MID-LOTHIAN

Edited by
David Hewitt
and
Alison Lumsden

EDINBURGH
University
Press

© The University Court of the University of Edinburgh 2004
Edinburgh University Press
22 George Square, Edinburgh

Typeset in Linotronic Ehrhardt
by Speedspools, Edinburgh
and printed and bound in Great Britain
by TJ Books Limited, Padstow

ISBN 0 7486 0570 3

A CIP record for this book is available from the British Library

FOREWORD

THE PUBLICATION of *Waverley* in 1814 marked the emergence of the modern novel in the western world. It is difficult now to recapture the impact of this and the following novels of Scott on a readership accustomed to prose fiction either as picturesque romance, 'Gothic' quaintness, or presentation of contemporary manners. For Scott not only invented the historical novel, but gave it a dimension and a relevance that made it available for a great variety of new kinds of writing. Balzac in France, Manzoni in Italy, Gogol and Tolstoy in Russia, were among the many writers of fiction influenced by the man Stendhal called 'notre père, Walter Scott'.

What Scott did was to show history and society in motion: old ways of life being challenged by new; traditions being assailed by counter-statements; loyalties, habits, prejudices clashing with the needs of new social and economic developments. The attraction of tradition and its ability to arouse passionate defence, and simultaneously the challenge of progress and 'improvement', produce a pattern that Scott saw as the living fabric of history. And this history was rooted in *place*; events happened in localities still recognisable after the disappearance of the original actors and the establishment of new patterns of belief and behaviour.

Scott explored and presented all this by means of stories, entertainments, which were read and enjoyed as such. At the same time his passionate interest in history led him increasingly to see these stories as illustrations of historical truths, so that when he produced his final *Magnum Opus* edition of the novels he surrounded them with historical notes and illustrations, and in this almost suffocating guise they have been reprinted in edition after edition ever since. The time has now come to restore these novels to the form in which they were presented to their first readers, so that today's readers can once again capture their original power and freshness. At the same time, serious errors of transcription, omission, and interpretation, resulting from the haste of their transmission from manuscript to print can now be corrected.

DAVID DAICHES

EDINBURGH
University
Press

CONTENTS

ACKNOWLEDGEMENTS

The Scott Advisory Board and the editors of the Edinburgh Edition of the Waverley Novels wish to express their gratitude to The University Court of the University of Edinburgh *for its vision in initiating and supporting the preparation of the first critical edition of Walter Scott's fiction. Those Universities which employ the editors have also contributed greatly in paying the editors' salaries, and awarding research leave and grants for travel and materials. In the case of* The Heart of Mid-Lothian *particular thanks are due to the* University of Aberdeen.

Although the edition is the work of scholars employed by universities, the project could not have prospered without the help of the sponsors cited below. Their generosity has met the direct costs of the initial research and of the preparation of the text of the novels appearing in this edition.

BANK OF SCOTLAND
The collapse of the great Edinburgh publisher Archibald Constable in January 1826 entailed the ruin of Sir Walter Scott who found himself responsible for his own private debts, for the debts of the printing business of James Ballantyne and Co. in which he was co-partner, and for the bank advances to Archibald Constable which had been guaranteed by the printing business. Scott's largest creditors were Sir William Forbes and Co., bankers, and the Bank of Scotland. On the advice of Sir William Forbes himself, the creditors did not sequester his property, but agreed to the creation of a trust to which he committed his future literary earnings, and which ultimately repaid the debts of over £120,000 for which he was legally liable.

In the same year the Government proposed to curtail the rights of the Scottish banks to issue their own notes; Scott wrote the 'Letters of Malachi Malagrowther' in their defence, arguing that the measure was neither in the interests of the banks nor of Scotland. The 'Letters' were so successful that the Government was forced to withdraw its proposal and to this day the Scottish Banks issue their own notes.

A portrait of Sir Walter appears on all current bank notes of the Bank of Scotland because Scott was a champion of Scottish banking, and because he was an illustrious and honourable customer not just of the Bank of Scotland itself, but also of three other banks now incorporated within it—the British Linen Bank which continues today as the merchant banking arm of the Bank of Scotland, Sir William Forbes and Co., and Ramsays, Bonars and Company.

Bank of Scotland's *support of the EEWN continues its long and fruitful involvement with the affairs of Walter Scott.*

THE BRITISH ACADEMY AND THE ARTS AND HUMANITIES
RESEARCH BOARD
Between 1992 and 1998 the EEWN was greatly assisted by the British Academy through the award of a series of research grants which provided most of the support required for employing a research fellow, without whom steady progress could not have been maintained. In 2000 the AHRB awarded the EEWN with a major grant which ensured the completion of the Edition. To both of these bodies, the British Academy and the Arts and Humanities Research Board, the Advisory Board and the editors express their thanks.

OTHER BENEFACTORS
The Advisory Board and the editors also wish to acknowledge with gratitude the generous grants and gifts to the EEWN from the P. F. Charitable Trust, the main charitable trust of the Fleming family which founded the City firm which bears their name; the Edinburgh University General Council Trust, now incorporated within the Edinburgh University Development Trust; Sir Gerald Elliott; the Carnegie Trust for the Universities of Scotland, which awarded a personal research grant to David Hewitt; and the Robertson Trust whose help has been particularly important in the preparation of this volume.

THE MODERN HUMANITIES RESEARCH ASSOCIATION
In 1993 an MHRA grant led to the appointment of Dr Alison Lumsden as MHRA Research Associate, and during the period of the grant she conducted the basic textual investigation for this edition. The editors wish to thank the MHRA for its support, and acknowledge with gratitude its commitment to facilitating fundamental research.

THE HEART OF MID-LOTHIAN
The manuscript of The Heart of Mid-Lothian, *as well as most of the relevant publishing archives, are owned by the National Library of Scotland. We wish to acknowledge our immense indebtedness not only to the National Library as an institution, but also to the professional staff of the Library, particularly Dr Murray Simpson, Dr Iain Brown, and Sheila Mackenzie who have done so much to facilitate the editing of* The Heart of Mid-Lothian.

One leaf of The Heart of Mid-Lothian *is owned by the South African Library, and one gathering of the proofs of the novel (bound into a printed edition) is owned by Yale University Library. The Longman Archive is in Reading University Library. We extend our thanks to all three libraries.*

Many individuals have assisted the editors, and for practical help, advice, and much information we wish to thank Dr Barbara Bell, Dr Gerard Carruthers, Dr Richard Cox, Professor Angelo Forte, Michelle Gait and the staff of the Special Libraries in the University of Aberdeen, the late James Gilhooley, Elizabeth Johnstone, Professor William Johnstone, Professor

Douglas Mack, Pamela McNicol of Edinburgh City Archives, Professor Donald Meek, Dr Athol Murray, the late Professor Roger Robinson, Dr Henry Sefton, M. R. G. Spiller, Jill Starkey of the Newark Information Centre, Angus Stewart QC, *Rev. Dr A. S. Todd, the late Dr Archie Turnbull, and Dr Janet Williams.*

We owe much to immediate colleagues on the Edinburgh Edition of the Waverley Novels: Dr J. H. Alexander, Professor Peter Garside, and G. A. M. Wood. Thanks are also due to our consultants, Professor John Cairns, Professor Thomas Craik, and Roy Pinkerton. Those who have processed the text, checked the references, and read the proofs, are essential to the business of publishing a reliable scholarly edition, and we wish to acknowledge with immense gratitude the parts played by Rev. Dr Ian Clark, Dr Sheena Ford, Audrey Inglis, and Harry McIntosh. And finally we wish to say thank you to Professor Claire Lamont and to Tony Inglis whose editions of The Heart of Mid-Lothian *for World's Classics and Penguin Books respectively supported the editors of this edition, and established the standards which we had to aim to surpass.*

What has the Edinburgh Edition of the Waverley Novels achieved? The original version of this General Introduction said that many hundreds of readings were being recovered from the manuscripts, and commented that although the individual differences were often minor, they were 'cumulatively telling'. Such an assessment now looks tentative and tepid, for the textual strategy pursued by the editors has been justified by spectacular results.

In each novel up to 2000 readings never before printed are being recovered from the manuscripts. Some of these are major changes although they are not always verbally extensive. The restoration of the pen-portraits of the Edinburgh literati in *Guy Mannering*, the reconstruction of the way in which Amy Robsart was murdered in *Kenilworth*, the recovery of the description of Clara Mowbray's previous relationship with Tyrrel in *Saint Ronan's Well*—each of these fills out what was incomplete, or corrects what was obscure. A surprising amount of what was once thought loose or unidiomatic has turned out to be textual corruption. Many words which were changed as the holograph texts were converted into print have been recognised as dialectal, period or technical terms wholly appropriate to their literary context. The mistakes in foreign languages, in Latin, and in Gaelic found in the early printed texts are usually not in the manuscripts, and so clear is this manuscript evidence that one may safely conclude that Friar Tuck's Latin in *Ivanhoe* is deliberately full of errors. The restoration of Scott's own shaping and punctuating of speech has often enhanced the rhetorical effectiveness of dialogue. Furthermore, the detailed examination of the text and supporting documents such as notes and letters has revealed that however quickly his novels were penned they mostly evolved over long periods; that although he claimed not to plan his work yet the shape of his narratives seems to have been established before he committed his ideas to paper; and that each of the novels edited to date has a precise time-scheme which implies formidable control of his stories. The Historical and Explanatory Notes reveal an intellectual command of enormously diverse materials, and an equal imaginative capacity to synthesise them. Editing the texts has revolutionised the editors' understanding and appreciation of Scott, and will ultimately generate a much wider recognition of his quite extraordinary achievement.

The text of the novels in the Edinburgh Edition is normally based on the first editions, but incorporates all those manuscript readings which were lost through accident, error, or misunderstanding in the process of converting holograph manuscripts into printed books. The Edition is the first to investigate all Scott's manuscripts and proofs, and all the printed editions to have appeared in his lifetime, and it has adopted the textual strategy which best makes sense of the textual problems.

It is clear from the systematic investigation of all the different states of Scott's texts that the author was fully engaged only in the early stages (manuscripts and proofs, culminating in the first edition), and when preparing the last edition to be published in his lifetime, familiarly known as the Magnum Opus (1829–33). There may be authorial readings in some of the many intermediate editions, and there certainly are in the third edition of *Waverley*, but not a single intermediate edition of any of the nineteen novels so far investigated shows evidence of sustained authorial involvement. There are thus only two stages in the textual development of the Waverley Novels which might provide a sound basis for a critical edition.

Scott's holograph manuscripts constitute the only purely authorial state of the texts of his novels, for they alone proceed wholly from the author. They are for the most part remarkably coherent, although a close examination shows countless minor revisions made in the process of writing, and usually at least one layer of later revising. But the heaviest revising was usually done by Scott when correcting his proofs, and thus the manuscripts could not constitute the textual basis of a new edition; despite their coherence they are drafts. Furthermore, the holograph does not constitute a public form of the text: Scott's manuscript punctuation is light (in later novels there are only dashes, full-stops, and speech marks), and his spelling system though generally consistent is personal and idiosyncratic.

Scott's novels were, in theory, anonymous publications—no title page ever carried his name. To maintain the pretence of secrecy, the original manuscripts were copied so that his handwriting should not be seen in the printing house, a practice which prevailed until 1827, when Scott acknowledged his authorship. Until 1827 it was these copies, not Scott's original manuscripts, which were used by the printers. Not a single leaf of these copies is known to survive but the copyists probably began the tidying and regularising. As with Dickens and Thackeray in a later era, copy was sent to the printers in batches, as Scott wrote and as it was transcribed; the batches were set in type, proof-read, and ultimately printed, while later parts of the novel were still being written. When typesetting, the compositors did not just follow what was before them, but supplied punctuation, normalised spelling, and corrected minor errors. Proofs were first read in-house against the transcripts, and, in addition to the normal checking for mistakes, these proofs were used to improve the punctuation and the spelling.

When the initial corrections had been made, a new set of proofs went to James Ballantyne, Scott's friend and partner in the printing firm which bore his name. He acted as editor, not just as proof-reader. He drew Scott's attention to gaps in the text and pointed out inconsistencies in detail; he asked Scott to standardise names; he substituted nouns for pronouns when they occurred in the first sentence of a paragraph, and inserted the names of speakers in dialogue; he changed incorrect punctuation, and added punctuation he thought desirable; he corrected grammatical errors; he removed close verbal repetitions; and in a cryptic correspondence in the margins of the proofs he told Scott when he could not follow what was happening, or when he particularly enjoyed something.

These annotated proofs were sent to the author. Scott usually accepted Ballantyne's suggestions, but sometimes rejected them. He made many more changes; he cut out redundant words, and substituted the vivid for the pedestrian; he refined the punctuation; he sometimes reworked and revised passages extensively, and in so doing made the proofs a stage in the creative composition of the novels.

When Ballantyne received Scott's corrections and revisions, he transcribed all the changes on to a clean set of proofs so that the author's hand would not be seen by the compositors. Further revises were prepared. Some of these were seen and read by Scott, but he usually seems to have trusted Ballantyne to make sure that the earlier corrections and revisions had been executed. When doing this Ballantyne did not just read for typesetting errors, but continued the process of punctuating and tidying the text. A final proof allowed the corrections to be inspected and the imposition of the type to be checked prior to printing.

Scott expected his novels to be printed; he expected that the printers would correct minor errors, would remove words repeated in close proximity to each other, would normalise spelling, and would insert a printed-book style of punctuation, amplifying or replacing the marks he had provided in manuscript. There are no written instructions to the printers to this effect, but in the proofs he was sent he saw what Ballantyne and his staff had done and were doing, and by and large he accepted it. This assumption of authorial approval is better founded for Scott than for any other writer, for Scott was the dominant partner in the business which printed his work, and no doubt could have changed the practices of his printers had he so desired.

It is this history of the initial creation of Scott's novels that led the editors of the Edinburgh Edition to propose the first editions as base texts. That such a textual policy has been persuasively theorised by Jerome J. McGann in his *A Critique of Modern Textual Criticism* (1983) is a bonus: he argues that an authoritative work is usually found not in the artist's manuscript, but in the printed book, and that there is a collective responsibility in converting an author's manuscript into print, exercised by author, printer and publisher, and governed by the nature of the understanding between the author and the other parties. In Scott's case the exercise of such a collective responsibility produced the first editions of the Waverley Novels. On the whole Scott's printers fulfilled his expectations. There are normally in excess of 50,000 variants in the first edition of a three-volume novel when compared with the manuscript, and the great majority are in accordance with Scott's general wishes as described above.

But the intermediaries, as the copyist, compositors, proof-readers, and James Ballantyne are collectively described, made mistakes; from time to time they misread the manuscripts, and they did not always understand what Scott had written. This would not have mattered had there not also been procedural failures: the transcripts were not thoroughly checked against the original manuscripts; Scott himself does not seem to have read the proofs against the manuscripts and thus did not notice transcription errors which made sense in their context; Ballantyne continued his editing in post-authorial proofs. Furthermore, it has become increasingly evident that, although in theory Scott as partner in the printing firm could get what he wanted, he also succumbed to the pressure of printer and publisher. He often had to accept mistakes both in names and the spelling of names because they were enshrined in print before he realised what had happened. He was obliged to accept the movement of chapters between volumes, or the deletion or addition of material, in the interests of equalising the size of volumes. His work was subject to bowdlerisation, and to a persistent attempt to have him show a 'high example' even in the words put in the mouths of his characters; he regularly objected, but conformed nonetheless. From time to time he inserted, under protest, explanations of what was happening in the narrative because the literal-minded Ballantyne required them.

The editors of modern texts have a basic working assumption that what is written by the author is more valuable than what is generated by compositors and proof-readers. Even McGann accepts such a position, and argues that while the changes made in the course of translating the manuscript text into print are a feature of the acceptable 'socialisation' of the authorial text, they have authority only to the extent that they fulfil the author's expectations about the public form of the text. The editors of the Edinburgh Edition normally choose the first edition of a novel as base-text, for the first edition usually represents the culmination of the initial creative process, and usually seems closest to the form of his work Scott wished his public to have. But they also recognise the failings of the first editions, and thus after the careful collation of all pre-publication materials, and in the light of their investigation into the factors governing the writing and printing of the Waverley Novels, they incorporate into the base-text those manuscript readings which were lost in the production process through accident, error, misunderstanding, or a misguided attempt to 'improve'. In certain cases they also introduce into the base-texts revisions found in editions published almost immediately

after the first, which they believe to be Scott's, or which complete the
intermediaries' preparation of the text. In addition, the editors correct
various kinds of error, such as typographical and copy-editing mistakes
including the misnumbering of chapters, inconsistencies in the naming
of characters, egregious errors of fact that are not part of the fiction, and
failures of sense which a simple emendation can restore. In doing all this
the editors follow the model for editing the Waverley Novels which was
provided by Claire Lamont in her edition of *Waverley* (Oxford, 1981):
her base-text is the first edition emended in the light of the manuscript.
But they have also developed that model because working on the Waverley Novels as a whole has greatly increased knowledge of the practices
and procedures followed by Scott, his printers and his publishers in
translating holograph manuscripts into printed books. The result is an
'ideal' text, such as his first readers might have read had the production
process been less pressurised and more considered.

The Magnum Opus could have provided an alternative basis for a
new edition. In the Advertisement to the Magnum Scott wrote that his
insolvency in 1826 and the public admission of authorship in 1827
restored to him 'a sort of parental control', which enabled him to re-
issue his novels 'in a corrected and . . . an improved form'. His assertion
of authority in word and deed gives the Magnum a status which no
editor can ignore. His introductions are fascinating autobiographical
essays which write the life of the Author of Waverley. In addition, the
Magnum has a considerable significance in the history of culture. This
was the first time all Scott's works of fiction had been gathered together,
published in a single uniform edition, and given an official general title,
in the process converting diverse narratives into a literary monument,
the Waverley Novels.

There were, however, two objections to the use of the Magnum as the
base-text for the new edition. Firstly, this has been the form of Scott's
work which has been generally available for most of the nineteenth and
twentieth centuries; a Magnum-based text is readily accessible to anyone who wishes to read it. Secondly, a proper recognition of the Magnum does not extend to approving its text. When Scott corrected his
novels for the Magnum, he marked up printed books (specially prepared by the binder with interleaves, hence the title the 'Interleaved
Set'), but did not perceive the extent to which these had slipped from
the text of the first editions. He had no means of recognising that, for
example, over 2000 differences had accumulated between the first edition of *Guy Mannering* and the text which he corrected, in the 1822
octavo edition of the *Novels and Tales of the Author of Waverley*. The
printed text of *Redgauntlet* which he corrected, in the octavo *Tales and
Romances of the Author of Waverley* (1827), has about 900 divergences
from the first edition, none of which was authorially sanctioned. He
himself made about 750 corrections to the text of *Guy Mannering* and

200 to *Redgauntlet* in the Interleaved Set, but those who assisted in the production of the Magnum were probably responsible for a further 1600 changes to *Guy Mannering*, and 1200 to *Redgauntlet*. Scott marked up a corrupt text, and his assistants generated a systematically cleaned-up version of the Waverley Novels.

The Magnum constitutes the author's final version of his novels and thus has its own value, and as the version read by the great Victorians has its own significance and influence. To produce a new edition based on the Magnum would be an entirely legitimate project, but for the reasons given above the Edinburgh editors have chosen the other valid option. What is certain, however, is that any compromise edition, that drew upon both the first and the last editions published in Scott's lifetime, would be a mistake. In the past editors, following the example of W. W. Greg and Fredson Bowers, would have incorporated into the first-edition text the introductions, notes, revisions and corrections Scott wrote for the Magnum Opus. This would no longer be considered acceptable editorial practice, as it would confound versions of the text produced at different stages of the author's career. To fuse the two would be to confuse them. Instead, Scott's own material in the Inter-leaved Set is so interesting and important that it will be published separately, and in full, in the two parts of Volume 25 of the Edinburgh Edition. For the first time in print the new matter written by Scott for the Magnum Opus will be wholly visible.

The Edinburgh Edition of the Waverley Novels aims to provide the first reliable text of Scott's fiction. It aims to recover the lost Scott, the Scott which was misunderstood as the printers struggled to set and print novels at high speed in often difficult circumstances. It aims in the Historical and Explanatory Notes and in the Glossaries to illuminate the extraordinary range of materials that Scott weaves together in creating his stories. All engaged in fulfilling these aims have found their en-quiries fundamentally changing their appreciation of Scott. They hope that readers will continue to be equally excited and astonished, and to have their understanding of these remarkable novels transformed by reading them in their new guise.

DAVID HEWITT
January 1999

TALES OF MY LANDLORD,

Second Series,

COLLECTED AND REPORTED

BY

JEDIDIAH CLEISHBOTHAM,

PARISH-CLERK AND SCHOOLMASTER OF GANDERCLEUGH.

Hear, Land o' Cakes and brither Scots,
Frae Maidenkirk to Jonny Groats',
If there's a hole in a' your coats,
　　　I rede ye tent it,
A chiel's amang you takin' notes,
　　　An' faith he'll prent it.
　　　BURNS.

IN FOUR VOLUMES.

VOL. I.

EDINBURGH:

PRINTED FOR ARCHIBALD CONSTABLE AND COMPANY.

1818.

Ahora bien, dixo el Cura, traedme, senor huésped, aquesos libros, que los quiero ver.
Que me place, respondió el, y entrando, en su aposento, sacó dél una maletilla vieja
cerrada con una cadenilla, y abriéndola, halló en ella tres libros grandes y unos papeles de
muy buena letra escritos de mano.—DON QUIXOTE, Parte I. Capitulo 32.

It is mighty well, said the priest; pray, landlord, bring me those books, for I
have a mind to see them. With all my heart, answered the host; and, going to his
chamber, he brought out a little old cloke-bag, with a padlock and chain to it,
and opening it, he took out three large volumes, and some manuscript papers
written in a fine character.—JARVIS'S *Translation.*

TO THE BEST OF PATRONS,

A PLEASED AND INDULGENT READER,

JEDIDIAH CLEISHBOTHAM

WISHES HEALTH, AND INCREASE, AND CONTENTMENT.

COURTEOUS READER,

IF INGRATITUDE comprehendeth every other vice, surely so foul a stain worst of all beseemeth him whose life has been devoted to instructing youth in virtue and in humane letters. Therefore have I chosen, in this prolegomen, to unload my burden of thanks at thy feet, for the favour with which thou hast kindly entertained the Tales of my Landlord. Certes, if thou hast chuckled over their facetious and festivous descriptions, or hast had thy mind fulfilled with pleasure at the strange and pleasing turns of fortune which they record, verily, I have also simpered when I beheld a second story with atticks, that has arisen on the basis of my small domicile at Gandercleugh, the walls having been aforehand pronounced by Deacon Barrow to be capable of enduring such an elevation. Nor has it been without delectation, that I have endued a new coat, (snuff-brown, and with metal buttons), having all nether garments corresponding thereto. We do therefore lie, in respect of each other, under a reciprocation of benefits, whereof those received by me being the most solid, (in respect that a new house and a new coat are better than a new tale and an old song,) it is meet that my gratitude should be expressed with the louder voice and more preponderating vehemence. And how should it be so expressed?—Certainly not in words only, but in act and deed. It is with this sole purpose, and disclaiming all intention of purchasing that pendicle or pofle of land called the Carlinescroft, lying adjacent to my garden, and measuring seven acres, three roods, and four perches, that I have committed to the eyes of those who thought well of the former tomes, these four additional volumes of the Tales of my Landlord. Not the less, if Peter Prayfort be minded to sell the said pofle, it is at his own choice to say so; and, peradventure, he may meet with a purchaser: unless (gentle reader) the

3

*pleasing pourtraictures of Peter Pattieson, now given unto thee in particular,
and unto the public in general, shall have lost their savour in thine eyes,
whereof I am no way distrustful. And so much confidence do I repose in thy
continued favour, that should thy lawful occasions call thee to the town of
Gandercleugh, a place frequented by most at one time or other in their lives,
I will enrich thine eyes with a sight of those precious manuscripts whence thou
hast derived so much delectation, thy nose with a snuff from my mull, and
thy palate with a dram from my bottle of strong waters, called by the learned
of Gandercleugh, the Dominie's dribble of drink.*

    *It is there, O highly esteemed and beloved reader, thou wilt be able to bear
testimony, through the medium of thine own senses, against the children of
vanity, who have sought to identify thy friend and servant with I know not
what inditer of vain fables; who hath cumbered the world with his devices,
but shrunken from the responsibility thereof. Truly, this hath been well
termed a generation hard of faith; since what can man do to assert his
property in a printed tome, saving to put his name in the title-page thereof,
with his description, or designation as the lawyers term it, and place of
abode? Truly, I would have such sceptics remember how they themselves
would brook to have their works ascribed to others, their names and professions imputed as forgeries, and their very existence brought into question;
even although, peradventure, it may be it is of little consequence to any but
themselves, not only whether they are living or dead, but even whether they
ever lived or no. Yet have my maligners carried their uncharitable censures
yet farther.*

    *These cavillers have not only doubted mine identity, although thus plainly
proved, but they have impeached my veracity and the authenticity of my
historical narratives! Truly, I can only say in answer, that I have been
cautelous in quoting mine authorities. It is true, indeed, that if I had
hearkened with only one ear, I might have rehearsed my tale with more
acceptation from those who love to hear but half the truth. It is, it may hap,
not altogether to the discredit of our kindly nation of Scotland, that we are
apt to take an interest, warm, yea partial, in the deeds and sentiments of our
fore-fathers. He whom his adversaries describe as a perjured prelatist, is
desirous that his predecessors should be held moderate in their power, and just
in their execution of its privileges, when, truly, the unimpassioned peruser of
the Annals of these times shall deem them sanguinary, violent, and tyrannical. Again, the representatives of the suffering non-conformists desire
that their ancestors, the Cameronians, shall be represented not simply as
honest enthusiasts, oppressed for conscience-sake, but as persons of fine
breeding and valiant heroes. Truly, the historian cannot gratify these predilections. He must needs describe the cavaliers as proud and high-spirited,
cruel, remorseless, and vindictive; the suffering party as honourably tenacious of their opinions under persecution; their own tempers being, how-*

ever, sullen, fierce, and rude; their opinions absurd and extravagant, and their whole course of conduct that of persons whom hellebore would better have suited than prosecutions unto death for high-treason. Natheless, while such and so preposterous were the opinions on either side, there were, it cannot be doubted, men of virtue and worth on both, to entitle either party to claim merit from its martyrs. It has been demanded of me, Jedidiah Cleishbotham, by what right I am entitled to constitute myself an impartial judge of these discrepancies of opinion, seeing (as it is stated) that I must necessarily have descended from one or other of the contending parties, and be, of course, wedded for better or for worse, according to the reasonable practice of Scotland, to its dogmata or opinions, and bound, as it were, by the tie matrimonial, or, to speak without metaphor, ex jure sanguinis, to maintain them in preference to all others.

But, nothing denying the rationality of the rule, which calls on all now living to rule their political and religious opinions by those of their great-grandfathers, and inevitable as seems the one or the other horn of the dilemma betwixt which my adversaries conceive they have pinned me to the wall, I yet spy some means of refuge, and claim a title to write and speak of both parties with impartiality. For, O ye powers of logic! when the prelatists and presbyterians of old times went together by the ears in this unlucky country, my ancestor (venerated be his memory!) was one of the people called Quakers, and suffered severe handling from either side, even to the extenuation of his purse and the incarceration of his person.

Craving thy pardon, gentle Reader, for these few words concerning me and mine, I rest, as above expressed, thy sure and obligated friend,

J. C.

GANDERCLEUGH,
this 1st of April, 1818.

THE
HEART OF MID-LOTHIAN

Chapter One

Being Introductory

So, down thy hill, romantic Ashbourn, glides
The Derby dilly, carrying three insides.
                                    FRERE

THE TIMES have changed in nothing more (we follow as we are wont
the manuscript of Peter Pattieson,) than in the rapid conveyance of
intelligence and communication betwixt one part of Scotland and
another. It is not above twenty or thirty years, according to the evidence of many credible witnesses now alive, since a little miserable
horse-cart, performing with difficulty a journey of thirty miles *per
diem*, carried our mails from the capital of Scotland to its extremity.
Nor was Scotland much more deficient in these accommodations,
than our richer sister had been about eighty years before. Fielding, in
his Tom Jones, and Farquhar, in a little farce called the Stage-Coach,
have ridiculed the slowness of these vehicles of public accommodation. According to the latter authority, the highest bribe could only
induce the coachman to promise to anticipate by half an hour the
usual time of his arrival at the Bull and Mouth.

But in both countries these ancient, slow, and sure modes of conveyance are now alike unknown; mail-coach races against mail-coach,
and high-flyer against high-flyer, through the most remote districts
of Britain. And in our village alone, three post-coaches, and four
coaches with men armed, and in scarlet cassocks, thunder through the
streets each day, and rival in brilliancy and noise the invention of the
celebrated tyrant,

> *Demens, qui nimbos et non imitabile fulmen,*
> *Ære et cornipedum pulsu, simularat, equorum.*

Now and then, to complete the resemblance, and to correct the presumption of the venturous charioteers, it does certainly happen that the career of these dashing rivals of Salmoneus meets with as undesirable and violent a termination as that of their prototype. It is upon such occasions that the Insides and Outsides, to use the appropriate vehicular phrases, have reason to rue the exchange of the slow and safe motion of the ancient Fly-coaches, which, compared with the chariots of Mr Palmer, so ill deserve the name. The ancient vehicle used to settle quietly down, like a ship scuttled and left to sink by the gradual influx of the waters, while the modern is smashed to pieces with the velocity of the same vessel hurled against breakers, or rather with the fury of a bomb bursting at the conclusion of its career through the air. The late ingenious Mr Pennant, whose humour it was to set his face in stern opposition to these speedy conveyances, had collected, I have heard, a formidable list of such casualties, which, joined to the imposition of innkeepers, whose charges the passenger has no time to dispute; the sauciness of the coachman, and the uncontrouled and despotic authority of the tyrant called the Guard, held forth a picture of horror, to which murder, theft, fraud, and peculation lent all their dark colouring. But that which gratifies the impatience of the human disposition will be practised in the teeth of danger, and in defiance of admonition. And, in despite of the Cambrian Antiquary, Mail-coaches not only roll their thunders round the base of Penmen-Maur and Cader-Edris, but

> Frighted Skiddaw hears afar
> The rattling of the unscythed car

and perhaps the echoes of Ben-Nevis may soon be awakened by the bugle, not of a warlike chieftain, but of the guard of a mail-coach.

It was a fine summer day, and our little school had obtained a half holiday by the intercession of a good-humoured visitor.* I expected by the coach a new number of an interesting periodical publication, and walked forward on the highway to meet it, with the impatience which Cowper has described as actuating the resident in the country when longing for intelligence from the mart of news:

> ———————The grand debate,
> The popular harangue,—the tart reply,—
> The logic, and the wisdom, and the wit,
> And the loud laugh,—I long to know them all;—
> I burn to set the imprisoned wranglers free,
> And give them voice and utterance again.

It was with such feelings that I eyed the approach of the new coach, lately established on our road, and known by the name of the Somer-

---

* His Honour Gilbert Goslinn of Gandercleugh; for I love to be precise in matters of importance.—J. C.

set, which, to say truth, possesses some interest for me, even when it conveys no such important information. The distant tremulous sound of its wheels was heard just as I gained the summit of the gentle ascent, called Goslin-brae, from which you command an extensive view down the valley of the river Gander. The public road, which comes up the side of that stream, and crosses it at a bridge about a quarter of a mile from the place where I was standing, runs partly through enclosures and plantations, and partly through open pasture land. It is a childish amusement perhaps,—but my life has been spent with children, and why should not my pleasures be like theirs?—childish as it is then, I must own I have had great pleasure in watching the approach of the carriage, where the openings of the road permit it to be seen. The gay glancing of the equipage, its diminished and toy-like appearance at a distance, contrasted with the rapidity of its motion, its appearance and disappearance at intervals, and the progressively increasing sounds that announce its nearer approach, have all to the idle and listless spectator, who has nothing more important to attend to, something of awakening interest. The ridicule may attach to me, which is flung upon many an honest citizen, who watches from the window of his villa the passage of the stage-coach; but it is a very natural source of amusement notwithstanding, and many of those who join in the laugh are perhaps not unused to practise it in secret.

On the present occasion, however, fate had decreed that I should not enjoy the consummation of the amusement, by seeing the coach rattle past me as I sat on the turf, and hearing the hoarse grating voice of the guard as he skimmed forth for my grasp the expected packet, without the carriage checking its course for an instant. I had seen the vehicle thunder down the hill that leads to the bridge with more than its usual impetuosity, glittering all the while by flashes from a cloudy tabernacle of the dust which it had raised, and leaving a train behind it on the road resembling a wreath of summer mist. But it did not appear on the top of the nearer bank within the usual space of three minutes, which frequent observation had enabled me to ascertain was the medium time for crossing the bridge and mounting the ascent. When double that space had elapsed, I became alarmed, and walked hastily forward. As I came in sight of the bridge, the cause of delay was too manifest, for the Somerset had made a summerset in good earnest, and over-turned so completely, that it was literally resting upon the ground, with the roof undermost, and the four wheels in the air. The "exertions of the guard and coachman," both of whom were gratefully commemorated in the newspapers, having succeeded in disentangling the horses by cutting the harness, were now proceeding to extricate the *insides* by a sort of summary and Cæsarean process of delivery, forcing the hinges from one of the doors which they could not open otherwise. In this manner were two disconsolate damsels set at liberty from the womb of the leathern conveniency. As they immediately began to settle their clothes, which were a little deranged, as may be presumed, I concluded they had received no injury, and did not venture to obtrude my services at their toilette, for which, I understand, I have since been reflected upon by the fair sufferers. The *outsides*, who must have been discharged from their elevated situation by a shock resembling the springing of a mine, escaped, nevertheless, with the usual allowance of scratches and bruises, excepting three, who, having been pitched into the river Gander, were dimly seen contending with the tide, like the reliques of Æneas's shipwreck,—

Rari apparent nantes in gurgite vasto.

I applied my poor exertions where they seemed to be most needed, and, with the assistance of one or two of the company who had escaped unhurt, easily succeeded in fishing out two of the unfortunate passengers, who were stout active young fellows; and but for the preposterous length of their great-coats, and the equally fashionable latitude and longitude of their Wellington trowsers, would have required little assistance from any one. The third was sickly and elderly, and might have perished but for the efforts used to preserve him.

When the two great-coated gentlemen had extricated themselves from the river, and shaken their ears like huge water-dogs, a violent altercation ensued between them and the coachman and guard, concerning the cause of their overthrow. In the course of the squabble, I discovered that both my new acquaintances belonged to the law, and that their professional sharpness was like to prove an overmatch for the surly and official tone of the guardians of the vehicle. The dispute ended in the guard assuring the passengers that they should have seats in a heavy coach which should pass that spot in less than half an hour, providing it was not full. Chance seemed to favour this arrangement, for when the expected vehicle arrived there were only two places occupied in a carriage which professed to transport six. The two ladies who had been disinterred out of the fallen vehicle were readily admitted, yet positive objections were stated by those previously in possession to the admittance of the two lawyers, whose wetted garments being much of the nature of well-soaked spunges, there was every reason to believe they would refund a considerable part of the water they had collected, to the inconvenience of their fellow-passengers. On the other hand, the lawyers rejected a seat on the roof, alleging that they had only taken that station for pleasure for one stage, but

were entitled in all respects to free egress and regress from the interior, to which their contract positively referred. After some altercation,
in which something was said upon the edict *Nautæ caupones stabularii*,
the coach went off, leaving the learned gentlemen to abide by their
action of damages.

They immediately applied to me to guide them to the next village
and the best inn; and from the account I gave them of the Wallace-
head, declared they were much better pleased to stop there than to go
forward upon the terms of that impudent scoundrel the guard of the
Somerset. All they now wanted was a lad to carry their travelling bags,
who was easily procured from an adjoining cottage; and they prepared
to walk forward, when they found there was another passenger in the
same deserted situation with themselves. This was the elderly and
sickly-looking person, who had been precipitated into the river along
with the two young lawyers. He, it seems, had been too modest to push
his own plea against the coachman when he saw that of his betters
rejected, and now remained behind with a look of dejected anxiety,
plainly intimating that he was deficient in those means of recommendation which are necessary passports to the hospitality of an inn.

I ventured to call the attention of the two dashing young blades, for
such they seemed, to the desolate condition of their fellow-traveller.
They took the hint with ready good-nature.

"O true, Mr Dunover," said one of the youngsters, "you must not
remain on the pavé here; you must go and have some dinner with us—
Halkit and I must have a post-chaise to go on, at all events, and we will
set you down wherever suits you best."

The poor man, for such his dress, as well as his diffidence, bespoke
him, made the sort of acknowledging bow by which a Scotsman says,
"It is too much honour for the like of me;" and followed humbly a few
paces behind his gay patrons, all three besprinkling the dusty road as
they walked along with the moisture of their drenched garments, and
exhibiting the singular and somewhat ridiculous appearance of three
persons suffering from the opposite extreme of humidity, while the
summer sun was at its height, and every thing else around them had
the expression of heat and drought. The ridicule did not escape
the young gentlemen themselves, and they had made what might be
received as one or two tolerable jests on the subject before they had
advanced far on their peregrination.

"We cannot complain, like Cowley," said one of them, "that Gideon's fleece remains dry, while all around is moist; this is the reverse
of the miracle."

"We ought to be received with gratitude in this good town; we bring
a supply of what they seem to need most," said Halkit.

"And distribute it with unparalleled generosity," replied his companion; "performing the part of three water-carts for the benefit of their dusty roads."

"We come before them too," said Halkit, "in full professional force —counsel and agent"—

"And client," said the young advocate, looking behind him, and then added, lowering his voice, "that looks as if he had kept such dangerous company too long."

It was, indeed, too true, that the humble follower of the gay young men had the thread-bare appearance of a worn-out litigant, and I could not but smile at the conceit, though anxious to conceal my mirth from the object of it.

When we arrived at the Wallace Inn, the elder of the Edinburgh gentlemen, and whom I understand to be a barrister, insisted that I should remain and take part of their dinner; and their enquiries and demands speedily put my landlord and his whole family in motion to produce the best cheer which the larder and cellar afforded, and proceed to cook it to the best advantage, a science in which our entertainers seemed to be admirably skilled. In other respects, they were lively young men in the hey-day of youth and good spirits, playing the part which is common to the higher classes of the law at Edinburgh, and which nearly resembles that of the young templars in the days of Steele and Addison. An air of giddy gaiety mingled with the good sense, taste, and information which their conversation exhibited; and it seemed to be their object to unite the character of men of fashion and lovers of the polite arts. A fine gentleman, bred up in the thorough idleness and inanity of pursuit, which I understand is absolutely necessary to the formation of the character in perfection, would in all probability have traced a tinge of professional pedantry which marked the barrister in spite of his efforts, and something of active bustle in his companion, and would certainly have detected more than a fashionable mixture of information and animated interest in the language of both. But to me, who had no pretensions to be so critical, my companions seemed to form a very happy mixture of good breeding and liberal information, with a disposition to lively rattle, pun, and jest, amusing to a grave man, because it is what he himself can least easily command.

The thin pale-faced man, whom their good nature had brought into their society, looked out of place, as well as out of spirits, sate on the edge of his seat, and kept the chair at two feet distance from the table, thus incommoding himself considerably in conveying the victuals to his mouth, as if by way of penance for partaking of them in the company of his superiors. A short time after dinner, declining all entreaty to partake of the wine, which circulated freely round, he informed himself of the hour when the chaise had been ordered to attend; and, saying he would be in readiness, modestly withdrew from the apartment.

"Jack," said the barrister to his companion, "I remember that poor fellow's face; you spoke more truly than you were aware of; he really is one of my clients, poor man."

"Poor man!" echoed Halkit—"I suppose you mean he is your one and only client."

"That's not my fault, Jack," replied the other, whose name I discovered was Hardie. "You are to give me all your business, you know; and if you have none, the learned gentleman here knows nothing can come of nothing."

"You seem to have brought something to nothing though, in the case of that honest man. He looks as if he were just about to honour with his residence the HEART OF MID-LOTHIAN."

"You are mistaken—it is quite the reverse—he is just delivered from it—our friend here looks for an explanation. Pray, Mr Pattieson, have you been in Edinburgh?"

I answered in the affirmative.

"Then you must have passed, occasionally at least, though probably not so faithfully as I am doomed to do, through a narrow intricate passage, leading out of the north-west corner of the Parliament-square, and passing by a high and antique building, with turrets and iron grates,

> Making good the saying odd,
> Near the church and far from God"—

Mr Halkit broke in upon his learned counsel, to contribute his moiety to the riddle—"Having at the door the sign of the Red Man"——

"And being on the whole," resumed the counsellor, interrupting his friend in his turn, "a sort of place where misfortune is happily confounded with guilt, where all who are in wish to get out"——

"And where none who have the good luck to be out wish to get in," added his companion.

"I conceive you, gentlemen," replied I; "you mean the prison."

"The prison," added the young lawyer—"you have hit it—the very reverend tolbooth itself; and let me tell you, you are obliged to us for describing it with so much modesty and brevity; for with whatever amplifications we might have chosen to decorate the subject, you lay entirely at our mercy, since the Fathers Conscript of our city have decreed, that the venerable edifice itself shall not remain in existence to confirm or to confute us."

"Then the tolbooth of Edinburgh is called the Heart of Mid-Lothian," said I.

"So termed and reputed, I assure you."

"I think," said I, with the bashful diffidence with which a man lets slip a pun in presence of his superiors, "the metropolitan county may, in that case, be said to have a sad heart."

"Right as my glove, Mr Pattieson," added Mr Hardie; "and a close heart, and a hard heart—Keep it up, Jack."

"And a wicked heart, and a poor heart," answered Halkit, keeping up the ball.

"And yet it may be called in some sort a strong heart, and a high heart," rejoined the advocate. "You see I can put you both out of heart."

"I have played all my hearts," said the writer.

"Then we'll have another lead," answered his companion.—"And as to the old and condemned tolbooth, what pity the same honour cannot be done to it as has been done to many of its inmates. Why should not the Tolbooth have its 'Last Speech, Confession, and Dying Words?' The old stones would be just as conscious of the honour, as many a poor devil who has dangled like a tassel at the west end of it, while the hawkers were shouting a confession the culprit had never heard of."

"I am afraid," said I, "if I might presume to give my opinion, it would be a tale of unvaried sorrow and guilt."

"Not entirely, my friend," said Hardie; "a prison is a world within itself, and has its own business, griefs, and joys peculiar to its circle. Its inmates are sometimes short-lived, but so are soldiers on service; they are poor relatively to the world without, but there are degrees of wealth and poverty among them, and so some are relatively rich also. They cannot stir abroad, but neither can the garrison of a besieged fort, or the crew of a ship at sea; and they are not under a dispensation quite so despotic as either, for they may have as much food as they have money to buy, and are not obliged to work whether they have food or not."

"But what variety of incident," said I, (not without a secret view to my present task), "could possibly be derived from such a work as you are pleased to talk of?"

"Infinite," replied the young advocate. "Whatever of guilt, crime, imposture, folly, unheard-of misfortune, and unlooked-for change of fortune, can be found to chequer life, my Last Speech of the Tolbooth should illustrate with examples sufficient to gorge even the public's all-devouring appetite for the wonderful and horrible. The inventor of fictitious narratives has to rack his brains for means to diversify his

tale, and after all can hardly hit upon characters or incidents which
have not been used again and again, until they are familiar to
the eye of the reader, so that the elopement, the *enlèvement*, the
desperate wound of which the hero never dies, the burning fever from
which the heroine is sure to recover, become a mere matter of course.
I join with my honest friend Crabbe, and have such an unlucky propensity to hope when hope is lost, and to rely upon the cork-jacket,
which carries the heroes of romance safe through all the billows of
affliction." He then declaimed the following passage, rather with too
much than too little emphasis:

> "Much have I fear'd, but am no more afraid,
> When some chaste beauty, by some wretch betray'd,
> Is drawn away with such distracted speed,
> That she anticipates a dreadful deed.
> Not so do I—Let solid walls impound
> The captive fair, and dig a moat around;
> Let there be brazen locks and bars of steel,
> And keepers cruel, such as never feel;
> With not a single note the purse supply,
> And when she begs, let men and maids deny;
> Be windows there from which she dares not fall,
> And help so distant, 'tis in vain to call;
> Still means of freedom will some Power devise,
> And from the baffled ruffian snatch his prize.

"The end of uncertainty," he concluded, "is the death of interest,
and hence it happens that no one now reads novels."

"Hear him, ye gods!" returned his companion. "I assure you, Mr
Pattieson, you will hardly visit this learned gentleman, but you are
likely to find the new novel most in repute lying on his table, snugly
intrenched, however, beneath Stair's Institutes, or an open volume of
Morrison's Decisions."

"Do I deny it?" said the hopeful jurisconsult, "or wherefore
should I, since it is well known these Dalilahs seduce my wisers and
my betters? May they not be found lurking amidst the multiplied
memorials of our most distinguished counsel, and even peeping from
under the cushion of a judge's arm-chair? Our seniors at the bar,
within the bar, and even on the bench, read novels, and, if not belied,
some of them have written novels into the bargain. I only say, that I
read from habit and from indolence, not from real interest; that, like
Ancient Pistol devouring his leek, I read and swear till I get to the end
of the narrative. But not so in the real records of human vagaries—not
so in the State-trials, or in the Books of Adjournal, where every now
and then you read new pages of the human heart, and turns of fortune
far beyond what the boldest novelist ever attempted to produce from
the coinage of his brain!"

"And for such narratives," I asked, "you suppose the History of the Prison of Edinburgh might afford appropriate materials?"

"In a degree unusually ample, my dear sir," said Hardie—"fill your glass, however, in the meanwhile. Was it not for many years the place in which the Scottish parliament met—was it not Jamie's place of refuge, when the mob, inflamed by a seditious preacher, broke forth on him with the cries of 'The sword of the Lord and of Gideon—bring forth the wicked Haman?' Since that time how many hearts have throbbed within these walls, as the tolling of the neighbouring bell announced to them how fast the sands of their life were ebbing. How many must have sunk at the sound—how many were supported by stubborn pride and dogged resolution—how many by the consolations of religion? Have there not been some, who, looking back on the motives of their crimes, were scarce able to understand how they should have had such temptation as to seduce them from virtue? and have there not, perhaps, been others, who, sensible of their innocence, were divided between indignation at the undeserved doom which they were to undergo, consciousness that they had not deserved it, and racking anxiety to discover some way in which they might yet vindicate themselves? Do you suppose any of these deep, powerful, and agitating feelings can be recorded and perused without exciting a corresponding depth of deep, powerful, and agitating interest?—O! do but wait till I publish the *Causes Célèbres* of Caledonia, and you will find no want of a novel or a tragedy for some time to come. The true thing will triumph over the brightest inventions of the most ardent imagination. *Magna est veritas et prævalebit.*"

"I have understood," said I, encouraged by the affability of my rattling entertainer, "that less of this interest must attach to Scottish jurisprudence than to that of any other country. The general morality of our people, their sober and prudent habits"—

"Secure them," said the barrister, "against any great increase of professional thieves and depredators, but not against wild and wayward starts of fancy and passion, producing crimes of an extraordinary description, which are precisely those to the detail of which we listen with thrilling interest. England has been much longer a highly civilized country; her subjects have been very long strictly amenable to laws administered without fear or favour; a complete division of labour has taken place among her subjects, and the very thieves and robbers form a distinct class in society, subdivided among themselves according to the subject of their depredations, and the mode in which they carry them on, acting upon regular habits and principles, which can be calculated and anticipated at Bow-Street, Hatton-Garden, or the Old-Bailey. Our sister kingdom is like a cultivated field,—the farmer expects that, in spite of all his care, a certain number of weeds will rise with the corn, and can tell you before hand their names and appearance. But Scotland is like one of her own Highland glens, and the moralist who reads the records of her criminal jurisprudence, will find as many curious and anomalous facts in the history of mind, as the botanist will detect rare specimens among her dingles and cliffs."

"And that's all the good you have obtained from three perusals of the Commentaries on Scottish Criminal Jurisprudence?" said his companion. "I suppose the learned author very little thinks that the facts which his erudition and acuteness have accumulated for the illustration of legal doctrines, might be so arranged as to form a sort of chapel of ease to the half-bound and slip-shod volumes of the circulating library."

"I'll bet you a pint of claret," said the elder lawyer, "that he will not feel sore at the comparison. But as we say at the bar, 'I beg I may not be interrupted;' I have much more to say upon my Scottish collection of *Causes Célèbres*. You will please recollect the scope and motive given for the contrivance and execution of many extraordinary and daring crimes, by the long continued civil dissentions of Scotland—by the hereditary jurisdictions, which, until 1748, vested the investigation of crimes in judges, ignorant, partial, or interested—by the habits of the gentry, shut up in their distant and solitary mansion-houses, nursing their revengeful passions just to keep their blood from stagnating—not to mention that amiable national qualification, called the *perfervidum ingenium Scotorum*, which our lawyers join in alledging as a reason for the severity of some of our enactments. When I come to treat of matters so mysterious, deep, and dangerous, as these circumstances have given rise to, the blood of each reader shall be curdled, and his epidermis crisped into goose skin.—But 'st—here comes the landlord, with tidings, I suppose, that the chaise is ready."

It was no such thing—it was tidings that no chaise could be had this evening, for Sir Peter Plyem had carried forward my landlord's two pair of horses that morning to the ancient royal borough of Bubbleburgh, to look after his interest there. But as Bubbleburgh is only one of a set of five boroughs which club their shares for a member of parliament, Sir Peter's adversary had judiciously watched his departure, in order to commence a canvass in the no less royal borough of Bitem, which, as all the world knows, lies at the very termination of Sir Peter's avenue, and has been held in leading strings by him and his ancestors for time immemorial. Now Sir Peter was thus placed in the situation of an ambitious monarch, who, after having commenced a daring inroad into his enemies' territories, is suddenly recalled by an invasion of his own hereditary dominions. He was obliged in consequence to return from the half-won borough of Bubbleburgh, to look after the half-lost borough of Bitem, and the two pair of horses which had carried him that morning to Bubbleburgh, were now forcibly detained to transport him, his agent, his valet, his jester, and his hard-drinker, across the country to Bitem. The cause of this detention, which to me was of as little consequence as it may be to the reader, was important enough to my companions to reconcile them with the delay. Like eagles, they smelled the battle afar off, ordered a magnum of claret and beds at the Wallace, and entered at full career into the Bubbleburgh and Bitem politics, with all the probable "petitions and complaints" to which they were likely to give rise.

In the midst of an anxious, animated, and, to me, most unintelligible discussion concerning provosts, baillies, deacons, sets of boroughs, leets, town-clerks, burgesses resident and non-resident, all of a sudden the lawyer recollected himself. "Poor Dunover, we must not forget him;" and the landlord was dispatched in quest of the *pauvre honteux*, with an earnestly civil invitation to him for the rest of the evening. I could not help asking the young gentlemen if they knew the history of this poor man, and the counsellor applied himself to his pocket to recover the memorial or brief from which he had stated his cause.

"He has been a candidate for our *remedium miserabile*," said Mr Hardie, "commonly called a cessio bonorum. As there are divines who have doubted the eternity of future punishments, so the Scottish lawyers seem to have thought that the crime of poverty might be atoned for by something short of perpetual imprisonment. After a month's confinement, you must know, he is entitled, on a sufficient statement to our supreme court, setting forth the amount of his funds, and the nature of his misfortunes, and surrendering all his effects to his creditors, to claim to be discharged from prison."

"I had heard," I replied, "of such a humane regulation."

"Yes," said Halkit, "and the beauty of it is, as the foreign fellow said, you may get the *cessio* when the *bonorums* are all spent—But what, are you puzzling in your pockets to seek out your only memorial among old play bills, letters requesting a meeting of the Faculty, rules of the Speculative Society, syllabus of lectures—all the miscellaneous contents of a young lawyer's pocket, which contains every thing but brieves and bank-notes? Can you not state a case of cessio without your memorial? Why it is done every Saturday. The events follow each other as regularly as clock-work, and one form of condescendence might suit every one of them."

"This is very unlike the variety of distress which this gentleman stated to fall under the consideration of your judges," said I.

"True," replied Halkit; "but Hardie spoke of criminal jurisprudence, and this business is purely civil. I could plead a cessio myself without the inspiring honours of a gown and three-tailed periwig—Listen.—My client was bred a journeyman weaver—made some little money—took a farm—(for conducting a farm, like driving a gig, comes by nature)—late severe times—induced to sign bills with a friend, for which he had no value—landlord sequestrates—creditors accept a composition—pursuer sets up a public-house—fails a second time—is incarcerated for a debt of ten pounds, seven and sixpence—his debts amount to blank—his losses to blank—his funds to blank—leaving a balance of blank in his favour. There is no opposition; your lordships will please grant commission to take his oath."

Hardie now renounced this ineffectual search, in which there was perhaps a little affectation, and told us the tale of poor Dunover's distresses, with a tone in which a degree of feeling, which he seemed ashamed of as unprofessional, mingled with his attempts at wit, and did him more honour. It was one of those tales which seem to argue a sort of ill luck or fatality attached to the hero. A well informed, industrious, and blameless, but poor and bashful man, had in vain essayed all the usual means by which others acquire independence, yet had never succeeded beyond the attainment of bare subsistence. During a brief gleam of hope, rather than of actual prosperity, he had added a wife and family to his cares, but the dawn was speedily overcast. Every thing retrograded with him towards the mouth of the miry Slough of Despond, which yawns for insolvent debtors; and after catching at each twig, and experiencing the protracted agony of feeling them one by one elude his grasp, he actually sunk into the miry pit whence he had been extricated by the professional exertions of Hardie.

"And, I suppose, now you have dragged this poor devil ashore, you will leave him half naked on the beach to provide for himself?" said Halkit. "Hark ye,"—and he whispered something in his ear, of which the penetrating and insinuating word, "Interest," alone reached mine.

"It is *pessimi exempli*," said Hardie, laughing, "to provide for a ruined client; but I was thinking of what you mention, providing it can be managed—But hush! here he comes."

The recent relation of the poor man's misfortunes had given him, I was pleased to observe, a claim to the attention and respect of the young men, who treated him with great civility, and gradually engaged him in conversation, which, much to my satisfaction, again turned upon the *Causes Célèbres* of Scotland. Emboldened by the kindness with which he was treated, Mr Dunover began to contribute his share to the amusement of the evening. Jails, like other places, have their ancient traditions, known only to the inhabitants, and handed down from one set of the melancholy lodgers to the next who occupy their cells. Some of these, which Dunover mentioned, were interesting, and served to illustrate the narratives of remarkable trials, which Hardie had at his fingers-ends, and which his companion was also well skilled in. This sort of conversation passed away the evening till the early hour when Mr Dunover chose to retire to rest, and I also retreated to take down memorandums of what I had learned, in order to add another narrative to those which it had been my chief amusement to collect, and to write out in detail. The two young men ordered a broiled bone, Madeira negus, and a pack of cards, and commenced a game at picquet.

Next morning the travellers left Gandercleugh. I afterwards learned from the papers that both have been since engaged in the great political cause of Bubbleburgh and Bitem, a summary case, and entitled to particular dispatch; but which, it is thought, nevertheless, may outlast the duration of the parliament to which the contest refers. Mr Halkit, as the newspapers informed me, acts as agent or solicitor; and Mr Hardie opened for Sir Peter Plyem with singular ability, and to such purpose, that I understand he has since had fewer play-bills and more briefs in his pocket. And both the young gentlemen deserve their good fortune; for I learned from Dunover, who called on me some weeks afterwards, and communicated the intelligence with tears in his eyes, that their interest had availed to obtain him a small office for the decent maintenance of his family; and that, after a train of constant and uninterrupted misfortune, he could trace a dawn of prosperity to his having the good fortune to be flung from the top of a mail-coach into the river Gander, in company with an advocate and a writer to the signet. The reader will not perhaps deem himself equally obliged to the accident, since it brings upon him the following narrative, founded upon the conversation of the evening.

Chapter Two

Whoe'er's been at Paris must needs know the Grève,
The fatal retreat of the unfortunate brave,
Where honour and justice most oddly contribute,
To ease heroes' pains by an halter and gibbet.

There death breaks the shackles which force had put on,
And the hangman completes what the judge but began;
There the squire of the pad, and the knight of the post,
Find their pains no more baulked, and their hopes no more cross'd.

PRIOR

IN FORMER TIMES, England had her Tyburn, to which the devoted victims of justice were conducted in solemn procession, up what is now called Oxford-Road. In Edinburgh, a large open street, or rather oblong square, surrounded by high houses, called the Grassmarket, was used for the same melancholy purpose. It was not ill chosen for such a scene, being of considerable extent, and therefore fit to accommodate a great number of spectators, such as are usually assembled by this melancholy spectacle. On the other hand, few of the houses which surround it were, even in early times, inhabited by persons of fashion; so that those likely to be offended or over deeply affected by such unpleasant exhibitions, were not in the way of having their quiet disturbed by them. The houses in the Grassmarket are, generally speaking, of a mean description; yet the place is not without some features of grandeur, being overhung by the southern side of the huge rock on which the castle stands, and by the moss-grown battlements and turretted walls of that ancient fortress.

It was the custom, until within these five-and-twenty years, or thereabouts, to use this esplanade for the scene of public executions. The fatal day was announced to the public, by the appearance of a huge black gallows-tree towards the eastern end of the Grassmarket. This ill-omened apparition was of great height, with a scaffold surrounding it, and a double ladder placed against it, for the ascent of the unhappy criminal and the executioner. As this apparatus was always arranged before dawn, it seemed as if the gallows had grown out of the earth in the course of one night, like the production of some foul demon; and I well remember the fright with which the school-boys, when I was one of their number, used to regard these ominous signs of deadly preparation. On the night after the execution the gallows again disappeared, and was conveyed in silence and darkness to the place where it was usually deposited, which was one of the vaults under the Parliament-house, or courts of justice. This mode of execution is now exchanged for one similar to that in front of Newgate,—with what beneficial effect is uncertain. The mental sufferings of the pannel are indeed shortened. He no longer walks between the attendant clergy-men, dressed in his graves-clothes, through a considerable part of the city, looking in gait, dress, and features like a moving and walking corpse, while yet an inhabitant of this world. But, as the ultimate purpose of punishment has in view the prevention of crimes, it may at least be doubted, whether, in abridging the melancholy ceremonial, we have not in part diminished that appalling effect upon the spec-tators which is the useful end of all such inflictions, and in considera-tion of which alone, unless in very particular cases, capital sentences can be altogether justified.

Upon the 8th day of September, 1736, these ominous preparations for execution were descried in the place we have described, and at an early hour the space around began to be occupied by several groupes, who gazed on the scaffold and gibbet with a stern and vindictive shew of satisfaction very seldom testified by the populace, whose good-nature, in most cases, forgets the crimes of the condemned person, and dwells only on his misery. But the act of which the expected culprit had been convicted was of a description calculated nearly and closely to awaken and irritate the resentful feelings of the multitude. The tale is well known; yet it is necessary to recapitulate its leading circumstances, for the better understanding what is to follow; and the narrative may prove long, but I trust not uninteresting, even to those who have heard its general issue. At any rate, some detail is necessary, in order to render intelligible the subsequent events of our narrative.

Contraband trade, though it strikes at the root of legitimate govern-ment, by encroaching on its revenues,—though it injures the fair trader, and debauches the minds of those engaged with it,—is not usually looked upon, either by the vulgar or by their betters, in a very heinous point of view. On the contrary, in those counties where it prevails, the cleverest, boldest, and most intelligent of the peasantry, are uniformly engaged in illicit transactions, and very often with the sanction of the farmers and the inferior gentry. Smuggling was almost universal in Scotland in the reigns of George I. and II.; for the people, unaccustomed to imposts, and regarding them as an unjust aggression upon their ancient liberties, made no scruple to elude them wherever it was possible to do so.

The county of Fife, bounded by two firths on the south and north, and by the sea on the east, and having a number of small sea-ports, was long famed for maintaining successfully a contraband trade; and, as there were many seafaring men residing there, who had been pirates and buccaneers in their youth, there were not wanting a sufficient number of daring men to carry it on. Among these, a fellow, called Andrew Wilson, originally a baker in the village of Pathhead, was particularly obnoxious to the revenue officers. He was possessed of great personal strength, courage, and cunning, perfectly acquainted with the coast, and capable of conducting the most desperate enterprizes. On several occasions he succeeded in baffling the pursuit and researches of the king's officers. But he became so much the object of their suspicious and watchful attention, that at length he was totally ruined by repeated seizures. The man became desperate. He considered himself as robbed and plundered; and took it into his head, that he had a right to make reprisals, as he could find opportunity. Where the heart is prepared for evil, opportunity seldom is long wanting. This Wilson learned, that the Collector of the customs at Kirkaldy had come to Pittenweem, in the course of his official round of duty, with a considerable sum of public money in his custody. As the amount was greatly within the value of the goods which had been seized from him, he felt no scruples of conscience in resolving to reimburse himself for his losses, at the expence of the Collector and the revenue. He associated with himself one Robertson, and other two idle young men, whom, having been concerned in the same illicit trade, he persuaded to view the transaction in the same justifiable light in which he himself considered it. They watched the motions of the Collector; they broke forcibly into the house where he lodged,— Wilson, with two of his associates, entering the Collector's apartment, while Robertson, the fourth, kept watch at the door with a drawn cutlass in his hand. The officer of the customs, conceiving his life in danger, escaped out of his bed-room window, and fled in his shirt, so that the plunderers, with much ease, possessed themselves of about two hundred pounds of public money. This robbery was committed in a very audacious manner, for several persons were passing in the street at the time. But Robertson, representing the noise they heard as a dispute or fray betwixt the Collector and the people of the house, the worthy citizens of Pittenweem felt themselves no way called on to interfere in behalf of the obnoxious revenue officer; so, satisfying themselves with this very superficial account of the matter, like the Levite in the parable, they passed on the opposite side of the way. An alarm was at length given, military were called in, the depredators were pursued, the booty recovered, and Wilson and Robertson tried and condemned to death, chiefly on the evidence of an accomplice.

Many thought, that in consideration of the men's erroneous opinions of the nature of the action they had committed, justice might have been satisfied with a less forfeiture than that of two lives. On the other hand, from the audacity of the fact, a severe example was judged necessary, and such was the opinion of the government. When it became apparent that the sentence of death was to be executed, files and other implements necessary for their escape, were transmitted secretly to the culprits by a friend from without. By these means they sawed a bar out of one of the prison-windows, and might have made their escape, but for the obstinacy of Wilson, who, as he was daringly resolute, was doggedly pertinacious of his opinion. His comrade, Robertson, a young and slender man, proposed to make the experiment of passing the foremost through the gap they had made, and enlarging it from the outside, if necessary, to allow Wilson free passage. Wilson, however, insisted on making the first experiment, and being a robust and lusty man, he not only found it impossible to get through betwixt the bars, but, by his struggles, he jammed himself so fast, that he was unable to draw his body back again. In these circumstances discovery became unavoidable, and sufficient precautions were taken by the gaoler to prevent any repetition of the same attempt. Robertson uttered not a word of reflection on his companion for the consequences of his obstinacy; but it appeared from the sequel, that Wilson's mind was deeply impressed with the recollection, that, but for him, his comrade, over whose mind he exercised considerable influence, would not have engaged in the criminal enterprise which had terminated thus fatally; and that now he had become his destroyer a second time, since, but for his obstinacy, Robertson might have effected his escape. Minds like Wilson's, even when exercised in evil practices, sometimes retain the power of thinking and resolving with enthusiastic generosity. His whole mind was now bent on the possibility of saving Robertson's life, without the least respect to his own. The resolution which he adopted, and the manner in which he carried it into effect, were striking and unusual.

Adjacent to the tolbooth or city gaol of Edinburgh, is one of the three churches into which the Cathedral of Saint Giles is now divided, called, from its vicinity, the Tolbooth Church. It was the custom, that criminals under sentence of death were brought to this church, with a sufficient guard, to hear and join in public worship on the Sabbath before execution. It was supposed that the hearts of these unfortunate persons, however hardened before against feelings of devotion, could not but be accessible to them upon uniting their thoughts and voices, for the last time, along with their fellow-mortals, in addressing their Creator. And to the rest of the congregation, it was thought it could not but be impressive and affecting, to find their devotions mingling with those, who, sent by the doom of an earthly tribunal to appear where the whole earth is judged, might be considered as beings trembling on the verge of eternity. The practice, however edifying, has been discontinued since the incident we are about to detail.

The clergyman, whose duty it was to officiate in the Tolbooth Church, had concluded an affecting discourse, part of which was particularly directed to the unfortunate men, Wilson and Robertson, who were in the pew set apart for the persons in their unhappy situation, each secured betwixt two soldiers of the City Guard. The clergyman had reminded them, that the next congregation they must join would be that of the just, or of the unjust: that the psalms they now heard must be exchanged, in the space of two brief days, for eternal hallelujahs, or eternal lamentations; and that this fearful alternative must depend upon the state to which they might be able to bring their minds before the moment of awful preparation: that they were not to despair on account of the suddenness of the summons, but rather to feel this comfort in their misery, that, though all who now lifted the voice, or bent the knee in conjunction with them, lay under the same sentence of certain death, they only had the advantage of knowing the precise moment at which it should be executed upon them. "Wherefore," urged the good man, his voice trembling with emotion, "redeem the time, my unhappy brethren, which is yet left, and remember, that, with the grace of Him to whom time and space are but as nothing, the work of salvation may yet be assured, even in the pittance of delay which the laws of your country afford you."

Robertson was observed to weep at these words; but Wilson seemed as one whose brain had not entirely received their meaning, or whose thoughts were deeply impressed with some different subject; —an expression so natural to a person in his situation, that it excited neither suspicion nor surprise.

The benediction was pronounced as usual, and the congregation were dismissed, many lingering to indulge their curiosity with a more fixed look at the two criminals, who now, as well as their guards, rose up, as if to depart when the crowd should permit them. A murmur of compassion was heard to pervade the spectators, the more general, perhaps, on account of the alleviating circumstances of the case. When all at once, Wilson, who, we have noticed, was a very strong man, seized two of the soldiers, one with each hand, and calling at the same time to his companion, "Run, Geordie, run!" threw himself on a third, and fastened his teeth on the collar of his coat. Robertson stood for a second as if thunderstruck, and unable to avail himself of the opportunity of escape. But the cry of "Run, run," being echoed from many around, whose feelings surprised them into a very natural interest in his behalf, he shook off the grasp of the remaining soldier, threw himself over the pew, mixed with the dispersing congregation, none of whom felt inclined to stop a poor wretch taking this last chance for his life, gained the door of the church, and was lost to all pursuit.

The generous intrepidity which Wilson had displayed on this occasion augmented the feeling of compassion which attended his fate. The public, who, where their own prejudices are not concerned, are easily engaged on the side of disinterestedness and humanity, admired Wilson's behaviour, and rejoiced in Robertson's escape. This general feeling was so great, that it excited a vague report that Wilson would be rescued at the place of execution, either by the mob or by some of his old associates, or by some second extraordinary and unexpected exertion of strength and courage on his own part. The magistrates thought it their duty to provide against the possibility of disturbance. They ordered out, for protection of the execution of the sentence, the greater part of their own City Guard, under the command of Captain Porteous, a man whose name became too memorable from the melancholy circumstances of the day and subsequent events. It may be necessary to say a word about this person, and the corps which he commanded. But the subject is of importance sufficient to deserve another chapter.

Chapter Three

And thou, great god of aqua-vitæ!
Wha sways the empire of this city,
(When fou we're sometimes capernoity,)
            Be thou prepared,
To save us frae that black banditti,
            The City Guard!
        FERGUSSON's *Daft Days*

CAPTAIN JOHN PORTEOUS, a name memorable in the traditions of Edinburgh, as well as in the records of criminal jurisprudence, was the son of a citizen of Edinburgh, who endeavoured to breed him up to his own mechanical trade. The youth, however, had a wild and irreclaimable propensity to dissipation, which finally sent him to serve in the corps long maintained in the service of the States of Holland, and called the Scotch-Dutch. Here he learned military discipline; and, returning afterwards, in the course of an idle and wandering life, to his native city, his services were required by the magistrates of Edinburgh in the disturbed year 1715, for disciplining their City Guard, in which he shortly after received a captain's commission. It was only by his military skill, and an alert and resolute character, that he merited this promotion, for he is said to have been a man of profligate habits, an unnatural son, and a brutal husband. He was, however, useful in his station, and his harsh and fierce habits rendered him formidable to rioters or disturbers of the public peace.

The corps in which he held his command is, or perhaps we should rather say *was*, a body of about one hundred and twenty soldiers, divided into three companies, and regularly armed, clothed, and embodied. It was chiefly veterans who enlisted in this corps, having the benefit of working at their trades when they were off duty. These men had the charge of preserving public order, repressing riots and street robberies, and attending on all public occasions where confusion or popular disturbance might be expected. Poor Fergusson, whose irregularities sometimes led him into unpleasant rencontres with these military conservators of public order, and who mentions them so often that he may be termed their poet laureate, thus admonishes his readers, warned doubtless by his own experience:

> Gude folk, as ye come frae the fair,
> Bide yont frae this black squad;
> There's nae sic savages elsewhere
> Allowed to wear cockad.

In fact, the soldiers of the City Guard, being, as we have said, in general discharged veterans, who had strength enough remaining for this municipal duty, and being, moreover, in general Highlanders, were neither by birth or education and former habits, trained to endure with much patience the insults of the rabble, truants, schoolboys, and idle debauchees of all descriptions, with whom their occupation brought them into contact. On the contrary, the temper of the poor old fellows was soured by the indignities with which the mob distinguished them on many occasions, and frequently might have required the soothing strains of the poet we have just quoted—

> O soldiers! for your ain dear sakes,
> For Scotland's love, the Land o' Cakes,
> Gie not her bairns sic deadly paiks,
> > Nor be sae rude,
> Wi' firelock or Lochaber axe,
> > As spill their bluid.

On all occasions when holiday licenses some riot and irregularity, a skirmish with these veterans was a favourite recreation with the rabble of Edinburgh. These pages may perhaps see the light when many have in fresh recollection such onsets as we allude to. But the venerable corps, with whom the contention was held, may now be considered as totally extinct. Of late the gradual diminution of these civic soldiers reminds one of the abatement of King Lear's hundred knights. The edicts of each succeeding set of magistrates, like those of Goneril and Regan, have diminished this venerable band with the similar question, "What need we five-and-twenty?—ten?—or five?" And it is now nearly come to, "What need one?" A spectre may indeed here and there still be seen of an old grey-headed and grey-bearded High-lander, with war-worn features, but bent double by age; dressed in an old-fashioned cocked-hat, bound with white tape instead of silver lace; and in coat, waistcoat, and breeches of a muddy-coloured red, bearing in his withered hand an ancient weapon, called a Lochaber-axe, a long pole namely, with an axe at the extremity and a hook at the back of the axe. Such a phantom of former days still creeps, I have been informed, round the statue of Charles the Second, in the Parlia-ment-Square, as if the image of a Stuart were the last refuge for any memorial of our ancient manners; and one or two others are supposed to glide around the door of the guard-house assigned to them in the Luckenbooths, when their ancient refuge in the High-street was laid low. But the fate of manuscripts bequeathed to friends and executors is so uncertain, that these frail memorials of the old Town-Guard of Edinburgh, who, with their grim and valiant corporal, John Dhu, (the fiercest looking fellow I ever saw,) were, in my boyhood, the alternate terror and derision of the petulant brood of the High School, may perhaps only come to light when all memory of the institution has faded away, and then serve as an illustration of Kay's caricatures, who has preserved the features of some of their heroes. In the preceding generation, when there was a perpetual alarm for the plots and activity of the Jacobites, some pains was taken by the magistrates of Edin-burgh to keep this corps, though composed always of such materials as we have noticed, in a more effective state than was afterwards judged necessary, when their most dangerous service was to skirmish with the rabble on the king's birth-day. They were, therefore, more the object of hatred, and less that of scorn, than they afterwards were accounted.

To Captain John Porteous, the honour of his command and of his corps seems to have been a matter of high interest and importance. He was exceedingly incensed against Wilson for the affront which he construed him to have put upon his soldiers, in the effort he made for the liberation of his companion, and expressed himself most violently on the subject. He was no less indignant at the report, that there was an intention to rescue Wilson himself from the gallows, and uttered many threats and imprecations upon that subject, which were after-wards remembered to his disadvantage. In fact, if a good deal of determination and promptitude rendered Porteous, in one respect, fit to command guards designed to suppress popular commotion, he seems, on the other, to have been disqualified for a charge so delicate, by a hot and surly temper, always too ready to come to blows and violence; a character void of principle; and a disposition to regard the rabble, who seldom failed to regale him and his soldiers with some marks of their displeasure, as declared enemies, upon whom it was natural and justifiable that he should seek opportunities of vengeance. Being, however, the most active and trust-worthy among the captains of the City Guard, he was the person to whom the magistrates entrusted the command of the soldiers appointed to keep the peace at the time of Wilson's execution. He was ordered to guard the gallows and scaffold, with about eighty men, all the disposable force that could be spared for that duty.

But the magistrates took farther precautions, which affected Porteous's pride very deeply. They requested the assistance of part of a regular infantry regiment, not to attend upon the execution, but to remain drawn up upon the principal street of the city, during the time that it went forward, in order to intimidate the multitude, in case they should be disposed to be unruly, with a display of force which could not be resisted without desperation. It may sound ridiculous in our ears, considering the fallen state of this ancient civic corps, that its officer should have felt punctiliously jealous of its honour. Yet so it was. Captain Porteous resented, as an indignity, the fetching the Welch Fusileers within the city, and into a street where no drums but his own were allowed to be struck, without the special command or permission of the magistrates. As he could not show his ill humour to his patrons the magistrates, it increased his indignation and his desire to be revenged on the unfortunate criminal Wilson, and all who favoured him. These internal emotions of jealousy and rage wrought a change on the man's mien and bearing, visible to all who saw him on the fatal morning when Wilson was appointed to suffer. Porteous's ordinary appearance was rather favourable. He was about the middle size, stout, and well made, having a military air, and yet rather a gentle and mild countenance. His complexion was brown, his face something fretted with the scars of the small-pox, his eyes rather languid than keen or fierce. On the present occasion, however, it seemed to those who saw him as if he were agitated by some evil demon. His step was irregular, his voice hollow and broken, his countenance pale, his eyes staring and wild, his speech imperfect and confused, and his whole appearance so disordered, that many remarked he seemed to be *fey*, a Scottish expression, meaning the state of those who are driven on to their impending fate by the strong impulse of some irresistible necessity.

One part of his conduct was truly diabolical, if, indeed, it has not been exaggerated by the general prejudice entertained against his memory. When Wilson, the unhappy criminal, was delivered to him by the keeper of the prison, in order that he might be conducted to the place of execution, Porteous, not satisfied with the usual precautions to prevent escape, ordered him to be manacled. This might be justifiable from the character and bodily strength of the malefactor, as well as from the apprehensions so generally entertained of an expected rescue. But the handcuffs which were produced being found too small for the wrists of a man so big-boned as Wilson, Porteous proceeded with his own hands, and by great exertion of strength, to force them till they clasped together, to the exquisite torture of the unhappy criminal. Wilson remonstrated against such barbarous usage, declaring that the pain distracted his thoughts from the subjects of meditation proper to his unhappy condition.

"It signifies little," replied Captain Porteous; "your pain will be soon at an end."

"Your cruelty is great," answered the sufferer. "You know not how soon you yourself may have occasion to ask the mercy, which you are now refusing to a fellow creature. May God forgive you."

These words, long afterwards quoted and remembered, were all that passed between Porteous and his prisoner; but as they took air, and became known to the people, they greatly increased the popular compassion for Wilson, and excited a proportional degree of indignation against Porteous; against whom, as strict, and even violent in the discharge of his unpopular office, the common people had some real, and many imaginary causes of complaint.

When the painful procession was completed, and Wilson, with the escort, arrived at the scaffold in the Grassmarket, there appeared no signs of that attempt to rescue him which had occasioned such precautions. The multitude, in general, looked on with deeper interest than at ordinary executions; and there might be seen, on the countenances of many, a stern and indignant expression, like that with which the ancient Cameronians might be supposed to witness the execution of their brethren, who glorified the covenant upon the same occasion, and at the same spot. But there was no attempt at violence. Wilson himself seemed disposed to hasten over the space that divided time from eternity. The devotions proper and usual on such occasions were no sooner finished than he submitted to his fate, and the sentence of the law was executed.

He had been suspended on the gibbet so long as to be totally deprived of life, when at once, as if occasioned by some newly-received impulse, there arose a tumult among the multitude. Many stones were thrown at Porteous and his guards; some mischief was done; and the mob continuing to press forward with whoops, shrieks, howls, and exclamations, a young fellow, with a sailor's cap slouched over his face, sprung on the scaffold, and cut the rope by which the criminal was suspended. Others approached to carry off the body, either to secure for it a decent grave, or to try, perhaps, some means of resuscitation. Captain Porteous was wrought by this appearance of insurrection against his authority into a rage so headlong as made him forget, that, the sentence having been fully executed, it was his duty not to engage in hostilities with the misguided multitude, but to draw off his men as fast as possible. He sprung from the scaffold, snatched a musket from one of his soldiers, commanded the party to give fire, and, as several eye-witnesses concurred in swearing, set them the example by discharging his piece, and shooting a man dead on the spot. Several soldiers obeyed his commands or followed his example; six or seven people were slain, and a great many more hurt and wounded.

After this act of violence, the Captain proceeded to withdraw his men towards their guard-house in the High-street. The mob were not so much intimidated as incensed by what had been done. They pursued the soldiers with execrations, accompanied by vollies of stones. As they pressed on them, the rear-most soldiers turned, and again fired with fatal aim and execution. It is not accurately known whether Porteous commanded this second act of violence; but of course the odium of the whole transactions of the fatal day attached to him, and to him alone. He arrived at his guard-house, dismissed his soldiers, and went to make his report to the magistrates concerning the unfortunate events of the day.

Apparently by this time Captain Porteous had begun to doubt the propriety of his own conduct, and the reception he met with from the magistrates was such as to make him still more anxious to gloss it over. He denied that he had given orders to fire; he denied he had fired with his own hand: he even produced the fusee which he carried as an officer for examination—it was found still loaded—of three cartridges which he was seen to put in his pouch that morning, two were still there—a white handkerchief was thrust into the muzzle of the piece, and returned unsoiled or blackened. To this it was answered, that he had not used his own piece, but had been seen to take one from a soldier. Among the many who had been killed and wounded by the unhappy fire, there were several of better rank; for even the humanity of such soldiers as fired over the heads of the mere rabble around the scaffold, proved in some instances fatal to persons who were stationed in windows, or observed the melancholy scene from a distance. The voice of public indignation was loud and general; and, ere men's temper had time to cool, the trial of Captain Porteous took place before the High Court of Justiciary. After a long and patient hearing, the jury had the difficult duty of balancing the positive evidence of many persons, and those of respectability, who deposed positively to the prisoner's commanding his soldiers to fire, and himself firing his piece, of which some swore that they saw the smoke and flash, and beheld a man drop at whom it was pointed, with the negative testimony of others, who, though well stationed for seeing what had passed, neither heard Porteous give orders to fire, nor saw him fire himself; but, on the contrary, averred that the first shot was fired by a soldier who stood close by him. A great part of his defence was also founded upon the turbulence of the mob, which witnesses, according to their feelings, their predilections, and their opportunities of observation, represented differently; some describing as a formidable riot, what others represented as a trifling disturbance, such as always used to take place on the like occasions, when the executioner of the law, and the men commissioned to protect him in his task, were generally exposed to some indignities. The verdict of the jury sufficiently shews how the evidence preponderated in their mind. It declared that John Porteous fired a gun among the people assembled at the execution; that he gave orders to his soldiers to fire, by which many persons were killed and wounded; but, at the same time, that the prisoner and his guard had been wounded and beaten, by stones thrown at them by the multitude. Upon this verdict, the Lords of Justiciary passed sentence of death against Captain John Porteous, adjudging him, in common form, to be hanged on a gibbet at the common place of execution, on Wednesday, 8th September, 1736, and all his moveable property to be forfeited to the king's use, according to the Scottish law in cases of wilful murder.

Chapter Four

The hour's come, but not the man.
Kelpie

ON THE DAY when the unhappy Porteous was expected to suffer the sentence of the law, the place of execution, extensive as it is, was crowded almost to suffocation. There was not a window in all the lofty tenements around it, or in the steep and crooked street called the Bow, by which the fatal procession was to descend from the High-Street, which was not absolutely filled with spectators. The uncommon height and antique appearance of these houses, some of which were formerly the property of the Knights Templars, and Knights of Saint John, and still exhibit on their fronts and gables the iron cross of these orders, gave additional effect to a scene in itself so striking. The area of the Grassmarket resembled a huge dark lake or sea of human heads, in the centre of which arose the fatal tree, tall, black, and ominous, from which dangled the deadly halter. Every object takes interest from its purpose and associations, and the erect beam and empty noose, things so simple in themselves, became objects, on such an occasion, of terror and of solemn interest.

Amid so numerous an assembly there was scarce a word spoken, save in whispers. The thirst of vengeance was in some degree allayed by its supposed certainty; and even the populace, with deeper feeling than they are wont to entertain, suppressed all clamorous exultation, and prepared to enjoy the scene of retaliation in triumph, silent and decent, though stern and relentless. It seemed as if the depth of their hatred to the unfortunate criminal despised to display itself in any thing resembling the more noisy current of their ordinary feelings. Had a stranger consulted only the evidence of his ears, he might have supposed that so vast a multitude were assembled for some purpose which affected them with the deepest sorrow, and stilled those noises which, upon all ordinary occasions, arise from such a concourse. But if he gazed upon their faces, he would have been instantly undeceived. The compressed lip, the bent brow, the stern and flashing eye of almost every one on whom he gazed, conveyed the expression of men come to glut their sight with triumphant revenge. It is probable that the appearance of the criminal might have somewhat changed the temper of the populace in his favour, and that they might in the moment of death have forgiven the man against whom their resentment had been so fiercely heated. It had, however, been destined, that the mutability of their sentiments was not to be exposed to this trial.

The usual hour for producing the criminal had been past for many minutes, yet the spectators observed no symptom of his appearance. "Would they venture to defraud public justice?" was the question which men began anxiously to ask at each other. The first answer in every case was bold and positive. "They dare not." But when the point was farther canvassed, other opinions were entertained, and various causes of doubt were suggested. Porteous had been a favourite officer of the magistracy of the city, which, being a numerous and fluctuating body, requires for its support a degree of energy in its functionaries, which the individuals who compose it cannot at all times alike be supposed to possess in their own persons. It was remembered, that in the Information for Porteous, (the paper, namely, in which his case was stated to the judges of the criminal court), he had been described by his counsel as the person on whom the magistrates chiefly relied in all emergencies of uncommon difficulty. It was argued too, that his conduct upon the unhappy occasion of Wilson's execution, was capable of being attributed to an imprudent excess of zeal in the execution of his duty, a motive for which those under whose authority he acted might be supposed to have great sympathy. And as these considerations might move the magistrates to make a favourable representation of Porteous's case, there were not wanting others in the higher departments of government, which would make such suggestions favourably listened to.

The mob of Edinburgh, when thoroughly excited, had been at all times one of the fiercest which could be found in Europe; and of late years they had risen repeatedly against the government, and sometimes not without success. They were conscious, therefore, that they were no favourites with the rulers of the period, and that if Captain Porteous's violence was not altogether regarded as good service, it might certainly be thought, that to visit it with a capital punishment would render it both delicate and dangerous for future officers, in the same circumstances, to act with effect in repressing tumults. There is also a natural feeling, on the part of all members of government, for the general maintenance of authority; and it seemed not unlikely, that what to the relatives of the sufferers appeared a wanton and unprovoked massacre, should be otherwise viewed in the cabinet of Saint James's. It might be there supposed, that, upon the whole matter, Captain Porteous was in the exercise of a trust delegated to him by the lawful civil authority; that he had been assaulted by the populace, and several of his men hurt; and that, in finally repelling force by force, his conduct could be fairly imputed to no other motive than self-defence in the discharge of his duty.

These considerations, of themselves very powerful, induced the spectators to apprehend the possibility of a reprieve; and to the various causes which might interest the rulers in his favour, the lower part of the rabble added one which was peculiarly well adapted to their comprehension. It was averred, in order to increase the odium against Porteous, that while he repressed with the utmost severity the slightest excesses of the poor, he not only overlooked the licence of the young nobles and gentry, but was very willing even to lend them the countenance of his official authority, in execution of such loose pranks as it was chiefly his duty to have restrained. This suspicion, which was perhaps much exaggerated, made a deep impression on the minds of the populace; and when several of the higher rank joined in a petition, recommending Porteous to the mercy of the crown, it was generally supposed he owed their favour not to any conviction of the hardship of his case, but to the fear of losing a convenient accomplice in their debaucheries. It is scarce necessary to say how much this suspicion augmented the people's detestation of this obnoxious criminal, as well as their fear of his escaping the sentence pronounced against him.

While these arguments were stated and replied to, and canvassed and supported, the hitherto silent expectation of the people became changed into that deep and agitating murmur, which is sent forth by the ocean before the tempest begins to howl. The crowded populace, as if the motions had corresponded with the unsettled state of their minds, fluctuated to and fro without any visible cause of impulse, like the agitation of the waters, called by sailors the ground-swell. The news, which the magistrates had almost hesitated to communicate to them, was at length announced, and spread among the spectators with a rapidity like lightning. A reprieve from the Secretary of State's office, under the hand of his Grace the Duke of Newcastle, had arrived, intimating the pleasure of Queen Caroline, (regent of the kingdom during the absence of George II. on the continent,) that the execution of the sentence of death pronounced against John Porteous, late Captain-lieutenant of the City Guard of Edinburgh, present prisoner in the tolbooth of that city, be respited for six weeks from the time appointed for his execution.

The assembled spectators, of almost all degrees, whose minds had been wound up to the pitch which we have described, uttered a groan, or rather a roar of indignation and disappointed revenge, similar to that of a tyger from whom his meal has been rent by his keeper when he was just about to devour it. This fierce exclamation seemed to forebode some immediate explosion of popular resentment, and, in fact, such had been expected by the magistrates, and the necessary measures had been taken to repress it. But the shout was not repeated; nor did any sudden tumult ensue, such as it seemed to announce. The populace appeared to be ashamed of having expressed their disappointment in a vain clamour, and the sound changed, not into the silence which had preceded the arrival of these stunning news, but into stifled mutterings, which each groupe maintained among themselves, and which were blended into one deep and hoarse murmur which floated above the assembly. Yet still, though all expectation of the execution was over, the mob remained assembled, stationary, as it were, through very resentment, and gazing on the preparations for death, which had now been made in vain, and stimulating their feelings, by recalling the various claims which Wilson might have had on royal mercy, from the mistaken motives on which he acted, as well as from the generosity he had displayed towards his accomplice. "This man," they said,—"the brave, the resolute, the generous, was executed to death without mercy for stealing a purse of gold, which in some sense he considered as a fair reprisal; while the profligate satellite, who took advantage of a trifling tumult, inseparable from such occasion, to shed the blood of twenty of his fellow-citizens, is deemed a fitting object for the exercise of the royal prerogative of mercy. Is this to be borne?—would our fathers have borne it? Are not we, like them, Scotsmen and burghers of Edinburgh?"

The officers of justice began now to remove the scaffold, and other preparations which had been made for the execution, in hopes, by doing so, to accelerate the dispersion of the multitude. The measure had the desired effect; for no sooner had the fatal tree been unfixed from the large stone pedestal or socket in which it was secured, and sunk slowly down upon the wain intended to remove it to the place where it was usually deposited, than the populace, after giving vent to their feelings in a second shout of rage and mortification, began slowly to disperse to their usual abodes and occupations.

The windows were in like manner gradually deserted, and groupes of the more decent class of citizens formed themselves, as if waiting to return homewards when the streets should be cleared of the rabble. Contrary to what is frequently the case, this description of persons agreed in general with the sentiments of their inferiors, and considered the cause as common to all ranks. Indeed, as we have already noticed, it was by no means amongst the lowest class of the spectators, or those most likely to be engaged in the riot at Wilson's execution, that the fatal fire of Porteous's soldiers had taken effect. Several persons were killed who were looking out at windows at the scene, who could not of course belong to the rioters, and were persons of decent rank and condition. The burghers, therefore, resenting the loss which had fallen on their own body, and proud and tenacious of their rights, as the citizens of Edinburgh have at all times been, were greatly exasperated at the unexpected respite of Captain Porteous.

It was noticed at the time, and afterwards more particularly remembered, that, while the mob were in the act of dispersing, several individuals were seen busily passing from one place and one groupe of people to another, remaining long with none, but whispering for a little time with those who appeared to be declaiming most violently against the conduct of government. These active agents had the appearance of men from the country, and were generally supposed to be old friends and confederates of Wilson, whose minds were of course highly excited against Porteous.

If, however, it was the intention of these men to stir the multitude to any sudden act of mutiny, it seemed for the time to be fruitless. The rabble, as well as the more decent part of the assembly, dispersed, and went home peaceably; and it was only by observing the moody discontent on their brows, or catching the tenor of the conversation they held with each other, that a stranger could estimate the state of their minds. We will give the reader this advantage, by associating ourselves with one of the numerous groupes who were painfully ascending the steep declivity of the West Bow to return to their dwellings in the Lawn-market.

"An unco thing this, Mrs Howden," said old Peter Plumdamas to his neighbour the rouping-wife, or saleswoman, as he offered her his arm to assist her in the toilsome ascent, "to see the grit folk at Lunnon set their face against law and gospel, and let loose sic a reprobate as Porteous upon a peaceable town."

"And to think o' the weary walk they hae gi'en us in a burning day like this," answered Mrs Howden, with a groan; "and sic a comfortable window as I had gotten, too, just within a penny-stane-cast of the scaffold—I could hae heard every word the minister said—and to pay twal pennies for my stand, and a' for naething!"

"I am judging," said Mr Plumdamas, "that this reprieve wadna stand gude in the auld Scots law, when the kingdom was a kingdom."

"I dinna ken muckle about the law," answered Mrs Howden; "but I ken, that when we had a king, and a chancellor, and parliament-men o' our ain, we could aye peeble them wi' stanes when they were na gude bairns—But naebody's nails can reach the length o' Lunnon."

"Weary on Lunnon, and a' that e'er came out o't!" said Miss Grizell Damahoy, an ancient seamstress; "they hae ta'en awa' our parliament, and they hae oppressed our trade. Our gentles will hardly allow that a Scots needle can sew ruffles on a sark, or lace on an owerlay."

"Ye may say that, Miss Damahoy, and I ken o' them that hae gotten raisins frae Lunnon by forpits at ance," responded Plumdamas; "and then sic an host of idle English gaugers and excisemen as hae come down to vex and torment us, that an honest man canna fetch sae muckle as a bit anker o' brandy frae Leith to the Lawn-market, but he's like to be robbit o' the very gudes he's bought and paid for.— Weel, I winna justify Andrew Wilson for pitting hand on what wasna his; but if he took nae mair than his ain, there's an awfu' difference between that and the fact that this man stands for."

"If ye speak about the law," said Mrs Howden, "here comes Mr Saddletree, that can settle it as weel as ony on the bench."

The party she mentioned, a grave elderly person, with a superb periwig, dressed in a decent suit of sad-coloured clothes, came up as she spoke, and courteously gave his arm to Miss Grizell Damahoy.

It may be necessary to mention, that Mr Bartholine Saddletree kept an excellent and highly-esteemed shop for harness, saddles, &c. &c. at the sign of the Golden Nag, at the head of Bess-Wynd. His genius, however, (as he himself and most of his neighbours conceived,) lay towards the weightier matters of the law, and he failed not to give frequent attendance upon the pleadings and arguments of the lawyers and judges in the neighbouring square, where, to say the truth, he was oftener to be found than would have consisted with his own emolument; but that his wife, an active pains-taking person, could, in his absence, make an admirable shift to please the customers and scold the journeymen. This good lady was in the habit of letting her husband take his way, and go on improving his stock of legal knowledge without interruption, but, as if in requital, she insisted upon having her own will in the domestic and commercial departments which he abandoned to her. Now, as Bartholine Saddletree had a considerable gift of words, which he mistook for eloquence, and conferred more liberally upon the society in which he lived than was at all times gracious and acceptable, there went forth a saying, with which wags used sometimes to interrupt his rhetoric, that, as he had a golden nag at his door, so he had a grey mare in his shop. This reproach induced Mr Saddletree, upon all occasions, to assume rather a haughty and stately tone towards his good woman, a circumstance by which she seemed very little affected, unless when he attempted to exercise any real authority, when she never failed to fly into open rebellion. But this extremity Bartholine seldom provoked; for, like gentle King Jamie, he was fonder of talking of authority than really exercising it. This turn of mind was, on the whole, lucky for him; since his substance was increased without any trouble on his part, or any interruption of his favourite studies.

This word in explanation has been thrown in to the reader, while Saddletree was laying down, with great precision, the law upon Porteous's case, by which he arrived at this conclusion, that, if Porteous had fired five minutes sooner, before Wilson was cut down, he would have been *versans in licito*, engaged, that is, in a lawful act, and only liable to be punished *propter excessum*, or for lack of discretion, which might have mitigated the punishment to *pœna ordinaria*.

"Discretion!" echoed Mrs Howden, on whom it may well be supposed the fineness of this distinction was entirely thrown away. "Whan had Jock Porteous either grace, discretion, or gude manners? —I mind when his father"——

"But, Mrs Howden," said Saddletree——

"And I," said Miss Damahoy, "mind when his mother"——

"Miss Damahoy," entreated the interrupted orator——

"And I," said Plumdamas, "mind when his wife"——

"Mr Plumdamas—Mrs Howden—Miss Damahoy," again implored the orator, "mind the distinction—as Counsellor Crossmyloof says, 'I,' says he, 'take a distinction.' Now, the body of the criminal being cut down, and the execution ended, Porteous was no longer official; the act which he came to protect and guard being done and ended, he was no better than *cuivis ex populo*."

"*Quivis—quivis*, Mr Saddletree, craving your pardon," said (with a prolonged emphasis on the first syllable) Mr Butler, the deputy schoolmaster of a parish near Edinburgh, who at that moment came up behind them as the false Latin was uttered.

"What signifies interrupting me, Mr Butler?—but I am glad to see ye notwithstanding—I speak after Counsellor Crossmyloof, and he said *cuivis*."

"If Counsellor Crossmyloof used the dative for the nominative, I would have crossed *his* loof with a tight leathern strap, Mr Saddletree; there is not a boy on the booby form but should have been scourged for such a solecism in grammar."

"I speak Latin like a lawyer, Mr Butler, and not like a schoolmaster," retorted Saddletree.

"Scarce like a school-boy, I think," rejoined Butler.

"It matters little," said Bartholine; "all I mean to say is, that Porteous has become liable to the *pœna extra ordinem*, or capital punishment; which is to say, in plain Scotch, the gallows, simply because he did not fire when he was in office, but waited till the body was cut down, the execution whilk he had in charge to guard implemented, and he himself exonered of the public trust imposed on him."

"But, Mr Saddletree," said Plumdamas, "do ye really think John Porteous's case wad hae been better if he had begun firing before ony stanes were flung at a'?"

"Indeed do I, neighbour Plumdamas," replied Bartholine, confidently, "he being then in point of trust and in point of power, the execution being but inchoat, or, at least, not implemented, or finally ended; but after Wilson was cut down it was a' ower—he was clean exauctorate, and had nae mair ado but get awa' wi' his guard up this West Bow as fast as if there had been a caption after him—And this is Law, for I heard it laid down by Lord Vincovincentem."

"Vincovintem?—Is he a lord of state, or a lord of seat?" enquired Mrs Howden.

"A lord of seat—a lord of the Session.—I fash mysell little wi' lords o' state; they vex me wi' a whin idle questions about their saddles, and curpels, and holsters, and horse-furniture, and what they'll cost, and whan they'll be ready—a wheen gallopping geese—my wife may serve the like o' them."

"And so might she, in her day, hae served the best lord in the land, for as little as ye think o' her, Mr Saddletree," said Mrs Howden, somewhat indignant at the contemptuous way in which her gossip was mentioned; "when she and I were twa gilpies, we little thought to hae

sitten doun wi' the like o' my auld Davie Howden, or you either, Mr
Saddletree."

While Saddletree, who was not bright at a reply, was cudgelling his
brains for an answer to this home-thrust, Miss Damahoy broke in on
him.

"And as for the lords of state," said Miss Damahoy, "ye suld mind
the riding o' the parliament, Mr Saddletree, in the gude auld time
before the Union,—a year's rent o' mony a gude estate gaed for graith
and harnessing, forbye broidered robes and foot-mantles, that wad
hae stude by their lane wi' gold and brocade, and that were muckle in
my ain line."

"Ay, and than the lusty banquetting, with sweet-meats and comfits
wet and dry, and dried fruits of divers sorts," said Plumdamas. "But
Scotland was Scotland in these days."

"I'll tell ye what it is, neighbours," said Mrs Howden, "I'll ne'er
believe Scotland is Scotland ony mair, if our kindly Scots sit doun wi'
the affront they hae gi'en us this day. It's not only the blude that *is*
shed, but the blude that might hae been shed, that's required at our
hands; there was my daughter's wean, little Eppie Daidle—my oe, ye
ken, Miss Grizell—had played the truant frae the school, as bairns will
do, ye ken, Mr Butler"——

"And for which," interjected Mr Butler, "they should be soundly
scourged by their well-wishers."

"And had just cruppin to the gallows' foot to see the hanging, as was
natural for a wean; and what for might na she hae been shot as weel as
the rest o' them, and where wad we a' hae been then? I wonder how
Queen Carline (if her name be Carline), wad hae liked to hae had ane
o' her ain bairns in sic a venture?"

"Report says," answered Butler, "that such a circumstance would
not have distressed her majesty beyond endurance."

"Aweel," said Mrs Howden, "the sum o' the matter is, that, were I a
man, I wad hae amends o' Jock Porteous, be the upshot what like o't, if
a' the carles and carlines in England had sworn to the nay-say."

"I would claw down the tolbooth door wi' my nails," said Mrs
Grizell, "but I wad be at him."

"Ye may be very right, ladies," said Butler, "but I would not advise
you to speak so loud."

"Speak!" exclaimed both the ladies together, "there will be naething else spoken about frae the Weigh-house to the Water-port, till
this is either ended or mended."

The females now departed to their respective places of abode.
Plumdamas joined the other two gentlemen in taking their *meridian* (a
bumper-dram of brandy), as they passed the well-known low-browed

shop in the Lawn-market, where they were wont to take that refreshment. Mr Plumdamas then departed towards his shop, and Mr Butler, who happened to have some particular occasion for the rein of an old bridle, (the truants of that busy day could have anticipated its application,) walked down the Lawn-market with Mr Saddletree, each talking as he could get a word thrust in, the one on the laws of Scotland, the other on those of syntax, and neither listening to a word which his companion uttered.

Chapter Five

Elswhair he colde right weel lay down the law,
But in his house was meke as is a daw.
                            DAVIE LINDSAY

"THERE HAS BEEN Jock Driver the carrier here, speering about his new graith," said Mrs Saddletree to her husband, as he crossed his threshold, not with the purpose by any means of consulting him upon his own affairs, but merely to intimate, by a gentle recapitulation, how much duty she had gone through in his absence.

"Weel," replied Bartholine, and deigned not a word more.

"And the laird of Girdingburst has had his running footman here, and caa'd himsell (he's a civil pleasant young gentleman), to see when the broidered saddle-cloth for his sorrel horse will be ready, for he wants it again the Kelso races."

"Weel, a-weel," replied Bartholine, as laconically as before.

"And his lordship, the Earl of Blazonburry, Lord Flash and Flame, is like to be clean daft, that the harness for the six Flanders mares, wi' the crests, coronets, housings, and mountings conform, are no sent hame according to promise gi'en."

"Weel, weel—weel, weel—weel, gude-wife," said Saddletree, "if he gangs daft, we'll hae him cognosced—it's a' very weel."

"It's weel that ye think sae, Mr Saddletree," answered his helpmate, rather nettled at the indifference with which her report was received; "there's mony ane wad hae thought themselves affronted, if sae mony customers had caa'd and naebody to answer them but women-folk, for a' the lads were aff sae sune as your back was turned to see Porteous hanged, that might be counted upon; and sae, you no being at hame"——

"Houts, Mrs Saddletree," said Bartholine, with an air of consequence, "dinna deave me wi' your nonsense. I was under the necessity of being elsewhere—*non omnia*—as Mr Crossmyloof said, when he was called by two macers at ance, *non omnia possumus—potimus—*

possimis—I ken our law-latin offends Mr Butler's ears, but it means naebody, an' it were the Lord President himsell, can do twa turns at ance."

"Very right, Mr Saddletree," answered his careful helpmate, with a sarcastic smile, "and nae doubt it's a decent thing to leave your wife to look after young gentlemen's saddles and bridles, when ye gang to see a man, that never did ye nae ill, raxing a halter."

"Woman," said Saddletree, assuming an elevated tone, to which the *meridian* had somewhat contributed, "desist,—I say forbear from intromitting with affairs thou can'st not understand. D'ye think I was born to sit here brogging an elshin through bend leather, when sic men as Duncan Forbes, and that other Arniston child there, without muckle greater parts, if the close-head speak true, than mysell, maun be Presidents and King's Advocates nae doubt, and wha but they? Whereas, were favour equally distribute, as in the days of the wight Wallace"——

"I ken naething we wad hae gotten by the wight Wallace," said Mrs Saddletree, "unless, as I hae heard the auld folk tell, that they fought in thae days wi' bend-leather guns, and than it's a chance but what if he bought them, he might forget to pay for them. And as for the greatness of your parts, Bartley, the folk in the close-head maun ken mair about them than I do, if they make sic a report of them."

"I tell ye, woman," said Saddletree, in high dudgeon, "that ye ken naething about these matters—in Sir William Wallace's days, there was nae man pinned down to sic a slavish wark as a sadler's, for they got ony leather graith that they had ready-made out o' Holland."

"Well," said Butler, who was, like many of his profession, something of an humourist and a dry joker, "if that be the case, Mr Saddletree, I think we have changed for the better since we make our own harness, and only import our lawyers from Holland."

"It's too true, Mr Butler," answered Bartholine with a sigh; "if I had had the luck—or rather, if my father had had the sense to send me to Leyden and Utrecht to learn the Substitutes and Pandex"——

"You mean the Institutes—Justinian's Institutes, Mr Saddletree," said Butler.

"Institutes and substitutes are synonymous words, Mr Butler, and used indifferently as such in deeds of tailzie, as you may see in Balfour's Practiques, or Dallas' Stiles. I understand these things pretty weel, I thank God; but I own I should have studied in Holland."

"To comfort you, you might not have been further forward than you now are, Mr Saddletree," replied Mr Butler; "for our Scottish advocates are an aristocratic race—Their brass is of the right Corinthian quality and—*Non cuivis contigit adire Corinthum*—aha, Mr Saddletree?"

"And aha, Mr Butler," rejoined Bartholine, upon whom, as may well be supposed, the jest was lost, and all but the sound of the words, "ye said a gliff syne it was *quivis*, and now I heard ye say *cuivis* with my ain ears, as plain as ever I heard a word at the fore-bar."

"Give me your patience, Mr Saddletree, and I'll explain the discrepancy in three words," said Butler, as pedantic in his own department, though with infinitely more judgment and learning, as Bartholine was in his self-assumed profession of the law—"Give me your patience for a moment—You'll grant that the nominative case is that by which a person or thing is nominated or designed, and which may be called the primary case, all others being formed from it by alterations of the termination in the learned languages, and by prepositions in our modern Babylonian jargons—You'll grant me that, I suppose, Mr Saddletree?"

"I dinna ken whether I will or no—*ad avisandum*, ye ken—naebody should be in a hurry to make admissions, either in point of law or in point of fact," said Saddletree, looking, or endeavouring to look, as if he understood what was said.

"And the dative case," continued Butler——

"I ken what a tutor dative is brawly," said Saddletree, readily enough.

"The dative case," resumed the grammarian, "is that in which any thing is given or assigned to as property as belonging to a person, or thing—You cannot deny that, I am sure."

"I am sure I'll no grant it though," said Saddletree.

"Then, what the *deevil* do ye take the nominative and the dative cases to be?" said Butler, hastily, and surprised at once out of his decency of expression and accuracy of pronounciation.

"I'll tell you that at leisure, Mr Butler," said Saddletree, with a very knowing look; "I'll take a day to see and answer every article of your condescendence, and then I'll hold ye to confess or deny as accords."

"Come, come, Mr Saddletree," said his wife, "we'll have nae confessions and condescendences here; let them deal in thae sort o' wares that are paid for them—they suit the like o' us as ill as a demipique saddle would set a draught ox."

"Aha!" said Mr Butler, "*Optat ephippia bos piger*—nothing new under the sun—But it was a fair hit of Mrs Saddletree, however."

"And it wad far better become ye, Mr Saddletree," continued his helpmate, "since ye say ye hae skeel o' the law, to try if ye can do ony thing for Effie Deans, puir thing, that's lying up in the tolbooth yonder, cauld and hungry and comfortless—a servant lass of ours, Mr Butler, and as innocent a lass to my thinking, and as usefu' in the chop

—When Mr Saddletree gangs out, and ye're aware he's seldom at hame when there's ony o' the plea-houses open, poor Effie used to help me to tumble the bundles o' barkened leather up and doun, and range out the gudes, and suit a' body's humours—And troth, she could please the customers better than mysell wi' her answers, for she was aye civil, and a bonnier lass wasna in Auld Reekie. And I am no sae young as I hae been, Mr Butler, and a wee bit short in the temper into the bargain. When there's ower mony folks crying on me at anes, and nane but ae tongue to answer them, folk maun speak hastily or they'll ne'er get through wark—Sae I miss Effie daily"—

"*De die in diem*," added Saddletree.

"I think," said Butler, after a good deal of hesitation, "I have seen the girl in the shop—a modest-looking, black-haired girl?"

"Ay, ay, that's just puir Effie," said her mistress. "How she was abandoned to hersell, or whether she was sackless o' the sinfu' deed, God in Heaven kens; but if she be guilty, she's been sair tempted, and I wad amaist take my bible-aith she hasna been hersell at the time."

Butler had by this time become much agitated; he fidgetted up and down the shop, and shewed the greatest agitation that a person of such strict decorum could be supposed to give way to. "Was not this girl," he said, "the daughter of David Deans, that has the parks at Saint Leonard's taken? and has she not a sister?"

"In troth has she—puir Jeanie Deans, ten years elder than hersel; she was here greeting a wee while syne about her sister. And what could I say to her, but that she behoved to come and speak to Mr Saddletree when he was at hame? It wasna that I thought Mr Saddletree could do her or ony other body muckle good or ill, but it wad aye serve to keep the puir thing's heart up for a wee while; and let sorrow come when sorrow maun."

"Ye are mista'en though, gudewife," said Saddletree scornfully, "for I could hae gien her great satisfaction; I could hae proved to her that her sister was indicted upon the statute sixteen hundred and ninety, chapter twenty-one—For the mair ready prevention of child-murder—for concealing her pregnancy, and giving no account of the child which she had borne."

"I hope," said Butler,—"I trust in a gracious God, that she can clear herself."

"And sae do I, Mr Butler," replied Mrs Saddletree. "I am sure I wad hae answered for her as my ain daughter; but, waes my heart, I had been tender a' the simmer, and scarce ower the door o' my room for twal weeks. And as for Mr Saddletree, he might be in a lying-in hospital, and ne'er find out what the women cam there for. Sae I could see little or naething o' her, or I wad hae had the truth o' her situation out o' her, I'se warrant ye—But we a' think her sister maun be able to speak something to clear her."

"The haill Parliament-house were speaking o' naething else," said Saddletree, "till this job o' Porteous's put it out o' head—It's a beautiful point of presumptive murder, and there's been nane like it in the Justiciar Court since the case of Luckie Smith the howdie, that suffered in the year saxteen hundred and seventy-nine."

"But what's the matter wi' you, Mr Butler," said the good woman; "ye are looking as white as a sheet; will ye take a dram?"

"By no means," said Butler, compelling himself to speak. "I walked in from Dumfries yesterday, and this is a warm day."

"Sit down," said Mrs Saddletree, laying hands on him kindly, "and rest ye—ye'll kill yoursell, man, at that rate—and are we to wish ye joy o' getting the scule, Mr Butler?"

"Yes—no—I do not know."

"Ye dinna ken whether ye're to get the free scule o' Dumfries or no, after hinging on and teaching it a' the simmer?"

"No, Mrs Saddletree—I am not to have it," replied Butler. "The Laird of Blackatthebane had a natural son bred to the kirk that the presbytery could not be prevailed on to license; and so"——

"Ay, ye need say nae mair about it; if there was a laird that had a puir kinsman or bastard that it wad suit, there's eneugh said.—And ye're e'en come back to Libberton to wait for dead men's shoon—and, for as frail as Mr Whackbairn is, he may live as lang as you, that are his assistant and successor."

"Very like," replied Butler with a sigh; "I do not know if I should wish it otherwise."

"Nae doubt it's a very vexing thing," continued the good lady, "to be in that dependent station; and you that hae right and title to sae muckle better, I wonder how ye bear these crosses."

"*Quos diligit castigat*," answered Butler; "even the pagan Seneca could see an advantage in affliction. The Heathens had their philosophy, and the Jews their revelation, Mrs Saddletree, and they endured their distresses in their day. Christians have a better dispensation than either—but doubtless"——

He stopped and sighed bitterly.

"I ken what ye mean," said Mrs Saddletree, looking toward her husband; "there's whiles we lose patience in spite of baith book and Bible—But ye are na ganging awa, and looking sae poorly—ye'll stay and tak some kale wi' us?"

Mr Saddletree laid aside Balfour's Practiques, (his favourite study, and much good may it do him,) to join in his wife's hospitable importunity. But the teacher declined all entreaty, and took his leave upon the spot.

"There's something in a' this," said Mrs Saddletree, looking after him as he walked up the street; "I wonder what makes Mr Butler sae distressed about Effie's misfortune—there was nae acquaintance atween them that ever I saw or heard of; but they were neighbours when David Deans was on the Laird of Dumbiedikes' land. Mr Butler wad ken her father, or some o' her folk.—Get up, Mr Saddletree—ye have set yoursell down on the very brecham that wants stitching—And here's little Willie, the prentice.—Ye little rin-there-out de'il that ye are that I should say sae, what taks you raking through the gutters to see folk hangit?—how wad ye like when it cums to be your ain chance, as I winna ensure ye, if ye dinna mend your manners?—and what are ye maundering and greeting for, as if a word was breaking your banes? —gang in bye, and be a better bairn another time, and tell Peggy to gi'e ye a bicker o' broth, for ye'll be as gleg as a gled, I'se warrant ye.—It's a fatherless bairn, Mr Saddletree, and motherless, whilk in some cases may be waur, and ane wad take care o' him, if they could—it's a Christian duty."

"Very true, goodwife," said Saddletree in reply, "we are in *loco parentis* to him during his years of pupillarity, and I hae had thoughts o' applying to the Court for a commission as factor *loco tutoris*, seeing there is nae tutor nominate, and the tutor-at-law declines to act; but only I fear the expence of the procedure wad not be in *rem versam*, for I am not aware that Willie has ony effects whereof to assume the administration."

He concluded this sentence with a self-important cough, as one who has laid down the law in an indisputable manner.

"Effects!" said Mrs Saddletree, "what effects has the puir wean?— he was naked when his mother died; and the blue polonie that Effie made for him out of an auld mantle o' my ain, was the first decent dress the bairn ever had on. Poor Effie!!! Can ye tell me na really, wi' a' your law, will her life be in danger, Mr Saddletree, when they are no able to prove that ever there was a bairn ava?"

"Whoy," said Mr Saddletree, delighted at having for once in his life seen his wife's attention arrested by a topic of legal discussion. "Whoy, there are two sorts of *murdrum* or *murdragium*, or what you *populariter et vulgariter* call murther. I mean there are many sorts; for there's your murthrum *per vigilias et insidias*, and your *murthrum* under trust."

"I am sure that's the way the gentry murder us merchants, and whiles makes us shut the booth up—but that has naething to do wi' Effie's misfortune."

"The case of Effie (or Euphemia) Deans," resumed Saddletree, "is one of those cases of murder presumptive, that is, a murder of the law's construing or construction, being derived from certain *indicia* or grounds of suspicion."

"So that," said the good woman," unless poor Effie has communicated her situation, she'll be hanged by the neck, if the bairn was stillborn, or if it be alive at this moment?"

"Assuredly," said Saddletree, "it being a statute made by our sovereign Lord and Lady, to prevent the horrid delict of bringing forth children in secret—the crime is rather a favourite of the law, this species of murther being one of its ain creation."

"Then, if the Law makes murders," said Mrs Saddletree, "the Law should be hanged for them; or if they wad hang a lawyer instead, the country wad find nae faut."

A summons to their frugal dinner interrupted the further progress of the conversation, which was otherwise like to take a turn much less favourable to the science of jurisprudence and its professors, than Mr Bartholine Saddletree, the fond admirer of both, had at its opening anticipated.

Chapter Six

But up then raise all Edinburgh,
They all rose up by thousands three.
Johnie Armstrang's Goodnight

BUTLER, on his departure from the sign of the Golden Nag, went in quest of a friend of his connected with the law, at whom he wished to make particular enquiries concerning the circumstances in which the unfortunate young woman mentioned in the last chapter was placed, having, as the reader has probably already conjectured, reasons much deeper than those dictated by mere humanity, for interesting himself in her fate. He found the person he sought absent from home, and was equally unfortunate in one or two other calls which he made upon acquaintances whom he hoped to interest in her story. But every body was, for the moment, stark-mad on the subject of Porteous, and engaged busily in attacking or defending the measures of government in reprieving him; and the ardour of dispute had excited such universal thirst, that half the young lawyers and writers, together with their very clerks, the class whom Butler was looking after, had adjourned the debate to some favourite tavern. It was computed by an experienced arithmetician, that there was as much twopenny ale consumed on the discussion as would have floated a first rate man of war.

Butler wandered about until it was dusk, resolving to take that opportunity of visiting the unfortunate young woman, when his doing so might be least observed; for he had his own reasons for avoiding the remarks of Mrs Saddletree, whose shop-door opened at no great distance from that of the jail, though on the opposite or south side of the street, and a little higher up. He passed, therefore, through the narrow and partly covered passage leading from the north-west end of the Parliament Square.

He stood now before the Gothic entrance of the ancient prison, which, as is well known to all men, rears its ancient front in the very middle of the High-street, forming, as it were, the termination to a huge pile of buildings called the Luckenbooths, which, for some inconceivable reason, our ancestors have jammed into the midst of the principal street of the town, leaving for passage a narrow street on the north, and on the south, into which the prison opens, a narrow crooked lane, winding betwixt the high and sombre walls of the tol-booth and the adjacent houses on the one side, and the buttresses and projections of the old Cathedral upon the other. To give some gaiety to this sombre passage, (well known by the name of the Krames,) a number of little booths, or shops, after the fashion of coblers' stalls, are plaistered, as it were, against the Gothic projections and abut-ments, so that it seems as if the traders have occupied with nests, bearing the same proportion to the building, every buttress and coign of vantage, as the martlett did in Macbeth's Castle. Of later years these booths have degenerated into mere toy-shops, where the little loiterers chiefly interested in such wares are tempted to linger, enchanted by the rich display of hobby-horses, babies, and Dutch toys, arranged in artful and gay confusion; yet half-scared by the cross-looks of the withered pantaloon, or spectacled old lady, by whom these tempting stores are watched and superintended. But, in the times we write of, the hosiers, the glovers, the hatters, the mercers, the milliners, and all who dealt in the miscellaneous wares now termed haberdasher's goods, were to be found in this narrow alley.

To return from our digression. Butler found the outer turnkey, a tall, thin, old man, with long silver hair, in the act of locking the outward door of the jail. He addressed himself to this person, and asked admittance to see Effie Deans, confined upon accusation of child-murther. The turnkey looked at him earnestly, and, civilly touching his hat out of respect to Butler's black coat and clerical appearance, replied it was impossible any one could be admitted at present.

"You shut up earlier than usual, probably on account of Captain Porteous's affair?" said Butler.

The turnkey, with the true mystery of a person in office, gave two grave nods, and withdrawing from the wards a ponderous key of about two feet in length, he proceeded to shut a strong plate of steel, which folded down above the key-hole, and was secured by a steel-spring and catch. Butler stood still instinctively while the door was made fast, and then looking at his watch, walked briskly up the street, muttering to himself almost unconsciously—

> *Porta adversa, ingens, solidoque adamante columnæ;*
> *Vis ut nulla virum, non ipsi exscindere ferro*
> *Cælicolæ valeant—Stat ferrea turris ad auras.* *

Having wasted some more time in a second fruitless attempt to seek out his legal friend and adviser, he thought it time to leave the city and return to his place of residence, in a small village, about two miles and a half to the southward of Edinburgh. The city was at this time surrounded by a high wall, with battlements and flanking projections at some intervals, and the access was through gates, called in the Scottish language *ports*, which were regularly shut at night. A small fee to the keepers would indeed procure egress and ingress at any time, through a wicket left for that purpose in the large gate, but it was of some importance to a man so poor as Butler, to avoid even this slight pecuniary mulct; and fearing he might be near the hour of shutting the gates, he made for that to which he found himself nearest, although, by doing so, he somewhat lengthened his walk homewards. Bristo-port was that by which his direct road lay, but the West-port, which leads out of the Grassmarket, was the nearest of the city gates to the place where he found himself, and to that, therefore, he directed his course. He reached the port in ample time to pass the circuit of the walls, and enter a suburb called Portsburgh, chiefly inhabited by the lower order of artizans and mechanics. Here he was unexpectedly interrupted.

He had not gone far from the gate before he heard the sound of a drum, and, to his great surprise, met a number of persons, sufficient to occupy the whole front of the street, and form a considerable mass behind, moving on with great speed towards the gate he had just come from, and having in front of them a drum beating to arms. While he considered how he should escape a party so assembled, as it might be presumed, for no lawful purpose, they came full on him and stopped him.

---

* Wide is the fronting gate, and raised on high,
With adamantine columns threats the sky;
Vain is the force of man, and Heaven's as vain,
To crush the pillars which the pile sustain;
Sublime on these a tower of steel is reared.
DRYDEN's *Virgil*, Book vi.

"Are you a clergyman?" one questioned him.

Butler replied that he was in orders, but was not a placed minister.

"It's Mr Butler of Libberton," said a voice from behind; "he'll discharge the duty as weel as ony man."

"You must turn back with us, sir," said the first speaker, in a tone civil but peremptory.

"For what purpose, gentlemen?" said Mr Butler. "I live at some distance from town—the roads are unsafe by night—you will do me a serious injury by stopping me."

"You shall be seen safely home—no man shall touch a hair of your head—but you must, and shall come along with us."

"But to what purpose or end, gentlemen?" said Butler. "I hope you will be so civil as to explain that to me."

"You shall know that in good time. Come along—for come you must, by force or fair means; and I warn you to look neither to the right hand nor the left, and to take no notice of any man's face, but consider all that is passing before you as a dream."

"I would it were a dream I could awaken from," said Butler to himself; but, having no means to oppose the violence with which he was threatened, he was compelled to turn round and march in front of the rioters, two men partly supporting and partly holding him. During this parley the insurgents had made themselves masters of the West-port, rushing upon the waiters (so the people were called who had the charge of the gate), and possessing themselves of the keys. They bolted and barred the folding doors, and commanded the person, whose duty it usually was, to secure the wicket, of which they did not understand the fastenings. The man, terrified at an incident so totally unexpected, was unable to perform his usual office, and gave the matter up, after several attempts. The rioters, who seemed to have come prepared for every emergency, called for torches, by the light of which they nailed up the wicket with long nails, which, it seemed probable, they had provided on purpose.

While this was going on, Butler could not, even if he had been willing, have avoided making remarks on the individuals who seemed to lead this singular mob. The torch light, while it fell on their forms and left him in the shade, gave him an opportunity to do so without their observing him. Several of those who seemed most active were dressed in sailors' jackets, trowsers, and sea-caps; others in large loose-bodied great-coats, and slouched hats; and there were several, who, judging from their dress, should have been called women, whose rough deep voices, uncommon size, and masculine deportment and mode of walking, forbade their being so interpreted. They moved as if by some well-concerted plan of arrangement. They had signals by which they knew, and nick-names by which they distinguished each other. Butler remarked, that the name of Wildfire was used among them, to which one stout Amazon seemed to reply.

The rioters left a small party to observe the West-port, and directed the waiters, as they valued their lives, to remain within their barrack, and make no attempt for that night to repossess themselves of the gate. They then moved with rapidity along the low street called the Cow-gate, the mob every where rising at the sound of their drum, and joining them. When they arrived at the Cowgate-port, they secured it with as little opposition as the former, made it fast, and left a small party to observe it. It was afterwards remarked, as an instance of prudence and precaution, singularly combined with audacity, that the parties left to guard these gates did not remain stationary on their posts, but flitted to and fro, keeping so near the gates as to see that no efforts were made to open them, yet not remaining so long as to have their persons observed. The mob, at first only about a hundred strong, now amounted to thousands, and was increasing every moment. They divided themselves so as to ascend with more speed the various narrow lanes which lead up from the Cowgate to the High Street; and still beating to arms as they went, and calling on all true Scotsmen to join them, they now filled the principal street of the city.

The Netherbow-port might be called the Temple-bar of Edinburgh, as, intersecting the High Street at its termination, it divided Edinburgh, properly so called, from the suburb called the Canongate, as Temple-bar divides London from Westminster. It was of the utmost importance to the rioters to possess themselves of this pass, because there was quartered in the Canongate at that time a regiment of infantry, commanded by Colonel Moyle, which might have occupied the city by advancing through this gate, and totally defeated the purpose of the rioters. The leaders therefore hastened to the Nether-bow-port, which they secured in the same manner, and with as little trouble, as the other gates, leaving a party to watch it, strong in proportion to the importance of the post.

The next object of these hardy insurgents was at once to disarm the City Guard, and to procure arms for themselves; for scarce any weapons but staves and bludgeons had been yet seen among them. The Guard-house was a long, low, ugly building, (removed in 1787,) which to a fanciful imagination might have suggested the idea of a long black snail crawling up the middle of the High Street and deforming its beautiful esplanade. This formidable insurrection had been so unexpected, that there were no more than the ordinary serjeant's guard of the city-corps upon duty. Even they were left without any supply of powder and ball; and sensible enough what had raised the storm, and which way it was rolling, could hardly be supposed very desirous to expose themselves by a valiant defence to the animosity of so numerous and desperate a mob, to whom they were on the present occasion much more than usually obnoxious.

There was a centinel upon guard, who (that one town-guard soldier might do his duty on that eventful evening,) presented his piece, and desired the foremost of the rioters to stand off. The young amazon, whom Butler had observed particularly active, sprung upon the soldier, seized his musket, and after a struggle succeeded in wrenching it from him, and throwing him down on the causeway. One or two soldiers who endeavoured to turn out to the support of their centinel, were in the same manner seized and disarmed, and the mob without difficulty possessed themselves of the Guard-house, disarming and turning out the rest of the men on duty. It was remarked, that notwithstanding the city soldiers had been the instruments of the slaughter which this riot was designed to revenge, no ill usage or even insult was offered to them. It seemed as if the vengeance of the people disdained to stoop at any head meaner than that which they considered as the source and origin of their injuries.

On possessing themselves of the guard, their first act was to destroy the drums by which they supposed an alarm might be conveyed to the garrison in the castle; for the same reason they now silenced their own, which was beaten by a young fellow, son to the drummer of Portsburgh, whom they had forced upon that service. Their next business was to distribute among the boldest of the rioters the guns, bayonets, partizans, halberts, and battle or Lochaber axes. Until this period the principal rioters had preserved silence on the ultimate object of their rising, as being that which all knew, but none expressed. Now, however, having accomplished all the preliminary parts of their design, they raised a tremendous shout of "Porteous! Porteous! To the tolbooth! To the tolbooth!"

They proceeded with the same prudence when the object seemed to be nearly in their grasp, as they had done hitherto when success was more dubious. A strong party of the rioters, drawn up in front of the Luckenbooths, and facing down the street, prevented all access from the eastward, and the west end of the Luckenbooths was secured in the same manner; so that the tolbooth was completely surrounded, and those who undertook the task of breaking it open effectually protected from the risk of interruption.

The magistrates, in the meanwhile, had taken the alarm, and assembled in a tavern, with the purpose of raising some strength to subdue the rioters. The deacons, or presidents of the trades, were applied to, but declared there was little chance of their being useful where it was the object to save a man so obnoxious. Mr Lindsay, member of parliament for the city, volunteered the perilous task of carrying a verbal message from the Lord Provost to Colonel Moyle, the commander of the regiment lying in the Canongate, requesting him to force the Netherbow-port, and enter the city to put down the tumult. But Mr Lindsay declined to charge himself with any written order, which, if found on his person by an enraged mob, might have cost him his life. And the issue of the matter was, that Colonel Moyle, having no written requisition from the civil authorities, and having the fate of Porteous before his eyes as an example of the severe construction put by a jury on the proceedings of military men acting on their own responsibility, declined to encounter the risk to which the Provost's measures invited him.

More than one messenger was dispatched by different ways to the Castle, to require the commanding officer to march down his troops, to fire a few cannon-shot, or even to throw a shell among the mob, for the purpose of clearing the streets. But so strict and watchful were the various patroles whom the rioters had established in different parts of the street, that none of the emissaries of the magistrates could reach the gate of the Castle. They were, however, turned back without either injury or insult, and with nothing more of menace than was necessary to deter them from again attempting to carry their errand.

The same vigilance was used to prevent every body of the higher, and those which, in this case, might be deemed the more suspicious orders of society, from appearing in the street, and observing the movements, or distinguishing the persons, of the rioters. Every person in the garb of a gentleman was stopped by small parties of two or three of the mob, who partly exhorted, partly required of them, that they should return to the place from whence they came. Many a quadrille table was spoiled that memorable evening; for the sedan chairs of ladies, and even of the highest rank, were interrupted in their passage from one point to another, in despite of the laced footmen and the blazing flambeaux. This was uniformly done with a deference and attention to the feelings of the ladies, which could hardly have been expected from the videttes of a mob so desperate. Those who stopped the chair usually made the excuse, that there was much disturbance on the street, and that it was absolutely necessary for the lady's safety that the chair should turn back. They offered themselves to escort the chairs which they had thus interrupted in their progress, from the apprehension, probably, that some of those who had casually united themselves to the riot might disgrace their systematic and determined plan of vengeance, by those acts of general insult and licence which are common on similar occasions.

Persons are yet living who remember to have heard from the mouths of ladies thus interrupted on their journey in the manner we have described, that they were escorted to their lodgings by the young men who stopped them, and even handed out of their chairs, with a polite attention far beyond what was consistent with their dress, which was apparently that of journeymen mechanics. It seemed as if the conspirators, like those who assassinated the Cardinal Beatoun in former days, had entertained the opinion, that the work about which they went was a judgment of Heaven, which, though unsanctioned by the usual authorities, ought to be proceeded in with order and gravity.

While their outposts continued thus vigilant, and suffered themselves neither from fear nor curiosity to neglect the part of the duty assigned to them, and while the main guards to the east and west secured them against interruption, a select body of the rioters thundered at the door of the jail, and demanded instant admission. No one answered, for the outer keeper had prudently made his escape with the keys at the commencement of the riot, and was nowhere to be found. The door was instantly assailed with sledge-hammers, iron-crows, and the coulters of ploughs, ready provided for the purpose, with which they prized, heaved, and battered for some time with little effect, the door being of double oak planks, clenched both end-long and athwart with iron, studded besides with broad-headed nails, and so hung and secured as to offer no means of forcing by any degree of violence, without the expenditure of much time. The rioters, however, were determined to force admittance. Gang after gang relieved each other at the exercise, for, of course, only a few could work at a time; but gang after gang retired, exhausted with their violent exertions, without making much progress at forcing the prison-door. Butler had been led up near to this the principal scene of action; so near, indeed, that he was almost deafened by the unceasing clang of the heavy forehammers against the iron-bound portals of the prison. He began to entertain hopes, as the task seemed protracted, that the populace might give it over in despair, or that some rescue might arrive to disperse them. There was a moment at which the latter seemed probable.

The magistrates, having assembled their officers, and some of the citizens who were willing to hazard themselves for the public tranquillity, now sallied forth from the tavern where they held their sitting, and approached the point of danger. Their officers went before them with links and torches, with a herald to read the riot-act, if necessary. They easily drove before them the outposts and videttes of the rioters; but when they approached the line of guards which the mob, or rather, we should say, the conspirators, had drawn across the street in the front of the Luckenbooths, they were received with an unintermitted volley of stones, and menaced, on their nearer approach, with the pikes, bayonets, and Lochaber-axes, of which the populace had possessed themselves. One of their ordinary officers, a strong resolute fellow, went forwards, seized a rioter, and took from him a musket; but, being unsupported, he was instantly thrown on his back in the street, and disarmed in his turn. The officer was too happy to be permitted to rise and run away without receiving any farther injury; which afforded another remarkable instance of the mode in which these men had united a sort of moderation towards all others, with the most inflexible inveteracy against the object of their resentment. The magistrates, after vain attempts to make themselves heard and obeyed, possessing no means of enforcing their authority, were constrained to abandon the field to the rioters, and retreat in all speed from the showers of missiles which whistled around their ears.

The passive resistance of the tolbooth door promised to do more to baffle the purpose of the mob than the active interference of the magistrates. The heavy sledge-hammers continued to din against it without intermission, and with a noise which, echoed from the lofty buildings around the spot, seemed enough to have alarmed the garrison in the Castle. It was circulated among the rioters, that the troops would march down to disperse them, unless they could execute their purpose without loss of time; or that, even without quitting the fortress, the garrison might attain the same end by throwing a bomb or two upon the street.

Urged by such motives for apprehension, gang after gang eagerly relieved each other at the labour of assailing the tolbooth door. Yet such was its strength, that it still defied their efforts. At length, a voice was heard to pronounce the words, "Try it with fire." The rioters, with an unanimous shout, called for combustibles, and as all their wishes seemed to be instantly supplied, they were soon in possession of two or three empty tar-barrels. A huge red glaring bonfire soon arose against the door of the prison, sending up a tall column of smoke and flame against its antique turrets and strongly grated windows, and illuminating the ferocious faces and wild gestures of the rioters who surrounded the place, as well as the pale and anxious groupes of those who, from windows in the vicinage, watched the progress of this alarming scene. The mob fed the flames with whatever they could find fit for the purpose. They roared and crackled among the heaps of nourishment piled on the fire, and a terrible shout soon announced that the door had kindled, and was in the act of being destroyed. The fire was suffered to decay, but, long ere it was quite extinguished, the most forward of the rioters rushed, in their impatience, one after another, over its yet smouldering remains. Thick showers of sparkles rose high in the air, as man after man bounded over the glowing embers and disturbed them in their passage. It was now obvious to Butler, and all others who were present, that the rioters would be instantly in possession of their victim, and have it in their power to work their pleasure upon him, whatever that might be.

Chapter Seven

The evil you teach us, we will execute; and it shall go
hard but we will better the instruction.
Merchant of Venice

THE UNHAPPY OBJECT of this remarkable disturbance had been that day delivered from the apprehension of a public execution, and his joy was the greater, as he had some reason to question whether government would have run the risk of unpopularity by interfering in his favour, after he had been legally convicted by the verdict of a jury, of a crime so very obnoxious. Relieved from this doubtful state of mind, his heart was merry within him, and he thought, in the emphatic words of Scripture on a similar occasion, that surely the bitterness of death was past. Some of his friends, however, who had watched the manner and behaviour of the crowd when they were made acquainted with the reprieve, were of a different opinion. They augured, from the unusual sternness and silence with which they bore their disappoint-ment, that the populace nourished some scheme of sudden and desperate vengeance, and they advised Porteous to lose no time in petitioning the proper authorities, that he might be conveyed to the Castle under a sufficient guard, to remain there in security until his ultimate fate should be determined. Habituated, however, by his office, to despise and overawe the rabble of the city, Porteous could not suspect them of an attempt so audacious as to storm a strong and defensible prison; and, despising the advice by which he might have been saved, he spent the afternoon of this eventful day in giving an entertainment to some friends who visited him in jail, several of whom, by the indulgence of the Captain of the Tolbooth, with whom he had an old intimacy, arising from their official connection, were even permitted to remain to supper with him, though contrary to the rules of the jail.

It was, therefore, in the hour of unalloyed mirth, when this unfortu-nate wretch was "full of bread," hot with wine, and high in mistimed and ill-grounded confidence, and alas! with all his sins full blown, when the first distant shouts of the rioters mingled with the song of merriment and intemperance. The hurried call of the jailor to the guests, requiring them instantly to depart, and his yet more hasty intimation that a dreadful and determined mob had possessed themselves of the city gates and guard-house, were the first explanation of these fearful clamours.

Porteous might, however, have eluded the fury from which the force of authority could not protect him, had he thought of slipping on some disguise, and leaving the prison along with his guests. It is probable that the jailor might have connived at his escape, or even that in the hurry of this alarming contingence he might not have observed it. But Porteous and his friends alike wanted presence of mind to suggest or execute such a plan of escape. The latter hastily fled from a place where their own safety seemed compromised, and the former, in a state resembling stupefaction, awaited in his apartment the termination of the enterprize of the rioters. The cessation of the clang of the instruments with which they had at first attempted to force the door, gave him momentary relief. The flattering hopes, that the military had marched into the city, either from the Castle or from the suburbs, and that the rioters were intimidated and dispersing, were soon destroyed by the broad and glaring light of the flames, which, illuminating through the grated window every corner of his apartment, plainly showed that the mob, determined on their fatal purpose, had adopted a means of forcing entrance equally desperate and certain.

The sudden glare of light suggested to the stupified and astonished object of popular hatred the possibility of concealment or escape. To rush to the chimney, to ascend it at the risk of suffocation, was the only means which seems to have occurred to him; but his progress was speedily stopped by one of those iron gratings, which are, for the sake of security, usually placed across the vents of buildings designed for imprisonment. The bars, however, which impeded his farther progress, served to support him in the situation which he had gained, and he seized them with the tenacious grasp of one who esteemed himself clinging to his last hope of existence. The lurid light, which had filled the apartment, lowered and died away; the sound of shouts was heard within the walls, and on the narrow and winding stair, which, cased within one of the turrets, gave access to the upper apartments of the prison. The huzza of the rioters was answered by a shout wild and desperate as their own, the cry, namely, of the imprisoned felons, who, expecting to be liberated in the general confusion, welcomed the mob as their deliverers. By some of these the apartment of Porteous was pointed out to his enemies. The obstacle of the lock and bolts was soon overcome, and from his hiding-place the unfortunate man heard his enemies search every corner of the apartment, with oaths and maledictions which would but shock the reader if we recorded them, but which served to prove, could it have admitted of doubt, the settled purpose of soul with which they sought his destruction.

A place of concealment so obvious to suspicion and scrutiny as that which Porteous had chosen, could not long screen him from detection. He was dragged from his lurking place, with a violence which seemed to argue an intention to put him to death on the spot. More than one weapon was directed towards him, when one of the rioters, the same whose female disguise had been particularly noticed by Butler, interfered in an authoritative tone. "Are ye mad?" he said, "or would ye execute an act of justice as if it were a crime and a cruelty?—this sacrifice will lose half its savour if we do not offer it at the very horns of the altar. We will have him die where a murderer should die, on the common gibbet—we will have him die where he spilled the blood of so many innocents!"

A loud shout of applause followed the proposal, and the cry, "To the gallows with the murderer!—To the Grassmarket with him!" echoed on all hands.

"Let no man hurt him," continued the speaker; "let him make his peace with God, if he can; we do not kill both his soul and body."

"What time did he gi'e better folk for preparing their account?" answered several voices. "Let us mete to him with the same measure he gi'ed to them."

But the opinion of the spokesman better suited the temper of those he addressed, a temper rather stubborn than impetuous, and desirous of imposing upon their cruel and revengeful action a shew of justice and moderation.

For an instant this man quitted the prisoner, whom he consigned to a selected guard, with instructions to permit him to give his money and property to whomsoever he pleased. A person confined in the jail for debt received this last deposit from the trembling hand of the victim of popular fury, who was at the same time permitted to make some other brief arrangements to meet his approaching fate. The felons, and all others who wished to leave the jail, were now at full liberty to do so; not that their liberation made any part of the settled purpose of the rioters, but it followed as almost a necessary consequence of their forcing the jail doors. With wild cries of jubilee they joined the mob, or disappeared among the narrow lanes to seek out the concealed receptacles of vice and infamy, where they were accustomed to lurk and conceal themselves from justice. Two persons, a man about fifty years old, and a girl about eighteen, were all who continued within the fatal walls, excepting two or three debtors, who probably saw no advantage in attempting their escape. The persons we have mentioned remained in the strong-room of the prison, now deserted by all others. One of their late companions in misfortune called out to the man to make his escape, in the tone of an acquaintance. "Rin for it, Ratcliffe—the road's clear."

"It may be sae, Willie," answered Ratcliffe, composedly, "but I have ta'en a fancy to leave aff trade, and set up for an honest man."

"Stay then, and be hanged for a donnard auld deevil," said the other, and ran down the prison-stair.

The person whom we have distinguished as one of the most active rioters, was about the same time at the ear of the young woman. "Flee, Effie, flee," was all he had time to whisper. She turned towards him an eye of mingled fear, affection, and upbraiding, all contending with a sort of stupified surprise. He again repeated, "Flee, Effie, flee, for the sake of a' that's gude and dear to ye."—Again she gazed on him, but was unable to answer—A loud noise was now heard, and the name of Madge Wildfire was repeatedly called from the bottom of the staircase—"I am coming,—I am coming," said the person who answered to that appellative; and then reiterating hastily, "For God's sake—for your ain sake—for my sake, flee, or they'll take your life!" he left the strong-room.

The girl gazed after him for a moment, and after faintly muttering, "Better tyne life, since tint is gude fame," she sunk her head upon her hand, and remained, seemingly, unconscious as a statue of the noise and tumult which passed around her.

That tumult was now transferred from the inside to the outside of the tolbooth. The mob had brought their destined victim forth, and were about to conduct him to the common place of execution, which they had fixed as the scene of his death. The leader, whom they distinguished by the name of Madge Wildfire, had been summoned to assist at the procession by the impatient shouts of his confederates.

"I will ensure you five hundred pounds," said the unhappy man, grasping Wildfire's hand—"five hundred pounds for to save my life."

The other answered in the same undertone, and returning his grasp with one equally convulsive, "Five hundred-weight of coined gold should not save you—Remember Wilson."

A deep pause of a minute ensued, when Wildfire added, in a more composed tone, "Make your peace with Heaven—Where is the clergyman?"

Butler, who, in great terror and anxiety, had been detained within a few yards of the tolbooth door, to wait the event of the search after Porteous, was now brought forward, and commanded to walk by the prisoner's side, and to prepare him for immediate death. His answer was a supplication that the rioters would consider what they did. "You are neither judges nor jury," said he. "You cannot have, by the laws of God or man, power to take away the life of a human creature, however deserving he may be of death. If it is murder even in a lawful magistrate to execute an offender otherwise than in the place, time, and manner which his sentence prescribes, what must it be in you, who have no warrant for your interference but your own wills? In the name of Him who is all Mercy! shew mercy to this unhappy man, and do not dip your hands in his blood, nor rush into the very crime which you are desirous of avenging."

"Cut your sermon short—you are not in your pulpit," answered one of the rioters.

"If we hear more of your clavers," said another, "we are like to hang you up beside him."

"Peace—hush!" said Wildfire. "Do the good man no skaith—he discharges his conscience, and I like him the better."

He then addressed Butler. "Now, sir, we have patiently heard you, and we just wish you to understand, in the way of answer, that you may as well argue to the ashler-wark and iron-staunchels of the tolbooth as think to change our purpose. Blood must have Blood. We have sworn to each other by the deepest oaths were ever pledged, that Porteous shall die the death he deserves sae richly; therefore, speak no more to us, but prepare him for death as weel as the briefness of his change will permit."

They had suffered the unfortunate Porteous to put on his night-gown and slippers, as he had thrown off his coat and shoes, in order to facilitate his attempted escape up the chimney. In this garb he was now mounted on the hands of two of the rioters, clasped together, so as to form what is called in Scotland, "the king's cushion." Butler was placed close to his side, and repeatedly urged to perform a duty always the most painful which can be imposed on a clergyman deserving of the name, and now rendered more so by the peculiar and horrid circumstances of the criminal's case. Porteous at first uttered some supplications for mercy, but when he found there was no chance that these would be attended to, his military education, and the natural stubbornness of his disposition, combined to support his spirits.

"Are you prepared for this dreadful end?" said Butler, in a faultering voice. "O turn to Him, in whose eyes time and space have no existence, and to whom a few minutes are as a life-time, and a life-time as a minute."

"I believe I know what you would say," said Porteous, sullenly. "I was bred a soldier; if they will murder me without time, let my sins as well as my blood lie at their door."

"Who was it," said the stern voice of Wildfire, "that said to Wilson at this very spot, when he could not pray, owing to the galling agony of his fetters, that his pains would soon be over?—I say to you to take your own tale home; and if you cannot profit by the good man's lessons, blame not them that are still more merciful to you than you to others."

The procession now moved forward with a slow and determined pace. It was enlightened by many blazing links and torches; for the actors of this work were so far from affecting any secrecy on the occasion, that they seemed even to court observation. Their principal leaders kept close to the person of the prisoner, whose pallid yet stubborn features were seen distinctly by the torch-light, as his person was raised considerably above the concourse which thronged around him. Those who bore swords, muskets, and battle-axes, marched on each side, as if forming a regular guard to the procession. The windows, as they went along, were filled with the inhabitants, whose slumbers had been broken by this unusual disturbance. Some of the spectators muttered accents of encouragement, but in general they were so much appalled by a sight so strange and audacious, that they looked on with a sort of stupified astonishment. No one offered, by act or word, the slightest interruption.

The rioters, on their part, continued to act with the same air of deliberate confidence and security which had marked all their proceedings. When the object of their resentment dropped one of his slippers, they stopped, sought for it, and replaced it upon his foot with great deliberation. As they descended the Bow towards the fatal spot where they designed to complete their purpose, it was suggested that there should be a rope kept in readiness. For this purpose the booth of a man who dealt in cordage was forced open, a coil of rope fit for their purpose was selected to serve as a halter, and the dealer next morning found that a guinea had been left on his counter in exchange; so anxious were the perpetrators of this daring action to shew that they meditated not the slightest wrong or infraction of law, excepting so far as Porteous was himself concerned.

Leading, or carrying along with them, in this determined and regular manner, the object of their vengeance, they at length reached the place of common execution, the scene of his crime, and destined spot of his sufferings. Several of the rioters (if they should not rather be described as conspirators) endeavoured to remove the stone which filled up the socket in which the end of the fatal tree was sunk when it was erected for its fatal purpose; others sought for the means of constructing a temporary gibbet, the place in which the gallows itself was deposited being reported too secure to be forced, without much loss of time. Butler endeavoured to avail himself of the delay afforded by these circumstances, to turn the people from their desperate design. "For God's sake," he exclaimed, "remember it is the image of your Creator which you are about to deface in the person of this unfortunate man! Wretched as he is, and wicked as he may be, he has a share in every promise of Scripture, and you cannot destroy him in impenitence without blotting his name from the Book of Life—Do not destroy soul and body—give him time for preparation."

"What time had they," returned a stern voice, "whom he murdered on this very spot?—The laws both of God and man call for his death."

"But what, my friends," insisted Butler, with a generous disregard to his own safety—"what hath constituted you his judges?"

"We are not his judges," replied the same person; "he has been already judged and condemned by lawful authority. We are those whom Heaven, and our righteous anger, have stirred up to execute judgment, when a corrupt government would have protected a murderer."

"I am none," said the unfortunate Porteous; "that which you charge upon me fell out in self-defence, in the lawful exercise of my duty."

"Away with him—away with him!" was the general cry. "Why do you trifle away time in making a gallows?—that dyester's pole is good enough for the homicide."

The unhappy man was forced to his fate with remorseless rapidity. Butler, separated from him by the press, escaped the last horrors of his struggles. Unnoticed by those who had hitherto detained him as a sort of prisoner, he fled from the fatal spot, without much caring in what direction his course lay. A loud shout proclaimed the stern delight with which the agents of this deed regarded its completion. Butler then, at the opening into the low street called the Cowgate, cast back a terrified glance, and, by the red and dusky light of the torches, he could discern a figure wavering and struggling as it hung suspended above the heads of the multitude. The sight was of a nature to double his horror, and to add wings to his flight. The street down which he ran opens to one of the eastern ports or gates of the city. Butler did not stop till he reached it, but found it still shut. He waited nearly an hour, walking up and down in inexpressible perturbation of mind. At length he ventured to call out, and rouse the attention of the terrified keepers of the gate, who now found themselves at liberty to resume their office without interruption. Butler requested them to open the gate. They hesitated. He told them his name and occupation.

"He is a preacher," said one; "I have heard him preach in Haddo's-hole."

"A fine preaching has he been at the night," said another; "but maybe least said is sunest mended."

Opening then the wicket in one of the leaves of the main-gate, the keepers suffered Butler to depart, who hastened to carry his horror and fear from beyond the walls of Edinburgh. His first purpose was, instantly to take the road homeward; but other fears and cares, connected with the news he had learned in that remarkable day, induced him to linger in the neighbourhood of Edinburgh until daybreak. More than one groupe of persons passed him as he was whiling away the hours of darkness that yet remained, whom, from the stifled tones of their discourse, the unwonted hour at which they travelled, and the hasty pace at which they walked, he conjectured to have been engaged in the late fatal transaction.

Certain it was, that the sudden and total dispersion of the rioters, when their vindictive purpose was accomplished, seemed not the least remarkable feature of this singular affair. In general, whatever may be the impelling motive by which a mob is at first raised, the attainment of their object has usually been only found to lead the way to farther excesses. But not so in the present case. They seemed completely satiated with the vengeance they had prosecuted with such staunch and sagacious activity. When they were fully satisfied that life had abandoned their victim, they dispersed in every direction, throwing down the weapons which they had only assumed to enable them to carry through their purpose. At daybreak there remained not the least token of the events of the night, excepting the corpse of Porteous, which remained suspended in the place where he had suffered, and the arms of various kinds which the rioters had taken from the city guard-house, and which remained scattered about the streets as they had thrown them from their hands, when the purpose for which they had seized them was accomplished.

The ordinary magistrates of the city resumed their power, not without trembling at the late experience of the fragility of its tenure. To march troops into the city, and commence a severe enquiry into the transactions of the preceding night, were the first marks of returning energy which they displayed. But these events had been conducted on so secure and well-calculated a plan of safety and secrecy, that there was little or nothing learned to throw light upon the authors or principal actors in a scheme so audacious. An express was dispatched to London with the tidings, where they excited great indignation and surprise in the council of regency, and particularly in the bosom of Queen Caroline, who considered her own authority as exposed to contempt by the success of this singular conspiracy. Nothing was spoke of for some time save the measure of vengeance which should be taken, not only on the actors of this tragedy, so soon as they should be discovered, but upon the magistrates who had suffered it to take place, and upon the city which had been the scene where it was exhibited. Upon this occasion, it is still recorded in popular tradition, that her Majesty, in the height of her displeasure, told the celebrated John, Duke of Argyle, that, sooner than submit to such an insult, she would make Scotland a hunting-field. "In that case, madam," answered that high-spirited nobleman, with a profound bow, "I will take leave of your Majesty, and go down to my own country to get my hounds ready."

The import of the reply had more than met the ear; and as most of the Scottish nobility and gentry seemed actuated by the same national spirit, the royal displeasure was necessarily checked in mid-volley, and milder courses were recommended and adopted, to some of which we may hereafter have occasion to advert.

Chapter Eight

Arthur's-Seat shall be my bed,
 The sheets shall ne'er be press'd by me;
Saint Anton's wall shall be my drink,
 Sin' my true-love's forsaken me.
Old Song

IF I WERE TO CHUSE a spot from which the rising or setting sun could be seen to the greatest possible advantage, it would be that wild walk winding betwixt the foot of the high belt of semi-circular rocks, called Salusbury Crags, and the steep descent which slopes down into the glen on the south-eastern side of the city of Edinburgh. The prospect, in its general outline, commands a close-built high-piled city, stretching itself out beneath in a form, which, to a romantic imagination, may be supposed to represent that of a dragon; now, a noble arm of the sea, with its rocks, islets, distant shores, and boundary of mountains; and now a fair and fertile champaign country, varied with hill, dale, and rock, and skirted by the varied and picturesque ridge of the Pentland Mountains. But as the path gently circles around the base of the cliffs, the prospect, composed as it is of these enchanting and sublime subjects, changes at every step, and presents them blended with or divided from each other, in every possible variety which can gratify the eye and the imagination. When a piece of scenery so beautiful, yet so varied, so exciting by its intricacy, and yet so sublime, is lighted up by the tints of morning or of evening, and all that variety of shadowy depth, exchanged with brilliancy, which gives character even to the tamest of landscapes, the effect approaches nearer to enchantment. This path used to be my favourite evening and morning resort, when engaged with a favourite author, or new subject of study. It is, I am informed, now become totally impassable; a circumstance which, if true, reflects little credit on the taste of the Good Town or its leaders.

It was from this fascinating path,—the scene to me of so much delicious musing, when life was young and promised to be happy, that I have been unable to pass it over without an episodical description—it was, I say, from this romantic path that Butler saw the morning arise the day after the murder of Porteous. It was possible for him with ease to have found a much shorter road to the house to which he was directing his course, and, in fact, that which he chose was extremely circuitous. But to compose his own spirits, as well as to while away the time, until a proper hour for visiting the family without surprise or disturbance, he was induced to extend his circuit by the foot of the rocks, and to linger upon his way until the morning should be considerably advanced. While, now standing with his arms across, and waiting the slow progress of the sun above the horizon, now sitting upon one of the numerous fragments which storms had detached from the rocks above him, he is meditating, now upon the horrible catastrophe which he had witnessed, now upon the melancholy, and to him most interesting, news which he had learned at Saddletree's, we will give the reader to understand who Butler was, and by what his fate was connected with that of Effie Deans, the unfortunate handmaiden of the careful Mrs Saddletree.

Reuben Butler was of English extraction, though born in Scotland. His grandfather was a trooper in Monk's army, and one of that party of dismounted dragoons which formed the forlorn-hope at the storm of Dundee in 1651. Stephen Butler (called, from his talents in reading and expounding, Scripture Stephen and Bible Butler,) was a staunch independent, and received in its fullest comprehension the promise that the saints should inherit the earth. As hard knocks were what had chiefly fallen to his share hitherto in the division of this common property, he lost not the opportunity which the storm and plunder of a commercial place afforded him, to appropriate as large a share of the better things of this world as he could possibly compass. It would seem that he had succeeded indifferently well, for his exterior circumstances appear, in consequence of this event, to have been much mended.

The troop to which he belonged was quartered at the village of Dalkeith, as forming the body guard of Monk, who, in the capacity of general for the Commonwealth, resided in the neighbouring castle. When, on the eve of the Restoration, the general commenced his march from Scotland, a measure pregnant with such important consequences, he new-modelled his troops, and most especially those immediately about his person, in order that they might consist entirely of individuals devoted to himself. Upon this occasion Scripture Stephen was weighed in the balance, and found wanting. It was supposed he felt no call to any expedition which might endanger the reign of the military sainthood, and that he did not consider himself as free in conscience to join with any party which might ultimately acknowledge the interest of Charles Stuart, the son of the "last man," as Charles I. was familiarly and unreverently termed by them in their common discourse, as well as in their more elaborate predications and harangues. As the time did not admit of cashiering such dissidents, Stephen Butler was only advised in a friendly way to give up his horse and accoutrements to one of Middleton's old troopers, who possessed an accommodating conscience of a military stamp, and which squared itself chiefly upon those of the colonel and pay-master. As this hint came recommended by a certain sum of arrears presently payable, Stephen had carnal wisdom enough to embrace the proposal, and with great indifference saw his old corps depart for Coldstream, on their route for the south, to establish the tottering government of England on a new basis.

The *zone* of the ex-trooper, to use Horace's phrase, was weighty enough to purchase a cottage and two or three fields (still known by the name of Beersheba,) within about a Scottish mile of Dalkeith; and there did Stephen establish himself with a youthful helpmate, chosen out of the said village, whose disposition to a comfortable settlement on this side of the grave reconciled her to the gruff manners, serious temper, and weather-beaten features of the martial enthusiast. Stephen did not long survive the falling on "evil days and evil tongues," of which Milton, in the same predicament, so mournfully complains. At his death his consort remained an early widow, with a male child of three years old, which, in the sobriety wherewith it demeaned itself, in the old-fashioned and even grim cast of its features, and in its sententious mode of expressing itself, would sufficiently have vindicated the honour of the widow of Beersheba, had any one thought proper to challenge the babe's descent from Bible Butler.

Butler's principles had not descended to his family, or extended themselves among his neighbours. The air of Scotland was alien to the growth of independence, however favourable to fanaticism under other colours. But, nevertheless, they were not forgotten; and a certain neighbouring laird, who piqued himself upon the loyalty of his principles "in the worst of times," though I never heard they exposed him to more peril than that of a broken head, or a night's lodging in the main guard, when wine and cavalierism predominated in his upper story, had found it a convenient thing to rake up all matter of accusation against the deceased Stephen. In this enumeration his religious principles made no small figure, as, indeed, they must have seemed of the most exaggerated enormity to one whose own were so small and so faintly traced, as to be well nigh imperceptible. In these circumstances, poor Widow Butler was supplied with her full proportion of fines for non-conformity, and all the other oppressions of the time, until Beersheba was fairly wrenched out of her hands, and became the property of the laird who had so wantonly, as it had hitherto appeared, persecuted this poor forlorn woman. When his purpose was fairly achieved, he shewed some remorse or moderation, or whatever the reader may please to term it, in permitting her to occupy her husband's cottage, and cultivate, on no very heavy terms, a croft of land adjacent. Her son, Benjamin, in the meanwhile, grew up to man's estate, and, moved by that impulse which makes men seek marriage, even when its end can only be the perpetuation of misery, he married and brought a wife, and, eventually, a son, Reuben, to share the poverty of Beersheba.

The Laird of Dumbiedikes had hitherto been moderate in his exactions, perhaps because he was ashamed to tax too highly the miserable means of support which remained to the Widow Butler. But when a stout active young fellow appeared as the labourer of the croft in question, Dumbiedikes began to think so broad a pair of shoulders might bear an additional burthen. He regulated, indeed, his management of his dependents (who fortunately were but few in number,) much upon the principle of the carters whom he observed loading their carts at a neighbouring coal hill, and who never failed to clap an additional brace of hundred-weights on their burthen, so soon as by any means they had compassed a new horse of somewhat superior strength to that which had broken down the day before. However reasonable this practice appeared to the Laird of Dumbiedikes, he ought to have observed, that it might be overdone, and then infer the destruction and loss both, of horse, cart, and loading. Even so it befell when the additional "prestations" came to be demanded of Benjamin Butler. A man of few words, and few ideas, but attached to Beersheba with a feeling like that which a vegetable entertains to the spot in which it chances to be planted, he neither remonstrated with the Laird, nor endeavoured to escape from him, but toiled night and day to accomplish the terms of his task-master, fell into a burning fever and died. His wife did not long survive him, and, as if it had been the fate of this family to be left orphans, our Reuben Butler was, about the year 1704–5, left in the same circumstances in which his father had been placed, and under the same guardianship, being that of his grandmother, the widow of Monk's old trooper.

The same prospect of misery hung over the head of another tenant of this hard-hearted lord of the soil. This was a tough true-blue presbyterian, called Deans, who, though most obnoxious to the Laird on account of principles in church and state, contrived to maintain his ground upon the estate by regular payment of mail duties, kain, arriage, carriage, dry multure, lock, gowpen, and knaveship, and all the various exactions now commuted for money, and summed up in the emphatic word RENT. But the years 1700 and 1701, long remembered in Scotland for dearth and general distress, subdued the stout heart of the agricultural whig. Citations by the ground-officer, decreets of the Baron Court, sequestrations, poindings of outsight and insight, flew about his ears as fast as ever the tory bullets whistled around those of the Covenanters at Pentland, Bothwell Brigg, or Airdsmoss. Struggle as he might, and he struggled gallantly, "douce David Deans" was routed horse and foot, and lay at the mercy of his grasping landlord just at the time that Benjamin Butler died. The fate of each family was anticipated, but they who prophesied their expulsion to beggary and ruin, were disappointed by an accidental circumstance.

On the very term-day when their ejection should have taken place, when all their neighbours were prepared to pity, and not one to assist them, the minister of the parish, as well as a doctor from Edinburgh, received a hasty summons to attend the Laird of Dumbiedikes. Both were surprised, for his contempt for both faculties had been pretty commonly his theme over an extra bottle, that is to say, at least once every day. The leech for the soul and he for the body alighted in the court of the little old manor-house at almost the same time, and when they had gazed a moment at each other with some surprise, both in the same breath expressed their conviction that Dumbiedikes must needs be very ill indeed, since he summoned them both to his presence at once. Ere the servant could usher them to his apartment the party was augmented by a man of law, Nichil Novit, writing himself procurator before the Sheriff-court, for in these days there were no solicitors. This latter personage was first summoned to the apartment of the Laird, where, after some short space, the soul-curer and the body-curer were invited to join him.

Dumbiedikes had been by this time transported into the best bed-room, used only upon occasions of death and marriage, and called, from the former of these occupations, the Dead-Room. There were in this apartment, besides the sick person himself and Mr Novit, the son and heir of the patient, a tall, gawky, silly-looking boy of fourteen or fifteen, and a house-keeper, a good buxom figure of a woman, betwixt forty and fifty, who had kept the keys and managed matters at Dumbiedikes since the lady's death. It was to these attendants that Dumbiedikes addressed himself pretty nearly in these words; temporal and spiritual matters, the care of his health and his affairs, being strangely jumbled in a head which was never one of the clearest.

"These are sair times wi' me, gentlemen and neibours! amaist as ill as at the aughty-nine, when I was rabbled by the collegeaners.—They mistook me muckle—they ca'd me a papist, but there was never a papist bit about me, minister.—Jock, ye'll take warning—it's a debt we maun a' pay, and there stands Nichil Novit that will tell ye I was never gude at paying debts in my life.—Master Novit, ye'll no forget to draw the annual rent that's due on the yerl's band—if I pay debt to other folk, I think they suld pay it to me—that's but equals aquals.—Jock, when ye hae naething else to do, ye may be aye sticking in a tree; it will be growing, Jock, when ye're sleeping. My father tauld me sae forty years syne, but I ne'er fand time to mind him—Jock, ne'er drink brandy in the morning, it files the stamach sair; gin ye take a morning's draught, let it be aqua mirabilis; Jenny there makes it weel.— Doctor, my breath is growing as scant as a broken-winded piper's, when he has played for twenty-four hours at a penny-wedding— Jenny, pit the cod aneath my head—but it's a' needless!—Mass John, could ye think o' rattling ower some bit short prayer—it wad do me gude maybe, and keep some queer thoughts out o' my head.—Say something, man."

"I cannot use a prayer like a rat-rhyme," answered the honest clergyman; "and if you wad have your soul redeemed like a prey from the fowler, Laird, you must needs shew me your state of mind."

"And shoudna ye ken that without my telling you?" answered the patient. "What have I been paying stipend and teind parsonage and vicarage for, ever sin' the aughty-nine, an' I canna get a spell of a prayer for't, the only time I ever asked for ane in my life?—Gang awa' wi' your whiggery, if that's a' ye can do; auld Curate Kiltstoup wad hae read half the Prayer-Book to me by this time—Awa w'ye!—Doctor, let's see if ye can do ony thing better for me."

The Doctor, who had obtained some information in the meanwhile from the house-keeper on the state of his complaints, assured him the medical art could not prolong his life many hours.

"Then damn Mass John and you baith!" cried the furious and intractable patient. "Did ye come here for naething but to tell me that ye canna help me at the pinch? Out wi' them, Jenny—out o' the house! and, Jock, my curse, and the curse of Cromwell go wi' ye, if ye gie them either fee or bountith, or sae muckle as a black pair o' cheverons."

The clergyman and doctor made a speedy retreat out of the apartment, while Dumbiedikes fell into one of those transports of violent and profane language, which had procured him the surname of Damn-me-dikes—"Bring me the brandy bottle, Jenny, ye b——," he cried, with a voice in which passion contended with pain. "I can die as I have lived, without fashing ony o' them. But there's ae thing," he said, sinking his voice—"there's ae fearful thing hings about my heart, and an anker of brandy winna wash it away—The Deans at Woodend! —I roupit them out in the dear years, and now they are to flitt they'll starve—and that Beersheba, and that auld trooper's wife and his oe, they'll starve—they'll starve!—Look out, Jock; what night is't?"

"Onding o' snaw, father," answered Jock, after having opened the window, and looked out with great composure.

"They'll perish in the drift," said the expiring sinner—"they'll perish wi' cauld!—but I'll be het aneugh, gin a' tales be true."

This last observation was made under breath, and in a tone which made the very attorney shudder. He tried his hand at ghostly advice, probably for the first time in his life, and recommended, as an opiate for the agonized conscience of the laird, reparation of the injuries he had done to these distressed families, which, he observed by the way, the civil law called *restitutio in integrum*. But Mammon was struggling with Remorse for retaining his place in a bosom he had so long possessed; and he partly succeeded, as an old tyrant proves often too strong for his insurgent rebels.

"I canna do't," he answered, with a voice of despair. "It would kill me to do't—how can ye bid me pay back siller, when ye ken how I want it? or dispone Beersheba, when it lies sae weel into my ain plaid-nuik? Nature made Dumbiedikes and Beersheba to be ae man's land—she did by——. Nichil, it wad kill me to part them."

"But ye maun die whether or no, Laird," said Mr Novit; "and maybe ye wad die easier—it's but trying. I'll scroll the disposition in nae time."

"Dinna speak o't, sir, or I'll fling the stoup at your head.—But, Jock, lad, ye see how the warld warstles wi' me on my death-bed—be kind to the puir creatures the Deanses and the Butlers—be kind to them, Jock —dinna let the warld get a grip o' ye, Jock—but keep the gear thegither! and whate'er ye do, dispone Beersheba at no rate. Let the creatures stay at a moderate mailing, and hae bite and soup; it will maybe be the better wi' your father whare he's gaun, lad."

After these contradictory instructions, the Laird felt his mind so much at ease that he drank three bumpers of brandy continuously, and "soughed awa," as Jenny expressed it, in an attempt to sing, "De'il stick the minister."

His death made a revolution in favour of the distressed families. John Dumbie, now Dumbiedikes, in his own right, seemed to be close and selfish enough; but wanted the grasping spirit and active mind of his father; and his guardian happened to agree with him in opinion, that his father's dying recommendation should be attended to. The tenants, therefore, were not actually turned out of doors among the snow wreaths, and were allowed wherewith to procure butter-milk and pease bannocks, which they eat under the full force of the original malediction. The cottage of Deans, called Woodend, was not very distant from that at Beersheba. Formerly there had been little intercourse between the families. Deans was a sturdy Scotchman, with all sort of prejudices against the southron, and the spawn of the southron. Moreover, Deans was, as we have said, a staunch presbyterian, of the most rigid and unbending adherence to what he conceived to be the only possible straight line, as he was wont to express himself, between right-hand heats and extremes, and left-hand defections; and, therefore, he held in high dread and horror all independents, and whomsoever he supposed allied to them.

But, notwithstanding these national prejudices and religious prepossessions, Deans and the Widow Butler were placed in such a situation latterly, as naturally created some intimacy between the families. They had shared a common danger and a mutual deliverance. They needed each other's assistance, like a company, who, crossing a mountain stream, are compelled to cling close together, lest the current should be too powerful for any who are not thus supported.

On nearer acquaintance, too, Deans abated some of his prejudices. He found Mrs Butler, though not thoroughly grounded in the extent and bearing of the real testimony against the defections of the times, had no opinions in favour of the independent party; neither was she an Englishwoman. Therefore, it was to be hoped, that, though she was the widow of an enthusiastic corporal of Cromwell's dragoons, it was possible her grandson might be neither schismatic nor anti-national, two qualities concerning which Goodman Deans had as wholesome a terror as about papists and malignants. Above all, (for Douce Davie Deans had his weak side,) he perceived that Widow Butler looked up to him with reverence, listened to his advice, and compounded for an occasional fling at the doctrines of her deceased husband, to which, as we have seen, she was by no means warmly attached, in consideration of the valuable counsels which the presbyterian afforded her for the management of her little farm. These usually concluded with, "they may do otherwise in Ingland, neighbour Butler, for aught I ken;" or, "it may be different in foreign parts;" or, "they wha think differently on the great foundation of our covenanted reformation, overturning and mishguggling the government and discipline of the Kirk, and breaking down the carved work of our Zion, might be for sawing the craft wi' aits; but I say pease, pease." And as his advice was shrewd and sensible, though conceitedly given, it was received with gratitude, and followed with respect.

The intercourse which took place betwixt the families at Beersheba and Woodend became strict and intimate, at a very early period, betwixt Reuben Butler, with whom the reader is already in some degree acquainted, and Jeanie Deans, the only child of Douce Davie Deans by his first wife, "that singular Christian woman," as he was wont to express himself, "whose name was savoury to all that knew her for a desirable professor, Christian Menzies in Hochmagirdle." The manner of which intimacy, and the consequences thereof, we now proceed to relate.

Chapter Nine

Reuben and Rachel, though as fond as doves,
Were yet discreet and cautious in their loves,
Nor would attend to Cupid's wild commands,
Till cool reflection bade them join their hands.
When both were poor, they thought it argued ill
Of hasty love to make them poorer still.
CRABBE's *Parish Register*

WHILE WIDOW BUTLER and Widower Deans struggled with poverty, and the hard and sterile soil of those "parts and portions" of the lands of Dumbiedikes which it was their lot to occupy, it became gradually apparent that Deans was to gain the strife, and his ally in the conflict was to lose it. The former was a man, and not much past the prime of life—Mrs Butler a woman, and declined into the vale of years. This, indeed, ought in time to have been balanced by the circumstance, that Reuben was growing up to assist his grandmother's labours, and that Jeanie Deans, as a girl, could be only supposed to add to her father's burthens. But Douce Davie Deans knew better things, and so schooled and trained the young minion, as he called her, that from the time she could walk upwards, she was daily employed in some task or other suitable to her age and capacity, a circumstance which, added to her father's daily instructions and lectures, tended to give her mind, even when a child, a grave, serious, firm, and reflecting cast. An uncommonly strong and healthy temperament, free from all nervous affection and every other irregularity, which, attacking the body in its more noble functions, so often influences the mind, tended greatly to establish this firmness, simplicity, and decision of character.

On the other hand, Reuben was weak in constitution, and, though not timid in temper, might be safely pronounced anxious, doubtful, and apprehensive. He partook of the temperament of his mother, who had died of a consumption in early age. He was a pale, thin, feeble, sickly boy, and somewhat lame, from an accident in early youth. He was, besides, the child of a doting grandmother, whose over-solicitous attention to him soon taught him a sort of diffidence in himself, with a disposition to over-rate his own importance, which is one of the very worst consequences that children deduce from over-indulgence.

Still, however, the two children clung to each other's society, not more from habit than from taste. They herded together the handful of sheep, with the two or three cows, which their parents turned out rather to seek food than actually to feed upon the uninclosed common of Dumbiedikes. It was there that the two urchins might be seen seated beneath a blooming bush of whin, their little round faces laid close together under the shadow of the same plaid drawn over both their heads, while the landscape around was embrowned by an overshadowing cloud, big with the shower which had driven the children to shelter. Upon other occasions they went together to school, the boy receiving that encouragement and example from his companion, in crossing the little brooks which intersected their path, and encountering cattle, dogs, and other perils, upon their journey, which the male sex in such cases usually consider it as their prerogative to extend to the weaker. But when, seated on the benches of the school-house, they began to con their lesson together, Reuben, who was as much superior to Jeanie Deans in acuteness of intellect, as inferior to her in firmness of constitution, and that insensibility to fatigue and danger which depends on the conformation of the nerves, was able fully to requite the kindness and countenance with which, in other circumstances, she used to regard him. He was decidedly the best scholar at the little parish school, and so gentle was his temper and disposition, that he was rather admired than envied by the little mob who occupied the noisy mansion, although he was the declared favourite of the master. Several girls, in particular, (for in Scotland they are taught with the boys) longed to be kind to, and comfort the sickly lad, who was so much cleverer than his companions. The character of Reuben Butler was so calculated as to offer scope both for their sympathy and their admiration, the feelings, perhaps, through which the female sex (the more deserving part of them at least) is most easily attached.

But Reuben, naturally reserved and distant, improved none of these advantages; and only became more attached to Jeanie Deans, as the enthusiastic approbation of his master assured him of fair prospects in future life, and awakened his ambition. In the mean time, every advance that Reuben made in learning (and, considering his opportunities, they were uncommonly great) rendered him less capable of attending to the domestic duties of his grandmother's farm. While studying the *pons asinorum* in Euclid, he suffered every *cuddie* upon the common to trespass upon a large field of pease belonging to the Laird, and nothing but the active exertions of Jeanie Deans, with her little dog Dustiefoot, could have saved great loss and consequent punishment. Similar miscarriages marked his progress in his classical studies. He read Virgil's Georgics till he did not know bear from barley; and had nearly destroyed the crofts of Beersheba, while attempting to cultivate them according to the practice of Columella and Cato the Censor.

These blunders occasioned grief to his grand-dame, and disconcerted the good opinion which her neighbour, Davie Deans, had for some time entertained of Reuben.

"I see naething ye can make of that silly callant, neighbour Butler," said he to the old lady, "unless ye train him to the wark o' the ministry. And ne'er was there mair need of poorfu' preachers than e'en now in this cauld Gallio days, when men's hearts are hardened like the nether mill-stone, till they regard none of these things. It's evident this puir callant of your's will never be able to do an usefu' day's wark, unless it be as an embassador from our Master; and I will make it my business to procure a licence when he is fit for the same, trusting he will be a shaft cleanly polished, and meet to be used in the body of the kirk; and that he will not turn again, like the sow, to wallow in the mire of heretical extremes and defections, but shall have the wings of a dove, though he hath lain among the pots."

The poor widow gulped down the affront to her husband's principles, implied in this caution, and hastened to take Butler from the High-School, and encourage him in the pursuit of mathematics and divinity, the only physics and ethics that chanced to be in fashion at the time.

Jeanie Deans was now compelled to part from the companion of her labour, her study, and her pastime, and it was with more than childish feeling that both children regarded the separation. But they were young, and hope was high, and they separated like those who hope to meet again at a more auspicious hour.

While Reuben Butler was acquiring at the University of Saint Andrews the knowledge necessary for a clergyman, and macerating his body with the privations which were necessary in seeking food for his mind, his grand-dame became daily less able to struggle with her little farm, and was at length obliged to throw it up to the new Laird of Dumbiedikes. That great personage was no absolute Jew, and did not cheat her in making the bargain more than was tolerable. He even gave her permission to tenant the house in which she had lived with her husband, as long as it should be "tenantable," only he protested against paying for a farthing of repairs, any benevolence which he had being of the passive, but by no means of the active mood.

In the meanwhile, from superior shrewdness, skill, and other circumstances, some of them purely accidental, Davie Deans gained a footing in the world, the possession of some wealth, the reputation of more, and a growing disposition to preserve and increase his store; for which, when he thought upon it seriously, he was inclined to blame himself. From his knowledge in agriculture, as it was then practised, he became a sort of favourite with the Laird, who had no pleasure either in active sports or in society, and was wont to end his daily saunter by calling at the cottage of Woodend.

Being himself a man of slow ideas and confused utterance, he used to sit or stand for half an hour with an old laced hat of his father's upon his head, and an empty tobacco-pipe in his mouth, with his eyes following Jeanie Deans, or "the lassie," as he called her, through the course of her daily domestic labour, while her father, after exhausting the subject of bestial, of ploughs, and of harrows, often took an opportunity of going full sail into controversial subjects, to which discussions the dignity listened with much seeming patience, but without making any reply, or, indeed, as most people thought, without understanding a single word of what the orator was saying. Deans, indeed, denied this stoutly, as an insult at once to his own talents for expounding hidden truths, of which he was a little vain, and to the Laird's capacity of understanding them. He said, "Dumbiedikes was nane of these flashy gentles, wi' lace on their skirts and swords at their tails, that were rather for riding on horseback to hell than ganging barefooted to Heaven. He wasna like his father—nae profane company-keeper—nae swearer—nae drinker—nae frequenter of play-house, or music-house, or dancing-house—nae Sabbath-breaker—nae imposer of aiths, or bonds, or denyer of liberty to the flock.—He clave to the warld, and the warld's gear, a wee ower muckle, but than there was some breathing of a gale upon his spirit," &c. &c. All this honest Davie Deans said and believed.

It is not to be supposed, that, as a father and a man of sense and observation, the constant direction of the Laird's eyes towards Jeanie was altogether unnoticed. This circumstance, however, made a much greater impression upon another member of his family, a second help-mate, to wit, whom he had chosen to take to his bosom ten years after the death of the first. Some people were of opinion, that Douce Davie had been rather surprised into this step, for in general he was no friend to marriages or giving in marriage, and seemed rather to regard that state of society as a necessary evil,—a thing lawful, and to be tolerated in the imperfect state of our nature, but which clipped the wings with which we ought to soar upwards, and tethered the soul to its mansion of clay, and the creature-comforts of wife and bairns. His own practice, however, had in this material point varied from his principles, since, as we have seen, he twice knitted for himself this dangerous and ensnaring entanglement.

Rebecca, his spouse, had by no means the same horror of matrimony, and as she made marriages in imagination for every neighbour round, she failed not to indicate a match betwixt Dumbiedikes and her step-daughter Jeanie. The gudeman used regularly to frown and pshaw whenever this topic was touched upon, but usually ended by taking his bonnet and walking out of the house to conceal a certain gleam of satisfaction, which, at such a suggestion, involuntarily diffused itself over his austere features.

The more youthful part of my readers may naturally ask, whether Jeanie Deans was deserving of this mute attention of the Laird of Dumbiedikes; and the historian, with due regard to veracity, is compelled to answer, that her personal attractions were of no uncommon description. She was short, and rather too stoutly made for her size, had grey eyes, light-coloured hair, a round good-humoured face, much tanned with the sun, and her only peculiar charm was an air of inexpressible serenity, which a good conscience, kind feelings, contented temper, and the regular discharge of all her duties, spread over her features. There was nothing, it may be supposed, very appalling in the form or manners of this rustic heroine; yet, whether from sheepish bashfulness, or from want of decision and imperfect knowledge of his own mind on the subject, the Laird of Dumbiedikes, with his old laced hat and empty tobacco-pipe, came and enjoyed the beatific vision of Jeanie Deans day after day, week after week, year after year, without proposing to accomplish any of the prophesies of Rebecca, the step-mother.

This good lady began to grow doubly impatient on the subject, when, after having been some years married, she herself presented Douce Davie with another daughter, who was named Euphemia, by corruption, Effie. It was then that Rebecca began to turn impatient with the slow pace at which the Laird's wooing proceeded, judiciously arguing, that, as Lady Dumbiedikes would have but little occasion for tocher, the principal part of her gudeman's substance would naturally descend to the child by the second venture. Other step-dames have tried less laudable means for clearing the way to the succession of their own children; but Rebecca, to do her justice, only sought little Effie's advantage through the promotion, or which must generally have been accounted such, of her elder sister. She therefore tried every female art within the compass of her simple skill to bring the Laird to a point; but had the mortification to perceive that her efforts, like those of an unskilful angler, only scared the trout she meant to catch. Upon one occasion, in particular, when she joked with the Laird on the propriety of giving a mistress to the house of Dumbie-dikes, he was so effectually startled, that neither laced hat, tobacco-pipe, nor the intelligent proprietor of these moveables, visited Woodend for a fortnight. Rebecca was therefore compelled to leave the Laird to proceed at his own snail's pace, convinced, by experience, of the grave-digger's aphorism, that your dull ass will not mend his pace for beating.

Reuben, in the meantime, pursued his studies at the university, supplying his wants by teaching to younger lads the knowledge he himself acquired, and thus at once gaining the means of maintaining himself at the seat of learning, and fixing in his mind the elements of what he had already obtained. In this manner, as is usual among the poorer students of divinity at Scottish universities, he contrived, not only to maintain himself according to his simple wants, but even to send considerable assistance to his sole remaining parent, a sacred duty, of which the Scotch are seldom negligent. His progress in knowledge of a general kind, as well as in the studies proper to his profession, was very considerable, but less marked from the retired modesty of his disposition, which in no respect qualified him to set off his learning to the best advantage. And thus, had Butler been a man given to make complaints, he had his tale to tell, like others, of unjust preferences, bad luck, and hard usage.

He obtained his licence as a preacher of the gospel, with some compliments from the presbytery by whom it was bestowed; but this did not lead to any preferment, and he found it necessary to make the cottage at Beersheba his residence for some months, with no other income than was afforded by the precarious occupation of teaching in one or two neighbouring families. After having greeted his aged grandmother, his first visit was to Woodend, where he was received by Jeanie with warm cordiality, arising from recollections which had never been dismissed from her mind, by Rebecca with good-humoured hospitality, and by old Davie in a mode peculiar to himself.

Highly as Douce Deans honoured the clergy, it was not upon each individual of the cloth that he bestowed his approbation; and, a little jealous, perhaps, at seeing his youthful acquaintance erected into the dignity of a teacher and preacher, he instantly attacked him upon various points of controversy, in order to discover whether he might not have fallen into some of the snares, defections, and desertions of the time. Butler was not only a man of staunch presbyterian principles, but was also willing to avoid giving pain to his old friend by disputing upon points of little importance; and therefore he might have hoped to have come like refined gold out of the furnace of Davie's interrogatories. But the result on the mind of that strict investigator was not altogether so favourable as might have been hoped and anticipated. Old Judith Butler, who had hobbled that evening as far as Woodend, in order to enjoy the congratulations of her neighbours upon Reuben's return, and upon his high attainments, of which she was herself not a little proud, was somewhat mortified to find that her old friend Deans did not enter into the subject with the warmth she expected. At first, instead, he seemed rather silent than dissatisfied; and it was not till Judith had essayed the subject more than once that it led to the following dialogue.

"Aweel, neibor Deans, I thought ye wad hae been glad to see Reuben amang us again, poor fallow."

"I am glad, Mrs Butler," was the neighbour's concise answer.

"Since he has lost his grandfather and his father, (praised be Him that giveth and taketh!) I ken nae friend he has in the world that's been sae like a father to him as the sell o' ye, neibor Deans."

"God is the only father of the fatherless," said Deans, touching his bonnet and looking upwards. "Give honour where it is due, gudewife, and not to an unwordy instrument."

"Aweel, that's your way o' turning it, and nae doubt ye ken best; but I hae kenned ye, Davie, send a forpit o' meal to Beersheba when there was na a bow left in the meal-ark at Woodend; ay, and I hae kenned ye"——

"Gudewife," said Davie, interrupting her, "these are but idle tales to tell me; fit for naething but to puff up our inward man wi' our ain vain acts. I stude beside blessed Alexander Peden, when I heard him call the death and testimony of our happy martyrs but draps of blude and scarts of ink; and what suld I think of ony thing the like o' me could do?"

"Weel, neibor Deans, ye ken best; but I maun say that, I am sure you are glad to see my bairn again—the halt's clean gane now, unless he has to walk ower mony miles at a stretch; and he has a wee bit colour in his cheek, that glads my auld een to see it; and he has as decent a black-coat as the minister, and"——

"I am very heartily glad he is weel and thriving," said Mr Deans, with a gravity that seemed intended to cut short the subject; but a woman who is bent upon a point is not easily pushed aside from it.

"And," continued Mrs Butler, "he can wag his head in a pulpit now, neibor Deans, think but of that—my ain oe—and a'body maun sit still and listen to him, as if he were the Paip o' Rome."

"The what?—the who?—woman?" said Deans, with a sternness far beyond his usual gravity, as soon as these offensive words had struck upon the tympanum of his ear.

"Eh, guide us!" said the poor woman; "I had forgot what an ill will ye had aye at the Paip, and sae had my puir gudeman, Stephen Butler. Mony an afternoon he wad sit and tak up his testimony again the Paip, and again baptizing of bairns, and the like."

"Woman!" reiterated Deans, "either speak about what ye ken something o', or be silent. I say that independency is a foul heresy, and anabaptism a damnable and deceiving error, whilk suld be rooted out of the land wi' the fire o' the spiritual, and the sword o' the civil magistrate."

"Weel, weel, neibor, I'll no say that ye mayna be right. I am sure ye are right about the sawing and the mawing, the sheering and the leading, and what for suld ye no be right about kirk-wark too?—But concerning my oe, Reuben Butler"——

"Reuben Butler, gudewife, is a lad I wish heartily weel to, even as if he were mine ain son—but I doubt there will be outs and ins in the tract of his walk. I muckle fear his gifts will get the heels of his grace. He has ower muckle human wit and learning, and thinks as muckle about the form of the bicker as he does about the healsomeness of the food—he maun broider the marriage-garment with lace and passments, or it's no gude aneugh for him. And it's like he's something proud o' his human gifts and learning, whilk enable him to dress up his doctrine in that fine airy dress. But," added he, moved at seeing the old woman's uneasiness at his discourse, "affliction may gi'e him a jagg, and let the wind out o' him as out o' a cow that's eaten wet clover, and the lad may do weel, and be a burning and a shining light; and I trust it will be yours to see, and his to feel it, and that soon."

Widow Butler was obliged to retire, unable to make any thing more of her neighbour, whose discourse, though she did not comprehend it, filled her with undefined apprehensions on her grandson's account, and greatly depressed the joy with which she had welcomed him on his return. And it must not be concealed, in justice to Mr Deans's discernment, that Butler, in their conference, had made a greater display of his learning than the occasion called for, or than was like to be acceptable to the old gentleman, who, accustomed to consider himself as a person pre-eminently entitled to dictate upon theological subjects of controversy, felt rather humbled and mortified when learned authorities were placed in array against him. In fact, Butler had not escaped the tinge of pedantry which naturally flowed from his education, and was apt, on many occasions, to make parade of his knowledge, when there was no need of such vanity.

Jeanie Deans, however, found no fault with this display of learning, but, on the contrary, admired it; perhaps on the same score that her sex are said to admire men of courage, on account of their own deficiency in that qualification. The circumstances of their families threw the young people constantly together; their old intimacy was renewed, though upon a footing better adapted to their age; and it became at length understood betwixt them, that their union should be deferred no longer than until Butler should obtain some steady means of support, however humble. This, however, was not a matter speedily to be accomplished. Plan after plan was formed, and plan after plan failed. The good-humoured cheek of Jeanie lost the first flush of juvenile freshness; Reuben's brow assumed the gravity of manhood, yet the means of attaining a settlement seemed remote as ever. Fortunately for the lovers, their passion was of no ardent or enthusiastic cast, and a sense of duty on both sides induced them to bear, with patient fortitude, the protracted interval which divided them from each other.

In the meanwhile, time did not roll on without effecting his usual changes. The widow of Stephen Butler, so long the prop of the family of Beersheba, was gathered to her fathers; and Rebecca, the careful spouse of our friend Davie Deans, was also summoned from her plans of matrimony and domestic economy. The morning after her death, Reuben Butler went to offer his mite of consolation to his old friend and benefactor. He witnessed, on this occasion, a remarkable struggle betwixt the force of natural affection, and the religious stoicism, which the sufferer thought it was incumbent upon him to maintain under each earthly dispensation, whether of weal or woe.

On his arrival at the cottage, Jeanie, with her eyes overflowing with tears, pointed to the little orchard, "in which," she whispered with broken accents, "my poor father has been since his misfortune." Somewhat alarmed at this account, Butler entered the orchard, and advanced slowly towards his old friend, who, seated in a small rude arbour, appeared to be sunk in the extremity of his affliction. He lifted his eyes somewhat sternly as Butler approached, as if offended at the interruption; but as the young man hesitated whether he ought to retreat or advance, he arose, and came forwards to meet him, with a self-possessed, and even a dignified air.

"Young man, lay it not to heart, though the righteous perish and the merciful are removed, seeing, it may well be, that they are taken away from the evils to come. Woe to me, were I to shed a tear for the wife of my bosom, when I might weep rivers of water for this afflicted Church, cursed as it is with carnal seekers, and with the dead of heart."

"I am happy," said Butler, "that you can forget your private affliction in your regard for public duty."

"Forget? Reuben," said poor Deans, putting his handkerchief to his eyes, "she's not to be forgotten on this side of time; but He that gives the wound can send the ointment. I declare there have been times during this night when my meditation has been so rapt, that I knew not of my heavy loss. It has been with me as with the worthy John Semple, called Carspharn John, upon a like trial,—I have been this night on the banks of Ulai, plucking an apple here and there."

Notwithstanding the assumed fortitude of Deans, which he conceived to be the discharge of a great Christian duty, he had too good a heart not to suffer deeply under this heavy loss. Woodend became altogether distasteful to him; and as he had obtained both substance and experience by his management of that little farm, he resolved to employ them as a dairy farmer, or cow-feeder, as they are called in Scotland. The situation he chose for his new settlement was at a place called Saint Leonard's Crags, lying betwixt Edinburgh and the mountain called Arthur's Seat, and adjoining to the extensive sheep pasture still named the King's Park, from its having been formerly dedicated to the preservation of the royal game. Here he rented a small lonely house, then nearly half a mile distant from the nearest point of the city, but the site of which, with all the adjacent ground, is now occupied by the buildings which form the south-eastern suburb. An extensive pasture-ground adjoining, which Deans rented from the Keeper of the Royal Park, enabled him to feed his milk-cows; and the unceasing industry and activity of Jeanie, his eldest daughter, was exerted in making the most of their produce.

She had now less frequent opportunities of seeing Reuben, who had been obliged, after various disappointments, to accept the subordinate situation of assistant in a parochial school of some eminence, at three or four miles' distance from the city. Here he distinguished himself, and became acquainted with several respectable burgesses, who, for health, or other reasons, chose that their children should commence their education in this little village. His prospects were thus gradually brightening, and upon each visit which he paid at Saint Leonard's he had an opportunity of gliding a hint to this purpose into Jeanie's ear. These visits were necessarily rare, on account of the demands which the duties of the school made upon Butler's time. Nor did he dare to make them even altogether so frequent as these avocations would permit. Deans received him with civility indeed, and even with kindness; but Reuben, as is usual in such cases, imagined that he read his purpose in his eyes, and was afraid too premature an explanation on the subject would draw down his positive disapproval. Upon the whole, therefore, he judged it prudent to call at Saint Leonard's just so frequently as old acquaintance and neighbourhood seemed to authorise, and no oftener. There was another person who was more regular in his visits.

When Davie Deans intimated to the Laird of Dumbiedikes his purpose of "quitting wi' the land and house at Woodend," the Laird stared and said nothing. He made his usual visits at the usual hour without remark, until the day before the term, when, observing the bustle of moving furniture already commenced, the great east-country *awmrie* dragged out of its nook, and standing with its shoulder to the company, like an awkward booby about to leave a room, the Laird again stared mightily, and was heard to ejaculate, "Hegh, sirs!" Even after the day of departure was past and gone, the Laird of Dumbiedikes, at his usual hour, which was that at which David Deans was wont to "loose the pleugh," presented himself before the closed door of the cottage at Woodend, and seemed as much astonished at finding it shut against his approach as if it was not exactly what he had to expect. On this occasion he was heard to ejaculate, "Gude guide us!" which, by those who knew him, was considered as a very unusual mark of emotion. From that moment forward, Dumbiedikes became an altered man, and the regularity of his movements, hitherto so exemplary, was as totally disconcerted as those of a boy's watch when he has broken the main-spring. Like the index of the said watch, did Dumbiedikes spin round the whole bounds of his little property, which may be likened unto the dial of the time-piece, with unwonted velocity. There was not a cottage into which he did not enter, nor scarce a maiden on whom he did not stare. But so it was, that although there were better farm-houses on the land than Woodend, and certainly much prettier girls than Jeanie Deans, yet it did somehow befall that the blank in the Laird's time was not so pleasantly filled up as it had been. There was no seat accommodated him so well as the "bunker" at Woodend, and no face he loved so much to gaze on as Jeanie Deans's. So, after spinning round and round his little orbit, and then remaining stationary for a week, it seems to have occurred to him, that he was not pinned down to circulate on a pivot, like the hands of the watch, but possessed the power of shifting his central point, and extending his circle if he thought proper. To realize which power of change of place, he bought a poney from a Highland drover, and with its assistance and company stepped, or rather stumbled, as far as Saint Leonard's Crags.

Jeanie Deans, though so much accustomed to the Laird's staring that she was sometimes scarce conscious of his presence, had nevertheless some occasional fears lest he should call in the organ of speech to back those expressions of admiration which he bestowed on her through his eyes. Should this happen, farewell, she thought, to all chance of an union with Butler. For her father, however stout-hearted and independent in civil and religious principle, was not without that respect for the laird of the land so deeply imprinted in the Scottish tenantry of the period. Moreover, if he did not positively dislike Butler, yet his fund of carnal learning was often the object of sarcasms on David's part, which were perhaps founded in jealousy, and which certainly indicated no partiality for the party against whom they were launched. And, lastly, the match with Dumbiedikes would have presented irresistible charms to one who used to complain that he felt himself apt to take "ower grit an armfu' o' the warld." So that, upon the whole, the Laird's diurnal visits were disagreeable to Jeanie from apprehension of future consequences, and it served much to console her, upon removing from the spot where she was bred and born, that she had seen the last of Dumbiedikes, his laced hat, and tobacco-pipe. The poor girl no more expected he could muster courage to follow her to Saint Leonard's Crags, than that any of the apple-trees or cabbages which she had left rooted in the "yard" at Woodend, would spontaneously, and unaided, have undertaken the same journey. It was, therefore, with much more surprise than pleasure that, on the sixth day after their removal to Saint Leonard's, she beheld Dumbiedikes arrive, laced hat, tobacco-pipe, and all, and, with the self same greeting of "how's a' wi' ye, Jeanie?—Whare's the gudeman?" assume as nearly as he could the same position in the cottage at Saint Leonard's which he had so long and so regularly occupied at Woodend. He was no sooner, however, seated, than with an unusual exertion of his powers of conversation, he added, "Jeanie—I say, Jeanie woman," here he extended his hand towards her shoulder with all the fingers spread out as if to clutch it, but in so bashful and awkward a manner, that when she whisked herself beyond its reach, the paw remained suspended in the air with the palm open, like the claw of a heraldic griffin—"Jeanie," continued the swain, in this moment of inspiration, —"I say, Jeanie, it's a braw day out bye, and the roads are no that ill for boot-hose."

"The de'il's in the daidling body," muttered Jeanie between her teeth; "wha wad hae thought o' his daikering out this length?" And she afterwards confessed that she threw a little of this ungracious sentiment into her accent and manner, for her father being abroad, and the "body," as she irreverently termed the landed proprietor, "looking unco gleg and canty, she didna ken what he might be coming out wi' next."

Her frowns, however, acted as a complete sedative, and the Laird relapsed from that day into his former taciturn habits, visiting the cow-feeder's cottage three or four times every week, when weather permitted, with apparently no other purpose than to stare at Jeanie Deans, while Douce Davie poured forth his eloquence upon the controversies and testimonies of the day.

Chapter Ten

> Her air, her manners, all who saw admired,
> Courteous, though coy, and gentle, though retired;
> The joy of youth and health her eyes display'd,
> And ease of heart her every look convey'd.
> CRABBE

THE VISITS of the Laird thus again sunk into matters of ordinary course, from which nothing was to be expected or apprehended. If a lover could have gained a fair one as a snake is said to fascinate a bird, by pertinaciously gazing on her with great stupid greenish eyes, which began now to be occasionally aided by spectacles, unquestionably Dumbiedikes would have been the person to perform the feat. But the art of fascination seems among the *artes perditæ*, and I cannot learn that this most pertinacious of starers produced any effect by his attentions beyond an occasional yawn.

In the meanwhile, the object of his gaze was gradually attaining the verge of youth, and approaching to what is called in females the middle age, which is impolitely held to begin a few years earlier with their more fragile sex than with men. Many people would have been of opinion, that the Laird would have done better to have transferred his glances to an object possessed of far superior charms to Jeanie's, even when Jeanie's were in their bloom, who began now to be distinguished by all who visited the cottage at Saint Leonard's Crags.

Effie Deans, under the tender and affectionate care of her sister, had now shot up into a beautiful and blooming girl. Her Grecian-shaped head was profusely rich in waving ringlets of dark hair, which, confined by a blue snood of silk, and shading a laughing Hebe countenance, seemed the picture of health, pleasure, and contentment. Her brown russet short-gown set off a shape, which time, perhaps, might be expected to render too robust, the frequent objection to

Scottish beauty, but which, in her present early age, was slender and taper, with that graceful and easy sweep of outline, which at once indicates health and beautiful proportion of parts.

These growing charms, in all their juvenile profusion, had no power to shake the stedfast mind, or divert the fixed gaze, of the constant Laird of Dumbiedikes. But there was scarce another eye that could behold this living picture of health and beauty, without pausing on it with pleasure. The traveller stopped his weary horse on the eve of entering the city which was the end of his journey, to gaze at the sylph-like form that tripped by him, with her milk-pail poised on her head, bearing herself so erect, and stepping so light and free under her burthen, that it seemed rather an ornament than an encumbrance. The lads of the neighbouring suburb, who held their evening rendezvous for putting the stone, casting the hammer, playing at long bowls, and other athletic exercises, watched the motions of Effie Deans, and contended with each other which should have the good fortune to attract her attention. Even the rigid presbyterians of her father's persuasion, who held each indulgence of the eye and sense to be a snare at least, if not a crime, were surprised into a moment's delight while gazing on a creature so exquisite,—instantly checked by a sigh, reproaching at once their own weakness, and mourning that a creature so fair should share in the common and hereditary guilt and imperfection of our nature. She was currently entitled the Lily of Saint Leonard's, a name which she deserved as much by her guileless purity of thought, speech, and action, as by her uncommon loveliness of face and person.

Yet there were points in Effie's character, which gave rise not only to strange doubt and anxiety on the part of Douce David Deans, whose ideas were rigid, as may easily be supposed, upon the subject of youthful amusements, but even of serious apprehension to her more indulgent sister. The children of the Scotch of the inferior classes are usually spoiled by the early indulgence of their parents: how, wherefore, and to what degree, the lively and instructive narrative of the amiable and accomplished authoress of "Glenburnie"* has saved me and all future scribblers the trouble of recording. Effie had had a double share of this inconsiderate and misjudged kindness. Even the strictness of her father's principles could not condemn the sports of infancy and childhood; and to the good old man, his younger daughter, the child of his old age, seemed a child for some time after she attained the years of womanhood, was still called the "bit lassie" and "little Effie," and was permitted to run up and down uncontrolled, unless upon the Sabbath, or at the times of family worship.

* Mrs Elizabeth Hamilton, now no more.—*Editor.*

Her sister, with all the love and care of a mother, could not be supposed to possess the same authoritative influence, and that which she had hitherto exercised became gradually limited and diminished as Effie's advancing years entitled her, in her own conceit at least, to the right of independence and free agency. With all the innocence and goodness of disposition, therefore, which we have described,the Lily of Saint Leonard's possessed a little fund of self-conceit and obstinacy, and some warmth and irritability of temper, partly natural per-haps, but certainly much increased by the unrestrained freedom of her childhood. Her character will be best illustrated by a cottage evening scene.

The careful father was absent in his well-stocked byre, foddering those useful and patient animals on whose produce his living depended; the summer evening was beginning to close in; and Jeanie Deans began to be very anxious for the appearance of her sister, and to fear that she would not reach home before their father returned from the labour of the evening, when it was his custom to have "family exercise," and she knew that Effie's absence would give him the most serious displeasure. These apprehensions hung heavier upon her mind, because, for several preceding evenings, Effie had disappeared about the same time, and her stay, at first so brief as scarce to be noticed, had been gradually protracted to half an hour, and an hour, and on the present occasion had considerably exceeded even this last limit. And now, Jeanie stood at the door, with her hand before her eyes to avoid the rays of the level sun, and looked alternately along the various tracts which led towards their dwelling, to see if she could descry the nymph-like form of her sister. There was a wall and a stile which separated the King's Park, as it is called, from the public road; and to this she frequently directed her attention, when she saw two persons appear there somewhat suddenly, as if they had walked close by the side of the wall to screen themselves from observation. One of them, a man, drew back hastily; the other, a female, crossed the stile, and advanced towards her—it was Effie. She met her sister with that affected liveliness of manner, which, in her rank, and sometimes in those above it, females occasionally assume to hide surprise or confusion; and she carolled as she came—

> "The elfin knight sate on the brae,
>   The broom grows bonnie, the broom grows fair;
> And by there came lilting a ladie so gay,
>   And we daurna gang down to the broom nae mair."

"Whisht, Effie," said her sister; "our father's coming out o' the byre."—The damsel stinted in her song.—"Whare hae ye been sae late at e'en?"

"It's no late, lass," answered Effie.

"It's chappit eight on every clock o' the town, and the sun's gaun down ahint the Corstorphine hills—Whare can ye hae been sae late?"

"Nae gate," answered Effie.

"And wha was that parted wi' you at the stile?"

"Naebody," replied Effie once more.

"Nae gate? naebody? I wish it may be a right gate, and a right body, that keeps folk out sae late at e'en, Effie!"

"What needs ye be aye speering then at folk?" retorted Effie. "I am sure, if ye'll ask nae questions, I'll tell ye nae lees. I never ask what brings the Laird of Dumbiedikes glowering here like a wull-cat, (only his een are greener, and no sae gleg,) day after day, till we are a' like to gaunt our chafts aff."

"Because ye ken very weel he comes to see our father," said Jeanie, in answer to this pert remark.

"And Dominie Butler—Does he come to see my father, that's sae taen wi' his Latin words?" said Effie, delighted to find that, by carrying the war into the enemy's country, she could divert the threatened attack upon herself, and with the petulance of youth she pursued her triumph over her prudential elder sister. She looked at her with a sly air, in which there was something like irony, as she chaunted, in a low but marked tone, a scrap of an old Scotch song—

> "Through the kirk-yard
> I met wi' the Laird,
> The silly puir body he said me nae harm;
> But just ere 'twas dark
> I met wi' the clerk"——

Here the songstress stopped, looked full at her sister, and, observing the tear gather in her eyes, she suddenly flung her arms round her neck, and kissed them away. Jeanie, though hurt and displeased, was unable to resist the caresses of this untaught child of nature, whose good and evil seemed to flow rather from impulse than from reflection. But as she returned the sisterly kiss, in token of perfect reconciliation, she could not suppress the gentle reproof—"Effie, if ye will learn fule sangs, ye might make a kinder use of them."

"And so I might, Jeanie," continued the girl, clinging to her sister's neck; "and I wish I had never learned ane o' them—and I wish we had never come here—and I wish my tongue had been blistered or I had vexed ye."

"Never mind that, Effie," replied her affectionate sister; "I canna be muckle vexed wi' ony thing ye say to me—but O dinna vex our father!"

"I will not—I will not," replied Effie; "and if there were as mony dances the morn's night as there are merry dancers in the north firmament on a frosty e'en, I winna budge an inch to gang near ane o' them."

"Dance?" echoed Jeanie Deans in astonishment. "O, Effie, what could tak ye to a dance?"

It is very possible, that, in the communicative mood into which the Lily of Saint Leonard's was now surprised, she might have given her sister her unreserved confidence, and saved me the pain of telling a melancholy tale. But at the moment the word *dance* was uttered, it reached the ear of old David Deans, who had turned the corner of the house, and came upon his daughters ere they were aware of his presence. The word *prelate*, or even the word *pope*, could hardly have produced so appalling an effect upon David's ear; for, of all exercises, that of dancing, which he termed a voluntary and regular fit of distraction, he deemed most destructive of serious thoughts, and a ready inlet to all sort of licentiousness; and he accounted the encouraging, and even permitting, assemblies or meetings, whether among those of high or low degree, for this fantastic and absurd purpose, or for that of dramatic representation, as one of the most clamant proofs of defection and causes of wrath. The pronouncing of the word Dance by his own daughters, and at his own door, now drove him beyond the verge of patience. "Dance!" he exclaimed. "Dance?—dance, said ye? I daur ye, limmers that ye are, to name sic a word at my door-cheek! It's a dissolute profane pastime, practised by the Israelites only at their base and brutish worship of the Golden Calf at Bethel, and by the unhappy lass wha danced aff the head of John the Baptist, upon whilk chapter I will exercise this night for your farther instruction, since ye need it sae muckle, nothing doubting that she has cause to rue the day, lang or this time, that ere she suld hae shook a limb on sic an errand. Better for her to hae been born a cripple, and carried frae door to door, like auld Bessie Bowie, begging for bawbees, than to be a king's daughter, fiddling and flinging the gate she did. I hae aften wondered that ony ane that ever bent a knee for the right purpose, should ever daur to crook a hough to fyke and fling at piper's wind and fiddler's squealing. And I bless God, (with that singular worthy, Peter Walker the packman at Bristo-port,) that ordered my lot in my dancing days, so that fear of my head and throat, dread of bloody rope and swift bullet, and trenchant swords and pain of boots and thumbikins, cauld and hunger, wetness and weariness, stopped the lightness of my head, and the wantonness of my feet. And now, if I hear ye, quean lassies, sae muckle as name dancing, or think there's sic a thing in this warld as flinging to fiddler's sounds and piper's springs, as sure as my father's spirit is with the just, ye shall be no more either charge or concern of

mine! Gang in, then—gang in, then, hinnies," he added, in a softer
tone, for the tears of both daughters, but especially those of Effie,
began to flow very fast,—"Gang in, dears, and we'll seek grace to
preserve us frae all manner of profane folly, whilk causeth to sin, and
promoteth the kingdom of darkness, warring with the kingdom of
light."

The objurgation of David Deans, however well meant, was unhappily timed. It created a diversion of feelings in Effie's bosom, and
deterred her from her intended confidence in her sister. "She wad
haud me nae better than the dirt below her feet," said Effie to herself,
"were I to confess I hae danced wi' him four times on the green down
bye, and anes at Maggie Macqueen's; and she'll maybe hing it ower
my head that she'll tell my father, and than she wad be mistress and
mair. But I'll no gang back there again. I am resolved I'll no gang back.
I'll lay in a leaf of my Bible, and that's very near as if I had an aith, that I
winna gang back." And she kept her vow for a week, during which she
was unusually cross and fretful, blemishes which had never before
been observed in her temper, except during a moment of contradiction.

There was something in all this so mysterious as considerably to
alarm the prudent and affectionate Jeanie, the more so as she judged it
unkind to her sister to mention to their father grounds of anxiety
which might arise from her own imagination. Besides, her respect for
the good old man did not prevent her from being aware that he was
both hot-tempered and positive, and she sometimes suspected that he
carried his dislike to youthful amusements beyond the verge that
religion and reason demanded. Jeanie had sense enough to see that a
sudden and severe curb upon her sister's hitherto unrestrained freedom might be rather productive of harm than good, and that Effie, in
the headstrong wilfulness of youth, was likely to make what might be
overstrained in her father's precepts an excuse to herself for neglecting them altogether. In the higher classes, a damsel, however giddy, is
still under the dominion of etiquette, and subject to the surveillance of
mammas and chaperones; but the country girl, who snatches her
moment of gaiety during the intervals of labour, is under no such
guardianship or restraint, and her amusement becomes just so much
the more hazardous. Jeanie saw all this with much distress of mind,
when a circumstance occurred which appeared calculated to relieve
her anxiety.

Mrs Saddletree, with whom our readers have already been made
acquainted, chanced to be a distant relation of Douce David Deans,
and as she was a woman orderly in her life and conversation, and,
moreover, of good substance, a sort of acquaintance was formally kept

up between the families. Now, this careful dame, about a year and a half before our story commenced, chanced to need in the line of her profession a better sort of servant, or rather shop-woman. "Mr Saddletree," she said, "was never in the shop when he could get his nose within the Parliament House, and it was an awkward thing for a woman-body to be staring amang bundles o' barkened leather her lane, selling saddles and bridles; and she had cast her eyes upon her far awa' cousin Effie Deans, as just the very sort of lassie she would want to keep her in countenance on such occasions."

In this proposal there was much that pleased old David,—there was bed, board, and bountith—it was a decent situation—the lassie would be under Mrs Saddletree's eye, who had an upright walk, and lived close by the Tolbooth Kirk, in which might still be heard the comforting doctrines of one of those few ministers of the Kirk of Scotland who had not bent the knee unto Baal, according to David's expression, or become accessary to the course of national defections,—union, toleration, patronages, and a bundle of prelatical Erastian oaths which had been imposed on the church since the Revolution, and particularly in the reign of "the late woman," (as he called Queen Anne), the last of that unhappy race of Stuarts. In the good man's security concerning the soundness of the theological doctrine which his daughter was to hear, he was nothing disturbed on account of the snares of a different kind, to which a creature so beautiful, young, and wilful, might be exposed in the centre of a populous and corrupted city. The fact is, that he thought with so much horror on all approaches to irregularities of the nature most to be dreaded in such cases, that he would as soon have suspected and guarded against Effie's being induced to become guilty of the crime of murder. He only regretted that she should live under the same roof with such a worldly-wise man as Bartholine Saddletree, whom David never suspected of being an ass, but considered as endowed with all the legal knowledge to which he made pretension, and only liked him the worse for possessing it. The lawyers, especially those amongst them who sate as ruling elders in the General Assembly of the Kirk, had been forward in promoting the measures of patronage, of the abjuration oath, and others, which, in the opinion of David Deans, were a breaking down of the carved work of the sanctuary, and an intrusion upon the liberties of the Kirk. Upon the dangers of listening to the doctrines of a legalized formalist, such as Saddletree, David gave his daughter many lectures; so much so, that he had time to touch but slightly on the dangers of chambering, company-keeping, and promiscuous dancing, to which, at her time of life, most people would have thought Effie more exposed, than to the risk of theoretical error in her religious faith.

Jeanie parted with her sister, with a mixed feeling of regret, and apprehension, and hope. She could not be so confident concerning Effie's prudence as her father, for she had observed her more narrowly, had more sympathy with her feelings, and could better estimate the temptations to which she was exposed. On the other hand, Mrs Saddletree was an observing, shrewd, notable woman, entitled to exercise over Effie the full authority of a mistress, and likely to do so strictly, yet with kindness. Her removal to Saddletree's, it was most probable, would also serve to break off some idle acquaintances, which Jeanie suspected her sister to have formed in the neighbouring suburb. Upon the whole, then, she viewed her removal from Saint Leonard's with pleasure, and it was not until the very moment of their parting for the first time in their lives, that she felt the full force of sisterly sorrow. While they repeatedly kissed each other's cheeks, and wrung each other's hands, Jeanie took that moment of affectionate sympathy, to press upon her sister the necessity of the utmost caution in her conduct while residing in Edinburgh. Effie listened, without once raising her large dark eye-lashes, from which the drops fell so fast as almost to resemble a fountain. At the conclusion she sobbed again, kissed her sister, and promised to recollect all the good counsel she had given her, and they parted.

The first week or two, Effie was all that her kinswoman expected, and even more. But with time there came a relaxation of that early zeal which she manifested in Mrs Saddletree's service. To borrow once again from the poet, who so correctly and beautifully describes living manners,—

> Something there was, what, none presumed to say,—
> Clouds lightly passing on a summer's day;
> Whispers and hints, which went from ear to ear,
> And mixed reports no judge on earth could clear.

During this interval, Mrs Saddletree was sometimes displeased by Effie's lingering, when she was sent upon errands about the shop business, and sometimes by a little degree of impatience which she manifested at being rebuked on such occasions. But she good-naturedly allowed, that the first was very natural to a girl to whom every thing in Edinburgh was new, and the other was only the petulance of a spoiled child, when subjected to the yoke of domestic discipline for the first time. Attention and submission could not be learned at once—Holy-Rood was not built in a day—use would make perfect.

It seemed as if the considerate old lady had presaged truly. Ere many months had passed, Effie became almost wedded to her duties, though she no longer discharged them with the laughing cheek and light step, which at first had attracted every customer. Her mistress sometimes observed her in tears, but they were signs of secret sorrow, which she concealed as often as she saw them attract notice. Time wore on, her cheek grew pale, and her step heavy. The cause of these changes could not have escaped the matronly eye of Mrs Saddletree, but she was chiefly confined by indisposition to her bed-room for several months during the latter part of Effie's service. This interval was marked by symptoms of anguish almost amounting to despair. The utmost efforts of the poor girl to command her fits of hysterical agony were often totally unavailing, and the mistakes which she made in the shop the while were so numerous and so provoking, that Bartholine Saddletree, who, during his wife's illness, was obliged to take closer charge of the business than consisted with his study of the weightier matters of the law, lost all patience with the girl, who, in his law Latin, and without much respect to gender, he declared ought to be cognosced by inquest of a jury, as *fatuus, furiosus*, and *naturaliter idiota*. Neighbours, also, and fellow-servants, remarked, with malicious curiosity or degrading pity, the disfigured shape, loose dress, and pale cheeks of the once beautiful and still interesting girl. But to no one would she grant her confidence, answering all taunts with bitter sarcasm, and all serious expostulation with sullen denial, or with floods of tears.

At length, when Mrs Saddletree's recovery was likely to permit her wonted attention to the regulation of her household, Effie Deans, as if unwilling to face an investigation made by the authority of her mistress, asked permission of Bartholine to go home for a week or two, assigning indisposition, and the wish of trying the benefit of repose and change of air, as the motives of her request. Sharp-eyed as a lynx (or conceiving himself to be so) in the nice, sharp quillets of legal discussion, Bartholine was as dull at drawing inferences from the occurrences of common life as any Dutch professor of mathematics. He suffered Effie to depart without much suspicion, and without any enquiry.

It was afterwards found that a period of a week intervened betwixt her leaving her master's house and arriving at Saint Leonard's. She made her appearance before her sister in a state rather resembling the spectre than the living substance of the gay and beautiful girl, who had left her father's cottage for the first time scarce seventeen months before. The lingering illness of her mistress had, for the last few months, given her a plea for confining herself entirely to the dusky precincts of the shop in the Lawn-market, and Jeanie was so much occupied, during the same period, with the concerns of her father's household, that she had rarely found leisure for a walk into the city,

and a brief and hurried visit to her sister. The young women, therefore, had scarcely seen each other for several months, nor had a single
scandalous surmise reached the ears of the secluded inhabitants of the
cottage at Saint Leonard's. Jeanie, therefore, terrified to death at her
sister's appearance, at first overwhelmed her with enquiries, to which
the unfortunate young woman returned for a time incoherent and
rambling answers, and finally fell into a hysterical fit. Rendered too
certain of her sister's misfortune, Jeanie had now the dreadful alternative of communicating her ruin to her father, or of endeavouring to
conceal it from him. To all questions concerning the name or rank of
her seducer, and the fate of the being to whom her fall had given birth,
Effie remained mute as the grave, to which she seemed hastening;
and indeed the least allusion to either seemed to drive her to distraction. Her sister, in distress and in despair, was about to repair to Mrs
Saddletree to consult her experience, and at the same time to obtain
what lights she could upon this most unhappy affair, when she was
saved that pains by a new stroke of fate, which seemed to carry misfortune to the uttermost.

David Deans had been alarmed at the state of health in which his
daughter returned to her paternal residence; but Jeanie had contrived
to divert him from particular and specific enquiries. It was, therefore,
like a clap of thunder to the poor old man, when, just as the hour of
noon had brought the visit of the Laird of Dumbiedikes as usual, other
and sterner, as well as most unexpected guests, arrived at the cottage
of Saint Leonard's. These were the officers of justice, with a warrant
of justiciary to search for and apprehend Euphemia, or Effie, Deans,
accused of the crime of child-murther. The stunning weight of a blow
so totally unexpected bore down the old man, who had in his time
resisted the brow of military and of civil tyranny, though backed with
swords and guns, tortures and gibbets. He fell extended and senseless
upon his own hearth; and the men, happy to escape from the scene of
his awakening, raised, with rude humanity, the object of their warrant
from her bed, and placed her in a coach, which they had brought with
them. The hasty remedies which Jeanie had applied to bring back her
father's senses were scarce begun to operate, when the noise of the
wheels in motion recalled her attention to her miserable sister. To run
shrieking after the carriage was the first vain effort of her distraction,
but she was stopped by one or two female neighbours, assembled, by
the extraordinary appearance of a coach in that sequestered place,
who almost forced her back to her father's house. The deep and
sympathetic affliction of these poor people, by whom the little family
at Saint Leonard's were held in high regard, filled the house with
lamentation. Even Dumbiedikes was moved from his wonted apathy,

and, groping for his purse as he spoke, ejaculated— "Jeanie woman! Jeanie woman! dinna greet—it's sad wark but siller will help it;" and he drew out his purse as he spoke.

The old man had now raised himself from the ground, and, looking about him as if he missed something, seemed gradually to recover the sense of his wretchedness. "Where," he said, with a voice that made the roof ring, "where is the vile harlot, that has disgraced the blood of an honest man?—Where is she, that has no place among us, but has come foul with her sins, like the Evil One, among the children of God? —Where is she, Jeanie?—Bring her before me, that I may kill her wi' a word and a look."

All hastened around him with their appropriate sources of consola- tion—the Laird with his purse, Jeanie with burnt feathers and strong waters, and the women with their exhortations. "O neighbour—O, Mr Deans, it's a sair trial, doubtless—but think of the Rock of Ages, neighbour—think of the promise!"

"And I do think of it, neighbours—and I bless God that I can think of it, even in the wrack and ruin of a' that's nearest and dearest to me —But to be the father of a cast-a-away—a profligate—a bloody Zip- porah—a mere murderess!—O, how will the wicked exult in the high places of their wickedness!—the prelatists, and the latitudinarians, and the hand-waled murderers, whose hands are hard as horn wi' hauding the slaughter-weapons—they will push out the lip, and say that we are even such as themselves. Sair, sair I am grieved, neigh- bours, for the poor cast-away—for the child of mine own old age—but sairer for the stumbling-block and scandal it will be to all tender and honest souls!"

"Davie—winna siller do't?" insinuated the Laird, still proffering his green purse, which was full of guineas.

"I tell ye, Dumbiedikes," said Deans, "that if telling down my haill substance could hae saved her frae this black snare, I wad hae walked out wi' naething but my bonnet and my staff to beg an awmous for God's sake, and ca'd mysell an happy man—But if a dollar, or a plack, or the nineteenth part of a boddle, wad save her open guilt and open shame frae open punishment, that purchase wad David Deans never make!—Na, na—an eye for an eye, a tooth for a tooth, life for life, blood for blood—it's the law of God and it's the law of man.—Leave me, sirs—leave me—I maun warstle wi' this trial in privacy and on my knees."

Jeanie, now in some degree restored to the power of thought, joined in the same request. The next day found the father and daughter still in the depth of affliction, but the father sternly supporting his load of ill through a proud sense of religious duty, and the daughter anxiously suppressing her own feelings to avoid again awakening his. Thus was it with the afflicted family until the morning after Porteous's death, a period at which we are now arrived.

Chapter Eleven

Is all the counsel that we two have shared,
The sisters' vows, the hours that we have spent
When we have chid the hasty-footed time
For parting us—Oh! and is all forgot?
                    Midsummer Night's Dream

WE HAVE BEEN a long while in conducting Butler to the door of the cottage at Saint Leonard's. Yet the space which we have occupied in the preceding narrative does not exceed in length that which he actually spent on Salusbury Crags upon the morning which succeeded the execution done upon Porteous by the rioters. For this delay he had his own motives. He wished to collect his thoughts, strangely agitated as they were, first by the melancholy news of Effie Deans's situation, and afterwards by the frightful scene which he had witnessed. In the situation also in which he stood with respect to Jeanie and her father, some ceremony, at least some choice of fitting time and season, was necessary to wait upon them. Eight in the morning was then the ordinary hour for breakfast, and he resolved that it should arrive before he made his appearance in their cottage.

Never did hours pass so heavily. Butler shifted his place, and enlarged his circle to while away the time, and heard the huge bell of Saint Giles's toll each successive hour in swelling tones, which were instantly attested by those of the other steeples in succession. He had heard seven struck in this manner, when he began to think he might venture to approach nearer to Saint Leonard's, from which he was still a mile distant. Accordingly he descended from his lofty station as low as the bottom of the valley which divides Salusbury Crags from those small rocks which take their name from Saint Leonard. It is, as many of my readers may know, a deep, wild, grassy valley, scattered with huge rocks and fragments which have descended from the cliffs and steep ascent to the east. This sequestered dell, as well as other places of the open pasturage of the King's Park, was, about this time, often the resort of the gallants of the time who had affairs of honour to discuss with the sword. Duels were then very common in Scotland, for the gentry were at once idle, haughty, fierce, and addicted to intemperance, so that there lacked neither provocation, nor inclination to resent it when given; and the sword, which was part of every gentleman's dress, was the only weapon used for the decision of such differences. When, therefore, Butler observed a young man, skulking, apparently to avoid observation, among the scattered rocks at some distance from the footpath, he was naturally led to suppose that he had sought this lonely spot upon that evil errand. He was so strongly impressed with this, that, notwithstanding his own distress of mind, he could not, according to his sense of duty as a clergyman, pass this person without speaking to him. There are times, thought he to himself, when the slightest interference may avert a great calamity—when a word spoken in season may do more for prevention than the eloquence of Tully could do for remedying evil—And for my own griefs, be they as they may, I shall feel them the lighter, if they divert me not from the prosecution of my duty.

Thus thinking and feeling, he quitted the ordinary path, and advanced nearer the object he had noticed. The man at first directed his course towards the hill, as if to avoid him; but when he saw that Butler seemed disposed to follow him, he adjusted his hat fiercely, turned round, and came forwards, as if to meet and defy scrutiny.

Butler had an opportunity of accurately studying his features as they advanced slowly to meet each other. The stranger seemed about twenty-five years old. His dress was of a kind which could hardly be said to indicate his rank with certainty, for it was such as young gentlemen sometimes wore while on active exercise in the morning, and which, therefore, was imitated by those of the inferior ranks, as young clerks and tradesmen, because its cheapness rendered it attainable, while it approached more nearly to the apparel of youths of fashion than any other which the manners of the times permitted them to wear. If his air and manner could be trusted, however, this person seemed rather to be dressed under than above his rank; for his carriage was bold and somewhat supercilious, his step easy and free, his manner daring and unconstrained. His stature was of the middle size, or rather above it, his limbs well proportioned and strong, yet not so strong as to infer the reproach of clumsiness. His features were uncommonly handsome, and all about him would have been interesting and prepossessing, but for that indescribable expression which habitual dissipation gives to the countenance, joined with a certain audacity in voice and manner, of that kind which is often assumed as a mask for confusion and apprehension.

Butler and the stranger met—surveyed each other—when, as the latter, slightly touching his hat, was about to pass by him, Butler, while he returned the salutation, observed, "A fine morning, sir—You are on the hill early."

"Sir, I have business here," said the young man, in a tone meant to repress further enquiry.

"I do not doubt it, sir," said Butler. "I trust you will forgive my hoping that it is of a lawful kind."

"Sir," said the other, with marked surprise, "I never forgive impertinence, nor can I conceive what title you have to hope any thing about what no ways concerns you."

"I am a soldier, sir," said Butler, "and have a charge to arrest evil-doers in the name of my Master."

"A soldier?" said the young man, stepping back, and fiercely laying his hand on his sword—"A soldier, and arrest me? Did you reckon what your life was worth before you took the commission upon you?"

"You mistake me, sir," said Butler gravely; "neither my warfare nor my warrant are of this world—I am a preacher of the gospel, and have power, in my Master's name, to command the peace upon earth and good will towards men, which was proclaimed with the gospel."

"A minister!" said the stranger, carelessly, and with an expression approaching to scorn. "I know the gentlemen of your cloth in Scotland claim a strange right of intermeddling with men's private affairs. But I have been abroad, and know better than to be priest-ridden."

"Sir, if it be true that any of my cloth, or, it might be more decently said, of my calling, interfere with men's private affairs, for the gratification either of idle curiosity, or for worse motives, you cannot have learned a better lesson abroad than to contemn such practices. But, in my Master's work, I am called to be busy in season and out of season, and, conscious as I am of a pure motive, it were better for me to incur your contempt for speaking, than the correction of my own conscience for being silent."

"In the name of the devil," said the young man impatiently, "say what you have to say, then; though whom you take me for, or what earthly concern you can have with me, a stranger to you, or with my actions and motives, of which you can know nothing, I cannot conjecture for an instant."

"You are about," said Butler, "to violate one of your country's wisest laws—you are about, which is much more dreadful, to violate a law, which God himself has implanted within our nature, and written, as it were, in the table of our hearts, to which every thrill of our nerves is responsive."

"And what is the law you speak of?" said the stranger, in a hollow and somewhat disturbed accent.

"Thou shalt do no MURDER," said Butler, with a deep and solemn voice.

The young man visibly started, and looked considerably appalled. Butler perceived he had made a favourable impression, and resolved to follow it up. "Think," he said, "young man," laying his hand kindly upon the stranger's shoulder, "what an awful alternative you voluntarily chuse for yourself, to kill or be killed. Think what it is, to rush uncalled into the presence of an offended Deity, your heart fermenting with evil passions, your hand hot from the steel you had been urging, urging with your best skill and malice, against the breast of a fellow-creature. Or, suppose yourself the scarce less wretched survivor, with the guilt of Cain, the first murderer, in your heart, with his stamp upon your brow—that stamp, which struck all who gazed on him with unutterable horror, and by which the murderer is made manifest to all who look upon him. Think——"

The stranger gradually withdrew himself from under the hand of his monitor; and, pulling his hat over his brows, thus interrupted him. "Your meaning, sir, I dare say, is excellent, but you are throwing your advice away. I am not in this place with violent intentions against any one. I may be bad enough—you priests say all men are so—but I am here for the purpose of saving life, not of taking it away. If you wish to spend your time rather in doing a good action than in talking about you know not what, I will give you an opportunity. Do you see yonder crag to the right, over which appears the chimney of a lone house? Go thither, enquire for one Jeanie Deans, the daughter of the gudeman; let her know that he she wots of remained here from day-break till this hour, expecting to see her, and that he can abide no longer. Tell her, she *must* meet me at the Hunter's Bog to-night, as the moon rises behind Saint Anthony's Hill, or that she will make a desperate man of me."

"Who, or what are you," replied Butler, exceedingly and most unpleasantly surprised, "who charge me with such an errand?"

"I am the devil!" answered the young man hastily.

Butler stepped instinctively back, and commended himself internally to Heaven; for, though a wise and strong-minded man, he was neither wiser nor more strong-minded than those of his age and education, with whom, to disbelieve witchcraft or spectres, was held an undeniable proof of atheism.

The stranger went on without observing his emotion. "Yes—call me Apollyon, Abaddon—whatever name you shall chuse, as a clergyman acquainted with the upper and lower circles of spiritual denomination, to call me by, you shall not name a name more odious to him that bears it, than is mine own."

This sentence was spoken with the bitterness of self-upbraiding, and a contortion of visage absolutely demoniacal. Butler, though a stout-hearted man, was overawed; for intensity of mental distress has in it a sort of sublimity which repels and over-awes all men, but especially those of kind and sympathetic dispositions. The stranger turned abruptly from Butler as he spoke, but instantly returned, and, coming up to him closely and boldly, said, in a fierce determined tone, "I have told you who and what I am—who, and what are you? What is your name?"

"Butler," answered the person to whom this abrupt question was addressed, surprised into answering it by the sudden and fierce manner of the querist—"Reuben Butler, a preacher of the gospel."

At this answer the stranger again plucked more deep over his brows the hat which he had thrown back in his former agitation. "Butler?" he repeated,—"the assistant of the schoolmaster at Libberton?"

"The same," answered Butler composedly.

The stranger covered his face with his hand, as if on sudden reflection, and then turned away, but stopped when he had walked a few paces, turned back, and seeing Butler follow him with his eyes, called out in a stern yet suppressed tone, just as if he had exactly calculated that his accents should not be heard a yard beyond the spot on which Butler stood. "Go your way, and do mine errand. Do not look after me. I will neither descend through the bowels of these rocks, nor vanish in a flash of fire. And yet the eye that seeks to trace my motions shall have reason to curse it was ever shrouded by eye-lid or eye-lash. Begone, and look not behind you. Tell Jeanie Deans, that when the moon rises I shall expect to meet her at Nicol Muschat's Cairn, beneath Saint Anthony's Chapel."

As he uttered these words, he turned and took the road against the hill, with a haste that seemed as peremptory as his tone of authority.

Dreading he knew not what of additional misery to a lot which seemed little capable of receiving augmentation, and desperate at the idea that any living man should dare to send so extraordinary a request, couched in terms so peremptory, to the half-betrothed object of his early and only affection, Butler strode hastily towards the cottage, in order to ascertain how far this daring and rude gallant was actually entitled to press on Jeanie Deans a request which no prudent, and scarce any modest young woman was likely to comply with.

Butler was by nature neither jealous nor superstitious; yet the feelings which lead to these moods of the mind were rooted in his heart, as a portion derived from the common stock of humanity. It was maddening to think that a profligate gallant, such as the manner and tone of the stranger evinced him to be, should have it in his power to command forth his future bride and plighted true love, at a place so improper, and an hour so unseasonable. Yet the tone in which the stranger spoke had nothing of the soft half-breathed voice proper to the seducer who solicits an assignation; it was bold, fierce, and imperative, and had less of love in it than of menace and intimidation.

The suggestions of superstition seemed more plausible, had Butler's mind been very accessible to them. "Was this indeed the Roaring Lion, who goeth about seeking whom he may devour?" This was a question which pressed itself on Butler's mind with an earnestness that cannot be conceived by those who live in the present day. The fiery eye, the abrupt demeanour, the occasionally harsh, and yet studiously subdued tone of voice,—the features, whose perfect beauty was now clouded with pride, now disturbed by suspicion, now inflamed with passion—those dark hazel eyes which he sometimes shaded with his cap, as if he were averse to have them seen while they were occupied with keenly observing the motions and bearing of others—those eyes that were now turbid with melancholy, now gleaming with scorn, and now sparkling with fury—was it the passions of a mere mortal they expressed, or the emotions of a fiend, who seeks, and seeks in vain, to conceal his fiendish designs under the borrowed mask of masculine beauty? The whole partook of the mien, language, and port of the archangel; and, imperfectly as we have been able to describe it, the effect of the interview upon Butler's nerves, shaken as they were at the time by the horrors of the preceding night, was greater than his understanding warranted, or his pride cared to submit to. The very place where he had met this singular person was desecrated, as it were, and unhallowed, owing to many violent deaths, both in duels and by suicide, which had in former times taken place there; and the place which he had named as a rendezvous at so late an hour, was held in general to be accursed, from a frightful and cruel murder which had been there committed by the wretch Nicol Muschat from whom the place took its name, upon the person of his own wife. It was in such places, according to the belief of that period (when the laws against witchcraft were still in fresh observance, and had even lately been acted upon), that evil spirits had power to make themselves visible to human eyes, and to practise upon the feelings and senses of mankind. Suspicions, founded on such circumstances, rushed on Butler's mind, unprepared as it was, by any previous course of reasoning, to deny that which all of his time, country, and profession, believed; but common sense rejected these vain ideas as inconsistent, if not with possibility, at least with the general rules by which the universe is governed,—a deviation from which, as Butler well argued with himself, ought not to be admitted as probable upon any but the plainest and most incontrovertible evidence. An earthly lover, however, or a young man, who, from whatever cause, had the right of exercising such summary and unceremonious authority over the object of his long-settled, and apparently sincerely returned affection, was an object scarce less appalling to his mind, than those which superstition suggested.

His limbs exhausted with fatigue, his mind harassed with anxiety, and with painful doubts and recollections, Butler dragged himself up the ascent from the valley to Saint Leonard's Crags, and presented himself at the door of Deans's habitation, with feelings much akin to the miserable reflections and fears of its inhabitants.

Chapter Twelve

Then she stretched out her lily hand,
And for to do her best;
"Hae back thy faith and troth, Willie,
God gi'e thy soul good rest."
Old Ballad

"COME IN," answered the low and sweet-toned voice he loved best to hear, as Butler tapped at the door of the cottage. He lifted the latch, and found himself under the roof of affliction. Jeanie was unable to trust herself with more than one glance toward her lover, whom she now met under circumstances so agonizing to her feelings, and at the same time so humbling to her honest pride. It is well known, that much, both of what is good and bad in the Scottish national character, arises out of the intimacy of their family connections. "To be come of honest folk," that is, of people who have borne a fair and unstained character, is an advantage as highly prized amongst the lower Scotch, as the emphatic counterpart, "to be come of a good family," is valued among their gentry. The worth and respectability of one member of a family is always accounted by themselves and others, not only a matter of honest pride, but a guarantee for the good conduct of the whole. On the contrary, such a melancholy stain as was now flung on one of the children of Deans, extended its disgrace to all connected with him, and Jeanie felt herself lowered at once, in her own eyes, and in those of her lover. It was in vain that she repressed this feeling, as far subordinate and too selfish to be mingled with her sorrow for her sister's calamity. Nature prevailed; and while she shed tears for her sister's distress and danger, there mingled with them bitter drops of grief for her own degradation.

As Butler entered, the old man was seated by the fire with his well-worn pocket Bible in his hands, the companion of the wanderings and dangers of his youth, and bequeathed to him on the scaffold by one of those, who, in the year 1688, sealed their enthusiastic principles with their blood. The sun sent its rays through a small window at the old man's back, and, "shining motty through the reek," to use the expression of a bard of that time and country, illuminated the grey hairs of the old man, and the sacred page which he studied. His features, far from handsome, and rather harsh and severe, from their expression of habitual gravity and contempt for earthly things, had an expression of stoical dignity amidst their sternness. He boasted, in no small degree, the attributes which Southey ascribes to the ancient Scandinavians, whom he terms "firm to resolve, and stubborn to endure." The whole formed a picture, of which the lights might have been given by Rembrandt, but the outline would have required the force and vigour of Michael Angelo.

Deans lifted his eye as Butler entered, and instantly withdrew it, as from an object which gave him at once surprise and sudden pain. He had assumed such high ground with this carnal-witted scholar, as he had in his pride termed Butler, that to meet him of all men, under feelings of humiliation, aggravated his misfortune, and was a consummation like that of the dying chief in the old ballad—"Earl Peircy sees my fall."

Deans raised the Bible with his left hand, so as partly to screen his face, and putting back his right as far as he could, held it towards Butler in that position, at the same time turning his body from him, as if to prevent his seeing the working of his countenance. Butler clasped the extended hand which had supported his orphan infancy, wept over it, and in vain endeavoured to say more than the words,—"God comfort you, God comfort you!"

"He will—he doth, my friend," said Deans, assuming firmness as he discovered the agitation of his guest; "he doth now, and he will yet more, in his own gude time. I have been ower proud of my sufferings in a gude cause, Reuben, and now I am to be tried with those whilk will turn my pride and glory into a reproach and a hissing. How muckle better I hae thought mysell than them that lay saft, fed sweet, and drank deep, whan I was in the moss-haggs and moors, wi' precious Donald Cameron, and worthy Mr Blackadder, called Guess-again; and how proud I was o' being made a spectacle to men and angels afore I was fifteen, when I was found worthy to be scourged by the same bloody hands that quartered the dear body of James Renwick and cut off those hands which were the first to raise up the down-fallen banner of the testimony—and how I was even preferred to stand on the pillory at the Canongate cross for twa hours during a cauld nor-east blast, and might hae been hangit by the neck had I been twa years elder, for the cause of a deserted covenant. To think Reuben, that I, wha hae been sae honoured and exalted in my youth, nay, when I was but a hafflins callant, and that hae borne testimony again the defections o' the times yearly, monthly, daily, hourly, minutely, striving and testifying with uplifted hand and voice, crying aloud, and sparing not, against all great national snares, as the nation-wasting and church-sinking abomination of union, toleration, and patronage, imposed by the last woman of that unhappy race of Stewarts; also against the infringements and invasions of the just powers of eldership, where-anent I uttered my paper, called a 'Cry of an Howl in the Desart,' printed at the Bowhead, and sold by all flying stationers in town and county—and *now*——"

Here he paused. It may well be supposed that Butler, though not absolutely coinciding in all the good old man's ideas about church government, had too much consideration and humanity to interrupt him, while he reckoned up with conscious pride his sufferings, and the constancy of his testimony. On the contrary, when he paused under the influence of the bitter recollections of the moment, Butler instantly threw in his mite of encouragement.

"You have been well known, my old and reverend friend, a true and tried follower of the Cross; one who, as Saint Jerome hath it, '*per infamiam et bonam famam grassari ad immortalitatem*,' which may be freely rendered, 'who rusheth on to immortal life, through bad report and good report.' You have been one of those to whom the tender souls and fearful cry during the midnight solitude,—'Watchman, what of the night?—Watchman, what of the night?'—And, assuredly, this heavy dispensation, as it comes not without Divine permission, so it comes not without its special commission and use."

"I do receive it as such," said poor Deans, returning the grasp of Butler's hand, "and, if I have not been taught to read the Scripture in any other tongue but my native Scottish, (even in his distress Butler's Latin quotation had not escaped his notice,) I have, nevertheless, so learned them, that I trust to bear even this crook in my lot with submission. But O, Reuben Butler, the Kirk, of whilk, though unworthy, I have yet been thought a polished shaft, and meet to be a pillar, holding, from my youth upward, the place of ruling elder— What will the light-headed and profane think of the guide that cannot keep his own family from stumbling? how will they take up their song and their reproach, when they see that the children of professors are liable to as foul back-sliding as the offspring of Belial! But I will take up my cross with the comfort, that whatever shewed like goodness in me or mine, is but like the light that shines frae the creeping insects on the brae-side in a dark night—it kythes bright to the ee, because all is dark around it; but when the morn comes on the mountains, it is but a puir crawling kail-worm after a'. And sae it shows, wi' ony rag of human righteousness, or formal law-work, that we may pit round us to cover our shame."

As he pronounced these words, the door again opened, and Mr Bartholine Saddletree entered, his three-pointed hat set far back on his head, with a silk handkerchief beneath it, to keep it in that cool position, his gold-headed cane in his hand, and his whole deportment that of a wealthy burgher, who might one day look to have a share in the magistracy, if not actually to hold the curule chair itself.

Rochefoucault, who has torn the veil from so many foul gangrenes of the human heart, says, we find something not altogether unpleasant to us in the misfortunes of our best friends. Mr Saddletree would have been very angry had any one told him that he felt pleasure in the disaster of poor Effie Deans, and the disgrace of her family; and yet there is great question whether the gratification of playing the person of importance, inquiring, investigating, and laying down the law on the whole affair, did not offer, to say the least, full consolation for the pain which pure sympathy gave him on account of his wife's kinswoman. He had now got a piece of real judicial business by the end, instead of being obliged, as was his common case, to intrude his opinion where it was neither wished nor wanted; and felt as happy in the exchange as a boy when he gets his first new watch, which actually goes when wound up, and has real hands and a true dial-plate. But besides this subject for legal disquisition, Bartholine's brains were also overloaded with the affair of Porteous, his violent death, and all its probable consequences to the city and community. It was what the French call *l'embarras des richesses*, the confusion arising from too much mental wealth. He walked in with a consciousness of double importance, full fraught with the superiority of one who possesses more information than the company into which he enters, and who feels a right to discharge his learning on them without mercy. "Good morning, Mr Deans,—good-morrow to you, Mr Butler,—I was not aware that you were acquainted with Mr Deans."

Butler made some slight answer: his reasons may be readily imagined for not making his connection with the family, which, in his eyes, had something of tender mystery, a frequent subject of conversation with indifferent persons, such as Saddletree.

The worthy burgher, in the plenitude of self-importance, now sate down upon a chair, wiped his brow, collected his breath, and made the first experiment of the restored pith of his lungs, in a deep and dignified sigh, resembling a groan in sound and intonation—"Awfu' times these, neighbour Deans, awfu' times."

"Sinfu', shamefu', heaven-daring times," answered Deans, in a lower and more subdued tone.

"For my part," continued Saddletree, swelling with importance, "what between the distress of my friends, and of my puir auld country, ony wit that ever I had may be said to have abandoned me, sae that I sometimes think mysell as ignorant as if I were *inter rusticos*. Here when I arise in the morning, wi' my mind just arranged touching what's to be done in puir Effie's misfortune, and hae gotten the hale statute at my finger-ends, the mob maun get up and string Jock Porteous to a dyester's beam, and ding a' thing out of my head again."

Deeply as he was distressed with his own domestic calamity, Deans could not help expressing some interest in the news. Saddletree immediately entered on details of the insurrection and its consequences, while Butler took the occasion to seek some private conversation with Jeanie Deans. She gave him the opportunity he sought, by leaving the room, as if in prosecution of some part of her morning labour. Butler followed her in a few minutes, leaving Deans so closely engaged by his busy visitor, that there was little chance of his observing their absence.

The scene of their interview was an outer apartment, where Jeanie was used to busy herself in arranging the productions of her dairy. When Butler found an opportunity of stealing after her into this place, he found her silent, dejected, and ready to burst into tears. Instead of the active industry with which she had been accustomed, even while in the act of speaking, to employ her hands in some useful branch of household business, she was seated listless in a corner, sinking apparently under the weight of her own thoughts. Yet the instant he entered, she dried her eyes, and, with the simplicity and openness of her character, immediately entered on the conversation.

"I am glad you have come in, Mr Butler," said she, "for—for—for I wished to tell ye, that all maun be ended between you and me—it's best for baith our sakes."

"Ended?" said Butler, in surprise; "and for what should it be ended?—I grant this is a heavy dispensation, but it lies neither at your door nor mine—it's an evil of God's sending, and it maun be borne; but it canna break plighted troth, Jeanie, while they that plighted their word wish to keep it."

"But, Reuben," said the young woman, looking at him affectionately, "I ken weel that ye wad think mair of me than yourself; and, Reuben, I can only in requital think mair of your weal than of my ain. Ye are a man of spotless name, bred to God's ministry, and a' men say that ye will some day rise high in the Kirk, though poverty keeps ye down e'en now. Poverty is a bad back-friend, Reuben, and that ye ken ower weel; but ill fame is a waur ane, and that is a truth ye sall never learn through my means."

"What do ye mean?" said Butler, eagerly and impatiently; "or how do you connect your sister's guilt, if guilt there be, which, I trust in God, may be yet disproved, with our engagement?—how can that affect you or me?"

"How can you ask me that, Mr Butler? Will this stain, d'ye think, ever be forgotten as lang as our heads are abune the grund? Will it not stick to us, and to our bairns, and to their very bairns' bairns? To hae been the child of an honest man, might hae been saying something for me and mine; but to be the sister of a —— O, my God!"—With this exclamation her resolution failed, and she burst into a passionate fit of tears.

Her lover used every effort to induce her to compose herself, and at length succeeded; but she only resumed her composure to express herself with the same positiveness as before. "No, Reuben, I'll bring disgrace hame to nae man's hearth; my ain distresses I can bear, and I maun bear, but there is nae occasion for buckling them on other folks' shouthers. I will bear my load alone—the back is made for the burthen."

A lover is by charter wayward and suspicious; and Jeanie's readiness to renounce their engagement, under pretence of zeal for his peace of mind and respectability of character, seemed to poor Butler to form a portentous combination with the commission of the stranger he had met with that morning. His voice faultered as he asked, "Whether nothing but a sense of her sister's present distress occasioned her to talk in that manner?"

"And what else can do sae?" she replied with simplicity. "Is it not ten long years since we spoke together in this way?"

"Ten years?" said Butler. "It is a long time—sufficient perhaps for a woman to weary"——

"To weary of her auld gown," said Jeanie, "and to wish for a new ane, if she likes to go brave, but not long enough to weary of a friend— The eye may wish change, but the heart never."

"Never?" said Reuben,—"that is a bold promise."

"But not more bauld than true," said Jeanie, with the same quiet simplicity which attended her manner in joy and grief, in ordinary affairs, and in those which most interested her feelings.

Butler paused, and, looking at her fixedly—"I am charged," he said, "with a message to you, Jeanie."

"Indeed? from whom or what can ony ane have to say to me?"

"It is from a stranger," said Butler, affecting to speak with an indifference which his voice belied—"A young man whom I met this morning in the Park."

"My God!" said Jeanie eagerly; "and what did he say?"

"That he could not see you at the hour he proposed, but required you should meet him alone at Muschat's Cairn this next night, so soon as the moon rises."

"Tell him," said Jeanie hastily, "I shall certainly come."

"May I ask," said Butler, his suspicions increasing at the ready alacrity of the answer, "who this man is to whom you are so willing to give the meeting at a place and hour so uncommon?"

"Folk maun do muckle they hae little will to do, in this world," replied Jeanie.

"Granted," said her lover; "but what compels you to this?—who is this person? What I saw of him was not very favourable—who, or what is he?"

"I do not know," replied Jeanie composedly.

"You do not know," said Butler, stepping impatiently through the apartment—"You propose to meet a young man whom you do not know, at such a time, and in a place so lonely—you say you are compelled to do this—and yet you say you do not know the person who exercises such an influence over you!—Jeanie, what am I to think of this?"

"Think only, Reuben, that I speak truth, as if I were to answer at the last day.—I do not ken this man—I do not even ken that I ever saw him, and yet I must give him the meeting he asks—there's life and death upon it."

"Will you not tell your father, or take him with you?" said Butler.

"I cannot," said Jeanie; "I have no permission."

"Will you let *me* go with you? I will wait in the Park till nightfall, and join you when you set out."

"It is impossible," said Jeanie; "there maunna be mortal creature within hearing of our conference."

"Have you considered well the nature of what you are going to do? —the time—the place—an unknown and suspicious character?— Why, if he had asked to see you in this house, your father sitting in the next room, and within call, at such an hour, you should have refused to see him."

"My weird maun be fulfilled, Mr Butler; my life and my safety are in God's hands, but I'll not spare to risk either of them on the errand I am ganging to do."

"Then, Jeanie," said Butler, much displeased, "we must indeed break short off, and bid farewell. When there can be no confidence betwixt a man and his plighted wife on such a momentous topic, 'tis a sign she has no longer the regard for him that makes their engagement safe and suitable."

Jeanie looked at him and sighed. "I thought," she said, "that I had brought myself to bear this parting—but—but—I did not ken that we were to part in unkindness. But I am a woman and you a man—it may be different wi' you—if your mind is made easier by thinking sae hardly of me, I would not ask you to think otherwise."

"You are," said Butler, "what you have always been—wiser, better, and less selfish in your native feelings, than I can be, with all the helps that philosophy can give to a Christian.—But why—why will you persevere in an undertaking so desperate? Why will you not let me be your assistant—your protector, or at least your adviser?"

"Just because I cannot, and I dare not," answered Jeanie.—"But hark, what's that? Surely my father is no ill?"

In fact, the voices in the next room became obstreperously loud of a sudden, the cause of which vociferation it is necessary to explain before we go farther.

When Jeanie and Butler retired, Mr Saddletree entered upon the business which chiefly interested the family. In the commencement of their conversation he found old Deans, who, in his usual state of mind, was no granter of propositions, so much subdued by a deep sense of his daughter's danger and disgrace, that he heard without replying to, or perhaps without understanding, one or two learned disquisitions on the nature of the crime imputed to her charge, and on the steps which ought to be taken in consequence. His only answer at each pause was, "I am no misdoubting that ye wuss us weel—your wife's our far awa' cousin."

Encouraged by these symptoms of acquiescence, Saddletree, who, as an amateur of the law, had a supreme deference for all constituted authorities, again recurred to his other topic of interest, the murder, namely, of Porteous, and pronounced a severe censure on the parties concerned.

"These are kittle times—kittle times, Mr Deans, when the people take the power of life and death out of the hands of the rightful magistrate into their ain rough grip. I am of opinion, and so I believe will Mr Crossmyloof and the Privy-Council, that this rising in effeir of war, to take away the life of a reprieved man, will prove little better than perduellion."

"If I hadna that on my mind that's ill to bear, Mr Saddletree," said Deans, "I wad make bold to dispute that point wi' you."

"How could ye dispute what's plain law, man?" said Saddletree, somewhat contemptuously; "there's no a callant that e'er carried a pock wi' a process in't, but will tell ye that perduellion is the warst and maist virulent kind of treason, being an open convocating of the king's lieges against his authority, (mair especially in arms, and by touk of drum, to baith whilk accessories my een and lugs bore witness,) and muckle warse than lese-majesty, or the concealment of a treasonable purpose. It winna bear a dispute, neighbour."

"But it will though," retorted Douce David Deans; "I tell ye it will bear a dispute. I never like your cauld, legal, formal doctrines, neighbour Saddletree. I haud unco little by the Parliament-house, since the awfu' downfall of the hopes of honest folk that followed the Revolution."

"But what wad ye hae had, Mr Deans?" said Saddletree impatiently; "did na ye get baith liberty and conscience made fast, and settled by tailzie on you and your heirs for ever?"

"Mr Saddletree," retorted Deans, "I ken ye are ane of those that are wise after the manner of this world, and that ye haud your part, and cast in your portion wi' the lang-heads and lang-gowns, and keep with the smart witty-pated lawyers of this our land—Weary on the dark and dolefu' cast that they hae gi'en this unhappy kingdom, when their black hand of defection was clasped in the red hand of our sworn murtherers: when those who had numbered the towers of our Zion, and marked the bulwarks of our reformation, saw their hope turn into a snare, and their rejoicing into weeping."

"I canna understand this, neighbour," answered Saddletree. "I am an honest presbyterian of the Kirk of Scotland, and stand by her and the General Assembly, and the due administration of justice by the fifteen Lords o' Session and the five Lords o' Justiciary."

"Out upon ye, Mr Saddletree!" exclaimed David, who, in an opportunity of giving his testimony on the offences and backslidings of the land, forgot for a moment his own domestic calamity—"out upon your General Assembly, and the back of my hand to your Court o' Session!—What is the tane but a waefu' bunch o' cauldrife professors and ministers, that sate bien and warm when the persecuted remnant were warstling wi' hunger, and cauld, and fear of death, and danger of fire and sword, upon wet brae-sides, peat-haggs, and flow-mosses, and that now creep out of their holes, like blue-bottles in a blink of sunshine, to take the pu'pits and places of better folk—of them that witnessed, and testified, and fought, and endured pit, prison-house, and transportation beyond seas—A bonny bike there's o' them!— And for your Court o' Session"——

"Ye may say what ye will o' the General Assembly," said Saddletree, interrupting him, "and let them clear them that kens them; but as for the Lords o' Session, forbye that they are my next door neighbours, I would have ye ken, for your ain regulation, that to raise scandal anent them, whilk is termed, to *murmur* again them, is a crime *sui generis*—*sui generis*, Mr Deans—ken ye what that amounts to?"

"I ken little o' the language of anti-christ," said Deans; "and I care less than little what carnal courts will call the speeches of honest men.

And as to murmur again them, it's what a' the folk that losses their pleas, and nine-tenths o' them that win them, will be gay sure to be guilty in. Sae I wad hae ye ken that I haud a' your gleg-tongued advocates, that sell their knowledge for pieces of silver, and your warldly-wise judges, that will gi'e three days of hearing in presence to a debate about the peeling of an ingan, and no ae half-hour to the gospel testimony, as legalists, formalists, countenancing, by sentences, and quirks, and cunning turns of law, the late begun courses of national defections—union, toleration, patronages, and Yerastian prelatic oaths. As for the soul and body-killing Court o' Justiciary"——

The habit of considering his life as dedicated to bear testimony in behalf of what he deemed the suffering and deserted cause of true religion, had swept honest David along with it thus far; but with the mention of the criminal court, the recollection of the disastrous condition of his daughter rushed at once on his mind; he stopped short in the midst of his triumphant declamation, pressed his hands against his forehead, and remained silent.

Saddletree was somewhat moved, but apparently not so much so as to induce him to relinquish the privilege of prosing in his turn, afforded him by David's sudden silence. "Nae doubt, neighbour," he said, "it's a sair thing to hae to do wi' courts of law, unless it be to improve ane's knowledge and practique, by waiting on as a hearer; and touching this unhappy affair of Effie—ye'll hae seen the dittay doubtless?" He dragged out of his pocket a bundle of papers, and began to turn them over. "This is no it—this is the information of Mungo Marsport, of that ilk, against Captain Lackland, for coming on his lands of Marsport with hawks, hounds, lying-dogs, nets, guns, cross-bows, hagbuts of found, or other engines more or less for destruction of game, sic as red-deer, fallow-deer, capper-cailzies, grey-fowl, moor-fowl, paitricks, herons, and sic like; he the said defender not being ane qualified person in terms of the statute sixteen hundred and twenty-ane; that is, not having ane plough-gate of land. Now the defences proposed say, that *non constat* at this present what is a plough-gate of land, whilk uncertainty is sufficient to elide the conclusions of the libel. But then the answers to the defences, (they are signed by Mr Crossmyloof, but Mr Younglad drew them,) they propone, that it signifies naething, *in hoc statu*, what or how muckle a plough-gate of land may be, in respect the defender has nae lands whatsoe'er, less or mair. 'Sae grant a plough-gate'" (here Saddletree read from the paper in his hand,) "'to be less than the nineteenth part of a guse's grass' (I trow Mr Crossmyloof put in that—I ken his style,) —'of a guse's grass, what the better will the defender be, seeing

he hasna a divot-cast of land in Scotland?—*Advocatus* for Lackland
duplies, that *nihil interest de possessione*, the pursuer must put his case
under the statute'—now, this is worth your notice, neighbour,—'and
must show, *formaliter et specialiter*, as well as *generaliter*, what is the
qualification that the defender Lackland does not possess—let him
tell me what a plough-gate of land is, and I'll tell him if I have one or
no. Surely the pursuer is bound to understand his own libel, and his
own statute that he founds upon. *Titius* pursues *Mævius* for recovery
of ane *black* horse lent to Mævius—surely he shall have judgment; but
if Titius pursue Mævius for recovery of ane *scarlet* or *crimson* horse,
surely he shall be bound to show that there is sic ane animal in *rerum
natura*. No man can be bound to plead to nonsense—that is to say, to a
charge which cannot be explained or understood'—(he's wrang there
—the better the pleading the fewer understand them,)—'and so the
reference unto this undefined and unintelligible measure of land is, as
if a penalty was inflicted by statute for any man who suld hunt or halk,
or use lying-dogs, without having about him ane'——But I am wearying you, Mr Deans, we'll pass to your ain business,—though this case
of Marsport against Lackland has made an unco din in the Outer-
house. Weel, here's the dittay against puir Effie: 'Whereas it is humbly meant and shown to us,' &c. (they are words of mere style,) 'that
where, by the laws of this and every other well-regulated realm, the
murder of any one, more especially of an infant child, is a crime of ane
high nature, and severely punishable: And whereas, without prejudice to the foresaid generality, it was, by ane act made in the second
session of the First Parliament of our most High and Dread Sover-
eigns William and Mary, especially enacted, that ane woman who shall
have concealed her condition, and shall not be able to show that she
hath called for help at the birth, in case that the child shall be found
dead or amissing, shall be deemed and held guilty of the murder
thereof; and the said facts of concealment and pregnancy being found
proven or confessed, shall sustain the pains of law accordingly; yet,
nevertheless, you Effie, or Euphemia Deans'"——

"Read no further," said Deans, raising his head up; "I would rather
ye thrust a sword into my heart than read a word farther."

"Weel, neighbour," said Saddletree, "I thought it wad hae comforted ye to ken the best and the warst o't. But the question is, what's to
be dune?"

"Nothing," answered Deans firmly, "but to abide the dispensation
that the Lord sees meet to send us. O if it had been His will to take
the grey head to rest before this awful visitation on my house and
name! But His will be done. I can say that yet, though I can say little
mair."

"But, neighbour," said Saddletree, "ye'll retain advocates for the puir lassie? it's a thing maun needs be thought of."

"If there was ae man of them," answered Deans, "that had held fast his integrity—but I ken them weel, they are a' carnal, crafty, and warld-hunting self-seekers, Yerastians, and Arminians, every ane o' them."

"Hout tout, neighbour, ye maunna take the warld at its word," said Saddletree; "the very de'il is no sae ill as he's ca'd; and I ken mair than ae advocate that may be said to hae some integrity as weel as their neighbours; that is, after a sort o' fashion o' their ain."

"It is indeed but a fashion of integrity that ye will find amang them," replied David Deans, "and a fashion of wisdom, and a fashion of carnal learning—gazing, glancing-glasses they are, fit only to fling the glaiks in folk's een, wi' their pawky policy, and earthly ingine, their flights and refinements and periods of eloquence, frae heathen emperors and popish canons, and canna, in that daft trash ye were reading to me, sae muckle as ca' men that are sae ill-starred as to be amang their hands, by ony name o' the dispensation o' grace, but maun new baptize them by the names of the accursed Titus, wha was made the instrument of burning the holy Temple, and other sic like heathens."

"It's Tishius," interrupted Saddletree, "and no Titus. Mr Crossmyloof cares as little about Titus or the Latin learning as ye do.—But it's a case of necessity—she maun hae counsel. Now I could speak to Mr Crossmyloof—he's weel kenned for a round-spun presbyterian, and a ruling-elder to boot."

"He's a rank Yerastian," replied Deans; "one of the public and polititious warldly-wise men that stude up to prevent ane general owning of the cause in the day of power."

"What say ye to the Laird of Cuffabout?" said Saddletree; "he whiles thumps the dust out of a case gay and weel."

"He? the fause lown!" answered Deans—"he was in his bandaliers to hae joined the ungracious Hielanders in 1715, an' they had ever had the luck to cross the Firth."

"Arniston? there's a clever child for ye," said Bartholine, triumphantly.

"Ay, to bring popish medals in till their very library from that schismatic woman in the north, the Duchess of Gordon."

"Weel, weel, but somebody ye maun hae—Kittlepunt?"

"He's an Arminian."

"Woodsetter?"

"He's, I doubt, a Cocceian."

"Auld Whulliewhaw?"

"He's ony thing ye like."

"Young Næmmo?"

"He's naething at a'."

"Ye're ill to please, neighbour," said Saddletree; "I hae run ower the pick o' them for you, ye maun e'en choose for yersell; but bethink ye that in the multitude of counsellors there's safety.—What say ye to try young Mackenyie? he has a' his uncle's practiques at the tongue's end."

"What, sir, wad ye speak to me," exclaimed the sturdy presbyterian in excessive wrath, "about a man that has the blood o' the saints at his fingers' end? Didna his eme die and gang to his place wi' the name of the Bluidy Mackenyie? and winna he be kenned by that name sae lang as there's a Scots tongue to speak the word? If the life of the dear bairn that's under a suffering dispensation, and Jeanie's, and my ain, and a' mankind's, depended on my asking sic a slave o' Satan to speak a word for me or them, they should a' gae down the water thegither for Davie Deans."

It was the exalted tone in which he spoke this last sentence that broke up the conversation between Butler and Jeanie, and brought them both "ben the house," to use the language of the country. Here they found the poor old man half frantic, between grief, and zealous ire against Saddletree's proposed measures, his cheek inflamed, his hand clenched, and his voice raised, while the tear in his eye, and the occasional quiver of his accents, shewed that his utmost efforts were inadequate to shaking off the consciousness of his misery. Butler, apprehensive of the consequences of his agitation to an aged and feeble frame, ventured to utter to him a recommendation to patience.

"I *am* patient," returned the old man, sternly,—"more patient than any one who is alive to the woeful backslidings of a miserable time can be patient; and in so much, that I need neither sectarians, nor sons nor grandsons of sectarians, to instruct my grey hairs how to bear my cross."

"But, sir," continued Butler, taking no offence at the slur cast on his grandfather's faith, "we must use human means. When you call in a physician, you would not, I suppose, question him on the nature of his religious principles?"

"Wad I *no?*" answered David—"But I wad though; and if he didna satisfy me that he had a right sense of the right-hand and left-hand defections of the day, not a goutte of his physic should gang through my father's son."

It is a dangerous thing to trust to an illustration. Butler had done so and miscarried; but, like a gallant soldier when his musket misses fire, he stood his ground, and charged with the bayonet.—"This is too rigid an interpretation of your duty, sir. The sun shines, and the rain descends on the just and unjust, and they are placed together in life in circumstances which frequently render intercourse between them indispensable, perhaps that the evil may have an opportunity of being converted by the good, and perhaps, also, that the righteous might, among other trials, be subjected to that of occasional converse with the profane."

"Ye're a silly callant, Reuben," answered Deans, "with your bits of argument. Can a man touch pitch and not be defiled? Or what think ye of the brave and worthy champions of the Covenant, that wadna sae muckle as hear a minister speak, be his gifts and graces as they would, that hadna witnessed against the enormities of the day? Nae lawyer shall ever speak for me and mine that hasna concurred in the testimony of the scattered, yet lovely remnant, which abode in the clifts of the rocks."

So saying, and as if fatigued, both with the arguments and presence of his guests, the old man arose, and seeming to bid them adieu with a motion of his head and hand, went to shut himself up in his sleeping apartment.

"It's thrawing his daughter's life awa," said Saddletree to Butler, "to hear him speak in that daft gate. Where will he ever get a Cameronian advocate? Or wha ever heard of a lawyer's suffering either for ae religion or another? The lassie's life is clean flung awa."

During the latter part of this debate, Dumbiedikes had arrived at the door, dismounted, hung the poney's bridle on the usual hook, and sunk down on his ordinary settle. His eyes, with more than their usual animation, followed first one speaker, then another, till he caught the melancholy sense of the whole from Saddletree's last words. He rose from his seat, stumped slowly across the room, and, coming close up to Saddletree's ear, said, in a tremulous and anxious voice, "Will— will siller do naething for them, Mr Saddletree?"

"Umph!" said Saddletree, looking grave,—"siller will certainly do it in the Parliament-house, if ony thing *can* do it; but whare's the siller to come frae? Mr Deans, ye see, will do naething; and though Mrs Saddletree's their far-awa friend, and right gude weel-wisher, and is weel disposed doubtless to assist, yet she wadna like to stand to be bound *singuli in solidum* to such an expensive wark. An' ilka friend wad bear a share o' the burthen, something might be dune—ilk ane to be liable for their ain input—I wadna like to see the case fa' through without being pled—it wadna be creditable, for a' that daft whig body says."

"I'll—I will—yes," (assuming fortitude,) "I *will* be answerable," said Dumbiedikes, "for a score of punds sterling,"—and he was silent, staring in astonishment at finding himself capable of such unwonted resolution and excessive generosity.

"God Almighty bless ye, Laird!" said Jeanie in a transport of gratitude.

"Ye may ca' the twenty punds thretty," said Dumbiedikes, looking bashfully away from her and towards Saddletree.

"That will do bravely," said Saddletree, rubbing his hands; "and ye sall hae a' my skeel and knowledge to gar the siller gang far—I'll tape it out weel—I ken how to gar the birkies tak short fees, and be glad o' them too—it's only garring them trow ye hae twa or three cases of importance coming on, and they'll work cheap to get custom. Let me alane for whullying an advocate;—it's nae sin to get as muckle frae them for our siller as we can—after a', it's but the wind o' their mouth —it costs them naething; whereas, in my wretched occupation of a saddler, horse-milliner, and harness-maker, we are out unconscionable sums just for barkened hides and leather."

"Can I be of no use?" said Butler. "My means, alas! are only worth the black coat I wear; but I am young—I owe much to the family—Can I do nothing?"

"Ye can help to collect evidence, sir," said Saddletree; "if we could but find ony ane to say she had gi'en the least hint o' her condition, she wad be brought aff wi' a wat finger—Mr Crossmyloof tell'd me sae. The crown, says he, canna be craved to prove a positive—was't a positive or a negative they couldna be ca'd to prove?—it was the tane or the tither o' them, I am sure, and it maksna muckle whilk. Wherefore, says he, the libel maun be redargued by the pannel proving her defences. And it canna be done otherwise."

"But the fact, sir," argued Butler, "the fact that this poor girl has borne a child; surely the crown lawyers must prove that?" said Butler.

Saddletree paused a moment, while the visage of Dumbiedikes, which traversed, as if it had been placed on a pivot, from the one spokesman to the other, assumed a more blithe expression.

"Ye—ye—ye—es," said Saddletree, after some grave hesitation; "unquestionably that is a thing to be proved, as the Court will more fully declare by an interlocutor of relevancy in common form; but I fancy that job's done already, for she has confessed her guilt."

"Confessed the murder?" exclaimed Jeanie, with a scream that made them all start.

"Na, I didna say that," replied Bartholine. "But she confessed bearing the babe."

"And what became of it then?" said Jeanie; "for not a word could I get from her but bitter sighs and tears."

"She says it was taken away from her by the woman in whose house it was born, and who assisted her at the time."

"And who was that woman?" said Butler. "Surely by her means the truth might be discovered.—Who was she? I will fly to her directly—*ocior ventis—ocior Euro*."

"I wish," said Dumbiedikes, "I were as young and as supple as you, and had the gift of the gab as weel."

"Who is she?" again reiterated Butler impatiently.—"Who could that woman be?"

"Ay, wha kens that but hersell," said Saddletree; "she deponed further, and declined to answer that interrogatory."

"Then to herself will I instantly go," said Butler; "farewell, Jeanie;" then coming close up to her.—"Take no *rash step* till you hear from me; farewell." And he immediately left the cottage.

"I wad gang too," said the landed proprietor, in an anxious, jealous, and repining tone, "but my powney winna for the life o' me gang ony other road than just frae Dumbiedikes to this house-end, and sae straight back again."

"Ye'll do better for them," said Saddletree, as they left the house together, "by sending me the thretty punds."

"Thretty punds?" hesitated Dumbiedikes, who was now out of the reach of those eyes which had inflamed his generosity; "I only said *twenty* punds."

"Ay; but," said Saddletree, "that was under protestation to add and eik; and so ye craved leave to amend your libel, and made it thretty."

"Did I? I dinna mind that I did," answered Dumbiedikes. "But whatever I said I'll stand to." Then bestriding his steed, with some difficulty he added, "Dinna ye think poor Jeanie's een wi' the tears in them glanced like lamour beads, Mr Saddletree?"

"I kenna muckle about women's een, Laird," replied the insensible Bartholine; "and I care just as little. I wuss I were as weel free o' their tongues; though few wives," he added, recollecting the necessity of keeping up his character for domestic rule, "are under better command than mine, Laird. I allow neither perduellion nor læse-majesty against my sovereign authority."

The Laird saw nothing so important in this observation as to call for a rejoinder, and when they had exchanged a mute salutation, they parted in peace upon their different errands.

Chapter Thirteen

I'll warrant that fellow from drowning, were the ship
no stronger than a nut-shell.

The Tempest

BUTLER FELT NEITHER fatigue nor want of refreshment, although from the mode in which he had spent the night he might well have been overcome with either. But in the earnestness with which he hastened to the assistance of the sister of Jeanie Deans, he forgot both.

In his first progress he walked with so rapid a pace as almost approached to running, when he was surprised to hear behind him a call upon his name, contending with an asthmatic cough, and half-drowned amid the resounding trot of an Highland poney. He looked behind, and saw the Laird of Dumbiedikes making after him with what speed he might, for it happened fortunately for the Laird's purpose of conversing with Butler, that his own road homeward was for about two hundred yards the same with that which led by the nearest way to the city. Butler stopped when he heard himself thus summoned, internally wishing no good to the panting equestrian who thus retarded his journey.

"Uh! uh! uh!" ejaculated Dumbiedikes, as he checked the hobbling pace of the poney by our friend Butler. "Uh! uh! it's a hard-set willyard beast this o' mine." He had in fact just overtaken the object of his chase at the very point beyond which it would have been absolutely impossible for him to have continued the pursuit, since there Butler's road parted from that leading to Dumbiedikes, and no means of influence or compulsion which the rider could possibly have used towards his Bucephalus could have induced the Celtic obstinacy of Rory Bean (such was the poney's name,) to have diverged a yard from the path that conducted him to his own paddock.

Even when he had recovered from the shortness of breath occasioned by a trot much more rapid than Rory or he were accustomed to, the high purpose of Dumbiedikes seemed to stick as it were in his throat and impede his utterance, so that Butler stood for nearly three minutes ere he could utter a syllable, and when he did find voice, it was only to say, after one or two efforts, "Uh! uh! uhm! I say, Mr—Mr Butler, it's a braw day for the harst."

"Fine day, indeed," said Butler impatiently. "I wish you good morning, sir."

"Stay—stay a bit," rejoined Dumbiedikes; "that was no what I had gotten to say."

"Then pray be quick, and let me have your commands," rejoined Butler; "I crave your pardon, but I am in haste, and *Tempus nemini*—you know the proverb."

Dumbiedikes did not know the proverb, nor did he even take the trouble to endeavour to look as if he did, as others in his place would have done. He was concentrating all his intellects for one grand proposition, and could not afford any detachment to defend outposts.

"I say, Mr Butler," said he, "ken ye if Mr Saddletree's a grit lawyer?"

"I have no person's word for it but his own," answered Butler drily; "but undoubtedly he best understands his own qualities."

"Umph!" replied the taciturn Dumbiedikes, in a tone which seemed to say, "Mr Butler, I take your meaning." "In that case," he pursued, "I'll employ my ain man o' business, Michel Novit (auld Nichil's son, and amaist as gleg as his father) to agent Effie's plea."

And having thus displayed more sagacity than Butler expected from him, he courteously touched his gold-laced cocked hat, and by a punch on the ribs, conveyed to Rory Bean, it was his rider's pleasure that he should forthwith proceed homewards; a hint which the quadruped obeyed with that degree of alacrity, with which men and animals interpret and obey suggestions that entirely correspond with their own inclinations.

Butler resumed his pace, not without a momentary revival of that jealousy, which the honest Laird's attention to the family of Deans, had at different times excited in his bosom. But he was too generous long to nurse any feeling, which was allied to selfishness. "He is," said Butler to himself, "rich in what I want; why should I feel vexed that he has the heart to dedicate some of his pelf to render them services, which I can only form the empty wish of executing? In God's name, let us each do what we can. May she be but happy!—saved from the misery and disgrace that seems impending—Let me but find the means of preventing the fearful experiment of this evening, and farewell to other hopes, though my heart-strings break in parting with them."

He redoubled his pace, and soon stood before the door of the tolbooth, or rather before the entrance where the door had formerly been placed. His interview with the mysterious stranger, the message to Jeanie, his agitating conversation with her on the subject of breaking off their mutual engagements, and the interesting scene with old Deans, had so entirely occupied his mind as to drown recollection even of the tragical event which he had witnessed the preceding evening. His attention was not recalled to it by the groupes who

stood scattered on the street in conversation, which they hushed
when strangers approached, or by the bustling search of the agents of
the city police, supported by small parties of the military, or by the
appearance of the Guard-House, before which were treble sentinels,
or, finally, by the subdued and intimidated looks of the lower orders of
society, who, conscious that they were liable to suspicion, if they were
not guilty of accession to a riot likely to be strictly enquired into, glided
about with an humble and dismayed aspect, like men whose spirits
being exhausted in the revel and the dangers of a desperate debauch
over night, are nerve-shaken, timorous, and unenterprizing on the
succeeding day.

None of these symptoms of alarm and trepidation struck Butler,
whose mind was occupied with a different, and to him still more
interesting subject, until he stood before the entrance to the prison,
and saw it defended by a double file of grenadiers, instead of bolts and
bars. Their "Stand, stand," the blackened appearance of the door-
less gate-way, and the winding stair-case and apartments of the tolbooth, now open to the public eye, recalled the whole proceedings of
the eventful night. Upon his requesting to speak with Effie Deans, the
same tall, thin, silver-haired turnkey, whom he had seen on the preceding evening, made his appearance.

"I think," he replied to Butler's request of admission, with true
Scottish indirection, "ye will be the same lad that was for in to see her
yestreen?"

Butler admitted he was the same person.

"And I am thinking," pursued the turnkey, "ye speered at me
when we locked up, and if we locked up earlier on account of
Porteous?"

"Very likely I might make some such idle observation," said Butler;
"but the question now is, can I see Effie Deans?"

"I dinna ken—gang in bye, and up the turnpike stair, and turn till
the ward on the left hand."

The old man followed close behind him, with his keys in his hand,
not forgetting even that huge one which had once opened and shut the
outward gate of his dominions, though at present it was but an idle and
useless burthen. No sooner had Butler entered the room to which he
was directed, than the experienced hand of the warder selected the
proper key and locked it on the outside. At first Butler conceived this
manœuvre was only an effect of the man's habitual and official caution and jealousy. But when he heard the hoarse command, "Turn out
the guard," and immediately afterwards heard the clash of a centinel's
arms, as he was posted at the door of his apartment, he again called out
to the turnkey, "My good friend, I have business of some consequence

with Effie Deans, and I beg to see her as soon as possible." No answer was returned. "If it be against your rules to admit me," repeated Butler, in a still louder tone, "to see the prisoner, I beg you will tell me so, and let me go about my business.—*Fugit irrevocabile tempus!*" muttered he to himself.

"If ye had business to do, you suld hae dune it before ye cam here," replied the man of keys from the outside; "ye'll find it's easier winning in than winning out here—there's sma' likelihood o' another Porteous-mob coming to rabble us again—the law will haud her ain now, neighbour, and that ye'll find to your cost."

"What do ye mean by that, sir?" retorted Butler. "You must mistake me for some other person. My name is Reuben Butler, preacher of the gospel."

"I ken that weel eneugh," said the turnkey.

"Well then, if you know me, I have a right to know from you in return, what warrant you have for detaining me: that, I know, is the right of every British subject."

"Warrant?" said the jailor—"the warrant's awa to Libberton wi' twa sheriff officers seeking ye. If ye had staid at hame, as honest men should do, ye wad hae seen the warrant; but if ye come to be incarcerated of your ain accord, wha can help it, my jo?"

"So I cannot see Effie Deans, then," said Butler; "and you are determined not to let me out?"

"Troth will I no, neighbour," answered the old man, doggedly; "as for Effie Deans, ye'll hae eneugh ado to mind your ain business, and let her mind hers; and for letting ye out, that maun be as the magistrate will determine. And fare ye weel for a bit, for I maun see Deacon Sawyers pitt on ane or twa o' the doors that your quiet folk broke down yesternight, Mr Butler."

There was something in this exquisitely provoking, but there was also something darkly alarming. To be imprisoned, even on a false accusation, has something in it disagreeable and menacing even to men of more constitutional courage than Butler had to boast, for although he had much of that resolution which arises from a sense of duty and an honourable desire to discharge it, yet as his imagination was lively, and his frame of body delicate, he was far from possessing that cool insensibility to danger which is the happy portion of men of stronger health, more firm nerves, and less acute sensibility. An indistinct idea of danger, which he could neither understand nor ward off, seemed to float before his eyes. He tried to think over the events of the preceding night, in hopes of discovering some means of explaining or vindicating his conduct for appearing among the mob, since it immediately occurred to him that his detention must be founded on that circumstance. And it was with anxiety that he found he could not recollect to have been under the observation of any disinterested witness in the attempts that he made from time to time to expostulate with the rioters, and to prevail on them to release him. The distress of the Deans family, the dangerous rendezvous which Jeanie had formed, and which he could not now hope to interrupt, had also their share in his unpleasant reflections. Yet impatient as he was to receive an eclaircissement upon the cause of his confinement, and if possible to obtain his liberty, he was affected with a trepidation which seemed no good omen; when, after remaining an hour in this solitary apartment, he received a summons to attend the sitting magistrate. He was conducted from prison strongly guarded by a party of soldiers, with a parade of precaution, that, however ill-timed and unnecessary, is generally displayed *after* an event, which, if used in time, such caution might have prevented.

He was introduced into the Council Chamber, as the place is called where the magistrates hold their sittings, and which was then at a little distance from the prison. One or two of the senators of the city were present, and seemed about to engage in the examination of an individual who was brought forward to the foot of the long green-covered table round which the council usually assembled. "Is that the preacher?" said one of the magistrates, as the city officer in attendance introduced Butler. The man answered in the affirmative. "Let him sit down there an instant: we will finish this man's business very briefly."

"Shall we remove Mr Butler?" queried the assistant.

"It is not necessary—Let him remain where he is."

Butler accordingly sate down on a bench at the bottom of the apartment, attended by one of his keepers.

It was a large room, partially and imperfectly lighted, but by chance, or by the skill of the architect, who might happen to remember the advantage which might occasionally be derived from such an arrangement, one window was so placed as to throw a strong light upon the foot of the table at which prisoners were usually posted for examination, while the upper end, where the examinants sate, was thrown into shadow. Butler's eyes were instantly fixed on the person whose examination was at present proceeding, in the idea that he might recognize some one of the conspirators of the former night. But though the features of this man were sufficiently marked and striking, he could not recollect that he had ever seen them before.

The complexion of this person was dark, and his age somewhat advanced. He wore his own hair, combed smooth down, and cut very short. It was jet black, slightly curled by nature, and already mottled with grey. The man's face expressed rather knavery than vice, more a disposition to sharpness, cunning, and roguery, than the traces of stormy and indulged passions. His sharp, quick, black eyes, acute features, ready sardonic smile, promptitude, and effrontery, gave him altogether what is called among the vulgar a *knowing* look, which generally implies a tendency to knavery. At a fair or market, you could not for a moment have doubted that he was a horse-jockey, intimate with all the tricks of his trade; yet had you met him on a moor, you would not have apprehended any violence from him. His dress was also that of a horse-dealer—a close buttoned jockey-coat, or wrap-rascal, as it was then termed, with huge metal buttons, coarse blue upper stockings, called boot-hose, because supplying the place of boots, and a slouched hat. He wanted only a loaded whip under his arm, and a spur upon one heel, to complete the dress of the character he seemed to present.

"Your name is James Ratcliffe?" said the magistrate.

"Ay—always wi' your honour's leave."

"That is to say, you could find me another name, if I did not like that ane?"

"Twenty to pick and chuse upon, always with your honour's leave," resumed the respondent.

"But James Ratcliffe is your present name—what is your trade?"

"I canna just say, distinctly, that I have what ye wad ca' preceesely a trade."

"But," repeated the magistrate, "what are your means of living—your occupation?"

"Hout tout—your honour, wi' your leave, kens that as weel as I do," replied the examined.

"No matter, I want to hear you describe it," said the examinant.

"Me describe?—and to your honour?—far be it from Jemmie Ratcliffe," responded the prisoner.

"Come, sir, no trifling—I insist on an answer."

"Weel, sir," replied the declarant, "I maun make a clean breast, for ye see, (wi' your leave) I am looking for favour—Describe my occupation, quo' ye?—troth it will be ill to do that, in a feasible way, in a place like this—but what is't again that the aught command says?"

"Thou shalt not steal," answered the magistrate.

"Are ye sure o' that?—Troth, than, my occupation, and that command, are sair at odds, for I aye read it, thou *shalt* steal, and that makes an unco difference, though there's but ae wee bit word left out."

"To cut the matter short, Ratcliffe, you have been a most notorious thief," said the examinant.

"I believe Highlands and Lawlands ken that, sir, forbye England and Holland," replied Ratcliffe, with the greatest composure and effrontery.

"And what d'ye think the end o' your calling will be?" said the magistrate.

"I could have gi'en a brave guess yesterday—but I dinna ken sae weel the day," answered the prisoner.

"And what would you have said would be your end, had you been asked the question yesterday?"

"Just the gallows," replied Ratcliffe, with the same composure.

"You are a daring rascal, sir," said the magistrate; "and how dare ye hope times are mended with you to-day?"

"Dear, your honour!" answered Ratcliffe, "there's muckle difference between lying in prison under sentence of death, and staying there of ane's ain proper accord, when it would have cost a man naething to get up and rin awa—what was to hinder me frae stepping out quietly, when the rabble walked awa' wi' Jock Porteous yestreen? —and does your honour really think I staid on purpose to be hanged?"

"I do not know what you may have proposed to yourself; but I know," said the magistrate, "what the law proposes for you, and that is to hang you next Wednesday eight days."

"Na, na, your honour," said Ratcliffe firmly, "craving your honour's pardon, I'll ne'er believe that till I see it. I have kenn'd the Law this mony a year, and mony a thrawart job I hae had wi' her first and last; but the auld jaud is no sae ill as that comes to—I aye fand her bark waur than her bite."

"And if you do not expect the gallows, to which you are condemned, (for the fourth time to my knowledge) may I beg the favour to know," said the magistrate, "what it is that you *do* expect in consideration of your not having taken your flight with the rest of the jail-birds, which I do admit was what was to have been expected?"

"I would never have thought for a moment of staying in that auld gousty toom house," answered Ratcliffe, "but that use and wont had just gi'en me a fancy to the place, and I'm just expecting a bit post in't."

"A post!" exclaimed the magistrate; "a whipping-post, I suppose, you mean?"

"Na, na, sir, I had nae thoughts o' a whuppin-post. After having been four times doomed to hang by the neck till I was dead, I think I am far beyond being whuppit."

"Then, in Heaven's name, what *did* you expect?"

"Just the post of under-turnkey, for I understand there's a

vacancy," said the prisoner; "I wadna think of asking the lock-man's* place ower his head; it wadna suit me sae weel as ither folk, for I never could pit a beast out o' the way, much less deal wi' a man."

"That's something in your favour," said the Baillie, making exactly the inference to which Ratcliffe was desirous to lead him, though he mantled his art with an affectation of oddity. "But," continued the magistrate, "how do you think you can be trusted with a charge in the prison, when you hae broken at your ain hand half the jails in Scotland?"

"Wi' your honour's leave," said Ratcliffe, "if I kenn'd sae weel how to win out mysel, it's like I wad be a' the better a hand to keep other folks in. I think they wad ken their business weel that keepit me in when I wanted to be out, or wan out when I wanted to keep them in."

The remark seemed to strike the magistrate, but he made no further immediate remark, only desired Ratcliffe to be removed.

When this daring, and yet sly free-booter was out of hearing, the magistrate asked the city-clerk, "what he thought of the fellow's assurance?"

"It's no for me to say, sir," replied the clerk; "but if James Ratcliffe be inclined to turn to good, there is not a man e'er came within the ports of the burgh could be of sae muckle use to the Good Town in the thief and lock-up line of business. I'll speak to Mr Sharpitlaw about him."

Upon Ratcliffe's retreat, Butler was placed at the table for examination. The magistrate conducted his enquiry civilly, but yet in a manner which gave him to understand that he laboured under strong suspicion. With a frankness which at once became his calling and character, Butler avowed his involuntary presence at the murder of Porteous, and, at the request of the magistrate, entered into a minute detail of the circumstances which attended that unhappy affair. All the particulars, such as we have narrated, were taken minutely down by the clerk from Butler's dictation.

When the narrative was concluded the cross examination commenced, which it is a painful task even for the most candid witness to undergo, since a story, especially if connected with agitating and alarming incidents, can scarce be so clearly and distinctly told, but that

---

* *Hangman*, so called from the small quantity of meal (Scottice, *lock*) which he was entitled to take out of every boll exposed to market in the city. In Edinburgh the duty has been very long commuted; but in Dumfries the finisher of the law still exercises, or did lately exercise, his privilege, the quantity taken being regulated by a small iron ladle, which he uses as the measure of his perquisite. The expression *lock* for a small quantity of any readily divisible dry substance, as corn, meal, flax, or the like, is still preserved, not only popularly, but in a legal description, as the *lock* and *gowpen*, or small quantity and handful, payable in thirlage cases, as in-town multure.

some ambiguity and doubt may be thrown upon it by a string of successive and minute interrogatories.

The magistrate commenced, by observing, that Butler had said his object was to return to the village of Libberton, but that he was interrupted by the mob at the West-port. "Is the West-port your usual way of leaving town when you go to Libberton?" said the magistrate with a sneer.

"No, certainly," answered Butler, with the haste of a man anxious to vindicate the accuracy of his evidence; "but I chanced to be nearer that port than any other, and the hour of shutting the gates was on the point of striking."

"That was unlucky," said the magistrate drily. "Pray, being, as you say, under coercion and fear of the lawless multitude, and compelled to accompany them through scenes disagreeable to all men of humanity, and more especially irreconcileable to the profession of a minister, did you not attempt to struggle, resist, or escape from their violence?"

Butler replied that their numbers prevented him from attempting resistance, and their vigilance from effecting his escape.

"That was unlucky," again repeated the magistrate, in the same dry inacquiescent tone of voice and manner. He proceeded with decency and politeness, but with a stiffness which argued his continued suspicion, to ask many questions concerning the behaviour of the mob, the manners and dress of the ringleaders; and when he conceived that the caution of Butler, if he was deceiving him, must be lulled asleep, the magistrate suddenly and artfully returned to former parts of his declaration, and required a new recapitulation of the circumstances, to the minutest and most trivial point which attended each part of the melancholy scene. No confusion or contradiction, however, occurred, that could countenance the suspicion which he seemed to have adopted against Butler. At length the train of his interrogatories reached Madge Wildfire, at whose name the magistrate and town-clerk exchanged significant glances. If the fate of the Good Town had depended on her careful magistrate knowing the features and dress of this personage, his enquiries could not have been more particular. But Butler could say almost nothing of this person's features, which were disguised apparently with red paint and soot, like an Indian going to battle, besides the projecting shade of a curch or coif, which muffled the hair of the supposed female. He declared that he thought he could not know this Madge Wildfire, if placed before him in a different dress, but that he believed he might recognize his voice.

The magistrate requested him next to state by what gate he left the city.

"By the Cowgate-port," replied Butler.

"Was that the nearest road to Libberton?"

"No," answered Butler, with embarrassment; "but it was the nearest way to extricate myself from the mob."

The clerk and magistrate again exchanged glances.

"Is the Cowgate-port a nearer way to Libberton from the Grassmarket, than Bristo-port?"

"No," replied Butler with hesitation; "but—I had to visit a friend."

"Indeed?" said the interrogator—"You were in a hurry to tell the sight you had witnessed, I suppose?"

"Indeed I was not," replied Butler; "nor did I speak on the subject the whole time I was at Saint Leonard's Crags."

"Which road did you take to Saint Leonard's Crags?"

"By the foot of Salusbury Crags," was the reply.

"Indeed?—you seem partial to circuitous routes," again said the magistrate. "Whom did you see after you left the city?"

One by one he obtained a description of every one of the groups who had passed Butler, as already noticed, their numbers, demeanour, and appearance; and, at length, came to the circumstance of the mysterious stranger in the King's Park. On this subject Butler would fain have remained silent. But the magistrate had no sooner got a slight hint concerning the incident, than he seemed bent to possess himself of the most minute particulars.

"Look ye, Mr Butler," said he, "you are a young man, and bear an excellent character; so much I will myself testify in your favour. But we are aware there has been, at times, a sort of bastard and fiery zeal in some of your order, and those, men irreproachable in other points, which has led them into doing and countenancing great irregularities, by which the peace of the country is liable to be shaken.—I will deal plainly with you. I am not at all satisfied with this story, of your setting out again and again to seek your dwelling by two several roads, which were both circuitous. And, to be frank, no one whom we have examined on this unhappy affair could trace in your appearance any thing like your acting under compulsion. Moreover, the waiters at the Cowgate-port observed something like the trepidation of guilt in your conduct, and declare that you were the first to command them to open the gate, in a tone of authority, as if still presiding over the guards and outposts of the rabble, who had besieged them the whole night."

"God forgive them!" said Butler; "I only asked free passage for myself; they must have much misunderstood, if they did not wilfully misrepresent me."

"Well, Mr Butler," resumed the magistrate, "I am inclined to judge the best and hope the best, as I am sure I wish the best; but you must

be frank with me, if you wish to secure my good opinion, and
lessen the risk of inconvenience to yourself. You have allowed you
saw another individual in your passage through the King's Park
to Saint Leonard's Crags—I must know every word which passed
betwixt you."

Thus closely pressed, Butler, who had no reason for concealing
what passed at that meeting, unless because Jeanie Deans was concerned in it, thought it best to tell the whole truth from beginning to
end.

"Do you suppose," said the magistrate, pausing, "that the young
woman will accept an invitation so mysterious?"

"I fear she will," replied Butler.

"Why do you use the word *fear* it," said the magistrate.

"Because I am apprehensive for her safety, in meeting, at such a
time and place, one who had something of the manner of a desperado,
and whose message was of a character so inexplicable."

"Her safety shall be cared for," said the magistrate. "Mr Butler, I
am concerned I cannot immediately discharge you from confinement,
but I hope you will not be long detained.—Remove Mr Butler, and let
him be provided with decent accommodation in all respects."

He was conducted back to the prison accordingly; but, in the food
offered to him, as well as in the apartment in which he was lodged, the
recommendation of the magistrate was strictly attended to.

END OF VOLUME FIRST

THE
HEART OF MID-LOTHIAN

VOLUME II

Chapter One

Dark and eerie was the night,
And lonely was the way,
As Janet, wi' her green mantell,
To Miles' Cross she did gae.
Old Ballad

LEAVING BUTLER to all the uncomfortable thoughts attached to his
new situation, among which the most predominant was his feeling that
he was, by his confinement, deprived of all possibility of assisting the
family at Saint Leonard's in their greatest need, we return to Jeanie
Deans, who had seen him depart, without an opportunity of further
explanation, in all that agony of mind with which the female heart bids
adieu to the complicated sensations so well described by Coleridge,—

Hopes, and fears that kindle hope,
An undistinguishable throng;
And gentle wishes long subdued—
Subdued and cherish'd long.

It is not the firmest heart (and Jeanie, under her russet rokelay, had
one that would not have disgraced Cato's daughter,) that can most
easily bid adieu to these soft and mingled emotions. She wept for a few
minutes bitterly, and without attempting to refrain from this indulgence of passion. But a moment's recollection induced her to check
herself for a grief selfish and proper to her own affections, while her
father and sister were plunged in such deep and irremediable affliction. She drew from her pocket the letter which had been that
morning flung into her apartment through an open window, and the
contents of which were as singular as the expression was violent and
energetic. "If she would save a human being from the most damning

guilt, and all its desperate consequences,—if she desired the life and honour of her sister to be saved from the bloody fangs of an unjust law, —if she desired not to forfeit peace of mind here, and happiness hereafter," such was the frantic style of the conjuration, "she was entreated to give a sure, secret, and solitary meeting to the writer. She alone could rescue him," so ran the letter, "and he only could rescue her." He was in such circumstances, the billet further informed her, that an attempt to bring any witness of their conference, or even to mention to her father, or any other person whatsoever, the letter which requested it, would inevitably prevent its taking place, and insure the destruction of her sister. The letter concluded with incoherent but violent protestations, that in obeying this summons she had nothing to fear personally.

The message delivered to her by Butler from the stranger in the Park tallied exactly with the contents of the letter, but assigned a later hour and a different place of meeting. Apparently the writer of the letter had been compelled to let Butler so far into his confidence, for the sake of announcing this change to Jeanie. She was more than once on the point of producing the billet, in vindication of herself from her lover's half-hinted suspicions. But there is something in stooping to justification which the pride of innocence does not at all times willingly submit to, besides that the threats contained in the letter, in case of her betraying the secret, hung heavy on her heart. It is probable, however, that had they remained longer together, she might have taken the resolution to submit the whole matter to Butler, and be guided by him as to the line of conduct which she should adopt. And when, by the sudden interruption of their conference, she lost the opportunity of doing so, she felt as if she had been unjust to a friend, whose advice might have been highly useful, and whose attachment deserved her full and unreserved confidence.

To have recourse to her father upon this occasion, she considered as highly imprudent. There was no possibility of conjecturing in what light the matter might strike old David, whose manner of acting and thinking in extraordinary circumstances depended upon feelings and principles peculiar to himself, and the operation of which could not be calculated upon even by those best acquainted with him. To have requested some female friend to accompany her to the place of rendezvous, would perhaps have been the most eligible expedient; but the threats of the writer, that betraying his secret would prevent their meeting (on which her sister's safety was said to depend,) from taking place at all, would have deterred her from making such a confidence, even had she known a person in whom she thought it could with safety have been reposed. But she knew none such. Their acquaintance with the cottagers in the vicinity had been very slight, and limited to little trifling acts of good neighbourhood. Jeanie knew little of them, and what she knew did not greatly incline her to trust any of them. They were of the order of loquacious good-humoured gossips usually found in their situation of life; and their conversation had at all times few charms for a young woman, to whom nature and the circumstance of a solitary life had given a depth of thought and force of character superior to the frivolous part of her sex, whether in high or low degree.

Left alone and separated from all earthly counsel, she had recourse to a friend and adviser, whose ear is open to the cry of the poorest and most afflicted of his people. She knelt, and prayed with fervent sincerity, that God would please to direct her what course to follow in her arduous and distressing situation. It was the belief of the time and sect to which she belonged, that special answers to prayer, differing little in their character from divine inspiration, were, as they expressed it, "borne in upon their minds" in answer to their earnest petitions in a crisis of difficulty. Without entering into an abstruse point of divinity, one thing is plain; namely, that the person who lays open his doubts and distresses in prayer, with feeling and sincerity, must necessarily, in the act of doing so, purify his mind from the dross of worldly passions and interests, and bring it into that state, when the resolutions adopted are likely to be selected rather from a sense of duty, than from any inferior motive. Jeanie arose from her devotions, with her heart fortified to endure affliction, and encouraged to face difficulties.

"I will meet with this unhappy man," she said to herself—"unhappy he must be, since I doubt he has been the cause of poor Effie's misfortune—but I will meet him, be it for good or ill. My mind shall never cast up to me, that, for fear of what might be said or done to me, I left a thing undone that might even yet be the rescue of her."

With a mind greatly composed since the adoption of this resolution, she went to attend her father. The old man, firm in the principles of his youth, did not, in outward appearance at least, permit a thought of his family distress to interfere with the stoical reserve of his countenance and manners. He even chid his daughter for having neglected, in the distress of the morning, some trifling domestic duties which fell under her department.

"Why, what meaneth this, Jeanie?" said the old man—"The brown four-year-auld's milk is not seiled yet, nor the bowies put up on the bink. If ye neglect your warldly duties in the day of affliction, what confidence have I that ye mind the greater matters that concern salvation? God knows, our bowies, and our pipkins, and our draps o' milk, and our bits o' bread, are nearer and dearer to us than the bread of life."

Jeanie, not unpleased to hear her father's thoughts thus expand themselves beyond the sphere of his immediate distress, obeyed him, and proceeded to put her household matters in order; while old Deans moved from place to place about his ordinary employments, scarce shewing, unless by a nervous impatience at remaining long stationary, an occasional convulsive sigh, or twinkle of the eye-lid, that he was labouring under the yoke of such bitter affliction.

The hour of noon came on, and the father and child sat down to their homely repast. In his petition for a blessing on the meal, the poor old man added to his usual supplication, a prayer that the bread eaten in bitterness, and the waters of Merah, might be made as nourishing as those which had been poured forth from a full cup and a plentiful basket and store; and having concluded his benediction, and resumed the bonnet which he had laid "reverently aside," he proceeded to exhort his daughter to eat, not by example indeed, but at least by precept.

"The man after God's own heart," he said, "washed and anointed himself, and did eat bread, in order to express his submission under a dispensation of suffering, and it did not become a Christian man or woman so to cling to creature-comforts of wife or bairns,"—(here the words became too great, as it were, for his utterance)—"as to forget the—first duty—submission to the Divine will."

To add force to his precept, he took a morsel on his plate, but nature proved too strong even for the powerful feelings with which he endeavoured to bridle it. Ashamed of his weakness, he started up, and ran out of the house, with haste very unlike the deliberation of his usual movements. In less than five minutes he returned, having successfully struggled to recover his usual composure of mind and countenance, and affected to colour over his late retreat, by muttering that he thought he heard the "young staig loose in the byre."

He did not again trust himself with the subject of his former conversation, and his daughter was glad to see that he seemed to avoid further discourse on that agitating topic. The hours glided on, as on they must and do pass, whether winged with joy or laden with affliction. The sun set beyond the dusky eminence of the Castle, and the screen of western hills, and the close of evening summoned David Deans and his daughty to the family duty of the evening. It came bitterly upon Jeanie's recollection, how often, when this hour of worship approached, she used to watch the lengthening shadow, and look out from the door of the house, to see if she could spy her sister's return homeward. Alas! this idle and thoughtless waste of time, to what evils had it not finally led? and was she altogether guiltless, who, noticing Effie's turn to idle and light society, had not called in her father's authority to restrain her?—But I acted for the best, she again reflected, and who could have expected such a flood of evil, from one grain of human leaven, in a disposition so kind, and candid, and generous?

As they sate down to the "exercise," as it is called, a chair happened accidentally to stand in the place which Effie usually occupied. David Deans saw his daughter's eyes swim in tears as they were directed towards this object, and pushed it aside, with a gesture of some impatience, as if desirous to destroy every memorial of earthly interest when about to address the Deity. The portion of Scripture was read, the psalm was sung, the prayer was made; and it was remarkable that, in discharging these duties, the old man avoided all passages and expressions, of which scripture affords so many, that might be considered as applicable to his own domestic misfortunes. In doing so it was perhaps his intention to spare the feelings of his daughter, as well as to maintain, in outward show at least, that stoical appearance of patient endurance of all the evil which earth could bring, which was, in his opinion, essential to the character of one who rated all earthly things at their own just estimate of nothingness. When he had finished the duty of the evening, he came up to his daughter, wished her good-night, and, having done so, continued to hold her by the hands for half a minute; then drawing her towards him, kissed her forehead, and ejaculated, "The God of Israel bless you, even with the blessings of the promise, my dear bairn!"

It was not either in the nature or habits of David Deans to seem a fond father; nor was he often known to experience, or at least to evince, that fullness of the heart which seeks to expand itself in tender expressions or caresses even to those who were dearest to him. On the contrary, he used to censure this as a degree of weakness in several of his neighbours, and particularly in poor Widow Butler. It followed, however, from the rarity of such emotions in this self-denied and reserved man, that his children attached to occasional marks of his affection and approbation a degree of high interest and solemnity; well considering them as evidences of feelings which were only expressed when they became too intense for suppression or concealment.

With deep emotion, therefore, did he bestow, and his daughter receive, this benediction and paternal caress. "And you, my dear father," exclaimed Jeanie, when the door had closed upon the venerable old man, "may you have purchased and promised blessings multiplied upon you—upon *you*, who walk in this world as you were not of the world, and hold all which it can give or take away but as the *midges* that the sun-blink brings out, and the evening wind sweeps away!"

She now made preparations for her night-walk. Her father slept in another part of the dwelling, and, regular in all his habits, seldom or never left his apartment when he had betaken himself to it for the evening. It was therefore easy for her to leave the house unobserved, so soon as the time approached at which she was to keep her appointment. But the step she was about to take had difficulties and terrors in her own eyes, though she had no reason to apprehend her father's interference. Her life had been spent in the quiet, uniform, and regular seclusion of their peaceful and monotonous household. The very hour which some damsels of the present day, as well of her own as of higher degree, would consider as the natural period of commencing an evening of pleasure, had, in her opinion, a sort of solemnity in it; and the resolution she had taken had a strange, daring, and adventurous character, to which she could hardly reconcile herself when the moment approached for putting it into execution. Her hands trembled as she snooded her fair hair beneath the ribband, then the only ornament or cover which young unmarried women wore on their head, and as she adjusted the scarlet tartan screen or muffler made of plaid, which the Scottish women wore, much in the fashion of the black silk veils still a part of female dress in the Netherlands. A sense of impropriety as well as of danger pressed on her as she lifted the latch of her paternal mansion to leave it on so wild an expedition, and at so late an hour, unprotected and without the knowledge of her natural guardian.

When she found herself abroad and in the open fields, additional subjects of apprehension crowded upon her. The dim cliffs and scattered rocks, interspersed with green sward, through which she had to pass to the place of appointment, as they glimmered before her in the clear autumn night, recalled to her memory many a deed of violence, which, according to tradition, had been done and suffered among them. In earlier days they had been the haunt of robbers and assassins, the memory of whose crimes is preserved in the precautionary edicts which the council of the city, and even the parliament of Scotland, had passed for dispersing their bands, and insuring safety to the lieges, so near the precincts of the city. The names of these criminals, and of their atrocities, were still remembered in traditions of the scattered cottages and the neighbouring suburb. In latter times, as we have already noticed, the sequestered and broken character of the ground rendered it a fit theatre for duels and rencontres among the fiery youth of the period. Two or three of these incidents, all sanguinary, and one of them fatal in its termination, had happened since Deans came to live at Saint Leonard's. His daughter's recollections, therefore, were of blood and horror as she pursued the small scarce-tracked solitary path, every step of which conveyed her to a greater distance from help, and deeper into the ominous seclusion of these unhallowed precincts.

As the moon began to peer forth on the scene with a doubtful, flitting, and solemn light, Jeanie's apprehensions took another turn, too peculiar to her rank and country to remain unnoticed. But to trace its origin will require another chapter.

Chapter Two

——The spirit I have seen
May be the devil. And the devil has power
To assume a pleasing shape.
Hamlet

WITCHCRAFT and dæmonology, as we have had already occasion to remark, were at this period believed in by almost all ranks, but more especially among the stricter classes of presbyterians, whose government, when at the head of the state, had been much sullied by their eagerness to enquire into, and persecute these imaginary crimes. Now, in this point of view also, Saint Leonard's Crags and the adjacent Chase were a dreaded and ill-reputed district. Not only had witches held their meetings there, but even of very late years the enthusiast, or impostor, mentioned in Baxter's Worlds of Spirits, had, among the recesses of these romantic cliffs, found his way into the hidden retreats where the fairies revel in the bowels of the earth.

With all these legends Jeanie Deans was too well acquainted, to escape that strong impression which they usually make on the imagination. Indeed, relations of this ghostly kind had been familiar to her from her infancy, for they were the only relief which her father's conversation afforded from controversial argument, or the gloomy history of the strivings and testimonies, escapes, captures, tortures, and executions of those martyrs of the covenant, with whom it was his chiefest boast to say he had been acquainted. In the recesses of mountains, in caverns, and in morasses, to which these persecuted enthusiasts were so ruthlessly pursued, they conceived they had often to contend with the visible assaults of the Enemy of Mankind, as in the cities, and in the cultivated fields, they were exposed to those of the tyrannical government and their soldiery. Such were the terrors which made one of their gifted seers exclaim, when his companion returned to him, after having left him alone in a haunted cavern in Sorn in Galloway, "It is hard living in this world—incarnate devils above the earth, and devils under the earth! Satan has been here since ye went away, but I have dismissed him by resistance; we will be no more troubled with him this night." David Deans believed this, and many other such ghostly encounters and victories, on the faith of the

Ansars, or auxiliaries of the banished prophets. This event was beyond David's remembrance. But he used to tell with great awe, yet not without a feeling of proud superiority to his auditors, how he himself had been present at a field-meeting at Crochmade, when the duty of the day was interrupted by the apparition of a tall black man, who, in the act of crossing a ford to join the congregation, lost ground, and was carried down apparently by the force of the stream. All were instantly at work to assist him, but with so little success, that ten or twelve stout men, who had hold of the rope which they had cast in to his aid, were rather in danger to be dragged into the stream, and lose their own lives, than likely to save that of the supposed perishing man. "But famous John Semple of Carsphairn," David Deans used to say with exultation, "saw the whaup in the rape,—'Quit the rope,' he cried to us, (for I that was but a callant had a haud o' the rape mysell;) 'it is the Great Enemy; he will burn, but not drown; his design is to disturb the good wark, by raising wonder and confusion in your minds; to put off from your spirits all that ye hae heard and felt.'—Sae we let go the rape," said David, "and he went adown the water screeching and bullering like a Bull of Bashan, as he is ca'd in scripture."

Trained in these and similar legends, it was no wonder that Jeanie began to feel an ill-defined apprehension, not merely of the phantoms which might beset her way, but of the quality, nature, and purpose of the being who had thus appointed her a meeting, at a place and hour of horror, and at a time when her mind must be necessarily full of those tempting and ensnaring thoughts of grief and despair, which were supposed to lay sufferers particularly open to the temptations of the Evil One. If such an idea had crossed even Butler's well-informed mind, it was calculated to make a much stronger impression upon her's. Yet firmly believing the possibility of an encounter so terrible to flesh and blood, Jeanie, with a degree of resolution of which we cannot sufficiently estimate the merit, because the incredulity of the age has rendered us strangers to the nature and extent of her feelings, persevered in her determination not to omit an opportunity of doing something towards saving her sister, although in the attempt to avail herself of it she might be exposed to dangers so dreadful to her imagination. So, like Christiana in the Pilgrim's Progress, when traversing with a timid yet resolved step the terrors of the Valley of the Shadow of Death, she glided on by rock and stone, "now in glimmer and now in gloom," as her path lay through moonlight or shadow, and endeavoured to overpower the suggestions of fear, sometimes by fixing her mind upon the distressed condition of her sister, and the duty she lay under to afford her aid, should that be in her power; and more frequently by recurring in mental prayer to the protection of that

Being to whom night is as noon-day.

Thus drowning at one time her fears by fixing her mind on a subject of overpowering interest, and arguing them down at others by referring herself to the protection of the Deity, she at length approached the place assigned for this mysterious conference.

It was situated in the depth of the valley behind Salusbury Crags, which has for a back ground the north-western shoulder of the mountain called Arthur's Seat, on whose descent still remain the ruins of what was once a chapel, or hermitage, dedicated to Saint Anthony the Eremite. A better site for such a building could hardly have been selected; for the chapel, situated among the rude and pathless cliffs, lies in a desert, even in the immediate vicinity of a rich, populous, and tumultuous capital: and the hum of the metropolis might mingle with the orisons of the recluses, conveying as little of worldly interest as if it had been the roar of the distant ocean. Beneath the steep ascent on which these mouldering ruins are still visible, was, and perhaps is still pointed out, the place where the wretch Nicol Muschat, who has been already mentioned in these pages, had closed a long scene of cruelty towards his unfortunate wife, by murdering her, with circumstances of uncommon barbarity. The execration in which the man's crime was held extended itself to the place where it was perpetrated, which was marked by a small *cairn*, or heap of stones, composed of those which each chance passenger had thrown there in testimony of abhorrence, and on the principle, it would seem, of the ancient British malediction, "May you have a cairn for your burial-place!"

As our heroine approached this ominous and unhallowed spot, she paused and looked to the moon, now rising broad on the north-east, and shedding a more distinct light than it had afforded during her walk thither. Eyeing the planet for a moment, she then slowly and fearfully turned her head towards the cairn, from which it was at first averted. She was disappointed. Nothing was visible beside the little pile of stones, which shone grey in the moonlight. A multitude of confused suggestions rushed on her mind. Had her correspondent deceived her, and broken his appointment?—was he too tardy at the appointment he had made?—or had some strange turn of fate prevented him from appearing as he proposed?—or if he were an unearthly being, as her secret apprehensions suggested, was it his object merely to delude her with false hopes, and put her to unnecessary toil and terror, as was the nature, she had heard, of those wandering dæmons whose purpose seems rather hazing than malevolent?—or did he propose to blast her with the sudden horrors of his presence when she had come closer to the place of rendezvous? These anxious reflections did not prevent her approaching to the cairn with a pace that, though slow, was determined.

When she was within two yards of the heap of stones, a figure rose suddenly up from behind it, and Jeanie scarce forbore to scream aloud at what seemed the realization of the most frightful of her anticipations. She constrained herself to silence, however, and, making a dead pause, suffered the figure to open the conversation, which he did, by asking, in a voice which agitation rendered tremulous and hollow, "Are you the sister of that ill-fated young woman?"

"I am—I am the sister of Effie Deans!" exclaimed Jeanie. "And O, as ever you hope God will hear you at your need, tell me, if you can tell, what can be done to save her!"

"I do *not* hope God will hear me at my need," was the singular answer. "I do not deserve—I do not expect he will." This desperate language he uttered in a tone calmer than that with which he had at first spoken, probably because the shock of first addressing her was what he felt most difficult to overcome. Jeanie remained mute with horror to hear language expressed so utterly foreign to all which she had ever been acquainted with, that it sounded in her ears rather that of a fiend than of a human being. The stranger pursued his address to her without seeming to notice her surprise. "You see before you a wretch, predestined to evil here and hereafter."

"For the sake of Heaven, that hears and sees us," said Jeanie, "dinna speak in this desperate fashion! The gospel is sent to the chief of sinners—to the maist miserable among the miserable."

"Then should I have my own share therein," said the stranger, "if you call it sinful to have been the destruction of the mother that bore me—of the friend that loved me—of the woman that trusted me—of the innocent child that was born to me. If to have done all this is to be a sinner, and to survive it is to be miserable, then am I most guilty and most miserable indeed."

"Then you are the wicked cause of my sister's ruin?" said Jeanie, with a natural touch of indignation expressed in her tone of voice.

"Curse me for it, if you will," said the stranger; "I have well deserved it at your hand."

"It is fitter for me," said Jeanie, "to pray to God to forgive you."

"Do as you will, how you will, or what you will," he replied, with vehemence; "only promise to obey my directions, and save your sister's life."

"I must first know," said Jeanie, "the means you would have me use in her behalf."

"No!—you must first swear—solemnly swear, that you will employ them, when I make them known to you."

"Surely, it is needless to swear that I will do a' that is lawful to a Christian, to save the life of my sister?"

"I will have no reservation!" thundered the stranger; "lawful or unlawful, Christian or heathen, you shall swear to do my hest, and act by my counsel, or—you little know whose wrath you provoke!"

"I will think on what you have said," said Jeanie, who began to get much alarmed at the frantic vehemence of his manner, and disputed in her own mind, whether she spoke to a maniac, or an apostate spirit incarnate. "I will think on what you say, and let you ken to-morrow."

"To-morrow?" exclaimed the man, with a laugh of scorn—"And where will I be to-morrow?—or, where will you be to-night, unless you swear to walk by my counsel!—There was one accursed deed done at this spot before now; and there shall be another to match it, unless you yield yourself up to my guidance, body and soul."

As he spoke, he offered a pistol at the unfortunate young woman. She neither fled nor fainted, but sunk on her knees, and asked him to spare her life.

"Is that all you have to say?"

"Do not dip your hands in the blood of a defenceless creature that has trusted to you," said Jeanie, still on her knees.

"Is that all you can say for your life?—Have you no promise to give? —Will you destroy your sister, and compel me to shed more blood?"

"I can promise nothing," said Jeanie, "which is unlawfu' for a Christian."

He cocked the weapon, and held it towards her.

"May God forgive you!" she said, pressing her hands forcibly against her eyes.

"D—n!" muttered the man; and, turning aside from her, he uncocked the pistol, and replaced it in his pocket—"I am a villain," he said, "steeped in guilt and wretchedness, but not wicked enough to do you any harm! I only wished to terrify you into my measures— She hears me not—she is gone!—Great God! what a wretch am I become!"

As he spoke, she recovered herself from an agony which partook of the bitterness of death; and, in a minute or two, through the strong exertion of her natural sense and courage, collected herself sufficiently to understand he intended her no personal injury.

"No!" he repeated; "I would not add to the murder of your sister, and of her child, that of any one belonging to her!—Mad, frantic, as I am, and unrestrained by either fear or mercy, given up to the possession of some evil being, and forsaken by all that is good, I would not hurt you, were the world offered me for a bribe! But, for the sake of all that is dear to you, swear you will follow my counsel. Take this weapon, shoot me through the head, and with your own hand revenge your sister's wrongs, only follow the course—the only course, by which her life can be saved."

"Alas! is she innocent or guilty?"

"She is guiltless—guiltless of every thing, but of having trusted a villain!—Yet had it not been for those that were worse than I am— yes, worse than I, though I am bad enough—this misery had not befallen."

"And my sister's child—does it live?" said Jeanie.

"No; it was murdered—the new-born infant was barbarously murdered," he uttered in a low, yet stern and sustained voice;—"but," he added hastily, "not by her knowledge or consent."

"Then, why cannot the guilty be brought to justice, and the innocent freed?"

"Torment me not with questions which can serve no purpose," he sternly replied—"The deed was done by those who are far enough from pursuit, and safe enough from discovery!—No one can save Effie but yourself."

"Woes me! how is it in my power?" asked Jeanie, in despondency.

"Harken to me!—You have sense—you can apprehend my meaning—I will trust you—Your sister is innocent of the crime charged against her"——

"Thank God for that!" said Jeanie.

"Be still, and harken. The person who assisted her in her illness— murdered the child; but it was without the mother's knowledge or consent—She is therefore guiltless, as guiltless as the unhappy innocent, that but gasped a few minutes in this miserable world—the better was its hap to be so soon at rest. She is innocent as that infant, and yet she must die—it is impossible to clear her of the law!"

"Cannot the wretches be discovered and given up to punishment?" said Jeanie.

"Do you think, you will persuade those that are hardened in guilt, to die to save another?—Is that the reed you would lean to?"

"But you said there was a remedy," again gasped out the terrified young woman.

"There is," answered the stranger, "and it is in your own hands. The blow which the law aims cannot be broken by directly encountering it, but it may be turned aside. You saw your sister during the period preceding the birth of her child—what is so natural as that she should have mentioned her condition to you? The doing so would, as their cant goes, take the case from under the statute, for it removes the quality of concealment. I know their jargon, and have had sad cause to know it; and the quality of concealment is essential to this statutory offence. Nothing is so natural as that Effie should have mentioned her condition to you—think—reflect—I am positive that she did."

"Woes me!" said Jeanie, "she never spoke to me on the subject, but grat sorely when I spoke to her about her altered looks, and the change on her spirits."

"You asked her questions on the subject?" said he, eagerly. "You *must* remember her answer was, a confession that she had been ruined by a villain—yes, lay a strong emphasis on that—a cruel, false villain called—the name is unnecessary; and that she bore under her bosom the consequences of his guilt and her folly; and that he had assured her he would provide safely for her approaching illness.—Well he kept his word!" These last words he spoke as it were to himself, and with a violent gesture of self-accusation, and then calmly proceeded, "You will remember all this?—That is all that is necessary to be said."

"But I cannot remember," answered Jeanie, with simplicity, "that which Effie never told me."

"Are you so dull—so very dull of apprehension!" he exclaimed, suddenly grasping her arm, and holding it firm in his hand. "I tell you," (speaking between his teeth, and under his breath, but with great energy,) "you *must* remember that she told you all this, whether she ever said a syllable of it or no. You must repeat this tale, in which there is no falsehood, except in so far as it was not told to you, before these Justices—Justiciary—whatever they call their blood-thirsty court, and save your sister from being murdered, and them from becoming murderers. Do not hesitate—I pledge life and salvation, that in saying what I have said, you will only speak the simple truth."

"But," replied Jeanie, whose judgment was too accurate not to see the sophistry of this argument, "I shall be man-sworn in the very thing in which my testimony is wanted, for it is the concealment for which poor Effie is blamed, and you would make me tell a falsehood anent it."

"I see," he said, "my first suspicions of you were right, and that you will let your sister, innocent, fair, and guiltless, except in trusting a villain, die the death of a murderess, rather than bestow the breath of your mouth and the sound of your voice to save her."

"I wad ware the best blood in my body to keep her skaithless," said Jeanie, weeping in bitter agony, "but I canna change right into wrang, or make that true which is false."

"Foolish, hard-hearted girl," said the stranger, "are you afraid of what they may do to you? I tell you, even the retainers of the law, who course life as greyhounds do hares, will rejoice at the escape of a creature so young—so beautiful; that they will not suspect your tale;

that, if they did suspect it, they would consider you as deserving, not only of forgiveness, but of praise for your natural affection."

"It is not man I fear," said Jeanie, looking upward; "the God, whose name I must call on to witness the truth of what I say, he will know the falsehood."

"And he will know the motive," said the stranger, eagerly; "he will know that you are doing this—not for lucre of gain, but to save the life of the innocent, and prevent the commission of a worse crime than that which the law seeks to avenge."

"He has given us a law," said Jeanie, "for the lamp of our path; if we stray from it, we err against knowledge—I may not do evil, even that good may come out of it. But you—you that ken all this to be true, which I must take on your word,—you that, if I understood what you said e'en now, promised her shelter and protection in her travail, why do not *you* step forward, and bear leal and soothfast evidence in her behalf, as ye may with a clear conscience?"

"To whom do you talk of a clear conscience, woman?" said he, with a sudden fierceness which renewed her terrors,—"to *me?*—I have not known one for many a year. Bear witness in her behalf?—a proper witness, that, even to speak these few words to a woman of so little consequence as yourself, must chuse such an hour and such a place as this. When you see owls and bats fly abroad, like larks, in the sunshine, you may expect to see such as I am in the assemblies of men.—Hush —listen to that."

A voice was heard to sing one of those wild and monotonous strains so common in Scotland, and to which the natives of that country chaunt their old ballads. The sound ceased—then came nearer, and was renewed; the stranger listened attentively, still holding Jeanie by the arm, (as she stood by him in motionless terror) as if to prevent her interrupting the strain by speaking or stirring. When the sounds were renewed, the words were distinctly audible:

> "When the gledd's in the blue cloud,
>   The lavrock lies still;
> When the hound's in the green-wood,
>   The hind keeps the hill."

The person who sung kept a strained and powerful voice at its very highest pitch, so that it could be heard at a very considerable distance. As the song ceased, they might hear a stifled sound, as of steps and whispers of persons approaching them. The song was again raised, but the tune was changed:

> "O sleep ye sound, Sir James, she said,
>   When ye suld rise and ride?
> There's twenty men, wi' bow and blade,
>   Are seeking where ye hide."

"I dare stay no longer," said the stranger; "return home, or remain till they come up—you have nothing to fear—but do not tell you saw me—your sister's fate is in your hands." So saying, he turned from her, and with a swift, yet cautiously noiseless step, plunged into the darkness on the side most remote from the sounds which they heard approaching, and was soon lost to her sight. Jeanie remained by the cairn terrified beyond expression, and uncertain whether she ought to fly homeward with all the speed she could exert, or wait the approach of those who were advancing towards her. This uncertainty detained her so long, that she now distinctly saw two or three figures already so near to her, that a precipitate flight would have been equally fruitless and impolitic.

Chapter Three

——She speaks things in doubt,
That carry but half sense: her speech is nothing,
Yet the unshaped use of it doth move
The hearers to collection; they aim at it,
And botch the words up fit to their own thoughts.
Hamlet

LIKE THE DIGRESSIVE poet Ariosto, I find myself under the necessity of connecting the branches of my story, by taking up the adventures of another of the characters, and bringing them down to the point at which we have left those of Jeanie Deans. It is not, perhaps, the most artificial way of telling a story, but it has the advantage of sparing the necessity of resuming what a knitter (if stocking-looms have left such a person in the land,) might call our "dropped stitches;" a labour in which the author generally toils much, without getting credit for his pains.

"I could risk a sma' wad," said the clerk to the magistrate, "that this rascal Ratcliffe, if he was once insured of his neck's safety, could do more than ony ten of our police-people and constables, to help us to get out of this scrape of Porteous. He is weel acquent wi' a' the smugglers, thieves, and banditti about Edinburgh; and, indeed, he may be called the father of a' the misdoers in Scotland, for he has passed amang them for these twenty years by the name of Daddie Rat."

"A bonny sort of a scoundrel," replied the magistrate, "to expect a place under the city!"

"Begging your honour's pardon," said the city's procurator-fiscal, upon whom the duties of superintendant of police devolved, "Mr Fairscrieve is perfectly in the right. It is just sic as Ratcliffe that the town needs in my department, an' it sae be that he's disposed to turn his knowledge to the city service—Ye'll get nae saints to be searchers for uncustomed goods, or for thieves and sic like;—and your decent sort of men, religious professors, and broken tradesmen, that are put into the like o' sic trust, can do nae gude ava. They are feared for this, and they are scrupulous about that, and they are no free to tell a lie, though it may be for the benefit of the city; and they dinna like to be out at irregular hours, and in a dark cauld night, and they like a clout ower the croun far waur; and sae between the fear o' God, and the fear o' man, and the fear o' getting a sair throat, or sair banes, there's a dozen o' our city-folks, baith waiters, and officers, and constables, that can find out naething but a wee-bit skulduddery for the benefit of the Kirk-treasurer. Jock Porteous, that's stiff and stark, puir fallow, was worth a dozen o' them; for he never had ony fears, or scruples, or doubts, or conscience, about ony thing your honours bade him."

"He was a gude servant o' the town," said the Baillie, "though he was an ower free-living man. But if you really think this rascal Ratcliffe could do us ony service in discovering these malefactors, I would insure life, reward, and promotion. It's an awsome thing this mischance for the city, Mr Fairscrieve. It will be very ill tane wi' abune stairs. Queen Caroline, God bless her, is a woman—at least I judge sae, and it's nae treason to speak my mind sae far—and ye maybe ken as weel as I do, for ye hae a housekeeper, though ye are nae married man, that women are wilfu', and downa bide a slight. And it will sound ill in her ears, that sic a confused mistake suld hae come to pass, and naebody sae muckle as to be put in the tolbooth about it."

"If ye thought that, sir," said the procurator-fiscal, "we could easily clap into the prison a few blackguards upon suspicion. It will have a gude active look, and I hae aye plenty on my list, that wadna be a hair the waur of a week or twa's imprisonment; and if ye thought it no strickly just, ye could be just the easier wi' them the neist time they did ony thing to deserve it; they arena the sort to be lang o' geeing ye an opportunity to clear scores wi' them on that accompt."

"I doubt that will hardly do in this case, Mr Sharpitlaw," returned the town-clerk; "they'll run their letters, and be a' adrift again, before ye ken whare ye are."

"I will speak to the Lord Provost," said the magistrate, "about Ratcliffe's business. Mr Sharpitlaw, you will go with me and receive instructions—something may be made too out of this story of Butler's and his unknown gentleman—I know no business any man has to swagger about in the King's Park, and call himself the devil, to the terror of honest folks, who dinna care to hear mair about the devil than is said from the pulpit on the Sabbath. I cannot think the preacher himsell wad be heading the mob, though the time has been, they hae been as forward in a bruilzie as their neighbours."

"But these times are lang bye," said Mr Sharpitlaw. "In my father's time, there was mair search for silenced ministers about the Bow-head and the Covenant-close, and all the tents of Kedar, as they ca'd the dwellings o' the godly in those days, than there's now for thieves and vagabonds in the Laigh-Calton and the back o' the Canongate. But that time's weel bye, an' it bide. And if the Baillie will get me directions and authority from the Provost, I'll speak wi' Daddie Rat mysell; for I am thinking I'll make mair out o' him than ye'll do."

Mr Sharpitlaw, being necessarily a man of high trust, was accordingly empowered, in the course of the day, to make such arrangements, as might seem in the emergency most advantageous for the Good Town. He went to the jail accordingly, and saw Ratcliffe in private.

The relative positions of a police-officer and a professed thief bear a different complexion, according to circumstances. The most obvious simile of a hawk pouncing upon his prey, is often least applicable. Sometimes the guardian of justice has the air of a cat watching a mouse, while he suspends his purpose of springing upon the pilferer, and taking care so to calculate his motions that he shall not get beyond his power. Sometimes, more passive still, he uses the art of fascination ascribed to the rattle-snake, and contents himself with glaring on the victim, through all his devious flutterings; certain that his terror, confusion, and disorder of ideas, will bring him into his jaws at last. The interview betwixt Ratcliffe and Sharpitlaw had an aspect different from all these. They sate for five minutes silent, on opposite sides of a small table, and looked fixedly at each other, with a sharp, knowing, and alert cast of countenance, not unmingled with an inclination to laugh, and resembled, more than any thing else, two dogs, who, preparing for a game at romps, are seen to couch down, and remain in that posture for a little time, watching each other's movements, and waiting which shall begin the game.

"So, Mr Ratcliffe," said the officer, conceiving it suited his dignity to speak first, "you give up business, I find?"

"Yes, sir," replied Ratcliffe; "I shall be on that lay nae mair—and I think that will save your fo'k some trouble, Mr Sharpitlaw?"

"Which Jock Dalgleish" (then finisher of the law in the Scottish metropolis,) "wad save them as easily," returned the procurator-fiscal.

"Ay; if I waited in the tolbooth here to have him fit my cravat—but that's an idle way o' speaking, Mr Sharpitlaw."

"Why, I suppose you know you are under sentence of death, Mr Ratcliffe?" replied Sharpitlaw.

"Ay, so are we a', as that worthy minister said in the Tolbooth Kirk the day Robertson wan off; but naebody kens whan it will be executed. Gude faith, he had better reason to say sae than he dreamed of, before the play was played out that morning."

"This Robertson," said Sharpitlaw, in a lower, and something like a confidential tone, "do ye ken, Rat—that is, can ye gie us ony inkling where he's to be heard tell o'?"

"Troth, Mr Sharpitlaw, I'll be frank wi' ye; Robertson is rather a cut abune me—a wild deevil he was, and mony a daft prank he played; but except the Collector's job that Wilson led him into, and some tuilzies about run goods wi' the gaugers and the waiters, he never did ony thing that came near our line o' business."

"Umph! that's singular, considering the company he kept."

"Fact, on my honour and credit," said Ratcliffe, gravely. "He keepit out o' our little bits of affairs, and that's mair than Wilson did; I hae dune business wi' Wilson afore now. But the lad will come on in time; there's nae fear o' him; naebody will live the life he has led, but what he'll come to sooner or later."

"Who or what is he, Ratcliffe? you know, I suppose?" said Sharpitlaw.

"He's better born, I judge, than he cares to let on; he's been a soldier, and he's been a play-actor, and I watna what he has been or hasna been, for as young as he is, sae that it had daffing and nonsense about it."

"Pretty pranks he has played in his time, I suppose?"

"Ye may say that," said Ratcliffe, with a sardonic smile; "and," (touching his nose,) "a deevil amang the lasses."

"Like enough," said Sharpitlaw. "Weel, Ratcliffe, I'll no stand niffering wi' ye; ye ken the way that favour's gotten in my office; ye maun be usefu'."

"Certainly, sir, to the best of my power—naething for naething—I ken the rule of the office," said the ex-depredator.

"Now the principal thing in hand e'en now," said the official person, "is this job of Porteous's; an ye can gi'e us a lift—why, the inner turnkey's office to begin wi', and the captainship in time—ye understand my meaning?"

"Ay, troth do I, sir; a wink's as gude as a nod to a blind horse; but Jock Porteous's job—Lord help ye, I was under sentence the hale time. God! but I couldna help laughing when I heard Jock skirling for mercy in the lads' hands! Mony a het skin ye hae gi'en me, neighbour, thought I, tak ye what's ganging; time about's fair play;

ye'll ken now what hanging's gude for."

"Come, come, this is all nonsense, Rat. Ye canna creep out at that hole, lad; you must speak to the point—the point—you understand me, if you want favour; gif-gaf makes gude friends, ye ken."

"But how can I speak to the point, as your honour ca's it," said Ratcliffe, demurely, and with an air of great simplicity, "when ye ken I was under sentence, and in the strong-room a' the while the job was going on?"

"And how can we turn you loose on the public again, Daddie Rat, unless ye do or say something to deserve it?"

"Weel then, d—n it!" answered the criminal, "since it maun be sae, I saw Geordie Robertson amang the boys that brake the jail; I suppose that will do me some gude?"

"That's speaking to the purpose, indeed," said the office-bearer; "and now, Rat, where think ye we'll find him?"

"De'il haet o' me kens," said Ratcliffe; "he'll no likely gang back to ony o' his auld howffs; he'll be off the country by this time. He has gude friends some gate or other, for a' the life he's led; he's been weel educate."

"He'll grace the gallows the better," said Sharpitlaw; "a desperate dog, to murther an officer of the city for doing his duty! Wha kens wha's turn it might be next?—But you saw him plainly?"

"As plainly as I see you."

"How was he dressed?" said Sharpitlaw.

"I couldna weel see; something of a woman's bit mutch on his head; but ye never saw sic a ca'-throw. Ane couldna hae een to a' thing."

"But did he speak to no one?" said Sharpitlaw.

"They were a' speaking and gabbling through other," said Ratcliffe, who was obviously unwilling to carry his evidence farther than he could possibly help.

"This will not do, Ratcliffe," said the procurator; "you must speak *out—out—out*," tapping the table emphatically as he repeated that impressive monosyllable.

"It's very hard sir; and but for the under-turnkey's place"——

"And the reversion of the Captaincy—the Captaincy of the Tolbooth, man—that is, in case of gude behaviour."

"Ay, ay," said Ratcliffe, "gude behaviour!—there's the deevil. And than it's waiting for dead folks' shoon into the bargain."

"But Robertson's head will weigh something," said Sharpitlaw; "something gay and heavy, Rat; the town maun show cause—that's right and reason—and than ye'll hae freedom to enjoy your gear honestly."

"I dinna ken," said Ratcliffe; "it's a queer way of beginning the trade of honesty—but de'il ma care. Weel, then, I heard and saw him speak to the wench Effie Deans, that's up there for child-murder."

"The de'il ye did? Rat, this is finding a mare's nest wi' a witness.— And the man that spoke to Butler in the Park—And that was to meet wi' Jeanie Deans at Muschat's Cairn—whew! lay that and that the-gither. As sure as I live he's been the father of the lassie's wean."

"There hae been waur guesses than that, I'm thinking," observed Ratcliffe, turning his quid of tobacco in his cheek, and squirting out the juice. "I heard something a while syne about his drawing up wi' a bonny quean about the Pleasaunts, and that it was a' Wilson could do to keep him frae marrying her."

Here a city officer entered, and told Sharpitlaw that they had the woman in custody whom he had directed them to bring before him.

"It's little matter now," said he, "the thing is taking another turn; however, George, ye may bring her in."

The officer retired, and introduced upon his return, a tall, strap-ping wench of eighteen or twenty, dressed fantastically, in a sort of blue riding jacket, with tarnished lace, her hair clubbed like that of a man, a Highland bonnet, and a bunch of broken feathers, a riding skirt (or petticoat,) of scarlet camlet, embroidered with tarnished flowers. Her features were coarse and masculine, yet at a little distance, by dint of very bright wild-looking black eyes, an aquiline nose, and a commanding profile, appeared rather handsome. She flourished the switch she held in her hand, dropped a curtsy as low as a lady at a birth-night introduction, recovered herself seemingly according to Touchstone's directions to Audrey, and opened the conversation without waiting till any questions were asked.

"God gi'e your honour gude e'en, and mony o' them, bonny Mr Sharpitlaw—Gude e'en to ye, Daddie Ratton—they tauld me ye were hanged, man; or did ye get out o' John Dalgleish's hands like half-hangit Maggie Dickson?"

"Whisht, ye daft jaud," said Ratcliffe, "and hear what's said to ye."

"Wi' a' my heart, Ratton. Great preferment for poor Madge to be brought up the street wi' a grand man, wi' a coat a' passemented wi' worset-lace, to speak wi' provosts, and baillies, and town-clerks, and prokitors, at this time o' day—and the hale town looking at me too— This is honour on earth for anes!"

"Ay, Madge," said Mr Sharpitlaw, in a coaxing tone; "and ye're dressed out in your braws, I see; these are not your every-day's claiths ye have on."

"De'il be in my fingers, then," said Madge—"Eh, sirs!" (observing Butler come into the apartment,) "there's a minister in the tolbooth—

wha will ca' it a graceless place, now?—I'se warrant he's in for the
gude auld cause—but it's be nae cause o' mine," and off she went into
song.

> "Hey for cavaliers, ho for cavaliers,
>   Dub a dub, dub a dub;
>   Have at old Beelzebub,—
> Oliver's rinning for fear."—

"Did you ever see that mad-woman before?" said Sharpitlaw to
Butler.

"Not to my knowledge, sir," replied Butler.

"I thought as much," said the procurator-fiscal, looking towards
Ratcliffe, who answered his glance with a nod of acquiescence and
intelligence.

"But that is Madge Wildfire, as she calls herself," said the man of
law to Butler.

"Ay, that I am," said Madge, "and that I have been—ever since I
was something better—Heigh ho"—(and something like melancholy
dwelt on her features for a minute)—"But I canna mind when that
was—it was lang syne, at ony rate, and I'll ne'er fash my thumb about
it.—

> I glance like the wildfire through country and town;
> I'm seen on the causeway—I'm seen on the down;
> The lightning that flashes so bright and so free,
> Is scarcely so blithe or so bonny as me."

"Haud yer tongue, ye skirling limmer," said the officer, who had
acted as master of the ceremonies to this extraordinary performer, and
who was rather scandalized at the freedom of her demeanour before a
person of Mr Sharpitlaw's importance—"haud your tongue, or I'se
gie ye something to skirl for."

"Let her alone, George," said Sharpitlaw; "dinna put her out o'
tune; I hae some questions to ask her—But first, Mr Butler, take
another look at her."

"Do sae, minister—do sae," cried Madge; "I am as weel worth
looking at as ony book in your aught.—And I can say the single
carritch, and the double carritch, and justification, and effectual calling, and the assembly of divines at Westminster, that is," (she added
in a low tone) "I could say them anes—but it's lang syne—and ane
forgets, ye ken." And poor Madge heaved another deep sigh.

"Weel, sir," said Mr Sharpitlaw to Butler, "what think ye now?"

"As I did before," said Butler; "that I never saw the poor demented
creature in my life before."

"Then she is not the person whom you said the rioters last night
described as Madge Wildfire?"

"Certainly not," said Butler. "They might be near a height, for they are both tall, but I see little other resemblance."

"Their dress, then, is not alike?" said Sharpitlaw.

"Not in the least," said Butler.

"Madge, my bonny woman," said Sharpitlaw, in the same coaxing manner, "what did ye do wi' your ilka day's claiths yesterday?"

"I dinna mind," said Madge.

"Where was ye yesterday at e'en, Madge?"

"I dinna mind ony thing about yesterday," answered Madge; "ae day is aneugh for ony body to win ower wi' at a time, and ower muckle sometimes."

"But maybe, Madge, ye wad mind something about it, if I was to gie ye this half-crown?" said Sharpitlaw, taking out the piece of money.

"That might gar me laugh, but it couldna gar me mind."

"But, Madge," continued Sharpitlaw, "were I to send you to the wark-house in Leith-Wynd, and gar Jock Dalgleish lay the tawse on your back"—

"That wad gar me greet," said Madge, sobbing, "but it couldna gar me mind, ye ken."

"She is ower far past reasonable folk's motives, sir," said Ratcliffe, "to mind siller, or John Dalgleish, or the cat and nine tails either; but I think I could gar her tell us something."

"Try her then, Ratcliffe," said Sharpitlaw, "for I am tired of her crazy pate, and be d—d to her."

"Madge," said Ratcliffe, "hae ye ony joes now?"

"An onybody ask ye, say ye dinna ken.—Set him up to be speaking of my joes, auld Daddie Ratton!"

"I dare say, ye hae de'il ane?"

"See if I haena than," said Madge, with the toss of the head of affronted beauty—"there's Rob the Ranter, and Will Fleming, and then there's Geordie Robertson, lad—that's Gentleman Geordie—what think ye o' that?"

Ratcliffe laughed, and, winking to the procurator-fiscal, pursued the enquiry in his own way. "But, Madge, the lads only like ye when ye hae on your braws—they wadna touch ye wi' a pair o' tangs when ye are in your auld ilka day rags."

"Ye're a leeing auld sorrow than," said Madge indignantly; "for Gentle Geordie Robertson put my ilka day's claiths on his ain bonnie sell yestreen, and gaed a' through the town wi' them; and gawsie and grand he lookit, like ony queen in the land."

"I dinna believe a word o't," said Ratcliffe, with another wink to the procurator. "Thae duds were a' o' the colour o' moonshine in the water, I'm thinking, Madge—The gown wad be a sky-blue scarlet, I'se warrant ye?"

"It was nae sic thing," said Madge, whose unretentive memory let out, in the eagerness of contradiction, all that she would have most wished to keep concealed, had her judgment been equal to her inclination. "It was neither scarlet nor sky-blue, but my ain auld brown threshie-coat of a shirt gown, and my mother's auld mutch, and my red rokelay—and he gaed me a croun and a kiss for the use o' them, blessing on his bonnie face—though it's been a dear ane to me."

"And whare did he change his clothes again, hinnie?" said Sharpit-law, in his most conciliatory manner.

"The procurator's spoiled a'," observed Ratcliffe, drily.

And it was even so; for the question, put in so direct a shape, immediately awakened Madge to the propriety of being reserved upon those very topics on which Ratcliffe had indirectly seduced her to become communicative.

"What was't ye were speering at us, sir?" she resumed, with an appearance of stolidity so speedily assumed, as shewed there was a good deal of knavery mixed with her folly.

"I asked you," said the procurator, "at what hour, and to what place, Robertson brought back your clothes."

"Robertson?—Lord haud a care o' us, what Robertson?"

"Why, the fellow we were speaking of, Gentle Geordie, as you call him."

"Geordie Gentle?" answered Madge, with well-feigned amaze-ment—"I dinna ken naebody they ca' Geordie Gentle."

"Come, my jo," said Sharpitlaw, "this will not do; you must tell us what you did wi' these clothes of your's."

Madge Wildfire made no answer, unless the question may seem connected with the snatch of a song with which she indulged the embarrassed investigator:—

> "What did ye wi' the bridal ring—bridal ring—bridal ring?
> What did ye wi' your wedding ring, ye little cutty quean, O
> I gied it till a sodger, a sodger, a sodger,
> I gied it till a sodger, an auld true love o' mine, O."

Of all the mad-women who have sung and said, since the days of Hamlet the Dane, if Ophelia be the most affecting, Madge Wildfire was the most provoking.

The procurator-fiscal was in despair. "I'll take some measure with this d——d Bess of Bedlam," said he, "that shall make her find her tongue."

"Wi' your favour, sir," said Ratcliffe, "better let her mind settle a little—Ye have aye made out something."

"True," said the official person; "a brown shirt-gown, mutch, red rokelay—that agrees with your Madge Wildfire, Mr Butler?" Butler agreed that it did so. "Yes, there was a sufficient motive for taking this crazy creature's dress and name, while he was about such a job."

"And I am free to say *now*," said Ratcliffe——

"When you see it has come out without you," interrupted Sharpit-law.

"Just sae, sir," reiterated Ratcliffe. "I am free to say, now since it's come out otherwise, that these were the clothes I saw Robertson wearing last night in the jail, when he was at the head of the rioters."

"That's direct evidence," said Sharpitlaw; "stick to that, Rat—I will report favourably of you to the provost, for I have business for you to-night. It wears late; I must hame and get a snack, and I'll be back in the evening. Keep Madge with you, Ratcliffe, and try to get her into a good tune again." So saying, he left the prison.

Chapter Four

And some they whistled—and some they sang,
And some did loudly say,
Whenever Lord Barnard's horn it blew,
"Away, Musgrave, away!"—
Ballad of Little Musgrave

WHEN THE MAN of office returned to the Heart of Mid-Lothian, he resumed his conference with Ratcliffe, of whose experience and assistance he now held himself secure. "You must speak with this wench, Rat—this Effie Deans—you must sift her a wee bit; for as sure as a tether she will ken Robertson's haunts—till her, Rat—till her, without delay."

"Craving your pardon, Mr Sharpitlaw," said the turnkey elect, "that's what I am not free to do."

"Free to do, man? what the de'il ails ye now?—I thought we had settled a' that."

"I dinna ken, sir," said Ratcliffe; "I hae spoken wi' this Effie—she's strange to this place and to its ways, and to a' our ways, Mr Sharpitlaw; and she greets, the silly tawpie, and she's breaking her heart already about this wild chield; and were she the means o' taking him, she wad break it outright."

"She winna hae time, lad," said Sharpitlaw; "the woodie will hae his ain o' her before that—a woman's heart takes a lang time o' breaking."

"That's according to the stuff they are made o', sir," replied Rat-cliffe—"But to mak a lang tale short, I canna undertake the job. It gangs against my conscience."

"Your conscience, Rat?" said Sharpitlaw, with a sneer, which the reader will probably think very natural upon the occasion.

"Ou ay, sir," answered Ratcliffe calmly, "just my conscience; a'body has a conscience, though it may be ill winning at it. I think mine's as weel out o' the gate as maist folks' are; and yet it's just like the noop of my elbow, it whiles gets a bit dirl on a corner."

"Weel, Rat," replied Sharpitlaw, "since ye are nice, I'll speak to the hussey mysell."

Sharpitlaw, accordingly, caused himself to be introduced into the little dark apartment tenanted by the unfortunate Effie Deans. The poor girl was seated on her little flock-bed, plunged in a deep reverie. Some food stood on the table, of a quality better than is usually supplied to prisoners, but it was untouched. The person under whose care she was more particularly placed, said, "that sometimes she tasted naething from the tae end of the four-and-twenty hours to the t'other, except a drink of water."

Sharpitlaw took a chair, and, commanding the turnkey to retire, he opened the conversation, endeavouring to throw into his tone and countenance as much commiseration as they were capable of expressing, for the one was sharp and harsh, the other sly, acute, and selfish.

"How's a' wi' ye, Effie?—How d'ye find yoursell, hinny?"

A deep sigh was the only answer.

"Are the folk civil to ye, Effie?—it's my duty to enquire."

"Very civil, sir," said Effie, compelling herself to answer, yet hardly knowing what she said.

"And your victuals," continued Sharpitlaw, in the same condoling tone—"do ye get what ye like?—or is there ony thing ye would particularly fancy, as your health seems but silly?"

"It's a' very weel, sir, I thank ye," said the poor prisoner, in a tone how different from the sportive vivacity of those of the Lily of Saint Leonard's!—"it's a' very gude—ower gude for me."

"He must have been a great villain, Effie, who brought you to this pass," said Sharpitlaw.

The remark was dictated partly by a natural feeling, of which even he could not divest himself, though accustomed to practise on the passions of others, and keep a most heedful guard over his own, and partly by his wish to introduce the sort of conversation which might best serve his immediate purpose. Indeed, upon the present occasion, these mixed motives of feeling and cunning harmonized together wonderfully; for, said Sharpitlaw to himself, the greater rogue Robertson is, the more will be the merit of bringing him to justice. "He must have been a great villain, indeed," he again reiterated; "and I wish I had the skelping o' him."

"I may blame mysell mair than him," said Effie; "I was bred up to ken better, but he, poor fallow,"——(She stopped.)

"Was a thorough blackguard a' his life, I dare say," said Sharpitlaw. "A stranger he was in this country, and a companion of that lawless vagabond, Wilson, I think, Effie."

"It wad hae been dearly telling him that he had ne'er seen Wilson's face."

"That's very true that you are saying, Effie," said Sharpitlaw. "Where was't that Robertson and you were used to howff thegither? Somegate about the Laigh Calton, I am thinking."

The simple and dispirited girl had thus far followed Mr Sharpitlaw's lead, because he had artfully adjusted his observations to the thoughts he was pretty certain must be passing through her own mind, so that her answers became a kind of thinking aloud, a mood into which those who are either constitutionally absent in mind, or are rendered so by the temporary pressure of misfortune, may be easily led by a skilful train of suggestions. But the last observation of the procurator-fiscal was too much of the nature of a direct interrogatory, and it broke the charm accordingly.

"What was it that I was saying?" said Effie, starting up from her reclining posture, seating herself upright, and hastily shading her dishevelled hair back from her wasted, but still beautiful countenance. She fixed her eyes boldly and keenly upon Sharpitlaw;—"You are too much of a gentleman, sir—too much of an honest man, to tak ony notice of what a poor creature like me says, that can hardly ca' my senses my ain—God help me!"

"Advantage!—I would be of some advantage to you if I could," said Sharpitlaw, in a soothing tone; "and I ken naething sae likely to serve ye, Effie, as gripping this rascal, Robertson."

"O dinna misca' him, sir, that never misca'd you!—Robertson?—I am sure I had naething to say against ony man o' the name, and naething will I say."

"But if ye do not heed your own misfortune, Effie, you should mind what distress he has brought on your family."

"O, Heaven help me!" exclaimed poor Effie—"My poor father—my dear Jeanie—O, that's sairest to bide of a'—o sir, if you hae ony kindness—if ye hae ony touch of compassion—for a' the folk I see here are as hard as the wa'-stanes—if ye wad but bid them let my sister Jeanie in the next time she ca's! for when I hear them pit her awa' frae the door, and canna climb up to that high window to see sae muckle as her gown-tail, it's like to pit me out o' my judgment." And she looked on him with a face of entreaty so earnest, yet so humble, that she fairly shook the steadfast purpose of his mind.

"You shall see your sister," he began, "if you'll tell me,"—then interrupting himself, he added, in a more hurried tone,—"no, d—n it, you shall see your sister whether you tell me any thing or no." So saying, he rose up and left the apartment.

When he had rejoined Ratcliffe, he observed, "You were right, Ratton; there's no making much of that lassie. But ae thing I have cleared—that is, that Robertson has been the father of the bairn, and so I will wager a boddle it will be him that's to meet wi' Jeanie Deans this night at Muschat's Cairn, and there we'll nail him, Rat, or my name is not Gideon Sharpitlaw."

"But," said Ratcliffe, perhaps because he was in no hurry to see any thing which was like to be connected with the discovery and apprehension of Robertson, "an that were the case, Mr Butler wad hae kenn'd the man in the King's Park to be the same person wi' him in Madge Wildfire's claise, that headed the mob."

"That makes nae difference, man," replied Sharpitlaw—"the dress, the light, the confusion, and maybe a touch o' a blackit cork, or a slake o' paint. Hout, Ratton, I have seen ye dress your ainsell, that the deevil ye belang to durstna hae made oath t'ye."

"And that's true, too," said Ratcliffe.

"And besides, ye donnard carle," continued Sharpitlaw triumphantly, "the minister *did* say, that he thought he knew something of the features of the birkie that spoke to him in the Park, though he could not charge his memory with where or when he had seen them."

"It's evident, than, your honour will be right," said Ratcliffe.

"Then, Rat, you and I will go with the party oursells this night, and see him in grips or we are done wi' him."

"I seena muckle use I can be o' to your honour," said Ratcliffe, reluctantly.

"Use?" answered Sharpitlaw—"You can guide the party—you ken the ground. Besides, I do not intend to quit sight o' you, my good friend, till I have him in hand."

"Weel, sir," said Ratcliffe, but in no joyful tone of acquiescence; "Ye maun hae it your ain way—but mind he's a desperate man."

"We shall have that with us," answered Sharpitlaw, "will settle him, if it's necessary."

"But, sir," answered Ratcliffe, "I am sure I couldna undertake to guide ye to Muschat's Cairn in the night-time; I ken the place, as mony ane does, in fair day-light, but how to find it by moonshine, amang sae mony crags and stanes, as like to each other as the collier to the de'il, is mair than I can tell. I might as soon seek moonshine in water."

"What's the meaning o' this, Ratcliffe?" said Sharpitlaw, while he fixed his eye on the recusant, with a fatal and ominous expression,

——"Have you forgotten that you're still under sentence of death?"

"No, sir," said Ratcliffe, "that's a thing no easily put out o' memory; and if my presence be judged necessary, nae doubt I maun gang wi' your honour. But I was ganging to tell your honour of ane that has mair skeel o' the gate than me, and that's e'en Madge Wildfire."

"The devil she has!—Do you think me as mad as she is, to trust to her guidance on such an occasion?"

"Your honour is best judge," answered Ratcliffe; "but I ken I can keep her in tune, and gar her haud the straight path—she aften sleeps out or rambles about amang thae hills the hale simmer night, the daft limmer."

"Well, Ratcliffe," replied the procurator-fiscal, "if you think she can guide us the right way—but take heed to what you are about—your life depends on your behaviour."

"It's a sair judgment on a man," said Ratcliffe, "when he has ance gane sae far wrang as I hae done, that de'il a bit he can be honest, try't whilk way he will."

Such was the reflection of Ratcliffe, when he was left for a few minutes to himself, while the retainer of justice went to procure a proper warrant, and give the necessary directions.

The rising moon saw the whole party free from the walls of the city, and entering upon the open ground. Arthur's Seat, like a couchant lion of immense size—Salusbury Crags, like a huge belt or girdle of granite, were dimly visible. Holding their path along the southern side of the Canongate, they gained the Abbey of Holyrood-House, and from thence found their way by step and stile into the King's Park. They were at first four in number—an officer of justice and Sharpitlaw, who were well armed with pistols and cutlasses; Ratcliffe, who was not trusted with weapons, lest he might, peradventure, have used them on the wrong side; and the female. But at the last stile, when they entered the Chase, they were joined by other two officers, whom Sharpitlaw, desirous to secure sufficient force for his purpose, and at the same time to avoid observation, had directed to wait for him at this place. Ratcliffe saw this accession of strength with some disquietude, for he had hitherto thought it likely that Robertson, who was a bold, stout, and active young fellow, might have made his escape from Sharpitlaw and the officer, by force or agility, without his being implicated in the matter. But the present strength of the followers of justice was overpowering, and the only mode of saving Robertson, (which the old sinner was well disposed to do, providing always he could accomplish his purpose without compromising his own safety), must be by contriving that he should have some signal of their approach. It was probably with this view that Ratcliffe had requested the addition of Madge to the party, having considerable confidence in her propensities to exert her lungs. Indeed, she had already given them so many specimens of her clamorous loquacity, that Sharpitlaw half determined to send her back with one of the officers, rather than carry forward in his company a person so extremely ill qualified to be a guide in a secret expedition. It seemed, too, as if the open air, the approach to the hills, and the ascent of the moon, supposed to be so potent over those whose brain is infirm, made her spirits rise in a degree tenfold more loquacious than she had hitherto exhibited. To silence her by fair means seemed impossible; authoritative commands and coaxing entreaties she set alike at defiance, and threats only made her sulky, and altogether intractable.

"Is there no one of you," said Sharpitlaw, impatiently, "that knows the way to this cursed place—this Nicol Muschat's Cairn—excepting this mad clavering idiot?"

"De'il ane o' them kens it, except mysell," exclaimed Madge; "how suld they, the puir fule cowards? But I hae sat on the grave frae bat-fleeing time till cock-crow, and had mony a fine crack wi' Nicol Muschat and Ailie Muschat, that are lying sleeping below."

"The devil take your crazy brain," said Sharpitlaw; "will you not allow the men to answer a question?"

The officers, obtaining a moment's audience while Ratcliffe diverted Madge's attention, declared that, though they had a general knowledge of the spot, they could not undertake to guide the party to it by the uncertain light of the moon, with such accuracy as to insure success to their expedition.

"What shall we do, Ratcliffe?" said Sharpitlaw; "if he sees us before we see him,—and that's what he is certain to do, if we go strolling about, without keeping the strait road,—we may bid gude day to the job; and I wad rather lose an hundred pounds, baith for the credit of the police, and because the Provost says somebody maun be hanged for this job o' Porteous, come o't what likes."

"I think," said Ratcliffe, "we maun just try Madge; and I'll see if I can get her keepit in ony better order. And at ony rate, if he suld hear her skirling her auld ends o' sangs, he's no to ken for that that there's ony body wi' her."

"That's true," said Sharpitlaw; "and if he thinks her alone he's as like to come to her as to rin frae her. So set forward—we have lost ower muckle time already—see to get her to keep the right road."

"And what sort o' house do Nicol Muschat and his wife keep now?" said Ratcliffe to the mad-woman, by way of humouring her vein of folly; "they were but thrawn folk lang syne, an' a' tales be true."

"Ou, ay, ay, ay—but a's forgotten now," replied Madge, in the

confidential tone of a gossip giving the history of her next-door neighbour—"Ye see I spoke to them mysell, and tauld them byganes suld
be byganes—her throat's sair misguggled and mashackered though;
she wears her corpse-sheet drawn weel up to hide it, but that canna
hinder the bluid seiping through, ye ken. I wussed her to wash it in
Saint Anthony's Well, and that will cleanse, if ony thing can—But they
say bluid never bleaches out o' linen claith—Deacon Sanders's new
cleansing draps winna do't—I tried them mysell on a bit rag we hae at
hame that was mailed wi' the bluid of a bit skirling wean that was hurt
some gate, but out it winna come—Weel, ye'll say that's queer; but I
will bring it out to Saint Anthony's blessed Well ae braw night just like
this, and I'll cry up Ailie Muschat, and she and I will hae a grand
bouking-washing, and bleach our claise in the beams of the bonny
Lady Moon, that's far pleasanter to me than the sun—the sun's ower
het, and ken ye, cummers, my harns are het aneugh already. But the
moon, and the dew, and the night-wind, they are just like a callar kail-
blade laid on my brow; and whiles I think the moon just shines on
purpose to pleasure me, when naebody sees her but mysell."

This raving discourse she continued with prodigious volubility,
walking on at a great pace, and dragging Ratcliffe along with her, while
he endeavoured, in appearance at least, if not in reality, to induce her
to moderate her voice.

All at once, she stopped short upon the top of a little hillock, gazed
upward fixedly, and said not one word for the space of five minutes.
"What the devil is the matter with her now?" said Sharpitlaw to
Ratcliffe—"Can you not get her forward?"

"Ye maun just take a grain o' patience wi' her, sir," said Ratcliffe.
"She'll no jee a foot faster than she likes hersel."

"D—n her, I'll take care she has her time in Bedlam or Bridewell,
or both, for she's both mad and mischievous." In the meanwhile,
Madge, who had looked very pensive when she first stopped, suddenly
burst into a vehement fit of laughter, then paused and sighed bitterly,
—then was seized with a second fit of laughter,—then fixed her eyes
on the moon, lifted up her voice, and sung,—

> "Good even, good fair moon, good even to thee;
> I prithee, dear moon, now show to me
> The form and the features, the speech and degree,
> Of the man that true lover of mine shall be.

"But I need not ask that o' the bonny Lady Moon—I ken that weel
aneugh mysel—*true*-lover though he wasna—But naebody shall say
that I ever tauld a word about the matter—But whiles I wish the
bairn had lived—Weel, God guide us, there's a heaven aboon us a'"
—(here she sighed bitterly) "and a bonny moon, and sterns in it

forbye," (and here she laughed once more).

"Are we to stand here all night?" said Sharpitlaw, very impatiently. "Drag her forward."

"Ay, sir," said Ratcliffe, "if we kenn'd whilk way to drag her, that would settle it at ance.—Come, Madge, hinny," addressing her, "we'll no be in time to see Nicol and his wife, unless ye show us the road."

"In troth and that I will, Ratton," said she, seizing him by the arm, and resuming her route with huge strides, considering it was a female who took them. "And I'll tell ye, Ratton, blithe will Nicol be to see ye, for he says he kens weel there is nae sic a villain out o' hell as ye are, and he wad be ravished to hae a crack wi' you—like to like, ye ken— it's a proverb never fails—and ye are baith a pair o' the deevil's peats, I trow—hard to ken whilk deserves the hettest nook o' his ingle-side."

Ratcliffe was conscience-struck, and could not forbear making an involuntary protest against this classification. "I never shed blood," he replied.

"But ye hae sauld it, Ratton—ye hae sauld blood mony a time. Folk kill wi' the tongue as weel as wi' the hand—wi' the word as weel as wi' the gulley,—

> It is the bonny butcher lad,
> That wears the sleeves of blue,
> He sells the flesh on Saturday,
> On Friday that he slew."

"And what is this that I am doing now?" thought Ratcliffe. "But I'll hae nae wyte of Robertson's young bluid, if I can help it;" then speaking apart to Madge, he asked her, "Whether she didna remember ony o' her auld sangs?"

"Mony a dainty ane," said Madge; "and blithely can I sing them, for lightsome sangs make merry gate." And she sang,—

> "When the gledd's in the blue cloud,
> The lavrock lies still;
> When the hound's in the green-wood,
> The hind keeps the hill."

"Silence her cursed noise, if you should throttle her," said Sharpit-law; "I see somebody yonder.—Keep close, my boys, and creep round the shoulder of the height. George Poinder, stay you with Ratcliffe and that mad bitch; and you other two, come with me round under the shadow of the brae."

And he crept forward with the stealthy pace of an Indian savage, who leads his band to surprise an unsuspecting party of some hostile tribe. Ratcliffe saw them glide off, avoiding the moonlight, and keeping as much in the shade as possible. "Robertson's done up," said he to himself; "thae young lads are aye sae thoughtless. What deevil could he hae to say to Jeanie Deans, or to ony woman on earth, that he suld gang awa and get his neck raxed for her? And this mad quean, after cracking like a pen-gun, and skirling like a pea-hen for the hale night, behoves just to hae hadden her tongue when her clavers might have done some gude! But it's aye the way wi' women; if they ever haud their tongue ava', ye may swear it is for mischief. I wish I could set her on again without this blood-sucker kenning what I am doing. But he's as gleg as Mackeachan's elshin, that ran through sax plies of bend-leather and half an inch into the king's heel."

He then began to hum, but in a very low and suppressed tone, a ballad which was a favourite of Madge Wildfire's and the words of which bore some distant analogy with the situation of Robertson, trusting that the power of association would not fail to bring the rest to her mind:

> "There's a bloodhound ranging Tinwald Wood,
>   There's harness glancing sheen;
> There's a maiden sits on Tinwald brae,
>   And she sings loud between."

Madge had no sooner received the catch-word, than she vindicated Ratcliffe's sagacity by setting off at score with the song:

> "O sleep ye sound, Sir James, she said,
>   When ye suld rise and ride?
> There's twenty men, wi' bow and blade,
>   Are seeking where ye hide."

Though Ratcliffe was at a considerable distance from the spot called Muschat's Cairn, yet his eyes, practised like those of a cat to penetrate darkness, could mark that Robertson had caught the alarm. George Poinder, less keen of sight, or less attentive, was not aware of his flight any more than Sharpitlaw and his assistants, whose view, though they were considerably nearer to the cairn, was intercepted by the broken nature of the ground under which they were screening themselves. At length, however, after the interval of five or six minutes, they also perceived that Robertson had fled, and rushed hastily towards the place, while Sharpitlaw called out aloud, in the harshest tones of a voice which resembled a saw-mill at work, "Chase, lads— chase—haud the brae—I see him on the edge of the hill." Then hollowing back to the rear-guard of his detachment, he issued his farther orders: "Ratcliffe, come here, and detain the woman— George, run and kepp at the stile at the Duke's Walk—Ratcliffe, come here directly—but first knock out that mad bitch's brains."

"Ye had better rin for it, Madge," said Ratcliffe, "for it's ill dealing wi' an angry man."

Madge Wildfire was not so absolutely void of common sense as not to understand this inuendo; and while Ratcliffe, in seemingly anxious haste of obedience, hastened to the spot where Sharpitlaw waited to deliver up Jeanie Deans to his custody, she fled with all the dispatch she could exert in an opposite direction. Thus the whole party were separated, and in rapid motion of flight or pursuit, excepting Ratcliffe and Jeanie, whom, although making no attempt to escape, he held fast by the cloak, and who remained standing by Muschat's Cairn.

Chapter Five

You have paid the heavens your function, and the
prisoner the very debt of your calling.
Measure for Measure

JEANIE DEANS,—for here our story unites itself with that part of the narrative which broke off at the end of chapter II.,—while she watched, in terror and amazement, the hasty advance of three or four men towards her, was yet more startled at their suddenly breaking asunder, and giving chase in different directions to the late object of her terror, who became at that moment, though she could not well assign a reasonable cause, rather the cause of her interest. One of the party (it was Sharpitlaw,) came straight up to her, and saying, "Your name is Jeanie Deans, and you are my prisoner," immediately added, "but if you'll tell me which way he ran I will let you go."

"I dinna ken, sir," was all the poor girl could utter; and indeed it is the phrase which rises most readily to the lips of any person in her rank, as a temporary reply to any embarrassing question.

"But ye *ken* wha it was ye were speaking wi', my leddy, on the hill side, and midnight sae near; ye surely ken *that*, my bonny woman?"

"I dinna ken, sir," again iterated Jeanie, who really did not comprehend in her terror the nature of the questions which were so hastily put to her in this moment of surprise.

"We will try to mend your memory by and bye, hinny," said Sharpitlaw, and shouted, as we have already told the reader, to Ratcliffe, to come up and take charge of her, while he himself directed the chase after Robertson, which he still hoped might be successful. As Ratcliffe approached, Sharpitlaw pushed the young woman towards him with some rudeness, and betaking himself to the more important objects of his quest, began to scale crags and scramble up steep banks, with an agility of which his profession and his general gravity of demeanour would previously have argued him incapable. In a few minutes there was no one within sight, and only a distant halloo from one of the pursuers to the other, faintly heard on the side of the hill, argued that there was any one within hearing. Jeanie Deans was left in the clear moonlight, standing under the guard of a person of whom she knew nothing, and, what was worse, concerning whom, as the reader is well aware, she could have learned nothing that would not have increased her terror.

When all in the distance was silent, Ratcliffe for the first time addressed her, and it was in that cold sarcastic indifferent tone familiar to habitual depravity, whose crimes are instigated by custom rather than by passion. "This is a braw night for ye, dearie," he said, attempting to pass his arm across her shoulder, "to be on the green hill wi' your jo." Jeanie extricated herself from his grasp, but did not make any reply. "I think lads and lasses," continued the ruffian, "dinna meet at Muschat's Cairn at midnight to crack nuts," and he again attempted to take hold of her.

"If ye are an officer of justice, sir," said Jeanie, again eluding his attempt to seize her, "ye deserve to have your coat stripped from your back."

"Very true, hinny," said he, succeeding forcibly in his attempt to seize her, "but suppose I should strip your cloak off first?"

"Ye are more a man, I am sure, than to hurt me, sir," said Jeanie; "for God's sake, have pity on a half-distracted creature!"

"Come, come," said Ratcliffe, "you're a good-looking wench, and shouldna be cross-grained. I was going to be an honest man—but the devil has this very day flung first a lawyer, and then a woman, in my gate. I'll tell you what, Jeanie, they are out on the hill-side—if you'll be guided by me, I'll carry you to a wee bit corner in the Pleasance, that I ken o' in an auld wifie's, that a' the prokitors in Scotland wot naething o', and we'll send Robertson word to meet us in Yorkshire, for there is a set o' braw lads about the midland counties, that I hae dune business wi' before now, and sae we'll leave Mr Sharpitlaw to whistle on his thumb."

It was fortunate for Jeanie, in an emergence like the present, that she possessed presence of mind and courage, so soon as the first hurry of surprise had enabled her to rally her recollection. She saw the risk she was in from a ruffian, who not only was such by profession, but had that evening been stupifying, by means of strong liquors, the internal aversion which he felt at the business on which Sharpitlaw had resolved to employ him.

"Dinna speak sae loud," said she, in a low voice, "he's up yonder."

"Who?—Robertson?" said Ratcliffe, eagerly.

"Ay," replied Jeanie; "up yonder;" and she pointed to the ruins of the hermitage and chapel.

"By G—d, then!" said Ratcliffe, "I'll make my ain of him, either one way or other—wait for me here."

But no sooner had he set off, as fast as he could run, towards the chapel, than Jeanie started in an opposite direction, over high and low, on the nearest path homeward. Her juvenile exercise as a herds-woman, had put "life and mettle" in her heels, and never had she followed Dustiefoot, when the cows were in the corn, with half so much speed as she now cleared the distance betwixt Muschat's Cairn and her father's cottage at Saint Leonard's. To lift the latch—to enter —to shut, bolt, and double bolt the door—to draw against it a heavy article of furniture, (which she could not have moved in a moment of less energy,) so as to make yet further provision against violence, was almost the work of a moment, yet done with such silence as equalled the celerity.

Her next anxiety was upon her father's account, and she drew silently to the door of his apartment, in order to satisfy herself whether he had been disturbed by her return. He was awake,—probably had slept but little; but the constant presence of his own sorrows, the distance of his apartment from the outer-door of the house, and the precautions which Jeanie had taken to conceal her departure and return, had prevented him from being sensible of either. He was engaged in his devotions, and Jeanie could distinctly hear him use these words: "And for the other child thou hast given me to be a comfort and stay to my old age, may her days be long in the land, according to the promise thou hast given to those who shall honour father and mother; may all purchased and promised blessings be multiplied upon her; keep her in the watches of the night, and in the uprising of the morning, that all in this land may know thou hast not utterly hid thy face from them that seek thee in truth and in sincerity." He was silent, but probably continued his petition in the strong fer-vency of mental devotion.

His daughter retired to her apartment, comforted, that while she was exposed to danger, her head had been covered by the prayers of the just as by an helmet, and under the strong confidence, that while she walked worthy of the protection of Heaven, she would experience its countenance. It was in that moment that a vague idea first darted across her mind, that something might yet be achieved for her sister's safety, conscious as she now was of her innocence of the unnatural murther with which she stood charged. It came, as she described it, on her mind like a sun-blink on a stormy sea; and although it instantly vanished, yet she felt a degree of composure which she had not experi-enced for many days, and could not help being strongly persuaded, that, by some means or other, she would be called upon, and directed, to work out her sister's deliverance. She went to bed, not forgetting her usual devotions, the more fervently made on account of her late deliverance, and she slept soundly in spite of her agitation.

We must return to Ratcliffe, who had started, like a greyhound from the slips when the sportsman cries halloo, so soon as Jeanie had pointed to the ruins. Whether he meant to aid Robertson's escape, or to assist his pursuers, may be very doubtful; perhaps he did not know himself, but had resolved to be guided by circumstances. He had no opportunity, however, of doing either; for he had no sooner surmounted the steep ascent, and entered under the broken arches of the ruins, than a pistol was presented at his head, and a harsh voice commanded him, in the king's name, to surrender himself prisoner. "Mr Sharpitlaw," said Ratcliffe, surprised, "is this your honour?"

"Is it only you, and be d——d to you?" answered the fiscal, still more disappointed—"what made you leave the woman?"

"She told me she saw Robertson go into the ruins, so I made what haste I could to cleek the callant."

"It's all over now," said Sharpitlaw; "we shall see no more of him to-night; but he shall hide himsell in a bean-hool, if he remains on Scottish ground without my finding him.—Call back the people, Ratcliffe."

Ratcliffe hollowed to the dispersed officers, who willingly obeyed the signal; for probably there was no individual among them who would have been much desirous of a rencontre hand to hand, and at a distance from his comrades, with such an active and desperate fellow as Robertson.

"And where are the two women?" said Sharpitlaw.

"Both made their heels serve them, I suspect," replied Ratcliffe, and he hummed the end of the old song—

> "Then hey play up the rin awa' bride,
> For she has ta'en the gee."

"One woman," said Sharpitlaw,—for, like all rogues, he was a great calumniator of the fair sex,—"is enough to dark the fairest ploy that ever was planned; and how could I be such a cuddie as to expect to carry through a job that had two in it? But we know how to come by them both, if they are wanted, that's one good thing."

Accordingly, like a defeated general, sad and sulky, he led back his discomfited forces to the metropolis, and dismissed them for the night.

The next morning early he was under the necessity of making his report to the sitting magistrate of the day. The gentleman who occupied the chair of office on this occasion (for the baillies, *Anglice* aldermen, take it by rotation) was a different and more intelligent person than him by whom Butler was committed, and was very generally respected among his fellow-citizens. Something he was of a humourist, and rather deficient in general education; but acute, patient, and upright, possessed of a fortune acquired by honest industry, which made him perfectly independent; and, in short, very happily qualified to support the respectability of the office which he held.

Mr Middleburgh had just taken his seat, and was debating, in an animated manner, with one of his colleagues, the doubtful chances of a game at golf which they had played the day before, when a letter was delivered to him, addressed "For Baillie Middleburgh; These: to be forwarded with speed." It contained these words:—

"SIR,

"I know you to be a sensible and a considerate magistrate, and one who, as such, will be content to worship God, though the devil bid you. I therefore expect that, notwithstanding the signature of this letter acknowledges my share in an action, which, in a proper time and place, I would not fear either to avow or to justify, you will not on that account reject what evidence I place before you. The clergyman, Butler, is innocent of all but involuntary presence at an action which he wanted spirit to approve of, and from which he endeavoured, with his best set phrases, to dissuade us. But it was not for him that it is my hint to speak. There is a woman in your jail, fallen under the edge of a law so cruel, that it has hung by the wall, like unscoured armour, for twenty years, and is now brought down and whetted to spill the blood of the most beautiful and most innocent creature whom the walls of a prison ever girdled in. Her sister knows of her innocence, as she communicated to her that she was betrayed by a villain.—O that high Heaven

> Would put in every honest hand a whip,
> To scourge me such a villain through the world!

"I write distractedly—But this girl—this Jeanie Deans, is a peevish puritan, superstitious and scrupulous after the manner of her sect; and I pray your honour, for so my phrase must go, to press upon her, that her sister's life depends upon her testimony. But though she should remain silent, do not dare to think that the young woman is guilty—far less to permit her execution. Remember the death of Wilson was fearfully avenged; and those yet live who can compel you to drink the dregs of your poisoned chalice.—I say, remember Porteous,—and say that you had good counsel from

"ONE OF HIS SLAYERS."

The magistrate read over this extraordinary letter twice or thrice. At first he was tempted to throw it aside as the production of a madman, so little did "the scraps from play-books," as he termed the poetical quotation, resemble the correspondence of a rational being. On a re-perusal, however, he thought that, amid its incoherence, he could discern something like a tone of awakened passion, though expressed in a manner quaint and unusual.

"It is a cruelly severe statute," said the magistrate to his assistant, "and I wish the girl could be taken from under the letter of it. A child may have been born, and it may have been conveyed away while the mother was insensible, or it may have perished for want of that relief which the poor creature herself,—helpless, terrified, distracted, despairing, and exhausted,—may have been unable to afford to it. And yet it is certain, if the woman is found guilty under the statute, execution will follow. The crime has been too common, and examples are become necessary."

"But if this other wench," said the city-clerk, "can speak to her sister communicating her situation, it will take the case from under the statute."

"Very true; and I will walk out one of these days to Saint Leonard's, and examine the girl myself. I know something of their father Deans— an old true-blue Cameronian, who would see house and family go to wreck ere he would disgrace his testimony by a sinful complying with the defections of the times; and such he will probably uphold the taking an oath before a civil magistrate. If they are to go on and flourish in their bull-headed obstinacy, the legislature must pass an act to take their affirmation, as in the case of Quakers. But surely neither a father nor a sister will scruple in a case of this kind. As I said before, I will go speak with them myself, when the hurry of this Porteous investigation is somewhat over; their pride and spirit of contradiction will be far less alarmed, than if they were called into a court of justice at once."

"And I suppose Butler is to remain incarcerated?" said the city-clerk.

"For the present, certainly," said the magistrate. "But I hope soon to set him at liberty upon bail."

"Do you rest upon the testimony of that light-headed letter?" said the clerk.

"Not very much," answered the baillie; "and yet there is something striking about it too—it seems the letter of a man beside himself, either from great agitation, or great sense of guilt."

"Yes," said the town-clerk, "it is very like the letter of a mad strolling play-actor, who deserves to be hanged with all the rest of his gang, as your honour justly observes."

"I was not quite so blood-thirsty," continued the magistrate. "But to the point. Butler's private character is excellent; and I am given to understand, by some enquiries I have been making this morning, that he did actually arrive in town only the day before yesterday, so that it was impossible he could have been concerned in any previous machinations of these unhappy rioters, and it is not likely that he should have joined them on a suddenty."

"There's no saying anent that—zeal catches fire at a slight spark as fast as a brunstane match," observed the secretary. "I hae kenn'd a minister wad be fair gud-day and fair gud-e'en wi' ilka man in the parochine, and hing just as quiet as a rocket on a stick, till ye mentioned the word abjuration-oath, or patronage, or sic like, and then, whiz, he was off, and up in the air an hundred miles beyond common manners, common sense, and common comprehension."

"I do not apprehend," answered the burgher-magistrate, "that this young man Butler's zeal is of so inflammable a character. But I will make farther investigation. What other business is there before us?"

And they proceeded to minute investigations concerning the affair of Porteous's death, and other affairs through which this history has no occasion to trace them.

In the course of their business they were interrupted by an old woman of the lower rank, who thrust herself into the council-room. "What do ye want, goodwife?—Who are you?"

"What do I want!" replied she, in a sulky tone—"I want my bairn, or I want naething frae nane o' ye, for as grand's ye are." And she went on muttering to herself, with the wayward spitefulness of age—"They maun hae lordships and honours nae doubt—set them up, the gutter-bloods! and de'il a gentleman amang them."—Then again addressing the sitting magistrate, "Will *your honour* gi'e back my puir crazy bairn? —his honour!—I hae kenn'd the day when less wad ser'd him, the oe of a Campvere skipper."

"Good woman," said the magistrate to this shrewish supplicant,— "tell us what it is that you want, and do not interrupt the court."

"That's as muckle as till say, Bark, Batie, and be dune wi't!—I tell ye," raising her termagant voice, "I want my bairn! is na that braid Scots?"

"Who *are* you?—who is your bairn?" demanded the magistrate.

"Wha am I?—wha suld I be, but Meg Murdockson, and wha suld my bairn be but Magdalen Murdockson?—Your guard-soldiers, and your constables, and your officers, ken us weel aneugh when they rive the bits o' duds aff our backs, and take what penny o' siller we hae, and hurle us to the Correction-house in Leith Wynd, and pettle us up wi' bread and water, and siclike sunkets."

"Who is she?" said the magistrate, looking round to some of his people.

"Other than a good ane, sir," said one of the city-officers, shrugging his shoulders and smiling.

"Will ye say sae?" said the termagant, her eye gleaming with impotent fury; "an I had ye amang the Frigate-Whins, wadna I set my ten commandments in your wizend face for that very word?" And she spread her long skinny fingers garnished at the extremities with claws which a goss-hawk might have coveted.

"What does she want here?" said the impatient magistrate—"Can she not tell her business or go away?"

"It's my bairn!—it's Magdalen Murdockson that I am wantin," answered the beldame, screaming at the highest pitch of her cracked and mistuned voice—"havena I been telling ye sae this half-hour? and if ye are deaf, what needs ye sit cockit up there, and keep folks scraughin' t'ye this gate?"

"She wants her daughter, sir," said the same officer whose interference had given the hag such offence before—"her daughter, who was taken up again last night—Madge Wildfire, as they ca' her."

"Madge HELLFIRE, as they ca' her!" echoed the beldame; "and what business has a blackguard like you to ca' an honest woman's bairn out o' her ain name?"

"An *honest* woman's bairn, Maggie!" answered the peace-officer, smiling and shaking his head with an ironical emphasis upon the adjective, and a calmness calculated to provoke to madness the furious old shrew.

"If I am no honest now, I was honest anes," she replied; "and that's mair than ye can say, ye born and bred thief, that never kenn'd ither folk's gear frae your ain since the day ye was cleckit. Honest! say ye?—ye pykit your mother's pouch o' twal-pennies Scots when ye were five years auld, just as she was taking leave o' your father at the fit o' the gallows."

"She has ye there, George," said the assistants, and there was a general laugh; for the wit was fitted for the meridian of the place where it was uttered. This general applause somewhat gratified the angry passions of the old hag; "the grim feature" smiled, and even laughed—but it was a laugh of bitter scorn. She condescended, however, as if appeased by the success of her sally, to explain her business more distinctly, when the magistrate, commanding silence, again desired her either to speak out her errand, or to leave the place.

"Her bairn," she said, "*was* her bairn, and she came to fetch her out of ill haft and waur guiding. If she wasna sae wise as ither folks, few ither folks had suffered as muckle as she had done; forbye that she could fend the waur for hersell within the four wa's of a jail. She could prove by fifty witnesses, and fifty to that, that her daughter had never seen Jock Porteous, alive or dead, since he had gien her a loundering wi' his cane, the neger that he was, for driving a dead cat at the provost's wig on the Elector of Hanover's birth-day."

Notwithstanding the wretched appearance and violent demeanour of this woman, the magistrate felt the justice of her argument, that her child might be as dear to her as to a more fortunate and more amiable mother. He proceeded to investigate the circumstances which had led to Madge Murdockson's (or Wildfire's,) arrest, and as it was clearly shown that she had not been engaged in the riot, he contented himself with directing that an eye should be kept upon her by the police, but that for the present she should be allowed to return home with her mother. During the interval of fetching Madge from the jail, the magistrate endeavoured to discover whether her mother had been privy to the change of dress betwixt that young woman and Robertson. But on this point he could obtain no light. She persisted in declaring, that she had never seen Robertson since his remarkable escape during service-time; and that if her daughter had changed clothes with him, it must have been during her absence at a hamlet about two miles out of town, called Duddingstone, where she could prove that she passed that eventful night. And, in fact, one of the town-officers, who had been searching for stolen linen at the cottage of a washer-woman in that village, gave his evidence, that he had seen Maggie Murdockson there, whose presence had considerably increased his suspicion of the house in which she was a visitor, in respect that he considered her as a person of no good reputation.

"I tauld ye sae," said the hag; "see now what it is to hae a character, gude or bad!—Now, maybe after a', I could tell ye something about Porteous that you council-chamber bodies never could find out, for as muckle stir as ye mak."

All eyes were turned towards her—all ears were alert. "Speak out," said the magistrate.

"It will be for your ain gude," insinuated the town-clerk.

"Dinna keep the baillie waiting," urged the assistants.

She remained doggedly silent for two or three minutes, casting around a malignant and sulky glance, that seemed to enjoy the anxious suspense with which they waited her answer. And then she broke forth at once,—"A' that I ken about him is, that he was neither soldier nor gentleman, but just a thief and a blackguard, like maist o' yoursels, dears—What will ye gie me for that news now?—He wad hae served the Gude Town lang or provost or baillie wad hae fund that out, my jo!"

While these matters were in discussion, Madge Wildfire entered, and her first exclamation was, "Eh! see if there isna our auld ne'er-do-weel, deevil's buckie o' a mither—Hegh, sirs! but we are a hopefu' family, to be twa o' us in the Guard at anes—But there were better days wi' us anes—were there na, mither?"

Old Maggie's eyes had glistened with something like an expression of pleasure when she saw her daughter set at liberty. But either her natural affection, like that of the tigress, could not be displayed without a strain of ferocity, or there was something in the ideas which Madge's speech awakened, that again stirred her cross and savage temper. "What signifies what we were, ye street-raking limmer!" she exclaimed, pushing her daughter before her to the door, with no gentle degree of violence. "I'se tell thee what thou is now—thou's a crazed hellicat Bess o' Bedlam, that sall taste naething but bread and water for a fortnight, to serve ye for the plague ye hae gien me, and ower gude for ye, ye idle tawpie."

Madge, however, escaped from her mother at the door, ran back to the foot of the table, dropped a very low and fantastic curtesy to the judge, and said, with a giggling laugh,—"Our minnie's sair mis-set, after her ordinar, sir—She'll hae had some quarrel wi' her auld gudeman—that's Satan, ye ken, sirs." This explanatory note she gave in a low confidential tone, and the spectators of that credulous generation did not hear it without an involuntary shudder. "The gudeman and her disna aye gree weel, and then I maun pay the piper; but my back's broad aneugh to bear't a'—An' if she hae nae havings, that's nae reason why wiser folk suldna hae some." Here another deep curtesy. The ungracious voice of her mother was heard.

"Madge, ye limmer! If I come to fetch ye!"

"Hear till her," said Madge. "But I'll win out a gliff the night for a' that, to dance in the moonlight, when her and the gudeman will be whirrying through the blue lift on a broom-shank, to see Jean Jap, that they hae putten intill the Pettycur tolbooth—ay, they will hae a merry sail ower Inchkeith, and a' the bits o' bonny waves that are poppling and plashing against the rocks in the gowden glimmer o' the moon, ye ken.—I'm coming, mother—I'm coming," she concluded, on hearing a scuffle at the door betwixt the beldame and the officers, who were endeavouring to prevent her re-entrance. Madge then waved her hand wildly towards the ceiling, sung, at the topmost pitch of her voice,—

> "Up in the air,
> On my bonnie grey mare,
> And I see, and I see, and I see her yet."

and with a hop, skip, and jump, sprung out of the room, as the witches in Macbeth used, in less refined days, to seem to fly upwards from the stage.

Chapter Six

SOME WEEKS intervened before Mr Middleburgh, agreeably to his benevolent resolution, found an opportunity of taking a walk towards Saint Leonard's, in order to discover whether it might be possible to obtain the evidence hinted at in the anonymous letter respecting Effie Deans.

In fact, the anxious perquisitions made to discover the murderers of Porteous, occupied the attention of all concerned with the administration of justice.

In the course of these enquiries, two circumstances happened material to our story. Butler, after a close investigation of his conduct, was declared innocent of accession to the death of Porteous; but, as having been present during the whole transaction, was obliged to find bail not to quit his usual residence at Libberton, that he might appear as a witness when called upon. The other incident regarded the disappearance of Madge Wildfire and her mother from Edinburgh. When they were sought, with the purpose of subjecting them to some further interrogatories, it was discovered by Mr Sharpitlaw that they had eluded the observation of the police, and left the city so soon as dismissed from the council-chamber. No efforts could trace the place of their retreat.

In the meanwhile the excessive indignation of the council of regency, at the slight put upon their authority by the murther of Porteous, had dictated measures, in which their own extreme desire of detecting the actors in that conspiracy were consulted, in preference to the temper of the people, and the character of their churchmen. An act of parliament was hastily passed, offering two hundred pounds reward to those who should inform against any person concerned in the deed, and the penalty of death, by a very unusual and severe enactment, was denounced against those who should harbour the guilty. But what was chiefly accounted exceptionable, was a clause, appointing the act to be read in churches by the officiating clergyman, upon the first Sunday of every month, for a certain period, immediately before the sermon. The ministers who should refuse to comply with this injunction were declared, for the first offence, incapable of sitting or voting in any church judicature, and for the second, incapable of holding any ecclesiastical preferment in Scotland.

This last order united in a common cause those who might privately rejoice in Porteous's death, though they dared not vindicate the manner of it, with the more scrupulous presbyterians, who held that even the pronouncing the name of the "Lords Spiritual" in a Scottish pulpit was, *quodammodo*, an acknowledgment of prelacy, and that the injunction of the legislature was an interference of the civil government with the *jus divinum* of presbytery, since to the General Assembly alone, as representing the invisible Head of the Kirk, belonged the sole and exclusive right of regulating whatever belonged to public worship. Very many also of different political or religious sentiments, and therefore not much moved by these considerations, thought they saw, in so violent an act of parliament, a more vindictive spirit than became the legislature of a great country, and something like an attempt to trample upon the rights and independence of Scotland. The various steps adopted for punishing the city of Edinburgh, by taking away her charter and liberties, for what a violent and overmastering mob had done within her walls, were resented by many, who thought a pretext was too hastily taken for degrading the ancient metropolis of Scotland. In short, there was much heart-burning, discontent, and disaffection, occasioned by these ill-considered measures.

Amidst these heats and dissensions, the trial of Effie Deans, after many weeks' confinement, was at length about to be brought forward, and Mr Middleburgh found leisure to enquire into the evidence concerning her. For this purpose he chose a fine day for his walk towards her father's house.

The excursion into the country was somewhat distant, in the opinion of a burgess of these days, although many of the present inhabit suburban villas considerably beyond the spot to which we allude. Three quarters of an hour's walk, however, even at a pace of magisterial gravity, conducted our benevolent office-bearer to the Crags of Saint Leonard, and the humble mansion of David Deans.

The old man was seated on the deas, or turf-seat, at the end of his cottage, busied in mending his cart-harness with his own hands; for in those days any sort of labour which required a little more skill than usual fell to the share of the goodman himself, and that even when he was well to pass in the world. With stern and austere gravity he persevered in his task, after having just raised his head to notice the advance of the stranger. It would have been impossible to have discovered, from his countenance and manner, the internal feelings of agony with which he contended. Mr Middleburgh waited an instant, expecting Deans would in some measure acknowledge his presence, and lead into conversation; but, as he seemed determined to remain silent, he was himself obliged to speak first.

"My name is Middleburgh—Mr James Middleburgh, one of the present magistrates of the city of Edinburgh."

"It may be sae," answered Deans laconically, and without interrupting his labour.

"You must understand," he continued, "that the duty of a magistrate is sometimes an unpleasant one."

"It may be sae," replied David; "I hae naething to say in the contrair;" and he was again doggedly silent.

"You must be aware," pursued the magistrate, "that persons in my situation are often obliged to make painful and disagreeable enquiries at individuals, merely because it is their bounden duty."

"It may be sae," again replied Deans; "I hae naething to say anent it, either the tae way or the t'other. But I do ken there was ance in a day a just and God-fearing magistracy in yon town o' Edinburgh, that did not bear the sword in vain, but were a terror to evil doers, and a praise to such as kept the path. In the glorious days of auld, worthy, faithfu' Provost Dick, when there was a true and faithfu' General Assembly of the Kirk, walking hand in hand with the real noble Scottish-hearted barons, and with the magistrates of this and other towns, gentles, burgesses, and commons of all ranks, seeing with one eye, hearing with one ear, and upholding the ark with their united strength—And than folk might see men deliver up their silver to the states' use, as if it had been as muckle sclate stanes. My father saw them toom the sacks of dollars out o' Provost Dick's window intill the carts that carried them to the army at Dunselaw; and if ye winna believe his testimony, there is the window itsell still standing in the Luckenbooths—I think it's a claith-merchant's booth the day—at the airn stanchells, five doors abune Gossford's Close—But now we hae nae sic spirit amang us; we think mair about the warst wally-draggle in our ain byre, than about the blessing which the angel of the covenant gave to the Patriarch even at Peniel and Mahanaim, or the binding obligation of our national vows; and we wad rather gi'e a pund Scots to buy an unguent to clear our auld rannell-trees and our beds o' the English bugs as they ca' them, than we wad gi'e a plack to rid the land of the swarms of Arminian caterpillars, Socinian pismires, and deistical Miss Katies, that have ascended out of the bottomless pit, to plague this perverse, insidious, and lukewarm generation."

It happened to David Deans on this occasion as it has done to many other habitual orators: when once he became embarked on his favourite subject, the stream of his own enthusiasm carried him forward in spite of his mental distress, while his well exercised memory supplied him amply with all the types and tropes of rhetoric peculiar to his sect and cause.

Mr Middleburgh contented himself with answering—"All this may be very true, my friend; but, as you said just now, I have nothing to say to it at present, either one way or other.—You have two daughters, I think, Mr Deans?"

The old man winced, as one whose smarting sore is suddenly galled, but instantly composed himself, resumed the work which, in the heat of his declamation, he had laid down, and answered with sullen resolution, "Ae daughter, sir—only *ane*."

"I understand you," said Mr Middleburgh; "you have only one daughter here at home with you—but this unfortunate girl who is a prisoner—she is, I think, your youngest daughter?"

The presbyterian sternly raised his eyes. "After the world, and according to the flesh, she is my daughter; but when she became a child of Belial, and a company-keeper, and a traitor in guilt and iniquity, she ceased to be bairn of mine."

"Alas, Mr Deans," said Middleburgh, sitting down by him, and endeavouring to take his hand, which the old man proudly withdrew. "We are ourselves all sinners; and the errors of our offspring, as they ought not to surprise us, being the portion which they derive of a common portion of corruption inherited through us, so they do not entitle us to cast them off because they have lost themselves."

"Sir," said Deans, impatiently, "I ken a' that as weel as—I mean to say," he resumed, checking the irritation he felt at being school'd,—a discipline of the mind, which those most ready to bestow it on others, do themselves most reluctantly submit to receive—"I mean to say, that what ye observe may be just and reasonable—But I hae nae freedom to enter into my ain private affairs wi' strangers—And now, in this great national emergency, when there's the Porteous Act has come doun frae London, that is a deeper blow to this poor sinfu' Kingdom and suffering Kirk, than ony that has been heard of since the foul and fatal Test—at a time like this"——

"But, goodman," interrupted Mr Middleburgh, "you must think of your own household first, or else you are worse even than the infidels."

"I tell ye, Baillie Middleburgh," retorted David Deans, "if ye be a baillie, as there is little honour in being ane in these evil days—I tell ye, I heard the gracious Sanders Peden—I wotna whan it was; but it was in killing time, when the plowers were drawing long their furrows on the back of the Kirk of Scotland—I heard him tell his hearers, gude and waled Christians they were too, that some o' them wad greet mair for a bit drowned calf or stirk, than for a' the defections and oppressions of the day; and that they were some o' them thinking o' ae thing, some o' anither, and there was Lady Hundelslope thinking o' greeting Jock at the fire-side! And the lady confessed in my hearing, that a drow of anxiety had come ower her for her son that she had left at hame weak of a decay—And what wad he hae said of me, if I had ceased to think of the gude cause for a cast-away—a—it kills me to think what she is—"

"But the life of your child, goodman—think of that, if her life could be saved," said Middleburgh.

"Her life!" exclaimed David—"I wadna gi'e ane o' my grey hairs for her life, if her gude name be gane—And yet," said he, relenting and retracting as he spoke, "I would—I would mak the niffer, Mr Middleburgh—I wad gi'e a' these grey hairs that she has brought to shame and sorrow—I wad gi'e the auld head they grow on for her life, and that she might hae time to amend and return, for what hae the wicked beyond the breath of their nosthrils—But I'll never see her mair.—No!—that—that I am determined in—I'll never see her mair." His lips continued to move for a minute after his voice ceased to be heard, as if he were repeating the same vow internally.

"Well, sir," said Mr Middleburgh, "I speak to you as a man of sense; if you would save your daughter's life, you must use human means."

"I understand what ye mean; but Mr Novit, who is the procurator and doer of an honourable person, the Laird of Dumbiedikes, is to do what carnal wisdom can do for her in the circumstances. Mysell am not clear to trinquet or traffic wi' courts o' justice, as they are now constituted; I have a tenderness and a scruple on my mind anent them."

"That is to say," said Middleburgh, "that you are a Cameronian, and do not acknowledge the authority of our courts of judicature or present government?"

"Sir, under your favour," replied David, who was too proud of his own polemical knowledge, to call himself the follower of any one, "ye tak me up before I fall down. I canna see why I suld be termed a Cameronian, especially now that ye hae given the name of that famous and savoury sufferer, not only until a regimented band of souldiers, whereof I am told many can now curse, swear, and use profane language, as fast as ever Richard Cameron could preach or pray; but also because ye have, in as far as it is in your power, rendered that martyr's name vain and contemptible, by pipes, drums, and fifes, playing the vain carnal spring, called the Cameronian Rant, which too many professors of religion dance to—a practice maist unbecoming a professor to dance to any tune whatsoever, more especially promiscuously, that is, with the female sex. A brutish fashion it is, whilk is the beginning of defection with many, as I may hae as muckle cause as maist folk to testify."

"Well, but Mr Deans," replied Mr Middleburgh, "I only meant to say you were a Cameronian or MacMillanite, one of the society people, in short, who think it inconsistent to take oaths under a government where the Covenant is not ratified."

"Sir," replied the controversialist, who forgot even his present distress in such discussions as these, "you cannot fickle me sae easily as ye opine. I am *not* a MacMillanite, or a Russelite, or a Hamiltonian, or a Harleyite, or a Howdenite—I will be led by the nose by none—and take my name as a Christian from no vessel of clay. I have my own principles and practice to answer for, and am an humble pleader for the gude auld cause in a legal way."

"That is to say," said Middleburgh, "that you are a *Deanite*, and have opinions peculiar to yourself."

"It may please you to say sae," replied David Deans; "but I have maintained my testimony before as great folks, and in sharper times; and though I will neither exalt myself nor pull down others, I wish every man and woman in this land had keepit the true testimony, and the middle and strait path, as it were, on the rigg of a hill, where wind and water shears, avoiding right-hand snares and extremes, and left-hand way-slidings, sae weel as Johnny Dodds of Farthing's Acre, and ae man mair that shall be nameless."

"I suppose," replied the magistrate, "that is as much as to say, that Johnny Dodds of Farthing's Acre, and David Deans of Saint Leonard's, constitute the only members of the true, real, unsophisticated Kirk of Scotland?"

"God forbid that I suld mak sic a vain-glorious speech, when there are sae mony professing Christians," answered David; "but this I maun say, that all men act according to their gifts and their grace, sae that it is nae marvel that"——

"This is all very fine," interrupted Mr Middleburgh, "but I have no time to spend in hearing it. The matter in hand is this—I have directed a citation to be lodged in your daughter's hands—If she appears on the day of trial and gives evidence, there is reason to hope she may save her sister's life—if, from any constrained scruples about the legality of her performing the office of an affectionate sister and a good subject, by appearing in a court held under the authority of the law and government, you become the means of deterring her from the discharge of this duty, I must say, though the truth may sound harsh in your ears, that you, who gave life to this unhappy girl, will become the means of her losing it by a premature and violent death."

So saying, Mr Middleburgh turned to leave him.

"Bide awee—bide awee, Mr Middleburgh," said Deans, in great perplexity and distress of mind; but the baillie, who was probably sensible that protracted discussion might diminish the effect of his best and most forcible argument, took a hasty leave, and declined entering further into the controversy.

Deans sunk down upon his seat, stunned with a variety of conflicting emotions. It had been a great source of controversy among those holding his opinions in religious matters, how far the government which succeeded the Revolution could be, without sin, acknowledged by true presbyterians, seeing that it did not recognize the great national testimony of the Solemn League and Covenant? And latterly, those agreeing in this general doctrine, and assuming the sounding title of the anti-popish, anti-prelatic, anti-erastian, anti-sectarian, true presbyterian remnant, were divided into many petty sects among themselves, even as to the extent of submission to the existing laws and rulers which constituted such an acknowledgement.

At a very stormy and tumultuous meeting, held in 1682, to discuss these important and delicate points, the testimonies of the faithful few were found utterly inconsistent with each other. The place where this conference took place was remarkably well adapted for such an assembly. It was a wild and very sequestered dell in Tweeddale, surrounded by high hills, and far remote from human habitation. A small river, or rather a mountain torrent, called the Talla, breaks down the glen with great fury, dashing successively over a number of small cascades, which has procured the spot the name of Talla-Linns. Here the leaders among the scattered adherents to the Covenant, men who, in their banishment from human society, and in the recollection of the severities to which they had been exposed, had become at once sullen in their temper, and fantastic in their religious opinions, met with arms in their hands, and by the side of the torrent discussed, with a turbulence which the noise of the stream could not drown, points of controversy as empty and unsubstantial as its foam.

It was the fixed judgment of most of the meeting, that all payment of cess or tribute to the existing government was utterly unlawful, and a sacrificing to idols. About other impositions and degrees of submission there were various opinions; and perhaps it is the best illustration of the spirit of these military fathers of the church to say, that while all allowed it was impious to pay the cess employed for maintaining the standing army and militia, there was a fierce controversy on the lawfulness of paying the duties levied at ports and bridges, for maintaining roads and other necessary purposes; that there were some who, repugnant to these imposts for turnpikes and pontages, were nevertheless free in conscience to make payment of the usual freight at public ferries, and that a person of exceeding and punctilious zeal, James Russel, one of the slayers of the Archbishop of Saint Andrews, had given his testimony with great warmth even against this last faint

shade of subjection to constituted authority. This ardent and enlightened person and his followers had also great scruples about the lawfulness of bestowing the ordinary names upon the days of the week
and the months of the year, which savoured in their nostrils so strongly
of paganism, that at length they arrived at the conclusion that they who
owned such names as Monday, Tuesday, January, February, and so
forth, "served themselves heirs to the same, if not greater punishment,
than had been denounced against the idolaters of old."

David Deans had been present on this memorable occasion,
though too young to be a speaker among the polemical combatants.
His brain, however, had been thoroughly heated by the noise, clamour, and metaphysical ingenuity of the discussion, and it was a controversy to which his mind had often returned; and though he carefully
disguised his vacillation from others, and perhaps from himself, he
had never been able to come to any precise line of decision on the
subject. In fact, his natural sense had acted as a counterpoise to his
controversial zeal. He was by no means pleased with the quiet and
indifferent manner in which King William's government slurred over
the errors of the times, when, far from restoring the presbyterian Kirk
to its former supremacy, they passed an act of oblivion even to those
who had been its persecutors, and bestowed on many of them
titles, favours, and employments. When, in the first General Assembly which succeeded the Revolution, an overture was made for the
revival of the League and Covenant, it was with horror that Douce
David heard the proposal eluded by the men of carnal wit and policy,
as he called them, as being inapplicable to the present times, and not
falling under the modern model of the church. The reign of Queen
Anne had increased his conviction, that the Revolution government
was not one of the true presbyterian complexion. But then, more
sensible than the bigots of his sect, he did not confound the moderation and tolerance of these two reigns with the active tyranny and
oppression exercised in those of Charles II. and James II. The
presbyterian form of religion, though deprived of the weight formerly
attached to its sentences of excommunication, and compelled to
tolerate the co-existence of episcopacy, and of sects of various
descriptions, was still the National Church; and though the glory of
the second temple was far inferior to that which had flourished from
1639 till the battle of Dunbar, still it was a structure that, wanting the
strength and the terrors, retained at least the form and symmetry of
the original model. Then came the insurrection in 1715, and David
Deans's horrors for the revival of the popish and prelatical faction
reconciled him greatly to the government of King George, although
he grieved that that monarch might be suspected of a leaning unto

Erastianism. In short, moved by so many different considerations, he had shifted his ground at different times concerning the degree of freedom which he felt in adopting any act of immediate acknowledgment or submission to the present government, which, however mild and paternal, was still uncovenanted; and now he felt himself called upon by the most powerful motive conceivable, to authorize his daughter's giving testimony in a court of justice, which all who have been since called Cameronians, accounted a step of lamentable and direct defection. The voice of nature, however, exclaimed loud in his bosom against the dictates of fanaticism; and his imagination, fertile in the solution of polemical difficulties, devised an expedient for extricating himself from the fearful dilemma, in which he saw, on the one side, a falling off from principle, and, on the other, a scene from which a father's thoughts could not but turn in shuddering horror.

"I have been constant and unchanged in my testimony," said David Deans; "but then who has said it of me, that I have judged my neighbour over closely, because he hath had more freedom in his walk than I have found in mine? I never was a separatist, nor for quarrelling with tender souls about mint, cummin, or other the lesser tithes. My daughter Jean may have a light in this matter that is hid frae my auld een—it is laid on her conscience and not on mine—If she hath freedom to gang before this judicatory and hold up her hand for this poor cast-away, surely I will not say she steppeth over her bounds; and if not"——He paused in his mental argument, while a pang of unutterable anguish convulsed his features, yet, shaking it off, he firmly resumed the strain of his reasoning—"And IF NOT—God forbid that she should go into defection at bidding of mine! I winna fret the tender conscience of one bairn—no, not to save the life of the other."

A Roman would have devoted his daughter to death from different feelings and motives, but not upon a more heroic principle of duty.

Chapter Seben

To man, in this his trial state,
The privilege is given,
When tost by tides of human fate,
To anchor fast on heaven.
WATTS's *Hymns*

IT WAS WITH A FIRM STEP that Deans sought his daughter's apartment, determined to leave her to the light of her own conscience in the dubious point of casuistry in which he supposed her to be placed.

The little room had been the sleeping apartment of both sisters, and there still stood there a small occasional bed which had been made for Effie's accommodation, when, complaining of illness, she had declined to share, as in happier times, her sister's pillow. The eyes of Deans rested involuntarily, on entering the room, upon this little couch, with its dark-green coarse curtains, and the ideas connected with it rose so thick upon his soul as almost to incapacitate him from opening his errand to his daughter. Her occupation broke the ice. He found Jeanie gazing on a slip of paper, which contained a citation to her to appear as a witness upon her sister's trial in behalf of the accused. For the worthy magistrate, determined to omit no chance of doing Effie justice, and to leave her sister no apology for not giving the evidence which she was supposed to possess, had caused the ordinary citation, or *sub-pœna*, of the Scottish criminal court, to be served upon her by an officer during his conference with David.

This precaution was so far favourable to Deans, that it saved him the pain of entering upon a formal explanation with his daughter; he only said, with a hollow and tremulous voice, "I perceive ye are aware of the matter."

"O father, we are cruelly sted between God's laws and man's laws —What will we do?—What will we do?"

Jeanie, it must be observed, had no scruples whatever about the mere act of appearing in a court of justice. She might have heard the point discussed by her father more than once; but we have already noticed, that she was accustomed to listen with reverence to much which she was incapable of understanding, and that subtle arguments of casuistry found her a patient, but unedified hearer. Upon receiving the citation, therefore, her thoughts did not turn upon the chimerical scruples which alarmed her father's mind, but to the language which had been held to her by the stranger at Muschat's Cairn. In a word, she never doubted but she was to be dragged forward into the court of justice, in order to place her in the cruel position of either sacrificing her sister by telling the truth, or committing perjury in order to save her life. And so strongly did her thoughts run in this channel, that she applied her father's words, "Ye are aware of the matter," to his acquaintance with the advice that had been so fearfully enforced upon her. She looked up with anxious surprise, not unmingled with a cast of horror, which his next words, as she interpreted and applied them, were not qualified to remove.

"Daughter," said David, "it has ever been my mind, that in things of ane doubtful and controversial nature, ilk Christian's conscience suld be his ain guide—Wherefore descend into yourself, try your ain mind with sufficiency of soul exercise, and as ye sall finally find yourself clear to do in this matter—even so be it."

"But, father," said Jeanie, whose mind revolted at the construction which she naturally put upon his language, "can this—THIS be a doubtful or controversial matter?—Mind, father, the ninth command —'Thou shalt not bear false witness against thy neighbour.'"

David Deans paused; for, still applying her speech to his own preconceived difficulties, it seemed to him, as if *she*, a woman, and a sister, was scarce entitled to be scrupulous upon this occasion, where *he*, a man, exercised in the testimonies of that testifying period, had given indirect countenance to her following what must have been the natural dictates of her own feelings. But he kept firm his purpose, until his eyes involuntarily rested upon the little settle-bed, and recalled the form of the child of his old age, as she sate upon it, pale, emaciated, and broken-hearted. His mind, as the picture arose before him, involuntarily conceived, and his tongue involuntarily uttered— but in a tone how different from his usual dogmatical precision, arguments for the course of conduct likely to insure his child's safety.

"Daughter," he said, "I did not say that your path was free from stumbling—and, questionless, this act may be in the opinion of some a transgression, since he who beareth witness unlawfully, and against his conscience, doth in some sort bear false witness against his neighbour. Yet in matters of compliance, the guilt lieth not in the compliance sae muckle, as in the mind and conscience of him that doth comply. And, therefore, although my testimony hath not been spared upon public defections, I haena felt freedom to separate mysell from the communion of many who have been clear to hear those ministers who have taken the fatal indulgence, because they might get good of them, though I could not."

When David had proceeded thus far, his conscience reproved him, that he might be indirectly undermining the purity of his daughter's faith, and smoothing the way for her falling off from strictness of principle. He, therefore, suddenly stopped, and changed his tone:— "Jeanie, I perceive that our vile affections,—so I call them in respect of doing the will of our Father,—cling too heavily to me in this hour of trying sorrow, to permit me to keep sight of my ain duty, or to airt you to yours. I will speak nae mair anent this over-trying matter.—Jeanie, if ye can, wi' God and gude conscience, speak in favour of this puir unhappy"—(here his voice faultered)—"she is your sister in the flesh —worthless and cast-away as she is, she is the daughter of a saint in Heaven, that was a mother to you, Jeanie, in place of your ain—but if ye arena free in conscience to speak for her in the court of judicature —follow your conscience, Jeanie, and let God's will be done." After this adjuration, he left the apartment, and his daughter remained in a state of great distress and perplexity.

It would have been no small addition to the sorrows of David Deans, even in this extremity of suffering, had he known that his daughter was applying the casuistical arguments which he had been using, not in the sense of a permission to follow her own opinion on a dubious and disputed point of controversy, but rather as an encouragement to transgress one of those divine commandments which Christians of all sects and denominations unite in holding most sacred.

"Can this be?" said Jeanie, as the door closed on her father—"Can these be his words that I have heard, or has the Enemy taken his voice and features to give weight unto the counsel which causeth to perish! —A sister's life, and a father pointing ane how to save it!—O God deliver me!—this is a fearfu' temptation."

Roaming from thought to thought, she at one time imagined her father understood the ninth commandment literally, as prohibiting false witness *against* our neighbour, without extending the denunciation against falsehood uttered in favour of the criminal. But her clear and unsophisticated power of discriminating between good and evil, instantly rejected an interpretation so limited, and so unworthy of the Author of the law. She remained in a state of the most agitating terror and uncertainty—afraid to communicate her thoughts freely to her father, lest she should draw forth an opinion with which she could not comply,—wrung with distress on her sister's account, rendered the more acute by reflecting that the means of saving her were in her power, but were such as her conscience prohibited her from using,— tossed, in short, like a vessel in an open roadstead during a storm, and, like that vessel, resting only on one sure cable and anchor,—faith in Providence, and a resolution to discharge her duty.

Butler's affection and strong sense of religion would have been her principal support in these distressing circumstances, but he was still under restraint, which did not permit him to come to Saint Leonard's Crags; and her distresses were of a nature, which, with her indifferent habits of scholarship, she found it impossible to express in writing. She was therefore compelled to trust for guidance to her own unassisted sense of what was right or wrong.

It was not the least of her distresses, that, although she hoped and believed her sister to be innocent, she had not had the means of receiving that assurance from her own mouth.

The double-dealing of Ratcliffe in the matter of Robertson had not prevented his being rewarded, as double-dealers frequently have been, with favour and preferment. Sharpitlaw, who found in him something of a kindred genius, had been intercessor in his behalf with the magistrates, and the circumstance of his having voluntarily remained in the prison, when the doors were forced by the mob, would have made it a hard measure to take the life which he had such easy means of saving. He received a full pardon; and soon afterwards, James Ratcliffe, the greatest thief and housebreaker in Scotland, was, upon the faith, perhaps, of an ancient proverb, selected as a person fit to be entrusted with the custody of other delinquents.

When Ratcliffe was thus placed in a confidential situation, he was repeatedly applied to by the sapient Saddletree and others, who took some interest in the Deans family, to procure an interview between the sisters. But the magistrates, who were extremely anxious for the apprehension of Robertson, had given strict orders to the contrary, hoping that, by keeping them separate, they might, from the one or the other, extract some information respecting that fugitive. On this subject Jeanie had nothing to tell them: she informed Mr Middleburgh, that she knew nothing of Robertson, except having met him that night by appointment to give her some advice respecting her sister's concern, the purport of which, she said, was betwixt God and her conscience. Of his motions, purposes, or plans, past, present, or future, she knew nothing, and so had nothing to communicate.

Effie was equally silent, though from a different cause. It was in vain that they offered a commutation and alleviation of her punishment, and even a free pardon, if she would confess what she knew of her lover. She answered only with tears; unless, when driven into pettish sulkiness by the persecution of the interrogators, she made them abrupt and disrespectful answers.

At length, after her trial had been delayed for many weeks, in hopes she might be induced to speak out on a subject infinitely more interesting to the magistracy than her own guilt and innocence, their patience was worn out, and even Mr Middleburgh finding no ear lent to further intercession in her behalf, the day was fixed for the trial to proceed.

It was now, and not sooner, that Sharpitlaw, recollecting his promise to Effie Deans, or rather being dinned into compliance by the unceasing remonstrances of Mrs Saddletree, who was his next door neighbour, and who declared it was heathen cruelty to keep the twa broken-hearted creatures separate, issued the important mandate, permitting them to see each other.

On the evening which preceded the eventful day of trial, Jeanie was permitted to see her sister—an awful interview, and occurring at a most distressing crisis. This, however, formed a part of the bitter cup which she was doomed to drink, to atone for crimes and follies to which she had no accession; and at twelve o'clock noon, being the time appointed for admission to the jail, she went to meet, for the first time for several months, her guilty, erring, and most miserable sister, in that abode of guilt, error, and utter misery.

Chapter Eight

———Sweet sister, let me live;
What sin you do to save a brother's life,
Nature dispenses with the deed so far,
That it becomes a virtue.
                              Measure for Measure

JEANIE DEANS was admitted into the jail by Ratcliffe. This fellow, as void of shame as of honesty, as he opened the now trebly secured door, asked her, with a leer which made her shudder, "whether she remembered him?"

A half-pronounced and timid "No," was her answer.

"What! not remember moonlight, and Muschat's Cairn, and Rob and Rat?" said he, with the same sneer;—"Your memory needs redding up, my jo."

If Jeanie's distresses had admitted of aggravation, it must have been to find her sister under the charge of such a profligate as this man. He was not, indeed, without something of good to balance so much that was evil in his character and habits. In his misdemeanours he had never been blood-thirsty or cruel; and in his present occupation, he had shown himself, in a certain degree, accessible to touches of humanity. But these good qualities were unknown to Jeanie, who, remembering the scene at Muschat's Cairn, could scarce find voice to acquaint him, that she had an order from Baillie Middleburgh, permitting her to see her sister.

"I ken that fu' weel, my bonny doo; mair by token, I have a special charge to stay in the ward with you a' the time ye are thegither."

"Must that be sae?" asked Jeanie, with an imploring voice.

"Hout, ay, hinny!" replied the turnkey; "and what the waur will you and your titty be of Jem Ratcliffe hearing what ye hae to say to ilk other?—De'il a word ye'll say that will gar him ken your kittle sex better than he kens them already; and another thing is, that if ye dinna speak o' breaking the tolbooth, de'il a word will I tell ower, either to do ye gude or ill."

Thus saying, Ratcliffe marshalled her the way to the apartment where Effie was confined.

Shame, fear, and grief, had contended for mastery in the poor prisoner's bosom during the whole morning, while she had looked forward to this meeting; but when the door opened, all gave way to a confused and strange feeling that had a tinge of joy in it, as, throwing herself on her sister's neck, she ejaculated, "My dear Jeanie!—my dear Jeanie! it's lang since I hae seen ye." Jeanie returned the embrace with an earnestness that partook almost of rapture, but it was only a flitting emotion, like a sun-beam unexpectedly penetrating betwixt the clouds of a tempest, and obscured almost as soon as visible. The sisters walked together to the side of the pallet bed, and sate down side by side, took hold of each other's hands, and looked each other in the face, but without speaking a word. In this posture they remained for a minute, while the gleam of joy gradually faded from their features, and gave way to the most intense expression, first of melancholy, and then of agony, till, throwing themselves again into each other's arms, they, to use the language of Scripture, lifted up their voice and wept bitterly.

Even the hard-hearted turnkey, who had spent his life in scenes calculated to stifle both conscience and feeling, could not witness this scene without a touch of human sympathy. It was shown in a trifling action, but which had more of delicacy in it than seemed to belong to Ratcliffe's character and station. The unglazed window of the miserable chamber was open, and the beams of a bright sun fell right upon the bed where the sufferers were seated. With a gentleness that had something of reverence in it, Ratcliffe partly closed the shutter, and seemed thus to throw a veil over a scene so sorrowful.

"Ye are ill, Effie," were the first words Jeanie could utter, "ye are very ill."

"O what wad I gi'e to be ten times waur, Jeanie," was the reply—"what wad I gi'e to be cauld dead afore the ten o'clock bell the morn! And our father—but I amna his bairn langer now—O I hae nae friend left in the warld!—O that I were lying dead at my mother's side, in Newbattle Kirkyard!"

"Hout, lassie," said Ratcliffe, willing to show the interest which he absolutely felt, "dinna be sae dooms down-hearted as a' that; there's mony a tod hunted that's no killed. Advocate Fairbrother has brought folk through waur snappers than a' this, and there's no a cleverer agent than Michel Novit e'er drew a bill of suspension. Hanged or unhanged, they are weel aff has sic an agent and counsel; ane's sure o' fair play. Ye are a bonny lass too, an' ye wad busk up your cockernonie a bit; and a bonny lass will find favour wi' judge and jury, when they would strap up a grewsome carle like me for the very fifteenth part of a flea's hide and tallow, d—n them!"

To this homely strain of consolation the mourners returned no answer; indeed they were so much lost in their own sorrows as to have become insensible of Ratcliffe's presence. "O Effie," said her elder sister, "how could ye conceal your situation frae me! O, woman, had I deserved this at your hand?—had ye spoke but ae word—sorry we might hae been, and shamed we might hae been, but this awfu' dispensation had never come ower us."

"And what gude wad that hae dune?" answered the prisoner. "Na, na, Jeanie, a' was ower when ance I forgot what I promised when I faulded down the leaf of my Bible. See," she said, producing the sacred volume, "the book opens aye at the place o' itsell. O see, Jeanie, what a fearfu' scripture!"

Jeanie took her sister's Bible, and found that the fatal mark was made at this impressive text in the book of Job: "He hath stripped me of my glory, and taken the crown from my head. He hath destroyed me on every side, and I am gone. And mine hope hath he removed like a tree."

"Isna that ower true a doctrine?" said the prisoner—"Isna my crown—my honour removed? And what am I but a poor wasted wanthriven tree, dug up by the roots, and flung out to waste in the highway, that man and beast may tread it under foot? I thought o' the bonny bit thorn that our father rooted out o' the yard last May, when it had a' the flush o' blossoms on it; and then it lay in the court till the beasts had dung them a' to pieces wi' their feet. I little thought, when I was wae for the bit silly green bush and its flowers, that I was to gang the same gate mysel."

"O, if ye had spoken a word," again sobbed Jeanie,—"if I were free to swear that ye had said but ae word of how it stude wi' ye, they couldna hae touched your life this day."

"Could they na?" said Effie, with something like awakened interest —for life is dear even to those who feel it as a burthen—"Wha tauld ye that, Jeanie?"

"It was ane that kenned what he was saying weel aneugh," replied Jeanie, who had a natural reluctance at mentioning even the name of her sister's seducer.

"Wha was it?—I conjure ye to tell me," said Effie, seating herself upright.—"Wha could tak interest in sic a cast-bye as I am now?— Was it—was it *him?*"

"Hout," said Ratcliffe, "what signifies keeping the poor lassie in a swither?—I'se uphaud it's been Robertson that learned ye that doctrine when ye saw him at Muschat's Cairn."

"Was it him?" said Effie, catching eagerly at his words—"was it him, Jeanie, indeed?—O, I see it was him—poor lad, and I was thinking his heart was as hard as the nether millstane—and him in sic danger on his ain part—poor George!"

Somewhat indignant at this burst of tender feeling towards the author of her misery, Jeanie could not help exclaiming,—"O, Effie, how can ye speak that gate of sic a man as that?"

"We maun forgi'e our enemies, ye ken," said poor Effie, with a timid look and a subdued voice, for her conscience told her what a different character the feelings with which she still regarded her seducer bore, compared with the Christian charity under which she attempted to veil it.

"And ye hae suffered a' this for him, and ye can think of loving him still?" said her sister, in a voice betwixt pity and blame.

"Love him?" answered Effie—"If I had na loved as woman seldom loves, I had nae been within these waa's this day; and trow ye, that love sic as mine is lightly forgotten?—Na, na—ye may hew down the tree, but ye canna chainge its bend—And O, Jeanie, if ye wad do gude to me at this moment, tell me every word that he said, and whether he was sorry for poor Effie or no."

"What needs I tell ye ony thing about it," said Jeanie. "Ye may be sure he had ower muckle to do to save himself, to speak lang or muckle about ony body beside."

"That's no true, Jeanie, though a saunt had said it," replied Effie, with a sparkle of her former lively and irritable temper. "But ye dinna ken, though I do, how far he pat his life in venture to save mine." And looking at Ratcliffe, she checked herself and was silent.

"I fancy," said Ratcliffe, with one of his familiar sneers, "the lassie thinks that naebody has een but hersell—Didna I see when Gentle Geordie was seeking to get other folk out of the tolbooth forbye Jock Porteous? but ye were o' my mind, hinny—better sit and rue, than flit and rue—Ye needna look in my face sae mazed. I ken mair things than that maybe."

"O my God! my God!" said Effie, springing up and throwing herself down on her knees before him—"D'ye ken whare they hae putten my bairn?—O my bairn! my bairn! the poor sackless innocent new-born wee ane—bone of my bone, and flesh of my flesh!—O, man, if ye wad e'er deserve a portion in Heaven, or a broken-hearted creature's blessing upon earth, tell me whare they hae put my bairn—the sign of my shame, and the partner of my suffering—tell me wha has ta'en't away, or what they hae dune wi't!"

"Hout tout!" said the turnkey, endeavouring to extricate himself from the firm grasp with which she held him, "that's taking me at my word wi' a witness—Bairn, quo' she? How the de'il suld I ken ony thing of your bairn, hizzy? Ye maun ask that at auld Meg Murdockson, if ye dinna ken ower muckle about it yoursell."

As his answer destroyed the wild and vague hope which had suddenly gleamed upon her, the unhappy prisoner let go her hold of his coat, and fell with her face on the pavement of the apartment in a strong convulsion fit.

Jeanie Deans possessed, with her excellently clear understanding, the concomitant advantage of promptitude of spirit, even in the extremity of distress.

She did not suffer herself to be overcome by her own feelings of exquisite sorrow, but instantly applied herself to her sister's relief, with the readiest remedies which circumstances afforded; and which, to do Ratcliffe justice, he shewed himself anxious to suggest, and alert in procuring. He had even the delicacy to withdraw to the farthest corner of the room, so as to render his official attendance upon them as little intrusive as possible, when Effie was composed enough again to resume her conference with her sister.

The prisoner once more, in the most earnest and broken tones, conjured Jeanie to tell her the particulars of the conference with Robertson, and Jeanie felt it was impossible to refuse her this gratification.

"Do ye mind," she said, "Effie, when ye were in the fever afore we left Woodend, and how angry your mother, that's now in a better place, was at me for gi'eing ye milk and water to drink, because ye grat for it? Ye were a bairn than, and ye are a woman now, and should ken better than to ask what canna but hurt ye—But come weal or woe, I canna refuse ye ony thing that ye ask me wi' the tear in your ee."

Again Effie threw herself into her arms, and kissed her cheek and forehead, murmuring, "O, if ye kenn'd how lang it is since I heard his name mentioned,—if ye but kenn'd how muckle good it does me but to ken ony thing o' him, that's like gudeness or kindness, ye wadna wonder that I wish to hear o' him."

Jeanie sighed, and commenced her narrative of all that had passed betwixt Robertson and her, making it at the first as brief as possible. Effie listened in breathless anxiety, holding her sister's hand in hers, and keeping her eye fixed upon her face, as if devouring every word she uttered. The interjections of "Poor fellow,"—"poor George," which escaped in whispers, and betwixt sighs, were the only sounds with which she interrupted the story. When it was finished she made a long pause.

"And this was his advice?" were the first words she uttered.

"Just sic as I hae tell'd ye," replied her sister.

"And he wanted you to say something to yon folks, that wad save my young life?"

"He wanted," answered Jeanie, "that I suld be mansworn."

"And you tauld him," said Effie, "that ye wadna hear o' coming between me and the death that I am to die, and me no aughteen year auld yet?"

"I told him," replied Jeanie, who now trembled at the turn which her sister's reflections seemed about to take, "that I dared na swear to an untruth."

"And what do ye ca' an untruth?" said Effie, again shewing a touch of her former spirit—"Ye are muckle to blame, lass, if ye think a mother would, or could, murther her ain bairn—Murther?—I wad hae laid down my life just to see a blink o' its ee."

"I do believe," said Jeanie, "that ye are as innocent of sic a purpose, as the new-born babie itsell."

"I am glad ye do me that justice," said Effie, haughtily; "it's whiles the faut of very good folk like you, Jeanie, that they think a' the rest of the warld are as bad as the warst temptations can mak them."

"I dinna deserve this frae ye, Effie," said her sister, sobbing, and feeling at once the injustice of the reproach, and compassion for the state of mind which dictated it.

"Maybe no, tittie," said Effie. "But ye are angry because I loe Robertson—How can I help looing him, that loos me better than body and soul baith?—Here he put his life in a niffer, to break the prison to let me out; and sure am I, had it stood wi' him as it stands wi' you"— here she paused and was silent.

"O, if it stude wi' me to save ye wi' risk of *my* life!" said Jeanie.

"Ay, lass," said her sister, "that's lightly said, but no sae lightly credited, frae ane that winna ware a word for me; and if it be a wrang word, ye'll hae time aneugh to repent o't."

"But that word is a grievous sin, and it's a deeper offence when it's a sin wilfully and presumptuously committed."

"Weel, weel, Jeanie," said Effie, "I mind a' about the sins o' presumption in the questions—we'll speak nae mair about this matter, and ye may save your breath to say your carritch; and for me, I'll soon hae nae breath to waste on ony body."

"I must needs say," interposed Ratcliffe, "that it's d—d hard, that when three words of your mouth would give the girl the chance to nick Moll Blood,* that you mak such scrupling about rapping† to them. D —n me, if they would take me, if I would not rap to all Whadye-callum's fables for her life—I am used to't, b—t me, for less matters. Why, I have smacked calf-skin‡ fifty times in England for a keg of brandy."

"Never speak mair o't," said the prisoner. "It's just as weel as it is— and gude day, sister; ye keep Mr Ratcliffe waiting on—Ye'll come back and see me I reckon, before——" here she stopped, and became deadly pale.

"And are we to part in this way," said Jeanie, "and you in sic deadly

* The Gallows.   † Swearing.   ‡ Kissed the book.

peril? O, Effie, look but up, and say what ye wad hae me do, and I could find in my heart amaist to say that I wad do't."

"No, Jeanie," replied her sister, after an effort, "I am better minded now. At my best, I was never half sae gude as ye were, and what for suld you begin to mak yoursell waur to save me, now that I am na worth saving? God knows, that, in my sober mind, I wadna wuss ony living creature to do a wrang thing to save my life. I might have fled frae this tolbooth on that awfu' night wi' ane wad hae carried me through the warld, and friended me, and fended for me. But I said than let life gang when gude fame is gane before it. But this lang imprisonment has broken my spirit, and I am whiles sair left to mysell, and then I wad gi'e the Indian mines of gold and diamonds, just for life and breath— for I think, Jeanie, I have such roving fits as I used to hae in the fever; but instead of the fiery een, and wolves, and Widow Butler's bull-segg, that I used to see spieling up on my bed, I am aye thinking now about a high black gibbet, and me standing up, and such seas of faces all looking up at poor Effie Deans, and asking if it be her that George Robertson used to call the Lily of Saint Leonard's—And then they stretch out their faces, and make mouths, and girn at me, and which ever way I look, I see a face laughing like Meg Murdockson, when she tauld me she had seen the last of my wean. God preserve us, Jeanie, that carline has a fearsome face." She clapped her hands before her eyes as she uttered this exclamation, as if to secure herself against seeing the fearful object she had alluded to.

Jeanie Deans remained with her sister for two hours, during which she endeavoured, if possible, to extract something from her that might be serviceable in her exculpation. But she had nothing to say beyond what she had declared on her first examination, with the purport of which the reader will be made acquainted in proper time and place. "They wadna believe her," she said, "and she had naething mair to tell them."

At length Ratcliffe, though reluctantly, informed the sisters that there was a necessity they should part. "Mr Novit," he said, "was to see the prisoner, and maybe Mr Fairbrother too.—Fairbrother likes to look at a bonny lass, whether in prison or out o' prison."

Reluctantly, therefore, and slowly, after many a tear, and many an embrace, Jeanie retired from the apartment, and heard its jarring bolts turned upon the dear being from whom she was separated. Somewhat familiarized now even with her rude conductor, she offered him a small present in money, with a request he would do what he could for her sister's accommodation. To her surprise he declined the fee. "I wasna bloody when I was on the pad," he said, "and I winna be greedy —that is, beyond what's right and reasonable,—now that I am in the lock.—Keep the siller; and for civility, your sister sall hae sic as I can bestow; but I hope you'll think better on it, and rap an oath for her—de'il a hair ill there is in it, if ye are rapping again the crown. I kenn'd a worthy minister, as gude a man, bating the deed they deposed him for, as ever ye heard claver in a pu'pit, that rapped to a hogshead of pigtail tobacco, just for as muckle as filled his spleuchan. But maybe ye are keeping your ain council—weel, weel, there's nae harm in that.—As for your sister, I'se see she gets her meat clean and warm, and I'll try to gar her lie down and take a sleep after dinner, for de'il a ee she'll close the night.—I hae gude experience of these matters. The first night is aye the warst o't. I hae never heard o' ane that sleepit the night afore trial, but of mony a ane that sleepit as sound as a tap the night before their necks were straughted. And it's nae wonder—the warst may be tholed when it is kenn'd—Better a finger aff as aye wagging."

Chapter Nine

Yet though thou may'st be dragg'd in scorn
To yonder ignominious tree,
Thou shalt not want one faithful friend
To share the cruel fates' decree.
                              Jemmy Dawson

AFTER SPENDING the greater part of the morning in his devotions, for his benevolent neighbours had kindly insisted upon discharging his task of ordinary labour, David Deans entered the apartment when the breakfast meal was prepared. His eyes were involuntarily cast down, for he was afraid to look at Jeanie, uncertain as he was whether she might feel herself at liberty, with a good conscience, to attend the Court of Justiciary that day, to give the evidence which he understood that she possessed, in order to her sister's exculpation. At length, after a minute of apprehensive hesitation, he looked at her dress to discover whether it seemed to be in her contemplation to go abroad that morning. Her apparel was neat and plain, but such as conveyed no exact intimation of her intentions to go abroad. She had exchanged her usual garb for morning labour, for one something inferior to that with which, as her best, she was wont to dress herself for church, or any more rare occasion of going into society. Her sense taught her, that it was respectful to be decent in her apparel on such an occasion, while her feelings induced her to lay aside the use of the very few and simple personal ornaments, which, on other occasions, she permitted herself to wear. So that there occurred nothing in her external appearance which could mark out to her father, with any thing like certainty, her intentions on this occasion.

The preparations for their humble meal were that morning made in vain. The father and daughter sate, each assuming the appearance of eating, when the other's eyes were turned to them, and desisting from the effort with disgust, when the affectionate imposture seemed no longer necessary.

At length these moments of constraint were removed. The sound of Saint Giles's heavy toll announced the hour previous to the commencement of the trial; Jeanie arose, and, with a degree of composure for which she herself could not account, assumed her plaid, and made her other preparations for a distant walking. It was a strange contrast between the firmness of her demeanour, and the vacillation and cruel uncertainty of purpose indicated in all her father's motions; and one unacquainted with both could scarce have supposed that the former was, in her ordinary habits of life, a docile, quiet, gentle, and even timid country-maiden, while her father, with a mind naturally proud and strong, and supported by religious opinions, of a stern, stoical, and unyielding character, had in his time undergone and withstood the most severe hardship, and the most imminent peril, without depression of spirit, or subjugation of his constancy. The secret of this difference was, that Jeanie's mind had already anticipated the line of conduct which she must adopt, with all its natural and necessary consequences; while her father, ignorant of every other circumstance, tormented himself with imagining what the one sister might say or swear, or what effect her testimony might have upon the awful event of the trial.

He watched his daughter, with a faultering and indecisive look, until she looked back upon him, with a look of unutterable anguish, as she was about to leave the apartment.

"My dear lassie," said he, "I will—" His action, hastily and confusedly searching for his worsted *mittans* and staff, shewed his purpose of accompanying her, though his tongue failed distinctly to announce it.

"Father," said Jeanie, replying rather to his action than his words, "ye had better not."

"In the strength of my God," answered Deans, assuming firmness, "I will go forth."

And, taking his daughter's arm under his, he began to walk from the door with a step so hasty, that she was almost unable to keep up with him. A trifling circumstance, but which marked the perturbed state of his mind, checked his course,—"Your bonnet, father?" said Jeanie, who observed he had come out with his grey hairs uncovered. He turned back with something like a blush on his cheek, as if ashamed to have been detected in an omission which indicated so much mental confusion, assumed his large blue Scottish bonnet, and with a step slower, but more composed, as if the circumstance had obliged him to summon up his resolution, and collect his scattered ideas, again placed his daughter's arm under his, and resumed the way to Edinburgh.

The courts of justice were then, and are still held, in what is called the Parliament-Close, or, according to modern phrase, the Parliament-Square, and occupied the buildings intended for the accommodation of the Scottish Estates. This edifice, though in an imperfect and corrupted style of architecture, had then a grave, decent, and, as it were, a judicial aspect, which was at least entitled to respect from its antiquity. For which venerable front, I observed, on my last occasional visit to the metropolis, that modern taste had substituted, at great apparent expence, a pile so utterly inconsistent with every monument of antiquity around, and in itself so clumsy at the same time and fantastic, that it may be likened to the decorations of Tom Errand the porter, in the Trip to the Jubilee, when he appears bedizened with the tawdry finery of Beau Clincher. *Sed transeat cum cæteris erroribus.*

The small quadrangle, or Close, if we may presume still to give it that appropriate, though antiquated title, which at Litchfield, Salisbury, and elsewhere, is properly applied to designate the enclosure adjacent to a cathedral, already evinced tokens of the fatal scene which was that day to be acted. The soldiers of the City Guard were on their posts, now enduring, and now rudely repelling with the butts of their musquets, the motley crew who thrust each other forward, to catch a glance at the unfortunate object of trial, as she should pass from the adjacent prison to the Court in which her fate was to be determined. All must have occasionally observed with disgust, the apathy with which the vulgar gaze on scenes of this nature, and how seldom, unless when their sympathies are called forth by some striking and extraordinary circumstance, they evince any interest deeper than that of callous, unthinking bustling, and brutal curiosity. They laugh, jest, quarrel, and push each other to and fro, with the same unfeeling indifference as if they were assembled for some holiday sport, or to see an empty procession. Occasionally, however, this demeanour, so natural to the degraded populace of a large town, is exchanged for a temporary touch of human affections; and so it chanced on the present occasion.

When Deans and his daughter presented themselves in the Close, and endeavoured to make their way forward to the door of the Courthouse, they became involved in the mob, and subject, of course, to their insolence. As Deans repelled with some force the rude pushes which he received on all sides, his figure and antiquated dress caught the attention of the rabble, who often shew an intuitive sharpness in ascribing the proper character from external appearance.—

"Ye're welcome, whigs,
Frae Bothwell briggs,"

sung one fellow, (for the mob of Edinburgh were at that time jacobitically disposed, probably because that was the line of sentiment most diametrically opposite to existing authority.)

"Mess David Williamson,
Chosen of twenty,
Run up the pu'pit stair,
And sang Killiecrankie,"

chaunted a syren, whose profession might be guessed by her appearance. A tattered cadie, or errand porter, whom David Deans jostled in his attempt to extricate himself from the vicinity of these scorners, exclaimed in a strong north-country tone, "Ta de'il ding out her Cameronian een—what gi'es her titles to dunch gentlemans about?"

"Make room for the ruling elder," said yet another; "he comes to see a precious sister glorify God in the Grassmarket."

"Whisht; shame's in ye, sirs," said the voice of a man very loudly, which, as quickly sinking, said in a low but distinct tone, "It's her father and sister."

All fell back to make way for the sufferers; and all, even the very rudest and most profligate, were struck with shame and silence. In the space thus abandoned to them by the mob, Deans stood, holding his daughter by the hand, and said to her, with a countenance strongly and sternly expressive of his internal emotion, "Ye hear with your ears, and see with your eyes, where and to whom the back-slidings and defections of professors are ascribed by the scoffers. Not to themselves alone, but to the Kirk of whilk they are members, and to its blessed and invisible Head. Then, weel may we take wi' patience our share and our portion of this out-spreading reproach."

The man who had spoken, no other than our old friend Dumbiedikes, whose mouth, like that of the prophet's ass, had been opened by the emergency of the case, now joined them, and, with his usual taciturnity, escorted them into the Court-house. No opposition was offered to their entrance, either by the guards or door-keepers; and it is even said, that one of the latter refused a shilling of civility-money, tendered him by the Laird of Dumbiedikes, who was of opinion that "siller wad mak a' easy." But this last incident wants confirmation.

Admitted within the precincts of the Court-house, they found the usual number of busy office-bearers, and idle loiterers, who attend on these scenes by choice, or from duty. Burghers gaped and stared; young lawyers sauntered, sneered, and laughed, as in the pit of the theatre; while others apart sat on a bench retired, and reasoned highly on the doctrines of constructive crime, and the true import of the statute. The bench was prepared for the arrival of the judges: the jurors were in attendance. The crown-counsel, employed in looking over their briefs and notes of evidence, looked grave, and whispered with each other. They occupied one side of a large table placed beneath the bench; on the other, sat the advocates, whom the humanity of the Scottish law (in this particular much more liberal than that of her sister country), not only permits, but enjoins, to appear and assist with their advice and skill all persons under trial. Mr Michel Novit was seen actively instructing the counsel for the pannel, (so the prisoner is called in Scottish law-phraseology,) busy, bustling, and important. When they entered the Court-room, Deans asked the Laird, in a tremulous whisper, "Where will *she* sit?"

Dumbiedikes whispered Novit, who pointed to a vacant space at the bar, fronting the judges, and was about to conduct Deans towards it.

"No!" he said; "I cannot sit by her—I cannot own her—not as yet at least—I will keep out of her sight, and turn mine own eyes elsewhere—better for us baith."

Saddletree, whose repeated interference with the counsel had procured him one or two rebuffs, and a special request that he would concern himself with his own matters, now saw with pleasure an opportunity of playing the person of importance. He bustled up to the poor old man, and proceeded to exhibit his consequence, by securing, through his interest with the bar-keepers and macers, a seat for Deans, in a situation where he was hidden from the general eye by the projecting corner of the bench.

"It's gude to have a friend at court," he said, continuing his heartless harangues to the passive auditor, who neither heard nor replied to them; "few folk but mysel could hae sorted ye out a seat like this—the Lords will be here incontinent, and proceed *instanter* to trial. They winna fence the court as they do at the Circuit—The High Court of Justiciary is aye fenced.—But Lord's sake, what's this o't?—Jeanie, ye are a cited witness—Macer, this lass is a witness—she maun be inclosed—she maun on nae account be at large.—Mr Novit, suldna Jeanie Deans be inclosed?"

Novit answered in the affirmative, and offered to conduct Jeanie to the apartment, where, according to the scrupulous practice of the Scottish Court, the witnesses remain in readiness to be called into court to give evidence; and separated, at the same time, from all who might influence their testimony, or give them information concerning that which was passing upon the trial.

"Is this necessary?" said Jeanie, still reluctant to quit her father's hand.

"A matter of absolute needcessity," said Saddletree; "wha ever heard of witnesses no being inclosed?"

"It is really a matter of necessity," said the younger counsellor, retained for her sister; and Jeanie reluctantly followed the macer of the court to the place appointed.

"This, Mr Deans," said Saddletree, "is ca'd sequestering a witness; but it's clean different (whilk maybe ye wadna fund out o' yoursel), frae sequestrating ane's estate or effects. I hae aften been sequestered as a witness, for the Sheriff is in the use whiles to cry me in to witness the declarations at precognitions, and so is Mr Sharpitlaw; but I was ne'er like to be sequestrated o' land and gude but ance, and that was lang syne, afore I was married. But whisht, whisht! here's the Court coming."

As he spoke, the five Lords of Justiciary, in their long robes of scarlet, faced with white, and preceded by their mace-bearer, entered with their usual formalities, and took their places upon the bench of judgment.

The audience rose to receive them; and the bustle occasioned by their entrance was hardly composed, when a great noise and confusion of persons struggling, and forcibly endeavouring to enter at the doors of the Court-room and of the galleries, announced that the prisoner was about to be placed at the bar. This tumult takes place when the doors, at first only opened to those either having right to be present, or to the better and more qualified ranks, are at length laid open to all whose curiosity induces them to be present on the occasion. With inflamed countenances and dishevelled dresses, struggling with, and sometimes tumbling over each other, in rushed the rude multitude, while a few soldiers, forming, as it were, the centre of the tide, could scarce, with all their efforts, clear a passage for the prisoner to the place which she was to occupy. By the authority of the Court, and the exertions of its officers, the tumult among the spectators was at length appeased, and the unhappy girl brought forward, and placed betwixt two centinels with drawn bayonets, as a prisoner at the bar, where she was to abide her deliverance for good or evil, according to the issue of her trial.

Chapter Ten

We have strict statutes, and most biting laws—
The needful bits, and curbs for headstrong steeds—
Which, for these fourteen years, we have let sleep,
Like to an o'ergrown lion in a cave,
That goes not out to prey.
Measure for Measure

"EUPHEMIA DEANS," said the presiding Judge, in an accent in which pity was blended with dignity, "stand up, and listen to the criminal indictment now to be preferred against you."

The unhappy girl, who had been stupified by the confusion through which her guards had forced a passage, cast a bewildered look on the multitude of faces around her, which seemed to tapestry, as it were, the walls, in one broad slope from the ceiling to the floor, with human countenances, and instinctively obeyed a command, which rung in her ears like the trumpet of the judgment-day.

"Put back your hair, Effie," said one of the macers. For her beautiful and abundant tresses of long dark hair, which, according to the costume of the country, unmarried women were not allowed to cover with any sort of cap, and which, alas! Effie dared no longer confine with the snood or ribband, which implied purity of maiden-fame, now hung unbound and dishevelled over her face, and almost concealed her features. On receiving this hint from the attendant, the unfortunate young woman, with a hasty, trembling, and apparently mechanical compliance, shaded back from her face her luxuriant locks, and showed to the whole court, excepting one individual, a countenance, which, though pale and emaciated, was so lovely amid its agony, that it called forth an universal murmur of compassion and sympathy. Apparently the expressive sound of human feeling recalled the poor girl from the stupor of fear, which predominated at first over every other sensation, and awakened her to the no less painful sense of shame and exposure attached to her present situation. Her eye, which had at first glanced wildly around, was turned on the ground; her cheek, at first so deadly pale, began gradually to be overspread with a faint blush, which increased so fast, that, when in an agony of shame she strove to conceal her face, her temples, her brow, her neck, and all that her slender fingers and small palms could not cover, became of the deepest crimson.

All marked and were moved by these changes, excepting one. It was old Deans, who, motionless in his seat, and concealed, as we have said, by the corner of the bench, from seeing or being seen, did nevertheless keep his eyes firmly fixed on the ground, as if determined that, by no possibility whatsoever, would he be made an ocular witness of the shame of his house.

"Ichabod!" he said to himself—"Ichabod! my glory is departed."

While these reflections were passing through his mind, the indictment, which set forth in technical form the crime of which the pannel stood accused, was read as usual, and the prisoner was asked if she was Guilty, or Not Guilty.

"Not guilty of my poor bairn's death," said Effie Deans, in an accent corresponding in plaintive softness of tone to the beauty of her features, and which was not heard by the audience without emotion.

The Court next directed the counsel to plead to the relevancy; that is, to state on either part the arguments in point of law, and evidence in point of fact, against and in favour of the criminal; after which it is the form of the Court to pronounce a preliminary judgment, sending the case to the cognizance of the jury or assize.

The counsel for the crown briefly stated the frequency of the crime of infanticide, which had given rise to the special statute under which the pannel stood indicted. He mentioned the various instances, many of them marked with circumstances of atrocity, which had at length induced the King's Advocate, though with great reluctance, to make the experiment, whether by strictly enforcing the Act of Parliament which had been made to prevent such enormities, their occurrence might be prevented. "He expected," he said, "to be able to establish by witnesses, as well as by the declaration of the pannel herself, that she was in the state described by the statute. According to his information, the pannel had communicated her pregnancy to no one, nor did she allege in her own declaration that she had done so. This secrecy was the first requisite in support of the indictment. The same declaration admitted, that she had borne a male child, in circumstances which gave but too much reason to believe it had died by the hands, or at least with the knowledge or consent, of the unhappy mother. It was not, however, necessary for him to bring positive produce that the pannel was accessory to the murther, nay, nor even to prove that the child was murthered at all. It was sufficient to support the indictment, that it could not be found. According to the stern, but necessary severity of this statute, she who should conceal her pregnancy, who should omit to call that assistance which is most necessary on such occasions, was held already to have meditated the death of her offspring, as an event most likely to be the consequence of her culpable and cruel concealment. And if, under such circumstances, she could not alternatively shew by proof that the infant had died a natural death, or produce it still in life, she must, under the construction of the Law, be held to have murthered it, and suffer death accordingly."

The counsel for the prisoner, a man of considerable fame in his profession, did not pretend directly to combat the arguments of the King's Advocate. "It was enough for their Lordships," he observed, "to know, that such was the law, and he admitted the Advocate had a right to call for the usual interlocutor of relevancy." But he stated, "that when he came to establish his case by proof, he trusted to make out circumstances which would satisfactorily elide the charge in the libel. His client's story was a short, but most melancholy one. She was bred up in the strictest tenets of religion and virtue, the daughter of a worthy and conscientious person, who in evil times had established a character for courage and religion, by becoming a sufferer for conscience-sake."

David Deans gave a convulsive start at hearing himself thus mentioned, and then resumed the situation, in which, with his face stooped against his hands, and both resting against the corner of the elevated bench on which the Judges sate, he had hitherto listened to the procedure in the trial. The whig lawyers seemed to be interested; the tories put up their lip.

"Whatever may be our difference of opinion," resumed the lawyer, whose business it was to carry his whole audience with him if possible, "concerning the peculiar tenets of these people," (here Deans groaned deeply) "it is impossible to deny them the praise of sound, and even rigid morals, or the merit of training up their children in the fear of God; and yet it was the daughter of such a person whom a jury would shortly be called upon, in the absence of evidence, and upon mere presumptions, to convict of a crime, more probably belonging to an heathen, or a savage, than to a Christian and civilized country. It was true," he admitted, "that the excellent nurture and early instruction which this poor girl had received, had not been sufficient to preserve her from guilt and error. She had fallen a sacrifice to an inconsiderate affection for a young man of prepossessing manners, as he had been informed, but of a very dangerous and desperate character. She was seduced under promise of marriage—a promise, which the fellow might have, perhaps, done her justice by keeping, had he not at that time been called upon by the law to atone for another deed, violent and desperate in itself, but which became the preface to an eventful history, every step of which was marked by blood and guilt, and the final termination of which had not even yet arrived. He believed that no one would hear him without surprise, when he stated that the father of this infant now amissing, and said by the learned Advocate to have been murthered, was no other than the notorious George Robertson, the accomplice of Wilson, the hero of the memorable escape from the Tolbooth-Church, and, as no one knew better than his learned friend the Advocate, the principal actor in the Porteous conspiracy."—

"I am sorry to interrupt a counsel in such a case as the present," said the presiding Judge; "but I must remind the learned gentleman, that he is travelling out of the case before us."

The counsel bowed, and resumed. "He only judged it necessary," he said, "to mention the name and situation of Robertson, because the circumstances in which that character was placed, went a great way in accounting for the silence on which his Majesty's counsel had laid so much weight, as affording proof that his client proposed to allow no fair play for its life, to the helpless being whom she was about to bring into the world. She had not announced to her friends that she had been seduced from the path of honour—and why had she not done so?—Because she expected daily to be restored to character, by her seducer doing her that justice which she knew to be in his power, and believed to be in his inclination. Was it natural—was it reasonable—was it fair, to expect that she should, in the interim, become *felo de se* of her own character, and proclaim her frailty to the world, when she had every reason to expect, that, by concealing it for a season, it might be veiled for ever? Was it not, on the contrary, pardonable, that a young woman, in such a situation, should be found far from disposed to make a confidante of every prying gossip, who, with sharp eyes, and eager ears, pressed upon her for an explanation of suspicious circumstances, which females in the lower—he might say which females of all ranks are so alert in noticing, that they sometimes discover them where they do not exist? Was it strange, or was it criminal, that she should have repelled their inquisitive impertinence, with petulant denials? The sense and feeling of all who heard him, would answer directly in the negative. But although his client had thus remained silent towards those to whom she was not called upon to communicate her situation,—to whom," said the learned gentleman, "I will add, it would have been unadvised and improper to her to have done so; yet, I trust, I shall remove this case most triumphantly from under the statute, and obtain the unfortunate young woman an honourable dismission from your Lordships' bar, by shewing that she did, in due time and place, and to a person most fit for such confidence, mention the calamitous circumstances in which she found herself. This occurred after Robertson's conviction, and when he was lying in prison in expectation of the fate which his comrade Wilson afterwards suffered, and from which he himself so strangely escaped. It was then, when all hopes of having her honour repaired by wedlock vanished from her eyes,—when an union with one in Robertson's situation, if still practicable, might, perhaps, have been regarded rather as an addition to her disgrace—it was *then*, that I trust to be able to prove, that the prisoner communicated and consulted with her sister, a young woman several years older than herself, the daughter of her father, if I mistake not, by a former marriage, upon the perils and distress of her unhappy situation."

"If, indeed, you are able to instruct *that* point, Mr Jem," said the presiding Judge——

"If I am indeed able to instruct that point, my Lord," resumed Mr Fairbrother, "I trust not only to serve my client, but to relieve your Lordships from that which I know you feel the most painful duty of your high office; and to give all who now hear me the exquisite pleasure of beholding a creature so young, so ingenuous, and so beautiful, as she that is now at the bar of your Lordships' Court, dismissed from thence in safety and in honour."

This address seemed to affect many of the audience, and was followed by a slight murmur of applause. Deans, as he heard his daughter's beauty and innocent appearance appealed to, was involuntarily about to turn his eyes towards her; but, recollecting himself, he bent them again on the ground with stubborn resolution.

"Will not my learned brother, on the other side of the bar," continued the advocate, after a short pause, "share in this general joy, since I know, while he discharges his duty in bringing an accused person here, no one rejoices more in their being freely and honourably sent hence? My learned brother shakes his head doubtfully, and lays his hand on the pannel's declaration. I understand him perfectly—he would insinuate that the facts now stated to your Lordships are inconsistent with the confession of Euphemia Deans herself. I need not remind your Lordships, that her present defence is no whit to be narrowed within the bounds of her former confession; and that it is not by any account which she may formerly have given of herself, but by what is now to be proved for or against her, that she must ultimately stand or fall. I am not under the necessity of accounting for her chusing to drop out of her declaration the circumstance of her confession to her sister. She might not be aware of its importance; she might be afraid of implicating her sister; she might even have forgot the circumstance entirely, in the terror and distress of mind incidental to the arrest of so young a creature on a charge so heinous. Any of these reasons are sufficient to account for her having suppressed the truth in this instance, at whatever risk to herself; and I incline most to her erroneous fear of criminating her sister, because I observe she has had a similar tenderness towards her lover, (however undeserved on his part), and has never once mentioned Robertson's name from beginning to end of her declaration.

"But, my Lords," continued Fairbrother, "I am aware the King's Advocate will expect me to shew, that the proof I offer is consistent with the other circumstances of the cause, which I do not and cannot deny. He will demand of me how Effie Deans's confession to her sister, previous to her delivery, is reconcileable with the mystery of the birth,—with the disappearance, perhaps the murther (for I will not deny a possibility which I cannot disprove), of the infant. My Lords, the explanation of this is to be found in the placability, perchance, I may say, in the facility and pliability, of the female sex. The *dulcis Amaryllidis irae*, as your Lordships well know, are easily appeased; nor is it possible to conceive a woman so atrociously offended by the man whom she has loved, but what she will retain a fund of forgiveness, upon which his penitence, whether real or affected, may draw largely, with a certainty that his bills will be answered. We can prove, by a letter produced in exculpation, that this villain Robertson, from the bottom of the dungeon whence he already probably meditated the escape, which he afterwards accomplished by the assistance of his comrade, contrived to exercise authority over the mind, and to direct the motions, of this unhappy girl. It was in compliance with his injunctions, expressed in that letter, that the pannel was prevailed upon to alter the line of conduct which her own better thoughts had suggested; and, instead of resorting, when her time of travail approached, to the protection of her own family, was induced to confide herself to the charge of some vile agent of this nefarious seducer, and by her conducted to one of those solitary and secret purlieus of villainy, which, to the shame of our police, still are suffered to exist in the suburbs of this city, where, with the assistance, and under the charge, of a person of her own sex, she bore a male-child, under circumstances which added treble bitterness to the woe denounced against our original mother. What purpose Robertson had in all this, it is hard to tell or even to guess. He may have meant to marry the girl, for her father is a man of substance. But, for the termination of the story, and the conduct of the woman whom he had placed about the person of Euphemia Deans, it is still more difficult to account. The unfortunate young woman was visited by the fever incidental to her situation. In this fever she appears to have been deceived by the person that waited on her, and, on recovering her senses, she found that she was childless in that abode of misery. Her infant had been carried off, perhaps for the worst purposes, by the wretch that waited on her. It may have been murthered for what I can tell."

He was here interrupted by a piercing shriek, uttered by the unfortunate prisoner. She was with difficulty brought to compose herself.

Her counsel availed himself of the tragical interruption, to close his pleading with effect.

"My Lords," said he, "in that piteous cry you heard the eloquence of maternal affection, far surpassing the force of my poor words—Rahel weeping for her children! Nature herself bears testimony in favour of the tenderness and acuteness of the prisoner's parental feelings. I will not dishonour her plea by adding a word more."

"Heard ye ever the like o' that, Laird?" said Saddletree to Dumbiedikes, when the Counsel had ended his speech. "There's a cheel that can spin a muckle pirn out of a wee tait of tow! De'il haet he kens mair about it than what's in the declaration, and a surmise that Jeanie Deans suld hae been able to say something about her sister's situation, whilk surmise, Mr Crossmyloof says, rests on sma' authority.—And he's cleckit this great muckle bird out o' that wee egg—and when poor Effie skirled, sae clever as he clinked it intill his pleading! He could wile the very flounders out o' the Firth.—What garr'd my father no send me to Utrecht?—But whisht, the Court is gaun to pronounce their interlocutor of relevancy."

And accordingly the Judges, after a few words, recorded their judgment, which bore, that the indictment, if proved, was relevant to infer the pains of law: And that the defence, that the pannel had communicated her situation to her sister, was a relevant defence: And, finally, appointed the said indictment and defence to be submitted to the judgment of an assize.

Chapter Eleven

> Most righteous judge! a sentence.—Come, prepare.
> *Merchant of Venice*

IT IS BY NO MEANS my intention to describe minutely the forms of a Scottish criminal trial, nor am I sure that I could draw up an account so intelligible and accurate as to abide the criticism of the gentlemen of the long robe. It is enough to say that the jury was impannelled, and the case proceeded. The prisoner was again required to plead to the charge, and she again answered with the same heart-thrilling Not Guilty.

The crown counsel then called two or three female witnesses, by whose testimony it was established, that Effie's situation had been remarked by them, that they had taxed her with the fact, and that her answers had amounted to an angry and petulant denial of what they charged her with. But, as very frequently happens, the declaration of the pannel or accused party herself was the evidence which bore hardest upon her case.

In case these Tales should ever find their way across the Border, it may be proper to apprize the southern reader that it is the practice in Scotland, on apprehending a suspected person, to subject him to a judicial examination before a magistrate. He is not compelled to answer any of the questions asked at him, but may remain silent if he sees it his interest to do so. But whatever answers he chuses to give are formally written down, and being subscribed by himself and the magistrate, are produced against the accused in case of his being brought to trial. It is true, that these declarations are not produced as being in themselves evidence properly so called, but only as *adminicles* of testimony, tending to corroborate what is considered as legal and proper evidence. Notwithstanding this nice distinction, however, introduced by lawyers to reconcile this procedure to their own general rule, that a man cannot be required to bear witness against himself, it nevertheless usually happens that these declarations become the means of condemning the accused, as it were, out of their own mouths. The prisoner, upon these previous examinations, has indeed the privilege of remaining silent if he pleases. But every man necessarily feels that a refusal to answer natural and pertinent interrogatories, put by judicial authority, is in itself a strong proof of guilt, and will certainly lead to his being committed to prison; and few can renounce the hope of obtaining liberty, by giving some specious account of themselves, and shewing apparent frankness in explaining their motives and accounting for their conduct. It, therefore, seldom happens that the prisoner refuses to give a judicial declaration, in which, either by letting out too much of the truth, or by endeavouring to substitute a fictitious story, he almost always exposes himself to suspicion and to contradiction, which weigh heavily in the minds of the jury.

The declaration of Effie Deans was uttered on other principles, and the following is a sketch of its contents, given in the judicial form, in which they may still be found in the Books of Adjournal.

The declarant admitted a criminal intrigue with an individual whose name she desired to conceal. "Being interrogated what her reason was for secrecy on this point? She declared, that she had no right to blame that person's conduct more than she did her own, and that she was willing to confess her own faults, but not to say any thing which might criminate the absent. Interrogated, if she confessed her situation to any one, or made any preparation for her confinement? Declares, she did not. And being interrogated why she forbore to take steps which her situation so peremptorily required? Declares, she was ashamed to tell her friends, and she trusted the person she has mentioned would provide for her and the infant. Interrogated, if he did so?

Declares, that he did not do so personally; but that it was not his fault, for that the declarant is convinced he would have laid down his life sooner than the bairn or she had come to harm. Interrogated, what prevented him from keeping his promise? Declares, that it was impossible for him to do so, and declines farther answer to this question. Interrogated, where she was from the period she left her master, Mr Saddletree's family, until her appearance at her father's, at Saint Leonard's, the day before she was apprehended? Declares, she does not remember. And, on the interrogatory being repeated, declares, she does not mind muckle about it, for she was very ill. On the question being again repeated, she declares, she will tell the truth, if it should be the undoing of her, so long as she is not asked to tell on other folk; and admits, that she passed that interval of time in the lodging of a woman, an acquaintance of that person who had wished her to that place to be delivered, and that she was there delivered accordingly of a male child. Interrogated, what was the name of that person? Declares and refuses to answer this question. Interrogated, where she lives? Declares, she has no certainty, for that she was taken to the lodging aforesaid under cloud of night. Interrogated, if the lodging was in the city or suburbs? Declares and refuses to answer that question. Interrogated, whether, when she left the house of Mr Saddletree, she went up or down the street? Declares and refuses to answer the question. Interrogated, whether she had ever seen this woman before she was wished to her, as she termed it, by the person whose name she refuses to answer? Declares, and replies, not to her knowledge. Interrogated, whether this woman was introduced to her by the said person verbally, or by writing? Declares, she has no freedom to answer this question. Interrogated, if the child was alive when it was born? Declares, that—God help her and it!—it certainly was alive. Interrogated, if it died a natural death after birth? Declares, not to her knowledge. Interrogated, where it now is? Declares, that she would give her right hand to ken, but that she never hopes to see mair than the banes of it. And being interrogated, why she supposes it is now dead? the declarant wept bitterly, and made no answer. Interrogated, if the woman, in whose lodging she was, seemed to be fit person to be with her in that situation? Declares, she might be fit enough for skill, but that she was an hard-hearted bad woman. Interrogated, if there was any other person in the lodging excepting themselves two? Declares, that she thinks there was another woman, but her head was so carried with pain of body and trouble of mind, that she minded her very little. Interrogated, when the child was taken away from her? Declared, that she fell in a fever, and was light-headed, and when she came to her own mind, the woman tauld her the bairn was dead; and that the declarant answered, if it was dead it had had foul play. That, thereupon, the woman was very sair on her, and gave her much ill-language; and that the deponent was frightened, and crawled out of the house when her back was turned, and went home to Saint Leonard's Crags, as weel as a woman in her condition dought. Interrogated, why she did not tell her story to her sister and father, and get force to search the house for her child, dead or alive? Declares, it was her purpose to do so, but she had not time. Interrogated, why she conceals the name of the woman, and the place of her abode now? The declarant remained silent for a time, and then said, that to do so could not repair the skaith that was done, but might be the occasion of mair. Interrogated, whether she had herself, at any time, had any purpose of putting away the child by violence? Declares, Never; so might God be merciful to her—and then again declares Never, when she was in her perfect senses; but what bad thoughts the Enemy might put into her brain when she was out of herself, she cannot answer for. And again solemnly interrogated, declares, that she would have been drawn with wild horses, rather than have touched the bairn with an unmotherly hand. Interrogated, declares, that among the ill language the woman gave her, she did say sure enough that the declarant had hurt the bairn when she was in the brain-fever; but that the declarant does not believe that she said this from any other cause than to frighten her, and make her be silent. Interrogated, what else the woman said to her? Declares, that when the declarant cried loud for her bairn, and was like to raise the neighbours, the woman threatened her, that they that could stop the wean's skirling would stop her's, if she did not keep a' the lounder. And that this threat, with the manner of the woman, made the declarant conclude, that the bairn's life was gone, and her own in danger, for that the woman was a desperate bad woman, as the declarant judged, from the language she used. Interrogated, declares, that the fever and delirium were brought on her by hearing bad news, suddenly told to her, but refuses to say what the said news related to. Interrogated, why she does not now communicate these particulars, which might, perhaps, enable the magistrate to ascertain whether the child is living or dead; and requested to observe, that her refusing to do so, exposes her own life, and leaves the child in bad hands; as also, that her present refusal to answer on such points, is inconsistent with her alleged intention to make a clean breast to her sister? Declares, that she kens the bairn is now dead, or, if living, there is one that will look after it; that for her own living or dying, she is in God's hands, who knows her innocence of harming her bairn with her will or knowledge; and that she has altered her resolution of speaking out, which she entertained when she left the woman's lodging, on account of a matter which she has since learned. And declares, in general, that she is wearied, and will answer no more questions at this time."

Upon a subsequent examination, Euphemia Deans adhered to the declaration she had formerly made, with this addition, that a paper found in her trunk being shewn to her, she admitted that it contained the credentials, in consequence of which she resigned herself to the conduct of the woman at whose lodging she was delivered of the child. Its tenor ran thus:—

"DEAREST EFFIE,

"I have gotten the means to send to you by a woman who is well qualified to assist you in your approaching streight—She is not what I could wish her, but I cannot do better for you in my present condition. I am obliged to trust to her in this calamity, for myself and you too. I hope for the best, though I am now in a sore pinch. Yet thought is free —I think Handie Andie and I may queer the stifler* for all that is come and gone. You will be angry with me for writing this, to my little Cameronian Lily; but if I can but live to be a comfort to you, and a father to your babie, you will have plenty of time to scold.—Once more let none know your counsel—my life depends on this hag, d—n her—she is both deep and dangerous, but she has more wiles and wit than ever were in a beldame's head, and has cause to be true to me. Farewell, my Lily—Do not droop on my account—in a week I will be yours, or no more my own."

Then followed a postscript. "If they must truss me, I will repent of nothing so much, even at the last hard pinch, as of the injury I have done my Lily."

Effie refused to say from whom she had received this letter, but enough of the story was now known, to ascertain that it came from Robertson; and from the date, it appeared to have been written about the time when Andrew Wilson and he were meditating their first abortive attempt to escape, which miscarried in the manner mentioned in the beginning of this history.

The evidence for the Crown being concluded, the counsel for the prisoner began to lead a proof in her defence. The first witnesses were examined upon the girl's character. All gave her an excellent one, but none with more feeling than worthy Mrs Saddletree, who, with the tears on her cheeks, declared, that she could not have had a higher opinion of Effie Deans, or a more sincere regard for her, if she had been her own daughter. All present gave the honest woman credit for

* Avoid the gallows.

her goodness of heart, excepting her husband, who whispered to Dumbiedikes, "That Michel Novit of yours is but a raw hand at leading evidence, I'm thinking. What signified his bringing a woman here to snotter and snivel, and bather their Lordships? He should hae ceeted me, sir, he should hae ceeted me, and I should hae gien them sic a screed o' testimony, they shouldna hae touched a hair o' her head."

"Hadna ye better get up and try't yet," said the Laird. "I'll mak a sign to Novit."

"Na, na," said Saddletree, "thank ye for naething, neighbour—that would be ultroneous evidence, and I ken what belangs to that; but Michel Novit suld hae had me ceeted *debito tempore*." And wiping his mouth with his silk handkerchief with great importance, he resumed the port and manner of an edified and intelligent auditor.

Mr Fairbrother now premised, in a few words, "that he meant to bring forward his most important witness, upon whose evidence the cause must in a great measure depend. What his client was, they had learned from the preceding witnesses, and so far as general character, given in the most forcible terms, and even with tears, could interest every one in her fate, she had already gained that advantage. It was necessary, he admitted, that he should produce more positive testimony of her innocence than arose out of general character, and this he undertook to do by the mouth of the person to whom she had communicated her situation—by the mouth of her natural counsellor and guardian—her sister.—Macer, call into court, Jean, or Jeanie Deans, daughter of David Deans, cowfeeder, at Saint Leonard's Crags."

When he uttered these words, the prisoner at the bar instantly started up, and stretched herself half-way over the bar, towards the side at which her sister was to enter. And when, slowly following the officer, the witness advanced to the foot of the table, Effie, with the whole expression of her countenance altered, from that of confused shame and dismay, to an eager, imploring, and almost extatic earnestness of entreaty, with outstretched hands, hair streaming back, eyes raised eagerly to her sister's face, and glistening through tears, exclaimed, in a tone which went through the heart of all who heard her—"O Jeanie, Jeanie, save me, save me!"

With a different feeling, yet equally appropriate to his proud and self-dependent character, old Deans drew himself back still farther under cover of the bench, so that when Jeanie, as she entered the court, cast a timid glance towards the place at which she had left him seated, his venerable figure was no longer visible. He sate down on the other side of Dumbiedikes, wrung his hand hard, and whispered, "Ah, Laird, this is warst of a'—if I can but win ower this part—I feel my head unco dizzy; but my Master is strong in his servant's weakness." After a moment's mental prayer, he again started up, as if impatient of continuing in any one posture, and gradually edged himself forwards towards the place he had just quitted.

Jeanie in the meantime had advanced to the bottom of the table, when, unable to resist the impulse of affection, she suddenly extended her hand to her sister. Effie was just within the distance that she could seize it with both hers, press it to her mouth, cover it with kisses, and bathe it in tears, with the fond devotion that a Catholic would pay to a guardian saint descended for his safety; while Jeanie, hiding her own face with her other hand, wept bitterly. The sight would have moved a heart of stone, much more of flesh and blood. Many of the spectators shed tears, and it was some time before the presiding Judge himself could so far subdue his own emotion, as to request the witness to compose hers, and the prisoner to forbear those marks of eager affection, which, however natural, could not be permitted at that time, and in that presence.

The solemn oath,—"the truth to tell, and no truth to conceal, as far as she knew or should be asked at," was then administered by the Judge "in the name of God, and as the witness should answer to God at the Great Day of Judgment;" an awful adjuration, which seldom fails to make some impression even on the most hardened character, and to strike with fear even the most upright. Jeanie, educated in the most severe reverence for the name and attributes of the Deity, was, by the solemnity of a direct appeal to his person and justice, awed, but at the same time elevated above all considerations, save those which she could, with a clear conscience, call HIM to witness. She repeated the form in a low and reverent, but distinct tone of voice, after the Judge, to whom, and not to any inferior officer of the Court, the task is assigned in Scotland of directing the witness in that solemn appeal, which is the sanction of his testimony.

When the Judge had finished the established form, he added in a feeling, but yet a monitory tone, an advice, which the circumstances appeared to him to call for.

"Young woman," these were his words, "you come before this Court in circumstances, which it would be worse than cruel not to pity and to sympathize with. Yet it is my duty to tell you, that the Truth, whatever its consequences may be, the Truth is what you owe to your country, and to that God whose word is truth, and whose name you have now invoked. Use your own time in answering the questions that gentleman" (pointing to the counsel) "shall put to you—But remember, that what you may be tempted to say beyond what is the actual truth, you must answer both here and hereafter."

The usual questions were then put to her: Whether any one had instructed her what evidence she had to deliver? Whether any one had given or promised her any good deed, hire, or reward, for her testimony? Whether she had any malice or ill-will at his Majesty's Advocate, being the party against whom she was cited as a witness? To which questions she successively answered by a quiet negative. But their tenor gave great scandal and offence to her father, who was not aware that they are put to every witness as a matter of form.

"Na, na," exclaimed he, loud enough to be heard, "my bairn is no like the widow of Tekoah—nae man has putten words into her mouth."

One of the Judges, better acquainted, perhaps, with the Books of Adjournal than with the Book of Samuel, was disposed to make some instant enquiry after this Widow Tekoah, who, as he construed the matter, had been tampering with the evidence. But the presiding Judge, better versed in Scripture history, whispered to his learned brother the necessary explanation; and the pause occasioned by this mistake, had the good effect of giving Jeanie Deans time to collect her spirits for the painful task she had to perform.

Fairbrother, whose practice and intelligence were considerable, saw the necessity of letting the witness compose herself. In his heart he suspected that she came to bear false witness in her sister's cause.

"But that is her own affair," thought Fairbrother; "and it is my business to see that she has plenty of time to regain composure, and to deliver her evidence, be it true, or be it false—*valeat quantum.*"

Accordingly, he commenced his interrogatory with uninteresting questions, which admitted of instant reply.

"You are, I think, the sister of the prisoner?"

"Yes, sir."

"Not the full sister, however?"

"No, sir,—we are by different mothers."

"True; and you are, I think, several years older than your sister?"

"Yes, sir," &c.

After the advocate had conceived that, by these preliminary and unimportant questions, he had familiarized the witness with the situation in which she stood, he asked, "whether she had not remarked her sister's state of health to be altered during the latter part of the term, when she had lived with Mrs Saddletree?"

Jeanie answered in the affirmative.

"And she told you the cause of it, my dear, I suppose," said Fairbrother, in an easy, and, as one may say, an inductive sort of tone.

"I am sorry to interrupt my brother," said the Crown Counsel, rising, "but I am in your Lordships' judgment, whether this be not a leading question."

"If this point is to be debated," said the presiding Judge, "the witness must be removed."

For the Scottish lawyers regard with a sacred and scrupulous horror, every question so shaped by the counsel examining, as to convey to a witness the least intimation of the nature of the answer which is desired from him. These scruples, though founded on an excellent principle, are sometimes carried to an absurd pitch of nicety, especially as it is generally easy for a lawyer who has his wits about him, to elude the objection. Fairbrother did so in the present case.

"It is not necessary to waste the time of the Court, my Lord; since the King's Counsel think it worth while to object to the form of my question, I will shape it otherwise.—Pray, young woman, did you ask your sister any question when you observed her looking unwell?— take courage—speak out."

"I asked her," replied Jeanie, "what ailed her."

"Very well—take your own time—and what was the answer she made?" continued Mr Fairbrother.

Jeanie was silent, and looked deadly pale. It was not that she at any one instant entertained an idea of the possibility of prevarication—it was the natural hesitation to extinguish the last spark of hope that remained for her sister.

"Take courage, young woman," said Fairbrother.—"I asked what your sister said ailed her when you inquired?"

"Nothing," answered Jeanie, with a faint voice, which was yet heard distinctly in the most distant corner of the Court-room,—such an awful and profound silence had been preserved during the anxious interval, which had interposed betwixt the lawyer's question and the answer of the witness.

Fairbrother's countenance fell; but with that ready presence of mind, which is as useful in civil as in military emergencies, he immediately rallied.—"Nothing?—True; you mean nothing at *first*—but when you asked her again, did she not say what ailed her?"

The question was put in a tone meant to make her comprehend the importance of her answer, had she not been already aware of it. The ice was broken, however, and, with less pause than at first, she now replied,—"Alack! alack! she never breathed word to me about it."

A deep groan passed through the Court. It was echoed by one deeper and more agonized from the unfortunate father. The hope, to which unconsciously, and in spite of himself, he had still secretly clung, had now dissolved, and the venerable old man fell forwards senseless on the floor of the Court-house, with his head at the foot of his terrified daughter. The unfortunate prisoner, with impotent passion, strove with the guards, betwixt whom she was placed. "Let me gang to my father—I *will* gang to him—I *will* gang to him—he is dead —he is killed—I hae killed him!—" she repeated in frenzied tones of grief, which those who heard them did not speedily forget.

Even in this moment of agony and general confusion, Jeanie did not lose that superiority, which a deep and firm mind assures to its possessor, under the most trying circumstances.

"He is my father—he is our father," she mildly repeated to those who endeavoured to separate them as she stooped,—shaded aside his grey hairs, and began assiduously to chafe his temples.

The Judge, after repeatedly wiping his eyes, gave directions that they should be transported into a neighbouring apartment, and carefully attended. The prisoner, as her father was borne from the Court, and her sister slowly followed, pursued them with her eyes so earnestly fixed, as if they would have started from their socket. But when they were no longer visible, she seemed to find, in her despairing and deserted state, a courage which she had not yet exhibited.

"The bitterness of it is now passed," she said, and then boldly addressed the Court. "My Lords, if it is your pleasure to gang on wi' this matter, the weariest day will hae its end at last."

The Judge, who, much to his honour, had shared deeply in the general sympathy, was surprised at being recalled to his duty by the prisoner. He collected himself, and requested to know if the pannel's counsel had more evidence to produce. Fairbrother replied, with an air of dejection, that his proof was concluded.

The King's Counsel addressed the jury for the crown. He said in few words, that no one could be more concerned than he was for the distressing scene which they had just witnessed. But it was the necessary consequence of great crimes to bring distress and ruin upon all connected with the perpetrators. He briefly resumed the proof, in which he showed that all the circumstances of the case concurred with those required by the act under which the unfortunate prisoner was tried: That the counsel for the pannel had totally failed in proving, that Euphemia Deans had communicated her situation to her sister: That, respecting her previous good character, he was sorry to observe, that it was females who possessed the world's good report, and to whom it was justly valuable, who were most strongly tempted, by shame and fear of the world's censure, to the crime of infanticide: That the child was murdered, he professed to entertain no doubt. The vacillating and inconsistent declaration of the prisoner herself, marked as it was by numerous refusals to speak the truth on subjects, when, according to her own story, it would have been natural, as well as advantageous, to have been candid; even this imperfect declaration left no doubt in his mind as to the fate of the unhappy infant. Neither could he doubt that the pannel was a partner in this guilt. Who else had an interest in a deed so inhuman? Surely neither Robertson, nor Robertson's agent, in whose house she was delivered, had the least temptation to commit such a crime, unless upon her account, with her connivance, and for the sake of saving her reputation. But it was not required of him, by the law, that he should bring precise proof of the murder, or of the prisoner's accession to it. It was the very purpose of the statute to substitute a certain chain of presumptive evidence in place of a probation, which, in such cases, it was peculiarly difficult to obtain. The jury might peruse the statute itself, and they had also the libel and the interlocutor of relevancy to direct them in point of law. He put it to the conscience of the jury, that under both he was entitled to a verdict of Guilty.

The charge of Fairbrother was much cramped by his having failed in the proof which he expected to lead. But he fought his losing cause with courage and constancy. He ventured to arraign the severity of the statute under which the young woman was tried. "In all other cases," he said, "the first thing required of the criminal prosecutor was, to prove unequivocally that the crime libelled had actually been committed, which lawyers called proving the *corpus delicti*. But this statute, made doubtless with the best intentions, and under the impulse of a just horror for the unnatural crime of infanticide, run the risk of itself occasioning the worst of murders, the death of an innocent person, to atone for a murder which may never have been committed by any one. He was so far from acknowledging the alleged probability of the child's violent death, that he could not even allow that there was evidence of its having ever lived."

The King's Counsel pointed to the woman's declaration; to which the counsel replied—"A production concocted in a moment of terror and agony, and which approached to insanity," he said, "his learned brother well knew was no sound evidence against the party who emitted it. It was true, that a judicial confession, in presence of the Justices themselves, was the strongest of all proof, in so much that it is said in law, that '*in confitentem nullæ sunt partes judicis.*' But this was true of judicial confession only, by which Law meant that which was made in presence of the justices, and the sworn inquest. Of extra-judicial confession, all authorities held with the illustrious Farinaceus, and Mattheus, '*confessio extrajudicialis in se nulla est, et quod nullum est, non potest adminiculari.*' It was totally inept, and void of all strength and effect from the beginning; incapable, therefore, of being bolstered up or supported, or, according to the law-phrase, adminiculated, by other presumptive circumstances. In the present case, therefore, letting the extra-judicial go, as it ought to go, for nothing," he contended, "the prosecutor had not made out the second quality of the statute, that a live child had been born; and *that*, at least, ought to be established before presumptions were received that it had been murdered. If any of the assize," he said, "should be of opinion that this was dealing rather narrowly with the statute, they ought to consider that it was in its nature highly penal, and therefore entitled to no favourable construction."

He concluded a learned speech, with an elegant peroration on the scene they had just witnessed, during which Saddletree fell fast asleep.

It was now the presiding Judge's turn to address the jury. He did so briefly and distinctly.

"It was for the jury," he said, "to consider whether the prosecutor had made out his plea. For himself, he sincerely grieved to say, that a shadow of doubt remained not upon his mind concerning the verdict which the inquest had to bring in. He would not follow the prisoner's counsel through the impeachment which he had brought against the statute of King William and Queen Mary. He and the jurors were sworn to judge according to the laws as they stood, not to criticise, or to evade, or even to justify them. In no civil case would a counsel have been permitted to plead his client's case in the teeth of the law; but in the hard situation in which counsel were often placed in the Criminal Court, as well as out of favour to all presumptions of innocence, he had not inclined to interrupt the learned gentleman, or narrow his plea. The present law, as it now stood, had been instituted by the wisdom of their fathers, to check the alarming progress of a dreadful crime; when it was found too severe for its purpose, it would doubtless be altered by the wisdom of the legislature; at present it was the law of the land, the rule of the court, and, according to the oath which they had taken, it must be that of the jury. This unhappy girl's situation could not be doubted; that she had borne a child, and that the child had disappeared, were certain facts. The learned counsel had failed to show that she had communicated her situation. All the requisites of the situation required by the statute were therefore before the jury. The learned gentleman had, indeed, desired them to throw out of consideration the pannel's own confession, which was the plea usually urged, in penury of all others, by counsel in his situation, who usually felt that the declarations of their clients bore hard on them. But that the Scottish law designed that a certain weight should be laid on these declarations, which, he admitted, were *quodammodo* extrajudicial, was evident from the universal practice by which they were always produced and read, as part of the prosecutor's probation. In the present case, no person, who had heard the witnesses describe the appearance of the young woman before she left Saddletree's house, and contrasted it with that of her state and condition at her return to her father's, could have any doubt that the fact had been as set forth in her own declaration, which was, therefore, not a solitary piece of testimony, but adminiculated and supported by the strongest circumstantial proof.

"He did not," he said, "state the impression upon his own mind with the purpose of biassing theirs. He had felt no less than they had done from the scene of domestic misery which had been exhibited before them; and if they, having God and a good conscience, the sanctity of their oath, and the regard due to the law of the country, before their eyes, could come to a conclusion favourable to this unhappy prisoner, he should rejoice as much as any one in Court; for never had he found his duty more distressing than in discharging it that day, and glad he would be to be relieved from the still more painful task, which would otherwise remain for him."

The jury, having heard the Judge's address, bowed and retired, preceded by a macer of Court, to the apartment destined for their deliberations.

Chapter Twelve

Law, take thy victim—May she find the mercy
In yon mild Heaven, which this hard world denies her.

IT WAS AN HOUR ere the jurors returned, and as they traversed the crowd with slow steps, as men about to discharge themselves of a heavy and painful responsibility, the audience was hushed into profound, earnest, and awful silence.

"Have you agreed on your chancellor, gentlemen?" was the first question of the Judge.

The foreman, called in Scotland the chancellor of the jury, usually the man of best rank and estimation among the assizers, stepped forward, and, with a low reverence, delivered to the Court a sealed paper, containing the verdict, which, until of late years, that verbal returns are in some instances permitted, was always couched in writing. The jury remained standing while the Judge broke the seals; and having perused the paper, handed it, with an air of mournful gravity, down to the clerk of Court, who proceeded to engross in the record the yet unknown verdict, of which, however, all omened the tragical contents. A form still remains, trifling and unimportant in itself, but to which imagination adds a sort of solemnity, from the awful occasion upon which it is used. A lighted candle is placed on the table, the original paper containing the verdict is inclosed in a sheet of paper, and, sealed with the Judge's own signet, is transmitted to the Crown-office, to be preserved among other records of the same kind. As all this is transacted in profound silence, the producing and extinguishing of the candle seems a type of the human spark which is shortly afterwards doomed to be quenched, and excites in the spectators something of the same effect which in England is obtained by the Judge assuming the fatal cap of judgment. When these preliminary forms had been gone through, the Judge required Euphemia Deans to attend to the verdict to be read.

After the usual words of style, the verdict set forth, that the Jury having made choice of John Kirk, Esq. to be their chancellor, and Thomas Moore, merchant, to be their clerk, did, by a plurality of voices, find the said Euphemia Deans GUILTY of the crime libelled; but, in consideration of her extreme youth, and the cruel circumstances of her case, did earnestly entreat that the Judge would recommend her to the mercy of the Crown.

"Gentlemen," said the Judge, "you have done your duty—and a painful one it must have been to men of humanity like you. I will, undoubtedly, transmit your recommendation to the throne. But it is my duty to tell all who now hear me, but especially to inform that unhappy young woman, in order that her mind may be settled accordingly, that I have not the least hope of a pardon being granted in the present case. You know the crime has been increasing in this land, and I know farther, that this has been ascribed to the lenity in which the laws have been exercised, and that there is therefore no hope whatever of obtaining a remission for this offence." The Jury bowed again, and, released from their painful office, dispersed themselves among the mass of byestanders.

The Court then asked Fairbrother, whether he had any thing to say, why judgment should not follow on the verdict? The counsel had spent some time in perusing, and re-perusing the verdict, counting the letters in each juror's name, and weighing every phrase, nay every syllable, in the nicest scales of legal criticism. But the clerk of the jury had understood his business too well. No flaw was to be found, and Fairbrother mournfully intimated, that he had nothing to say in arrest of judgment.

The presiding Judge then addressed the unhappy prisoner:— "Euphemia Deans, attend to the sentence of the Court now to be pronounced against you."

She rose from her seat, and with composure far greater than could have been augured from her demeanour during some parts of the trial, abode the conclusion of the awful scene. So nearly does the mental portion of our feelings resemble those which are corporeal, that the first severe blows which we receive bring with them a stunning apathy, which renders us indifferent to those that follow them. So said Mandrin, when he was undergoing the punishment of the wheel; and so have all felt, upon whom successive afflictions have descended with continuous and reiterated violence.

"Young woman," said the Judge, "it is my painful duty to tell you, that your life is forfeited under a law, which, if it may seem in some degree severe, is yet wisely so, to render those of your unhappy situation aware what risk they run, by concealing, out of pride or false shame, their lapse from virtue, and making no preparation to save the lives of the unfortunate infants whom they are to bring into the world. When you concealed your situation from your mistress, your sister, and other worthy and compassionate persons of your own sex, in whose favour your former conduct had given you a fair place, you seem to me to have had in your contemplation, at least, the death of the helpless creature, for whose life you neglected to provide. How the child was disposed of—whether it was dealt upon by another, or by yourself—whether the extraordinary story you have told is partly false, or altogether so, is between God and your own conscience. I will not aggravate your distress by pressing on that topic, but I do most solemnly adjure you to employ the remaining space of your time in making your peace with God, for which purpose such reverend clergymen, as you yourself may name, shall have access to you. Notwithstanding the humane recommendation of the jury, I cannot afford to you, in the present circumstances of the country, the slightest hope that your life will be prolonged beyond the period assigned for the execution of your sentence. Forsaking, therefore, the thoughts of this world, let your mind be prepared by repentance for those of more awful moment—for death, judgment, and eternity.—Doomster, read the sentence."

When the Doomster shewed himself, a tall, hagard figure, arrayed in a fantastic garment of black and grey, passmented with lace, all fell back with a sort of instinctive horror, and made wide way for him to approach the foot of the table. As this office was held by the common executioner, men shouldered each other backwards to avoid even the touch of his garment, and some were seen to brush their own clothes, which had accidentally become subject to such contamination. A sound went through the court, produced by each person drawing in their breath hard, as men do when they expect or witness what is frightful, and at the same time affecting. The caitiff villain yet seemed, amid his hardened brutality, to have some sense of his being the object of public detestation, which made him impatient of being in public, as birds of evil omen are anxious to escape from day-light, and from pure air.

Repeating after the Clerk of Court, he gabbled over the words of the sentence, which condemned Euphemia Deans to be conducted back to the Tolbooth of Edinburgh, and detained there until Wednesday the —— day of ——; and upon that day, betwixt the hours of two and four o'clock afternoon, to be conveyed to the common place of execution, and there hanged by the neck upon a gibbet. "And this," said the Dempster, aggravating his harsh voice, "I pronounce for *doom*."

He vanished when he had spoken the last emphatic word, like a foul fiend after the purpose of his visitation has been accomplished; but the impression of horror excited by his presence and his errand, remained upon the crowd of spectators.

The unfortunate criminal, so she must now be termed, with more susceptibility, and more irritable feelings than her father and sister, was found, in this emergence, to possess a considerable share of their courage. She had remained standing motionless at the bar while the sentence was pronounced, and was observed to shut her eyes when the Doomster appeared. But she was the first to break silence when that evil form had left his place.

"God forgive ye, my Lords," she said, "and dinna be angry wi' me for wishing it—we a' need forgiveness.—As for myself I canna blame ye, for ye act up to your lights; and if I havena killed my poor infant, ye may witness a' that hae seen it this day, that I hae been the means of killing my grey-headed father—I deserve the warst frae man, and frae God too—But God is mair mercifu' to us than we are to each other."

With these words the trial concluded. The crowd rushed, rearing and shouldering each other, out of the court, in the same tumultuary mode in which they had entered; and, in the excitation of animal motion and animal spirits, soon forgot whatever they had felt as impressive in the scene which they had witnessed. The professional spectators, whom habit and theory had rendered as callous to the distress of the scene as medical men are to those of a surgical operation, walked homeward in groupes, discussing the general principle of the statute under which the young woman was condemned, the nature of the evidence, and the arguments of the counsel, without considering even that of the Judge as exempt from their criticism.

The female spectators, more compassionate, were loud in exclamation against that part of the Judge's speech which seemed to cut off the hope of pardon.

"Set him up, indeed," said Mrs Howden, "to tell us that the puir lassie behoved to die, when Mr John Kirk, as civil a gentleman as is within the ports of the town, took the pains to prigg for her himself."

"Ay, but neighbour," said Miss Damahoy, drawing up her thin maidenly form to its full height of prim dignity—"I really think this unnatural business of having bastard-bairns should be putten a stop to —There isna a hizzy now on this side of thirty that ye can bring within your doors, but there will be chields—writer-lads, prentice-lads, and what not—coming traiking after them for their destruction, and discrediting ane's honest house into the bargain—I hae nae patience wi' them."

"Hout, neighbour," said Mrs Howden, "we suld live and let live— we hae been young oursells, and we are no aye to judge the warst when lads and lasses forgather."

"Young oursells? and judge the warst?" said Miss Damahoy. "I amna sae auld as that comes to, Mrs Howden; and as for what ye ca' the warst—I ken neither gude nor bad about the matter, I thank my stars."

"Ye are thankfu' for sma' mercies, then," said Mrs Howden, with a toss of her head; "and as for you and young—I trow ye were doing for yoursell at the last riding of the Scots Parliament, and that was in the gracious year seven, sae ye can be nae sic chicken at ony rate."

Plumdamas, who acted as squire of the body to the two contending dames, instantly saw the hazard of entering into such delicate points of chronology, and being a lover of peace and good neighbourhood, lost no time in bringing back the conversation to its original subject.

"The Judge didna tell us a' he could hae tell'd us, if he had liked, about the application for pardon, neighbours," said he; "there is aye a wimple in a lawyer's clew; but it's a wee bit of a secret."

"And what is't?—what is't, neighbour Plumdamas?" said Mrs Howden and Miss Damahoy at once, the acid fermentation of their dispute being at once neutralized by the powerful alkali implied in the word secret.

"Here's Mr Saddletree can tell ye that better than me, for it was him that tauld me," said Plumdamas as Saddletree came up, with his wife hanging on his arm, and looking very disconsolate.

When the question was put to Saddletree he laughed scornfully. "They speak about stopping the frequency of child murther," said he, in a contemptuous tone; "do ye think our auld enemies of Ingland, as honest Glendook aye ca's them in his printed Statutebook, care a boddle whether we didna kill ane anither, skin and birn, horse and foot, man, woman, and bairns, all and sindry, *omnes et singulos*, as Mr Crossmyloof says? Na, na, it's no that hinders frae pardoning the bit lassie. But here is the pinch of the plea. The king and queen is sae ill pleased with that mistak about Porteous, that de'il a kindly Scot will they ever pardon again, either by reprieve or remission, if the haill town o' Edinburgh suld be a' hanged on ae tow."

"De'il that they were back at their German kale-yard then, as my neighbour MacRoskie ca's it," said Mrs Howden; "an that's the way they are gaun to guide us."

"They say for certain," said Miss Damahoy, "that King George flang his periwig in the fire when he heard o' the Porteous mob."

"He has done that, they say," replied Saddletree, "for less thing."

"Aweel," said Miss Damahoy, "he might keep mair wit in his anger —but it's a' the better for his wig-maker, I'se warrant."

"The queen tore her biggonets for perfect anger,—ye'll hae heard that too?" said Plumdamas. "And the king, they say, kickit Sir Robert Walpole for no keeping down the mob of Edinburgh; but I dinna believe he wad behave sae ungenteel."

"It's dooms truth, though," said Saddletree; "and he was for kickin the Duke of Argyle too."

"Kickin the Duke of Argyle!" exclaimed the hearers at once, in all the various combined keys of utter astonishment.

"Ay, but Maccallanmore's blood wadna sit down wi' that; there was risk of Andro Ferrara coming in thirdsman."

"The duke is a real Scotsman—a true friend to the country," answered Saddletree's hearers.

"Ay, troth is he, to king and country baith, as ye sall hear," continued the orator, "if ye will come in bye to our house, for it's safest speaking of sic things *inter parietes*."

When they entered his shop he thrust the prentice boy out of it, and, unlocking his desk, took out, with an air of grave and complacent importance, a dirty and crumpled piece of printed paper; he observed, "This is new corn—it's no every body could shew ye the like of this. It's the duke's speech about the Porteous mob, just promulgated by the hawker. Ye shall hear what Ian Roy Cean says for himsell. My correspondent bought it in the Palace-yard, that's like just under the king's nose—I think he claws up their mittans.—It came in a letter about a foolish bill of exchange that the man wants me to renew for him. I wish ye wad see about it, Mrs Saddletree."

Honest Mrs Saddletree had hitherto been so sincerely distressed about the situation of her unfortunate protegée, that she had suffered her husband to proceed in his own way, without attending to what he was saying. The words *bill* and *renew*, had, however, an awakening sound in them; and she snatched the letter which her husband held towards her, and wiping her eyes, and putting on her spectacles, endeavoured, as fast as the dew which collected on her glasses would permit, to get at the meaning of the needful part of the epistle; while her husband, with pompous elocution, read an extract from the speech.

"I am no minister, I never was a minister, and I never will be one"——

"I didna ken his grace was ever designed for the ministry," interrupted Mrs Howden.

"He disna mean a minister of the gospel, Mrs Howden, but a minister of state," said Saddletree with condescending goodness, and then proceeded: "Time was when I might have been a piece of a minister, but I was too sensible of my own incapacity to engage in any state affair. And I thank God that I had always too great a value for these few abilities which nature has given me, to employ them in doing any drudgery, or any job of what kind soever. I have, ever since I set out in the world, (and I believe few have set out more early,) served my prince with my tongue; I have served him with any little interest I had, and I have served him with my sword, and in my profession of arms. I have held employments which I have lost, and were I to be to-morrow deprived of those which still remain to me, and which I have endeavoured honestly to deserve, I would still serve him to the last acre of my inheritance, and to the last drop of my blood."

Mrs Saddletree here broke in upon the orator.—"Mr Saddletree, what *is* the meaning of a' this? Here are ye clavering about the Duke of Argyle, and this man Martingale ganging to break on our hands, and lose us gude sixty pounds—I wonder what duke will pay that, quotha —I wish the Duke of Argyle would pay his ain accounts—He is in a thousand punds Scots on thae very books when he was last at Roystoun—I am no saying but he's a just nobleman, and that it's gude siller—but it wad drive ane daft to be confeised wi' deukes and drakes, and thae distressed folk upstairs, that's Jeanie Deans and her father. And than, pitting the very callant that was sewing the curpel out o' the shop, to play wi' blackguards in the close—Sit still, neighbours, it's no that I mean to disturb you; but what between courts o' law and courts o' state, and upper and under parliaments, and parliament-houses, here and in London, the gudeman's gane clean gyte, I think."

The gossips understood civility, and the rule of doing as they would be done by, too well, to tarry upon the slight invitation implied in the conclusion of this speech, and therefore made their farewells and departure as fast as possible, Saddletree whispering to Plumdamas that he would meet him at MacRoskie's, (the low-browed shop in the Luckenbooths, already mentioned), "in the hour of cause, and put

Maccallanmore's speech in his pocket, for a' the gudewife's din."

When Mrs Saddletree saw the house freed of her importunate visitors, and the little boy reclaimed from the pastimes of the wynd to the exercise of the awl, she went to visit her unhappy relative, David Deans, and his elder daughter, who had found in her house the nearest place of friendly refuge.

Chapter Thirteen

Alas! what poor ability's in me
To do him good?
—— Assay the power you have.
Measure for Measure

WHEN MRS SADDLETREE entered the apartment in which her guests had shrouded their misery, she found the window darkened. The feebleness which followed his long swoon had rendered it necessary to lay the old man in bed. The curtains were drawn around him, and Jeanie sate motionless by the side of the bed. Mrs Saddletree was a woman of kindness, nay, of feeling, but not of delicacy. She opened the half-shut window, drew aside the curtain, and taking her kinsman by the hand, exhorted him to sit up, and bear his sorrow like a good man, and a Christian man, as he was. But when she quitted his hand, it fell powerless by his side, nor did he attempt the least reply.

"Is all over?" asked Jeanie, with lips and cheeks as pale as ashes,— "And is there nae hope for her?"

"Nane, or next to nane," said Mrs Saddletree; "I heard the Judge-carle say it with my ain ears—It was a burning shame to see sae mony o' them set up yonder in their red gowns and black gowns, and a' to take the life o' a bit senseless lassie. I had never muckle broo o' my gudeman's gossips, and now I like them waur than ever. The only wiselike thing I heard ony body say was decent Mr John Kirk of Kirk-knowe, and he wussed them just to get the king's mercy, and nae mair about it. But he spake to unreasonable folk—he might just hae keepit his breath to hae blawn on his porridge."

"But *can* the king gie her mercy?" said Jeanie, earnestly. "Some folk tell me that he canna gie mercy in cases of mur——in cases like her's."

"*Can* he gie mercy, hinny?—Ay, weel I wot he *can*, when he likes. There was young Singlesword, that stickit the Laird of Ballencleuch, and Captain Hackum, the Englishman, that killed Lady Colgrain's gudeman, and the Master of St Clair, that shot the twa Shaws, and mony mair in my time—to be sure they were gentle blude, and had their kin to speak for them—And there was Jock Porteous the other day—I'se warrant there's mercy an folk could win at it."

"Porteous!" said Jeanie; "very true—I forget a' that I suld maist mind.—Fare ye weel, Mrs Saddletree; and may ye never want a friend in the hour o' distress."

"Will ye no stay wi' your father, Jeanie, bairn?—Ye had better," said Mrs Saddletree.

"I will be wanted ower yonder," indicating the tolbooth with her hand, "and I maun leave him now, or I will never be able to leave him. I fearna for his life—I ken how strong-hearted he is—I ken it," she said, laying her hand on her bosom, "by my ain heart at this minute."

"Weel, hinny, if ye think it's for the best, better he stay here and rest him, than gang back to Saint Leonard's."

"Muckle better—muckle better—God bless ye—God bless ye.— At no rate let him gang till ye hear frae me," said Jeanie.

"But ye'll be back belive?" said Mrs Saddletree, detaining her; "they winna let ye stay yonder, hinny."

"But I maun gang to Saint Leonard's—there's muckle to be dune, and little time to do it in—And I have friends to speak to—God bless you—take care of my father."

She had reached the door of the apartment, when, suddenly turning, she came back, and knelt down by the bedside.—"O father, gie me your blessing—I dare not go till ye bless me. Say but God bless ye, and prosper ye, Jeanie—try but to say that."

Instinctively, rather than by an exertion of intellect, the old man murmured a prayer, that "purchased and promised blessings might be multiplied upon her."

"He has blessed mine errand," said his daughter, rising from her knees; "and it is borne in upon my mind that I shall prosper."

So saying, she left the room.

Mrs Saddletree looked after her, and shook her head. "I wish she binna roving, poor thing—There is something queer about a' thae Deanses. I dinna like folk to be sae muckle better than other folk— seldom comes gude o't. But if she is ganging to look after the kye at Saint Leonard's, that's another story, to be sure they maun be sorted. —Grizz, come up here and tak tent to the honest auld man, and see he wants naething.—Ye silly tawpie," (addressing the maid-servant as she entered,) "what garr'd ye busk up your cockernony that gate?—I think there's been aneugh the day to gie an awfu' warning about your cockups and fal-lal duds—see what they a' come to," &c. &c. &c.

Leaving the good lady to her lecture upon worldly vanities, we must transport our reader to the cell in which the unfortunate Effie Deans was now immured, being restricted of several liberties which she had enjoyed before her sentence was pronounced.

When she had remained about an hour in the state of stupified horror so natural in her situation, she was disturbed by the opening of the jarring bolts of her place of confinement, and Ratcliffe shewed himself. "It's your sister," he said, "wants to speak t'ye, Effie."

"I canna see naebody," said Effie, with the hasty irritability which misery had rendered more acute—"I canna see naebody, and least of a' her—bid her take care o' the auld man—I am naething to ony o' them now, nor them to me."

"She says she maun see ye though," said Ratcliffe; and Jeanie, rushing into the apartment, threw her arms around her sister's neck, who writhed to extricate herself from her embrace.

"What signifies coming to greet ower me, when you have killed me? —killed me, when a word of your mouth would have saved me—killed me, when I am an innocent creature—innocent of that guilt at least— and me that wad hae wared body and soul to save your finger from being hurt!"

"You shall not die," said Jeanie, with enthusiastic firmness; "say what ye like o' me—think what ye like o' me—only promise—for I doubt your proud heart—that ye winna harm yoursell—And you shall not die this shameful death."

"A *shameful* death I will not die, Jeanie, lass. I have that in my heart —though it has been ower kind a ane—that winna bide shame. Gae hame to our father, and think nae mair on me—I have eat my last earthly meal."

"O this was what I feared!" said Jeanie.

"Hout tout! hinnie," said Ratcliffe; "it's but little ye ken o' thae things. Ane aye thinks at the first dinnle o' the sentence, they hae heart aneugh to die rather than bide out the sax weeks; but they aye bide the sax weeks out for a' that. I ken the gate o't weel; I hae fronted the doomster three times, and here I stand, Jem Ratcliffe, for a' that. Had I tied my napkin strait the first time, as I had a great mind till't—and it was a' about a bit grey cowt, wasna worth ten punds sterling—where would I have been now?"

"And how *did* you escape?" said Jeanie, the fates of this man, at first so odious to her, having acquired a sudden interest in her eyes from their correspondence with those of her sister.

"*How* did I escape?" said Ratcliffe, with a knowing wink,—"I tell ye I scapit the way that naebody will escape from this tolbooth while I keep the keys."

"My sister shall come out in the face of the sun," said Jeanie; "I will go to London, and beg her pardon from the king and queen. If they pardoned Porteous, they may pardon her; and if a sister asks a sister's

life on her bended knees, they *will* pardon her—they *shall* pardon her
—and they shall win a thousand hearts by it."

Effie listened in bewildered astonishment, and so earnest was her
sister's enthusiastic assurances, that she almost involuntarily caught a
gleam of hope, but it instantly faded away.

"Ah, Jeanie! the king and queen live in London, a thousand
miles from this—far ayont the saut sea; I'll be gane before ye win
there."

"You are mista'en," said Jeanie; "it is no sae far, and they go to it by
land; I learned something about thae things from Reuben Butler."

"Ah, Jeanie, ye never learned ony thing but what was gude frae the
folk ye keepit wi'; but I—but I—;" she wrang her hands, and wept
bitterly.

"Dinna think on that now," said Jeanie; "there will be time for that
if the present space be redeemed.—Fare ye weel. Unless I die by the
road, I will see the King's face that gies grace.—O, sir," (to Ratcliffe)
"be kind to her—She ne'er kenn'd what it was to need stranger's
kindness till now—Fareweel—fareweel, Effie—Dinna speak to me—
I maunna greet now—my head is ower dizzy already."

She tore herself from her sister's arms, and left the cell. Ratcliffe
followed her, and beckoned her into a small room. She obeyed his
signal, but not without trembling.

"What's the fule thing shaking for?" said he; "I mean nothing but
civility to you—D—n me, I respect you, and I can't help it. You have
so much spunk, that, d—n me, but I think there's some chance of your
carrying the day. But you must not go to the king till you have
made some friend; try the duke—try Maccallanmore; he's Scotland's
friend—I ken that the great folks dinna muckle like him—but they
fear him, and that will serve your purpose as weel. Do ye ken naebody
wad gie ye a letter to him?"

"Duke of Argyle?" said Jeanie, recollecting herself suddenly—
"what was he to that Argyle that suffered in my father's time—in the
persecution?"

"His son or grandson, I am thinking," said Ratcliffe; "but what o'
that?"

"Thank God!" said Jeanie, devoutly clasping her hands.

"You whigs are aye thanking God for something," said the ruffian.
"But hark ye, hinny, I'll tell ye a secret. Ye may meet wi' rough
customers on the Border, or in the Midland, afore ye get to Lunnon.
Now de'il ane o' them will touch an acquaintance o' Daddie Ratton's;
for though I am retired frae public practice, yet they ken I can do a
gude or an ill turn yet—and de'il a gude fellow that has been but a
twelvemonth on the lay, be he ruffler or padder, but he knows my

gybe* as well as the jark† of e'er a queer cuffin‡ in England—and there's rogue's Latin for you."

It was, indeed, totally unintelligible to Jeanie Deans, who was only impatient to escape from him. He hastily scrawled a line or two on a dirty piece of paper, and said to her, as she drew back when he offered it, "Hey! what the de'il—it winna bite you, my lass—if it does nae gude, it can do nae ill. But I wish ye to show it, if you have ony fasherie wi' ony o' Saint Nicholas's clerks."

"Alas!" said she, "I do not understand what ye mean?"

"I mean if ye fall amang thieves, my precious,—that is a Scripture phrase, if ye will hae ane—the bauldest of them will ken a scart o' my guse feather.—And now awa' wi' ye—and stick to Argyle; if ony body can do the job, it maun be him." He then conducted her to the door of the prison and permitted her to depart.

After casting one anxious look at the grated windows and blackened walls of the old tolbooth, and another scarce less anxious at the hospitable lodging of Mrs Saddletree, Jeanie turned her back on that quarter, and soon after on the city itself. She reached Saint Leonard's Crags without meeting any one whom she knew, which, in the state of her mind, she considered as a great blessing. "I must do naething," she thought, as she went along, "that can soften or weaken my heart—it's ower weak already for what I hae to do. I will think and act as firmly as I can, and speak as little."

There was an ancient servant or rather cottar of her father's, who had lived under him for many years, and whose fidelity was worthy of full confidence. She sent for this woman, and explaining to her that the circumstances of her family required that she should undertake a journey, which would detain her for some weeks from home, she gave her full instructions concerning the management of the domestic concerns in her absence. With a precision, which, upon reflection, she herself could not help wondering at, she described and detailed the most minute steps which were to be taken, and especially such as were necessary for her father's comfort. "It was probable," she said, "that he would return to Saint Leonard's to-morrow; certain that he would return very soon—all must be in order for him. He had eneugh to distress him, without being fashed about warldly matters."

In the meanwhile she toiled busily, along with May Hettly, to leave nothing unarranged.

It was deep in the night when all these matters were settled; and when they had partaken of some food, the first which Jeanie had tasted on that eventful day, May Hettly, whose usual residence was a cottage at a little distance from Deans's house, asked her young mistress,

* Pass.   † Seal.   ‡ Justice of Peace.

whether she would not permit her to remain in the house all night? "Ye hae had an awfu' day," she said, "and sorrow and fear are but bad companions in the watches of the night, as I hae heard the gudeman say himsell."

"They are ill companions, indeed," said Jeanie; "but I maun learn to abide their presence, and better begin in the house than in the field."

She dismissed her aged assistant accordingly,—for so slight was the gradation in their rank of life, that we can hardly term May a servant, —and proceeded to make a few preparations for her journey.

The simplicity of her education and country made these preparations very brief and easy. Her tartan screen served all the purposes of a riding-habit, and of an umbrella; a small bundle contained such changes of linen as were absolutely necessary. Barefooted, as Sancho says, she had come into the world, and barefooted she proposed to perform her pilgrimage; and her clean shoes and snow-white thread stockings were to be reserved for special occasions of ceremony. She was not aware, that the English habits of *comfort* attach an idea of abject misery to the idea of a barefooted traveller; and if the objection of cleanliness had been made to the practice, she would have been apt to vindicate herself upon the very frequent ablutions to which, with Mahometan scrupulosity, a Scottish damsel of some condition usually subjects herself. Thus far, therefore, all was well.

From an oaken press or cabinet, in which her father kept a few old books, and two or three bundles of papers, besides his ordinary accounts and receipts, she sought out and extracted from a parcel of notes of sermons, calculations of interest, records of dying speeches of the martyrs, and the like, one or two documents which she thought might be of some use to her upon her mission. But the most important difficulty remained behind, and it had not occurred to her until that very evening. It was the want of money, without which it was impossible she should undertake so distant a journey as she now meditated.

David Deans, as we have said, was easy, and even opulent in his circumstances. But his wealth, like that of the patriarchs of old, consisted in his flocks and herds, and two or three sums lent out at interest to neighbours or relatives, who, far from being in circumstances to pay anything to account of the principal sums, thought they did all that was incumbent on them when, with considerable difficulty, they discharged "the annual rent." To these debtors it would be in vain, therefore, to apply, even with her father's concurrence; nor could she hope to obtain such concurrence, or assistance in any mode, without such a series of explanations and debates as she felt might deprive her totally of the power of taking the step, which, however daring and hazardous, she felt was absolutely necessary for trying the last chance in favour of her sister. Without departing from filial reverence, Jeanie had an inward conviction that the feelings of her father, however just, and upright, and honourable, were too little in unison with the spirit of the time to admit of his being a good judge of the measures to be adopted in this crisis. Herself more flexible in manner, though no less upright in principle, she felt that to ask his consent to her pilgrimage would be to encounter the risk of drawing down his positive prohibition, and under that she believed her journey could not be blessed in its progress and event. Accordingly, she had determined upon the means by which she might communicate to him her undertaking and its purpose, shortly after her actual departure. But it was impossible to apply to him for money without altering this arrangement, and discussing fully the propriety of her journey; pecuniary assistance from that quarter, therefore, was laid out of the question.

It now occurred to Jeanie that she should have consulted with Mrs Saddletree on this subject. But, besides the time that must now necessarily be lost in recurring to her assistance, Jeanie internally revolted from it. Her heart acknowledged the goodness of Mrs Saddletree's general character, and the kind interest she took in their family misfortunes; but still she felt that Mrs Saddletree was a woman of an ordinary and worldly way of thinking, incapable, from habit and temperament, of taking a keen or enthusiastic view of such a resolution as she had formed, and to debate the point with her, and to rely upon her conviction of its propriety for the means of carrying it into execution, would have been gall and wormwood.

Butler, whose assistance she might have been assured of, was greatly poorer than herself. In these circumstances she formed a singular resolution for the purpose of surmounting this difficulty, the execution of which will form the subject of the next volume.

END OF VOLUME SECOND

THE
HEART OF MID-LOTHIAN

VOLUME III

Chapter One

'Tis the voice of the sluggard, I've heard him complain,
"You have waked me too soon, I must slumber again;"
As the door on its hinges, so he on his bed,
Turns his side, and his shoulders, and his heavy head.

DR WATTS

THE MANSION-HOUSE of Dumbiedikes, to which we are now to
introduce our readers, lay three or four miles—no matter for the exact
topography—to the southward of Saint Leonard's. It had once borne
the appearance of some little celebrity; for the "auld laird," whose
humours and pranks were often mentioned in the ale-houses for
about a mile round it, wore a sword, kept a good horse, and a brace of
grey-hounds; brawled, swore, and betted at cock-fights and horse-
matches; followed Somerville of Drum's hawks, and the Lord Ross's
hounds, and called himself *point device* a gentleman. But the line had
vailed its splendour in the present proprietor, who cared for no rustic
amusement, and was as saving, timid, and retired, as his father had
been at once grasping and selfishly extravagant,—daring, wild, and
intrusive.

Dumbiedikes was what is called in Scotland a *single* house; that
is, having only one room occupying its whole breadth, each of which
single apartments was illuminated by six or eight cross lights, whose
diminutive panes and heavy frames permitted scarce so much light
to enter as shines through one well-constructed modern window.
This inartificial edifice, exactly such as a child would build with cards,
had a steep roof flagged with coarse grey-stones instead of slates. A
half-circular turret, battlemented, or, to use the appropriate phrase,

bartizan'd on the top, served as a case for a narrow turnpike-stair, by which an ascent was gained from storey to storey; and at the bottom of the said turret was a door studded with large-headed nails. There was no lobby at the bottom of the tower, and scarce a landing-place opposite to the doors which gave access to the apartments. One or two low and dilapidated out-houses, connected by a court-yard wall equally ruinous, surrounded the mansion. The court had been paved, but the flags being partly displaced, and partly removed, a gallant crop of docks and thistles sprung up between them, and the small garden, which opened by a postern through the wall, seemed not to be in a much more orderly condition. Over the low-arched gateway, which led into the yard, there was a carved stone, exhibiting some attempt at armorial bearings; and above the inner entrance hung, and had hung for many years, the mouldering hatchment, which announced that umquhile Laurence Dumbie, of Dumbiedikes, had been gathered to his fathers in Newbattle kirk-yard. The approach to this palace of pleasure, was by a road formed by the rude fragments of stone gathered from the land, and it was surrounded by ploughed, but uninclosed land. Upon a baulk, that is an unploughed ridge of land interposed among the corn, the Laird's trusty palfrey was tethered by the head, and picking a meal of grass. The whole argued neglect and discomfort; the consequences, however, of idleness and indifference, not of poverty.

In this inner court, not without a sense of bashfulness and timidity, stood Jeanie Deans, at an early hour in a fine spring morning. She was no heroine of romance, and therefore looked with some curiosity and interest on the mansion-house and domains, of which, it might at that moment occur to her, a little encouragement, such as women of all ranks know by instinct how to apply, might have made her mistress. Moreover, she was no person of taste beyond her time, rank, and country, and certainly thought the house of Dumbiedikes, though inferior to Holyroodhouse, or the palace at Dalkeith, was still a stately structure in its way, and the land a "very bonnie bit, if it were better seen to and done to." But Jeanie Deans was a plain, true-hearted, honest girl, who, while she acknowledged all the splendour of her old admirer's habitation and the value of his property, never for a moment harboured a thought of doing the Laird, Butler, or herself, the injustice, which many ladies of higher rank would not have hesitated to do to all three, on much less temptation.

Her present errand being with the Laird, she looked round the offices to see if she could find any domestic to announce that she wished to see him. As all was silence, she ventured to open one door; —it was the old Laird's dog-kennel, now deserted, unless when occupied, as one or two tubs seemed to testify, as a washing-house. She tried another—it was the roofless shade where the hawks were once kept, as appeared from a perch or two not yet completely rotten, and a lure and jesses which hung mouldering on the wall. A third door led to the coal-house, which was well stocked. To keep a very good fire, was one of the few points of domestic management in which Dumbiedikes was positively active; in all other matters of domestic economy he was completely passive, and at the mercy of his house-keeper, the same buxom dame whom his father had long since bequeathed to his charge, and who, if fame did her no injustice, had feathered her nest pretty well at his expence.

Jeanie went on opening doors, like the second Calender wanting an eye, in the castle of the hundred obliging damsels, until, like the said prince errant, she came to a stable. The Highland Pegasus, Rory Bean, to which belonged the single entire stall, was her old acquaint-ance whom she had seen grazing on the baulk, as she failed not to recognize by the well-known ancient riding furniture and demi-pique saddle, which half hung on the walls, half trailed on the litter. Beyond the "treviss," which formed one side of the stall, stood a cow, who turned her head and lowed when Jeanie came into the stable, an appeal which her habitual occupations enabled her perfectly to under-stand, and with which she could not refuse complying, by shaking down some fodder to the animal, which had been neglected like most things else in the castle of the sluggard.

While she was accommodating "the milky mother" with the food which she should have received two hours sooner, a slip-shod wench peeped into the stable, and perceiving that a stranger was employed in discharging the task which she, at length, and reluctantly, had quitted her slumbers to perform, ejaculated, "Eh, sirs! the Brownie! the Brownie!" and fled, yelling as if she had seen the devil.

To explain her terror, it may be necessary to notice, that the old house of Dumbiedikes had, according to report, been long haunted by a Brownie, one of those familiar spirits, who were believed in ancient times to supply the deficiencies of the ordinary labourer—

Whirl the long mop, and ply the airy flail.

Certes, the convenience of such a supernatural assistant could have been nowhere more sensibly felt, than in a family where the domestics were so little disposed to personal activity; yet this serving maiden was so far from rejoicing in seeing a supposed aerial substitute dis-charging a task which she should have long since performed herself, that she proceeded to raise the family by her screams of horror, uttered as thick as if the Brownie had been flaying her. Jeanie, who had immediately resigned her temporary occupation, and followed the yelling damsel into the court-yard, in order to undeceive and appease her, was there met by Mrs Janet Balchristie, the favourite sultana of the last laird, as scandal went—the house-keeper of the present. The good-looking, buxom woman, betwixt forty and fifty, (for such we described her at the death of the last laird) was now a fat, red-faced, old dame of seventy, or thereabouts, fond of her place, and jealous of her authority. Conscious that her place of administration did not rest on so sure a basis as in the time of the old proprietor, this considerate lady had introduced into the family the screamer afore-said, who added good features and bright eyes to the powers of her lungs. She made no conquest of the Laird, however, who seemed to live as if there was not another woman in the world but Jeanie Deans, and to bear no very ardent or overbearing affection even to her. Mrs Janet Balchristie, notwithstanding, had her own uneasy thoughts upon the almost daily visits to Saint Leonard's Crags, and often, when the Laird looked at her wistfully and paused, according to his custom before utterance, she expected him to say, "Jenny, I am gaun to change my condition;" but she was relieved by "Jenny, I am ganging to change my shoon."

Still, however, Mrs Balchristie regarded Jeanie Deans with no small portion of malevolence, the customary feeling of such persons towards any one who they think has the means of doing them an injury. But she had also a general aversion to any female, tolerably young, and decently well-looking, who shewed a wish to approach the house of Dumbiedikes and the proprietor thereof. And as she had raised her mass of mortality out of bed two hours earlier than usual, to come to the rescue of her clamorous niece, she was in such extreme bad humour against all and sundry, that Saddletree would have pro-nounced, that she harboured *inimicitiam contra omnes mortales*.

"Wha the de'il are ye?" said the fat dame to poor Jeanie, whom she did not immediately recognize, "scouping about a decent house at sic an hour in the morning?"

"It was ane wanting to speak to the Laird," said Jeanie, who felt something of the instinctive terror which she had formerly entertained for this termagant, when she was occasionally at Dumbiedikes on business of her father's.

"Ane?—And what sort of an ane are ye?—hae ye nae name?—D'ye think his honour has naething else to dae than to speak wi' ilka idle tramper that comes about the loan, and him in his bed yet, honest man?"

"Dear, Mrs Balchristie," replied Jeanie, in a submissive tone, "d'ye no mind me?—d'ye no mind Jeanie Deans?"

"Jeanie Deans!!!" said the termagant, in accents affecting the utmost astonishment; then, taking two strides nearer to her, she peered into her face with a stare of curiosity, equally scornful and malignant—"I say Jeanie Deans indeed—Jeanie Deevil, they had better hae caa'd ye!—A bonnie spot o' wark your tittie and you hae made on't, murdering ae puir wean, and your light limmer of a sister to be hangit for't, as weel she deserves!—And the like o' you to come to ony honest man's house, and want to be into a decent bachelor gentleman's room at this time in the morning, and him in his bed?— gae wa', gae wa'."

Jeanie was struck mute with shame at the unfeeling brutality of this accusation, and could not even find words to justify herself from the vile construction put upon her visit, when Mrs Balchristie, seeing her advantage, continued in the same tone, "Come, come, bundle your pipes and tramp awa' wi' ye!—ye may be seeking a father to another wean for ony thing I ken. If it waurna that your father, auld David Deans, had been a tenant on our land, I would cry up the men-folk, and hae ye dookit in the burn for your impudence."

Jeanie had already turned her back, and was walking towards the door of the court-yard, so that Mrs Balchristie, to make her last threat impressively audible to her, had raised her stentorian voice to its utmost pitch. But, like many a general, she lost the engagement by pressing her advantage too far.

The Laird had been disturbed in his morning slumbers by the tones of Mrs Balchristie's objurgation, sounds in themselves by no means uncommon, but very remarkable, in respect to the early hour at which they were now heard. He turned himself on the other side, however, in hopes the squall would blow by, when, in the course of Mrs Balchristie's second explosion of wrath, the name of Deans distinctly struck the tympanum of his ear. As he was, in some degree, aware of the small portion of benevolence with which his housekeeper regarded the family at Saint Leonard's, he instantly conceived that some message from thence was the cause of this untimely ire, and getting out of bed, he slipt as speedily as possible into an old brocaded night-gown, and some other necessary garments, clapped on his head his father's gold-laced hat, (for though he was seldom seen without it, yet it is proper to contradict the popular report, that he slept in it, as Don Quixote did in his helmet), and opening the window of his bed-room, beheld, to his great astonishment, the well-known figure of Jeanie Deans herself retreating from his gate; while his housekeeper, with arms a-kimbo, fist clenched and extended, body erect, and head shaking with rage, sent after her a volley of Billingsgate oaths. His choler rose in proportion to the surprise, and, perhaps, to the disturbance of his repose. "Hark ye," he exclaimed from the window, "ye auld limb of Satan—wha the de'il gies you commission to guide an honest man's daughter that gate?"

Mrs Balchristie was completely caught in the manner. She was aware, from the unusual warmth with which the Laird expressed himself, that he was quite serious in this matter, and she knew that, with all his indolence of nature, there were points on which he might be provoked, and that, being provoked, he had in him something dangerous, which her wisdom taught her to fear accordingly. She began, therefore, to retract her false step as fast as she could. "She was but speaking for the house's credit, and she couldna think of disturbing his honour in the morning sae early, when the young woman might as weel wait or call again; and to be sure, she might make a mistake between the twa sisters, for ane o' them wasna sae creditable an acquaintance."

"Haud your peace, ye auld jade," said Dumbiedikes; "the warst quean e'er stude in their shoon may ca' you cousin, an' a' be true that I have heard.—Jeanie, my woman, gang into the parlour—but stay, that winna be redd up yet—wait there a minute till I come doun and let ye in—Dinna mind what Jenny says to ye."

"Na, na," said Jenny, with a laugh of affected heartiness, "never mind me, lass—a' the warld kens my bark's waur than my bite—if ye had had an appointment wi' the Laird, ye might hae tauld me—I am nae uncivil person—gang your ways in bye, hinny," and she opened the door of the house with a master-key.

"But I had no appointment wi' the Laird," said Jeanie, drawing back; "I want just to speak twa words to him, and I wad rather do it standing here, Mrs Balchristie."

"In the open court-yard?—Na, na, that wad never do, lass; we maunna guide ye that gate neither—And how's that douce honest man, your father?"

Jeanie was saved the pain of answering this hypocritical question by the appearance of the Laird himself.

"Gang in and get breakfast ready," said he to his housekeeper—"and, d'ye hear, breakfast wi' us yoursell—ye ken how to manage thae porringers of tea-water—and, hear ye—see abune a' that there is a gude fire.—Weel, Jeanie, my woman, gang in bye—gang in bye, and rest ye."

"Na, Laird," Jeanie replied, endeavouring as much as she could to express herself with composure, notwithstanding she still trembled, "I canna gang in—I have a lang day's darg afore me—I maun be twenty mile o' gate the night yet, if feet will carry me."

"Guide and deliver us!—twenty mile—twenty mile on your feet!"

ejaculated Dumbiedikes, whose walks were of a very circumscribed diameter,—"Ye maun never think o' that—come in bye."

"I canna do that, Laird," replied Jeanie; "the twa words I hae to say to ye I can say here; forbye that Mrs Balchristie"—

"The de'il flee awa' wi' Mrs Balchristie," said Dumbiedikes, "and he'll hae a heavy lading o' her. I tell ye, Jeanie Deans, I am a man of few words, but I am laird at hame, as weel as in the fields; de'il a brute or body about my house but I can manage when I like, except Rory Bean, my powney; but I can seldom be at the plague, an' it binna when my bluid's up."

"I was wanting to say to ye, Laird," said Jeanie, who felt the necessity of entering upon her business, "that I was ganging a lang journey, outbye of my father's knowledge."

"Outbye his knowledge, Jeanie!—Is that right?—Ye maun think o't again—it's no right," said Dumbiedikes, with a countenance of great concern.

"If I were anes at Lunnon," said Jeanie, in exculpation, "I am amaist sure I could get means to speak to the queen about my sister's life."

"Lunnon—and the queen—and her sister's life!" said Dumbiedikes, whistling for very amazement—"the lassie's demented."

"I am no out o' my mind," said she, "and, sink or swim, I am determined to gang to Lunnon, if I suld beg my way frae door to door —and so I maun, unless ye wad lend me a small sum to pay my expences—little thing will do it; and ye ken my father's a man of substance, and wad see nae man, far less you, Laird, come to loss by me."

Dumbiedikes, on comprehending the nature of this application, could scarce trust his ears—he made no answer whatever, but stood with his eyes rivetted on the ground.

"I see ye are no for assisting me, Laird," said Jeanie; "sae fare ye weel—and gang and see my poor father as aften as ye can—he will be lonely aneugh now."

"Whare is the silly bairn ganging?" said Dumbiedikes; and, laying hold of her hand, he led her into the house. "It's no that I didna think o't before," he said, "but it aye stack in my throat."

Thus speaking to himself, he led her into an old-fashioned parlour, shut the door behind them, and fastened it with a bolt. While Jeanie, surprised at this manœuvre, remained as near the door as possible, the Laird quitted her hand, and pressed upon a spring lock fixed in an oak-pannel in the wainscot, which instantly slipped aside. An iron strong-box was discovered in a recess of the wall; he opened this also, and pulling out two or three drawers, shewed that they were filled with leathern-bags, full of gold and silver coin.

"This is my bank, Jeanie lass," he said, looking first at her, and then at the treasure, with an air of great complacence,—"nane o' your goldsmith's bills for me,—they bring folk to ruin."

Then suddenly changing his tone, he resolutely said,—"Jeanie, I will make ye Lady Dumbiedikes afore the sun sets, and ye may ride to Lunnon in your ain coach, if ye like."

"Na, Laird," said Jeanie, "that can never be—my father's grief— my sister's situation—the discredit to you"—

"That's *my* business," said Dumbiedikes; "ye wad say naething about that if ye were na a fule—and yet I like ye the better for't—ae wise body's aneugh in the married state. But if your heart's ower fu', tak what siller will serve ye, and let it be when ye come back again—as gude syne as sune."

"But, Laird," said Jeanie, who felt the necessity of being explicit with so extraordinary a lover, "I like another man better than you, and I canna marry ye."

"Another man better than me, Jeanie?" said Dumbiedikes—"how is that possible?—It's no possible, woman—ye hae kenn'd me sae lang."

"Ay but, Laird," said Jeanie, with persevering simplicity, "I kenn'd him langer."

"Langer?—It's no possible. It canna be; ye were born on the land. O Jeanie woman, ye haena lookit—ye haena seen the half o' the gear." He drew out another drawer—"A' gowd, Jeanie, and there's bands for siller lent—And the rental book, Jeanie—clear three hunder sterling —de'il a wadset, heritable band, or burthen—Ye haena lookit at them, woman—And than my mother's wardrope, and my grandmother's forbye—silk gowns wad stand on their ends their lane—pearlin-lace as fine as spiders' webs, and rings and ear-rings to the boot of a' that— they are a' in the chamber of deas—Oh, Jeanie, gang up the stair, and look at them."

But Jeanie held fast her integrity, though beset with temptations, which perhaps the Laird of Dumbiedikes did not greatly err in supposing were those most affecting to her sex.

"It canna be, Laird—I have said it—and I canna break my word till him, if ye wad gie me the haill barony of Dalkeith, and Lugton into the bargain."

"Your word to *him*," said the Laird, somewhat pettishly; "but wha is he, Jeanie?—wha is he?—I haena heard his name yet—Come now, Jeanie, ye are but queering us—I am no trowing that there is sic a ane in the warld—ye are but making fashion—What is he?—wha is he?"

"Just Reuben Butler, that's schule-master at Libberton," said Jeanie.

"Reuben Butler! Reuben Butler!" echoed the Laird of Dumbiedikes, pacing the apartment in high disdain,—"Reuben Butler, the
dominie at Libberton—and a dominie-depute too!—Reuben, the son
of my cottar!—Very weel, Jeanie lass, wilfu' woman will hae her way—
Reuben Butler! he hasna in his pouch the value o' the auld black coat
he wears—but it disna signify." And, as he spoke, he shut successively, and with vehemence, the drawers of his treasury. "A fair offer,
Jeanie, is nae cause of feud—Ae man may bring a horse to the water,
but twenty winna gar him drink—And as for wasting my substance on
other folk's joes"——

There was something in the last hint that nettled Jeanie's honest
pride.—"I was begging nane frae your honour," she said; "least of a'
on sic a score as ye pit it on.—Gude morning to ye, sir; ye hae been
kind to my father, and it isna in my heart to think otherwise than kindly
of you."

So saying, she left the room without listening to a faint "But, Jeanie
—Jeanie—stay, woman!" And traversing the court-yard with a quick
step, she set out on her forward journey, her bosom glowing with that
natural indignation and shame, which an honest mind feels at having
subjected itself to ask a favour, which had been unexpectedly refused.
When out of the Laird's ground, and once more on the public road,
her pace slackened, her anger cooled, and anxious anticipations of the
consequence of this unexpected disappointment began to influence
her with other feelings. Must she then actually beg her way to London? for such seemed the alternative; or must she turn back, to solicit
her father for money; and by doing so lose time, which was precious,
besides the risk of encountering his positive prohibition respecting
her journey? Yet she saw no medium between these alternatives; and,
while she walked slowly on, was still meditating whether it were not
better to return.

While she was thus in uncertainty, she heard the clatter of a horse's
hoofs, and a well-known voice calling her name. She looked round,
and saw advancing towards her on a poney, whose bare back and
halter assorted ill with the night-gown, slippers, and laced cocked-hat
of the rider, a cavalier of no less importance than Dumbiedikes himself. In the energy of his pursuit, he had overcome even the Highland
obstinacy of Rory Bean, and compelled that self-willed palfrey to
canter the way his rider chose; which Rory, however, performed with
all symptoms of reluctance, turning his head aside, and accompanying
every bound he made in advance with a side-long motion, which
indicated his extreme wish to turn round,—a manœuvre which nothing but the constant exercise of the Laird's heels and cudgel could
possibly have counteracted.

When the Laird came up with Jeanie, the first words he uttered were,—"Jeanie, they say ane shouldna aye take a woman at her first word?"

"Ay, but ye maun take me at mine," said Jeanie, looking on the ground, and walking on without a pause.—"I hae but ae word to bestow on ony ane, and that's aye a true ane."

"Then," said Dumbiedikes, "at least ye suldna aye take a man at *his* first word. Ye maunna gang this wilfu' gate sillerless, come o't what like."—He put a purse into her hand. "I wad gie you Rory too, but he's as wilfu' as yoursell, and he's ower weel used to a gate that maybe he and I hae gaen ower aften, and he'll gang nae road else."

But, Laird," said Jeanie, "though I ken my father will satisfy every penny of this siller, whatever there's o't, yet I wad like ill to borrow it frae ane that maybe thinks of something mair than the paying o't back again."

"There's just twenty-five guineas o't," said Dumbiedikes, with a gentle sigh, "and whether your father pays or disna pay, I make ye free till't without another word; gang where ye like—do what ye like—and marry a' the Butlers in the country, gin ye like—And sae, gude morning to you, Jeanie."

"And God bless you, Laird, wi' mony a gude morning," said Jeanie, her heart more softened by the unwonted generosity of this uncouth character, than perhaps Butler might have approved, had he known her feelings at that moment; "and comfort, and the Lord's peace, and the peace of the world, be with you, if we suld never meet again!"

Dumbiedikes turned and waved his hand; and his poney, much more willing to return than he had been to set out, hurried him homewards so fast, that, wanting the aid of a regular bridle, as well as of saddle and stirrups, he was too much puzzled to keep his seat to permit of his looking behind, even to give the parting glance of a forlorn swain. I am ashamed to say, that the sight of a lover, run away with in night-gown and slippers and a laced-hat, by a bare-backed Highland poney, has something in it of a sedative, even to a grateful and deserved burst of affectionate esteem. The figure of Dumbiedikes was too ludicrous not to confirm Jeanie in the original sentiments she entertained towards him.

"He is a gude creature," said she, "and a kind—it's pity he has sae willyard a powney."

And she immediately turned her thoughts to the important journey which she had commenced, reflecting with pleasure, that, according to her habits of life and of undergoing fatigue, she was now amply or even superfluously provided with the means of encountering

the expences of the road, up and down from London, and all other
expences whatever.

Chapter Two

What strange and wayward thoughts will slide
Into a lover's head:
"O mercy!" to myself I cried,
"If Lucy should be dead!"
WORDSWORTH

IN PURSUING her solitary journey, our heroine, shortly after passing
the house of Dumbiedikes, gained a gentle eminence, from which, on
looking to the eastward down a little prattling brook, whose meanders
were shaded with straggling willows and alder trees, she could see the
cottages of Woodend and Beersheba, the haunts and habitation of her
early life, and could distinguish the common on which she had so
often herded sheep, and the recesses of the rivulet where she had
pulled rushes with Butler, to plait crowns and sceptres for her sister
Effie, then a beautiful, but spoiled child, of about three years old. The
recollections which the scene brought with them were so bitter, that,
had she indulged them, she would have sate down and relieved her
heart with tears.

"But I kenn'd," said Jeanie, "that greeting would do but little good,
and that it was mair beseeming to thank the Lord, that had shewed me
kindness and countenance by means of a man, that mony caa'd a
Nabal and a churl, but wha was free of his gudes to me as ever the
fountain was free of the stream. And I minded the Scripture about the
sin of Israel at Meribah, when the people murmured, although Moses
had brought water from the dry rock that the congregation might
drink and live. Sae, I wad not trust mysell with another look at poor
Woodend, for the very blue reek that came out of the lum-head pat me
in mind of the change of market-days with us."

In this resigned and Christian temper she pursued her journey,
until she was beyond this place of melancholy recollections, and not
distant from the village where Butler dwelt, which, with its old-fashioned church and steeple, rises among a tuft of trees, occupying the
ridge of an eminence to the south of Edinburgh. At a quarter of a
mile's distance is a clumsy square tower, the residence of the laird,
who, in former times, with the habits of the predatory chivalry of
Germany, is said frequently to have annoyed the city of Edinburgh, by
intercepting the supplies and merchandize which came to the town
from the southward.

This village, its tower, and its church, did not lie precisely in

Jeanie's road towards England; but they were not much aside from it, and the village was the abode of Butler. She had resolved to see him in the beginning of her journey, because she conceived him the most proper person to write to her father concerning her resolution and her hopes. There was probably another reason latent in her affectionate bosom. She wished once more to see the object of so early and so sincere an attachment, before commencing a pilgrimage, the perils of which she did not disguise from herself, although she did not allow them so to press upon her mind as to diminish the strength and energy of her resolution. A visit to a lover from a young person in a higher rank of life than Jeanie's, would have something forward and improper in its character. But the simplicity of her rural habits was inconsistent with these punctilious ideas of decorum, and no notion, therefore, of impropriety crossed her imagination, as, setting out upon a long journey, she went to bid adieu to an early friend.

There was still another motive that pressed on her mind with additional force as she approached the village. She had looked anxiously for Butler in the court-house, and had expected that certainly, in some part of that eventful day, he would have appeared to bring such countenance and support as he could give to his old friend, and the protector of his youth, even if her own claims were laid aside. She knew, indeed, that he was under a certain degree of restraint; but she still had hoped he would have found means to emancipate himself from it, at least for one day. In short, the wild and wayward thoughts which Wordsworth has described as rising in an absent lover's imagination, suggested as the only explanation of his absence, that Butler must be very ill. And so much had this wrought on her imagination, that when she approached the cottage in which her lover occupied a small apartment, and which had been pointed out to her by a maiden with a milk-pail on her head, she trembled at anticipating the answer she might receive on enquiring for him.

Her fears in this case had, indeed, only hit upon the truth. Butler, whose constitution was naturally feeble, did not soon recover the fatigue of body and distress of mind which he had suffered, in consequence of the tragical events with which our narrative commenced. The painful idea that his character was breathed on by suspicion, was an aggravation to his distress.

But the most cruel addition, was the absolute prohibition laid by the magistrates on his holding any communication with Deans or his family. It had unfortunately appeared likely to them, that some intercourse might be again attempted with that family by Robertson, through the medium of Butler, and this they were anxious to intercept, or prevent if possible. The measure was not meant as a harsh or

injurious severity on the part of the magistrates; but, in Butler's circumstances, it pressed cruelly hard. He felt he must be suffering
under the bad opinion of the person who was dearest to him, from an
imputation of unkind desertion, the most alien to his nature.

This painful thought, pressing on a frame already injured, brought
on a succession of slow and lingering feverish attacks, which greatly
impaired his health, and at length rendered him incapable even of the
sedentary duties of the school, on which his bread depended. Fortunately, old Mr Whackbairn, who was the principal of the little parochial establishment, was sincerely attached to Butler. Besides that he
was sensible of his merits and value as an assistant, which had greatly
raised the credit of his little school, the ancient pedagogue, who had
himself been tolerably educated, retained some taste for classical lore,
and would gladly relax after the drudgery of the school was over, by
conning a few pages of Horace or Juvenal with his usher. A similarity
of taste begot kindness, and he, accordingly, saw Butler's increasing
debility with great compassion, roused up his own energies to teaching the school in the morning hours, insisted upon his assistant's
reposing himself at that period, and, besides, supplied him with such
comforts as the patient's situation required, and his own means were
inadequate to compass.

Such was Butler's situation, scarce able to drag himself to the place
where his daily drudgery must gain his daily bread, and racked with a
thousand fearful anticipations concerning the fate of those who were
dearest to him in the world, when the trial and condemnation of Effie
Deans put the cope-stone upon his mental misery.

He had a particular account of these events from a fellow student,
who resided in the same village, and who, having been present on
the melancholy occasion, was able to place it in all its agony of
horrors before his excruciated imagination. That sleep should have
visited his eyes, after such a curfew-note, was impossible. A thousand dreadful visions haunted his imagination all night, and in the
morning he was awaked from a feverish slumber, by the only circumstance which could have added to his distress—the visit of an intrusive ass.

This unwelcome visitant was no other than Bartholine Saddletree.
The worthy and sapient burgher had kept his appointment at Mac-
Roskie's, with Plumdamas and some other neighbours, to discuss the
Duke of Argyle's speech, the justice of Effie Deans's condemnation,
and the improbability of her obtaining a reprieve. The sage conclave
disputed high and drank deep, and on the next morning Bartholine
felt, as he expressed it, as if his head was like a "confused progress of
writts."

To bring his reflective powers to their usual serenity, Saddletree resolved to take a morning's ride upon a certain hackney, which he, Plumdamas, and another honest shopkeeper, combined to maintain by joint subscription, for occasional jaunts for the purpose of business or exercise. As Saddletree had two children boarded with Whack-bairn, and was, as we have seen, rather fond of Butler's society, he turned his palfrey's head towards Libberton, and came, as we have already said, to give the unfortunate usher that additional vexation, of which Imogene complains so feelingly when she says,

> I'm sprighted with a fool—
> Sprighted and angered worse.——

If any thing could have added gall to bitterness, it was the choice which Saddletree made of a subject for his prosing harangues, being the trial of Effie Deans, and the probability of her being executed. Every word fell on Butler's ear like the knell of a death-bell, or the note of a screech-owl.

Jeanie paused at the door of her lover's humble abode upon hearing the loud and pompous tones of Saddletree sounding from the inner apartment, "Credit me, it will be sae, Mr Butler.—Brandy cannot save her.—She maun gang down the Bow wi' the lad in the pioted coat at her heels.—I am sorry for the lassie—But the law, sir, maun hae its course.

> Vivat Rex,
> Currat Lex,

as the poet has it, in whilk of Horace's odes I know not."

Here Butler groaned, in utter impatience of the brutality and ignorance which Bartholine had contrived to amalgamate into one sentence. But Saddletree, like other prosers, was blessed with a happy obtuseness of perception concerning the unfavourable impression which he sometimes made on his auditors. He proceeded to deal forth his scraps of legal knowledge without mercy, and concluded by asking Butler, "Was it na a pity my father didna send me to Utrecht? Havena I missed the chance to turn out as *clarissimus* an *ictus*, as auld Grunwiggin himsell?—Whatfor dinna ye speak, Mr Butler? Wad I no hae been a *clarissimus ictus?*—Eh, man?"

"I really do not understand you, Mr Saddletree," said Butler, thus pushed hard for an answer. His faint and exhausted tone of voice was instantly drowned in the sonorous bray of Bartholine.

"No understand me, man?—*Ictus* is Latin for a lawyer, is it not?"

"Not that ever I heard of," answered Butler, in the same dejected tone.

"The de'il ye didna!—See, man, I got the word but this morning out of a memorial of Mr Crossmyloof's—see there it is, *ictus clarissi-*

mus et perti—peritissimus—it's a' Latin, for it's printed in the Italian types."

"O you mean *juris-consultus.—Ictus* is an abbreviation for *juris-consultus.*"

"Dinna tell me, man," persevered Saddletree, "there's nae abbreviates except in adjudications; and this is a' about a servitude of stillicide—that is to say, water-drap, (maybe ye'll say that's no Latin neither) in Mary King's Close, in the High Street."

"Very likely," said poor Butler, overwhelmed by the noisy perseverance of his visitor. "I am not able to dispute with you."

"Few folks are—few folks are, Mr Butler, though I say it, that should na say it," returned Bartholine, with great complacence. "Now it will be twa hours yet or ye're wanted in the schule, and as ye arena weel, I'll sit wi' you to divert ye, and explain to ye the nature of a stillicide. Ye maun ken the pursuer, Mrs Crombie, a very decent woman, is a friend of mine, and I hae stude her friend in this case, and brought her wi' credit into the court, and I doubtna, that in due time she will win out o' it wi' credit, win she or lose she. Ye see, being an inferior tenement or laigh-house, we grant ourselves to be burthened wi' the *stillicide*, that is, that we are obligated to receive the natural water-drap of the superior tenement, sae far as the same fa's frae the heavens, on the roof of our neighbour's house, and from thence by the gutters or eaves upon our laigh tenement. But the other night comes a Highland quean of a lass, and she flashes, God kens what, out at the eastmost window of Mrs MacPhail's house, that's the superior tenement. I believe the auld women wad hae greed, for Luckie MacPhail sent down the lass to tell my friend Mrs Crombie that she had made the gardy-loo out of the wrang window, out o' respect for twa Highlandmen that were speaking Gaelic in the close below the right ane. But luckily for Mrs Crombie, I just chanced to come in in time to break aff the communing, for it's a pity the point suldna be tried. We had Mrs MacPhail into the Ten-Mark Court—The hieland limmer of a lass wanted to swear hersell free—but haud ye there, says I"—

The detailed account of this important suit might have lasted until poor Butler's hour of rest was completely exhausted, had not Saddletree been interrupted by the noise of voices at the door. The woman of the house where Butler lodged, on returning with her pitcher from the well, whence she had been fetching water for the family, found our heroine Jeanie Deans standing at the door, impatient of the prolix harangue of Saddletree, yet unwilling to enter until he should have taken his leave.

The good woman abridged the period of hesitation by enquiring, "Was ye wanting the gudeman or me, lass?"

"I wanted to speak with Mr Butler, if he's at leasure," replied Jeanie.

"Gang in bye then, my woman," answered the goodwife; and opening the door of the room, she announced this additional visitor, with "Mr Butler, here's a lass wants to speak t'ye."

The surprise of Butler was extreme, when Jeanie, who seldom stirred half a mile from home, entered his apartment upon this annunciation.

"Good God!" he said, starting from his chair, while alarm restored to his cheek the colour of which sickness had deprived it; "some new misfortune must have happened."

"None, Mr Reuben, but what ye must hae heard of—but O ye are looking ill yoursell!"—for not even the "hectic of a moment" had concealed from her affectionate eye the ravages which lingering disease and anxiety of mind had made in her lover's person.

"No: I am well—quite well," said Butler, with eagerness; "if I can do anything to assist you, Jeanie—or your father."

"Ay, to be sure," said Saddletree; "the family may be considered as limited to them twa now, just as if Effie had never been in the tailzie, puir thing. But Jeanie, lass, what brings you out to Libberton sae air in the morning, and your father lying ill in the Luckenbooths?"

"I had a message frae my father to Mr Butler," said Jeanie, with embarrassment; but instantly feeling ashamed of the fiction to which she had resorted, for her love of and veneration for truth was almost quaker-like, she corrected herself—"that is to say, I wanted to speak with Mr Butler about some business of my father's and puir Effie's."

"Is it law business?" said Bartholine; "because if it be, ye had better tak my opinion on the subject than his."

"It is not just law business," said Jeanie, who saw considerable inconvenience might arise from letting Mr Saddletree into the secret purpose of her journey; "but I want Mr Butler to write a letter for me."

"Very right," said Mr Saddletree; "and if ye'll tell me what it is about, I'll dictate to Mr Butler as Mr Crossmyloof does to his clerk. Get your pen and ink *in initialibus*, Mr Butler."

Jeanie looked at Butler, and wrung her hands with vexation and impatience.

"I believe, Mr Saddletree," said Butler, who saw the necessity of getting rid of him at all events, "that Mr Whackbairn will be somewhat affronted, if you do not hear your boys called up to their lessons."

"Indeed, Mr Butler, and that's as true; and I promised to ask a half-play-day to the schule, so that the bairns might gang and see the hanging, which canna but have a pleasing effect on their young minds, seeing there is no knowing what they may come to themselves.—Odd

so, I didna mind ye were here, Jeanie Deans; but ye maun use yoursell
to hear the matter spoken o'.—Keep Jeanie here till I come back, Mr
Butler; I winna bide ten minutes."

And with this unwelcome assurance of an immediate return, he
relieved them of the embarrassment of his presence.

"Reuben," said Jeanie, who saw the necessity of using the interval
of his absence in discussing what had brought her there, "I am bound
on a lang journey—I am ganging to Lunnon to ask Effie's life at the
king and at the queen."

"Jeanie! you are surely not yourself," answered Butler, in the
utmost surprise; "*you* go to London—*you* address the king and
queen!"

"And what for no, Reuben?" said Jeanie, with all the composed
simplicity of her character; "it is but speaking to a mortal man and
woman when a' is done. And their hearts maun be made o' flesh and
blood like other folk's, and Effie's story wad melt them were they
stane. Forbye, I hae heard that they are no sic bad folks as what the
jacobites ca's them."

"Yes, Jeanie," said Butler; "but their magnificence—their retinue
—the difficulty of getting audience?"

"I have thought of a' that, Reuben, and it shall not break my spirit.
Nae doubt their claes will be very grand, wi' their crowns on their
heads, and their sceptres in their hands, like the great King Ahasuerus
when he sate upon his royal throne foranent the gate of his house, as
we are told in Scripture. But I have that within me that will keep my
heart from failing, and I am amaist sure that I will be strengthened to
speak the errand I came for."

"Alas! alas!" said Butler, "the kings now-a-days do not sit in the
gate to administer justice, as in patriarchal times. I know as little of
courts as you do, Jeanie, by experience; but by reading and report, I
know that the King of Britain does every thing by means of his ministers."

"And if they be upright, God-fearing ministers," said Jeanie, "it's
sae muckle the better chance for Effie and me."

"But you do not even understand the most ordinary words relating
to a court," said Butler; "by the ministry is meant the king's official
servants."

"Nae doubt," returned Jeanie, "he maun hae a great number mair, I
dare to say, than the duchess has at Dalkeith, and great folk's servants
are aye mair saucy than themselves. But I'll be decently put on, and I'll
offer them a trifle o' siller, as if I came to see the palace. Or if they
scruple that, I'll tell them I am come on a business of life and death,
and then they will surely bring me to speech of the king and queen?"

Butler shook his head. "O, Jeanie, this is entirely a wild dream. You can never see them but through some great lord's intercession, and I think it is scarce possible even then."

"Weel, but maybe I can get that too," said Jeanie, "with a little helping from you."

"From me! Jeanie, this is the wildest imagination of all."

"Ay; but it is not, Reuben—Havena I heard you say, that your grandfather (whom my father never likes to hear about) did some gude turn langsyne to the forbear of this Maccallanmore, when he was Lord of Lorn?"

"He did so," said Butler, eagerly, "and I can prove it.—I will write to the Duke of Argyle—report speaks him a good kindly man, as he is known for a brave soldier and true patriot—I will conjure him to stand between your sister and this cruel fate. There is but a poor chance of success, but we will try all means."

"We *must* try all means," replied Jeanie; "but writing winna do it—a letter canna look, and pray, and beg, and beseech, as the human voice can do to the human heart. A letter's like the music that the leddies have for their spinets—naething but black scores, compared to the same tune played or sung. It's word of mouth maun do't, or naething, Reuben."

"You are right," said Reuben, recollecting his firmness, "and I will hope that Heaven has suggested to your kind heart and firm courage the only possible means of saving the life of this unfortunate girl. But, Jeanie, ye must not take this most perilous journey alone; I have an interest in you, and I will not agree that my Jeanie throws herself away. You must even, in the present circumstances, give me a husband's right to protect you, and I will go with you myself on this journey, and assist ye to do your duty by your family."

"Alas, Reuben!" said Jeanie in her turn, "this must not be; a pardon will not gie my sister her fair fame again, or make me a bride fitting for an honest man and an usefu' minister. Wha wad mind what he said in the pu'pit, that had to wife the sister of a woman that was condemned for sic wickedness?"

"But, Jeanie," pleaded her lover, "I do not believe, and I cannot believe, that Effie has done this deed."

"Heaven bless you for saying sae, Reuben," answered Jeanie; "but she maun bear the blame o't after all."

"But that blame, were it justly laid on her, does na fa' on you?"

"Ah, Reuben, Reuben," replied the young woman, "ye ken it is a blot that spreads to kith and kin.—Ichabod—as my poor father says—the glory is departed from our house; for the poorest man's house has a glory, where there are true hands, a devout heart, and an honest fame—And the last has gaen frae us."

"But, Jeanie, consider your word and plighted faith to me; and wad ye go and undertake such a journey without a man to protect you, and what should that protector be but your husband?"

"You are kind and good, Reuben, and wad take me wi' a' my shame, I doubt na. But ye canna but own that this is no time to marry or be given in marriage. Na, if that suld ever be, it maun be in another and a better season.—And, dear Reuben, ye speak of protecting me on my journey—Alas! who will protect and take care of you—your very limbs tremble with standing for ten minutes on the floor; how could you undertake a journey as far as Lunnon?"

"But I am strong—I am well," continued Butler, sinking in his seat totally exhausted, "at least I will be quite well to-morrow."

"Ye see, and ye ken, ye maun just let me depart," said Jeanie, after a pause; and then taking his extenuated hand, and gazing kindly in his face, she added, "It's e'en a grief the mair to me to see you in this way. But ye maun keep up your heart for Jeanie's sake, for if she isna your wife, she will never be the wife of living man. And now gie me the paper for Maccallanmore, and bid God speed me on my way."

There was something of romance in Jeanie's venturous resolution; yet, on consideration, as it seemed impossible to alter it by persuasion, or to give her assistance but by advice, Butler, after some further debate, put into her hands the paper she desired, which, with the muster-roll in which it was folded up, were the sole memorials of the stout and enthusiastic Bible Butler, his grandfather. While Butler sought this document, Jeanie had time to take up his pocket Bible. "I have marked a scripture," she said, as she again laid it down, "with your kylevine pen, that will be useful to us baith. And ye maun tak the trouble, Reuben, to write a' this to my father, for, God help me, I have neither hand nor head for lang letters at ony time, forbye now; and I trust him entirely to you, and I trust you you'll soon win to see him. And, Reuben, when ye do win to the speech o' him, mind a' the auld man's bits o' ways for Jeanie's sake; and dinna speak o' Latin or English terms to him, for he's o' the auld warld, and downa bide to be fashed wi' them, though I dare say he may be wrang. And dinna ye say muckle to him, but set him on speaking himsell, for he'll bring himsell mair comfort that way. And O, Reuben, the poor lassie in yon dungeon—but I needna bid your kind heart—gie her what comfort ye can sae soon as they will let ye see her—tell her—but I winna speak mair about her, for I maunna take leave o' ye wi' the tear in my ee, for that wadna be canny.—God bless ye, Reuben!"

To avoid so ill an omen she left the room hastily, while her features yet retained the mournful and affectionate smile which she had compelled them to wear, in order to support Butler's spirits.

It seemed as if the power of sight, of speech, and of reflection, had left him as she disappeared from the room, which she had entered and retired from so like an apparition. Saddletree, who entered immediately afterwards, overwhelmed him with questions, which he answered without understanding them, and with legal disquisitions, which conveyed to him no iota of meaning. At length the learned burgess recollected that there was a Baron Court to be held at Loanhead that day, and though it was hardly worth while, "he might as weel go to see if there was ony thing doing, as he was acquainted with the baron-baillie, who was a decent man, and would be glad of a word of legal advice."

So soon as he had departed, Butler flew to the Bible, the last book which Jeanie had touched. To his extreme surprise, a paper, containing two or three pieces of gold, dropped from the book. With a black lead pencil, she had marked the sixteenth and twenty-fifth verses of the thirty-seventh Psalm,—"A little that a righteous man hath is better than the riches of many wicked."—"I have been young and now am old, yet have I not seen the righteous forsaken, nor his seed begging bread."

Deeply impressed with the affectionate delicacy which shrouded its own generosity under the cover of a providential supply to his wants, he pressed the gold to his lips with more ardour than ever the metal was greeted by a miser. To emulate her devout firmness and confidence seemed now the pitch of his ambition, and his first task was to write an account to David Deans of his daughter's resolution and journey southward. He studied every sentiment, and even every phrase, which he thought could reconcile the old man to her extraordinary resolution. The effect which this epistle produced will be hereafter adverted to. Butler committed it to the charge of an honest clown, who had frequent dealings with Deans in the sale of his dairy produce, and who readily undertook a journey to Edinburgh, to put the letter into his own hands.*

Chapter Three

My native land, good night.
LORD BYRON

IN THE PRESENT DAY, a journey from Edinburgh to London is a matter at once safe, brief, and simple, however inexperienced or

---

* By dint of assiduous research I am enabled to certiorate the reader, that the name of this person was Saunders Broadfoot, and that he dealt in the wholesome commodity called kirn-milk, (*Anglice,* butter-milk).—J. C.

unprotected the traveller. Numerous coaches of different rates of charge, and as many packets, are perpetually passing and repassing betwixt the capital of Britain and her northern sister, so that the most timid or indolent may execute such a journey upon a few hours' notice. But it was different in 1737. So slight and infrequent was the intercourse betwixt London and Edinburgh, that men still alive remember that upon one occasion the mail from the former city arrived at the General Post-Office in Scotland, with only one letter in it. The usual mode of travelling was by means of post-horses, the traveller occupying one and his guide another, in which manner, by relays of horses from stage to stage, the journey might be accomplished in a wonderfully short time by those who could endure fatigue. To have their bones shaken to pieces by a constant change of those hacks, was a luxury for the rich—the poor were under the necessity of using the mode of conveyance with which nature had provided them.

With a strong heart, and a frame patient of fatigue, Jeanie Deans, travelling at the rate of twenty miles a-day, and sometimes farther, traversed the southern part of Scotland, and advanced as far as Durham.

Hitherto she had been either among her own country-folks, or those to whom her bare feet and tartan screen were objects too familiar to attract much attention. But as she advanced, she perceived that both circumstances exposed her to sarcasms and taunts, which she might otherwise have escaped; and, although in her heart she thought it unkind, and unhospitable, to sneer at a passing stranger on account of the fashion of her attire, yet she had the good sense to alter those parts of her dress which attracted ill-natured observation. Her checked screen was deposited carefully in her bundle, and she conformed to the national extravagance of wearing shoes and stockings for the whole day.

She confessed afterwards, that "besides the wastrife, it was lang or she could walk sae comfortably with the shoes as without them, but there was often a bit saft heather by the road-side, and that helped her weel on." The want of the screen, which was drawn over the head like a veil, she supplied by a *bon-grace*, as she called it; a large straw bonnet, like those worn by the English maidens when labouring in the fields. "But I thought unco shame o' mysell," she said, "the first time I pat on a married woman's *bon-grace*, and me a single maiden."

With these changes she had little, as she said, to make "her kenspeckle when she didna speak," but her accent and language drew down on her so many jests and gibes, couched in a worse *patois* by far than her own, that she soon found it was her interest to speak as little and as seldom as possible. She answered, therefore, civil salutations of

chance passengers with a civil curtesy, and chose, with anxious circumspection, such places of repose as looked at once most decent
and most sequestered. She found the common people of England,
although inferior in courtesy to strangers, such as was then practised
in her own more unfrequented country, yet, upon the whole, by no
means deficient in the real duties of hospitality. She readily obtained
food, and shelter, and protection at a very moderate rate, which sometimes the generosity of mine host altogether declined, with a blunt
apology,—"Thee hast a lang way afore thee, lass; and I'se ne'er take
penny out of single woman's purse; it's the best friend thou canst have
o' th' road."

It often happened, too, that mine hostess was struck with "the tidy,
nice, Scotch body," and procured her an escort or a cast in a waggon
for some part of the way, or gave her useful advice and recommendation respecting her resting-places.

At York, our pilgrim stopped for the best part of a day, partly to
recruit her strength,—partly because she had the good luck to obtain a
lodging in an inn kept by a country-woman,—partly to indite two
letters to her father and Reuben Butler; an operation of some little
difficulty, her habits being by no means those of literary composition.
That to her father was in the following words:

DEAREST FATHER,

"It makes my present pilgrimage heavy and burthensome more
than through the sad occasion to reflect that it is without your knowledge, which, God knows, was far contrary to my heart. For Scripture
saith that the vow of the daughter should not be binding without
consent of the father, wherein it may be I have been guilty to tak this
wearie journey without your consent. Nevertheless, it was borne in
upon my minde that I should be an instrument to help my poor sister
in this extremity of needcessity, otherwise I wald not, for wealth or for
world's gear, or for the hail lands of Da'keith and Lugton, have done
the like o' this, without your free will and knowledge. O, deer father,
as ye wad desire a blessing upon my journey, and upon your househald, speak a word or write a line of comfort to yon poor prisoner. If
she has sinned, she has sorrowed and suffered, and ye ken better than
me, that we maun forgie others, as we pray to be forgi'en. Dear father,
forgive my saying this muckle, for it doth not become a young head to
instruct grey hairs; but I am sae far frae ye, that my heart yearns to ye
a', and fain wad I hear that ye had forgi'en her trespass, and sae I nae
dout say mair than may become me. The folk here are civil, and, like
the barbarians unto the holy Apostle, hae shown me much kindness;
and there are a sort of chosen people in the land, for they hae some

kirks without orguns that are like ours, and are called meeting-houses, where the minister preaches without a gown. But most of the country are prelatists, whilk is awfu' to think; and I saw twae men that were ministers following hunds, as bauld as Roslin or Driden, the young Laird of Loupthedike, or ony wild gallant in Lothian. A sorrowfu' sight to behold! O, dear father, may a' blessings be with your down-lying and uprising, and remember in your prayers your affectionate daughter to command,

"JEAN DEANS."

A postscript bore, "I learned from a decent woman, a grazier's widow, that they hae a cure for the mur-ill in Cumberland, whilk is ane pint, as they ca't, of yill, whilk is a drible in comparison of our gawsie Scots pint, and hardly a muchkin, boil'd wi' sape and hartes-horn draps, and teemed doun the creature's throat wi' ane whorn. Ye might try it on the bauson-faced year-auld quey—An it does nae gude, it can do nae ill.—She was a kind woman, and seemed skeely about horned beasts. When I reach Lunnon, I intend to gang to our cousin Mistress Glass, the tobacconist, at the sign o' the Thistle, wha is so ceevil as to send you down your spleuhan-fu' anes a-year, and as she must be well kenn'd in Lunnon, I dout not easily to find out whare she bides."

Being seduced into betraying our heroine's confidence thus far, we will stretch our communication a step beyond, and impart to the reader her letter to her lover.

"MR REUBEN BUTLER,

"Hoping this will find you better, this comes to say, that I have reached this great town safe, and am not wearied with walking, but the better for it. And I have seen many things which I trust to tell you one day, also the muckle Kirk of this place; and all around the city are milns, whilk havena muckle-wheels nor miln-dams, but gang by the wind—strange to behold. Ane millar asked me to gang in and see it work, but I wald not, for I am not com to the south to mak acquaint-ance wi' strangers. I keep the straight road, and just beck if ony speaks to me ceevilly, and answer naebody with the tong but women of mine ain sect. I wish, Mr Butler, I kend ony thing that wad mak ye weel, for thae hae mair medicines in this town of York than wad cure a' Scot-land, and surely some of them wad be gude for your complaints. If ye had a kindly motherly body to nurse ye, and no to lute ye waste yoursell wi' reeding—whilk ye read mair than aneugh with the bairns in the scule—and to gie ye warm milk in the morning, I wad be mair easy for ye. Dear Mr Butler, keep a gude heart, for we are in the hands of ane that kens better what is gude for us than we ken what is for our-sells. I haena doubt to do that for which I am come—I canna doubt it—I winna think to doubt it—because, if I haena full assurance, how shall I bear myself with earnest entreaties in the great folk's presence. But to ken that ane's purpose is right, and to make their heart strong, is the way to get through the warst day's dargue. The bairns' rime says, that the warst blast of the borrowing days couldna kill the three silly poor hog-lams. And if it be God's pleasure, we that are sindered in sorrow may meet again in joy, even on this hither side of Gordan. I dinna bid ye mind what I said at our partin' anent my poor father and that misfortunate lassie, for I ken you will do sae for the sake of cristian charity, whilk is mair than the entreaties of her that is your servant to command,

"JEAN DEANS."

This letter also had a postscript. "Dear Reuben, if ye think that it wad hae been right for me to have said mair and kinder things to ye, just think that I hae written sae, since I am sure I wish a' that is kind and right to ye and by ye. Ye will think I am turned waster, for I wear clean hose and shoon every day; but it's the fashion here for decent bodies, and ilk land has its ain laugh. Ower and aboon, if laughing days were e'er to come back again till us, ye wad laugh weel to see my round face at the far end of a strae bongrace, that looks as muckle and round as the middell aisle in Libberton Kirk. But it sheds the sun weel aff, and keeps unceevil folk frae staring as if ane were a worrycow. I sall tell ye by writ how I come on wi' the Deuke of Argyle, whan I win up to Lunnon. Direct a line, to say how ye are, to me, to the charge of Mrs Margaret Glass, tobacconist, at the sine of the Thistell, Lunnon, whilk, if it assures me of your health, will make my mind sae muckell easier. Excuse bad spelling and writing, as I have ane ill pen."

The orthography of these epistles may seem to the southron to require a better apology than the letter expresses; but, on behalf of the heroine, I would have them to know, that, thanks to the care of Butler, Jeanie Deans wrote and spelled fifty times better than half the women of rank in Scotland at that period, whose strange orthography and singular diction form the strongest contrast to the good sense which their correspondence usually intimates.

For the rest, in the tenor of these epistles, Jeanie expressed, per-haps, more hopes, a firmer courage, and better spirits, than she actu-ally felt. But this was with the amiable idea of relieving her father and lover from apprehensions on her account, which she was sensible must greatly add to their other troubles. "If they think me weel, and like to do weel," said the poor pilgrim to herself, "my father will be kinder to Effie, and Butler will be kinder to himsell. For I ken weel that they will think mair o' me, than I do o' mysell."

Accordingly, she sealed her letters carefully, and put them into the post-office with her own hand, after many enquiries concerning the time in which they were likely to reach Edinburgh. When this duty was performed, she readily accepted her landlady's pressing invitation to dine with her, and remain till the next morning. The hostess, as we have said, was her country-woman, and the eagerness with which Scottish people meet, communicate, and, to the extent of their power, assist each other, although it is often objected to us, as a prejudice and narrowness of sentiment, seems, on the contrary, to arise from a most justifiable and honourable feeling of patriotism, combined with a conviction, which, if undeserved, would long since have been confuted by experience, that the habits and principles of the nation are a sort of guarantee for the character of the individual. At any rate, if the extensive influence of this national partiality be considered as an additional tie, binding man to man, and calling forth the good offices of such as can render them to the countryman who happens to need them, we think it must be found to exceed, as an active and efficient motive to generosity, that more impartial and wider principle of general benevolence, which we have sometimes seen pleaded as an excuse for assisting no individual whatever.

Mrs Bickerton, lady of the ascendant of the Seven Stars, in the Castle-gate, York, was deeply infected with the unfortunate prejudices of her country. Indeed, she displayed so much kindness to Jeanie Deans, (because, she herself, being a Merse woman, *marched* with Mid-Lothian, in which Jeanie was born,) shewed such motherly regard to her, and such anxiety for her farther progress, that Jeanie thought herself safe, though by temper sufficiently cautious, in communicating her whole story to her.

Mrs Bickerton raised her hands and eyes at the recital, and exhibited much wonder and pity. But she also gave some effectual good advice.

She required to know the strength of Jeanie's purse, reduced by her deposit at Libberton, and the necessary expence of her journey to about fifteen pounds. "This," she said, "would do very well, providing she could carry it a' safe to London."

"Safe?" answered Jeanie; "I'se warrant my carrying it safe, bating the needful expences."

"Ay, but highwaymen, lassie," said Mrs Bickerton; "for ye are come into a more civilized, that is to say, a more dangerous country than the north, and how ye are to get forward, I do not profess to know. If ye could wait here eight days, our waggons would go up, and I would recommend you to Joe Broadwheel, who would see you safe to the Swan and two Necks. And dinna sneeze at Joe, if he should be for drawing up wi' you" (continued Mrs Bickerton, her acquired English mingling with her national and original dialect), "he's a handy boy, and a wanter, and no lad better thought on o' th' road; and the English make good husbands enough, witness my poor man, Moses Bickerton, as is i' th' kirk-yard."

Jeanie hastened to say, that she could not possibly wait for the setting forth of Joe Broadwheel, being internally by no means gratified with the idea of becoming the object of his attention during the journey.

"Aweel, lass!" answered the good landlady, "then thou must pickle in thine ain poke-nook, and belt thine girdle thine ain gate. But take my advice, and hide thy gold in thy stays, and keep a piece or two and some silver, in case thou be'st spoke withal; for there's as wud lads haunts within a day's walk from hence, as on the Braes of Doun in Perthshire. And, lass, thou maunna gang staring through Lunnon, asking wha kens Mrs Glass at sign o' th' Thistle; marry, they would laugh thee to scorn. But gang thou to this honest man," and she put a direction into Jeanie's hand, "he kens maist part of the sponsible Scottish folks in the city, and he will find out your friend for thee."

Jeanie took the little introductory letter with sincere thanks; but, something alarmed on the subject of the highway robbers, her mind recurred to what Ratcliffe had mentioned to her, and briefly narrating the circumstances which placed a document so extraordinary in her hands, she put the paper he had given her into the hand of Mrs Bickerton.

The Lady of the Seven Stars did not, indeed, ring a bell, because such was not the fashion of the time, but she whistled on a silver-call, which was hung by her side, and a tight serving-maiden entered the room.

"Tell Dick Ostler to come here," said Mrs Bickerton.

Dick Ostler accordingly made his appearance;—a queer, knowing, shambling animal, with a hatchet-face, a squint, a game-arm, and a limp.

"Dick Ostler," said Mrs Bickerton, in a tone of authority that showed she was (at least by adoption) Yorkshire too, "thou knowst most people and most things o' th' road."

"Eye, eye, God help me, mistress," said Dick, shrugging his shoulders betwixt a repentant and a knowing expression—"Eye! I ha' know'd a thing or twa i' ma day, mistress." He looked sharp and laughed—looked grave and sighed, as one who was prepared to take the matter either way.

"Ken'st thou this wee bit paper amang the rest, man?" said Mrs Bickerton, handing him the protection which Ratcliffe had given Jeanie Deans.

When Dick had looked at the paper, he winked with one eye, extended his grotesque mouth from ear to ear, like a navigable canal, scratched his head powerfully, and then said, "Ken?—ay—maybe we ken summat, an' it were for nae harm to him, mistress?"

"None in the world," said Mrs Bickerton; "only a dram of Hollands to thyself, man, an' thou wilt speak."

"Why then," said Dick, giving the head-band of his breeches a knowing hoist with one hand, and kicking out one foot behind him to accommodate the adjustment of that important habiliment, "I dares to say the pass will be kenn'd weel aneugh on the road, an that be all."

"But what sort of a lad was he?" said Mrs Bickerton, winking to Jeanie, as proud of her knowing ostler.

"Why, what ken I?—Jem the Rat—why he was Cock o' the North within this twelmonth—he and Scotch Wilson, Handie Dandie, as they called him—but he's been out o' this country a while, as I rackon; but ony gentleman, as keeps the road o' this side Stamford, will respect Jem's pass."

Without asking further questions, the landlady filled Dick Ostler a bumper of Hollands. He ducked with his head and shoulders, scraped with his more advanced hoof, bolted the alcohol, to use the learned phrase, and withdrew to his own domains.

"I would advise thee, Jean," said Mrs Bickerton, "an thou meetst with ugly customers o' th' road, to show them this bit paper, for it will serve thee, assure thyself."

A neat little supper concluded the evening. The exported Scotswoman, Mrs Bickerton by name, eat heartily of one or two seasoned dishes, drank some sound old ale, and a glass of stiff negus; while she gave Jeanie a history of her gout, admiring how it was possible that she, whose fathers and mothers for many generations had been farmers in Lammermoor, could have come by a disorder so totally unknown to them. Jeanie did not chuse to offend her friendly landlady, by speaking her mind on the probable origin of this complaint, but she thought on the flesh-pots of Egypt, and, in spite of all entreaties to better fare, made her evening meal upon vegetables, with a glass of fair water.

Mrs Bickerton assured her, that the acceptance of any reckoning was entirely out of the question, furnished her with credentials to her correspondent in London, and to several inns upon the road where she had some influence or interest, reminded her of the precautions she should adopt for concealing her money, and as she was to depart early in the morning, took leave of her very affectionately, taking her word that she would visit her on her return to Scotland, and tell her how she had managed, and that *summum bonum* for a gossip, "all how and about it." This Jeanie faithfully promised.

Chapter Four

And Need and Misery, Vice and Danger, bind,
In sad alliance, each degraded mind.

AS OUR TRAVELLER set out early on the ensuing morning to pro-secute her journey, and was in the act of leaving the inn-yard, Dick Ostler, who either had risen early or neglected to go to bed, either circumstance being equally incident to his calling, hollo'd out after her,—"The top of the morning to you, Moggie. Have a care o' Gumoorsbury Hill, young one. Robin Hood's dead and gwone, but there be takers yet in the vale of Bever." Jeanie looked at him as if to request a further explanation, but, with a leer, a shuffle, and a shrug, inimitable, (unless by Emery,) Dick turned again to the raw-boned steed, which he was currying, and sung as he employed the comb and brush,—

"Robin Hood was a yeoman right good,
    And his bow was of trusty yew;
And if Robin bid stand on the King's lea-land,
    Pray, why should not we say so too?"

Jeanie pursued her journey without further enquiry, for there was nothing in Dick's manner that inclined her to prolong their confer-ence. A painful day's journey brought her to Ferrybridge, the best inn, then and since, upon the great northern road; and an introduction from Mrs Bickerton, added to her own simple and quiet manners, so propitiated the landlady of the Swan in her favour, that the good dame procured her the convenient accommodation of a pillion and post-horse then returning to Tuxford, so that she accomplished, upon the second day after leaving York, the longest journey she had yet made. She was a good deal fatigued by a mode of travelling to which she was less accustomed than to walking, and it was considerably later than usual on the ensuing morning that she felt herself able to resume her pilgrimage. At noon the hundred-armed Trent, and the blackened ruins of Newark Castle, demolished in the great civil war, lay before her. It may easily be supposed, that Jeanie had no curiosity to make antiquarian researches, but, entering the town, went straight to the inn to which she had been directed at Ferrybridge. While she pro-cured some refreshment, she observed that the girl who brought it to her, looked at her several times with fixed and peculiar interest, and at last, to her infinite surprise, enquired if her name was not Deans, and if she was not a Scotchwoman, going to London upon justice business. Jeanie, with all her simplicity of character, had some of the caution of her country, and, according to Scottish universal custom, she answered the question by another, requesting the girl would tell her why she asked these questions?

The Maritornes of the Saracen's Head, Newark, replied, "Two women has passed that morning, who had made enquiries after one Jeanie Deans, travelling to London on such an errand, and could scarce be persuaded that she had not passed on."

Much surprised, and somewhat alarmed, (for what is inexplicable is usually alarming,) Jeanie questioned the wench about the particular appearance of these two women, but could only learn that the one was aged, and the other young; that the latter was the taller, and that the former spoke most, and seemed to maintain an authority over her companion, and that both spoke with the Scottish accent.

This conveyed no information whatever, and with an indescribable presentiment of evil designed towards her, Jeanie adopted the resolution of taking post-horses for the next stage. In this, however, she could not be gratified. Some accidental circumstances had occasioned what is called a run upon the road, and the landlord could not accommodate her with a guide and horses. After waiting some time, in hopes that a pair which had gone southward would return in time for her use, she at length, feeling ashamed of her own pusillanimity, resolved to prosecute her journey in her usual manner.

"It was all plain road," she was assured, "except a high mountain called Gunnersbury Hill, about three miles from Grantham, which was her stage for the night."

"I'm glad to hear there's a hill," said Jeanie, "for baith my sight and my very feet are weary o' sic tracks o' level ground—it looks a' the way between this and York as if a' the land had been trenched and levelled, whilk is very wearisome to my Scots een. When I lost sight of a muckle blue hill they ca' Ingleboro', I thought I hadna a friend left in this strange land."

"For the matter of that, young woman," said mine host, "an you be so fond o' hills, I carena an thou could'st carry Gunnersbury away with thee in thy lap, for it's a murther to post-horses. But here's to thy good journey, and may'st thou win well through it, for thou is a bold and a canny lass."

So saying, he took a powerful pull at a solemn tankard of home-brewed ale.

"I hope there is nae bad company on the road, sir?" said Jeanie.

"Why, when it's clean without them I'll thatch Groby pool wi' pancakes. But there arena sae mony now; and since they lost Jem the

Rat, they hold together no better than the men of Marsham when they lost their common. Take a drop ere thou goest," he concluded, offering her the tankard; "thou wilt get naething at night save Grantham gruel, nine grots, and a gallon of water."

Jeanie courteously declined the tankard, and enquired what was her "lawing?"

"Thy lawing? Heaven help thee, wench, what ca'st thou that?"

"It is—I was wanting to ken what's to pay," replied Jeanie.

"Pay? Lord help thee!—why nought, woman—we hae drawn no liquor but a gill o' beer, and the Saracen's Head can spare a mouthful o' meat to a stranger like o' thee, that cannot speak Christian language. So here's to thee once more. The same again, quoth Mark of Bellgrave," and he took another profound pull at the tankard.

The travellers who have visited Newark more lately, will not fail to remember the remarkable civil and gentlemanly manners of the person who now keeps the principal inn there, and may find some amusement in contrasting them with those of his more rough precessor. But we believe it will be found that the polish has worn off none of the real worth of the metal.

Taking leave of her Lincolnshire Gaius, Jeanie resumed her solitary walk, and was somewhat alarmed when evening and twilight overtook her in the open ground which extends to the foot of Gunnersbury Hill, and is intersected with patches of copse and with swampy spots. The extensive commons on the north road, most of which are now enclosed, and in general a relaxed state of police, exposed the traveller to highway robbery in a degree which is now unknown, excepting in the immediate vicinity of the metropolis. Aware of this circumstance, Jeanie mended her pace when she heard the trampling of a horse behind, and instinctively drew to one side of the road, as if to allow as much room for the rider to pass as might be possible. When the animal came up, she found that it was bearing two women, the one placed on a side-saddle, the other on a pillion behind her, as may be still occasionally seen in England.

"A braw gude night to ye, Jeanie Deans," said the foremost female as the horse passed our heroine; "What think ye o' yon bonny hill yonder, lifting its brow to the moon? Trow ye yon's the gate to Heaven ye are sae fain of?—maybe we'll win there the night, God sain us, though our minny here's rather driegh in the upgang."

The speaker kept changing her seat in the saddle, and half-stopping the horse, as she brought her body round, while the woman that sate behind her on the pillion seemed to urge her on in words which Jeanie heard but imperfectly.

"Haud your tongue, ye moon-raised b——, what is your business with . . . or with heaven or hell either?"

"Troth, mither, no muckle wi' heaven, I doubt, considering wha I carry ahint me—and as for hell, it will fight its ain battle at its ain time, I'se be bound.—Come, naggie, hist awa, man, as an thou wert a broomstick, for a witch rides thee—

With my curtch on my foot, and my shoe on my hand,
I glance like the wildfire through brugh and through——"

The tramp of the horse, and the increasing distance, drowned the rest of her song, but Jeanie heard for some time the inarticulate sounds ring along the waste.

Our pilgrim remained stupified with undefined apprehension. The being named by her name in so wild a manner, and in a strange country, without further explanation or communing, by a person who thus strangely flitted forward and disappeared before her, came near to the supernatural sounds in Comus:—

The airy tongues, which syllable men's names
On sands, and shores, and desert wildernesses.

And although widely different in features, deportment, and rank, from the lady of that enchanting masque, the continuation of the passage may be happily applied to Jeanie Deans upon this singular alarm:—

These thoughts may startle well, but not astound
The virtuous mind, that ever walks attended
By a strong siding champion—Conscience.

In fact, it was, with the recollection of the affectionate and dutiful errand on which she was engaged, her right, if such a word could be applicable, to expect protection in a task so meritorious. She had not advanced much further, with a mind calmed by these reflections, when she was disturbed by a new and more instant subject of terror. Two men, who had been lurking among some copse, started up as she advanced, and met her on the road in a menacing manner. "Stand and deliver," said one of them, a short stout fellow, in a smock-frock, such as are worn by waggoners.

"The woman," said the other, a tall thin figure, "does not understand the words of action.—Your money, my precious, or your life."

"I have but very little money, gentlemen," said poor Jeanie, tendering that portion which she had separated from her principal stock, and kept apart for such an emergence; "but if you're determined to have it, to be sure you must have it."

"This won't do, my girl. D—n me, if it shall pass," said the shorter ruffian; "do ye think gentlemen are to hazard their lives on the road to be cheated in this way? We'll have every farthing you have got, or we will strip you to the skin, curse me."

His companion, who seemed to have something like compassion for the horror which Jeanie's countenance now expressed, said, "No, no, Tom, this is one of the precious sisters, and we'll take her word, for once, without putting her to the stripping proof.—Hark ye, my lass, if you'll look up to Heaven, and say, this is the last penny you have about ye, why, hing it, we'll let you pass."

"I am not free," answered Jeanie, "to say what I have about me, gentlemen, for there's life and death depends on my journey; but if you leave me as much as will find me in bread and water, I'll be satisfied, and thank you, and pray for you."

"D—n your prayers," said the short fellow, "that's a coin won't pass with us;" and at the same time made a motion to seize her.

"Stay, gentlemen," said Jeanie, Ratcliffe's pass suddenly occurring to her; "perhaps you know this paper."

"What devil is she after now, Frank?" said the more savage ruffian —"Do you look at it, for, d—n me, if I could read it, if it were for the benefit of my clergy."

"This is a jark from Jem Ratcliffe," said the taller, having looked at the bit of paper. "The wench must pass by our cutter's law."

"I say no," answered his companion; "Rat is left the lay and turned blood-hound, they say."

"We may need a good turn from him all the same," said the taller ruffian again.

"But what are we to do then?" said the shorter man.—"We promised, you know, to strip the wench, and send her begging back to her own beggarly country, and now you are for letting her go on."

"I did not say that," said the other fellow, and whispered to his companion, who replied, "Be alive about it then, and don't keep chattering till some travellers come up to nab us."

"You must follow us off the road, young woman," said the taller.

"For the love of God!" exclaimed Jeanie, "as you were born of woman, dinna ask me to leave the road; rather take all I have in the world."

"What the devil is the wench afraid of?" said the other fellow. "I tell you you shall come to no harm; but if you will not leave the road and come with us, d—n me, but I beat your brains out where you stand."

"Thou art a rough bear, Tom," said his companion.—"An ye touch her, I'll give thee a shake by the collar shall make the Leicester beans rattle in thy guts.—Never mind him, girl, I will not allow him to lay a finger on you, if you walk quietly on with us; but if you keep jabbering there, d—n me, but I leave him to settle it with you."

This threat conveyed all that is terrible to the imagination of poor Jeanie, who saw in him that "was of milder mood" her only protection from the most brutal treatment. She, therefore, not only followed him, but even held him by the sleeve, lest he should escape from her; and the fellow, hardened as he was, seemed something touched by those marks of confidence, and repeatedly assured her, that he would suffer her to receive no harm.

They conducted their prisoner in a direction leading more and more from the public road, but she observed that they kept a sort of track or bye-path, which relieved her from some part of her apprehensions, which would have been greatly increased had they not seemed to follow a determined and ascertained route. After about half an hour's walking, all three in profound silence, they approached an old barn, which stood on the edge of some cultivated ground, but remote from every thing like habitation. It was itself, however, tenanted, for there was light in the windows.

One of the foot-pads scratched at the door, which was opened by a female, and they entered with their unhappy prisoner. An old woman, who was preparing food by the assistance of a stifling fire of lighted charcoal, asked them, in the name of the devil, what they brought the wench there for, and why they did not strip her and turn her adrift on the common?

"Come, come, Mother Blood," said the tall man, "we'll do what's right to oblige you, and we'll do no more; we are bad enough, but such as you would make us devils incarnate."

"She has got a *jark* from Jem Ratcliffe," said the short fellow, "and Frank here won't hear of our putting her through the mill."

"No, that will I not, by G—d," answered Frank; "but if old Mother Blood could keep her here for a little while, or send her back to Scotland without hurting her, why, I see no harm in that—not I."

"I'll tell you what, Frank Levitt," said the old woman, "if you call me Mother Blood again, I'll paint this gulley (and she held a knife up as if about to make good her threat,) in the best blood in your body, my bonnie boy."

"The price of oatmeal must be up in the north," said Frank, "that puts Mother Blood so much out of humour."

Without a moment's hesitation the fury darted her knife at him with the vengeful dexterity of a wild Indian. As he was on his guard, he avoided the missile by a sudden motion of his head, but it whistled past his ear, and stuck in the clay wall of a partition behind.

"Come, come, mother," said the robber, seizing her by both wrists, "I shall teach you who's master;" and so saying, he forced the hag, who strove vehemently, backwards by main force, until she sunk on a bunch of straw, and then letting go her hands, he held up his finger toward her in the menacing posture by which a maniac is intimidated by his keeper. It appeared to produce the desired effect; for she did not attempt to rise from the seat on which he had placed her, or to resume any measures of actual violence, but wrung her withered hands with impotent rage, and brayed and howled like a demoniac.

"I will keep my promise with you, you old devil," said Frank; "the wench shall not go forward on the London road, but I will not have you touch a hair of her head, if it were but for your insolence."

This intimation seemed to compose in some degree the vehement passion of the old hag; and while her exclamations and howls sunk into a low, maundering, growling tone of voice, another personage was added to this singular party.

"Eh, Frank Levitt," said this new-comer, who entered with a hop, step, and jump, which at once conveyed her from the door into the centre of the party, "were ye killing our mother? or were ye cutting the gruntler's weasand that Tam brought in this morning? or have ye been reading your prayers backward, to bring up my auld acquaintance the de'il amang ye?"

The tone of the speaker was so particular, that Jeanie immediately recognised the woman who had rode foremost of the pair which passed her just before she met the robbers; a circumstance which greatly increased her terror, as it served to shew that the mischief designed against her was premeditated, though by whom, or for what cause, she was totally at a loss to conjecture. From the style of her conversation, the reader also may probably acknowledge in this female, an old acquaintance in the earlier part of our narrative.

"Out, ye mad devil," said Tom, whom she had disturbed in the midst of a draught of some liquor with which he had found means of accommodating himself; "betwixt your Bess of Bedlam pranks, and your dam's frenzies, a man might live quieter in the devil's ken than here."—And he again resumed the broken jug out of which he had been drinking.

"And wha's this o't?" said the mad woman, dancing up to Jeanie Deans, who, although in great terror, yet watched the scene with a resolution to let nothing pass unnoticed which might be serviceable in assisting her escape, or informing her as to the true nature of her situation, and the danger attending it,—"Wha's this o't!" again exclaimed Madge Wildfire. "Douce Davie Deans, the auld doited whig body's daughter in a gypsey's barn, and the night setting in; this is a sight for sair een!—Eh sirs, the falling off o' the godly!—And the t'other sister's i' the tolbooth at Edinburgh; I am very sorry for her, for my share—it's my mother wusses ill to her, and no me—though maybe I hae as muckle cause."

"Hark ye, Madge," said the taller ruffian, "you have not such a touch of the devil's blood as the hag your mother, who may be his dam for what I know—take this young woman to your kennel, and do not let the devil enter, though he should ask in God's name."

"Ow ay; that I will, Frank," said Madge, taking hold of Jeanie by the arm, and pulling her along; "for it's no for decent Christian young leddies, like her and me, to be keeping the like o' you and Tyburn Tam company at this time o' night. Sae gudeen t'ye, sirs, and mony o' them; and may ye a' sleep till the hangman wauken ye, and then it will be weel for the country."

She then, as her wild fancy seemed suddenly to prompt her, walked demurely towards her mother, who, seated by the charcoal fire, with the reflection of the red light on her withered and distorted features marked by every evil passion, seemed the very picture of Hecate at her infernal rites; and suddenly dropping on her knees, said, with the manner of a child six years old, "Mammie, hear me say my prayers before I go to bed, and say God bless my bonny face, as ye used to do lang syne."

"The de'il flay the hide o' it to sole his brogues wi'," said the old lady, aiming a buffet at the suppliant, in answer to her pious request.

The blow missed Madge, who, being probably acquainted by experience with the mode in which her mother was wont to confer her maternal benedictions, slipt out of arm's length with great dexterity and quickness. The hag then starting up, and, seizing a pair of old fire-tongs, would have amended her motion, by beating out the brains either of her daughter or of Jeanie, (she did not seem greatly to care which), when her hand was once more arrested by the man whom they called Frank Levitt, who, seizing her by the shoulder, flung her from him with great violence, exclaiming, "What, Mother Damnable— again, and in my sovereign presence!—Hark ye, Madge of Bedlam, get to your hole with your play-fellow, or we shall have the devil to pay here, and nothing to pay him with."

Madge took Levitt's advice, retreating as fast as she could, and dragging Jeanie along with her into a sort of recess, partitioned off from the rest of the barn, and filled with straw, from which it appeared that it was intended for the purpose of slumber. The moonlight shone through an open hole upon a pillion, a pack-saddle, and one or two wallets, the travelling furniture of Madge and her amiable mother.— "Now, saw ye e'er in your life," said Madge, "sae dainty a chamber of deas? see as the moon shines down sae caller on the fresh strae! There isna a pleasanter cell in Bedlam, for as braw a place as it is on the outside.—Were ye ever in Bedlam?"

"No," answered Jeanie faintly, appalled by the question, and the way in which it was put, yet willing to sooth her insane companion, being in circumstances so unhappily precarious and suspicious, that even the society of this gibbering mad-woman seemed a species of protection.

"Never in Bedlam?" said Madge, as if with some surprise.—"But ye'll hae been in the cells at Edinburgh?"

"Never," repeated Jeanie.

"Weel, I think thae daft carles the magistrates send naebody to Bedlam but me—they maun hae an unco respect for me, for whenever I am brought to them, they aye hae me back to Bedlam. But troth, Jeanie, (this she said in a very confidential tone,) to tell ye my private mind about it, I think ye are at nae great loss; for the keeper's a cross patch, and he maun hae it a' his ain gate, to be sure, or he makes the place waur than hell. I often tell him he's the daftest in a' the house.— But what are they making sic a skirling for?—De'il ane o' them's get in here—it wadna be mensefu'! I will sit wi' my back again the door; it winna be that easy stirring me."

"Madge!"—"Madge!"—"Madge Wildfire!"—"Madge devil! what have ye done with the horse?" was repeatedly asked by the men without.

"He's at his supper, puir thing," answered Madge; "de'il an ye were at yours, an it was scauding brimstane, and then we wad hae less o' your din."

"His supper?" answered the more sulky ruffian—"What d'ye mean by that?—Tell me where he is, or I will knock your Bedlam brains out!"

"He is in Gaffer Gabblewood's wheat-close, an ye maun ken."

"His wheat-close, you crazed jilt!" answered the other, with an accent of great indignation.

"O, dear Tyburn Tam, man, what ill will the blades of the young wheat do to the puir nag?"

"That is not the question," said the other robber; "but what the country will say to us to-morrow, when they see him in such quarters. —Go, Tom, and bring him in; and avoid the soft ground, my lad; leave no hoof-track behind you."

"I think you give me always the fag of it, whatever is to be done," grumbled his companion.

"Leap, Laurence, you're long enough," said the other; and the fellow left the barn accordingly, without farther remonstrance.

In the meanwhile, Madge had arranged herself for repose in the straw; but still in a half-sitting posture, with her back resting against the door of the hovel, which, as it opened inwards, was in this manner kept shut by the weight of her person.

"There's mair shifts bye stealing, Jeanie," said Madge Wildfire;

"though whiles I can hardly get our mother to think sae. Whae wad
hae thought but mysell of making a bolt of my ain back-bane! But it's
no sae strong as thae that I hae seen in the tolbooth at Edinburgh. The
hammermen of Edinburgh are to my mind afore the world for making
stancheons, ring-bolts, fetter-bolts, bars, and locks. And they arena
that bad at girdles for carcakes neither; though the Cu'ross hammermen have the gree for that. My mother had ance a bonny Cu'ross
girdle, and I thought to have baked carcakes on it for my puir wean
that's dead and gane, nae fair way—but we maun a' dee, ye ken, Jeanie
—You Cameronian bodies ken that brawlies; and ye're for making life
a hell upon earth that ye may be less unwullin to part wi' it. But as
touching Bedlam that ye were speaking about, I'se ne'er recommend
it muckle the tae gate or the tother, be it right—be it wrang. But ye ken
what the sang says." And, pursuing the unconnected and fluent wanderings of the mind, she sung aloud—

> "In the bonnie cells of Bedlam,
> Ere I was one and twenty,
> I had hempen bracelets strong,
> And merry whips, ding-dong,
> And prayer and fasting plenty.

"Weel, Jeanie, I am something herse the night, and I canna sing
muckle mair; and troth, I think, I am ganging to sleep."

She drooped her head on her breast, a posture from which Jeanie,
who would have given the world for an opportunity of quiet to consider the means and the probability of her escape, was very careful not
to disturb her. After nodding, however, for a minute or two, with her
eyes half closed, the unquiet and restless spirit of her malady again
assailed Madge. She raised her head, and spoke, but with a lowered
tone, which was again gradually overcome by drowsiness, to which the
fatigue of a day's journey on horseback had probably given unwonted
occasion. "I dinna ken what makes me sae sleepy—I amaist never
sleep till my bonny Lady Moon gangs till her bed—mair by token,
when she's at the full, ye ken, rowing aboon us yonder in her grand
silver coach—I have danced to her my lane sometimes for very joy—
and whiles dead folk came and danced wi' me—the like o' Jock Porteous, or ony body that I had kenn'd when I was living—for ye maun
ken I was ance dead mysell." Here the poor maniac sung in a low and
wild tone,

> "My banes are buried in yon kirk-yard
> Sae far ayont the sea,
> And it is but my blithesome ghaist
> That's speaking now to thee.

"But after a', Jeanie, my woman, naebody kens weel wha's living and wha's dead. Or wha's gane to Fairyland—there's another question. Whiles I think my puir bairn's dead—ye ken very weel it's buried —but that signifies naething. I have had it on my knee a hundred times, and a hunder till that, since it was buried—and how could that be were it dead, ye ken—it's mere impossible."—And here, some conviction half-overcoming the reveries of her imagination, she burst into a fit of crying and ejaculation, "Waes me! waes me! waes me!" till at length she moaned and sobbed herself into a deep sleep, which was soon intimated by her breathing hard, leaving Jeanie to her own melancholy reflections and observations.

Chapter Five

Bind her quickly; or, by this steel,
I'll tell, although I truss for company.
FLETCHER

THE IMPERFECT LIGHT which shone into the window enabled Jeanie to see that there was scarcely any chance of making her escape in that direction, for the aperture was high in the wall, and so narrow, that, could she have climbed up to it, she might well doubt whether it would have admitted her to pass her body through it. An unsuccessful attempt to escape would be sure to draw down worse treatment than she now received, and she, therefore, resolved to watch her opportunity carefully ere making such a perilous effort. For this purpose she applied herself to the ruinous clay partition, which divided the hovel in which she now was from the rest of the waste barn. It was decayed and full of cracks and chinks, one of which she enlarged with her fingers, cautiously and without noise, until she could obtain a plain view of the old hag and the taller ruffian, whom they called Levitt, seated together beside the decayed fire of charcoal, and apparently engaged in close conference. She was at first terrified by the sight, for the features of the old woman had a hideous cast of hardened and inveterate malice and ill-humour, and those of the man, though naturally less unfavourable, were such as corresponded well with licentious habits, and a lawless profession.

"But I remembered," said Jeanie, "my worthy father's tales of a winter evening, how he was confined with the blessed martyr Mr James Renwick, who lifted up the fallen standard of the true Reformed Kirk of Scotland, after the worthy and renowned Daniel Cameron, our last blessed bannerman, had fallen among the swords of the wicked at Airds-moss, and how the very hearts of the wicked malefactors and murtherers, whom they were confined withal, were melted like wax at the sound of their doctrine: and I bethought mysell, that the same help that was wi' them in their strait, wad be wi' me in mine, an' I could but watch the Lord's time and opportunity for delivering my feet from their snare; and I minded the Scripture of the blessed Psalmist, whilk he insisteth on, as weel in the forty-second as in the forty-third Psalm, 'Why art thou cast down, O my soul, and why art thou disquieted within me? Hope in God, for I shall yet praise Him, who is the health of my countenance, and my God.'"

Strengthened in a mind naturally calm, sedate, and firm, by the influence of religious confidence, this poor captive was enabled to attend to, and comprehend, a great part of an interesting conversation which passed betwixt those into whose hands she had fallen, notwithstanding that their meaning was partly disguised by the occasional use of cant terms, of which Jeanie knew not the import, and partly by the low tone in which they spoke, and by their mode of supplying their broken phrases by shrugs and signs, as is usual amongst those of their disorderly profession.

The man opened the conversation by saying, "Now, dame, you see I am true to my friend.—I have not forgot that you *planked a chury*,* which helped me through the bars of the Castle of York, and I came to do your work without asking questions, for one good turn deserves another. But now that Madge, who is as loud as Tom of Lincoln, is somewhat still, and this same Tyburn Neddie is shaking his gallows-heels after the old nag, why you must tell me what all this is about, and what's to be done—for d—n me if I touch the girl, or let her be touched, and she with Jem Rat's pass too."

"Thou art an honest lad, Frank," answered the old woman, "but e'en too kind for thy trade; thy tender heart will get thee into trouble. I will see ye gang up Holbourn Hill backward, and a' on the word of some silly lown that could never hae rapped to ye had ye drawn your knife across his weasand."

"You may be bilked there, old one," answered the robber; "I have known many a pretty lad cut short in his first summer upon the road, because he was something hasty with his flats and sharps. Besides, a man would fain live out his two years with a good conscience. So, tell me what all this is about, and what's to be done for you that one can do decently."

"Why, you maun know, Frank—but first taste a snap of right Hollands." She drew a flask from her pocket, and filled the fellow a large bumper, which he pronounced to be the right thing.—"You must know then, Frank—winna ye mend your hands?" again offering the flask.

* Concealed a knife.

"No, no—when a woman wants mischief from you she always begins by filling you drunk.—D—n all Dutch courage.—What I do I do soberly—I'll last the longer for that too."

"Well, then, you must know," resumed the old woman, without any further attempts at propitiation, "that this girl is going to London."

Here Jeanie could only distinguish the word sister.

The robber answered in a louder tone, "Fair enough that; and what the devil is your business with it?"

"Business enough, I think. If the b— queers the noose, that silly cull will marry her."

"Well—and who cares if he does," said the man.

"Who cares, ye donnard Neddie? *I* care; and I will strangle her with my own hand, rather than she should come to Madge's preferment."

"Madge's preferment? Does your old blind eye see no further than that? If he is as you say, d'ye think he'll ever marry a moon-calf like Madge? Ecod that's a good one—Marry Madge Wildfire!"

"Hark ye, ye crack-rope padder, born beggar and bred thief! suppose he never marries the wench, is that a reason he should marry another, and that other to hold my daughter's place, and she crazed, and I a beggar, and all along of him? But I know that of him will hang him—I know that of him will hang him, if he had a thousand lives—I know that of him will hang—hang—hang him!"

She grinned as she repeated and dwelt upon the fatal monosyllable, with the emphasis of a vindictive fiend.

"Then why don't you hang—hang—hang him?" said Frank, repeating her words contemptuously. "There would be more sense in that, than in wreaking yourself here upon two wenches that have done you and your daughter no ill."

"No ill?" answered the old woman—"and he to marry this jail-bird, if ever she gets her foot loose!"

"But as there is no chance of his marrying a bird of your brood, I cannot, for my soul, see what you have to do with all this," again replied the robber, shrugging his shoulders. "Where there is aught to be got, I'll go as far as my neighbours, but I hate mischief for mischief's sake."

"And would you go nae length for revenge?" said the hag—"for revenge, the sweetest morsel to the mouth that ever was cooked in hell!"

"The devil may keep it for his own eating then," said the robber; "for hang me if I like the sauce he dresses it with."

"Revenge!" continued the old woman; "why it is the best reward the devil gives us for our time here and hereafter. I have wrought hard for it—I have suffered for it, and I have sinned for it—And I will have it, or there is neither justice in heaven nor in hell!"

Levitt had by this time lighted a pipe, and was listening with great composure to the frantic and vindictive ravings of the old hag. He was too much hardened by his course of life to be shocked with them —too indifferent, and probably too stupid, to catch any part of their animation or energy. "But, mother," he said, after a pause, "still I say, that if revenge is your wish, you should take it on the young fellow himself."

"I wish I could," she said, drawing in her breath, with the eagerness of a thirsty person while mimicking the action of drinking—"I wish I could—but no—I cannot—I cannot."

"And why not?—You would think little of peaching and hanging him for this Scotch affair.—Rat me, one might have milled the Bank of England, and less noise about it."

"I have nursed him at this withered breast," answered the old woman, folding her hands on her bosom, as if pressing an infant to it, "and though he has proved an adder to me—though he has been the destruction of me and mine—though he has made me company for the devil, if there be a devil, and food for hell, if there be such a place, yet I cannot take his life—No, I cannot," she continued, with an appearance of rage against herself; "I have thought of it—I have tried it—but, Francis Levitt, I canna gang through wi't!—Na, na—he was the first bairn I ever nurst—ill I had been—and man can never ken what woman feels for the bairn she has held first to her bosom."

"To be sure," said Levitt, "we have no experience; but, mother, they say you ha'nt been so kind to other *bairns* as you call them, that have come in your way.—Nay, d—n me, never lay your hand on the whittle, for I am captain and leader here, and I will have no rebellion."

The hag, whose first motion had been, upon hearing the question, to grasp the haft of a large knife, now unclosed her hand, stole it away from the weapon, and suffered it to fall by her side, while she proceeded with a sort of smile—"Bairns! ye are joking, lad, wha wad touch bairns? Madge, puir thing, had a misfortune wi' ane—and the t'other—" Here her voice sunk so much, that Jeanie, though anxiously upon the watch, could not catch a word she said, until she raised her tone at the conclusion of the sentence—"so Madge, in her daffin', threw it into the Nor'-Loch, I trow."

Madge, whose slumbers, like those of most who labour under mental malady, had been short and were easily broken, now made herself heard from her place of repose.

"Indeed, mother, that's a great lie, for I did nae sic thing."

"Hush, thou hellicat devil," said her mother—"By Heaven! the other wench will be waking too."

"That may be dangerous," said Frank, and he rose and followed Meg Murdockson across the floor.

"Rise," said the hag to her daughter, "or I sall drive the knife between the planks into the Bedlam-back of thee!"

Apparently she at the same time seconded her threat, by pricking her with the point of a knife, for Madge, with a faint scream, changed her place, and the door opened.

The old woman held a candle in one hand, and a knife in the other. Levitt appeared behind her; whether with a view of preventing, or assisting her in any violence she might meditate, could not be well guessed. Jeanie's presence of mind stood her friend in this dreadful crisis. She had resolution enough to maintain the attitude and manner of one who sleeps profoundly, and to regulate even her breathing, notwithstanding the agitation of instant terror, so as to correspond with her attitude.

The old woman passed the light across her eyes; and although Jeanie's fears were so powerfully awakened by this movement, that she often declared afterwards, that she thought she saw the figures of her destined murtherers through her closed eyelids, she had still the resolution to maintain the feint on which her safety, perhaps, depended.

Levitt looked at her with fixed attention; he then turned the old woman out of the place, and followed her himself. Having regained the outer apartment, and seated themselves, Jeanie heard the highwayman say, to her no small relief, "She's as fast as if she were in Bedfordshire.—Now, old Meg, d—n me, if I can understand a glim of this story of yours, or what good it will do you to hang the one wench, and torment the other; but, rat ye, I will be true to my friend, and serve ye the way ye like it. I see it will be a bad job; but I do think I could get her down to Surfleet on the Wash, and so on board Tom Moonshine's neat lugger, and keep her out of the way three or four weeks, if that will please ye?—But d—n me if any one shall harm her, unless they have a mind to choke on a brace of blue plums.—It's a cruel bad job, and I wish you and it, Meg, were both at the devil."

"Never mind, hinny Levitt," said the old woman; "you are a ruffler, and will have a' your ain gate—She shanna gang to heaven an hour sooner for me; I carena whether she live or die—it's her sister—ay, her sister!"

"Well, well, no more about it, I hear Tom come in. We'll couch a hogshead,* and so better had you." They retired to repose, accordingly, and all was silent in this asylum of iniquity.

Jeanie lay for a long time awake. At break of day she heard the two

_____
* Lay ourselves down to sleep.

ruffians leave the barn, after whispering with the old woman for some time. The sense that she was now guarded only by persons of her own sex, gave her some confidence, and irresistible lassitude at length threw her into slumber.

When the captive awakened, the sun was high in heaven, and the morning considerably advanced. Madge Wildfire was still in the hovel which had served them for the night, and immediately bid her good morning, with her usual air of insane glee. "And d'ye ken, lass," said Madge, "there's queer things chanced since ye hae been in the land of Nod. The constables hae been here, lass, and they met my minnie at the door, and they hae whirled her awa to the Justice's about the man's wheat.—Dear! thae English churles think as muckle o' a blade of wheat or grass, as a Scots laird does about his maukins and his muirpoots. Now, lass, if ye like, we'll play them a fine jink; we will awa' out and tak a walk—they will make an unco wark when they miss us, but we can easily be back by dinner time, or before dark night at ony rate, and it will be some fun and fresh air.—But maybe ye wad like to take some breakfast, and than lie down again; I ken by mysell, there's whiles I can sit wi' my head on my hand the hale day, and havena a word to cast at a dog—and other whiles that I canna sit still a moment. That's when the folk think me warst, but I am aye canny enough—ye needna be feared to walk wi' me."

Had Madge Wildfire been the most raging lunatic, instead of possessing a doubtful, uncertain, and twilight sort of rationality, varying, probably, from the influence of the most trivial causes, Jeanie would hardly have objected to leave a place of captivity where she had so much to apprehend. She eagerly assured Madge that she had no occasion for farther sleep, no desire whatever for eating; and hoping internally that she was not guilty of sin in doing so, she flattered her keeper's crazy humour for walking in the woods.

"It's no a'thegether for that neither," said poor Madge; "but I am judging ye will win the better out o' thae folk's hands; no that they are a' thegither bad folks neither, but they have queer ways wi' them, and I whiles dinna think it has been ever very weel wi' my mother and me since we kept sic like company."

With the haste, the joy, the fear, and the hope of a liberated captive, Jeanie snatched up her little bundle, followed Madge into the free air, and eagerly looked round her for a human habitation; but none was to be seen. The ground was partly cultivated, and partly left in its natural state, according as the fancy of the slovenly agriculturists had decided. In its natural state, it was waste, in some places covered with dwarf trees and bushes, in others swamp, and elsewhere firm and dry downs or pasture grounds.

Jeanie's active mind next led her to conjecture which way the high road lay, whence she had been forced. If she regained that public road, she imagined she must soon meet some person, or arrive at some house, where she might tell her story, and request protection. But after a glance around her, she saw with regret that she had no means whatever of directing her course with any degree of certainty, and that she was still in dependence upon her crazy companion. "Shall we not walk upon the high road?" said she to Madge, in such a tone as a nurse uses to coax a child. "It's brawer walking on the road than amang thae wild bushes and whins."

Madge, who was walking very fast, stopped at this question, and looked at Jeanie with a sudden and scrutinizing glance that seemed to indicate complete acquaintance with her purpose. "Aha, lass!" she exclaimed, "are ye ganging to guide us that gate?—Ye'll be for making your heels save your hands, I am judging."

Jeanie hesitated for a moment, at hearing her companion thus express herself, whether she had not better take the hint, and try to outstrip and get rid of her. But she knew not in which direction to fly; she was by no means sure that she would prove the swiftest, and perfectly conscious that, in the event of her being pursued and over-taken, she would be inferior to the mad-woman in strength. She therefore gave up thoughts for the present of attempting to escape in that manner, and, saying a few words to allay Madge's suspicions, she followed in anxious apprehension the wayward path by which her guide thought proper to lead her. Madge, infirm of purpose, and easily reconciled to the present scene, whatever it was, began soon to talk with her usual diffuseness of ideas.

"It's a dainty thing to be in the woods on a fine morning like this—I like it far better than the towns, for there isna a wheen duddie bairns to be crying after ane, as if ane were a warld's wonder, just because ane maybe is a thought bonnier and better put-on than their neighbours—though, Jeanie, ye suld never be proud o' braw claiths, or beauty neither—waes me! they're but a snare.—I anes thought better o' them, and what came o't?"

"Are ye sure ye ken the way ye are taking us?" said Jeanie, who began to imagine that she was getting deeper into the woods, and more remote from the high road.

"Do I ken the road?—Wasna I mony a day living here, and what for shouldna I ken the road?—I might hae forgotten too, for it was afore my accident; but there are some things ane can never forget, let them try it as muckle as they like."

By this time they had gained the deepest part of a patch of wood-land. The trees were a little separated from each other, and at the foot of one of them, a beautiful poplar, was a hillock of moss, such as the poet of Grasmere has described. So soon as she arrived at this spot, Madge Wildfire, joining her hands above her head, with a loud scream that resembled laughter, flung herself all at once upon the spot, and remained lying there motionless.

Jeanie's first idea was to take the opportunity of flight; but her desire to escape yielded for a moment to apprehension for the poor insane being, who, she thought, might perish for want of relief. With an effort, which, in her circumstances, might be termed heroic, she stooped down, spoke in a soothing tone, and endeavoured to raise up the forlorn creature. She effected this with difficulty, and, as she placed her against the tree in a sitting posture, she observed with surprise, that her complexion, usually florid, was now deadly pale, and that her face was bathed in tears. Notwithstanding her own extreme danger, Jeanie was affected by the situation of her companion; and the rather, that through the whole train of her wavering and inconsistent state of mind and line of conduct, she discerned a general colour of kindness towards herself, for which she felt gratitude.

"Let me alane!—let me alane!" said the poor young woman, as her paroxysm of sorrow began to abate—"Let me alane—it does me good to weep. I canna shed tears, but maybe anes or twice a-year, and I aye come to wet this turf with them, that the flowers may grow fair, and the grass may be green."

"But what is the matter with you?" said Jeanie—"Why do you weep so bitterly?"

"There's matter enow," replied the lunatic,—"mair than ae puir mind can bear, I trow. Stay a bit, and I'll tell you a' about it; for I like ye, Jeanie Deans—a' body spoke weel about ye when we lived in the Pleasaunts—And I mind aye the drink o' milk ye gae me yon day, when I had been on Arthur's Seat for four-and-twenty hours, looking for the ship that somebody was sailing in."

These words recalled to Jeanie's recollection, that, in fact, she had been one morning much frightened by meeting a crazy young woman near her father's house at an early hour, and that as she appeared to be harmless, her apprehension had been changed into pity, and she had relieved the unhappy wanderer with some food, which she devoured with the haste of a famished person. The incident, trifling in itself, was at present of great importance, if it should be found to have made a favourable and permanent impression in her favour on the mind of the object of her charity.

"Yes," said Madge, "I'll tell ye a' about it, for ye are a decent man's daughter—Douce Davie Deans, ye ken—and maybe ye'll can teach me to find out the narrow way, and the strait path, for I have been burning bricks in Egypt, and walking through the weary wilderness of Sinai, for lang and mony a day. But whenever I think about mine errors, I am like to cover my lip for shame."—Here she looked up and smiled.—"It's a strange thing now—I hae spoke mair gude words to you in ten minutes, than I wad speak to my mother in as mony years— it is no that I dinna think on them—and whiles they are just at my tongue's end, but then comes the Devil, and brushes my lips with his black wing, and lays his broad black loof on my mouth—for a black loof it is, Jeanie—and sweeps away a' my gude thoughts, and dits up my gude words, and pits a wheen fule sangs and idle vanities in their place."

"Try, Madge," said Jeanie,—"try to settle your mind and make your breast clean, and you'll find your heart easier—Just resist the devil, and he will flee from you—and mind that, as my worthy father tells me, there is nae devil sae deceitfu' as our ain wandering thoughts."

"And that's true too, lass," said Madge, starting up; "and I'll gang a gate where the devil daurna follow me; and it's a gate that you will like dearly to gang—but I'll keep fast o' your arm, for fear Apollyon should stride across the path, as he did in the Pilgrim's Progress."

Accordingly she got up, and, taking Jeanie by the arm, began to walk forward at a great pace; and soon, to her companion's no small joy, came into a marked path, with the meanders of which she seemed perfectly acquainted. Jeanie endeavoured to bring her back to the confessional, but the fancy was gone by. In fact, the mind of this deranged being resembled nothing so much as a quantity of dry leaves, which may for a few minutes remain still, but are instantly discomposed and put in motion by the first casual breath of air. She had now got John Bunyan's parable into her head, to the exclusion of every thing else, and on she went with great volubility.

"Did ye never read the Pilgrim's Progress? And you shall be the woman Christiana, and I will be the maiden Mercy, for ye ken Mercy was of the fairer countenance, and the more alluring than her companion—and if I had my little messan dog here, it would be Great-heart their guide, ye ken, for he was e'en as bauld, that he wad bark at ony thing twenty times his size; and that was e'en the death of him, for he bit Corporal MacAlpine's heels ae morning when they were hauling me to the guard-house, and Corporal MacAlpine killed the bit faithfu' thing wi' his Lochaber axe—de'il pike the Highland banes o' him!"

"O fie, Madge," said Jeanie, "ye should not speak such words."

"It's very true," said Madge, shaking her head; "but then I maunna think on my puir bit doggie Snap, when I saw it lying dying in the gutter. But it is just as weel, for it suffered baith cauld and hunger when it was living, and in the grave there is rest for a' things—rest for the doggie, and my puir bairn, and me."

"Your bairn?" said Jeanie, conceiving that by speaking on such a topic, supposing it to be a real one, she could not fail to bring her companion to a more composed temper.

She was mistaken, however, for Madge coloured, and replied with some anger, "*My* bairn? ay, to be sure, my bairn. Whatfor shouldna I hae a bairn, and lose a bairn too, as weel as your bonnie tittie, the Lily of Saint Leonard's?"

The answer struck Jeanie with some alarm, and she was anxious to sooth the irritation she had unwittingly given occasion to. "I am very sorry for your misfortune"——

"Sorry? what wad ye be sorry for?" answered Madge. "The bairn was a blessing—that is, Jeanie, it wad hae been a blessing if it hadna been for my mother; but my mother's a queer woman.—Ye see, there was an auld carle wi' a bit land, and a gude clat o' siller besides, just the very picture of old Mr Feeblemind or Mr Ready-to-halt, that Great-heart delivered from Slaygood the giant, when he was rifling him, and about to pick his bones, for Slaygood was of the nature of the flesh-eaters—and Greatheart killed Giant Despair too—but I am doubting Giant Despair's come alive again, Jeanie, for a' the story book—I find him busy at my heart whiles."

"Weel, and so the auld carle," said Jeanie, for she was painfully interested in getting to the truth of Madge's history, which she could not but suspect was in some extraordinary way linked and entwined with the fate of her sister. She was also desirous, if possible, to engage her companion in some narrative which might be carried on in a lower tone of voice, for she was in great apprehension lest the elevated notes of Madge's conversation should direct her mother or the robbers in search of them.

"And so the auld carle," said Madge, repeating her words—"I wish ye had seen him stoiting about, aff ae leg on to the other, wi' a kind o' dot-and-go-one sort o' motion, as if ilk ane o' his twa legs had belanged to sindry folk—But Gentle George could take him aff brawly—Eh as I used to laugh to see George gang hip-hop like him. —I dinna ken, I think I laughed heartier then than what I do now, though maybe no just sae muckle."

"And who was Gentle George?" said Jeanie, endeavouring to bring her back to her story.

"O, he was Geordie Robertson, ye ken, when he was in Edinburgh; but that's no his right name neither—His name is——But what is your business wi' his name?" said she, as if upon sudden recollection.

"What have ye to do asking for folk's names?—Have ye a mind I should scour my knife between your ribs, as my mother says?"

As this was spoken with a menacing tone and gesture, Jeanie hastened to protest her total innocence of design in the accidental question which she had asked, and Madge Wildfire went on somewhat pacified.

"Never ask folk's names, Jeanie—it's no civil—I hae seen half a dozen o' folk in my mother's at anes, and ne'er ane o' them ca'd the ither by his name; and Daddie Ratton says, it is the maist uncivil thing may be, because these baillie bodies are aye asking fashious questions, whan ye saw sic a man, or sic a man; and if ye dinna ken their names, ye ken there can be nae mair about it."

In what strange school, thought Jeanie to herself, has this poor creature been bred up, where such remote precautions are taken against the pursuits of justice? What would my father or Reuben Butler think, if I were to tell them there are sic folk in the world? And to abuse the simplicity of this demented creature! O, that I were but safe at hame amang mine ain leal and true people! and I'll bless God, while I have breath, that placed me mongst those who live in his fear, and under the shadow of his wing.

She was interrupted by the insane laugh of Madge Wildfire, as she saw a magpie hop across the path.

"See there—that was the gate my auld joe used to cross the country, but no just sae lightly—he hadna wings to help his auld legs, I trow; but I behoved to have married him for a' that, Jeanie, or my mother wad hae been the dead of me. But than came in the story of my poor bairn, and my mother thought he wad be deaved wi' its skirling, and she pat it away in below the bit bourock of turf yonder, just to be out o' the gate; and I think she buried my best wits with it, for I have never been just mysell yet. And only think, Jeanie, after my mother had been at a' this pains, the auld doited body Johnny Drottle turned up his nose, and wadna hae aught to say to me! But it's little I care for him, for I have led a merry life ever since, and ne'er a braw gentleman looks at me but ye wad think he was ganging to drop off his horse for mere love of me. I have kenn'd some o' them put their hand in their pocket, and gie me as muckle as sixpence at a time, just for my weel-fa'ard face."

This speech gave Jeanie a dark insight into Madge's history. She had been courted by a wealthy suitor, whose addresses her mother had favoured, notwithstanding the objections of old age and deformity. She had been seduced by some profligate, and, to conceal her shame and promote the advantageous match she had planned, her mother had not hesitated to destroy the offspring of their intrigue.

That the consequence should be the total derangement of a mind which was constitutionally unsettled by giddiness and vanity, was extremely natural; and such was, in fact, the history of Madge Wildfire's insanity.

Chapter Six

So free from danger, free from fear,
They cross'd the court—right glad they were.
CHRISTABEL

PURSUING THE PATH which Madge had chosen, Jeanie Deans observed, to her no small delight, that marks of more cultivation appeared, and the thatched roofs of houses, with their blue smoke arising in little columns, were seen embosomed in a tuft of trees at some distance. The track led in that direction, and Jeanie, therefore, resolved, while Madge continued to pursue it, that she would ask her no questions; having had the penetration to observe, that by doing so she ran the risk of irritating her guide, or awakening suspicions, to the impressions of which, persons in Madge's unsettled state of mind are particularly liable.

Madge, therefore, uninterrupted, went on with the wild disjointed chat which her rambling imagination suggested; a mood in which she was much more communicative as to her own history, and that of others, than when there was any attempt made, by direct queries, or cross examination, to extract information on these subjects.

"It's a queer thing," she said, "but whiles I can speak about the bit bairn and the rest of it, just as if it had been another body's, and no my ain; and whiles I am like to break my heart about it—Had you ever a bairn, Jeanie?"

Jeanie replied in the negative.

"Ay; but your sister had though—and I ken what came o't too."

"In the name of heavenly mercy," said Jeanie, forgetting the line of conduct which she had hitherto adopted, "tell me but what became of that unfortunate babe, and"——

Madge stopped, looked at her gravely, and fixedly, and then burst into a great fit of laughing—"Aha, lass!—catch me if ye can—I think it's easy to gar ye trow ony thing.—How suld I ken ony thing o' your sister's wean? Lasses suld hae naething to do wi' weans till they are married—and then a' the gossips and cummers come in and feast as if it were the blithest day in the warld.—They say maidens' bairns are weel guided. I wot that wasna true of your tittie's and mine; but these are sad tales to tell—I maun just sing a bit to keep up my heart—It's a

sang that Gentle George made on me lang syne, when I went with him
to Lockington wake, to see him act upon a stage, in fine clothes, with
the player folks. He might have dune waur than married me that night
as he promised—better wed over the mixen* as over the moor, as they
say in Yorkshire—he may gang farther and fare waur—But that's a'
ane to the sang,——

> I'm Madge of the country, I'm Madge of the town,
> And I'm Madge of the lad I am blithest to own—
> The Lady of Beever in diamonds may shine,
> But has not a heart half so lightsome as mine.
>
> I am Queen of the Wake, and I'm Lady of May,
> And I lead the blithe ring round the May-pole to-day:
> The wild-fire that flashes so fair and so free
> Was never so bright, or so bonnie as me.

"I like that the best o' a' my sangs," continued the maniac, "because he
made it. I am often singing it, and that's maybe the reason folks ca' me
Madge Wildfire. I aye answer to the name, though it's no my ain, for
what's the use of making a fash?"

"But ye shouldna sing upon the Sabbath at least," said Jeanie, who,
amid all her distress and anxiety, could not help being scandalized at
the deportment of her companion, especially as they now approached
near to the little village or hamlet.

"Ay! is this Sunday?" said Madge. "My mother leads sic a life, wi'
turning night into day, that ane loses a' count o' the days o' the week,
and disna ken Sunday frae Saturday. Besides, it's a' your whiggery—
in England, folks sing when they like—And then, ye ken, you are
Christiana, and I am Mercy—and ye ken, as they went on their way
they sang."—And she immediately raised one of John Bunyan's dit-
ties:—

> "He that is down need fear no fall,
>   He that is low no pride;
> He that is humble ever shall
>   Have God to be his guide.
>
> Fulness to such a burthen is
>   That go on pilgrimage;
> Here little, and hereafter bliss,
>   Is best from age to age.

"And ye ken, Jeanie, I think there's much truth in that book the
Pilgrim's Progress. The boy that sings that song, was feeding his
father's sheep in the valley of humiliation, and Mr Greatheart says,
that he lived a merrier life, and had more of the herb called hearts-

* A homely proverb, signifying, better wed a neighbour than one fetched from a distance.—Mixen, signifies dunghill.

ease in his bosom, than they that wear silk and velvet like me, and are as bonny as I am."

Jeanie Deans had never read the fanciful and delightful parable to which Madge alluded. Bunyan was, indeed, a rigid Calvinist, but then he was also a member of a Baptist congregation, so that his works had no place on David Deans's shelf of divinity. Madge, however, at some time of her life, had been well acquainted, as it appeared, with the most popular of his performances, which, indeed, rarely fails to make a deep impression upon children and people of the lower rank.

"I am sure," she continued, "I may weel say I am come out of the City of Destruction, for my mother is Mrs Bat's-eyes, that dwells at Deadman's corner; and Frank Levitt, and Tyburn Tam, they may be likened to Mistrust and Guilt, that came galloping up and struck the poor pilgrim to the ground with a great club, and stole a bag of silver, which was most of his spending money, and so have they done to many, and will do to more. But now we will gang to the Interpreter's house, for I ken a man that will play the Interpreter right weel; for he has eyes lifted up to Heaven, the best of books in his hand, the law of truth written on his lips, and he stands as if he pleaded wi' men—O if I had minded what he said to me, I had never been the cast-away creature that I am!—But it is all over now.—But we'll knock at the gate, and then the keeper will admit Christiana, but Mercy will be left out—and then I'll stand at the door trembling and crying, and then Christiana—that's you, Jeanie,—will intercede for me. And then Mercy,—that's me, ye ken,—will faint; and then the Interpreter— yes, the Interpreter, that's Mr Staunton himself, will come out and take me—that's poor, lost, demented me—by the hand, and give me a pomegranate, and a piece of honeycomb, and a small bottle of spirits, to stay my fainting—and then the good times will come back again, and we'll be the happiest folk you ever saw."

In the midst of the confused assemblage of ideas indicated in this speech, Jeanie thought she saw a serious purpose on the part of Madge, to endeavour to obtain the pardon and countenance of some one whom she had offended; an attempt the most likely of all others to bring them once more into contact with law and legal protection. She, therefore, resolved to be guided by her while she was in so hopeful a disposition, and act for her own safety according to circumstances.

They were now close by the village, one of those beautiful scenes which are so often found in merry England, where the cottages, instead of being built in two straight lines, one on each side of a dusty high-road, stand in detached groupes, interspersed not only with large oaks and elms, but with fruit-trees, so many of which were at this time in flourish, that the grove seemed enamelled with their crimson and white blossoms. In the centre of the hamlet the parish church reared its little Gothic tower, from which at present was heard the Sunday chime of bells.

"We will wait here until the folks are a' in the church—they ca' the kirk a church in England, Jeanie, be sure you mind that—for if I was ganging forward amang them, a' the gaitts o' boys and lassies wad be crying at Madge Wildfire's tail, the little hell-rakers, and the beadle would be as hard upon us as if it was our fault. I like their skirling as ill as he does, I can tell him that; I often wish there was a het peat doun their throats when they set them up that gate."

Conscious of the disorderly appearance of her own dress after the adventure of the preceding night, and of the grotesque habit and demeanour of her guide, and sensible how important it was to secure an attentive and patient audience to her strange story from some one who might have the means to protect her, Jeanie readily acquiesced in Madge's proposal to rest under the trees, by which they were still somewhat screened, until the commencement of service should give them an opportunity of entering the hamlet without attracting a crowd around them. She made the less opposition, that Madge had intimated that this was not the village where her mother was in custody, and that the two squires of the pad were absent in a different direction.

She sate herself down, therefore, at the foot of an oak, and by assistance of a placid fountain which had been dammed up for the use of the villagers, and which served her as a natural mirror, she began— no uncommon thing with a Scottish maiden of her rank,—to arrange her toilette in the open air, and bring her dress, soiled and rumpled as it was, into such order as the place and circumstances admitted.

She soon perceived reason, however, to regret that she had set about this task, however decent and necessary, in the present time and society. Madge Wildfire, who, among other indications of insanity, had a most over-weening opinion of those charms, to which, in fact, she had owed her misery, and whose mind, like a raft upon a lake, was agitated and driven about at random by each fresh impulse, no sooner beheld Jeanie begin to arrange her hair, place her bonnet in order, rub the dust from her shoes and clothes, adjust her neck-handkerchief and mittans, and so forth, than with imitative zeal she began to bedizen and trick herself out with shreds and remnants of beggarly finery, which she took out of a little bundle, and which, when disposed around her person, made her appearance ten times more fantastic and apish than it had been before.

Jeanie groaned in spirit, but dared not interfere in a matter so delicate. Across the man's cap or riding-hat which she wore, Madge placed a broken and soiled white feather, intersected with one which had been shed from the train of a peacock. To her dress, which was a kind of riding-habit, she stitched, pinned, and otherwise secured, a large furbelow of artificial flowers, all crushed, wrinkled, and dirty, which had first bedecked a lady of quality, then descended to her Abigail, and dazzled the inmates of the servants-hall. A tawdry scarf of yellow silk, trimmed with tinsel and spangles, which had seen as hard service, and boasted as honourable a transmission, was next flung over one shoulder, and fell across her person in the manner of a belt or baldrick. Madge then stripped off the coarse ordinary shoes which she wore, and replaced them by a pair of dirty satin ones, spangled and embroidered to match the scarf, and furnished with very high heels. She had cut a willow switch in her morning's walk, almost as long as a boy's fishing-rod. This she set herself seriously to peel, and when it was transformed into such a wand as the Treasurer or High Steward bears on public occasions, she told Jeanie that she thought they now looked decent, as young women should do, upon the Sunday morning, and that as the bells had done ringing, she was willing to conduct her to the Interpreter's house.

Jeanie sighed heavily, to think it should be her lot on the Lord's day, and during kirk-time too, to parade the street of an inhabited village with so very grotesque a comrade; but necessity had no law, since, without a positive quarrel with the mad-woman, which, in the circumstances, would have been very unadvisable, she could see no means of shaking herself free of her society.

As for poor Madge, she was completely puffed up with personal vanity, and the most perfect satisfaction concerning her own dazzling dress, and superior appearance. They entered the hamlet without being observed, except by one old woman, who, being nearly "high-gravel blind," was only conscious that something very fine and glittering was passing by, and dropped as deep a reverence to Madge as she would have done to a countess. This filled up the measure of Madge's self-approbation. She minced, she ambled, she smiled, she simpered, and waved Jeanie Deans forward with the condescension of a noble *chaperone*, who has undertaken the charge of a country miss on her first journey to the capital.

Jeanie followed in patience, and with her eyes fixed on the ground, that she might save herself the mortification of seeing her companion's absurdities; but she started when, ascending two or three stone steps, she found herself in the church-yard, and saw that Madge was making straight for the door of the church. As Jeanie had no mind to enter the congregation in such company, she walked aside from the path-way, and said in a decided tone, "Madge, I will wait here till the church comes out—you may go in by yourself, if you have a mind."

As she spoke these words, she was about to seat herself upon one of the grave-stones.

Madge was a little before Jeanie when she turned aside; but suddenly changing her course, she made after her with long strides, and, with every feature inflamed with passion, overtook and seized her by the arm. "Do ye think, ye ungratefu' wretch, that I am ganging to let ye sit doun upon my father's grave? The de'il settle ye doun, if ye dinna rise and come into the Interpreter's house, that's the house of God, wi' me, but I'll rive every dud aff your back!"

She adapted the action to the phrase; for with one clutch she stripped Jeanie of her straw bonnet and a handful of her hair to boot, and threw it up into an old yew tree, where it stuck fast. Jeanie's first impulse was to scream, but conceiving she might receive deadly harm before she could obtain the assistance of any one, notwithstanding the vicinity of the church, she thought it wiser to follow the mad-woman into the congregation, where she might find some means of escape from her, or at least be secured against her violence. But when she meekly intimated her consent to follow Madge, her guide's uncertain brain had caught another train of ideas. She held Jeanie fast with one hand, and with the other pointed to the inscription on the grave-stone, and commanded her to read it. Jeanie obeyed, and read these words:—

"THIS MONUMENT WAS ERECTED TO THE MEMORY OF DONALD MURDOCKSON OF THE KING'S XXVI, OR CAMERONIAN REGIMENT, A SINCERE CHRISTIAN, A BRAVE SOLDIER, AND A FAITHFUL SERVANT, BY HIS GRATEFUL AND SORROWING MASTER, ROBERT STAUNTON."

"It's very weel read, Jeanie; it's just the very words," said Madge, whose ire had now faded into deep melancholy, and with a step, which, to Jeanie's great joy, was uncommonly quiet and mournful, she led her companion towards the door of the church.

It was one of those old-fashioned Gothic parish churches which are frequently to be met with in England, the most cleanly, decent, and reverential places of worship that are, perhaps, any where to be found in the Christian world. Yet, notwithstanding the decent solemnity of its exterior, Jeanie was too faithful to the directory of the Presbyterian Kirk to have entered a prelatic place of worship, and would, upon any other occasion, have thought that she beheld in the porch the venerable figure of her father waving her back from the entrance, and pronouncing in a solemn tone, "Cease, my child, to hear the instruction which causeth to err from the words of knowledge." But in her present agitating and alarming situation, she took for safety to this forbidden place of assembly, as the hunted animal will sometimes seek shelter from imminent danger in the human habitation, or in other places of refuge most alien to its nature and habits. Not even the sound of the organ, and of one or two flutes which accompanied the psalmody, prevented her from following her guide into the chancel of the church.

No sooner had Madge put her foot upon the pavement, and become sensible that she was the object of attention to the spectators, than she resumed all the fantastic extravagance of deportment which some transient touch of melancholy had banished for an instant. She swam rather than walked up the centre aisle, dragging Jeanie after her, whom she held fast by the hand. She would, indeed, have fain slipped aside into the pews nearest to the door, and left Madge to ascend in her own manner and alone to the high places of the synagogue; but this was impossible, without a degree of violent resistance, which seemed to her inconsistent with the time and place, and she was accordingly led in captivity the whole length of the church by her grotesque conductress, who, with half-shut eyes, a prim smile upon her lips, and a mincing motion with her hands, which corresponded with the delicate and affected pace at which she was pleased to move, seemed to take the general stare of the congregation, which such an exhibition necessarily excited, as a high compliment, and which she returned by nods and half curtsies to individuals amongst the audience, whom she seemed to distinguish as acquaintances. Her absurdity was enhanced in the eyes of the spectators by the strange contrast which she formed to her companion, who, with dishevelled hair, downcast eyes, and a face glowing with shame, was dragged as it were in triumph after her.

Madge's airs were at length fortunately cut short by her encountering in her progress the looks of the clergyman, who fixed upon her a glance at once steady, compassionate, and admonitory. She hastily opened an empty pew which happened to be near her, and entered, dragging in Jeanie after her. Kicking Jeanie on the shins, by way of hint that she should imitate her example, she sunk her head upon her hand for the space of a minute. Jeanie, to whom this posture of mental devotion was entirely new, did not attempt to do the like, but looked round her with a bewildered stare, which her neighbours, judging from the company in which they saw her, very naturally ascribed to insanity. Every person in their immediate vicinity drew back from this extraordinary couple as far as the limits of their pew permitted, but one old man could not get beyond Madge's reach, ere she had snatched the prayer-book from his hand, and ascertained the lesson of the day. She then turned up the ritual, and, with the most overstrained enthusiasm of gesture and manner, shewed Jeanie the passages as they were read in the service, making at the same time her own responses so loud as to be heard above those of every other person.

Notwithstanding the shame and vexation which Jeanie felt in being thus exposed in a place of public worship, she could not and durst not omit rallying her spirits so as to look around her, and consider to whom she ought to appeal for protection so soon as the service should be concluded. Her first ideas naturally fixed upon the clergyman, and she was confirmed in the resolution by observing that he was an aged gentleman, of a dignified appearance and deportment, who read the service with an undisturbed and decent gravity, which brought back to becoming attention those younger members of the congregation who had been disturbed by the extravagant behaviour of Madge Wildfire. To the clergyman, therefore, Jeanie resolved to make her appeal when the service was over.

It is true she felt disposed to be shocked at his surplice, of which she had heard so much, but which she had never witnessed upon the person of a preacher of the word. Then she was confused by the change of posture adopted in different parts of the ritual, the more so as Madge Wildfire, to whom they seemed familiar, took the opportunity to exercise authority over her, pulling her up and pushing her down with a bustling assiduity, which Jeanie felt must make them both the objects of painful attention. But notwithstanding these prejudices, it was her sensible resolution, in this dilemma, to imitate as nearly as she could what was done around her. The prophet, she thought, permitted Naaman the Syrian to bow even in the house of Rimmon.—Surely if I, in this streight, worship the God of my fathers in mine own language, although the manner thereof be strange to me, the Lord will pardon me in this thing.

In this resolution she became so much confirmed, that, withdrawing herself from Madge as far as the pew permitted, she endeavoured to evince, by serious and composed attention to what was passing, that her mind was composed to devotion. Her tormentor would not long have permitted her to remain quiet, but fatigue overpowered her, and she fell asleep in the other corner of the pew.

Jeanie, though her mind in her own despite sometimes reverted to her situation, compelled herself to give attention to a sensible, energetic, and well-composed discourse, upon the practical doctrines of Christianity, which she could not help approving, although it was every word written down and read by the preacher, and although it was delivered in a tone and gesture very different from those of Boanerges Stormheaven, who was her father's favourite preacher. The serious and placid attention with which Jeanie listened did not escape the clergyman. Madge Wildfire's entrance had rendered him apprehensive of some disturbance, to provide against which, as far as possible, he often turned his eyes to the part of the church where Jeanie and she were placed, and became soon aware that, notwithstanding the loss of her head-gear, and the awkwardness of her situation, had given an uncommon and wild appearance to the features of the former, yet she was in a state of mind very different from that of her companion. When he dismissed the congregation, he observed her look around with a wild and terrified look, as if uncertain what course she ought to adopt, and noticed that she approached one or two of the most decent of the congregation, as if to address them, and then shrunk back timidly, on observing that they seemed to shun and to avoid her. The clergyman was satisfied there must be something extraordinary in all this, and as a benevolent man, as well as a good Christian pastor, he resolved to enquire into the matter more minutely.

Chapter Seven

——There govern'd in that year,
A stern, stout churl—an angry overseer.
                                        CRABBE

WHILE MR STAUNTON, for such was this worthy clergyman's name, was laying aside his gown in the vestry, Jeanie was in the act of coming to an open rupture with Madge.

"We must return to Mummer's barn directly," said Madge; "we'll be ower late, and my mother will be angry."

"I am not going back with you, Madge," said Jeanie, taking out a guinea, and offering it to her; "I am much obliged to you, but I maun gang my ain road."

"And me coming a' this way out o' my gate to pleasure you, ye ungratefu' cutty," answered Madge; "and me to be brained by my mother when I gang hame, and a' for your sake—but I will gar ye as good—"

"For God's sake!" said Jeanie to a man who stood beside them, "keep her off—she is mad."

"Ey—ey," answered the boor; "I hae some guess of that, and I trow thou be'st a bird of the same feather. Howsomever, Madge, I read thee keep hand off her, or I'se lend thee a whister-poop."

Several of the lower class of the parishioners now gathered round the strangers, and the cry arose among the boys, that "there was a-going to be a fit between mad Madge Murdockson and another Bess of Bedlam." But while the fry assembled with the humane hope of seeing as much of the fun as possible, the laced cocked-hat of the beadle was discerned among the multitude, and all made way for that person of awful authority. His first address was to Madge.

"What's brought thee back again, thou silly donnot, to plague this parish? Has thou brought na more bastards wi' thee to lay to honest men's doors? or does thou think to burthen us with this goose, that's as gare-brained as thysel, as if rates were no up enow? Away wi' thee to thy thief of a mother; she's fast in the stocks yonder at Barkston town-end—Away wi' ye out o' parish, or I'se be at ye wi' the rattan."

Madge stood sulky for a minute; but she had been too often taught submission to the beadle's authority by ungentle means, to feel courage enough to dispute it.

"And my mother—my puir auld mother, is in the stocks at Barkston!—This is a' your wyte, Miss Jeanie Deans; but I'll be upsides wi' you, as sure as my name's Madge Wildfire—I mean Murdockson—God help me, I forget my very name in this confused waste."

So saying, she turned upon her heel, and went off, followed by all the mischievous imps of the village, some crying, "Madge, canst tell thy name yet?" some pulling the skirts of her dress, and all, to the best of their strength and ingenuity, exercising some device or other to exasperate her into frenzy.

Jeanie saw her departure with infinite delight, though she wished, that, in some way or other, she could have requited the service Madge had conferred upon her.

In the meantime, she applied to the beadle to know, whether "there was any house in the village where she could be civilly entertained for her money, and whether she could be permitted to speak to the clergyman?"

"Ay, ay, we'se ha' reverend care on thee; and I think," answered the man of constituted authority, "that, unless thou answer the rector all the better, we'se spare thy money, and gie thee lodging at the parish charge, young woman."

"Where am I to go, then?" said Jeanie, in some alarm.

"Why, I am to take thee to his Reverence, in the first place, to gie an account o' thyself, and to see thou come na to be a burthen upon parish."

"I do not wish to burthen any one," replied Jeanie; "I have enough for my own wants, and only wish to get on my journey safely."

"Why, that's another matter," replied the beadle; "an' if it be true—and I think thou doest not look so polrumptious as thy play-fellow yonder—thou wouldst be a nittle lass enow, an thou wert snog and snod a bit better. Come thou away then—the Rector is a good man."

"Is that the minister," said Jeanie, "who preached"——

"The minister? Lord help thee! What kind o' presbyterian art thou?—Why, 'tis the Rector—the Rector's sell, woman, and there isna the like o' him in the county, nor the four next to it. Come away—away with thee—we munna bide here."

"I am sure I am very willing to go to see the minister," said Jeanie; "for, though he read his discourse, and wore that surplice, as they call it here, I canna but think he must be a very worthy God-fearing man, to preach the root of the matter in the way he did."

The disappointed rabble, finding that there was like to be no sport, had by this time dispersed, and Jeanie, with her usual patience, followed her consequential and surly, but not brutal, conductor towards the rectory.

This clerical mansion was large and commodious, for the living was an excellent one, and the advowson belonged to a very wealthy family in the neighbourhood, who had usually bred up a son or nephew to the church, for the sake of inducting him, as opportunity offered, into this very comfortable provision. In this manner the rectory of Willingham had always been considered as a direct and immediate appanage of Willingham-hall; and as the rich baronets to whom the latter belonged, had usually a son, or brother, or nephew settled in the living, the utmost care had been taken to render their habitation not merely respectable and commodious, but even dignified and imposing.

It was situated about four hundred yards from the village, and on a rising ground which sloped gently upward, covered with small enclosures, or closes, laid out irregularly, so that the old oaks and elms which were planted in hedge-rows, fell into perspective and were blended together in beautiful irregularity. When they approached nearer to the house, a handsome gate-way admitted them into a lawn, of narrow dimensions indeed, but which was interspersed with large sweet-chesnut trees and beeches, and kept in handsome order. The front of the house was irregular. Part of it seemed very old, and had, in fact, been the residence of the incumbent in Romish times. Successive occupants had made considerable additions and improvements, each in the taste of his own age, and without much regard to symmetry. But these incongruities of architecture were so graduated and happily mingled, that the eye, far from being displeased with the combination of various styles, saw nothing but what was interesting in the varied and intricate pile which they displayed. Fruit-trees displayed on the southern wall, outer stair-cases, various places of entrance, a combination of roofs and chimneys of different ages, united to render the front, not indeed beautiful or grand, but intricate, perplexed, or, to use Mr Price's appropriate phrase, picturesque. The most considerable addition was that of the present Rector, who "being a bookish man," as the beadle was at the pains to inform Jeanie, to augment, perhaps, her reverence for the person before whom she was to appear, had built a handsome library and parlour, and no less than two additional bed-rooms.

"Mony men would ha scrupled such expence," continued the parochial officer, "seeing as the living mun go as pleases Sir Edmund to will it; but his Reverence has a canny bit land of his own, and need not look on two sides of a penny."

Jeanie could not help comparing the irregular yet extensive and commodious pile of building before us, to the "Manses," in her own country, where a set of penurious heritors, professing all the while the devotion of their lives and fortunes to the presbyterian establishment, strain their inventions to discover what may be nipped, and clipped, and pared from a building which forms but a poor accommodation even for the present incumbent, and, despite the superior advantage of stone masonry, must, in the course of forty or fifty years, again burthen their descendants with an expence, which, once liberally and handsomely employed, ought to have freed their estates from the recurrence of it for more than a century at least.

Behind the Rector's house the ground sloped down to a small river, which, without possessing the romance, vivacity and rapidity of a northern stream, was, nevertheless, by its occasional appearance through the ranges of willows and poplars that crowned its banks, a very pleasing accompaniment to the landscape. "It was the best trouting stream," said the beadle, whom the patience of Jeanie, and especially the assurance that she was not about to become a burthen to the parish, had rendered rather communicative, "the best trouting stream in all Lincolnshire, for when you got lower down, there was nought to be done wi' fly-fishing."

Turning aside from the principal entrance, he conducted Jeanie towards a sort of portal connected with the older part of the building, which was chiefly occupied by servants, and knocking at the door, it was opened by a servant in grave purple livery, such as befitted a wealthy and dignified clergyman.

"How doest do, Tummas?" said the beadle—"and how's young Measter Staunton?"

"Why, but poorly—but poorly, Measter Stubbs.—Are you wanting to see his Reverence?"

"Ay, ay, Tummas; please to say I ha' brought up the young woman

as came to sarvice to-day with mad Madge Murdockson—she seems
to be a decentish koind of body; but I ha' asked her never a question.
Only I can tell his Reverence that she is a Scotchwoman, I judge, and
as flat as the fens of Holland."

Tummas honoured Jeanie Deans with such a stare, as the pam-
pered domestics of the rich, whether spiritual or temporal, usually
esteem it part of their privilege to bestow upon the poor, and then
desired Mr Stubbs and his charge to step in till he informed his master
of their presence.

The room into which he shewed them was a sort of steward's
parlour, hung with a county map or two, and three or four prints of
eminent persons connected with the county, as Sir William Monson,
James York the blacksmith of Lincoln, and the famous Peregrine,
Lord Willoughby, in complete armour, looking as when he said, in the
words of the legend below the engraving,—

> Stand to it, noble pikemen,
>   And face ye well about;
> And shoot ye sharp, bold bowmen,
>   And we will keep them out.
> Ye musqueteers and callivers,
>   Do you prove true to me,
> I'll be the foremost man in fight,
>   Said brave Lord Willoughbee.

When they had entered this apartment, Tummas as a matter of
course offered, and as a matter of course Mr Stubbs accepted, a
"summat" to eat and drink, being the respectable reliques of a gammon of bacon, and a *whole whiskin*, or black pot of sufficient double
ale. To these eatables Mr Beadle seriously inclined himself, and (for
we must do him justice) not without an invitation to Jeanie, in which
Tummas joined, that his prisoner or charge would follow his good
example. But although she might have stood in need of refreshment,
considering she had tasted no food that day, the anxiety of the
moment, her own sparing and abstemious habits, and a bashful aversion to eat in company of the two strangers, induced her to decline
their courtesy. So she sate in a chair apart, while Mr Stubbs and Mr
Tummas, who chose to join his friend in consideration that dinner
was to be put back till after the afternoon service, made a hearty
luncheon, which lasted for half an hour, and might not then have
concluded, had not his Reverence rung his bell, so that Tummas was
obliged to attend his master. Then, and no sooner, to save himself the
labour of a second journey to the other end of the house, he
announced to his master the arrival of Mr Stubbs, with the other mad
woman, as he chose to designate Jeanie, as an event which had just
taken place. He returned with an order that Mr Stubbs and the young

woman should be instantly ushered up to the library.

The beadle bolted in haste his last mouthful of fat bacon, washed down the greasy morsel with the last rinsings of the pot of ale, and immediately marshalled Jeanie through one or two intricate passages which led from the more ancient to the modern buildings, into a handsome little hall, or anti-room, adjoining to the library, and out of which a glass door opened to the lawn.

"Stay here," said Stubbs, "till I tell his Reverence you are come."

So saying, he opened a door and entered the library.

Without wishing to hear their conversation, Jeanie, as she was circumstanced, could not avoid it; for as Stubbs stood by the door, and his Reverence was at the upper end of a large room, their conversation was necessarily audible in the anti-room.

"So you have brought the young woman here at last, Mr Stubbs. I expected you some time since. You know I do not wish such persons to remain in custody a moment without some enquiry into their situation."

"Very true, your Reverence," replied the beadle; "but the young woman had eat nought to-day, and soa Measter Tummas did set down a drap of drink and a morsel, to be sure."

"Mr Thomas was very right, Mr Stubbs; and what has become of the other most unfortunate being?"

"Why," replied Mr Stubbs, "I did think the sight on her would but vex your Reverence, and soa I did let her go her ways back to her muther, who is in trouble in the next parish."

"In trouble?—that signifies in prison, I suppose?" said Mr Staunton.

"Ay, truly; something like it, an' it like your Reverence."

"Wretched, unhappy, incorrigible woman!" said the clergyman. "And what sort of person is this companion of her's?"

"Why, decent enow, an' it like your Reverence," said Stubbs; "for aught I sees of her, there's no harm of her, and she says she has cash enow to carry her out of the county."

"Cash? that is always what you think of, Stubbs—But, has she sense?—has she her wits?—has she the capacity of taking care of herself?"

"Why, your Reverence," replied Stubbs, "I cannot just say—I will be sworn she was not born at Witt-ham;* for Gaffer Gibbs looked at her all the time of sarvice, and he says she could not turn up a single lesson like a Christian, even though she had Madge Murdockson to help her—But then, as to fending for herself, why, she's a bit of a

* A proverbial and punning expression in that county, to express that a person is not very witty.

Scotchwoman, your Reverence, and they say the worst donnot of them can look out for their own turn—and she is decently put on enow, and not behounched like t'other."

"Send her in here then, and do you remain below, Mr Stubbs."

This colloquy had engaged Jeanie's attention so deeply, that it was not until it was over that she observed that the sashed door, which, we have said, led from the anti-room into the garden, was opened, and that there entered, or rather was borne in by two assistants, a young man, of a very pale and sickly appearance, whom they lifted to the nearest couch, and placed there, as if to recover from the fatigue of an unusual exertion. Just as they were making this arrangement, Stubbs came out of the library, and summoned Jeanie to enter it. She obeyed him not without tremor, for besides the novelty of the situation to a girl of her secluded habits, she felt also as if the successful prosecution of her journey was to depend upon the impression she should be able to make on Mr Staunton.

It is true, it was difficult to suppose on what pretext a person travelling on her own business, and at her own charge, could be interrupted upon her route. But the violent detention she had already undergone was sufficient to show that there existed persons at no great distance who had the interest, the inclination, and the audacity forcibly to stop her journey, and she felt the necessity of having some countenance and protection, at least till she should get beyond their reach. While these things passed through her mind, much faster than our pen and ink can record, or even the reader's eye collect the meaning of its traces, Jeanie found herself in a handsome library, and in presence of the Rector of Willingham. The well-furnished presses and shelves which surrounded the large and handsome apartment, contained more books than Jeanie imagined existed in the world, being accustomed to consider as an extensive collection two fir shelves, each about three feet long, which contained her father's treasured volumes, the whole pith and marrow, as he used sometimes to boast, of modern divinity. An orrery, globes, a telescope, and some other scientific implements, conveyed to Jeanie an impression of admiration and wonder not unmixed with fear, for, in her ignorant apprehension, they seemed rather adapted for magical purposes than any other; and a few stuffed animals (as the Rector was fond of natural history,) added to the impressive character of the apartment.

Mr Staunton spoke to her with great mildness. He observed, that although her appearance at church had been uncommon, in strange, and, he must add, discreditable society, and calculated, upon the whole, to disturb the congregation during divine worship, he wished, nevertheless, to hear her own account of herself before taking any steps which his duty might seem to demand. He was a justice of peace, he informed her, as well as a clergyman.

"His honour" (for she would not say his reverence,) "was very civil and kind," was all that poor Jeanie could at first bring out.

"Who are you, young woman?" said the clergyman, more peremptorily—"and what do you do in this country, and in such company?— We allow no strollers or vagrants here."

"I am not a vagrant or a stroller, sir," said Jeanie, a little roused by the supposition. "I am a decent Scots lass, travelling through the land on my own business and my own expences; and I was so unhappy as to fall in with bad company, and was stopped a' night on my journey. And this puir creature, who is something light-headed, let me out in the morning."

"Bad company!" said the clergyman. "I am afraid, young woman, you have not been sufficiently anxious to avoid them."

"Indeed, sir," returned Jeanie, "I have been brought up to shun evil communication. But these wicked people were thieves, and stopped me by violence and mastery."

"Thieves?" said Mr Staunton; "then you charge them with robbery, I suppose?"

"No, sir; they did not take so much as a bodle from me," answered Jeanie; "nor did they use me ill, otherwise than by confining me."

The clergyman enquired into the particulars of her adventure, which she told him from point to point.

"This is an extraordinary, and not a very probable tale, young woman," resumed Mr Staunton. "Here has been, according to your account, a great violence committed without any adequate motive. Are you aware of the law of this country—that if you lodge this charge you will be bound over to prosecute this gang?"

Jeanie did not understand him, and he explained that the English law, in addition to the inconvenience sustained by persons who have been robbed or injured, has the goodness to entrust to them the care and the expence of appearing as prosecutors.

Jeanie said, "that her business at London was express; all she wanted was, that any gentleman would, out of Christian charity, protect her to some town where she could hire horses and a guide; and, finally," she thought, "it would be her father's mind that she was not free to give testimony in an English court of justice, as the land was not under a direct gospel dispensation."

Mr Staunton stared a little, and asked if her father was a Quaker.

"God forbid, sir," said Jeanie—"He is nae schismatic nor sectary, nor ever treated for sic black commodities as their's, and that's weel kenn'd o' him."

"And what is his name, pray?" said Mr Staunton.

"David Deans, sir, the cow-feeder at Saint Leonard's Crags, near Edinburgh."

A deep groan from the anti-room prevented the rector from replying, and, exclaiming, "Good God! that unhappy boy," he left Jeanie alone, and hastened into the outer apartment.

Some noise and bustle was heard, but no one entered the library for the best part of an hour.

Chapter Eight

Fantastic passions! maddening brawl!
And shame and terror over all!
Deeds to be hid which were not hid,
Which all confused, I could not know
Whether I suffered or I did,
For all seemed guilt, remorse, or woe;
My own, or other's, still the same
Life-stifling fear, soul-stifling shame.
                              COLERIDGE

DURING THE INTERVAL while she was thus left alone, Jeanie anxiously revolved in her mind what course was best for her to pursue. She was impatient to continue her journey, yet she feared she could not safely adventure to do so while the old hag and her assistants were in the neighbourhood, without risking a repetition of their violence. She thought she could collect from the conversation which she had partly overheard, and also from the wild confessions of Madge Wildfire, that her mother had a deep and revengeful motive for obstructing her journey if possible. And from whom could she hope for assistance if not from Mr Staunton? His whole appearance and demeanour seemed to encourage her hopes. His features were handsome, though marked with a deep cast of melancholy; his tone and language were gentle and encouraging; and, as he had served in the army for several years during his youth, his air retained that easy frankness which is peculiar to the profession of arms. He was, besides, a minister of the gospel; and although only a worshipper, according to Jeanie's notions, in the Court of the Gentiles, and so benighted as to wear a surplice, read the Common Prayer, and write over every word of his sermon before delivering it; and though he was, moreover, in strength of lungs, as well as pith and marrow of doctrine, vastly inferior to Boanerges Stormheaven, Jeanie still thought he must be a very different person from Curate Kiltstoup, and other prelatical divines of her father's earlier days, who used to get drunk in their canonical dress, and hound out the dragoons against the wandering Cameronians.

The house seemed to be in some disturbance, but as she could not suppose she was altogether forgotten, she thought it better to remain quiet in the apartment where she had been left, till some one should take notice of her.

The first who entered was, to her no small delight, one of her own sex, a motherly-looking aged person of a house-keeper. To her Jeanie explained her situation in a few words, and begged her assistance.

The dignity of a housekeeper did not encourage too much familiarity with a person who was at the Rectory on justice-business, and whose character might seem in her eyes somewhat precarious; but she was civil, although distant.

"Her young master," she said, "had had a bad accident by a fall from his horse, which made him liable to fainting fits; he had been taken very ill just now, and it was impossible his Reverence could see Jeanie for some time; but that she need not fear his doing all that was just and proper in her behalf the instant he could get her business attended to."—She concluded by offering to show Jeanie a room, where she might remain till his Reverence was at leisure.

Our heroine took the opportunity to request the means of adjusting and changing her dress.

The housekeeper, in whose estimation order and cleanliness ranked high among personal virtues, gladly complied with a request so reasonable; and the change of dress which Jeanie's bundle furnished, made so important an improvement in her appearance, that the old lady hardly knew the spoiled and disordered traveller, whose attire shewed the violence she had sustained, in the neat, clean, quiet-looking little Scotchwoman, who now stood before her. Encouraged by such a favourable alteration in her appearance, Mrs Dalton ventured to invite Jeanie to partake of her dinner, and was equally pleased with the decent propriety of her conduct during that meal.

"Thou canst read this book, canst thou, young woman?" said the old lady when their meal was concluded, laying her hand upon a hall-Bible.

"I hope sae, madam," said Jeanie, surprised at the question; "my father wad hae wanted mony things, ere I had wanted *that* schuling."

"The better sign of him, young woman. There are men here, well to pass in the world, would not want their share of a Leicestershire plover, and that's a bag-pudding, if fasting for three hours would make all their poor children read the Bible from end to end. Take thou the book, then, for my eyes are something dazed, and read where thou listest—it's the only book thou canst not happen wrong in."

Jeanie was at first tempted to turn up the parable of the good Samaritan, but her conscience checked her, as if it were an using of

Scripture, not for her own edification, but to work upon the minds of others for the relief of her worldly afflictions; and under this scrupulous sense of duty, she selected, in preference, a chapter of the prophet Isaiah, and read it, notwithstanding her northern accent and tone, with a devout propriety, which greatly edified Mrs Dalton.

"Ah," she said, "an' all Scotswomen were sic as thou!—but it was our luck to get born devils of thy country, I think—every one worse than t'other. If thou knowst of any tidy lass like thysell, that wanted a place, and could bring a good character, and would not go laiking about to wakes and fairs, and wore shoes and stockings all the day round—why, I'll not say but we might find room for her at the rectory. Hast no cousin or sister, lass, that such an offer would suit?"

This was touching upon a sore point, but Jeanie was spared the pain of replying by the entrance of the same man-servant she had seen before.

"Measter wishes to see the young woman from Scotland," was Tummas's address.

"Go to his Reverence, my dear, as fast as you can, and tell him all your story—his Reverence is a kind man," said Mrs Dalton. "I will fold down the leaf, and make you a cup of tea, with some nice muffin, against you come down, and that's what you seldom see in Scotland, girl."

"Measter's waiting for the young woman," said Tummas impatiently.

"Well, Mr Jack-Sauce, and what is your business to put in your oar? —And how often must I tell you to call Mr Staunton his Reverence, seeing as he is a dignified clergyman, and not be meastering, meastering him, as if he were a little petty squire?"

As Jeanie was now at the door and ready to accompany Tummas, the footman said nothing till he got into the passage, when he muttered, "There are moe masters than one in house, and I think we shall ha' a mistress too, an Dame Dalton curries it thus."

Tummas led the way through a more intricate range of passages than Jeanie had yet threaded, and ushered her into an apartment which was darkened by the closing of most of the window-shutters, and in which was a bed with the curtains partly drawn.

"Here is the young woman, sir," said Tummas.

"Very well," said a voice from the bed, but not that of his Reverence; "be ready to answer the bell, and leave the room."

"There is some mistake," said Jeanie, confounded at finding herself in the apartment of an invalid, "the servant told me that the minister"——

"Don't trouble yourself," said the invalid, "there is no mistake. I know more of your affairs than my father, and I can manage them better—Leave the room, Tom." The servant obeyed.—"We must not," said the invalid, "lose time, when we have little to lose. Open the shutter of that window."

She did so, and as he drew aside the curtain of his bed, the light fell on his pale countenance, as, turban'd with bandages, and dressed in a night-gown, he lay seemingly exhausted upon the bed.

"Look at me," he said. "Jeanie Deans, can you not recollect me?"

"No, sir," said she, full of surprise. "I was never in this country before."

"But I may have been in yours. Think—recollect. I would fain not name the name you are most dearly bound to loathe and to detest. Think—remember!"

A terrible recollection flashed on Jeanie, which every tone of the speaker confirmed, and which his next words rendered certainty.

"Be composed—remember Muschat's Cairn, and the moonlight night."

Jeanie sunk down on a chair, with clasped hands, and gasped in agony.

"Yes, here I lie," he said, "like a crushed snake, writhing with impatience at my incapacity of motion—here I lie, when I ought to have been in Edinburgh, trying every means to save a life that is dearer to me than my own.—How is your sister?—how fares it with her?—condemned to death, I know it, by this time! O, the horse that carried me safely on a thousand errands of folly and wickedness, that he should have broke down with me on the only good mission I have undertaken for years! But I must rein in my passion—my frame cannot endure it, and I have much to say. Give me some of the cordial which stands on that table—Why do you tremble? But you have too good cause.—Let it stand—I need it not."

Jeanie, however reluctant, approached him with the cup into which she had poured the draught, and could not forbear saying, "There is a cordial for the mind, sir, if the wicked will turn from their transgressions, and seek to the Physician of souls."

"Silence!" he said sternly—"and yet I thank you. But tell me, and lose no time in doing so, what you are doing in this country? Remember, though I have been your sister's worst enemy, yet I will serve her with the best of my blood, and I will serve you for her sake; and no one can serve you to such purpose, for no one can know the circumstances so well—So speak without fear."

"I am not afraid, sir," said Jeanie, collecting her spirits. "I trust in God; and if it pleases Him to redeem my sister's captivity, it is all I seek, whosoever be the instrument. But, sir, to be plain with you, I dare not use your counsel, unless I were enabled to see that it accords with the law which I must rely upon."

"The devil take the puritan!" said George Staunton, for so we must now call him. "I beg your pardon; but I am naturally impatient, and you drive me mad. What harm can it possibly do you to tell me in what situation your sister stands, and your own expectations of being able to assist her? It is time enough to refuse my advice when I offer any which you may think improper. I speak calmly to you, though 'tis against my nature;—but do not urge me to impatience—it will only render me incapable of serving Effie."

There was in the looks and words of this unhappy young man a sort of restrained eagerness and impetuosity which seemed to prey upon itself, as the impatience of a fiery steed fatigues itself with churning upon the bit. After a moment's consideration, it occurred to Jeanie that she was not entitled to withhold from him, whether on her sister's account or her own, the fatal account of the consequences of the crime which he had committed, nor to reject such advice, being in itself lawful and innocent, as he might be able to suggest in the way of remedy. Accordingly, in as few words as she could express it, she told the history of her sister's trial and condemnation, and of her own journey as far as Newark. He appeared to listen in the utmost agony of mind, yet repressed every violent symptom of emotion, whether by gesture or sound, which might have interrupted the speaker, and, stretched on his couch like the Mexican monarch on his bed of live coals, only the contortions of his cheek, and the quivering of his limbs, gave indication of his sufferings. To much of what she said he listened with stifled groans, as if he were only hearing those miseries confirmed, whose fatal reality he had known before; but when she pursued her tale through the circumstances which had interrupted her journey, extreme surprise and earnest attention appeared to succeed to the symptoms of remorse which he had before exhibited. He questioned Jeanie closely concerning the appearance of the two men, and the conversation which she had overheard between the taller of them and the woman.

When Jeanie mentioned the old woman having alluded to her foster-son—"It is too true," said he; "and the source from which I derived food, when an infant, must have communicated to me the wretched—the fated—propensity to vices that were strangers in my own family.—But go on."

Jeanie passed slightly over her journey in company with Madge, having no inclination to repeat what might be the effect of mere raving on the part of her companion, and therefore her tale was now closed.

Young Staunton lay for a moment in profound meditation, and at length spoke with more composure than he had yet displayed during their interview.—"You are a sensible, as well as a good young woman, Jeanie Deans, and I will tell you more of my story than I have told to any one.—Story did I call it?—it is a tissue of folly, guilt, and misery. —But take notice—I do it because I desire your confidence in return —that is, that you will act in this dismal matter by my advice and direction. Therefore do I speak."

"I will do what is fitting for a sister, and a daughter, and a Christian woman to do," said Jeanie; "but do not tell me any of your secrets—It is not good that I should come into your counsel, or listen to the doctrine which causeth to err."

"Simple fool!" said the young man. "Look at me. My head is not horned, my foot is not cloven, my hands are not garnished with talons; and, since I am not the very devil himself, what interest can any one else have in destroying the hopes with which you comfort or fool yourself? Listen to me patiently, and you will find that, when you have heard my counsel, you may go to the seventh heaven with it in your pocket, if you have a mind, and not feel yourself an ounce heavier in the ascent."

At the risk of being somewhat heavy, as explanations usually prove, we must here endeavour to combine into a distinct narrative, information which the invalid communicated in a manner at once too circumstantial, and too much broken by passion, to admit of our giving his precise words. Part of it, indeed, he read from a manuscript, which he had perhaps drawn up for the information of his relations after his decease.

"To make my tale short—this wretched hag—this Margaret Murdockson, was the wife of a favourite servant of my father;—she had been my nurse;—her husband was dead;—she resided in a cottage near this place. She had a daughter who grew up, and was then a beautiful but very giddy girl;—her mother endeavoured to promote her marriage with an old but wealthy churl in the neighbourhood;— the girl saw me frequently—She was familiar with me, as our connection seemed to permit—and I—in a word, I wronged her cruelly—it was not so bad as your sister's business, but it was sufficiently villainous: her folly should have been her protection. Soon after this I was sent abroad—to do my father justice, if I have turned out a fiend it is not his fault—he used the best means. When I returned, I found the wretched mother and daughter had fallen into disgrace, and were chased from this country.—My deep share in their shame and misery was discovered—my father used very harsh language—we quarrelled. I left his house, plunged into low dissipation, and led a life of strange adventure, resolving never again to see my father or my father's home.

"And now comes the story!—Jeanie, I put my life in your hands, and not only my own life, which, God knows, is not worth saving, but the happiness of a respectable old man, and the honour of a family of consideration. My love of low society, as such propensities as I was cursed with are usually termed, was, I think, of an uncommon kind, and indicated a nature, which, if not depraved by early debauchery, would have been fit for better things. I did not so much delight in the wild revel, the low humour, the unconfined liberty of those with whom I associated, as in the spirit of adventure, presence of mind in peril, and sharpness of intellect which they displayed in prosecuting their marauding upon the revenue, or similar adventures.——Have you looked round this rectory, Jeanie?—is it not a sweet and pleasant retreat?"

Jeanie, alarmed at this sudden change of subject, answered in the affirmative.

"Well! I wish it had been ten thousand fathom under ground, with its church-lands, and tythes, and all that belongs to it. Had it not been for this cursed rectory I would have been permitted to follow the bent of my own inclinations and the profession of arms, and half the courage and address that I have displayed among smugglers and deer-stealers would have secured me an honourable rank among my contemporaries. Why did I not go abroad when I left this house?—Why did I leave it at all?—why—But it is come to that point with me that it is madness to look back, and misery to look forward."

He paused, and then went on with more composure.

"The chances of a wandering life brought me unhappily to Scotland, to embroil myself in worse and more criminal actions than I had yet been concerned in. It was now I became acquainted with Wilson, a remarkable man in his station of life; quiet, composed, and resolute, firm in mind, and uncommonly strong in person, gifted with a sort of rough eloquence which raised him above his companions. Hitherto I had been

> As dissolute as desperate, yet through both
> Were seen some sparkles of a better hope.

But it was this man's misfortune, as well as mine, that, notwithstanding the difference of our rank and education, he acquired an extraordinary and fascinating influence over me, which I can only account for by the calm determination of his character being superior to the less sustained impetuosity of mine. Where he led I felt myself bound to follow; and strange was the courage and address which he displayed in his pursuits. While I was engaged in desperate adventures, under so strange and dangerous a preceptor, I became acquainted with your unfortunate sister at some sports of the young people in the suburbs, which she frequented by stealth—and her ruin proved an interlude to the tragic scenes in which I was now deeply engaged. Yet this let me say—the villainy was not premeditated, and I was firmly resolved to do her all the justice which marriage could do, so soon as I should be able to extricate myself from my unhappy course of life, and embrace some one more suited to my birth.—I had wild visions—visions of conducting her as if to some poor retreat, and introducing her at once to rank and fortune she never dreamed of. A friend, at my request, attempted a negociation with my father, which was protracted for some time, and renewed at different intervals. At length, and just when I expected my father's pardon, he learned by some means or other my infamy, painted in even exaggerated colours, which was, God knows, unnecessary—He wrote me a letter—how it found me out, I know not—enclosing me £100, and disowning me for ever.—I became desperate—I became frantic. I readily joined Wilson in a perilous smuggling adventure in which we miscarried, and was willingly blinded by his logic to consider the robbery of the officer of the customs in Fife, as a fair and honourable reprisal. Hitherto I had observed a certain line in my criminality, and steered free of assaults upon personal property, but now I felt a wild pleasure in disgracing myself as much as possible.

"The plunder was no object to me. I abandoned that to my comrades, and only asked the post of danger. I remember well, that when I stood with my drawn sword guarding the door while they committed the felony, I had not a thought of my own safety. I was only meditating on my sense of supposed wrong from my family, my impotent thirst of vengeance, and how it would sound in the haughty ears of the family of Willingham, that one of their descendants, and the heir apparent of their honours, should perish by the hands of the hangman for robbing a Scottish gauger. We were taken—I expected no less. We were condemned—that also I looked for. But death, as he approached nearer, looked grimly; and the recollection of your sister's destitute condition determined me on an effort to save my life. —I forgot to tell you, that in Edinburgh I again met the woman Murdockson and her daughter.—She had followed the camp when young, and had now, under pretence of a trifling traffic, resumed predatory habits, with which she had already been but too familiar. Our first meeting was stormy; but I was liberal of what money I had, and she forgot, or seemed to forget, the injury her daughter had received. The unfortunate girl herself seemed hardly even to know her seducer, far less to retain any sense of the injury she had received. Her mind is totally alienated, which, according to her mother's account, is sometimes the consequence of an unfavourable confinement. But it was *my doing*. Here was another stone knitted around my neck to sink me into the pit of perdition. Every look—every word of this poor creature—her false spirits—her imperfect recollections—her allusions to things which she had forgotten, but which were recorded in my conscience, were stabs of a poniard—stabs did I say? —they were tearing with hot pincers, and scalding the raw wound with burning sulphur—they were to be endured, however, and they *were* endured.—I return to my prison thoughts.

"It was not the least miserable of them that your sister's time approached. I knew her dread of you and of her father—She often said she would die a thousand deaths ere you should know her shame —yet her confinement must be provided for.—I knew this woman Murdockson was an infernal hag, but I thought she loved me, and that money would make her true. She had procured a file for Wilson, and a spring-saw for me; and she undertook readily to take charge of Effie during her illness, in which she had skill enough to give the necessary assistance.—I gave her the £100 note which my father had sent me— It was settled that she should receive Effie into her house in the meantime, and wait for farther directions from me, when I should effectuate my escape. I communicated this purpose, and recommended the old hag to poor Effie by a letter, in which I recollect that I endeavoured to support the character of Macheath under condemnation—a fine, gay, bold-faced ruffian, who is game to the last—Such, and so wretchedly poor, was my ambition! Yet I had resolved to forsake the course I had been engaged in, should I be so fortunate as to escape the gibbet. My design was to marry your sister, and go over to the West Indies. I had still some money left, and I trusted in one way or other to provide for myself and my wife.

"We made the attempt to escape, and by the obstinacy of Wilson, who insisted upon going first, it totally miscarried. The undaunted and self-denied manner in which he sacrificed himself to redeem his error, and accomplish my escape from the Tolbooth-Church, you must have heard of—all Scotland rang with it. It was a gallant and an extraordinary deed—All men spoke of it—all men, even those who most condemned the habits and crimes of this self-devoted man, praised the heroism of his friendship. I have many vices, but cowardice, or want of gratitude, are none of the number. I resolved to requite his generosity, and even your sister's safety became a secondary consideration with me for the time. To effect Wilson's liberation was my principal object, and I doubted not to find the means.

"Yet I did not forget Effie neither. The bloodhounds of the law were so close after me, that I dared not trust myself near any of my old haunts, but old Murdockson met me by appointment, and informed me that your sister had happily been delivered of a boy. I charged the hag to keep her patient's mind easy, and let her want for nothing that money could purchase, and I retreated to those places of concealment where the men engaged in Wilson's desperate trade are used to hide themselves and their uncustomed goods. Men who are disobedient both to human and divine laws, are not always insensible to the claims of courage and generosity. We were assured that the mob of Edinburgh, strongly moved with the hardship of Wilson's situation, and the gallantry of his conduct, would back any bold attempt that might be made to rescue him even from the foot of the gibbet. Desperate as the attempt seemed, upon my declaring myself ready to lead the onset on the guard, I found no want of followers who engaged to stand by me.

"I have no doubt I should have rescued him from the very noose that dangled over his head," he continued with animation, which seemed a flash of the interest which he had taken in such exploits; "but amongst other precautions, the magistrates had taken one, suggested, as we afterwards learned, by the unhappy wretch Porteous, which effectually disconcerted my measures. They anticipated, by half an hour, the ordinary period for execution; and, as it had been resolved amongst us, that, for fear of observation from the officers of justice, we should not show ourselves upon the street until the time of action approached, it followed that all was over before our attempt at a rescue commenced. It did commence, however, and I gained the scaffold and cut the rope with my own hands. It was too late! The bold, stout-hearted, generous criminal was no more—and vengeance was all that remained to us—a vengeance, as I then thought, doubly due from my hand, to whom Wilson had given life and liberty when he could as easily have secured his own."

"O, sir," said Jeanie, "did the Scripture never come into your mind, 'Vengeance is mine, saith the Lord, and I will repay it?'"

"Scripture? Why, I had not opened a Bible for five years," answered Staunton.

"Waes me, sirs," said Jeanie—"and a minister's son too!"

"It is natural for you to say so; yet do not interrupt me, but let me finish my most accursed history. The beast, Porteous, who kept firing on the people long after it had ceased to be necessary, became the object of their hatred for having over-done his duty, and of mine for having done it too well. We—that is, I and other determined friends of Wilson, resolved to be avenged—but caution was necessary. I thought I had been marked by one of the officers, and therefore continued to lurk about the vicinity of Edinburgh, but without daring to venture within the walls. At length I visited, at the hazard of my life, the place where I hoped to find my future wife and my son—they were both

gone. Dame Murdockson informed me that so soon as Effie heard of
the miscarriage of the attempt to rescue Wilson, and the hot pursuit
after me, she fell into a brain fever; and that being one day obliged to
go out on some necessary business and leave her alone, she had taken
that opportunity to escape, and she had not seen her since. I loaded
her with reproaches, to which she listened with the most provoking
and callous composure; for it is one of her attributes, that, violent and
fierce as she is upon most occasions, there are some in which she
shews the most imperturbable calmness. I threatened her with justice;
she said I had more reason to fear justice than she had. I felt she was
right, and was silenced. I threatened her with vengeance; she replied
in nearly the same words, that, to judge by injuries received, I had
more reason to fear her vengeance, than she to dread mine. She was
again right, and I was left without an answer. I flung from her in
indignation, and employed a comrade to make enquiry in the neighbourhood of Saint Leonard's concerning your sister; but ere I
received his answer, the opening quest of a well-scented terrier of the
law drove me from the vicinity of Edinburgh to a more distant and
secluded place of concealment. A secret and trusty emissary at length
brought me the account of Porteous's condemnation, and of your
sister's imprisonment on a criminal charge; thus astounding one of
mine ears, while he gratified the other.

"I again ventured to the Pleasance—again charged Murdockson
with treachery to the unfortunate Effie and her child, though I could
conceive no reason, save that of appropriating the whole of the money
I had lodged with her. Your narrative throws light on this, and shews
another motive, not less powerful because less evident—the desire of
wreaking vengeance on the seducer of her daughter,—the destroyer
at once of her reason and reputation. Great God! how I wish that,
instead of the revenge she made choice of, she had delivered me up to
the cord!"

"But what account did the wretched woman gie of Effie and the
bairn?" said Jeanie, who, during this long and agitating narrative, had
firmness and discernment enough to keep her eye on such points as
might throw light on her sister's misfortunes.

"She would give none," said Staunton; "she said the mother made
a moonlight flitting from her house, with the infant in her arms—that
she had never seen either of them since—that the lass might have
thrown the child into the North Loch or the Quarry-Holes, for what
she knew, and it was like enough she had done so."

"And how came you to believe that she did not speak the fatal
truth?" said Jeanie, trembling.

"Because, on this second occasion, I saw her daughter, and I understood from her, that, in fact, the child had been removed or destroyed during the illness of the mother. But all knowledge to be got from her is so uncertain and indirect, that I could not collect any further circumstances. Only the diabolical character of old Murdockson makes me augur the worst."

"The last account agrees with that given by my poor sister," said Jeanie; "but gang on wi' your ain tale, sir."

"Of this I am certain," said Staunton, "that Effie, in her senses, and with her knowledge, never injured living creature—But what could I do in her exculpation?—Nothing— and, therefore, my whole thoughts were turned toward her safety. I was under the cursed necessity of suppressing my feelings towards Murdockson; my life was in the hag's hand—that I cared not for; but on my life hung that of your sister. I spoke the wretch fair; I appeared to confide in her; and to me, so far as I was personally concerned, she gave proofs of extraordinary fidelity. I was at first uncertain what measures I ought to adopt for your sister's liberation, when the general rage excited among the citizens of Edinburgh on account of the reprieve of Porteous, suggested to me the daring idea of forcing the jail, and at once carrying off your sister from the clutches of Danger, and bringing to condign punishment a miscreant, who had tormented the unfortunate Wilson, even in the hour of death, as if he had been a wild Indian taken captive by an hostile tribe. I flung myself among the multitude in the moment of fermentation—so did others among Wilson's mates, who had, like me, been disappointed in the hope of glutting their eyes with Porteous's execution. All was organized, and I was chosen for the captain. I felt not—I do not now feel, compunction for what was to be done, and has since been executed."

"O God forgive ye, sir, and bring you to a better sense of your ways!" exclaimed Jeanie, in horror at the avowal of such violent sentiments.

"Amen," replied Staunton, "if my sentiments are wrong. But I repeat, that, although willing to aid the deed, I could have wished them to have chosen another leader; because I foresaw that the great and general duty of the night would interfere with the assistance which I proposed to render Effie. I gave a commission, however, to a trusty friend to protect her to a place of safety, so soon as the fatal procession had left the jail. But for no persuasions which I could use in the hurry of the moment, or which my comrade employed at more length, after the mob had taken a different direction, could the unfortunate girl be prevailed upon to leave the prison. His arguments were all wasted upon the infatuated victim, and he was obliged to leave her in reverence to his own safety. Such was his account; but, perhaps, he persevered less steadily in his attempts to persuade her than I would have done."

"Effie was right to remain," said Jeanie; "and I love her the better for it."

"Why will you say so?" said Staunton.

"You cannot understand my reasons, sir, if I should render them," answered Jeanie, composedly; "they that thirst for the blood of their enemies have no taste for the well-spring of life."

"My hopes," said Staunton, "were thus a second time disappointed. My next efforts were to bring her through her trial by means of yourself. How I urged it, and where, you cannot have forgotten. I do not blame you for your refusal; it was founded, I am convinced, on principle, and not on indifference to your sister's fate. For me, judge of me as a man frantic; I knew not which hand to turn to, and all my efforts were unavailing. In this condition, and close beset on all sides, I thought of what might be done by means of my family, and their influence. I fled from Scotland—I reached this place—my miserably wasted and unhappy appearance procured me from my father that pardon, which a parent finds it so hard to refuse, even to the most undeserving son. And here I have awaited in anguish of mind, which the condemned criminal might envy, the event of your sister's trial."

"Without taking any steps for her relief?" said Jeanie.

"To the last I hoped her case might terminate more favourably; and it is only two days since that the fatal tidings reached me. My resolution was instantly taken. I mounted my best horse with the purpose of making the utmost haste to London, and there compounding with Sir Robert Walpole for your sister's safety, by surrendering to him, in the person of the heir of the family of Willingham, the notorious George Robertson, the accomplice of Wilson, the breaker of the Tolbooth prison, and the well-known leader of the Porteous mob."

"But would that save my sister?" said Jeanie, in astonishment.

"It would, as I should drive my bargain," said Staunton. "Queens love revenge as well as their subjects—Little as you seem to esteem it, it is a poison which pleases all palates, from the prince to the peasant. —The life of an obscure villager? Why, I might ask the best of the crown-jewels for laying the head of such an insolent conspiracy at the foot of her majesty, with a certainty of being gratified. All my other plans have failed, but this could not—Heaven is just, however, and would not honour me with making this voluntary atonement for the injury I have done your sister. I had not rode ten miles, when my horse, the best and most sure-footed animal in this country, fell with me on a level piece of road, as if he had been struck by a cannon-shot. I was greatly hurt, and was brought back here in the condition in which you now see me."

As young Staunton had come to this conclusion, the servant opened the door, and, with a voice which seemed intended rather for a signal, than merely the announcing of a visit, said, "His Reverence, sir, is coming upstairs to wait upon you."

"For God's sake, hide yourself, Jeanie," exclaimed Staunton, "in that dressing closet!"

"No, sir," said Jeanie; "as I am here for nae ill, I canna take the shame of hiding mysell frae the master o' the house."

"But, good Heavens!" exclaimed George Staunton, "do but consider"——

Ere he could complete the sentence, his father entered the apartment.

Chapter Nine

And now, will pardon, comfort, kindness, draw
The youth from vice? will honour, duty, law?
                                        CRABBE

JEANIE AROSE from her seat, and made her quiet reverence, when the elder Mr Staunton entered the apartment. His astonishment was extreme at finding his son in such company.

"I perceive, madam," said he, "I have made a mistake respecting you, and ought to have left the task of interrogating you, and of righting your wrongs, to this young man, with whom, doubtless, you have been formerly acquainted."

"It's unwitting on my part that I am here," said Jeanie; "the servant told me his master wished to speak with me."

"There goes the purple coat over my ears," murmured Tummas. "D——n her, must she needs speak the truth, and could have as well said any thing else she had a mind?"

"George," said Mr Staunton, "if you are still—as you have ever been—lost to all self-respect, you might at least have spared your father, and your father's house, such a disgraceful scene as this."

"Upon my life—upon my soul, sir!" said George, throwing his feet over the side of the bed, and starting from his recumbent posture.

"Your life, sir?" interrupted his father, with melancholy sternness,—"What sort of life has it been?—Your soul? alas! what regard have you ever paid to it? Take care to reform both ere offering either as pledges of your sincerity."

"On my honour, sir, you do me wrong," answered George Staunton; "I have been all you can call me that's bad, but in the present instance you do me injustice. By my honour, you do!"

"Your honour!" said his father, and turned from him, with a look of the most upbraiding contempt, to Jeanie. "From you, young woman, I neither ask nor expect any explanation; but, as a father alike and as a clergyman, I request your departure from this house. If your romantic story has been other than a pretext to find admission into it, (which, from the society in which you first appeared, I may be permitted to doubt,) you will find a justice of peace within two miles, with whom, more properly than with me, you may lodge your complaint."

"This shall not be," said George Staunton, starting up to his feet. "Sir, you are naturally kind and humane—you shall not become cruel and inhospitable on my account—Turn out that eaves-dropping rascal," pointing to Thomas, "and get what hartshorn drops, or better receipt you have against fainting, and I will explain to you in two words the connection betwixt this young woman and me. She shall not lose her fair character through me—I have done too much mischief to her family already, and I know too well what belongs to the loss of fame."

"Leave the room, sir," said the Rector to the servant; and when the man had obeyed, he carefully shut the door behind him, and then addressing his son, he said sternly, "Now, sir, what new proof of your infamy have you to impart to me?"

Young Staunton was about to speak, but it was one of those moments when those, who, like Jeanie Deans, possess the advantage of a steady courage and unruffled temper, can assume the superiority over more ardent but less determined spirits.

"Sir," she said to the elder Staunton, "ye have an undoubted right to ask your ain son to render a reason of his conduct. But respecting me, I am but a way-faring traveller, no ways obligated or indebted to you, unless it be for the meal of meat which, in my ain country, is willingly gien by rich or poor, according to their ability, to those who need it; and for which, forbye that, I am willing to make payment, if I didna think it would be an affront to offer siller in a house like this— only I dinna ken the fashions of the country."

"This is all very well, young woman," said the Rector, a good deal surprised, and unable to conjecture whether to impute Jeanie's language to simplicity or impertinence—"this may be all very well—but let me bring it to a point. Why do you stop this young man's mouth, and prevent his communicating to his father and his best friend, an explanation (since he says he has one) of circumstances which seem in themselves—a little suspicious?"

"He may tell of his ain affairs what he likes," answered Jeanie; "but my family and friends have nae right to hae ony stories told anent them without their express desire; and, as they canna be here to speak for themselves, I entreat ye wadna ask Mr George Rob—I mean Staunton, or whatever his name is, ony questions anent me or my folk; for I maun be free to tell you, that he will neither have the bearing of a Christian or a gentleman, if he answers you against my express desire."

"This is the most extraordinary thing I ever met with," said the Rector, as, after fixing his eyes keenly on the placid, yet modest countenance of Jeanie, he turned them suddenly upon his son. "What have you to say, sir?"

"That I feel I have been too hasty in my promise, sir," answered George Staunton; "I have no title to make any communications respecting the affairs of this young person's family without her assent."

The elder Mr Staunton turned his eyes from one to the other with marks of surprise.

"This is more, and worse, I fear," he said, addressing his son, "than one of your frequent and disgraceful connections—I insist upon knowing the mystery."

"I have already said, sir," replied his son, rather sullenly, "that I have no title to mention the affairs of this young woman's family without her consent."

"And I hae nae mysteries to explain, sir," said Jeanie, "but only to pray you, as a preacher of the gospel and a gentleman, to permit me to go safe to the next public-house on the Lunnon road."

"I shall take care of your safety," said young Staunton; "you need ask that favour from no one."

"Do you say so before my face?" said the justly incensed father. "Perhaps, sir, you intend to fill up the cup of disobedience and profligacy by forming a low and disgraceful marriage? But let me bid you beware."

"If you were feared for sic a thing happening wi' me, sir," said Jeanie, "I can only say, that not for all the land that lies between the twa ends of the rainbow wad I be the woman that should wed your son."

"There is something very singular in all this," said the elder Staunton; "follow me into the next room, young woman."

"Hear me speak first," said the young man. "I have but one word to say. I confide entirely in your prudence; tell my father as much or as little of these matters as you will, he shall know neither more or less from me."

His father darted at him a glance of indignation, which softened into sorrow as he saw him sink down on the couch, exhausted with the scene he had undergone. He left the apartment and Jeanie followed him, George Staunton raising himself as she passed the door-way, and pronouncing the word, "Remember!" in a tone as monitory as it was uttered by Charles I. upon the scaffold. The elder Staunton led the way into a small parlour, and shut the door.

"Young woman," said he, "there is something in your face and appearance that marks both sense and simplicity, and if I am not deceived, innocence also—Should it be otherwise, I can only say, you are the most accomplished hypocrite I have ever seen.—I ask to know no secret that you have unwillingness to divulge, least of all those which concern my son. His conduct has given me too much unhappiness to permit me to hope comfort or satisfaction from him. If you are such as I suppose you, believe me, that whatever unhappy circumstances may have connected you with George Staunton, the sooner you break through them the better."

"I think I understand your meaning, sir," replied Jeanie; "and as ye are sae frank as to speak o' the young gentleman in sic a way, I maun needs say that it is but the second time of my speaking wi' him in our lives, and what I hae heard frae him on these twa occasions has been such that I never wish to hear the like again."

"Then it is your real intention to leave this part of the country, and proceed to London?" said the Rector.

"Certainly, sir; for I may say, in one sense, that the avenger of blood is behind me; and if I were but assured against mischief by the way"——

"I have made enquiry," said the clergyman, "after the suspicious characters you described. They have left their place of rendezvous; but as they may be lurking in the neighbourhood, and as you say you have special reason to apprehend violence from them, I will put you under the charge of a steady person, who will protect you as far as Stamford, and see you into a light coach, which goes from thence to London."

"A coach is not for the like of me, sir," said Jeanie; to whom the idea of a stage-coach was unknown, as indeed they were then only used in the neighbourhood of London.

Mr Staunton briefly explained that she would find that mode of conveyance more commodious, cheaper, and more safe than travelling on horseback. She expressed her gratitude with so much singleness of heart, that he was induced to ask her whether she wanted the pecuniary means of prosecuting her journey. She thanked him, but said she had enough for her purpose, and indeed she had husbanded her stock with great care. This reply served also to remove some doubts, which naturally enough still floated in Mr Staunton's mind, respecting her character and real purpose, and satisfied him, at least, that money did not enter into her scheme of deception, if an impostor she should prove. He next requested to know what part of the city she wished to go to.

"To a very decent merchant, a cousin o' my ain, a Mrs Glass, sir, that sells snuff and tobacco, at the sign o' the Thistle, some-gate in the town."

Jeanie communicated this intelligence with a feeling that a connection so respectable ought to give her consequence in the eyes of Mr Staunton; and she was a good deal surprised when he answered, "And is this woman your only acquaintance in London, my poor girl? and have you really no better knowledge where she is to be found?"

"I was ganging to see the Duke of Argyle, forbye Mrs Glass," said Jeanie; "and if your honour thinks it would be best I could go there first, and get some of his Grace's folks to show me my cousin's shop"——

"Are you acquainted with any of the Duke of Argyle's people?" said the Rector.

"No, sir."

"Her brain must be something touched after all, or it would be impossible for her to rely on such introductions.—Well," said he aloud, "I must not enquire into the cause of your journey, and so I cannot be fit to give you advice how to manage it. But the landlady of the house where the coach stops, is a very decent person; and, as I use her house sometimes, I will give you a recommendation to her."

Jeanie thanked him for his kindness with her best courtesy, and said, "That with his honour's line, and ane from worthy Mrs Bickerton, that keeps the Seven Stars at York, she did not doubt to be well taken out in Lunnon."

"And now," said he, "I presume you will be desirous to set out immediately."

"If I had been in an inn, sir, or any suitable resting-place," answered Jeanie, "I wad not have presumed to use the Lord's day for travelling; but as I am on a journey of mercy, I trust my doing so will not be imputed."

"You may, if you chuse it, remain with Mrs Dalton for the evening; but I desire you will have no further correspondence with my son, who is not a proper counsellor for a person of your age, whatever your difficulties may be."

"Your honour speaks but ower truly in that," said Jeanie; "it was not with my will that I spoke wi' him just now, and—not to wish the gentleman ony thing but gude—I never wish to see him between the een again."

"If you please," added the Rector, "as you seem to be seriously-disposed, young woman, you may attend family worship in the hall this evening."

"I thank your honour," said Jeanie; "but I am doubtful if my attendance would be to edification."

"How!" said the Rector; "so young, and already unfortunate enough to have doubts upon the duties of religion!"

"God forbid, sir," replied Jeanie; "it is no for that; but I have been bred in the faith of the suffering remnant of the presbyterian doctrine in Scotland, and I am doubtful if I can lawfully attend upon your fashion of worship, seeing it has been testified against by many precious souls of our Kirk, and specially by my worthy father."

"Well, my good girl," said the Rector, with a good-humoured smile, "far be it from me to put any force upon your conscience; and yet you ought to recollect that the same divine grace dispenses its streams to other kingdoms as well as to Scotland. As it is as essential to our spiritual, as water to our earthly wants, its springs, various in character, yet alike efficacious in virtue, are to be found in abundance throughout the Christian world."

"Ah, but," said Jeanie, "though the waters may be alike, yet, with your worship's leave, the blessing upon them may not be equal. It would have been in vain for Naaman the Syrian leper to have bathed in Pharphar and Abana, rivers of Damascus, when it was only the waters of Jordan that were sanctified for the cure."

"Well," said the Rector, "we will not enter upon the great debate betwixt our national churches at present. We must endeavour to satisfy you, that, at least, amongst our errors, we preserve Christian charity, and a desire to assist our brethren."

He then ordered Mrs Dalton into his presence, and consigned Jeanie to her particular charge, with directions to be kind to her, and with assurances, that, early in the morning, a trusty guide and a good horse should be ready to conduct her to Stamford. He then took a serious and dignified, yet kind leave of her, wishing her full success in the objects of her journey, which he said he doubted not were laudable, from the soundness of thinking which she had displayed in conversation.

Jeanie was again conducted by the housekeeper to her own apartment. But the evening was not destined to pass over without further torment from young Staunton. A paper was slipped into her hand by the faithful Tummas, which intimated his young master's desire, or rather demand, to see her instantly, and assured her he had provided against interruption.

"Tell your young master," said Jeanie, openly, and regardless of all the winks and signs by which Tummas strove to make her comprehend that Mrs Dalton was not to be admitted into the secret of the correspondence, "that I promised faithfully to his worthy father that I would not see him again."

"Thomas," said Mrs Dalton, "I think you might be much more creditably employed, considering the coat you wear, and the house you live in, than to be carrying messages between your young master and girls that chance to be in this house."

"Why, Mistress Dalton, as to that, I was hired to carry messages, and not to ask any questions about them; and it's not for the like of me to refuse the young gentleman's bidding, if he were a little wildish or so.—If there's harm meant, there's no harm done, you see."

"However," said Mrs Dalton, "I gie you fair warning, Thomas Ditton, that an I catch thee at this work again, his Reverence shall make a clear house of you."

Thomas retired, abashed and in dismay. The rest of the evening past away without any thing worthy of notice.

Jeanie enjoyed the comforts of a good bed and a sound sleep with grateful satisfaction, after the perils and hardships of the preceding day; and such was her fatigue, that she slept soundly until six o'clock, when she was awakened by Mrs Dalton, who acquainted her that her guide and horse were ready, and in attendance. She hastily rose, and, after her morning devotions, was soon ready to resume her travels. The motherly care of the housekeeper had provided an early breakfast, and, after she had partaken of this refreshment, she found herself safe seated on a pillion behind a stout Lincolnshire peasant, who was, besides, armed with pistols, to protect her against any violence which might be offered.

They trudged along in silence for a mile or two by the country road, which conducted them, by hedge and gate-way, into the principal highway, a little beyond Grantham. At length her master of the horse asked her whether her name was not Jean, or Jane Deans. She answered in the affirmative, with some surprise. "Then here's a bit note as concerns you," said the man, handing it over his left shoulder. "It's from young master, as I judge, and every man about Willingham is fain to pleasure him either for love or fear; for he'll come to be landlord at last, let them say what they like."

Jeanie broke the seal of the note, which was addressed to her, and read as follows:

"You refuse to see me. I suppose you are shocked at my character: but, in painting myself such as I am, you should give me credit for my sincerity. I am, at least, no hypocrite. You refuse, however, to see me, and your conduct may be natural—but is it wise? I have expressed my anxiety to repair your sister's misfortunes at the expence of my honour, my family's honour, my own life; and you think me too debased to be admitted even to sacrifice what I have remaining of honour, fame, and life, in her cause. Well, if the offerer be despised, the victim is still equally at hand; and perhaps there may be justice in the decree of Heaven, that I shall not have the melancholy credit of appearing to make this sacrifice of my own free good-will. You, as you have declined my concurrence, must take the whole upon yourself. Go, then, to the Duke of Argyle, and, when other arguments fail you, tell him that you have it in your power to bring to condign punishment the most active conspirator in the Porteous mob. He will hear you on this topic, should he be deaf on every other. Make your own terms, for they will be at your own making. You know where I am to be found; and you may be assured that I will not give you the dark side of the hill, as at Muschat's Cairn; I have no thoughts of stirring from the house I was born in; like the hare, I shall be worried in the seat I started from. I repeat it—make your own terms. I need not remind you to ask your sister's life, for that you will do of course. But make terms of advantage for yourself—ask wealth and reward, office and income for Butler— ask any thing, you will get any thing—and all for delivering to the hands of the executioner a man most deserving of his office;—one who, though young in years, is old in wickedness, and whose most earnest desire is, after the storms of an unquiet life, to sleep and be at rest."

This extraordinary letter was subscribed with the initials G. S.

Jeanie read it over once or twice with great attention, which the slow pace of the horse, as he stalked through a deep lane, enabled her to do with facility.

When she had perused this billet, her first employment was to tear it into as small pieces as possible, and disperse these pieces in the air by a few at a time, so that a document containing so perilous a secret might not fall into any other person's hand.

The question how far, in point of extremity, she was entitled to save her sister's life by sacrificing that of a person who, though guilty towards the state, had done her no injury, formed the next earnest and most painful subject of consideration. In one sense, indeed, it seemed as if denouncing the guilt of Staunton, the cause of her sister's errors and misfortunes, would have been an act of just, and even providential retribution. But Jeanie, in the strict and severe tone of morality in which she was educated, had to consider not only the general aspect of a purposed action, but its justness and fitness in relation to the actor, before she could be, according to her own phrase, free to enter upon it. What right had she to make a barter between the lives of Staunton and of Effie, and to sacrifice the one for the safety of the other? The crime—that crime for which he was amenable to the laws—was a crime against the public indeed, but it was not against her.

Neither did it seem to her that his share in the death of Porteous, though her mind revolted at the idea of using violence to any one, was in the relation of a common murder, against the perpetrator of which every one is called to aid the public magistrate. That violent action was blended with many circumstances, which, in the eyes of those of Jeanie's rank in life, if they did not altogether deprive it of the character of guilt, softened, at least, its most atrocious features. The anxiety of the government to obtain conviction of some of the offenders, had but served to increase that public feeling which connected the action, though violent and irregular, with the idea of ancient national independence. The very rigorous measures adopted or proposed against the city of Edinburgh, the ancient metropolis of Scotland—the extremely unpopular and injudicious measure of compelling the clergy to promulgate from the pulpit the reward offered for discovery of the perpetrators of this slaughter, had produced on the public mind the opposite consequences from what were intended; and Jeanie felt conscious, that whoever should lodge information concerning that event, and for whatsoever purpose it might be done, it would be considered as an act of treason against the independence of Scotland. With the fanaticism of the Scotch presbyterians, there was always mingled a glow of national feeling, and Jeanie trembled at the idea of her name being handed down to posterity with that of the "fause Monteith," and one or two others, who, having deserted and betrayed the cause of their country, are damned to perpetual remembrance and execration among its peasantry. Yet, to part with Effie's life once more, when a word spoken might save it, pressed severely on the mind of her affectionate sister.

"The Lord support and direct me," said poor Jeanie, "for it seems to be his will to try me with difficulties far beyond my ain strength."

While this thought passed through Jeanie's mind, her guard, tired of silence, began to show some inclination to be communicative. He seemed a sensible steady peasant, but not having more delicacy or prudence than is common to those in his situation, he, of course, chose the Willingham family as the subject of his conversation. From this man Jeanie learned some particulars of which she had hitherto been ignorant, and which we will briefly recapitulate for the information of the reader.

The father of George Staunton had been bred a soldier, and during service in the West Indies, had married the heiress of a wealthy planter. By this lady he had an only child, George Staunton, the unhappy young man who has been so often mentioned in this narrative. He passed the first part of his early youth under the charge of a doting mother, and in the society of negro slaves, whose study it was to gratify his every caprice. His father was a man of worth and of sense; but as he alone retained tolerable health among the officers of the regiment he belonged to, he was much engaged with his duty. Besides, Mrs Staunton was beautiful and wilful, and enjoyed but delicate health; so that it was difficult for a man of affection, humanity, and a quiet disposition, to struggle with her on the point of her over-indulgence to an only child. Indeed, what Mr Staunton did do towards counteracting the baneful effects of his wife's system, only tended to render it more pernicious, for every restraint imposed on the boy in his father's presence, was compensated by treble license during his absence. So that George Staunton acquired, even in childhood, the habit of regarding his father as a rigid censor, from whose severity he was desirous of emancipating himself as soon and absolutely as possible.

When he was about ten years old, and his mind had received all the seeds of those evil weeds which afterwards grew apace, his mother died, and his father, half heart-broken, returned to England. To sum her imprudence and unjustifiable indulgence, she contrived to place a considerable part of her fortune at her son's exclusive controul or disposal. George Staunton had not been long in England till he learned his independence, and how to abuse it. His father had endeavoured to rectify the defects of his education by placing him in a well-regulated seminary. But although he showed some capacity for learning, his riotous conduct soon became intolerable to his teachers. He found means (too easily offered to all youths who have certain expectations) of procuring such a command of money as enabled him to anticipate in boyhood the frolics and follies of a more mature age, and, with these accomplishments, he was returned on his father's hands as a profligate boy, whose example might ruin an hundred.

The elder Mr Staunton, whose mind, since his wife's death, had been tinged with a melancholy, which certainly his son's conduct did not tend to dispel, had taken orders, and was inducted by his brother Sir William Staunton into the family living of Willingham. The revenue was a matter of consequence to him, for he derived little advantage from the estate of his late wife; and his own fortune was that of a younger brother.

He took his son to reside with him at the rectory, but he soon found that his disorders rendered him an intolerable inmate. And as the young men of his own rank would not endure the purse-proud insolence of the Creole, he fell into that taste for low society, which is worse than "pressing to death, whipping, or hanging." His father sent him abroad, but he only returned wilder and more desperate than before. It is true, this unhappy youth was not without his good qualities. He had lively wit, good temper, reckless generosity, and manners which, while he was under restraint, might pass well in society. But all these availed him nothing. He was so well acquainted with the turf, the gaming-table, the cock-pit, and worse rendezvouses of folly and dissipation, that his mother's fortune was spent before he was twenty-one, and he was soon in debt and in distress. His early history may be concluded in the words of our British Juvenal, when describing a similar character:—

> Headstrong, determined in his own career,
> He thought reproof unjust and truth severe.
> The soul's disease was to its crisis come,
> He first abused and then abjured his home;
> And when he chose a vagabond to be,
> He made his shame his glory, "I'll be free."

"And yet 'tis pity on Measter George, too," continued the honest boor, "for he has an open hand, and winna let a poor body want an' he has it."

The virtue of profuse generosity, by which, indeed, they themselves are most directly advantaged, is readily admitted by the vulgar as a cloak for many sins.

At Stamford our heroine was deposited in safety by her communicative guide. She obtained a place in the coach, which, although termed a light one, and accommodated with no fewer than six horses, only reached London on the afternoon of the second day. The recommendation of the elder Mr Staunton procured Jeanie a civil reception at the inn where the carriage stopped, and, by the aid of Mrs Bickerton's correspondent, she found out her friend and relative Mrs Glass, by whom she was kindly received and hospitably entertained.

Chapter Ten

> My name is Argyle, you may well think it strange,
> To live at the court and never to change.
>
> *Ballad*

FEW NAMES DESERVE more honourable mention in the history of Scotland during this period, than that of John, Duke of Argyle and Greenwich. His talents as a statesman and a soldier were generally admitted; he was not without ambition, but "without the illness that attends it"—without that irregularity of thought and aim, which often excites great men, in his peculiar situation, (for it was a very peculiar one) to grasp the means of raising themselves to power, at the risk of throwing a kingdom into confusion. Pope has distinguished him as

> Argyle, the state's whole thunder born to wield,
> And shake alike the senate and the field.

He was alike free from the ordinary vices of statesmen, falsehood, namely, and dissimulation, and from those of warriors, inordinate and violent thirst after self-aggrandizement.

Scotland, his native country, stood at this time in a very precarious and doubtful situation. She was indeed united to England, but the cement had not had time to acquire consistence. The irritation of ancient wrongs still subsisted, and betwixt the fretful jealousy of the Scottish, and the supercilious disdain of the English, quarrels repeatedly occurred, in the course of which the national league, so important to the safety of both, was in the utmost danger of being dissolved. Scotland had, besides, the disadvantage of being divided into intestine factions, which hated each other bitterly, and waited but a signal to break forth into action.

In such circumstances, another man, with the talents and rank of Argyle, but without a mind so happily regulated, would have sought to rise from the earth in the whirlwind, and direct its fury. He chose a course more safe and more honourable.

Soaring above the petty distinctions of faction, his voice was raised, whether in office or opposition, for those measures which were at once just and lenient. His high military talent enabled him, during the memorable year 1715, to render such services to the House of Hanover, as, perhaps, were too great to be either acknowledged or repaid. He had employed, too, his utmost influence in softening the consequences of that insurrection to the unfortunate gentlemen, whom a mistaken sense of loyalty had engaged in the affair, and was rewarded by the esteem and affection of his country in an uncommon degree. This popularity, with a discontented and warlike people, was supposed to be a subject of jealousy at court, where the power to become dangerous is sometimes of itself obnoxious, though the inclination is not united with it. Besides, the Duke of Argyle's independent and somewhat haughty mode of expressing himself in parliament, and acting in public, were ill calculated to attract royal favour. He was, therefore, always respected, and often employed, but he was not a favourite of George the Second, his consort, or his ministers. At several different periods in his life, the Duke might be considered as in absolute disgrace at court, although he could hardly be said to be a declared member of opposition. This rendered him the dearer to Scotland, because it was usually in her cause that he incurred the displeasure of her sovereign; and upon this very occasion of the Porteous mob, the animated and eloquent opposition which he had offered to the severe measures which were about to be adopted towards the city of Edinburgh, was the more gratefully received in that metropolis, as it was understood that the Duke's interposition had given personal offence to Queen Caroline.

His conduct upon this occasion, as indeed that of all the Scottish members of the legislature, with one or two unworthy exceptions, had been in the highest degree spirited. The popular tradition, concerning his reply to Queen Caroline, has been given already, and some fragments of his speeches against the Porteous Bill are still remembered. He retorted upon the Chancellor, Lord Hardwicke, the insinuation that he had stated himself in this case rather as a party than as a judge: —"I appeal," said Argyle, "to the House—to the nation, if I can be justly branded with the infamy of being a jobber, or a partizan. Have I been a briber of votes?—a buyer of boroughs?—the agent of corruption for any purpose, or in behalf of any party?—Consider my life; examine my actions in the field and in the cabinet, and see where there lies a blot that can attach to my honour. I have shewn myself the friend of my country—the loyal subject of my king. I am ready to do so again, without an instant's regard to the frowns or smiles of a court. I have experienced both, and am prepared with indifference for either. I have given my reasons for opposing this bill, and have made it appear that it is repugnant to the international treaty of union, to the liberty of Scotland, and, reflectively, to that of England, to common justice, to common sense, and to the public interest. Shall the metropolis of Scotland, the capital of an independant nation, the residence of a long line of monarchs, by whom that noble city was graced and dignified— shall such a city, for the fault of an obscure and unknown body of rioters, be deprived of its honours and its privileges—its gates and its guards?—and shall a native Scotsman tamely behold the havock? I glory, my Lords, in opposing such unjust rigour, and reckon it my dearest pride and honour to stand up in defence of my native country, while thus laid open to undeserved shame, and unjust spoliation."

Other statesmen and orators, both Scottish and English, used the same arguments, the bill was gradually stripped of its most oppressive and obnoxious clauses, and at length ended in a fine upon the city of Edinburgh in favour of Porteous's widow. So that, as somebody observed at the time, the whole of these fierce debates ended in making the fortune of an old cook-maid, such having been the good woman's original capacity.

The court, however, did not forget the baffle which they had received in this affair, and the Duke of Argyle, who had contributed so much to it, was thereafter considered as a person in disgrace. It is necessary to place these circumstances under the reader's observation, both because they are connected with the preceding and subsequent part of our narrative.

The Duke was alone in his study, when one of his gentlemen acquainted him, that a country-girl, from Scotland, was desirous of speaking with his Grace.

"A country-girl, and from Scotland!" said the Duke; "what can have brought the silly fool to London?—Some lover pressed and sent to sea, or some stock sunk in the South-Sea funds, or some such hopeful concern, I suppose, and then nobody to manage the matter but Maccallanmore.—Well, this same popularity has its inconveniencies.—However, show our country-woman up, Archibald—it is ill manners to keep her in attendance."

A young woman of rather low stature, and whose countenance might be termed very modest and pleasing in expression, though sunburned, somewhat freckled, and not possessing regular features, was ushered into the splendid library. She wore the tartan plaid of her country, adjusted so as partly to cover her head, and partly to fall back over her shoulders. A quantity of fair hair, disposed with great simplicity and neatness, appeared in front of her round and good-humoured face, to which the solemnity of her errand, and her sense of the duke's rank and importance, gave an appearance of deep awe, but not of slavish fear, or fluttered bashfulness. The rest of Jeanie's dress was in the style of Scottish maidens of her own class; but arranged with that scrupulous attention to neatness and cleanliness, which we often find united with that purity of mind, of which it is a natural emblem.

She stopped near the entrance of the room, made her deepest reverence, and crossed her hands upon her bosom, without uttering a syllable. The Duke of Argyle advanced towards her; and if she admired his graceful deportment and rich dress, decorated with the orders which had been deservedly bestowed on him, his courteous manner, and quick and intelligent cast of countenance, he on his part was not less, or less deservedly, struck with the quiet simplicity and modesty expressed in the dress, manners, and countenance of his humble countrywoman.

"Did you wish to speak with me, my bonnie lass?" said the Duke, using the encouraging epithet which at once acknowledged the connection betwixt them as country-folks; "or, did you want to see the Duchess?"

"My business is with your honour, my Lord—I mean your Lordship's Grace."

"And what is it, my good girl?" said the Duke, in the same mild and encouraging tone of voice. Jeanie looked at the attendant. "Leave us, Archibald," said the Duke, "and wait in the anti-room." The domestic retired. "And now sit down, my good lass," said the Duke; "take your breath—take your time, and tell me what you have got to say. I guess by your dress, you are just come up from poor old Scotland —Did you come through the streets in your tartan plaid?"

"No, sir," said Jeanie; "a friend brought me in ane o' their street coaches—a very decent woman," she added, her courage increasing as she became familiar with the sound of her own voice in such a presence; "your Lordship's Grace kens her—it's Mistress Glass, at the sign o' the Thistle."

"O my worthy snuff-merchant—I have always a chat with Mrs Glass when I purchase my Scots high-dried.—Well, but your business, my bonnie woman—time and tide, you know, wait for no one."

"Your Lordship—I beg your honour's pardon—I mean your Grace," for it must be noticed, that this matter of addressing the Duke by his appropriate title had been anxiously inculcated upon Jeanie by her friend Mrs Glass, in whose eyes it was a matter of such importance, that her last words, as Jeanie left the coach, were, "Mind to say your Grace;" and Jeanie, who had scarce ever in her life spoke to a person of higher quality than the Laird of Dumbiedikes, found great difficulty in arranging her language according to the rules of ceremony.

The Duke, who saw her embarrassment, said, with his usual affability, "Never mind my grace, lassie; just speak out a plain tale, and shew you have a Scots tongue in your head."

"Sir, I am muckle obliged—Sir, I am the sister of that poor unfortunate criminal, Effie Deans, who is ordered for execution at Edinburgh."

"Ah!" said the Duke, "I have heard of that unhappy story, I think— a case of child murder, under a special act of parliament—Duncan Forbes mentioned it at dinner the other day."

"And I was come up frae the north, sir, to see what could be done for her in the way of getting reprieve or pardon, sir, or the like of that."

"Alas! my poor girl," said the Duke, "you have made a long and a sad journey to very little purpose—Your sister is ordered for execution."

"But I am given to understand there is law for reprieving her, if it is in the king's pleasure," said Jeanie.

"Certainly there is," said the Duke; "but that is purely in the king's breast. The crime has been but too common—the Scots crown-lawyers think it is right there should be an example. Then the late disorders in Edinburgh have excited a prejudice in government against the nation at large, which they think can only be managed by measures of intimidation and severity. What argument have you, my poor girl, except the warmth of your sisterly affection, to offer against all this?—What is your interest?—What friends have you at court?"

"None, excepting God and your Grace," said Jeanie, still keeping her ground resolutely, however.

"Alas!" said the Duke, "I could almost say with old Ormond, that there could not be any, whose influence was smaller with kings and ministers. It is a cruel part of our situation, young woman—I mean of the situation of men in my circumstances, that the public ascribes to them influence which they do not possess; and that individuals are led to expect from them assistance, which we have no means of rendering. But candour and plain-dealing are in the power of every one, and I must not let you imagine you have resources in my influence, which do not exist, to make your distress the heavier—I have no means of averting your sister's fate—She must die."

"We must a' die, sir," said Jeanie; "it is our common doom for our father's transgression; but we shouldna hasten ilk other out o' the world, that's what your honour kens better than me."

"My good young woman," said the Duke, mildly, "we are all apt to blame the law under which we immediately suffer; but you seem to have been well educated in your line of life, and you must know that it is alike the law of God and man, that the murderer shall surely die."

"But, sir, Effie—that is my poor sister, sir—canna be proved to be a murderer; and if she be not, and if the law take her life notwithstanding, wha is it that is the murderer then?"

"I am no lawyer," said the Duke; "and I own I think the statute a very severe one."

"You are a law-maker though, sir, with your leave; and, therefore, ye have power over the law," answered Jeanie.

"Not in my individual capacity," said the Duke; "though, as one of a large body, I have a voice in the legislation. But that cannot serve you —nor have I at present, I care not who knows it, so much personal influence with the sovereign, as would entitle me to ask from him the most insignificant favour. What could tempt you, young woman, to address yourself to me?"

"It was yoursell, sir."

"Myself?" he replied—"I am sure you have never seen me before."

"No, sir; but a' the world kens that the Duke of Argyle is the country's friend and the poor man's friend; and that ye fight for the right, and speak for the right, and that there is nae name like your's in our present Israel, and so they that think themselves wranged draw to refuge under your shadow; and if ye winna stir to save the bluid of an innocent country-woman of your ain, what should we expect frae southerns and strangers? And maybe I had another reason for troubling your honour."

"And what is that?" asked the Duke.

"I hae understood frae my father, that your honour's House, and especially your gudesire and his father, laid down their lives on the scaffold in the persecuting time. And my father was honoured to gie his testimony baith in the cage and in the pillory, as is specially mentioned in the books of Peter Walker the packman, that your honour, I dare say, kens, for he uses maist partly the west-land of Scotland. And, sir, there's ane that takes concern in me, that wished me to gang to your Grace's presence, for his gudesire had done your gracious gudesire some gude turn, as ye will see frae these papers."

With these words, she delivered to the Duke the little parcel which she had received from Butler. He opened it, and, in the envelope, read with some surprise, "Muster-roll of the men serving in the troop of that godly gentleman, Captain Salathiel Bangtext.—Obadiah Muggleton, Sin-Despise Double-knock, Stand-fast-in-faith Gipps, Turn-to-the-right Thwack-away—What the deuce is this? A list of Praise-God Barebone's Parliament I think, or of old Noll's evangelical army—that last fellow should understand his wheelings to judge by his name.—But what does all this mean, my girl?"

"It was the other paper, sir," said Jeanie, somewhat abashed at the mistake.

"O! this is my unfortunate grandfather's hand sure enough—'To all who may have friendship for the House of Argyle, These are to certifie, that Benjamin Butler, of Monk's Regiment of Dragoons, having been, under God, the means of saving my life from four English troopers who were about to slay me, I, having no other present means of recompense in my power, do give him this acknowledgment, hoping that it may be useful to him or his during these troublesome times; and do conjure my friends, tenants, kinsmen, and whoever will do aught for me, either in the Highlands or Lowlands, to protect and assist the said Benjamin Butler, and his friends or family, in their lawful occasions, giving them such countenance, maintenance, and supply, as may correspond with the benefit he hath bestowed on me, witness my hand—

'LORNE.'

"This is a strong injunction—This Benjamin Butler was your grandfather I suppose?—You seem too young to have been his daughter."

"He wasna akin to me, sir—he was grandfather—to ane—to a neighbour's son—to a sincere well-wisher of mine, sir," dropping her little curtsey as she spoke.

"O, I understand," said the Duke—"a true-love affair. He was the grandsire of one you are engaged to?"

"One I *was* engaged to, sir," said Jeanie, sighing; "but this unhappy business of my puir sister"——

"What!" said the Duke, hastily,—"he has not deserted you on that account, has he?"

"No, sir; he wad be the last to leave a friend in difficulties," said Jeanie; "but I maun think for him, as weel as for mysell. He is a clergyman, sir, and it would not beseem him to marry the like of me, wi' this disgrace on my kindred."

"You are a singular young woman," said the Duke. "You seem to me to think of every one before yourself. And have you really come up from Edinburgh on foot, to attempt this hopeless solicitation for your sister's life?"

"It was not a'thegether on foot, sir," answered Jeanie; "for I sometimes got a cast in a waggon, and I had a horse from Ferrybridge, and then the coach"——

"Well, never mind all that," interrupted the Duke.—"What reason have you for thinking your sister innocent?"

"Because she has not been proved guilty, sir, as will appear from looking at these papers."

She put into his hand a note of the evidence, and copies of her sister's declaration. These papers Butler had procured after her departure, and Saddletree had them forwarded to London, to Mrs Glass's care, so that Jeanie found the documents, so necessary for supporting her suit, lying in readiness at her arrival.

"Sit down in that chair, my good girl," said the Duke, "until I glance over the papers."

She obeyed, and watched with the utmost anxiety each change in his countenance as he cast his eye through the papers briefly, yet with attention, and making memoranda as he went along. After reading them hastily over, he looked up, and seemed about to speak, yet changed his purpose, as if afraid of committing himself by giving too hasty an opinion, and read over again several passages which he had marked as being most important. All this he did in shorter time than can be supposed by men of ordinary talents; for his mind was of that acute and penetrating character which discovers with the glance of intuition what facts bear on the particular point that chances to be subjected to consideration. At length he rose after a few minutes' deep reflection.—"Young woman," said he, "your sister's case must certainly be termed a hard one."

"God bless you, sir, for that very word," said Jeanie.

"It seems contrary to the genius of British law," continued the

Duke, "to take that for granted which is not proved, or to punish with death for a crime, which, for aught the prosecutor has been able to show, may not have been committed at all."

"God bless you, sir, again," said Jeanie, who had risen from her seat, and, with clasped hands, eyes glittering through tears, and features which trembled with anxiety, drank in every word which the Duke uttered.

"But alas! my poor girl," he continued, "what good will my opinion do you, unless I could impress it upon those in whose hands your sister's life is placed by the law? Besides, I am no lawyer; and I must speak with some of our Scottish gentlemen of the gown about the matter."

"O but, sir, what seems reasonable to your honour, will certainly be the same to them," answered Jeanie.

"I do not know that," replied the Duke; "ilka man buckles his belt his ain gate—you know our old Scots proverb?—But you shall not have placed this reliance on me altogether in vain. Leave these papers with me, and you shall hear from me to-morrow or next day. Take care to be at home at Mistress Glass's, and ready to come to me at a moment's warning. It will be unnecessary for you to give Mrs Glass the trouble to attend you;—and, by the bye, you will please to be dressed just as you are at present."

"I wad hae putten on a cap, sir," said Jeanie, "but your honour kens it isna the fashion of my country for single women; and I judged that being sae mony hunderd miles frae hame, your Grace's heart wad warm to the tartan," looking at the corner of her plaid.

"You judged quite right," said the Duke. "I know the full value of the snood; and Maccallanmore's heart will be as cold as death can make it, when it does *not* warm to the tartan. Now, go away, and don't be out of the way when I send."

Jeanie replied,—"There is little fear of that, sir, for I have little heart to go to see sights amang this wilderness of black houses. But if I might say to your gracious honour, that if ye ever condescend to speak to ony ane that is of greater degree than yoursell, though maybe it isna civil in me to say sae, just if you would think there can be nae sic odds between you and them, as between poor Jeanie Deans from Saint Leonard's and the Duke of Argyle; and so dinna be chappit back or cast down wi' the first rough answer."

"I am not apt," said the Duke, laughing, "to mind rough answers much—Do not you hope too much from what I have promised. I will do my best, but God has the hearts of kings in his own hand."

Jeanie curtsied reverently and withdrew, attended by the Duke's gentleman, to her hackney-coach, with a respect which her appearance did not demand, but which was perhaps paid to the length of interview with which his master had honoured her.

Chapter Eleven

——ascend,
While radiant summer opens all its pride,
Thy hill, delightful Shene! Here let us sweep
The boundless landscape.
THOMSON

FROM HER KIND and officious, but somewhat gossipping friend, Mrs Glass, Jeanie underwent a very close catechism on their road to the Strand, where the Thistle of the good lady flourished in full glory, and, with its legend of *Nemo me impune*, distinguished a shop then well known to all Scottish folks of high and low degree.

"And were you sure aye to say your Grace to him?" said the good old lady; "for ane should make a distinction between Maccallanmore and the bits o' southern bodies that they ca' lords here—there are as mony o' them, Jeanie, as would gar ane think they maun cost but little fash in the making—some of them I wadna trust wi' sax pennies worth of black rappee—some of them I wadna gie mysell the trouble to put up a hapnyworth in brown paper for—But I hope you showed your breeding to the Duke of Argyle, for what sort of folks would he think your friends in London, if you had been lording him, and him a Duke?"

"He didna seem muckle to mind," said Jeanie; "he kenn'd that I was landward bred."

"Weel, weel," answered the good lady. "His Grace kens me weel; so I am the less anxious about it. I never fill his snuff-box but he says, 'How d'ye do, good Mrs Glass?—How are all our friends in the North?' or it maybe—'Have ye heard from the North lately?' And you may be sure, I make my best curtesy, and answer, My Lord Duke, I hope your Grace's noble Duchess, and your Grace's young ladies, are well; and I hope the snuff continues to give your Grace satisfaction. And then ye will see the people in the shop begin to look about them; and if there's a Scotsman there, as may be three or half a dozen, aff go the hats, and mony a look after him, and there goes the Prince of Scotland, God bless him. But ye have not told me yet the very words he said t'ye."

Jeanie had no intention to be quite so communicative. She had, as the reader may have observed, some of the caution and shrewdness, as well as of the simplicity of her country. She answered generally, that the Duke had received her very compassionately, and had promised to interest himself in her sister's affair, and to let her hear from him in the course of the next day, or the day after. She did not chuse to make any mention of his having desired her to be in readiness to attend him, far less of his hint, that she should not bring her landlady. So that honest Mrs Glass was obliged to remain satisfied with the general intelligence above mentioned, after having done all she could to extract more.

It may easily be conceived, that, on the next day, Jeanie declined all invitations and inducements, whether of exercise or curiosity, to walk abroad, and continued to inhale the close, and somewhat professional atmosphere of Mrs Glass's small parlour. The latter flavour it owed to a certain cupboard, containing, among other articles, a few cannisters of real Havannah, which, whether from respect to the manufacture, or out of a reverend fear of the excisemen, Mrs Glass did not care to trust in the open shop below, and which communicated to the room a scent, that, however fragrant to the nostrils of the connoisseur, was not very agreeable to those of Jeanie.

"Dear sirs," she said to herself, "I wonder how my cousin's silk manty, and her gowd watch, or ony thing in the world, can be worth sitting sneezing all her life in this little stifling room, and might walk on green braes if she liked."

Mrs Glass was equally surprised at her cousin's reluctance to stir abroad, and her indifference to the fine sights of London. "It would always help to pass away the time," she said, "to have something to look at, though ane was in distress." But Jeanie was unpersuadable.

The day after her interview with the Duke was spent in that "hope delayed, which maketh the heart sick." Minutes glided after minutes —hours fled after hours—it became too late to have any reasonable expectation of hearing from the Duke that day; yet the hope which she disowned, she could not altogether relinquish, and her heart throbbed, and her ears tingled, with every casual sound in the shop below. It was in vain. The day wore away in the anxiety of protracted and fruitless expectation.

The next morning commenced in the same manner. But before noon, a well-dressed gentleman entered Mrs Glass's shop, and requested to see a young woman from Scotland.

"That will be my cousin, Jeanie Deans, Mr Archibald," said Mrs Glass, with a curtesy of recognizance. "Have you any message to her from his Grace the Duke of Argyle, Mr Archibald? I will carry it up to her in a moment."

"I believe I must give her the trouble of stepping down, Mrs Glass."

"Jeanie—Jeanie Deans!" said Mrs Glass, screaming at the bottom of the little stair-case, which ascended from the corner of the shop to the higher regions. "Jeanie—Jeanie Deans, I say, come down stairs instantly; here is the Duke of Argyle's Groom of the Chambers desires to see you directly." This was announced in a voice so loud, as to make all who chanced to be within hearing, aware of the important communication.

It may easily be supposed, that Jeanie did not tarry long in adjusting herself to attend the summons, yet her feet almost failed her as she came down stairs.

"I must ask the favour of your company a little way," said Archibald, with civility.

"I am quite ready, sir," said Jeanie.

"Is my cousin ganging out, Mr Archibald? then I will hae to gang wi' her no doubt.—James Rasper—Look to the shop, James.—Mr Archibald," pushing a jar towards him, "you take his Grace's mixture, I think. Please to fill your box, for old acquaintance sake, while I get on my things."

Mr Archibald transposed a modest parcel of snuff from the jar to his own mull, but said he was obliged to decline the pleasure of Mrs Glass's company, as his message was particularly to the young person.

"Particularly to the young person?" said Mrs Glass; "is not that uncommon, Mr Archibald? But his Grace is the best judge; and you are a steady person, Mr Archibald. It is not every one that comes from a great man's house, I would trust my cousin with. But, Jeanie, you must not go through the streets with Mr Archibald with your tartan what d'ye call it there, upon your shoulders, as you had come up with a drove of Highland cattle. Wait till I bring you down my silk cloak. Why you will have the mob after you!"

"I have a hackney-coach in waiting, madam," said Mr Archibald, interrupting the officious old lady, from whom Jeanie might otherwise have found it difficult to escape, "and, I believe, I must not allow her time for any change of dress."

So saying, he hurried Jeanie into the coach, while she internally praised and wondered at the easy manner in which he shifted off Mrs Glass's officious offers and enquiries, without mentioning his master's orders, or entering into any explanation.

On entering the coach, Mr Archibald seated himself on the front seat, opposite to our heroine, and they drove on in silence. After they had driven nearly half an hour, without a word on either side, it occurred to Jeanie, that the distance and time did not correspond with that which had been occupied by her journey on the former occasion to, and from, the residence of the Duke of Argyle. At length she could not help asking her taciturn companion, "Whilk way they were going?"

"My Lord Duke will inform you himself, madam," answered Archibald, with the same solemn courtesy, which marked his whole demeanour. Almost as he spoke, the hackney-coach drew up, and the coachman dismounted and opened the door. Archibald got out and assisted Jeanie to get down. She found herself in a large turnpike road, without the bounds of London, upon the other side of which was drawn up a plain chariot and four horses, the pannels without arms, and the servants without liveries.

"You have been punctual, I see, Jeanie," said the Duke of Argyle, as Archibald opened the carriage door. "You must be my companion for the rest of the way. Archibald will remain here with the hackney-coach till your return."

Ere Jeanie could make answer, she found herself, to her no small astonishment, seated by the side of a duke, in a carriage which rolled forward at a rapid yet smooth rate, very different in both particulars from the lumbering, jolting vehicle which she had just left; and which, lumbering and jolting as it was, conveyed to one, who had only once been in a coach before, a certain feeling of dignity and importance.

"Young woman," said the Duke, "after thinking as attentively on your sister's case as is in my power, I continue to be impressed with the belief that great injustice may be done by the execution of her sentence. So are one or two liberal and intelligent lawyers of both countries whom I have spoken with.—Nay, pray hear me out before you thank me.—I have already told you my personal conviction is of little consequence, unless I could impress the same upon others. Now I have done for you, what I would certainly not have done to serve any purpose of my own—I have asked an audience of a lady whose interest with the king is deservedly very high. It has been allowed me, and I am desirous that you should see her and speak for yourself. You have no occasion to be abashed; tell your story simply as you did to me."

"I am much obliged to your Grace," said Jeanie, remembering Mrs Glass's charge, "and I am sure since I have had the courage to speak to your Grace, in poor Effie's cause, I have less reason to be shame-faced in speaking to a leddy. But, sir, I would like to ken what to ca' her, whether your grace, or your honour, or your leddyship, as we say to lairds' leddies in Scotland, and I will take care to mind it; for I ken leddies are full mair particular than gentlemen about their titles of honour."

"You have no occasion to call her any thing but Madam. Just say what you think is likely to make the best impression—look at me from time to time—if I put my hand to my cravat so—(shewing her the motion)—you will stop; but I shall only do this if you say any thing that is not likely to please."

"But, sir, your Grace," said Jeanie, "if it wasna ower muckle trouble, wad it na be better to tell me what I should say, and I could get it by heart?"

"No, Jeanie, that would not have the same effect—that would be like reading a sermon you know, which we good presbyterians think has less unction than when spoken without book," replied the Duke. "Just speak as plainly and boldly to this lady, as you did to me the day before yesterday; and if you can gain her consent, I'll wad ye a plack, as we say in the north, that you get this pardon from the king."

As he spoke, he took a pamphlet from his pocket, and began to read. Jeanie had good sense and tact, which constitute betwixt them that which is called natural good breeding. She interpreted the Duke's manœuvre as a hint that she was to ask no more questions, and she remained silent accordingly.

The carriage rolled rapidly onwards through fertile meadows, ornamented with splendid old oaks, and catching occasionally a glance of the majestic mirror of a broad and placid river. After passing through a pleasant village, the equipage stopped on a commanding eminence, where the beauty of English landscape was displayed in its utmost luxuriance. Here the Duke alighted, and desired Jeanie to follow him. They paused for a moment on the brow of the hill, to gaze on the unrivalled landscape which it presented. A huge sea of verdure, with crossing and intersecting promontories of massive and tufted groves, was tenanted by numberless flocks and herds, which seemed to wander unrestrained and unbounded through the richest pastures. The Thames, here turretted with villas, and there garlanded with forests, moved on slowly and placidly, like the mighty monarch of the scene, to whom all its other beauties were but accessories, and bore on his bosom an hundred barks and skiffs, whose white sails and gaily fluttering penons gave life to the whole.

The Duke of Argyle was, of course, familiar with this scene; but to a man of genius, it must be always new. Yet, as he paused and looked on this inimitable landscape, with the feeling of delight which it must give to the bosom of every admirer of nature, his thoughts naturally reverted to his own more grand, yet scarce less beautiful, domains of Inverary.—"This is a fine scene," he said to his companion, curious, perhaps, to draw out her sentiments; "we have nothing like it in Scotland."

"It's braw rich feeding for the cows, and they have a fine breed o' cattle here," replied Jeanie; "but I like just as weel to look at the crags of Arthur's Seat, and the sea coming in ayont them, as at a' thae muckle trees."

The Duke smiled at a reply equally professional and national, and made signal for the carriage to remain where it was. Then adopting an unfrequented footpath, he conducted Jeanie, through several complicated mazes, to a postern-door in a high brick wall. It was shut; but as the Duke tapped slightly at it, a person in waiting within, after reconnoitring through a small iron-grate contrived for the purpose, unlocked the door, and admitted them. They entered, and it was immediately closed and fastened behind them. This was all done quickly, the door so instantly closing, and the person who had opened it so suddenly disappearing, that Jeanie could not even catch a glance of his exterior.

They found themselves at the extremity of a deep and narrow alley, carpetted with the most verdant and close shaven turf, which felt like velvet under their feet, and screened from the sun by the branches of the lofty elms which united over the path, and caused it to resemble, in the solemn obscurity of the light which they admitted, as well as from the range of columnar stems, and intricate union of their arched branches, one of the narrow side aisles in an ancient Gothic cathedral.

Chapter Twelve

——I beseech you—
These tears beseech you, and these chaste hands woo you,
That never yet were heaved but to things holy—
Things like yourself—You are a God above us;
Be as a God, then, full of saving mercy!
The Bloody Brother

ENCOURAGED AS SHE WAS by the courteous manners of her noble countryman, it was not without a feeling of something like terror that Jeanie felt herself in a place apparently so lonely, with a man of such high rank. That she should have been permitted to wait on the Duke in his own house, and have been there received to a private interview, was in itself an uncommon and distinguished event in the annals of a life so simple as her's. But to find herself his travelling companion in a journey, and then suddenly to be left alone with him in so secluded a situation, had something in it of awful mystery. A romantic heroine might have suspected and doubted the power of her own charms; but Jeanie was too wise to let such a silly thought intrude on her mind. Still, however, she had a most eager desire to know where she now was, and to whom she was to be presented.

She remarked that the Duke's dress, though still such as indicated rank and fashion, (for it was not the custom for men of quality at that time to dress themselves like their own coachmen or grooms,) was nevertheless plainer than that in which she had seen him upon a former occasion, and was divested, in particular, of all those badges of external decoration which intimated superior consequence. In short, he was attired as plainly as any gentleman could then appear in the streets of London in a morning; and this circumstance helped to shake an opinion which Jeanie began to entertain, that, perhaps, he intended she should plead her cause in the presence of royalty itself. "But, surely," said she to herself, "he wad hae putten on his braw star and garter, an' he had thought o' coming before the face of Majesty— and after a', this is mair like a gentleman's policy than like a palace royal."

There was some sense in Jeanie's reasoning; yet she was not sufficiently mistress either of the circumstances of etiquette, or the particular relations which existed betwixt the government and the Duke of Argyle, to form an accurate judgment. The Duke, as we have said, was at this time in open opposition to the administration of Sir Robert Walpole, and was understood to be out of favour with the royal family, to whom he had rendered such important services. But it was a maxim of Queen Caroline, to bear herself towards her political friends with such caution, as if there was a possibility of their one day being her enemies, and towards political opponents with the same degree of circumspection, as if they might again become friendly to her measures. Since Margaret of Anjou, no queen-consort had exercised such weight in the political affairs of England, and the personal address which she displayed on many occasions, had no small share in reclaiming from their political heresy many of those determined tories, who, after the reign of the Stuarts had been extinguished in the person of Queen Anne, were disposed rather to transfer their allegiance to her brother the Chevalier de Saint George, than to acquiesce in the settlement of the crown on the Hanover family. Her husband, whose most shining quality was courage in the field of battle, and who endured the office of King of England, without ever being able to acquire English habits, or any familiarity with English dispositions, found the utmost assistance from the address of his partner, and while he jealously affected to do every thing according to his own will and pleasure, was in secret prudent enough to take and to follow the advice of his more adroit consort. He entrusted to her the delicate office of determining the various degrees of favour necessary to attach the wavering, or to confirm those who were already friendly, or to regain those whose good-will had been lost.

With all the winning address of an elegant, and, according to the times, an accomplished woman, Queen Caroline possessed the masculine soul of the other sex. She was proud by nature, and even her policy could not always temper her expressions of displeasure, although few were more ready at repairing any false step of this kind, when her prudence came up to the aid of her passion. She loved the real possession of power, rather than the shew of it, and whatever she did herself that was either wise or popular, she always desired that the king should have the full credit as well as the advantage of the measure, conscious that by adding to his respectability, she was most likely to maintain her own. And so desirous was she to comply with all his tastes, that, when threatened with the gout, she repeatedly had recourse to checking the fit, by the use of the cold bath, thereby endangering her life that she might be able to attend the king in his long walks.

It was a very consistent part of Queen Caroline's character, to keep up many private correspondencies with those to whom in public she seemed unfavourable, or who, for various reasons, stood ill with the court. By this means she kept in her hands the thread of many a political intrigue, and, without pledging herself to any thing, could often prevent discontent from becoming hatred, and opposition from exaggerating itself into rebellion. If by any accident her correspondence with such persons chanced to be observed or discovered, which she took all possible pains to prevent, it was represented as a mere intercourse of society, having no reference to politics; an answer with which even the prime minister, Sir Robert Walpole, was compelled to remain satisfied, when he discovered that the Queen had given a private audience to Pulteney, afterwards Earl of Bath, his most formidable and most inveterate enemy.

In thus maintaining occasional intercourse with several persons who seemed most alienated from the crown, it may readily be supposed, that Queen Caroline had taken care not to break entirely with the Duke of Argyle. His high birth, his great talents, the estimation in which he was held in his own country, the great services which he had rendered the House of Brunswick in 1715, placed him high in that rank of persons who were not to be rashly neglected. He had, almost by his single and unassisted talents, stopped the eruption of the banded force of all the Highland chiefs; there was little doubt but that with the slightest encouragement, he could put them all in motion, and renew a civil war; and it was well known that the most flattering overtures had been transmitted to the Duke from the court of Saint Germains. The character and temper of Scotland was still little known, and it was considered as a volcano, which might, indeed, slumber for a series of years, but was still liable, at a moment the most unexpected, to break out into a wasteful eruption. It was, therefore, of the highest importance to retain some hold over so important a personage as the Duke of Argyle, and Caroline preserved the means of doing so by means of a lady, with whom, as wife of George II., she might have been supposed to be on less intimate terms.

It was not the least instance of the Queen's address, that she had contrived that one of her principal attendants, Lady Suffolk, should unite in her own person the two apparently inconsistent characters of her husband's mistress, and her own very obsequious and complaisant confidante. By this dextrous management the Queen secured her power against the danger which might most have threatened it—the thwarting influence of an ambitious rival; and if she submitted to the mortification of being obliged to connive at her husband's infidelity, she was at least guarded against what she might think its most danger- ous effects, and was besides at liberty, now and then, to bestow a few civil insults upon "her good Howard," whom, however, in general, she treated with great decorum. Lady Suffolk lay under strong obligations to the Duke of Argyle, for reasons which may be collected from Horace Walpole's Reminiscences of that reign, and through her means the Duke had some occasional correspondence with Queen Caroline, much interrupted, however, since the part he had taken in the debate concerning the Porteous mob, an affair which the Queen was disposed to resent, rather as an intended and premeditated insol- ence to her own person and authority, than as a sudden ebullition of popular vengeance. Still, however, the communication remained open betwixt them, though it had been of late disused on both sides. These remarks will be found necessary to understand the scene which is about to be presented to the reader.

From the narrow alley which they had traversed, the Duke turned into one of the same character, but broader and still longer. Here, for the first time since they had entered these gardens, Jeanie saw persons approaching them.

They were two ladies; one of whom walked a little behind the other, yet not so much as to prevent her from hearing and replying to what- ever observation was addressed to her. As they advanced very slowly, Jeanie had time to study their features and appearance. The Duke also slackened his pace, as if to give her time to collect herself, and repeatedly desired her not to be afraid. The lady who seemed the principal had remarkably good features, though somewhat injured by the small-pox, that venomous scourge which each village Esculapius (thanks to Jenner,) can now tame as easily as their tutelary deity subdued the Python. The lady's eyes were brilliant, her teeth good, and her countenance formed to express at will either majesty or cour- tesy. Her form, though rather *en-bon-point*, was nevertheless graceful; and the elasticity and firmness of her step gave no room to suspect, what was actually the case, that she suffered occasionally from a disorder the most unfavourable to pedestrian exercise. Her dress was rather rich than gay, and her manner commanding and noble.

Her companion was of lower stature, with light-brown hair and expressive blue eyes. Her features, without being absolutely regular, were perhaps more pleasing than if they had been critically handsome. A melancholy, or at least a pensive expression, for which her lot gave too much cause, predominated when she was silent, but gave way to a pleasing and good-humoured smile whenever she spoke to any one.

When they were within twelve or fifteen yards of these ladies, the Duke made a sign that Jeanie should stand still, and stepping forward himself, with the grace which was natural to him, made a profound obeisance, which was formally, yet in a dignified manner, returned by the personage whom he approached.

"I hope," she said, with an affable and condescending smile, "that I see so great a stranger at court, as the Duke of Argyle has been of late, in as good health as his friends there and elsewhere could wish him to enjoy."

The Duke replied, "That he had been perfectly well;" and added, "that the necessity of attending to the public business before the House, as well as the time occupied by a late journey to Scotland, had rendered him less assiduous in paying his duty at the Levee and Drawing-room than he could have desired."

"When your Grace *can* find time for a duty so frivolous," replied the Queen, "you are aware of your title to be well received. I hope my readiness to comply with the wish which you expressed yesterday to Lady Suffolk, is a sufficient proof that one of the royal family, at least, has not forgotten ancient and important services, in resenting something which resembles recent neglect." This was said apparently with great good-humour, and in a tone which expressed a desire of conciliation.

The Duke replied, "That he would account himself the most unfortunate of men, if he could be supposed capable of neglecting his duty, in modes and circumstances when it was expected, and would have been agreeable. He was deeply gratified by the honour which her Majesty was now doing to him personally; and he trusted she would soon perceive, that it was in a matter essential to his Majesty's interest that he had the boldness to give her this trouble."

"You cannot oblige me more, my Lord Duke," replied the Queen, "than by giving me the advantage of your lights and experience on any point of the King's service. Your Grace is aware, that I can only be the medium through which the matter is subjected to his Majesty's superior wisdom; but if it is a suit which respects your Grace personally, it shall lose no support by being preferred through me."

"It is no suit of mine, madam," replied the Duke; "nor have I any to prefer for myself personally, although I feel in full force my obligation to your Majesty. It is a business which concerns his Majesty, as a lover of justice and of mercy, and which I am convinced may be highly useful in conciliating the unfortunate irritation which at present subsists amongst his Majesty's good subjects in Scotland."

There were two parts of this speech disagreeable to Caroline. In the first place, it removed the flattering notion she had adopted, that Argyle designed to use her personal intercession in making his peace with the administration, and recovering the employments of which he had been deprived; and then she was displeased that he should talk of the discontents in Scotland as irritations to be conciliated, rather than suppressed.

Under the influence of these feelings, she answered hastily, "That his Majesty has good subjects in England, my Lord Duke, he is bound to thank God and the laws—that he has subjects in Scotland, I think he may thank God and his sword."

The Duke, though a courtier, coloured slightly, and the Queen, instantly sensible of her error, added, without displaying the least change of countenance, and as if the words had been an original branch of the sentence—"And the swords of those real Scotchmen who are friends to the House of Brunswick, particularly that of his Grace of Argyle."

"My sword, madam," replied the Duke, "like that of my fathers, has been always at the command of my lawful king, and of my native country—I trust it is impossible to separate their real rights and interests. But the present is a matter of more private concern, and respects the person of an obscure individual."

"What is the affair, my Lord?" said the Queen. "Let us find out what we are talking about, lest we should misconstrue and misunderstand each other."

"The matter, madam," answered the Duke of Argyle, "regards the fate of an unfortunate young woman in Scotland, now lying under sentence of death, for a crime of which I think it highly probable that she is innocent. And my humble petition to your Majesty is, to obtain your powerful intercession with the King for a pardon."

It was now the Queen's turn to colour, and she did so over cheek and brow—neck and bosom. She paused a moment, as if unwilling to trust her voice with the first expressions of her displeasure; and assuming an air of dignity and an austere regard of controul, she at length replied, "My Lord Duke, I will not ask your motives for addressing to me a request, which circumstances have rendered such an extraordinary one. Your road to the king's closet, as a peer and a privy-counsellor entitled to request an audience, was open, without giving me the pain of this discussion. *I*, at least, have had enough of Scotch pardons."

The Duke was prepared for this burst of indignation, and he was not shaken by it. He did not attempt a reply while the Queen was in the first heat of displeasure, but remained in the same firm, yet respectful posture, which he had assumed during the interview. The Queen, trained from her situation to self-command, instantly perceived the advantage she might give against herself by yielding to passion; and added, in the same condescending and affable tone in which she had opened the interview, "You must allow me some of the privileges of the sex, my Lord; and do not judge uncharitably of me, though I am a little moved at the recollection of the gross insult and outrage done in your capital city to the royal authority, at the very time when it was vested in my unworthy person. Your Grace cannot be surprised that I should both have felt it at the time, and recollected it now."

"It is certainly a matter not speedily to be forgotten," answered the Duke. "My own poor thoughts of it have been long before your Majesty, and I must have expressed myself very ill if I did not convey my detestation of the murder which was committed under such extraordinary circumstances. I might, indeed, be so unfortunate as to differ with his Majesty's advisers on the degree in which it was either just or politic to punish the innocent instead of the guilty. But I trust your Majesty will permit me to be silent on a topic in which my sentiments have not the good fortune to coincide with those of more able men."

"We will not prosecute a topic on which we may probably differ," said the Queen. "One word, however, I may say in private—you know our good Lady Suffolk is a little deaf—the Duke of Argyle, when disposed to renew his acquaintance with his master and mistress, will hardly find many topics on which we should disagree."

"Let me hope," said the Duke, bowing profoundly to so flattering an intimation, "that I shall not be so unfortunate as to have found one on the present occasion."

"I must first impose on your Grace the duty of confession," said the Queen, "before I grant you absolution. What is your particular interest in this young woman? She does not seem (and she scanned Jeanie as she said this with the eye of a connoisseur) much qualified to alarm my friend the Duchess's jealousy."

"I think your Majesty," replied the Duke, smiling in his turn, "will allow my taste may be a pledge for me on that score."

"Then, though she has not much the air *d'une grande-dame*, I suppose she is some thirtieth cousin in the terrible chapter of Scottish genealogy."

"No, madam," said the Duke; "but I wish some of my nearer relations had half her worth, honesty, and affection."

"Her name must be Campbell at least?" said Queen Caroline.

"No, madam; her name is—not quite so distinguished, if I may be permitted to say so," answered the Duke.

"Ah! but she comes from Inverara or Argyleshire?" said the Sovereign.

"She has never been farther north in her life than Edinburgh, madam."

"Then my conjectures are all ended," said the Queen, "and your Grace must yourself take the trouble to explain the affair of your protegée."

With that precision and easy brevity which is only acquired by habitually conversing in the higher ranks of society, and which is the diametrical opposite of that protracted style of disquisition,

> Which squires call potter, and which men call prose,

the Duke explained the singular law under which Effie Deans had received sentence of death, and detailed the affectionate exertions which Jeanie had made in behalf of a sister, for whose sake she was willing to sacrifice all but truth and conscience.

Queen Caroline listened with attention; she was rather fond, it must be remembered, of an argument, and soon found matter in what the Duke told her for raising difficulties to his request.

"It appears to me, my Lord," she replied, "that this is a severe law. But still it is adopted upon good grounds, I am bound to suppose, as the law of the country, and the girl has been convicted under it. The very presumptions which the law construes into a positive proof of guilt exist in her case; and all that your Grace has said concerning the possibility of her innocence may be a very good argument for annulling the Act of Parliament, but cannot, while it stands good, be admitted in favour of any individual convicted upon the statute."

The Duke saw and avoided the snare, for he was conscious, that, by replying to the argument, he must have been inevitably led to a discussion, in the course of which the Queen was likely to be hardened in her own opinion, until she became obliged out of mere respect to consistency, to let the criminal suffer. "If your Majesty," he said, "would condescend to hear my poor countrywoman herself, perhaps she may find an advocate in your own heart, more able than I am to combat the doubts suggested by your understanding."

The Queen seemed to acquiesce, and the Duke made a signal for Jeanie to advance from the spot where she had hitherto remained watching countenances, which were too long accustomed to suppress all apparent signs of emotion, to convey to her any interesting intelligence. Her Majesty could not help smiling at the awe-struck manner in which the quiet demure figure of the little Scotchwoman advanced towards her, and yet more at the first sound of her broad northern accent. But Jeanie had a voice low and sweetly tuned, an admirable thing in woman, and she besought "her Leddyship to have pity on a poor misguided young creature," in tones so affecting, that, like the notes of some of her native songs, provincial vulgarity was lost in pathos.

"Stand up, young woman," said the Queen, but in a kind tone, "and tell me what sort of a barbarous people your countryfolks are, where child-murther is become so common as to require the restraint of laws like your's?"

"If your Leddyship pleases," answered Jeanie, "there are mony places besides Scotland where mothers are unkind to their ain flesh and blood."

It must be observed, that the disputes between George the Second, and Frederick, Prince of Wales, were then at the highest, and that the good-natured part of the public laid the blame on the Queen. She coloured highly, and darted a glance of a most penetrating character first at Jeanie, and then at the Duke. Both sustained it unmoved; Jeanie from total unconsciousness of the offence she had given, and the Duke from his habitual composure. But in his heart he thought, My unlucky protegée has, with this luckless answer, shot dead, by a kind of chance-medley, her only hope of success.

Lady Suffolk, good-humouredly and skilfully, interposed in this awkward crisis. "You should tell this lady," she said to Jeanie, "the particular causes which render this crime common in your country."

"Some thinks it's the kirk-session—that is—it's the—it's the cutty-stool, if your Leddyship pleases," said Jeanie, looking down, and curtseying.

"The what?" said Lady Suffolk, to whom the phrase was new, and who besides was rather deaf.

"That's the stool of repentance, madam, if it please your Leddyship," answered Jeanie, "for light life and conversation, and for breaking the seventh command." Here she raised her eyes to the Duke, saw his hand at his chin, and, totally unconscious of what she had said out of joint, gave double effect to the innuendo, by stopping short and looking embarrassed.

As for Lady Suffolk, she retired like a covering party, which, having interposed betwixt their retreating friends and the enemy, have suddenly drawn on themselves a fire unexpectedly severe.

The deuce take the lass, thought the Duke of Argyle to himself;

there goes another shot—and she has killed with both barrels right and left.

Indeed the Duke had himself his share of the confusion, for, having acted as master of ceremonies to this innocent offender, he felt much in the circumstances of a country-squire, who, having introduced his spaniel into a well-appointed drawing-room, is doomed to witness the disorder and damage which arises to china and to dress-gowns, in consequence of its untimely frolics. Jeanie's last chance-hit, however, obliterated the ill impression which had arisen from the first; for her Majesty had not so lost the feelings of a wife in those of a Queen, but what she could enjoy a jest at the expence of "her good Suffolk." She turned towards the Duke of Argyle with a smile, which marked that she enjoyed the triumph, and observed, "the Scotch are a rigidly moral people." Then again applying herself to Jeanie, she asked, how she travelled up from Scotland.

"Upon my foot mostly, madam," was the reply.

"What, all that immense way upon foot?—How far can you walk in a day?"

"Five and twenty miles and a bittock."

"And a what?" said the Queen, looking towards the Duke of Argyle.

"And about five miles more," replied the Duke.

"I thought I was a good walker," said the Queen, "but this shames me sadly."

"May your Leddyship never hae sae weary a heart, that ye canna be sensible of the weariness of the limbs," said Jeanie.

That came better off, thought the Duke; it's the first thing she has said to the purpose.

"And I didna just a'thegether walk the haill way neither, for I had whiles the cast of a cart; and I had the cast of a horse from Ferry-bridge, and divers other easements," said Jeanie, cutting short her story, for she observed the Duke made the sign he had fixed upon.

"With all these accommodations," answered the Queen, "you must have had a very fatiguing journey, and, I fear, to little purpose; since, if the King were to pardon your sister, in all probability it would do her little good, for I suppose your people of Edinburgh would hang her out of spite."

She will sink herself now outright, thought the Duke.

But he was wrong. The shoals on which Jeanie had touched in this delicate conversation lay under ground, and were unknown to her; this rock was above water, and she avoided it.

"She was confident," she said, "that baith town and country wad rejoice to see his Majesty taking compassion on a poor unfriended creature."

"His Majesty has not found it so in a late instance," said the Queen; "but I suppose my Lord Duke would advise him to be guided by the votes of the rabble themselves, who should be hanged and who spared?"

"No, madam," said the Duke; "but I would advise his Majesty to be guided by his own feelings and those of his royal consort; and thus, I am sure, punishment will attach itself only to guilt, and even then with cautious reluctance."

"Well, my Lord," said her Majesty, "all these fine speeches do not convince me of the propriety of so soon showing any mark of favour— to your—I suppose I must not say—rebellious—but, at least, your very disaffected and intractable metropolis. Why, the whole nation is in a league to screen the savage and abominable murtherers of that unhappy man; otherwise, how is it possible but that, of so many perpetrators, and engaged in so public an action for such a length of time, one at least must have been recognized? Even this wench, for aught I can tell, may be a depositary of the secret. Heark you, young woman; had you any friends engaged in the Porteous mob?"

"No, madam," answered Jeanie, happy that the question was so framed that she could, with a good conscience, answer it in the negative.

"But I suppose," continued the Queen, "if you were possessed of such a secret, you would hold it matter of conscience to keep it to yourself?"

"I would pray to be directed and guided what was the line of duty, madam," answered Jeanie.

"Yes, and take that which suited your own inclinations," replied her Majesty.

"If it like you, madam," said Jeanie, "I would hae gaen to the end of the earth to save the life of John Porteous, or of ony other unhappy man in his condition; but I might lawfully doubt how far I am called upon to be the avenger of his blood, though it may become the civil magistrate to do so. He is dead and gane to his place, and they that have slain him must answer for their ain act. But my sister—my puir sister Effie, still lives, though her days and hours are numbered!— She still lives, and a word of the King's mouth might restore her to a broken-hearted auld man, that never, in his daily and nightly exercise, forgot to pray that his Majesty might be blessed with a long and a prosperous reign, and that his throne, and the throne of his posterity, might be established in righteousness. O, madam, if ever ye kenn'd what it was to sorrow for and with a sinning and a suffering creature, whose mind is sae tossed that she can be neither ca'd fit to live or die, have some compassion on our misery!—Save an honest house from dishonour, and an unhappy girl, not eighteen years of age, from an early and dreadful death! Alas! it is not when we sleep soft and wake merrily ourselves that we think on other folk's sufferings. Our hearts are waxed high within us then, and we are for righting our ain wrangs and fighting our ain battles. But when the hour of trouble comes to the mind or to the body—and seldom may it visit your Leddyship—and when the hour of death comes, that comes to high and low—lang and late may it be yours—O, my Leddy, then it isna what we hae dune for oursells, but what we hae dune for others, that we think on maist pleasantly. And the thoughts that ye hae intervened to spare the puir thing's life will be sweeter in that hour, come when it may, than if a word of your mouth could hang the haill Porteous mob at the tail of ae tow."

Tear followed tear down Jeanie's cheeks, as, with features glowing and quivering with emotion, she pleaded her sister's cause with a pathos which was at once simple and solemn.

"This is eloquence," said her Majesty to the Duke of Argyle. "Young woman," she continued, addressing herself to Jeanie, "*I* cannot grant a pardon to your sister—but you shall not want my warm intercession with his Majesty. Take this housewife," she continued, putting a small embroidered needle-case into Jeanie's hands; "do not open it now, but at your leisure you will find something in it which will remind you that you have had an interview with Queen Caroline."

Jeanie, having her suspicions thus confirmed, dropped on her knees, and would have expanded herself in gratitude; but the Duke, who was upon thorns lest she should say more or less than just enough, touched his chin once more.

"Our business is, I think, ended for the present, my Lord Duke," said the Queen, "and, I trust, to your satisfaction. Hereafter I hope to see your Grace more frequently, both at Richmond and Saint James's. —Come, Lady Suffolk, we must wish his Grace good morning."

They exchanged their parting reverences, and the Duke, so soon as the ladies had turned their backs, assisted Jeanie to rise from the ground, and conducted her back through the avenue, which she trod with the feeling of one who walks in her sleep.

END OF VOLUME THIRD

THE
HEART OF MID-LOTHIAN

VOLUME IV

Chapter One

So soon as I can win the offended King
I will be known your advocate.
Cymbeline

THE DUKE OF ARGYLE led the way in silence to the small postern
by which they had been admitted into Richmond Park, so long the
favourite residence of Queen Caroline. It was opened by the same
half-seen janitor, and they found themselves beyond the precincts of
the royal demesne. Still not a word was spoken on either side. The
Duke probably wished to allow his rustic protegée time to recruit her
faculties, dazzled and sunk with colloquy sublime; and betwixt what
she had guessed, had heard, and had seen, Jeanie Deans's mind was
too much agitated to permit her to ask any questions.

They found the carriage of the Duke in the place where they had
left it; and when they had resumed their places, were soon advancing
rapidly on their return to town.

"I think, Jeanie," said the Duke, breaking silence, "you have every
reason to congratulate yourself on the issue of your interview with her
Majesty."

"And that leddy *was* the Queen hersell?" said Jeanie; "I mis-
doubted it when I saw that your honour didna put on your hat—And
yet I can hardly believe it, even when I heard her speak it hersell."

"It was certainly Queen Caroline," replied the Duke. "Have you no
curiosity to see what is in the little pocket-book?"

"Do you think the pardon will be in it, sir?" said Jeanie, with the
eager animation of hope.

"Why, no," replied the Duke; "that is unlikely. They seldom carry

343

these things about them, unless they were to be wanted; and besides, her Majesty told you it was the King, not she, who was to grant it."

"That is true too," said Jeanie; "but I am so confused in my mind— But does your honour think there is a certainty of Effie's pardon then?" she continued, still holding in her hand the unopened pocket-book.

"Why, kings are kittle cattle to shoe behind, as we say in the north," replied the Duke; "but his wife knows his trim, and I have not the least doubt that the matter is quite certain."

"O God be praised! God be praised!" ejaculated Jeanie; "and may the gude leddy never want the heart's ease she has gi'en me at this moment—And God bless you too, my Lord! without your help I wad ne'er hae won near her."

The Duke let her dwell upon this subject for a considerable time, curious, perhaps, to see how long the feelings of gratitude would continue to supersede those of curiosity. But so feeble was the latter feeling in Jeanie's mind, that his Grace, with whom, perhaps, it was for the time a little stronger, was obliged once more to bring forward the subject of the Queen's present. It was opened accordingly. In the inside of the case were the usual assortment of silk and needles, with scissars, tweazers, &c.; and in the pocket was a bank-bill for fifty pounds.

The Duke had no sooner informed Jeanie of the value of this last document, for she was unaccustomed to see notes for such sums, than she expressed her regret at the mistake which had taken place. "For the hussy itsell," she said, "was a very valuable thing for a keepsake, with the Queen's name written in the inside with her ain hand doubt-less—*Caroline*—as plain as could be, and a crown drawn aboon it."

She therefore tendered the bill to the Duke, requesting him to find some mode of returning it to the royal owner.

"No, no, Jeanie," said the Duke, "there is no mistake in the case. Her Majesty knows you have been put to great expence, and she wishes to make it up to you."

"I am sure she is even over gude," said Jeanie, "and it glads me muckle that I can pay back Dumbiedikes his siller, without distressing my father, honest man."

"Dumbiedikes? What, a freeholder of Mid-Lothian is he not?" said his Grace, whose occasional residence in that county made him acquainted with most of the heritors, as landed persons are termed in Scotland—"He has a house not far from Dalkeith, wears a black wig and a laced hat?"

"Yes, sir," answered Jeanie, who had her reasons for being brief in her answers upon this topic.

"Ah! my old friend Dumbie!" said the Duke; "I have thrice seen him fou, and only once heard the sound of his voice—Is he a cousin of yours, Jeanie?"

"No, sir, my Lord."

"Then he must be a well-wisher, I suspect?"

"Ye—yes,—my Lord, sir," answered Jeanie, blushing, and with hesitation.

"Aha! then, if the Laird starts, I suppose my friend Butler must be in some danger?"

"O no, sir!" answered Jeanie much more readily, but at the same time blushing much more deeply.

"Well, Jeanie," said the Duke, "you are a girl may be safely trusted with your own matters, and I shall enquire no further about them. But as to this same pardon, I must see to get it passed through the proper forms; and I have a friend in office who will, for auld lang syne, do me so much favour. And then, Jeanie, as I shall have occasion to send an express down to Scotland, who will travel with it safer and more swiftly than you can do, I will take care to have it put into the proper channel; meanwhile you may write to your friends by post of your good success."

"And does your Honour think," said Jeanie, "that will do as weel as I were to take my tap in my lap, and slip my ways hame again on my ain errand?"

"Much better, certainly," said the Duke. "You know the roads are not very safe for a single woman to travel."

Jeanie internally acquiesced in this observation.

"And I have a plan for you besides. One of the Duchess's attendants, and one of mine—your acquaintance Archibald—are going down to Inverara in a light calash, with four horses I have bought, and there is room enough in the carriage for you to go with them as far as Glasgow, where Archibald will find means of sending you safely to Edinburgh—And in the way, I beg you will teach the woman as much as you can of the mystery of cheese-making, for she is to have a charge in the dairy, and I dare swear you are as tidy about your milk-pail as about your dress."

"Does your Honour like cheese?" said Jeanie, with a gleam of conscious delight as she asked the question.

"Like it?" said the Duke, whose good-nature anticipated what was to follow,—"cakes and cheese are a dinner for an emperor, let alone a Highlandman."

"Because," said Jeanie, with modest confidence, and great and evident self-congratulation, "we have been thought particular in making cheese, that some folk think is as gude as the real Dunlop; and if your Honour's Grace wad but accept a stane or twa, blythe, and fain, and proud it wad make us. But maybe ye may like the ewe-milk or the Buckholmside cheeses better; or maybe the gait-milk, as ye come frae the Highlands—and I canna pretend just to the same skeel o' them; but my cousin Jean, that lives at Lockermaikus in Lammermoor, I could speak to her, and"——

"Quite unnecessary," said the Duke; "the Dunlop is the very cheese of which I am so fond, and I will take it as the greatest favour you can do me to send one to Caroline-Park. But remember, be on honour with it, Jeanie, and make it all yourself, for I am a real good judge."

"I am not feared," said Jeanie confidently, "that I may please your Honour; for I am sure you look as if you could hardly find fault wi' ony body that did their best; and weel is it my part, I trow, to do mine."

This discourse introduced a topic upon which the two travellers, though so different in rank and education, found each a good deal to say. The Duke, besides his other patriotic qualities, was a distinguished agriculturist, and proud of his knowledge in that department. He entertained Jeanie with his observations on the different breeds of cattle in Scotland, and their capacity for the dairy, and received so much information from her practical experience in return, that he promised her a couple of Devonshire cows in reward of the lesson. In short, his mind was so transported back to his rural employments and amusements, that he sighed when his carriage stopped opposite to the old hackney-coach, which Archibald had kept in attendance at the place where they had left it. While the coachman again bridled his lean cattle, which had been indulged with a bite of musty hay, the Duke cautioned Jeanie not to be too communicative to her landlady concerning what had passed. "There is," he said, "no use in speaking of matters till they are actually settled; and you may refer the good lady to Archibald, if she presses you hard with questions. She is his old acquaintance, and he knows how to manage with her."

He then took a cordial farewell of Jeanie, and told her to be ready in the ensuing week to return to Scotland—saw her safely established in her hackney-coach, and rolled off in his own carriage, humming a stanza of the ballad which he is said to have composed:—

> "At the sight of Dumbarton once again,
> I'll cock up my bonnet and march amain,
> With my claymore hanging down to my heel,
> To whang at the bannocks of barley meal."

Perhaps one ought to be actually a Scotchman to conceive how ardently, under all distinctions of rank and situation, they feel their mutual connexion with each other as natives of the same country.

There are, I believe, more associations common to the inhabitants of a rude and wild, than of a well cultivated and fertile country; their ancestors have more seldom changed their place of residence; their mutual recollections of remarkable objects is more accurate; the high and the low are more interested in each other's welfare; the feelings of kindred and relationship are more widely extended, and, in a word, the bonds of patriotic affection, always honourable even when a little too exclusively strained, have more influence on men's feelings and actions.

The rumbling hackney-coach which tumbled over the (then) execrable London pavement, at a rate very different from that which had conveyed the ducal carriage to Richmond, at length deposited Jeanie Deans and her attendant at the national sign of the Thistle. Mrs Glass, who had been in long and anxious expectation, now rushed, full of eager curiosity and open-mouthed interrogation, upon our heroine, who was positively unable to sustain the overwhelming cataract of her questions which burst forth with the sublimity of a grand gardyloo:— "Had she seen the Duke, God bless him—the Duchess—the young ladies?—Had she seen the King, God bless him—the Queen—the Prince of Wales—the Princess—or any of the rest of the royal family? —Had she got her sister's pardon?—Was it out and out—or only a commutation of punishment?—How far had she gone—Where had she driven to—Whom had she seen—What had been said—Who had kept her so long?"

Such were the various questions huddled upon each other with a curiosity so eager, that it could hardly wait for its own gratification. Jeanie would have been more than sufficiently embarrassed by this over-bearing tide of interrogations, had not Archibald, who had probably received from his master a hint to that purpose, advanced to her rescue. "Mrs Glass," said Archibald, "his Grace desired me particularly to say, that he would take it as a great favour if you would ask the young woman no questions, as he wishes to explain to you more distinctly than she can do how her affairs stand, and consult you on some matters which she cannot altogether so well explain. The Duke will call at the Thistle to-morrow or next day for that purpose."

"His Grace is very condescending," said Mrs Glass, her zeal for enquiry slaked for the present by the dexterous administration of this sugar-plumb—"his Grace is sensible that I am in a manner accountable for the conduct of my young kinswoman, and no doubt his Grace is the best judge how far he should entrust her or me with the management of her affairs."

"His Grace is quite sensible of that," answered Archibald with national gravity, "and will certainly trust what he has to say to the most discreet of the two; and therefore Mrs Glass, his Grace relies you will speak nothing to Mrs Jean Deans, either of her own affairs or her sister's, untill he sees you himself. He desired me to assure you, in the meanwhile, that all was going on as well as your kindness could wish, Mrs Glass."

"His Grace is very kind—very considerate, certainly, Mr Archibald —his Grace's commands shall be obeyed, and——But you have had a far drive, Mr Archibald, as I guess by the time of your absence, and I guess" (with an engaging smile) "you winna be the waur of a glass of right Rosa Solis."

"I thank you, Mrs Glass," said the great man's great man, "but I am under the necessity of returning to my Lord directly." And making his adieus civilly to both cousins, he left the shop of the Lady of the Thistle.

"I am glad your affairs have prospered so well, Jeanie, my love," said Mrs Glass; "though indeed there was little fear of them so soon as the Duke of Argyle was so condescending as to take them into hand. I will ask you no questions about them, because his Grace, who is most considerate and prudent in such matters, intends to tell me all that you ken yourself, dear, and doubtless a great deal more. So that any thing that may lie heavily on your mind may be imparted to me in the meantime, as you see it is his Grace's pleasure that I should be made acquainted with the whole matter forthwith, and whether you or he tells it, will make no difference in the world, ye ken. If I ken what he is going to say beforehand, I will be much more ready to give my advice, and whether you or he tell me about it, cannot much signify after all, my dear. So you may just say whatever you like, only mind I ask you no questions about it."

Jeanie was a little embarrassed. She thought that the communication she had to make was perhaps the only means she might have in her power to gratify her friendly and hospitable kinswoman. But her prudence immediately suggested that her secret interview with Queen Caroline, which seemed to pass under a certain sort of mystery, was not a proper subject for the gossip of a woman like Mrs Glass, of whose heart she had a much better opinion than of her prudence. She, therefore, answered in general, that the Duke had had the extraordinary kindness to make very particular enquiries into her sister's bad affair, and that he thought he had found the means of putting it a' straight again, but that he proposed to tell all that he thought about the matter to Mrs Glass herself.

This did not quite satisfy the penetrating Mistress of the Thistle. Searching as her own small rappee, she, in spite of her promise, urged Jeanie with still further questions. "Had she been a' that time at

Argyle-house? Was the Duke with her the whole time? and had she seen the Duchess? and had she seen the young ladies—and specially Lady Caroline Campbell?"—To these questions Jeanie gave the general reply, that she knew so little of the town that she could not tell exactly where she had been; that she had not seen the Duchess, to her knowledge; that she had seen two ladies, one of whom she understood bore the name of Caroline; and more, she said, she could not tell about the matter.

"It would be the Duke's eldest daughter, Lady Caroline Campbell —there is no doubt of that," said Mrs Glass; "but, doubtless, I shall know more particularly through his Grace.—And so, as the cloth is laid in the little parlour above stairs, and it is past three o'clock, for I have been waiting this hour for you, and I have had a snack myself, and, as they used to say in Scotland in my time—I do not ken if the word be used now—there is ill talking between a full body and a fasting."

Chapter Two

Heaven first sent letters to some wretch's aid—
Some banished lover, or some captive maid.
POPE

BY DINT OF UNWONTED LABOUR with the pen, Jeanie Deans contrived to indite, and give to the charge of the postman on the ensuing day, no less than three letters, an exertion altogether strange to her habits; insomuch so, that, if milk had been plenty, she would rather have made thrice as many Dunlop cheeses. The first of them was very brief. It was addressed to George Staunton, Esq. at the Rectory, Willingham, by Grantham; the address being part of the information which she had extracted from the communicative peasant who rode before her to Stamford. It was in these words:—

"SIR,

"To prevent farder mischieves, whereof there hath been enough, comes these: Sir, I have my sister's pardun from the Queen's Majesty, whereof, I do not dout, you will be glad, having had to say naut of matters whereof you know the purport. So, sir, I pray for your better welfare in bodie and saul, and that it will please the fisicyian to visit you in His good time. Allwaies, sir, I pray you will never come again to see my sister, whereof there has been too much. And so, wishing you no evil, but even your best good, that you may be turned from your iniquity, (for why suld ye die?) I rest your humble servant to command.
                                        "*Ye ken wha.*"

The next letter was to her father. It is too long altogether for subscription, so we only give a few extracts. It commenced—

"DEAREST AND TRULY HONOURED FATHER,

"This comes with my duty to inform you, that it has pleased God to redeem that captivitie of my poor sister, in respect the Queen's blessed Majeesty, for whom we are ever bound to pray, hath redeemed her soul from the slayer, granting the ransom of her blood, whilk is ane pardon or reprieve. And I spoke with the Queen face to face, and yet live; for she is not muckle differring from other grand leddies, saving that she hath a stately presence, and een like a blue huntin' hawk's, whilk gae throu' and throu' me like ane Hieland durk —And all this good was, alway under the Great Giver, to whom all are but instriments, wrought forth for us by the Duk of Argile, wha is ane native true-hearted Scotsman, and not pridefu', like other folks we ken of—And likewise skeely enow in bestial, whereof he has promised to gi'e me twa Denshire kye, of which he is enamoured, althou' I do still haud by the real hawkit Airshire breed—And I have promised him a cheese; and I wad wuss ye, if Gowans, the brockit cow, has a quey, that she suld suck her fill of milk, as I am given to understand he has none of that breed, and is not scornfu', but will take a thing frae a puir body, that it may lighten their heart of the loading of debit that they awe him. Also his Honor the duke will except ane of our Dunlap cheeses, and it sall be my faut if a better was ever yearned in Lowden." —[Here follow some observations respecting the breed of cattle, and the produce of the dairy, which it is our intention to forward to the Board of Agriculture.]—"Nevertheless, these are but matters of the after-harvest in respect of the great good which Providense hath gifted us with—and, in especial, poor Effie's life. And O, my dear father, since it hath pleesed God to be merciful to her, let her not want your free pardon, whilk will make her meet to be ane vessel of grace, and also a comfort to your ain graie hairs. Dear father, will ye let the Laird ken that we have had friends strangely raised up to us, and that the talent whilk he lended me shall be thankfully repaid. I hae some of it to the fore; and the rest of it is not knotted up in ane purse or napkin, but in ane wee bit paper, as is the fashion heir, whilk I am assured is gude for the siller. And, dear father, through Mr Butler's means I had gude friendship with the duke, for there had been kindness between their forbears in the auld troublesum time by-past. And Mrs Glass has been kind like my very mother. She has a braw house here, and lives bien and warm, wi' twa servant lasses, and a man and a callant in the shop. And she is to send you doun a pound of her hie-dried, and some other tobaka, and we maun think of some propine for her, since her kindness hath been great. And the duk is to send the pardun doun by an express messenger, in respeck that I canna travel sae fast; and I am to come doun wi' twa of his honor's servants—that is, John Archibald, a decent elderly gentleman, that says he has seen you lang syne when ye were buying beasts in the west frae the Laird of Auchtermuggitie— but maybe ye winna mind him—ony way, he's a civil man—and Mrs Dolly Dutton, that is to be dairy-maid at Inverara; and they bring me on as far as Glasgo', whilk will mak it nae pinch to win hame, whilk I desire of all things. May the Giver of all good things keep ye in your outgangings and incomings, whereof devoutly prayeth your loving dauter,

"JEAN DEANS."

The third letter was to Butler, and its tenor as follows:—

"MAISTER BUTLER.

"SIR,—It will be pleasure to you to ken, that all I came for is, thanks be to God, weel dune and to the gude end, and that your forbear's letter was right welcome to the duk of Argile, and that he wrote your name down with a kylevine pen in a leathern book, whereby it seems like he will do for you either wi' a scule or a kirk; he has enow of baith, as I am assured. And I have seen the Queen, which gave me a huzzy case out of her own hand. She had not her crown and skeptre, but they are laid bye for her, like the bairns' best claise, to be worn when she needs them. And they are keppit in a tour, whilk is not like the tour of Libberton, nor yet Craigmiller, but mair like to the castell of Edinbrugh, if it were taen and set down in the midst of the Nor'-Loch. Also the Queen was very bounteous, giving me a paper worth fiftie pounds, as I am assured, to pay my expences here and back agen—Sae, Maister Butler, as we were aye neibours bairns, forbye ony thing else that may hae been spoken between us, I trust ye winna skrimp yoursell in what is needfu' for your health, since it signifies not muckle whilk o' us has the siller, if the other wants it. And mind this is no meant to haud ye to ony thing whilk ye wad rather forget, if ye suld get a charge of a kirk or a scule, as above said. Only I hope it will be a scule, and not a kirk, because of these difficulties anent aiths and patronages, whilk might gang ill doun wi' my honest father. Only if ye could compass a harmonious call frae the parish of Skreegh-me-dead, as ye anes had hope of, I trow it wad please him weel; since I hae heard him say, that the root of the matter was mair deeply hafted in that wee murland parish than in the Canno'gate of Edinburgh. I wish I kend whaten books ye wanted, Mr Butler, for they hae haill houses of them here, and they are obliged to set sume out in the street, whilk are sauld cheap, doutless, to get them out o' the weather. It is a muckle place, and I hae seen sae muckle of it, that my poor head turns round—And ye ken langsyne I amna great pen-woman—and it is near ele'en o'clock o' the night. I am cumming down in gude company, and safe—and I had troubles ganging up, whilk makes me blyther of travelling wi' kend folk. My cousin, Mrs Glass, has a braw house here, but a' thing is sae poisoned wi' snuff, that I am like to be scomfished whiles. But what signifies these things, in comparison of the great deliverance whilk has been vouchsafed to my father's house, in whilk you, as our auld and dear well-wisher, will, I dout not, rejoice and be exceedingly glad. And I am, dear Mr Butler, your sincere well-wisher in temporal and eternal things,

"J.D."

After these labours of an unwonted kind, Jeanie retired to her bed, yet scarce could sleep a few minutes together, so often was she awakened by the heart-stirring consciousness of her sister's safety, and so powerfully urged to deposit her burthen of joy, where she had before laid her doubts and sorrows, in the warm and sincere exercises of devotion.

All the next, and all the succeeding day, Mrs Glass fidgetted about her shop in the agony of expectation, like a pea (to use a vulgar simile which her profession renders appropriate,) upon one of her own tobacco-pipes. With the third morning came the expected coach and six, with four servants clustered behind on the foot-board, in dark-brown and yellow liveries; the Duke in person, with laced coat, gold-headed cane, star and garter, all, as the story-book says, very grand.

He enquired for his little countrywoman at Mrs Glass, but without requesting to see her, probably because he was unwilling to give an appearance of personal intercourse betwixt them, which scandal might have misinterpreted. "The Queen," he said to Mrs Glass, "had taken the case of her kinswoman into her gracious consideration, and being specially moved by the affectionate and resolute character of the elder sister, had condescended to use her powerful intercession with his Majesty, in consequence of which a pardon had been dispatched to Scotland to Effie Deans, on condition of her banishing herself forth of Scotland for fourteen years. The king's advocate had insisted," he said, "upon this qualification of the pardon, having pointed out to his Majesty's ministers that within the course of only seven years, twenty-one instances of child murther had occurred in Scotland."

"Weary on him!" said Mrs Glass, "what for needed he to have telled that of his ain country, and to the English folk abune a'? I used

aye to think the advocate a douce decent man, but it is an ill bird—
begging your Grace's pardon for speaking of such a coorse bye-word.
And then what is the poor lassie to do in a foreign land?—Why, waes
me, it's just sending her to play the same pranks ower again, out of
sight or guidance of her friends."

"Pooh! pooh!" said the Duke, "that need not be anticipated. Why,
she may come up to London, or she may go over to America, and
marry well for all that is come and gone."

"In troth, and so she may, as your Grace is pleased to intimate,"
replied Mrs Glass; "and now I think upon it, there is my old correspondent in Virginia, Ephraim Buckskin, that has supplied the Thistle
this forty year with tobacco, and it is not a little that serves our turn,
and he has been writing to me this ten years to send him out a wife.
The carle is not above sixty, and hale and hearty, and well to pass in
the world, and a line from my hand would settle the matter, and Effie
Deans's misfortune (forbye that there is no special occasion to speak
about it) would be thought little of there."

"Is she a pretty girl?" said the Duke, "her sister does not get beyond
a good comely sonsy lass."

"Oh, far prettier is Effie than Jeanie," said Mrs Glass; "though it's
long since I saw her mysell, but I hear of the Deanses by all my
Lowden friends when they come—your Grace kens we Scots are
clannish bodies."

"So much the better for us," said the Duke, "and the worse for
those who meddle with us, as your good old-fashioned Scots sign says,
Mrs Glass. And now I hope you will approve of the measures I have
taken for restoring your kinswoman to her friends." These he detailed
at length, and Mrs Glass gave her unqualified approbation, with a
smile and a curtesy at every sentence. "And now, Mrs Glass, you must
tell Jeanie, I hope she will not forget my cheese when she gets down to
Scotland. Archibald has my orders to arrange all her expences."

"Begging your Grace's humble pardon," said Mrs Glass, "it is a pity
to trouble yourself about them; the Deanses are wealthy people in
their way, and the lass has money in her pocket."

"That's all very true," said the Duke; "but you know where Maccallanmore travels he pays all; it is our highland privilege to take from
all what *we* want, and to give to all what *they* want."

"Your Grace's better at giving than taking," said Mrs Glass.

"To shew you the contrary," said the Duke, "I will fill my box out of
this cannister without paying you a bawbee;" and again desiring to be
remembered to Jeanie, with his good wishes for her safe journey, he
departed, leaving Mrs Glass uplifted in heart and in countenance, the
proudest and happiest of tobacco and snuff dealers.

Reflectively, his Grace's good humour and affability had a favourable effect upon Jeanie's situation. Her kinswoman, though effectively kind to her, had acquired too much of London breeding to be perfectly satisfied with her cousin's rustic and national dress, and was, besides, something scandalized at the cause of her journey to London. Mrs Glass might, therefore, have been less sedulous in her attentions towards Jeanie, but for the interest which the foremost of the Scottish nobles (for such, in all men's estimation, was the Duke of Argyle) seemed to take in her fate. Now, however, as a kinswoman whose virtues and domestic affections had attracted the notice and approbation of royalty itself, Jeanie stood to her relative in a light very different and much more favourable, and was not only treated with kindness, but with actual observance and respect.

It depended upon herself alone to have made as many visits, and seen as many sights, as lay within Mrs Glass's power to compass. But, excepting that she dined abroad with one or two "far-away kinsfolk," and that she paid the same respect, on Mrs Glass's strong urgency, to Mrs Deputy Dabby, wife of the Worshipful Mr Deputy Dabby, of Farringdon Without, she did not avail herself of the opportunity. As Mrs Dabby was the second lady of great rank whom Jeanie had seen in London, she used sometimes afterwards to draw a parallel betwixt her and the Queen, in which she observed, that "Mrs Dabby was dressed twice as grand, and was twice as big, and spoke twice as loud, and twice as muckle as the Queen did, but she hadna the same goss-hawk glance that makes the skin creep, and the knee bend; and though she had very kindly gifted her with a loaf of sugar and twa punds of tea, yet she hadna a'thegether the sweet look that the Queen had when she put the needle-book into her hand."

Jeanie might have enjoyed the sights and novelties of this great city more, had it not been for the qualification added to her sister's pardon, which greatly grieved her affectionate disposition. On this subject, however, her mind was somewhat relieved by a letter which she received in return of post, in answer to that which she had written to her father. With his affectionate blessing, it brought his full approbation of the step which she had taken, as one inspired by the immediate dictates of Heaven, and which she had been thrust upon in order that she might become the means of safety to a perishing household.

"If ever a deliverance was dear and precious, this," said the letter, "is a dear and precious deliverance—and if life saved can be made more sweet and savoury, it is when it cometh by the hands of those whom we hold in the ties of affection. And do not let your heart be disquieted within you, that this victim, who is rescued from the horns of the altar, whereuntil she was fast bound by the chains of human law, is now to be driven beyond the bounds of our land. Scotland is a blessed land to those who love the ordinances of Christianity, and it is a fair land to look upon, and dear to them who have dwelt in it a' their days; and weel said that judicious Christian, worthy John Livingstone, a sailor in Borrowstounness, as the famous Patrick Walker reporteth his words, that howbeit he thought Scotland was a Gehennah of wickedness when he was at home, yet, when he was abroad, he accounted it ane paradise; for the evils of Scotland he found every where, and the good of Scotland he found no where. But yet we are to hold in remembrance that Scotland, though it be our native land, and the land of our fathers, is not like Goshen, in Egypt, on whilk the sun of the heavens and of the gospel shineth allenarly, and leaveth the rest of the world in utter darkness. Therefore, and also because this increase of profit at Saint Lennard's Craigs, may be a cauld waff of wind blawing from the frozen land of earthly self, where never plant of grace took root or grew, and because my concerns make me take something ower muckle a grip of the gear of the warld in mine arms, I receive this dispensation anent Effie as a call to depart out of Haran, as righteous Abraham of old, and leave my father's kindred and my mother's house, and the ashes and mould of them who have gone to sleep before me, and which wait to be mingled with these auld crazed banes of mine own. And my heart is lightened to do this, when I call to mind the decay of active and earnest religion in this land, and survey the height and the depth, the breadth and the length of national defections, and how the love of many is waxing lukewarm and cold; and I am strengthened in this resolution to change my domicile. Likewise I hear that store-farms are to be set at an easy mail in Northumberland, where there are many precious souls that are of our true, though suffering persuasion. And sic part of the kye or stock as I judge it fit to keep, may be driven thither without incommodity—say about Wooler, or that gate—keeping aye a shouther to the hills, and the rest might be sauld here to gude profit and advantage, if we had but grace weel to use and guide these gifts of the warld. The Laird has been a true friend on our unhappy occasions, and I have paid him back the siller for Effie's misfortune, whereof Mr Michel Novit returned him no balance, as the Laird and I did expect he wad hae done. But law licks up a', as the common folks say.—I have had the siller to borrow out of sax purses. Mr Saddletree advised to give the Laird of Lounsbeck a charge on his band for a thousand merks. But I hae nae broo' of charges, since that awfu' morning that a tout of a horn, at the cross of Edinburgh, blew half the faithfu' ministers of Scotland out of their pulpits.—However I sall raise an adjudication, whilk Mr

Saddletree says comes instead of the auld apprisings, and will not lose weel-won gear with the like of him if it may be helped. As for the Queen, and the credit whilk she hath done to a poor man's daughter, and the mercy and the grace ye found with her, I can only pray for her weel-being here and hereafter, for the establishment of her house now and for ever, upon the throne of these kingdoms. I doubt not but what you told her Majesty, that I was the same David Deans of whom there was a sport at the Revolution when I noited thegither the heads of twa false prophets, these ungracious Graces the prelates, as they stood on the Hie-street, after being expelled from the Convention-parliament. The Duke of Argyle is a noble and true-hearted noble-man, who pleads the cause of the poor, and those who have none to help them; verily his reward shall not be lacking unto him. I have been writing of many things, but not of that whilk lies nearest mine heart. I have seen the poor misguided thing; she will be at freedom the morn, on enacted caution that she shall leave Scotland in four weeks. Her mind is in an evil frame,—casting her eye backward on Egypt, I doubt, as if the bitter waters of the wilderness were harder to endure than the brick furnaces, by the side of which there were savoury flesh-pots. I need not bid you make hast down, for you are, excepting always my Great Master, my only comfort in these streights. I charge you to withdraw your feet from the delusions of that Vanity-fair in whilk ye are a sojourner, and not to go to their worship, whilk is but an ill mumbled mass, as it was weel termed by James the Sext, though he afterwards, with his unhappy son, strove to bring it ower back and belly into his native kingdom, wherethrough their race have been cut off as foam upon the water, and shall be as wanderers among the nations. See the prophecies of Hosea, ninth and seventeenth, and the same, tenth and seventh. But us and our house, let us say with the same prophet; 'Let us return to the Lord, for he hath torn and he will heal us—He hath smitten, and he will bind us up.'"

He proceeded to say, that he approved of her proposed mode of returning by Glasgow, and entered into sundry minute particulars not necessary to be quoted. A single line in the letter, but not the least frequently read by the party to whom it was addressed, intimated, that "Reuben Butler had been as a son to him in his sorrows." As David Deans scarce ever mentioned Butler before, without some gibe, more or less direct, either at his carnal gifts and learning, or at his grand-father's heresy, Jeanie drew a good omen from no such qualifying clause being added to this sentence respecting him.

A lover's hope resembles the bean in the nursery tale,—let it once take root, and it will grow so rapidly, that in the course of a few hours the giant Imagination builds a castle on the top, and by and bye comes

Disappointment with the "curtal axe," and hews down both the plant and the superstructure. Jeanie's fancy, though not the most powerful of her faculties, was lively enough to transport her to a wild farm in Northumberland, well stocked with milk-cows, yield beasts and sheep; a meeting-house hard by, frequented by serious presbyterians, who had united in a harmonious call to Reuben Butler to be their spiritual guide;—Effie restored, not to gaiety, but to cheerfulness at least;—their father, with his grey hairs smoothed down, and spectacles on his nose;—herself, with the maiden snood exchanged for a matron's curch—all arranged in a pew in the said meeting-house, listening to words of devotion, rendered sweeter and more powerful by the affectionate ties which combined them with the preacher. She cherished such visions from day to day, until her residence in London began to become unsupportable and tedious to her, and it was with no ordinary satisfaction that she received a summons from Argyle-house, requiring her in two days to be prepared to join their northward party.

Chapter Three

One was a female, who had grievous ill
Wrought in revenge, and she enjoyed it still;
Sullen she was, and threatening; in her eye
Glared the stern triumph that she dared to die.
CRABBE

THE SUMMONS of preparation arrived after Jeanie Deans had resided in the metropolis about three weeks.

On the morning appointed she took a grateful farewell of Mrs Glass, as that good woman's attention to her particularly required, placed herself and her moveable goods, which purchases and presents had greatly increased, in a hackney-coach, and joined her travelling companions in the housekeeper's apartment at Argyle-house. While the carriage was getting ready, she was informed that the Duke wished to speak with her; and upon being ushered into a splendid saloon, she was surprised to find that he wished to present her to his lady and daughters.

"I bring you my little countrywoman, Duchess," these were the words of the introduction; "With an army of young fellows, as gallant and steady as she is, and a good cause, I would not fear two to one."

"Ah, papa!" said a lively young lady, about twelve years old, "remember you were full one to two at Sheriff-moor, and yet," (singing the well known ballad)—

"Some say that we wan, and some say that they wan,
   And some say that nane wan at a', man;

But of ae thing I'm sure, that on Sheriff-moor
A battle there was that I saw, man."

"What, little Mary turned Tory on my hands?—This will be fine news for our countrywoman to carry down to Scotland!"

"We may all turn tories for the thanks we have gotten for remaining whigs," said the second young lady.

"Well, hold your peace, you discontented monkies, and go dress your babies; and as for the Bob of Dumblain,

If it wasna weel bobbit, weel bobbit, weel bobbit,
If it wasna weel bobbit, we'll bobb it again."

"Papa's wit is running low," said Lady Mary; "the poor gentleman is repeating himself—he sang that on the field of battle, when he was told the Highlanders had cut his left wing to pieces with their claymores."

A pull by the hair was the repartee to this sally.

"Ah! brave Highlanders and bright claymores," said the Duke, "well do I wish them, 'for a' the ill they hae done me yet,' as the song goes.—But come, madcaps, say a civil word to your countrywoman— I wish you had half her canny homely sense; I think you may be as leal and true-hearted."

The Duchess advanced, and, in few words, in which there was as much kindness as civility, assured Jeanie of the respect she had for a character so affectionate, and yet so firm, and added, "When you get home, you will perhaps hear from me."

"And from me." "And from me." "And from me, Jeanie," added the young ladies one after the other, "for you are a credit to the land we love so well."

Jeanie, overpowered with these unexpected compliments, and not aware that the Duke's investigation had made him acquainted with her behaviour on her sister's trial, could only answer by blushing, and curtseying round and around, and uttering at intervals, "Mony thanks! mony thanks!"

"Jeanie," said the Duke, "you must have *doch an' dorroch*, or you will be unable to travel."

There was a salver with cake and wine on the table. He took up a glass, drank "to all true hearts that lo'ed Scotland," and offered a glass to his guest.

Jeanie, however, declined it, saying, "that she had never tasted wine in her life."

"How comes that, Jeanie?" said the Duke,—"wine maketh glad the heart, you know."

"Ay, sir, but my father is like Jonadab the son of Rechab, who charged his children that they should drink no wine."

"I thought your father would have had more sense," said the Duke, "unless, indeed, he prefers brandy. But, however, Jeanie, if you will not drink, you must eat, to save the character of my house."

He thrust upon her a large piece of cake, nor would he permit her to break off a fragment, and lay the rest on the salver. "Put it in your pouch, Jeanie," said he; "you will be glad of it before you see Saint Mungo's steeple. I wish to heaven I were to see it as soon as you! and so my best service to all friends at and about Auld Reekie, and a blithe journey to you."

And, mixing the frankness of a soldier with his natural affability, he shook hands with his protegée, and committed her to the charge of Archibald, satisfied that he had provided sufficiently for her being attended to by his domestics, from the unusual attention with which he had himself treated her.

Accordingly, in the course of her journey, she found both her companions disposed to pay her every possible attention, so that her return, in point of ease and safety, formed a strong contrast to her journey to London.

Her heart also was disburthened of the weight of grief, shame, apprehension, and fear, which had loaded her before her interview with the Queen at Richmond. But the human mind is so strangely capricious, that, when freed from the pressure of real misery, it becomes open and sensitive to the apprehension of ideal calamities. She was now much disturbed in mind, that she had heard nothing from Reuben Butler, to whom the operation of writing was so much more familiar than it was to herself.

"It would have cost him sae little fash," she said to herself; "for I hae seen his pen gang as fast ower the paper, as ever it did ower the water when it was in the grey goose's wing. Waes me! maybe he may be badly—but then my father wad likely hae said something about it— Or maybe he may hae ta'en the rue, and kens na how to let me wot of his change of mind. He needna be at muckle fash about it,"—she went on, drawing herself up, though the tear of honest pride and injured affection gathered in her eye, as she entertained the suspicion,— "Jeanie Deans is no the lass to pu' him by the sleeve, or put him in mind of what he wishes to forget. I shall wish him weel and happy a' the same; and if he has the luck to get a kirk in our country, I sall gang and hear him just the very same, to show that I bear nae malice." And as she imagined the scene, the tear stole over her eye.

In these melancholy reveries, Jeanie had full time to indulge herself; for her travelling companions, servants in a distinguished and fashionable family, had, of course, many topics of conversation, in which it was absolutely impossible she could have either pleasure or portion. She had, therefore, abundant leisure for reflection, and even for self-tormenting, during the several days which, indulging the young horses which the Duke was sending down to the North with sufficient ease and short stages, they occupied in reaching the neighbourhood of Carlisle.

In approaching the vicinity of that ancient city, they discerned a considerable crowd upon an eminence at a little distance from the high road, and learned from some passengers who were gathering towards that busy scene from the southward, that the cause of the concourse was, the laudable public desire "to see a domned Scotch witch and thief get half of her due upo' Haribee broo' yonder, for she was only to be hanged; she should hae been boorned aloife, an' cheap on't."

"Dear Mr Archibald," said the dame of the dairy elect, "I never seed a woman hanged in a' ma loife, and only foive men, as made a goodly spectacle."

Mr Archibald, however, was a Scotchman, and promised himself no exuberant pleasure in seeing his countrywoman undergo "the terrible behests of law." Moreover, he was a man of sense and delicacy in his way, and the late circumstances of Jeanie's family, with the cause of her expedition to London, were not unknown to him; so that he answered drily, it was impossible to stop, as he must be early at Carlisle on some business of the Duke's, and he accordingly bid the postillions get on.

The road at that time passed at about a quarter of a mile's distance from the eminence, called Harabee or Hara-brow, which, though it is very moderate in size and height, is nevertheless seen from a great distance around, owing to the flatness of the country through which the Eden flows. Here many an outlaw, and border-rider of both kingdoms, had wavered in the wind during the wars, and scarce less hostile truces between the two countries. Upon Harabee, in later days, other executions had taken place with as little ceremony as compassion; for these frontier provinces remained long unsettled, and even at the time of which we write, were ruder than those in the centre of England.

The postillions drove on, wheeling, as the Penrith road led them, round the verge of the rising ground. Yet still the eager eyes of Mrs Dolly Dutton, which, with the head and substantial person to which they belonged, were all turned towards the scene of action, could discern plainly the outline of the gallows-tree, relieved against the clear sky, the darker shade formed by the persons of the executioner and the criminal upon the light rounds of the tall aerial ladder, until one of the objects, launched into air, gave unequivocal signs of mortal agony, though appearing in the distance not larger than a spider dependant at the extremity of his invisible thread, while the remaining form descended from its elevated situation, and regained with all speed an undistinguished place among the crowd. This termination of the tragic scene drew forth of course a squall from Mrs Dutton, and Jeanie, with instinctive curiosity, turned her head in the same direction.

The sight of a female culprit in the act of undergoing the fatal punishment from which her beloved sister had been so recently rescued, was too much, not perhaps for her nerves, but for her mind and feeling. She turned her head to the other side of the carriage, with a sensation of sickness, of loathing, and of faintness. Her female companion overwhelmed her with questions, with proffers of assistance, with requests that the carriage might be stopped—that a doctor might be fetched—that drops might be gotten—that burned feathers and assafœtida, fair water, and hartshorn might be procured, all at once, and without one instant's delay. Archibald, more calm and considerate, only desired the carriage to push forward, and it was not till they had got beyond sight of the fatal spectacle, that, seeing the deadly paleness of Jeanie's countenance, he stopped the carriage, and jumping out himself, went in search of the most obvious and most easily procured of Mrs Dutton's pharmacopeia—a draught, namely, of fresh water.

While Archibald was absent on this good-natured piece of service, damning the ditches which produced nothing but mud, and thinking upon the thousand bubbling springlets of his own mountains, the attendants on the execution began to pass the stationary vehicle in their way back to Carlisle.

From their half-heard and half-understood words, Jeanie, whose attention was involuntarily rivetted by them, as that of children is by ghost stories, though they know the pain with which they will afterwards remember them, Jeanie, I say, could discern that the present victim of the law had died *game*, as it is termed by those unfortunates, that is, sullen, reckless, and impenitent, neither fearing God, nor regarding man.

"A sture woife, and a dour," said one Cumbrian peasant, as he clattered by in his wooden brogues, with a noise like the trampling of a dray-horse.

"She has gone to ho master, with ho's name in her mouth," said another; "Shame the country should be harried wi' Scotch witches and Scotch bitches this gate—but I say hang and drown."

"Ay, ay, Gaffer Tramp, take awa' yealdon, take awa' low—hang the witch, and there will be less scathe amang us; myne owsen hae been reckan this two-mont."

"And mine bairns hae been crining too, mon," replied his neighbour.

"Silence wi' your fule tongues, ye churles," said an old woman, who hobbled past them, as they stood talking near the carriage; "this was nae witch, but a bluidy fingered thief and murtheress."

"Ay? was it e'en sae, Dame Hinchup?" said one in a civil tone, and stepping out of his place to let the old woman pass upon the foot-path—"Nay, you know best, sure—but at ony rate, we hae tint but a Scot of her, and that's a thing better lost than found."

The old woman passed on without making any answer.

"Eye, eye, neighbour," said Gaffer Tramp, "seeest thou hou one witch will speak for t'other?—Scots or English, the same to them."

His companion shook his head, and replied in the same subdued tone, "Eye, eye, when a Sark-foot wife gets on her broomstick, the dames of Allonby are ready to mount, just as sure as the bye word gangs o' the hills,

> If Skiddaw hath a cap,
> Criffel wots full weel of that."

"But," continued Gaffer Tramp, "thinkst thou the daughter o' yon hangit body isna as rank a witch as ho?"

"I kenna clearly," returned the fellow, "but the folks are speaking o' swumming her i' th' Eden." And they passed on their several roads, after wishing each other good morning.

Just as the clowns left the place, and as Mr Archibald returned with some fair water, a crowd of boys and girls, and some of the lower rabble of more mature age, came up from the place of execution, grouping themselves with many a yell of delight around a tall female fantastically dressed, who was dancing, leaping, and bounding in the midst of them. A horrible recollection pressed on Jeanie as she looked on this unfortunate creature, and the reminiscence was mutual, for by a sudden exertion of great strength and agility, Madge Wildfire broke out of the noisy circle of tormentors who surrounded her, and clinging fast to the door of the calash, uttered, in a sound betwixt laughter and screaming, "Eh, d'ye ken, Jeanie Deans, they hae hangit our mither?" Then suddenly changing her tone to that of the most piteous entreaty, she added, "O gar them let me gang to cut her down!—let me but cut her down!—she is my mother, if she was waur than the deil, and she'll be nae mair kenspeckle than half-hangit Maggie Dickson, that cried saut mony a day after she had been hangit; her voice was roupit and hoarse, and her neck was a wee agee, or ye wad hae kend nae odds on her frae ony other saut-wife."

Mr Archibald, embarrassed by the mad-woman's clinging to the carriage, and detaining around them her noisy and mischievous attendants, was all this while looking out for some constable or beadle, to whom he might commit this unfortunate creature. But seeing no such person of authority, he endeavoured to loosen her hold from the carriage, that they might escape from her by driving on. This, however, could hardly be achieved without some degree of violence; Madge held fast, and renewed her frantic entreaties to be permitted to cut down her mother. "It was but a tenpenny tow lost," she said, "and what was that to a woman's life?" There came up, however, a parcel of savage looking fellows, butchers and graziers chiefly, among whose cattle there had been of late a very general and fatal distemper, which their wisdom imputed to witchcraft. They laid violent hands on Madge, and tore her from the carriage, exclaiming—"What, doest stop fo'k o' king's highway? Hast no done mischief enow already, wi' thy murders and thy witcherings?"

"Oh Jeanie Deans—Jeanie Deans!" exclaimed the poor maniac, "save my mother, and I will take ye to the Interpreter's house again,— and I will teach ye a' my bonnie sangs,—and I will tell ye what came o' the"—— The rest of her entreaties were drowned in the shouts of the rabble.

"Save her, for God's sake!—save her from those people!" exclaimed Jeanie to Archibald. "She is mad, but quite innocent."

"She is mad, gentlemen," said Archibald; "do not use her ill, take her before the Mayor."

"Ay, ay, we'se hae care enow on her," answered one of the fellows; "gang thou thy gate, man, and mind thine own matters."

"He's a Scot by his tongue," said another; "and an' he will come out on his whirligig there, I'se gie him a tartan plaid fu' o' broken banes."

It was clear nothing could be done to rescue Madge, and Archibald, who was a man of humanity, could only bid the postillions hurry on to Carlisle, that he might obtain some assistance to the unfortunate woman. As they drove off, they heard the hoarse roar with which the mob preface acts of riot or cruelty, yet even above that deep and dire note, they could discern the screams of the unfortunate victim. They were soon out of hearing of the cries, but had no sooner entered the streets of Carlisle, than Archibald, at Jeanie's earnest and urgent entreaty, went to a magistrate, to state the cruelty which was likely to be exercised on this unhappy creature.

In about an hour and a half he returned and reported to Jeanie, that the magistrate had very readily gone in person, with some assistants, to the rescue of the unfortunate woman, and that he had himself accompanied him; that when they came to the muddy pool, in which the mob were ducking her, according to their favourite mode of punishment, the magistrate succeeded in rescuing her from their hands, but in a state of insensibility, owing to the cruel treatment which she had received. He added, that he had seen her carried to the work-house, and understood she had been brought to herself, and was expected to do well.

This last averment was a slight alteration in point of fact, for Madge Wildfire was not expected to survive the treatment she had received; but Jeanie seemed so much agitated, that Archibald did not think it prudent to tell her the worst at once. Indeed she appeared so fluttered and disordered by this alarming incident, that, although it had been their intention to proceed to Longtown that evening, her companions judged it most advisable to pass the night at Carlisle.

This was particularly agreeable to Jeanie, who resolved, if possible, to procure an interview with Madge Wildfire. Connecting some of her wild flights with the narrative of George Staunton, she was unwilling to omit the opportunity of extracting from her, if possible, some information concerning the fate of that unfortunate infant which had cost her sister so dear. Her acquaintance with the disordered state of poor Madge's mind, did not permit her to cherish much hope that she could acquire from her any useful intelligence; but then, since Madge's mother had suffered her deserts, and was silent for ever, it was her only chance of obtaining any kind of information, and she was loth to lose the opportunity.

She coloured her wish to Mr Archibald by saying, that she had seen Madge formerly, and wished to know, as a matter of humanity, how she was attended to under her present misfortunes. That complaisant person immediately went to the work-house, or hospital, in which he had seen the sufferer lodged, and brought back for reply, that the medical attendants positively forbade her seeing any one. When the application for admittance was repeated next day, Mr Archibald was informed that she had been very quiet and composed, insomuch that the clergyman, who acted as chaplain to the establishment, had thought it expedient to read prayers beside her bed, but that her wandering fit of mind had returned soon after his departure; however, her countrywoman might see her if she chose it. She was not expected to live above an hour or two.

Jeanie had no sooner received this intimation, than she hastened to the hospital, her companions attending her. They found the dying person in a large ward, where there were ten beds, of which the patient's was the only one occupied.

Madge was singing when they entered—singing her own wild snatches of songs and forgotten airs, with a voice no longer overstrained by false spirits, but softened, saddened, and subdued by bodily exhaustion. She was still insane, but was no longer able to express her wandering ideas in the wild notes of her former state of exalted imagination. There was death in the plaintive tones of her voice, which yet, in this moderated and melancholy mood, had something of the lulling sound with which a mother sings her infant asleep. As Jeanie entered, she heard first the air, and then a part of the chorus and words of what had been, perhaps, the song of a jolly harvest-home.

> "Our work is over—over now,
> The goodman wipes his weary brow,
> The last long wain wends slow away,
> And we are free to sport and play.
>
> "The night comes on when sets the sun,
> And labour ends when day is done.
> When Autumn's gone and Winter's come,
> We hold our jovial harvest-home."

Jeanie advanced to the bed-side when the strain was finished, and addressed Madge by her name. But it produced no symptom of recollection. On the contrary, the patient, like one provoked by interruption, changed her posture, and called out, with an impatient tone, "Nurse—nurse, turn my face to the wa', that I may never answer to that name ony mair, and never see mair of a wicked world."

The attendant on the hospital arranged her in her bed as she desired, with her face to the wall, and her back to the light. So soon as she was quiet in this new position, she began again to sing in the same low and modulated strains, as if she was recovering the state of abstraction which the interruption of her visitants had disturbed. The strain, however, was different, and rather resembled the music of the Methodist hymns, though the measure of the song was similar to that of the former.

> "When the fight of grace is fought,—
> When the marriage vest is wrought,—
> When Faith hath chased cold Doubt away,
> And Hope but sickens at delay,—
> When Charity, imprisoned here,
> Longs for a more expanded sphere,
> Doff thy robes of sin and clay;
> Christian, rise, and come away."

The strain was solemn and affecting, sustained as it was by the pathetic warble of a voice which had naturally been a fine one, and which weakness, if it diminished its power, had improved in softness. Archibald, though a follower of the court, and therefore a poco-curante by profession, was confused, if not affected; the dairy-maid blubbered; and Jeanie felt the tears rise spontaneously to her eyes.

Even the nurse, accustomed to all modes in which the spirit can pass, seemed considerably affected.

The patient was evidently growing weaker, as was intimated by an apparent difficulty of breathing, which seized her from time to time, and by the utterance of low listless moans, intimating that nature was succumbing in the last conflict. But the spirit of melody, which must originally have so strongly possessed this unfortunate young woman, seemed, at every interval of ease, to triumph over her pain and weakness. And it was remarkable, that there could always be traced in her songs something appropriate, though perhaps only obliquely or collaterally so, to her present situation. Her next seemed to be the fragment of some old ballad:

> "Cauld is my bed, Lord Archibald,
>   And sad my sleep of sorrow;
> But thine sall be as sad and cauld,
>   My fause true-love, to-morrow.
>
> "And weep ye not, my maidens free,
>   Though death your mistress borrow;
> For he for whom to-day I die,
>   Shall die for me to-morrow."

Again she changed the tune to one wilder, less monotonous, and less regular. But of the words only a fragment or two could be collected by those who listened to this singular scene.

> "Proud Maisie is in the wood,
>   Walking so early;
> Sweet Robin sits on the bush,
>   Singing so rarely.
>
> "'Tell me, thou bonny bird,
>   When shall I marry me?'—
> 'When six braw gentlemen
> Kirkward shall carry ye.'
>   *   *   *
> "'Who makes the bridal bed,
>   Birdie, say truly?'
> 'The grey-headed sexton
>   That delves the grave duly.'
>   *   *   *
> "The glow-worm o'er grave and stone
>   Shall light thee steady.
> The owl from the steeple sing,
>   'Welcome, proud lady.'"

Her voice died away with the last notes, and she fell into a slumber, from which the experienced attendant assured them she would never awaken at all, or only in the death-agony.

Her first prophecy was true. The poor maniac parted with existence, without again uttering a sound of any kind. But our travellers

did not witness this catastrophe. They left the hospital so soon as
Jeanie had satisfied herself that no elucidation of her sister's misfortunes was to be hoped from the dying person.

Chapter Four

Wilt thou go on with me?
The moon is bright, the sea is calm,
And I know well the ocean-paths....
Thou wilt go on with me.
Thalaba

THE FATIGUE AND AGITATION of these various scenes had agitated Jeanie so much, notwithstanding her robust strength of constitution, that Archibald judged it necessary that she should have a day's
repose at the village of Longtown. It was in vain that Jeanie herself
protested against any delay. The Duke of Argyle's man of confidence
was of course consequential; and as he had been bred to the medical
profession in his youth, (at least he used this expression to describe
his having, thirty years before, pounded for six months in the mortar of
old Mungo Mangelman, the surgeon at Greenock), he was obstinate
wherever a matter of health was in question.

In this case he discovered febrile symptoms, and having once made
a happy application of that learned phrase to Jeanie's case, all farther
resistance became in vain; and she was glad to acquiesce, and even to
go to bed, and drink water-gruel, in order that she might possess her
soul in quiet, and without interruption.

Mr Archibald was equally attentive in another particular. He
observed that the execution of the old woman, and the miserable fate
of her daughter, seemed to have made a more powerful effect upon
Jeanie's mind, than the usual feelings of humanity might naturally
have been expected to occasion. Yet she was obviously a strong-
minded, sensible young woman, and in no respect subject to nervous
affections; and therefore Archibald, being ignorant of any special
connection between his master's protegée and these unfortunate persons, excepting that she had seen Madge formerly in Scotland, naturally imputed the strong impression these events had made upon her,
to her associating them with the unhappy circumstances in which her
sister had so lately stood. He became anxious, therefore, to prevent
any thing occurring which might recal these associations to Jeanie's
mind.

Archibald had speedily an opportunity of exercising this precaution. A pedlar brought to Longtown that evening, amongst other
wares, a large broadside-sheet, giving an account of the "Last Speech

and Execution of Margaret Murdockson, and of the barbarous Murder of her Daughter, Magdalen or Madge Murdockson, called
Madge Wildfire; and of her pious Conversation with his Reverence
Arch-deacon Fleming;" which authentic publication had apparently
taken place on the day they left Carlisle, and being an article of a
nature peculiarly acceptable to such country-folks as were within
hearing of the transaction, the itinerant bibliopolist had forthwith
added them to his stock in trade. He found a merchant sooner than he
expected; for Archibald, much applauding his own prudence, purchased the whole lot for two shillings and ninepence; and the pedlar,
delighted with the profit of such a wholesale transaction, instantly
returned to Carlisle to supply himself with more.

The considerate Mr Archibald was about to commit his whole
purchase to the flames, but it was rescued by the yet more considerate
dairy-maid, who said, very prudently, it was a pity to waste so much
paper, which might crêpe hair, pin up bonnets, and serve many other
useful purposes. And she promised to put the parcel into her own
trunk, and keep it carefully out of the sight of Mrs Jeanie Deans:
"Though by the bye she had no great notion of folks being so very
nice. Mrs Deans might have heard enough of the gallows all this time
to endure a sight of it, without all this to do about it."

Archibald reminded the dame of the dairy of the Duke's very particular charge, that they should be attentive and civil to Jeanie; as also
they were to part company soon, and consequently would not be
doomed to observing any one's health or temper during the rest of the
journey. With which answer Mrs Dolly Dutton was obliged to hold
herself satisfied.

On the morning they resumed their journey, and prosecuted it
successfully, travelling through Dumfries-shire and part of Lanarkshire, until they arrived at the small town of Rutherglen, within about
four miles of Glasgow. Here an express brought letters to Archibald
from the principal agent of the Duke of Argyle in Edinburgh.

He said nothing of their contents that evening; but when they were
seated in the carriage the next day, the faithful squire informed Jeanie,
that he had received directions from the Duke's factor, to whom his
Grace had recommended her, to carry her if she had no objection, for
a stage or two beyond Glasgow. Some temporary causes of discontent
had occasioned tumults in that city and the neighbourhood, which
would render it unadviseable for Mrs Jeanie Deans to travel alone and
unprotected betwixt that city and Edinburgh; whereas by going forward a little farther, they would meet one of his Grace's sub-factors,
who was coming up from the Highlands to Edinburgh with his wife,
and under whose charge she might journey with comfort and in safety.

Jeanie remonstrated somewhat against this arrangement. "She had been lang," she said, "frae hame—her father and her sister behoved to be very anxious to see her—there were other friends she had that werena weel in health. She was willing to pay for man and horse at Glasgow, and surely naebody wad middle wi' sae harmless and feckless a creature as she was.—She was muckle obliged by the offer; but never hunted deer langed for its resting-place, as I do to find myself at Saint Leonard's."

The Groom of the Chambers exchanged a look with his female companion, which seemed so full of meaning, that Jeanie screamed aloud—"O Mr Archibald—Mrs Dutton, if ye ken of ony thing that has happened at Saint Leonard's, for God's sake—for pity's sake, tell me, and dinna keep me in suspense!"

"I really know nothing, Mrs Deans," said the Groom of the Chambers.

"And I—I—I am sure, I knows as little," said the dame of the dairy, while some communication seemed to tremble on her lips, which, at a glance of Archibald's eye, she appeared to swallow down, and compressed her lips thereafter into a state of extreme and vigilant primness, as if she had been afraid of its bolting out before she was aware.

Jeanie saw that there was something to be concealed from her, and it was only the repeated assurances of Archibald that her father—her sister—all her friends were, so far as he knew, well and happy, that at all pacified her alarm. From such respectable people as those with whom she travelled, she could apprehend no harm, and yet her distress was so obvious, that Archibald, as a last resource, pulled out, and put into her hand, a slip of paper, on which these words were written:—

"JEANIE DEANS—You will do me a favour by going with Archibald and my female domestic a day's journey beyond Glasgow, and asking them no questions, which will greatly oblige your friend,
                                        "ARGYLE & GREENWICH."

Although this laconic epistle, from a nobleman to whom she was bound by such inestimable obligations, silenced all Jeanie's objections to the proposed route, it rather added to than diminished the eagerness of her curiosity. The proceeding to Glasgow seemed now no longer to be an object with her fellow travellers. On the contrary, they kept the left hand side of the river Clyde, and travelled through a thousand beautiful and changing views down the side of that noble stream, till ceasing to hold its inland character, it began to assume that of a navigable river.

"You are not for ganging intill Glasgow then?" said Jeanie, as she observed that the drivers made no motion for inclining their horses' heads towards the ancient bridge which was then the only mode of access to Saint Mungo's capital.

"No," replied Archibald; "there is some popular commotion, and as our Duke is in opposition to the court, perhaps we might be too well received; or they might take it in their heads to remember that the captain of Carrick came down upon them with his highlandmen in the time of Shawfield's mob in 1725, and then we would be too ill received. And at any rate, it is best for us, and for me in particular, who may be supposed to possess his Grace's mind upon many particulars, to leave the good people of the Gorbals to act according to their own imaginations, without either provoking or encouraging them by my presence."

To reasoning of such tone and consequence, Jeanie had nothing to reply, although it seemed to her to contain fully as much self-import-ance as truth.

The carriage meantime rolled on; the river expanded itself, and gradually assumed the dignity of an œstuary, or arm of the sea. The influence of the advancing and retiring tides, became more and more evident, and in the beautiful words of him of the laurel wreath, the river waxed

> A broader and a broader stream.
> *   *   *   *
> The Cormorant stands upon its shoals,
>   His black and dripping wings
>   Half opened to the wind.

"Which way lies Inverary?" said Jeanie, gazing on the dusky ocean of Highland hills, which now, piled above each other, and intersected by many a lake, stretched away on the opposite side of the river to the northward. "Is yon high castle the Duke's hoose?"

"That, Mrs Deans?—Lud help thee," replied Archibald, "that's the old Castle of Dumbarton, the strongest place in Europe, be the other what it may. Sir William Wallace was governor of it in the old wars with the English, and his Grace is governor just now. It is always entrusted to the best man in Scotland."

"And does the Duke live on that high rock, then?" demanded Jeanie.

"No, no, he has his deputy-governor who commands in his absence; he lives in the white house you see at the bottom of the rock —His Grace does not live there himself."

"I think not indeed," said the dairy-woman, upon whose mind the road, since they had left Dumfries, had made no very favourable impression; "for if he did, he might go whistle for a dairy-woman, an' he were the only duke in England. I did not leave my place and my friends to come down to see cows starve to death upon hills as they be at that pig-stye of Elfinfoot, as you called it, Mister Archibald, or to be perched up on the top of a rock, like a squirrel in his cage, hung out of a three pair of stairs window."

Inwardly chuckling that these symptoms of recalcitration had not taken place until the fair malcontent was, as he mentally termed it, under his thumb, Archibald coolly replied, "That the hills were none of his making, nor did he know how to mend them. But as to lodging, they would soon be in a house of the Duke's in a very pleasant island called Roseneath, where they went to wait for shipping to take them to Inverary, and would meet the company with whom Jeanie was to return to Edinburgh."

"An island?" said Jeanie, who in the course of her various and adventurous travels had never quitted terra firma, "then I am doubting we maun gang in ane of these boats; they look unco sma', and the waves are something rough, and"—

"Mr Archibald," said Mrs Dutton, "I will not consent to it; I was never engaged to leave the country, and I desire you will bid the boys drive round by the other way to the Duke's house."

"There is a safe pinnace belonging to his Grace, ma'am, close by," replied Archibald, "and you need be under no apprehensions whatsoever."

"But I *am* under apprehensions," said the damsel; "and I insist upon going round by land, Mr Archibald, were it ten miles about."

"I am sorry I cannot oblige you, madam, as Roseneath happens to be an island."

"If it were ten islands," said the incensed dame, "that's no reason why I should be drowned in going over the seas to it."

"No reason why you should be drowned, certainly madam," answered the unmoved Groom of the Chambers, "but an admirable good one why you cannot proceed to it by land." And, fixed his master's mandates to perform, he pointed with his hand, and the drivers, turning off the high-road, proceeded towards a small hamlet of fishing huts, where a shallop, somewhat more gaily decorated than any which they had yet seen, having a flag which displayed a boar's-head, crested with a ducal coronet, waited with two or three seamen, and as many Highlanders.

The carriage stopped, and the men began to unyoke their horses, while Mr Archibald gravely superintended the removal of the baggage from the carriage to the little vessel. "Has the Caroline been long arrived?" said Archibald to one of the seamen.

"She has been here in five days from Liverpool, and she's lying down at Greenock," answered the fellow.

"Let the horses and carriage go down to Greenock then," said Archibald, "and be embarked there for Inverara when I send notice —they may stand in my cousin, Duncan Archibald the stabler's.— Ladies," he added, "I hope you will get yourselves ready, we must not lose the tide."

"Mrs Deans," said the Cowslip of Inverary, "you may do as you please—but I will sit here all night, rather than go into that there painted egg-shell—Fellow—fellow" (this was addressed to a Highlander who was lifting a travelling trunk) "that trunk is *mine*, and that there band-box, and that pillion mail, and those seven bundles, and the paper bag, and if you ventures to touch one of them, it shall be at your peril."

The Celt kept his eye fixed on the speaker, then turned his head towards Archibald, and receiving no countervailing signal, he shouldered the portmanteau, and without further notice of the distressed damsel, or paying any attention to remonstrances, which probably he did not understand, and would certainly have equally disregarded whether he understood them or not, moved off with Mrs Dutton's wearables, and deposited the trunk containing them safely in the boat.

The baggage being stowed in safety, Mr Archibald handed Jeanie out of the carriage, and, not without some tremor on her part, she was transported through the surf and placed in the boat. He then offered the same civility to his fellow servant, but she was resolute in her refusal to quit the carriage, in which she now remained in solitary state, threatening all concerned or unconcerned with actions for wages and board-wages, damages and expences, and numbering on her fingers the gowns and other habiliments, from which she seemed in the act of being separated for ever. Mr Archibald did not give himself the trouble of making many remonstrances, which, indeed, seemed only to aggravate the damsel's indignation, but spoke two or three words to the Highlanders in Gaelic; and the wily mountaineers, approaching the carriage cautiously, and without giving the slightest intimation of their intentions, at once seized the recusant so effectually fast that she could neither resist nor struggle, and hoisting her on their shoulders in nearly an horizontal posture, rushed down with her to the beach, and through the surf, and, with no other inconvenience than ruffling her garments a little, deposited her in the boat; but in a state of surprise, mortification, and terror at her sudden transportation, which rendered her absolutely mute for two or three minutes. The men jumped in themselves, one tall fellow remaining till he had pushed off the boat, and then tumbling in upon his companions. They took their oars and began to pull from the shore, then spread their sail, and drove merrily across the firth.

"You Scotch villain," said the infuriated damsel to Archibald, "how dare you use a person like me in this way?"

"Madam," said Archibald, with infinite composure, "it's high time you should know you are in the Duke's country, and that there is not one of these fellows, but would throw you out of the boat as readily as into it, if such were his Grace's pleasure."

"Then the Lord have marcy on me!" said Mrs Dutton. "If I had had any on myself, I would never have engaged with you."

"It's something of the latest to think of that now, Mrs Dutton," said Archibald; "but I assure you, you will find the Highlands have their pleasures. You will have a dozen of cow-milkers under your own authority at Inverary, and you may throw any of them into the lake, if you have a mind, for the Duke's head people are almost as great as himself."

"This is a strange business, to be sure, Mr Archibald," said the lady; "but I suppose I must make the best on't.—Are you sure the boat will not sink? it leans terribly to one side, in my poor mind."

"Fear nothing," said Mr Archibald, taking a most important pinch of snuff; "this same ferry on Clyde knows us very well, or we know it, which is all the same; no fear of any of our people meeting with any accident. We should have crossed from the opposite shore, but for the disturbances at Glasgow, which made it improper for his Grace's people to pass through the city."

"Are you not afeard, Mrs Deans," said the dairy-maid, addressing Jeanie, who sat, not in the most comfortable state of mind, by the side of Archibald, who himself managed the helm;—"Are you not afeard of these wild men with their naked—knees, and of this nut-shell of a thing, that seems bobbing up and down like a skimming dish in a milk pail?"

"No—no—madam," answered Jeanie, with some hesitation, "I am not feared; for I hae seen Hielandmen before, though I never was sae near them; and for the danger of the deep waters, I trust there is a Providence by sea as weel as by land."

"Well," said Mrs Dutton, "it is a beautiful thing to have learned to write and read, for one can always say such fine words whatever should befall them."

Archibald, rejoicing in the impression which his vigorous measure had made upon the intractable damsel, now applied himself, as a sensible and good-natured man, to secure by fair means the ascendancy which he had obtained by some wholesome violence; and he succeeded so well in representing to her the idle nature of her fears, and the impossibility of leaving her upon the beach, enthroned in an empty carriage, that the good understanding of the party was completely revived ere they landed at Roseneath.

Chapter Five

— Did Fortune guide,
Or rather Destiny, our bark, to which
We could appoint no port, to this blest place?
FLETCHER

THE ISLANDS in the Firth of Clyde, which the daily passage of so many smoke-pennoned steam-boats now renders so easily accessible, were, in our fathers' times, secluded spots, frequented by no travellers, and few visitants of any kind. They are of exquisite, yet varied beauty. Arran, a mountainous region, or Alpine island, abounds with the grandest and most romantic highland scenery. Bute is of a softer and more woodland character. The Cumrays, as if to exhibit a contrast to both, are green, level, and bare, forming the links of a sort of natural bar, which is drawn along the mouth of the Firth, leaving large intervals, however, of ocean. Roseneath lies much higher up the Firth, and towards its western shore, near the opening of the lake called the Gare-Loch, and not far from Loch-Long and Loch-Seant, or the Haly-Loch, which wind from the mountains of the western Highlands to join the œstuary of the Clyde.

In these isles the severe frost winds, which tyrannize over the vegetable creation during a Scottish spring, are comparatively little felt; nor, excepting the gigantic strength of Arran, are they much exposed to the Atlantic storms, lying land-locked and protected to the westward by the shores of Argyleshire. Accordingly, the weeping-willow, the weeping-birch, and other trees of early and pendulous shoots, flourish in these favoured recesses in a degree unknown in our eastern districts; and the air is also said to possess that mildness which is favourable to consumptive cases.

The picturesque beauty of the island of Roseneath, in particular, had such recommendations, that the Earls and Dukes of Argyle, from an early period, made it their occasional residence, and had their temporary accommodation in a fishing or hunting-lodge, which succeeding improvements have since transformed into a palace. It was in its original simplicity, when the little bark, which we left traversing the Firth at the end of the last chapter, was approaching its shores.

When they touched the landing-place, which was partly shrouded by some old low but wide-spreading oak-trees, intermixed with hazel-bushes, two or three figures were seen as if awaiting their arrival. To these Jeanie paid little attention, so that it was with a shock of surprise almost electrical, that, upon being carried by the rowers out of the boat to the shore, she was received in the arms of her father!

It was too wonderful to be believed—too much like a happy dream to have the stable feeling of reality—She extricated herself from his close and affectionate embrace, and held him at arm's length to satisfy her mind that it was no illusion. But the form was indisputable—Douce David Deans himself, in his best light-blue Sunday's coat, with broad metal-buttons, and waist-coat and breeches of the same, his strong gramashes or leggins of thick grey cloth—the very copper-buckles—the broad Lowland blue bonnet, thrown back as he lifted his eyes to Heaven in speechless gratitude—the grey locks that straggled from beneath it down his weather-beaten "haffets"—the bald and furrowed forehead—the clear blue eye, that, undimmed by years, gleamed bright and pale from under its shaggy grey pent-house—the features, usually so stern and stoical, now melted into the unwonted expression of rapturous joy, affection, and gratitude—were all those of David Deans; and so happily did they assort together, that, should I ever again see my friends Wilkie or Allan, I will beg, borrow or steal from them a sketch of this very scene.

"Jeanie—my ain Jeanie—my best—my maist dutiful bairn—the Lord of Israel be thy father, for I am hardly worthy of thee! Thou hast redeemed our captivity—brought back the honour of our house—Bless thee, my bairn, with mercies promised and purchased!—But He *has* blessed thee in the good of which He has made thee the instrument."

These words broke from him not without tears, though David was of no melting mood. Archibald had, with delicate attention, withdrawn the spectators from this interview, so that the wood and setting sun alone were witnesses of the expansion of their feelings.

"And Effie?—and Effie, dear father?" was an interjectional question which Jeanie repeatedly threw in among her expressions of joyful thankfulness.

"Ye will hear—ye will hear," said David hastily, and ever and anon renewed his grateful acknowledgments to Heaven for sending Jeanie safe down from the land of prelatic deadness and schismatic heresy; and having delivered her from the dangers of the way, and the lions that were in the path.

"And Effie?" repeated her affectionate sister again and again. "And—and—(fain would she have said Butler, but she modified the direct enquiry)—and Mr and Mrs Saddletree—and Dumbiedikes—and a' friends?"

"A' weel—a' weel, praise to His name."

"And—and Mr Butler—he wasna weel whan I gaed awa'?"

"He is quite mended—quite weel."

"Thank God—but O, dear father, Effie?—Effie?"

"You will never see her mair, my bairn," answered Deans in a solemn tone—"You are the ae and only leaf now left on the auld tree —heal be your portion."

"She is dead!—She is dead!—It has come ower late!" exclaimed Jeanie, wringing her hands.

"No, Jeanie," returned Deans, in the same grave melancholy tone. "She lives in the flesh, and is at freedom from earthly restraint; if she were as much alive in faith, and as free from the bonds of Satan."

"The Lord protect us!" said Jeanie.—"Can the unhappy bairn hae left you for that villain?"

"It is ower truly spoken," said Deans—"She has left her auld father, that has wept and prayed for her—She has left her sister, that travailed and toiled for her like a mother—She has left the bones of her mother, and the land of her people, and she is ower the march wi' that son of Belial—She has made a moonlight flitting of it." He paused, for a feeling betwixt sorrow and strong resentment choked and impeded his utterance.

"And wi' that man?—that fearfu' man?" said Jeanie. "And she has left us a' to gang aff wi' him?—O Effie, Effie, wha could hae thought it, after sic a deliverance as you had been gifted wi'!"

"She went out from us, my bairn, because she was not of us," replied David. "She is a withered branch will never bear fruit of grace —a scape-goat gone forth into the wilderness of the world, to carry wi' her, as I trust, the sins of our little congregation. The peace of the warld gang wi' her, and a better peace when she has the grace to turn to it. If she is of His elected, His ain hour will come. What would her mother have said, that famous and memorable matron, Rebecca Mac-Naught, whose memory is like a flower of sweet savour in Newbattle, and a pot of frankincense in Lugton?—But be it sae—let her part—let her gang her gate—let her bite on her ain bridle—The Lord kens his time—She was the bairn of prayers, and may not prove an utter cast-away. But never, Jeanie—never more let her name be spoken between you and me—She hath passed from us like the brook which vanisheth when the summer waxeth warm, as patient Job saith—let her pass, and be forgotten."

There was a melancholy pause which followed these expressions. Jeanie would fain have asked more circumstances relating to her sister's departure, but the tone of her father's prohibition was positive. She was about to mention her interview with Staunton at his father's rectory; but, on hastily running over the particulars in her memory, she thought that, on the whole, they were more likely to aggravate than diminish his distress of mind. She turned, therefore, the discourse from this painful subject, resolving to suspend farther enquiry until she should see Butler, from whom she expected to learn the particulars of her sister's elopement.

But when was she to see Butler? this was a question she could not forbear asking herself, especially when her father, as if eager to escape from the subject of his youngest daughter, pointed to the opposite shore of Dumbarton-shire, and asking Jeanie "if it werena a pleasant abode? declared to her his intention of removing his earthly tabernacle to that country, in respect he was solicited by his Grace the Duke of Argyle, as one weel skilled in country-labour, and a' that appertained to flocks and herds, to superintend a store-farm, whilk his Grace had ta'en into his ain hand for the improvement of stock."

Jeanie's heart sunk within her at this declaration. "She allowed it was a goodly and pleasant land, and sloped bonnily to the western sun; and she doubtedna that the pasture might be very gude, for the grass looked green, for as drouthy as the weather had been. But it was far frae hame, and she thought she wad be aften thinking on the bonny spots of turf, sae fu' of gowans and yellow king-cups, amang the Craigs at Saint Leonard's."

"Dinna speak on't, Jeanie," said her father; "I wish never to hear it named mair—that is, after the rouping is ower, and the bills paid. But I brought a' the beasts ower bye that I thought ye wad like best. There is Gowans, and there's your ain brockit cow, and the wee hawkit ane, that ye ca'd—I needna tell ye how ye ca'd it—but I couldna bid them sell the creature, though the sight o't may sometimes gie us a sair heart —it's no the puir dumb creature's fault—And ane or twa beasts mair I hae reserved, and I caused them to be driven before the other cattle, that men might say, as when the son of Jesse returned from battle, 'This is David's spoil.'"

Upon more particular enquiry, Jeanie found new occasion to admire the active beneficence of her friend the Duke of Argyle. While establishing a sort of experimental farm on the skirts of his immense Highland estates, he had been somewhat at a loss to find a proper person in whom to vest the charge of it. The conversation his Grace had upon country matters with Jeanie Deans during their return from Richmond, had impressed him with a belief that the father, whose experience and success she so frequently quoted, must be exactly the sort of person whom he wanted. When the condition annexed to Effie's pardon rendered it highly probable that David Deans would chuse to change his place of residence, this idea again occurred to the Duke more strongly, and as he was an enthusiast equally in agriculture and in benevolence, he imagined he was serving the purposes of both, when he wrote to the gentleman in Edinburgh entrusted with his affairs, to enquire into the character of David Deans, cow-feeder, and so forth, at Saint Leonard's Crags; and if he found him such as he had been represented, to engage him without delay, and on the most liberal terms, to superintend his fancy-farm in Dumbartonshire.

The proposal was made to old David by the gentleman so commissioned, on the second day after his daughter's pardon had reached Edinburgh. His resolution to leave Saint Leonard's had been already formed; the honour of an express invitation from the Duke of Argyle to superintend a department where so much skill and diligence was required, was in itself extremely flattering; and the more so, because honest David, who was not without an excellent opinion of his own talents, persuaded himself that, by accepting this charge, he would in some sort repay the great favour he had received at the hands of the Argyle family. The appointments, including the right of sufficient grazing for a small stock of his own, were amply liberal; and David's keen eye saw that the situation was convenient for trafficking to advantage in Highland cattle. There was risk of "her'ship" from the neighbouring mountains, indeed; but the awful name of the Duke of Argyle would be a great security, and a trifle of *black mail* would, David was aware, assure his safety.

Still, however, there were two points on which he boggled. The first was the character of the clergyman with whose worship he was to join; and on this delicate point he received, as we will presently show the reader, perfect satisfaction. The next obstacle was the condition of his younger daughter, obliged as she was to leave Scotland for so many years.

The gentleman of the law smiled, and said, "There was no occasion to interpret that clause very strictly—that if the young woman left Scotland for a few months, or even weeks, and came to her father's new residence by sea from the western side of England, nobody would know of her arrival, or at least nobody who had either the right or inclination to give her disturbance. The extensive heritable jurisdictions of his Grace excluded the interference of other magistrates with those living on his estates, and they who were in immediate dependence on him would receive orders to give the young woman no disturbance. Living on the verge of the Highlands, she might, indeed, be said to be out of Scotland, that is, beyond the bounds of ordinary law and civilization."

Old Deans was not quite satisfied with this reasoning; but the elopement of Effie, which took place on the third night after her liberation, rendered his residence at Saint Leonard's so detestable to him, that he closed at once with the proposal which had been made him, and entered with pleasure into the idea of surprising Jeanie, as had been proposed by the Duke, to render the change of residence more striking to her. The Duke had apprized Archibald of these circumstances, with orders to act according to the instructions he should receive from Edinburgh, and by which accordingly he was directed to bring Jeanie to Roseneath.

The father and daughter communicated these matters to each other, now stopping, now walking slowly to the Lodge, which showed itself among the trees, at about half a mile's distance from the little bay in which they had landed.

As they approached the house, David Deans informed his daughter, with somewhat like a grim smile, which was the utmost advance he ever made towards a mirthful expression of visage, that "there was baith a worshipful gentleman, and ane reverend gentleman, residing therein. The worshipful gentleman was his honour the Laird of Knocktarlitie, who was baillie of the lordship under the Duke of Argyle, ane Hieland gentleman, tarr'd wi' the same stick," David doubted, "as mony of them, namely, a hasty and choleric temper, and a neglect of the higher things that belong to salvation, and also a gripping unto the things of this world, without muckle distinction of property—but, however, ane gude hospitable gentleman, with whom it would be a part of wisdom to live on a good understanding—(for Hielandmen were hasty, ower hasty.)—As for the reverend person of whom he had spoken, he was candidate by favour of the Duke of Argyle (for David would not for the universe have called him presentee) to the kirk of the parish in which their farm was situated, and he was likely to be highly acceptable unto the Christian souls of the parish, who were hungering for spiritual manna, having been fed but upon sour Hieland sowens by Mr Duncan MacDonought, the last minister, who began the morning duly, Sunday and Saturday, with a mutchkin of usquebaugh. But I need say the less about the present lad," said David, again grimly grimacing, "as I think ye may hae seen him afore; and here he is come to meet us."

She had indeed seen him before, for it was no other than Reuben Butler himself.

Chapter Six

No more shalt thou behold thy sister's face;
Thou hast already had her last embrace.
Elegy on Mrs Anne Killigrew

THIS SECOND SURPRISE had been accomplished for Jeanie Deans by the rod of the same benevolent enchanter, whose power had transplanted her father from the crags of Saint Leonard's to the banks of the Gare-Loch. The Duke of Argyle was not a person to forget the hereditary debt of gratitude, which had been bequeathed to him by his grandfather, in favour of the grandson of old Bible Butler. He had internally resolved to provide for Reuben Butler in this Kirk of Knocktarlitie, of which the incumbent had just departed this life. Accordingly, his agent received the necessary instructions for that purpose, under the qualifying condition always that the learning and character of Reuben Butler should be found proper for the charge. Upon enquiry, these were found as highly satisfactory as had been reported in the case of David Deans himself.

By this preferment, the Duke of Argyle more essentially benefited his friend and protegée, Jeanie, than he himself was aware of, since he contributed to remove objections in her father's mind to the match, which he had no idea had been in existence.

We have already noticed that Deans had something of a prejudice against Butler, which was, perhaps, in some degree owing to his possessing a sort of consciousness that the poor usher looked with eyes of affection upon his elder daughter. This, in David's eyes, was a sin of presumption, even though it should not be followed by any overt act, or actual proposal. But the lively interest which Butler had displayed in his distresses, since Jeanie set forth on her London expedition, and which David therefore ascribed to personal respect for himself individually, had greatly softened the feelings of irritability with which he sometimes regarded him. And, while he was in this good disposition towards Butler, another incident took place which had great influence on the old man's mind.

So soon as the shock of Effie's second elopement was over, it was Deans's early care to collect and refund to the Laird of Dumbiedikes the money which he had lent for Effie's trial, and for Jeanie's travelling expences. The Laird, the poney, the cocked hat, and the tobacco-pipe, had not been seen at Saint Leonard's Crags for many a day; so that, in order to pay this debt, David was under the necessity of repairing in person to the mansion of Dumbiedikes.

He found it in a state of unexpected bustle. There were workmen pulling down some of the old hangings, and replacing them with others, altering, repairing, scrubbing, painting, and white-washing. There was no knowing the old house, which had been so long the mansion of sloth and silence. The Laird himself seemed in some confusion, and his reception, though kind, lacked something of the reverential cordiality with which he used to greet David Deans. There was a change also, David did not very well know what, about the exterior of this landed proprietor—an improvement in the shape of his garments, a spruceness in the air with which they were put on, that were both novelties. Even the old hat looked smarter; the cock had been newly pointed, the lace had been refreshed, and instead of slouching backward or forwards on the Laird's head, as it happened to be thrown on, it was adjusted with a knowing inclination over one eye.

David Deans opened his business, and told down the cash. Dumbiedikes inclined his ear to the one, and counted the other with great accuracy, interrupting David, while he was talking of the redemption of the captivity of Judah, to ask him whether he did not think one or two of the guineas looked rather light. When he was satisfied on this point, had pocketted his money, and had signed a receipt, he addressed David with some little hesitation,—"Jeanie wad be writing ye something, gudeman?"

"About the siller?" replied David—"Nae doubt, she did."

"And did she say nae mair about me?" asked the Laird.

"Nae mair but kind and Christian wishes—what suld she hae said," replied David, fully expecting that the Laird's long courtship (if his dangling after Jeanie deserves so active a name,) was now coming to a point. And so indeed it was, but not to that point which he wished or expected.

"Aweel, she kens her ain mind best, Gudeman. I hae made a clean house o' Jenny Balchristie and her niece. They were a bad pack—steal'd meat and mault, and loot the carters magg the coals—I'm to be married the morn, and kirkit on Sunday."

Whatever David felt, he was too proud and too steady-minded to show any unpleasant surprise in his countenance and manners.

"I wuss ye happy, sir, through Him that gies happiness—marriage is an honourable state."

"And I am wedding into an honourable house, David—the Laird of Lickpelf's youngest daughter—she sits next us in the kirk, and that's the way I came to think on't."

There was no more to be said, but again to wish the Laird joy, to taste a cup of his liquor, and to walk back again to Saint Leonard's, musing on the mutability of human affairs and human resolutions.

The expectation that, one day or other, Jeanie would be Lady Dumbiedikes, had, in spite of himself, kept a more absolute possession of David's mind than he himself was aware of. At least, it had hitherto been an union at all times within his daughter's reach, whenever she chose to give her silent lover any degree of encouragement, and now it was vanished for ever. David returned, therefore, in no very gracious humour for so good a man. He was angry with Jeanie for not having encouraged the Laird—he was angry with the Laird for requiring encouragement—and he was angry with himself for being angry at all on the occasion.

On his return he found the gentleman who managed the Duke of Argyle's affairs was desirous of seeing him, with a view to completing the arrangement between them. Thus, after a brief repose, he was obliged to set off anew for Edinburgh, so that old May Hettly declared, "That a' this was to end with the master just walking himsel aff his feet."

When the business respecting the farm had been talked over and arranged, the professional gentleman acquainted David Deans, in answer to his enquiries concerning the state of public worship, that it was the pleasure of the Duke to put an excellent young clergyman, called Reuben Butler, into the parish, which was to be his future residence.

"Reuben Butler!" exclaimed David—"Reuben Butler, the usher at Libberton?"

"The very same," said the Duke's commissioner; "his Grace has an excellent character of him, and has some hereditary obligations to him besides—few ministers will be so comfortable as I am directed to make Mr Butler."

"Obligations?—The Duke?—Reuben Butler?—Reuben Butler a placed minister of the Kirk of Scotland?" exclaimed David, in interminable astonishment, for somehow he had been led by the bad success which Butler had hitherto met with in all his undertakings, to consider him as one of those step-sons of Fortune, whom she treats with unceasing rigour, and ends with disinheriting altogether.

There is, perhaps, no time at which we are disposed to think so highly of a friend, as when we find him standing higher than we expected in the esteem of others. When assured of the reality of Butler's change of prospects, David expressed his great satisfaction at his success in life, which, he observed, was entirely owing to himself. "I advised his puir grandmother, who was but a silly woman, to breed him up to the ministry; and I prophesied that, with a blessing on his endeavours, he would become a polished shaft in the temple. He was something ower proud o' his carnal learning, but a gude lad, and has the root of the matter—as ministers gang now, where ye'll find ane better, ye'll find ten waur than Reuben Butler."

He took leave of the man of business, and walked homeward, forgetting his weariness in the various speculations to which this wonderful piece of intelligence gave rise. Honest David had now, like other great men, to go to work to reconcile his speculative principles with existing circumstances; and, like other great men, when they set seriously about that task, he was tolerably successful.

"Ought Reuben Butler in conscience to accept of this preferment in the Kirk of Scotland, subject as David at present thought that establishment was to the Erastian encroachments of the civil power?" This was the leading question, and he considered it carefully. "The Kirk of Scotland was shorn of its beams, and deprived of its full artillery and banners of authority; but still it contained zealous and fructifying pastors, attentive congregations, and, with all her spots and blemishes, the like of the Kirk was no where else to be seen upon earth."

David's doubts had been too many and too critical to permit him ever unequivocally to unite himself with any of the dissenters, who, upon various accounts, absolutely seceded from the national church. He had often joined in communion with such of the established clergy as approached nearest to the old presbyterian model and principles of 1640. And although there were many things to be amended in that system, yet he remembered that he, David Deans, had himself ever been a humble pleader for the good old cause in a legal way, but without rushing into right-hand excesses, divisions, and separations. But, as an enemy to separation, he might join the right hand of fellowship with a minister of the Kirk of Scotland in its present model. *Ergo*, Reuben Butler might take possession of the parish of Knocktarlitie, without forfeiting his friendship or favour—Q. E. D. But, secondly, came the trying point of lay-patronage, which David Deans had ever maintained to be a coming in by the window, and over the wall, a cheating and starving the souls of a whole parish, for the purpose of clothing the back and filling the belly of the incumbent.

This presentation, therefore, from the Duke of Argyle, whatever was the worth and high character of that nobleman, was a limb of the brazen image, a portion of the evil thing, and with no kind of consistency could David bend his mind to favour such a transaction. But if the parishioners themselves joined in a general call to Reuben Butler to be their pastor, it did not seem quite so evident that the existence of this unhappy presentation was a reason for his refusing them the comforts of his doctrine. If the presbytery admitted him to the kirk, in virtue rather of that act of patronage, than of the general call of the congregation, that might be their error, and David allowed it was a heavy one. But if Reuben Butler accepted of the cure as tendered to him by those whom he was called to teach, and who had expressed themselves desirous to learn, David, after considering and reconsidering the matter, came, through the great virtue of IF, to be of opinion that he might safely so act in that matter.

There remained a third stumbling-block—the oaths to government exacted from the established clergymen, in which they acknowledged an Erastian king and parliament, and homologated the incorporating Union between England and Scotland, through which the latter kingdom had become part and portion of one wherein prelacy, the sister of popery, had made fast her throne, and elevated the horns of her mitre. These were symptoms of defection which had often made David cry out, "My bowels—my bowels!—I am pained at the very heart!" And he remembered that a godly Bow-head matron had been carried out of the Tolbooth Church in a swoon, beyond the reach of brandy and burned feathers, merely on hearing those fearful words, "It is enacted by the Lords *spiritual* and temporal," pronounced from a Scottish pulpit, in the proem to the Porteous Proclamation. These oaths were, therefore, a deep compliance and dire abomination—a sin and a snare, and a danger and a defection. But this Shibboleth was not always exacted. Ministers had respect to their own tender consciences, and those of the brethren; and it was not till a later period that the reins were taken up tight by the General Assemblies and Presbyteries. The peace-making particle came again to David's assistance. *If* an incumbent was not called upon to make such compliances, and *if* he got a right entry into the church without intrusion, and by orderly appointment, why, upon the whole, David Deans came to be of opinion, that he might lawfully enjoy the spirituality and temporality of the cure of souls at Knocktarlitie, with stipend, manse, glebe, and all thereunto appertaining.

The best and most upright-minded men are so strangely influenced by existing circumstances, that it would be somewhat cruel to enquire too nearly what weight paternal affection gave to these ingenious trains of reasoning. Let David Deans's situation be considered. He was just deprived of one daughter, and his eldest, to whom he owed so much, was cut off, by the sudden resolution of Dumbiedikes, from the high hope which David had entertained, that she might one day be mistress of that fair lordship. Just while this disappointment was bearing heavy on his spirits, Butler comes before his imagination—no longer the half-starved, thread-bare usher—but fat and sleek and fair, the beneficed minister of Knocktarlitie, beloved by his congregation,—exemplary in his life,—powerful in his doctrine,—doing the duty of the Kirk as never Highland minister did it before,—turning sinners as a colley dog turns sheep,—a favourite of the Duke of Argyle, and drawing a stipend of eight hundred punds Scots, and four chalder of victual. Here was a match, making up, in David's mind, in a tenfold degree the disappointment in the case of Dumbiedikes, in so far as the goodman of Saint Leonard's held a powerful minister in much greater admiration than a mere landed proprietor. It did not occur to him, as an additional reason in favour of the match, that Jeanie might herself have some choice in the matter; for the idea of consulting her feelings never once entered into the honest man's head, any more than the possibility that her inclination might perhaps differ from his own.

The result of his meditations was, that he was called upon to take the management of the whole affair into his own hand, and give, if it should be possible without sinful compliance, or backsliding, or defection of any kind, a worthy pastor to the Kirk of Knocktarlitie. Accordingly, by the intervention of the honest dealer in butter-milk who dwelt in Libberton, David summoned to his presence Reuben Butler. Even from this worthy messenger he was unable to conceal certain swelling emotions of dignity, in so much, that, when the carter had communicated his message to the usher, he added, that "Certainly the gudeman of Saint Leonard's had some grand news to tell him, for he was as uplifted as a midden-cock upon pattens."

Butler, it may readily be conceived, immediately obeyed the summons. His was a plain character, in which worth, good sense and simplicity were the principal ingredients; but love, on this occasion, gave him a certain degree of address. He had received an intimation of the favour designed him by the Duke of Argyle, with what feelings those only can conceive, who have experienced a sudden prospect of being raised to independence and respect, from penury and toil. He resolved, however, that the old man should retain all the consequence of being, in his own opinion, the first to communicate the important intelligence. At the same time, he also determined that in the expected conference he would permit David Deans to expatiate at length upon the proposal, in all its bearings, without irritating him either by interruption or contradiction. This last plan was the most prudent he could have adopted; because, although there were many doubts which David Deans could himself clear up to his own satisfaction, yet he might have been by no means disposed to accept the solution of any other person; and to engage him in an argument would have been certain to confirm him at once and for ever in the opinion which Butler chanced to impugn.

He received Reuben with an appearance of important gravity,

which real misfortune had long compelled him to lay aside, and which belonged to those days of awful authority in which he predominated over Widow Butler, and dictated the mode of cultivating the crofts at Beersheba. He acquainted his young friend at great prolixity with the prospect of his changing his present residence for the charge of the Duke of Argyle's stock-farm in Dumbartonshire, enumerated the various advantages of the situation with obvious self-congratulation; but assured the patient hearer, that nothing had so much moved him to acceptance, as the sense that, by his skill in bestial, he could render the most important services to his Grace the Duke of Argyle, to whom, "in the late unhappy circumstance," (here a tear dimmed the sparkle of pride in the old man's eye,) he had been sae muckle obliged.

"To put a rude Hielandman into sic a charge, what could be expected but that he suld be sic a chiefest herdsman, as wicked Doeg the Edomite; whereas, while this grey head is to the fore, not a cloot o' them but sall be as weel cared for as if they were the fatted kine of Pharaoh.—And now, Reuben, lad, seeing we maun remove our tent to a strange country, ye will be casting a dolefu' look after us, and thinking with whom ye are to hold council anent your government in thae slippery and backsliding times; and nae doubt remembering, that the auld man, Davie Deans, was made the instrument to bring ye out of the mire of schism and heresy, wherein your father's house delighted to wallow; aften also, nae doubt, when ye are pressed wi' insnaring trials and tentations and heart-plagues, you, that are like a recruit that is marching for the first time to the took of drum, will miss the auld, bauld and experienced veteran soldier, that has felt the brunt of mony a foul day, and heard the bullets whistle as aften as he has hairs left on his auld pow."

It is very possible that Butler might internally be of opinion, that the reflection on his ancestor's peculiar tenets might have been spared, or that he might be presumptuous enough even to think, that, at his years and with his own lights, he might be able to hold his course without the pilotage of honest David. But he only replied, by expressing his regret, that any thing should separate him from an ancient, tried, and affectionate friend.

"But how can it be helped, man?" said David, twisting his features into a sort of smile—"How can we help it?—I trow ye canna tell me that—Ye maun leave that to ither folk—to the Duke of Argyle and me, Reuben. It's a gude thing to hae friends in this warld—how muckle better to hae an interest beyond it!"

And David, whose piety, though not always quite rational, was as sincere as it was habitual and fervent, looked reverentially upward, and paused. Mr Butler intimated the pleasure with which he would receive his friend's advice on a subject so important, and David resumed.

"What think ye now, Reuben, of a kirk—a regular kirk under the present establishment?—Were sic offered to ye, wad ye be free to accept it, and under whilk provisions?—I am speaking but by way o' query."

Butler replied, "That if such a prospect were held out to him, he would probably first consult whether he was likely to be useful to the parish he should be called to; and if there appeared a fair prospect of his being so, his friend must be aware, that, in every other point of view, it would be highly advantageous for him."

"Right, Reuben, very right, lad—your ain conscience is the first thing to be satisfied—for how sall he teach others that has himsel sae ill learned the Scriptures, as to grip for the lucre of foul earthly preferment, sic as gear and manse, money and victual, that which is not his in a spiritual sense—or wha makes his kirk a stalking-horse to tak aim at his stipend? But I look for better things of you—and specially ye maun be minded not to act altogether on your ain judgment, for therethrough comes sair mistakes, backslidings, and defections, on the left and on the right. If there were sic a day of trial put to you, Reuben, ye, who are a young lad, although it maybe ye are gifted wi' the carnal tongues, and those whilk were spoken at Rome, whilk is now the seat of the scarlet abomination, and by the Greeks, to whom the gospel was as foolishness, yet nae-the-less ye may be entreated by your weel-wishers to take the counsel of those prudent and resolved and weather-withstanding professors, wha hae kenned what it was to lurk in banks and in mosses, in bogs and in caverns, and to risk the peril of the head against the honesty of the heart."

Butler replied, "That certainly, possessing such a friend as he hoped and trusted he had in the goodman himself, who had seen so many changes in the preceding century, he should be much to blame if he did not avail himself of his experience and friendly counsel."

"Eneugh said—eneugh said, Reuben," said David Deans, with internal exultation; "and say that ye were in the predicament whereof I hae spoken, of a surety I would deem it my duty to gang to the root o' the matter, and lay bare the ulcers and the imposthumes, and the sores and the leprosies, of this our time, crying aloud and sparing not."

David Deans was now in his element. He commenced his examination of the doctrines and belief of the Christian Church with the very Culdees, from whom he passed to John Knox,—from John Knox to the recusants in James the Sixth's time,—Bruce, Black, Blair and Livingstone,—from them to the brief, and at length triumphant period of the presbyterian church's splendour, until it was over-run by the English independents. Then followed the dismal times of prelacy, the indulgences, seven in number, with all their shades and bearings, until he arrived at the reign of King James, in which he himself had been, in his own mind, neither an obscure actor nor an obscure sufferer. Then was Butler doomed to hear the most ornate and annotated edition of what he had so often heard before—David Deans's confinement, namely, in the iron cage in the Canongate tolbooth, and the cause thereof.

We should be very unjust to our friend David Deans, if we should "pretermit," to use his own expression, a narrative which he held essential to his fame. A drunken trooper of the Royal Guard, Francis Gordon by name, had chased five or six of the skulking whigs, among whom was our friend David; and after he had compelled them to stand, and was in the act of brawling with them, one of their number fired a pocket-pistol, and shot him dead. David used to sneer and shake his head when any one asked him whether *he* had been the instrument of removing this wicked persecutor from the face of the earth. In fact, the merit of the deed lay between him and his friend Patrick Walker, the pedlar, whose works he was so fond of quoting. Neither of them cared directly to claim the merit of silencing Mr Francis Gordon of the Life Guards, there being some wild cousins of his about Edinburgh who might have been even yet addicted to revenge, but yet neither of them chose to disown or yield to the other the merit of this active defence of their religious rites. David Deans said, that if he had fired a pistol then, it was what he never did after or before. And as for Patrick Walker, he has left it upon record, that his great surprise was, that so small a pistol could kill so big a man. These are the words of that venerable biographer, whose trade had not taught him by experience, that an inch was as good as an ell. "He got a shot in his head out of a pocket-pistol, rather fit for diverting a boy than killing such a furious, mad, brisk man, which notwithstanding killed him dead!"

Upon the extensive foundation which the history of the Kirk afforded, during its short-lived triumph and long tribulation, David, with length of breath and of narration, which would have astounded any one but a lover of his daughter, proceeded to lay down his own rules for guiding the conscience of his friend, as an aspirant to serve in the ministry. Upon this subject, the good man went through such a variety of nice and casuistical problems, supposed so many extreme cases, made the distinctions so critical and nice betwixt the right hand and the left hand—betwixt compliance and defection—holding back and stepping aside—slipping and stumbling—snares and errors—

that at length, after having limited the path of truth to a mathematical line, he was brought to the broad admission, that each man's conscience, after he had gained a certain view of the difficult navigation which he was to encounter, would be the best guide for his pilotage. He stated the examples and arguments for and against the acceptance of a kirk on the present revolution model, with much more impartiality to Butler than he had been able to place them before his own view. And he concluded, that he ought to think upon these things, and be guided by the voice of his own conscience, whether he could take such an awful trust as the charge of souls, without doing injury to his own intimate conviction of what is right or wrong.

When David had concluded his very long harangue, which was only interrupted by monosyllables, or little more, on the part of Butler, the orator himself was greatly astonished to find that the conclusion, at which he very naturally wished to arrive, seemed much less decisively attained than when he had argued the case in his own mind.

In this particular, David's current of thinking and speaking only illustrated the very important and general proposition concerning the excellence of the publicity of debate. For, under the influence of any partial feeling, it is certain, that most men can much more easily reconcile themselves to any favourite measure, when agitating it in their own mind, than when obliged to expose its merits to a third party, when the necessity of seeming impartial procures for the opposite arguments a much more fair statement than that which they afford it in tacit meditation. Having finished what he had to say, David thought himself obliged to be more explicit, and to explain that this was no hypothetical case, but one on which, (by his own influence and that of the Duke of Argyle,) Reuben Butler would soon be called upon to decide.

It was even with something like apprehension that David Deans heard Butler announce, in return to this communication, that he would take that night to consider on what he had said with such kind intentions, and return him an answer the next morning. The feelings of the father mastered David on this occasion. He pressed Butler to spend the evening with him—He produced, most unusual at his meals, one, nay, two bottles of aged strong ale.—He spoke of his daughter—of her merit—her housewifery—her thrift—her affection. He led Butler so decidedly up to a declaration of his feelings towards Jeanie, that, before night-fall, it was distinctly understood she was to be the bride of Reuben Butler; and if they thought it indelicate to abridge the period of deliberation which Reuben had stipulated, it seemed to be sufficiently understood betwixt them, that there was a strong probability of his becoming minister of Knocktarlitie, providing the congregation were as willing to accept of him, as the Duke to grant him the presentation. The matter of the oaths, they agreed, it was time enough to dispute about, whenever the Shibboleth should be tendered.

Many arrangements were adopted that evening, which were afterwards ripened by correspondence with the Duke of Argyle's man of business, who intrusted Deans and Butler with the benevolent wish of his principal, that they should all meet with Jeanie, on her return from England, at the Duke's hunting-lodge on Roseneath.

This retrospect, so far as the placid loves of Jeanie Deans and Reuben Butler are concerned, forms a full explanation of the preceding narrative up to their meeting on the island as already mentioned.

Chapter Seven

"I come," he said, "my love, my life,
And—nature's dearest name—my wife:
Thy father's house and friends resign,
My home, my friends, my sire are thine."
                                        LOGAN

THE MEETING of Jeanie and Butler, under circumstances promising to crown an affection so long delayed, was rather affecting from its simple sincerity than from its uncommon vehemence of feeling. David Deans, whose practice was sometimes a little different from his theory, appalled them at first, by giving them the opinion of sundry of the suffering preachers and champions of his younger days, that marriage, though honourable by the laws of Scripture, was yet a state over-rashly coveted by professors, and specially by young ministers, whose desire, he said, was at whiles too inordinate for kirks, stipends, and wives, which had frequently occasioned over-ready compliances with the general defections of the time. He made them aware also, that hasty wedlock had been the bane of many a savoury professor—that the unbelieving wife had too often revenged the text, and perverted the believing husband—that when the famous Donald Cargill, being then hiding in Lee-Wood, in Lanarkshire, it being killing-time, did, upon importunity, marry Robert Marshal of Starry Shaw, he had thus expressed himself: "What hath induced Robert to marry this woman? Her ill will overcome his good—he will not keep the way long—his thriving days are done." To the sad accomplishment of whilk prophecy David said he was himself a living witness, for Robert Marshal having fallen into foul compliances with the enemies, went home and heard the curates, declined into other steps of defection, and became lightly esteemed. Indeed he observed, that the great upholders of the standard, Cargill, Peden, Cameron, and Renwick, had less delight in tying the bonds of matrimony than in any other piece of their ministerial work. And although they would neither dissuade nor refuse their office, they considered the being called to it as an evidence of indifference on the part of those between whom it was solemnized to the many grievous things of the day. Notwithstanding, however, that marriage was a snare unto many, David was of opinion (as, indeed, he had showed in his practice,) that it was in itself honourable, especially if times were such that honest men could be secure against being shot, hanged, or banished, and had ane competent livelihood to maintain themselves, and those that might come after them. "And therefore," as he concluded something abruptly, addressing Jeanie and Butler, who, with faces as high-coloured as crimson, had been listening to his lengthened argument for and against the holy state of matrimony, "I will leave ye to your ain cracks."

As their private conversation, however interesting to themselves, might probably be very little so to the reader, so far as it respected their present feelings and future prospects, we shall pass it over, and only mention the information which Jeanie received from Butler concerning her sister's elopement, which contained many particulars that she had been unable to extract from her father.

Jeanie learned, therefore, that, for three days after her pardon had arrived, Effie had been the inmate of her father's house at Saint Leonard's—that the interviews betwixt David and his erring child, which had taken place before she was liberated from prison, had been touching in the extreme; but Butler could not suppress his opinion, that, when he was freed from the apprehension of losing her in a manner so horrible, her father had tightened the bands of discipline, so as, in some degree, to gall the feelings and aggravate the irritability of a spirit naturally impatient and petulant, and now doubly so from the sense of merited disgrace.

On the third night, Effie disappeared from Saint Leonard's, leaving no tracks whatever of the route she had taken. Butler, however, set out in pursuit of her, and with much trouble traced her towards a little landing-place, formed by a small brook which enters the sea betwixt Musselburgh and Edinburgh. This place, which has been since made into a small harbour, and surrounded by many small villas and lodging houses, is now termed Portobello. At this time it was surrounded by a waste common, covered with furze, and unfrequented, save by fishing-boats, and now and then a smuggling lugger. A vessel of this description had been hovering in the Firth at the time of Effie's elopement, and, as Butler ascertained, a boat had come ashore in the evening on which the fugitive had disappeared, and had carried on board a female. As they made sail immediately, and landed no part of their cargo, there seemed little doubt that they were accomplices of the notorious Robertson, and that that vessel had only come into the Frith to carry off his paramour.

This was made clear by a letter which Butler himself soon afterwards received by post, signed E. D., but without any place or date. It was miserably ill written and spelled; sea-sickness having apparently aided the derangement of Effie's very irregular orthography and mode of expression. In this epistle, however, as in all that that unfortunate girl said or did, there was something to praise as well as much to blame. She said, in her letter, "That she could not endure that her father and sister should go into banishment, or be partakers of her shame—that if her burthen was a heavy one, it was of her own binding, and she had the more right to bear it alone,—that in future they could not be a comfort to her, or she to them, since every look and word of her father put her in mind of her transgression, and was like to drive her mad,—that she had nearly lost her judgment during the three days she was at Saint Leonard's—her father meant weel by her, and all men, but he did not know the dreadful pain he gave her in casting up her sins. If Jeanie had been at hame, it might hae dune better—Jeanie was ane, like the angels in Heaven, that rather weep for sinners, as reckon their transgressions. But she should never see Jeanie ony mair, and that was the thought that gave her the sairest heart of a' that had come and gane yet. On her bended knees would she pray for Jeanie, night and day, baith for what she had done, and what she had scorned to do, in her behalf; for what a thought it would have been to her at that moment o' time, if that upright creature had made a fault to save her. She desired her father would give Jeanie a' the gear—her ain (*i. e.* Effie's) mother's and a'—She had made a deed, giving up her right, and it was in Mr Novit's hands—Warld's gear was henceforward the least of her care, nor was it like to be muckle her mister—She hoped this would make it easy for her sister to settle; and immediately after this expression, she wished Butler himself all good things, in return for his kindness to her. For herself," she said, "she kenn'd her lot would be a waesome ane, but it was of her own framing, sae she deserved the less pity. But, for her friends' satisfaction, she wished them to know that she was ganging nae ill gate —that they who had done the maist wrong were now willing to do her what justice was in their power; and she wad, in some respects, be far better aff than she deserved. But she desired her family to remain satisfied with this assurance, and give themselves no trouble in making farther enquiries after her."

To David Deans and to Butler this letter gave very little comfort;

for what was to be expected from this unfortunate girl's uniting her
fate to that of a character so notorious as Robertson, who they readily
guessed was alluded to in the last sentence, excepting that she should
become the partner and victim of his future crimes. Jeanie, who knew
George Staunton's character, and real rank, saw her sister's situation
under a ray of better hope. She augured well of the haste he had shewn
to reclaim his interest in Effie, and she trusted he had made her his
wife. If so, it seemed improbable that, with his expected fortune, and
high connections, he should again resume the life of criminal adventure which he had led, especially since, as matters stood, his life
depended upon his keeping his own secret, which could only be done
by an entire change of his habits, and particularly by avoiding all those
who had known the heir of Willingham in the character of the audacious, criminal, and condemned Robertson.

She thought it most likely they would go abroad for a few years, and
not return to England until the affair of Porteous was totally forgotten.
Jeanie, therefore, saw more hopes for her sister than Butler or her
father had been able to perceive; but she was not at liberty to impart
the comfort which she felt in believing that she would be secure from
the pressure of poverty, and in little risk of being seduced into the
paths of guilt. She could not have explained this without making
public what it was essentially necessary for Effie's chance of comfort
to conceal, the identity namely of George Staunton and George Robertson. After all, it was dreadful to think that Effie had united herself
to a man condemned for felony, and liable to trial for murder, whatever were his rank in life, and the degree of his remorse. Besides, it
was melancholy to reflect, that, she herself being in possession of the
whole dreadful secret, it was most probable he would, out of respect to
his own feelings, and fear for his safety, never again permit her to see
poor Effie. After perusing and re-perusing her sister's valedictory
letter, she gave ease to her feelings in a flood of tears, which Butler in
vain endeavoured to check by every blandishment in his power. She
was obliged, however, at length, to look up and wipe her eyes, for her
father, thinking he had allowed the lovers time enough for conference,
was now advancing towards them from the Lodge, accompanied by
the Captain of Knockdunder, or, as his friends called him for brevity's
sake, Duncan Knock, a title which some youthful exploits had rendered peculiarly appropriate.

This Duncan of Knockdunder was a person of first-rate importance in the island of Roseneath, and the continental parishes of
Knocktarlitie, Kilmun, and so forth; nay, his influence extended as far
as Cowal, where, however, it was obscured by that of another factor.
The Tower of Knockdunder still occupies, with its remains, a cliff

over-hanging the Holy-Loch. Duncan swore it had been a royal castle; if so, it was of the smallest, the space within only forming a square of sixteen feet, and bearing therefore a ridiculous proportion to the thickness of the walls, which was ten feet at least. Such as it was, however, it had long given the title of Captain, equivalent to that of Chatellain, to the ancestors of Duncan, who were retainers of the house of Argyle, and held a hereditary jurisdiction under them, of little extent indeed, but which had great consequence in their eyes, and was usually administered with a vigour somewhat beyond the law.

The present representative of that ancient family was a stout short man about fifty, whose pleasure it was to unite in his own person the dress of the Highlands and Lowlands, wearing on his head a black tie-wig, surmounted by a fierce cocked-hat, deeply guarded with gold lace, while the rest of his dress consisted of the plaid and philabeg. Duncan superintended a district which was partly Highland, partly Lowland, and therefore might be supposed to combine their national habits, in order to show his impartiality to Trojan or Tyrian. The incongruity, however, had a whimsical and ludicrous effect, as it made his head and body look as if belonging to different individuals; or, as some one said who had seen the executions of the insurgent prisoners in 1715, it seemed as if some Jacobite enchanter, having recalled the sufferers to life, had clapped, in his haste, an Englishman's head on a Highlander's body. To finish the portrait, the bearing of the gracious Duncan was brief, bluff, and consequential, and the upward turn of his short copper-coloured nose indicated that he was somewhat addicted to wrath and usquebaugh.

When this dignitary had advanced up to Butler and to Jeanie, "I tak the freedom, Mr Deans," he said, "to salute your daughter, whilk I presume this young lass to be—I kiss every pretty girl that comes to Roseneath, in virtue of my office." Having made this gallant speech, he took out his quid, saluted Jeanie with a hearty smack, and bade her welcome to Argyle's country. Then addressing Butler, he said, "Ye maun gang ower and meet the carle ministers yonder the morn, for they will want to do your job, and synd it down with some usquebaugh doubtless—they seldom make dry wark in this kintra."

"And the Laird"—said David Deans.

"The Captain, man," interrupted Duncan; "folk winna ken wha ye are speaking aboot, unless ye gie shentlemens their proper title."

"The Captain, then," said David, "assures me that the call is unanimous on the part of the parishioners—a real harmonious call, Reuben."

"I pelieve," said Duncan, "it was as harmonious as could pe expected, whan the tae half o' the bodies were clavering Sassenach, and the t'other skirling Gaelic, like sea-maws and claik-geese before a storm. Ane wad hae needed the gift of tongues to ken preceesely what they said—but I pelieve the best end of it was, 'Long live Maccallan-more and Knockdunder.'—And as to its being an unanimous call, I wad be glad to ken fat business the carles have to call ony thing or ony body but what the Duke and mysell likes."

"Nevertheless," said Mr Butler, "if any of the parishioners have any scruples, which sometimes arise in the mind of sincere professors, I should be happy of an opportunity of trying to remove"——

"Never fash your peard about it, man," interrupted Duncan Knock —"Leave it a' to me—Scruple! de'il o' them has been bred up to scruple ony thing that they're bidden do—And if sic a thing suld happen as ye speak o', ye sall see the sincere professor, as ye ca' him, towed at the stern of my boat for a few furlongs.—I'll try if the water of the Haly-Loch winna wash off scruples as weel as fleas—Cot tamn!——"

The rest of Duncan's threat was lost in a growling, gurgling sort of sound, which he made in his throat, and which menaced recusants with no gentle means of conversion. David Deans would certainly have given battle in defence of the right of the Christian congregation to be consulted in the choice of their own pastor, which, in his estima-tion, was one of the choicest and most inalienable of their privileges. But he had again engaged in close conversation with Jeanie, and, with more interest than he was in use to take in affairs foreign alike to his occupation and to his religious tenets, was inquiring into the particu-lars of her London journey. This was, perhaps, fortunate for the new formed friendship betwixt him and the Captain of Knockdunder, which rested, in David's estimation, upon the proofs he had given of his skill in managing stock, but, in reality, upon the special charge transmitted to Duncan from the Duke and his agent, to behave with the utmost attention to Deans and his family.

"And now, sirs," said Duncan, in a commanding tone, "I am to pray ye a' to come in to your supper, for yonder is Mr Archibald half famished, and a Saxon woman, that looks as if her een were fleeing out o' her head wi' fear and wonder, as if she had never seen a shentleman in a philabeg pefore."

"And Reuben Butler," said David, "will doubtless desire instantly to retire, that he may prepare his mind for the exercise of to-morrow, that his work may suit the day, and be an offering of a sweet savour in the nostrils of the reverend presbytery."

"Hout tout, man, it's put little ye ken about them," interrupted the Captain. "Teil a ane o' them wad gie the savour of the hot venison pasty which I smell (turning his squab nose up in the air,) a' the way frae the lodge, for a' that Mr Putler, or you either, can say to them."

David groaned, but judging he had to do with a Gallio, as he said, did not think it worth his while to give battle. They followed the Captain to the house, and arranged themselves with great ceremony round a well-loaded supper-table. The only other circumstance of the evening worthy to be recorded is, that Butler pronounced the blessing, that Knockdunder found it too long, and David Deans censured it as too short, from which the charitable reader may conclude that it was exactly the proper length.

Chapter Eight

Now turn the Psalms of David ower,
And lilt wi' holy clangor;
Of double verse come gie us four,
And skirl up the Bangor.
BURNS

THE NEXT WAS THE IMPORTANT DAY, when, according to the forms and ritual of the Scottish Kirk, Reuben Butler was to be ordained minister of Knocktarlitie by the Presbytery of——. And so eager were the whole party, that all, excepting Mrs Dutton, the destined Cowslip of Inverary, were stirring at an early hour.

Their host, whose appetite was as quick and keen as his temper, was not long in summoning them to a substantial breakfast, where there were at least a dozen of different preparations of milk, plenty of cold meat boiled and roasted, eggs, a huge cag of butter, herrings boiled and broiled, fresh and salt, and tea and coffee for them that liked it, which, as their landlord assured them, with a nod and a wink, pointing, at the same time, to a little cutter which seemed dodging under the lee of the island, cost them little beside the fetching ashore.

"Is the contraband trade permitted here so openly?" said Butler. "I should think it very unfavourable to the people's morals."

"The Duke, Mr Putler, has gi'en nae orders concerning the putting of it down," said the magistrate, and seemed to think that he had said all that was necessary to justify his connivance.

Butler was a man of prudence, and aware that real good can only be obtained by remonstrance when remonstrance is well-timed; so for the present he said nothing more on the subject.

When breakfast was half over, in flounced Mrs Dolly as fine as a blue sacque and cherry-coloured ribbands could make her.

"Good morrow to you, madam," said the master of ceremonies; "I trust your early rising will not skaith ye."

The dame apologized to Captain Knockunder—as she was pleased to term their entertainer; "but, as we say in Cheshire," she added, "I was like the Mayor of Altringham, who lies in bed while his breeches are amending, for the girl did not bring up the right bundle to my room, till she had brought up all the others by mistake one after t'other.—Well, I suppose we are all for church to-day, as I understand—Pray may I be so bold as to ask, if it is the fashion for you North-country gentlemen to go to church in your petticoats, Captain Knockunder?"

"Captain of Knockdunder, madam, if you please, for I knock under to no man; and in respect of my garb, I shall go to church as I am, at your sarvice, madam; for if I were to lie in bed, like your Major What-d'ye-callum, till my preeches were mended, I might lie there all my life, seeing I never had a pair of them on my person but twice in my life, which I am pound to remember, it peing when the Duke brought his Duchess here, when her Grace pehoved to be pleasured, and so I e'en porrowed the minister's trews for the twa days her Grace was pleased to stay—but I will put myself under sic confinement again for no man on earth, or woman either, but her Grace being always excepted, as in duty pound."

The mistress of the milking-pail stared, but, making no answer to this round declaration, immediately proceeded to show, that the alarm of the preceding evening had in no degree injured her appetite.

When the meal was finished, the Captain proposed to them to take boat, in order that Mistress Jeanie might see her new place of residence, and that he himself might enquire whether the necessary preparations had been made, there and at the Manse, for receiving the future inmates of these mansions.

The morning was delightful, and the huge mountain-shadows slept upon the mirror'd wave of the Firth, almost as little disturbed as if it had been an inland lake. Even Mrs Dutton's fears no longer annoyed her. She had been informed by Archibald, that there was to be some sort of junketting after the sermon, and that was what she loved dearly; and as for the water, it was so still that it would look quite like a party on the Thames.

The whole party being embarked, therefore, in a large boat, which the captain called his coach and six, and attended by a smaller one termed his gig, the gallant Duncan steered strait upon the little tower of the old-fashioned church of Knocktarlitie, and the exertions of six stout rowers sped them rapidly on their voyage. As they neared the land, the hills appeared to recede from them, and a little valley, formed by the descent of a small river from the mountains, evolved itself as it were upon their approach. The style of the country on each side was simply pastoral, and resembled, in appearance and character, the description of a forgotten Scottish poet, which runs nearly thus:—

> The water gently down a level slid,
> With little din, but couthy what it made;
> On ilka side the trees grew thick and lang,
> And wi' the wild birds' notes were a' in sang;
> On either side, a full bow-shot and mair,
> The green was even, gowany, and fair;
> With easy slope on every hand the braes
> To the hills' feet with scattered bushes raise;
> With goats and sheep aboon, and kye below,
> The bonnie banks all in a swarm did go.*

They landed in this Highland Arcadia, at the mouth of the small stream which watered the delightful and peaceable valley. Inhabitants of several descriptions came to pay their respects to the Captain of Knockdunder, an homage which he was very peremptory in exacting, and to see the new settlers. Some of these were men after David Deans's own heart, elders of the kirk-session, zealous professors, from the Lennox, Lanarkshire, and Ayrshire, to whom the preceding Duke of Argyle had given *rooms* in this corner of his estate, because they had suffered for joining his father the unfortunate Earl during his ill-fated attempt in 1685. These were cakes of the right leaven for David's regaling himself with; and had it not been for this circumstance, he has been heard to say, "that the Captain of Knockdunder would have swore him out of the country in twenty-four hours, sae awsome it was to ony thinking soul to hear his imprecations, upon the slightest temptation that crossed his humour."

Besides these, there were a wilder set of parishioners, mountaineers from the upper glen and adjacent hills, who spoke Gaelic, went about armed, and wore the Highland dress. But the strict commands of the Duke had established such good order in this part of his territories, that the Gael and Saxons lived upon the best possible terms of good neighbourhood.

They first visited the *Manse*, as the parsonage is termed in Scotland. It was old, but in good repair, and stood snugly embosomed in a grove of sycamore, with a well-stocked garden in front, bounded by the small river, which was partly visible from the windows, partly concealed by the bushes, trees, and bounding hedge. Within, the house looked less comfortable than it might have been, for it had been neglected by the late incumbent; but workmen had been labouring under the directions of the Captain of Knockdunder, and at the expence of the Duke of Argyle, to put it into some order. The old "plenishing" had been removed, and neat, but plain household furniture had been sent down by the Duke in a brig of his own, called the Caroline, and was now ready to be placed in order in the apartments.

* Ross's Fortunate Shepherdess. Edit. 1778, p. 23.

The gracious Duncan, finding matters were at a stand among the workmen, summoned before him the delinquents, and impressed all who heard him with a sense of his authority, by the penalties with which he threatened them for their delay. Mulcting them in half their charge, he assured them, would be the least of it; for, if they were to neglect his pleasure and the Duke's, "he would be tamn'd if he paid them the t'ither half either, and they might seek law for it where they could get it." The work-people humbled themselves before the offended dignitary, and spake him soft and fair; and at length, upon Mr Butler recalling to his mind, that it was the ordination-day, and that the workmen were probably thinking of going to church, Knockdunder agreed to forgive them out of respect to their new minister.

"But an I catch them neglecking my duty again, Mr Putler, the teil pe in me if the kirk shall be an excuse; for what has the like o' them rapparees to do at the kirk ony day put Sundays, or then either, if the Duke and I has the necessitous uses for them?"

It may be guessed with what feelings of quiet satisfaction and delight Butler looked forward to spending his days, honoured and useful as he trusted to be in this sequestered valley, and how often an intelligent glance was exchanged betwixt him and Jeanie, whose good-humoured face looked positively handsome, from the expression of modesty, and, at the same time, of satisfaction, which she wore when visiting the apartments of which she was soon to call herself mistress. She was left at liberty to give more open indulgence to her feelings of delight and admiration, when, leaving the Manse, the company proceeded to examine the destined habitation of David Deans.

Jeanie found with pleasure that it was not above a musket-shot from the Manse; for it had been a bar to her happiness to think that she might be obliged to reside at a distance from her father, and she was aware that there were strong objections to his actually living in the same house with Butler. But this brief distance was the very thing which she could have wished.

The farm-house was on the plan of an improved cottage, and contrived with great regard to convenience; an excellent little garden, an orchard, and a set of offices complete, according to the best ideas of the time, combined to render it a most desirable habitation for the practical farmer, and far superior to the hovel at Woodend, and the small house at Saint Leonard's Crags. The situation was considerably higher than that of the Manse, and fronted to the west. The windows commanded an enchanting view of the little vale over which the mansion seemed to preside, the windings of the stream, and the Firth, with its associated lakes and romantic islands. The hills of Dumbartonshire, once possessed by the fierce clan of MacFarlanes, formed a crescent behind the valley, and far to the right were seen the dusky and more gigantic mountains of Argyleshire, with a seaward view of the shattered and thunder-splitten peaks of Arran.

But to Jeanie, whose taste for the picturesque, if she had any by nature, had never been awakened or cultivated, the sight of the faithful old May Hettly, as she opened the door to receive them in her clean toy, Sunday's russet-gown, and blue apron, nicely smoothed down before her, was worth the whole varied landscape. The raptures of the faithful old creature at seeing Jeanie were equal to her own, as she hastened to assure her "that baith the gudeman and the beasts had been as weel seen after as she possibly could contrive." Separating her from the rest of the company, May then hurried her young mistress to the offices, that she might receive the compliments she expected for her care of the cows. Jeanie rejoiced, in the simplicity of her heart, to see her charge once more; and the mute favourites of our heroine, Gowans, and the others, acknowledged her presence by lowing, turning round their broad and decent brows when they heard her well-known "Pruh, my leddy—pruh, my woman," and, by various indications, known only to those who have studied the animals' habits, shewing sensible pleasure as she approached to caress them in their turn.

"The very brute beasts are glad to see ye again," said May; "but nae wonder, Jeanie, for ye were aye kind to beast and body. And I maun learn to ca' ye *mistress* now, Jeanie, since ye hae been up to Lunnon, and seen the Duke, and the King, and a' the braw folk. But wha kens," added the old dame slily, "what I'll hae to ca' ye forbye mistress, for I am thinking it winna lang be Deans."

"Ca' me aye your ain Jeanie, May, and then ye can never gang wrang."

In the cow-house which they examined, there was one young animal, which Jeanie looked at till the tears gushed into her eyes. May, who had watched her with a sympathizing expression, immediately observed, in an under tone, "The gudeman aye sorts that beast him-sel, and is kinder to it than ony beast in the byre; and I noticed he was that e'en when he was angriest, and had maist cause to be angry.—Eh sirs! a parent's heart's a queer thing!—Mony a warstle he has had for that puir lassie—I am thinking that he petitions mair for her than for yoursel, hinny; for what can he plead for you but just to wish ye the blessing ye deserve? And when I sleepit ayont the hallan, when we came first here, he was often earnest a' night, and I could hear him come ower and ower again wi', 'Effie—puir blinded misguided thing!' it was aye 'Effie! Effie!'—If that puir wandering lamb comena into the sheepfauld in the Shepherd's ain time, it will be an unco wonder, for I wot she has been a child of prayers. O, if the puir prodigal wad return, sae blithely as the goodman wad kill the fatted calf!—though Brockie's calf will no be fit for killing this three weeks yet."

And then, with the discursive talent of persons of her description, she got once more afloat in her account of domestic affairs, and left this delicate and affecting topic.

Having looked at every thing in the offices and the dairy, and expressed her satisfaction with the manner in which matters had been managed in her absence, Jeanie rejoined the rest of the party, who were surveying the interior of the house, all excepting David Deans and Butler, who had gone down to the church to meet the kirk-session and the clergymen of the presbytery, and arrange matters for the duty of the day.

In the interior of the cottage all was clean, neat, and suitable to the exterior. It had been originally built and furnished by the Duke, as a retreat for a favourite domestic of the higher class, who did not long enjoy it, and had been dead only a few months, so that every thing was in excellent taste and good order. But in Jeanie's bed-room was a neat trunk, which had greatly excited Mrs Dutton's curiosity, for she was sure that the direction, "For Mrs Jean Deans, at Auchingower, parish of Knocktarlitie," was the writing of Mrs Semple, the Duchess's own woman. May Hettly produced the key in a sealed parcel, which bore the same address, and attached to the key was a label, intimating that the trunk and its contents were "a token of remembrance to Jeanie Deans, from her friends the Duchess of Argyle and the young ladies." The trunk, hastily opened as the reader will not doubt, was found to be full of wearing apparel of the best quality, suited to Jeanie's rank in life; and to most of the articles the names of the particular donors were attached, as if to make Jeanie sensible not only of the general, but the individual interest she had excited in the noble family. To name the various articles by their appropriate names, would be to attempt things unattempted yet in prose or rhyme; besides, that the old-fashioned terms of manteaus, sacks, kissing-strings, and so forth, would convey but little information even to the milliners of the present day. I shall deposit, however, an accurate inventory of the contents of the trunk with my kind friend, Miss Martha Buskbody, who has promised, should the public curiosity seem interested on the subject, to supply me with a professional glossary and commentary. Suffice it to say, that the gift was such as became the donors, and was suited to the situation of the receiver; that every thing was handsome and appropriate, and nothing forgotten which belonged to the wardrobe of a young person in Jeanie's situation in life, the destined bride of a respectable clergyman.

Article after article was displayed, commented upon, and admired, to the wonder of May, who declared, "she didna think the Queen had mair or better claise," and somewhat to the envy of the northern Cowslip. This unamiable, but not very unnatural, disposition of mind, broke forth in sundry unfounded criticisms to the disparagement of the articles, as they were severally exhibited. But it assumed a more direct character, when, at the bottom of all, was found a dress of white silk, very plainly made, but still of white silk, and French silk to boot, with a paper pinned to it, bearing, that it was a present from the Duke of Argyle to his travelling companion, to be worn on the day when she should change her name.

Mrs Dutton could forbear no longer, but whispered into Mr Archibald's ear, that it was a clever thing to be a Scotchwoman; "She supposed all *her* sisters, and she had half a dozen, might have been hanged, without any one sending her a present of a pocket-handkerchief."

"Or without your making any exertion to save them, Mrs Dolly," answered Archibald drily.—"But I am surprised we do not hear the bell yet," said he, looking at his watch.

"Fat ta teil, Mr Archibald," answered the Captain of Knockdunder, "wad ye hae them ring the bell before I am ready to gang to kirk?—I wad gar the bedral eat the bell-rope, if he took ony sic freedom. But if ye want to hear the bell, I'll just shew mysell on the knowe-head, and it will begin jowing forthwith."

Accordingly, so soon as they sallied out, and as the gold-laced hat of the Captain was seen rising like Hesper above the dewy verge of the rising ground, the clash (for it was rather a clash than a clang) of the bell was heard from the old moss-grown tower, and the clapper continued to thump its cracked sides all the while they advanced towards the kirk, Duncan exhorting them to take their own time, "for teil ony sport wad be till he came."

Accordingly, the bell only changed to the final and impatient chime when they crossed the stile; and "rung in," that is, concluded its mistuned summons, when they had entered the Duke's seat in the little kirk, where the whole party arranged themselves with Duncan at their head, excepting David Deans, who already occupied a seat among the elders.

The business of the day, with a particular detail of which it is unnecessary to trouble the reader, was gone through according to the established form, and the sermon pronounced upon the occasion had the good fortune to please even the critical David Deans, though it was only an hour and a quarter long, which David termed a short allowance of spiritual provender.

The preacher, who was a divine that held many of David's opinions, privately apologized for his brevity by saying, "That he observed the Captain was gaunting grievously, and that if he had detained him longer, there was no knowing how long he might be in paying the next term's victual stipend."

David groaned to find that such carnal motives could have influence upon the mind of a powerful preacher. He had, indeed, been scandalized by another circumstance during the service.

So soon as the congregation were seated after prayers, and the clergyman had read his text, the gracious Duncan, after rummaging the leathern-purse which hung in front of his petticoat, produced a short tobacco-pipe made of iron, and observed, almost aloud, "I hae forgotten my spleuchan—Lachlan, gang down to the Clachan, and bring me up a pennyworth of twist." Six arms, the nearest within reach, presented, with an obedient start, as many tobacco-pouches to the man of office. He made choice of one with a nod of acknowledgment, filled his pipe, lighted it with the assistance of his pistol-flint, and smoked with infinite composure during the whole time of the sermon. At the end of the discourse he knocked the ashes out of his pipe, replaced it in his sporran, returned the tobacco-pouch or spleuchan to its owner, and joined in the prayer with decency and attention.

At the end of the service, when Butler had been admitted minister of the Kirk of Knocktarlitie, with all its spiritual immunities and privileges, David, who had frowned, groaned, and murmured at Knockdunder's irreverent demeanour, communicated his plain thoughts of the matter to Isaac Micklehose, one of the elders, with whom a reverential aspect and huge grizzle wig had especially disposed him to seek fraternization. "It didna become a wild Indian," David said, "much less a Christian, and a gentleman, to sit in the kirk puffing tobacco reek, as if he were in a change-house."

Micklehose shook his head, and allowed it was "far frae beseeming —But what will ye say? The Captain's a queer hand, and to speak to him about that or ony thing else that crosses the maggot, wad be to set the kiln a-low. He keeps a high hand ower the country, and we couldna deal wi' the Hielandmen without his protection, sin' a' the keys o' the kintra hings at his belt; and he's no an ill body in the main, and maistry, ye ken, maws the meadows doun."

"That may be a' very true, neighbour," said David; "but Reuben Butler isna the man I tak him to be, if he disna learn the Captain to fuff his pipe some other gate than in God's house, or the quarter be ower."

"Fair and softly gangs far," said Micklehose; "and if a fule may gie a wise man a counsel, I wad hae him think twice or he mells wi'

Knockdunder—He suld hae a lang-shankit spune that wad sup kail wi' the de'il. But they are a' away to their dinner to the change-house, and if we dinna mend our pace, we'll come short at meal-time."

David accompanied his friend without answer; but began to feel from experience, that the glen of Knocktarlitie, like the rest of the world, was haunted by its own special subjects of regret and discontent. His mind was so much occupied by considering the best means of converting Duncan of Knock to a sense of reverential decency during public worship, that he altogether forgot to enquire, whether Butler was called upon to subscribe the oaths to government.

Some have insinuated, that his neglect on this head was, in some degree, intentional; but I think this explanation inconsistent with the simplicity of my friend David's character. Neither have I ever been able by the most minute enquiries to know, whether the *formula*, at which he so much scrupled, had been exacted from Butler, aye or no. The books of the kirk-session might have thrown some light on this matter; but unfortunately they were destroyed in the year 1746, by one Donacha Dhu na Dunaigh, at the instance, it was said, or at least by the connivance, of the gracious Duncan of Knock, who had a desire to obliterate the records of the foibles of a certain Kate Finlayson.

Chapter Nine

Now butt an' ben the change-house fills
Wi' yill-caup commentators,—
Here's crying out for bakes and gills,
And there the pint-stoup clatters.
While thick and thrang, and loud and lang,—
Wi' logic and wi' scripture,
They raise a din that in the end
Is like to breed a rupture,
      O' wrath that day.
         BURNS

A PLENTIFUL ENTERTAINMENT, at the Duke of Argyle's cost, regaled the reverend gentlemen who had assisted at the ordination of Reuben Butler, and almost all the respectable part of the parish. The feast was, indeed, such as the country itself furnished; for plenty of all the requisites for "a rough and round" dinner, were always at Duncan of Knock's command. There was the beef and mutton on the braes, the fresh and salt-water fish in the lochs, the brooks, and firth; game of every kind, from the deer to the leveret, were to be had for the killing, in the Duke's forests, moors, heaths, and mosses; and for liquor, home-brewed ale flowed as freely as water; brandy and usquebaugh both were had in these happy times without duty; even white wine and claret were got for nothing, since the Duke's extensive rights of admiralty gave him a title to all the quantity of liquors in cask, which often come ashore on the western coast and isles of Scotland, when shipping have suffered by severe weather. In short, as Duncan boasted, the entertainment did not cost Maccallanmore a plack out of his sporran, and was nevertheless not only liberal, but overflowing.

The Duke's health was solemnized in a *bona fide* bumper, and David Deans himself added perhaps the first huzza that his lungs had ever uttered, to swell the shout with which the pledge was received. Nay, so exalted in heart was he upon this memorable occasion, and so much disposed to be indulgent, that he expressed no dissatisfaction when three bag-pipers struck up, "The Campbells are coming." The health of the reverend minister of Knocktarlitie was received with similar honours; and there was a roar of laughter, when one of his brethren slyly subjoined the addition of, "A good wife to our brother, to keep the Manse in order." On this occasion David Deans was delivered of his first-born joke; apparently the parturition was accompanied with many throes, for sorely did he twist about his physiognomy, and much did he stumble in his speech, before he could express his idea, "That the lad being new wedded to his spiritual bride, it was hard to threaten him with ane temporal spouse in the saam day." He then laughed a hoarse and brief laugh, and was suddenly grave and silent, as if abashed at his own vivacious effort.

After another toast or two, Jeanie, Mrs Dolly, and such of the female natives as had honoured the feast with their presence, retired to David's new dwelling at Auchingower, and left the gentlemen to their potations.

The feast proceeded with great glee. The conversation, where Duncan had it under his direction, was not indeed always strictly canonical, but David escaped any risk of being scandalized, by engaging with one of his neighbours in a recapitulation of the sufferings of Ayrshire and Lanarkshire, during what was called the invasion of the Highland Host; the prudent Mr Micklehose from time to time cautioning them to lower their voices, for "that Duncan Knock's father had been at that onslaught, and brought back muckle gude plenishing, and that Duncan was no unlikely to hae been there himsell, for what he kenn'd."

Meanwhile, as the mirth and fun grew fast and furious, the graver members of the party began to escape as well as they could. David Deans accomplished his retreat, and Butler anxiously watched an opportunity to follow him. Knockdunder, however, desirous, he said, of knowing what stuff was in the new minister, had no intention to part with him so easily, but kept him pinned to his side, watching him sedulously, and with obliging violence filling his glass to the brim, so often as he could seize an opportunity of doing so. At length, as the evening was wearing late, a venerable brother chanced to ask Mr Archibald when they might hope to see the Duke, *tam carum caput*, as he would venture to term him, at the Lodge of Roseneath. Duncan of Knock, whose ideas were somewhat conglomerated, and who, it may be believed, was no great scholar, catching up some imperfect sound of the words, conceived the speaker was drawing a parallel between the Duke and Sir Donald Gorme of Sleat; and being of opinion that such comparison was odious, snorted thrice, and prepared himself to be in a passion.

To the explanation of the venerable divine, the Captain answered, "I heard the word Gorme myself, sir, with my ain ears. D'ye think I do not know Gaelic from Latin?"

"Apparently not, sir;"—so the clergyman, offended in his turn, and taking a pinch of snuff, answered with great coolness.

The copper nose of the gracious Duncan now became heated like the bull of Phalaris, and while Mr Archibald mediated betwixt the offended parties, and the attention of the company was engaged by their dispute, Butler took an opportunity to effect his retreat.

He found the females at Auchingower, very anxious for the breaking up of the convivial party; for it was a part of the arrangement, that although David Deans was to remain at Auchingower, and Butler was that night to take possession of the Manse, yet Jeanie, for whom complete accommodations were not yet provided in her father's house, was to return for a day or two to the Lodge at Roseneath, and the boats had been held in readiness accordingly. They waited, therefore, for Knockdunder's return, but twilight came, and they still waited in vain. At length Mr Archibald, who, as a man of decorum, had taken care not to exceed in his conviviality, made his appearance, and advised the females strongly to return to the island under his escort; observing, that from the humour in which he had left the Captain, it was a great chance whether he budged out of the public-house that night, and it was absolutely certain that he would not be very fit company for ladies. The gig was at their disposal, he said, and there was still pleasant twilight for a party on the water.

Jeanie, who had considerable confidence in Archibald's prudence, immediately acquiesced in this proposal; but Mrs Dolly positively objected to the small boat. If the big boat could be gotten, she agreed to set out, otherwise she would sleep on the floor, rather than stir a step. Reason with Dolly was out of the question, and Archibald did not think the difficulty so pressing as to require compulsion. He observed, it was not using the Captain very politely to deprive him of his coach and six; "but as it was in the ladies' service," he gallantly said, "he would use so much freedom—besides the gig would serve the Captain's purpose better, as it could come off at any hour of the tide; the large boat should, therefore, be at Mrs Dolly's service."

They walked to the beach accordingly, accompanied by Butler. It was some time before the boatmen could be assembled, and ere they were well embarked, and ready to depart, the pale moon was come over the hill, and flinging a trembling reflection on the broad and glittering waves. But so soft and pleasant was the night, that Butler, in bidding farewell to Jeanie, had no apprehension for her safety; and what is yet more extraordinary, Mrs Dolly felt no alarm for her own. The air was soft, and came over the cooling wave with something of summer fragrance. The beautiful scene of headlands, and capes, and bays, around them, with the broad blue chain of mountains, seemed to sleep in the moonlight; while every dash of the oars made the waters glance and sparkle with the brilliant phenomenon called the sea-fire.

This last circumstance filled Jeanie with wonder, and served to amuse the mind of her companion, until they approached the little bay, which seemed to stretch its dark and wooded arms into the sea as if to welcome them.

The usual landing-place was at a quarter of a mile's distance from the Lodge, and although the tide did not admit of the large boat coming quite close to the jetty of loose stones which served as a pier, Jeanie, who was both bold and active, easily sprung ashore; but Mrs Dolly positively refusing to commit herself to the same risk, the complaisant Mr Archibald ordered the boat round to a more regular landing-place, at a considerable distance along shore. He then prepared to land himself, that he might, in the meanwhile, accompany Jeanie to the Lodge. But as there was no mistaking the woodland lane, which led from thence to the shore, and as the moonlight shewed her one of the white chimneys rising out of the wood which embosomed the building, Jeanie declined this favour with thanks, and requested him to proceed with Mrs Dolly, who being "in a country where the ways were strange to her, had mair need of countenance."

This was indeed a fortunate circumstance, and might even be said to save poor Cowslip's life, if it was true, as she herself used solemnly to aver, that she must positively have expired for fear, if she had been left alone in the boat with six wild Highlanders in kilts.

The night was so exquisitely beautiful, that Jeanie, instead of immediately directing her course towards the Lodge, stood looking after the boat as it again put off from the side, and rowed out into the little bay, the dark figures of her companions growing less and less distinct as they diminished in the distance, and the jorram, or melancholy boat-song of the rowers, coming on the ear with softened and sweeter sound, until the boat rounded the headland, and was lost to her observation.

Still Jeanie remained in the same posture, looking out upon the sea. It would, she was aware, be some time ere her companions could reach the Lodge, as the distance by the more convenient landing-place was considerably greater than from the point where she stood, and she was not sorry to have an opportunity to spend the interval by herself.

The wonderful change which a few weeks had wrought in her situation, from shame and grief, and almost despair, to honour, joy, and a fair prospect of future happiness, passed before her eyes with a sensation which brought the tears into them. Yet they flowed at the same time from another source. As human happiness is never perfect, and as well constructed minds are never more sensible of the distresses of those whom they love, than when their own situation forms a contrast with them, Jeanie's affectionate regrets turned to the fate of her poor sister—the child of so many hopes—the fondled nursling of so many years—now an exile, and, what was worse, dependent on the will of a man, of whose habits she had every reason to entertain the worst opinion, and who, even in his fiercest paroxysms of remorse, had appeared too much a stranger to the feelings of real penitence.

While her thoughts were occupied with these melancholy reflections, a shadowy figure seemed to detach itself from the copse-wood on her right hand. Jeanie started, and the stories of apparitions and wraiths, seen by solitary travellers in wild situations, at such times, and in such an hour, suddenly came full upon her imagination. The figure glided on, and as it came betwixt her and the moon, she was aware that it had the appearance of a woman. A soft voice twice repeated, "Jeanie —Jeanie!"—Was it indeed—could it be the voice of her sister?—Was she still among the living, or had the grave given up its tenant?—Ere she could state these questions to her own mind, Effie, alive, and in the body, had clasped her in her arms, and was straining her to her bosom, and devouring her with kisses. "I have wandered here," she said, "like a ghaist, to see you, and nae wonder ye take me for ane—I thought but to see ye gang by, or to hear the sound of your voice; but to speak to yoursell again, Jeanie, was mair than I deserved, and mair than I durst pray for."

"O Effie! how cam ye here alone, and at this hour, and on the wild sea-beach?—Are ye sure it's your ain living sell?"

There was something of Effie's former humour in her practically answering the question by a gentle pinch, more beseeming the fingers of a fairy than of a ghost. And again the sisters embraced, and laughed and wept by turns.

"But ye maun gang up wi' me to the Lodge, Effie," said Jeanie, "and tell me a' your story—I hae gude folk there that will make ye welcome for my sake."

"Na, na, Jeanie," replied her sister sorrowfully,—"ye hae forgotten what I am—a banished outlawed body, scarce escaped the gallows by your being the bauldest and the best sister that ever lived—I'll gae near nane o' your grand friends, if there was nae danger to me."

"There is nae danger—there shall be nae danger," said Jeanie eagerly. "O Effie, dinna be wilfu'—be guided for anes—we will be sae happy a'thegither!"

"I have a' the happiness I deserve on this side of the grave, now that I hae seen you," answered Effie; "and whether there were danger to mysell or no, naebody shall ever say that I come with my cheat-the-gallows face to shame my sister amang her grand friends."

"I hae nae grand friends," said Jeanie; "nae friends but what are friends of yours—Reuben Butler and my father.—O, unhappy lassie, dinna be dour, and turn your back on your happiness again! We winna see another acquaintance—Come hame to us, your ain dearest friends—it's better sheltering under an auld hedge than under a new planted wood."

"It's in vain speaking, Jeanie—I maun drink as I hae browed—I am married, and I maun follow my husband, for better for worse."

"Married, Effie!" exclaimed Jeanie—"Misfortunate creature! and to that awfu'"——

"Hush, hush," said Effie, clapping one hand on her mouth, and pointing to the thicket with the other, "he is yonder."

She said this in a tone which shewed her husband had found means to inspire her with awe, as well as affection. At this moment a man issued from the wood.

It was young Staunton. Even by the imperfect light of the moon, Jeanie could observe that he was handsomely dressed, and had the air of a person of rank.

"Effie," he said, "our time is well nigh spent—the skiff will be aground in the creek, and I dare not stay here longer—I hope your sister will permit me to salute her." But Jeanie shrunk back from him with a feeling of internal abhorrence. "Well," said he, "it does not much signify; if you keep up the feeling of ill-will, at least you do not act upon it, and I thank you for your respect to my secret, when a word (which in your place I would have spoken at once) would have cost me my life. People say, you should keep from the wife of your bosom the secret that concerns your neck—my wife and her sister both know mine, and I shall not sleep a wink less sound."

"But are you really married to my sister, sir?" asked Jeanie, in great doubt and anxiety; for the haughty careless tone in which he spoke seemed to justify her worst apprehensions.

"I really am legally married, and by my own name," replied Staunton, more gravely.

"And your father—and your friends?"—

"And my father and my friends must just reconcile themselves to that which is done and cannot be undone," replied Staunton. "However, it is my intention, in order to break off dangerous connections, and to let my friends come to their temper, to conceal my marriage for the present, and stay abroad for some years. So that you will not hear of us for some time, if you ever hear of us again at all. It would be dangerous, you must be aware, to keep up the correspondence, for all would guess that the husband of Effie was the—what shall I call myself?—the slayer of Porteous."

Hard-hearted light man! thought Jeanie—to what a character she has intrusted her happiness!—She has sown the wind, and maun reap the whirlwind.

"Dinna think ill o' him," said Effie, breaking away from her husband, and leading Jeanie a step or two out of hearing,—"dinna think *very* ill o' him—he's gude to me, Jeanie—as gude as I deserve—And he is determined to gie up his bad courses.—Sae, after a', dinna greet for Effie; she is better off than she has wrought for.—But you—O you!—how can you be happy eneugh?—never till ye get to Heaven, where a' body is as gude as yoursel.—Jeanie, if I live and thrive, ye shall hear of me—if not, just forget sic a creature ever lived to vex ye—fare ye weel—fare—fare ye weel!"

She tore herself from her sister's arms, rejoined her husband—they plunged into the copsewood, and she saw them no more. The whole scene had the effect of a vision, and she could almost have believed it such, but that, very soon after they quitted her, she heard the sound of oars, and a skiff was seen on the Firth, pulling swiftly towards the small smuggling sloop which lay in the offing. It was on board of such a vessel that Effie had embarked at Portobello, and Jeanie had no doubt that the same conveyance was destined, as Staunton had hinted, to transport them to a foreign country.

Although it was impossible to determine whether this interview, while it was passing, gave more pain or pleasure to Jeanie Deans, yet the ultimate impression which remained on her mind was decidedly favourable. Effie was married—made, according to the common phrase, an honest woman—that was one main point; it seemed also as if her husband were about to abandon the path of gross vice, in which he had run so long and so desperately—that was another;—for his final and effectual conversion, he did not want understanding, and God knew his own hour.

Such were the thoughts with which Jeanie endeavoured to console her anxiety respecting her sister's future fortune. On her arrival at the Lodge, she found Archibald in some anxiety at her stay, and about to walk out in quest of her. A headache served as apology for retiring to rest, in order to conceal her visible agitation of mind from her companions.

By this secession also, she escaped another scene of a different sort. For as if there was danger in all gigs, whether by sea or land, that of Knockdunder had been run down by another boat, an accident owing chiefly to the drunkenness of the captain, his crew, and passengers. Knockdunder, and two or three guests, whom he was bringing along with him to finish the conviviality of the evening at the Lodge, got a sound ducking, but, being rescued by the crew of the boat which endangered them, there was no ultimate loss, excepting that of the captain's laced hat, which, greatly to the satisfaction of the Highland part of the district, as well as to the improvement of the uniformity of his own personal appearance, he replaced by a smart Highland bonnet next day. Many were the vehement threats of vengeance which, on the succeeding morning, the gracious Duncan threw out against the boat which had upset him; but as neither she, nor the small smuggling vessel to which she belonged, was any longer to be seen in the Firth, he was compelled to sit down with the affront. This was the more hard, he said, as he was assured the mischief was done on purpose, these scoundrels having lurked about after they had landed every drop of brandy, and every bag of tea they had on board; and he understood their coxswain had been on shore, making particular enquiries concerning the time when his boat was to cross over, and to return, and so forth.

"Put the neist time they meet me on the Firth," said Duncan, with great majesty, "I will teach the moonlight rapscallions and vagabonds to keep their ain side of the road, and be tamn'd to them."

Chapter Ten

Lord! who would live turmoiled in a court,
And may enjoy such quiet walks as these?
SHAKESPEARE

WITHIN A REASONABLE TIME after Butler was safely and comfortably settled in his living, and Jeanie had taken up her abode at

Auchingower with her father, the precise extent of which interval we request each reader to settle according to his own sense of what is decent and proper upon the occasion; and after due proclamation of banns, and all other formalities, the long wooing of this worthy pair was ended by their union in the holy bands of matrimony. On this occasion, David Deans stoutly withstood the iniquities of pipes, fiddles, and promiscuous dancing, to the great wrath of the Captain of Knockdunder, who said, if he "had guessed it was to be sic a tamned Quakers' meeting, he wad hae seen them peyont the cairn before he wad hae darkened their doors."

And so much rancour remained on the spirits of the gracious Duncan upon this occasion, that various "picqueerings," as David called them, took place upon the same and similar topics; and it was only in consequence of an accidental visit of the Duke to his Lodge at Roseneath, that they were put a stop to. But upon that occasion his Grace shewed such particular respect to Mr and Mrs Butler, and such favour even to old David, that Knockdunder held it prudent to change his course towards the latter. He, in future, used to express himself among friends, concerning the minister and his wife, as "very worthy decent folk, just a little ower strict in their notions; put it was pest for thae plack cattle to err on the safe side." And respecting David, he allowed that "he was an excellent judge of nowt and sheep, and a sensible aneugh carle, an' it werena for his tamned Cameronian nonsense, whilk it is not worth while of a shentleman to knock out of an auld silly head, either by force of reason, or otherwise." So that, by avoiding topics of dispute, the personages of our tale lived in great good habits with the gracious Duncan, only that he still grieved David's soul, and set a perilous example to the congregation, by sometimes bringing his pipe to the church during a cold winter-day, and almost always sleeping during sermon in the summer-time.

Mrs Butler, whom we must no longer, if we can help it, term by the familiar name of Jeanie, brought into the married state the same firm mind and affectionate disposition,—the same natural and homely good sense, and spirit of useful exertion,—in a word, all the domestic good qualities of which she had given proof during her maiden life. She did not indeed rival Butler in learning; but then no woman more devoutly venerated the extent of her husband's erudition. She did not pretend to understand his expositions of divinity; but no minister of the presbytery had his humble dinner so well arranged, his clothes and linen in equal good order, his fire-side so neatly swept, his parlour so clean, and his books so well dusted.

If he talked to Jeanie of what she did not understand,—and (for the man was mortal, and had been a schoolmaster,) he sometimes did harangue more scholarly and wisely than was necessary,—she listened in placid silence; and wherever the point referred to common life, and was such as came under the grasp of a strong natural understanding, her views were more forcible, and her observations more acute, than his own. In acquired politeness of manners, when it happened that she mingled a little in society, Mrs Butler was, of course, judged deficient. But then she had that obvious wish to oblige, that real and natural good-breeding which depends on good sense and good humour, to which she joined a considerable degree of archness and liveliness of manner, so that her behaviour was acceptable to all with whom she was called upon to associate. Notwithstanding her strict attention to all domestic affairs, she always appeared the neat, clean, well-dressed mistress of the house, never the sordid household drudge. When complimented on this occasion by Duncan Knock, who swore "that he thought the fairies must help her, since her house was always clean, and nobody ever saw any body sweeping it," she modestly replied that much might be done by "timing ane's turns."

Duncan replied, "He heartily wished she could teach that art to the huzzies at the Lodge, for he could never discover that the house was washed at a', except now and then by breaking his shins over the pail—Cot tamn the jauds!"

Of lesser matters there is not occasion to speak much. It may easily be believed that the Duke's cheese was carefully made, and so graciously accepted, that the offering became annual. Remembrances and acknowledgments of past favours were sent to Mrs Bickerton and to Mrs Glass, and an amicable intercourse maintained from time to time with these two respectable and benevolent persons.

It is especially necessary to mention, that in the course of five years, Mrs Butler had three children, two boys and a girl, all stout healthy babes of grace, fair-haired, blue-eyed, and strong-limbed. The boys were named David and Reuben, an order of nomenclature which was much to the satisfaction of the old hero of the Covenant, and the girl, by her mother's special desire, was christened Euphemia, rather contrary to the wish both of her father and husband, who nevertheless loved Mrs Butler too well, and were too much indebted to her for their hours of happiness, to withstand any request which she made with earnestness, and as a gratification to herself. But from some feeling, of I know not what kind, the child was never distinguished by the name of Effie, but by the abbreviation of Femie, which in Scotland is equally commonly applied to persons called Euphemia.

In this state of quiet and unostentatious enjoyment, there were, besides the ordinary rubs and ruffles which disturb even the most uniform life, two things which particularly chequered Mrs Butler's happiness. "Without these," she said to our informer, "her life would have been but too happy; and perhaps she had need of some crosses in this world to remind her that there was a better to come behind it."

The first of these related to certain polemical skirmishes betwixt her father and her husband, which, notwithstanding the mutual respect and affection they entertained for each other, and their great love for her,—notwithstanding also their general agreement in strictness, and even severity of Presbyterian principle,—often threatened unpleasant weather between them. David Deans, as our readers must be aware, was sufficiently opinionative and intractable, and having prevailed on himself to become a member of a kirk-session under the established church, he felt doubly obliged to evince, that in so doing, he had not compromised any whit of his former profession, either in practice or principle. Now Mr Butler, doing all credit to his father-in-law's motives, was frequently of opinion that it were better to drop out of memory points of division and separation, and to act in the manner most likely to attract and unite all parties who were serious in religion. Moreover, he was not pleased, as a man and a scholar, to be always dictated to by his unlettered father-in-law; and as a clergyman, he did not think it fit to seem for ever under the thumb of an elder of his own kirk-session. A proud but honest thought carried his opposition now and then a little farther than it would otherwise have gone. "My brethren," he said, "will suppose I am flattering and conciliating the old man for the sake of his succession, if I defer and give way to him on every occasion; and, besides, there are many on which I neither can nor will conscientiously yield to his notions. I cannot be persecuting old women for witches, or ferretting out matter of scandal among the young ones, which might otherwise have remained concealed."

From this difference of opinion it happened, that in many cases of nicety, such as in owning certain defections, and failing to testify against certain backslidings of the time, in not always and severely tracing forth little matters of scandal and *fama clamosa*, which David called a loosening of the reins of discipline, and in failing to demand clear testimonies in other points of controversy which had, as it were, drifted to leeward with the change of times, Butler incurred the censure of his father-in-law; and sometimes the disputes betwixt them turned eager and almost unfriendly. In all such cases Mrs Butler was a mediating spirit, who endeavoured, by the alkaline smoothness of her own disposition, to neutralize the acidity of theological controversy. To the complaints of both she lent an unprejudiced and attentive ear, and sought always rather to excuse than absolutely to defend the other party.

She reminded her father that Butler had not "his experience of the

auld and wrastling times, when folk were gifted wi' a far look into
eternity, to make up for the oppressions whilk they suffered here
below in time. She freely allowed that many devout ministers and
professors in times past had enjoyed downright revelation, like the
blessed Peden, and Lundie, and Cameron, and Renwick, and John
Caird the tinkler, wha entered into the secrets, and Elizabeth Melvill,
Lady Culross, wha prayed in her bed, surrounded by a great many
Christians in a large room, in whilk it was placed on purpose, and that
for three hours' time, with wonderful assistance; and Lady Robertland, whilk got sic rare outgates of grace, and mony others in times
past; and of a specialty, Mr John Scrimgeour, minister of Kinghorn,
who having a beloved child sick to death of the crewels,* was free to
expostulate with his Maker with such impatience of displeasure, and
complaining so bitterly, that at length it was said unto him, that he was
heard for this time, but that he was requested to use no such boldness
in time coming; so that when he returned he found the child sitting up
in the bed heal and fere, with all its wounds closed, and supping its
parritch, whilk babe he had left at the time of death. But though these
things might be true in these needful times, she contended that those
ministers who had not seen such vouchsafed and especial mercies,
were to seek their rule in the records of ancient times; and therefore
Reuben was carefu' both to search the Scriptures and the books
written by wise and good men of old; and sometimes in this way it wad
happen that twa precious saints might pu' sundry wise, like twa cows
riving at the same hay-band."

To this David used to reply, with a sigh, "Ah, hinny, thou kenn'st
little o't; but that saam John Scrimgeour, that blew open the gates of
heaven as an it had been wi' a sax-pund cannon-ball, used devoutly to
wish that most part of books were burned except the Bible. Reuben's a
gude lad and a kind—I have aye allowed that; but as to his not allowing
enquiry anent the scandal of Margery Kittledoop and Rory MacRand,
under pretence that they hae southered sin wi' marriage, it's clear
again the Christian discipline o' the kirk. And then there is Aily
MacClure of Deepheugh, that practises her abominations, spaeing
folks' fortunes wi' egg-shells and mutton-banes, and dreams and
divinations, whilk is a scandal to ony Christian land to suffer a witch to
live; and I'll uphaud that in a' judicatures, civil or ecclesiastical."

"I dare say ye are very right, father," was the general style of Jeanie's
answer; "but ye maun come down to the Manse to your dinner the
day. The bits o' bairns, puir things, are wearying to see their luckie-
dad; and Reuben never sleeps weel, nor I neither, when you and he
hae had ony bit outcast."

* King's-evil.

"Nae outcast, Jeanie; God forbid I suld cast out wi' thee, or aught that is dear to thee." And he put on his Sunday's coat, and came to the Manse accordingly.

With her husband, Mrs Butler had a more direct conciliatory process. Reuben had the utmost respect for the old man's motives, and affection for his person, as well as gratitude for his early friendship. So that, upon any such occasion of accidental irritation, it was only necessary to remind him with delicacy of his father-in-law's age, of his scanty education, strong prejudices, and family distresses. The least of these considerations always inclined Butler to measures of conciliation, in so far as he could accede to them without compromising principle; and thus our simple and unpretending heroine had the merit of those peace-makers, to whom it is pronounced as a benediction, that they shall inherit the earth.

The second crook in Mrs Butler's lot, to use the language of her father, was the distressing circumstance, that she had never heard of her sister's safety, or of the circumstances in which she found herself, though betwixt four and five years had elapsed since they had parted on the beach of the island of Roseneath. Frequent intercourse was not to be expected—not to be desired, perhaps, in their relative situations; but Effie had promised, that, if she lived and prospered, her sister should hear from her. She must then be no more, or sunk into some abyss of misery, since she had never redeemed her pledge. Her silence seemed strange and portentous, and wrung from Jeanie, who could never forget the early years of their intimacy, the most painful anticipations concerning her fate. At length, however, the veil was drawn aside.

One day, as the Captain of Knockdunder had called in at the Manse, on his return from some business in the Highland part of the parish, and had been accommodated, according to his special request, with a mixture of milk, brandy, honey, and water, which he said Mrs Butler compounded "petter than ever a woman in Scotland,"—for, in all innocent matters, she studied the taste of every one around her,— he said to Butler, "Py the pye, minister, I have a letter here either for your canny pody of a wife or you, which I got when I was last at Glasco; the postage comes to fourpence, which ye may either pay me forthwith, or give me tooble or quitts in a hitt at pack-cammon."

The playing at back-gammon and draughts had been a frequent amusement of Mr Whackbairn, Butler's principal, when at Libberton school. The minister, therefore, still piqued himself on his skill at both games, and occasionally practised them, as strictly canonical, although David Deans, whose notions of every kind were more rigorous, used to shake his head, and groan grievously, when he espied the tables lying in the parlour, or the children playing with the dice-boxes or back-gammon men. Indeed Mrs Butler was sometimes chidden for removing these implements of pastime into some closet or corner out of sight. "Let them lie where they are, Jeanie," would Butler say upon such occasions; "I am not conscious of following this, or any other trifling relaxation, to the interruption of my more serious studies, and still more serious duties. I will not, therefore, have it supposed, that I am indulging by stealth, and against my conscience, in an amusement which, using it so little as I do, I may well practise openly, and without any check of mind—*Nil conscire sibi*, Jeanie, that is my motto; which signifies, my love, the honest and open confidence which a man ought to entertain, when he is acting openly, and without any sense of doing wrong."

Such being Butler's humour, he accepted the Captain's defiance to a twopenny-hit at back-gammon, and handed the letter to his wife, observing, the post-mark was York, but, if it came from her friend Mrs Bickerton, she had considerably improved her hand-writing, which was uncommon at her years.

Leaving the gentlemen to their game, Mrs Butler went to order something for supper, for Captain Duncan had proposed kindly to stay the night with them, and then carelessly broke open her letter. It was not from Mrs Bickerton, and, after glancing over the first few lines, she soon found it necessary to retire into her own bed-room, to read the document at leisure.

Chapter Eleven

Happy thou art! then happy be,
Nor envy me my lot;
Thy humble state I envy thee,
And peaceful cot.
Anonymous

THE LETTER, which Mrs Butler, when retired into her own apartment, perused with anxious wonder, was certainly from Effie, although it had no other signature than the letter E.; and although the orthography, style, and penmanship, were very far superior not only to any thing which Effie could produce, who, though a lively girl, had been a remarkably careless scholar, but even to her more considerate sister's own powers of composition and expression. The manuscript was a fair Italian hand, though something stiff and constrained—the spelling and the diction that of a person who had been accustomed to read good composition and mix in good society.

The tenor of the letter was as follows:

"My Dearest Sister,

"At many risks I venture to write to you, to inform you that I am still alive, and, as to worldly situation, that I rank higher than I could expect or merit. If wealth, and distinction, and an honourable rank, could make a woman happy, I have them all; but you, Jeanie, whom the world might think placed far beneath me in all these respects, are far happier than I am. I have had means of hearing of your welfare, my dearest Jeanie, from time to time—I think I should have broken my heart otherwise. I have learned with great pleasure of your increasing family. We have not been worthy of such a blessing; two infants have been successively removed, and we are now childless—God's will be done. But, if we had a child, it would perhaps divert him from the gloomy thoughts which make him terrible to himself and others. Yet do not let me frighten you, Jeanie; he continues to be kind, and I am far better off than I deserve. You will wonder at my better scholarship; but when I was abroad, I had the best teachers, and I worked hard because my progress pleased him. He is kind, Jeanie, only he has much to distress him, especially when he looks backward. When I look backward myself, I have always a ray of comfort; it is in the generous conduct of a sister, who forsook me not when I was forsaken by every one. You have had your reward. You live happy in the esteem and love of all who know you, and I drag on the life of a miserable impostor, indebted for the marks of regard I receive to a tissue of deceit and lies, which the slightest accident may unravel. He has produced me to his friends, since the estate opened to him, as the daughter of a Scotchman of rank, banished on account of the Viscount of Dundee's wars— that is, our Fr's old friend Clavers, you know—and he says I was educated in a Scotch convent; indeed I lived in such a place long enough to enable me to support the character. But when a countryman approaches me, and begins to talk, as they all do, of the various families engaged in Dundee's affair, and to make enquiries into my connections, and when I see *his* eye bent on mine with such an expression of agony, my terror brings me to the very risk of detection. Good-nature and politeness have hitherto saved me, as they prevented people from pressing on me with distressing questions. But how long—O how long, will this be the case!—And if I bring that disgrace on him, he will hate me—he will kill me, for as much as he loves me; he is as jealous of his family honour now, as ever he was careless about it. I have been in England four months, and have often thought of writing to you; and yet, such are the dangers that might arise from an intercepted letter, that I have hitherto forborne. But now I am obliged to run the risk. Last week I saw your great friend, the D. of A. He came to my box, and sate by me; and something in the play

put him in mind of you—Gracious Heaven! he told over your whole
London journey to all who were in the box, but particularly to the
wretched creature who was the occasion of it all. If he had known—if
he could have conceived, beside whom he was sitting, and to whom
the story was told!—I suffered with courage, like an Indian at the
stake, while they are rending his fibres and boring his eyes, and while
he smiles applause at each well-imagined contrivance of his torturers.
It was too much for me at last, Jeanie—I fainted; and my agony was
imputed partly to the heat of the place, and partly to my extreme
sensibility; and, hypocrite all over, I encouraged both opinions—any
thing but discovery. Luckily he was not there. But the incident has led
to more alarms. I am obliged to meet your great man often; and he
seldom sees me without talking of E. D. and J. D., and R. B. and D.
D., as persons in whom my amiable sensibility is interested. My amiable sensibility!!!—And then the cruel tone of light indifference with
which persons in the fashionable world speak together on the most
affecting subjects! To hear my guilt, my folly, my agony, the foibles
and weaknesses of my friends—even your heroic exertions, Jeanie,
spoken of in the drolling style which is the present tone in fashionable
life—Scarce all that I formerly endured is equal to this state of
irritation—then it was blows and stabs—now it is pricking to death
with needles and pins.—He, I mean the D., goes down next month to
spend the shooting-season in Scotland; he says, he makes a point of
always dining one day at the Manse—be on your guard, and do
not betray yourself, should he mention me—Yourself, alas! *you* have
nothing to betray, nothing to fear—It is E. whose life is once more in
your hands—it is E. whom you are to save from being plucked of her
borrowed plumes, discovered, branded, and trodden down, first by
him, perhaps, who has raised her to this dizzy pinnacle!—The inclos-
ure will reach you twice a-year—do not refuse it—it is out of my own
allowance, and may be twice as much when you want it. With you it
may do good, with me it never can.

"Write to me soon, Jeanie, or I shall remain in the agonizing apprehension that this has fallen into wrong hands—Address simply to L.
S., under cover, to the Reverend George Whiterose, in the Minster-
Close, York. He thinks I correspond with some of my noble jacobite
relations who are in Scotland. How high-church and jacobitical
zeal would burn in his cheeks, if he knew he was the agent, not of
Euphemia Seton, of the honourable house of Winton, but of E.
D., daughter of a Cameronian cow-feeder!—Jeanie, I can laugh yet
sometimes—but God protect you from such mirth.—My father—I
mean your father, would say it was like the idle crackling of fire among
thorns; but the thorns keep their poignancy, they remain unconsumed

—Farewell, my dearest Jeanie—Do not show this even to Mr Butler, much less to any one else—I have every respect for him, but his principles are over strict, and my case will not endure severe handling. —I rest your affectionate sister, E."

In this long letter there was much to surprise as well as to distress Mrs Butler. That Effie—her sister Effie, should be mingling freely in society, and apparently on not unequal terms, with the Duke of Argyle, sounded like something so extraordinary, that she even doubted if she read truly. Nor was it less marvellous, that, in the space of four years, her education should have made such progress. Jeanie's humility readily allowed that Effie had always, when she chose it, been smarter at her book than she herself was, but then she was very idle, and, upon the whole, had made much less proficiency. Love, or fear, or necessity, however, had proved an able school-mistress, and completely supplied all her deficiencies.

What Jeanie least liked in the tone of the letter was a smothered degree of egotism. "We should have heard little about her," thought Jeanie to herself, "but that she was feared the Duke might come to learn wha she was, and a' about her puir friends here; but Effie, puir thing, aye took her ain way, and folks that do that think mair o' themselves than of their neighbours.—I am no clear about keeping her siller," she added, taking up a 5ol. note which had fallen out of the paper to the floor. "We hae aneugh, and it looks unco like theft-boot, or hush-money, as they ca' it; she might hae been sure that I wad say naething wad harm her, for a' the gowd in Lunnon. And I maun tell the minister about it. I dinna see that she suld be sae feared for her ain bonnie bargain of a gudeman, and that I shouldna reverence Mr Butler just as much; and sae I'll e'en tell him, when that tippling body the Captain has ta'en boat in the morning.——But I wonder at my ain state of mind," she added, turning back, after she had made a step or two to the door to join the gentlemen; "surely I am no sic a fule as to be angry that Effie's a braw leddy, while I am only a minister's wife?— and yet I am as petted as a bairn, when I should bless God, that has redeemed her from shame, and poverty, and guilt, as ower likely she might hae been plunged into."

Sitting down upon a stool at the foot of the bed, she folded her arms upon her bosom, saying within herself, "From this place will I not rise till I am in a better frame of mind;" and so placed, by dint of tearing the veil from the motives of her little temporary spleen against her sister, she compelled herself to be ashamed of them, and to view as blessings the advantages of her sister's lot, while its embarrassments were the necessary consequences of errors long since committed. And thus she fairly vanquished the feeling of pique which she naturally enough entertained, at seeing Effie, so long the object of her care and her pity, soar suddenly so high above her in life, as to reckon amongst the chief objects of her apprehension the risk of their relationship being discovered.

When this unwonted burst of *amour propre* was thoroughly subdued, she walked down to the little parlour where the gentlemen were finishing their game, and heard from the Captain a confirmation of the news intimated in her letter, that the Duke of Argyle was shortly expected at Roseneath.

"He'll find plenty of moor-powts and plack-cock on the moors of Auchingower, and he'll pe nae doubt for taking a late dinner, and a ped at the Manse, as he has done pefore now."

"He has a gude right, Captain," said Jeanie.

"Teil ane better to ony ped in the kintra," answered the Captain. "And ye had petter tell your father, puir pody, to get his beasts a' in order, and put his tamned Cameronian nonsense out o' his head for twa or three days, if he can pe so opliging; for fan I speak to him apout prute pestial, he answers me out o' the Pible, whilk is not using a shentleman weel, unless it pe a person of your cloth, Mr Putler."

No one better understood than Jeanie the merit of the soft answer, which turneth away wrath; and she only smiled, and hoped his Grace would find every thing that was under her father's care to his entire satisfaction.

But the Captain, who had lost the whole postage of the letter at back-gammon, was in the pouting mood not unusual to losers, and which, says the proverb, must be allowed to them.

"And, Master Putler, though you know I never meddle with the things of your kirk-sessions, yet I must pe allowed to say that I will not pe pleased to allow Ailie MacClure of Deepheugh to pe poonished as a witch, in respect she only spaes fortunes, and does not lame, or plind, or pedevil any persons, or coup cadgers' carts, or ony sort of mischief; but only tells people good fortunes, as anent our poats killing so many seals and doug-fishes, whilk is very pleasant to hear."

"The woman," said Butler, "is, I believe, no witch, but a cheat; and it is only on that head that she is summoned to the kirk-session, to cause her to desist in future from practising her impostures upon ignorant persons."

"I do not know," replied the gracious Duncan, "what her practices or her postures are, but I pelieve that if the poys take hould on her to duck her in the Clachan-purn, it will be a very sorry practice— and I pelieve, moreover, that if I come in thirdsman among you at the kirk-sessions, you will pe all in a tamn'd pad posture indeed."

Without noticing this threat, Mr Butler replied, "That he had not attended to the risk of ill usage which the poor woman might undergo at the hands of the rabble, and that he would give her the necessary admonition in private, instead of bringing her before the assembled session."

"This," Duncan said, "was speaking like a reasonable shentleman;" and so the evening passed peaceably off.

Next morning, after the Captain had swallowed his morning draught of Athole brose, and departed in his coach and six, Mrs Butler anew deliberated upon communicating to her husband her sister's letter. But she was deterred by the recollection, that in doing so she would unveil to him the whole of a dreadful secret, of which, perhaps, his public character might render him an unfit depositary. Butler knew indeed that Effie had eloped with that same Robertson who had been a leader in the Porteous mob, and who lay under sentence of death for the robbery at Kirkaldy. But he did not know his identity with George Staunton, a man of birth and fortune, who had now apparently re-assumed his natural rank in society, and no good could arise to any one from imparting it to him. Jeanie had respected Staunton's own confession as sacred, and upon reflection she considered the letter of her sister as equally so, and resolved to mention the contents to no one.

On re-perusing the letter, she could not help observing the staggering and unsatisfactory condition of those who have risen to distinction by undue paths, and the outworks and bulwarks of fiction and falsehood, by which they are under the necessity of surrounding and defending their precarious advantages. But she was not called upon, she thought, to unveil her sister's original history—it would restore no right to any one, for she was usurping none—it would only destroy her happiness, and degrade her in the public estimation. Had she been wise, Jeanie thought she would have chosen seclusion and privacy, in place of public life and gaiety; but the power of choice might not be hers. The money she thought could not be returned without seeming haughty and unkind. She resolved, therefore, upon re-considering this point, to employ it as occasion should serve, either in educating her children better than her own means could compass, or to save it for their future portion. Her sister had enough, was strongly bound to assist Jeanie by any means in her power, and the arrangement was so natural and proper, that it ought not to be declined out of fastidious or romantic delicacy. Jeanie accordingly wrote to her sister, acknowledging her letter, and requesting to hear from her as often as she could. In entering into her own little details of news, chiefly respecting domestic affairs, she experienced a singular vacillation of ideas; for sometimes she apologized for mentioning things unworthy the notice of a lady of rank, and then recollected that every thing which concerned her should be interesting to Effie. Her letter, under the cover of Mr Whiterose, she committed to the post-office at Glasgow, by the intervention of a parishioner who had business at that city.

The next week brought the Duke to Roseneath, and shortly afterwards he intimated his intention of sporting in their neighbourhood, and taking his bed at the Manse, an honour which he had once or twice done to its inmates on former occasions.

Effie proved to be perfectly right in her anticipations. The Duke had hardly set himself down at Mrs Butler's right hand, and taken upon himself the task of carving the excellent "barn-door chucky," which had been selected as the high dish upon this honourable occasion, before he began to speak of Lady Staunton of Willingham in Lincolnshire, and the great noise which her wit and beauty made in London. For much of this Jeanie was, in some measure, prepared— but Effie's wit! that would never have entered into her imagination, being ignorant how exactly raillery in the higher ranks resembles flippancy among their inferiors.

"She has been the ruling belle—the blazing star—the universal toast of the winter," said the Duke; "and is really the most beautiful creature that was seen at court upon the birth-day."

The birth-day! and at court!—Jeanie was annihilated, remembering well her own presentation, all its extraordinary circumstances, and particularly the cause of it.

"I mention this lady particularly to you, Mrs Butler," said the Duke, "because she has something in the sound of her voice, and cast of her countenance, that reminded me of you—not when you look so pale though—you have over fatigued yourself—you must pledge me in a glass of wine."

She did so, and Butler observed, "It was dangerous flattery in his Grace to tell a poor minister's wife that she was like a court-beauty."

"Oho! Mr Butler," said the Duke, "I find you are growing jealous; but it's rather too late in the day, for you know how long I have admired your wife. But seriously, there is betwixt them one of those inexplicable likenesses which we see in countenances, that do not otherwise resemble each other."

"The perilous part of the compliment has flown off," said Mr Butler.

His wife, feeling the awkwardness of silence, forced herself to say, "That, perhaps, the lady might be her countrywoman, and the language might make some resemblance."

"You are quite right," replied the Duke. "She is a Scotchwoman, and speaks with a Scotch accent, and now and then a provincial word drops out so prettily, that it is quite Doric, Mr Butler."

"I should have thought," said the clergyman, "that would have sounded vulgar in the great city."

"Not a bit," replied the Duke; "you must suppose, though, it is not the broad coarse Scotch that is spoke in the Cowgate of Edinburgh, or in the Gorbals. This lady has been very little in Scotland, in fact—She was educated in a convent abroad, and speaks that pure court-Scottish, which was common in my younger days; but it is so generally disused now, that it sounds like a different dialect, entirely distinct from our modern *patois*."

Notwithstanding her anxiety, Jeanie could not help admiring within herself, how the most correct judges of life and manners can be imposed on by their own preconceptions, while the Duke proceeded thus: "She is of the unfortunate house of Winton, I believe; but, being bred abroad, she had missed the opportunity of learning her own pedigree, and was obliged to me for informing her, that she comes of the Setons of Windygoul. I wish you could have seen how prettily she blushed at her own ignorance. Amidst her noble and elegant manners, there is now and then a little touch of bashfulness and conventual rusticity, if I may call it so, that makes her quite enchanting. You see at once the rose that has bloomed untouched amid the chaste precincts of the cloister, Mr Butler."

True to the hint, Mr Butler failed not to start with his

Ut flos in septis secretus nascitur hortis, &c.

while his wife could hardly persuade herself that all this was spoken of Effie Deans, and by so competent a judge as the Duke of Argyle; and had she been acquainted with Catullus, would have thought the fortunes of her sister had reversed the whole passage.

She was, however, determined to obtain some indemnification for the anxious feelings of the moment, by gaining all the intelligence she could; and therefore ventured to make some enquiry about the husband of the lady his Grace admired so much.

"He is very rich," replied the Duke; "of an ancient family, and has good manners; but he is far from being such a favourite as his wife.— Some people say he can be very pleasant—I never saw him so; but should rather judge him reserved, and gloomy and capricious. He was very wild in his youth, they say, and has bad health; yet he is a young good-looking man enough—a great friend of your Lord High Commissioner of the Kirk, Mr Butler."

"Then he is the friend of a very worthy and honourable nobleman," said Butler.

"Does he admire his lady as much as other people do?" said Jeanie, in a low voice.

"Who—Sir George? They say he is very fond of her," said the Duke; "but I observe she trembles a little when he fixes his eye on her, and that is no good sign—But it is strange how I am haunted by this resemblance of your's to Lady Staunton, in look and tone of voice. One would almost swear you were sisters."

Jeanie's distress became uncontroulable, and beyond concealment. The Duke of Argyle was much disturbed, good-naturedly ascribing it to his having unwittingly recalled to her remembrance her family misfortunes. He was too well-bred to attempt to apologize; but hastened to change the subject, and arrange the points of dispute which had occurred betwixt Duncan of Knock and the minister, acknowledging that his worthy substitute was sometimes a little too obstinate, as well as too energetic, in his executive measures.

Mr Butler admitted his general merits; but said, "He would presume to apply to the worthy gentleman the words of the poet to Marrucinus Asinius,

> *Manu——*
> *Non belle uteris in joco atque vino."*

The discourse being thus turned on parish-business, nothing farther occurred that can interest the reader.

Chapter Twelve

> Upon my head they placed a fruitless crown,
> And put a barren sceptre in my gripe,
> Thence to be wrench'd by an unlineal hand,
> No son of mine succeeding.
> *Macbeth*

AFTER THIS PERIOD, but under the most strict precautions against discovery, the sisters corresponded occasionally, exchanging letters about twice every year. Those of Lady Staunton spoke of her husband's health and spirits as being deplorably uncertain; her own seemed also to be sinking, and one of the topics on which she most frequently dwelt, was their want of family. Sir George Staunton, always violent, had taken some aversion at the next heir, whom he suspected of having irritated his friends against him during his absence; and he declared, he would bequeath Willingham and all its lands to a hospital, ere that fetch and carry tell-tale should inherit an acre of it.

"Had he but a child," said the unfortunate wife, "or had that luckless infant survived, it would be some motive for living and for exertion. But Heaven has denied us a blessing which we have not deserved."

Such complaints, in varied form, but turning frequently on the same topic, filled the letters which passed from the spacious but melancholy halls of Willingham, to the quiet and happy parsonage at Knocktarlitie. Years meanwhile rolled on amid these fruitless repinings. John Duke of Argyle and Greenwich died in the year 1743, universally lamented, but by none more than by the Butlers, to whom his benevolence had been so distinguished. He was succeeded by his brother Duke Archibald, with whom they had not the same intimacy; but who continued the protection which his brother had extended towards them. This, indeed, became more necessary than ever; for, after the breaking out and suppression of the rebellion in 1745, the peace of the country, adjacent to the Highlands, was considerably disturbed. Marauders, or men that had been driven to that desperate mode of life, quartered themselves in the fastnesses nearest to the Lowlands, which were their scene of plunder; and there is scarce a glen in the romantic and now peaceable highlands of Perth, Stirling, and Dumbarton shires, where one or more did not take up their residence.

The prime pest of the parish of Knocktarlitie was a certain Donacha Dhu na Dunaigh, or Black Duncan the Mischievous, whom we have already casually mentioned. This fellow had been originally a tinkler or *caird*, many of whom stroll about these districts; but when all police was disorganized by the civil war, he threw up his profession, and from half thief became whole robber; and being generally at the head of three or four active young fellows, and he himself artful, bold, and well acquainted with the passes, he plied his new profession with emolument to himself, and infinite plague to the country.

All were convinced that Duncan of Knock could have put down his namesake Donacha any morning he had a mind; for there were in the parish a set of stout young men, who had joined Argyle's banner in the war under our old friend, and behaved very well upon several occasions. And as for their leader, as no one doubted his courage, it was generally supposed that Donacha had found out the mode of conciliating his favour, a thing not very uncommon in that age and country. This was the more readily believed, as David Deans's cattle (being the property of the Duke) were left untouched on the night when the minister's cows were carried off by the thieves. Another attempt was made to renew the same act of rapine, and the cattle were in the act of being driven off, when Butler, laying his profession aside in a case of such necessity, put himself at the head of some of his neighbours, and rescued the creagh, an exploit at which Deans attended on the occasion, notwithstanding his extreme old age, mounted on a Highland poney, and girded with an old broadsword, likening himself (for he failed not to arrogate the whole merit of the expedition) to David, the son of Jesse, when he recovered the spoil of Ziklag from the Amalekites. This spirited behaviour had so far a good effect, that Donacha Dhu na Dunaigh kept his distance for some time to come; and, though his distant exploits were frequently spoken of, he did not exercise any depredations in that part of the country. He continued to flourish, and to be heard of occasionally, until the year 1751, when, if the fear of the second David had kept him in check, fate released him from that restraint, for the venerable patriarch of Saint Leonard's was in that year gathered to his fathers.

David Deans died full of years and of honour. He is believed, for the exact time of his birth is not known, to have lived upwards of ninety years; for he used to speak of events, as falling under his own knowledge, which happened about the time of the battle of Bothwell-Bridge. It was said that he even bore arms there; for once, when a drunken Jacobite laird wished for a Bothwell-Brigg whig, that "he might stow the lugs out of his head," David informed him with a peculiar austerity of countenance, that if he liked to try such a prank, there was ane at his elbow; and it required the interference of Butler to preserve the peace.

He expired in the arms of his beloved daughter, thankful for all the blessings which Providence had vouchsafed to him while in this valley of strife and trial—and thankful also for the trials he had been visited with; having found them, he said, needful to mortify that spiritual pride and confidence in his own gifts, which was the side on which the wily Enemy did most sorely beset him. He prayed in the most affecting manner for Jeanie, her husband, and her family, and that her affectionate duty to the puir auld man might purchase her length of days here, and happiness hereafter; then, in a pathetic petition, too well understood by those who knew his family circumstances, he besought the Shepherd of souls, while gathering his flock, not to forget the little one that had strayed from the fold, and even then might be in the hands of the ravening wolf.—He prayed for the national Jerusalem, that peace might be in her land and prosperity in her palaces—for the welfare of the honourable House of Argyle, and for the conversion of Duncan of Knockdunder. After this he was silent, being exhausted, nor did he again utter any thing distinctly. He was heard indeed to mutter something about national defections, right-hand extremes, and left-hand fallings off; but, as May Hettly observed, his head was carried at the time: and it seems probable that these expressions occurred to him merely out of general habit, and that he died in the full spirit of charity with all men. About an hour afterwards he slept in the Lord.

Notwithstanding her father's advanced age, his death was a severe shock to Mrs Butler. Much of her time had been dedicated to attending to his health and his wishes, and she felt as if part of her business in the world was ended, when the good old man was no more. His wealth, which came nearly to fifteen hundred pounds, in disposable capital, served to raise the fortunes of the family at the Manse. How to dispose of this sum for the best advantage of his family, was matter of anxious consideration to Butler.

"If we put it on heritable band, we will maybe lose the interest (for there's that band ower Lounsbeck's land, your father could neither get principal nor interest for't); if into the funds, we will maybe lose the principal and all, as many did in the South-sea scheme. The little estate of Craigsture is in the market—it lies within two miles of the Manse, and Knock says his Grace has no thought to buy it. But they ask £2,500, and they may, for it is worth the money; and were I to borrow the balance, the creditor might call it up suddenly, or in case of my death my family might be distressed."

"And so, if we had mair siller, we might buy that bonnie pasture-ground, where the grass comes sae early?" asked Jeanie.

"Certainly, my dear; and Knockdunder, who is a good judge, is strongly advising me to it.—To be sure it is his nephew that is selling."

"Aweel, Reuben," said Jeanie, "ye maun just look up a text in Scripture, as ye did when ye wanted siller before—just look up a text in the Bible."

"Ah, Jeanie," said Butler, laughing and pressing her hand kindly at the same time, "the best people in these times can only work miracles once."

"We will see," said Jeanie composedly; and, going to the closet in which she kept her honey, her sugar, her pots of jelly, her vials of the more useful medicines, and which served her, in short, as a sort of store-room, she jangled vials and gallipots, till, from out the darkest nook, well flanked by a triple row of bottles and jars, which she was under the necessity of displacing, she brought a cracked brown cann, with a piece of leather tied over the top. Its contents seemed to be written papers, thrust in disorder into this uncommon secretaire. But from amongst these Jeanie brought an old clasped Bible, which had been David Deans's companion in his early wanderings, and which he had given to his daughter when the failure of his eyes had compelled him to use one of a larger print. This she gave to Butler, who had been

looking at her motions with some surprise, and desired him to see
what that book could do for him. He opened the clasps, and to his
astonishment a parcel of £50 bank-notes dropped out from betwixt
the leaves, where they had been separately lodged, and fluttered upon
the floor. "I didna think to hae tauld ye o' my wealth, Reuben," said his
wife, smiling at his surprise, "till on my death-bed, or maybe at some
family pinch; but it wad be better laid out on yon bonny grass-holms,
than lying useless here in the wame of the auld pigg."

"How on earth came ye be that siller, Jeanie?—Why, here is more
than a thousand pounds," said Butler, lifting up and counting the
notes.

"If it were ten thousand, it's a' honestly come by," said Jeanie; "and
troth I kenna how muckle there is o't, but it's a' there that ever I got.—
And as for how I came by it, Reuben—it's weel come by, and honestly,
as I said before—And it's mair folk's secret than mine, or ye wad hae
kenned about it lang syne; and as for ony thing else, I am not free to
answer mair questions about it, and ye maun just ask me nane."

"Answer me but one," said Butler. "Is it all freely and indisputably
your own property, to dispose of as you think fit?—Is it possible no
one has a claim in so large a sum except you?"

"It *was* mine, free to dispose of it as I like," answered Jeanie; "and I
have disposed of it already, for now it is yours, Reuben—You are
Bible Butler now, as weel as your forbear, that my puir father had sic
an ill will at. Only if ye like, I wad wish Femie to get a gude share o't
when you are gane."

"Certainly, it shall be as you chuse—But who on earth ever pitched
on such a hiding-place for temporal treasures?"

"That is just ane o' my auld-fashioned gates, as you ca' them,
Reuben. I thought if Donacha Dhu was to make an outbreak upon us,
the Bible was the last thing in the house he wad meddle wi'—but an'
ony mair siller should drap in, as is not unlikely, I shall e'en pay it ower
to ye, and ye may lay it out your ain way."

"And I positively must not ask you how you have come by all this
money?" said the clergyman.

"Indeed, Reuben, you must not; for if you were asking me very sair
I wad maybe tell you, and then I am sure I would do wrang."

"But tell me," said Butler, "is it any thing that distresses your own
mind?"

"There is baith weal and woe come aye wi' warld's gear, Reuben;
but ye maun ask me naething mair—This siller binds me to naething,
and can never be speered back again."

"Surely," said Mr Butler, when he had again counted over the
money, as if to assure himself that the notes were real, "there was

never man in the world had a wife like mine—a blessing seems to follow her."

"Never," said Jeanie, "since the enchanted princess in the bairns' fairy tale, that kamed gold nobles out o' the tae side of her haffit locks, and Dutch dollars out o' the tother. But gang away now, minister, and put by the siller, and dinna keep the notes wampishing in your hand that gate, or I will wish them in the brown pigg again, for fear we get a black cast about them—we're ower near the hills in these times to be thought to hae siller in the house. And, besides, ye maun gree wi' Knockdunder, that has the selling o' the lands; and dinna you be simple and let him ken o' this windfa', but keep him to the very barest penny, as if ye had to borrow siller to mak the price up."

In the last admonition Jeanie showed distinctly, that, although she did not understand how to secure the money which came into her hands otherwise than by saving and hoarding it, yet she had some part of her father David's shrewdness, even upon worldly subjects. And Reuben Butler was a prudent man, and went and did even as his wife had advised him.

The news quickly went abroad into the parish that the minister had bought Craigsture; and some wished him joy, and some "were sorry it had gane out of the auld name." However, his clerical brethren understanding that he was under the necessity of going to Edinburgh about the ensuing Whitsunday, to get together David Deans's cash to make up the purchase-money of his new acquisition, took the opportunity to name him their delegate to the General Assembly, or Convocation of the Scottish Church, which takes place yearly in the latter end of the month of May.

Chapter Thirteen

> But who is this? what thing of sea or land—
> Female of sex it seems—
> That so bedeck'd, ornate, and gay,
> Comes this way sailing?
>
> MILTON

NOT LONG AFTER the incident of the Bible and the bank-notes, Fortune showed that she could surprise Mrs Butler as well as her husband. The minister, in order to accomplish the various pieces of business, which his unwonted visit to Edinburgh rendered necessary, had been under the necessity of setting out from home in the latter end of the month of February, concluding justly, that he would find the space betwixt his departure and the term of Whitsunday (15th May) short enough for the purpose of bringing forward those various

debtors of old David Deans, out of whose purses a considerable part
of the price of his new purchase was to be made good.

Jeanie was thus in the unwonted situation of inhabiting a lonely
house, and she felt it yet more solitary from the death of the good old
man, who used to divide her cares with her husband. Her children
were her principal resource, and to them she paid constant attention.

It happened, a day or two after Butler's departure, that, while she
was engaged in some domestic duties, she heard a dispute among the
young folks, which, being maintained with obstinacy, appeared to call
for her interference. All came to their natural umpire with their complaints. Femie, not yet ten years old, charged Davie and Reubie with
an attempt to take away her book by force; and David and Reuben
replied, the elder, "That it was not a book for Femie to read," and
Reuben, "That it was about a bad woman."

"Where did ye get the book, ye little hempie?" said Mrs Butler.
"How dare ye touch papa's books when he is away?"

But the little lady, holding fast a printed sheet of crumpled paper,
declared, "It was nane o' papa's books, and May Hettly had taken it aff
the muckle cheese which came from Inverara;" for, as was very natural to suppose, a friendly intercourse, with interchange of mutual
civilities, was kept up from time to time between Mrs Dolly Dutton,
now Mrs MacCorkindale, and her former friends.

Jeanie took the subject of contention out of the child's hand, to
satisfy herself of the propriety of her studies; but how much was she
struck when she read upon the title of the broadside sheet, "Last
Speech and Execution of Margaret Murdockson, and of the barbarous Murder of her Daughter, Magdalen or Madge Murdockson,
called Madge Wildfire; and of her pious Conversation with his Reverence Arch-deacon Fleming." It was, indeed, one of those papers
which Archibald had bought at Longtown, when he monopolized the
pedlar's stock, which Dolly had thrust into her trunk out of sheer
economy. One or two copies, it seems, had remained in her reposit-
ories at Inverara, till she chanced to need them in packing a cheese,
which, as a very superior production, was sent, in the way of civil
challenge, to the dairy at Knocktarlitie.

The title of this paper, so strangely fallen into the very hands from
which, in well-meant respect to her feelings, it had been so long
detained, was of itself sufficiently startling; but the narrative itself was
so interesting, that Jeanie, shaking herself loose from the children, ran
upstairs to her own apartment, and bolted the door, to peruse it
without interruption.

The narrative, which appeared to have been drawn up, or at least
corrected, by the clergyman who attended this unhappy woman,

stated the crime for which she suffered to have been "her active part in that atrocious robbery and murder, committed two years since near Haltwhistle, for which the notorious Frank Levitt was committed for trial at Lancaster assizes. It was supposed the evidence of the accomplice, Thomas Tuck, commonly called Tyburn Tom, upon which the woman had been convicted, would weigh equally heavily against him; although many were inclined to think it was Tuck himself who had struck the fatal blow, according to the dying statement of Meg Murdockson."

After a circumstantial account of the crime for which she suffered, there was a brief sketch of Margaret's life. It was stated, that she was a Scotchwoman by birth, and married a soldier in the Cameronian regiment—that she had long followed the camp, and doubtless acquired in fields of battle, and similar scenes, that ferocity and love of plunder for which she had been afterwards distinguished—that her husband, having obtained his discharge, became servant to a beneficed clergyman of high situation and character in Lincolnshire, and that she acquired the confidence and esteem of that honourable family. She had lost this many years after her husband's death, it was stated, in consequence of conniving at the irregularities of her daughter with the heir of the family, added to the suspicious circumstances attending the birth of a child, which was strongly suspected to have met with foul play, in order to preserve, if possible, the girl's reputation. After this, she had led a wandering life both in England and Scotland, under colour sometimes of telling fortunes, sometimes of driving a trade in smuggled wares, but, in fact, receiving stolen goods, and occasionally actively joining in the exploits by which they were obtained. Many of her crimes she had boasted of after conviction, and there was only one circumstance for which she seemed to feel a mixture of joy and occasional compunction. When she was residing in the suburbs of Edinburgh during the preceding summer, a girl, who had been seduced by one of her confederates, was entrusted to her charge, and in her house delivered of a male infant. Her daughter, whose mind was in a state of derangement ever since she had lost her own child, according to the criminal's account, carried off the poor girl's infant, taking it for her own, of the reality of whose death she at times could not be persuaded.

Margaret Murdockson stated, that she, for some time, believed her daughter had actually destroyed the infant in her mad fits, and that she gave the father to understand so, but afterwards learned that a female stroller had got it from her. She showed some compunction at having separated mother and child, especially as the mother had nearly suffered death, being condemned, on the Scotch law, for the supposed murther of her infant. When it was asked what possible interest she could have had in exposing the unfortunate girl to suffer for a crime she had not committed, she asked, if they thought she was going to put her own daughter into trouble to save another? she did not know what the Scotch law would have done to her for carrying the child away. This answer was by no means satisfactory to the clergyman, and he discovered, by close examination, that she had a deep and revengeful hatred against the young person whom she had thus injured. But the paper intimated, that, whatever besides she had communicated upon this subject, was confided by her in private to the worthy and reverend Arch-Deacon who had bestowed such particular pains in affording her spiritual assistance. The broadside went on to intimate, that after her execution, of which the particulars were given, her daughter, the insane person mentioned more than once, and who was generally known by the name of Madge Wildfire, had been very ill used by the populace, under the belief that she was a sorceress, and an accomplice in her mother's crimes, and had been with difficulty rescued by the prompt interference of the police.

Such (for we omit moral reflections, and all that may seem unnecessary to the explanation of our story,) was the tenor of the broadside. To Mrs Butler it contained intelligence of the highest importance, since it seemed to afford unequivocal proof of her sister's innocence respecting the crime for which she had so nearly suffered. It is true, neither she nor her husband, nor even her father, had ever believed her capable of touching her infant with an unkind hand when in possession of her reason; but there was a darkness on the subject, and what might have happened in a moment of insanity was dreadful to think upon. Besides, whatever was their own conviction, they had no means of establishing Effie's innocence to the world, which, according to the tenor of this fugitive publication, was now at length completely manifested by the dying confession of the person chiefly interested in concealing it.

After thanking God for a discovery so dear to her feelings, Mrs Butler began to consider what use she should make of it. To have shown it to her husband would have been her first impulse, but, besides that he was absent from home, and the matter too delicate to be the subject of correspondence by an indifferent penwoman, Mrs Butler recollected that he was not possessed of the information necessary to form a judgment upon the occasion, and that, adhering to the rule which she had considered as most advisable, she had best transmit the information immediately to her sister, and leave her to adjust with her husband the mode in which they should avail themselves of it. Accordingly she dispatched a special messenger to Glasgow, with a packet, inclosing the broadside Confession of Margaret Murdockson, addressed, as usual, under cover, to Mr Whiterose of York. She expected, with anxiety, an answer, but none arrived in the usual course of post, and she was left to imagine how many various causes might account for Lady Staunton's silence. She began to be half sorry that she had parted with the printed paper, both for fear of its having fallen into bad hands, and from the desire of regaining the document, which might be essential to establish her sister's innocence. She was even doubting whether she had not better commit the whole matter to her husband's consideration, when other incidents occurred to divert her purpose.

Jeanie (she is a favourite, and we beg her pardon for still using the familiar title) had walked down to the sea-side with her children one morning after breakfast, when the boys, whose sight was more discriminating than her's, exclaimed, that "the Captain's coach and six was coming right for the shore, with ladies in't." Jeanie instinctively bent her eyes on the approaching boat, and became soon sensible that there were two females in the stern, seated beside the gracious Duncan, who acted as pilot. It was a point of politeness to walk towards the landing-place, in order to receive them, especially as she saw that the Captain of Knockdunder was upon honour and ceremony. His piper was in the bow of the boat, sending forth music, of which one half sounded better that the other was drowned by the waves and the breeze. Moreover, he himself had his brigadier wig newly frizzed, his bonnet (he had abjured the cocked hat) decorated with Saint George's red cross, his uniform mounted as a captain of militia, the Duke's flag with the boar's head displayed—all intimated parade and gala.

As Mrs Butler approached the landing-place, she observed the Captain hand the ladies ashore with marks of great attention, and the party advanced towards her, the Captain a few steps before the two ladies, of whom the latter and elder leaned on the shoulder of the other, who seemed to be an attendant or servant.

As they met, Duncan, in his best, most important, and deepest tone of Highland civility, "pegged leave to introduce to Mrs Putler, Lady—eh—eh—I hae forgotten your leddyship's name."

"Never mind my name, sir," said the lady; "I trust Mrs Butler will be at no loss. The Duke's letter"——And, as she observed Mrs Butler looked confused, she said again to Duncan, something sharply, "Did you not send the letter last night, sir?"

"In troth and I didna, and I crave your leddyship's pardon; but you see, matam, I thought it would do as weel to-tay, pecause Mrs Putler is never taen out o' sorts—never—and the coach was out fishing—and the gig was gaen to Greenock for a cag of prandy—and——Put here's his Grace's letter."

"Give it me, sir," said the lady, taking it out of his hand; "since you have not found it convenient to do me the favour to send it before me, I will deliver it myself."

Mrs Butler looked with great attention, and a certain dubious feeling of deep interest on the lady, who thus expressed herself with authority over the man of authority, and to whose mandates he seemed to submit, resigning the letter with a "Just as your leddyship is pleased to order it."

The lady was rather above the middle size, beautifully made, though something *en bon point*, with a hand and arm exquisitely formed. Her manner was easy, dignified, and commanding, and seemed to evince high birth and the habits of elevated society. She wore a travelling dress—a grey beaver hat, and a veil of Flanders lace. Two footmen, in rich liveries, who got out of the barge, and lifted out a trunk and a portmanteau, appeared to belong to her suite.

"As you did not receive the letter, madam, which should have served for my introduction—for I presume you are Mrs Butler—I will not present it to you till you are so good as to admit me into your house without it—so, if you please, you will have the goodness to admit me—as a friend of the Duke's."

"To pe sure, matam," said Knockdunder, "ye canna doubt Mrs Putler will do that.—Mrs Putler, this is Lady—Lady—these tamn'd Southern names rin out o' my hieland head like a stane trowling down hill—put I pelieve she is a Scottish woman porn—the mair our credit —and I presume her leddyship is of the house of"——

"The Duke of Argyle knows my family very well, sir," said the lady, in a tone which seemed designed to silence Duncan, or, at any rate, which had that effect completely.

There was something about the whole of this stranger's address, and tone and manner, which acted upon Jeanie's feelings like the illusions of a dream, that teaze us with a puzzling approach to reality. Something there was of her sister in the gait and manner of the stranger, as well as in the sound of her voice, and something also, when, lifting her veil, she shewed features, to which, changed as they were in expression and in complexion, she could not but attach many remembrances.

The stranger was turned of thirty certainly; but so well were her personal charms assisted by the power of dress, and arrangement of ornament, that she might well have passed for one-and-twenty. And her behaviour was so steady and so composed, that as often as Mrs Butler perceived anew some point of resemblance to her unfortunate sister, so often the sustained self-command and absolute composure of the stranger destroyed the ideas which began to arise in her imagination. She led the way silently towards the Manse, lost in a confusion of reflections, and trusting the letter with which she was to be there entrusted, would afford her satisfactory explanation of what was a most puzzling and embarrassing scene.

The lady maintained in the meanwhile the manners of a stranger of rank. She admired the various points of view like one who has studied nature, and the best representations of art. At length she took notice of the children.

"These are two fine young mountaineers—Your's, madam, I presume?"

Jeanie replied in the affirmative. The stranger sighed, and sighed once more as they were presented to her by name.

"Come here, Femie," said Mrs Butler, "and hold your head up."

"What is your daughter's name, madam?" said the lady.

"Euphemia, madam," answered Mrs Butler.

"I thought the ordinary Scottish contraction of the name had been Effie?" replied the stranger in a tone which went to Jeanie's heart; for in that single word there was more of her sister—more of *lang syne* ideas—than in all the reminiscences which her own heart had anticipated, or the features and manner of the stranger had suggested.

When they reached the Manse, the lady gave Mrs Butler the letter which she had taken out of the hands of Knockdunder; and as she gave it she pressed her hand, adding aloud, "Perhaps, madam, you will have the goodness to get me a little milk."

"And me a drap of the grey-peard, if you please, Mrs Putler," added Duncan.

Mrs Butler withdrew, but deputing to May Hettly and to David the supply of the strangers' wants, she hastened into her own room to read the letter. The envelope was addressed in the Duke of Argyle's hand, and requested Mrs Butler's attentions and civility to a lady of rank, a particular friend of his late brother, Lady Staunton of Willingham, who being recommended to drink goats' whey by the physicians, was to honour the Lodge at Roseneath with her residence, while her husband made a short tour in Scotland. But within the same cover, which had been given to Lady Staunton unsealed, was a letter from that lady, intended to prepare her sister for meeting her, and which, but for the Captain's negligence, she ought to have received on the preceding evening. It stated that the news in Jeanie's last letter had been so interesting to her husband, that he was determined to enquire farther into the confession made at Carlisle, and the fate of that poor innocent, and that as he had been in some degree successful, she had by the most earnest entreaties extorted rather than obtained his permission, under promise of observing the most strict incognito, to spend a week or two with her sister, or in her neighbourhood, while he was prosecuting researches, to which (though it appeared to her very vainly) he seemed to attach some hope of success.

There was a postscript, desiring that Jeanie would trust to Lady S. the management of their intercourse, and be contented with assenting to what she should propose. After reading and again reading the letter, Mrs Butler hurried down stairs, divided betwixt the fear of betraying her secret, and the desire to throw herself upon her sister's neck. Effie received her with a glance at once affectionate and cautionary, and immediately proceeded to speak.

"I have been telling Mr ——, Captain ——, this gentleman, Mrs Butler, that if you could accommodate me with an apartment in your house, and a place for Ellis to sleep, and for the two men, it would suit me better than the Lodge, which his Grace has so kindly placed at my disposal. I am advised I should reside as near where the goats feed as possible."

"I have peen assuring my Lady, Mrs Putler," said Duncan, "that though it could not discommode you to receive any of his Grace's visitors or mine, yet she had mooch petter stay at the Lodge; and for the gaits, the creatures can be fetched there, in respect it is mair fitting they suld wait upon her Leddyship, than she upon the like of them."

"By no means derange the goats for me," said Lady Staunton; "I am certain the milk must be much better here." And this she said with languid negligence, as one whose slightest intimation of humour is to bear down all argument.

Mrs Butler hastened to intimate, that her house, such as it was, was heartily at the disposal of Lady Staunton; but the Captain continued to remonstrate.

"The Duke," he said, "had written"—

"I will settle all that with his Grace"—

"And there were the things had been sent down frae Glasco—"

"Any thing necessary might be sent over to the Parsonage—She would beg the favour of Mrs Butler to shew her an apartment, and of the Captain to have her remaining trunks, &c. sent over from Roseneath."

So she curtsied off poor Duncan, who departed, saying in his secret soul, "Cot tamn her English impudence!—she takes possession of the minister's house as an it were her ain—and speaks to shentlemens as if they were pounden servants, an pe tamn'd to her!—And there's the deer that was shot too—but we will send it ower to the Manse, whilk will pe put civil, seeing I hae prought worthy Mrs Putler sic a fliskmahoy"—And with these kind intentions, he went to the shore to give his orders accordingly.

In the meantime, the meeting of the sisters was as affectionate as it was extraordinary, and each evinced her feelings in the way proper to her character. Jeanie was so much overcome by wonder, and even by awe, that her feelings were deep, stunning, and almost overpowering. Effie, on the other hand, wept, laughed, sobbed, screamed, and clapped her hands for joy, all in the space of five minutes, giving way at once, and without reserve, to a natural excessive vivacity of temper, which no one, however, knew better how to restrain under the rules of artificial breeding.

After an hour had passed like a moment in their expressions of mutual affection, Lady Staunton observed the Captain walking with impatient steps below the window. "That tiresome Highland fool has returned upon our hands," she said. "I will pray him to grace us with his absence."

"Hout no! hout no!" said Mrs Butler, in a tone of entreaty; "ye maunna affront the Captain."

"Affront?" said Lady Staunton; "nobody is ever affronted at what I do or say, my dear. However, I shall endure him, since you think it proper."

The Captain was accordingly graciously requested by Lady Staunton to remain during dinner. During this visit his studious and punctilious complaisance towards the lady of rank was happily contrasted by the cavalier air of civil familiarity in which he indulged towards the minister's wife.

"I have not been able to persuade Mrs Butler," said Lady Staunton to the Captain, during an interval when Jeanie had left the parlour, "to let me talk of making any recompence for storming her house, and garrisoning it in the way I have done."

"Doubtless, matam," said the Captain, "it wad ill pecome Mrs Putler, wha is a very decent pody, to make any such sharge to a lady who comes from my house, or his Grace's, which is the same thing.— And, speaking of garrisons, in the year forty-five, I was poot with a garrison of twenty of my lads in the house of Inver-Garry, whilk had near been unhappy for"—

"I beg your pardon, sir—But I wish I could think on some way of indemnifying this good lady."

"O, no need of intemnifying at all—no trouble for her, nothing at all —So, peing in the house of Inver-Garry, and the people about being uncanny, I doubted the warst, and"—

"Do you happen to know, sir," said Lady Staunton, "if any of these two lads, these young Butlers, I mean, show any turn for the army?"

"Could not say, indeed, my leddy," replied Knockdunder—"So, I knowing the people to be unchancy, and not to lippen to, and hearing a pibroch in the wood, I pegan to pid my lads look to their flints, and then"—

"For," said Lady Staunton, with the most ruthless disregard to the narration which she mangled by these interruptions, "if that should be the case, it would cost Sir George but the asking a pair of colours for one of them at the War-office, since we have always supported government, and never had occasion to trouble ministers."

"And if you please, my leddy," said Duncan, who began to find some savour in this proposal, "as I hae a braw weel grown lad of a nevoy, ca'd Duncan MacGilligan, that is as pig as paith the Putler pairns putten thegether, Sir George could ask a pair for him at the same time, and it wad pe put ae asking for a'."

Lady Staunton only answered this hint with a well-bred stare, which gave no sort of encouragement.

Jeanie, who now returned, was lost in amazement at the wonderful difference betwixt the helpless and despairing girl, whom she had seen stretched on a flock-bed in a dungeon, expecting a violent and disgraceful death, and last as a forlorn exile upon the midnight beach, with the elegant, well-bred, beautiful woman before her. The features, now that her sister's veil was laid aside, did not appear so extremely different, as the whole manner, expression, look, and bearing. In outside show, Lady Staunton seemed completely a creature too soft and fair for sorrow to have touched; so much accustomed to have all her whims complied with by those around her, that she seemed to expect she should even be saved the trouble of forming them; and so totally unacquainted with contradiction, that she did not even use the tone of self-will, since to breathe a wish was to have it fulfilled. She made no ceremony in ridding herself of Duncan so soon as the evening approached; but complimented him out of the house under pretext of fatigue, with the utmost *non-chalance*.

When they were alone, her sister could not help expressing her wonder at the self-possession with which Lady Staunton sustained her part.

"I dare say you are surprised at it," said Lady Staunton, composedly; "for you, my dear Jeanie, have been truth itself from your cradle upwards; but you must remember that I am a Lie of fifteen years' standing, and therefore must by this time be used to my character."

In fact, during the feverish tumult of feelings excited during the two or three first days, Mrs Butler thought her sister's manner was completely contradictory of the desponding tone which pervaded her correspondence. She was moved to tears, indeed, by the sight of her father's grave, marked by a modest stone, recording his piety and integrity. But lighter impressions and associations had also power over her. She amused herself with visiting the dairy, in which she had so long been assistant, and was so near discovering herself to May Hettly, by betraying her acquaintance with the celebrated receipt for Dunlop cheese, that she compared herself to Bedreddin Hassan, whom the vizier, his father-in-law, discovered by his superlative skill in composing cream-tarts with pepper in them. But when the novelty of such avocations ceased to amuse her, she showed to her sister but too plainly, that the gaudy colouring with which she veiled her unhappiness afforded as little real comfort, as the gay uniform of the soldier when it is drawn over his mortal wound. There were moods and moments, in which her despondence seemed to exceed even that which she herself had described in her letters, and which too well convinced Mrs Butler how little her sister's lot, which in appearance was so brilliant, was, in reality, to be envied.

There was one source, however, from which Lady Staunton derived a pure degree of pleasure. Gifted in every particular with a higher degree of imagination than that of her sister, she was an admirer of the beauties of nature, a taste which compensates many evils to those who happen to enjoy it. Here her character of a fine lady stopped short, where she ought to have

> Scream'd at ilk cleugh, and screech'd at ilka how,
> As loud as she had seen the worrie-cow.

On the contrary, with the two boys for her guides, she undertook long and fatiguing walks among the neighbouring mountains, to visit glens, lakes, water-falls, and whatever scenes of natural wonder or beauty lay concealed among their recesses. It is Wordsworth, I think, who, talking of an old man under difficulties, remarks, with singular attention to nature,

> ——whether it was care that spurred him,
> God only knows; but to the very last,
> He had the lightest foot in Ennerdale.

In the same manner, languid, listless, and unhappy, at times even indicating something which approached near to contempt of the homely accommodations of her sister's house, although she instantly endeavoured, by a thousand kindnesses, to atone for such ebullitions of spleen, Lady Staunton appeared to feel interest and energy while in the open air, and amid the mountain landscapes, and in society with the two boys, whose ears she delighted with stories of what she had seen in other countries, and what she had to show them at Willingham Manor. And they, on the other hand, exerted themselves in doing the

honours of Dumbartonshire to the lady who seemed so kind, insomuch that there was scarce a glen in the neighbouring hills to which
they did not introduce her.

Upon one of these excursions, while Reuben was otherwise
engaged, David alone acted as Lady Staunton's guide, and promised
to show her a cascade in the hills, grander and higher than any they
had yet visited. It was a walk of five long miles, and over rough ground,
varied, however, and cheered by mountain views, and peeps now of
the Frith and its islands, now of distant lakes, now of rocks and
precipices. The scene itself, too, when they reached it, amply
rewarded the labour of the walk. A single shoot carried a considerable
stream over the face of a black rock, which contrasted strangely in
contour with the white foam of the cascade, and fell down to the depth
of about seventy feet when a huge rock intercepted the view of the
bottom of the fall. The water, wheeling out at great depth, swept
round the crag, which thus bounded their view, and tumbled down the
rocky glen in a torrent of foam. Those who love nature always desire to
penetrate into its utmost recesses, and Lady Staunton asked David
whether there was not some mode of gaining a view of the abyss at the
foot of the fall. He said that he knew a station on a shelf on the further
side of the intercepting rock, from which the whole waterfall was
visible, but the road to it was steep and slippery and dangerous. Bent,
however, on gratifying her curiosity, she desired him to lead the way;
and accordingly he did so over crag and stone, anxiously pointing out
to her the resting-places where she ought to step, for their mode of
advancing soon ceased to be walking, and became scrambling.

In this manner, clinging like sea-birds to the face of the rock, they
were enabled at length to turn round it, and came full in front of the
fall, which here had a most tremendous aspect, boiling, roaring, and
thundering with unceasing din, into a black cauldron, a hundred feet
at least below them, which resembled the crater of a volcano. The din,
the dashing of the waters, which gave an unsteady appearance to all
around them, the trembling even of the huge crag on which they
stood, the precariousness of their footing, for there was scarce room
for them to stand on the shelf of rock which they had thus attained,
had so powerful an effect on the senses and imagination of Lady
Staunton, that she called out to David she was falling, and would in
fact have dropped from the crag had he not caught hold of her. The
boy was bold and stout of his age—still he was but fourteen years old,
and as his assistance gave no confidence to Lady Staunton, she felt her
situation become really perilous. The chance was, that, in the appalling novelty of the circumstances, he might have caught the infection
of her panic, in which case it is likely that both must have perished.

She now screamed with terror, though without hope of calling any one to her assistance. To her amazement, the scream was answered by a whistle from above, of a tone so clear and shrill, that it was heard even amid the noise of the waterfall.

In this moment of terror and perplexity, a human face, black, and having grizzled hair hanging down over the forehead and the cheeks, and mixing with moustaches and a beard of the same colour, and as much matted and tangled, looked down on them from a broken part of the rock above.

"It is The Enemy!" said the boy, who had nearly become incapable of supporting Lady Staunton.

"No, no," she exclaimed, inaccessible to supernatural terrors, and restored to the presence of mind of which she had been deprived by the danger of her situation, "it is a man—for God's sake, my friend, help us!"

The face glared at them, but made no answer; in a second or two afterwards, another, that of a young lad, appeared beside the first, equally swart and begrimed, but having tangled black hair, descending in elf locks, which gave an air of wildness and ferocity to the whole expression of the countenance. Lady Staunton repeated her entreaties, clinging to the rock with more energy, as she found that from the superstitious terror of her guide he became incapable of supporting her. Her words were probably drowned in the roar of the falling stream, for, though she observed the lips of the younger being whom she supplicated move as he spoke in reply, not a word reached her ear.

A moment afterwards it appeared he had not mistaken the nature of her supplication, which, indeed, was easy to be understood from her situation and gestures. The younger apparition disappeared, and immediately after lowered a ladder of twisted osiers, about eight feet in length, and made signs to David to hold it fast while the lady ascended. Despair gives courage, and finding herself in this fearful predicament, Lady Staunton did not hesitate to risk the ascent by the precarious means which this accommodation afforded; and, carefully assisted by the person who had thus providentially come to her aid, she reached the summit in safety. She did not, however, even look around her until she saw her nephew lightly and actively follow her example, although there was now no one below to hold the ladder fast. When she saw him safe she looked round, and could not help shuddering at the place and company in which she found herself.

They were on a sort of platform of rock, surrounded on every side by precipices, or overhanging cliffs, and which it would have been scarce possible for any research to have discovered, as it did not seem to be commanded by any accessible position. It was partly covered by a huge fragment of stone, which, having fallen from the cliffs above, had been intercepted by others in its descent, and jammed so as to serve for a sloping roof to the further part of the broad shelf or platform on which they stood. A quantity of withered moss and leaves, strewed beneath this rude and wretched shelter, shewed the lairs,—they could not be termed the beds,—of those who dwelt in this eyrie, for it deserved no other name. Of these, two were before Lady Staunton. One, the same who had afforded such timely assistance, stood upright before them, a tall, lathy, young savage; his dress a tattered plaid and philabeg, no shoes, no stockings, no hat or bonnet, the place of the last being supplied by his hair twisted and matted like the *glibbe* of the ancient wild Irish, and, like theirs, forming a natural thickset, stout enough to bear off the cut of a sword. Yet the eyes of the lad were keen and sparkling; his gesture free and noble, like that of all savages. He took little notice of David Butler, but gazed with wonder on Lady Staunton, as a being different probably in dress, and superior in beauty, to any thing he had ever beheld. The old man, whose face they had first seen, remained recumbent in the same posture as when he had first looked down on them, only his face was turned towards them as he lay and looked up with a lazy and listless apathy, which belied the general expression of his dark and rugged features. He seemed a very tall man, but was scarce better clad than the younger. He had on a loose Lowland great coat, and ragged tartan trews or pantaloons.

All around looked singularly wild and unpropitious. Beneath the brow of the recumbent rock was a charcoal fire, on which there was a still working, with bellows, pincers, hammers, a moveable anvil, and other smith's tools; three guns, with two or three sacks and barrels, were disposed against the wall of rock, under shelter of the superincumbent crag; a dirk or two, swords, and a Lochaber-axe, lay scattered around the fire, of which the red glare cast a ruddy tinge on the precipitous foam and mist of the cascade. The lad, when he had satisfied his curiosity with staring at Lady Staunton, fetched an earthen jar and a horn cup, into which he poured some spirits, apparently hot from the still, and offered them successively to the lady and to the boy. Both declined, and the young savage quaffed off the draught, which could not amount to less than three ordinary glasses. He then fetched another ladder from the corner of the cavern, if it could be termed so, adjusted it against the transverse rock, which served as a roof, and made signs for the lady to ascend it while he held it fast below. She did so, and found herself on the top of a broad rock, near the brink of the chasm into which the brook precipitates itself. She could see the crest of the torrent flung loose down the rock like the mane of a wild horse, but without having any view of the lower platform from which she had ascended.

David was not suffered to mount so easily; the lad, from sport or love of mischief, shook the ladder a good deal as he ascended, and seemed to enjoy the terror of young Butler, so that, when they had both come up, they looked on each other with no friendly eyes. Neither, however, spoke. The young caird, or tinker, or gypsey, with a good deal of attention, assisted Lady Staunton up a very perilous ascent which she had still to encounter, and they were followed by David Butler, untill all three stood free of the ravine on the side of a mountain, whose sides were covered with heather and sheets of loose shingle. So narrow was the chasm out of which they ascended, that, unless when they were on the very verge, the eye passed to the other side without perceiving the existence of a rent so fearful, and nothing was seen of the cataract, though its deep hoarse voice was still heard.

Lady Staunton, freed from the danger of rock and river, had now a new subject of anxiety. Her two guides confronted each other with angry countenances; for David, though younger by two years at least, and much shorter, was a stout, well-set, and very bold boy.

"You are the black-coat's son of Knocktarlitie," said the young caird; "if you come here again, I'll pitch you down the linn like a football."

"Ay, lad, ye are very short to be sae lang," retorted young Butler undauntedly, and measuring his opponent's height with an undismayed eye; "I am thinking you are a gillie of Black Donacha; if you come down the glen, we'll shoot you like a wild buck."

"You may tell your father," said the lad, "that the leaf on the timber is the last he shall see—we will hae amends for the mischief he has done to us."

"I hope he will live to see mony simmers, and do ye muckle mair," answered David.

More might have passed, but Lady Staunton stepped between them with her purse in her hand, and, taking out a guinea, of which it contained several, visible through the net-work, as well as some silver in the opposite end, offered it to the caird.

"The white siller, lady—the white siller," said the young savage, to whom the value of gold was probably unknown.

Lady Staunton poured what silver she had into her hand, and the juvenile savage snatched it greedily, and made a sort of half inclination of acknowledgment and adieu.

"Let us make haste now, Lady Staunton," said David, "for there will be little peace wi' them since they hae seen your purse."

They hurried on as fast as they could; but they had not descended the hill a hundred yards or two before they heard a halloo behind them, and looking back, saw both the old man and the young one pursuing them with great speed, the former with a gun on his shoulder. Very fortunately, at this moment a sportsman, a game-keeper of the Duke, who was engaged in stalking deer, appeared on the face of the hill. The bandits stopped on seeing him, and Lady Staunton hastened to put herself under his protection. He readily gave them his escort home, and it required his athletic form and loaded rifle to restore to the lady her usual confidence and courage.

Donald listened with much gravity to the account of their adventure; and answered with great composure to David's repeated enquiries, whether he could have suspected that the cairds had been lurking there: "Indeed, Master Tavie, I might hae had some guess that they were there, or thereabout, though maybe I had nane. But I am aften on the hill; and they are like wasps—they sting only them that fashes them; sae, for my part, I make a point not to see them, unless I were ordered out on the preceese errand by Maccallanmore or Knockdunder, whilk is a clean different case."

They reached the Manse late; and Lady Staunton, who had suffered much both from fright and fatigue, never suffered her love of the picturesque to carry her so far among the mountains without a stronger escort than David, though she acknowledged he had won the stand of colours by the intrepidity he had displayed, so soon as assured he had to do with an earthly antagonist. "I couldna, maybe, hae made muckle o' a bargain wi' yon lang callant," said David, when thus complimented on his valour; "but when ye deal wi' thae fo'k, it is tyne heart tyne a'."

Chapter Fourteen

————What see you there,
That hath so cowarded and chased your blood
Out of appearance?

Henry the Fifth

WE ARE UNDER the necessity of returning to Edinburgh, where the General Assembly of the Kirk of Scotland was now sitting. It is well known, that some Scottish nobleman is usually deputed as High Commissioner, to represent the person of the King in this convocation; that he has allowances for the purpose of maintaining a certain outward show and solemnity, and supporting the hospitality of the representative of Majesty. Whoever is distinguished by rank, or office, in or near the capital, usually attend the morning levees of the Lord

Commissioner, and walk with him in procession to the place where the Assembly meets.

The nobleman who held this office chanced to be particularly connected with Sir George Staunton, and it was in his train that he ventured to tread the High-Street of Edinburgh for the first time since the fatal night of Porteous's execution. Walking at the right-hand of the representative of Sovereignty, covered with lace and embroidery, and with all the paraphernalia of wealth and rank, the handsome though wasted form of the English stranger attracted all eyes. Who could have recognized in a form so aristocratic the plebeian convict, that, disguised in the rags of Madge Wildfire, had led the formidable rioters to their destined revenge! There was no possibility that this could happen, even if any of his ancient acquaintances, a race of men whose lives are so brief, had happened to survive the span commonly allotted to evil doers. Besides, the whole affair had long fallen asleep, with the angry passions in which it originated. Nothing was more certain than that persons known to have had a share in that formidable riot, and to have fled from Scotland on that account, had made money abroad, returned to enjoy it in their native country, and lived and died undisturbed by the law.* The forbearance of the magistrate was in these instances wise, certainly, and just; for what good impression could be made on the public mind by punishment, when the memory of the offence was obliterated, and all that was remembered was the recent inoffensive, or perhaps exemplary conduct of the sufferer?

Sir George Staunton might, therefore, tread the scene of his former audacious exploits, free from the apprehension of the law, or even of discovery or suspicion. But with what feelings his heart that day throbbed, must be left to those of the reader to imagine. It was an object of no common interest which had brought him to encounter so many painful remembrances.

In consequence of Jeanie's letter to Lady Staunton, transmitting the confession, he had visited the town of Carlisle, and had found Archdeacon Fleming still alive, by whom that confession had been received. This reverend gentleman, whose character stood deservedly very high, he so far admitted into his confidence, as to own himself the father of the unfortunate infant which had been spirited away by Madge Wildfire, representing the intrigue as a matter of juvenile extravagance on his own part, for which he was now anxious to atone, by tracing, if possible, what had become of the child. After some recollection of the circumstances, the clergyman was able to call to memory, that the unhappy woman had written a letter to George

* See Arnot's Criminal Trials, 4to ed. p. 235.

Staunton, Esq. younger, Rectory, Willingham, by Grantham; that he had forwarded it to the address accordingly, and that it had been returned, with a note from the Reverend Mr Staunton, Rector of Willingham, saying, he knew no such person as him to whom the letter was addressed. As this had happened just at the time when George had, for the last time, absconded from his father's house to carry off Effie, he was at no loss to account for the cause of the resentment, under the influence of which his father had disowned him. This was another instance in which his ungovernable temper had occasioned his misfortune; had he remained at Willingham but a few days longer, he would have received Margaret Murdockson's letter, in which was exactly described the person and haunts of the woman, Annaple Bailzou, to whom she had parted with the infant. It appeared that Meg Murdockson had been induced to make this confession, less from any feelings of contrition, than from the desire of obtaining, through George Staunton or his father's means, protection and support for her daughter Madge. The letter said, "That, while the writer lived, her daughter would have needed nought from any body, and that she would never have meddled in these affairs, except to pay back the ill that George had done to her and hers. But she was to die, and her daughter would be destitute, and without reason to guide her. She had lived in the world long enough to know that people did nothing for nothing;—so she had told George Staunton all he could wish to know about his wean, in hopes he would not see the demented young creature he had ruined perish for want. As for her motives for not telling them sooner, she had a lang account to reckon for in the next world, and she would reckon for that too."

The clergyman said, that Meg had died in the same desperate state of mind, occasionally expressing some regret about the child which was lost, but oftener sorrow that the mother had not been hanged— her mind at once a chaos of guilt, rage, and apprehension for her daughter's future safety, a sort of instinctive feeling of parental anxiety —it, in common with the she-wolf and lioness, being the last shade of kindly affection which deserted a mind equally savage.

The melancholy catastrophe of Madge Wildfire was occasioned by her taking the confusion of her mother's execution, as affording an opportunity of leaving the work-house to which the clergyman had sent her, and presenting herself to the mob in their fury, to perish in the way we have already seen. When Dr Fleming found the convict's letter was returned from Lincolnshire, he wrote to a friend in Edinburgh, to enquire into the fate of the unfortunate girl whose child had been stolen, and was informed by his correspondent, that she had been pardoned, and with all her family had retired to some distant part of Scotland, or left the kingdom entirely. And here the matter rested, untill, at Sir George Staunton's application, the clergyman looked out, and produced Margaret Murdockson's returned letter, and the other memoranda which he had kept concerning the affair.

Whatever might be Sir George Staunton's feelings in ripping up this miserable history, and listening to the tragical fate of the unhappy girl whom he had ruined, he had so much of his ancient wilfulness of disposition left, as to shut his eyes on every thing, save the prospect which seemed to open itself of recovering his son. It was true it would be difficult to produce him, without telling much more of the history of his birth, and the misfortunes of his parents, than it was prudent to make known. But let him once be found, and, being found, let him but prove worthy of his father's protection, and many ways might be fallen upon to avoid such risk. Sir George Staunton was at liberty to adopt him as his heir, if he pleased, without communicating the secret of his birth; or an act of parliament might be obtained, declaring him legitimate, and allowing him the name and arms of his father. He was, indeed, already a legitimate child according to the law of Scotland, by the subsequent marriage of his parents. Wilful in every thing, Sir George's sole desire now was to see this son, even should his recovery bring with it a new series of misfortunes, as dreadful as those which followed on his being lost.

But where was the youth who might eventually be called to the honours and estates of this ancient family? On what heath was he wandering, and shrouded by what mean disguise? Did he gain his precarious bread by some petty trade, by menial toil, by violence, or by theft? These were questions on which Sir George's anxious investigations could obtain no light. Many remembered this Annaple Bailzou wandering through the country as a beggar and fortune-teller, or spae-wife—some remembered that she had been seen with an infant in 1737 or 1738, but for more than ten years, she had not travelled that district; and that she had been heard to say she was going to a distant part of Scotland, of which country she was a native. To Scotland, therefore, came Sir George Staunton; having parted with his lady at Glasgow, and his arrival at Edinburgh happening to coincide with the sitting of the General Assembly of the Kirk, his acquaintance with the nobleman who held the office of Lord High Commissioner forced him more into public than suited either his views or inclinations.

At the public table of this nobleman, Sir George Staunton was placed next to a clergyman of respectable appearance, and well-bred, though plain demeanour, whose name he discovered to be Butler. It had been no part of Sir George's plan to take his brother-in-law into his confidence, and he had rejoiced exceedingly in the assurances he received from his wife, that Mrs Butler, the very soul of integrity and honour, had never suffered the account he had given of himself at Willingham Rectory to transpire, even to her husband. But he was not sorry to have an opportunity to converse with so near a connection, without being known to him, and to form a judgment of his character and understanding. He saw much, and heard more, to raise Butler very high in his opinion. He found he was generally respected by those of his own profession, as well as by the laity who had seats in the Assembly. He had made several public appearances in the Assembly, distinguished by good sense, candour, and ability; and he was followed and admired as a sound, and, at the same time, an eloquent preacher.

This was all very satisfactory to Sir George Staunton's pride, which had revolted at the idea of his wife's sister being obscurely married. He now began, on the contrary, to think the connection so much better than he had expected, that, if it should be necessary to acknowledge it, in consequence of the recovery of his son, it would sound well enough that Lady Staunton had a sister, who, in the decayed state of the family, had married a Scottish clergyman, high in the opinion of his countrymen, and a leader in the church.

It was with these feelings, that, when the Lord High Commissioner's company broke up, Sir George Staunton, under pretence of prolonging some enquiries concerning the constitution of the Church of Scotland, requested Butler to go home to his lodgings in the Lawnmarket, and drink a cup of coffee. Butler agreed to wait upon him, providing Sir George would permit him, in passing, to call at a friend's house where he resided, and make his apology for not coming to partake her tea. They proceeded up the High-Street, entered the Krames, and passed the begging-box, placed to remind those at liberty of the distresses of the poor prisoners. Sir George paused there one instant, and next day a L.20 note was found in that receptacle for public charity.

When he came up to Butler again, he found him with his eyes fixed on the entrance of the tolbooth, and apparently in deep thought.

"That seems a very strong door," said Sir George, by way of saying something.

"It is so, sir," said Butler, turning off and beginning to walk onward, "but it was my misfortune upon one occasion to see it prove greatly too weak."

At this moment, looking at his companion, he asked him whether he felt himself ill, and Sir George Staunton admitted, that he had been so foolish as to eat ice, which sometimes disagreed with him. With kind officiousness, that would not be gainsaid, and ere he could find out where he was going, Butler hurried Sir George into the friend's house, near to the prison, in which he himself had lived since he came to town, being indeed no other than that of our old friend Bartholine Saddletree, in which Lady Staunton had served a short noviciate as a shop-maid. This recollection rushed on her husband's mind, and the blush of shame which it excited over-powered the sensation of fear which had produced his former paleness. Good Mrs Saddletree, however, bustled about to receive the rich English baronet as the friend of Mr Butler, and requested an elderly female in a black gown to sit still, in a way which seemed to imply a wish, that she would clear the way for her betters. In the meanwhile, understanding the state of the case, she ran to get some cordial waters, sovereign, of course, in all cases of faintishness whatever. During her absence, her visitor, the female in black, made some progress out of the room, and might have left it altogether, had she not stumbled at the threshold, so near Sir George Staunton, that he, in point of civility, raised her and assisted her to the door.

"Mrs Porteous is turned very doited now, puir body," said Mrs Saddletree, as she returned with her bottle in her hand—"She isna sae auld, but she early got a sair back-cast wi' the slaughter o' her husband—Ye had some trouble about that job, Mr Butler.—I think, sir," to Sir George, "ye had better drink out the haill glass, for to my een ye look waur than whan ye came in."

And indeed he grew as pale as a corpse, at recollecting who it was that his arm had so lately supported—the widow whom he had so large a share in making such.

"It is a prescribed job that case of Porteous now," said old Saddletree, who was confined to his chair by the gout—"clean prescribed and out of date."

"I am no clear of that, neighbour," said Plumdamas, "for I have heard them say twenty years should rin, and this is but the fifty-ane— Porteous's mob was in thretty-seven."

"Ye'll no teach me law, I think, neighbour—me that has four ganging pleas, and might hae had fourteen, an it hadna been the gudewife. I tell ye if the foremost of the Porteous-mob were standing there where that gentleman stands, the King's Advocate wadna meddle wi' him—it fa's under the negative prescription."

"Haud your din, carles," said Mrs Saddletree, "and let the gentleman sit down and get a dish of tea."

But Sir George had had quite enough of their conversation; and Butler, at his request, made an apology to Mrs Saddletree, and accompanied him to his lodgings. Here they found another guest waiting Sir George Staunton's return. This was no other than our reader's old acquaintance Ratcliffe.

This man had exercised the office of turnkey with so much vigilance, acuteness, and fidelity, that he gradually rose to be governor, or Captain of the Tolbooth. And it is yet remembered in tradition, that young men, who rather sought amusing than select society in their merry meetings, used sometimes to request Ratcliffe's company, in order that he might regale them with legends of his extraordinary feats in the way of robbery and escape.* But he lived and died without resuming his original vocation, otherwise than in his narratives over a bottle.

Under these circumstances, he had been recommended to Sir George Staunton by a man of the law in Edinburgh, as a person likely to answer any questions he might have to ask about Annaple Bailzou, who, according to the colour which Sir George Staunton gave to his cause of enquiry, was supposed to have stolen a child in the west of England, belonging to a family in which he was interested. The gentleman had not mentioned his name, but only his official title; so that Sir George Staunton, when told that the Captain of the Tolbooth was waiting for him in his parlour, had no idea of meeting his former acquaintance Jem Ratcliffe.

This, therefore, was another new and most unpleasant surprise, for he had no difficulty in recollecting this man's remarkable features. The change, however, from George Robertson to Sir George Staunton, baffled even the penetration of Ratcliffe, and he bowed very low to the baronet and his guest, hoping Mr Butler would excuse his recollecting that he was an old acquaintance.

"And once rendered my wife a piece of great service," said Mr Butler, "for which she sent you a token of grateful acknowledgment, which I hope came safe and was welcome."

"De'il a doubt o't," said Ratcliffe, with a knowing nod; "but ye are muckle changed for the better since I saw ye, Maister Butler."

"So much so, that I wonder you knew me."

"Aha, then!—De'il a face I see I ever forget," said Ratcliffe; while Sir George Staunton, tied to the stake, and incapable of escaping, internally cursed the accuracy of his memory. "And yet, sometimes," continued Ratcliffe, "the sharpest hand will be ta'en in. There is a face in this very room, if I might presume to be sae bauld, that if I didna ken the honourable person it belangs to—I might think it had

---

* There seems an anachronism in the history of this person. Ratcliffe, among other escapes from justice, was released by the Porteous-mob when under sentence of death. And he was again under the same predicament when the Highlanders made a similar jail delivery in 1745. He was too sincere a whig to embrace liberation at the hands of the jacobites, and in reward was made one of the keepers of the tolbooth. So at least runs a constant tradition.

some cast of an auld acquaintance."

"I should not be much flattered," answered the Baronet sternly, and roused by the risk in which he saw himself placed, "if it is to me you mean to apply that compliment."

"By nae manner of means, sir," said Ratcliffe, bowing very low; "I am come to receive your honour's commands, and no to trouble your honour wi' my poor observations."

"Well, sir," said Sir George, "I am told you understand police matters—So do I.—To convince you of which, here are ten guineas of retaining fee—I make them fifty when you can find me certain notice of a person, living or dead, whom you will find described in that paper.—I shall leave town presently—you may send your written answer to me to the care of Mr ——," (naming his highly respectable agent,) "or of his Grace the Lord High Commissioner." Ratcliffe bowed and withdrew.

"I have angered the proud peat now," he said to himself, "by finding out a likeness—but if George Robertson's father had lived within a hundred miles of his mother, d—n me if I should not know what to think, for as high as he carries his head."

When he was left alone with Butler, Sir George Staunton ordered tea and coffee, which were brought by his valet, and then, after considering with himself for a moment, asked his guest whether he had lately heard from his wife and family. Butler, with some surprise at the question, replied, "that he had received no letter for some time; his wife was a poor pen-woman."

"Then," said Sir George Staunton, "I am the first to inform you there has been an invasion of your quiet premises since you left home. My wife, whom the Duke of Argyle had the goodness to permit to use Roseneath-Lodge, while she was spending some weeks in your country, has sallied across and taken up her quarters in the Manse, as she says, to be nearer the goats, whose milk she is using; but I believe, in reality, because she prefers Mrs Butler's company to that of the respectable gentleman who acts as seneschal on the Duke's domains."

Mr Butler "had often heard the late Duke and the present speak with high respect of Lady Staunton, and was happy if his house could accommodate any friend of theirs—it would be but a very slight acknowledgment of the many favours he owed them."

"That does not make Lady Staunton and myself the less obliged to your hospitality, sir," said Sir George. "May I enquire if you think of returning home soon?"

"In the course of two days," Mr Butler said, "his duty in the Assembly would be ended; and the other matters he had in town being all finished, he was desirous of returning to Dumbartonshire as soon as he could—but he was under the necessity of transporting a considerable sum in bills and money with him, and therefore wished to travel in company with one or two of his brethren of the clergy."

"My escort will be more safe," said Sir George Staunton, "and I think of setting off to-morrow or next day.—If you will give me the pleasure of your company, I will undertake to deliver you and your charge safe at the Manse, provided you will admit me along with you."

Mr Butler gratefully accepted of this proposal; the appointment was made accordingly, and by dispatches with one of Sir George's servants, who was sent forward for the purpose, the inhabitants of the Manse of Knocktarlitie were made acquainted with the intended journey; and the news rung through the whole vicinity, "that the minister was coming back wi' a braw English gentleman, and a' the siller that was to pay for the estate of Craigsture."

This sudden resolution of going to Knocktarlitie had been adopted by Sir George Staunton, in consequence of the incidents of the evening. In spite of his present consequence, he felt he had presumed too far in venturing so near the scene of his former audacious acts of violence, and he knew, from past experience, the acuteness of a man like Ratcliffe, too well again to encounter him. The next two days he kept his lodgings, under pretence of indisposition, and took leave, by writing, of his noble friend, the High Commissioner, alleging the opportunity of Mr Butler's company as a reason for leaving Edinburgh sooner than he had proposed. He had a long conference with his agent on the subject of Annaple Bailzou; and the professional gentleman, who was the agent also of the Argyle family, had directions to collect all the information which Ratcliffe or others might be able to obtain concerning the fate of that woman and the unfortunate child, and, so soon as any thing transpired which had the least appearance of being important, that he should send an express with it instantly to Knocktarlitie. These instructions were backed with a deposit of money, and a request that no expence might be spared; so that Sir George Staunton had little reason to apprehend negligence on the part of the persons entrusted with the commission.

The journey, which the brothers made in company, was attended with more pleasure, even to Sir George Staunton, than he had ventured to expect. His heart lightened in spite of himself when they lost sight of Edinburgh; and the easy, sensible conversation of Butler was well calculated to withdraw his thoughts from painful reflections. He even began to think whether there could be much difficulty in removing his wife's connections to the Rectory of Willingham; it was only on his part procuring some still better preferment for the present incumbent, and on Butler's, that he should take orders according to the English church, to which he could not conceive a possibility of his making objection, and then he had them residing under his wing. No doubt there was pain in seeing Mrs Butler, acquainted, as he knew her to be, with the full truth of his evil history—But then her silence, though he had no reason to complain of her indiscretion hitherto, was still more absolutely ensured. It would keep his lady, also, both in good temper and in more subjection, for she was sometimes troublesome to him, by insisting on remaining in town when he desired to retire to the country, alleging the total want of society at Willingham. "Madam, your sister is there," would, he thought, be a sufficient answer to this ready argument.

He sounded Butler on this subject, asking what he would think of an English living of twelve hundred pounds yearly, with the burthen of affording his company now and then to a neighbour whose health was not strong, or his spirits equal. "He might meet," he said, "occasionally, a very learned and accomplished gentleman, who was in orders as a Catholic priest, but he hoped that would be no insurmountable objection to a man of his liberality of sentiment. What," he said, "would Mr Butler think of as an answer, if the offer should be made to him?"

"Simply that I could not accept of it," said Mr Butler. "I have no mind to enter into the various debates between the churches; but I was brought up in mine own, have received her ordination, am satisfied of the truth of her doctrines, and will die under the banner I have enlisted to."

"What may be the value of your preferment?" said Sir George Staunton, "unless I am asking an indiscreet question."

"Probably one hundred a–year, one year with another, besides my glebe and pasture-ground."

"And you scruple to exchange that for twelve hundred a–year, without alleging any damning difference of doctrine betwixt the two churches of England and Scotland?"

"On that, sir, I have reserved my judgment; there may be much good, and there are certainly saving means in both, but every man must act according to his own lights. I hope I have done, and am in the course of doing, my Master's work in this Highland parish; and it would ill become me, for the sake of lucre, to leave my sheep in the wilderness. But, even in the temporal view which you have taken of the matter, Sir George, this hundred pounds a–year of stipend hath fed and clothed us, and left us nothing to wish for; my father-in-law's succession, and other circumstances, have added a small estate of about twice as much more, and how we are to dispose of it I do not know—So I leave it to you, sir, to think if I were wise, not having the wish or opportunity of spending three hundred a-year, to covet the possession of four times that sum."

"This is philosophy," said Sir George; "I have heard of it, but I never saw it before."

"It is common sense," replied Butler, "which accords with philosophy and religion more frequently than pedants or zealots are apt to admit."

Sir George turned the subject, and did not again resume it. Although they travelled in Sir George's chariot, he seemed so much fatigued with the motion, that it was necessary for him to remain for a day at a small town called Mid-Calder, which was their first stage from Edinburgh. Glasgow occupied another day, so slow were their motions.

They travelled on to Dumbarton, where they had resolved to leave the equipage, and to hire a boat to take them to the shores near the Manse, as the Gare-Loch lay betwixt them and that point, besides the impossibility of travelling in that district with wheel-carriages. Sir George's valet, a man of trust, accompanied them, as also a footman; the grooms were left with the carriage. Just as this arrangement was completed, which was about four o'clock in the afternoon, an express arrived from Sir George's agent in Edinburgh, with a packet, which he opened and read with great attention, appearing much interested and agitated by the contents. The packet had been dispatched very soon after their leaving Edinburgh, but the messenger had missed the travellers by passing through Mid-Calder in the night, and over-shot his errand by getting to Roseneath before them. He was now on his return, after having waited more than four-and-twenty hours. Sir George Staunton instantly wrote back an answer, and rewarding the messenger liberally, desired him not to sleep till he placed it in his agent's hands.

At length they embarked in the boat, which had waited for them some time. During their voyage, which was slow, for they were obliged to row the whole way, and often against the tide, Sir George Staunton's enquiries ran chiefly on the subject of the Highland banditti who had infested that country since the year 1745. Butler informed him that many of them were not native Highlanders, but gypsies, tinkers, and other men of desperate fortunes, who had taken advantage of the confusion introduced by the civil war, the general discontent of the mountaineers, and the unsettled state of police, to practise their plundering trade with more audacity. Sir George next enquired into their lives, their habits, whether the violences which they committed were not sometimes atoned for by acts of generosity, and whether they did not possess the virtues, as well as the vices, of savage tribes?

Butler answered, that certainly they did sometimes show sparks of generosity, of which even the worst class of malefactors are seldom utterly divested; but that their evil propensities were certain and regular principles of action, while any occasional burst of virtuous feeling was only a transient impulse not to be reckoned upon, and excited probably by some singular and unusual concatenation of circumstances. In discussing these enquiries, which Sir George pursued with an apparent eagerness that rather surprised Butler, the latter chanced to mention the name of Donacha Dhu na Dunaigh, with which the reader is already acquainted. Sir George caught the sound up eagerly, and as if it conveyed particular interest to his ear. He made the most minute enquiries concerning the man whom he mentioned, the number of his gang, and even the appearance of those who belonged to it. Upon these points Butler could give little answer. The man had a name among the lower class, but his exploits were considerably exaggerated; he had always one or two fellows with him, but never aspired to the command of above three or four. In short, he knew little about him, and the small acquaintance he had, had by no means inclined him to desire more.

"Nevertheless, I should like to see him one of these days."

"That would be a dangerous meeting, Sir George, unless you mean we are to see him receive his deserts from the law, and then it were a melancholy one."

"Use every man according to his deserts, Mr Butler, and who shall escape whipping? But I am talking riddles to you. I will explain them more fully to you when I have spoken over the subject with Lady Staunton.—Pull away, my lads," he added, addressing himself to the rowers; "the clouds threaten us with a storm."

In fact, the dead and heavy closeness of the air, the huge piles of clouds which assembled in the western horizon, and glowed like a furnace under the influence of the setting sun—that awful stillness in which nature seems to expect the thunder-burst, as a condemned soldier waits for the platoon-fire which is to stretch him on the earth, all betokened a speedy storm. Large broad drops fell from time to time, and induced the gentlemen to assume the boat-cloaks; but the rain again ceased, and the oppressive heat, so unusual in Scotland in the end of May, inclined them to throw them aside. "There is something solemn in this delay of the storm," said Sir George; "it seems as if it suspended its peal till it solemnized some important event in the world below."

"Alas!" replied Butler, "what are we, that the laws of nature should correspond in their march with our ephemeral deeds or sufferings? The clouds will burst when surcharged with the electric fluid, whether a goat is falling at that instant from the cliffs of Arran, or a hero expiring on the field of battle he has won."

"The mind delights to deem it otherwise," said Sir George Staunton; "and to dwell on the fate of humanity as on that which is the prime central movement of the mighty machine. We love not to think that we shall mix with the ages that have gone before us, as these broad black rain-drops mingle with the waste of waters, making a trifling and momentary eddy, and are then lost for ever."

"For *ever!*—we are not—we cannot be lost for ever," said Butler, looking upward; "death is to us change, not consummation; and the commencement of a new existence, corresponding in character to the deeds which we have done in the body."

While they agitated these grave subjects, to which the solemnity of the approaching storm naturally led them, their voyage threatened to be more tedious than they had expected, for gusts of wind, which rose and fell with sudden impetuosity, swept the bosom of the Firth, and impeded the efforts of the rowers. They had now only to double a small head-land, in order to get to the proper landing-place in the mouth of the small river; but in the state of the weather, and the boat being heavy, this was like to be a work of time, and in the meanwhile they must necessarily be exposed to the storm.

"Could we not land on this side of the head-land," asked Sir George, "and so gain some shelter?"

Butler knew of no landing-place, at least none affording a convenient or even practicable passage up the rocks which surrounded the shore.

"Think again," said Sir George Staunton; "the storm will soon be violent."

"Hout, ay," said one of the boatmen, "there's the Caird's Cove; but we dinna tell the minister about it, and I am no sure if I can steer the boat to it, the bay is sae fu' o' shoals and sunk rocks."

"Try," said Sir George, "and I will give you half-a-guinea."

The old fellow took the helm, and observed, "that if they could get in, there was a steep path up from the beach, and half-an-hour's walk from thence to the Manse."

"Are you sure you know the bay?" said Butler to the old man.

"I maybe kenn'd it a wee better fifteen years syne, when Dand Wilson was in the Firth with his clean-ganging lugger. I mind Dand had a wild young Englisher wi' him, that they ca'd"——

"If you chatter so much," said Sir George Staunton, "you will have the boat on the Grindstone—bring that white rock in a line with the top of the steeple."

"By G——," said the veteran, staring, "I think your honour kens the bay as weel as me.—Your honour's nose has been on the Grindstane ere now, I'm thinking."

As they spoke thus they approached the little cove, which, concealed behind crags, and defended in every point by shallows and sunken rocks, could scarce be discovered or approached, except by those intimate with the navigation. An old shattered boat was already drawn up on the beach within the cove, close beneath the trees, and with precautions for concealment.

Upon observing this vessel, Butler remarked to his companion, "It is impossible for you to conceive, Sir George, the difficulty I have had with my poor people, in teaching them the guilt and the danger of this contraband trade—yet they have perpetually before their eyes all its dangerous consequences. I do not know any thing that more effectually depraves and ruins their moral and religious principles."

Sir George forced himself to say something in a low voice, about the spirit of adventure natural to youth, and that unquestionably many would become wiser as they grew older.

"Too seldom, sir," replied Butler. "If they have been deeply engaged, and especially if they have mingled in the scenes of violence and blood to which their occupation naturally leads, I have observed, that, sooner or later, they come to an evil end. Experience, as well as Scripture, teaches us, Sir George, that mischief shall hunt the violent man, and that the blood-thirsty man shall not live half his days—but take my arm to help you ashore."

Sir George needed assistance, for he was contrasting in his altered thought the different feelings of mind and frame with which he had formerly frequented the same place. As they landed, a low growl of thunder was heard at a distance.

"That is ominous, Mr Butler," said Sir George.

"*Intonuit lævum*—it is ominous of good, then," answered Butler, smiling.

The boatmen were ordered to make the best of their way round the head-land to the ordinary landing-place; the two gentlemen, followed by the servant, sought their way by a blind and tangled path through a close copsewood to the Manse of Knocktarlitie, where their arrival was anxiously expected.

The sisters had in vain expected their husbands' return on the preceding day, which was that appointed by Sir George's letter. The delay of the travellers at Calder had occasioned this breach of appointment. The inhabitants of the Manse began even to doubt whether they would arrive on the present day. Lady Staunton felt this hope of delay as a brief reprieve, for she dreaded the pangs which her husband's pride must undergo at meeting with a sister-in-law, to whom the whole of his unhappy and dishonourable history was too well known. She knew, whatever force or constraint he might put on his feelings in public, that she herself must be doomed to see them display themselves in full vehemence in secret,—consume his health, destroy his temper, and render him at once an object of dread and compassion. Again and again she cautioned Jeanie to display no tokens of recognition, but to receive him as a perfect stranger,—and again and again Jeanie renewed her promise to comply with all her wishes.

Jeanie herself could not fail to bestow an anxious thought on the awkwardness of the approaching meeting; but her conscience was ungalled—and then she was cumbered with many household cares of an unusual nature, which, joined to the anxious wish once more to see Butler, after an absence of unusual length, made her extremely desirous that the travellers should arrive as soon as possible. And—why should I disguise the truth?—ever and anon a thought stole across her mind that her gala dinner had now been postponed for two days; and how few of the dishes, after every art of her simple *cuisine* had been exerted to dress them, could with any credit or propriety appear again upon the third; and what was she to do with the rest!—Upon this last subject she was saved the trouble of farther deliberation, by the sudden appearance of the Captain, at the head of half-a-dozen stout fellows, dressed and armed in the Highland fashion.

"Goot-morrow morning to ye, Leddy Staunton, and I hope I hae the pleasure to see ye weel—And goot-morrow to you, goot Mrs Putler—I do peg you will order some victuals and ale and prandy for the lads, for we hae peen out on firth and moor since afore day-light, and a' to no purpose neither—Cot tamn!"

So saying, he sate down, pushed back his brigadier wig, and wiped his head with an air of easy importance; totally regardless of the look of well-bred astonishment by which Lady Staunton endeavoured to make him comprehend that he was assuming too great a liberty.

"It is some comfort, when one has had a sair tassell," continued the Captain, addressing Lady Staunton, with an air of gallantry, "that it is in a fair leddy's service, or in the service of a gentleman whilk has a fair leddy, whilk is the same thing, since serving the husband is serving the wife, as Mrs Putler does very weel know."

"Really, sir," said Lady Staunton, "as you seem to intend this compliment for me, I am at a loss to know what interest Sir George or I can have in your movements this morning."

"O Cot tamn!—that is too cruel, my leddy—as if it was not py special express from his Grace's honourable agent and commissioner at Edinburgh, with a warrant conform, that I was to seek for and apprehend Donacha Dhu na Dunaigh, and pring him pefore myself and Sir George Staunton, that he may have his deserts, that is to say, the gallows, whilk he has doubtless merited, py peing the means of frightening your leddyship, as weel as for some things of less importance."

"Frightening me?" said her ladyship; "Why, I never wrote to Sir George about my alarm at the water-fall."

"Then he must have heard it otherwise; for what else can give him sic an earnest tesire to see this rapscallion, that I maun ripe the haill mosses and murs in the country for him, as if I were to get something for finding him, when the pest o't might pe a pall through my prains?"

"Can it be really true, that it is on Sir George's account that you have been attempting to apprehend this fellow?"

"Py Cot, it is for no other cause that I know than his honour's pleasure; for the creature might hae gone on in a decent quiet way for me, sae lang as he respectit the Duke's pounds—put reason goot he suld be ta'en, and hangit to poot, if it may pleasure ony honourable shentleman, that is the Duke's friend—Sae I got the express over night, and I caused warn half a score of pretty lads, and was up in the morning pefore the sun, and I garr'd the lads take their kilts and short coats."

"I wonder you did that, Captain," said Mrs Butler, "when you know the act of parliament against wearing the Highland dress."

"Hout-tout, ne'er fash your thumb, Mrs Putler—The law is put twa-three years auld yet, and is ower young to hae come our length; and pesides, how is the lads to climb the praes wi' thae tamned breekens on them?—it makes me sick to see them—Put ony how, I thought I kenn'd Donacha's haunts gay and weel, and I was at the place where he had nested yestreen; for I saw the leaves the limmers had lain on, and the ashes of their fire; by the same token there was a pit greeshoch purning yet. I am thinking they got some word out o' the island what was intended—I sought every glen and cleuch, as if I had been deer-stalking, but teil a waff of his coat-tail could I see—Cot tamn!"

"He'll be away down the Firth to Cowal," said David; and Reuben, who had been out early that morning a-nutting, observed, "That he had seen a boat making for the Caird's Cove," a place well known to the boys, though their less adventurous father was ignorant of its existence.

"Py Cot," said Duncan, "then I will stay here no longer than to trink this horn of prandy and water, for it is fery possible they will pe in the wood. Donacha's a clever fellow, and maype thinks it pest to sit next the chimley when the lum reeks. He thought naebody would look for him sae near hand. I peg your leddyship will excuse my aprupt departure, as I will return forthwith, and I will either pring you Donacha in life, or else his head, whilk I dare to say will be as satisfactory. And I hope to pass a pleasant evening with your leddyship; and I hope to have mine revenges on Mr Putler at packgammon, for the four pennies whilk he won, for he will pe surely home soon, or else he will have a wet journey, seeing it is apout to pe a scud."

Thus saying, with many scrapes and bows, and apologies for leaving them, which were very readily received, and reiterated assurances of his speedy return, (of the sincerity whereof Mrs Butler entertained no doubt, so long as her best grey-beard of brandy was upon duty,) Duncan left the Manse, collected his followers, and began to scour the close and entangled wood which lay between the little glen and the Caird's Cove. David, who was a favourite with the Captain, on account of his spirit and courage, took the opportunity of escaping, to attend the investigations of that great man.

Chapter Fifteen

————I did send for thee,
*   *   *   *   *   *   *   *
That Talbot's name might be in thee reviv'd,
When sapless age, and weak unable limbs,
Should bring thy father to his drooping chair.
But,—O malignant and ill-boding stars!—
First Part of Henry the Sixth

DUNCAN AND HIS PARTY had not proceeded very far in the direction of the Caird's Cove before they heard a shot, which was quickly followed by two others. "Some tamn'd villains among the roe-deer," said Duncan; "look sharp out, lads."

The clash of swords was next heard, and Duncan and his myrmidons hastening to the spot, found Butler and Sir George Staunton's servant in the hands of four ruffians. Sir George himself lay stretched on the ground, with his drawn sword in his hand. Duncan, who was brave as a lion, instantly fired his pistol at the leader of the band, unsheathed his sword, cried out to his men, *Claymore!* and run his weapon through the body of the fellow whom he had previously wounded, and who was no other than Donacha Dhu na Dunaigh himself. The other banditti were speedily overpowered, excepting one young lad, who made wonderful resistance for his years, and was at length secured with difficulty.

Butler, so soon as he was liberated from the ruffians, ran to raise Sir George Staunton, but life had wholly left him.

"A creat misfortune," said Duncan; "I think it will pe pest that I go forward to intimate it to the coot leddy.—Tavie, my dear, you hae smelled pouther for the first time this day—take my sword and hack off Donacha's head, whilk will pe coot practice for you against the time you may wish to do the same kindness to a living shentleman—or hould, as your father does not approve, you may leave it alone, as he will be a greater object of satisfaction to Leddy Staunton to see him entire; and I hope she will do me the credit to pelieve that I can afenge a shentleman's plood fery speedily and well."

Such was the observation of a man too much accustomed to the ancient state of manners in the Highlands, to look upon the issue of such a skirmish, as any thing worthy of wonder or emotion.

We will not attempt to describe the very contrary effect which the unexpected disaster produced upon Lady Staunton, when the bloody corpse of her husband was brought to the house, where she expected to meet him alive and well. All was forgotten, but that he was the lover of her youth; and whatever were his faults to the world, that he had towards her exhibited only those that arose from the inequality of spirits and temper, incidental to a situation of unparalleled difficulty. In the vivacity of her grief she gave way to all the natural irritability of her temper; shriek followed shriek, and swoon succeeded to swoon. It required all Jeanie's watchful affection to prevent her from making known, in these paroxysms of affliction, much which it was of the highest importance that she should keep secret.

At length silence and exhaustion succeeded to frenzy, and Jeanie stole out to take counsel with her husband, and to exhort him to anticipate the Captain's interference, by taking possession, in Lady Staunton's name, of the private papers of her deceased husband. To the utter astonishment of Butler, she now, for the first time, explained the relation betwixt herself and Lady Staunton, which authorized, nay, demanded, that he should prevent any stranger from being unnecessarily made acquainted with her family affairs. It was in such a crisis that Jeanie's active and undaunted habits of virtuous exertion were most conspicuous. While the Captain's attention was still engaged by a prolonged refreshment, and a very tedious examination, in Gaelic and English, of all the prisoners, and every other witness of the fatal transaction, she had the body of her unhappy brother-in-law undressed and properly disposed.—It then appeared, from the crucifix, the beads, and the shirt of hair which he wore next his person, that his sense of guilt had induced him to receive the dogmata of a religion, which pretends, by the maceration of the body, to expiate the crimes of the soul. In the packet of papers, which the express had brought to Sir George Staunton from Edinburgh, and which Butler, authorized by his connection with the deceased, did not scruple to examine, he found new and astounding intelligence, which gave him reason to thank God he had taken that measure.

Ratcliffe, to whom all sort of misdeeds and misdoers were familiar, instigated by the promised reward, soon found himself in a condition to trace the infant of these unhappy parents. The woman to whom Meg Murdockson had sold that most unfortunate child, had made it the companion of her wanderings and her beggary, until he was about seven or eight years old, when, as Ratcliffe learned from a companion of hers, then in the Correction-house of Edinburgh, she sold him in her turn to Donacha Dhu na Dunaigh. This man, to whom no art of mischief was unknown, was occasionally an agent in a horrible trade then carried on betwixt Scotland and America, for supplying the plantations with servants, by means of *kidnapping*, as it was termed, both men and women, but especially children under age. Here Ratcliffe lost sight of the boy, but had no doubt that Donacha Dhu could give an account of him. The gentleman of the law, so often mentioned, dispatched therefore an express, with a letter to Sir George Staunton, and another covering a warrant for apprehension of Donacha, with instructions to the Captain of Knockdunder to exert his utmost energy for that purpose.

Possessed of this information, and with a mind agitated by the most gloomy apprehensions, Butler now joined the Captain, and obtained from him with some difficulty a sight of the examinations. These, with a few questions to the elder of the prisoners, soon confirmed the most dreadful of Butler's anticipations. We give the heads of the information without descending into minute details.

Donacha Dhu had indeed purchased Effie's unhappy child, with the purpose of selling it to the American traders, whom he had been in the habit of supplying with human flesh. But no opportunity occurred for some time; and the boy, who was known by the name of "The Whistler," made some impression on the heart and affections even of this rude savage, perhaps because he saw in him flashes of a spirit as fierce and vindictive as his own. When Donacha struck or threatened him—a very common occurrence—he did not answer with complaints and entreaties like other children, but with oaths and efforts at revenge—he had all the wild merit, too, by which Woggarwolfe's arrow-bearing page won the hard heart of his master;

> Like a wild cub, rear'd at the ruffian's feet,
> He could say biting jests, bold ditties sing,

And quaff his foaming bumper at the board,
With all the mockery of a little man.*

In short, as Donacha Dhu said, the Whistler was a born imp of
Satan, and *therefore* he should never leave him. Accordingly, from his
eleventh year forward, he was one of the band, and often engaged in
acts of violence. The last of these was more immediately occasioned
by the researches which the Whistler's real father made, after him
whom he was taught to consider as such. Donacha Dhu's fears had
been for some time excited by the strength of the means which began
now to be employed against persons of his description. He was sensible he existed only by the precarious indulgence of his namesake,
Duncan of Knockdunder, who was used to boast that he could put
him down or string him up when he had a mind. He resolved to leave
the kingdom by means of one of those sloops which were engaged in
the traffic of his old kidnapping friends, and which was about to sail
for America; but he was desirous first to strike a bold stroke.

The ruffian's cupidity was excited by the idea that a wealthy
Englishman was coming to the Manse—he had neither forgotten the
Whistler's report of the gold he had seen in Lady Staunton's purse,
nor his old vow of revenge against the minister. And, to bring the
whole to a point, he conceived the hope of appropriating the money,
which, according to the general report of the country, the minister was
to bring from Edinburgh to pay for his new purchase. While he was
considering how he might best accomplish his purpose, he received
the intelligence from one quarter, that the vessel in which he proposed
to sail, was to sail immediately from Greenock; from another, that the
minister and a rich English lord, with a great many thousand pounds,
were expected the next evening at the Manse; and from a third, that
he must consult his safety by leaving his ordinary haunts as soon as
possible, for the Captain had ordered out a party to scour the glens for
him at break of day. Donacha laid his plans with promptitude and
decision. He embarked with the Whistler and two others of his gang,
(whom, by the bye, he meant to sell to the kidnappers,) and set sail for
the Caird's Cove. He intended to lurk till night-fall in the wood
adjoining to this place, which he thought was too near the habitation of
men to excite the suspicion of Duncan Knock, then break into Butler's peaceful habitation, and flesh at once his appetite for plunder and
for revenge. When his villainy was accomplished, his boat was to
convey him to the vessel, which, according to previous agreement with
the master, was instantly to set sail.

This desperate design would probably have succeeded, but for
the ruffians being discovered in their lurking-place by Sir George

* Ethwald.

Staunton and Butler, in their accidental walk from Caird's Cove towards the Manse. Finding himself detected, and at the same time observing that the servant carried a casket, or strong-box, Donacha conceived that both his prize and his victims were within his power, and attacked the travellers without hesitation. Shots were fired and swords drawn on both sides; Sir George Staunton offered the bravest resistance, till he fell, as there was too much reason to believe, by the hand of a son, so long sought, and now at length so unhappily discovered.

While Butler was half-stunned with this intelligence, the hoarse voice of Knockdunder added to his consternation.

"I will take the liberty to take down the pell-ropes, Mr Putler, as I must pe taking order to hang these idle people up to-morrow morning, to teach them more consideration in their doings in future."

Butler entreated him to remember the act abolishing the heritable jurisdictions, and that he ought to send them to Glasgow or Inverary, to be tried by the Circuit. Duncan scorned the proposal.

"The Jurisdiction Act," he said, "had nothing to do put with the rebels, and specially not with Argyle's country, and he would hang the men up all three in one row before coot Leddy Staunton's windows, which would be a creat comfort to her in the morning to see that the coot gentleman, her husband, had been suitably afenged."

And the utmost length that Butler's most earnest entreaties could prevail, was, that he would reserve "the twa pig carles for the circuit, but as for him they ca'd the Fustler, he should try how he could fustle in a swinging tow, for it suld ne'er be said that a shentleman, friend to the Duke, was killed in his country, and his people didna take at least twa lives for ane."

Butler entreated him to spare the victim, for his soul's sake. But Knockdunder answered, "that the soul of such a scum had been long the tefil's property, and that, Cot tamn! he was determined to gif the tefil his due."

All persuasion was in vain, and Duncan issued his mandate for execution on the succeeding morning. The child of guilt and misery was separated from his companions, strongly pinioned, and committed to a separate room, of which the Captain kept the key.

In the silence of the night, however, Mrs Butler arose, resolved, if possible, to avert, at least to delay, the fate which hung over her nephew, especially if, upon conversing with him, she should see any hope of his being brought to better temper. She had a master-key that opened every lock in the house; and at midnight, when all was still, she stood before the eyes of the astonished young savage, as, hard-bound with cords, he lay, like a sheep designed for slaughter, upon a quantity of the refuse of flax which filled a corner in the apartment. Amid features sun-burnt, tawny, grimed with dirt, and obscured by his shaggy hair of a rusted black colour, Jeanie tried in vain to trace the likeness of either of his very handsome parents. Yet how could she refuse compassion to a creature so young and so wretched,—so much more wretched even than he himself could be aware of, since the murther he had too probably committed with his own hand, but in which he had at any rate participated, was in fact a parricide. She placed food on a table near him, raised him, and slacked the cords on his arms, so as to permit him to feed himself. He stretched out his hands, still smeared with blood, perhaps that of his father, and he ate voraciously and in silence.

"What is your first name?" said Jeanie, by way of opening the conversation.

"The Whistler."

"But your Christian name, by which you were baptized?"

"I never was baptized that I know of—I have no other name than the Whistler."

"Thou poor unhappy abandoned lad!" said Jeanie; "What would ye do if ye could escape from this place, and the death you are to die to-morrow morning?"

"Join wi' Rob Roy, or wi' Serjeant More Cameron, (noted free-booters at that time,) and revenge Donacha's death on all and sun-dry."

"O ye unhappy boy," said Jeanie, "do ye no ken what will come o' ye when ye die?"

"I shall neither feel cauld nor hunger more," said the youth dog-gedly.

"To let him be execute in this dreadful state of mind would be to destroy baith body and saul—and to let him gang I dare not—what will be done?—But he is my sister's son—my own nephew—our flesh and blood—and his hands and feet are yerked as tight as cords can be drawn.—Whistler, do the cords hurt you?"

"Very much."

"But, if I were to slacken them, you would hurt me?"

"No, I would not—you never hurt me or mine."

"There may be good in him yet," thought Jeanie—"I will try fair play with him."

She cut his bonds—he stood upright, looked round him with a laugh of wild exultation, clapped his hands together, and sprung from the ground, as if in transport on finding himself at liberty. He looked so wild, that Jeanie trembled at what she had done.

"Let me out," said the young savage.

"I winna, unless you promise"——

"Then I'll make you glad to let us both out."

He seized the lighted candle and threw it among the flax, which was momentarily in a flame. Jeanie screamed, and ran out of the room; the prisoner rushed past her, threw open a window in the passage, jumped into the garden, sprung over its enclosure, bounded through the woods like a deer, and gained the sea-shore. Meantime, the fire was extinguished, but the prisoner was sought in vain. As Jeanie kept her own secret, the share she had in his escape was not discovered. But they learned his fate some time afterwards—it was as wild as his life had hitherto been.

The anxious enquiries of Butler at length learned that the youth had gained the ship in which his master, Donacha, had designed to embark. But the avaricious shipmaster, inured by his evil trade to every species of treachery, and disappointed of the rich booty which Donacha had proposed to bring aboard, secured the person of the fugitive, and having transported him to America, sold him as a slave, or indented servant, to a Virginian planter, far up the country. When these tidings reached Butler, he sent over to America a sufficient sum to redeem the lad from slavery, with instructions that measures should be taken for improving his mind, restraining his evil propensities, and encouraging whatever good might appear in his character. But his aid came too late. The young man had headed a conspiracy in which his inhuman master was put to death, and had then fled to the next tribe of wild Indians. He was never more heard of; and it may therefore be presumed that he lived and died after the manner of that savage people, with whom his previous habits had well fitted him to associate.

All hopes of the young man's reformation being now ended, Mr and Mrs Butler agreed it could serve no purpose to explain to Lady Staunton a history so full of horror. She remained their guest more than a year, during the greater part of which period her grief was excessive. In the latter months, it assumed the appearance of listlessness and low spirits, which the monotony of her sister's quiet establishment afforded no means of dissipating. Effie, from her earliest youth, was never formed for a quiet low content. Far different from her sister, she required the dissipation of society to divert her sorrow, or enhance her joy. She left the seclusion of Knocktarlitie with tears of sincere affection, and after heaping its inmates with all she could think of that might be valuable in her eyes. But she *did* leave it, and when the anguish of the parting was over, her departure was a relief to both sisters.

The family at the Manse of Knocktarlitie, in their own quiet happiness, heard of the well-dowered and beautiful Lady Staunton resuming her place in the fashionable world. They learned it by more substantial proofs; for David received a commission, and as the military spirit of Bible Butler seemed to have revived in him, his good behaviour qualified the envy of five hundred young Highland cadets, "come of good houses," who were astonished at the rapidity of his promotion. Reuben followed the law, and rose more slowly, yet surely. Euphemia Butler, whose fortune, augmented by her aunt's generosity, and added to her own beauty, rendered her no small prize, married a Highland laird, who never asked the name of her grandfather, and was loaded on the occasion with presents from Lady Staunton, which made her the envy of all the beauties in Dumbarton and Argyle-shires.

After blazing nearly ten years in the fashionable world, and hiding, like many of her compeers, an aching heart with a gay demeanour; —after declining repeated offers of the most respectable kind for a second matrimonial engagement, Lady Staunton betrayed the inward wound by retiring to the continent, and taking up her abode in the convent where she had received her education. She never took the veil, but lived and died in severe seclusion, and in the practice of the Roman Catholic religion, in all its formal observances, vigils, and austerities.

Jeanie had so much of her father's spirit as to sorrow bitterly for this apostacy, and Butler joined in her regret. "Yet any religion, however imperfect," he said, "was better than cold scepticism, or the hurrying din of dissipation, which fills the ear of worldlings, until they care for none of these things."

Meanwhile, happy in each other, in the prosperity of their family, and the love and honour of all who knew them, this simple pair lived beloved, and died lamented.

———

READER—This tale will not be told in vain, if it shall be found to illustrate the great truth, that guilt, though it may attain temporal splendour, can never confer real happiness; that the evil consequences of our crimes long survive the commission, and, like the ghosts of the murdered, for ever haunt the steps of the malefactor; and that the paths of virtue, though seldom those of worldly greatness, are always those of pleasantness and peace.

L'Envoy, *by* JEDIDIAH CLEISHBOTHAM.

THUS concludeth the Tale of "THE HEART OF MID-LOTHIAN," *which hath filled more pages than I opined. The Heart of Mid-Lothian is now no more, or rather it is transferred to the extreme side of the city, even as the Sieur Jean Baptiste Poquelin called Molière saith, in his pleasant comedy called* Le Medecin Malgré lui, *where the simulated doctor wittily replieth to a charge, that he had placed the heart on the right side, instead of the left,* "Cela étoit autrefois ainsi, mais nous avons changé tout cela." *Of which witty speech, if any reader shall demand the purport, I have only to respond, that I teach the French as well as the Classical tongues, at the easy rate of five shillings per quarter, as my advertisements are periodically making known to the public.*

FINIS

ESSAY ON THE TEXT

1. THE GENESIS OF *TALES OF MY LANDLORD*, second series (*The Heart of Mid-Lothian*) 2. THE COMPOSITION OF *TALES OF MY LANDLORD*, second series: the Timetable; the Manuscript; from Manuscript to First Edition; the First Edition 3. THE LATER EDITIONS: 'Second' and 'Third' Editions; the Carey Edition; *Novels and Tales of the Author of Waverley* octavo (1819), duodecimo (1821), octavo (1822), 18mo (1823), duodecimo (1825); the Interleaved Set and the Magnum 4. THE PRESENT TEXT: verbal emendations; mistakes in normalising the text; punctuation; volume and chapter divisions; proper names; defects; omitted manuscript material; inconsistencies; conclusion.

The following conventions are used in transcriptions from Scott's manuscript and proofs: deletions are enclosed ⟨thus⟩ and insertions ↑thus↓; superscript letters are lowered without comment. The same conventions are used as appropriate for indicating variants between the printed editions.

1. THE GENESIS OF *THE HEART OF MID-LOTHIAN*

Scott's fifth work of fiction, *Rob Roy*, was published on 30 December 1817.[1] According to his biographer Lockhart 'as soon as he came in view of the completion of Rob Roy' Scott asked his agent John Ballantyne to propose to the Edinburgh publishers Constable and Co. a second series of *Tales of My Landlord*, in four volumes, to be ready for publication by 'the King's birth-day', 4 June 1818.[2]

This account of the genesis of *The Heart of Mid-Lothian* is seriously misleading. The immediate inspiration, as recounted by Scott in the Introduction to the Magnum Opus edition of 1830,[3] was the story of Helen Walker which he received from Helen Goldie, the wife of Thomas Goldie of Craigmuie, Commissary of Dumfries. Helen Walker, says Mrs Goldie,

> had been left an orphan with the charge of a sister considerably younger than herself, and who was educated and maintained by her exertions. Attached to her by so many ties therefore it will not be easy to conceive her feelings when she found that this only sister must be tried by the laws of her country for child murder, and upon being called as principal witness against her! The counsel for the prisoner told Helen that if she could declare that her sister had made any preparations however slight or had given her any intimation on the subject, that such a statement would save her sister's life, as she was the principal witness against her. Helen said It is impossible for me to swear to a falsehood, and, whatever may be the consequence I will give my oath according to my conscience."

The trial came on, and the sister was found guilty and condemned but, in Scotland, six weeks must elapse between the sentence and its execution, and Helen Walker availed herself of it. The
very day of her sisters condemnation she got a petition drawn up,
stating the peculiar circumstances of the case, and that very night
set out on foot to London.

Without introduction or recommendation, with her simple
(perhaps ill expressed petition drawn up by some inferior clerk of
the court) she presented herself in her tartan plaid and country
attire to the late Duke of Argyle, who immediately procured the
pardon she petitioned for, and Helen returned with it on her feet
just in time to save her sister.[4]

This is the stuff of folk tale: it is most unlikely that the Duke of Argyle
'immediately procured the pardon'; and Helen Walker was not the
bearer when she returned to Scotland on foot. (A royal pardon was intimated by warrant and was sent by a Secretary of State to the Lord
Justice Clerk, Scotland's senior criminal judge, who then issued appropriate instructions to the relevant magistrates; this is what happened in
the Walker case: Historical Note, 589). However, it is clear that Mrs
Goldie's story, and her account of Helen Walker living quietly and
respectably near the Abbey of Lincluden in her old age, formed both the
immediate inspiration for *The Heart of Mid-Lothian*, and its broad narrative thrust.

In the Magnum Opus Helen Goldie's communication is undated, but
the original, in Edinburgh University Library, is postmarked 31 January
1817. Scott must therefore have read it early in February. At very nearly
the same time he must also have read the second part of a highly critical
review in *The Edinburgh Christian Instructor* of the first series of *Tales of
My Landlord* which had been published on 2 December 1816. In the
first part, published in January 1817, Thomas McCrie had accused
Scott of '*gross* partiality and injustice'[5] in his presentation of the Covenanters, commenting:

The good people of Scotland, who inherit any portion of the spirit
of their fathers, will no doubt be amazed to see those whom they
have been accustomed to revere as patriots, and to venerate as
confessors and martyrs for truth, now held up to derision as mad
enthusiasts, and reviled as hypocritical and murderous ruffians.[6]

In the second part, which appeared in February, McCrie put great
emphasis on the Covenanters' commitment to truth-telling, quoting
Isabel Alison who, while under interrogation in January 1681, said:

I asked them if they would have me to lie. I would not quite [give
up] one truth though it would purchase my life 1000 years, which
ye cannot purchase, nor promise me an hour.[7]

The beginnings of *The Heart of Mid-Lothian* can therefore be dated to
early February 1817 when Scott received Helen Goldie's letter and

probably read McCrie's account of Isabel Alison. Indeed, it might be argued that the story of Helen Walker offered Scott a way of replying to McCrie's accusations.

Scott had awarded publication of the original *Tales of My Landlord* to William Blackwood in Edinburgh and John Murray in London. By April 1817 he was thoroughly fed up with being 'mucked about' by Blackwood: 'I am really tired of being supposed to receive favours when I am in fact conferring them',[8] he wrote to James Ballantyne on the 16th. He even suggested that if his preferred publisher, Archibald Constable, were to take over responsibility for new editions of the first *Tales* from Blackwoods he would 'probably give him four volumes more by next season'. This is the very first hint of *The Heart of Mid-Lothian*. However, in a letter to John Ballantyne later in the month (the letter is just dated 'Monday', and could be either 21 or 28 April) he said that there might be 'some delicacy'[9] in giving a new series of Jedidiah's tales to Constable when the original series had been published by Blackwood and Murray, and so he offered Constable *Rob Roy* instead. The contract was agreed on Monday 5 May.[10]

It seems certain that ideas for *The Heart of Mid-Lothian* were developing in the spring of 1817. In fact it is possible that the first chapter of *The Heart of Mid-Lothian* was written in April 1817. In the manuscript the first chapter is on slightly smaller paper than the main text, and most of the last leaf of the chapter is blank.[11] As Scott's normal manuscript practice was to run-on chapters, the evidence suggests that Chapter 1 was written separately. It was probably written before the main text: there are 13 manuscript leaves to the first chapter, and when Scott started Chapter 2 he numbered the page 13, a mistake which is fairly common in his manuscripts, but one which always indicates that he was conscious of preceding material but did not have it by him. In addition, the heading 'Chapter II' is in the same pen and ink as the text that follows, and is not altered in any way; thus when he wrote 'Chapter II' there was already a Chapter I. Of course Scott could have begun writing in the knowledge that he was going to write an introductory chapter later, but this is improbable, if only because he obviously knew (roughly) the length of the first chapter.

Scott might have written the first chapter at any time before January 1818, but April 1817 seems the most likely date because in that month he had not yet begun *Rob Roy*, was suggesting a contract with Constable for a new series of *Tales*, and was still negotiating for materials from the tolbooth (which was in process of being demolished) for use in Abbotsford. In letters he began talking about obtaining stones from the tolbooth in the autumn of 1816, but he was specifying particular stones in April 1817 when he wrote on the subject to Robert Johnstone, the Dean of Guild in Edinburgh.[12] The first chapter constitutes an eloquent lament for the demolition of the tolbooth, and it is not fanciful to think that it might have been written at the same time as he sought to obtain relics of Edinburgh's history.

As discussed below, a contract with Constable for a new series of *Tales of My Landlord* in four volumes (which was expected to contain two stories as in the first series), was agreed with Constable on 15 September, long before he had finished *Rob Roy*. That negotiation seems to have been prompted by non-literary considerations, but by 10 November Scott had a title and, writing to Constable, said: 'Depend on it, that, barring unforeseen illness or death, these will be the best volumes which have appeared. I pique myself on the first tale which is called "The Heart of Midlothian" '.[13] It is absolutely clear from this amazing declaration that Scott had planned, conceptualised, and imagined *The Heart of Mid-Lothian*. *Rob Roy* was a distraction from what Scott proclaims to be his *chef d'oeuvre*.

If the story of Helen Walker, and the criticism of Thomas McCrie, were the immediate stimuli of *The Heart of Mid-Lothian*, the broader conception of the novel owes much to the context of Scott's own life. Scott was anxious to move away from the ground covered by *Waverley* and *Rob Roy* and their descriptions of Highland life. In September 1817 in a letter to James Ballantyne, his friend, partner and printer, he comments 'you are aware the Highlands are rather a worn out subject'.[14] In this new novel he planned to describe a very different Scotland, one grounded in the Lowland traditions of Edinburgh, and encapsulating not Jacobite but Covenanting dissent.

Another source of inspiration for the novel, and indeed its title, came from Scott's physical environment. During the composition of the novel the old town of Edinburgh was being redesigned, and in *The Heart of Mid-Lothian* Scott chronicles his home city as it had existed in the previous century and his own early years. The ancient city of Edinburgh is given a life of its own in the novel's powerful early scenes, and the passing of its edifices, institutions and traditions is a recurrent topic expressed, for example, in these comments on the City Guard:

> Such a phantom of former days still creeps, I have been informed, round the statue of Charles the Second, in the Parliament-Square, as if the image of a Stuart were the last refuge for any memorial of our ancient manners; and one or two others are supposed to glide around the door of the guard-house assigned to them in the Luckenbooths, when their ancient refuge in the High-street was laid low. (28.7–13)

In November 1817 (the same month in which the title of the new novel is first mentioned) Scott wrote to Johnstone: 'I embrace your kind offer of once more troubling you for another *rake* of the Old Heart of Midlothian & for Creeches lintel whereof you gave me so entertaining an account'.[15] (Creech was a bookseller with a shop in the Luckenbooths which, like the tolbooth, were demolished in 1817.) In February 1818

Scott told Lady Compton that Abbotsford is 'a sort of pic-nic dwelling for its ornaments have been pillaged from all sort of old buildings—I shall only mention Galashiels old Kirk and the tolbooth of Edinburgh the cross of the one and the gate-way of the other being now transported to the banks of Tweed'.[16] Just as Scott's home was being turned into a repository of artefacts from Scotland's past, so too his fiction, and particularly *The Heart of Mid-Lothian*, was being created as a means of preserving ancient stories and traditions.

Another source of inspiration for this novel lay in the day-to-day business of Scott's life. In the first, Introductory, chapter of the novel he adds a witty aside, playing, as he often does, with his own role as an anonymous author, and with the personae he has created for himself: 'Our seniors at the bar, within the bar, and even on the bench, read novels, and, if not belied, some of them have written novels into the bargain' (15.36–38). But the young advocate who is speaking goes on to disparage novels and to propose that there is a greater human interest 'in the real records of human vagaries', namely 'in the State-trials, or in the Books of Adjournal, where every now and then you read new pages of the human heart, and turns of fortune far beyond what the boldest novelist ever attempted to produce from the coinage of his brain!' (15.41–45). Scott, as a lawyer working in the courts, must have come into almost daily contact with stories of this sort and in *The Heart of Mid-Lothian* he draws on this material to provide the 'Last Speech, Confession, and Dying Words' of the Tolbooth (14.18–19). But the novel is also deeply reflexive, interrogating the legal system it describes. From the early scenes in which the Porteous rioters take the law into their own hands, to the legal injustice which lies at the heart of Jeanie and Effie's story and which was drawn to Scott's attention in the story of Helen and Isobel Walker, this is a novel which reflects on the very legal processes which formed the day-to-day business of Scott's professional life. Scott had a simple story which, as he created from it a chronicle of Scottish life spanning a century, drew upon the whole range of his professional and literary life. As Saddletree says to Dumbiedikes in the course of Effie's trial: 'There's a cheel can spin a muckle pirn out of a wee tait of tow!' (203.9–10).

If by the autumn of 1817 Scott had clearly imagined and conceptualised *The Heart of Mid-Lothian*, the details of its publication were much more difficult to settle. On 6 September Scott told John Ballantyne that he wanted to raise £4000 'to pay off the Bond'.[17] In 1809 Scott and the brothers Ballantyne had signed a deed of copartnery setting up John Ballantyne and Co. as a publishing business to rival Archibald Constable and Co. By 1813 John Ballantyne and Co. was insolvent, and was only saved from bankruptcy by a loan to Scott from a private individual, guaranteed by the Duke of Buccleuch, which Scott used to buy back his copyrights from John Ballantyne and Co., thus injecting £4000 into the insolvent company. Scott now wanted to retire the bond. In his letter to John Ballantyne he says that if Longman, Hurst, Rees, Orme and Brown, the great London publishers, were unable to make an agreement, 'I must . . . enter into treaty with Constable . . . for the continuation Tales of My L[andlor]d 4 vols. which will make the £4000 forth coming'.[18] His irritation with Blackwood had grown yet further, and the £4000 would be 'forth coming', he wrote, 'especially if I change the publishers of the first four volumes'. For Scott the primary financial objective in writing a new book was to repay the debt represented by the bond and to release the Duke of Buccleuch from his obligation.

Although Lockhart claims that Scott asked John Ballantyne to write to Constable and Co. proposing the new series of *Tales of My Landlord* in fact it was James in a letter dated 14 September who was asked to do this.[19] It appears that on 15 September[20] Constable agreed in principle to the terms proposed by James, and by 2 October the details of the contract had been defined. John Ballantyne then wrote to Constable:

> Referring to the terms of your letter to my brother of the 15th. September, the following are the terms upon which we have agreed with the Author of the Tales of my landlord for a continuation of that work in four volumes 12mo. You will observe that the terms are in all respects the same with those accepted by you of that date, excepting that the various shares are now distinctly ascertained.
> 1. The Tales 4 vols 10,000 copies, to be ready by whitsunday *at farthest*.
> 2. The Author retains the option of finding Paper.
> 3. Acceptances must be granted for author's profits at 6 months as in former cases and particularly in that of Rob Roy.
> 4. In consideration of being preferred to the work Messrs Constable & Co take the whole remaining stock of John Ballantyne & Co on the same terms of discount & acceptances as formerly, but as this is a heavy list the author impowers us to aid you with such renewals of credit as may be agreed on as reasonable at your expence.
> 5. The work is to be divided in exactly the same manner and proportions as Rob Roy viz one third to Constable & Co with the management one third to Longman & Co and one third to John Ballantyne.
> 6. The Author proposes to give the next edition of the original Tales of my Landlord, say Four thousand Copies upon the same terms and to be divided in the same manner as the present.
> 7. From four to five thousand pounds must be forthcoming to account, to the Author, from the three parties before Martinmas first.[21]

Item 4, which details that Constable and Co. would take the remaining stock of John Ballantyne and Co., was a heavy provision, and Lockhart gives one version of the details behind it. Archibald Constable, he states, had been disappointed to see the first series of *Tales* published by

Murray and Blackwood and, knowing this, John Ballantyne took an early opportunity to mention the proposal for the 'New Tales' as if casually to Constable.[22] Constable was to be given the impression that it was Scott's intention to give the second series once more to Murray and Blackwood, but Constable was so eager to publish the series that 'He agreed on the instant to do all that John seemed to shrink from asking—and at one sweep cleared the Augean stable in Hanover Street of unsaleable rubbish to the amount of L.5270! . . . Burthened with this heavy condition', Lockhart concludes, 'the agreement for the sale of 10,000 copies of the embryo series was signed before the end of November, 817'.[23] Lockhart is wrong about the date of the contract, and his account of this negotiation belies a far more complex, and in fact more bitter, series of negotiations concerning the publication of the proposed series.

The matter of John Ballantyne's stock seems to have been first raised in early September 1817, for on the 10th Scott wrote to James Ballantyne:

> I have an important communication from John [who was in London] announcing that Longmans people are willing to clear our hands of the whole remaining stock on getting the next Tales. But I presume our freind at the Cross [Archibald Constable whose shop was on the north side of the High Street, opposite the town cross] will be willing to do the same a point which you must lose no time in ascertaining. Mr. Constable will not I am sure wish or expect me to be a loser by my preference of him.[24]

Even at this stage, however, there seem to have been tensions with Longman and Co., for Scott goes on to state that 'Longman have proposed to take it by valuation but to this I will not consent: indeed they did not make a condition but only a suggestion to that effect to which assuredly I shall not listen'. In essence, Scott was looking for normal trade terms; Longman was looking for remainder terms. John, however, seems to have taken the matter further than Scott expected, for in the letter of 14 September Scott told James that Longman and Co. were willing to come into the contract on the terms outlined by Scott, and should be included in the agreement James was to discuss with Constable: Longmans, he wrote,

> cannot therefore be left out entirely and the Tales (say 10000 copies) must be divided as in the case of Rob Roy Constable taking the uncontrold management. I should have been well pleased to have let Constable have the whole but besides that it would be using Longmans ill to shut them out of a bargain which has been mentioned to them by an authorized agent.[25]

On 27 September Scott told John Ballantyne that they had to settle some things together before meeting Constable, saying emphatically 'we *must* have London Bills'[26] (meaning that if Longmans were coming into the bargain they would have to pay Scott directly, and that this would have to be a condition of the agreement with Constable), but by the 30th negotiations with Longmans had evidently disintegrated as Scott disapproved of 'their proposal of referring the price to arbitration'; Constable, he says, 'should settle the terms on which he proposes to give them their share'.[27] By 8 November Scott clearly believed Longman and Co. was no longer to be a direct part of the bargain, leaving any negotiations with them to Constable: 'Mr. Constable takes upon the same terms as the others the share reserved for them in consequence of their finally rejecting it but whatever share he may be disposed to admit them to whether with or without stock you will be happy to consent to on the part of the author'.[28] He then wrote to Constable, who was at the time in London, stating:

> I was not desirous to fling the door in their [Longmans] face, though indifferent to their thinking proper to shut it upon themselves. Their ultimate answer intimated a desire to take the share retained *without* any part of the stock on the terms settled with you. I have desired J. B. to reply that they having definitely declined the share and terms proposed, the whole bargain was in consequence taken up by your house who would be the proper persons to deal with as to the share and terms they might wish. So you have the staff in your own hand and as you are on the spot can manage it your own way.[29]

Constable and Co. were certainly eager to publish the novel but they were clearly anxious that such an agreement would leave them with very little profit from the transaction. On 11 November 1817 Robert Cadell, Constable's junior partner, wrote to his senior saying:

> You have ... state of our own quire stock, also of J Ballantyne, as copied from JB's list received last week, on mature consideration I think we should get Longman & Co to join in the undertaking, the weight of our own and John Bs share of the Stock is too much for our share of the advantages to cover, from Mr Ss letter you can contract with L & Co as you may see best, and this change may turn to our own advantage, it will take all the management we are capable of to get out of this transaction with profit.[30]

On 17 November Cadell wrote again:

> So far as I can calculate at present, the 10,000 Copies of Rob Roy will yield a profit of say £5000 say that the Tales will yield ¼ more being 4 vols 6250 add to this the profit of 4000 of the old Tales say £2,500 leaves us the gross of ⅙ of £8,750—with £1,458—if Joh B & Co stock amounts to 4000 our ⅓ is 1353—being our profit on the new bargain for the Tales—so that it would appear distressing and annoying as it is, that we will make little but the name by this new publication of Mr S.[31]

The calculation is difficult to follow, but his point is broadly sound: half the profit (receipts less direct costs) from a novel went to Scott, and so if the rest of the profits were to be divided between Constables, John

Ballantyne, and Longmans, then Constables received only one sixth overall (£1458). John Ballantyne's stock was offered at £4000, and if they also purchase John Ballantyne's old stock, Cadell is arguing, then they have to produce another £1353 (presumably he meant to write £1333), Longman and John Ballantyne also having to purchase a third each in accordance with the agreement above. It is no wonder that he continues: 'I have not given, nor will I give, John B a Bill of any sort for the Tales'.[32] Had he done so, Scott would have immediately presented the bill to the bank and got his cash, while it would have become another of Constable's liabilities, payable in six months' time.

Constable and Co. did not accept John Ballantyne's, or Scott's, proposals as eagerly as Lockhart's version implies, and were keen to bring Longmans into the bargain to offset some of the cost to themselves. By 22 November, Constable and Co. were clearly of the opinion that they had resolved the problem by striking a deal with Longmans. Cadell writes:

> I feel relieved at the portion Longman & Co have taken of the Tales it was too much for us to have the whole stock of J B & Co taking it in that view—at present nothing is stirring in the matter, and I think the most politic way is to say as little as possible to them . . . how would it do, to get L & Co *to join* in buying John out of the market, this will halve our risk of Loss . . . our most prudent course may be to confine our object to getting rid of John Ballantynes portion of the Stock striving at the same time to get the abatement from it at as low a rate as possible[33]

Another of Cadell's worries is registered in this letter: John Ballantyne's one-third share. It was a source of worry because John had no intention of putting up any money, and was relying on selling on to Constable his shares in both the new *Tales* and of his old stock. Indeed Constable had agreed as much on 29 September when Ballantyne wrote to Archibald Constable detailing this arrangement:

> Having been admitted one fourth sharer in the New Tales of my Landlord, & of the ⟨first⟩ republication of the present Tales; I beg to offer you all the books attaching to the ⟨first⟩ number agreed to be printed of the New Tales, & to the ⟨first⟩ republication of the old, on *precisely the same terms* under which you have come in our agreement for Rob Roy[34]

Why Ballantyne says 'one fourth' when he should have said 'one third' or perhaps 'one sixth' is not clear, but the letter is endorsed by Archibald Constable as being accepted on these terms. Cadell was therefore keen to get Longman and Co. back into the bargain so as to take a share in the risks.

A further source of worry was that on this occasion Scott was asking for £4000 (his share of the profit on publishing the second series of *Tales of My Landlord*) to be fully paid in advance in order to retire the bond;

previously he had received only an advance. So on 20 November and again on 22 November Cadell presses Constable to see if Longman would pay up front: 'If you could close with L & Co a regular agreement as to the Tales—perhaps they would grant for their ⅓ of £4000—*now*, and so much more for profits—or agree to account subject to after arrangements but the truth is I can show no face in this Bond business without something of this kind in hand to make me confident.'[35] And there was yet a further cause of anxiety, Scott's health. On 20 November Cadell wrote to Constable: 'I say *to you* and to *no one else* will even I hint it, that W S is not long for this world . . . My fears of W. S. are great, great . . . were any thing to happen to this person we would suffer most cruelly . . . Mr S may promise but these spasms assail him almost daily— and he cannot proceed'.[36]

However, matters began to improve. On Saturday 22 November Cadell and Scott agreed to postpone paying off the bond until Whitsun- day (15 May) the following year—and as Scott had promised the second series of *Tales* for 4 June Constable and Co. could look forward to getting money in from the sales of the novel at roughly the same time as it had to make payments to the author. The cost to Cadell and Constable as partners in Archibald Constable and Co. was six months' interest on the £4000. Cadell was delighted with his success; he told Constable on 24 November 'you *could* not have done it—for you *would* not have done it'.[37] The agreement was concluded and signed on the 25th.[38] Exactly why Cadell was so pleased with himself becomes appar- ent in a letter to Constable of the 28th, where Cadell argues that as Scott had said he held himself paid (having got an agreement in which he would be paid the following May), his statement would be evidence in the event of his death that he had indeed been paid. The Duke of Buccleuch would then have to pay off the £4000 bond.[39] As Cadell is here proposing to defraud both Scott's estate and the Duke of Buc- cleuch, it is no wonder that he says that Constable would not have done what he had done.

When signing the agreement on 25 November Scott was reported as looking 'remarkably well',[40] and the major anxiety about his health was alleviated on 11 December by Constable and Co. taking out a £5000 assurance policy on Scott's life at an annual cost of £206 5s.,[41] thus covering the firm for any loss should the author die before completing novels contracted for. 'God send he may live a while, but this at any rate keeps us very snug', wrote Cadell, 'and the longer he lives the surer are we of recovering the sum'.[42] On the 12th Cadell reported to Constable that he had worked out how to deal with John Ballantyne: take his share of the stock, try to sell it for him, and then when it does not sell well get him to reduce the price for the rest.[43]

Meanwhile, Longman and Co. were far more ambivalent about the whole transaction than Cadell appears to have believed, balking, as

Scott's own letters imply, at the condition of the stock. On 29 October
they had written:

> Our Mr Orme having returned to town, we have to acquaint you
> that his recollection of the Agreement concerning the Tales of My
> landlord &c is precisely the same as Mr Longman's, that the
> Agreement was conclusive without the slightest allusion to any
> reference whatever; and further that you appeared to be particu-
> larly pleased with the arrangement. We have determined however
> only to request you will submit this circumstance to the author and
> to beg he will favour us, through you, with his opinion whether he
> thinks we have been properly treated, and whether he would not
> suggest some mode by which he could be connected ⟨with⟩ in the
> works without taking the stock on the terms which we could not
> accept & have declined.[44]

And on 15 November they had further written: 'After consulting with
the author concerning the Stock, we shall hope to hear satisfactorily
from you. We should be truly grieved to be separated from him. In the
mean time we will talk the ⟨letter⟩ matter over with Mr. Constable, who
is now in London'.[45] But by 4 December Cadell was also certain that
they could expect no immediate help from Longmans, and wrote to
Constable to say: 'I am *now* quite of your opinion that we cannot at this
time get any thing from Longman and Co. on account of the Tales, it
will come in very well for the payment we have to make in May'.[46]

The initial contract had been for four volumes, although by 5 January
1818 there was a hint that this might be increased to five.[47] By 21
January Cadell was suggesting that this might be increased to six, confident that the first tale would be published in May, and that by increasing the number of volumes included in the bargain they would recoup
some of the losses they would sustain in taking the Ballantyne's stock:

> I fondly expect we will have the Tales in three volumes first, and
> afterwards in two or three more, the three first *tis said* positively in
> May, if this turns out so, we will do yet—Mr. H. M. Buchanan is
> very ill, and Mr Scott on that account gives up all intention of going
> to the Continent this season, which he planned, therefore I think
> there can be little doubt of the 2nd Tales in the Autumn, I have a
> plan in hand as to the stock, which I think you will approve of—and
> it will please Mr Scott—it is not to ask any abatement, but shew him
> candidly and honestly the loss we will sustain upon it, and trust that
> he will give us the next Book to make up the deficiency—I am sure
> he will do it—and we will thus get easily out, he will say I have little
> doubt you shall have 6 volumes in place of 4—which might do so far
> we should ask more—[48]

And by 22 January 1818 Cadell had resolved in his own mind that it
would be more profitable to dissuade Longman and Co. from coming
into the bargain:

> I set to work upon the Tales of My Landlord and enclosed you have

a general calculation as far as they occur to me . . . by which you will
notice that upon the whole it is more favourable for us to keep the
whole stock of John B & Co . . . I am aware you have a verbal
understanding with L & Co but they have taken into their heads so
much haughtiness about Rob Roy—that I would not be greatly
surprised were they to be dry as to the Tales,— . . . A good deal of
thought as to this has brought up some ideas as to Ballantynes
stock, which I have little doubt but you will approve of—it is, to
possess it without any delay and immediately print a *Cheap* List or
Catalogue of the whole of it . . . and circulate this throughout the
whole Kingdom . . . by these plans we may reduce this said stock,
and get our own money for a considerable portion of it—and pack
the balance off at what it will bring—we will thus lay a strong claim
on the Author of the Novels to prefer us to all those in time coming
—and shew him that L & Co will make no exertion for his behoof[49]

However, while Cadell may now have been happy to release Longman and Co. from taking any share in Ballantyne's stock it is clear that
he used their reluctance on this issue as an excuse to exclude them,
finally, from the whole transaction concerning the New Tales. While the
London company were no doubt relieved to be no party to the sale of
John's stock they were unaware that they had been cut out of the bargain
completely until near the publication of *The Heart of Mid-Lothian*. In
June Cadell was in London discussing the situation with them directly:

The Conversation at Longman Co yday took place in consequence
of my stating to Rees with candour that the course we had now
taken as to the Tales, arose from the whole bargain being left on
our hands, he said *there had been a misunderstanding* and referred to
their letters, and said explicitly that they understood themselves to
have accepted all our terms *in toto*—to construe it as they *now* wish
it. I allowed there appeared a misunderstanding of each others
meaning, but I convinced both Mr L and him, that we could not
have construed it in any other way, and took the measure we are
now pursuing in consequence of having so considered it, and that,
till the receipt of their letters wherein they alluded to ours of the 5th
and theirs of the 9th being quite at one completely, we had no
doubt of their refusal, and had taken our measures accordingly—
they said nothing to this, and I added very little. Mr L followed by
alluding to our dealings with the author in a tone I did not relish,
such as—"the bargain is in our eyes no great bargain—our agreement with John Ballantyne would have been £4000 better for the
stock is not worth £1000—" (this is not far from truth, they shewed
me J B's agt) again—"You seem to give the author every thing he
asks"—and, "have you any better hold on him by taking all the
Stock? I think not, by giving him so much money you enable him to
ask high terms in future, and perhaps he may not stay with you"—
and so on—I felt my heated side getting up at all this—but scarcely
said more, the matter is done I believe I said[50]

It is impossible to determine how much of this situation actually arose from misunderstanding, how much from Longmans' offhand treatment of Constables, and how much from double dealing on the part of Constable and Co. Given the inherent dishonesty in Cadell's view of the bargain that he and Scott had reached on 22 November and signed on the 25th, it is not unreasonable to think that his treatment of Longmans might also be dishonest. At any rate, Longman and Co. had no share in the novel's publication; the Edinburgh firm of Archibald Constable and Co. was to be sole publisher.

In certain respects this made no difference: Scott's contract with Constables gave them the management of the project, and so they were responsible for promotion. Thus, they advertised widely, and, as with *Rob Roy* before, they planted an article designed to generate interest prior to the publication of the novel: 'Remarks on the Tumult at Edinburgh, Commonly Called the Porteous Mob' appeared in the *Edinburgh Magazine and Literary Miscellany* for June 1818,[51] and an early remark prognosticates that the Porteous affair was 'destined to be speedily restored to popular interest as the ground-work of one of the New Tales of my Landlord'.[52] Promotion was easy, but selling was difficult for as Constable and Co. now had no London partners Cadell was left to trawl around various London booksellers (publishers, but here acting as retailers) to subscribe the novel (i.e. to obtain wholesale orders). In a letter of 8 June 1818 Cadell wrote to Constable: 'I rather incline to your opinion not to call to subscribe the Tales say for a few days—I think Thursday may start nearest the Row'.[53] On 11 June he wrote: 'You will give me credit for a short letter to day—when I tell you that I totally changed my plan of delaying the subscription of Tales—the *dissolution* of Parliament yesterday will for some time create a great bustle—and I resolved to let it not increase, which I fear it will do in a weeks time I therefore assailed the people this morning and up to this time have subscribed about 3230 Tales'.[54] On that day alone he had visited 'the Row folk—Cheapside—Exchange Cornhill . . . and fleet Street as Temple Bar' and claims 'I am now like to drop with heat and fatigue (5 oclock)'. Sales were reasonably good; Longman and Co. for example took a thousand copies, but he complained 'the price bear most heavily against me', and that 'the title New Tales is rather awkward'.[55] Cadell's grudge against Longmans evidently persisted: 'Longman & Co must require many more' he wrote 'which they shall *pay for* through the nose'.[56] Cadell continued to traverse London on foot on 12 and 13 June, aware that circumstances required urgency in getting the book subscribed. 'I am pushing through with all the dispatch I possibly can' he writes on the 12th. 'The folk are flying off to the country and electioneering at such a rate I have not an hour to loose, otherwise the Trade will be all disrupted'.[57]

In spite of all his efforts, Cadell claimed he met with 'many very many aflictions and most particularly as to price, the title, and whether the genuine thing'.[58] The quarrel with Longmans was also debilitating. They refused to take more than a thousand copies, while Cadell argued that they probably needed double that number, and this figure on Cadell's list put off, according to his letter of 13 June, other buyers. Several did not like the terms of the subscription and took smaller numbers than Cadell had hoped, claiming that they would 'lean on the Row for their supplies' unaware that Longmans had the book only in small quantities and on the same terms as themselves.[59] Not surprisingly, in Cadell's complaints the author is also blamed. 'The late season of bringing out the book, and the circumstance of the general election, are together at least £200 against us on this subscription' he concludes; 'had it been ready in May, matters might have been different'.[60]

The novel, perhaps because of the unusual length of the final volume, was further delayed, and was not shipped for London until Friday 17 July 1818. It was published on the 25 July in Edinburgh and was announced as 'now ready for delivery' in London on the 28th.[61] It sold for a price of £1 12s., to great acclaim according to Lockhart:

> From the choice of localities, and the splendid blazoning of tragical circumstances that had left the strongest impression on the memory and imagination of every inhabitant, the reception of this tale in Edinburgh was a scene of all-engrossing enthusiasm, such as I never witnessed there on the appearance of any other literary novelty. But the admiration and delight were the same all over Scotland. Never before had he seized such really noble features of the national character as were canonized in the person of his homely heroine: no art had ever devised a happier running contrast than that of her and her sister—or interwoven a portraiture of lowly manners and simple virtues, with more graceful delineations of polished life, or with bolder shadows of terror, guilt, crime, remorse, madness, and all the agony of the passions.[62]

2. THE COMPOSITION OF *THE HEART OF MID-LOTHIAN*

The Timetable. *Rob Roy* was published on 30 December 1817. Scott commonly left a gap of several weeks between finishing one novel and beginning another, but because of his illness, particularly acute around 20 November, he submitted the final copy for *Rob Roy* only on 23 December.[63] On 31 December he wrote to Constable to tell him 'I am resting myself here [Abbotsford] a few days before commencing my new labours, which will be untrodden ground, and, I think, pretty likely to succeed'.[64]

However, Scott seems to have allowed himself at least three weeks' rest before embarking on his new project, for on 12 January the Ballantynes' mother died and in a letter of 15 January Cadell told Constable that 'he is to begin the New Tales immediately after the funeral'.[65] While Scott may not have begun actually to pen the novel until the second half of January he was already intellectually engaged with his new work of fiction, for, Cadell continues, Scott 'was in great glee' and 'he wants all the tracts, pamphlets &c &c that we can get him about Capt Porteous Mob—for the Tale "The Heart of Mid-Lothian"'. At the end of January, Cadell wrote to Constable: 'It gives me no small pleasure to inform you that the *New Tales of My Landlord are at Press*!!!!! and what is more a considerable portion of them ... the Author says that he feels himself very strong with what he has now on hand, the report of such being forthcoming is gaining ground—but the Author does not wish them announced for a long time yet—and I dout he is right'.[66]

In the early stages of writing the novel Scott was also re-exploring aspects of the Covenanters. At the request of the *Quarterly Review* he undertook to review *The Secret and True History of the Church of Scotland* by the Covenanting minister James Kirkton which had been edited by his friend Charles Kirkpatrick Sharpe.[67] In a letter of 23 March 1818 to the London publisher John Murray who owned the *Quarterly*, he said: 'I laid Kirkton aside half finished, from a desire to get the original edition of the lives of Cameron, &c., by Patrick Walker, which I had not seen since a boy, and now I have got it, and find, as I suspected, that some curious *morceaux* have been cut out by subsequent editors'.[68] *The Heart of Mid-Lothian* owes a little to Kirkton, and much to Patrick Walker. In addition, in February a Mr Grieve, a Cameronian preacher, proposed taking up residence at one of the cottages on the Abbotsford estate. The idea both pleased and amused Scott,[69] and in a letter to William Laidlaw, his steward at Abbotsford, he writes:

> I cannot tell you how delighted I am with the account Hogg gives me of Mr. Grieve. The great Cameron was chaplain in the house of my great something grandfather, and so I hope Mr. Grieve will be mine ... I have a pair of thumbikins also much at his service, if he requires their assistance to glorify God and the Covenant.[70]

He elaborates in a letter of 26 February to his friend Lady Compton: 'He is in his way a very sensible and rather well informed man but as mad on the subject of the solemn league and covenant as if one of the Grassmarket martyrs had risen from the dead'.[71]

The reading undertaken by Scott as he wrote *The Heart of Mid-Lothian* is documented, but there is little evidence about the way in which the composition of the novel proceeded. Scott had to attend to his duties in the Court of Session from 15 January to 11 March; he then went to Abbotsford, and was back in Edinburgh again from 12 May. While these are the actual court dates, letters confirm his movements.[72] This means that for two-thirds of the time he was writing the novel, he was in Edinburgh; there are therefore few notes to James of the sort he would normally have attached to copy being sent from Melrose, and so few documents by which to chart progress. However, in an undated letter to James Ballantyne Scott indicates that he had got to the end of Volume 2, and he adds: 'You need not disturb yourself tomorrow. I shall call on you on tuesday after the court rises'.[73] He offers to call on Tuesday probably because the Court did not sit on a Monday, giving Scott a complete writing day which he does not want James to disturb. 'Tomorrow' would therefore be Monday. It is therefore probable that the letter was written on a Sunday, and that the conclusion of Volume 2, sent off to James 'yesterday', was finished on a Saturday. The Court would normally have risen for the Easter vacation on 11 March, but 11 March was a Wednesday in 1818, and the Teind Court sat every second Wednesday; thus in practice the Court of Session rose on Tuesday 10th. It is therefore probable that this letter was written on Sunday 8 March, and that Scott had completed the first two volumes of *The Heart of Mid-Lothian* by 7 March 1818.

It is evident that for some time the idea persisted that, following the model of the first series, the new *Tales* would consist of two novels, the first of which was to be *The Heart of Mid-Lothian*. On 14 January Scott wrote to John B. S. Morritt that he had 'two stories on the anvil (a continuation of the Tales of My Landlord) far superior to Rob Roy in point of interest'.[74] The second tale, according to Cadell on 6 February, was to be 'the "*Regalia*"'.[75] The Scottish regalia were located in Edinburgh Castle by a party including Scott on 4 February 1818,[76] but in a letter to Daniel Terry on 8 February Scott makes clear that the second tale was to have been about the hiding of the Scottish regalia from Cromwell and his troops in 1652 in Kinneff Church in Kincardineshire. 'A beautiful drama might be made on the concealment of the Scotch regalia during the troubles', he wrote, but added that such a story 'would interfere with the democratic spirit of the times, and would probably . . . "be hooted from the stage"'.[77] Scott's caution over the use of this material for a play may also have discouraged him from attempting a novel. Still, the plan for a second Tale seems to have persisted well into the composition of the novel, for as late as 30 April Scott wrote to Daniel Terry suggesting that the novel he was writing could be dramatised:

> There is in Jedediah's present work a thing capable of being woven out a Bourgeoise tragedy. I think of contriving that it shall be in your hands some time before the public see it, that you may try to operate upon it yourself. This would not be difficult, as vol. 4, and part of 3d contain a different story.[78]

These remarks are puzzling, for if Scott had finished Volume 2 by 7 March then he should have passed the middle of Volume 3 by 30 April especially as in the letter of 8 March he clearly knew where he was going. In response to some criticism passed by Ballantyne he writes:

> I would be sorry the difference you complain of did not exist. You are to consider R. writes his letter in the strong hope of escaping himself in the resolution of at least dying game. In short like a blackguard as he is. The circumstances of his friends death his own escape & the affair of Porteous stir up those latent energies which

give him a [very] different & more striking character. If he had been a man of a regularly dignified cast of mind he could not have been in the scrape. He is a Poins by nature & habit by strong circumstance a Moor or a Bertram.[79]

This clearly anticipates Robertson's confession in Volume 3. However, as the source of the text of the letter of 30 April to Terry is Lockhart's *Life*, neither the text nor the dating can be implicitly trusted. And there are real reasons for doubt: Lockhart erroneously says that the second tale was to have been *The Bride of Lammermoor*; the division between stories sounds suspiciously like that between *The Bride* and *A Legend of the Wars of Montrose*; and the phrase 'Bourgeoise tragedy' better fits *The Bride* than *Mid-Lothian*. But perhaps Scott's progress did just slow once he got to Abbotsford: he was preoccupied with work on building his extension, and had so many visitors that in his letter to Terry he talks of keeping 'open house'.[80]

It is also not known when Scott decided that *The Heart of Mid-Lothian* must take four volumes, and that the second tale should be abandoned. Scott was contracted to write four volumes, and there is neither manuscript nor external documentary evidence of any kind to suggest that he was just filling up space. The tone of the fourth volume changes, admittedly, but the change in tone may be read as another change in the narrative mode, similar to the change which occurs at the beginning of Volume 3 as Jeanie sets out for London. If it cannot now be determined *when* Scott realised that all four volumes had to be taken up by *The Heart of Mid-Lothian*, by the end of May the four-volume format was an established fact, since Constable and Co. wrote to Hurst, Robinson in Leeds telling them that 'the third volume is now in press' and that 'we shall send you a sett of Vols 1, 2 & 3 the moment it is ready & Vol 4th the moment it is concluded'.[81] On 13 June they wrote 'I hope I may be able to send you 3 vols Tales of my Landlord next week, & the 4th when ready'.[82] On 17 June Scott told Terry that he would 'very soon receive some private sheets from me', presumably *The Heart of Mid-Lothian*,[83] although it was not until 10 or 11 July that he sent the first three volumes, with the proofs of Volume 4 following the next day.[84]

The Manuscript. The manuscript of *The Heart of Mid-Lothian* is owned by the National Library of Scotland.[85] It is complete apart from three sections, the first corresponding to 127.1–24 ('if you wish . . . FIRST'), the second to 231.13–33.42 ('obliging damsels . . . Billingsgate'), and the third to 452.23–55.34 ('heard from . . . to row the'). Only one leaf has been located elsewhere: folio 73 of Volume 2, corresponding to 232.27–33.42 ('of mortality . . . Billingsgate'), is owned by the South African Library in Cape Town.[86] The National Library of Scotland manuscript is bound in red morocco with gilt tooling, probably dating from the early nineteenth century. The paper on which the novel is written has no watermark and, in general, measures approximately 27cm by 20cm. The first 17 leaves, containing the Prolegomen (ff. 1–4) and the opening chapter (numbered by Scott 1–13, and by the library 5–17), are written on paper of a smaller size, measuring 24cm by 20cm.

It was Scott's normal procedure to send portions of his novels off to James Ballantyne in folded batches, using the outside of the last sheet as a cover. As a result the editors of the Edinburgh Edition of the Waverley Novels have in some cases been able to identify points at which Scott broke off writing and sent material to his copyist. However, the manuscript of *The Heart of Mid-Lothian* is remarkably clean and the versos of the sheets comparatively fresh, suggesting either that Scott wrote long sections before handing over material, or that he transmitted the manuscript sheets to the copyist or James Ballantyne by some other means: he was in Edinburgh during much of the time when he was writing the novel and so may have handed over copy personally. There are places where a packet break can be identified however: the verso of the sheet following the end of Volume 1 in the manuscript is, for example, very dirty and there is evidence of a fold in the sheet at f. 125, just as the letter from Robertson reaches the magistrates. There is a clear fold in f. 143 after Jeanie has visited Effie in prison and the verso of f. 238 at the end of Volume 3 is very grubby. There is also an apparent end of packet at f. 306, just after Butler's conversation with Staunton on the boat as they approach Roseneath, suggesting that the last sections of the novel were being dealt with by James very quickly.

The physical condition of the manuscript offers one further interesting piece of evidence about how Scott himself was preparing his text for print. At f. 169, just before Jeanie visits the house of Dumbiedikes, Scott initially contemplated a volume break, writing 'this difficulty the execution of which will form the subject of the next ⟨chapter⟩ Volume. ⟨Here the vol; may end.⟩'. The paper has then been ripped in half following the last line of text, and he presumably intended to send the material to James. However, Scott changed his mind about the volume division and deleted the words 'Here the vol; may end' and the '1' following the next chapter heading. The two halves of the sheet have then been glued onto a second sheet of paper to make them one again, and the text follows consecutively. Scott later writes 'End of Vol II' somewhat emphatically on f. 174, at the end of the chapter in which Dumbiedikes gives Jeanie the silver. That the first edition and the EEWN does not follow this volume-break is because Scott wrote to Ballantyne saying: 'I think Vol. II should stop at the end of the Chapter p. 70 of copy sent yesterday. This will give about seven pages to Vol: III'.[87] In this instruction Scott restores his original intention.

Once Scott put pen to paper he proceeded in what, by the time of this his sixth work of fiction, had become an established pattern. The rectos of each folio of *The Heart of Mid-Lothian* are closely covered, with writing occupying the whole of the page. There is an average of 48 lines on each. The versos were initially left blank, but were put to use as Scott revised and expanded his text. Scott seems to have written fluently, occasionally altering words as he wrote, but more frequently reading over the work of the previous day as he started the next morning, revising, altering and supplementing as his thoughts developed. *The Heart of Mid-Lothian* demonstrates thousands of such changes, ranging from single words to quite extensive additions.

In many cases, changes of even single words demonstrate Scott striving for precision, or for the specific word which will illuminate his story. For example, many hearts are described as having '⟨beaten⟩ ↑throbd↓' (16.9) within the Heart of Mid-Lothian. Mrs Howden and her associates are first described as '⟨ladies⟩' and then, to avoid a repetition a few lines before, as '↑females↓' (40.41) and Butler first attends '⟨Edinburgh⟩' and then only as an afterthought '↑St Andrews↓' University (74.41–42), a more appropriate institution in the eighteenth century for someone of his social status and orthodox theology. Ratcliffe has at first only been condemned to death for a '⟨third⟩' time, but Scott increases his culpability to make it a '↑fourth↓' time (123.29; see note to 59.3). Madge's jacket is at first '⟨red⟩', but becomes a '↑blue riding↓' jacket (148.19). Madge herself at first describes a rag as '⟨staind⟩' with blood, but then as the more evocative '↑maild↓' (158.9). The court at Dumbiedikes is at first paved with '⟨stones⟩' but then with the '↑flags↓' (230.8) more appropriate to its ancient Scottish character. As Jeanie enters York she only becomes '↑our pilgrim↓' (250.16) as an afterthought, and the shoes which form part of Madge's outfit outside the village church are initially only 'embroidered' before becoming, more ludicrously, '↑spangled &↓ embroidered' (281.11–12). Queen Caroline's description of the Scottish people as '↑barbarous↓' (338.11) is added in the margin, and her comment on Jeanie's journey is altered to read 'that ↑immense↓ way' (339.17) as if to remind the reader of the distance Jeanie has travelled. These small changes often show Scott striving to find the most appropriate word; David, for example, first imagines Butler drawing a '⟨salary⟩' but then '↑stipend↓' (385.3), the correct term for ministerial pay, while it is not the old '⟨furniture⟩' of the manse which has been replaced, but the '↑plenishing↓' (398.42).

In *The Heart of Mid-Lothian* several of Scott's small changes involve names. Butler, for example, is at first called 'Tawse', the Scots word for the leather belt once used to chastise children in school, thus implying that Scott initially envisaged him simply as a generic schoolmaster, a fitting colleague for his senior 'Whackbairn'. However, as the character began to develop Scott altered his plans and the name 'Tawse' gave way to 'Butler' in Chapter 6 of Volume 1, when Scott writes: 'The young lawyers and writers together with their clerks, the class whom ⟨Tawse⟩

Butler was looking after had adjourned the debate to some favourite tavern' (47.35–37). Here the change is made immediately, in the line of text, and thereafter appears as the constant way of referring to this character. Earlier in the volume the name has been altered, at times in the hand of one of the intermediaries, above the line of text in the manuscript. That this correction appears in the manuscript indicates that the earlier part of Scott's manuscript had not yet been copied, and this would be in line with his normal practice in which he would have written about half of the first volume before handing over anything to be copied and typeset.

Some of Scott's changes involve short phrases which elaborate upon the details of his story and provide further insight into the nature of his characters. For example, the scene in which the Grassmarket of Edinburgh gradually clears after the non-appearance of Porteous is enhanced by the alteration on the facing verso of the single word '⟨Groupes⟩' to read '↑The windows were in like manner gradually deserted & groupes↓' (36.13), and Mrs Howden's description of the robes worn before the Union is given more force by the added detail that they '↑wad hae stude by their lane wi' gold & brocade↓' (40.9–10). The identification of Robertson's disguise with that of Madge Wildfire is similarly added on the facing verso as Scott writes '↑and the name of Madge Wildfire was repeatedly calld from the bottom of the staircase↓' (59.15–17). The ambiguous nature of David's character and our equally ambiguous response to him are interestingly developed when he is visited by Mr Middleburgh. For example, the passage ↑His lips continued to move for a minute after his voice ceased to be heard, as if he were repeating the same vow internally↓ (175.14–15) is added on the facing verso, providing his character with extra pathos, while his stubbornness is also enhanced by the additional information that he is '↑too proud of his own polemical knowlege to call himself the followr of any one↓' (175.28–29). Effie's petulance when Jeanie visits her in prison is also expanded in revision; her bitter chiding '↑and if it be a wrang word ye'll hae time aneugh to repent o't↓' (189.23–24) and her sulky '↑we'll speak nae mair about this matter↓' (189.28) both appear as additions. And it is not only Scott's major characters which engage him in this way. The innkeeper's action of taking '↑a powerful pull at a solemn tankard of home-brewd ale↓' (257.39–40) which underlines his sympathies with Jeanie's situation is an addition, as is Mrs Howden's comment '↑I didna ken his Grace was ever designd for the ministry↓' (221.8) which she makes on the Duke of Argyle's speech in the House of Lords where he declares 'I am no minister, I never was a minister, and I never will be one' (221.6–7): Mrs Howden creates a moment of almost Shakespearean comedy after the pathos of Effie's trial. Even towards the end of the novel Scott demonstrates that minor characters from the early scenes are still sharply conceived; at first he writes that on meeting Staunton Mrs Saddletree '⟨received him⟩' but remembering the nature of this woman, he alters his text to read, more appropriately, that she ' ↑ bustled about to receive the rich English baronet ↓ ' (450.8).

Most of these examples involve only single words and phrases, but Scott also engaged in a more complex process of revision. Structurally, the most significant of such changes involve chapter divisions, and Scott frequently alters where these are to be placed. At 26.27, for example, he begins to write about the character of John Porteous but, realising the seriousness of this task, decides to begin a new chapter, indicating the break on the facing verso. A new chapter break is added at 357.17 prior to Jeanie's summons to meet the queen, and again at 417.25 when Jeanie retreats into her bedroom to read Effie's letter. The break between the penultimate and last chapters of the novel at 461.20 when Duncan advances to the cove where Staunton is to meet his fate, is again added, to dramatic effect, in revision.

Scott also alters the beginning and ends of chapters. At 171.1 he began a new chapter when embarking on his description of Mr Middleburgh's visit to David Deans, but then decided to expand adding a lengthy passage on the facing verso which details what has happened in the intervening period, including all the material up to 172.23. (In the first edition, the new material was taken in, but the chapter break was overlooked by the intermediaries, even though the material clearly requires a new chapter, a mistake remedied for the first time in this edition.) The opening of Chapter 7 of Volume 2, down to and including 'he found Jeanie gazing' (179.32–180.9), is also added in revision. On the other hand Chapter 9 in Volume 3 is given a stronger conclusion by the addition of the quotation from Crabbe and the horseman's sympathetic view of George Staunton (316.11–30).

Some longer revisions develop characters. For example, several passages supply additional and accumulating information concerning John Porteous (see 26.37–27.2; 32.7–14; 34.14–24; 169.24–39), the last being Meg Murdockson's heated commentary on him. The entire passage which first introduces David Deans (68.3–24) is also added on the facing verso, while Deans's emphatic denunciation of all the lawyers who might defend Effie also appears as a revision:

> Nae lawyer shall ever speak for me and mine that hasna concurred in the testimony of the scattered, yet lovely remnant, which abode in the clifts of the rocks."
>
> So saying, and as if fatigued, both with the arguments and presence of his guests, the old man arose, and seeming to bid them adieu with a motion of his head and hand, went to shut himself up in his sleeping apartment. (114.12–19)

Several of the passages in which Madge identifies herself and Jeanie as characters from *The Pilgrim's Progress* are additions (for example

274.21–30; 275.19–21; 279.12–16) while Madge's account of George Robertson's promise of marriage, and the extent to which she has been wronged by him, also appears on the facing verso (278.3–5). In the case of Jeanie herself, her reasons for not telling Butler about Effie's letter are outlined in a long insert at 422.11–24.

In some instances Scott also uses these longer additions to clarify points which could otherwise seem obscure and to explain more clearly the legal issues which lie at the centre of the novel. For example, the early word-play on the 'sad heart' of the Heart of Mid-Lothian at 14.4–16 is added on a paper apart, while the legal description of the court in which Effie is tried is enhanced at 195.3–10, perhaps to add clarity for a non-Scottish audience. At 198.26–29 a passage is added which emphasises how crucial Jeanie's testimony is to Effie's defence, while at 201.38–202.1 Scott elaborates on the particulars of Effie's case.

Several of the changes to the manuscript involve the time scheme, as Scott apparently considers and re-considers the inter-relationship between the novel's events.[88] For example, when he first introduces the Deans sisters, he writes that Jeanie is '⟨a wee bit⟩ older than Effie' (44.24), but on second thoughts changes this to '↑ ten years ↓' a figure much closer to the difference which must exist between them but one which is still not long enough (see Historical Note, 597). Effie, he writes, has been out in 'the evening', but on reflection Scott adds that it is a '↑ summer ↓' evening, again locating the events of his story specifically in time (86.14). Initially, Scott writes that Mrs Saddletree had been looking for an assistant in the shop 'a year before' the time of the story, but again, realising that this will not leave enough time to accommodate Effie's seduction and pregnancy, adds '↑ & a half ↓' to the span he has given (90.1–2). At 172.19–20 he adds that Effie's trial was about to be brought forward '↑ after many weeks confinement ↓' again adding time so that Jeanie's pilgrimage can take place in March and April, and at 413.28 he alters his text to relate that Jeanie has had her children in the course of not '⟨four⟩' years but '↑ five ↓'.

While these improvements, refinements and expansions accumulate into a significant and impressive revision of the earliest level of writing, none suggests a major change of direction in the plot of *The Heart of Mid-Lothian*; Scott, it seems, had the entire story clearly in his mind throughout its composition. Only one alteration, at the very end of this long work of fiction, suggests a minor twist in the details of the plot. At first there is some ambiguity concerning whether or not Staunton has been killed by his son: 'Sir George Staunton offerd the bravest resistance—⟨He was killd by a shot but as several ↑ more than one ↓ were fired—it was not positively certain—but there were the strongest grounds to be⟩' (465.6–7). As Scott wrote, however, he clearly decided to dispense with this ambiguity and replaced the passage with one which reads: 'till he fell as there was too much reason to believe by the hand of a son so long sought and now at length so unhappily discoverd' (465.7–9). Thus he creates the tragic dénouement.

However, categorising Scott's revisions and alterations and treating them as above actually prevents a recognition of their full literary effect, which can only be seen through an analysis of the ways in which different kinds of change work together in a specific context. One of the finest pieces of writing in the novel is the passage at the beginning of Volume 1, Chapter 7, where the rioters break into the prison to find Porteous, a passage which is not heavily revised, but demonstrates well the kinds of change Scott was continually making. The detail that Porteous had petitioned the authorities to be conveyed to the castle and kept '↑in security↓' for example, is added above the line of text, to somewhat ironic effect (56.26). Porteous has not just '⟨some⟩' intimacy with the captain of the Tolbooth, but '↑an old↓' intimacy (56.34). An allusion to Hamlet (Porteous was captured '↑"full of bread"↓'), is added on the facing verso (56.38), and Scott changes his mind about the mob which he intially describes as '⟨fearful &⟩ determined', and then decides that 'dreadful & determined' might be more appropriate (57.3). Porteous and his friends are described as wanting the presence of mind to try some plan of '⟨safety⟩ ↑escape↓' (57.12), while they entertain the '⟨idea⟩ ↑hopes↓' (57.17) that relief might come from the castle. Porteous is 'one who ⟨one holds his hand ⟨his⟩ the sole support betwixt⟩' before Scott alters the metaphor so that the passage reads 'one who esteemed himself clinging to his last hope of existence' (57.32–33). And the light which fills his apartment is qualified by the wonderfully evocative adjective '↑lurid↓' (57.33). One of the rioters is described as having not simply a disguise, but a '↑female↓' disguise (58.9), a detail which comes from Scott's sources (see explanatory note), and which is crucial to the subsequent story. Here one can almost see the plot in evolution. The leader of the mob reiterates the sacred nature of what they are doing by stating at first 'we do not make it in' but then 'we do not offer it at the very horns of the altar' (58.12–13). Finally, Scott struggles for the most appropriate phrase as he begins to write 'we do not war with his body but with' and then rephrases the passage to read 'we do not ↑kill both↓ his ↑soul & body↓' (58.20).

Collectively, these thousands of changes show the work of a craftsman, indeed a meticulous craftsman, who pays close attention to detail in controlling the huge and complex plot of a hundred-year chronicle. They demonstrate the great care which Scott took, something which generations of critics denied in their accusations of slap-dash writing. They also reveal him as the quintessential romantic novelist. In the Introductory Epistle to *The Fortunes of Nigel* the Author of Waverley says that there is 'a dæmon who seats himself on the feather of my pen . . . Characters expand under my hand; incidents are multiplied.'[89] That description describes well the pattern of unconscious creativity which one can see in the enlivening and sharpening details of Scott's revisions and expansions.

From Manuscript to First Edition. *The Heart of Mid-Lothian* was converted from holograph to print following exactly the same procedures as other novels written in the period before 1827. As explained in the General Introduction (xii–iii above) Scott's novels appeared anonymously. To prevent his handwriting being seen in the printing office, and so to preserve his anonymity, Scott sent his manuscript in batches to a copyist, who, in the case of *The Heart of Mid-Lothian*, has not been identified. As we have seen, Scott sent about half of Volume 1 to the copyist before the end of January 1818. Printer's copy for *The Heart of Mid-Lothian*, as with all the rest of Scott's novels, has not survived. The compositors received the transcripts, not Scott's manuscript, and proceeded to put the text into type, and while doing so inserted most marks of punctuation, normalised spelling, and corrected small errors. They pulled proofs which, to judge from the only gathering of pre-author proofs to have survived for any novel by Scott,[90] must have needed much extra work, probably supplied by Ballantyne's foreman Daniel Mac-Corkindale, to bring them up to the standard expected of printed books. After MacCorkindale's corrections had been taken in a new proof would have been pulled, sent first to James Ballantyne, and then on to Scott.

The one extant gathering of author's proofs for *The Heart of Mid-Lothian*, corresponding to 110.37–18.4, show that these were indeed the procedures.[91] There are a few corrections by Ballantyne, but most are by Scott, although it is not always possible to decide who effected minor improvements such as the addition of commas. Scott corrects mistakes in Latin, indicates that phrases under discussion such as the black and scarlet horses in Saddletree's summary of the case of Marsport *versus* Lackland (111.9–10) should be italicised, adds a number of speech-markers, changes, in a narrative passage, the Scots 'pin' to 'hook' (114.25), and alters 'stamped' (a clear misreading of the manuscript) to 'stumped' (114.29). He also improves. There are no extensive additions in these sixteen pages of proof, but the addition of 'holy' to 'burning the holy Temple' (112.20), and of 'warldly-wise men' to 'one of the public and polititious warldly-wise men' (112.27–28), to choose only two examples, not only improves the cadence of each phrase but makes Saddletree and Deans's language more vivid. The process of revising the manuscript, which is analysed above, thus continued in the proofs. There is only one example of an exchange of comments; Ballantyne must have written that he could not understand a piece of Latin which appeared in print as '*Sempus nemini*' (118.2), and Scott replied: 'I am sure as printed neither do I—you must always return my MS where latin occurs—O I have it—but', presumably meaning that even if he had now got the sense (he corrected the Latin to '*Tempus nemini*') he still wanted to get his manuscript back.

Although no later proofs have survived, the normal practice was that corrections were copied onto fresh sheets (to preserve anonymity) and that these fresh sheets went back to the compositors, the type was corrected, and a new proof was drawn and read in-house.

The First Edition. Given the pressures of time and the nature of the nineteenth-century printing processes, the 'intermediaries' as the copyist, the compositors, the proof-readers including MacCorkindale, and James Ballantyne, have come to be known by the Edinburgh Edition, made a remarkable job of turning Scott's manuscript into a readable text. Thousands of changes take place between the manuscript and the first edition, most certainly produced by the intermediaries who were responding to hypothetical 'standing orders' to provide suitable punctuation, to normalise spelling, to eliminate the repetition of words in close proximity, and to sort out any apparent muddles in Scott's text. For example, in the first volume of the novel, typical changes, probably by the intermediaries, include the change from 'burthen' to 'burden' (3.9) and from 'pleasing' to 'pleasant' (3.12), the upgrading of Scott's punctuation from a semicolon at 3.30 and at 7.20, in the first instance to a colon and in the second to a full stop, and the alteration of the word 'mingle' at 12.25 to 'unite' in order to avoid a repetition within a few lines. A repetition is also avoided at 17.10 by a change from 'learning' to 'erudition' while there is a typical movement towards Scots at 44.25, 29 and 30 where the words 'since', 'poor', and 'must' in the manuscript appear as 'syne', 'puir', and 'maun' in the first edition. In the passage where revisions were considered earlier, there is evidence that the intermediaries have altered the manuscript material in typical ways. Scott's spellings such as 'risque' at 56.14 have been modernised, and a coherent punctuation system has been put in place. Repetitions, such as that of 'proper' at 56.25 and 26, have been eliminated by the substitution of 'sufficient' in the second instance, and the repetition of 'cling' caused by Scott's manuscript revision of the passage at 57.32 by the alteration of 'clung' to 'seized'. Scott's ampersands have been expanded throughout.

There are of course many changes between manuscript and first edition which arise not from the intermediaries but from Scott's own revision of proofs. Only a small part of these survives, but even though there is little evidence, many of the changes between manuscript and first edition must have been Scott's own. For example, at 4.28 it is most improbable that the change from the word 'cautious' to 'cautelous' is other than Scott's own, and at 13.10–11 there is an addition of a speech indicator typical of the kind of change Scott usually made. At 21.30 the position of the gallows tree is given specifically as 'towards the eastern end of the Grassmarket'; at 213.2–7 a passage is added giving extra force to the case against Effie; and at 292.1–2 a sentence is inserted clarifying Mr Staunton's legal position in relation to Jeanie's plight: 'He was a justice of peace, he informed her, as well as a clergyman'. In the Porteous passage discussed above Scott's biggest intervention was to add the motto at the head of the chapter (56.8–9); in *The Heart of Mid-Lothian* twenty-four of the mottoes are added post-manuscript. These changes are characteristic of the kind of activity which takes place between manuscript and first edition, as the intermediaries 'socialise' Scott's text for its appearance in print, and as Scott takes yet another opportunity to adjust, to expand, and to clarify.

However, even though the intermediaries on the whole made an excellent job of translating Scott's manuscript into a printed text, there must have been problems in the production process for *The Heart of Mid-Lothian* is perhaps the most poorly produced of all of the Waverley fictions. The text is riddled with compositors' errors. In the novel as a whole there are 36 missing apostrophes (the contracted form of 'it is' appears as *its* on many occasions), and 14 wrongly positioned apostrophes, such as *Dumbiedike's* at 46.7, *dy'e* at 268.15, and *stair's* at 371.6. This excludes all issues about how to represent manuscript readings in print (for example should the manuscript *its* be 'it is' or 'it's'). There are many examples where a list which normally comes without commas in the manuscript is still without commas in the first edition: 'coat waistcoat and breeches' (28.4) is the first instance of this kind. In Volume 3 alone there are at least eleven glaring printing errors, such as an inverted letter appearing in the word 'supposing' at 236.33 (found in all copies examined), and two missing letters in the word 'reluctance' at 237.39 (found in some of the copies examined). There is an uncommonly high number of instances of slipped print, and this is a pattern which persists throughout the four volumes. Most of these many errors would normally have been caught in the process of proof-reading; why they were missed in the case of *The Heart of Mid-Lothian* has not been determined.

More problematically for the present editors, internal literary errors persist. It was normally Ballantyne's job to catch such errors, but the failings in this novel are many and extraordinary. For example, in the first edition Effie's counsel is called 'Langtale' (185.33), but later becomes 'Fairbrother'. At 328.17–18 Scott added—presumably at proof stage—a phrase stating that Jeanie had never been in a coach, seemingly forgetting, as he re-enters his text, that she had travelled in one earlier in the novel. More importantly, Effie, we are told initially, is 'a modest-looking, black-haired girl' (44.13), but at 84.36 Effie has a 'Grecian-shaped head' that is 'profusely rich in waving ringlets of brown hair'. At 91.18 Effie has 'large dark eye-lashes', yet at her trial she is told to pull back her 'beautiful and abundant tresses of long fair hair' (197.17). Most muddled of all, on the night when Robertson meets

Jeanie at Arthur's Seat, we are told that Madge escapes on Ratcliffe's hint 'with all the dispatch she could exert' (161.1–2); however, the next day, when her mother comes to look for her at the Tolbooth, we are told that she is fetched 'from the jail' (169.10), Scott apparently forgetting that he has set her free the previous evening.

When dealing with texts where proofs survive, such as *Quentin Durward* or *Redgauntlet*, the editors of the Edinburgh Edition of the Waverley Novels have found a careful attention to detail and production quality, but their customary processes seem to have gone awry in the case of *The Heart of Mid-Lothian*. The small portion of proofs which survives offers no illumination about what went wrong. It is not uncommon for Scott to make mistakes over details such as the varying colour of Effie's hair, or Madge's escape and inexplicable reappearance; it is, however, unusual for the normally pedantic James not to have noticed them and not to have called Scott's attention to them in the proofs, for these are precisely the kinds of detail he usually pointed out to Scott. Even the carelessness of the mechanical processes suggests that there was a lack of heed being taken in the Ballantyne printing-house at this time. Certainly, Constable and Co. chide them for a problem over the paper on which the novel is printed. On 29 July 1818 they write:

> The complaints of the Paper on which the Tales of My Landlord, *Second Series* are printed, continue to such an extent, that we are compelled however reluctantly to request you to pause before you settle Messrs Cowans' account—the quality is in no respect equal to the price charged … the disgrace attending all who are connected with the publication is so considerable that no deduction can compensate the loss of character attending the production of these celebrated books—when they appear in an inferior and unbusiness like style the charge of 24/- made by Messrs Cowans is totally out of the question[92]

No complaints are recorded as to the preparation and printing of the book, but it would seem that more was wrong than the quality of paper.

It is impossible to account for this lack of attention to detail, although it is possible that the death of James and John Ballantyne's mother early in the novel's composition had disturbed the normally successfully cooperative relationship between James and Scott. That James was paying some attention to the contents of the text is evident in the letter about Robertson's character quoted above, but the kind of alteration which takes place between manuscript and first edition actually implies that Scott was responding to the proofs in a more mechanical way than we would normally expect. Two passages in particular demonstrate this. At some point between the manuscript and the first edition Scott adds a passage to explain why Jeanie has not visited Effie while she has been working at Mrs Saddletree's shop:

> The lingering illness of her mistress had, for the last few months,

given her a plea for confining herself entirely to the dusky precincts of the shop in the Lawn-market, and Jeanie was so much occupied, during the same period, with the concerns of her father's household, that she had rarely found leisure for a walk into the city, and a brief and hurried visit to her sister. The young women, therefore, had scarcely seen each other for several months, nor had a single scandalous surmise reached the ears of the secluded inhabitants of the cottage at Saint Leonard's. (92.39–93.4)

Later, he adds another passage of this 'explanatory' kind to justify Staunton's account of his life to Jeanie:

At the risk of being somewhat heavy, as explanations usually prove, we must here endeavour to combine into a distinct narrative, information which the invalid communicated in a manner at once too circumstantial, and too much broken by passion, to admit of our giving his precise words. Part of it, indeed, he read from a manuscript, which he had perhaps drawn up for the information of his relations after his decease. (298.20–26)

These two passages are heavy indeed; they exhibit an unusual degree of awkwardness, clumsiness, and flat-footed pedantry. As readers we accept details of the plot such as Jeanie's ignorance of Effie's pregnancy; if they are not entirely realistic they have narrative coherence and we go along with them. And we do not need to be told that the narrator will 'endeavour to combine into a distinct narrative, information which the invalid communicated in a manner at once too circumstantial, and too much broken by passion, to admit of our giving his precise words'. This is, after all, a narrative convention without which the novel form could hardly exist. Experience of proofs suggests that these passages may have been prompted by precisely the kind of literal-mindedness which James often expresses—acting as the 'normal' reader to suggest that Scott clarify details which might seem obscure to those more dull than himself. While Scott is often induced to adjust his text, he is equally likely to resist suggestions for change in a piece of good-humoured banter of the kind quoted above. In this novel, however, he has responded to the hypothetical queries by adding these awkward and clumsy passages. Of course James has a point. John Sutherland has written memorably on the improbability of Effie managing to conceal her pregnancy from her sister: 'What is unlikely is that a woman, in any normal social situation, should be able to disguise her altered physical shape in the last months of pregnancy, or that she should be able to deliver her own child without the assistance of a midwife'.[93] John Sutherland is wrong: the records of the trials for child murder show all too clearly that some young women were successful in hiding their condition, and did attempt to give birth in secret. But history is not always probable, and it is that lack of probability that Scott has addressed in this added passage. Yet even if constrained by the pressure of this realisation to add an explanation, why was it a totally unconvincing, circumstantial explanation rather than a cultural one, such as the disparity in the sisters' ages, the general lack of frankness on such subjects in a time when the Church punished fornication, the fear of her father, and even the nature of eighteenth-century clothes which could easily have concealed the pregnancy of a young and slim girl until the last few weeks?

Ironically, while *The Heart of Mid-Lothian* is marred by failure in the production process, even at the most mechanical of levels, the novel also demonstrates a failure in the transmission from manuscript to printed text caused by an over-zealousness on the part of the intermediaries. In the novel Jeanie Deans writes two sets of letters, the first when she stops off in York, and the second when she has seen the queen and obtained Effie's pardon. In the first edition, each set of these letters contains a number of odd orthographical variants, seemingly justifying Jeanie's apology that she has 'ane ill pen' (252.29) and Scott's statement on the poor state of her orthography (252.30–36). However, in Scott's manuscript, the letters contain many more spelling variants, including the words 'orguns' for 'organs', 'reeding' for 'reading', 'dout' for 'doubt', 'cristian' for 'Christian', 'sine' for 'sign', and 'Thistell' for 'Thistle'. It was, of course, part of the role of the intermediaries to normalise Scott's spelling; his spellings of 'turnd' for 'turned' or 'sinderd' for 'sindered' in the letters, for example, are also normal features of Scott's holograph. Equally, it is common to find in Scott's hand, as we do here, the spellings 'knowlege' and 'comparaison' and the normalisation of the spelling of these words is accepted by the editors of the Edinburgh Edition as part of the process of socialising the text. However, Jeanie's letters contain spellings quite distinct from what would normally be expected; for example, while the word 'mickle' appears 53 times in the manuscript and as 'muckle' 27 times, it appears as 'muckell' in Jeanie's letters only. The words 'pardun', 'instriments', and 'Edinbrugh' are also not found elsewhere in the manuscript of *The Heart of Mid-Lothian*, nor in the manuscripts of other novels. It is clear that the intermediaries, in their zealousness to normalise Scott's spelling for the first edition, obscured the full difference of Jeanie's orthography and the impact of the social and intellectual points implied by it. While this provides a textual justification for restoring the spelling of Jeanie's letters as proposed by the manuscript, Scott also offers a cultural justification: 'Jeanie Deans wrote and spelled fifty times better than half the women of rank in Scotland at that period' (252.33–34). The claim 'fifty times better than half the women' cannot be verified, of course, but the point is just. There was no fixed orthography for Scots, and those learning to write used forms which approximated to the sounds which they were uttering. The finest example is to be found in Lady Grisell Baillie's household accounts which she kept from the time of her marriage in 1692 until her death in 1746.[94] The real woman was rather older than the fictional, but she still illustrates well the way in which spelling for that generation of women was roughly phonetic, unlike modern British spelling which since Samuel Johnson has been determined and fixed by etymologies.

To the editors of the Edinburgh Edition of the Waverley Novels this example is particularly satisfying; it both illuminates the processes involved in converting a Waverley Novel from manuscript to first edition, and by demonstrating the ways in which these normally successful processes might go awry justifies both their return to the manuscript as a source of emendation and the editorial procedures followed in interpreting the manuscript.

Examination of the press figures of the first edition have shown some variation, but collation of the relevant gatherings has demonstrated that there is only one state of the first edition. Basic typographical errors in the text, such as turned letters, are not corrected indicating that corrections were probably not made in the course of printing, although this could only be determined definitively by collating a large number of copies. Some copies of the novel exist with the information 'Vol 1' and the signature 'A' at the foot of page 1 while others lack these, but collation has shown there is no textual variation in the gathering. A copy in the National Library of Scotland having this information contains a note which identifies it as the 'second state', but this variant alone does not justify the appellation.[95] The four pages of preliminaries exist in two states; no doubt they were set in duplicate, but there is no textual variation. It is a truism to say that no copy of a hand-set text is identical to any other; this is probably true of *The Heart of Mid-Lothian*, but the variation between copies that has been observed can all be attributed to the printing process, and nothing indicates interventions in the text in the course of printing.

3. THE LATER EDITIONS

Library catalogues imply that there were second and third editions of *The Heart of Mid-Lothian*, but in fact between the first and the last editions to be published in Scott's lifetime the novel was reissued in Britain only as part of the *Novels and Tales of the Author of Waverley*, which had five editions between 1819 and 1825: two octavo editions in 1819 and 1822, two duodecimo editions in 1822 and 1825, and one 18mo in 1823. The first American edition was published by Carey and Son of Philadelphia in 1818. The textual relationship of these various editions is described in the text below and represented in the stemma on the next page.

The Second and Third Editions. Examination of press figures shows that copies of the novel which profess to be second and third editions consist of first-edition sheets with new title pages. Some 10,000 copies of *Rob Roy* had been published and sold out within a fortnight,

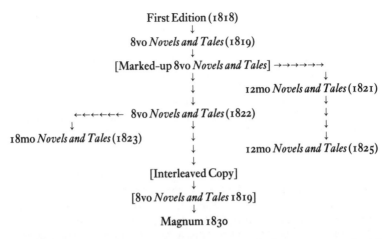

First Edition (1818)
↓
8vo *Novels and Tales* (1819)
↓
[Marked-up 8vo *Novels and Tales*] → → → → → →
↓   ↓
↓   12mo *Novels and Tales* (1821)
↓   ↓
← ← ← ← ← ← 8vo *Novels and Tales* (1822)   ↓
↓   ↓   ↓
18mo *Novels and Tales* (1823)   ↓   ↓
↓   12mo *Novels and Tales* (1825)
↓
[Interleaved Copy]
↓
[8vo *Novels and Tales* 1819]
↓
Magnum 1830

and optimism was equally high for the new novel, since 10,000 copies of that were also printed. However, demand did not match the optimism; sales were slower. This may have been due to the time of year, the election, the title, and the price, as Cadell laments, but Constable and Co.'s quarrel with Longman and Co. was the principal cause. In his desire to maximise the return to Constables, Cadell had sacrificed their distribution system, and there was confusion among London booksellers who did not realise that for this title Longmans was only a retailer, not a wholesaler. And when there was a shortage of books in the south Constables responded with some churlishness, on 7 August refusing to sell them to Longmans at a reduced price, and stating, against all later evidence, that 'the book is almost gone'.[96] This was clearly a lie. It seems that Constables was issuing 'second-edition' copies at some point before November (the profits for the 'second edition' were entered in Constable and Co.'s accounts in August and September 1818).[97] As late as 25 November 1818 Cadell recounts having told James Ballantyne that they had 1931 copies of the novel remaining,[98] and on 26 November he wrote that 'a sale should reduce 750 of them at least'.[99]

The Carey Edition (1818). In 1996 Jane Millgate established that Robinson and Co. of Leeds, who later moved to London to become Hurst, Robinson and Co., had been supplying American outlets with surplus stock from Constables, and that in 1817 they agreed to supply early proofs of works by Scott. The first fruits of this arrangement was *Rob Roy* which was dispatched to America on 19 December 1817.[100] The first American edition of *The Heart of Mid-Lothian* was published by Matthew Carey in 1818, but the collation of that edition shows that it was derived not from early proofs, but either final proofs or the first edition. There are only 69 verbal variants; a few correct mistakes in the first edition (the date set for Porteous's hanging and the date of his lynching appears as 8 September) but the rest are their own straightforward mistakes—single words omitted, added, or substituted, a few misunderstandings such as Ratcliffe saying that they would have to get Madge to guide them through the Park, adding 'I'll see if I can get her keepit in ony better order', which in the Carey edition becomes 'I'll see if I can get her keep it in ony better order' (157.33–34). This was the first Scott novel to be published by Carey, and is historically important, but it has no significance for the transmission of the text of *The Heart of Mid-Lothian*.

The Octavo *Novels and Tales* (1819). Constable and Co.'s squabble with Longman and Co. had left them without London partners and rather than patch up their relationship with what Cadell called 'a selfish set' they decided, after the publication of *The Heart of Mid-Lothian* and the trouble its distribution had caused them, to enter into a new arrangement with Hurst, Robinson and Co.[101] In the November following the publication of *The Heart of Mid-Lothian* Cadell wrote to Constable: 'The more I consider the arrangements so near a conclusion with H & R I am the more convinced of the great utility they will be to us—and looking to such a transaction as the ground work of our future ease and prosperity'.[102] One of the first fruits of this new relationship was the preparation and publication of the *Novels and Tales of the Author of Waverley*, a collected edition of Scott's novels which was eventually issued in three different formats and which would establish, they hoped, a new and expanded market for Scott's fiction, and, of course, a new source of profit.

In 1819 Constable purchased the copyrights of the first seven novels and proceeded to plan his collected editions. The first of these, the octavo *Novels and Tales*, was clearly well under way by May 1819, for on the 7th Constable and Co. wrote to Hurst, Robinson and Co., saying:

> We send you with this two of the drawings for Illustrations of the works of the Author of Waverley, which we would be obliged by your getting us an estimate of the expence of engraving in twelve prints, such as we have already described to you. The other drawings will be ready and forwarded gradually from this time till the beginning of October when we hope the whole will be finished...
> ... The illustrations of Waverly &c are intended to suit both 8vo & the original 12mo of the Works. The drawings now sent are too large for the small size, and must we presume be reduced a little. We are anxious to see the Specimens of the Illustrations which are doing for some similar works.[103]

As David Hewitt has argued, part of Constable and Co.'s motive in producing the collected editions was to move the printing away from James Ballantyne and Co.[104] While Scott's intervention on 19 April prevented them doing so, they were clearly unhappy with being tied to the one (expensive) printer, and on 21 September 1819 wrote to Ballantyne to suggest that the firm could not fulfil its printing obligations:

> but as you say *you cannot* do them and do Ivanhoe, the matter comes to this, that we must relieve you of two or three Volumes of the Octavo Novels—and you must do your utmost with the foolscap poetry—of the Octavo Novels there are still *five* Volumes to do in time, which it is a matter of *utter impossibility* your accomplishing ... but as Ivanhoe—the Octavo ⟨volumes⟩ Novels, and the foolscap poetry *must* all be ready at the same time, why what can we do but get foreign aid ... this then is the upshot—we shall get the 2nd Tales managed.[105]

They wrote the next day giving more specific information:

> I now state how the Book [8vo Novels] stands in your printing House
>
> There are seven of the twelve Vols finished, and of the remaining *five* only 14 sheets are done.
>
> There are finished, consequently little more than half of the Job, and Six weeks only to spare This will never do. We have therefore in conformity with the conversation we had with you this morning put Vols 9 & 10 into another office Vols 1, 2, 3, 4, 5—11 & 12 are done. You have thus only 6, 7, & 8 to complete—and to these do pray bend your whole force.[106]

On 24 November 1819 they wrote to James Ballantyne: 'Now that the 8o Novels are within some sheets of being completed at press I hope you will be able to deliver us half of the impression within a week—your doing so would much oblige us'.[107] On 26 November they wrote to Ballantyne: 'I am glad to find that the 8vo Novels are so nearly ready, and shall reckon on one half of the Impression being ready for packing and sending up here on the morning of the day you name'.[108] And on the same day they wrote to Hurst, Robinson: 'The 12 Vols Novels and Tales will be shipped on the 3 dec. you should push them during the last weeks of the year as much as possible'.[109] On 3 December 1819 they wrote again to Hurst, Robinson informing them: 'We annex Invoice of 650 Nov'ls & Tales'.[110] The edition was published in Edinburgh on 9 December 1819. On 18 December 1819 Hurst, Robinson wrote to Constable and Co.: 'The 12 Vols Novels 8vo arrived on Wednesday and are all delivered to the Trade'.[111] Publication was announced in the *Edinburgh Evening Courant* of 9 December 1819 and in London on the 28th.[112]

The Heart of Mid-Lothian occupies volumes 9 and 10 of the 1819 octavo, the two volumes which were farmed out to another printer, even though the colophon specifies James Ballantyne and Co. The edition shows little sign of intellectual engagement with Scott's text. It corrects the mechanical failures of the first edition such as turned letters and slipped print. It shows a tendency to modernise Scott's spelling ('shew' becomes 'show' on many occasions), and street names assume their modern form ('High Street' replacing 'High-street', for example). There is an increase in capitalisation: words like 'presbyterian' which usually begin with a lower case letter in the first edition are consistently capitalised in the 1819 octavo. There are many instances of changes in hyphenation. In the Porteous passage discussed above, the 1819 octavo alters the wrongly numbered chapter of the first edition (56.7), adds a comma after 'even that' at 57.9, and another at 57.10 after 'contingency' (now emended to 'contingence'). It alters the spelling of 'enterprize' to 'enterprise' at 57.15, and 'showed' to 'shewed' at 57.22 (usually the change is in the reverse direction). It closes the gap between 'turrets' and the comma which follows (57.36), adds a hyphen in 'lurking place' at 58.6 and deletes one in 'Grassmarket' at 58.17. Such minor changes are typical. In all there are some 45 verbal changes: most are mistakes, but the only bloomer is its transformation of Mrs Crombie (who is suing her neighbour) from a 'pursuer' into a 'prisoner' (243.15). Some 182 commas are added and 125 deleted; there are 93 further alterations in punctuation, many of which correct first-edition errors such as providing missing apostrophes, but others destroy the first-edition indicator of interrupted speech, namely closing inverted commas followed by a dash, by substituting a dash followed by inverted commas which the manuscript and first edition use to indicate speech that trails away. There are also 163 changes in spelling, and 34 in capitalisation. This was a competently-executed 'copy-typing' job, and as such confirms that it was not printed by James Ballantyne and Co., which could not resist 'improving' Scott's text.

The Duodecimo *Novels and Tales* (1821). The first duodecimo edition of *Novels and Tales of the Author of Waverley* in 16 volumes was announced in the *Edinburgh Evening Courant* on 31 March 1821.[113] *The Heart of Mid-Lothian* occupies part of Volume 11, the whole of Volumes 12 and 13, and part of Volume 14; 1500 copies were ordered.[114]

The 1821 duodecimo has variants which it shares with the 1819 octavo: 'filled' for 'fulfilled' (3.11); 'lessons' for 'lesson' (73.28); 'obtaining' for 'attaining' (80.19); 'she replied' for 'replied she' (167.20); and 'accident' for 'incident' (364.11). In the Porteous passage there is a comma after 'even that' at 57.9, and 'contingence' at 57.10, 'showed' is changed to 'shewed' at 57.22, a hyphen is added to 'lurking place' (58.6), and the hyphen removed from 'Grassmarket' (58.17). Trivial though these examples are, they are typical of the many variants that are to be found in both the 1819 octavo and the 1821 duodecimo, and prompt the conclusion that the latter was set from the former.

The 1821 edition also shares variants with the 1822 octavo edition which are not found in the 1819 version. This might suggest that the

1822 octavo was set from the 1821 duodecimo, but there are readings in 1821 that are not found in 1822. As 1821 and 1822 share variants that are not in 1819, and as both have variants that they do not share, it is probable that both the duodecimo of 1821, and the octavo of 1822 were set independently of each other from a marked-up copy of the 1819 octavo edition of *Novels and Tales of the Author of Waverley*. A comparison of the two editions of 1821 and 1822 shows that what they have in common (in addition to the readings taken in from 1819) is almost entirely confined to Volumes 1 and 2 (Volume 9 in the octavo *Novels and Tales*); thus only one of the two volumes was marked up. A new footnote on Salisbury Crags at 65.9 is dated 1820 ('A beautiful and solid pathway has now been formed around these romantic rocks.—1820'), and this suggests that the marking-up was done in 1820; it is almost as though Ballantyne, annoyed at losing the contract to print Volumes 9 and 10, got hold of them and went through the first of them indicating what his firm would have done better.

The hypothetical marked-up 1819 edition attends to some clear errors, most notably at 44.13 where the colour of Effie's hair becomes 'fair', and at 44.22 where 'Andrew Deans' is corrected to 'David Deans'. At 10.40 'the inconvenience' becomes 'the manifest inconvenience', while 'too' is added after 'client' at 12.6. Butler's 'Fine day' is altered to 'A fine day' (117.37), 'expressed' to 'exhibited' (133.35), and 'away' to 'from you' (133.42), both the latter two to remove repetition. It attempts to distinguish Scots and English more emphatically. For instance, it begins to remove Scots from Robertson's speech while he is in his Wildfire disguise (this was probably a mistake—would Robertson have wanted to be identified as English while leading an Edinburgh mob?) and so 'flee' becomes 'fly' on five occasions (59.10, 11, 13, 19), 'ain' becomes 'own' (59.19), and 'skaith' becomes 'violence' (60.14). It makes the speech of Scots speakers more Scots—Saddletree's 'It's too true, Mr Butler' becomes 'It's ower true' (42.32). Speech marks are occasionally inserted (such as 'said the agent' after 'honest man' at 13.15). In the Porteous passage a semicolon replaces the comma after 'execution' (56.12); 'seem' becomes 'seemed' (57.27), thus correcting a first-edition fault sensibly for it could not be known that Scott had written 'seems' in the manuscript; 'gi'e' becomes 'gie' (58.21); and those who were accustomed to 'conceal' now 'shroud' or 'shrowd' themselves from justice (58.40). These examples are shared by both 1821 and 1822, and are characteristic of the corrections inscribed in the putative marked-up copy of the 1819 octavo: they are light, unsystematic, and brief—the footnote is the longest addition. Although Scott was perfectly capable of executing all of these corrections, the absence of any imaginative enhancement superior to the substitution of 'shroud' for 'conceal' suggests that it was not he who annotated that copy of the 1819 edition.

There are many changes in the 1821 duodecimo which are not shared with 1822. The majority are marks of punctuation, and the verbal changes more often look like accidents than deliberate revisions. In the Porteous passage a comma is deleted after 'us' in the motto on page 56, commas appear after 'convicted' (56.15) and 'justice' (58.11), and 'gi'ed' is replaced by 'gave' (58.23). The 1821 edition has a tendency to add commas, and to upgrade existing commas to semicolons; it also exhibits a fondness for exclamation marks. It shows some degree of intellectual engagement, but the changes are not creative, and none suggests the author.

The Octavo *Novels and Tales* (1822). By 5 July 1821 there were only 25 copies of the first edition of the octavo *Novels and Tales* left in Edinburgh.[115] A new edition was ordered; it was shipped to London in January 1822 and publication was announced in the *Edinburgh Evening Courant* on 2 February.[116]

The 1822 octavo has all the changes which apparently derive from the 'marked-up copy' previously discussed. In its own right it demonstrates a greater involvement in the text than its 1819 and 1821 predecessors, but not one which is creative, or authorial. It too has a tendency to add commas and modernise spelling. It makes changes of a more substantive nature by continuing the role of the intermediaries in altering words to avoid verbal repetition. It does, from time to time, correct inherited errors, guessing, for example, the correct reading 'cure' as the word for a minister's parochial charge instead of 'care' (384.2). In the Porteous passage it accepts the changes of the 1819 octavo, and adds further changes of its own. It deletes a comma after 'office' at 56.28, and after 'door' at 57.16. It resolves a first-edition muddle at 57.11–15, where the first edition reads:

> But Porteous and his friends alike wanted presence of mind to suggest or execute such a plan of escape. The former hastily fled from a place where their own safety seemed compromised, and the latter, in a state resembling stupefaction, awaited in his apartment the termination of the enterprize of the rioters.

There is clearly confusion between the referents of the 'former' and 'latter', which the 1822 octavo resolves through a complete reorganisation of the sentence:

> But Porteous and his friends alike wanted presence of mind to suggest or execute such a plan of escape. The former, in a state resembling stupefaction, awaited in his apartment the termination of the enterprize of the rioters, and the latter hastily fled from a place where their own safety seemed compromised.

It changes the spelling of 'farther' to 'further' at 57.30. In addition, it continues the anglicisation of Robertson's speech by altering the word 'ye' twice at 58.10–11. It removes an apostrophe in 'gi'ed' at 58.23.

Including the changes coming from the hypothetical marked-up copy, there are 191 verbal differences from 1819; 242 commas are added and 186 deleted; there are 172 other changes in punctuation, and 334 in spelling; capitals are raised on 57 occasions and lowered on 34; there are about 50 other changes. All the figures are indicative rather than precise, and what they indicate is a large volume of inconsequential, often fairly random, change. And some of it is just careless: for example, the path which is 'pursued' in the editions of 1818 and 1819 is here 'perused' (134.42); when Sharpitlaw bets that it is Robertson whom Jeanie is to meet in the Park, he (amusingly) wagers a 'bottle' rather than Scott's 'boddle' (155.7); and the proverb 'ilk land has its ain laugh' is perverted into 'ilka land has its ain law' (252.20).

The 18mo *Novels and Tales* (1823). Constable forecast a new market for Scott's work with a small inexpensive edition. Hurst, Robinson and Co. was clearly impressed, for in a letter of 14 August 1821 they ordered 5000 copies, which were to be delivered for publication on 10 October 1822, and which were to be printed by Ballantynes 'in their best style on a new Type'.[117] Work on preparing the edition had begun by April 1822; printing was completed in mid-August 1823, and the last consignment was sent to London on 5 September.[118] The new 'miniature edition' at £4 4s. (£4.20) was advertised in the *Morning Chronicle* in London on 11 September and in the *Edinburgh Evening Courant* on 20 September 1823.[119]

The Heart of Mid-Lothian occupies Volumes 9 and 10 in this edition. A copy of the 1822 octavo was used as copy-text, probably because the volume divisions in the octavo and the 18mo editions are the same. That it was the 1822 edition on which the 18mo was based is established by collation evidence. For instance, at 26.4–6 the first edition reads:

> The public, where their own prejudices are not concerned, are
> easily engaged on the side of disinterestedness and humanity,
> admired Wilson's behaviour, and rejoiced in Robertson's escape.

The 1821 duodecimo, recognising that something is wrong, resolves it by altering the 'are' to read 'who', a change also found in the 1825 duodecimo. The 1822 octavo and the 18mo, however, resolve the same difficulty by changing the word to 'being'. The 18mo resolves the muddled sentences at 57.11–15 in the same way as the 1822 octavo. It also keeps two of the mistakes of 1822 listed above: the path is still 'perused' (134.42), and Sharpitlaw bets his 'bottle' (155.7).

Of all the *Novels and Tales* editions the 1823 18mo shows the greatest signs of having been dealt with in an intelligent way. In a letter of 16 September 1822 Scott told James Ballantyne: 'I send two proofs and Copy also last Vol: of novels. I shall wish to correct the succeeding volumes also of the new edition.'[120] The date suggests that he is referring to the 1823 18mo, and the reference to a volume suggests that he has marked up what we have deduced was an 1822 octavo volume. But it is not clear which of the twelve volumes he has 'corrected', nor whether he ever got as far as *The Heart of Mid-Lothian*. Internal evidence offers no proof of Scott's involvement in these volumes of the 18mo, for without exception every change could have been effected by a sympathetic editor such as James Ballantyne. The accumulation of punctuation continues; the compositor seems fond of using dashes and semicolons. There is a tendency to modernise spelling; 'groupes' becomes 'groups', for example, at 37.1. There is also, however, a greater willingness to alter the text in substantive ways, although only occasionally can this be said to result in improvement rather than change for its own sake. At times the changes even result in a deterioration such as at 33.33, where the elimination of the words 'which, being' leaves a sentence with no connection between its clauses. At 44.42–43 Mrs. Saddletree's 'be in a lying-in hospital' is altered to read 'live a week in a lying-in hospital', a change which may clarify, but is not necessary.

The Porteous passage in the 18mo absorbs the changes that had accumulated in the 1819 and 1822 octavos, and adds its own. A comma is added after 'convicted' at 56.15. At 56.24 Porteous's friends do not 'advise' him, but 'desired' him to ask to be transferred to the Castle. The spelling of 'connection' is altered to 'connexion' at 56.34, and a comma is added after the second 'and' on 56.40. A comma is upgraded to a semicolon after 'overcome' at 57.42. 'This sacrifice' becomes 'The sacrifice' at 58.12, and 'spilled' becomes 'spilt' at 58.14. A dash is added after 'justice' at 58.40.

The Duodecimo *Novels and Tales* (1825). The second duodecimo edition appeared unheralded in the spring of 1825. The print-order is unknown.

The 1825 duodecimo is based upon the edition of 1821, shares its changes, and adds many variants of its own. The substitution of the word 'character' for 'habits' at 26.39 to avoid a repetition that occurs two lines later is one of the latter, although this only produces another, and closer repetition on the previous line; the 1822 octavo is the only other of the *Novels and Tales* editions to deal with this and, somewhat more successfully, changes the second occurrence of the word at 26.41 to 'manners'. The 1825 edition shows signs of James's literal-mindedness, explaining, for example, Porteous's phrase 'they will murder me without time' by adding 'for repentance' (60.41) without recognising that 'without time' is an established idiom. In the Porteous passage the 1825 duodecimo adds to the 1821 variants an alteration in the spelling of 'connection' to 'connexion' at 56.35, and a comma between 'and' and 'alas' at 56.40. It resolves the muddle at 57.11–15 in a simple way, but one unique to itself, by exchanging the words 'former' and 'latter' so that the passage reads:

But Porteous and his friends alike wanted presence of mind to suggest or execute such a plan of escape. The latter hastily fled from a place where their own safety seemed compromised, and the former, in a state resembling stupefaction, awaited in his apartment the termination of the enterprize of the rioters.

There is no question but that the 1825 duodecimo was based upon the 1821 edition. However, the alteration in the spelling of 'connection' at 56.35, and the insertion of a comma between 'and' and 'alas' at 56.40, were also features of the 1823 edition. Such changes could well be coincidental. In addition, the 1825 duodecimo shares substantive variants with the 1823 18mo, such as the addition of the phrase 'the descendants of one' in place of 'He' at 4.33. There is no obvious explanation: 1825 does not systematically gather in material new to 1823—the footnote to 65.9 is different in 1823 from how it appears in both 1821 and 1825. Maybe the best explanation is that Scott did write a few corrections into the volumes of the 1822 octavo edition which were used as copy for the 1823 18mo, and that these volumes were referred to when 1825 was being typeset.

The 1825 duodecimo is just another version of *The Heart of Mid-Lothian*. It was reasonably well executed, but it has no textual merits, and no textual authority. It leads nowhere, never having been used for another edition. It is a textual dead end. But it does exhibit yet again the extraordinary assumption of the Ballantyne printing business that it could 'improve' what an author had written.

The Interleaved Set and the Magnum. In 1823 Archibald Constable proposed a collected edition of all Scott's fiction, corrected and annotated by the author, and to facilitate its preparation he had prepared an interleaved set of the novels. Scott demurred, came round to the idea in 1825, but, as the financial crash of January 1826 put in doubt the ownership of the copyrights, he spent the next two years on other literary activities. In 1827 Robert Cadell, who had become Scott's sole publisher, resurrected the scheme for a complete, annotated version of the Waverley Novels, and it was finally published in 48 volumes, a volume a month, between 1 June 1829 and 3 May 1833. The full story of the making of the 'Magnum Opus', or just 'Magnum' as the final edition is known, is to be found in Jane Millgate's *Scott's Last Edition* (Edinburgh, 1987). The first 12 volumes of the Interleaved Set are based on the 1822 octavo *Novels and Tales*.

The interleaved copy of *The Heart of Mid-Lothian* may be found in mss 23009 and 23010 in the National Library of Scotland. In it Scott makes approximately 250 verbal changes to the text, discounting those places where he indicates that notes should be added. The great majority of these changes occur in the first half of the novel, and in particular in the opening chapters, suggesting that to some extent he lost interest in the process of revision; indeed the text corresponding to the last two volumes of the first edition exhibits very few changes. Typical changes include the clarification of who is speaking, such as 'answerd the young man vaguely' (45.16) or 'said David with solemnity' (79.22). Scott does make more creative contributions, such as the details that the City Guard were 'acting in short as a armd police' (27.6) and that Meg Murdockson is 'extremely haggard in looks and wretched in her apparel' (167.18). The description of Porteous's suspended body as Butler retreats from the scene and the additional comment that he 'could even observe men striking at it with their Lochaber-axes & partizans' (62.33) is a disturbing detail present in Scott's sources but which he suppressed in his original account of the riot. At times, however, the changes seem to show a lack of real engagement with the text. At 22.3, for example, he changes 'walks' to 'stalks' when talking of the condemned prisoner being led to his death; normally one would imagine the new word to be an interesting alternative, but in this context it makes little sense. At 302.3, 302.12, and 305.35 during Staunton's long explanatory speech he further elaborates upon the details of 'Robertson's' movements around the time of Effie's confinement, and on what Jeanie might gain by giving him over to the state; but while these passages may provide extra information, it is arguably the case that they also add to the pedantry which had crept into these scenes between manuscript and first edition.

By far Scott's longest intervention in the interleaved copy occurs at 199.4 in the present text where he recognises that Effie's counsel is mistakenly named as 'Mr Fairbrother', when the night before Ratcliffe implies that 'Mr Langtale' will be acting. Rather than a simple change of name, Scott adds a passage which reads as follows:

> He began by lamenting that his senior at bar Mr Langtale had
> been calld suddenly to the county of which he was Sheriff and
> that he had been hastily calld upon to give the pannell his assistance
> in this intersting cause. He had had little time he said to make up
> for his inferiority ⟨in⟩ to his learned brother by long & minute
> research & he was afraid he might give a specimen of his ⟨ca⟩
> incapacity by being compelld to admit the ⟨relevancy of the indict-
> ment⟩ accuracy of the Indictment under the statute (Interleaved
> Copy, 9.408)

This material is, with standard normalisations, reproduced in the Magnum text (Magnum, 12.128–29). While it may resolve a relatively straightforward muddle (and one which would not have perhaps occurred if the novel had, in its first manifestation, been edited as rigorously as normal) it arguably demonstrates Scott is no longer in full sympathy with the text. In the first edition Effie's trial is scrupulously conducted, but the law by which she is judged and condemned is manifestly unjust; this new material suggests a hint of malpractice thus subtly shifting the balance of the narrative, and marring the point of Scott's original tale.

The normal practice during the production of the Magnum Opus edition was for Robert Cadell to incorporate Scott's revisions into the new text. Cadell gives an account of his activities on the Magnum throughout September and October 1829 in his diary.[121] He first mentions that he is 'busy all this evening copying notes to Tales of My Landlord' on 31 March 1829,[122] but does not specify which series. It is unlikely to be *The Heart of Mid-Lothian*, as he refers to the novel specifically by name on Friday 11 September when he 'revised part of Heart of Mid Lothian'.[123] He records having done so on Wednesday 16, Thursday 17, Friday 18, Monday 21, and Tuesday 22 September.[124] He notes on Wednesday 23 September that he has 'resumed revise of Heart of Mid Lothian',[125] and on Friday 2 October that he has 'finished the revisal of Heart of Mid Lothian'.[126] Of Scott's more than 250 verbal changes the Magnum includes all but 21, although those longer than a single word often had to undergo a process of 'socialisation' similar to that which takes place between manuscript and first edition. Ironically, the largest discrepancy between the interleaved copy and the Magnum occurs in Scott's ill-fated rendition of Jeanie's letters; in the second set at 349–52 Scott makes six substantive changes to the text of the letters, none of which is incorporated into the Magnum text.

The Magnum edition, of which *The Heart of Mid-Lothian* comprises part of Volume 11, Volume 12 and part of Volume 13, also produces approximately 330 semantic variants of its own, along with many more new variants in punctuation and spelling. It should be remembered that Scott was not responding to the first edition text, but to that of the 1822 octavo. However Cadell in preparing copy for the press copied and edited Scott's revisions and corrections into a copy of the 1819 octavo, and so achieved a fortuitous restoration of earlier readings. Thus the Magnum regains Robertson's 'Flee . . . Flee' (59.10, 11, 13, 19), the word 'expressed' (133.35), and 'boddle' in place of 'bottle' (155.7). Cadell, however, has none of Scott's creative inspiration, and does not even show James Ballantyne's pedantic common sense; his revisions, while they at times resolve such muddles as altering the statement that Jeanie had never been in a coach (328.17) to read 'seldom', or such confusions as the reference to the hillock of moss which 'the poet of Grasmere has described in the motto to our chapter' (273.1–2), his alterations to the Magnum edition are never inspired and sometimes wrong.

The Heart of Mid-Lothian appeared, therefore, in seven British editions in Scott's lifetime—in 1819 and 1822 as the octavo *Novels and Tales of the Author of Waverley*, in 1821 and 1825 as the duodecimo *Novels and Tales*, in 1823 as the 18mo *Novels and Tales*, and in 1830 as part of the Magnum Opus edition. While Constable and Co. clearly took some care with the physical appearance of these books, it was generally less concerned with the production of the text. Ballantyne, on the other hand, was very concerned with the text, but was committed to a false idea of 'improvement'. None of these later editions, with the exception of the Magnum, shows any real intellectual engagement with the novel or its text; each may correct mistakes but each also contributes to an increasing textual deterioration.

4. THE PRESENT TEXT

The only critical edition of the Waverley Novels is the Edinburgh Edition, but two novels, *Waverley*, edited by Claire Lamont, and *The Heart of Mid-Lothian*, edited by Tony Inglis, have been subject to modern textual scrutiny. Tony Inglis's edition of *The Heart of Mid-Lothian*[127] is a fine achievement. Like the editors of the EEWN, he chooses the first edition as his base text, and emends that text with readings from the manuscript which appear 'to arise from misreading, rather than intentional amendment'; but unlike the editors of the EEWN he then follows a classic Greig-Bowers procedure of adopting readings from Scott's interleaved copy, as well as readings from later editions (1819, 1821, 1822, 1823, 1825) which 'correct actual mistakes or appear to make improvements in line which those that Scott made himself'.[128]

The present edition is different in that it aims to be an ideal first edition; it is based upon a copy of the first edition, but it incorporates manuscript and proof readings which were lost through misreading, misunderstanding or straightforward transcription error during the process of converting the holograph text into four printed books. It is also the argument of the editors, an argument based on exhaustive study of the evidence, that none of the five editions published between 1819 and 1825 incorporates new material that can be identified as authorial, or even probably authorial, and that there is only minimal external evidence to suggest that Scott may have contributed to the 1823 18mo. Consequently, this edition does not draw upon these later editions except on those comparatively few occasions (in all 92) when they address manifest error (including the missing apostrophes discussed above) which was not noticed in the process of producing the first edition. The interleaved copy does of course contain Scott's revisions and notes, but because this edition of *The Heart of Mid-Lothian* is an ideal first edition it makes no use of new Scott material in the interleaved copy, except when it too corrects manifest error.

There are two main differences between this edition and that edited by Tony Inglis. Firstly, this text belongs almost entirely to 1818, the year in which *The Heart of Mid-Lothian* was created by Walter Scott. Secondly, the present edition confronts the problems created by the many 'copy-editing' failures. In doing this the editors are acting as the intermediaries ought to have done in 1818: while always respecting precisely what Scott wrote they develop means of establishing his intentions and preferences whenever these have been represented ineffectively in print, and emend appropriately in a way which involves minimal disturbance to what was written by the author.

Verbal Emendations. The vast majority of verbal emendations are derived from the manuscript, for the misreading, or misinterpretation, of even single letters, words or marks of punctuation can frequently make substantial differences to the reading of Scott's text. For example, in Scott's hand it is often difficult to distinguish between the long 's' and 'f' and in one instance, at 4.2, this difficulty results in a misreading whereby Jedidiah worries that his tales will have lost their 'favour' rather than their 'savour' with the public; in the current edition the word 'savour' is restored, thus reinstating Scott's Biblical reference. (Often recognising a literary reference is the clinching evidence of what Scott wrote.) Similarly, at 49.28 Scott writes that the Edinburgh district of Portsburgh is inhabited by the 'lower order of artizans and mechanics'. However, the word 'artizans' was misread as the far more neutral 'citizens', a mistake which spoils the sociological point Scott makes, and which creates a phrase that while intelligible conveys little. When Saddletree visits Butler in Liberton after Effie's trial, we are told that his account of the case of stillicide 'might have rested until poor Butler's hour of rest was completely exhausted' (243.34), but the manuscript in fact reads 'might have lasted', a phrase making greater immediate sense. When David Deans considers his move to Roseneath we read that there are two points on which he 'haggled' (378.23); the manuscript, however, reads 'boggled'. At 413.12 the first edition describes Jeanie as 'the real clean well-dressed mistress', but the manuscript reads 'the neat clean well-dressed mistress'. At 460.32 Scott writes that Donacha and his band have 'nested' the day before, a word misread in the transmission from manuscript to printed text as the far weaker 'rested'. At 441.12–13 two misreadings in close proximity result in the alteration of Scott's description in the manuscript of the landscape visited by Effie and David Butler as one where the rock 'contrasted strangely in contour' with the white foam of the cascade, to one where in the first edition it contrasts 'strongly in colour'. In each of these instances the stronger manuscript readings have been restored.

Later in the text a confusion between an 'n' and an 's' also results in a weakened, or even nonsensical reading; in a facing verso insert Scott writes that some of the Covenanters found the imposts for 'turnpikes and pontages' repugnant; the word which appears in the first edition, however, is 'postages' (177.39). This alteration in the first edition may have resulted purely from a confusion of letters, but it is also possible that the less familiar word 'pontages' was misunderstood by the intermediaries who consequently replaced it by a more familiar reading. This is a process which can be seen in operation repeatedly in the transmission of the text between the manuscript and the first edition. For example, at 17.11 Scott discusses the relationship between the law and fictional writing, and argues that it forms a 'sort of chapel of ease' to the volumes of the circulating library; in the first edition, however, 'chapel of ease' is replaced by 'appendix' as if an intermediary had failed to grasp the sense Scott intended, or perhaps even disapproved of his use of a religious metaphor. Later, the first edition informs us that David Deans considered dancing as 'one of the most flagrant proofs of defection and causes of wrath' (88.19); Scott's word in holograph, however, is in fact 'clamant'. At 175.32 Scott writes that David objects to the use of Richard Cameron's name for a 'regimented band of souldiers', a phrase rendered in print as a 'regimental band'. When Jeanie visits Dumbiedikes the manuscript tells us that she looks in the 'roofless shade where the hawks were once kept' (231.2–3), but the word in print is the more commonplace 'shed', as if the intermediary has failed to understand the more unusual Scots word for a shelter for birds. A similar failure in understanding seems to have resulted in the change of the manuscript description of Butler's hand as 'extenuated'—shrunken and emaciated through illness—to the more pedestrian account of it as 'extended' (247.15). A failure to understand Scott's sense when he wrote that Effie was 'a Lye of fifteen years standing' results in the far less loaded description of her as 'a liar' (439.38). In each case, what Scott wrote in manuscript has been restored. It would be hard to argue that these changes result from misreading alone; as all result in a weakened or more neutral text they seem to reflect a failure on the part of the intermediaries to understand the full range and complexity of Scott's language.

Elsewhere, Scott's text is diminished by a misreading which is made worse by a subsequent attempt to correct without reference to the manuscript. At 375.19, for example, he writes that if he sees his friends Wilkie or Allan he will 'beg borrow or steal from them a sketch'. However, the word 'beg' is misread as 'try' and the word 'to' added after it to make sense of the new reading. At 229.20 Scott writes in manuscript that the line of Dumbiedikes 'had vaild of its splendour in the present proprietor'; in print 'vaild' (meaning lowered) appears as 'veiled', and 'been' was added, but whoever effected the changes did not deal with the unidiomatic and intrusive 'of' (there is no support in the *OED* for 'of' with either verb). This pattern whereby misreading results in subsequent change is a common one, and not only moves the sense away from what Scott wrote, but reduces the force of his conception. These mistakes involve a failure of recognition; the intermediaries do not seem to grasp the meaning of particular words.

Defects also arise from the simple failure to notice material in the manuscript. The omission of single words can have a real impact upon the sense: at 45.37, for example, the phrase 'sighed bitterly' appears only as 'sighed', while at 40.9 Miss Damahoy reflects on the 'robes and foot-mantles that ↑ wad hae stude by their lane wi' gold & brocade and that ↓ were muckle in my ain line'. The ampersand was overlooked, significantly altering the meaning of the first-edition text. At other places the intermediaries failed to spot material on the facing verso. Early in the novel Hardie states: 'You are mistaken—it is quite the reverse—he is just delivered from it' (13.17–18); the phrase '—it is quite the reverse—' appears on the facing verso and was omitted in the first edition. At 22.5 the condemned prisoner walking to the gallows is described as 'looking in gait dress and features like a moving and walking corpse'; the phrase 'in gait dress and features' is on the facing verso and again fails to appear. At 226.13–14 the sentence 'He then conducted her to the door of the prison and permitted her to depart.' appears on the facing verso and seems simply to have been overlooked. Without it, Jeanie never leaves the Tolbooth.

The above examples are emended in the present edition; most result from the misreading or misunderstanding of letters, words or short phrases, or from the failure to assimilate material into the first-edition text.

Mistakes in Normalising the Text. It is a basic working assumption of the editors of the Edinburgh Edition of the Waverley Novels that the manuscript offers 'instructions' about how Scott's text ought to be realised in print, and it is the understanding of these 'instructions' that at times goes awry. Perhaps the most striking instance in *The Heart of Mid-Lothian* is the treatment of Jeanie's letters by the intermediaries. While it is clear that the intermediaries were acting in their expected fashion by normalising Scott's own spellings, it is also clear (as explained above) that there are failures in responding to Scott's 'instructions' as formulated in what he actually wrote in the folios where the letters appear. Here Scott's writing is unusually distinct and well-formed; while writing both sets of letters Scott sharpened his pen several times, giving his holograph unusual clarity. In addition, Scott places 'hooks' over the letter 'u' in words such as 'orguns', thus indicating that the letter is 'u', and not any other vowel. Such activity implies that Scott was anxious to write clearly and that implies that he expected what he wrote to be followed. But what he wrote was overlooked and Jeanie's spelling was normalised, at least to an extent. The decision has been taken to restore Jeanie's inconsistent and idiosyncratic orthography, which involves the inclusion of spellings such as 'orguns' (251.1), 'milns' (251.30), 'Thistell' (252.27), and 'cristian' (252.11).

Sometimes mistakes come from a failure to grasp the broader meaning. At several points in the novel, the intermediaries do not seem to have grasped Scott's wish to imply a particular dialect or ideolect; for example, at 254.18 Scott's 'at sign' appears in print as 'at the sign' while at 360.15 Dolly Dutton's 'ma loife' appears as 'my life'. These are examples of the intermediaries responding to their 'standing orders' too well, or at least too mechanically. At other times they are over-enthusiastic in eliminating verbal repetition, and do not recognise the rhetorical force of repetition. For example, at 54.25 Scott writes that 'gang after gang' of the Porteous mob relieve each other as they try to beat down the tolbooth door, and a few paragraphs later he writes that 'Urged by such motives for apprehension gang after gang eagerly relieved each other at the labour of assailing the tolbooth door' (55.26). However, perceiving the repetition as unfortunate rather than for dramatic effect, the second 'gang after gang' is altered to 'they' (55.26). A much more unfortunate instance occurs at 98.38 where the elimination of the repetition in Staunton's melodramatic 'name a name' results in the phrase 'find an appellation'.

Punctuation. Another source of emendation arises from a failure to interpret correctly Scott's intentions in respect of the punctuation of the text. Scott's holograph is very lightly punctuated and one of the roles of the intermediaries was to provide printed-book style punctuation. In most cases the intermediaries did well, but in some instances a failure in punctuating Scott's text can distort the sense. Often these failures are as simple as the misplacing of a comma, or the replacement of one mark of punctuation for another. At 12.38–43, for example, Scott, rather unusually, supplies a comma in the manuscript, which reads:

> The thin pale-faced man whom their good nature had brought into
> their society lookd out of place as well as out of spirits, sate on the
> edge of his ⟨chair⟩ ↑ seat ↓ and kept the ⟨ ↑ said ↓ ⟩ chair at two
> feet distance from the table thus incommoding himself considerably in conveying the victuals to his mouth as if by way of penance
> for partaking ↑ of ↓ them in the company of his superiors.

As is often the case, Scott's comma is 'upgraded' in the first edition into a semicolon. The first edition then supplies a semicolon at 12.40 between 'table' and 'thus' where Scott himself offers no punctuation. The appropriate punctuation in both instances is a comma, and these appear in the Edinburgh Edition text. Sometimes, punctuation is simply misplaced: at 13.3 the base text supplies the punctuation 'and saying, he would be in readiness, modestly'. Clearly, the punctuation should be 'and, saying he would be in readiness, modestly', and this is what appears in this edition.

Given the lightness of Scott's manuscript punctuation it is important that where he does supply punctuation it ought to be rendered in print. At 46.32, for example, Scott writes in manuscript 'Poor Effie!!!' but only one exclamation mark appears in the first edition; here Scott's triple level of exclamation has been restored. As with the case of semantic errors, sometimes a failure to understand what Scott has written results in the alteration of the punctuation in the text; at 236.28 for example, Scott writes 'silk gowns wad stand on their ends their lane— lace as fine as spiders webs'. However, the intermediary fails to notice, or to understand, Scott's phrase 'their lane' and in order to make sense of Scott's text supplies a comma and omits Scott's 'lane—' to produce 'wad stand on their ends, their pearlin-lace as fine as spider's webs'. Scott's sense has been restored in this edition. Elsewhere, faulty punctuation indicates misinterpretation of Scott's text. At 328.36, for example, the intermediaries make sense of Jeanie's speech on how she should address the queen by printing 'as we say to lairds and leddies in Scotland'. However, Scott had written 'lairds leddies' in manuscript, and the insertion of a simple apostrophe to produce 'lairds' leddies' more accurately interprets the point Jeanie is making. At 259.7 Jeanie hears Madge Wildfire's song, which in manuscript tails off 'through brugh & through'. However, failing to notice the context, whereby Scott tells us that 'The tramp of the horse, and the increasing distance, drowned the rest of her song', the intermediaries complete the line to produce 'and through land'. The correct interpretation would have been to supply the punctuation 'through——', thus indicating speech that trails off, and this is what is done in the present text. Finally, a failure to insert the correct punctuation can also result in an altogether more straight-faced text than that in Scott's imagination. In manuscript, for example, Dolly Dutton asks Jeanie if she is not afraid 'of these wild men with their naked—knees' (373.29). The first edition, however, ignores this dash, although it is emphatic in holograph, thus failing to transmit Scott's hint of bawdy.

Volume and Chapter Divisions. The Edinburgh Edition text of *The Heart of Mid-Lothian* accepts the manuscript divisions between Volumes 1 and 2, thus moving one chapter back from Volume 2 to Volume 1. Almost certainly the chapter was moved into the second volume in the first edition because the first would otherwise have been longer than normal; the move was made to equalise the size of volumes, but there is no doubt but that the drama of the novel is better served by Scott's original volume breaks.[129] Of course this critical point is not the reason for the change; what Scott indicates in the manuscript is more important than the desire of the printing house and the publisher for volumes of approximately equal length.

This edition also follows the manuscript in supplying a chapter break at 171.1, a break which was overlooked when the extensive passage added on the facing verso was incorporated into the main text. As a result, this becomes the only chapter in the novel to lack a motto. As explained above Scott added many of the mottoes later, and so when the chapter break was overlooked so was the motto. The bald appearance of page 171 is regrettable, but the chapter division which was in the manuscript is a greater need and its omission has never previously been corrected.

Proper Names. Standardising the forms of names was one of the tasks expected of the intermediaries, but they did not do well in *The Heart of Mid-Lothian*. On his first appearance, David Deans was called Andrew (44.22); that name got into the first edition and was not corrected until the 1821 duodecimo. The lawyer who attends to the dying Dumbiedikes is called 'Nichil Novit', meaning 'he knows nothing'; his son whose services are volunteered for Effie by the next Dumbiedikes is called in the manuscript 'Michel Novit' ('he knows much') on six occasions, plain 'Novit' on six, and 'Nemo' ('nobody') once. While correcting 'Nemo', the first edition manages to miss the fact that the two lawyers are distinguished from each other by their Christian names. The second lawyer is given his own name for the first time in this edition. Similarly May Hettly is so spelled on each of the five occasions her name appears in the manuscript, but she twice appears as 'Hettley' in the first edition. Mrs MacRoskie becomes Mrs MacCroskie; the difference is slight, but one is Scott's form and the other is not. Ratcliffe is called 'Jem' or 'Jemmie' on eight occasions in the manuscript, and twice 'Jim', but in the first edition is 'Jim' on eight out of the ten occurrences of the name. Each of these instances is a particular version of the misreading of single letters or words. More subtly, the intermediaries miss the fact that 'Widow' is used as part of the name 'Widow Butler' on every instance but one on which it occurs in the manuscript, that the Good Town is a name for Edinburgh, and that in the manuscript 'Inverara' is consistently the spoken form, and 'Inverary' the narrative form, a distinction restored in this edition.

The first edition can also be grossly inconsistent. Over a twenty-eight page section of the first volume it spells Saddletree's Christian name 'Bartoline' (37.39–47.17 in the EEWN text), but from 90.30 the form is always 'Bartholine'. In those first 28 pages Scott swithered: he used six 't' forms and six 'th'. From 90.30 he uses only the 'th' form. He was not pushed into this by print as the first edition's normalisation used the 't' form, and so the ultimate adoption of the 'th' form (which appears 21 times in manuscript) represents Scott's decision and is adopted accordingly in this edition.

'Salusbury', the form used by Scott when the first edition has 'Salisbury', represents a different problem. Scott is wholly consistent about this spelling in the manuscript but writes 'Salisbury' when he refers to the English city; he must, therefore, be making a point. It is clear from Stuart Harris's *The Place Names of Edinburgh*[130] that Scott's spelling has no historic precedent, yet it also seems from the examples cited by Harris that the name ought to be pronounced as four syllables, not three as in the English pronunciation of 'Salisbury' in which the 'i' is redundant. Because Scott is consistent, and because there seems a reason for his unusual spelling, 'Salusbury' has been preferred in this edition. Another normalisation where intermediary practice may be questioned concerns 'Maccallanmore', one of the names of the Duke of Argyle. The first edition regularly prints 'MacCullummore', but this form (discounting hyphens and the interior capital) is only used three times out of twelve by Scott in manuscript. In his edition Tony Inglis says that 'Scott's late and previously unadopted variation of *MacCullumore* to *MacCallanmore* has been followed where Gaelic speakers are being quoted or reported, but not introduced elsewhere',[131] but the distinction has no basis in manuscript evidence as, besides Argyle who may be presumed to command Gaelic, only two other Gaelic speakers use the name, and between the three of them they employ four different forms. There is no pattern about the form used by particular speakers. Scott clearly had difficulty in deciding on an appropriate form, but the current editors have decided that the standard should be 'Maccallanmore', because this is the form of the name on which Scott attempts to normalise in the interleaved copy of the novel, a form which he also adopted in *Tales of the Wars of Montrose*, and, in its Gaelic form, in *Chronicles of the Canongate*.

Finally, Scott is consistent about 'tolbooth' beginning with a lower-case letter, except where it is clear that a proper name is in question such as the Tolbooth Kirk; and indeed this can be seen to be right if 'prison' is substituted—the Edinburgh tolbooth is just the prison in Edinburgh. There are of course occasions when a capital is proper, as when Hardie asks 'Why should not the Tolbooth have its "Last Speech, Confession, and Dying Words?"' (14.18–19). And when the Church of Scotland is referred to as the 'Kirk' Scott is again almost entirely consistent. In both cases Scott's manuscript distinctions are preferred in this edition.

Defects in the First Edition. In spite of James Ballantyne's activity as copy-editor, and in spite of the input of several proof-readings, and in spite of the proofs being read by Scott himself, there are still many errors in the first edition. Later editions sometimes resolve problems, and where they suggest suitable solutions those solutions have been used as the basis of emendation in the present text, and when they have different ways of resolving a crux the one that involves the least intervention has been preferred. In the Porteous passage discussed previously, the present text adopts the elegant solution offered by the 1825 duodecimo by switching the words 'former' and 'latter' (57.12–13). At 205.27 the present edition accepts the 18mo's resolution of the first edition's odd statement that Effie was introduced to Meg Murdockson 'verbally, or by word of mouth'. Recognising that no contrast is being offered here, the 18mo alters 'word of mouth' to 'writing'. The 1821 duodecimo resolves the difficulty produced at 328.17 when Jeanie is said to have 'never' been in a coach by supplying the alternative 'only once', a solution again accepted here. Later editions may also correct factual errors; the 1821 duodecimo, for example, corrects the first-edition statement that Effie leaves Edinburgh by 'a little landing-place, formed by a small brook which enters the sea betwixt Dalkeith and Edinburgh' (391.34–36) by changing 'Dalkeith' to 'Musselburgh', a solution also accepted by this edition—a necessary change as Dalkeith is inland. Similarly, the Magnum alters the rather alarming statement in the first edition concerning Lady Culross, 'wha prayed in her bed, surrounded by a great many Christians in a large bed' (415.7–8) to suggest that the second 'bed' should be replaced by 'room'. 'Room' also happens to be the word used in Scott's source (see note to 415.6–9), and so 'room' is the reading incorporated here.

Another problem resulting from lack of attention at the first-edition stage also caused the current editors some dilemma. In the manuscript there is no motto at the opening of Volume 3, Chapter 5 (266.11), but in the text Scott refers to 'a hillock of moss, such as the poet of Grasmere has described in the motto to our chapter' (273.1–2). It would appear that he intended the motto to come from Wordsworth's 'The Thorn'. However, in the first edition the given motto is a quotation from Fletcher. The problem was noted in the 18mo where the phrase 'such as the poet of Grasmere has described in the motto to our chapter' was removed. The loss of the Wordsworthian reference is a real loss and the lesser remedy of merely cutting 'in the motto to our chapter' has been preferred here. A more radical step would have been to insert a motto from 'The Thorn', but the current edition, taking the first edition not the manuscript as its base text, opts for the more conservative solution.

Errors in punctuation are frequently noticed in later editions of the novel and often resolved appropriately; where this is the case, the later edition which first resolves the problem is cited as the model for the emendation in the Emendation List. The 1822 octavo, for example, notices and resolves the problem of the misplaced comma at 13.3. The 18mo, similarly, supplies a comma absent in the first edition at 217.34 where the Doomster is 'a tall, hagard figure'. Similarly, all the 36 missing apostrophes are to be found in their proper place in later editions.

Reconsidering omitted Manuscript Material. In the manuscript of *The Heart of Mid-Lothian* there are a number of passages which were omitted in the first edition, possibly because they suffer from some defect. For instance, the first edition at 1.292.14–18 reads:

> made a spectacle to men and angels, having stood on their pillory at the Canongate afore I was fifteen years old, for a cause of a national covenant. To think

The manuscript, however, reads:

made a spectacle to men and angels afore I was fifteen when I was
found worthy to be scourged by the same bloody hands that quar-
terd the dear body of James Renwick & cut off those hands that
were the first to raise up the down-fallen banner of the testimony—
and how I, was even preferd to stand on the pillory at the Canongate cross for twa hours during a cauld nor-east blast and might hae
been hangit by the neck had I been twa years older for the cause of a
deserted covenant—To think (f. 72/79)

It is possible that the manuscript reading was rejected because of a
possible confusion relating to the repeated word 'hands', but a simple
edit ('which' for 'that') makes the sense clear. The EEWN text now
reads:

made a spectacle to men and angels afore I was fifteen, when I was
found worthy to be scourged by the same bloody hands that quartered the dear body of James Renwick and cut off those hands
which were the first to raise up the down-fallen banner of the
testimony—and how I was even preferred to stand on the pillory
at the Canongate cross for twa hours during a cauld nor-east blast,
and might hae been hangit by the neck had I been twa years elder,
for the cause of a deserted covenant. To think (102.33–40)

Elsewhere the reasons for omission seem more ambiguous; at
422.19–20 an omitted sentence reads: 'He did not know this fact and
no good could arise to any one from imparting it to him'. The material is
on the facing verso, but within a large revision, most of which has been
incorporated: there is no reason to suspect the missing sentence had not
been noticed. A possible reason for its omission is that this information
(concerning Butler's knowledge, or rather lack of knowledge, of the
identity of Robertson and Staunton) is already known by the reader and
so may have been perceived as repetitious. Further, the sentence itself
introduces verbal repetition. It is therefore possible to see reasons for
the omission, but the current editors consider the formulation to be
rhetorical, an emphatic suggestion to the reader that Jeanie is no longer
the innocent she was. It has therefore been restored here, adjusted, as
the Emendation List comments, in order to avoid the verbal repetition
that Scott and the intermediaries would surely have removed. Similarly,
at 116.4 Butler's speech ends in manuscript with a Latin quotation,
seemingly in keeping with his character: 'ocior ventis—ocior Euro', an
adaptation of a phrase from Horace. It appeared in the proof as 'Ocior
ventes—ocior Euro', and was deleted in proof probably by Scott, and
probably because as it stands it does not make sense. Notwithstanding
Scott's delete sign it has been restored in this edition. Just two leaves
later in the proofs, Scott wrote, no doubt in reply to some Ballantyne
comment now lost about being unable to understand the Latin: 'I am
sure as printed neither do I—you must always return my MS where latin
occurs—O I have it—but'. In the light of this comment it seems likely

that Scott simply could not recover the sense of the wrong Latin that appeared in the print, and opted to delete it rather than correct it.

Inconsistencies. Such emendations are problematic, but even if the editors' reasoning is wrong, what the reader now has is something that Scott wrote. However, there are still problems; it is absolutely clear that the production process of *The Heart of Mid-Lothian* at times went seriously awry, and the editors have had to confront issues of factual accuracy and matters of internal consistency which later editions ignored or avoided. In addressing these the editors have taken the view that nothing should be changed which is not demonstrably a mistake. Two historical dates at 101.39 and 398.21 have been emended because both were supplied by one of Scott's helpers, and both were wrong, but at 450.32 where Plumdamas recalls that the Porteous mob was 'in thretty-seven', no emendation has been made even though both in fact and in fiction the riot was in 1736, for the mistake may be attributable to Plumdamas rather than the author.

The reverse problem concerns the date in the fiction on which Porteous dies. The manuscript and first edition give the day on which the crowd gathers to witness the execution of Porteous as the '7th day of September, 1736' (22.13), but when the sentence on Porteous is pronounced the date for the execution is fixed for 8 September (32.23). The reason for the discrepancy is that Porteous was indeed lynched on 7 September, the day before that set for his execution. That the crowd in the novel had gathered and then was frustrated, with the lynching a consequence of the general disappointment, is dramatic, but it does involve an alteration of the historical record, and required an adjustment of dates, an adjustment which was not effected. The discrepancy has remained uncorrected until now, and the editors have chosen 8 September because standardising on that date requires minimal editorial intervention—only the figure '7' needs to be emended.

In the manuscript and first edition the title of the chapbook recording the details of Meg Murdockson's death is given first as 'Last Speech and Execution of Margaret Murdockson, and of the barbarous Murder of her Daughter, Magdalen or Madge Murdockson, called Madge Wildfire; and of her pious Conversation with his Reverence Arch-deacon Fleming.' (Ed1, 4.75.16–21), and later as 'The Last Speech, Confession, and Dying Words of Margaret MacCraw, or Murdockson, executed on Harabee-hill, near Carlisle, the—day of——1737.' (Ed1, 4.263.19–23). As the title is being read in both cases, Scott must have intended it to be the same, and would have expected it to be standardised, and so at 431.25–29 in the present edition it *is* standardised in line with its first appearance at 367.41–68.4. Effie's counsel has two names, Langtale and Fairbrother. Scott often tests names before settling on one as he did with 'Tawse' and 'Butler'; in the new edition 'Langtale' is suppressed (it was only used three times), because the dominant appellation is Fairbrother. The problem about Madge escaping one night, only to be produced 'from prison' the next morning, is resolved by the insertion of 'again' so that now she is 'taken up again last night' at 168.15. At 437.36 the first edition tells us that Effie begs the favour of the Captain 'to have her trunks, &c. sent over from Roseneath'; but Effie's trunks have already been unloaded as she arrived. The present text resolves this inconsistency by emending the text to read 'her remaining trunks', thus resolving an error noted by no earlier edition. These solutions address clear and unmistakable errors, errors which have been noticed not just by pernickety editors but also by their students; they require minimal editorial intervention, and what has been done has been guided by that conservative requirement.

A possibly more controversial decision has been made over the problem of Effie's hair. This involves four passages in the base text: a reference to her as 'black-haired' at 1.119.16 in the first edition (44.13), a reference to her 'waving ringlets of brown hair' at 1.240.20 (84.37), a description of her 'large dark eye-lashes' at 1.259.4 (91.18), and a final reference to her 'long fair hair' during her trial at 2.231.5 (197.18). Later editions of the text do recognise this problem and attempt to resolve it, all except the 1819 octavo altering the initial 'black-haired' to read 'fair-haired'; none, however, makes any attempt to bring the reference to her brown ringlets, or to her dark eye-lashes into line. Scott ignores the issue in the interleaved copy.

The present editors were not satisfied with the solution of turning 'black-haired' into 'fair-haired' because it does not address all the problems, and so they reconsidered all the evidence. There are strong suggestions that Scott conceived of Effie with dark hair. The majority of references to her colouring make her dark. At 84.36–37 Effie has a 'Grecian-shaped head' and at 84.38–9 'a laughing Hebe countenance'; there is a strong Greek image here, which *might* suggest black hair. In addition, at 377.25–26 David Deans, telling Jeanie of the cows he has taken to Roseneath, states that he took 'the wee hawkit ane, that ye ca'd —I needna tell ye how ye ca'd it'. The cow must be called 'Effie' and a 'hawkit' cow is spotted or streaked with white; in other words it is a dark-haired cow with white markings. Later, after her marriage to Staunton, she is described as 'the ruling belle—the blazing star . . . and is really the most beautiful creature that was seen at court upon the birth-day' (423.22–24). In the mid-forties, fashionable beauty was black-haired with a white complexion (compare Sophia Western). It is also the case that Scott is fond of contrasting sisters (compare Minna and Brenda Troil in *The Pirate*), and throughout the novel Effie is contrasted with Jeanie. The latter definitely has fair hair: she is given 'light-coloured hair' at 76.25, and a 'quantity of fair hair' at 319.18. The current editors have therefore concluded that Effie should have black hair. The first reference in the base text at 44.13 must, of course, be left as it is. At 84.37 the word 'black' does not work in the context, so the editors have chosen 'dark' used elsewhere by Scott in relation to Effie's eye-lashes. The word 'dark' is chosen again for 197.18.

The editors of the current text have also reconsidered the problems posed by the clumsy explanatory passages added in proof (see particularly 92.39–93.4, and 298.20–26), and which have been discussed above. However, no matter how much these passages may irritate, the Edinburgh Edition of the Waverley Novels takes the first edition as its base text, and consequently the editors must accept material that was probably added by Scott between manuscript and first edition. There is no evidence to suggest the passages were written by anyone else or added by Scott under protest. James Ballantyne complained of the 'mournful tone',[132] and it is possible that a few inept jokes which were added in proof such as 'It was computed by an experienced arithmetician, that there was as much twopenny ale consumed on the discussion as would have floated a first rate man of war.' (47.37–39) were put in to lighten the tone as a response to James. But there is no evidence to support this. In the present text, therefore, these passages remain: the editors are bound by their own code of practice.

Conclusion. *The Heart of Mid-Lothian* is undoubtedly one of the most powerfully written and intellectually fascinating of all the Waverley texts. It is also one of the most loved of all Scott's novels. For reasons which are not now entirely clear it appeared in its first-edition format in a manner unworthy of the status it holds in the Waverley canon. The present edition has attempted to do what it can within the bounds of its editorial policy to present undimmed of the splendour of the text. *The Heart of Mid-Lothian* is the work of a writer at the height of his powers, envisaging and controlling a narrative of over 1300 pages which chronicles the history of a family and of the Scottish nation. The editors of the Edinburgh Edition hope that their text does justice to the ambition of Scott's narrative and the humanity of his understanding.

NOTES

All manuscripts referred to are in the National Library of Scotland (NLS) unless otherwise stated.

1   William B. Todd and Ann Bowden, *Sir Walter Scott: A Bibliographical History 1796–1832* (New Castle, Delaware, 1998), 439; MS 322, f. 244v.
2   J. G. Lockhart, *Memoirs of the Life of Sir Walter Scott, Bart.*, 7 vols (Edinburgh, 1837), 4.108.
3   Magnum, 11.141–47.
4   Edinburgh University Library, MS La.III.584, ff. 91–94. Helen Goldie's memorandum is on ff. 91–93, and her note to Scott on f. 94. The text of

the original document was reproduced in the Magnum with reasonable fidelity, but was tidied and punctuated for publication. Neither memorandum nor note is dated, but to judge from the handwriting they were written on separate occasions; the note is in a more spidery and slightly shaky hand. The paper is watermarked 'H. SALMON 1809', which means that the memorandum cannot have been written earlier than 1809. The postmark 31 January 1817 probably dates the note to Scott.

5   [Thomas McCrie], review of *Tales of My Landlord*, *The Edinburgh Christian Instructor*, 14 (1817), 41–73, 100–40, 170–201 (61).

6   McCrie, 103.

7   McCrie, 122.

8   *The Letters of Sir Walter Scott*, ed. H. J. C. Grierson and others, 12 vols (London, 1932–37), 4.431.

9   *Letters*, 1.514.

10   *Letters*, 1.514–15.

11   MS 1548, ff. 5–17 (library); ff. [1]–13 (Scott).

12   *Letters*, 4.286, 289, 302, 335, 336, 337; 432.

13   *Letters*, 5.13.

14   *Letters*, 4.504.

15   *Letters*, 5.14–15.

16   *Letters*, 5.91.

17   *Letters*, 1.516.

18   *Letters*, 1.516–17.

19   *Letters*, 4.510–12.

20   This letter from Constable does not appear to be extant; the date is derived from the letter of John Ballantyne quoted below.

21   MS 21001, f. 257 r–v.

22   Lockhart, 4.109.

23   Lockhart, 4.110.

24   *Letters*, 4.507.

25   *Letters*, 4.511.

26   *Letters*, 4.530.

27   *Letters*, 4.532–33.

28   *Letters*, 5.10–11.

29   *Letters*, 5.12–13.

30   MS 322, f. 150r–v.

31   MS 322, f. 171r–v.

32   MS 322, f. 171v.

33   MS 322, f. 174r–v.

34   MS 21001, f. 255r.

35   MS 322, f. 186r.

36   MS 322, f. 178r–79v.

37   MS 322, f. 188v.

38   MS 322, f. 192v; Cadell to Constable, 25 November 1817.

39   MS 322, f. 196v–97r.

40   MS 322, f. 192v.

41   MS 322, f. 226r.

42   MS 322, f. 226r; Robert Cadell to Archibald Constable, 12 December 1817.

43   MS 322, f. 229r.
44   Reading University Library, Longman MS 1, 100, no. 149.
45   Reading University Library, Longman MS 1, 100, no. 171.
46   MS 322, f. 208r.
47   MS 322, f. 269r.
48   MS 322, f. 290r–v.
49   MS 322, ff. 292r–93v.
50   MS 322, ff. 321r–22r.
51   *Edinburgh Magazine and Literary Miscellany*, 81 (Part 1, 1818), 543–47.
52   *Edinburgh Magazine and Literary Miscellany*, 81 (Part 1, 1818), 543.
53   MS 322, f. 320r.
54   MS 322, f. 325r.
55   MS 322, f. 325v.
56   MS 322, f. 325v–26r.
57   MS 322, f. 327r.
58   MS 322, f. 329v.
59   MS 322, f. 330r.
60   MS 322, f. 330v.
61   MS 790, f. 221; Todd and Bowden, 467.
62   Lockhart, 4.180.
63   MS 322, f. 250r.
64   *Letters*, 5.37.
65   MS 322, 280v.
66   MS 322, f. 306r–v.
67   Lockhart, 4.121.
68   *Letters*, 5.108.
69   See Lockhart, 4.131.
70   *Letters*, 5.73.
71   *Letters*, 5.92.
72   See *Letters*, 5.99; Lockhart, 4.142.
73   *Letters*, 5.67.
74   *Letters*, 5.50.
75   MS 322, f. 313v.
76   For a full description of the recovery of the Regalia see Lockhart,
      4.111–20.
77   *Letters*, 5.78.
78   Lockhart, 4.140.
79   *Letters*, 5.67.
80   Lockhart, 4.138. The letter is found only in Lockhart (4.138–40), and
      the wrong reference to *The Bride of Lammermoor* is at 4.143.
81   MS 790, f. 209.
82   MS 790, f. 209.
83   *Letters*, 5.165.
84   *Letters*, 5.169. The official date for the rising of the Court of Session was
      11 July, a Saturday; this letter is therefore most probably dated 11 or 12
      July, not the 11 or 18 July given in *Letters*.
85   MS 1548.
86   South African Library, MSA 20.
87   *Letters*, 5.67.

88 For a full discussion of the time scheme in the novel see the Historical Note, 594–98.

89 Walter Scott, *The Fortunes of Nigel*, ed. Frank Jordan, EEWN 13 (Edinburgh, 2004), 10.22–24.

90 MS 23135.

91 *The Heart of Mid-Lothian*, Yale University Library, Sco86 818t 1. The proofs are bound into Volume 1 of a first edition of *The Heart of Mid-Lothian*, between pages 314 and 315. They are numbered 315–34, but two leaves, pp. 317–18, and 331–32, are missing.

92 MS 790, f. 236.

93 John Sutherland, *Is Heathcliff a Murderer? Great Puzzles in Nineteenth-Century Literature* (Oxford, 1996), 20.

94 *The Household Book of Lady Grisell Baillie 1692–1733*, ed. Robert Scott-Moncrieff (Edinburgh, 1911).

95 This copy is held at NLS NG.1178.d.4.

96 MS 790, f. 242.

97 MS 322, f. 406v.

98 MS 322, f. 444r.

99 MS 322, f. 447v.

100 Jane Millgate, 'Archibald Constable and the Problem of London', *The Library*, 6th series, 18 (1996), 110–23.

101 MS 322, f. 433r.

102 MS 322, f. 401r.

103 MS 790, ff. 483–84.

104 David Hewitt, 'Essay on the Text', *The Antiquary* (EEWN 3), 373.

105 MS 790, ff. 645–46.

106 MS 790, ff. 648–49.

107 MS 790, f. 685.

108 MS 790, f. 686.

109 MS 790, f. 689.

111 MS 790, f. 692.

111 MS 326, f. 23v.

112 Todd and Bowden, 772.

113 Todd and Bowden, 783.

114 MS 23232, f. 60r.

115 MS 323, f. 208r.

116 Todd and Bowden, 778.

117 MS 326, f. 42r.

118 MS 323, f. 245v; MS 792, p. 138; MS 320, f. 160r.

119 Todd and Bowden, 792.

120 *Letters*, 7.245.

121 MS 21019, ff. 37v–46r.

122 MS 21019, f. 15v.

123 MS 21019, f. 39r.

124 MS 21019, ff. 39v–40v.

125 MS 21019, f. 40v.

126 MS 21019, f. 42r.

127 Sir Walter Scott, *The Heart of Mid-Lothian*, ed. Tony Inglis (London, 1994).

128   *The Heart of Mid-Lothian*, ed. Inglis, 680.
129   Tony Inglis argues (*The Heart of Mid-Lothian*, ed. Inglis, xlix–l) that the
      'decision in early May to make *The Heart of Mid-Lothian* the whole of the
      new *Tales* entailed changes, at once drastic and ingeniously minimal, in
      what had already been written. The Prolegomen and the Introductory
      Chapter were apparently written and inserted at this stage.' Tony Inglis's
      Introduction is learned and perceptive, but his interpretation of the biblio-
      graphical evidence is mistaken. When Scott decided, or found that he had
      to devote all four volumes to *The Heart of Mid-Lothian* cannot be deter-
      mined (there is no evidence although May seems probable), but that
      decision or discovery, whenever it was, had no implications for the trans-
      fer of chapters from one volume to another. As discussed earlier, the first
      matter to be written was the first chapter, for that is where Scott's page
      numbers begin. The last chapter of the first volume in the manuscript was
      transferred to Volume 2 before Scott completed Volume 2, because, with
      the chapter transferred, the first two volumes are of roughly equal length;
      in other words, Scott took the transfer into account when writing Volume
      2. The manuscript indicates that Scott originally intended to end the
      second volume where it now ends, but changed his mind (on f. 70 he
      wrote and then deleted 'Here the Vol; may end.'), and carried on to write
      another chapter, which covers Jeanie's visit to Dumbiedikes prior to her
      journey to London. But the next day Scott changed his mind again,
      writing to James Ballantyne 'I think Vol. II should stop at the end of the
      Chapter p. 70 of copy sent yesterday. This will give about seven pages to
      Vol: III' (*Letters*, 5.67). That this was indeed a next-day decision can be
      seen in his beginning to number the pages in Volume 3 in the manuscript
      at 8, thus allowing for the transfer of the 7 pages. He originally thought of
      ending Volume 3 before the interview with the Queen, writing and delet-
      ing 'End of Vol III' at the end of Chapter 11, but added what is now
      Chapter 12 before inserting afresh 'End of Vol: III.'. Scott's foliation of
      Volume 3 continues uninterrupted up to f. 70 at the end of the twelfth
      chapter, and begins afresh at f. 1 for the first chapter of Volume 4, thus
      indicating that Scott changed his mind as he wrote, and before he had
      written any of Volume 4. An 'entire chapter of 32 pages' (*The Heart of
      Mid-Lothian*, ed. Inglis, xl) was not moved 'from its original position in
      Volume 4 into Volume 3 at a late stage of production'. The Prolegomen
      was written after Scott had begun the novel, for its pages have a separate
      numbering sequence; when it was written is not known—the date 'this 1st
      of April, 1818' (5.28) is clearly a joke. Devoting all four volumes to *The
      Heart of Mid-Lothian* had no implications for volume divisions. Nor did it
      have financial implications: Scott contracted for a four-volume work, and
      was paid for a four-volume work. The other tale, 'The Regalia', was never
      written.
130   Stuart Harris, *The Place Names of Edinburgh* (Edinburgh, 1996).
131   *The Heart of Mid-Lothian*, ed. Inglis, 681.
132   *Letters*, 5.67.

EMENDATION LIST

The base-text for this edition of *The Heart of Mid-Lothian* is a specific copy of the first edition, owned by the Edinburgh Edition of the Waverley Novels. All emendations to this base-text, whether verbal, orthographic, or punctuational, are listed below, with the exception of certain general categories of emendation described in the next paragraph, and of those errors which result from accidents of printing such as a letter dropping out, provided always that evidence for the 'correct' reading has been found in at least one other copy of the first edition.

The following proper names have been standardised throughout on the authority of Scott's preferred usage as deduced from the manuscript (see Essay on the Text, 518–19): Argyle-house, Bartholine, Dalgleish, Donacha Dhu na Dunaigh, Greatheart, Grizell, Groom of the Chambers, Grassmarket, Gunnersbury, Hettly, Jem (Ratcliffe), Lawn-market, Maccallanmore, MacRoskie, Michel (Novit), Micklehose, Plumdamas, the names of Edinburgh's city gates, Saint, Salusbury, Seton, Widow (Butler), and Winton. Inverted commas are sometimes found in the first edition for displayed verse quotations, sometimes not; the present text has standardised the inconsistent practices of the base-text by eliminating such inverted commas, except when they occur at the beginning or end of direct speech. The presentation of direct speech quoted within letters, and of speech quoted by another speaker, has been standardised by the consistent use of single quotation marks within double. Chapter numbering has been normalised. The typographic presentation of volume and chapter headings, of the opening words of volumes and chapters, of letters quoted in the primary text, has been standardised. Ambiguous end-of-line hyphens in the base-text have been interpreted in accordance with the following authorities (in descending order of priority): predominant first-edition usage; octavo *Novels and Tales* (1819); Magnum; MS.

Each entry in the list below is keyed to the text by page and line number; the reference is followed by the new, EEWN reading, then in brackets the reason for the emendation, and after the slash the base-text reading that has been replaced. Occasionally, some explanation of the editorial thinking behind an emendation is required, and this is provided in a brief note.

The great majority of emendations are derived from the manuscript. Most merely involve the replacement of one reading by another, and these are listed with the simple explanation '(MS)'. The spelling and punctuation of some emendations from the manuscript have been normalised in accordance with the prevailing conventions of the base-text. And although as far as possible emendations have been fitted into the existing base-text punctuation, at times it has been necessary to provide emendations with a base-text style of punctuation. Where the manuscript reading adopted by the EEWN has required editorial intervention to normalise spelling or punctuation, the exact manuscript reading is given in the form: '(MS actual reading)'. Where the new reading has required editorial interpretation of the manuscript, e.g. when interpreting a homophone, or supplying a missing word, or distinguishing between Scott's hand and those who marked-up Scott's manuscript, the explanation is given in the form '(MS derived: actual reading)'. In transcriptions from Scott's manuscript, deletions are enclosed ⟨thus⟩ and insertions ↑thus↓; superscript letters are lowered without comment.

In spite of the care taken by the intermediaries, some local confusions in the manuscript persisted into the first edition. When straightening these, the editors have studied the manuscript context so as to determine Scott's original intention, but sometimes problems cannot be rectified in this way. In these circumstances, Scott's own corrections and revisions in the Interleaved Set have more authority than the proposals of other editions, but if the autograph portions of the Interleaved Set have nothing to offer, the reading from the earliest edition to offer a satisfactory solution is adopted as the neatest means of rectifying a fault. The later editions, the Interleaved Set, and the Magnum are indicated by '(8vo 1819)', etc., '(ISet)' or '(Magnum)'. Emendations which have not been anticipated by a contemporaneous edition are indicated by '(Editorial)'.

1.3   REPORTED (Editorial) / ARRANGED
       The series *Tales of My Landlord* was initiated with *The Black Dwarf*, and
       The Tale of Old Mortality in 1816. The title at the head of Jedidiah's
       Introduction in the manuscript, and the title as reported by William
       Blackwood on 22/23 August 1816, have 'collected and reported',
       'Jedidiah', and 'Parish-clerk and Schoolmaster', and it is improbable that
       Scott saw a proof of the title-page before its publication. See *The Black
       Dwarf*, ed. P. D. Garside, EEWN 4a, 173–74.
1.5   JEDIDIAH (Editorial) / JEDEDIAH
       See note above.
1.6   PARISH-CLERK AND SCHOOLMASTER (Editorial) / SCHOOL-
       MASTER AND PARISH CLERK
       See note above.
2.4   Parte (Editorial) / Part
       The Spanish was corrected in Ed4 of *Tales of My Landlord*, first series.
3.3   JEDIDIAH (MS) / JEDEDIAH
3.6   In Ed1 Cleishbotham's dedication is set in Roman type but is here set in
       italics to bring its typographical presentation into conformity with *Tales
       of My Landlord*, first series: see *The Black Dwarf*, ed. P. D. Garside,
       EEWN 4a, 5–9, and *The Tale of Old Mortality*, ed. Douglas Mack,
       EEWN 4b, 353.
3.6   every other vice (MS) / every vice
3.12   pleasing (MS) / pleasant
4.2   savour (MS) / favour
4.15   can man (MS) / can a man
4.39   but as persons (MS) / but persons

5.6	Jedidiah (MS) / Jedediah
5.7	these (MS) / their
5.8	discrepancies (MS) / descrepancies
5.8	opinion (MS) / opinions
5.18	title (MS) / privilege
5.27	GANDERCLEUGH (MS) / GANDERCLEUCH
7.7	three (MS) / six
	The source and the manuscript both read 'three'; in addition light mail coaches carried only three inside passengers.
7.9	are (MS) / were
7.13	credible (MS) / creditable
8.2	does certainly happen (MS) / does happen
8.4	prototype (Editorial) / proto-type
	The word is hyphenated over a line-end in each of Ed1, 8vo 1822, and the Magnum, and so the normal EEWN procedures for resolving whether an end-of-line hyphen is hard or soft cannot be applied. As the word appears as 'prototype' on the other two occasions it is used in Scott's fiction (in *Guy Mannering* and *The Monastery*), unusually it is emended on this occasion in the light of practice elsewhere in Scott first editions.
8.15	casualities (MS) / casualties
8.22	admonition. And (MS) / admonition; and
8.26	car [new line] and (MS) / car. [new line] And
9.4	called Goslin-brae (MS) / called the Goslin-brae
10.26	between (MS) / betwixt
10.28	discovered (MS discoverd) / observed
10.32	should pass (MS) / would pass
10.35	transport (MS) / carry
10.37	yet (MS) / but
11.10	All they (MS) / All that they
11.17	dejected (MS) / timid
11.28	a Scotsman says (MS) / says a Scotchman
11.29	It is (MS) / It's
11.29	humbly a few paces behind (MS) / humbly behind
12.6	him, and (MS him and) / him. And
12.14	understand (MS) / understood
12.28	the formation of the character (MS) / the character
12.29	would (MS) / might
12.39	spirits, (MS) / spirits;
12.40	table, thus (Editorial) / table; thus
	The two semicolons in the base-text unnaturally break up the sentence, and the MS comma after 'spirits' proposes a satisfactory way of punctuating this sentence.
13.3	and, saying he (8vo 1822) / and saying, he
13.17	—it is quite the reverse—he (MS — ↑ —it is quite the reverse ↓ —he) / —he
	The omitted phrase appears on the opposing verso.
13.37	"you (MS) / "You
13.38	tolbooth (MS) / Tolbooth
14.1	tolbooth (MS) / Tolbooth
14.1	Mid-Lothian," said (MS Mid-Lothian" said) / Mid-Lothian?" said
14.9	keeping up the ball (MS) / doing his best
14.14	writer (MS) / younger gentleman
14.16	tolbooth (MS) / Tolbooth
14.32	despotic (MS) / desperate

14.39   misfortune (MS misfortune⟨s⟩) / misfortunes
15.3   elopement, the *enlèvement* (MS elopement the enlevement) / develop-
        ment, *enlèvement*
15.6   have such an (MS) / have an
15.43   brain!" (MS) / brain. "
16.5   met—was (MS) / met? Was
16.5   Jamie's (MS) / James's
16.7   of "The (8vo 1819) / of "The [MS as Ed1]
16.8   Haman?' Since (8vo 1819) / Haman?" Since [MS as Ed1]
16.10   ebbing. How (MS) / ebbing; how
16.12   consolations (MS) / consolation
16.23   *Célèbres* (Magnum) / *Celebres*
16.26   *prævalebit.*" [new paragraph] (MS) / *prævalebit.*' [new paragraph]
16.36   very long strictly (MS) / very strictly
16.37   favour; a (MS derived: favour: a) / favour, a
        The MS has colons after 'country' (39.24), and 'favour'; both colons
        should have been treated in the same way.
17.5   curious and anomalous (MS) / curious anomalous
17.8   Scottish (MS) / Scotch
17.12   chapel of ease (MS) / appendix
17.17   *Célèbres* (Magnum) / *Celebres*
17.19   long continued civil (MS) / long civil
17.31   it was tidings (MS derived: it wath tidings) / the tidings bore, that
17.42   enemies' (MS enemies; 8vo 1819 enemies') / enemies
18.23   cessio bonorum (MS) / *cessio bonorum*
18.24   Scottish (MS) / Scotch
18.32   Halkit, "and (MS) / Halkit," and
18.34   seek out your (MS) / seek your
18.36   syllabus (MS) / syllabus'
18.38   cessio (MS) / *cessio*
19.2   cessio (MS) / *cessio*
19.9   seven and (MS) / seven shillings and
19.24   mouth (MS) / verge
19.33   word (MS) / words
19.33   "Interest," (MS) / "Interest with my Lord,"
19.40   in conversation (MS) / in a conversation
19.41   upon (MS) / up on
19.41   *Célèbres* (Magnum) / *Celebres*
20.5   fingers-ends (MS) / finger-ends
21.2   Grève (8vo 1819) / Grève
21.8   pad (MS and Prior) / poet
21.8   and the knight (MS and Prior) / and knight
22.5   looking in gait, dress, and features like (MS looking ↑ in gait dress and
        features ↓ like) / looking like
        The inserted phrase appears on the opposing verso in the MS.
22.6   world. But (MS) / world; but
22.8   ceremonial (MS) / ceremony
22.13   8th (Editorial) / 7th
        See Essay on the Text, 522, and note to 32.29.
22.18   crimes (MS) / crime
22.34   and the inferior (MS) / and inferior
22.37   wherever (MS) / whenever
22.39   firths (MS) / friths
23.2   originally (MS) / orginally
23.4   cunning, perfectly (MS cunning perfectly) / cunning,—was perfectly

23.7   officers. But (MS) / officers; but
23.12   seldom is (MS) / is seldom
23.17   scruples (MS) / scruple
23.40   opinions (MS) / opinion
24.30   of the three (MS) / of three
24.31   Cathedral (MS) / cathedral
25.6   City Guard (MS) / city guard
25.13   they were not to despair (MS derived: they not to despair) / they should
        not despair
25.18   Wherefore (MS) / Therefore
25.20   time and space (MS) / space and time
25.21   nothing, the work of salvation (MS) / nothing, salvation
25.29   were (MS) / was
25.33   case. When (MS) / case; when
25.39   escape. But (MS) / escape; but
26.4   public, who, where (12mo 1821) / public, where
26.26   FERGUSSON'S (MS) / Ferguson's
26.37   after (MS) / afterwards
27.9   Fergusson (MS) / Ferguson
27.21   birth or education and former (MS birth or education & former) / birth,
        education, or former
27.22   rabble, truants, schoolboys (MS rabble truants schoolboys) / rabble, or
        the provoking petulance of truant schoolboys
        The intermediaries seem to have understood the word 'truant' in its
        modern sense, rather than in its older sense of vagabond or idle
        person.
27.24   temper ... was (MS) / tempers ... were
27.33   bluid. (MS) / bluid!
        The MS follows the text of Fergusson's poem.
27.41   magistrates, like ... Regan, have diminished (MS derived: magistrates
        have like ... Regan have diminishd) / magistrates have, like ... Regan,
        diminished
        Scott changed his mind as to the construction of this sentence in the
        course of writing it but did not delete the first 'have'.
28.4   coat, waistcoat, and (8vo 1819) / coat waistcoat and
28.7   axe (MS) / hatchet
28.14   that these (MS) / that the narrative containing these
28.26   object (MS) / objects
28.27   afterwards were (MS) / were afterwards
28.32   violently (MS) / ardently
29.18   Welch Fusileers (MS) / Welsh fusileers
29.29   something (MS) / somewhat
30.19   proportional (MS) / proportionate
30.24   escort, arrived (MS) / escort, had arrived
30.40   continuing (MS continuing) / continued
30.41   exclamations, a young (MS exclamations a young) / exclamations. A
        young
31.10   commands (MS) / command
31.11   more (MS) / were
31.21   his (MS) / the
31.28   hand: (MS) / hand;
31.29   examination—it (MS) / examination; it
31.29   loaded—of (MS) / loaded. Of
31.31   there—a (MS) / there; a
32.8   upon (MS) / on

32.15   mind (MS) / minds
32.21   in common (MS) / in the common
32.36   and Knights (MS) / and the Knights
33.2   purpose (MS) / uses
33.16   concourse. But (MS) / concourse; but
34.32   willing even to (MS) / willing to
35.8   was (MS) / were
35.26   appeared (MS appear) / seemed
35.33   resentment, and gazing (MS) / resentment, gazing
35.40   considered (MS considerd) / might consider
37.9   us in a burning day like this," (MS) / us,"
37.13   twal pennies (MS) / twalpennies
37.17   ken, that when (MS) / ken, when
37.25   that, Miss Damahoy, and (MS derived and 8vo 1819) / that—Miss
          Damahoy and
          The MS reads: 'that Miss Damahoy" responded'; the clause 'and I ken
          . . . at ance' was added later. Obviously the subject is not 'Miss Dama-
          hoy and I'.
37.30   robbit (MS) / rubbit
37.31   hand (MS) / hands
38.19   this extremity (MS) / such extremes
38.20   like gentle (MS) / like the gentle
38.33   away. "Whan (MS away. Whan) / away,—"whan
38.41   orator, "mind (MS orator "mind) / orator,—"mind
38.41   distinction—as (MS) / distinction, as
38.42   says, 'I (MS) / says—'I
39.30   but get (MS) / but to get
39.32   Law (MS) / law
39.33   Vincovintem (MS) / Vincovincentem
39.35   of the Session (MS) / of session
39.36   whin (MS) / wheen
40.8   for graith (MS) / for horse-graith
40.10   gold and brocade (MS gold & brocade) / gold brocade
40.12   than (MS) / then
40.16   wi' (MS wi) / with
40.20   played (Magnum) / plaid
41.20   caa'd (MS) / ca'd
41.22   again (MS) / agane
41.23   a-weel (MS a-weil) / aweel
41.24   Blazonburry (MS) / Blazonbury
41.28   Weel, weel—weel, weel—weel (MS Weel weel—weel, weel—weel) /
          Weel, weel, weel—weel, weel
41.33   caa'd (MS) / caad
41.38   nonsense. I (MS) / nonsense; I
41.40   ance (MS) / once
41.40   *potimus* (MS) / *pessimus*
42.14   Presidents and King's Advocates (MS) / presidents and king's advoc-
          ates
42.18   tell, that they (MS) / tell, they
42.19   than (MS) / then
42.25   matters—in (MS) / matters. In
42.27   had ready-made (MS) / had use for ready-made
42.27   o' (MS) / of
42.29   and a dry (MS) / and dry
42.30   better since (MS) / better; since

42.39 Dallas' Stiles (MS Dallas ⟨of St Martins s⟩ Stiles) / Dallas of St Martin's Stiles

42.41 further (MS) / farther

43.1 quality and—*Non* (MS) / quality, and *Non*

43.22 is brawly," (MS) / is,"

43.22 readily enough. (MS) / "readily enough."

43.24 assigned to as property as belonging (MS) / assigned as properly belonging
The Ed1 reading probably arose from misreading 'property' as 'properly', which required a consequential adjustment.

43.27 do ye (MS) / d'ye

43.37 *piger*—nothing (MS) / *piger*, nothing

44.3 doun (MS) / down

44.5 could please (MS) / could aye please

44.5 customers better than mysell wi' (MS) / customers wi'

44.6 And I am (MS derived: And am) / And when folk were hasty and unreasonable, she could serve them better than me, that am
The omission of 'I' in the MS generated an elaboration that involves considerable repetition.

44.8 bargain. When (MS) / bargain. For when

44.8 folks (MS) / folk

44.16 kens (MS) / knows

44.16 she be guilty (MS) / she's been guilty

44.22 David (12mo 1821) / Andrew

44.22 has (MS) / had

44.31 Ye are (MS) / Ye're

44.34 twenty-one (MS twenty one) / one

45.4 Parliament-house were speaking o' naething else," said Saddletree, "till (MS Parliament-house were speaking o' naething else said Saddletree till) / Parliament-house," said Saddletree, "was speaking o' naething else, till

45.14 rate—and (MS) / rate.—And

45.17 ye're (MS) / ye are

45.20 Blackatthebane (MS) / Black-at-the-bane

45.21 license (MS) / licence

45.23 or bastard (MS) / or a bastard

45.24 shoon— (MS) / shoon?—

45.37 sighed bitterly. (MS) / sighed.

45.40 na ganging (MS) / no gaun

45.41 tak (MS) / take

46.7 Dumbiedikes' (8vo 1819) / Dumbiedike's

46.11 are that I should say sae, what (MS) / are, what

46.11 taks (MS) / takes

46.13 and (MS) / And

46.14 was (MS) / were

46.15 banes?—gang (MS) / banes? gang

46.21 o' (MS) / of

46.25 that (MS) / if

46.30 naked (MS) / in rags

46.31 o' (MS) / of

46.32 Effie!!! Can (MS) / Effie! can

46.33 no (MS) / na

46.36 discussion. "Whoy (MS) / discussion—"Whoy

47.1 murder of the (MS) / murder of of the

47.2 construing (MS) / inferring

47.11   Law (MS) / law
47.11   Law (MS) / law
47.22   *Johnie* (MS) / *Johnnie*
48.4   jail (MS) / gaol
48.15   tolbooth (MS) / Tolbooth
48.21   seems (Editorial) / seemed
         This emendation and the next complete the revision of tenses begun by
         Scott in the MS at 48.12 ('had' to 'have') and 48.20 ('were' to 'are'), and
         continued at 48.25 and 48.29 ('were' to 'are'). The effect of the changes is
         to place Pattieson's narration before the demolition of the Luckenbooths
         and the Tolbooth in 1817.
48.21   have (Editorial) / had
48.34   tall, thin, old (Magnum) / tall thin old
48.36   to see Effie (MS) / to Effie
48.37   child-murther (MS) / child-murder
48.39   replied it (MS) / replied, "It
48.40   present. [new paragraph] (MS) / present." [new paragraph]
49.8   *virum* (MS) / virûm
         The small mark Scott puts above the letter 'u' in foreign-language
         words to indicate that it is 'u' here turned up as a circumflex.
49.8   *exscindere* (MS) / exscindire
49.9   auras.* (MS) / auras—&c.*
49.10   wasted some more (MS) / wasted more
49.11   city (MS) / metropolis
49.28   artizans (MS) / citizens
49.33   moving on with (MS) / moving with
49.35   party so assembled (MS) / party, assembled
50.2   that he (MS) / that "he
50.2   minister. [new paragraph] (Editorial) / minister." [new para-
         graph]
50.3   of (MS) / from
50.13   me." (MS) / me?"
50.24   gate (MS) / gates
50.38   sailors' (8vo 1819) / sailors [MS as Ed1]
50.38   sea-caps (MS) / sea caps
50.42   their (MS) / them
51.5   barrack (MS) / lodge
51.8   the mob every (MS) / the mob of the city every
51.11   an instance (MS a ⟨singular⟩ instance) / a singular instance
51.13   these (MS) / those
51.16   a (MS) / one
51.17   was (MS) / were
51.42   duty. Even (MS duty ↑ Even) / duty; even
51.42   they were left without (MS) / these were without
52.20   their (MS) / the
52.31   tolbooth ... tolbooth (MS) / Tolbooth ... Tolbooth
52.36   the Luckenbooths (MS) / the defile formed by the Luckenbooths
52.37   tolbooth (MS) / Tolbooth
52.39   protected from (MS) / secured against the risk of
52.40   meanwhile (MS) / mean while
53.8   life. And (MS) / life; and
53.8   matter (MS) / application
53.33   and the blazing (MS) / and blazing
53.37   street (MS) / streets
54.12   the part (MS) / that part

54.18	door was (Magnum) / doors were
54.22	with iron, studded besides with broad-headed (MS with iron studded besides with broad headed) / with broad-headed
54.23	offer (MS) / yield to
54.23	forcing by any degree of violence, (MS) / forcing,
54.25	were (MS) / seemed
54.25	force (MS) / gain
54.28	at (MS) / in
54.42	guards (MS) / guard
55.2	and menaced, on their nearer approach, with the pikes (MS and menaced on their nearer approach ⟨with⟩ the pikes) / and, on their nearer approach, the pikes
	Why 'with' was deleted in the MS cannot be determined, but its omission in the printed proof must have occasioned the proof revision (see next emendation).
55.4	themselves. (MS) / themselves, were presented against them.
55.5	forwards (MS) / forward
55.15	which (MS) / that
55.16	tolbooth door promised (MS tolbooth door promised) / Tolbooth promised
55.24	attain (MS) / obtain
55.26	gang after gang (MS) / they
55.27	tolbooth door. Yet (MS) / Tolbooth door; yet
55.33	against (MS) / close to
55.38	flames (MS) / fire
55.39	They (MS) / The flames
56.31	this (MS) / the
57.10	contingence (MS) / contingency
57.12	latter (12mo 1825) / former
57.13	former (12mo 1825) / latter
57.27	seems (MS derived: seem [or] seems) / seem
57.36	turrets, gave (8vo 1819) / turrets ,gave
58.11	cruelty?—this (MS cruelty—this) / cruelty? This
58.14	gibbet—we (MS) / gibbet—We
58.20	do (MS) / will
58.31	victim of popular fury, (MS) / victim,
59.7	then (MS) / there
59.14	gude (MS) / good
59.14	ye."—Again (MS) / ye." Again
59.15	answer—A (MS) / answer. A
59.17	stair-case—"I (MS) / stair-case [new paragraph] "I
59.26	tolbooth (MS) / Tolbooth
59.40	tolbooth (MS) / Tolbooth
60.18	tolbooth (MS) / Tolbooth
60.19	purpose. (MS) / purpose—
60.19	have Blood (MS) / have blood
60.20	were ever (MS) / ever were
60.21	shall (MS) / should
60.22	weel (MS) / well
60.28	the king's cushion (MS) / The King's Cushion
60.33	found there (MS) / found that there
62.7	body—give (MS) / body; give
62.7	give him time (MS) / give time
62.27	a sort of prisoner (MS) / a prisoner
63.9	whiling (MS) / whileing

63.11   at which (MS) / when
64.18   ne'er (MS neer) / never
64.19   wall (MS) / well
64.24   betwixt (MS) / around
64.25   and the steep (MS) / and marking the verge of the steep
64.30   islets (MS) / isles
64.38   varied, so (MS varied so) / varied,—so
64.39   and all (MS) / and displays all
64.40   with brilliancy (MS) / with partial brilliancy
65.20   now upon (MS) / alternately, upon
65.21   now upon (MS) / and upon
66.2   most (MS) / more
66.9   the "last man" (MS) / "the last man"
66.10   unreverently (MS) / irreverently
66.22   ex-trooper (8vo 1819) / ex trooper
67.33   might be overdone, and then infer the destruction and loss both, of (MS
        might be overdone & then infer the destruction & loss both of) / may be
        overdone, and that it infers, as a matter of course, the destruction and
        loss of both
67.39   toiled (MS toild) / toiling
68.16   Airdsmoss (MS Airds moss) / Airdmoss
68.35   these (MS) / those
68.43   tall, gawky, silly-looking (12mo 1821) / tall gawky silly-looking
69.8   neibours (MS) / neighbours
69.13   Master (MS) / Mr
69.15   that's but equals (MS) / that equals
69.18   syne (MS) / sin'
69.22   twenty-four (MS twenty four) / four-and-twenty
69.24   prayer—it (MS) / prayer, it
69.28   wad (MS) / would
69.41   intractable (MS) / untractable
70.11   I roupit them out in (MS) / I sequestrated them in
70.12   his (MS) / her
70.16   drift (MS) / drifts
70.30   she (MS) / She
70.36   be (MS) / Be
70.37   Jock—dinna (MS) / Jock. Dinna
71.14   southron (MS) / southern
71.14   southron (MS) / southern
71.21   prepossessions (MS) / professions
71.23   situation latterly, as (MS) / situation, as
71.36   about (MS) / against
71.43   Ingland (MS) / England
72.3   Kirk (MS) / kirk
72.14   Hochmagirdle (MS) / Hochmaagirdle
72.25   Widower (MS) / widower
72.36   walk upwards (MS) / walk, upwards
73.42   most (MS) / more
74.23   this (MS) / these
74.23   they regard (MS) / they come to regard
74.25   embassador (MS) / ambassador
74.26   will (MS) / shall
75.1   grand-dame (8vo 1819) / grandame
        The MS reads 'mother'; 'grandame' was inserted in proof.
75.18   himself a man (MS) / a man himself

75.25	dignity (MS) / dignitary
75.32	ganging (MS) / gaun
75.37	than (MS) / then
75.39	Davie Deans said (MS) / Davie said
76.2	the (MS) / his
76.15	gudeman (MS) / goodman
76.35	of Rebecca, the (MS of Rebecca the) / of the
77.1	venture (MS) / marriage
77.4	generally have (MS) / have generally
77.18	to (MS) / the
78.12	upon (MS) / on
78.16	instead (MS) / indeed
78.21	am (MS) / *am*
78.27	unwordy (MS) / unworthy
78.29	forpit (MS) / forpet
78.36	o' (MS) / of
78.37	could (MS) / can
78.39	halt's clean gane (MS) / halt's gane
79.5	o' (MS) / of
79.11	tak (MS) / take
79.14	silent. (MS) / silent;
79.28	it's (8vo 1819) /its
79.28	it's (8vo 1819) /its
79.29	enable (MS) / enables
79.30	he, moved at (MS) / he, at
80.28	matrimony (MS) / matrimonial
80.42	forwards (MS) / forward
80.43	even a dignified (MS) / even dignified
81.2	be, that (MS) / be said, that
81.9	Forget? Reuben," (MS Forget? Reuben⟨?⟩") / Forget, Reuben?"
81.10	eyes, "she's (MS eyes "she's) / eyes,—"She's
81.12	rapt (MS) / wrapt
81.27	house, then nearly (MS) / house, nearly
81.37	miles' (18mo) / miles
81.39	for (MS) / on account of
81.43	necessarily rare (MS) / necessarily very rare
82.17	a room (MS) / the room
82.42	power (MS) / privilege
83.10	principle (MS) / principles
83.11	in (MS) / on
83.24	the apple-trees (MS) / her apple-trees
83.42	Jeanie (MS) / Jeany
84.8	when weather (MS) / when the weather
84.37	dark (Editorial) / brown
	See Essay on the Text, 523–24.
85.32	parents: (MS) / parents;
85.39	time (MS) / years
86.14	depended; the (MS depended the) / depended, the
86.14	in; and Jeanie (MS in and Jeanie) / in, when Jeanie
86.18	and she (MS) / and when she
86.26	tracts (MS) / tracks
86.28	the King's (MS) / the royal domain, or King's
86.29	and to this (MS) / to this pass
86.39	ladie (MS) / lady
87.7	gate? naebody? I (MS) / gate?—Naebody?—I

87.8   Effie!" (MS) / Effie."
87.9   I am (MS) / I'm
87.12   een are (MS) / een's
87.40   her (MS) / the
88.5   tak (MS) / take
88.9   tale. But (MS) / tale; but
88.9   *dance* (MS) / dance
88.15   a ready (MS) / the readiest
88.19   representation (MS) / representations
88.19   clamant (MS) / flagrant
88.20   Dance (MS) / *dance*
88.25   brutish (MS) / brutal
88.31   begging for bawbees (MS) / begging bawbees
88.32   aften (MS) / often
88.38   thumbikins (MS) / thumkins
89.8   diversion (MS) / division
89.12   anes (MS) / ance
89.13   than (MS) / then
89.14   I am (MS) / I'm
89.15   had an (MS) / had made an
89.36   becomes just so (MS) / becomes so
90.6   staring (MS) / standing
90.6   amang (MS) / among
90.11   bountith (MS) / bounteth
90.37   Kirk (MS) / kirk
92.28   and change (MS) / and the change
92.29   nice, sharp (Editorial) / nice sharp
92.29   quillets (MS) / quillits
93.21   enquiries (MS) / enquiry
93.28   time (MS) / early youth
93.29   and of civil (MS) / and civil
94.1   ejaculated— (MS) / ejaculated,
94.1   woman! Jeanie (MS) / woman—Jeanie
94.10   wi' (MS) / with
94.19   cast-a-away (MS) / cast-a-way
        The word is very clearly written in the MS, and must be intended to
        indicate a verbal hesitation as Deans speaks.
94.37   God ... man (MS) / man ... God
95.11   Leonard's. Yet (MS) / Leonard's; yet
95.34   east. This (MS) / east. [new paragraph] This
96.15   towards (MS) / toward
96.15   as if to (MS) / in order, as it appeared, to
96.17   forwards (MS) / forward
96.31   well proportioned and strong, yet (MS) / well-proportioned, yet
96.42   "Sir, I (MS "Sir I) / "I
97.2   kind." (MS) / kind?"
97.5   ways (MS) / way
98.6   urging, urging with (MS) / urging, with
98.21   gudeman (MS Gudeman) / goodman
98.24   rises behind (MS and 12mo 1825) / rises, behind
98.29   devil!" answered (MS) / devil!"——answered
98.35   Yes—call (MS) / Yes, call
98.36   Abaddon—whatever (MS) / Abaddon, whatever
98.38   name a name (MS) / find an appellation
99.10   Butler? (MS) / Butler!

99.11   —"the (MS) / —the
99.15   paces, turned back, and (MS paces turnd back and) / paces; and
99.20   fire. And (MS) / fire; and
99.31   towards (MS) / toward
99.36   these (MS) / those
100.7   harsh, and yet (MS) / harsh, yet
100.17   masculine (MS) / manly
100.20   was (Editorial) / were [MS as Ed1]
100.27   wretch Nicol Muschat from (MS wretch Nicol Muschit from) / wretch
         from
101.24   be come of (MS) / be of
101.25   a family (MS) / a peasant's family
         In the MS the term 'peasant' is used only of country-people in England,
         and thus its addition here in proof was an error.
101.39   1688 (Editorial) / 1686
         In the MS Scott wrote the first two digits, while the next two were
         written in by someone else. In view of Deans's description of his suffer-
         ing with Renwick (102.33–40) it seems probable that the year should
         have been that of Renwick's death.
102.1   illuminated (MS) / illumined
102.16   Peircy (MS) / Percy
102.24   you, God (MS) / you—God
102.31   whan (MS) / when
102.33   EEWN reading: angels afore I was fifteen, when I was found worthy to
         be scourged by the same bloody hands that quartered the dear body of
         James Renwick and cut off those hands which were the first to raise up
         the down-fallen banner of the testimony—and how I was even pre-
         ferred to stand on the pillory at the Canongate cross for twa hours
         during a cauld nor-east blast, and might hae been hangit by the neck
         had I been twa years elder, for the cause of a deserted covenant. To
         think
         MS reading: angels afore I was fifteen when I was found worthy to be
         scourged by the same bloody hands that quarterd the dear body of
         James Renwick & cut off those hands that were the first to raise up the
         down-fallen banner of the testimony—and how I, was even preferd to
         stand on the pillory at the Canongate cross for twa hours during a cauld
         nor-east blast and might hae been hangit by the neck had I been twa
         years elder for the cause of a deserted covenant—To think
         Ed1 reading: angels, having stood on their pillory at the Canongate
         afore I was fifteen years old, for the cause of a national covenant. To
         think
         It is possible that the MS reading was rejected because of a possible
         confusion relating to the repeated word 'hands', but a simple edit
         ('which' for 'that') makes the sense clear.
103.4   Stewarts (MS) / Stuarts
103.8   county (MS) / country
103.8   now——" (Editorial) / now"——
103.16   reverend (MS) / revered
103.20   tender souls and fearful (MS) / tender and fearful souls
103.30   Kirk (MS) / kirk
103.33   What (MS) / what
103.33   light-headed (MS) / lightsome
103.34   how (MS) / How
103.34   take up (MS) / bear
103.38   is (MS) / was

103.38 frae the creeping (MS) / frae creeping
103.38 insects on the brae-side in (MS) / insects, on the brae-side, in
104.30 were (MS) / was
104.31 answer: (MS) / answer;
104.37 restored (MS) / resolved
104.43 and of my (MS) / and my
104.43 puir (MS) / poor
105.2 mysell (MS) / myself
105.28 it's (12mo 1821) / its
105.30 Ended? (MS) / Ended!
105.36 ye wad think (MS) / ye think
105.39 Kirk (Editorial) / kirk
On all other occasions the word, when indicating the Church of Scotland, is capitalised.
105.39 keeps (MS) / keep
106.2 be yet (MS) / yet be
106.11 Her (MS) / The
106.30 go (MS) / be
106.35 feelings. (MS) / feelings,
106.38 Indeed? from whom or (MS) / Indeed! From whom? Or
107.1 this next night (MS) / this night
107.7 hae (MS) / have
107.14 propose (MS) / purpose
107.36 ganging (MS) / gaun
107.39 'tis (MS) / it is
107.40 sign she (MS) / sign that she
108.1 you a man (MS) / you are a man
108.5 helps that philosophy (MS) / helps philosophy
108.10 ill (MS) / weel
108.39 ye (MS) / you
108.42 een (MS) / ee n
109.1 purpose. It (MS) / purpose—It
109.2 Douce David (MS) / douce Davie
109.3 dispute. I (MS) / dispute—I
109.10 ane (MS) / one
109.15 hand (MS) / hands
109.15 hand (MS) / hands
109.43 will (MS) / may
110.5 warldly-wise (MS) / worldly-wise
110.7 legalists, formalists (MS) / legalists and formalists
110.8 turns (MS) / terms
111.5 that the defender (MS) / that defender
111.5 not (proofs) / *not*
111.10 for recovery of ane (MS) / for ane
111.11 surely (MS) / doubtless
111.14 pleading (MS) / pleadings
111.16 halk (MS) / hawk
111.20 Outer-house. Weel (MS) / Outer-house—Weel
111.34 further (MS) / farther
112.12 and a fashion of carnal (MS) / and fashion of carnal
112.14 folk's (12mo 1821) / folks
112.16 canons, and (MS canons and) / canons. They
112.17 as to be (MS) / as be
112.30 the Laird (MS) / the auld Laird
112.32 lown (MS) / loon

112.33   Hielanders (MS hielanders) / Highlanders
112.35   "Arniston (proofs) / "Weel, Arniston
112.39   hae—Kittlepunt (proofs) / hae—What think ye o' Kittlepunt
112.43   Whulliewhaw (MS) / Whilliewhaw
113.5   yersell (MS ye'rsell) / yoursell
113.10   o' (MS) / of
113.11   end? (MS) / ends?
114.4   indispensable (Magnum) / indispensible
         This word was added in proof, but the Ed1 spelling has no historical
         support.
114.30   tremulous and anxious (MS) / tremulous anxious
114.36   disposed doubtless to (MS) / disposed to
114.38   ilk (MS) / ilka
114.42   *will* be (MS) / will be
115.8   skeel (MS) / skill
115.12   whullying (MS) / whillying
115.25   muckle whilk (MS) / muckle matter whilk
115.29   borne (Magnum) / born
115.39   Na (MS) / No
116.3   directly—*ocior ventis*—*ocior Euro.*" (MS directly—ocior ventis—ocior
         Euro—") / directly."
         See Essay on the Text, 521–22.
116.12   *step* (MS) / *steps*
116.13   me; farewell." And (MS me farewell—" And) / me. Farewell," and
116.26   steed, with some difficulty he (proof correction) / steed with some
         difficulty, he
116.29   Laird (8vo 1819) / laird
         Ed1 adopts an initial capital for 'laird' at 116.33 and 116.35; this
         emendation completes the process.
117.1   Chapter Thirteen (MS Chapter .) / END OF VOLUME FIRST
117.36   harst (MS) / ha'rst
117.37   Butler impatiently. (MS) / Butler.
118.5   would (MS) / might
118.8   grit (MS) / great
118.14   Michel Novit (auld Nichil's son (MS Michel Novit (auld Nickils son) /
         Nichel Novit (auld Nickel's son
118.34   hopes (MS) / thoughts
118.37   tolbooth (MS) / Tolbooth
118.41   recollection even (MS) / even recollection
119.17   tolbooth (MS) / Tolbooth
119.23   indirection (MS) / indirectness
119.26   "ye (MS) / "that ye
119.27   whan (MS) / when
119.29   such idle observation (MS) / such observation
120.7   winning ... winning (MS) / wunnin ... wunnin
120.11   ye (MS) / you
120.16   me: (MS) / me;
120.28   pitt (MS) / put
121.5   of the Deans family (MS derived: of Deans family) / of Deans's family
121.14   caution (MS) / precaution
121.24   there an (MS) / there for an
121.24   instant: (MS) / instant;
121.31   or by the (MS) / or the
121.33   upon (MS) / at
121.40   he had ever (MS) / ever he had

122.1	grey (MS) / gray
122.3	quick, black (12mo 1821) / quick black
122.13	wanted only a (MS) / wanted a
122.15	present (MS) / represent
122.22	name— (MS) / name?—
122.39	than (MS) / then
122.40	I aye read (MS) / I read
122.41	ae (MS) / a
123.1	Lawlands (MS) / Lowlands
123.8	be (MS) / have been
123.11	ye (MS) / you
123.13	honour!" (MS) / honour,"
123.16	frae (MS) / from
123.31	I do admit was what was to (MS) / I will admit was a line of conduct little to
124.4	Baillie (MS) / magistrate
124.8	hae (MS) / have
124.8	ain (MS) / own
124.11	win (MS) / wun
124.12	keepit (MS) / held
124.13	whan (MS) / when
124.13	keep (MS) / haud
124.21	Good Town (MS Good town) / good town
	In the MS both words in this sobriquet for Edinburgh are capitalised on the other four occasions they appear.
125.17	replied that (MS) / replied, "that
125.18	escape. [new paragraph] (MS) / escape." [new paragraph]
125.33	magistrate (MS) / magistrate's
125.41	his (MS) / her
125.42	next (MS) / again
126.8	Butler with hesitation; (MS) / Butler;
126.8	but—I (MS) / but I
126.12	Crags." [new paragraph] (MS) / Crags. [new paragraph]
126.18	numbers (MS) / number
127.24	END OF VOLUME FIRST (Editorial) / [no text]
	The MS leaf ending Volume 1 is missing.
129.28	in (MS) / into
129.28	irremediable (MS) / irretrievable
130.7	further (MS) / farther
130.37	accompany (MS) / have accompanied
131.29	a thing (MS) / that
132.4	Deans (MS) / David
132.10	his usual supplication (MS) / his supplication
132.22	the—first (MS) / the first
132.37	daughty (MS) / daughter
132.38	this (MS) / the
132.39	shadow (MS) / shadows
133.41	as you (MS) / as though you
133.42	which (MS) / that
134.1	preparations (MS) / preparation
134.12	had, in her opinion, a sort of solemnity in it (MS) / brought, in her opinion, awe and solemnity in it
134.21	on (MS) / upon
134.27	the clear (MS) / a clear
134.31	is (12mo 1821) / are

134.31 precautionary (MS) / various
135.11 WITCHCRAFT (MS) / WICHTCRAFT
135.19 Worlds (MS) / World
137.13 metropolis (MS) / capital
137.16 these mouldering ruins (MS) / these ruins
137.17 Nicol (MS) / Nichol
137.28 north-east (Editorial) / north-west
        Scott's directions were often at fault: Jeanie is looking NE as she
        approaches from the SW, and, of course, the moon does not rise in the
        NW.
137.32 was disappointed (MS) / was at first disappointed
137.40 as was the nature, she (MS) / according to the nature, as she
137.41 dæmons whose purpose seems rather hazing than malevolent?—or
        (MS dœmons whose purpose seems rather hazing than malevolent or)
        / dæmons?—or
137.42 propose (MS) / purpose
137.43 closer (MS) / close
138.10 And O, as (MS And O as) / And as
138.19 rather that (MS) / rather like that
138.25 maist (MS) / most
139.1   a' (MS) / all
139.9   incarnate. "I (MS) / incarnate—"I
139.14 yield yourself up (MS) / yield up
139.14 guidance, body (MS derived: guidance body) / guidance body
139.23 unlawfu' (MS) / unlawful
139.41 some (MS) / an
140.7   than I, though (MS) / than I am, though
140.11 —"but (12mo 1821) / —but
140.24 harken. The (MS) / harken!—The
140.24 illness—murdered (MS) / illness, murdered
140.27 miserable (MS) / unhappy
140.32 that (MS) / who
141.6   said he (MS) / he said
141.9   called—the (MS calld—the) / call it—any other
141.23 whatever (MS) / whatsoever
141.35 murderess (MS) / murdress
143.30 was once insured (MS) / was insured
143.32 Porteous (MS) / Porteous's
143.35 name of Daddie (MS) / name Daddie
144.1   department, an' it (MS department an' it) / department; an' if
144.2   service— (MS) / service, ye'll no find a better man.—
        The extra phrase was added in proof to create a main clause, which was
        lacking as a result of misreading 'it' as 'if'.
144.6   no (MS) / na
144.11 city-folks (MS) / city-folk
144.19 insure life (MS) / insure him life
144.22 it's (8vo 1819) / its
144.25 suld hae come (MS) / suld come
144.26 in (MS) / into
144.26 tolbooth (MS) / Tolbooth
144.31 strickly (MS) / strictly
144.33 accompt (MS) / account
144.35 be a' adrift (MS) / be adrift
144.36 whare (MS) / where
145.10 I am (MS) / I'm

145.21 mouse, while (MS derived: mouse & ↑ while) / mouse, and, while
This and the next emendation rectify Scott's insertion of a caret taking
in a verso addition on the wrong side of a MS ampersand.
145.21 pilferer, and taking (MS derived: pilferer ↓ taking) / pilferer, taking
145.27 betwixt (MS) / between
145.38 fo'k (MS) / folk
145.42 tolbooth (Editorial) / Tolbooth
The phrase 'in the Tolbooth here' was added in proof, but in the MS
Scott does not normally capitalise the initial letter.
146.2 replied Sharpitlaw (MS) / replied Mr Sharpitlaw
146.4 whan (MS) / when
146.8 do ye (MS) / d'ye
146.9 he's (MS) / he is
146.16 on (MS) / upon
146.24 he's been a play-actor (MS) / he has been a play-actor
146.42 lads' (MS) / lads's
146.43 ganging (MS) / gaun
147.3 point—the point—you (MS) / point, you
147.10 it?" (MS) / it?'
147.11 Weel (MS) / Well
147.20 said Sharpitlaw (MS) / said Mr Sharpitlaw
147.36 Captaincy . . . Captaincy (MS) / captaincy . . . captaincy
147.39 than (MS) / then
147.39 folks' (8vo 1819) / folks
147.42 than (MS) / then
148.5 Park—And (MS) / Park, and
148.40 day's (18mo) / days'
148.43 tolbooth (MS) / Tolbooth
149.2 it's (12mo 1821) / its
149.2 into song (MS) / into a song
149.7 rinning (MS) / rnnning
149.14 herself," (MS herself") / herself?"
149.16 been—ever (MS) / been ever
149.25 yer (MS derived: ye're) / your
149.32 at (MS) / of
149.37 it's (8vo 1819) / its
149.44 might (MS) / may
149.44 a (MS) / the same
150.5 day's (12mo 1821) / days
150.5 claiths (Editorial) / claise
A MS lacuna was filled by an intermediary with 'claise', but the word
used by Scott at 148.40 and 150.37 is 'claiths'.
150.9 win (MS) / wun
150.25 him up to (MS) / him to
150.28 than (MS) / then
150.34 ye . . . ye (MS) / you . . . you
150.36 than," said Madge indignantly; "for (MS than" said Madge indignantly
"for) / then; for
150.37 claiths (MS) / claise
151.5 shirt (MS) / short
151.8 whare (MS) / where
151.26 wi' (MS) / with
151.37 measure (MS) / measures
151.42 shirt (MS) / short
152.11 hame (MS) / home

152.30 wi' (MS) / to
152.35 winna (MS) / wunna
152.39 mak (MS) / make
153.3 winning (MS) / wunnin
153.4 it's (8vo 1819) / its
153.26 ye...ye...ye (MS) / you...you...you
154.1 fallow (MS) / fellow
154.23 tak ony (MS) / take any
154.32 ye (MS) / you
154.33 distress he has (MS) / distre ss hehas
154.35 O,...a'—o sir, (MS) / O,...a'! O, sir,
154.37 if (MS) / If
154.38 pit (MS) / put
154.40 it's (12mo 1821) / its
155.4 were (MS) / are
155.7 him (MS) / he
155.17 paint. Hout (MS) / paint—hout
155.23 memory with where (MS) / memory where
155.24 than (MS) / then
155.34 "will (MS) / "that will
155.35 it's (MS its) / it is
155.37 ye (MS) / you
155.38 mony ane does (MS) / mony does
156.1 you're (MS youre) / you are
156.4 ganging (MS) / gaun
157.8 potent (MS) / portentous
157.14 cursed (MS) / accursed
157.17 puir (MS) / poor
157.29 strait (MS) / straight
157.30 an (MS) / one
157.38 to (MS) / towards
157.40 do (MS) / does
158.11 ae (MS) / some
158.15 harns (MS) / brains
158.28 jee (MS) / gae
158.39 o' (MS) / of
158.40 *true*-lover (MS) / *true*-love
159.9 Nicol be (MS) / Nicol Muschat be
159.10 is nae (MS) / isna
159.12 it's (8vo 1819) / its
159.13 nook (MS) / corner
159.24 is this that (MS) / is that
159.26 didna (MS did na) / did not
160.5 tongue (MS) / tongues
160.5 it is (MS) / it's
160.9 a ballad which was a favourite of Madge Wildfire's and the words...
Robertson, trusting (MS a ballad which was a favourite of Madge ↑ and
the words...Robertson ↓ Wildfires trusting) / the first stanza of a
favourite ballad of Wildfire's, the words...Robertson, trusting
A misplaced caret may have been a factor in provoking this revision.
160.38 kepp at the (MS) / kepp the
161.10 here our (MS) / her own
161.11 watched (MS watchd) / waited
161.19 you'll (MS) / you will
161.22 a temporary (MS) / the readiest

162.21 shouldna (MS should na) / should not
162.25 wifie's (MS wifies) / wife's
162.25 in (MS) / o'
162.27 midland (MS) / mid-land
162.30 emergence (MS) / emergency
163.9 further (MS) / farther
163.23 all purchased (MS) / all her purchased
163.25 know thou (MS) / know that thou
163.26 them (MS) / those
164.16 himsell (MS) / himself
164.31 a cuddie (MS) / an ass
164.40 was a different and more intelligent person than him by whom Butler was committed, and was (MS was a different and more intelligent person than him by whom Butler was committed and was) / chanced to be the same by whom Butler was committed, a person
166.1 discern (MS) / discover
166.10 are become necessary (MS) / are necessary
166.21 in (MS) / wi'
166.22 affirmation (MS) / affirmations
167.6 gud-day ... gud-e'en (MS) / gude day ... gude e'en
167.11 this (MS) / the
167.13 farther (MS) / further
167.19 ye (MS) / you
167.25 gi'e back (MS) / gi'e me back
167.26 his (MS) / *His*
167.29 is that you (MS) / is you
167.30 Batie (MS) / Bawtie
167.38 hurle (MS) / harle
168.3 commandments (MS) / talents
168.3 wizend (MS) / wuzzent
168.3 And she spread her long skinny fingers garnished at the extremities with claws which a goss-hawk might have coveted. (MS And spread her long skinny fingers garnishd at the extremities with claws which a goss-hawk might have coveted.) / and she suited the word to the action, by spreading out a set of claws resembling those of Saint George's dragon on a country sign-post.
       The restoration at 168.3 of the term 'commandments' (which was clearly misunderstood) requires the continuation of the original metaphor.
168.8 that I am (MS than I am) / I'm
168.11 folks (MS) / folk
168.15 taken up again last night (Editorial) / taken up last night
       See Essay on the Text, 523.
168.20 upon (MS) / on
168.25 Honest! (MS) / Honest,
168.26 Scots (MS) / Scotch
168.29 ye (MS) / you
168.31 the angry passions (MS) / the passions
169.38 Gude Town (MS Good Town) / gude town
169.39 jo (MS) / joe
169.41 ne'er-do-weel, deevil's (MS) / ne'er-do-weel deevil's
169.43 anes ... anes (MS) / ance ... ance
170.12 tawpie (MS) / taupie
170.14 curtesy (MS) / curtsey
170.21 An' (MS) / an'

170.22 suldna (MS) / shouldna
170.22 curtesy (MS) / curtsey
170.25 win (MS) / wun
170.28 Pettycur (MS Pit⟨enweems⟩ ↑ tycur ↓) / Kircaldy
It is possible that the name could not be deciphered and that an intermediary substituted 'Kircaldy'.
170.29 and a' (MS) / and ower a'
170.34 ceiling, sung (MS) / cieling, and sung
In addition to misspelling 'ceiling', the intermediaries did not notice
that this is the second clause in a list which concludes after Madge's
song, nor that a lower-case at 'and' is required to complete the sentence
(see next emendation).
170.39 and (Editorial) / And
170.40 in (MS) / of
171.1 Chapter Six (MS Chapter. V.) / [no chapter break]
Scott deleted the original opening to the chapter, but did not delete
'Chapter. V.'. There is a break in the story at this point which makes a
new chapter natural.
171.22 council of regency (MS) / Council of Regency
Accepting the MS form here standardises the form of the name: at
63.40 the intermediaries followed the MS.
171.23 murther (MS) / murder
172.5 Head of the Kirk (MS) / head of the kirk
172.20 weeks' (8vo 1819) / weeks
172.29 Leonard (MS) / Leonard's
173.14 auld, worthy, faithfu' (8vo 1819) / auld worthy faithfu'
173.20 than (MS) / then
173.26 hae nae (MS) / haena
173.27 wally-draggle (MS) / wally-draigle
173.32 swarms (MS) / swarm
173.37 orators: (MS) / orators;
174.13 be bairn (MS) / be a bairn
174.15 withdrew. "We (MS) / withdrew, "we
174.26 Porteous Act (MS) / Porteous' Act
174.27 Kingdom and suffering Kirk (MS Kingdom and suffering kirk) / kingdom and suffering kirk
174.35 Sanders (MS) / Saunders
174.36 long (MS) / alang
175.3 think what (MS) / think of what
175.8 would—I would mak the (MS) / would make the
175.19 ye (MS) / you
175.22 or (MS) / and
175.23 and a scruple on (MS) / and scruple in
175.28 who was too (Magnum) / who, too
175.32 regimented (MS) / regimental
176.1 say you (MS) / say that you
176.6 ye (MS) / you do
176.11 say," said (MS) / say, Mr Deans," said
176.13 replied (MS) / said
176.16 keept (MS) / kept
176.17 strait (MS) / straight
176.17 rigg (MS) / ridge
176.19 sae (MS) / as
176.25 mak (MS) / make
177.13 rulers which (MS) / rulers, which

177.13   acknowledgement. (MS) / acknowledgement as amounted to sin.
177.26   temper (MS) / tempers
177.39   pontages (MS) / postages
178.10   though (MS) / although
178.19   Kirk (MS) / kirk
178.41   horrors (MS) / horror
179.20   matter (MS) / subject
179.27   winna (MS) / wunna
180.9   Jeanie (MS) / her
180.43   ye (MS) / you
181.6   his own preconceived (MS) / his preconceived
181.24   comply. And (MS) / comply; and
182.13   ane (MS) / out
182.28   only on one (MS) / on one only
182.38   had not had the (MS) / had not the
183.6   person fit to (MS) / person to
183.10   Deans (12mo 1821) / Deans'
183.11   sisters. But (MS) / sisters; but
183.15   she (MS) / She
184.31   hinny! (MS) / hinny,
184.35   tolbooth (MS) / Tolbooth
185.8   other's (8vo 1822) / others
185.12   other's (18mo) / others
185.13   voice (MS) / voices
185.17   more of delicacy (MS) / more delicacy
185.33   Fairbrother (Editorial) / Langtale
185.35   Michel (MS) / Nichel
185.39   the very fifteenth (MS) / the fifteenth
185.40   them! (MS) / them.
186.1   ye (MS) / you
186.1   frae (MS) / from
186.16   crown—my (MS) / crown, my
186.21   dung them a' to pieces (MS) / trod them a' pieces
187.11   had nae been (MS) / hadna been
187.11   waa's (MS) / wa's
187.13   chainge (MS) / change
187.13   gude (MS) / good
187.25   tolbooth (MS) / Tolbooth
187.26   were o' (MS were o) / are of
187.27   mazed (MS) / amazed
187.35   suffering—tell (MS) / suffering! tell
187.37   tout! (MS) / tout,
187.40   hizzy (MS) / huzzy
188.16   gratification. (12mo 1821) / gratification."
188.17   afore (MS) / before
188.20   than (MS) / then
188.21   than to ask (MS) / than ask
188.26   gudeness (MS) / goodness
189.4   do ye (MS) / d'ye
189.6   murther (MS) / murder
189.6   Murther (MS) / Murder
189.7   ee (MS) / e'e
189.9   babie (MS) / babe
189.12   mak (MS) / make
189.16   tittie (MS) / sister

189.16 loe...looing...loos (MS) / love...loving...loves
189.25 it's (8vo 1819) / its
189.25 it's (8vo 1819) / its
189.34 Whadyecallum's (MS) / Whatd'yecallum's
189.35 fables (MS) / fabbs
189.40 before——" (MS) / before"——
190.9 than let (MS) / to them, let
190.15 am aye thinking (MS) / am thinking
190.21 she had (MS) / I had
190.33 necessity they (MS) / necessity that they
190.34 Fairbrother...Fairbrother (Editorial) / Langtale...Langtale
191.5 pu'pit (MS) / pulpit
191.8 see she (MS) / see that she
191.14 it is (MS) / it's
192.7 Giles's (MS) / Giles'
192.13 scarce (MS) / scarcely
192.18 hardship (MS) / hardships
192.29 will——" (MS) / will"——
193.18 cæteris (MS) / cœteris
193.23 City Guard (MS) / City-Guard
        This is the only occasion (out of 9) where City Guard is hyphenated in
        Ed1.
193.32 bustling (MS) / bustle
193.35 empty (MS) / idle
194.10 Run (MS) / Ran
194.13 Deans jostled (MS) / Deans had jostled
194.27 and see (MS) / and ye see
194.29 Kirk (MS) / kirk
194.29 whilk (MS) / which
194.31 and our portion (MS) / and portion
195.3 the jurors (MS) / The jurors
195.10 Michel (MS) / Nichel
195.33 winna (MS) / wunna
196.10 sequestrating (MS) / sequestering
196.13 sequestrated (MS) / sequestered
196.13 gude (MS) / gudes
197.12 her guards (MS) / the guards
197.18 dark (Editorial) / fair
        This emendation is discussed in the Essay on the Text, 523–24.
197.35 in an agony (MS) / in agony
198.2 he be made an (MS derived: he made an) / he be an
198.16 case (MS) / cause
198.33 produce (MS) / proof
198.43 Law (MS) / the law
199.27 probably (MS) / properly
199.30 this (MS) / the
199.37 another deed (MS) / a crime
199.38 an (MS) / another
199.42 murthered (MS murtherd) / murdered
200.9 circumstances (MS) / circumstance
200.21 that a young (Editorial) / that in such an emergency a young
        The phrase 'a young woman, in such a situation' was added in proof, but
        the necessary deletion of 'in such an emergency' was not effected.
201.7 Jem (MS) / Fairbrother
201.36 forgot (MS) / forgotten

202.4 with the other (MS) / with other
202.4 cause (MS) / case
202.7 murther (MS) / murder
202.16 exculpation (MS) / evidence
202.26 those (MS) / these
202.41 murthered (MS murtherd) / murdered
203.5 Rahel (MS Rahal) / Rachael
       Rahel is the spelling of the name in the quotation from Jeremiah 31.15.
203.9 cheel that can (MS) / chield can
203.14 that wee (MS) / this wee
203.14 egg—and when poor Effie skirled, sae clever as he clinked it intill his
       pleading! He (MS egg—and when poor Effie skirl'd sae clever as he
       clinkd it intill his pleading—he) / egg! He
       A verso addition was omitted.
203.18 their (MS) / the
203.33 answered with the same heart-thrilling Not Guilty. (MS answerd with
       the same heart-thrilling Not Guilty.) / replied, "Not Guilty," in the
       same heart-thrilling tone as before.
203.37 her answers (MS) / h a n swers
204.18 pleases. But (MS) / pleases; but
204.28 contradiction (MS) / contradictions
205.23 this woman (MS) / the woman
205.27 writing (18mo) / word of mouth
205.31 Declares, that she (MS) / Declares, she
205.35 be fit (MS) / be a fit
205.43 tauld (MS) / told
206.5 weel (MS) / well
206.12 mair (MS) / more
206.16 answer for. (MS) / answer.
207.8 lodging (MS) / lodgings
207.12 streight—She (MS) / streight; she
207.14 this calamity (MS) / this present calamity
207.15 pinch. Yet (MS pinch Yet) / pinch; yet
207.17 with me for (MS) / for me
207.35 for (MS) / of
208.2 Michel (MS) / Nichel
208.5 sir, he should hae ceeted me, and (MS sir ye should her ceeted me and)
       / sir, and
208.12 Michel (MS) / Nichel
208.22 than arose (MS) / than what arose
208.37 appropriate (MS) / appropriated
208.39 under cover (MS) / under the cover
209.4 forwards (MS) / forward
209.14 his own emotion (MS) / his emotion
209.15 hers (MS) / herself
209.21 Great Day of Judgment (MS Great day of Judgement) / great day of
       judgment
209.22 make some impression (MS) / make impression
209.22 character (MS) / characters
209.24 severe (MS) / devout
209.26 same time elevated (MS) / same elevated
209.28 reverent (MS) / reverend
209.37 Truth (MS) / truth
209.38 Truth (MS) / truth
210.9 exclaimed he (MS) / he exclaimed

210.27 interrogatory (MS) / interrogatories
211.33 Nothing?—True (MS) / Nothing? True
211.34 say (MS) / tell you
212.4 him!—" she (MS) / him!"—she
212.19 passed (MS passd) / past
212.31 resumed (MS) / reviewed
212.35 communicated (MS) / communinicated
      The syllable 'ni' was repeated after an end-of-line hyphen.
213.13 and the interlocutor (MS) / and interlocutor
213.37 Law (MS) / law
213.37 was made (MS) / is made
214.2 extra-judicial go (MS) / extra-judicial confession go
214.20 jurors (MS) / jury
215.5 fact had been as (MS) / fact of delivery had taken place, as
215.21 deliberations (MS) / deliberation
215.25 returned, and (8vo 1819) / returned,and
215.40 remains (MS derived: remain) / remained
216.2 is (MS) / was
216.3 is (MS) / was
216.4 is (MS) / was
216.6 extinguishing of the (MS) / extinguishing the
216.43 with composure (MS) / with a composure
217.3 corporeal (MS) / corporal
217.7 afflictions (MS aflictions) / inflictions
217.25 clergymen (MS) / clergyman
217.32 moment (MS) / moments
217.34 tall, hagard (18mo) / tall hagard
217.38 backwards (MS) / backward
218.11 Dempster (MS) / Doomster
218.30 rearing (MS) / bearing forward
219.1 puir (MS) / poor
219.7 hizzy (MS) / huzzy
219.16 amna (MS am na) / am no
219.17 warst—I (MS) / warst, I
219.17 gude (MS) / good
219.37 laughed scornfully (MS laughd scornfully) / looked very scornful
219.39 Ingland (MS) / England
219.40 as honest Glendook (MS) / as Glendook
219.41 care (MS) / cares
219.43 hinders frae (MS) / hinders them frae
220.2 is (MS) / are
220.3 they ever pardon (MS) / they pardon
220.4 suld (MS) / should
220.8 they are (MS) / they're
220.14 heard that (MS) / heard o' that
220.29 the (MS) / his
220.34 hawker (MS) / hawkers
220.37 wants (MS) / wanted
221.4 elocution (MS) / elevation
221.12 "Time (MS) / "The time
221.15 these (MS) / those
221.26 ganging (MS) / gaun
221.30 I am (MS) / I'm
221.32 upstairs (MS) / up stairs
221.33 than (MS) / then

221.33 pitting (MS) / putting
222.34 me that he (MS) / me he
222.36 Ay, weel (MS Ay weel) / I weel
222.39 St (MS St.) / Saint
223.3 Porteous! (MS) / Porteous?
223.8 tolbooth (MS) / Tolbooth
223.12 it's (8vo 1819) / its
223.14 ye...ye (MS) / you...you
223.17 winna (MS) / wunna
223.32 There is (MS) / There's
223.34 she is ganging (MS) / she's gaun
223.36 Grizz (MS) / Grizzie
223.36 tak (MS) / take
223.40 and fal-lal (MS) / and your fal-lal
224.1 her (MS) / the
224.11 around (MS) / round
224.20 winna (MS) / wunna
224.20 yoursell—And (MS) / yourself, and
224.23 winna (MS) / wunna
224.27 tout! (MS) / tout,
224.39 the (MS) / in a
224.43 her; and if (MS) / her; if
225.4 assurances (MS) / assurance
225.12 keepit wi' (MS) / keepit company wi'
225.12 I—;" (MS I—") / I"—
225.12 wrang (MS) / wrung
225.19 head is (MS) / head's
225.29 Do ye (MS) / D'ye
225.34 I am (MS) / I'm
225.40 Ratton (MS) / Rattan
226.6 winna (MS) / wunna
226.7 ye (MS) / you
226.9 ye (MS) / you
226.10 amang (MS) / among
226.13 him." He then conducted her to the door of the prison and permitted
       her to depart. [new paragraph] After (MS) / him." [new paragraph]
       After
       A verso insert was missed.
226.15 one (MS) / an
226.16 tolbooth (MS) / Tolbooth
227.16 and snow-white (MS) / and change of snow-white
227.35 flocks (MS) / kine
227.35 and two (MS) / and in two
228.30 volume (MS) / chapter
229.10 Watts (8vo 1819) / Watt
229.20 vailed (MS derived: vaild of) / been veiled of
229.21 amusement (MS) / amusements
229.30 had (18mo) / having
229.30 slates. A (MS) / slates; a
230.3 turret was (MS) / turret, was
230.8 removed (MS) / renewed
230.22 consequences (MS) / consequence
231.2 shade (MS) / shed
231.4 hung (MS) / were
231.15 acquaintance whom (MS) / acquaintance, whom

232.19 ganging (Editorial) / gaun
        The MS is not extant at this point, but Scott never uses gaun.
232.35 instinctive (MS) / intuitive
232.38 of an ane (MS) / of ane
232.39 to dae (MS derived: today) / to do
232.40 loan (MS) / town
232.42 Dear, Mrs (MS) / Dear Mrs
232.42 d'ye (MS dye) / D'ye
233.1   !!! (MS) / !!
233.5   caa'd (MS ca'ad) / ca'd
233.6   on't (MS) / out
233.6   sister to be hangit (MS) / sister's to be hanged
233.14 bundle your (MS) / bundle up your
233.21 stentorian (MS) / stentorean
233.34 of bed (MS) / of his bed
233.38 Quixote (MS) / Quixotte
234.19 doun and let (MS) / do unto let
234.36 ye—see (MS) / ye, see
234.36 there is (MS) / there's
235.2   o' (MS) / of
235.7   fields (MS) / field
235.12 ganging (MS) / gaun
235.31 ye (MS) / you
235.33 Whare (MS) / Where
235.33 ganging (MS) / gaun
235.35 it aye stack (MS) / it stack
236.8   you"—(MS) / you—"
236.12 tak (MS) / take
236.12 whan (MS) / when
236.27 than (MS) / then
236.28 ends their lane—pearlin (MS) / ends, their pearlin
236.29 spiders' (18mo) / spider's
236.33 supposing (MS) / supposiug
237.1   Butler!" echoed (MS) / Butler!' echoed
237.9   winna (MS) / wunna
237.21 on (MS) / upon
237.25 to (MS) / and
237.31 in uncertainty (MS) / in an uncertainty
237.39 all symptoms (MS) / all the symptoms
237.39 head aside, (MS) / head,
238.14 wad like ill (MS) / wadna like
238.19 word; gang (MS) / word. Gang
238.38 He is (MS) / He's
238.38 it's pity (MS) / it's a pity
238.39 powney." [new paragraph] And (MS powney"—And) / powney."
        And
        In the MS a dash after direct speech signals a new paragraph.
239.9   shortly (ms) / soon
239.10 gentle (MS) / little
239.11 a little prattling (MS) / a prattling
239.23 caa'd (MS) / ca'ed
239.24 and a churl (MS) / and churl
239.26 Meribah (MS) / Mirebah
240.5   hopes. There (MS hopes There) / hopes: There
240.11 have something (MS) / have had something

240.16 on (MS) / upon
240.23 hoped he (MS) / hoped that he
241.15 conning a (MS) / conning over a
241.26 the cope-stone (MS) / thecope-stone
241.40 The sage (MS) / This sage
242.21 lassie—But (MS) / lassie, but
242.22 course. (MS) / course—
242.32 Butler, "Was (MS) / Butler, with great self-complacency, "Was
243.7   servitude of stillicide—that is to say, water-drap, (maybe (MS servitude
        of Stillicide—that is to say water-drap (maybe) / servitude of water-
        drap—that is to say, *tillicidian*,* (maybe
243.7   [no footnote] (MS) / *He meant, probably, *stillicidium*
243.12 complacence (MS) / delight
243.13 arena (MS are na) / are no
243.14 to ye (MS) / t'ye
243.15 stillicide (MS) / *tillicidian*
243.18 o' it (MS) / o't
243.20 *stillicide* (MS) / *tillicide*
243.22 on (MS) / or
243.28 o' (MS) / of
243.33 hersell (MS her sell) / herself
243.34 lasted (MS) / rested
244.1   leasure (MS) / leisure
244.4   the room (MS) / a room
244.4   this (MS) / the
244.12 ye (MS) / you
244.13 for not even the . . . had concealed (MS) / for the . . . had not concealed
244.28 tak (MS) / take
245.3   winna (MS) / wunna
245.8   ganging (MS derived: going) / gaun
        Scott always writes 'ganging', and when Scoticising this is the form the
        intermediaries ought to have used.
245.14 it is (MS) / it's
245.17 folks (MS) / folk
245.22 claes (MS) / claiths
245.42 I am (MS) / I'm
246.6   me! Jeanie, this (MS me! Jeanie this) / me, Jeanie! this
246.8   whom (MS) / that
246.9   gude turn langsyne (MS) / gude langsyne
246.18 leddies (MS) / ladies
246.20 do't (MS) / do it
246.25 ye (MS) / you
246.29 ye (MS) / you
246.39 na fa' (MS) / not fall
246.43 devout (MS) / divine
247.1   gaen (MS) / gane
247.1   us." (MS) / us a'."
247.2   wad (MS) / would
247.3   ye go and undertake (MS) / ye undertake
247.4   what (MS) / who
247.15 extenuated (MS) / extended
247.22 further (MS) / farther
247.30 hand nor head (MS) / head nor hand
247.31 you'll soon win (MS) / you will soon be permitted
247.39 sae (MS) / as

247.39   winna (MS) / maunna
248.2   sight (MS) / light
248.13   he had departed (MS) / he departed
248.17   hath is (MS and the Authorised Version) / hath, is
248.18   many (MS and the Authorised Version) / the
248.18   now am (Editorial) / am now
248.19   begging bread (Editorial) / begging their bread
          As Butler is reading the Bible the text ought to be as written.
249.4   hours' (8vo 1822) / hours
249.13   their (MS) / the
249.23   sarcasms (MS) / sarcasm
249.28   checked (MS checkd) / checqued
249.37   pat (MS) / put
250.1   curtesy (MS) / curtsey
250.3   and most sequestered (MS) / and sequestered
250.10   of (MS) / o' a
250.10   canst have o' th' road (MS) / can have on the road
250.13   nice, Scotch (12mo 1821) / nice Scotch
250.23   It makes (MS) / I make
250.23   pilgrimage heavy (MS) / pilgrimage more heavy
250.23   burthensome more than through (MS) / burthensome, through
250.25   heart. For (MS) / heart; for
250.26   saith that the (MS) / says, that "the
250.27   father, wherein (MS) / father," wherein
250.29   minde (MS) / mind
          For this and the following emendations see Essay on the Text, 499, 515.
250.30   wald (MS) / wad
250.31   hail (MS) / hale
250.32   deer (MS) / dear
250.33   upon (MS) / on
250.33   househald (MS) / household
250.40   dout (MS) / doubt
250.41   Apostle (MS) / apostle
251.1   orguns (MS) / organs
251.3   twae (MS) / twa
251.5   Loupthedike (MS) / Loup-the-dike
251.6   a' blessings (MS a blessings) / a blessing
251.11   mur-ill (MS) / muir-ill
251.12   drible (MS) / dribble
251.13   a (Magnum) / half ane
          A Scots pint was equivalent to about three English pints; a mutchkin
          was about ¾ of an English pint.
251.13   muchkin (MS) / mutchkin
251.13   sape and harteshorn (MS) / sope and hartshorn
251.14   teemed (MS teemd) / toomed
251.15   quey—An (MS) / quey; an'
251.19   spleuhan-fu' (MS) / spleuchan-fu'
251.20   dout (MS) / doubt
251.20   whare (MS) / where
251.21   bides (MS) / lives
251.29   Kirk (MS) / kirk
251.30   milns (MS) / mills
251.30   miln-dams (MS) / mill-dams
251.31   millar (MS) / miller
251.32   wald (MS) / wad

251.32   com (MS) / come
251.32   mak (MS) / make
251.33   wi' (MS) / with
251.33   ony speaks (MS) / ony body speaks
251.34   answer (MS) / answers
251.35   kend (MS) / kenn'd
251.36   thae (MS) / they
251.38   lute (MS) / let
251.39   reeding (MS) / reading
251.40   scule (MS) / schule
251.41   gude (MS) / good
252.2   haena (MS hae na) / hae nae
252.4   folk's (8vo 1822) / folks
252.7   says, that the (MS) / says, the
252.11   cristian (MS) / Christian
252.14   JEAN (MS) / JEANIE
252.17   sure I (MS) / sure that I
252.20   ilk (MS) / ilka
252.20   aboon, if (MS) / aboon a', if
252.25   Deuke (MS) / Duke
252.25   whan I win (MS) / when I won
252.27   sine of the Thistell (MS) / sign of the Thistle
252.28   muckell (MS) / muckle
253.1   himsell (MS) / himself
254.5   on o' th' road (MS) / o' on the road
254.7   i' th' (MS) / i' the
254.12   lass!" (MS) / lass,"
254.13   belt (MS) / buckle
254.16   haunts (MS) / haunt
254.18   at sign (MS) / at the sign
254.18   th' Thistle (MS) / the Thistle
254.24   narrating (MS) / relating
254.37   knowst (MS) / knowest
254.38   th' road (MS) / the road
255.7   were for nae harm (MS) / werena for harm
255.9   wilt (18mo) / will't
255.16   Jem (MS) / Jim
255.20   Jem's (MS) / Jim's
255.21   further (MS) / farther
255.25   Jean (MS) / Jeanie
255.25   meetst (MS) / meetest
255.26   th' road (MS) / the road
255.33   Lammermoor (MS) / Lammer-muir
256.12   Gumoorsbury (MS) / Gunners'bury
         Scott consistently has 'Gunners' as the first element of the name on the
         other three occasions it appears; in this context, then, 'Gumoors' must
         be intended as a feature of Dick Ostler's speech.
256.20   bid (MS) / said
256.39   observed that the (MS) / observed the
257.19   gratified. Some (MS) / gratified; some
257.22   which (MS) / of horses that
257.34   "For (MS) / "As for
257.35   hills (MS) / hill
257.36   thy good journey (MS) / thy journey
257.43   they lost (MS) / they hae lost

257.43 Jem (MS) / Jim
258.8   what's (MS whats) / what was
258.17 precessor (MS) / predecessor
258.26 to highway (MS) / to a highway
258.37 Heaven ye (MS) / Heaven, that ye
258.37 we'll (MS) / we will
258.37 night, God (MS) / night yet, God
259.4   hist (MS) / trot
259.4   as an (MS) / an as
259.7   through——" (MS through") / through land."
        The intermediaries thought it necessary to complete the line, while the
        text makes clear that Jeanie is unable to hear more.
259.11 apprehension (MS) / apprehensions
259.28 further (MS) / farther
259.38 emergence (MS) / emergency
259.38 you're determined (MS youre determind) / you are resolved
260.6   hing (MS) / hang
260.9   as will find (MS) / as finds
260.11 short (MS) / shorter
260.11 coin won't (MS) / coin that won't
260.13 gentlemen," said Jeanie, Ratcliffe's (MS gentlemen" said Jeanie Rat-
        cliffes) / gentlemen," Ratcliffe's
260.18 Jem (MS) / Jim
260.20 is (MS) / has
260.36 I beat (MS) / I'll beat
260.38 thee (MS) / ye
260.41 I leave (MS) / I'll leave
261.8   from some part (MS) / from part
261.13 like habitation (MS) / like a habitation
261.19 adrift (MS) / abroad
261.22 but such (MS) / but not such
261.23 us devils (MS) / us—devils
261.33 oatmeal (MS) / ointment
261.40 hag, who strove vehemently, backwards by main force, until (MS hag
        who strove vehemently backwards by main force until) / hag backwards
        by main force, who strove vehemently until
261.43 toward (MS) / towards
262.15 gruntler's (MS) / grunter's
262.27 midst (MS) / middle
262.35 her escape (MS) / her to escape
262.40 i' (MS) / in
262.40 tolbooth (MS) / Tolbooth
263.4   Ow (MS) / Ou
263.7   gudeen (MS) / gude e'en
263.19 suppliant (MS) / supplicant
263.19 pious (MS) / duteous
263.23 starting (MS) / started
263.25 or of Jeanie (MS) / or Jeanie
263.40 There isna (MS There is na) / There's no
263.42 No," (18mo) / No;"
264.1   precarious and suspicious, that (MS) / precarious, that
264.4   Bedlam? (MS) / Bedlam!
264.10 Jeanie, (this she said . . .) (MS Jeanie (this she said . . .)) / Jeanie," (she
        said this . . .)
264.21 was (MS) / were

264.26 He is (MS) / He's
264.39 in (MS) / on
265.3   tolbooth (MS) / Tolbooth
265.4   Edinburgh are to (8vo 1819) / Edinburgh to
265.10 making life a (MS) / making a
265.14 fluent (MS) / floating
265.15 the mind (MS) / her mind
265.17 one (MS) / ane
265.22 ganging (MS) / gaun
265.31 occasion. "I (MS) / occasion,—"I
265.36 body that I (MS) / body I
265.38 wild tone (MS) / wild-tone
265.41 blithesome (MS) / blithesome
266.1   dead. Or (MS dead Or) / dead—or
266.4   hunder (MS) / hundred
266.5   mere (MS) / merely
266.19 admitted (MS) / permitted
266.37 Reformed (MS) / reformed
266.39 Airds-moss (MS) / Aird-moss
267.14 import, and partly by (MS) / import, by
267.23 gallows-heels (MS) / heels
267.26 Jem (MS) / Jim
267.30 lown (MS) / loon
267.32 bilked (MS bilkd) / baulked
267.38 maun (MS) / must
267.41 winna (MS) / wunna
267.41 hands (MS) / hand
268.2   I do soberly (MS) / I will do soberly
268.5   further (MS) / farther
268.11 "Well—and (MS) / "And
268.13 hand (MS) / hands
268.14 preferment? (MS) / preferment!
268.14 eye (MS) / eyes
268.14 further (MS) / farther
268.15 d'ye (8vo 1819) / dy'e [MS dye]
268.33 aught (Magnum) / ought
268.43 And I will (MS) / and I will
269.1   it, or (MS it or) / it,—or
269.34 t'other—" (MS) / t'other"—
270.19 murtherers (MS) / murderers
270.39 well, no (MS) / we'll say no
270.39 come (MS) / coming
271.8   lass (MS) / woman
271.10 met my (MS) / met wi' my
271.11 they hae whirled (MS) / they whirled
271.12 o' (MS) / about
271.15 tak (MS) / take
271.15 make an unco (MS) / make unco
271.17 fun (MS) / frolic
271.18 than (MS) / then
271.32 win (Editorial) / wun
        The word is not in the MS, but Scott does not use the 'wun' form.
271.32 folk's (12mo 1825) / folks
272.14 ganging (MS) / gaun
272.15 hands (MS) / head

272.29 towns (MS) / town
273.2 described. (18mo) / described in the motto to our chapter.
See Essay on the Text, 520.
274.6 it is (MS) / it's
274.19 keep fast o' (MS) / keep a fast haud o'
275.1 it is (MS) / it's
275.13 misfortune"—— (MS) / misfortune——"
275.22 again, Jeanie, for (MS again Jeanie for) / again, for
276.4 design (MS) / purpose
276.7 folk's (8vo 1819) / folks
276.9 maist (MS) / most
276.10 these (MS) / the
276.11 whan (MS) / when
276.12 mair about (MS) / mair speed about
276.19 mongst (MS) / amongst
276.26 than (MS) / then
276.34 ganging (MS derived: going) / gaun
Scott always writes 'ganging', and when Scoticising this is the form the
intermediaries ought to have used.
276.36 weel-fa'ard (MS) / weel-faur'd
276.40 objections (MS) / objection
277.21 as to (MS derived: as) / respecting
277.23 examination (MS) / examinations
277.33 burst (MS) / broke
277.34 lass! (MS) / lass,
277.35 ye (MS) / you
278.38 And ye (MS) / And do ye
279.11 City (MS) / city
279.20 he said (MS) / he had said
279.24 me. And (MS me—And) / me; and
279.40 straight (MS) / direct
279.40 lines, one (MS lines ↑ one ↓) / lines on
280.1 hamlet the parish church reared its (MS) / hamlet stood the parish
church and its
280.6 ganging (MS derived: going) / gaun
Scott always writes 'ganging', and when Scoticising this is the form the
intermediaries ought to have used.
280.6 lassies (MS) / lasses
280.9 him that; I (MS) / him; I'm sure I
280.27 rumpled (MS) / disordered
281.9 a belt (MS shouldbelt) / a shoulder-belt
It appears that Scott began to write 'shoulder', saw a repetition, but did
not delete the repeated matter.
281.26 puffed up (MS puffd up) / elated
281.39 three stone steps (MS) / three steps
282.5 made after (MS) / followed
282.7 ganging (MS derived: going) / gaun
Scott always writes 'ganging', and when Scoticising this is the form the
intermediaries ought to have used.
282.7 ye (MS) / you
282.9 into (MS) / in to
282.34 frequently to be met with in (MS) / frequent in
282.37 Presbyterian Kirk (MS) / presbyterian kirk
283.2 took (MS) / looked
283.15 pews (MS) / pew

283.19 captivity the (MS) / captivity up the
283.36 imitate (MS) / follow
284.7   place of public worship (MS) / place of worship
285.33 ye as (MS) / ye, as
285.34 good—" (MS) / good"—
285.38 read (MS) / redd
286.2   fit (MS) / fite
286.8   Has (MS) / Hast
286.8   na (MS) / ony
286.11 stocks yonder at (MS) / stocks at
286.12 out o' parish (MS) / out o' the parish
286.12 wi' the (MS) / with the
286.21 canst tell (MS) / canst thou tell
286.38 upon parish (MS) / upon the parish
287.1   nittle (MS) / mettle
287.34 sweet-chesnut trees (MS sweet chesnut trees; Magnum sweet-chestnut
        trees) / sweet chesnut-trees
287.41 combination (MS) / combinations
288.9   ha (MS) / hae
288.10 as pleases (MS) / as it pleases
288.22 the (MS) / a
288.25 romance, vivacity (MS) / romantic vivacity
288.32 lower down, (MS) / lower,
288.39 doest (MS) / dost
289.1   sarvice (MS) / service
289.2   of (MS) / o'
289.20 musqueteers and callivers (MS) / musquet and calliver-men
289.36 chose (MS) / had chosen
290.5   the more ancient to the modern (MS) / the ancient to the more modern
290.26 trouble? (MS) / trouble!
290.41 herself (MS) / hersell
291.3   behounched (MS behounchd) / bechounched
291.41 add, discreditable (MS) / add, in discreditable
292.19 Thieves? (MS) / Thieves!
293.34 although only a (MS) / although a
293.35 surplice, read (MS) / surplice, although he read
293.36 write over (MS) / wrote down
294.32 hall-Bible (MS) / large Bible
294.35 things (MS) / a thing
294.41 it's (8vo 1819) / its
294.43 using (MS) / use
295.1   minds (MS) / mind
295.8   knowst (MS) / knowest
295.8   any (MS) / ony
295.13 pain (MS) / pains
295.31 in house (MS) / in this house
295.32 ha' (MS) / have
295.32 curries (MS) / carries
296.11 fain not name (MS derived: faint not name) / faint did I name
296.40 So (MS) / so
297.9   do not (MS) / don't
297.36 said he (MS) / he said
298.30 place. She (MS place She) / place;—she
298.32 but (MS) / and
298.34 it (MS) / It

298.35 villainous: her (MS) / villainous—her
298.37 to (MS) / To
298.42 house, plunged into low dissipation, and (MS house plungd into low dissipation and) / house, and
299.1 in (MS) / into
299.11 marauding (MS) / maraudings
299.12 rectory, Jeanie? (MS rectory Jeanie) / rectory?
299.14 answered (MS answerd) / replied
299.18 would (MS) / should
299.23 is come (MS) / came
300.8 dreamed (MS dreamd) / dreamt
300.14 £100 (MS) / a sum of money
300.15 frantic. (MS) / frantic—
300.19 steered (MS steerd) / stood
300.37 been but too (MS) / been too
301.1 around (MS) / round
301.17 £100 note (MS) / money
301.20 effectuate (MS affectuate) / effect
301.25 course (MS) / courses
301.33 and an extraordinary (MS) / and extraordinary
302.24 hands (MS) / hand
302.30 mine, saith the Lord, and (MS mine saith the Lord and) / mine, and
303.14 flung from (MS) / flung myself from
303.32 gie (MS) / give
304.4 further (MS) / farther
304.20 Danger (MS) / the law
304.43 reverence (MS) / order to attend
305.1 attempts (MS) / attempt
305.7 thrist (MS) / thirst
305.14 which (MS) / what
306.3 this (MS) / the
306.6 upstairs (MS) / up stairs
306.22 madam," said he, "I (MS Madam" said he "I) / madam, I
306.29 her, must (MS) / her, why must
306.29 truth, and could (MS truth & could) / truth, when she could
306.36 sir? (MS) / sir!
306.37 soul? (MS) / soul!
307.1 all you (MS) / all that you
307.13 eaves-dropping (MS) / eves-dropping
307.14 or better (MS) / or what better
307.41 themselves—a (MS) / themselves not a
309.14 through them (MS) / them through
309.16 maun (MS) / must
309.24 way"——— (MS) / way———"
310.9 answered, "And (MS) / answered, [new paragraph] "And
310.12 ganging (MS) / gaun
310.13 I could (MS) / to
310.15 shop"——— (MS) / shop———"
310.35 chuse it, (MS) / chuse,
310.39 speaks but ower (MS) / speaks ower
310.43 be seriously disposed, young (MS be seriously disposed young) / be a seriously-disposed young
311.7 no (MS) / not
311.11 Kirk (MS) / kirk
312.4 Thomas (MS) / Tummas

312.8 Mistress (MS) / Mrs
312.11 there's (MS) / there was
312.12 Thomas (Editorial) / Tummas
As can be seen above at 312.4 Mrs Dalton addresses him as Thomas; the MS here reads 'John', and when correcting this error the intermediaries should have followed the form of the name used by Mrs Dalton.
312.28 by the (MS) / along a
312.32 bit note (MS) / bit of a note
313.1 honour, my family's honour, my (MS) / honour,—my family's honour
313.6 sacrifice of (MS) / sacrifice out of
313.9 him that you (MS) / him you
313.13 assured that I (MS) / assured I
313.17 course. But (MS) / course; but
313.18 reward, office (MS) / reward—office
313.19 thing, you (MS thing you) / thing—you
313.40 purposed (MS) / proposed
313.43 The crime ... crime (MS) / His guilt ... guilt
314.11 that (MS) / the
314.13 The very rigorous (MS) / The rigorous
314.16 for discovery (MS) / for the discovery
314.25 Monteith (MS) / Monteath
314.30 said poor Jeanie (MS) / said Jeanie
315.17 and his (MS) / and when his
315.19 sum her (MS) / sum up her
315.20 she contrived (MS) / she had contrived
315.22 disposal. George (MS) / disposal, in consequence of which management, George
315.27 offered (MS offerd) / afforded
316.6 and worse rendezvouses (MS and worse rendezvous's) / and every worse rendezvous
317.23 talent (MS) / talents
317.24 House (MS) / house
317.42 her sovereign (MS) / his sovereign
318.9 speeches (MS) / speech
318.15 in (MS) / on
318.29 Scotsman (MS) / Scotchman
318.40 baffle which they (MS) / baffle they
319.10 inconveniencies (MS) / inconveniences
319.14 sun-burned (MS sun-burnd) / sun-burnt
319.37 want (MS) / wish
320.8 it's (8vo 1819) / its
320.8 Mistress (MS) / Mrs
320.13 Lordship ... honour's (MS Lordship ... honours) / honour ... Lordship's
320.32 getting reprieve (MS) / getting a reprieve
320.36 understand there (MS) / understand that there
321.8 ascribes (MS) / ascribe
321.11 are (18mo) / is
321.24 and if the (MS) / and the
321.28 law-maker though, sir (MS) / law-maker, sir
321.39 country's friend and the poor man's friend; (MS country's freind and the poor mans freind;) / country's friend;
321.40 there is nae name like (MS) / there's nane like
321.42 winna (MS) / wunna
321.42 bluid (MS) / blood

322.4 House (MS) / house
322.12 gude (MS) / good
322.19 Barebone's (MS) / Barebones's
322.24 O! (MS) / O,
322.25 House ... These (MS) / house .... these
322.26 certifie (MS) / certify
322.26 Regiment of Dragoons (MS) / regiment of dragoons
322.33 in (MS) / on
322.41 wasna (MS was na) / was nae
322.41 grandfather—to (MS) / grandfather to
323.4 puir (MS) / poor
323.20 guilty, sir, as (MS guilty Sir as) / guilty, as
323.39 minutes' (18mo) / minutes
324.4 sir, again," said (MS sir again" said) / sir," again said
324.19 Mistress (MS) / Mrs
324.25 hunderd (MS) / hundred
324.34 isna (MS is na) / is nae
325.18 sax (MS) / six
325.30 curtesy (MS) / curtsey
325.34 Scotsman there, as may (MS Scotsman there as may) / Scotsman, as
        there may
326.14 excisemen (MS) / exciseman
326.38 curtesy (MS) / curtsey
326.38 to (MS) / for
326.39 it up to (MS) / it to
327.12 ganging (MS derived: gaing) / going
327.12 gang (MS) / go
327.26 bring you down (MS) / bring down
327.27 you will (MS) / we'll
327.36 on (MS) / in
328.6 which was (MS) / which road was
328.17 only once (12mo 1821) / never
        The passage 'and which, lumbering and jolting as it was, conveyed to
        one, who had never been in a coach before, a certain feeling of dignity
        and importance' was added in proof, but fails to remember what had
        been written previously: Jeanie travelled from Stamford to London in a
        coach, hence this emendation.
328.32 charge, "and (MS) / charge, and
328.36 lairds' leddies (MS lairds leddies) / lairds and leddies
328.42 if (MS) / when
329.9 this (MS) / the
329.21 the hill (MS) / a hill
329.25 richest (MS) / rich
329.40 crags (MS) / craigs
330.1 made signal (MS) / made a signal
330.31 her's. But (MS) / her's; but
330.34 doubted (MS) / dreaded
330.39 for (MS) / of
331.3 gentleman could (MS) / gentleman of fashion could
331.3 could then appear (MS) / could appear
331.9 than like a palace royal (MS) / than a royal palace
331.35 and to follow (MS) / and follow
332.2 passion (MS) / passions
332.8 she repeatedly (MS) / she had repeatedly
332.10 his long walks (MS) / his walks

332.13   correspondencies (MS) / correspondences
332.31   House (MS) / house
332.33   eruption (MS) / irruption
332.34   doubt but that (MS) / doubt, that
332.36   a (MS) / the
332.40   most (MS) / least
333.36   principal had (MS) / principal person had
334.8   whenever (MS) / when
334.21   Levee and Drawing-room (MS) / levee and drawing-room
335.6   amongst (MS) / among
335.29   Queen (MS) / Quee n
335.39   expressions (MS) / expression
335.39   and assuming (MS) / and on assuming
336.27   you (MS) / You
336.41   *grande-dame* (MS) / *grand-dame*
337.4   is—not (MS) / is not
338.5   tuned (MS) / toned
338.6   she (MS) / eke
338.29   kirk-session (Editorial) / Kirk-Session
         These words are not in the MS but they are given lower-case initial
         letters on every other occasion.
340.6   thus (MS) / then
340.7   attach itself only (MS) / only attach itself
340.10   favour—to (MS) / favour to
340.11   say—rebellious— (MS) / say rebellious?—
340.30   or of ony (MS) / or any
341.3   folk's (MS folks) / people's
341.4   high (MS) / light
341.14   with (MS) / her
341.20   housewife," (MS) / housewife case,"
343.19   they had resumed their places, were soon advancing (MS) / they re-
         sumed their places, soon began to advance
344.1   were to (MS) / were likely to
         The proof addition creates repetition.
344.5   she continued (MS) / continued she
345.4   Lord." (MS) / Lord.
345.10   sir!" (MS) / sir,"
345.42   thought particular (MS) / thought so particular
345.43   is (MS) / it
346.3   cheeses (MS) / cheese
346.5   Lockermaikus (MS) / Lockermachus
346.5   Lammermoor (MS) / Lammermuir
346.29   in (MS) / of
347.4   recollections (MS) / recollection
347.5   other's (8vo 1819) / others
347.21   or only (MS) / or was it only
347.22   Where ... Whom ... What ... Who (MS) / where ... whom ... what
         ... what
347.25   with (MS) / by
348.4   meanwhile (MS) / mean while
348.9   of right (MS) / of the right
348.20   more. So (MS) / more; so
348.32   immediately (MS immediatly) / instantly
349.32   pardun (MS) / pardon
349.33   dout (MS) / doubt

349.35 saul (MS) / soul
349.35 fisicyian (MS) / fisycian
349.36 Allwaies (MS) / Alwaies
349.39 command. [new line] "Ye (MS) / command, Ye
350.2   subscription (MS) / insertion
350.6   Majeesty (MS) / Majesty
350.7   her blood, whilk (MS) / her, whilk
350.9   differring (MS) / differing
350.11 gae (MS) / gaed
350.11 ane (MS) / a
350.13 instriments (MS) / instruments
350.15 And likewise (MS) / and likewise
350.16 Denshire (MS) / Devonshire
350.16 althou' (MS althou) / although
350.17 breed—And (MS) / breed—and
350.21 debit (MS) / debt
350.22 Honor (MS) / Honour
350.22 duke (MS) / Duke
350.22 except (MS) / accept
350.22 Dunlap (MS) / Dunlop
350.27 Providense (MS) / Providence
350.29 pleesed (MS) / pleased
350.33 lended (MS) / lent
350.33 shall (MS) / will
350.37 duke (MS) / Duke
350.37 there (MS) / their
350.38 troublesum (MS) / troublesome
350.38 by-past (MS) / bye-past
351.1   duk (MS) / Duk
351.2   respeck (MS) / respect
351.3   honor's (MS) / Honour's
351.5   Auchtermuggitie (MS) / Aughtermuggitie
351.8   mak (MS) / make
351.10 outgangings (MS) / outgauns
351.14 Maister (MS) / Master
351.17 duk (MS) / Duke
351.20 huzzy (MS) / hussy
351.23 keppit (MS) / keepit
351.24 Craigmiller (MS) / Craigmillar
351.24 Edinbrugh (MS) / Edinburgh
351.25 it (MS) / the buildings
351.27 Maister (MS) / Master
351.28 neibours (MS) / neebours
351.29 ye (MS) / you
351.29 in (MS) / for
351.35 compass (MS) / compas
351.38 wee murland (MS) / wild muirland
351.39 Canno'gate (MS) / Canogate
351.39 kend (MS) / had
351.41 sume (MS) / sum
352.1   doutless (MS) / doubtless
352.1   o' (MS) / of
352.3   amna (MS am na) / am nae
352.3   ele'en (MS) / eleven
352.4   gude (MS) / good

352.5   ganging (MS) / in gaun
352.23   coach and six, with (MS) / coach, with
353.4   it's (8vo 1819) / its
353.12   year (MS) / years
353.20   it's (MS its) / it is
353.29   curtesy (MS) / curtsey
353.32   it is (MS) / it's
354.2   effectively (MS) / civil and
355.4   fair (MS) / faer
355.10   But yet we (MS) / But we
355.15   Lennard's Craigs (MS Lennards craigs) / Leonard's Crags
355.23   banes (MS) / bones
355.25   breadth and the length (MS) / length and the breadth
355.27   domicile. Likewise I (MS) / domicile, likewise, as I
355.33   might (MS) / may
355.33   sauld here to (MS) / sauld to
355.33   had but grace (MS) / had grace
356.3   whilk (MS) / that
356.15   the poor misguided (MS) / the misguided
356.21   streights (MS) / straights
356.22   delusions (MS) / delusion
356.23   is but an (MS) / is an
356.27   upon the (MS) / uponthe
356.28   nations. See (MS) / nations—see
356.30   'Let (12mo 1821) / "Let
356.31   up.'" (12mo 1821) / up."
357.31   and upon being (MS) / and being
357.38   Sheriff-moor (MS) / Sheriff-muir
358.1   Sheriff-moor (MS) / Sheriff-muir
358.8   Dumblain (MS) / Dumblane
358.19   homely (MS) / hamely
358.22   respect she (MS) / respect which she
359.6   Saint Mungo's (MS) / St Giles's
         St Giles does not have a steeple.
359.8   all friends (MS) / all my friends
360.4   neighbourhood (12mo 1825) / vicinity
360.11   Haribee broo' (MS) / Haribee-broo'
360.12   aloife (MS) / aloive
360.15   ma loife (MS) / my life
360.15   foive (MS) / four
360.21   unknown to him (MS) / unknown to to him
360.26   Harabee or Hara-brow (MS) / Haribee or Harabee-brow
360.31   later (MS) / latter
360.34   those (MS) / these
360.37   the eager eyes (MS) / the eyes
360.41   darker (MS) / dark
360.43   into air (MS) / into the air
361.10   feeling (MS) / feelings
361.11   faintness (MS) / fainting
361.14   burned (MS burnd) / burnt
362.7   upon (MS) / along
362.8   tint but (MS) / but tint
362.11   Eye, eye (MS Eye eye) / Ay, ay
362.11   seeest (MS) / seest
362.11   hou (MS) / how

362.14 Eye, eye (MS Eye eye) / Ay, ay
362.18 that." [new line] (MS) / that. [new line]
362.19 thinkst (MS) / thinkest
362.21 folks (MS) / folk
362.22 swumming (MS) / swimming
362.22 th' Eden (MS) / the Eden
362.34 d'ye (8vo 1819) / dye [MS dye]
362.35 mither (MS) / mother
362.41 saut-wife." (MS) / saut-wife.'
363.2   all this (MS) / allthis
363.2   some (MS) / a
363.3   this (MS) / the
363.14 fo'k (MS) / folk
363.19 the"——— (MS) / the———"
363.22 Archibald. "She is mad, but quite innocent." [new paragraph] "She
        (MS Archibald. "She is mad, but quite innocent"—"She) / Archibald.
        [new paragraph] "She is mad, but quite innocent; she
        The absence of a dash after 'Archibald' indicates that the speaker has
        not changed.
363.28 on (MS) / o'
363.28 a (MS) / his
364.5   understood she (MS) / understood that she
364.9   that Archibald (MS) / that Mr Archibald
364.33 establishment, had thought (MS) / establishment, thought
364.38 intimation (MS) / information
364.43 forgotten (MS) / obsolete
365.19 symptom (MS) / symptoms
366.16 true-love, (MS) / true-love!
366.19 to-day I die (MS) / I die to-day
366.35 grey-headed (MS) / gray-headed
366.39 steady. (MS) / steady;
366.43 them she (MS) / them, that she
366.44 awaken (MS) / awake
367.19 wherever (MS) / whenever
368.2   Magdalen (MS) / Magdalene
368.15 dairy-maid (MS) / dairy-damsel
368.17 purposes. And she (MS) / purposes; and who
368.20 heard enough of (MS) / had enough to think about
368.36 recommended her, to carry her if (MS recommended her to carry her if)
        / recommended him to carry her, if
368.42 up (MS) / down
369.1   remonstrated somewhat against (MS) / remonstrated against
369.19 primness (MS) / firmness
369.21 something to be (MS) / to be something
369.25 her (MS) / his
370.1   ganging (MS) / gaun
370.2   horses' (8vo 1819) / horses
371.4   called (MS calld) / call
371.4   Mister (MS) / Mr
371.6   stairs (MS) / stair's
371.10 them. But (MS) / them; but
371.31 madam (MS) / ma'am
371.38 seamen (MS) / seaman
372.4   Inverara (MS) / Inverary
372.5   cousin (MS) / cousin's

372.13   ventures (MS) / venture
372.17   further (MS) / farther
372.35   intentions (MS) / intention
372.42   themselves, one (MS themselves one) / themselves; one
372.42   remaining . . . tumbling (MS) / remained . . . tumbled
373.9   marcy (MS) / mercy
373.26   dairy-maid (MS) / dairy-vestal
373.29   naked—knees (MS) / naked knees
373.35   weel (MS) / well
373.40   damsel (MS) / dairy-maid
374.14   romantic highland scenery (MS) / romantic scenery
374.18   Roseneath lies (MS) / Roseneath, a smaller isle, lies
374.21   Haly-Loch (MS) / Holy-Loch
374.27   Argyleshire (Editorial) / Ayrshire
         This error is in the MS and was not corrected in Scott's lifetime.
374.38   of the last (MS) / of last
374.38   its shores (MS) / the shores of the isle
375.10   grey (MS) / gray
375.19   beg, borrow (MS) / try to borrow
375.29   this (MS) / the
375.31   father? (MS) / father!
375.37   having (18mo) / had
376.1   whan (MS) / when
376.5   now left (MS) / left now
376.7   dead!—It (MS) / slain!—It
376.10   restraint; if (Editorial) / restraint, if
376.19   choked and impeded his (MS) / choked his
376.22   us a' to (MS) / us to
376.30   MacNaught (MS) / M'Naught
377.6   Butler? this was (MS) / Butler? was
377.7   when (MS) / while
377.12   weel (MS) / well
377.19   aften (MS) / often
377.20   amang (MS) / among
377.28   puir (MS) / poor
377.29   cattle (MS) / beasts
378.23   boggled (MS) / haggled
378.27   younger (MS) / youngest
379.9   to (MS) / towards
380.8   Gare-Loch (8vo 1819) / Gare Loch
         The name is not in the MS, being substituted for Loch-Long, but all
         other instances are hyphenated.
380.11   Kirk (Editorial) / kirk
         'Kirk of Knocktarlitie' is not in the MS, but Scott capitalises the initial K
         of 'Kirk' on the other two occasions on which he uses the phrase.
380.15   Reuben (MS) / Mr
380.26   though (MS) / although
380.29   which David therefore ascribed (MS) / which, therefore, he ascribed
380.31   he sometimes (MS) / David had sometimes
381.13   forwards (MS) / forward
381.23   David (MS) / Davie
381.31   Jenny (MS) / Jennie
382.4   been (MS) / seemed
382.5   chose (MS) / might chuse
382.25   has an (MS) / has heard an

382.29 Butler? (MS) / Butler!
382.30 Scotland? (MS) / Scotland!
383.16 the Kirk (MS) / this Kirk
384.2   cure (MS) / care
384.11 one wherein (MS) / the former, wherein
384.17 burned (MS burnd) / burnt
384.17 those (MS) / these
384.23 the brethren (MS) / their brethren
384.32 strangely (MS) / strongly
384.41 half-starved, thread-bare usher— (MS) / half-starved thread-bare
        usher,
385.1   Kirk (MS) / kirk
385.4   chalder (MS) / chalders
385.5   tenfold degree (MS) / tenfold, degree
385.15 be possible (MS) / be found possible
385.16 Kirk (MS) / kirk
385.25 worth, good (MS worth good) / worth and good
385.43 Reuben (Editorial) / his friend
386.4   his young friend (MS) / Reuben
386.16 cloot (MS) / clute
386.18 Pharaoh (8vo 1819) / Pharoah
386.22 Davie (MS) / David
386.23 ye (MS) / you
386.27 auld, bauld (12mo 1821) / auld bauld
387.6   o' (MS) / of
387.11 being (MS) / proving
387.22 ye (MS) / you
387.28 in banks (MS) / on banks
387.36 root (MS) / rute
387.37 and the imposthumes (MS) / and imposthumes
387.38 time, (MS) / time to you,
387.42 Blair and Livingstone (MS Blair & Livingstone) / Blair, Livingstone
388.6   ornate (MS) / detailed
388.8   tolbooth (MS) / Tolbooth
388.12 Guard (MS) / Guards
388.25 David Deans said (MS) / David said
388.27 for Patrick (MS) / for Mr Patrick
388.30 He got (MS) / He," (Francis Gordon,) "got
388.34 Kirk (MS) / kirk
389.11 intimate (MS) / internal
389.24 they afford (12mo 1821) / he affords
389.28 called upon to (MS) / called to
390.9   on (MS) / in
390.28 compliances (MS) / compliance
390.29 time (MS) / times
390.36 Her (MS) / her
390.38 whilk (MS) / which
390.39 enemies (MS) / enemy
391.3   work. And (MS) / work; and
391.33 tracks (MS) / traces
391.36 Musselburgh (12mo 1821) / Dalkeith
        Dalkeith is inland; the geographic description shows that Musselburgh
        was intended.
391.41 Firth (MS) / Frith
392.1   they (MS) / the vessel

392.6   without any place or date (MS) / without bearing any date of place or time

392.7   spelled (MS spelld) / spelt

392.10   as much to (MS) / as to

392.12   and sister (MS) / and her sister

392.26   it would (MS) / would it

392.30   Novit's (MS Novits) / Novitt's

392.30   hands (MS) / hand

392.31   like (MS) / likely

392.36   deserved (MS) / desired

392.37   ganging (MS) / gaun

392.38   the maist (MS) / her maist

392.39   wad (MS) / would

392.40   aff (MS) / off

392.42   farther (MS) / further

393.13   in (MS) / under

393.15   likely they (MS) / likely that they

393.28   respect (MS) / regard

393.32   blandishment (MS) / soothing attention

394.2   was of (MS) / was one of

394.27   tak (MS) / take

394.34   with some usquebaugh (MS) / with usquebaugh

394.43   whan (MS) / when

395.1   claik-geese (MS) / clack-geese

395.8   arise (MS) / happen

395.9   remove"—— (MS) / remove——"

395.12   bidden do (MS) / bidden to do

395.16   tamn (MS) / damn

395.22   privileges. But (MS) / privileges; but

395.41   put (MS) / but

396.8   conclude that it (MS) / conclude it

396.24   meat boiled and roasted, eggs (MS meat boiled and roasted eggs) / meat, scores boiled and roasted eggs
As 'roasted' is a word more appropriately applied to meat than eggs, it is clear that this passage was punctuated incorrectly; 'scores' was added in proof.

396.24   butter, herrings (MS) / butter, half a firkin herrings
The phrase 'half a firkin' was added in proof, but is inappropriate when the herrings are 'boiled and broiled, fresh and salt'.

397.3   amending (MS) / mending

397.11   sarvice (MS) / service

397.11   lie (MS) / be

397.15   pleasured, and so (MS) / pleasured, so

397.16   her (MS) / his

398.21   1685 (Editorial) / 1686
Scott gave the first two digits of the date; the rest was supplied in the MS by someone else, but it happens to be wrong.

398.22   David's (MS Davids) / David

398.28   hills (MS) / hill

398.33   *Manse* (MS) / Manse

399.7   t'ither (MS tither) / t'other

399.28   think that she (MS) / think she

400.27   winna (MS) / wunna

400.28   me aye your (MS) / me your

400.30   one young animal (MS) / one animal

400.35 that e'en (MS) / that way e'en
400.37 thinking that he (MS) / thinking he
400.38 wish ye (MS) / wish you
401.29 but the (MS) / but of the
402.23 I'll (MS) / I will
402.25 as (18mo) / that
402.33 rung (MS) / rang
403.24 Kirk (MS) / kirk
403.37 kintra (MS) / kintray
403.39 be a' very (MS) / be very
403.40 tak (MS) / take
404.22 an' (MS and Burns) / and
404.26 While (Editorial) / Wi'
        Quotations are not normally corrected in the EEWN, but the *Wi'* written
        by Scott (apparently quoting from memory) is not just a mistake but
        does not make sense.
405.3   quantity of liquors in cask, which often come (MS quantity of liquors in
        cask which often come) / wine in cask, which is drifted
405.12 dissatisfaction (MS) / dissastisfaction
405.31 David escaped (MS) / David Deans escaped
405.34 Micklehose from time to time cautioning them to (MS Meiklehose from
        time to time cautioning them to) / Meiklehose cautioning them from
        time to time to
405.37 himsell (MS) / himself
405.39 mirth and fun grew (MS) / mirth grew
407.15 seemed to sleep (MS seemd to sleep) / were dimly visible
407.28 along shore (MS) / along the shore
407.36 This was indeed (MS) / This, indeed, was
408.22 fiercest (MS) / strongest
408.36 ye (MS) / you
408.37 ye (MS) / you
408.40 cam (MS) / came
408.41 ye (MS) / you
409.14 whether there (MS) / whetherthe re
409.20 winna (MS) / wunna
409.23 browed (MS browd) / brewed
409.26 awfu'"——(MS) / awfu'——"
409.29 shewed her (MS) / shewed that her
409.36 stay here longer (MS) / stay longer
409.37 permit (MS) / allow
410.7   friends?"—(MS) / friends?—"
410.13 you ever (MS) / ever you
411.7   as apology (MS) / as an apology
411.11 was (MS) / were
411.19 uniformity (MS) / conformity
411.29 their (MS) / the
412.20 ower (MS) / over
412.22 nowt (MS) / nowte
413.2   wherever (MS) / whenever
413.12 neat, clean, well-dressed (MS neat clean well-dressd) / real clean well-
        dressed
413.17 replied that (MS) / replied, "That
413.17 done (MS) / dune
413.17 by "timing (MS) / by timing
413.25 and to Mrs (MS) / and Mrs

413.37 of I know not what (MS) / I know not of what
414.2 perhaps she (MS) / perhaps," she added, "she
414.13 profession (MS) / professions
414.31 always and severely (MS) / always severely
415.8 room, in (Magnum) / bed, on [MS as Ed1]
415.10 rare (MS) / sure
415.10 others (MS) / other
415.12 crewels,* was (MS) / crewels, was
415.17 heal and fere (MS derived: heal and fair) / hale and fair
    'Heal and fere' is a set phrase; 'fair' makes little sense in this context and so is probably a homophone.
415.31 Kittledoop (MS) / Kittlesides
415.32 hae (MS) / have
415.33 there is (MS) / there's
415.36 a witch (MS) / sic a wretch
415.43 *King's-evil. (MS) / [no footnote]
    The footnote is a verso addition which was missed.
416.26 anticipations (MS) / anticipation
416.36 ye (MS) / you
417.4 lie (MS) / be
417.28 humble (MS) / happy
417.40 composition (MS) / compositions
418.36 that (MS) / this
419.22 He, I mean the D., goes (MS He I mean the D. goes) / He—I mean the D.—goes
    The intermediaries supplied dashes where commas are appropriate and in so doing detracted from the force of Scott's own MS dashes.
419.23 Scotland; he (MS Scotland he) / Scotland—he
419.26 betray, nothing (MS betray nothing) / betray—nothing
419.32 good, with (MS good with) / good—with
419.42 of fire among thorns (MS) / of thorns
419.43 unconsumed— (MS) / unconsumed.—
420.17 thought (MS) / said
420.18 to learn (MS) / tolearn
420.20 took (MS) / looks
420.32 leddy (MS) / lady
421.11 moor-powts (MS) / moor-fowls
421.22 better understood (MS) / understood better
421.23 hoped his (MS) / hoped that his
421.31 Deepheugh (MS) / Deephaugh
422.1 pad (MS) / bad
422.14 Butler knew indeed (MS He knew indeed) / Butler already had reason to believe
422.19 society, and no good could arise to any one from imparting it to him. Jeanie (MS derived: Society. He did not know this fact and no good could arise to any one from imparting it to him. Jeanie) / society. Jeanie
    A whole MS sentence was omitted, but because of verbal repetition the omitted material cannot be assimilated unchanged into the text.
422.37 or to save it for (MS) / or for
424.7 a bit (MS) / at all
424.7 suppose, though, it (MS suppose though it) / suppose it
424.10 court-Scottish (MS court-Scotish) / court-Scotch
424.24 has (MS) / had
424.36 Duke; "of (MS) / Duke; of
425.14 the (MS) / certain

426.21 Dumbarton shires (MS Dunbarton Shires) / Dumbartonshire
426.35 our (MS) / his
426.40 untouched on the night when (MS) / untouched, when
427.2 attended on (MS) / attended in person on
427.6 Ziklag (12mo 1825) / Ziglag [MS as Ed1]
427.13 was in that (MS) / was that
427.23 ane (MS) / one
428.1 seems (MS) / is
428.13 band (MS) / bond
428.13 interest (for there's that band ower Lounsbeck's land, your father could neither get principal nor interest for't); if into (MS interest ↑ for there's that bond ower Lounsbeck's land your father could neither get principal nor interest for't." ↓ if into) / interest; for there's that bond over Lounsbeck's land, your father could neither get principal nor interest for it—If we bring it into
428.23 sae (MS) / so
428.25 selling." (MS) / selling it."
428.29 hand kindly at (MS) / hand at
428.34 useful (MS) / ordinary
428.40 amongst (MS) / among
428.41 early (MS) / earlier
429.5 ye (MS) / you
429.6 at (MS) / on
429.8 in the wame of the auld (MS) / in this auld
429.9 be (MS) / by
429.19 of as (MS) / of it as
429.24 o't (MS) / o 't
429.25 you (MS) / we
429.31 as is (MS) / as it is
429.32 ye (MS) / you
429.36 wrang (MS) / wrong
430.11 barest (MS) / lowest
430.12 mak (MS) / make
430.26 yearly (MS) / usually
430.40 15th (Editorial) / 24th (MS as Ed1)
It is not known why Scott wrote '24th'; he knew the Whitsunday term date (15 May), but the 24th is not the term day, nor the term day adjusted for the change in the calendar in 1752, nor Whitsunday (50 days after Easter day).
431.4 felt it yet (MS) / felt yet
431.17 a printed sheet (MS) / a sheet
431.18 aff (MS) / off
431.25 "Last Speech and Execution of Margaret Murdockson, and of the barbarous Murder of her Daughter, Magdalen or Madge Murdockson, called Madge Wildfire; and of her pious Conversation with his Reverence Arch-deacon Fleming." (Editorial) / "The Last Speech, Confession, and Dying Words of Margaret MacCraw, or Murdockson, executed on Harabee-hill, near Carlisle, the — day of —— 37."
This emendation standardises the name of the broadside by adopting that on 367.41–368.4.
431.40 upstairs (MS) / up stairs
432.2 committed two (MS) / committed near two
432.6 heavily (MS) / heavy
432.13 she had long (MS) / she long

432.13 and doubtless (MS) / and had doubtless
432.29 was only one (MS) / was one
433.22 afford unequivocal (MS derived: afford the ⟨most absolute proof⟩ unequivocal) / afford the most unequivocal
434.1 the broadside Confession (MS the broad-side Confession) / the Confession
434.16 in't (MS) / in it
434.23 sounded better (MS) / sounded the better
434.32 latter (MS) / taller
435.17 and a portmanteau (MS) / and portmanteau
435.21 it—so, if you please, you will have the goodness to admit me—as a friend of the Duke's." [new paragraph] (MS it—so if you please you will have the goodness to admit me—as a friend of the Dukes"—[run on]) / it." [new paragraph]
435.25 my hieland head (MS) / my head
435.26 pelieve (MS) / believe
435.27 of"——(MS) / of——"
435.37 and in complexion (MS) / and complexion
436.19 Effie?" (MS) / Effie,"
437.5 hope (MS) / hopes
437.7 contented (MS) / content
437.33 Glasco—" (MS) / Glasco"—
437.36 her remaining trunks (Editorial) / her trunks
       This error (trunks were unloaded as she arrived) has remained uncorrected in all editions.
438.18 maunna (MS) / mauna
438.28 an (MS) / the
438.33 his Grace's (MS) / hisGrace's
438.36 unhappy (MS) / unhappily
438.37 on (MS) / of
438.40 about being (MS) / about it being
439.6 narration (MS) / narrative
439.7 would (MS) / should
439.30 in (MS) / of
439.38 Lie (MS Lye) / liar
439.39 years' (8vo 1822) / years
440.3 integrity. But (MS) / integrity; but
440.21 taste which (MS) / tast ewhich
440.28 and (MS) / or
441.12 strangely in contour (MS) / strongly in colour
441.13 and fell down to the (MS) / and, at the
441.14 seventy feet when a huge rock (MS) / twenty feet, another rock
441.15 at great depth (MS) / far beneath
441.22 but the (MS) / but that the
442.6 and the cheeks (MS) / and cheeks
442.38 one below to (MS) / one to
443.26 recumbent (MS) / incumbent
443.30 dirk or two, swords (MS dirk or two swords) / dirk and two swords
444.10 free (MS) / clear
444.15 cataract (MS) / cararact
444.38 her (MS) / his
444.42 wi' (MS wi) / with
445.15 sting (MS) / stang
445.26 fo'k (MS) / folk
445.26 it is (MS) / it's

445.34 Assembly of the Kirk of Scotland was (MS) / Assembly was
446.8 paraphernalia (MS) / parapharnalia
446.17 was (MS) / is
447.17 The letter (MS) / Her letter to George Staunton
447.26 lang (MS) / long
447.32 safety, a sort of instinctive (MS safety a sort of instinctive) / safety;— that instinctive
447.32 anxiety—it, in (MS anxiety ↑ which she had ↓ it in) / anxiety which she had in
Scott added 'which she had' above the line, without deleting the 'it'. It looks as though Scott did not read the rest of the sentence when correcting; reversion to the original MS reading seems to be the best means of reducing the syntactic muddle.
447.34 which deserted a mind (MS) / that occupied a breast
447.43 and with all her family had (MS) / and that, with all her family, she had
448.28 this (MS) / that
448.29 wandering (MS) / wandered
448.34 Staunton; having (Editorial) / Staunton, having
449.16 he had expected (MS) / he expected
449.34 tolbooth (MS) / Tolbooth
449.37 onward (MS) / forward
449.38 upon one occasion (MS) / at one time
449.43 gainsaid (MS) / gainsayed
450.13 whatever (MS) / whatsoever
450.19 isna (MS is na) / is no
450.20 she early got (MS) / she got
450.23 whan (MS) / when
450.24 at (MS) / on
450.30 no (MS) / not
450.33 ganging (MS) / gaun
451.4 Captain (MS) / captain
451.18 Captain (MS) / captain
451.30 o't (MS) / on't
451.43 tolbooth (MS) / Tolbooth
452.5 nae (MS) / no
452.18 a hundred miles (MS) / a mile
452.22 moment (MS) / minute
456.22 one (MS) / some
457.11 For ever! (MS) / For ever!
457.39 bay (MS) / way
457.40 Dand (MS) / Dandie
457.41 Dand (MS) / Dandie
457.42 ca'd"——— (Editorial) / ca'd———"
Inverted commas followed by a dash is the normal manuscript convention for indicating interrupted speech, but 'that they ca'd———"' was added in proof.
458.1 the top of the steeple (MS) / the steeple
458.7 in (MS) / on
458.22 especially (MS) / espepecially
458.40 had in vain (MS) / in vain had
459.5 on (MS) / upon
459.11 with all her (MS) / with her
459.23 rest! (MS) / rest?
460.1 that (MS) / this
460.6 merited (MS) / deserved

460.7   some things (MS) / something
460.13 murs (MS) / muirs
460.32 nested (MS) / rested
460.33 their fire (MS) / them
460.38 Firth (MS) / Frith
461.1   this horn (MS) / this very horn
461.1   fery (MS) / very
461.9   surely home (MS) / surely at home
461.30 by two (MS) / by one or two
461.36 was brave (MS) / was as brave
461.39 wounded, and who (MS wounded & who) / wounded, who
462.22 incidental (MS) / incident
462.40 her unhappy brother-in-law (MS) / her brother-in-law
463.5   astounding (MS) / astonishing
463.14 art (MS) / act
464.17 idea (MS) / intelligence
464.20 minister. And (MS) / minister; and
464.30 for the (MS) / for that the
464.38 and for revenge (MS) / and revenge
465.1   from Caird's (MS) / from the Caird's
465.16 Inverary (MS) / Inverara
465.26 suld ne'er (MS) / suldna
466.6   even than (MS) / than even
466.7   murther (MS) / murder
466.10 himself. (MS) / himself?
466.19 "Thou poor (MS) / "Poor
466.25 ye no ken (MS) / ye ken
466.30 saul (MS) / soul
466.35 hurt (MS) / harm
466.36 hurt (MS) / harmed
466.39 round him with (MS) / round with
467.1   winna (MS) / wunna
467.4   momentarily (MS) / instantly
467.9   discovered. But (MS) / discovered; but
467.22 his (MS) / this
467.29 agreed (MS) / thought
467.39 her (MS) / their
468.24 ear (MS) / ears
468.33 the commission (MS) / their commission
469.1   In Ed1 the L'Envoy is set in Roman type but is here set in italics to bring
the typographical presentation of the utterances of Jedidiah Cleis-
botham into conformity with their treatment in *Tales of My Landlord*,
first series: see *The Black Dwarf*, ed. P. D. Garside, EEWN 4a, 5–9, and
The Tale of Old Mortality, ed. Douglas Mack, EEWN 4b, 353.
469.1   Jedidiah (Editorial) / Jedediah
      See note to title page.
469.6   *called Molière saith* (MS called Moliere saith) / hath it
469.7   Médecin (Magnum) / Medecin
469.7   Malgré (MS) / *Malgre*
469.14 FINIS (MS) / END OF VOLUME FOURTH

END-OF-LINE HYPHENS

All end-of-line hyphens in the present text are soft unless included in the list below. The hyphens listed are hard and should be retained when quoting.

HISTORICAL NOTE

Political Context. In 1736–37 George II (1683–1760; king 1727) was on the British throne, but on 7 September 1736, the night of the Porteous Riot, he was in Hanover, of which he was Elector (i.e. ruler and one of those who elected the Holy Roman Emperor). While he was abroad (from 22 May 1736 to 15 January 1737), his wife, Queen Caroline (1683–1737) acted as Regent. The Prime Minister was Sir Robert Walpole (1676–1745).

The Union of 1707 in which the Parliaments of England and of Scotland united to form the Parliament of Great Britain did not at first go well. The benefits of a single market were not initially realised, and, after the election of 1710, Parliament, inevitably dominated by English interests, acted provocatively in passing two measures, the Toleration Act and the Patronage Act, that were considered to be in breach of the terms of the Union and hostile to the Presbyterian Church of Scotland. The Toleration Act gave freedom of worship to Scottish Episcopalians provided that they prayed for the reigning monarch by name, while the Patronage Act restored to certain landowners the right to nominate the minister of a parish, a right which in 1690 had been vested in the kirk session and the congregation of each parish. In *The Heart of Mid-Lothian* David Deans repeatedly vocalises the widespread objections to these measures. Further, the Government felt that Scotland was not paying its due share of national expenditure, and it was appalled by the extent of smuggling and tax evasion. In 1713 it attempted to apply the malt tax to Scotland, and as the tax would have been in breach of the terms of the Union, and would have increased the price of ale, the measure provoked a furious reaction. In June a motion in the House of Lords to repeal the Union failed by only four votes. T. M. Devine argues:

> The view from Westminster was that the Scots were not paying their way through taxation because of the enormous scale of smuggling and systematic revenue fraud said to be endemic in Scottish society. London merchants, for instance, were infuriated by the level of evasion in the Glasgow tobacco trade, and modern research has confirmed that between 1707 and 1722 the Scots paid duty on only half their imports from Virginia and Maryland. Fraudulent practices existed on a similar scale in other trades.[1]

Attempts to levy taxes systematically were resisted: there were repeated acts of violence and small-scale riots which prevented customs officers from collecting dues. In 1725 Walpole, Prime Minister from 1721, again attempted to increase the duty on malt, this time by 3*d.* per bushel, and this led to rioting in Stirling, Dundee, Ayr, Elgin, Paisley and Glasgow. Disturbances were worst in Glasgow: the house of the local Member of Parliament who was suspected of supporting the measure was looted and burned; soldiers fired on the crowd, killing eight, and they were then driven out of the town; it required a combined force of cavalry and infantry under General Wade to restore order. Rosalind Mitchison has written that 'every sign points to this being a movement of national resistance'.[2] Walpole appointed the Earl of Islay, brother of the Duke of Argyle, to control Scotland on the government's behalf. Islay enforced the law against the Glasgow rioters. The provost and magistrates of Glasgow were arrested for failing to maintain order, and the town was fined. The officer commanding the troops which had fired on the crowd, having been tried for murder and found guilty, was pardoned. Under Islay tax collection became more systematic and was supported by a greater number of revenue officers. In the novel Plumdammas provides testimony to the effectiveness of measures to improve the revenue from Scotland while also articulating the general opposition: 'and then sic an host of idle English gaugers and excisemen as hae come down to vex and torment us, that an honest man canna fetch sae muckle as a bit anker o' brandy frae Leith to the Lawn-market, but he's like to be robbit o' the very gudes he's bought and paid for' (37.26–30). A more effective government of Scotland was achieved by Islay's political control. He used patronage extensively: the majority of judges and sheriffs were said to have been appointed by him, and there were a great number of minor political and governmental positions to fill. And within the church the system of lay patronage which had been brought in by the Patronage Act began to be exercised in favour of a less 'independent' body of clergy.

The Porteous Riot seemed a repeat of the events of 1725. By taking the law into its own hands a Scottish mob had again challenged the government's right to levy taxes and to maintain law and order. It again appeared that a riot had been tacitly supported by the provost and the magistrates of a Scottish city. However, the government's countermeasures were ill-advised, and included a proclamation to be read from pulpits whose terms were regarded as an affront to the Church of Scotland, and a bill which would have imposed drastic penalties on Edinburgh and its provost. The government's over-reaction and its direct involvement in the affairs of a semi-independent Scotland created a crisis.[3]

In 1689 those who had been in opposition to the rule of Charles II and James VII and II and their ministers benefited from the Revolution, but in practice there were more continuities than expected; David Deans, we are told, 'was by no means pleased with the quiet and indifferent manner in which King William's government slurred over the errors of the times, when, far from restoring the presbyterian Kirk to its former supremacy, they passed an act of oblivion even to those who had been its persecutors, and bestowed on many of them titles, favours, and employments' (178.17–22). The treatment of Covenanters by the governments of Charles II and his brother James II had created a class which was habituated to being oppositional. The National Covenant of 1638 was drawn up to consolidate opposition to the ecclesiastical innovations introduced by Charles I, and it led to a Presbyterian revolution and to a kind of Presbyterian theocracy that lasted until Cromwell's conquest of Scotland in 1650–51. There were high hopes that the Restoration of the monarchy in 1660 would lead to the re-establishment of Presbyterian government, but in 1662 Charles II repudiated the National Covenant which he had sworn to uphold, and initiated a series of measures, such as imposing episcopacy, and requiring recognition 'that the king's majesty is the only supreme governor of this realm, over all persons, and in all causes, as well ecclesiastical as civil' (Wodrow, 3.297). Many Presbyterians were unable to accept the king's view of his position in religious matters, and attempts to enforce recognition of the king as supreme governor on all who held public office and all ministers of the church led to dissent and ultimately armed resistance. These people were known as Covenanters. The total number of the people who participated in insurrection was not great and largely confined to the western and southern counties of Scotland, but arbitrary trials and executions created martyrs who seized the popular imagination. In addition, the habit of arguing their case led to the elaboration of a distinctive Covenanting rhetoric, and political opposition to the government in Scotland was linked to this tradition of dissent.

David Deans represents the continuation of this tradition in the eighteenth century, and even though he criticises sectarianism and remains an elder in the Church of Scotland, he uses the rhetoric of a body of people determined and accustomed to resist those in power, together with their way of thought and view of the world. Although Deans would never have participated in the riot, the attempt to coerce the church into supporting governmental measures following the riot created antagonism against the government, and helped to convert the riot from a local disturbance into a national articulation of opposition to England.

It is in this political context that Jeanie Deans seeks a royal pardon for her sister.

Table of Dates

1560   The Scottish Reformation. A struggle to decide whether the reformed Church of Scotland should be Presbyterian or Episcopal continued until 1690.

1603   The Union of the Crowns. On the death of Queen Elizabeth of England, James VI of Scotland became king of both countries, and ruled from London.

1638   The National Covenant, a manifesto opposing the religious innovations of Charles I, won widespread support in Scotland.

1639–50   A period of Presbyterian rule regarded by many including David Deans as the great age of the Church of Scotland.

1643   The Solemn League and Covenant. In this treaty between Scotland and England the Scottish Parliament promised military support to the English Parliament against Charles I in return for England's adopting Presbyterian church government.

1649   Execution of Charles I.

1650   Charles II crowned.

1650–51   Cromwell's conquest of Scotland.

1658   Death of Cromwell.

1660   Restoration of Charles II.

1662   Charles II renounced the National Covenant and reimposed Episcopacy. Around 300 ministers were ejected from their charges for refusing to recognise Charles as 'supreme governor' of the church. Support for the ousted ministers was particularly strong in the SW and Borders of Scotland, and the ministers and their people worshipped at open-air conventicles. The government tried to suppress such activity and employed increasingly arbitrary and oppressive measures which generated armed resistance.

1679   A Covenanting army defeated by royalist troops at Bothwell Bridge.

1681   The Test Act.

1684–85   The killing time when the summary execution of Covenanters in Scotland was at its height, but the name was often extended to the period 1681–85.

1685   Death of Charles II who was succeeded by his Roman Catholic brother James VII of Scots and II of England. Rebellions in England led by the Duke of Monmouth and in Scotland by the Earl of Argyle were suppressed and both leaders were executed.

1688   James VII and II fled to France.

1689   William of Orange and his consort Mary, protestant daughter of James VII and II, were invited to accept the thrones of the two kingdoms by the Parliaments of England and Scotland.

1690   Presbyterianism re-established by law in Scotland.

1696–99   The 'dear years', when there was widespread famine in Scotland; the phrase was also applied to the extended period 1694–1701.

1701   Act of Settlement determines a Protestant succession in England and Scotland.

1702   Death of William and accession of Queen Anne.

1707	Union of the Parliaments of England and Scotland. Subordinate legislation guaranteed Presbyterian governance of the Church of Scotland.
1712	Toleration and Patronage Acts.
1713	Excise Act.
1714	Death of Anne and accession of George I, Elector of Hanover.
1715	The supporters of James VII and II (known as Jacobites) in Scotland and northern England attempted to put his son on the throne. In Scotland a government army led by the 2nd Duke of Argyle prevented the Jacobite army from leaving the Highlands.
1725	Another Excise Act; Shawfield Riot in Glasgow.
1727	Death of George I and accession of George II and his consort Queen Caroline.
1736	Porteous Riot.
1745	Jacobite Rising, followed by severe legislative measures to prevent any repetition.

Historical Sources. The two central episodes of *The Heart of Mid-Lothian*, the Porteous Riot and the trial of Effie Deans, are based on historical fact, but Scott deals with the historical evidence in totally different ways. For Porteous he follows the record closely, but for Effie he departs wholly from it.

1] *The Porteous Riot.* The first edition of *The Heart of Mid-Lothian* contains an advertisement for *Criminal Trials, Illustrative of the Tale Entitled "The Heart of Mid-Lothian," Published from the Original Record*, which, according to the advertisement, appeared 'this day', in other words simultaneously with the novel, although, in fact, newspaper advertisements suggest a week's gap.[4] It was clearly a hurried job, in that it was printed not by James Ballantyne but by George Ramsay and Company whom Constable used when Ballantyne was unable to take further work, and in that an account of the life of Porteous, largely reprinted from a pamphlet of 1737, appears as Prefatory Notice when it should have been treated as text. There is no evidence of Scott being involved,[5] and he need not have been, but it seems inconceivable that he was unaware of what his publisher Constable intended. What is remarkable is that the simultaneous publication challenges a comparison of the novel with the archival documents on which it is based, and what it proves is Scott's consummate ability to make dull material interesting.

Between 2 and 11 March 1736, Andrew Wilson, William Hall and George Robertson were tried for robbing James Stark, Collector of Excise, in Pittenweem in Fife on 9 January 1736. They were found guilty and condemned to death, the date of execution being fixed for 14 April. They attempted to escape from the tolbooth on Friday 9 April;

the service in the Tolbooth Kirk at which Wilson ensured Robertson got away was on Sunday 11 April; on Wednesday 14 April Wilson was hanged, and Porteous and the City Guard fired on the crowd. Porteous's trial opened on 5 July 1736. The declaration as to relevancy (the procedures followed in a Scottish criminal trial of the day are explained in the note to 31.40–41) was made on 16 July; the debate before the jury took place on 19 July; Porteous was found guilty on 20 July and the day of execution was set for 8 September. On 26 August the Secretary of State signed a stay of execution for 6 weeks, and on 3 September the High Court issued a warrant instructing the magistrates of Edinburgh to delay the execution to 20 October. Porteous was lynched on 7 September. Scott takes some liberties with the record: he makes the reprieve arrive after the crowd has gathered to see the hanging, but he achieves a greatly enhanced drama by delaying the announcement until the morning set for Porteous's execution with his murder following that same night.[6]

Scott also investigated sources other than those detailed in *Criminal Trials*, including the Edinburgh Tolbooth Warding and Liberation Book (i.e. the register of those admitted and discharged from the tolbooth) where he found that one James Ratcliff was an actual prisoner in the tolbooth on the night of 7 September 1736. And although Ratcliff used the opportunity to escape (unlike the Ratcliffe of the novel) Scott must have noted that he came from 'Spaldon' (Spalding) in Lincolnshire; from that suggestion comes the novel's Lincolnshire scenes.[7]

Scott made selective use of these sources. For instance he ignores William Hall, presumably because Hall played no part in the exciting scenes in the Tolbooth Kirk and the Grassmarket, his sentence having been commuted to transportation. Detailed analysis shows that Scott summarises brilliantly, clarifying the action and the issues, intensifying the drama, and dramatising the responses of the people of Edinburgh. It also shows a systematic adjustment of the way in which the riot was usually understood.[8] David Hume, whose lectures enraptured Scott as a student,[9] makes a distinction in his *Commentaries on the Law of Scotland respecting the Description and Punishment of Crimes* between rioting and treason; he argues specifically that the Porteous mob was a mob because it had one particular aim, to hang Porteous, and that it was not rebellion in that it did not challenge the state.[10] The criminal records support his argument. But the 'compare and contrast' process which the publication of *Criminal Trials* invites us to undertake shows that the fictional narrative simplifies the events, ignores innumerable contradictions in details between various reports, and makes the whole proceedings less horrific. For instance, the Porteous rioters forced William Weir, aged 18, the son of the drummer of the Edinburgh suburb of Portsburgh, into service; Weir's testimony says that 'the rioters pushed and threatened . . . and tore his neck till the blood came, and thereby compelled him to beat the drum'.[11] Another witness, George Watson, testified that Porteous was three times hung up and twice let down again before he was dispatched, and added that he heard 'some of the mob make a proposal of cutting his ears out, and others proposed to geld him; and at the last time he was hung up, he saw some of the mob strike him upon the face with a Lochaber-axe'.[12] The indictment of the one man tried for participating in the Porteous Riot reads that when Porteous

> endeavoured to save himself, by catching hold of the rope with his hands, he, the said William Maclauchlane, or one or other of his vile associates, barbarously beat them down with a padle, or other instrument, and brutally struck him upon the face with a Lochaber-axe, or other weapon; and wantoning in their wickedness, making loose the rope that was fixed about the said dyer's tree, he, the said William Maclauchlane, or some of his accomplices, let him down to the ground, and pulled him up again, where he hung by the neck till he was dead.[13]

All the reports on the Porteous Riot indicate it was an ugly business, but in *The Heart of Mid-Lothian* Scott sanitises the mob. The mob is well organised; it is orderly and sober, and treats all but Porteous well. Porteous's execution is regularly undertaken, even although it is an extra-judicial killing; the rope used to hang him is paid for. The action of the fictional mob in its orderliness is made to appear closer to rebellion than to mobbing. In the historical analysis of the Porteous affair in Chapters 2 to 7 of Volume 1 of *The Heart of Mid-Lothian* the narrator identifies the root cause of the riot in the collision between, on the one hand, the state in maintaining its right to collect customs and excise duties (Robertson and Wilson robbed the collector in Pittenweem), protecting that right in law (Robertson and Wilson are condemned to death for their crime), and using due force to maintain that right (Porteous's error is to use undue force), and, on the other hand, the people in asserting their resistance to paying taxes and making known their sense of injustice. The narrator uses the terms 'insurgents' and 'conspirators', and such words suggest that the riot might well be considered open rebellion, as identified and characterised by Hume: the levying of war against the King 'embraces all those risings, which though not aimed directly at the person of the King, are however against his royal Majesty; that is against his Crown or royal dignity; against his prerogative, authority, or office'.[14] Certainly the Queen and the government see the riot to be a challenge to their authority (63.39–64.4), and the people at large, including Jeanie, feel that the whole affair has a national political dimension:

> The anxiety of the government to obtain conviction of some of the offenders, had but served to increase that public feeling which connected the action, though violent and irregular, with the idea of ancient national independence. The very rigorous measures

adopted or proposed against the city of Edinburgh, the ancient
metropolis of Scotland—the extremely unpopular and injudicious
measure of compelling the clergy to promulgate from the pulpit the
reward offered for discovery of the perpetrators of this slaughter,
had produced on the public mind the opposite consequences from
what were intended; and Jeanie felt conscious, that whoever
should lodge information concerning that event, and for whatsoever purpose it might be done, it would be considered as an act of
treason against the independence of Scotland. (314.9–21)

2] *Isobel Walker.* The Porteous riot was a known episode in history,
but in 1818 when *The Heart of Mid-Lothian* was published it appeared
that the rest was fiction. However the Jeanie and Effie story also had a
historical origin. In early February 1818 Scott received an anonymous 'communication' concerning Helen Walker, the prototype of Jeanie
Deans. That story (see Essay on the Text, 471–72) provided the central
narrative of *The Heart of Mid-Lothian*. The focus of the story is upon
Helen Walker, not her sister Isobel, and Scott's imagination clearly
seized on the idea of a woman walking to London to seek a reprieve for a
sister condemned to death, and he repeatedly mentioned this inspiration. On 23 March 1823, for instance, he wrote to Constable: 'one letter
I have somewhere remarkably well written but anonymous suggesting
indeed narrating the outline of Jenny Deans & her quiet unpretending
heroism'.[15] He tells the story again in the Introduction to *Chronicles of
the Canongate* (1827):

> Another debt, which I pay most willingly, is that which I owe to an
> unknown correspondent (a lady), who favoured me with the his-
> tory of the upright and high principled female, whom, in the Heart
> of Midlothian, I have termed Jeanie Deans. The circumstance of
> her refusing to save her sister's life by an act of perjury, and under-
> taking a pilgrimage to London to obtain her pardon, are both
> represented as true by my fair and obliging correspondent; and
> they led me to consider the possibility of rendering a fictitious
> personage interesting by mere dignity of mind and rectitude of
> principle, assisted by unpretending good sense and temper, with-
> out any of the beauty, grace, talent, accomplishment, and wit, to
> which a heroine of romance is supposed to have a prescriptive
> right. If the portrait was received with interest by the public, I am
> conscious how much it was owing to the truth and force of the
> original sketch, which I regret that I am unable to present to the
> public, as it was written with much feeling and spirit.[16]

In October 1827 he discovered that the story had been sent by Mrs
Helen Goldie, of Dumfries,[17] and he later obtained her family's consent
to reproducing her narrative in the Introduction to the Magnum edition
of *The Heart of Mid-Lothian* in 1830.[18]

Most of the known information about Helen Walker is contained in
Scott's Magnum introduction. There is so little there that Scott must

have felt quite free to develop the character of Jeanie Deans, deriving from Mrs Goldie's 'communication' only the ideas of her being unable to commit perjury to save her sister, and of her walking to London to obtain a pardon for her sister through the intercession of the Duke of Argyle. On the other hand, the misadventure of Isobel Walker is fully recorded in the legal records. The records were accessible to Scott, but he seems to have made no use of them: verbal connections are largely confined to legal terms, which Scott would have used in any case.

Isobel Walker of Cluden (4 km NW of Dumfries), in the parish of Irongray, then in the Stewartry of Kirkcudbright, was accused of concealing her pregnancy, or alternatively, of murdering her child on or about 24 October 1736. She made a declaration to magistrates on 28 October 1736, on which day the statements of witnesses were also gathered. She appeared before justices of the peace at the quarter sessions in Kirkcudbright on 1 March 1737 and the case was remitted to the High Court in Dumfries. At the High Court on 2 May 1737 the advocate for the defence, James Ferguson, younger of Craigdarroch, objected that the court could not hear the case as there was only one judge upon the bench (on circuit there should have been two judges: in Edinburgh all five Lords of Justiciary sat together), and so Lord Strichen who was presiding remitted the trial to be heard in the High Court in Edinburgh on 21 June. On 21 May Isobel Walker was sent to Edinburgh and admitted to the tolbooth. There is no record of the case having been heard in Edinburgh on 21 June, and on 6 April 1738 the accused was sent back to Dumfries. She, together with witnesses and jurymen, were summoned in April 1738 to appear before the High Court on 1 May. To escape trial she petitioned for banishment, but she was, nonetheless, tried on 1 May 1738, before Lords Grant and Mackenzie, the prosecution being led by Sir James Elphinstone, Advocate Depute, and the defence by James Ferguson and James Geddes. The assize (or jury) found that she had concealed her pregnancy and that the baby was either dead or missing. Isobel Walker was therefore found guilty and condemned to death, the execution to take place on 14 June. On 12 June the Lord Justice Clerk delivered a letter to the High Court from the Duke of Newcastle, Secretary of State, signifying the King's agreement that the sentence be respited for two months, and the magistrates in Dumfries were directed to postpone the execution until 15 August, but there is no evidence in the legal papers of how the reprieve was obtained. On 12 July the King pardoned Isobel Walker, on the condition that she should 'within the Space of Forty Days after being set at Liberty . . . transport her self forth of His Majesty's Dominions of Great Britain and Ireland, never to return thereto, without having first obtained a License for that purpose from His Majesty'.[19]

The details of the case accentuate the difference between the fictional tale of Effie Deans and of the real Isobel Walker. In her declaration on

28 October 1736 Walker acknowledges the birth of a still-born baby and admitted throwing the body into the Water of Cluden. A baby was found dead in the river with a ligature round its neck, the inference being that it had been strangled, but she claimed that the baby found in the river was not hers. A large number of witnesses gave statements which indicate that her condition was known but that she had refused to confess to her pregnancy, and at the trial a selected number of witnesses gave evidence that pointed to her culpability under the law of 1690. The jury duly found her guilty under the 1690 law, but the circumstantial evidence suggests that Isobel Walker may well have strangled her baby.[20]

Isobel Walker is not the model for Effie Deans, and her story is not Effie's. The fictional tale is relocated in time and place, and, unlike Isobel Walker about whom there can be suspicions, Effie did not murder her baby and is never thought by the reader to have done so. The argument for Effie's condemnation is that she concealed her pregnancy and asked for no assistance at the birth. The pathos of her situation is accentuated by the circumstances: there is no body (205.31–33); she suffered from puerperal fever (205.42), a condition recognised at the time but not so named; and, if Robertson had not been arrested for robbing the collector, Effie would never have found herself in the predicament which befalls her.

In addition, the fictional case does not typify the historical situation in the 1730s. In the text the Duke of Argyle reports that there were 21 instances of child murder in seven years (352.39–41); this figure accords with 21 recorded by Hugo Arnot for the period 1700–06 in *A Collection and Abridgement of Celebrated Trials in Scotland, From AD 1536, to 1784*, and some have suspected that Scott gleaned his information from that source.[21] In fact there *were* 21 cases brought under the 1690 Act in the years 1730 to 1737 inclusive; 24 for 1730 to 1739. Of the 24, three women were hanged; five cases were found not proven (Scottish juries pronounced cases proven or not proven); four were deserted. The remaining 12 women were banished.[22] For the most part they had petitioned the court prior to trial admitting that their behaviour was scandalous (i.e. that they had had a baby outside wedlock), but arguing that as they had not harmed their babies they would be prepared to accept banishment and transportation instead. In most cases the Lord Advocate accepted such petitions. Before the same court as tried Isobel Walker, Mary Douglas was found guilty of the same crime, but her petition that she be banished rather than hanged was supported by the Advocate Depute, Sir James Elphinstone, and immediately granted by the judges, without any recourse to the royal prerogative.[23] The difference between the two cases seems to have been that there was no evidence to suggest that Douglas killed her baby. In 1738 the normal practice was to accept such petitions for banishment, but where there was some reason to think that the baby had indeed been murdered there was a trial. Isobel Walker was one of those suspected of murder. Had Effie's been a real case it seems probable that she would have petitioned for banishment before trial, and been granted it.

Furthermore, although at Effie's trial the prosecution talks of 'the various instances, many of them marked with circumstances of atrocity, which had at length induced the King's Advocate, though with great reluctance, to make the experiment, whether by strictly enforcing the Act of Parliament which had been made to prevent such enormities, their occurrence might be prevented' (198.19–24), there is no evidence of an increase in the crime in the 1730s as the text suggests (216.26), and not much sign of 'circumstances of atrocity'. There is no evidence in the 1730s that there was any change in policy on the administration of the 1690 Act, and in the legal reports no prosecutor makes a statement like the one quoted above. This does not accord with what is said in works of Scottish history, but the review of the evidence leads to the conclusion that too often historians appear to have repeated without further enquiry statements which are wrong in fact and hysterical in tone.[24]

Scott, then, 'changes' history, and in so doing he makes the Effie case try the law by which she is condemned. The law of 1690 'anent Murthering of Children' was designed to prevent 'the frequent Murthers that have or may be committed upon Innocent Infants'. It is clear from the terms of the Act that its real objective was not to prevent *murder* as now understood, but what would now in Scots Law be called culpable homicide, that is a death which results from negligence or accident rather than design. The Act is directed against mothers who 'do conceal their being with Child, and do not call for necessary Assistance in the Birth, whereby the new born Child may be easily Stifled, or being left exposed in the condition it comes into the World, it must quickly perish'. It continues:

> if any woman shall conceal to being with Child, during the whole space, and shall not call for, and make use of help and assistance in the Birth, the child being found dead, or amissing, the Mother shall be holden and reputed the Murtherer of her own Child: ... and the Libel [charge] being remitted to the knowledge of an Inquest [trial by jury], it shall be sufficient ground for them [the judges] to return their Verdict, finding the Libel proven, and the Mother guilty of Murther, tho there be no appearance of Wound or Bruise upon the Body of a Child.[25]

In 1773 John Erskine of Carnock wrote that 'Where certain facts which do not of their own nature constitute murder, are by statute declared to be murder, the crime thence arising may be called *presumptive* or *statutory* murder'.[26] In the case of Effie Deans the enactment generates injustice and the verdict 'guilty' is a lie. The words and the processes of the state create a false reality on which Mrs Saddletree provides the most colourful and the most forceful indictment: 'Then, if the Law makes murders, . . . the Law should be hanged for them' (47.11–12).

Historical Characters. There are many historical characters in *The Heart of Mid-Lothian*: the Duke of Argyle, Queen Caroline, John Porteous, Wilson, Robertson, Ratcliffe, and many other figures, whose names are mentioned but who do not appear in the novel, such as the Duke of Newcastle, Patrick Lindsay (Member of Parliament for Edinburgh), and Colonel Moyle who commanded the regiment quartered in the Canongate at the time of the riot. The most notable of these historical characters is the Duke of Argyle (see note to 64.6), whom Scott interprets in accordance with his historical reputation, and whom he authenticates, at least in part, by quoting from his speeches in the House of Lords. He treats Queen Caroline and the Countess of Suffolk (see note to 333.4) similarly, drawing significantly upon Horace Walpole's 'Reminiscences' (see note to 333.16). The portrait of Porteous, who is allowed no direct speech, comes directly from his life as given in the 1737 pamphlet, reproduced in *Criminal Trials*. Scott develops other real people such as Robertson and Ratcliffe quite freely. Both were known Edinburgh criminals. The real and the fictional Robertson (see note to 23.19) were both condemned to death for robbing the collector in Pittenweem, and escaped from the Tolbooth Kirk, but the historical figure was not an upper-class Englishman in disguise. On the other hand, the historical Ratcliff was English, from Spalding (see note to 59.3): little else except the crimes for which he was tried is known about the man, but that he came from Lincolnshire (a fact recorded in the criminal records) permits the critical plot connection which Scott developed.

Literary and Linguistic Sources. The legal language, including Saddletree's partially-heard mimicry of it, is a greatly distinctive discourse of *The Heart of Mid-Lothian*, and most probably came directly from Scott's knowledge of the language and legal styles of the courts. That it is authentic can be seen from the written forms of evidence and formalised summaries of the proceedings of the High Court in trials of the period, as well as acts of Parliament.

Much of what David Deans says is informed by the Bible but the most colourful material comes from the popular historian Patrick Walker (*c.* 1666–1745), a Covenanter denounced as a rebel in 1682, and imprisoned and tortured in 1684 and 1685. He published lives of various Covenanters—Alexander Peden (1724; revised edn 1728), John Semple, John Welwood, and Richard Cameron (1727), and Daniel Cargill and others (1732).[27] Scott adopts many actual phrases from Walker, and makes use of the same or similar scriptural references, without his parodying Covenanting discourse. Even if David Deans is a fictional character, his rhetoric is a faithful reworking of authentic Covenanting accounts of their persecution in the seventeenth century. In addition, Walker, with other later writers of Covenanting lives such as John Howie (1735–93), whose *Biographica Scoticana; or . . . Scots Worthies* first appeared in 1775, provide models for the life of David Deans. Within the novel David Deans is marked as the tradition-bearer, transmitting Covenanting experience and legend into the eighteenth century, and that tradition is continued in Jeanie, who from time to time uses the language of her father but less insistently.

These languages draw upon particular linguistic corpora, which help to identify not just the individual characters and the social subgroups to which they belong, also different ways of seeing and understanding. The language of other characters, however, is much more literary. The thieves' cant used by Ratcliffe, and by his associates in Lincolnshire, comes from Francis Grose's *A Classical Dictionary of the Vulgar Tongue*, while the specifically Midland proverbs which help to make Lincolnshire 'foreign' to Jeanie are to be found in Grose's *A Provincial Glossary*.[28] Grose's dictionaries define cant words, providing two or three standard-English synonyms, but do not cite quotations as illustrations of usage. It follows, then, that one cannot be certain that the language of the criminal classes in *The Heart of Mid-Lothian* is authentic, but in basing it on Grose Scott convinces the reader of its probability.

Beyond these completely identifiable discourses there is a range of social dialects, recognisable in the contrasts between the speech of different characters. There are also individualising speech patterns. Effie, for instance, often uses a proverbial structure in formulating ideas, but normally her 'proverbs' are not true proverbs, shared formulations of traditional wisdom: is it possible to see in this a kind of linguistic deviance that parallels the impulsiveness of her life? Robertson's speeches during his encounter with Jeanie in the Park, and his long confession later in the Rectory, have been described as 'Byronic'[29] (but there are, in fact, only two direct quotations from Byron in the novel, 'midnight solitude' at 103.21, and the motto on 248). Further, linguistic accommodation can be seen in the way in which characters adjust their speech to the person they are addressing, as does Argyle when addressing Jeanie. Strictly speaking, the variety of language discernible in the novel does not have known sources; the society Scott 'imitates' had gone even when he wrote the novel. What Scott does is to use his understanding of the sociology of language in a way that convinces the reader of the social variety that the language is actually creating.

There is also an immense number of quotations, allusions and references identifiable in *The Heart of Mid-Lothian*, and detailed in the Explanatory Notes. Scott's uses of Shakespeare's *Measure for Measure*, Bunyan's *The Pilgrim's Progress*, Smollett's *Humphry Clinker*, Crabbe's poetry, and popular song, have been the subjects of specific study,[30] but these are only some areas among many. The range of reference continuously sets up different perspectives, and the intertextual dialogue comments upon and extends human experience and understanding. But it is more than just a question of identifying quotations, for in *The Heart of Mid-Lothian* there is an intertextuality that involves an apparent underpinning of the movement of the novel by specific literary texts (as Tony Inglis has argued about *Humphry Clinker*), and an intertextuality of ideas seen, for instance, in the debate between the legal ideas of the novel those of David Hume.[31]

The Narration. The manuscript of the second series of *Tales of My Landlord* was nominally prepared for the press by Jedidiah Cleishbotham, the schoolmaster of Gandercleugh, who dates his dedicatory epistle '1st of April, 1818' (5.28). The tale itself is represented as being written by Peter Pattieson, Cleishbotham's late assistant, and as dating from 1809. The narrator says that hangings in the Grassmarket stopped 25 years ago 'or thereabouts' (21.27–28); the actual date was 1784. The first chapter takes place in the context of an election, and it would be a neat fiction to see the Parliamentary election of 1807 as the context in which Pattieson first gets his ideas for a new novel, leading to its completion in 1809. But the most persuasive factor in recognising 1809 as the date of the narration is that in this year the 1690 Act on child murder was repealed.[32] Other references are less precise: for instance the first paragraph of Pattieson's story refers to the state of English public transport 'about eighty years before' (7.17), and comments that Fielding and Farquhar had ridiculed 'the slowness of these vehicles of public accommodation' (7.19–20); yet *Tom Jones* was published in 1749, and *The Stage-Coach* first performed in 1704. At 13.41–42 it is reported that the town councillors of Edinburgh had decided to demolish the Edinburgh tolbooth. The building was pulled down in 1817 but when the decision was made cannot be so easily determined: an act of Parliament of 1782 provided for a new prison, but as it was not built until 1815–17 the expectation of the tolbooth's demolition was around for thirty years. These references are imprecise, but they do not conflict with 1809 as the year in which Pattieson nominally completed his novel.

The Narrative. The central action of *The Heart of Mid-Lothian* extends over a mere nine months between September 1736 and May 1737. But the novel can be seen as a family saga for the reported action lasts the lifetime of David Deans, from his birth, probably in 1673, to his death in 1751. It is a family saga in Homeric mode: it opens *in medias res*; what happens in the period before 1736–37 is told in an imbedded retrospective narrative, while what happens after the central nine months is told in the final six chapters.

In the novel Porteous is due to be hanged on 8 September 1736

(22.13 and 32.23),[33] and he is murdered that night. Between the date given in Chapter 2 and the gathering of the crowd to witness his execution there is a retrospective narrative, without dates, in which we are told the stories of Wilson and Robertson, and of Porteous. Chapters 4 to 7 inclusive in Volume 1 return to September 1736, and cover the disappointment of the crowd, the subsequent rising of the mob, and the lynching of Porteous. As Butler, having escaped the mob, wanders in the King's Park waiting for a respectable hour of day before visiting Jeanie and her father, the reader is given a long three-chapter retrospective (65–95) in which the full story of the Deans and Butler families is told. On the morning of 9 September Butler meets Robertson, and when he reaches the cottage at St Leonard's he delivers Robertson's demand that Jeanie meet him in the Park that night, while Saddletree simultaneously tries to persuade Davie Deans that a lawyer will be required to defend Effie, and Dumbiedikes offers to underwrite the legal bills (Chapter 12). Butler is arrested and incarcerated (Chapter 13). In the first two chapters of Volume 2 Jeanie prepares for and then meets Robertson in the Park; meanwhile in Chapters 3 and 4 Sharpitlaw recruits Ratcliffe, interviews Madge Wildfire, and goes in search of Robertson.

On the morning of 10 September Middleburgh considers Effie's case (165.4–67.13) and interrogates Meg Murdockson and Madge. There is then a gap of 'some weeks' (171.2) before he goes to collect evidence from Jeanie and Davie Deans. Many more weeks go by (183.27) before the date of Effie's trial is fixed, during which time it is hoped that Effie will speak 'on a subject infinitely more interesting to the magistracy than her own guilt and innocence' (183.28–29). On the evening before the trial Jeanie is allowed into the prison to see Effie. The day after the trial Jeanie leaves for London. She calls on Dumbiedikes on a 'fine spring morning' (230.25), a description which sounds like March, and which would be compatible with the double lapse of several weeks. At 249.5 the year is specified as 1737.

Jeanie walks twenty miles a day (249.17), which, if Scots miles, would be roughly comparable to the 'Five and twenty miles and a bittock' (339.19) she reports to the Queen. She walks for 300 of the 400 miles to London (the 'cast in a wagon, and . . . a horse from Ferrybridge' (323.16) would make little difference to the overall speed), and would have taken 12 days to do so. She has a day off in York (250.16); she loses two nights in Lincolnshire, one in the Murdockson den and the other at the Rectory; she takes a coach from Stamford which arrives in London about 100 miles away 'on the afternoon of the second day' (316.26). Thus it takes Jeanie about 17 days to get to London.

No doubt Jeanie goes to the Argyle residence on the day immediately after her arrival. She spends the next at home awaiting a summons (326) and on the next again is collected by Archibald 'before noon'

(326.34–35). She returns from her audience after 3 o'clock (349.12). The Duke arrives to see Mrs Glass three days later (352.23), in other words, six days after Jeanie's arrival in London, and 23 days after leaving Edinburgh. Jeanie could have returned on foot bearing the pardon, and got there within the stipulated six-weeks between sentence and execution, but in fact the Duke has the pardon sent express to Edinburgh (351.1–2). In all, Jeanie spends about three weeks in London (357.24). The coach north takes 'several days' (360.2) but the journey is leisurely, conducted with 'ease and short stages' (360.4). Coaches would not have been exceeding 8 miles an hour (it takes one and a half days to go from Stamford to London and this confirms that speed), and so the 300 miles to Carlisle probably took five days. They have an overnight stop in Carlisle (364.13), spend a day recuperating in Longtown (367.12–13), a day going from Longtown to Rutherglen (368.28–30), and another from Rutherglen to Roseneath (369.30). All in all Jeanie has been away for nearly seven weeks, and she reaches Roseneath in May. Butler is inducted by the local Presbbytery to the parish of Knocktarlitie the day after Jeanie's arrival in Roseneath, and that night the two sisters meet and part. At this point the main action stops; it has extended over nine months.

David Deans stretches the story well back into the seventeenth century. He is said to have been present at Talla-linns (178.9), a historic gathering which took place in 1682, and to have at least witnessed the murder in the same year of Trooper Francis Gordon (388.10–33; see note to 388.12–13). He tells Butler about 'how proud I was o' being made a spectacle to men and angels afore I was fifteen, when I was found worthy to be scourged by the same bloody hands that quartered the dear body of James Renwick and cut off those hands which were the first to raise up the down-fallen banner of the testimony' (102.33–37). As Renwick was executed on 17 February 1688 it is implied that David was born in 1673. However, on his death in 1751 we are told that 'He is believed . . . to have lived upwards of ninety years' (427.16–17); the verbal form, as well as the report that he was at Bothwell Brig in 1679 (427.18–19), suggests that Davie Deans is being re-constructed as a folk hero, an embodiment of the collective memory of the Covenanting era, with the 'ninety years' as the age of a patriarch.

The history of the Deans and Butler families given in the long, three-chapter retrospective (65–95) also actualises the seventeenth century within the nine-month period of the main action. Reuben's grandfather was part of Monk's army at the sack of Dundee in 1651 (65.27–29), was discharged in 1660 (66.4–21), settled near Dalkeith, and married a young wife from the village (66.25). He died a few years later leaving a son, Benjamin, aged 3 (66.31–32), and a widow who was persecuted by the old laird of Dumbiedikes for non-conformity (67.7–11). In due course Benjamin married, and 'eventually' (67.18) had a son, Reuben, but he and his wife died early in 1705 (67.41–43), leaving Reuben to be brought up by his grandmother, who because of the laird and the years of famine was facing the loss of home, land and all means of survival.

In the 'dear years' (70.11) of 1700 and 1701, 'long remembered in Scotland for dearth and general distress' (68.10–11; see also note), David Deans too is ruined by a series of disasters and legal processes initiated by the same laird (68.3–21), and was to have been evicted from his cottage and land at Candlemas 1705. The year is 1705 because of the death of Reuben Butler's parents which was 'about the year 1704–05' (67.42–43), a form of date used to specify the year in both the old and new calendars. The date of their eviction would have been Candlemas, 2 February, for that is the only quarter day which could be in both 1704 (old style) and 1705 (new style), and because snow was falling heavily (70.14–16).

David Deans's first wife, Christian Menzies (72.14), had died before 1705, for there is no mention of her being evicted along with David. Jeanie was brought up by her father: we are told that 'from the time she could walk' (72.36) he was training her for some task. Thus Jeanie must have been born early in 1704 at the latest, and she is at least 33 at the time of Effie's trial. This is consistent with the suggestion that Jeanie was 'approaching to what is called in females the middle age' (84.28–29) when the novel opens. Ten years later, i.e. not later than 1714 (76.1–2), David married Rebecca MacNaught (376.30–31). After being 'some years married', Rebecca gave birth to Effie; this must have been in 1719, because in March 1737 Effie cries out to Jeanie 'and me no aughteen year auld yet' (188.42–43). Incompatible with these dates is the earlier statement by Mrs Saddletree that there are ten years, rather than fifteen, between the sisters (44.24); this is clearly a mistake but explicable as it was written before the three-chapter retrospective narrative giving the history of the Deans and Butler families.

Reuben Butler was at university at the time of Effie's birth (77.17); were he too born in 1704, he would have been at St Andrews around 1718–22; he had then another four years to undertake at the Divinity Hall before he obtained his license to preach (77.32), which would have been in 1726 or so. There are 10 years to 1736, and at 106.25–26 Jeanie asks 'Is it not ten long years since we spoke together in this way?', thus proving this chronology, and justifying the sense of wasted years:

> it became at length understood betwixt them, that their union should be deferred no longer than until Butler should obtain some steady means of support, however humble. This, however, was not a matter speedily to be accomplished. Plan after plan was formed, and plan after plan failed. The good-humoured cheek of Jeanie lost the first flush of juvenile freshness; Reuben's brow assumed the gravity of manhood, yet the means of attaining a settlement seemed remote as ever. (80.12–19)

The time scheme of the conclusion is also sound. David Deans dies in January 1751 (427.11); Butler sets off to Edinburgh 'in the latter end of the month of February' (430.38–39). Plumdamas confirms the year (450.31) when Reuben is in Edinburgh, and the boatman reassures Reuben that he knows the way by saying 'I maybe kenn'd it a wee better fifteen years syne, when Dand Wilson was in the Firth' (457.40–41). Effie turns up in Knocktarlitie in May 1751 after having been banished in April 1737 for 14 years (352.36). However, there are two contra-indications suggesting that the year is 1752, but both can be explained. Effie tells Jeanie that she is a 'Lie of fifteen years' standing' (439.38–39); but of course that 'fifteen' is a round figure—when did Effie's deceit begin? Secondly, David Butler is 'but fourteen years old' at the time of Effie's visit (441.39); as he could not have been born before 1738 this would make the year 1752, were it not for the practice of the period whereby someone in their fourteenth year would be called 'fourteen' (while someone who had just passed their fourteenth birth-day would be called 'fourteen complete'). The year is therefore 1751.

The chronology of *The Heart of Mid-Lothian* is complex, but it is controlled and precise. The few areas of vagueness such as the date of David Deans's birth can even be seen as deliberate for the vagueness facilitates the representation of David as a mythic figure. *The Heart of Mid-Lothian* is more of a chronicle than any other Scott novel, and when viewed this way it appears that while David Deans is not the primary focus of our interest, the revolution seen in his life and lifetime is at least one of the underlying subjects of the fiction.

NOTES

All manuscripts referred to are part of the National Archives of Scotland. For standard abbreviations see 601–02.

1   T. M. Devine, *The Scottish Nation 1700–2000* (London, 1999), 20.
2   Rosalind Mitchison, *A History of Scotland*, 2nd edn (London, 1982), 326.
3   This account is indebted to Rosalind Mitchison, *A History of Scotland*, 2nd edn (London, 1982), 323–27; and T. M. Devine, *The Scottish Nation 1700–2000* (London, 1999), 18–24.
4   William B. Todd and Ann Bowden, *Sir Walter Scott: a Bibliographical History* (New Castle, DE, 1998), 467, 474.
5   *Criminal Trials, Illustrative of the Tale Entitled "The Heart of Mid-Lothian,"* (Edinburgh, 1818) is not mentioned in Scott's correspondence, nor does it appear in the letter books of Archibald Constable and Co. However, it is clear that whoever put *Criminal Trials* together was very familiar with *The Heart of Mid-Lothian*. The note on the tolbooth which concludes the Prefatory Notice is in parts close to the wording of the note on the tolbooth in the Magnum (11.256), and the elegiac comment that 'This building, rendered so singularly interesting to the mind by a thousand historical associations, . . . surely deserved a better fate' (xxxv–vi) sounds like Scott. While these hints might suggest Scott's involvement they do not prove it.

6 *Criminal Trials*, 1–204. *Criminal Trials* reproduces the original records, now in the National Archives of Scotland, reasonably accurately, and, although there are some mistakes, differences are for the most part limited to formal matters such as spelling, and capitalisation.

7 NAS: HH.11/18, p. 173.

8 For a fuller version of this discussion see David Hewitt, '*The Heart of Mid-Lothian* and "The People" ', *European Romantic Review*, 13 (2002), 299–309.

9 Walter Scott, 'Memoirs', in *Scott on Himself*, ed. David Hewitt (Edinburgh, 1981), 42.

10 Hume, *Crimes*, 2.231–32.

11 *Criminal Trials*, 292.

12 *Criminal Trials*, 305.

13 *Criminal Trials*, 210–11.

14 Hume, *Crimes*, 2.428.

15 *Letters*, 7.360.

16 *Chronicles of the Canongate*, ed. Claire Lamont, EEWN 20, 5.20–34.

17 *Letters*, 10.297–98. See also *Letters*, 11.303–04; 12.33.

18 Magnum, 11.142–47.

19 NAS: Great Seal warrants C.7/43/50. Remission sealed and recorded in the Great Seal Register C.3/18 no. 82.

20 NAS: Justiciary Processes JC.26/126, and JC.26/127 D2049; South Circuit minute book JC.12/5; Books of Adjournal JC.3/22; Edinburgh Tolbooth warding and liberation book HH.11/18, p. 173; Great Seal warrants C.7/43/50.

21 Hugo Arnot, *A Collection and Abridgement of Celebrated Trials in Scotland, From AD 1536, to 1784* (Edinburgh, 1785), 311. See also note to 352.38–39.

22 NAS: for the High Court in Edinburgh, JC.3/17, 18, 19, 20, 21, 22, 23; the North Circuit JC.11/7, 8, 9, 10; the South Circuit JC.12/4, 5; the West Circuit JC.13/6, 7. In the figures given here Isobel Walker is included in the total of 12 who were banished; she was the only one to have been condemned to death and to have received a royal pardon.

23 NAS: JC.12/5.

24 Prevalent ideas about the application of the 1690 Act seem to be derived from Fountainhall, who covers the period to 1712: John Lauder of Fountainhall, *The Decisions of the Lords of Council and Session, from June 6th, 1678, to July 30th, 1712* (Edinburgh, 1759). They are repeated by Hugo Arnot, in *A Collection and Abridgement of Celebrated Criminal Trials in Scotland, From AD 1536, to 1784* (Edinburgh, 1785), 311. They continue to be recycled by historians to the present day, even although Arnot was talking only of the period 1700–06, and his hysteria about the moral controls of the church implies an agenda of his own. Further, in spite of what many commentators have implied, a law of this kind was not unique to Scotland: Henry II of France issued an edict in 1556, and the English law of child murder (21 James I, c. 27) was repealed only in 1803—that Scotland had to wait until 1809 merely reflects the neglect of the British Parliament.

25 'ACT anent Murthering of Children', 1690, c. 21, in *The Laws and Acts*

Made in the Second Session of the First Parliament of... William and Mary (Edinburgh, 1690), 282.

26 John Erskine of Carnock, *An Institute of the Law of Scotland*, 2 vols (Edinburgh, 1773), 718.

27 See Patrick Walker, *Seven Saints of the Covenant*, ed. D. Hay Fleming, 2 vols (London, 1901), where all are reprinted.

28 Francis Grose, *A Classical Dictionary of the Vulgar Tongue*, 3rd edn (Lonn, 1796: *CLA*, 156); *A Provincial Glossary* (London, 1787: *CLA*, 156).

29 See Fiona Robertson, *Legitimate Histories* (Oxford, 1994), 205–08.

30 D. Biggins, '*Measure for Measure* and *The Heart of Midlothian*', *Etudes Anglaises*, 14 (1961), 193–205; Thomas Crawford, *Scott*, 2nd edn (Edinburgh, 1982), 93–95; Tony Inglis, 'And an Intertextual Heart: Rewriting Origins in *The Heart of Mid-Lothian*', in *Scott and Carnival*, ed. J. H. Alexander and David Hewitt (Aberdeen, 1993), 216–31; Gavin Edwards, 'Scott and Crabbe: A Meeting at the Border', *Eighteenth Century Life*, 22 (1998), 123–40; C. M. Jackson-Houlston, *Ballads, Songs and Snatches* (Aldershot, 1999), 39–45.

31 David Hume, *Commentaries on the Law of Scotland respecting the Description and Punishment of Crimes*, 2 vols (Edinburgh, 1797); *Commentaries on the Law of Scotland respecting Trial for Crimes*, 2 vols (Edinburgh, 1800).

32 49 Geo. III, c. 14.

33 In the manuscript and Ed1 the date at 22.13 is given as 7 September. This date is at odds with the date of 8 September set by the judge at 32.23; the discrepancy was never corrected by any edition in Scott's lifetime. The mistake arose because the lynching of Porteous actually took place on 7 September, the day before the date of his execution as set by the judges, but Scott adjusted the historical record to create the more dramatic situation of a reprieve arriving after the crowd had gathered. An editorial emendation has harmonised the dates so that within the fiction the lynching of Porteous takes place on 8 September, preference being given to 8 September because of the textual simplicity of the change. That Wednesday was the day on which hangings took place (compare the sentence upon Effie at 218.7–8) is a 'bonus'.

EXPLANATORY NOTES

In these notes a comprehensive attempt is made to identify Scott's sources, and all quotations, references, historical events, and historical personages, to explain proverbs, and to translate difficult or obscure language. (Phrases are explained in the notes while single words are treated in the glossary.) The notes are brief; they offer information rather than critical comment or exposition. When a quotation has not been recognised this is stated: any new information from readers will be welcomed. References are to standard editions, or to the editions Scott himself used. Thus proverbs are normally identified both by reference to the third edition of Ray's *A Compleat Collection of English Proverbs*, and to *The Oxford Dictionary of English Proverbs*. Books in the Abbotsford Library are identified by reference to the appropriate page of the *Catalogue of the Library at Abbotsford*. When quotations reproduce their sources accurately, the reference is given without comment. Verbal differences in the source are indicated by a prefatory 'see', while a general rather than a verbal indebtedness is indicated by 'compare'. Biblical references are to the Authorised Version. Plays by Shakespeare are cited without authorial ascription, and references are to *William Shakespeare: The Complete Works*, edited by Peter Alexander (London and Glasgow, 1951, frequently reprinted).

The following publications are distinguished by abbreviations, or are given without the names of their authors:

Child   *The English and Scottish Popular Ballads*, ed. Francis James Child, 5 vols (Boston and New York, 1882–98).
CLA   [J. G. Cochrane], *Catalogue of the Library at Abbotsford* (Edinburgh, 1838).
Crabbe, *Poetical Works*   George Crabbe, *The Complete Poetical Works*, ed. Norma Dalrymple-Champneys and Arthur Pollard, 3 vols (Oxford, 1988).
Criminal Trials   [Anon.] *Criminal Trials, Illustrative of the Tale Entitled "The Heart of Mid-Lothian"* (Edinburgh, 1818).
EEWN   The Edinburgh Edition of the Waverley Novels (Edinburgh, 1993–).
Grant   James Grant, *Old and New Edinburgh*, 3 vols (London, 1882).
Grose, *A Classical Dictionary*   Francis Grose, *A Classical Dictionary of the Vulgar Tongue*, 3rd edn (London, 1796): *CLA*, 156.
Grose, *A Provincial Glossary*   Francis Grose, *A Provincial Glossary* (London, 1787): *CLA*, 156.
Herd   *Ancient and Modern Scottish Songs Heroic Ballads Etc*, ed. David Herd, 2nd edn, 2 vols (1776): *CLA*, 171.
Hume, *Crimes*   David Hume, *Commentaries on the Law of Scotland respecting the Description and Punishment of Crimes*, 2 vols (Edinburgh, 1797): *CLA*, 272. See also note to 17.8.
Hume, *Trial*   David Hume, *Commentaries on the Law of Scotland respecting Trial for Crimes*, 2 vols (Edinburgh, 1800): *CLA*, 272. See also note to 17.8.
Kelly   James Kelly, *A Compleat Collection of Scotish Proverbs Explained and made Intelligible to the English Reader* (London, 1721): *CLA*, 169.
Kinsley   *The Poems and Songs of Robert Burns*, ed. James Kinsley, 3 vols (Oxford, 1968).

Letters   *The Letters of Sir Walter Scott*, ed. H. J. C. Grierson and others, 12 vols (London, 1932–37).

Life of Porteous   [Anon.] *The Life and Death of Captain John Porteous* (London, 1737). *CLA*, 16.

Lockhart   J. G. Lockhart, *Memoirs of the Life of Sir Walter Scott, Bart.*, 7 vols (Edinburgh, 1837–38).

Magnum   Walter Scott, *Waverley Novels*, 48 vols (Edinburgh, 1829—33).

Minstrelsy   Walter Scott, *Minstrelsy of the Scottish Border*, ed. T. F. Henderson, 4 vols (Edinburgh, 1902).

ODEP   *The Oxford Dictionary of English Proverbs*, 3rd edn, rev. F. P. Wilson (Oxford, 1970).

OED   *The Oxford English Dictionary*, 12 vols (Oxford, 1933).

Percy   *Reliques of Ancient English Poetry*, [ed. Thomas Percy], 3 vols (London, 1765): see *CLA*, 172.

The Pilgrim's Progress   John Bunyan, *The Pilgrim's Progress*, ed. J. B. Wharey and Roger Sharrock, 2nd edn (Oxford, 1960): Part 1 originally published 1678, and Part 2 1684. See *CLA*, 179, 335.

Prose Works   *The Prose Works of Sir Walter Scott, Bart.*, 28 vols (Edinburgh, 1834–36).

Ramsay   Allan Ramsay, *A Collection of Scots Proverbs* (1737), in *The Works of Allan Ramsay*, 6 vols, Vol. 5, ed. Alexander M. Kinghorn and Alexander Law (Edinburgh and London: Scottish Text Society, 1972), 59–133.

Ray   J[ohn] Ray, *A Compleat Collection of English Proverbs*, 3rd edn (London, 1737): *CLA*, 169.

Roughead   William Roughead, *Trial of Captain Porteous* (Glasgow and Edinburgh, 1909).

SND   *The Scottish National Dictionary*, ed. William Grant and David D. Murison, 10 vols (Edinburgh 1931–76).

SMM   *The Scots Musical Museum*, ed. James Johnson, 6 vols (1787–1803).

TTM   *The Tea-Table Miscellany; or, A Collection of Choice Songs, Scots and English*, ed. Allan Ramsay, 10th edn, 4 vols with consecutive page numbering (London, 1740): see *CLA*, 171.

Walker   Patrick Walker, *Seven Saints of the Covenant*, ed. D. Hay Fleming, 2 vols (London, 1901).

Walpole   'Reminiscences', in *The Works of Horatio Walpole, Earl of Orford*, 5 vols (London, 1798), 4, 273–318: *CLA*, 234.

Wodrow   Robert Wodrow, *The History of the Sufferings of the Church of Scotland*, 2nd edn, 4 vols (Glasgow, 1835); originally published 1721–22: see *CLA*, 11.

Information derived from the notes of the late Dr J. C. Corson is indicated by '(Corson)', and information that would not otherwise have been found from the editions of *The Heart of Mid-Lothian* edited by Claire Lamont (Oxford, 1982) and by Tony Inglis (London, 1994) is acknowledged by '(Lamont)' and '(Inglis)' respectively.

1.1   Landlord   the landlord of the Wallace Inn in Gandercleugh, situated in the 'navel ... of Scotland': see *The Black Dwarf*, ed. P. D. Garside, EEWN 4a, 5.20–25.

1.2   Second Series   the first series of *Tales of My Landlord* was published in 1816, and consisted of *The Black Dwarf* and *The Tale of Old Mortality*.

1.3   collected and reported   *Tales of My Landlord* are purportedly written by the recently dead Peter Pattieson, Cleishbotham's assistant in the school, and edited for publication by Cleishbotham: see note to 4.1 below, and also *The Black Dwarf*, ed. P. D. Garside, EEWN 4a, 8–9.

1.5 Jedidiah Cleishbotham Jedidiah ('beloved of the Lord') is the name given to Solomon in 2 Samuel 12.25. 'Clashbottom' was a facetious name used by one of Joseph Train's corresponding 'Parish Clerks and Schoolmasters of Galloway', a name 'derived . . . from his using the Birch' (MS 3277, pp. 22–23); *clash* in Scots means 'strike' or 'flog'. For further discussion of the name and its origins, see *The Black Dwarf*, ed. P. D. Garside, EEWN 4a, 129–30.

1.6 Parish-clerk clerk to the kirk session, the lowest church court in the Presbyterian system (whereby the church is governed by a system of courts, kirk session, presbytery, synod, and General Assembly). The position was very often given to the schoolmaster.

1.6 Gandercleugh in Scots *cleugh* is a gorge or ravine; hence, 'goose-hollow'.

1.7–12 Hear, Land o' Cakes . . . prent it Robert Burns, 'On the Late Captain Grose's Peregrinations thro' Scotland, collecting the Antiquities of that Kingdom' (1789), lines 1–6 (Kinsley, no. 275).

1.7 Land o' Cakes Scotland. The name comes from one of Scotland's formerly staple foods, unleavened oat or barley-meal biscuits. In the *OED*, the first instance of the phrase in this sense is dated 1669 (*cake*, noun 1b).

1.8 Maidenkirk to Jonny Groats' the most southern and northern points of the Scottish mainland, in the SW and NE of the country respectively.

1.12 An' faith and by faith.

2.1–9 for the translated passage, see *The Life and Exploits of the Ingenious Gentleman Don Quixote De La Mancha Translated from the Original Spanish of . . . Cervantes . . . by Charles Jarvis, Esq.*, 2 vols (London, 1742), 1.204. The incident occurs in Part 1, Bk 4, Ch. 5 (or Part 1, Ch. 32: 'Which treats of what befel Don Quixote's whole company in the inn').

3.5 Courteous Reader in his own review of the first series of *Tales of My Landlord* Scott says that Jedidiah's opening piece 'is written in the quaint style of that prefixed by Gay to his *Pastorals*' (*Prose Works*, 19.22).

3.6 ingratitude comprehendeth every other vice compare *Twelfth Night*, 3.4.338–41.

3.8 prolegomen while clearly meaning 'prolegomenon' (a piece preliminary to a literary work), *prolegomen* is probably to be regarded as Cleishbotham's coinage.

3.10 Tales of my Landlord see notes to 1.1, 1.2, 1.3.

3.13 second story with atticks a facetious reference to the building of the first stage of Abbotsford, Scott's Border home, between 1817–19. What follows contains a series of teasing references to Scott, the supposedly unknown author.

3.15 Deacon Barrow a *deacon* is the chief official of a craft; he is called 'Barrow' because his trade is building.

3.21 new tale and an old song probably *Tales of My Landlord*, written and published in 1816, and *Harold the Dauntless*, begun probably in 1815, and published anonymously in 1817. The first Earl of Seafield, Chancellor of Scotland, said 'Now there's ane end of ane old song', as he signed the Treaty of Union in 1707; so Cleishbotham's remark is not only materialistic but suggests some contempt for the Scottish past.

3.24 purchasing in 1817 Scott was in frequent negotiations with his neighbour Nicol Milne of Faldonside about the purchase of land.

3.25 Carlinescroft i.e. the croft of the old woman; compare the Carline's Hole on the Abbotsford estate (*Letters*, 5.40; to William Laidlaw, January, 1818).

3.26 seven acres, three roods, and four perches *English measure* 2.83 hectares.

3.27–28 four additional volumes both the first series and second series of *Tales of My Landlord* originally appeared in four volumes.

3.29   Prayfort   i.e. Pray-for-it.

4.1   Peter Pattieson   the fictitious teacher of the lower classes at the Gandercleugh village school, and nominal author of the first, second and third series of *Tales of My Landlord* whose manuscripts are edited for publication by Cleishbotham. 'Patie' is a diminutive of Patrick; in Scots *paiter* means to 'chatter on endlessly'. See also *The Black Dwarf*, ed. P. D. Garside, EEWN 4a, note to 8.4.

4.2   lost their savour   see Matthew 5.13; Luke 14.34.

4.8   strong waters   whisky.

4.12–14   sought to identify ... inditer of vain fables ... shrunken from the responsibility   Scott's first three novels (*Waverley*, *Guy Mannering*, and *The Antiquary*) were published anonymously; *Tales of My Landlord* were nominally arranged by a different author, Jedidiah Cleishbotham.

4.15   generation hard of faith   i.e. a set of people resistant to belief. While the phrase itself is not biblical, each word is.

4.26–27   impeached ... the authenticity of my historical narratives   Scott's presentation of the Covenanters (see note to 4.42 below) in *The Tale of Old Mortality* was attacked by the Rev. Thomas McCrie in a series of papers published in January to March 1817: *The Edinburgh Christian Instructor*, 14 (1817), 41–73, 100–40, 170–201.

4.33   perjured prelatist   hostile name for those who supported episcopacy.

4.37   non-conformists   those who had seceded from the Church of Scotland in the course of the 18th century.

4.38   Cameronians   followers of Richard Cameron (1648–80), leader of the extreme wing of Presbyterianism, killed at Airds Moss (see note to 30.29 below) in 1680.

4.42   suffering party   Presbyterians, particularly those who refused to renounce the National Covenant of 1638 and take the oath of allegiance to the crown and who became known as Covenanters (see note to 30.30), suffered twenty-six years of persecution from 1662–88.

5.10   wedded for better or for worse   words from the English marriage service; see *The Book of Common Prayer* (1559, revised 1662).

5.12   ex jure sanguinis   *Latin, literally* by the law of blood; i.e. by blood ties. The phrase is common, but if there is a single source it might be Justinian's *Digest*, 1.7.23: *adoptio ... non ius sanguinis ... adfert* (adoption does not confer a legal blood-relationship). The *Digest* (compiled 530–33) is an anthology of writings by Roman lawyers.

5.16–17   horn of the dilemma   proverbial: see *ODEP*, 385.

5.21–22   ancestor ... Quakers   John Swinton of Swinton (d. 1679), and Walter Scott of Raeburn (d. before 1688), respectively Scott's maternal and paternal great-great-grandfathers, were both Quakers (members of the Religious Society of Friends, founded by George Fox between 1648–50), and both suffered for their faith before and after the Revolution of 1688–89 (see note to 90.16–18). There is a long note in Magnum, 11.157–61; see also *Letters*, 11.225–27; and *Redgauntlet*, ed. G. A. M. Wood with David Hewitt, EEWN 17, note to 55.23–25. Thomas McCrie in his review of *Tales of My Landlord* (1816) accused the author of 'gross partiality' towards 'the persecutors of the Presbyterians' (*The Edinburgh Christian Instructor*, 14 (1817), 200–01); these references to Scott's ancestors may be taken as a riposte.

5.28   1st of April   all fools' day. Scott began writing the novel in January 1818 and did not finish until the end of June; thus 1 April is probably a fictitious date.

7   motto   George Canning, John Hookham Frere, and George Ellis, 'The Love of the Triangles' (1798), lines 178–79, in *Poetry of the Anti-Jacobin*, ed. L. Rice-Oxley (Oxford, 1924), 102. These particular lines are by Canning. The

'Argument of the First Canto' introduces the motif of an overturned coach (91), but the poem was not finished and did not reach this part of the story. The text of the poem reads 'three insides'; Scott in his manuscript quotes Canning correctly; but Ed1 reads 'six insides'. It seems that someone counted the passengers on Scott's coach and counted wrongly, for there are five passengers, of whom only two are inside. In addition, light mail-coaches carried only three inside passengers.

7.12 twenty or thirty years 1779–89 as Pattieson is writing about 1809 (see notes to 21.14 and 21.27–28 below). Mail-coaches in place of stage-coaches as the means of distributing mail were proposed by John Palmer in 1782, and adopted by William Pitt, the Prime Minister, in 1784. They spread rapidly in England; the London to Edinburgh service was introduced in 1786, and the first purely Scottish service, Edinburgh to Glasgow, in 1788.

7.15 mails ... extremity 'extremity' is vague, but, when referring to postal services, may be taken as Aberdeen. The first light mail-coach service to Aberdeen from Edinburgh seems to have been in 1793 just before Scott first visited Aberdeen; the first proper mail-coach service was in 1798. For speeds before and after the advent of the mail-coach see A. R. B. Haldane, *Three Centuries of Scottish Posts* (Edinburgh, 1971), 48–49, 80.

7.17–18 Fielding ... Tom Jones Henry Fielding, *The History of Tom Jones* (1749), Bk. 10, Ch. 9.

7.18 Farquhar ... Stage-Coach George Farquhar and Peter Motteux, *The Stage Coach* (1704), Act 1.

7.22 Bull and Mouth inn in St-Martin's-le-Grand, the London terminus for many coach journeys. For an illustration see A. R. B. Haldane, *Three Centuries of Scottish Posts* (Edinburgh, 1971), facing 80.

7.25–26 the most remote districts of Britain in 1813 in Scotland there were mail-coach services from Edinburgh to Glasgow, Stirling, Aberdeen via Perth and Dundee, Inverness via Aberdeen and Banff or Huntly, Berwick, Carlisle, Dumfries, Portpatrick via Dumfries, and from Glasgow to Ayr, Carlisle and Edinburgh.

7.27 men armed on the introduction of the mail-coach service in 1784 (see note to 7.12) coach guards were armed.

7.30–31 Demens ... equorum the madman who with bronze and the beating of horn-footed horses had imitated the thunder clouds and the inimitable thunderbolt [of Zeus]: Publius Vergilius Maro (Virgil: 70–19 BC), *Aeneid*, 6.590–91.

8.3 Salmoneus in Greek legend a son of Aeolus, and king of Elis, who emulated Zeus in making a noise like thunder by driving around in a bronze chariot and throwing firebrands. According to Virgil, he was blasted by Zeus for this and put in Tartarus, a part of the underworld where the wicked are punished.

8.8 Mr Palmer see note to 7.12. A patent mail-coach was introduced by Besant in 1787, and for forty years he and his partner Vidler had a monopoly on building and maintaining mail-coaches which they leased to operators.

8.13 Mr Pennant Thomas Pennant (1726–98), Welsh naturalist, antiquary, and traveller, whose criticisms are contained in his *A Letter to a Member of Parliament on Mail-Coaches* (1792).

8.16–17 no time to dispute it appears that four horses were regularly changed within five minutes at a stage.

8.22 Cambrian Antiquary i.e. Thomas Pennant (see note to 8.13).

8.23–24 Penmen-Maur and Cader-Edris mountains in Wales.

8.25–26 Frighted Skiddaw ... car compare Samuel Taylor Coleridge, 'Kubla Khan' (written 1798; published 1816), lines 28–29: 'And mid this tumult Kubla heard from far / Ancestral voices prophesying war!'. Skiddaw

(931m) is in the Lake District in NW England. There is no other recorded use of 'unscythed', but the word appears to be an Enlightenment joke, which compares the war chariots of the ancient Britons with those of the modern era. Compare *The Black Dwarf*, ed. P. D. Garside, EEWN 4a, 44.41–42: 'Let Destiny drive forth her scythed car'.

8.27   Ben Nevis   highest mountain in Scotland (1343m), near Fort William, on the W coast.

8.35–40   The grand debate … again   see William Cowper, *The Task* (1785), 4.30–35.

8.42–9.1   Somerset   county in SW England, but the name was chosen to create an obvious pun (see text at 9.37).

8.43   Gilbert Goslinn   i.e. Gilbert Gosling. The villain of *Guy Mannering* (1815) is Gilbert Glossin; the similarity is a joke which links a novel by 'the Author of Waverley' with one 'collected and reported' by Jedidiah Cleishbotham.

9.29–30   cloudy tabernacle of the dust   i.e. hidden in a tent of dust. See Exodus 40.33–38. In Jewish history the *tabernacle* was the curtained tent which contained the Ark of the Covenant which the Jewish people carried with them while wandering in the desert and afterwards put in the temple in Jerusalem.

9.37   Somerset had made a summerset   compare Tobias Smollett, *The Expedition of Humphry Clinker* (1771), J. Melford to Sir Watkin Phillips, 24 May; ed. Thomas R. Preston (Athens and London, 1990), 75–76. Tony Inglis comments: 'In each case the vehicle overturns at a distance from the narrator, who hurries to the spot; in each case it has capsized completely, but without injury to anyone; in each, the coach doors are being torn from their hinges so that trapped "damsels" may be "delivered", apparently in both the chivalric and the obstetrical senses.' ('And an Intertextual Heart: Rewriting Origins in *The Heart of Mid-Lothian*', in *Scott and Carnival*, ed. J. H. Alexander and David Hewitt (Aberdeen, 1993), 222).

9.40   exertions of the guard and coachman   not identified, but it may be intended as a quotation from the newspapers. Mail-coaches carried an armed guard.

10.13   Rari … vasto   they appear swimming scattered widely over the vast deep: Virgil (70–19 BC), *Aeneid*, 1.118. The Trojans under Aeneas were wrecked and cast up on the shore of Carthage, in modern Tunisia.

10.18   preposterous length of their great-coats   i.e. they were in the Napoleonic style fashionable in the period.

10.19   Wellington trowsers   trousers cut wide in the lower part of the leg to be worn over boots; named after the Duke of Wellington (1769–1852).

10.31   heavy coach   stage-coach; the mail-coach carried a few passengers who were essentially ancillary to the mail, while the stage-coach was designed for passengers.

11.3   the edict Nautæ, caupones, stabularii   a Roman praetorian edict (*Edicta Praetorum*, 11.2) which allowed actions against three categories of people (boatmen, inn-keepers, and stablemen) in respect of the security of property in their care. See also Justinian (*c.* 482–565, Emperor from 527), *Digesta seu Pandectae* (533), *D.* 4.9, 47.5, where it is specified that the praetor imposed on these classes of individual a strict liability for the return of property put in their care.

11.7–8   Wallace-head   named after the Scottish national hero, Sir William Wallace (*c.* 1270–1305), for whom see note to 42.15–16.

11.13   deserted   term applied to a legal case that is given up.

11.39–40   Cowley … moist   Abraham Cowley (1618–67), who in 'The Complaint' uses the Gideon story (see note below) to complain about the uneven distribution of royal patronage, commenting 'And nothing but the Muse's fleece was dry' (lines 68–74).

11.40–41 reverse of the miracle see Judges 6.36–40: God shows that he will save Israel by wetting a fleece while all around is left dry; Gideon demands a second proof and on the next night the fleece is dry while all around is wet.

12.5 counsel and agent advocate (i.e. a barrister in Scotland) and solicitor.

12.18 to the best advantage so as to augment its quality by the greatest possible amount.

12.22–23 templars in the days of Steele and Addison barristers with chambers in the Inner or Middle Temple, off Fleet Street in London. 'The Templar' is one of the Club in *The Spectator* (1711–12), and represents the young men who ostensibly studied law but were in fact mainly interested in theatrical and fashionable life. See Joseph Addison (1672–1719) and Sir Richard Steele (1672–1729), *The Spectator*, no. 2 (1711), in *The Spectator*, ed. Donald F. Bond, 5 vols (1965), 1, 9.

13.12–13 nothing can come of nothing proverbial: see *ODEP*, 579; *King Lear*, 1.1.89, and 1.4.131–32.

13.16 Heart of Mid-Lothian the tolbooth, i.e. the Edinburgh prison. The first citation in the *SND* for the use of the phrase as a name for the prison is dated 1713 (Supplement of Addenda and Corrigenda). Built in 1430, it stood at the foot of the Lawnmarket, just NW of the High Kirk of Edinburgh (St Giles Cathedral): see maps, 771, 772, and the illustrations in Grant, 1.128 and 133. Originally it accommodated Parliament, the courts of justice, and a debtors prison; from 1640 its sole use was as a prison. See Magnum, 11.256–57, where, *inter alia*, Scott records that the gateway and the old door came to Abbotsford on the demolition of the tolbooth in 1817.

13.26–27 Making ... God proverbial: see *ODEP*, 557. The High Church (St Giles Cathedral) and the prison stood side-by-side on the N side of Parliament Square (see maps, 771, 772).

13.29–30 sign of the Red Man the form of words suggests an inn sign, but here refers to the member of the City Guard, whose uniform was 'a muddy-coloured red' (see text, 28.4), on watch outside the door of the prison.

13.41 Fathers Conscript translation of the Latin *patres conscripti*, meaning 'elected fathers', i.e. the members of the Roman senate; it refers here to the members of the Town Council of Edinburgh.

13.42 venerable edifice ... not remain in existence the replacement of the tolbooth as Edinburgh's prison was under discussion from 1785–86; it was finally demolished in 1817. See A. J. Youngson, *The Making of Classical Edinburgh* (Edinburgh, 1966), 122–23.

14.7 Right as my glove not recorded as a standard phrase, but also used in *The Antiquary*, ed. David Hewitt, EEWN 3, 238.40.

14.18–19 Last Speech ... Dying Words the traditional title of the supposedly autobiographical statements of condemned people, often sold as broadsides.

14.20–21 dangled ... at the west end of it public executions were transferred from the Grassmarket to the west end of the tolbooth in 1784.

14.32–33 food ... work prisoners purchased whatever food they could afford until the mid-19th century, and there was a system for providing for poor prisoners. For a comparison with food in the navy in 1797 see http://www.stvincent.ac.uk/Heritage/1797/Victory/food.htm. The idea that work could constitute a mode of rehabilitation for offenders developed during the 19th century.

14.41 fictitious narratives compare George Crabbe (1754–1832), writing to Scott on 5 March 1813: 'I have often thought I should love to read *Reports* that is, brief Histories of extraordinary Cases with the Judgements'

(*Selected Letters and Journals of George Crabbe*, ed. Thomas C. Faulkner with Rhonda L. Blair (Oxford, 1985), 90–91). In 'Scott and Crabbe: A Meeting at the Border', *Eighteenth Century Life*, 22 (1998), 123–40, Gavin Edwards analyses the mutual debts of Crabbe and Scott with particular reference to *The Heart of Mid-Lothian*.

15.11–24 Much have I fear'd ... snatch his prize George Crabbe (1754–1832), *The Borough* (1810), Letter 20, 'The Poor of the Borough— Ellen Orford', lines 78–91, in Crabbe, *Poetical Works*, 1.546.

15.29–30 new novel ... snugly intrenched ... beneath Stair's Institutes this is usually taken to be an anecdote about Scott himself; see Arthur Melville Clark, *Sir Walter Scott: the Formative Years* (Edinburgh and London, 1969), 244.

15.30 Stair's Institutes James Dalrymple, Viscount Stair (1619–95), twice Lord President of the Court of Session (1671–81 and 1689–95), but best known for his *Institutions of the Law of Scotland* (1681; see *CLA*, 263), in which modern Scots law was first given articulate form.

15.31 Morrison's Decisions W. M. Morison (d. 1821), *Decisions of the Court of Session from Its Institution until ... 1808*, 42 vols (Edinburgh, 1811).

15.33 Dalilahs Delilah is the woman whom Samson loved and who betrayed him in Judges 16. John Dryden refers to ranting passages in his earlier plays as 'those Dalilahs of the theatre' in his Dedication to *The Spanish Friar* (1681): *The Works of John Dryden*, ed. Walter Scott, 18 vols (Edinburgh, 1808), 6.377. Scott used the phrase of his childhood love of ballads in his 'Memoirs' (*Scott on Himself*, ed. David Hewitt (Edinburgh, 1981), 28), and of Abbotsford in *Letters*, 5.60. The normal English spelling of the name is *Delilah*; the spelling *Dalilah* originates in the Septuagint and is used in the Vulgate.

15.36–37 at the bar, within the bar, and even on the bench advocates, King's Counsel (the most senior advocates, appointed as counsel to the crown, who wear a silk instead of a stuff gown), and judges. The *bar* was originally the barrier separating the immediate precinct of the judge from the rest of the court, and at which prisoners were stationed for trial and sentence.

15.40 Ancient Pistol devouring his leek see *Henry V*, 5.1.14–63.

15.40 I read and swear see *Henry V*, 5.1.44.

15.42 State-trials trials for treason. Various collections were published in the 18th century. Scott owned *A Complete Collection of State Trials and Proceedings for High Treason*, ed. T. B. Howell, 32 vols (London, 1811–20); *CLA*, 30. Volumes 1–10 were published as *Cobbett's Complete Collection ...*; Vol. 33 and the index, ed. T. J. Howell, were published later.

15.42 Books of Adjournal the records of trials before the High Court of Justiciary (the highest criminal court in Scotland which tries the most serious offences).

15.45 coinage of his brain see *Hamlet*, 3.4.137.

16.4–5 the place in which the Scottish Parliament met the Scottish Parliament met in the tolbooth in 1438, and continued to meet there from time to time until 1639.

16.5–6 Jamie's place of refuge on 17 December 1596 James VI was conferring with the Lords of Session in the Tolbooth Kirk when a Protestant mob meeting in the Little Kirk (Haddo's Hole) rose up in the belief that the King's counsellors were intending to reintroduce Catholicism. The King retreated to the tolbooth for safety. See note to 24.31, and maps, 771, 772.

16.7 The sword of the Lord and of Gideon Judges 7.18, 20: the battle cry of Gideon, used to rally those who thought they fought for the Lord.

16.8 wicked Haman Esther 7.6. Haman sought to turn the Persian king against the Jews and was hanged on the gallows he had prepared for them.

16.10 sands of their life were ebbing Scott fuses the images of the sand in the hour-glass of life running out (compare *Pericles*, 5.2.1), and the *tide* of life (see *OED, tide*, 9).

16.23   Causes Célèbres of Caledonia   presumably a sequel to Hugo Arnot, *A Collection and Abridgement of Celebrated Criminal Trials in Scotland from AD 1536, to 1784* (Edinburgh, 1785). In 1813 Scott said that he had thought of publishing such a collection himself: see *Letters*, 3.257.

16.26   Magna est veritas et prævalebit   *Latin* great is truth and it will prevail: see 1 Esdras (in the Apocrypha) 4.41.

16.37–38   division of labour   the title given by Adam Smith to the first chapter of *The Wealth of Nations* (1776).

16.39   distinct class in society, subdivided among themselves   the formation of social classes was the subject of much discussion among figures of the Scottish Enlightenment: compare, for instance, Adam Ferguson, *An Essay on the History of Civil Society*, ed. Duncan Forbes (Edinburgh, 1966: originally published 1767), Part 4, Section 1 'Of the Separation of Arts and Professions', 180; John Millar, *Observations concerning the Distinction of Ranks in Society* (London, 1771).

16.42   Bow-Street   magistrates' court, at 4 Bow Street, London, 1740–1880.

16.42   Hatton-Garden   former magistrates' court at 52–53 Hatton Garden, London.

16.43   the Old-Bailey   chief criminal court for Greater London since 1539 when the first Old Bailey Sessions House was erected. It was rebuilt in 1774 and again in 1907.

17.8   Commentaries on Scottish Criminal Jurisprudence   David Hume, *Commentaries on the Law of Scotland respecting the Description and Punishment of Crimes*, 2 vols (Edinburgh, 1797), and *Commentaries on the Law of Scotland respecting Trial for Crimes*, 2 vols (Edinburgh, 1800): *CLA*, 272. The first two volumes cover criminal law and the cases illustrating and refining the application of law, whereas the second work concerns procedures in criminal cases. Hume (1757–1838), nephew of the philosopher, was Professor of Scots Law at Edinburgh University and later one of Scott's colleagues as Principal Clerk to the Court of Session 1812–22. Scott studied under Hume 1790–92, and was greatly impressed: 'I copied over his lectures twice with my own hand from notes taken in the class and when I have had occasion to consult them I can never sufficiently admire the penetration and clearness of conception which were necessary to the arrangement of the fabric of law' ('Memoirs', in *Scott on Himself*, ed. David Hewitt (Edinburgh, 1981), 42). The notes are still in Abbotsford.

17.12   chapel of ease   chapel built for the convenience of those who live far from the parish church.

17.12   slip-shod   *literally* wearing slippers; i.e. in a shabby condition (*OED, slipshod*, 1c).

17.12–13   circulating library   lending library financed by the subscriptions of the members. The first such library in Scotland was founded by Allan Ramsay in Edinburgh in 1726 and by the late 18th and early 19th centuries the circulating library was crucial in making fiction widely available.

17.14   pint of claret   either a Scots pint (1.7 litres) or an English (0.6 litres). Claret was a favourite drink with the Edinburgh upper classes in the 18th and early 19th centuries.

17.16–26   Scottish collection... enactments   compare Hugo Arnot, *A Collection and Abridgement of Celebrated Criminal Trials in Scotland from AD 1536, to 1784* (Edinburgh, 1785), xv: 'The Criminal Records of a Country are an historical monument of the ideas of a People, of their manners and jurisprudence: And in the days of ignorance and barbarism, they exhibit a striking, but hideous picture of human nature. The records of Scotland, in particular, present such a frequent display of the extravagance of the human mind, as amuses the fancy after the wearisome detail of form, and the disgusting representation of guilt.'

17.19 long continued civil dissentions of Scotland the civil wars, and the struggle for religious power, from 1543 to 1689.

17.20 hereditary jurisdictions until 1748 many legal offices were hereditary, and barons (landowners who held their land on a feu granted by the crown) had the right to try accused persons of all crimes committed in the area of their jurisdiction except murder, fire-raising, rape, and robbery with violence, as well as to hear civil actions. Sheriffs too were hereditary. The hereditary jurisdictions were abolished by 20 George II, c. 43, which was passed in 1747 and took effect from 25 March 1748. The Act was of the greatest significance in reducing the power of landowners over their feudal vassals and tenants, and in professionalising the law in Scotland.

17.20–21 vested the investigation of crimes in judges magistrates and sheriffs both investigated crimes and presided at trials.

17.24–25 perfervidum ingenium Scotorum *Latin* very fiery temper of the Scots. See George Buchanan (1506–82), *Rerum Scoticarum Historia* (1582), in his *Opera Omnia*, ed. Thomas Ruddiman, 2 vols (Edinburgh, 1715), 1.321: 'Scotorum praefervida ingenia'.

17.32 Plyem the name implies that he bribes voters with liberal supplies of alcohol.

17.32 had carried forward *probably* had taken the horses to a stage beyond the next which is where they would normally have been changed and then returned to their owner with the next coach.

17.35–36 five boroughs which club their shares for a member of parliament by the terms of the Union Scotland had 45 members of the House of Commons. By the act 1706, c. 8, 15 of these were elected by the royal burghs; Edinburgh elected one of these 15, and the other 14 were elected by 14 specified groups of 4 or 5 burghs.

17.39 leading strings child's reins.

18.7–8 Like eagles, they smelled the battle afar off see Job 39.25, 29–30. Scott fuses the idea of the war-horse which 'smelleth battle afar off', with the eagle which 'seeketh the prey, and her eyes behold afar off. / Her young ones also suck up blood: and where the slain are, there is she'.

18.10 petitions and complaints applications to the Court for redress of complaints about corrupt behaviour in officials, magistrates, judges, etc.

18.13–14 sets of boroughs the forms of municipal organisation in burghs as set down in their charters (*SND*, *set* II.6.(8)).

18.14 burgesses resident and non-resident it was common for the charters of royal burghs to require burgesses to be resident. The terms of such charters vary, but non-resident burgesses are likely to have had reduced privileges, including being unable to vote for a member of parliament.

18.16–17 pauvre honteux *French* apologetic pauper.

18.22 remedium miserabile *Latin* wretched remedy; i.e. wretched means of putting things right.

18.23 cessio bonorum *Latin* surrendering of goods, i.e. property. This was a legal proceeding in Scots Law by which a debtor could petition the Court of Session to be released from prison, if innocent of fraud, by surrendering his whole means and estate to his creditors.

18.27 month's confinement according to Stair a debtor had to be detained 'for a considerable time' to be eligible to petition for a *cessio bonorum*, and this reference implies that 'a considerable time' was to be interpreted as a month: James Dalrymple, Viscount Stair, *Institutions of the Law of Scotland*

(Edinburgh, 1681), 4.52.33 (*CLA*, 263).

18.32 foreign fellow not identified.

18.35 the Faculty Faculty of Advocates, the body which regulates advocates, those who are entitled to plead before the judges of the highest courts in Scotland, namely the High Court of Justiciary in criminal cases and the Court of Session in civil.

18.36 Speculative Society a debating society in the University of Edinburgh founded in 1769. Scott joined in 1790 and ceased to be an active member in 1795.

19.3 gown and three-tailed periwig the dress of an advocate.

19.6–8 induced to sign bills with a friend ... composition i.e. Dunover, the drawer, signed bills promising to pay the friend the sum stated on a specified date in the future, which the friend then took to the bank and for which the bank, relying on the trustworthiness of the drawer, gave cash (less a discount which was the bank's charge for the transaction). He received no value, i.e. he received no goods or services in exchange. When the due date came the friend did not return the money, and Dunover was unable to repay the bank, leading to his bankruptcy, and the sequestration of his property to satisfy creditors, who accepted a 'composition', i.e. a payment of so-much in the pound in return for which the debtor was released from his debts.

19.9–10 ten pounds, seven and sixpence £10.37½p.

19.12 grant commission to take his oath a judge's authorisation for someone to take the client's oath in a *cessio bonorum* (see note to 18.23). The preceding narrative is a comic version of the condescendence in which the debtor set out his property, and which was delivered to the court. The debtor next had to take an oath that the condescendence contained a true state of his affairs, and that he had made no conveyance of his property before or after imprisonment that prejudiced his creditors. It was necessary for the judge to grant a commission to administer this oath as the debtor was in prison. The debtor was then liberated.

19.24–25 miry Slough of Despond see *The Pilgrim's Progress*, Part 1, 14–16. The 'Miry Slough' is 'the descent whither the scum and filth that attends conviction for sin doth continually run, and therefore it is called the *Slough of Despond*: for still as the sinner is awakened about his lost condition, there ariseth in his soul many fears, and doubts, and discouraging apprehensions'. Christian falls into the Slough shortly after setting out on his pilgrimage and is helped out. Dunover and Hardie constitute a secular parallel.

19.33 Interest ability to influence because of family, financial or political connections.

19.34 pessimi exempli *Latin* a very bad precedent.

20.9–10 another narrative ... chief amusement to collect see note to 4.1.

20.11 broiled bone grilled meat (on the bone): see *OED*, bone, noun 6a.

20.11 Madeira negus mixture of Madeira (the amber-coloured fortified wine produced in the island of Madeira), hot water, spices and sugar. *Negus* takes its name from its inventor, Col. Francis Negus (d. 1732).

20.12 picquet piquet, a card game for two people, played with 32 cards (cards from 2–6 are excluded), in which points are scored on various combinations of cards and on tricks.

20.15 summary case *Scots law* case involving a simplified procedure and, in a pecuniary claim, with a low limit.

20.29 writer to the signet member of the most prestigious body of solicitors in Scotland. Writers to the Signet were originally the clerks by whom signet writs (i.e. writs and warrants of the Court of Session) were prepared; they now perform specialised functions for the Court.

21 motto see Matthew Prior (1664–1721), 'The Thief and the Cordelier', lines 1–8.

21.2 Grève Place de Grève, on the N bank of the Seine in Paris, formerly the place of public execution. In 1830 it became Place de l'Hôtel de Ville.

21.8 squire of the pad ... knight of the post footpad, someone on foot who robs travellers, called a squire to distinguish him from the highwayman (the knight) who is on horseback when he robs post-coaches, i.e. coaches carrying mail. While the quotation invites this interpretation of 'knight of the post', the *OED* definition is 'notorious perjurer; one who gets his living by swearing false evidence'.

21.11 Tyburn from 1388 to 1783 the site of the public gallows in London, at what is now called Marble Arch at the W end of Oxford St.

21.12–13 solemn procession ... Oxford-Road prisoners were taken for execution from Newgate Prison on the site of the Old Bailey in Newgate St, by High Holburn to Oxford Rd (now Oxford St) and on to Tyburn (see note above).

21.14 Grassmarket below the S side of Edinburgh Castle, the site of a weekly market from 1477. The E end of the Grassmarket was the place of public execution from after the Restoration in 1660 to 1784, when executions were transferred to the W end of the old tolbooth. For an illustration see Grant, 2.233.

21.27–28 five-and-twenty years, or thereabouts the last execution in the Grassmarket was in 1784. The block on which the gallows were mounted remained until 1823.

21.32 double ladder it was usual for prisoners to mount a ladder with the rope around their neck and jump off, but if fright prevented them they had to be 'turned off' by the hangman.

21.36–37 school-boys, when I was one of their number Scott (if 'I' is Scott and not Peter Pattieson) was a pupil of the High School of Edinburgh 1779–83.

21.41 Parliament-house, or courts of justice the complex of buildings on the S side of Parliament Sq. off the High Street. Parliament House was built between 1632 and 1639 for the Court of Session and the High Court of Justiciary, and for the meetings of the Estates, the Scottish Parliament, which took place in Parliament Hall. After the parliamentary Union with England in 1707, the south end of the Hall was used for sittings of the Outer House of the Court of Session; the other was occupied by stalls (as described by Scott in a footnote to *Redgauntlet*, ed. G. A. M. Wood with David Hewitt, EEWN 17, 3), and used for legal consultations. The court was given a new chamber in 1779, and Parliament Hall then became a general meeting place for advocates and others with business in the courts. The buildings were extensively remodelled in 1804–11, and given a new unified frontage.

22.1 Newgate see note to 21.12–13. From 1783 executions took place immediately outside the prison: see the illustration in *The London Encyclopædia*, ed. Ben Weinreb and Christopher Hibbert (London, 1983), 545.

22.3 He no longer walks the condemned prisoner walked from the tolbooth up the Lawnmarket, and down the West Bow to the E end of the Grassmarket. See map, 771.

22.13 8th day of September, 1736 see Historical Note, 522.

22.27 Contraband trade smuggling was endemic in 18th-century Scotland. The Union of 1707 created a single fiscal system for Great Britain, although the introduction of taxes on malt and salt in Scotland was to be delayed. However, customs and excise were levied at higher rates and on a wider range of goods in England than they had been in Scotland, and the collection had been more efficient. In Scotland resentment about rates of tax, particularly when rates discriminated in favour of English production or English tastes, about extending the malt tax to Scotland in 1713, about increasing the rate and extending its application in 1725, and about the increasing efficiency in collecting tax, all fuelled popular support for smuggling. See Bruce Lenman, *The Jacobite Risings in Britain 1689–1746* (London, 1980), 99–102.

22.35   reigns of George I. and II.   respectively 1714–27, and 1727–60.

22.39   two firths   the Firth of Forth to the S; the Firth of Tay to the N.

23.2   Pathhead   now part of Kirkcaldy, in Fife.

23.11   right to make reprisals   see *Life of Porteous*, 15.

23.13   Collector of the customs   senior customs officer in overall charge of an area and directly responsible to the Commissioners of Excise. The historical figure was James Stark.

23.14   Kirkaldy   Kirkcaldy, town on the N shore of the Firth of Forth, directly opposite Edinburgh.

23.14   Pittenweem   small port on the Fife coast, E of Kirkcaldy.

23.19   Robertson   the historical figure was George Robertson, an innkeeper in the Bristo area of Edinburgh, just outside the city gate. James Ratcliff when arrested (see note to 59.3) was accompanied by one James Robertson, who like Ratcliff came from Spalding in Lincolnshire. This probably helped to make the link in Scott's mind between the George Robertson of the novel and Lincolnshire.

23.35–36   like the Levite in the parable   who passed by on the other side in the parable of the Good Samaritan: see Luke 10.32. A *Levite* was a subordinate official of the Temple in Jerusalem.

23.37   military were called in   as there was no organised police force in most places, the army was used whenever force might be required.

24.31   three churches into which the Cathedral of Saint Giles is now divided   after the Reformation in 1560, the collegiate church of St Giles was subdivided at different times into various churches, a police office, and a meeting place for the General Assembly of the Church of Scotland (see note to 90.34). The places mentioned in the novel are: the Tolbooth Kirk in the SW corner of St Giles; the Little Kirk, also known as Haddo's Hole, in the NW corner; and the Preston Aisle in the SE corner, in which the General Assembly met (see maps, 771, 772).

25.6   City Guard   constituted in 1648, confirmed by the act 1690, c. 65, and disbanded 1817. It was composed originally of Edinburgh citizens, but by the 18th century was a corps of veterans recruited (for the most part) from the Highland regiments.

25.8   just, or of the unjust   see Matthew 5.45, and Acts 24.15.

25.19   redeem the time   save time from being lost, i.e. make good use of time: see Ephesians 5.16; Colossians 4.5.

25.34–37   Wilson ... collar of his coat   see *Life of Porteous*, 16. Scott here alters the historical record: the escape took place before the service had begun.

26   motto   see Robert Fergusson, 'The Daft Days' (1772), lines 61–66.

26.27–40   John Porteous ... brutal husband   see *Life of Porteous*, 5–12.

26.29   citizen of Edinburgh   Stephan Porteous, tailor, admitted as a burgess of Edinburgh 20 March 1695 (Roughead, 4).

26.32   States of Holland   the Dutch Parliament from the 15th century to 1796, consisting of the three estates, the clergy, the nobles and the commons.

26.33   Scotch-Dutch   the brigade of Scots soldiers that served the Estates of the Netherlands from the time of William the Silent in the 16th century until 1782. Porteous is said to have served until the Treaty of Utrecht (1713) which concluded the War of the Spanish Succession, at which time there were 6 Scots regiments in the service of the Dutch. See Vol. 2 (1698–1782) of *Papers Illustrating the History of the Scots Brigade in the Service of the United Netherlands*

1572–1782, ed. James Ferguson, 3 vols (London, 1899–1901).

26.35 services were required originally appointed as adjutant to the City Guard in 1715, Porteous served until 1716. He was reappointed in 1718, and made one of the 3 captain-lieutenants in 1726 (Roughead, 7–9).

26.36 disturbed year 1715 due to the Jacobite Rising from September 1715 to February 1716 (the Jacobites were followers of James VII and II, who vacated the throne in the Revolution of 1688–89, and of his descendants). The Earl of Mar began the rebellion in Braemar in September. In October a detachment from the main army crossed the Forth, and got to within two miles of Edinburgh. On 13 November 1715 at Sheriffmuir near Stirling they met government forces under John Campbell, 2nd Duke of Argyle (1678–1743), who features in this novel. The battle was inconclusive but it contained the rebellion and thus ensured its failure.

27.2–3 is, or perhaps we should rather say was the City Guard numbered only 75 in Scott's early years, and became yet smaller before its disbanding in 1817.

27.9 popular disturbance might be expected 'The Lord Provost was ex-officio commander and colonel of the corps, which might be increased to three hundred men when the times required it. No other drum but theirs was allowed to sound on the High Street between the Luckenbooths and the Netherbow' (Magnum, 11.199).

27.9 Poor Fergusson poet (1750–74). Fergusson's first poetry was published in 1771 in Thomas Ruddiman's *Weekly Magazine, or Edinburgh Amusement*; his first Scots poem, 'The Daft-Days', appeared in January 1772. In the 19th century it was believed that Fergusson's health problems were due to excessive drinking (hence 'irregularities').

27.14–17 Gude folk ... cockad Robert Fergusson, 'Hallow-Fair' (1772), lines 100–03.

27.28–33 O soldiers ... their bluid see Robert Fergusson, 'The King's Birth-Day in Edinburgh' (1772), lines 61–66.

27.29 Land o' Cakes see note to title-page.

27.32 Lochaber axe long-handled halbert; it combines spear and battle-axe and has a hook for catching fugitives etc.

27.40–44 Lear's hundred knights ... What need one? see *King Lear*, 2.4.200–62.

28.7 phantom see Alexander Pope, *Moral Essays* (1731–35), 2.241–42.

28.8 statue of Charles the Second erected in 1685, the statue stands in Parliament Sq.

28.11 glide around see Alexander Pope, *Moral Essays* (1731–35), 2.241–42.

28.12 Luckenbooths row of houses and shops between St Giles and the N side of the High St, demolished in 1817. At the E end of the Luckenbooths was Allan Ramsay's shop and circulating library; at the W end was the tolbooth. From 1785–1817 the guard-house was in the ground floor of the tolbooth. For illustrations see Grant, 1.128 and 153; for maps see 771, 772.

28.12 their ancient refuge in the High-street the original guard-house was in the middle of the High St between the Tron Kirk and the town cross; it was demolished in 1785. For illustrations see Grant, 1.136–37.

28.14 frail memorials see Thomas Gray, *An Elegy Written in a Country Churchyard* (first published London, 1751), line 78.

28.15 John Dhu i.e. John Black, *Dhu* being Gaelic for 'dark' or 'black'. See also note to 28.19.

28.17 High School the High School of Edinburgh, housed in a new building in Infirmary St from 1777.

28.19 Kay's caricatures 'cartoon' sketches of Edinburgh citizens done by

John Kay (1742–1826), owner of a print-shop in Parliament Close (now Square). They were published in book form after his death as *A Series of Original Portraits and Caricature Etchings by the Late John Kay* (1837–38). Dhu is the middle figure in the second etching, dated 1784.

28.21–22 perpetual alarm for the plots and activity of the Jacobites many Jacobites (see note to 26.36) maintained a correspondence with the exiled monarchy until after 1750, and were perpetually involved in plots to regain power, although most were not engaged in the risings of 1689, 1708, 1715, 1719 and 1745. The defeat of the Jacobites in April 1746 at the battle of Culloden, the subsequent military repression in the Highlands, the forfeiting of estates, and the acts ending heritable jurisdictions (the right of landowners and chiefs holding lands from the crown to act as judges for offences committed within their own areas), brought about the end of Jacobitism as a political force.

28.26 king's birth-day 4 June, birthday of George III (1738–1820; king 1760). The day was kept as a public holiday, celebrated 'with dinners and claret and squibs and crackers and Saturnalia' (*Journal*, 311). The populace of Edinburgh seems to have enjoyed throwing 'clarty unctions' (filth and mud) at the City Guard: see Robert Fergusson, 'The King's Birth-Day in Edinburgh' (1772).

29.11 upon the principal street of the city in the Lawnmarket.

29.18 Welch Fusileers formed in 1689, the regiment was designated the Royal Welch Fusileers in 1727.

29.19 no drums but his own were allowed to be struck among the privileges granted to free burghs was the right to regulate their own policing, and as one sign of their independence burghs prevented royal troops from marching with drums beating on city streets without their express permission. The City Guard took precedence over regular troops within Edinburgh. See also note to 27.9.

29.25–26 fatal morning when Wilson was appointed to suffer Wednesday, 14 April 1736. Wednesday was the normal day for executions.

29.26–31 ordinary appearance ... fierce see *Life of Porteous*, 6.

29.32–35 step was irregular ... disordered see *Life of Porteous*, 17.

30.7 exquisite torture *Life of Porteous*, 17.

30.11–15 It signifies little ... May God forgive you see *Life of Porteous*, 18.

30.29 Cameronians the extreme wing of Presbyterianism, named after Richard Cameron (1648–80). The Cameronians formed themselves into a separate religious and political party (see note to 176.1–2) after the defeat of the Covenanters (see note to 30.30) at Bothwell Brig in 1679, and in the Sanquhar Declaration (1680) rejected all compacts with the state. They are called 'ancient' because they attracted few new supporters after Cameron's death at Airds Moss, and so a Cameronian in 1736 is likely to have been at least 70.

30.29–30 execution of their brethren over 20 Cameronians were executed in the Grassmarket in 1680 and 1681.

30.30 glorified the covenant became martyrs in the Covenanting cause. The National Covenant of 1638 was a manifesto opposing the religious innovations of Charles; it had widespread support in Scotland. The Solemn League and Covenant of 1643 was a treaty by which the Scottish Parliament promised military support to the English Parliament against Charles I in return for what it believed would be England's adoption of Presbyterian church government (whereby the church is governed by a system of courts, kirk session, presbytery, synod, and General Assembly). In the period after 1662 those Scotsmen who continued to support the principles of the National Covenant, and who opposed Charles II's repudiation of the National Covenant and his forcible imposition of

Episcopacy on Scotland, became known as Covenanters.

30.41–42   young fellow ... cut the rope   a few witnesses (including the 2 bailies who were in official attendance) agreed that the body was cut down by someone other than the hangman (*Criminal Trials*, 117; Roughead, 277, 284) but the detail about dress may have been suggested by the first witness for the defence who testified that he saw a man 'with a silk napkin about his neck' (*Criminal Trials*, 187).

31.1   decent grave   i.e. in consecrated ground. Wilson was buried in Pathhead, now within Kirkcaldy, Fife, on 15 April 1736.

31.6–12   snatched a musket ... hurt and wounded   see *Life of Porteous*, 18; the full trial report is in *Criminal Trials*, 77–204. Porteous was tried for the murder of 6 people, and wounding 11, but the number of dead and wounded was not exactly determined. On 19 April 1736 the *Caledonian Mercury* said that it was informed that 'two or three' more had died in the country (Roughead, 237).

31.18–19   It is not accurately known whether Porteous commanded this second act of violence   Duncan Forbes, the Lord Advocate (see note to 42.12), leading for the prosecution, made this charge (*Criminal Trials*, 87), but the statements of witnesses do not support it.

31.24–32   Porteous ... blackened   see *Criminal Trials*, 122.

31.40–41   trial ... long and patient hearing   at a Scottish criminal trial in 1736 there were usually 5 judges who heard the libel, i.e. indictment, in open court and then required a written statement from the prosecution (the 'Information for His Majesty's Advocate'), and a written statement from the defence ('Information for John Porteous'). After considering the indictment and the legal arguments both oral and written they decided on relevancy: 'The proper question concerning the relevancy of the libel is only this: Is the form of the libel good? Does it set forth in the outset an offence which is known in the law of Scotland? Does it relate the fact with the necessary circumstances? And does the fact so related amount to the species of crime which is stated in the major proposition of the libel?' (Hume, *Trial*, 2.43). The judges gave their answer in an *interlocutor of relevancy*. They then required evidence to be heard before an assize, or jury, of 15 people. In this case the opening hearing was held on Monday 5 July 1736, and the judges ordered the 'Information' for the prosecution to be deposited with the Clerk of the Court by 6 pm on Friday 9th and for the defence by Tuesday 13th. The decision about relevancy was made on Friday 16th, and the trial was held on 19 and 20 July. Twenty-eight witnesses for the prosecution were called and 16 for the defence. Porteous was found guilty, and sentenced to be hanged on Wednesday 8 September 1736.

31.41   High Court of Justiciary   the highest criminal court in Scotland which tries the most serious offences.

31.42–32.14   positive evidence ... indignities   see *Criminal Trials*, 159–99.

32.14   verdict of the jury   see *Criminal Trials*, 200–01.

32.20   Lords of Justiciary   the judges of the High Court of Justiciary (see note to 31.41), who have the courtesy title 'lord'.

32.20   passed sentence   see *Criminal Trials*, 202.

32.23   moveable property   i.e. cash, investments, household goods, etc., excluding land, houses, commercial premises, etc. (real property).

32   motto   the words are associated with a water-spirit, the kelpie, who lures men to their death as they cross a ford: see *kelpies*, in Katherine Briggs, *A Dictionary of Fairies* (London, 1976). Although a recognised folk-motif (Stith Thompson, *Motif-Index of Folk Literature*, 6 vols (Indiana, 1955), D1311.11.1), the first written record of it in English seems to be in Scott's note to John Jamieson's poem 'Water Kelpie', in *Minstrelsy of the Scottish Border* (*Minstrelsy*, 4.346).

32.29 On the day Scott here departs from the historical record: the reprieve was signed on 26 August, and arrived in Edinburgh on 2 September; the next day the High Court instructed the magistrates to put off the execution until 20 October (*Criminal Trials*, 203–04; Roughead, 68). The actual date of Porteous's lynching was 7 September, and thus no crowd gathered on 8 September to witness the hanging.

32.36–37 property of the Knights Templars, and Knights of Saint John on the W side of the West Bow, near its junction with the Grassmarket. The Knights were originally orders formed to protect pilgrims to the Holy Land and to provide them with hospitality. The Templars came to Scotland during the reign of David I (1124–53). After the suppression of the order in 1312, these properties passed to the Knights of St John who held them until the Reformation. Robert Chambers writes: 'When any of their grounds were feued out to secular persons, it was strictly a part of the bargain, that the houses erected thereon should wear the badge of their order, in token of their superiority over the ground, and of the tenants being liable to answer only to their Courts' (*Traditions of Edinburgh*, 2 vols (Edinburgh, 1825), 1.148; *CLA*, 332).

33.26 usual hour between 2 and 4 pm.

33.37 Information for Porteous see note to 31.40–41. For the text see *Criminal Trials*, 107–54.

34.7–8 of late years they had risen repeatedly against the government e.g. in 1701 (over the Darien fiasco), 1705 (the Captain Green affair), 1706 (the Union), 1720 (food riots), 1724 (the Levellers Revolt over enclosures), 1725 (malt tax), and 1734 (the imprisonment of two apprentices): see Roughead, 254; and Kenneth J. Logue, *Popular Disturbances in Scotland 1780–1815* (Edinburgh, 1979), 2–7.

34.18–19 the cabinet of Saint James's the council-chamber in the Palace of St James in London, then the residence of the sovereign, and so, by extension, the body of people who met in the council chamber to advise the sovereign.

34.36 higher rank joined in a petition Roughead reproduces two petitions, one from Edinburgh and the Borders and the other from the north-east, supported by 69 signatures, including 14 peers (Roughead, 232–34). The almost identical wording suggests that one was derived from the other.

35.9 reprieve see note to 32.29.

35.10 under the hand of signed by.

35.10 Duke of Newcastle Thomas Pelham-Holles (1693–1768). Newcastle entered government as a minister in 1724, and was almost continuously in office until his resignation as First Lord of the Treasury in 1762. From 1725–42 Newcastle was one of the two Secretaries of State who had responsibility for both home and foreign affairs, one for the south, and the other for the north including the N of England and Scotland.

35.11 Queen Caroline Caroline of Anspach (1683–1737). She was appointed Regent when her husband, George II (1683–1760; king 1727), visited Hanover, of which he was Elector (i.e. ruler and one of those who elected the Holy Roman Emperor). On this occasion George was abroad from 22 May 1736 to 15 January 1737.

35.23 expected by the magistrates see *Life of Porteous*, vi; Roughead, 71–73, 243–44.

35.27 vain clamour compare 'vain words', a common biblical phrase (see e.g. 2 Kings 18.20).

35.39 executed to death the full (now obsolete) form of 'executed' (*OED*, execute, 6).

35.42–43 the blood of twenty of his fellow-citizens see note to 31.6–12.

36.34 men from the country see *Life of Porteous*, vi; Roughead, 71, 243.

37.4 Plumdamas the name is derived from a Scots word for a dried damson or plum, i.e. a prune.

37.7 against law and gospel i.e. against the law of the land and the law of God.

37.11 penny-stane-cast distance to which a penny-stane can be thrown, a penny-stane being a round, flat stone used as a quoit.

37.14–15 this reprieve wadna stand gude in the auld Scots law this is merely 'nationalist' prejudice; it always seems to have been open to the monarch to grant a reprieve.

37.15 when the kingdom was a kingdom Scotland and England united on 1 May 1707, and as a result Scotland ceased to be an independent country.

37.17 king, and a chancellor, and parliament-men James VI left Scotland in 1603, and although he (in 1617) and his successors Charles I (in 1633 and 1641) and Charles II (in 1650–51) visited Scotland no reigning monarch came again until 1822. The chancellor of Scotland was, in the 17th century, considered to be the first minister of Scotland, but the position was abolished by the Act of Union in 1707. After the Union, Parliament met only in London, and thus the 45 Scottish Members of Parliament in the House of Commons and 16 elected peers in the House of Lords were inaccessible.

37.19 naebody's nails can reach the length o' Lunnon see *ODEP*, 575, where this is the first recorded use, but it is probable that it is a proverb only by virtue of Scott's formulation.

37.20 Weary on the devil take.

37.21 Damahoy variant of Dalmahoy, but probably used here because Scots *damas* signifies damask.

37.22 oppressed our trade a common complaint following the Union. Modern historians are sceptical, although they admit that before 1740 all expectations of economic growth were disappointed: see T. C. Smout, *A History of the Scottish People 1560–1830* (London, 1969), 243–44, and Rosalind Mitchison, *A History of Scotland*, 2nd edn (Edinburgh, 1982), 324–30.

37.22–26 Our gentles . . . frae Lunnon the common complaints of uncompetitive economies. England was producing better and cheaper needles than Scotland, and it was easier to order luxuries from London than to obtain them in Edinburgh shops.

37.26 by forpits at ance 3½ lbs (1.5 kg) at a time.

37.27 English gaugers and excisemen gaugers or excisemen in Scotland gathered excise duties from producers in a specified area. The provisions of the Union allowed the gradual raising of custom and excise duties in Scotland to English levels. It became apparent that Scotland was not making a fair contribution to government revenues, and in 1725 a tax on malt of 3*d.* (1.25p) per bushel (53 litres) was introduced. In addition the collection of duties was notoriously lax, and after 1725 English customs officers were frequently appointed as a means of combating widespread connivance of smuggling. See Rosalind Mitchison, in *A History of Scotland*, 2nd edn (Edinburgh, 1982), 324–25.

37.29 Leith the port of Edinburgh.

37.37 sad-coloured clothes clothes of a sombre colour, a phrase used in the late 17th and early 18th centuries, with a probable reference to Don Quixote who was 'the knight of the sad countenance' (Part 1 (1605), Ch. 19).

37.39 Bartholine Saddletree *Barthol* is a Scots form of Bartholomew, and *Bartholine* means 'little Bartholomew'. Saddletree's Christian name may owe something to the apostle St Bartholomew who is supposed to have been flayed alive, and is thus patron saint of tanners. Martin M. Fritzen has identified a legal pedant called Bartoline in John Crowne, *City Politique* (first performed 1682; published 1683; *CLA*, 219): *The Scott Newsletter*, no. 38 (Spring 2001), 7. Tony

Inglis argues in a private communication that Saddletree is named after the Italian jurist Bartolus de Saxoferrato (Bartolo da Sassoferrato: 1314–57), who taught in Perugia, and who wrote commentaries on the Corpus Juris Civilis (i.e. Roman Law as codified under Justinian, *c.* 482–565, Emperor from 527), which were sometimes accorded an authority equal to the code itself. The specific connections cited by Inglis include Bartolo's views on *restitutio in integrum* (see note to 70.23), and his being criticised by Farinaceus (Prospero Farinacci: see note to 213.39–40) on the subject of extra-judicial confession (a debate in which the term *indicia* features: see note to 47.2–3). The *saddletree* is the framework over which leather is stretched when forming a saddle.

37.41 Bess-Wynd formerly on the S side of the Lawnmarket, leading down to the Cowgate, close to the SW corner of the tolbooth. It was demolished in 1809.

37.43 weightier matters of the law Matthew 23.23: 'Woe unto you, scribes and Pharisees, hypocrites! for ye . . . have omitted the weightier matters of the law, judgment, mercy, and faith'.

38.15 grey mare in his shop compare 'the grey mare is the better horse', meaning the wife rules the husband (Ray, 202; *ODEP*, 338).

38.20 gentle King Jamie James VI of Scotland and I of England (1566–1625; king of Scots 1567, and of England 1603). In *The True Law of Free Monarchies* (1598), attributed to James, he sets out his theory of the divine right of kings in reply to the argument in *De Jure Regni apud Scotos* of his once-tutor George Buchanan (1506–82) that kings are responsible to their people. As king, James was a wise and adept compromiser.

38.29 versans in licito *Latin* engaged in a lawful act. This is a common tag without a particular source.

38.30 propter excessum *Latin, literally* on account of excess, as a result of going too far. This is a tag without a particular source.

38.31 pœna ordinaria *Latin, literally* ordinary penalty. An ordinary penalty was one specified in law.

38.41–42 Crossmyloof Grease-my-palm.

39.2–3 cuivis ex populo . . . Quivis *Latin, literally* to or for whom you like from the people. As Butler indicates below, Saddletree uses the wrong case and should have said 'quivis ex populo', i.e. any other person. The phrase 'quivis ex populo' is used by Cicero (106–43 BC), in *Brutus*, 93.320, but as it appears to be a tag in use in the courts no reference to *Brutus* need be implied.

39.5 schoolmaster of a parish after the act of 1696 a school was established in every parish in lowland Scotland; the system was extended to the Highlands in the course of the later 18th century.

39.18 pœna extra ordinem *Latin* extraordinary punishment. An extraordinary punishment was one left to the discretion of the judge; Saddletree is wrong to say that it was capital punishment, although his might be a 'common-sense' interpretation.

39.31 caption warrant to arrest a debtor following his failure to pay up after being required to do so by the courts.

39.32–33 Lord Vincovincentem . . . Vincovintem *Latin, literally* I overcome (*vinco*) the one who overcomes (*vincentem*), i.e. I am victorious over the victor. Mrs Howden presumably mishears: the second element of what she says is without sense.

39.33 lord of state, or a lord of seat i.e. a peer of the realm (who are 'lords', or a judge of the Court of Session (Scotland's supreme court in civil cases), who have the courtesy title 'lord'.

39.35 Session the Court of Session, Scotland's supreme court in civil cases. The Court of Session was created in 1532. In 1736 there were 15 judges,

5 of whom were also judges in the High Court of Justiciary, Scotland's supreme court in criminal cases.

39.41   for as little as ye think o' her   even although you think little of her.

40.1   sitten doon   in addition to the literal sense of 'sat down', the phrase may also imply marriage: a *sittin-doon* is a marriage settlement (see *SND*, *sit*, verb I.B.2; see also *doonsit*, 1).

40.7   riding o' the parliament   the formal procession from the Palace of Holyrood to Parliament Hall which preceded the opening of a parliamentary session. The Canongate and High Street were lined with troops. The procession consisted of: two trumpeters; 157 Members of Parliament (called commissioners) on horseback accompanied each by two lackeys on foot; barons, viscounts and earls on horseback, each accompanied by three lackeys in livery; trumpeters and heralds; the sword, sceptre and crown; the Lord High Commissioner (representing the sovereign) accompanied by servants, pages and footmen; dukes with eight lackeys, and marquises with six; and a squadron of Horse Guards.

40.19   Daidle   see *SND*, *daidle*, *noun*, meaning 'bib' or 'pinafore'; or *verb*, meaning in the first sense 'to waste time', or in the second 'to fondle, dandle [a child]'.

40.25   and what for might na she   and why couldn't she.

40.27   Queen Carline   a pun: the spelling reflects the Scottish pronunciation of 'Caroline', and is also a derogatory Scots term for an old woman.

40.29–30   such a circumstance would not have distressed her majesty   Frederick Prince of Wales (1717–51) was on notoriously bad terms with his parents and had become a figurehead for the opposition to the government of Sir Robert Walpole (see note to 220.15–16).

40.32   be the upshot what like o'   whatever the outcome.

40.39   frae the Weigh-house to the Water-port   i.e. from one end of the town to the other. The weigh-house stood in the middle of the road in the Lawnmarket at its junction with the Bow, while the Water-port was the town gate at the foot of the Canongate.

40.40   ended or mended   proverbial: see *ODEP*, 525.

41   motto   not Sir David Lindsay of the Mount (*c.* 1486–1555) to whom proverbial sayings were commonly attributed in the 18th century but a pastiche of *1 Henry VI*, 2.4.17–18: 'But in these nice sharp quillets of the law, / Good faith, I am no wiser than a daw'.

41.19   Girdingburst   from *girding*, leather belt or strap, and *burst*.

41.19   running footman   footman who runs before a carriage. The best description is in *The Bride of Lammermoor*, ed. J. H. Alexander, EEWN 7a, 175.40–176.7.

41.24   Blazonburry   from *blazon*, a coat of arms, and, perhaps, *burry*, to overcome, overpower.

41.40–42.1   non omnia possumus—potimus—possimis   *Latin* we cannot [do] everything: Virgil (70–19 BC), *Eclogues* (37 BC), 8.63. Saddletree's classical Latin quotation is correct, but his 'law-latin' is wrong and as he struggles to get it right he gets it increasingly wrong. The verb *posse*, 'to be able', is irregular, and *potimus* is a reasonable guess although wrong; the third is quite plainly wrong in its confusion of noun and verb endings.

42.2   Lord President   the senior judge of the Court of Session.

42.7   raxing a halter   *literally* stretching a rope, i.e. getting hanged.

42.12   Duncan Forbes   of Culloden (1685–1747), Lord Advocate 1725–37, and Lord President of the Court of Session 1737–47. The Lord Advocate is the chief legal officer of the crown in Scotland and leads either himself or through deputies all criminal prosecutions before the High Court. Forbes conducted the prosecution case against Porteous.

42.12 Arniston Robert Dundas, Lord Arniston (1685–1753). Dundas was a member of Scotland's most successful political family in the 18th century and had himself a distinguished legal and political career: Lord Advocate 1720–25; MP for Midlothian 1722–37; Dean of the Faculty of Advocates 1725; Judge of the Court of Session 1737; Lord President of the Court of Session 1748.

42.13 muckle greater parts much greater ability.

42.13 if the close-head speak true if what is commonly said is true.

42.14 King's Advocates i.e. Lord Advocates (see note to 42.12).

42.14 wha but they? who in addition to them?

42.15–16 wight Wallace i.e. valiant Wallace, Scottish patriot and hero. Sir William Wallace (*c.* 1270–1305) led the opposition from 1297 against the attempt of Edward I of England to annex Scotland. He was captured in 1305 and sent to London where he was tried for treason and beheaded.

42.19 bend-leather guns light artillery, consisting of a light metal barrel, bound with rope and in a thick leather sheaf. First made in Zurich in 1622, many were subsequently produced in Britain. The best collection is in the Museum of Scotland, Edinburgh. See Geoffrey Parker, *The Military Revolution* (Camidge, 1988), 33–34. *Bend leather* is very thick leather, and used for the heels of shoes, etc.

42.19–20 it's a chance but what it's possible that.

42.21 as for the greatness of your parts in this context *parts* means 'abilities', but Mrs Saddletree seems to give an indecent turn to her husband's phrase at 42.13.

42.31 import our lawyers from Holland in the first half of the 18th century many Scots lawyers, including Duncan Forbes (see note to 42.12), were educated in the universities of Leiden or Utrecht in the Netherlands. The Scots, like the Dutch, placed greater emphasis upon the *principles* of Roman law than on custom.

42.34 Substitutes and Pandex Saddletree's erroneous titles for two legal works commissioned by the Roman Emperor Justinian (AD *c.* 482–565; emperor from 527), and known as the *Institutes* (533) and the *Digest* (533). (*Pandects* is an alternative name for the *Digest*, the full title being *Digesta seu Pandectae*.) The first is a short manual intended as a text-book for students, and the second a codification of the works of the classical jurists.

42.37 Institutes and substitutes are synonymous words in Scots law, the person named as inheritor under an entail is the *institute* while those listed under 'whom failing' are *substitutes*. Saddletree's claim that the terms are 'synonymous' is wrong, but has some justification in that all listed are potential heirs.

42.38 deeds of tailzie deeds of entail. An *entail* prescribed a specific line of inheritance, and which if broken usually involved forfeiture of the inheritance. New entails have been incompetent since 1912.

42.38–39 Balfour's Practiques Sir James Balfour, Lord Pettindreich (*c.* 1525–83), *Practicks: or a System of the more ancient Law of Scotland* (Edinburgh, 1754). His work was written *c.* 1574–83, and edited from his manuscripts in the 18th century.

42.39 Dallas' Stiles George Dallas of Saint-Martins (*c.* 1630–1702), *System of Stiles As now Practicable within the Kingdom of Scotland* (Edinburgh, 1697). The work covers the whole system of legal procedures, documentation and authorisations.

42.42–43 our Scottish advocates are an aristocratic race from the first establishment of the Scottish bar in the 16th century, legal dynasties rapidly developed; and from the Restoration in 1660 there was a strong tendency for advocates to be drawn from landed and titled families.

42.43–43.1 brass ... Corinthian quality alloy of gold, silver, and copper produced at Corinth and much prized in the ancient world as a material for costly ornaments.

43.1 Non cuivis contigit adire Corinthum *Latin* it has not been everyone's lot to visit Corinth: see Horace (65–8 BC), *Epistles*, 1.17.36. Corinth was a very prosperous society, particularly in the 3rd century BC.

43.13–14 all other being formed from it ... learned languages Greek and Latin (the learned languages) are inflected languages, i.e. the root remains constant and the work done by prepositions (of, to, by, with, from, etc.) in modern languages is effected by changing the word-end.

43.15 modern Babylonian jargons see Genesis 11.9: 'the name of it [is] called Babel; because the Lord did there confound the language of all the earth'. Butler means that while Latin and Greek were once *the* languages of Christendom they were replaced by separate modern languages each with its own rules.

43.17 ad avisandum *Scots law Latin* for further consideration.

43.18 make admissions make concessions, surrender points in an argument.

43.21 dative case the case of noun in Latin which indicates *to* or *for* whom something is done, or given, or spoken, etc.

43.22 tutor dative *tutor* is the technical term in Scots law for the guardian of a boy under 14 years complete and a girl under 12 years complete; the term *dative* indicates that the guardian is appointed by a court.

43.29 accuracy of pronounciation in other words Butler gives up speaking his educated Scots English.

43.31–32 every article of your condescendence *Scots law* every point in your statement of the facts of the case.

43.32 confess or deny as accords agree or reject as is agreeable and conformable to law.

43.37 Optat ephippia bos piger *Latin* the lazy ox desires the trappings of the horse, i.e. envies the horse: Horace (65–8 BC), *Epistles*, 1.14.43.

43.37–38 nothing new under the sun proverbial: see Ecclesiastes 1.9; *ODEP*, 580.

43.40 hae skeel o' have skill in, are learned in.

44.4 range out arrange, display.

44.6 Auld Reekie Old Smokey, a standard nickname for Edinburgh.

44.11 De die in diem *Latin* from day to day.

44.15 abandoned to hersell given herself to evil advice or influence.

44.22–23 Saint Leonard's on the western edge of the King's Park, about 1 km S of the Canongate; 'parks' are grass-fields used for grazing animals. See text, 81.22–31.

44.24 In troth in truth, indeed.

44.24 ten years elder see Historical Note, 597.

44.29–30 let sorrow come when sorrow maun *proverbial* grieve only when you have to, said of someone who is anticipating unhappiness: see Ramsay, 108; *ODEP*, 754.

44.33–34 statute sixteen hundred and ninety, chapter twenty-one see *The Laws and Acts Made in the Second Session of the First Parliament of ... William and Mary* (Edinburgh, 1690): 'ACT anent Murthering of Children'. For the text see Historical Note, 591. When reprinted in *The Acts of the Parliament of Scotland*, ed. Thomas Thomson, Vol. 9 (1822), 195, the Act was renumbered c. 50. The crime ceased to be capital in 1809 when Parliament substituted a maximum penalty of two years' imprisonment (49 George III, c. 14).

44.40 waes my heart *literally* woe is my heart, i.e. alas.

45.2 I'se warrant ye I promise you, I assure you.

45.6 presumptive murder see John Erskine of Carnock, *An Institute of the Law of Scotland*, 2 vols (Edinburgh, 1773), 718: 'Where certain facts which do not of their own nature constitute murder, are by statute declared to be murder, the crime thence arising may be called *presumptive* or *statutory* murder'.

45.7 Justiciar Court High Court of Justiciary; see note to 31.41.

45.7 the case of Luckie Smith the howdie a case of presumptive murder (decided on 10 March 1679) cited by John Lauder of Fountainhall (1646–1722), *The Decisions of the Lords of Council and Session, from June 6th, 1678, to July 30th, 1712* (Edinburgh, 1759), 47. Scott located some of Fountainhall's papers in the Advocates' Library around 1816–17 (see *Letters*, 4.33–34), subsequently editing them as *Chronological Notes of Scottish Affairs, from 1680 till 1701* (Edinburgh, 1822).

45.12 Dumfries 110 km SW of Edinburgh.

45.15 getting the scule following the act of 1696 a school was established in every parish in lowland Scotland (see note to 39.5). The schoolmaster was appointed by the heritors, who were the owners of heritable property (normally excluding houses) in the parish. In most country parishes there were few landowners and thus few heritors, and so it would have been easy for a laird (by definition a landowner) to have his natural son appointed schoolmaster.

45.17 free scule o' Dumfries i.e. the parish school in Dumfries.

45.20 bred to the kirk trained for the ministry of the Church of Scotland.

45.21 presbytery ... license presbytery, the second level of the ecclesiastical courts of the Presbyterian Church of Scotland, was responsible for the licensing of preachers, the first step on the road to ordination as a minister of religion. Many schoolmasters were either prospective or failed candidates for the ministry.

45.24 Libberton Liberton, then a village about 4 km S of Edinburgh, now a southern suburb.

45.24 to wait for dead men's shoon *proverbial* to wait for dead men's shoes: see Ray, 95; *ODEP*, 171.

45.25 Mr Whackbairn i.e. Mr Beat-the-child. In the MS Butler had a similar 'professional' name, being called 'Tawse' (the two or three-pronged leather belt formerly used to chastise children in Scottish schools). Scott began using 'Butler' on f. 6 of the MS (47.36) and the earlier references to 'Tawse' were retrospectively altered.

45.32 Quos diligit castigat *Latin* those whom he loves he chastises: see Hebrews 12.6 in the *Vulgate*, where the phrase reads: 'quem enim diligit Dominus, castigat' (for the person the Lord loves he chastises).

45.32 Seneca Lucius Annæus Seneca (*c.* 4 BC–AD 65), Roman philosopher and Stoic. Butler when referring to Seneca's seeing 'advantage in affliction' probably had in mind such dialogues as *De providentia*, which maintains that no evil can befall a good man, and *De consonantia sapientis*, on the self-possession of the wise man.

45.33–34 Heathens had their philosophy ... Jews their revelation Butler means that the Greeks and Romans were reconciled to disappointment and suffering through the teachings of Zeno (335–263 BC) and his followers the Stoics, of whom the most notable was the Roman philosopher Seneca (see note above) who taught that the good man would be indifferent to the tribulations of life. The Jews, on the other hand, were comforted by God's promise, and this can be seen in the Psalms of Lament (e.g. Psalm 22).

45.42 Balfour's Practiques see note to 42.38–39.

46.7 Dumbiedikes an invented name. 'Dumbie', pronounced 'Dummie', is Scots for a dumb person; 'dikes' (referring to the walls round a field or an estate) indicates a territorial designation—landowners were often known by the name of their land.

46.11 **that I should say** may God forgive me for saying so.

46.12–13 **how wad ... manners** how would you like it when it comes to be your own fate, for I can't guarantee against it unless you change your ways.

46.14 **as if a word was breaking your banes** proverbial: see Ray, 286; *ODEP*, 353.

46.15 **in bye** inside.

46.16 **gleg as a gled** keen (i.e. hungry) as a kite. This is not recorded as a proverb in *ODEP*, but it does appear as a set phrase in *SND* where the quoted example is this.

46.16 **I'se warrant ye** I'm sure.

46.20–21 **in loco parentis** *Latin* in the position of a parent.

46.21 **years of pupillarity** *Scots law* from birth to 14 years complete for a boy and to 12 years complete for a girl. The subjects were known as *pupils*.

46.22 **factor loco tutoris** *Latin literally* agent acting in place of a guardian, i.e. a person appointed by the court to manage the property of a pupil (see note above).

46.23 **tutor nominate** guardian nominated by the father by testament (i.e. in a will) or other writing.

46.23 **tutor-at-law** man entitled to be guardian by law, i.e. the closest male relative (the heir at law) on the father's side, over the age of 25, who becomes tutor (guardian) in default of one appointed by the father (see note above).

46.24 **in rem versam** *Latin literally* resulting in the matter being changed; thus the whole phrase 'wad not be in *rem versam*' means 'would not make any difference'.

46.30 **naked when his mother died** see Job 1.21. The phrase implies that Willie's mother died in childbirth.

46.32 **Can ye tell me na really** can't you really tell me.

46.37 **murdrum or murdragium** although *murdrum* does exist in medieval Latin, *murdragium* has not been found, and must indicate Saddletree's scrabbling to find plausible Latin.

46.37–38 **populariter et vulgariter** *Latin* in common and ordinary speech.

46.39 **murthrum per vigilias et insidias** murder by keeping watch and stratagems, i.e. premeditated murder. This does not seem to have existed as a specific crime.

46.39 **murthrum under trust** crime created by the statute of 1587, c. 51, to cover cases where the deceased had accepted hospitality or protection and voluntarily put himself in the killer's power. In 1709 the crime came to be considered aggravated murder under the statute 7 Anne, c. 21.

47.1 **murder presumptive** see note to 45.6.

47.2–3 **indicia or grounds of suspicion** commenting on the 1690 law, Hume writes that it 'authorises, or rather obliges, a jury to convict, on proof of certain *indicia* or presumptions of guilt, without direct evidence of murder' (Hume, *Crimes*, 1.463).

47.7–8 **our sovereign Lord and Lady** William and Mary, joint monarchs when the 1690 Act was passed. These are the opening words of the text of the 1690 act.

47 **motto** see Child, 169B, stanza 17.

47.37–39 **It was computed ... man of war** an example of a sentence added between Scott's writing the MS and the publication of Ed1. See Essay on the Text, 497–99.

48.11 Luckenbooths see note to 28.12.

48.18 Krames formerly a narrow passage between St Giles Cathedral in the S and the Luckenbooths (see note to 28.12) and the tolbooth to the N in the High Street of Edinburgh (see maps, 771, 772). *Krame* is Scots for a merchant's booth or stall.

48.22–23 every buttress and coign of vantage see *Macbeth*, 1.6.7.

48.23 martlett did in Macbeth's Castle see *Macbeth*, 1.6.3–9.

48.26–27 Dutch toys i.e. toys made in Germany. The German reputation for such wares was established in the 16th century.

49.7 Porta adversa ... ad auras Virgil (70–19 BC), *Aeneid*, 6.552–54; Virgil describes the door of Tartarus where the wicked were sent to be punished in their afterlife.

49.13–14 city ... surrounded by a high wall the Flodden Wall. A new wall surrounding the east, south and west of the city was built with great speed to keep out an expected English army after the overwhelming English victory at the Battle of Flodden in 1513; it was strengthened in 1540, 1560, 1591 and 1618.

49.23 Bristo-port ... West-port city gates at the S end of the modern George IV Bridge, and at the W end of the Grassmarket respectively.

49.34 drum beating to arms see the *Caledonian Mercury*, 13 September 1736, in Roughead, 239.

50.2 in orders in holy orders, i.e. an ordained minister of religion.

50.2 placed minister minister appointed by a presbytery to a parish ministry.

50.10–11 hair of your head see Psalm 40.12; Matthew 10.30; Luke 7.38, 44, and 12.7.

50.15–16 to the right hand nor the left common biblical phrase: see e.g. Deuteronomy 2.27, 5.32, 17.11, 20, and 28.14.

50.17 as a dream compare Genesis 41.7; 1 Kings 3.15.

50.39 slouched hats hats with a wide brim worn so that the brims cover the face.

50.40 should have been called women compare *Macbeth*, 1.3.39–47.

51.7–8 the low street called the Cowgate *low* because it is at the bottom of the steep slope down from the High St.

51.9 Cowgate-port city gate at the junction of the Cowgate and the modern St Mary's St.

51.22 Netherbow-port city gate, demolished in 1764, dividing Edinburgh from the Canongate. Brass plaques in the road where St Mary's Street and Jeffrey Street meet the Canongate indicate where it stood. For illustrations see Grant, 1.201, 221.

51.22 Temple-bar marked the W limit of the City of London, between Fleet Street and the Strand. The gate was removed in 1877–78.

51.28 Colonel Moyle commander of the 36th Regiment of Foot (the 2nd Battalion the Worcestershire Regiment) from 1723–37.

51.37 Guard-house see note to 28.12.

51.40 esplanade i.e. the square formed by the N and S sides of the High Street, and the Netherbow-port in the E and the Luckenbooths in the W.

51.41–42 ordinary serjeant's guard the City Guard was divided into 3 squads of 30 men, one under each lieutenant-captain. According to evidence given to the enquiry before the House of Lords (Roughead, 287–88) the squad on duty that evening had only 20 men and an officer, as 7 were suspended on account of suspicion of firing at Wilson's execution, and 3 were ill. Of these 21, 14 were on duty at the guard-house.

51.43 supply of powder and ball the evidence given to the House of Lords after the riot indicates that powder and ball were distributed to the guard by the City treasurer only when the magistrates believed a disturbance was likely: see Roughead, 273, 276.

52.5 a centinel see Examinations of the Witnesses before the House of Lords, Roughead, 288.

52.19 source and origin translation of the Latin *fons et origo*: compare Aulus Gellius (2nd century AD), *Noctes Atticae*, 10.20.7: 'totius huius rei iurisque ... caput ipsum et origo et quasi fons rogatio est' (the chief point itself, the origin and as it were the fount of this whole process of law is the appeal).

52.41 assembled in a tavern Clark's tavern, which was in Writer's Close on the north side of the High Street. The councillors were unable to get to their chamber because of its proximity (in Parliament Square) to the tolbooth.

53.1 Mr Lindsay Patrick Lindsay (d. 1753); Lord Provost of Edinburgh 1729–30 and 1733–34; Member of Parliament for Edinburgh 1734–41.

53.6–7 declined ... any written order this seems to be Scott's invention: in fact it was thought that a letter would take too long to write (see Examinations of the Witnesses before the House of Lords, Roughead, 282, 291).

53.9 having no written requisition from the civil authorities see Examinations of the Witnesses before the House of Lords, Roughead, 292, 297.

53.30–31 sedan chairs closed cabins seating one person and carried on two poles, one at each side, by two or four porters. In 18th-century Edinburgh the porters were commonly Highlanders. In the mid-18th century sedan chairs were more common than coaches being better adapted to the streets and closes of the Old Town. Although the number of coaches increased as the New Town developed from 1767, there were still 188 public sedan chairs for hire in 1779 and their use did not end until 1850. The number of private chairs is not known.

54.7 Cardinal Beatoun David Beaton (*c*. 1494–1546), Archbishop of St Andrews from 1539. He was leader of the pro-French party in Scotland and his anti-English policy and persecution of Protestants, especially the burning of George Wishart in 1546, led to his murder on 29 May 1546.

54.9 judgment of Heaven see John Knox on the murder of Cardinal Beaton in 1546, in *John Knox's History of the Reformation in Scotland*, ed. William Croft Dickinson, 2 vols (London and Edinburgh, 1949), 1.77–78: 'But James Melville ... said, "This work and judgment of God (although it be secret) ought to be done with greater gravity"; and presenting unto him the point of the sword, said, "Repent thee of thy former wicked life, but especially of the shedding of the blood of that notable instrument of God, Master George Wishart, which albeit the flame of fire consumed before men, yet cries it a vengeance upon thee, and we from God are sent to revenge it"'.

54.36–55.15 magistrates ... around their ears see extract from *The Gentleman's Magazine*, and Examinations of the Witnesses before the House of Lords, Roughead, 267–68, 278, 282.

54.40 read the riot-act read a specified portion of the act of 1714 (1 George I, c. 5) which came into force on 31 July 1715 and which declares that if twelve or more persons 'being unlawfully, riotously, and tumultuously assembled together' and refuse to disperse within an hour after the formula requiring them to do so is read by a competent person they shall be deemed felons.

55.21–22 troops would march down to disperse them an account in the Newcastle papers in the British Library indicates that troops armed with grenades were ready to march into the city from the Castle: Roughead, 244.

55.32 empty tar-barrels see the *Caledonian Mercury*, 13 September 1736, in Roughead, 239.

55.42 long ere it was quite extinguished see the *Caledonian Mercury*, 13 September 1736, in Roughead, 239.

56 motto see *The Merchant of Venice*, 3.1.61–62.

56.12 that day the fiction requires that the reprieve arrived on the day appointed for Porteous's execution, i.e. 8 September, but it had in fact come on 3 September.

56.17 heart was merry within him 1 Samuel 25.36, of Nabal, who was 'churlish and evil in his doings', and who was to die 10 days later.

56.18–19 surely the bitterness of death was past see 1 Samuel 15.32: the words of Agag immediately before being killed by Samuel.

56.31–32 afternoon... giving an entertainment it appears that 3 people dined with Porteous on the afternoon prior to his death, and that he had 2 other visitors including a minister, Robert Yetts, between 4 and 7 pm: see Roughead, 227–28.

56.38 full of bread *Hamlet*, 3.3.80.

56.39 with all his sins full blown see *Hamlet*, 3.3.81. *Full blown* means 'in full bloom'.

57.26–58.1 rush to the chimney... maledictions see the *Caledonian Mercury*, 13 September 1736, in Roughead, 239: 'before the prison door was near burnt down, severals [*sic*] rushed through the flames, up the stairs, demanded the keys from the keepers, and though they could scarce see one another for the smoke, got into Captain Porteous's apartment, calling *Where is the Buggar?* He is said to have answered, Gentlemen, I am here; but what are you to do with me?'

58.9 female disguise see *Criminal Trials*, 303.

58.12 sacrifice will lose half its savour on some 40 occasions in the Bible it is said that sacrifices are of 'a sweet savour' to God: e.g. see Genesis 8.20–21, and Ephesians 5.2.

58.12–13 very horns of the altar see Psalm 118.27. In the Jewish temple there were projections like horns at each corner of the altar. See also Leviticus 4.1–12 on sinning in ignorance, especially verse 7.

58.14–15 die where he spilled the blood of so many innocents see the *Caledonian Mercury*, 13 September 1736, in Roughead, 239; see 'Life and Death of Richard Cameron', in Walker, 1.254; and compare the common biblical phrase 'innocent blood'.

58.20 we do not kill both his soul and body see Matthew 10.28: 'rather fear him which is able to destroy both soul and body in hell', i.e. the devil.

58.22–23 mete to him with the same measure he gi'ed to them see Matthew 7.2; Mark 4.24; and Luke 6.38.

58.31 this last deposit in fact Porteous gave someone 23 guineas (£24.15) for his brother: see the *Caledonian Mercury*, 13 September 1736, in Roughead, 239–40.

58.33–34 felons... jail 17 prisoners are said to have escaped: see the *Caledonian Mercury*, 9 September 1736, in Roughead, 238. The 17 included the 7 members of the City Guard still in prison for firing on the crowd on 14 April 1736.

59.3 Ratcliffe James Ratcliff or Ratcliffe, of 'Spaldon' (Spalding) in Lincolnshire was an actual prisoner in the tolbooth, but took the opportunity to escape (see the Edinburgh Tolbooth Warding and Liberation Book, NAS HH.11/18, p. 173). Ratcliff was apprehended in Perth on 18 May 1731, but escaped from prison, using false keys, on 31 July. He was caught again in January 1736 after breaking into shops in Arbroath and stealing horses in Fife, was transferred to Edinburgh, but escaped on the night of 7–8 September during the Porteous riot. He was re-arrested in 1739, tried, and was condemned to be hanged on 1 August (NAS JC.3/22, 628–37), but on 21 July escaped once more. Caught again in April 1740, he was reported in the *Caledonian Mercury* of 14 April to have been told by the Captain of the tolbooth that 'it was now high

Time to think of a future state, which he must soon enter into', to which Ratcliff is reported to have replied 'that he would lay 5 Guineas against him, that he should not be hanged this Season'. On 29 December the *Mercury* reported that he had 'begun to write the history of his life, with an Account of all his Accomplices and their Receptacles', and that, no doubt, was one factor in granting the pardon which was signed on 23 January 1741. In September 1745 he was once more in the tolbooth, but got out after the Jacobites had taken the city: the Highlanders went off with the keys to the prison, and Ratcliff and others escaped 'having taken off the Lock to the outer door', out of fear of the Castle firing upon the city (NAS HH.11/22, p. 195). Finally in October he was re-arrested having 'gone about the Country since he last got out of Jail, and at the Head of a gang of Villains in Highland and Lowland Dress, with white Cockades' (*Caledonian Mercury*, 16 October 1745). He died in the tolbooth of Edinburgh on 19 June 1746 (NAS HH.11/22, p. 196). Ratcliff was notorious as thief and jail-breaker, but through its regular reporting on him the *Caledonian Mercury* built him into a villain-hero. The sources of Scott's information cannot be determined with certainty, but it would seem that he had read at least the report in the *Caledonian Mercury* of 14 April 1740, and based some of Ratcliffe's negotiation with Sharpitlaw upon it. Scott's note on Ratcliff on 451 is accurate on two points (that Ratcliff was in prison and escaped during the Porteous riot in 1736 and again during the Jacobite occupation of the city in 1745), but it seems certain that he was never one of the keepers of the tolbooth. However, Scott almost certainly knew of François-Eugène Vidocq (1775–1857), a French convict and jail-breaker, who in 1809 offered to use his knowledge of the criminal world in exchange for his freedom. His offer was accepted, and he set up a police department, the Sûreté, under Napoleon, and eventually became its head. In 1817, with only 12 full-time assistants, he is said to have been responsible for more than 800 arrests. Vidocq's memoirs were published in 1828 (*CLA*, 40).
59.10 at the ear of the young woman compare John Milton, *Paradise Lost* (1667), 4.800.
59.22 Better tyne life, since tint is gude fame *proverbial* it is best to lose life since my good name is lost: see 'Take away my good name and take away my life' (Ray, 139; *ODEP*, 322).
60.3–5 If it is murder ... his sentence prescribes compare Hume, *Crimes*, 1.288–90.
60.19 Blood must have Blood see *Macbeth*, 3.4.122, and *ODEP*, 69; compare Genesis 9.6; Exodus 21.23–25; Numbers 35.33 etc.
60.22 briefness of his change brief space of time before he passes from life (*OED*, *change*, 1d).
60.24–25 night-gown and slippers according to the *Caledonian Mercury*, 13 September 1736, Porteous was already in his night-gown and slippers when captured: see Roughead, 239.
60.28 king's cushion seat formed by two people each of whom grasps one of his own wrists and the opposite wrist of the other person (*CSD*, *king*).
60.34 military education Porteous served with the Scots Brigade in the Netherlands: see note to 26.33.
60.41 without time *probably* without giving me time for amendment of life.
60.41–42 sins ... lie at their door let them be responsible for my sins as well as for shedding my blood: see Genesis 4.7.
61.2–3 take your own tale home apply your words to yourself.
61.16 slumbers had been broken the mob was in the Grassmarket about 9.30 pm; it seized the Netherbow-port at 9.45, and obtained entry to the tolbooth about 11.30. Porteous was hanged at about 11.45.
61.27–28 booth ... forced open the story is in the report of the *Caledonian*

Mercury, 9 September 1736; see Roughead, 238, but the guinea (£1.05) seems to be a later accretion.

62.3   image of your Creator   see Genesis 1.26.

62.5   share in every promise of Scripture   the most important being the promise of eternal life: see e.g. 2 Peter 1.4.

62.6–7   blotting his name from the Book of Life   see Revelation 3.5.

62.7   Do not destroy soul and body   see note to 58.20.

62.21   Away with him—away with him   John 19.15: with these words the Jews demand the crucifixion of Christ.

62.22   dyester's pole   at the head of Hunter's Close at the SE corner of the Grassmarket.

62.25–26   the last horrors of his struggles   the details are to be found in *Criminal Trials*, 303–05.

62.42–43   Haddo's-hole   see note to 24.31.

63.2   least said is sunest mended   proverbial: see *ODEP*, 472.

63.22–23   throwing down the weapons   the immediate discarding of weapons is reported in the *Caledonian Mercury*, 13 September 1736, in Roughead, 240.

63.37–38   little or nothing learned . . . principal actors   at the end of Chapter 7 in the Magnum (11.274–82) Scott prints a long memorandum by the Solicitor General, Charles Erskine, on the extreme difficulty in getting evidence concerning the participants that could be used in a criminal trial. See also Roughead, 248–53. What may be the original document is bound into the Interleaved Copy of the novel (MS 23009).

63.40   council of regency   the council appointed to advise Queen Caroline while she was Regent in the absence of George II in Hanover (see note to 35.11), and identical with the Privy Council (see note to 108.32) which advised the King.

64.6   John, Duke of Argyle   John Campbell (1678–1743), 2nd Duke (succeeded 1703). Appointed Queen's Commissioner to the Scottish Parliament in 1705 (i.e. representative of Queen Anne), he supported the Union of England and Scotland (1707). He served as a general under the Duke of Marlborough in the War of the Spanish Succession (1701–13). In 1712 he was appointed commander-in-chief in Scotland, lost office in 1713, was re-appointed under a new government in 1714, and was responsible for checking the Jacobite Rising of 1715 (see note to 26.36). His achievement was not recognised, but he came back into favour in 1719 and was made Duke of Greenwich. He established his reputation as a Scottish patriot, 'a true friend to the country', in 1713 by his opposition to the imposition of the malt tax on Scotland and his strong support in the House of Lords for the dissolution of the Union (a motion which was lost by four votes). His support of Scottish causes repeatedly made him unpopular with the government and the court, but he also repeatedly resigned his offices when he did not get his own way. In the latter part of his life he and his brother the Earl of Islay came to control through corruption and patronage (standard features of 18th-century politics) about half the constituencies of Scotland and were thus Scotland's most important political managers in the period from 1725 to his death. See *Tales of a Grandfather*, 3rd Series, in *Prose Works*, 25.162–66.

64.6–7   sooner . . . hunting field   originally attributed to the Duke of York (later James VII and II): see Alexander Shiels, *A Hind Let Loose* (Edinburgh, 1687), 200 (*CLA*, 69, 72, 73); and Wodrow, 3.348.

64   motto   see 'Oh waly, waly up the bank', lines 17–20, in *TTM*, 170; Percy, 3.144–46; Herd, 1.81–82; *SMM*, no. 158.

64.17   Arthur's-Seat   hill (251m) now surrounded by Edinburgh, but in 1736 about 2 km SE of the city.

64.19 Saint Anton's wall well above St Anthony's Chapel, on the N slopes of Arthur's Seat.

64.25 Salusbury Crags Salisbury Crags, the circle of cliffs to the west of Arthur's Seat. The spelling *Salusbury*, consistently used by Scott in the MS, is not supported by Stuart Harris in *The Place Names of Edinburgh* (Edinburgh, 1996), but early forms of the name cited by Harris suggest that it had a four-syllable pronunciation; thus Scott's spelling probably represents the pronunciation before the spelling and pronunciation were assimilated to those of the English City.

64.33 Pentland Mountains the Pentland Hills, on the SW boundary of modern Edinburgh, stretching further SW for about 30 km.

65.1–3 This path ... new subject of study see Scott's 'Memoirs', in *Scott on Himself*, ed. David Hewitt (Edinburgh, 1981), 33.

65.3 totally impassable the path was reconstructed in 1820.

65.5 Good Town sobriquet for Edinburgh.

65.9 Butler saw the morning arise the path below Salisbury Crags looks W, but in Scott's day it continued round to the SE below the cliffs of Arthur's Seat, following the line of the road which was constructed in the late 19th century.

65.27 Monk's army troops under the command of General George Monk (1608–70) who after Cromwell's victory at Dunbar in 1650 completed the conquest of Scotland for the Commonwealth (see note to 65.42). He was appointed governor of Scotland in 1654, and in 1660, seeing the confusion into which the Commonwealth had fallen after Cromwell's death in 1658, led his army south to restore the monarchy.

65.28–29 storm of Dundee Dundee was taken and sacked, and many of its inhabitants massacred on 1 September 1651.

65.31 independent supporter of the system of church organisation later called Congregationalism which gives each congregation the right to organise itself, independently from any other congregation or organisation. From 1645 the Independents were the strongest party in English government.

65.31–32 promise that the saints should inherit the earth see Psalm 37.9, 11, and 22 where those 'that wait on the Lord', the meek, and 'such as be blessed' by God (collectively 'the saints') 'shall inherit the earth'. The 'fullest comprehension' of the promise implies that it is understood literally.

65.41 Dalkeith 10 km SE of Edinburgh. The castle was a medieval tower, acquired by the earls of Buccleuch in the 1640s.

65.42 Commonwealth the republican government of the British Isles, from 1649 following the execution of Charles I to 1660 when the monarchy was restored, with Oliver Cromwell (1599–1658) as Lord Protector from 1653.

65.43 Restoration the Restoration of the monarchy. Monk left Scotland late in 1659 and reached London in February. After a period of negotiation, Charles II returned as king, and arrived in London on 29 May 1660.

66.2 new-modelled here an ironic term in that the army organised by Cromwell in 1645 during the civil war was known as the 'new model army'; largely composed of cavalry, it combined strict discipline with religious zeal. Monk now looks for soldiers of a different persuasion.

66.5 weighed in the balance, and found wanting like Belshazzar: see Daniel 5.27.

66.14 Middleton John Middleton (*c.* 1608–74), 1st Earl of Middleton. Middleton fought for the Covenanting army and was second-in-command at the Battle of Philiphaugh (1645) when Montrose was defeated. He supported the agreement reached with Charles I in December 1647, and was in the Scottish army fighting for the newly-crowned King of Scots, Charles II, which was defeated by Cromwell at Worcester (1651). He was captured, but later escaped and joined the King in exile.

66.19 Coldstream town on the River Tweed on the Scottish side of the border with England.

66.22 zone ... to use Horace's phrase i.e. Butler's money-belt. Horace (65–8 BC) tells of a soldier who says 'ibit eo quo vis qui zonan perdidit' (a man who has lost his money-belt will go wherever you like): *Epistles*, 2.2.40.

66.24 Beersheba the place where Isaac having found water decided to settle: see Genesis 26.24–33.

66.24 Scottish mile 1977 yds (1.12 imperial miles; 1.8 km).

66.29 evil days and evil tongues see John Milton, *Paradise Lost* (1667), 7.26. Milton describes those who held power after the Restoration and who were implacably hostile to the Commonwealth (see note to 65.42) and its supporters.

66.38–39 air of Scotland was alien to the growth of independence in Scotland Presbyterianism whereby the church is governed by a system of courts (kirk session, presbytery, synod, and General Assembly) was dominant, and was hostile to independence (see note 65.31).

66.42 in the worst of times Sir Thomas Browne, *Christian Morals*, Part 1, paragraph 12, in *The Works of Sir Thomas Browne*, ed. Charles Sayle, 4 vols (Edinburgh 1912), 3.449. Although the context is apposite ('The worst of times afford imitable Examples of Virtue'), the inverted commas seem to point to a better known quotation.

67.1 main guard keep of a castle, cell.

67.1 cavalierism the political philosophy of the Cavaliers who supported the monarchy in the 1630s and during the civil war of 1642–49.

67.8 fines for non-conformity by a proclamation of 23 December 1662 fines of 20s. Scots were to be exacted on those who did not attend their own parish church each Sunday: see Wodrow, 1.285–86.

67.40 task-master term used in Exodus to describe those overseeing the forced labour of the Israelites during their captivity in Egypt: see Exodus 1.11; 3.7; 5.6, 10, 13, 14.

68.4 true-blue the Covenanters (see note to 30.30) wore blue in opposition to the red of royalty, their justification being Numbers 15.38 where the children of Israel are told to wear a 'ribband of blue'.

68.7–8 mail duties, kain, arriage, carriage, dry multure, lock, gow-pen, and knaveship payments and services required of feuars and tenants by landlords and feudal superiors: *mail* was rent; *kain* payment in kind, but chiefly poultry; *arriage* unspecified feudal service; *carriage* transportation provided free to the landlord or superior; *dry multure* proportion of corn ground at the landlord's mill; *lock* quantity of meal exacted as payment for grinding corn; *gowpen* the perquisite of the miller's assistant; *knaveship* small quantity of corn or meal exacted to pay the miller's servants.

68.8–9 all the various exactions now commuted for money the substitution of money rents in place of feudal services during the 18th century was one of the features of the agrarian revolution.

68.10–11 years 1700 and 1701 ... dearth and general distress crop failure led to famine in 1695–99, and 1700 and 1701 would not normally be regarded by modern historians as years of general distress. But Scott's dates have support in that the popular historian Patrick Walker (1666–1745), whose writings inform all the utterances of David Deans, says that King William's 'Seven Ill Years' lasted from 1694 to 1701: see 'Life and Death of Daniel Cargill', in Walker, 2.28–32.

68.12 Citations by the ground-officer legal demands made by the *ground-officer* (estate manager) that Deans pay his rent on the next term day

(Candlemas, 2 February; Whitsunday, 15 May; Lammas, 1 August; Martinmas, 11 November).

68.13–14 decreets of the Baron Court ... insight judicial orders regarding Deans's debts, issued by the Baron Court (i.e. the court pertaining to each estate held as a fief or feu direct from the crown: see note to 17.20) lead to the sequestration of Deans's property, and the *poinding* (seizure and sale) of *outsight* (moveable property such as farm animals and implements) and *insight* (household goods).

68.14 tory here used of the royalists in the religious struggles of 1662–88. In the 18th century it became the name of the political party which generally supported the principle of the hereditary succession to the crown and which was generally considered to have Jacobite sympathies.

68.15–16 Pentland, Bothwell Brigg, or Airdsmoss engagements in 1666, 1679, and 1680 in which Covenanters (see note to 30.30) were defeated by royalist forces.

68.17 routed horse and foot completely overwhelmed. The phrase is a military metaphor and literally means that both divisions of the army were routed.

68.22 term-day one of the four Scottish term-days, when rent became due and leases began and ended. For tenancies the crucial terms were Whitsunday, 15 May, and Martinmas, 11 November (1 William and Mary, c. 35).

68.34 Nichil Novit from the Latin, *nihil novit* (he knows nothing), used as a stock phrase in written records when potential witnesses to a criminal act have no relevant testimony.

68.34–35 procurator ... no solicitors solicitors entitled to act before the Supreme Court formed themselves into a society only in 1784; a *procurator* was entitled to act before the sheriff courts.

68.37–38 the soul-curer and the body-curer see *The Merry Wives of Windsor*, 3.1.90.

69.9 aughty-nine, when I was rabbled by the collegeaners before the Revolution of 1688–89, the students at Edinburgh College (Edinburgh University) were violently anti-Catholic. In 1681 they burned down Priestfield, or Prestonfield, House which belonged to the Lord Provost, a strong supporter of the Duke of York (later James VII and II) who was Catholic, and a persecutor of the Covenanters. They were involved in the destruction of the Chapel Royal at Holyrood in 1688 and took part in riots in 1688–89 before the establishment of a new government.

69.14 yerl's band earl's bond; i.e. Dumbiedikes has lent an earl a sum of money and the agreement specifies payment of interest at set intervals.

69.15 equals aquals equally balanced, fair.

69.16–17 it will be growing, Jock, when ye're sleeping Scott says this message 'was actually delivered ... by a Highland laird, while on his death-bed, to his son' (Magnum 11.294).

69.19 files the stamach upsets the digestion.

69.20 aqua mirabilis *Latin* 'The wonderful water, is prepared of cloves, galangals, cubebs, mace, cardomums, nutmegs, ginger, and spirit of wine, digested twenty-four hours, then distilled': Samuel Johnson, *A Dictionary of the English Language* (London, 1755).

69.23 Mass John familiar name for a minister of religion.

69.28–29 like a prey from the fowler see Psalm 91.3.

69.31–32 stipend and teind parsonage and vicarage the payment of the parish minister's stipend was the responsibility of the heritors (those possessed of landed property) in each parish. *Parsonage* and *vicarage* were originally teinds (tithes) paid to the parson or vicar, as appropriate, but in 18th-century Scotland both were a tax upon certain lands payable in kind (wheat, barley, oats, and peas in the case of parsonage teinds, and grass, kale, carrots, calves, lambs, butter, cheese and fish in the case of vicarage teinds), and from 1633 both were used to maintain the minister.

69.34–35 whiggery ... auld Curate ... the Prayer-Book Dumbiedikes sends away the minister (*whiggery* was an abusive term for Scots Presbyterianism), and compares him unfavourably to the former Episcopalian curate who had been a drinking companion ('Kiltstoup' literally interpreted means 'upturn the drinking flagon'). Some Episcopalians used the set prayers of the English *Book of Common Prayer* (1662), but in Presbyterian worship considerable reliance was put on extempore prayer. The curate probably lost his charge for refusing to take the oath of allegiance to William and Mary after the Revolution of 1688–89.

69.43 curse of Cromwell *proverbial: ODEP*, 162. The hatred felt for Cromwell in Ireland and Scotland as a result of his brutal conquest of the two countries makes this a powerful curse.

70.1 fee or bountith a set phrase: *fee* is the pay due to a servant and *bountith* a gift usually stipulated in the contract of employment.

70.6 b—— probably indicates 'bugger'. The MS form is also 'b——', and while this form might stand for 'bitch' Scott normally writes out that word in full (e.g. at 159.37).

70.11 dear years years in which the price of corn was high, as it was in 1696, 1698 and 1699, but the phrase might be applied to the whole period 1694–1701 (see note to 68.10–11).

70.23 restitutio in integrum *legal Latin* the restoration of a person to the same position as he would have occupied had the legal process not taken place.

70.23 Mammon term of opprobrium for wealth as an object of veneration.

70.29 when it lies sae weel into my ain plaid-nuik *literally* when it fits my own pocket so well; i.e. fits in so well with my own estate.

70.39 dispone Beersheba at no rate don't make over Beersheba in any circumstances.

70.40 bite and soup a small amount to eat and drink.

71.1 soughed awa breathed his last, gradually slipped away.

71.1–2 De'il stick the minister for words see C. M. Jackson-Houlston, *Ballads, Songs and Snatches* (Aldershot, 1999), 43. *De'il stick the minister* means 'may the devil do away with the minister'. The version of the song recorded in *Songs and Ballads of Northern England*, ed. John Stokoe and Samuel Reay (1893), Jackson-Houlston's source, seems to be a parallel version to Scott's source.

71.6 guardian as young Dumbiedikes is 'fourteen or fifteen' (see text, 69.1) he has a guardian who controls his property.

71.10 eat recognised 18th-century form of 'ate'.

71.10–11 original malediction i.e. Adam and Eve's expulsion from paradise: see Genesis 3.16–24.

71.17 only possible straight line after the Revolution of 1688–89 the Scottish Parliament abolished 'prelacy' (government of the church by bishops), restored the ministers excluded in 1662, and established Presbyterian church government, but it did not create a theocracy based on the covenants (see note to 30.30), Deans's 'straight line'. Many of the Covenanters were disaffected and considered the new church to be 'erastian', i.e. a church controlled by secular power and motivated by secular concerns (see note to 90.17).

71.18 right-hand heats and extremes, and left-hand defections common Covenanting terminology: see Patrick Walker, 'Life and Death of Alexander Peden', in Walker, 1.18–19, 102. See also note to 50.15–16. For Deans the defections were the Church of Scotland's compromises with the state (see note to 90.16–18), as well as the worldliness of the ruling classes.

71.30 defections of the times standard Covenanting phrase. See also notes to 71.17–18, and 90.16–18.

71.34 anti-national while it is not possible to be certain of the meaning of this term, the most probable signification is 'opposed to a national church'. The primary aim of the National Covenant in 1638 was the establishment in perpetuity of a single national Presbyterian church in Scotland, described in the National Covenant as the only 'true Christian Faith and Religion', but by the 18th century this concept was under attack: see e.g. note to 112.13.

72.2 covenanted reformation standard phrase in Covenanting literature (e.g. see James Renwick, quoted in Wodrow, 4.148–49). It was believed that the National Covenant of 1638 (see notes to 30.30 and 173.23) was a second Reformation which re-established the first Reformation on its proper and original foundation (see Wodrow, 1.1). As the Privy Council in 1639 had required the whole nation to subscribe to the National Covenant, it was also considered the promise to God made by the Scottish people, including their king, to maintain the reformed faith and the Presbyterian government of the church.

72.4 breaking down the carved work see Psalm 74.6.

72.4 our Zion the description of the ideal state created by the National Covenant; this idea of 'Zion' is common in Covenanting literature (e.g. see Walker, 1.259).

72.4–5 sawing the craft wi' aits . . . pease sowing the croft with oats, but I say peas. It was a common mode of literary mockery in a later era to make Covenanters invoke the whole Covenanting tradition to justify sensible advice.

72.12 that singular Christian woman see 'Life and Death of Alexander Peden', in Walker, 1.61.

72.13–14 whose name was savoury to all that knew her for a desirable professor who had a reputation for spirituality to all who knew her as a godly Christian. See 'Life and Death of Richard Cameron', in Walker, 1.285: 'Barbara Brice, and Marion Kinloch my first wife (whose names are savoury to all who knew them, for two desirable Christians)'.

72.14 Hochmagirdle fictitious place, meaning 'cause my girdle [belt holding up lower garments] to fall'.

72 motto George Crabbe (1754–1832), 'The Parish Register' (1807), Part 2, 'Marriages', lines 435–40, in Crabbe, *Poetical Works*, 1.249.

72.26 parts and portions standard phrase from a Scottish lease.

72.30–31 declined into the vale of years declined into old age, was old: *Othello*, 3.3.269–70.

73.16 uninclosed common land without fences or other divisions used by all members of a parish or locality for grazing livestock.

73.36 noisy mansion the phrase used of the school in Oliver Goldsmith, *The Deserted Village* (1770), line 195, in *Collected Works of Oliver Goldsmith*, ed. Arthur Friedman, 5 vols (Oxford, 1966), 4.295.

74.7 pons asinorum *Latin* the bridge of asses, a reference to the 5th proposition of the 1st book of the *Stoicheia*, by Euclid (lived *c.* 300 BC), which was found difficult by beginners; now proverbial: *ODEP*, 637.

74.12 Virgil's Georgics poem on agriculture in 4 books, written by Virgil 37–30 BC.

74.14 Columella Lucius Junius Moderatus, who wrote *De Re Rustica* ('About Rural Matters'), in 12 books, about AD 65.

74.15 Cato the Censor Marcus Porcius Cato (234–149 BC), called 'the Censor' because he was elected to that office (which was responsible for keeping the roll of citizens) in Rome. Although best known as a moralistic politician, he wrote a prose treatise on agriculture (*De Agri Cultura*) about 160 BC.

74.22 Gallio Lucius Annaeus Novatus, bother of the philosopher Seneca, who as proconsul of Achaea (on the N coast of the Peloponnese in Greece) *c*. AD 52 refused to consider the case put by the Jews against Paul, caring for 'none of those things': see Acts 18.12–17. Deans believes that the Revolution of 1688–89 has not re-established 'Zion', but created a worldly state.

74.22–23 hearts are hardened like the nether mill-stone see Job 41.15 in the Geneva Bible of 1560.

74.26 procure a licence from the Presbytery: see note to 45.21.

74.27 shaft cleanly polished see Isaiah 49.2: 'And he hath made my mouth like a sharp sword; in the shadow of his hand hath he hid me, and made me a polished shaft'. See also 'Life and Death of Walter Smith', in Walker, 2.64.

74.27 body of the kirk see Colossians 1.18.

74.28 sow, to wallow in the mire see 2 Peter 2.22.

74.29 extremes and defections see notes to 71.17–18, and 90.16–18.

74.29 the wings of a dove see Psalm 55.6: 'Oh that I had wings like a dove! for then would I fly away, and be at rest'; see also next note.

74.30 though he hath lain among the pots i.e. although he has suffered great hardship, *or* although he has been among dirty things (such as independency). See Psalm 68.13: 'Though ye have lien among the pots, yet shall ye be as the wings of a dove covered with silver, and her feathers with yellow gold'.

74.41–42 University of St Andrews Scotland's oldest university, founded in 1412. At this period it was known for its intellectual conservatism.

75.33–36 He wasna like his father ... flock Deans lists the characteristics of those who oppressed the Covenanters and the Presbyterian church, but most of the features seen in Old Dumbiedikes are subject to a biblical prohibition as explained below.

75.33–34 nae profane company-keeper see the marginal gloss to Proverbs 24.19 ('Keep not company with the wicked') and 1 Corinthians 5.11–13.

75.34 nae swearer see Matthew 5.34: 'But I say unto you, Swear not at all'.

75.34 nae drinker see Leviticus 10.9, etc.

75.34–35 nae frequenter of play-house, or music-house, or dancing-house sins comprehended within the seventh commandment, 'Thou shalt not commit adultery' (Exodus 20.14). See question 139 in 'The Larger Catechism' of 1647–48: 'The sins forbidden in the seventh commandment ... are: ... lascivious songs, books, pictures, dancing, stage plays; and all other provocations to, or acts of uncleanness, either in ourselves or others' (*The School of Faith: the Catechisms of the Reformed Church*, ed. Thomas F. Torrance (London, 1959), 217–18). For the *Catechisms* see notes to 149.34–36 and 149.36.

75.35 nae Sabbath-breaker see the fourth commandment: Exodus 20.8–10.

75.35–36 nae imposer of aiths in spite of Matthew 5.34–37 ('Swear not at all ... But let your communication be, Yea, yea; Nay, nay'), Covenanters did not refuse in principle to take oaths (unlike Quakers), but they did object to many of the oaths required of them by Charles II and James VII and II's governments as they involved recognising the monarch as the head of the church, a position which in Protestant theology is Christ's alone. It was this issue which drove Covenanters first into dissent and then into rebellion.

75.36 bonds in 1678 the Scottish Privy Council required sheriffs to summon all landholders within their jurisdiction and to have them subscribe to a bond promising to prevent all members of their families, their servants and their tenants from attending conventicles (field-preachings) and unauthorised meetings; this action led directly to the Covenanters' rising of 1679.

75.36 denyer of liberty to the flock this is probably less about the denying of religious liberties than civil: Covenanters, and any thought to sympathise with them, were subject to arbitrary fines, imprisonment, torture, and summary execution.

75.38 some breathing of a gale upon his spirit see 'Life and Death of

Richard Cameron', in Walker, 1.286: 'somewhat of a gale of young zeal upon my spirit'.

76.4–5 marriages ... necessary evil proverbial: see *ODEP*, 910. The proverb comes from the Greek comic dramatist Menander (*c.* 342–292 BC), *Minor Fragments*, 651: 'Marriage ... is an evil but a necessary evil'. Deans shares Paul's attitude to marriage: compare 1 Corinthians 7.8–9.

76.6–7 clipped the wings proverbial: see Ray, 182; *ODEP*, 127. *Clipping wings* involves cutting the flight feathers of a bird to prevent flight. For *wings* as the way to God see Isaiah 40.31.

76.8 mansion of clay combines the Tyndale translation of 2 Corinthians 5.1 ('Oure erthly mancion wherin we now dwell') and Job's references to the body as clay: see Job 10.9, 13.12, 33.6. See also Job 4.19 where God does not put trust 'in them that dwell in houses of clay', a formulation which may be metaphoric.

76.12 Rebecca in the Old Testament the wife of Isaac who 'waxed great ... For he had possession of flocks, and possession of herds': Genesis 26.12–14.

77.14 snail's pace proverbial: see Ray, 210; *ODEP*, 747.

77.15–16 your dull ass will not mend his pace for beating see the gravedigger in *Hamlet*, 5.1.56–57.

77.24 parent used here in the sense of 'progenitor'; Widow Butler was Reuben's grandmother.

77.32 licence as a preacher of the gospel see note to 45.21.

78.4 snares, defections, and desertions see notes to 71.17–18, and 90.16–18.

78.8–9 like refined gold out of the furnace of Davie's interrogatories compare Proverbs 17.3: 'The fining pot is for silver, and the furnace for gold: but the Lord trieth the hearts'.

78.22–23 Him that giveth and taketh see Job 1.21: 'the Lord gave, and the Lord hath taken away; blessed be the name of the Lord'.

78.25 father of the fatherless Psalm 68.5.

78.26 bonnet see note to 193.1.

78.26 Give honour where it is due see Romans 13.7.

78.30 bow bowl. Although the form *bow* is normally considered a spelling of 'boll', this cannot be the sense as a boll of meal would be 140 lbs. It seems more likely that a 'bowl' is meant, as that would make the gift of a forpit (1¾ lbs, or 2.25 litres) of meal seem generous in a time of general scarcity. As 'bowie' (a flat bowl for milk or porridge, also a water or milk pail) is probably a diminutive of 'bow' (from Old English *bolla* or Old Norse *bolli*, meaning 'bowl'), Scott may have recreated *bow* as the non-diminutive form, although it is not recorded as meaning 'bowl' in either *OED* or *SND*.

78.33 puff up see 1 Corinthians 4.6, 18, 19, 5.2; Colossians 2.18.

78.33 inward man see Romans 7.22; 2 Corinthians 4.16.

78.34 Alexander Peden 1626–86. Peden became the minister at New Luce in 1660, but in 1662 refused to take the oath which recognised Charles II as head of the church, and was deprived of his charge. He then led a wandering life, preaching at field conventicles and avoiding capture by royal forces until 1673, when he was sentenced to imprisonment on the Bass Rock in the Firth of Forth. He was liberated in 1678. His life by Patrick Walker was published in 1724: see Walker, 1.1–178.

78.35–36 draps of blude and scarts of ink see 'Life and Death of Alexander Peden', in Walker, 1.83: 'your bits of papers and your drops of blood (meaning our martyrs' testimonies and blood)'.

79.12 again baptizing of bairns as infant baptism was supported by Independency (see note to 65.31) Widow Butler here shows her theological muddle.

79.15 anabaptism system of belief which rejects infant baptism. *Anabaptist* is used as a general term for all the groups who in the 16th and 17th centuries refused to allow their children to be baptised and who reinstituted the baptism of believers. Such groups were denounced by both Luther and Calvin, and were persecuted by Roman Catholics and Protestants alike.

79.15–16 rooted out of the land see Psalm 52.5: 'God shall likewise destroy thee for ever, he shall take thee away, and pluck thee out of thy dwelling place, and root thee out of the land of the living'.

79.16 fire ... sword implies utter destruction. Deans draws on the phrase 'denunciation of fire and sword', which in Scots law was a legal order authorising a sheriff to dispossess an obstinate tenant by burning his house or to proceed against a delinquent of any sort by any means in his power.

79.23–24 outs and ins in the tract of his walk bad times and good times in his path of life. See 'Life and Death of John Welwood', in Walker, 1.207.

79.24 his gifts will get the heels of his grace his gifts will outrun his grace, i.e. his ability will be greater than his spirituality. See 'Life and Death of John Welwood', in Walker, 1.207.

79.27 marriage-garment see Matthew 22.11, where the phrase is 'wedding garment', and signifies the sinner's preparation for union with God.

79.32 let the wind out o' him Walker reports that John Semple prayed of too airy a preacher that God should 'brod [prick] him, and let out the wind of him' ('Life and Death of John Semple', in Walker, 1.189).

79.33 a burning and a shining light John 5.35. See also 'Life and Death of Alexander Peden', in Walker, 1.149; James Hog, Preface to Edward Fisher, *The Marrow of Modern Divinity* (1718), pages unnumbered; and Robert Burns, 'Holy Willie's Prayer' (written 1785; first published 1801), line 11 (Kinsley, no. 53), where Burns uses the phrase satirically.

80.5–6 when there was no need of such vanity see *Much Ado About Nothing*, 3.3.19.

80.26 gathered to her fathers see Judges 2.10; 2 Kings 22.20; 2 Chronicles 34.28.

81.1–2 the righteous perish and the merciful are removed see Isaiah 57.1.

81.4 rivers of water see Lamentations 3.48, where Jeremiah weeps for the destruction of Jerusalem and the captivity of Judah.

81.5 afflicted Church ... carnal seekers see note to 71.17.

81.5 carnal seekers, and with the dead of heart see Romans 8.6–7.

81.13–14 John Semple, called Carspharn John (1602–77) minister of Carsphairn, about 18 km NW of New Galloway in Dumfries and Galloway. Walker published his life in 1727: see Walker, 1.179–205.

81.14–15 I have been this night on the banks of Ulai, plucking an apple here and there Walker, 1.205; see also Magnum, 11.323. Ulai is where Daniel has his vision of the ram and the goat, a historical allegory that Deans might appropriately meditate upon: see Daniel Ch. 8. The significance of 'plucking an apple here and there' is clear neither in Walker nor here, although it suggests the fruits of meditation. Walker confusingly appends the story from which the sentence comes to the 'Life and Death of John Semple', but the person who meditates on the banks of Ulai on the night of his wife's death is actually John Welwood. Scott quotes the key passage from Walker in a Magnum note (11.323).

82.14 the term either Whitsunday (15 May), or Martinmas (11 Nov.), then the 2 Scottish term days on which tenancies began or ended.

82.21 loose the pleugh undo the fastenings of the plough, i.e. stop working, which, the text indicates later (93.22–23), was about noon.

82.24 Gude guide us God save us.

83.13   carnal learning   see Romans 8.6–7.

84   motto   George Crabbe (1754–1832), 'The Parish Register' (1807), Part 2, 'Marriages', lines 135–38, in Crabbe, *Poetical Works*, 1.241.

84.24   art of fascination   recorded as obsolete in the *OED* (*fascination*, 1), but Scott elides the idea of the snake fascinating (84.20) with the obsolete sense.

84.24   artes perditæ   *Latin* the lost arts.

84.29   middle age   Jeanie is now about 33; see Historical Note, 597.

84.36–37   Grecian-shaped head   perhaps best exemplified in Scott's age by Byron; a Grecian profile involved a nose that seemed to rise straight from the forehead, and a prominent jaw.

84.38–39   laughing Hebe countenance   compare John Milton, 'L'Allegro' (1631?), lines 28–29: 'Nods, and Becks, and Wreathed Smiles, / Such as hang on *Hebe's* cheek'. In Greek mythology Hebe, daughter of Zeus and Hera, poured out nectar for the gods and was associated with perpetual youth.

85.4–5   had no power to shake the stedfast mind   a relatively common sentiment in both love and religious poetry in the 17th and 18th centuries. Compare the second brother's belief in his sister when he says that darkness and noise will be unable to 'stir the constant mood of her calm thoughts': John Milton, *A Mask Presented at Ludlow Castle* [*Comus*] (performed 1634; published 1637), line 371.

85.14   putting the stone, casting the hammer   *athletics* shot putting and hammer throwing.

85.14–15   long bowls   ninepins; a game where heavy balls are thrown from the hand at pins or skittles.

85.18–19   indulgence of the eye . . . if not a crime   a position adopted by many Christian moralists on the basis of 1 John 2.15–16: 'Love not the world, neither the things that are in the world. If any man love the world, the love of the Father is not in him. . . . the lust of the flesh, and the lust of the eyes, and the pride of life, is not of the Father, but is of the world'.

85.22–23   common and hereditary guilt and imperfection   original sin. Adam and Eve's sin was held to be transmitted from generation to generation.

85.34   authoress of 'Glenburnie'   Elizabeth Hamilton (1758–1816). Her didactic novel *The Cottagers of Glenburnie* appeared in 1808.

85.36   double share   compare Deuteronomy 21.17; 2 Kings 2.9.

85.39   child of his old age   see Genesis 37.3: 'Now Israel loved Joseph more than all his children, because he was the son of his old age'.

85.42   the times of family worship   shortly after sunset: see text, 132.35–37. At 87.2 Jeanie says that it is after 8 o'clock.

86.4   in her own conceit   see Romans 12.16: 'Be not wise in your own conceits'.

86.5   free agency   an ambiguous phrase; in Fielding it was free-agency which led to the Fall, but in Scott's day it was used approvingly of the individual's right to self determination by such as Coleridge.

86.17–18   family exercise   family worship, consisting of prayer and Bible readings.

86.37–40   The elfin knight . . . broom nae mair   a composite song. For line 1 see 'The Elfin Knight', Child, 2; in ballads a supernatural lover commonly implies a sexual threat (compare Child, 2, 4, 39). The refrain (lines 2 and 4) is from 'The broom blooms bonie', *SMM*, no. 461; see also Child, 16B. Going to the woods and plucking flowers is an obvious metaphor for sexual adventure. Line 3 has no single source.

86.42–87.6   Whare hae ye been . . . Naebody   a formalised pattern of question and answer is a common form in many popular songs; compare Burns's 'Wha is that at my bower door?' (Kinsley, no. 356).

87.3 Corstorphine hills 6 km to the NW of the Old Town of Edinburgh.

87.10 if ye'll ask nae questions . . . lees proverbial: see *ODEP*, 20.

87.23–27 Through the kirk-yard . . . clerk see Herd, 2.231. The line which follows reads 'He gaed me my barm, barm'; *barm* is yeast and in the context of the song has sexual implications.

87.31 untaught child of nature the state of nature was a subject much debated in the 18th century. The model which Scott seems to envisage here is one in which the child has not been trained in the moral laws of contemporary society. Compare 'a State of Simplicity, in which Man can have so few Desires, and no Appetites, roving beyond the immediate Call of untaught Nature': Bernard Mandeville, *The Fable of the Bees: or, Private Vices, Publick Benefits*, ed. F. B. Kaye, 2 vols (Oxford, 1924), Part 2, Dialogue 6, 2.285. However, in the context of the Romantic period the phrase has a much more positive connotation.

87.38 I wish my tongue had been blistered see *Romeo and Juliet*, 3.2.90.

88.1 the morn tomorrow.

88.1 merry dancers the northern lights, aurora borealis.

88.4–5 what could tak ye to a dance see note to 75.34–35.

88.14–15 regular fit of distraction see 'Life and Death of Richard Cameron', in Walker, 1.239; quoted in Magnum, 11.345.

88.19 dramatic representation see note to 75.34–35.

88.21–22 drove him beyond the verge of patience see *1 Henry IV*, 1.3.200.

88.22–40 Dance . . . wantonness of my feet this speech is taken from Patrick Walker's 'Life and Death of Richard Cameron'. The passage refers to the golden calf and Salome, and the two sentences 'I hae aften wondered . . . wantonness of my feet' are near to direct quotation. See Walker, 1.239–40; Magnum, 11.344–46.

88.25 Golden Calf at Bethel see Exodus Ch. 32. The Israelites under Aaron made a golden calf to worship while Moses was up Mount Sinai receiving commandments from God. When Moses returned 'he saw the calf, and the dancing' (Exodus 32.19). The golden calf at Bethel, erected by King Jeroboam, is not linked to dancing: see 1 Kings 12.28–29.

88.25–26 unhappy lass . . . John the Baptist Salome, who as payment for her dancing before King Herod, asked him for the head of John the Baptist: see Matthew 14.6–10; Mark 6.20–28. In the Gospels the dancer is identified only as the daughter of Herodias, but is called Salome by Josephus.

88.35–36 Peter Walker . . . Bristo-port Patrick Walker (*c.* 1666–1745), a Covenanter denounced as a rebel in 1682, and imprisoned and tortured 1684–85. As a historian of the Covenanters, he published lives of Alexander Peden (1724; revised edn 1728), John Semple, John Welwood, and Richard Cameron (1727), and Daniel Cargill and others (1732): see Walker, where all are republished. He was probably not a 'packman', in spite of his being so described by many in the early 19th century (see Walker, 1.xxxvi–viii), but he did much walking in search of material for his lives. Walker's title pages indicate that he lived just inside the Bristo Port, at the end of the modern George IV Bridge. In calling him *Peter* Scott has not made a mistake as the names were interchangeable, the Celtic 'Patrick' being commonly anglicised as Peter in parish registers.

88.40 quean lassies young girls.

89.5–6 darkness . . . light a crucial biblical opposition.

89.12 Maggie Macqueen's not identified.

89.15 lay in a leaf of my Bible i.e. she will identify a relevant biblical text and turn over a corner of the leaf by way of making a resolution to refrain from dancing. Scott in a Magnum footnote wrote: 'This custom . . . is still held to be, in some sense, an appeal to Heaven for his or her sincerity' (Magnum, 11.333).

90.9 keep her in countenance keep her from being abashed or disconcerted.

90.12 had an upright walk lived in a moral, God-fearing way. In various forms 'upright walk' is a common biblical phrase, e.g. see Psalm 15.1–2: 'Lord, who shall abide in thy tabernacle? . . . He that walketh uprightly'. See also 1 Kings 3.6; Psalm 84.11; Proverbs 2.7, 10.9, 14.2, 15.21, 28.18; Micah 2.7.

90.13 Tolbooth Kirk see note to 24.31.

90.15 had not bent the knee unto Baal see 1 Kings 19.18; Romans 11.4. Deans follows Paul in Romans where the phrase refers to those who have not compromised with state religion. Baal was an Old Testament heathen god.

90.16–18 national defections . . . Revolution faced with mounting opposition and the army of William of Orange which had landed in Torbay in November 1688, James VII and II left Britain and sailed for France on 23 December. The Parliaments of both England and Scotland invited William of Orange and his wife Mary, James's daughter, to succeed him. In the course of 1689–90 the Scottish Parliament carried out a thorough legislative revolution, which included the re-establishment of Presbyterianism in the Church of Scotland. Deans identifies the various ways in which since the Revolution of 1688–89 Presbyterianism had been compromised in Scotland: the Union of Scotland and England in 1707 which made the Presbyterian Church of Scotland subject to the power of an essentially English legislature; the Toleration Act of 1712 which allowed Episcopalian clergy who used the liturgy of the Church of England to establish congregations in Scotland and to conduct worship provided they prayed for the sovereign by name; the Patronage Act of 1712 which restored to certain landowners the right to choose the parish minister, a right exercised by congregation and Presbytery from 1690; the oath of allegiance (and similar oaths) which after 1689 involved a promise to be 'faithfull and bear true allegiance to their Majesties King WILLIAM & Queen MARY', and the abjuration oath which from 1712 required all ministers to reject the Stewart dynasty. To Presbyterians of Deans's persuasion such oaths involved recognising the authority of the state in church matters. 'National defections' is a phrase repeatedly used by Walker who sees their source in the decisions of the Revolution Convention and of the General Assembly in 1690: see 'Vindication of Cameron's Name', in Walker, 1.254–60.

90.17 Erastian oaths for the oaths see note above. Erastians, called after the Swiss theologian Thomas Erastus (1504–83), believed in the ascendancy of the state over the church. Deans believes that what has happened in Scotland subordinates the church to the state.

90.20 unhappy race of Stuarts 'Life and Death of Richard Cameron', in Walker, 1.227, 257. The Stewarts were on the throne of Scotland from Robert II (reigned 1371–90), and of England from James I (reigned 1603–25), to the death of Queen Anne (reigned 1702–14). The word *unhappy* is used by Walker about the Stewarts both as a family and as individuals because of 'their usurping the royal prerogatives of King Christ' (Walker, 1.227).

90.33 ruling elders laymen chosen and ordained to take part in the business of the church courts (kirk session, presbytery, synod, and General Assembly), called *ruling* because their function is to govern the parish, in distinction to the minister who is the 'teaching elder'. The kirk session, the lowest court in Presbyterian churches (and thus in the Church of Scotland), has usually one minister and many elders, and is represented on higher courts by its minister and a single elder.

90.34 General Assembly of the Kirk the highest court of the Church of Scotland.

90.35 patronage . . . abjuration see note to 90.16–18.

90.36–37 carved work of the sanctuary see Psalm 74.6. Deans refers to the Presbyterian theocracy, established by the covenants, and which had flourished between 1638 and 1649.

90.38 legalized formalist see 'Life and Death of Alexander Peden', in Walker, 1.144.

90.40–41 chambering Romans 13.13: 'Let us walk honestly, as in the day; not in rioting and drunkenness, not in chambering [lewd behaviour] and wantonness, not in strife and envying'.

90.41 company-keeping see notes to 75.33–34, and 174.12.

90.41 promiscuous dancing dancing with the opposite sex; see Magnum, 11.346.

91.27–30 Something ... on earth could clear see George Crabbe (1754–1832), *The Borough* (1810), Letter 15, 'Inhabitants of the Alms-House—Clelia', lines 39–42, in Crabbe, *Poetical Works*, 1.500.

91.39 Holy-Rood was not built in a day proverbial, variant of 'Rome was not built in a day': see Ray, 152; *ODEP*, 683. Holyrood is the Abbey at the foot of the Canongate founded in 1138, and the adjoining palace, begun around 1500, and substantially remodelled in 1671.

91.39–40 use would make perfect proverbial: see *ODEP*, 856.

92.2 secret sorrow a phrase used in poetry from Spenser to Crabbe: see e.g. Edmund Spenser (*c.* 1552–99), *The Faerie Queene*, 1.7.38: *CLA*, 42, 187.

92.14 weightier matters of the law see note to 37.43.

92.16–17 fatuus, furiosus, and naturaliter idiota *Latin* stupid, mad, and a natural idiot. The phrase 'without much respect to gender' refers to the fact that when used of a female the first two words ought to be 'fatua, furiosa'. The terms are to be found in the brieves (warrants) authorising an inquiry into someone's mental state under Scots law. Saddletree correctly quotes from brieves of furiosity (madness) and idiotry ('fatuus et naturaliter idiota'). There then followed a procedure before all the judges of the Court of Session to determine the alleged insanity.

92.29–30 nice, sharp quillets of legal discussion see *1 Henry VI*, 2.4.17.

92.31 Dutch professor of mathematics while academics are traditionally considered to be unobservant, why a Dutch professor of mathematics should be thought particularly unobservant has not been determined.

92.39–93.4 The lingering illness ... Saint Leonard's this passage was added between Scott's writing the MS and the publication of Ed1. See Essay on the Text, 497–99.

93.25–26 officers of justice, with a warrant of justiciary i.e. officers of the High Court of Justiciary with a warrant issued by that court. Effie's condition has been noticed by 'neighbours' and 'fellow-servants' (see text, 92.17); the elders and beadles of the various kirk sessions would pick up and gather information about illicit relationships and the pregnancies of unmarried women with a view to disciplining those involved. In this case they would have passed their information to the civil authorities who would have acted as indicated.

93.29 resisted the brow of military and of civil tyranny for Deans as Covenanter see text, 102.29–103.8.

94.9 Evil One the Devil.

94.9 children of God phrase used 9 times in the New Testament: see e.g. Matthew 5.9.

94.13–14 burnt feathers and strong waters used to bring round someone who had fainted.

94.15 Rock of Ages God; the alternative (marginal) translation of Isaiah 26.4: 'Trust ye in the Lord for ever: for the Lord Jehovah is the rock of ages', and Scottish Paraphrase 22.4 (1781). The phrase seems to have gained currency in religious poetry and sermons in the 17th century.

94.16 the promise of eternal life. See 1 John 2.25.

94.19–20 bloody Zipporah see Exodus 4.25–26 where in the Authorised Version Zipporah calls Moses 'a bloody husband'.

94.20–21 wicked exult in the high places compare Ephesians 6.12.

94.22 hand-waled murderers see 'Life and Death of Richard Cameron', in Walker, 1.238.

94.23 push out the lip express derision or contempt: see Psalm 22.7.

94.26 stumbling-block word used in the Bible of the problems put in the way of those who consider themselves righteous; see e.g. Isaiah 8.14.

94.30 telling down counting out money in payment.

94.34 nineteenth part of a boddle i.e. the most minute sum imaginable: a *boddle* was a Scots coin worth two pence Scots (one sixth of a penny sterling).

94.36–37 an eye for an eye…blood see Exodus 21.23–25; Leviticus 24.20; Deuteronomy 19.21.

94.37 it's the law of God and it's the law of man but this Old Testament law was reversed by Jesus: see Matthew 5.38–48.

95 motto *A Midsummer Night's Dream*, 3.2.198–201.

95.19 fitting time and season see Ecclesiastes 3.1.

95.20 wait upon pay a respectful visit to.

95.36 affairs of honour duels.

96.9 word spoken in season see Proverbs 15.23; Isaiah 50.4.

96.10 Tully the great Roman orator and statesman, Marcus Tullius Cicero (106–43 BC). Cicero is remembered for his speeches in support of the constitution of the Roman republic against the absolutist tendencies of many contemporaries including Caesar, and on corruption in the administration of Rome and its provinces.

97.6 I am a soldier for 'soldier of Christ' see 2 Timothy 2.3.

97.6–7 arrest evil-doers in the name of my Master see 1 Peter 2.14.

97.14–15 peace upon earth and good will towards men see Luke 2.14.

97.20–21 cloth… calling Butler's distinction reflects differences between English and Scottish modes of referring to the profession of minister of religion.

97.24 in season and out of season see 2 Timothy 4.2.

97.40 Thou shalt do no Murder Matthew 19.18. This is the New Testament form of the sixth commandment (Exodus 20.13).

98.8 Cain, the first murderer see Genesis 4.3–8.

98.9 his stamp upon your brow the mark of Cain: Genesis 4.15.

98.16 I may be bad enough—you priests say all men are so i.e. all are original sinners: see Romans 5.12. Compare Robert Burns, 'Holy Willie's Prayer' (1785; first published 1801), lines 7–18 (Kinsley, no. 53).

98.17 the purpose of saving life, not of taking it away compare Mark 3.4; Luke 6.9, 9.56.

98.24 Hunter's Bog between Arthur's Seat and Salisbury Crags.

98.25 Saint Anthony's Hill presumably the N slopes of Arthur's Seat, below Hunter's Bog, where Saint Anthony's Chapel and Well are situated.

98.33 disbelieve witchcraft or spectres see note to 100.29–31.

98.36 Apollyon, Abaddon see Revelation 9.11: 'And they had a king over them, which is the angel of the bottomless pit, whose name in the Hebrew tongue is Abaddon but in the Greek tongue hath his name Appolyon'.

98.37–38 upper and lower circles of spiritual denomination i.e. heaven and hell.

99.23 Nicol Muschat's Cairn Muschat murdered his wife by cutting her throat on 17 October 1720, at a spot near St Anthony's Chapel. Scott remarks in a Magnum note that a cairn long marked the spot but is now 'almost totally removed, in consequence of an alteration on the road in that place' (Magnum, 11.359). See *Criminal Trials*, 323–44, and William Roughead, 'Nicol Muschet: His Crime and His Cairn', in *The Riddle of the Ruthvens and other Studies* (Edinburgh, 1919), 307–34.

100.3–4 Roaring Lion ... devour a description of the devil: see 1 Peter 5.8.

100.17–18 mien, language, and port of the archangel Satan, as described by John Milton, *Paradise Lost* (1667), 1.599–612.

100.29–31 laws against witchcraft ... acted upon the last execution for witchcraft in Scotland was in Dornoch in 1727; the laws were repealed in 1736. Legal scepticism about witchcraft was apparent through the Restoration period, and the 1736 repeal was the culmination of a revolution in thinking among lawyers and people of similar intellectual standing, but the popular belief in witches lingered through the 18th century: see Walter Scott, *Letters on Demonology and Witchcraft* (London, 1830), 339.

100.36 common sense an idea particularly associated with Scottish philosophy about what good observers could accept as the general experience of human beings.

100.36–39 inconsistent ... with the general rules by which the universe is governed ... ought not to be admitted as probable this passage summarises precisely David Hume's arguments on miracles: see David Hume, 'Of Miracles', in *An Enquiry Concerning Human Understanding* (originally published 1748), ed. Tom L. Beauchamp (Oxford, 2000), 83–99; compare particularly 'A miracle is a violation of the laws of nature' (86).

101 motto see 'Sweet William's Ghost' (Child, 77A), stanza 10, in *TTM*, 325; Percy, 3.128–31; Herd, 1.77; and *SMM*, no. 363.

101.14 low and sweet-toned voice compare *King Lear*, 5.3.272–73.

101.41 shining motty through the reek with dust seen shining in the smoky atmosphere: see Allan Ramsay (1684–1758), *The Gentle Shepherd* (1725), 5.2.4. In 1736 Ramsay, poet, dramatist, editor, was the most significant literary figure in Scotland.

102.7 firm to resolve, and stubborn to endure see Robert Southey, 'To A. S. Cottle', line 62, in A. S. Cottle, *Icelandic Poetry or the Edda of Saemund translated into English verse* (Bristol, 1797), xxxiv.

102.9 Rembrandt Rembrandt van Ryn (1606–69), the Dutch painter whose subjects are often dramatised by the way in which light strikes them.

102.10 Michael Angelo Michelangelo Buonarroti (1475–1564). It is probable that Scott had seen none of Michelangelo's paintings or sculpture, but that he had seen the drawings in the royal collection, which would explain his emphasis on 'outline'.

102.13 carnal-witted see Romans 8.6–7.

102.16–17 Earl Peircy sees my fall see 'Chevy Chase' (Child, 162B), in Percy, 1.231–46, line 148.

102.23–24 God comfort you, God comfort you see Isaiah 40.1.

102.27 ower proud see Robert Burns, 'Holly Willie's Prayer' (written 1785; first published 1801), line 57 (Kinsley, no. 53).

102.29 a reproach and a hissing Old Testament terms. Although they do not appear in conjunction both suggest the scorn felt by worldly men for the righteous: see e.g. Psalm 69.8–9 ('I am become a stranger unto my brethren ... and the reproaches of them that reproached thee are fallen upon me'), and Job 27.23 ('Men shall clap their hands at him, and shall hiss him out of his place').

102.30–31 lay saft ... moss-hags and moors see 'Life and Death of Alexander Peden', in Walker, 1.103.

102.32 Donald Cameron the name conflates those of Richard Cameron

(1648–80) who renounced the King's authority in 1680 and was killed that year at Airds Moss, and who gave his name to the Cameronians (see note to 30.29), and of Donald or Daniel Cargill (1619–81) who was associated with Cameron, and who was captured and executed in 1681. Their bitter attitude to those who had compromised with the state during Covenanting times cut them off from most of the movement. The lives of both were written by Patrick Walker.

102.32   Mr Blackadder, called Guess-again   see 'Life and Death of Richard Cameron', in Walker, 1.251. John Blackadder (1615–86), was deprived of his living in 1662, preached in conventicles, fled to Rotterdam in 1674 but returned in 1679, again to lead the wandering life of the outlawed preacher. He was captured in 1681, and imprisoned on the Bass Rock in the Firth of Forth, where he died.

102.33   made a spectacle   compare 'Life and Death of Richard Cameron', in Walker, 1.225.

102.35   James Renwick   (1662–88). Ordained in Holland he returned to Scotland in 1683 to minister to the Cameronians. He was the last Covenanter to be executed.

102.35–36   quartered the dear body . . . cut off those hands   such mutilation was often part of the punishment for those found guilty of rebellion, although strictly speaking this was not provided for in Scots law which specified hanging and the forfeiture of real and moveable estate.

102.36–37   the first to raise up the down-fallen banner of the testimony   i.e. Renwick rallied the Cameronians after the deaths of Cameron and Cargill (see note to 102.32). Compare 'Life and Death of Richard Cameron', in Walker, 1.224.

102.39–40   hangit by the neck had I been twa years elder   customarily capital punishment seems not to have been applied to those aged 16 and younger but there was no fixed age: see Hume, *Crimes*, 1.13–18.

102.41   exalted   see Robert Burns, 'Holy Willie's Prayer' (1785), line 14 (Kinsley, 53).

102.42–43   defections o' the times   see notes to 71.17–18, and 90.16–18.

103.1   with uplifted hand and voice, crying aloud, and sparing not   see Isaiah 58.1.

103.2–3   nation-wasting and church-sinking abomination . . . patronage   see 'Life and Death of Richard Cameron', in Walker, 1.270. For 'union, toleration, and patronage' see note to 90.16–18.

103.4   the last woman   Queen Anne.

103.4   unhappy race of Stewarts   see note to 90.20.

103.5   infringements and invasions of the just powers of eldership   many crimes and misdemeanours which formerly were in the cognisance of kirk sessions were 'taken over' or abolished by secular powers in the 18th century. This was particularly true of witchcraft (see note to 100.29–31), in which David Deans still believes.

103.6   Cry of an Howl in the Desart   Walker (writing in 1727) says: 'There are some of late have written *A Cry of an Howl in the Desert to all Elderships*' ('Life and Death of Richard Cameron', in Walker, 1.275), but no copy of the anonymous pamphlet now seems to be extant. Its title is derived from Psalm 102.6: 'I am like an owl of the desert'.

103.7   the Bowhead   the head of the Bow, i.e. where the West Bow, a precipitous street leading to the Grassmarket joined the Lawnmarket in Edinburgh. It is said to have been the dwelling place of many Covenanters.

103.7   flying stationers   *slang* itinerant stationers. In *A Classical Dictionary* Grose defines them as 'Ballad-singers and hawkers of penny histories'. The imprint page of some of the chapbooks collected by Scott as a boy (*CLA*, 159) include the phrase 'Printed for the Company of Flying Stationers'.

103.17 Saint Jerome (*c.* 342–420). Beginning in 382 he translated much of the Bible from Hebrew and Greek into Latin; in the 6th century his translations were gathered together to form the *editio vulgata*, i.e. the Vulgate.

103.17–18 per infamiam . . . ad immortalitatem the Vulgate version of 2 Corinthians 6.8 reads 'per infamiam, & bonam famam' (through ill repute and good repute); Butler adds 'grassari immortalitatem' (to approach immortality). The Latin verb implies more caution than does Butler's 'rusheth on'.

103.20–21 tender souls and fearful although this sounds like a quotation no source has been found.

103.21 midnight solitude Lord Byron, 'Remember Him, &c.' (written 1813; published 1814), line 20.

103.21–22 Watchman, what of the night? Isaiah 21.11; quoted in 'Life and Death of Alexander Peden', in Walker, 1.5.

103.23 dispensation the result of God's special dealing with a community, family or individual.

103.27 native Scottish as only the Authorised Version of the Bible was read in Scotland 'native Scottish' must refer to how the Bible sounded when read in Scotland.

103.29 crook in my lot turn in my affairs, misfortune, affliction. The phrase when used by Deans also refers to Thomas Boston (1676–1732), *The Crook in the Lot; or The Sovereignty and Wisdom of God Displayed in the Afflictions of Men* (1752).

103.31 polished shaft see note to 74.27.

103.32 pillar Revelation 3.12: 'Him that overcometh will I make a pillar in the temple of my God'.

103.32 ruling elder see note to 90.33.

103.36 back-sliding used 17 times in the Old Testament (13 in Jeremiah) of sinning or falling away from God.

103.36 offspring of Belial as sons or children of Belial, a common biblical expression denoting evil men who worship false gods, particularly sensuality: see Deuteronomy 13.13, etc.

104.6 curule chair ornamental seat used by the highest magistrates of Rome, hence the seat or office of Lord Provost of Edinburgh.

104.7–9 Rochefoucault . . . best friends see François, Duc de la Rochefoucault (1613–80), *Maximes*, ed. Jacques Truchet (Paris, 1967), 139: 'Dans l'adversité de nos meilleurs amis, nous trouvons toujours quelque chose qui ne nous déplaît pas'. The work was first published in Holland as *Sentences et Maximes de Morale* in 1664, and in France as *Réflexions ou Sentences et Maximes Morales* in 1665. This maxim appears only in the edition of 1665, where it is numbered 99; it was suppressed in later editions. In the English translation by L. W. Tancock (Harmondsworth, 1969) it is numbered 583.

104.16 got . . . by the end got command of.

104.24 l'embarras des richesses *French* embarrassment of riches, from the play by Léonor-Jean-Christine Soulas d'Allainval, *L'Embarras des Richesses* (1725). Arlequin is a poor but light-hearted gardener, who is given a fortune by Plutus; he then becomes suspicious, bad-tempered and miserable, until he realises his own deterioration and returns the treasure. He marries the girl he loves and lives poor but happy.

104.40 heaven-daring see 'Life and Death of Alexander Peden', in Walker, 1.22, 37.

105.2 inter rusticos *Latin* among peasants.

105.31 heavy dispensation see note to 103.23.

106.16–17 the back is made for the burthen proverbial: see *ODEP*, 312.

106.18 lover is by charter wayward and suspicious   i.e. the lover is wayward and suspicious in accordance with the rules of courtly love: compare Andreas Capellanus, *The Art of Courtly Love*, ed. and trans. John Jay Parry (New York, 1941), 185–86.

108.17 granter of propositions   i.e. one usually prepared to admit a proposition as true.

108.32 Privy-Council   the council which advises the monarch, and which in the 17th and early 18th centuries was the chief centre of executive power until the development of the cabinet system of government.

108.32–33 in effeir of war   in show of war.

108.33–34 will prove little better than perduellion   will prove little better than high treason. According to Hume 'the levying of war against the King... equally embraces all those risings, which... [are] against his prerogative, authority, or office' (Hume, *Crimes*, 2.427–28).

108.37 How could ye dispute what's plain law   Deans is right and Saddletree is wrong: that the situation is susceptible to various interpretations is central to *The Heart of Mid-Lothian*. Levying war against the king is perduellion or high treason (Hume, *Crimes*, 2.424), but Hume makes a distinction between 'projects of extensive and systematical resistance to the laws and Magistrates of the land', and those 'sudden and limited disturbances which arise from special grudge and provocation' (Hume, *Crimes*, 2.431). He argues specifically: 'it was plain, upon the whole circumstances of the case of *Porteous*, that there was no impeachment among the multitude of the royal prerogative of mercy, nor any project of opposition to it *generally*; but only a quarrel with the exercise of it in a particular instance, and on account of a special enmity to the person who was the object of mercy; the crime was therefore justly held not to be treason, but a case of riot only and murder' (Hume, *Crimes*, 2.431–32). 'Convocating the king's lieges... by touk of drum' and the bearing of arms in the street were certainly crimes, but could equally be considered characteristics of mobbing (see Hume, *Crimes*, 2.235). Significantly, the indictment of William Maclauchlane, the only man to be tried for participation in the Porteous Riot, accuses him of 'convocating the lieges by beat of drum; and their assembling themselves riotously and tumultuously together, armed with guns, Lochaber-axes, or other warlike weapons whatsoever' (*Criminal Trials*, 206).

108.39–40 perduellion is the warst and maist virulent kind of treason   for the various kinds of treason see Hume, *Crimes*, 2.406–83.

108.43 lese-majesty   *Scots law* untrue and slanderous statements such as are likely to prejudice relations between the king and his subjects, as defined by the laws of 1584, c. 134, 1585, c. 10, and 1703, c. 4. 'Leasing-making' was originally punishable by death; transportation (see note to 109.34) and a red-hot iron driven through the tongue were other punishments. The Act of 1703 restricted punishment to a fine, lashing or imprisonment, at the judge's discretion. The Scots law of treason was superseded by the English at the Union in 1707 and the uniform application of the law of treason throughout Great Britain was ensured by the Treason Act of 1708 (7 Anne, c. 21), which was effective from 1 July 1709.

108.43–109.1 concealment of a treasonable purpose   see Hume, *Crimes*, 2.411.

109.5–6 awfu' downfall... the Revolution   see notes to 71.17, and 90.16–18.

109.8 liberty and conscience made fast   Saddletree may refer to the Revolution settlement of 1689; the Claim of Right adopted by the Convention of Estates (the Scottish Parliament) on 11 April 1689 stated among other things that the royal prerogative could not override the law. He more probably refers to the Act of Settlement of 1706 in which the Presbyterian system of church government was guaranteed as a basic condition of Union, and later accepted as an integral part of the parliamentary Union of 1707. Saddletree conceives of the terms of the Union as an entail ('tailzie') as they were, in theory, unalterable.

109.11 **wise after the manner of this world** see 1 Corinthians 3.18.

109.11 **haud your part** legal metaphor implying ownership of a minor share of a bigger fief.

109.12 **cast in your portion** throw in your lot.

109.12 **keep with** keep company with, side with.

109.13 **Weary on** *expression of exasperation* may evil fall on, the devil take.

109.15–16 **black hand of defection ... red hand of our sworn mur-therers** see 'Life and Death of Alexander Peden', in Walker, 1.83.

109.16–17 **numbered the towers ... marked the bulwarks** see Psalm 48.12–13; 'Life and Death of Richard Cameron', in Walker, 1.259. *Zion*, the holy city, is here the theocracy envisaged by the Covenanters and which they thought had been achieved between 1639 and 1650 (see note to 178.38).

109.21 **General Assembly** see note to 90.34.

109.22 **fifteen Lords o' Session and the five Lords o' Justiciary** the judges of the Court of Session (the highest civil court of Scotland), and of the High Court of Justiciary, the highest criminal court.

109.23 **Out upon** interjection expressing reproach: see *OED*, *out*, interjection 2b.

109.26 **back of my hand** phrase expressing contempt or dismissal.

109.28 **persecuted remnant** Covenanters and Cameronians particularly of the period 1681–85 when persecution was at its worst (see notes to 4.38, 4.42 and 30.29). After the Revolution of 1688–89 the phrase 'suffering remnant' became common as a description of those who opposed the new establishment in church and state on conscientious grounds. See also note to 177.10–11.

109.31–34 **blue-bottles ... bonny bike** see 'Life and Death of Alexander Peden', in Walker, 1.83.

109.34 **transportation beyond seas** transportation to Europe was introduced in the early 17th century as a punishment for leasing-making (see note to 108.43), and to Virginia or Barbados for other crimes before 1675.

109.37 **let them clear them that kens them** let those people explain or expound things that know about them.

109.40 **scandal ... murmur** slandering or murmuring a judge was made a crime in the act 1540, c. 104; see Hume, *Crimes*, 2.207.

109.41 **sui generis** *Latin* of its own kind.

109.42 **language of anti-christ** language of the papacy, i.e. Latin.

110.4 **sell their knowledge for pieces of silver** as Judas did Jesus: see Matthew 26.14–16; 27.3–10.

110.5 **in presence** before the judge himself, and not by written submission.

110.9–10 **union ... oaths** see note to 90.16–18. For *Yerastian* see note to 90.17.

110.10 **soul and body-killing** the High Court of Justiciary kills souls because its oaths recognised the legitimacy of the Hanoverian regime, and kills bodies because it had the power to sentence criminals to death.

110.23 **waiting on** attending.

110.27 **of that ilk** of that place, i.e. of Marsport. The phrase was often used as a designation among the Scots landed gentry.

110.29 **hagbuts of found** early kind of portable firearm made of cast metal.

110.32–33 **qualified person ... plough-gate of land** hunting was restricted to those who owned a plough-gate of land by the Act 1621, c. 31. A *plough-gate* was the amount of land which a plough, pulled by 8 oxen, could till in a year, calculated to be 104 Scots acres but inevitably varying considerably.

110.34–36 defences . . . libel the defence put forward argues that there is no agreement as to what constitutes a plough-gate of land, and that that uncertainty is sufficient to dispose of the charge.

110.34 non constat *Latin* it is not settled, it is not established.

110.38 in hoc statu *Latin* in this statute.

110.42 guse's grass as much land as would form pasturage for a goose.

111.2 nihil interest de possessione *Latin literally* nothing matters about possession, i.e. ownership is not an issue.

111.4 formaliter et specialiter, as well as generaliter *Latin* formally and in particular detail (i.e. with specific reference to this case), as well as in general.

111.8 Titius . . . Mævius fictitious litigants used in arguments in Roman legal writings.

111.11–12 in rerum natura *Latin* in the nature of things, i.e. in nature.

111.19–20 Outer-house in 1736 the Court of Session was organised into Outer and Inner Houses; in the Outer House each judge (except the Lord President) presided separately as a judge of first instance; cases could be remitted to the Inner House for final decision, or to seek rulings on particular legal issues. However, Saddletree may be referring to the place where the Outer-house sat, for which see note to 21.41.

111.25–27 act . . . William and Mary see note to 44.33–34.

111.41 visitation God's coming in judgment. The term is frequently used in the Bible: e.g. see Jeremiah 8.12, 10.15, 46.21.

111.42 His will be done see Matthew 26.42, words used by Jesus while praying in Gethsemane, before his betrayal, trial and murder. See also the Lord's Prayer, Matthew 6.10, Luke 11.2.

112.5 Yerastians see note to 90.17.

112.5 Arminians followers of the Dutch reformed theologian Jacobus Arminius (Jakob Hermans, 1560–1609). Arminius came to doubt Calvinist doctrines of predestination, and argued that God's sovereignty was compatible with free will in man. Arminian doctrines were formalised in the Remonstrance of 1610.

112.8 the very de'il is no sae ill as he's ca'd proverbial: see *ODEP*, 182.

112.13 gazing, glancing-glasses Walker writes 'glazing glancing-glass' ('Life and Death of Richard Cameron', in Walker, 1.277), a slighting reference to James Glas (1695–1773), minister of Tealing, near Dundee, and his followers, the Glassites. In 1727 Glas published a work arguing that the idea of a national church is unscriptural, and that the reformed churches' pursuit of secular power in support of spiritual authority was unlawful; he was deposed from his charge in 1730. See also 'Life and Death of Walter Smith', in Walker, 2.69.

112.14 fling the glaiks in folk's een dazzle, deceive, delude someone.

112.15 flights and refinements and periods of eloquence rhetorical terms. When Milton says that he 'with no middle flight intends to soar / Above th' Aonian Mount' (*Paradise Lost*, 1.14–15) he means that he will not use the middle style and forms of poetry but the highest epic style. *Refinement*, originally an alchemical term, means purification by reduction, and when used rhetorically it implies the elimination of vulgar language from one's utterance. A *period* is a 'stopping point', i.e. the end of a sentence, but also carried the sense of a well-rounded utterance.

112.15–16 frae heathen emperors and popish canons Scots lawyers frequently used Latin in their pleas, quoting the two sources of Scots law, the jurists who codified Roman law under the Emperor Justinian (AD 482–565; emperor from 527), and medieval canon law. But Deans probably refers both to the legal content, and the mode of utterance, for canons of criticism illustrating how one should write and speak were published from the Renaissance.

112.17 Yerastian see note to 90.17.

112.19–20 Titus...Temple Deans picks up Saddletree's reference to Titius at 111.8, and thinks that it refers to the Roman Emperor Titus (AD 39–81; emperor 79–81), who captured Jerusalem in 70, and destroyed the Temple.

112.25 round-spun presbyterian 'Life and Death of John Welwood', in Walker, 1.208. *Round-spun* would appear to mean 'genuine' in this context, but as the term is derived from weaving, and means 'coarsely spun in weave or texture', there may be an ironic implication in Saddletree's use of it.

112.26 to boot in addition.

112.27–28 one of the public and polititious warldly-wise men see 'Life and Death of Richard Cameron', in Walker, 1.256.

112.31 gay and weel very well.

112.32 in his bandaliers...1715 i.e. Cuffabout was wearing a soldier's shoulder-belt, and was ready to join the Jacobite rebels in 1715. The Jacobites, as supporters of the Stewart monarchy under which both Covenanters and the Covenanting cause had suffered, are intolerable to Deans.

112.35 Arniston Robert Dundas, Lord Arniston (1685–1753). Dundas became a judge in 1737: see note to 42.12.

112.37–38 popish medals...Gordon in 1711 James Dundas of Arniston presented a Jacobite medal to the Faculty of Advocates on behalf of the Roman Catholic Duchess of Gordon; the Faculty made some difficulty over accepting it because of its political implications. It was the subject of a pamphlet by Daniel Defoe, *The Scotch Medal Decipher'd* (1711).

112.39 Kittlepunt *literally* tricky point.

112.40 Arminian see note to 112.5.

112.42 Cocceian follower of Johannes Cocceius (1603–69), a professor in Leyden in the Netherlands from 1650. He opposed strict Calvinist theology and argued for a personal covenant between the individual and God. James Renwick is quoted as using the term in 'Mr James Renwick', in John Howie (1735–93), *Biographica Scoticana; or... Scots Worthies*, 4th edn (Glasgow, 1813; originally published 1775), 430 (*CLA*, 71).

112.43 Whulliewhaw i.e. a flatterer who deceives by wheedling and cajoling.

113.2 Næmmo from Latin *nemo*, meaning 'nobody'.

113.6 in the multitude of counsellors there's safety see Proverbs 11.14, 24.6.

113.7 young Mackenyie in practice this is a fictional character, like the rest of the list of possible defenders for Effie. Sir George Mackenzie (see note to 113.12) did have an advocate nephew, Simon Mackenzie, but he was born in 1664 and died in 1730. The 'z' in modern versions of Mackenzie is a false transliteration of the medieval letter yogh.

113.7 practiques *Scots law* collections of legal material made for their utility, *or*, the recorded decisions of the Court of Session, forming a system of case-law. Saddletree probably has in mind Sir George Mackenzie's *Laws and Customs of Scotland in Matters Criminal* (1678) rather than the better known *Institutions of the Law of Scotland* (1684), because the meaning of *practique* is 'customary usage, usual practice'.

113.12 Bluidy Mackenyie Sir George Mackenzie of Rosehaugh (1636–91), who as Lord Advocate 1677–86, and 1688, led the legal prosecution of the Covenanters, for which he earned the epithet *Bluidy* ('Bloody'). He is regarded as the founder of the Advocates' Library (1689), and was the author of legal works (see note above), a novel *Aretina* (1660), and *A Vindication of the Government of Scotland during the Reign of King Charles II* (1683), among others.

113.16 **gae down the water** go to wreck or perdition.

113.20 **ben the house** through to the other room.

113.30–31 **sectarians, nor sons nor grandsons of sectarians** Butler's grandfather was an Independent. The term *sectarian* was used abusively by Presbyterians of Independents (see note to 65.31) in the 17th century.

113.38–39 **right-hand and left-hand defections** see notes to 71.18, and 90.16–18.

114.1–2 **sun shines, and the rain descends on the just and unjust** see Matthew 5.45.

114.9 **Can a man touch pitch and not be defiled** proverbial: see Ecclesiasticus 13.1 in the Apocrypha; *ODEP*, 834.

114.14 **scattered...remnant** see note to 109.28.

114.14–15 **clifts of the rocks** see Exodus 33.22; Song of Solomon 2.14; Isaiah 2.21, 57.5; Jeremiah 49.16; Obadiah 3; 'Life and Death of Daniel Cargill', in Walker, 2.49.

114.37 **singuli in solidum** *Latin* singly for the entire sum. As usual Saddletree's Latin is not correct: when referring to Mrs Saddletree he should have said *singulae*.

115.22 **wi' a wat finger** *proverbial* with the utmost ease: see Ray, 215; *ODEP*, 881.

115.25 **maksna muckle** it is of no consequence, it doesn't matter.

115.35 **interlocutor of relevancy** judicial pronouncement that the charges are relevant: see note to 31.40–41.

116.4 **ocior ventis—ocior Euro** *Latin* faster than the winds, faster than the southeast wind: see Horace (65–8 BC), *Odes*, 2.16.23: 'ocior cervis et agente nimbos / ocior Euro' (faster than the deer and faster than the south-east wind that drives along the storm-clouds).

116.6 **gift of the gab** *proverbial* gift of being able to talk well and convincingly, a stock phrase often used in a slightly mocking manner: *ODEP*, 301.

116.23 **protestation** *Scots Law* procedure by which a defender in the Court of Session compels the pursuer either to proceed with an action or end it. However, while Saddletree's legal language is designed to make Dumbiedikes's offer appear binding, in this context *protestation* seems to be used in a non-technical way, to mean that Dumbiedikes had formally requested a change in what he had submitted.

116.23–24 **add and eik** make an addition to a formal legal document.

116.33 **perduellion nor læse-majesty** see notes to 108.37 and 108.43.

117 **motto** see *The Tempest*, 1.1.43–44.

117.27 **Bucephalus** horse of Alexander the Great, Alexander III of Macedon (356–23 BC).

117.28 **Rory Bean** *Rory* is an anglicised form of the Gaelic Ruairidh (Roderick), which is often used as a generic name for a Highlander. The whole name may be a joke derived from *Sawney Bean*, by tradition a 15th-century cannibal who lived on the coast of Ayrshire near Ballantrae. However, as *Sawney* (a diminutive of Alexander) was used in England in the 17th and 18th centuries as a generic (and hostile) name for Scotsmen, and as the first accounts of Sawney Bean emerge in English broadsides in the 17th century, it is possible that the name *Rory Bean* is meant to suggest that this portrait of a wilful pony is a caricature of the breed.

118.2 **Tempus nemini** *Latin* time [waits] for no-one. Proverbial: see *ODEP*, 822.

118.14 **Michel Novit** combination of Scots and Latin meaning 'he knows much', unlike his father (see note to 68.34).

118.18 **cocked hat** three-cornered hat with the brim permanently turned up.

119.23 was for in wanted to.

119.31 in bye inside, into the interior.

119.34 that huge one immense keys, said to be the keys of the Edinburgh tolbooth (demolished in 1817), may be seen hanging in the hall in Abbotsford.

120.4 Fugit irrevocabile tempus *Latin* time flies and cannot be recalled. See Virgil, (70–19 BC), *Georgics*, 3.284.

120.19 sheriff officers officers who fulfilled the orders of the sheriff court.

120.24 Troth will I no I certainly will not.

121.16–18 Council Chamber . . . at a little distance from the prison in the SW corner of Parliament Square. It was the width of St Giles from the tolbooth.

121.18 senators members of the Roman senate, here used jocularly of town councillors.

122.13 slouched hat hat with a wide brim worn so that the brim covers the face.

122.13 loaded whip whip weighted with lead.

122.16 James Ratcliffe see note to 59.3.

122.36 aught command eighth commandment: 'Thou shalt not steal' (Exodus 20.15).

122.40 thou shalt steal compare *Measure for Measure*, 1.2.7–11, and the 'Wicked Bible' (1632) in which the word 'not' was omitted from the seventh commandment, making it 'Thou shalt commit adultery'.

123.22 next Wednesday eight days a week on Wednesday; i.e. 22 September 1736.

123.26 the auld jaud is no sae ill as that comes to the law is not so bad that it comes to a hanging. Law (as well as fortune) is often personified as a wilful horse.

123.26–27 her bark waur than her bite proverbial: see *ODEP*, 30.

124.3 pit a beast out o' the way kill an animal.

124.13 wan out got out, escaped.

124.21 Good Town sobriquet for Edinburgh.

124.22 Sharpitlaw i.e. Sharpened-law.

124.39 the finisher of the law the hangman.

124.44 in-town multure payment levied for grinding corn at the superior's mill; tenants and feuars were usually obliged by the terms of their tenancy or feu to use the superior's mill.

126.25 bastard and fiery zeal see 'Vindication of Cameron's Name', in Walker, 1.284.

129 motto see 'The Young Tamlane', in *SMM*, no. 411, stanza 39 (Child, 39A); *Minstrelsy*, 2.401, stanza 51 (Child, 39I).

129.18–21 Hopes . . . cherish'd long Samuel Taylor Coleridge, 'Love' (1799), lines 73–76.

129.23 Cato's daughter Porcia (d. 43 BC), daughter of Marcus Portius Cato Uticensis (95–46 BC). She shared the republican ideals of her father and her husband Brutus (*c.* 85–42 BC), but Porcia as the image of resolution in the face of suffering probably owes more to Shakespeare's portrayal than to classical literature: see *Julius Caesar*, 2.1.234–309.

131.39 day of affliction Jeremiah 16.19: 'O Lord, my strength, and my fortress, and my refuge in the day of affliction'.

131.42–43 the bread of life Jesus, and his teachings: John 6.35, 48.

132.7 yoke of such bitter affliction common phrase, expanding the biblical 'yoke', used in sermons and exegetical literature about the need to accept the trials and tribulations of life as part of God's purpose.

132.11 waters of Merah see Exodus 15.23: 'they could not drink of the waters of Marah, for they were bitter'.

132.12 full cup compare Psalm 23.5. Deans here uses the biblical image of God as the host at a feast who distributes meat and drink to his guests as he sees fit.

132.13 basket and store see Deuteronomy 28.5, 17; Robert Burns, 'Holy Willie's Prayer' (written 1785; first published 1801), line 77 (Kinsley, no. 53). The phrase is used of the daily supply of food and provisions.

132.14 bonnet... "reverently aside" see Robert Burns, 'The Cotter's Saturday Night' (1786), line 104 (Kinsley, no. 72).

132.17 The man after God's own heart David: see 1 Samuel 13.14.

132.17–18 washed and anointed himself, and did eat bread see 2 Samuel 12.20.

132.33–34 hours... winged with joy compare William Hamilton of Gilbertfield (c.1665–1751), *A New Edition of the Life and Heroick Actions of the Renoun'd Sir William Wallace* (1722), 6.55–56; Robert Burns, 'Tam o' Shanter' (1791), lines 55–56 (Kinsley, no. 321).

133.3 grain of human leaven compare 1 Corinthians 5.6–8.

133.23 God of Israel phrase used 29 times in the Authorised Version; see e.g. Psalm 72.18, Luke 1.68.

133.23–24 blessings of the promise the favour and kindness of God resulting from his promise to Abram in Genesis 12.1–3 and Ch. 15, interpreted in the New Testament as a promise that God will send the Messiah (Romans 4.13, 14; Galatians 3.16), and that through faith man will be saved (Romans 9.8; Galatians 4.28; Hebrews 6.12–16).

133.27 fullness of the heart state of being full of emotion.

133.40 purchased and promised blessings blessings of salvation purchased by Jesus's death on the cross and promised to Abram (see note to 133.23–24); see 'Life and Death of Alexander Peden', in Walker, 1.31, 85; and 'Life and Death of Walter Smith', in Walker, 2.99.

133.41–42 as you were not of the world see John 17.14, 16.

134.16 the ribband unmarried women wore a ribbon which went over the front of the head and tied over the hair at the back of the neck: see e.g. David Allan's painting 'The Highland Dance' on loan to the National Galleries of Scotland.

134.18–20 the scarlet tartan screen... Netherlands a kind of large headsquare worn round the back of the neck and down the front; the point of comparison with the Netherlands has not been determined.

134.31–33 precautionary edicts which the council of the city, and even the parliament of Scotland, had passed for dispersing their bands none has been traced.

135 motto see *Hamlet*, 2.2.594–96.

135.13–15 presbyterians, whose government... imaginary crimes it is estimated that as many as 4000 people were executed for witchcraft in Scotland between 1560 and 1707, but the narrator is wrong in implying that witchcraft trials were specifically the product of Presbyterianism: of the 4 witch-craft 'epidemics' (1590–97, the late 1620s, the 1640s, and 1660–63) only that of the 1640s took place under Presbyterian government. See T. C. Smout, *A History of the Scottish People 1560–1830* (London, 1969), 198–207.

135.19 Baxter's Worlds of Spirits Richard Baxter, *Certainty of the World of Spirits* (London, 1691): *CLA*, 146. As Scott confesses in a Magnum note (12.19), the story on which this passage is based actually comes from Captain George Burton whose report appears in Richard Bovett, *Pandæmonium, or the Devil's Cloyster* (London, 1684), 172–75: *CLA*, 143. The story, 'The Fairy Boy of Leith', concerns a lad who acts as drummer for fairies meeting under the

Calton Hill in Edinburgh; it is reproduced in Magnum, 12.19–20.

135.35 one of their gifted seers Alexander Peden: see note to 78.34.

135.36 Sorn in Ayshire, 25 km E of Ayr.

135.37–40 It is hard living ... this night 'Life and Death of Alexander Peden', in Walker, 1.79.

136.1 Ansars helpers, auxiliaries; specifically the citizens of Medina who offered Mohammed refuge and assistance when he fled from Mecca.

136.4 Crochmade not identified.

136.5–17 apparition of a tall black man ... heard and felt see 'Life and Death of John Semple', in Walker, 1.194–95.

136.12 John Semple of Carsphairn see note to 81.13–14.

136.13 the whaup in the rape *proverbial* what was amiss: see Kelly, 305; Ramsay, 114; *ODEP*, 881. A *whaup* is a 'kink'.

136.14–15 the Great Enemy the Devil.

136.18–19 adown the water screeching and bullering see an editorial footnote on Satan in Robert Law, *Memorialls ... from 1638 to 1684*, ed. Charles Kirkpatrick Sharpe (Edinburgh, 1818), 8. Scott was involved in editing this work: see *Letters*, 4.538–39.

136.19 Bull of Bashan see Psalm 22.12–13. In a Magnum note Scott remarks that the 'gloomy, dangerous, and constant wanderings of the persecuted sect of Cameronians' naturally led to their believing that they were persecuted 'by the secret wiles and open terrors of Satan' (Magnum, 12.20–21).

136.36–38 like Christiana in the Pilgrim's Progress ... Death see *The Pilgrim's Progress*, Part 2, 241–46.

136.37–38 Valley of the Shadow of Death Psalm 23.4.

136.38–39 now in glimmer and now in gloom Samuel Taylor Coleridge, 'Christabel', Part 1 (written 1798; published 1816), line 169.

137.1 night is as noon-day see Job 5.14; Isaiah 58.10, 59.10.

137.9–10 St Anthony the Eremite d. 356. He spent most of his life in solitude in desert places in Egypt, engaged in prayer, study and manual labour, and confronting violent sexual temptations. Because he organised the hermits attracted by his example into loose-knit communities St Anthony is regarded as the founder of monasticism.

137.17–18 Nicol Muschat see note to 99.23.

137.25 ancient British i.e. pertaining to the Britons of Strathclyde (who spoke what would now be called Welsh). Variants of the saying appear in both Welsh and Gaelic (see next note).

137.25–26 May you have a cairn for your burial-place proverbial. See A65 in Donald MacIntosh, *A Collection of Gaelic Proverbs and Familiar Phrases* (Edinburgh, 1819; originally published 1785): 'Am fear nach meudaich an carn, g'a meudaich e chroich', translated as 'The man who will not increase the cairn, may he augment the gallows'. Alexander Nicolson, editor of the edition of 1881, comments: 'It was an ancient Celtic custom to erect a cairn, or pile of stones, as a memorial to the ... infamy of the person buried beneath it' (23). Scott owned both editions: *CLA*, 86, 175.

138.22 predestined to evil here and hereafter i.e. the speaker is despairing: Jeanie articulates the orthodox position that mercy is available to all.

138.24–25 chief of sinners see 1 Timothy 1.15.

139.1 needless to swear ... lawful see Matthew 5.34–37.

139.8–9 apostate spirit incarnate one of the angels who fell with Satan, appearing here as human.

139.12 walk by my counsel see Psalm 1.1.

139.34–35 agony ... bitterness of death compare Job 6.2–4; Psalm 88.1–7.

139.35 bitterness of death 1 Samuel 15.32.

140.33   reed you would lean to   compare Isaiah 36.6; *ODEP*, 88.

140.38–39   You saw your sister . . . preceding the birth   see text, 92.43–93.2.

140.41   take the case from under the statute   i.e. the law on child-murder would not be applicable to this case. The phrase is common in legal books of the period.

140.43   the quality of concealment is essential   see Hume, *Crimes*, 1.466–71; Magnum 12.21.

141.35–36   breath of your mouth   see Job 15.30; Psalm 33.6.

142.3–4   God . . . witness the truth of what I say   more than just a court procedure: in the Bible God is frequently called upon to witness (i.e. to see and to give testimony about) people's dealings with each other.

142.7   lucre of gain   the phrase is 'frequent in 17th c[entury]' (*OED, lucre*, 2). Compare 1 Timothy 3.3, 8; Titus 1.7, 11; 1 Peter 5.2.

142.10   He has given us a law . . . for the lamp of our path   a common biblical concept. Compare e.g. Proverbs 6.23: 'For the commandment is a lamp; and the law is a light; and reproofs of instruction are the way of life'.

142.11   err against knowledge   i.e. ignore knowledge of God's will and the way of salvation.

142.14–15   why do not you step forward   it had not been established in law that a woman's confession of pregnancy to the father would 'take her case from under the statute': see Hume, *Crimes*, 1.468–69.

142.32–35   When the gledd's . . . the hill   probably by Scott.

142.41–44   O sleep ye sound . . . where ye hide   not directly from any ballad, but the idea of a man rising from his bed to escape from great odds is balladic: compare 'The Baron of Brackley' (Child, 203C), and 'Young Johnstone' (Child, 88C), stanza 22.

142   motto   see *Hamlet*, 4.5.6–10.

143.20   the digressive poet Ariosto   Ludovico Ariosto (1474–1533), author of *Orlando furioso* (1516–32), one of the great works of the Italian Renaissance. Written in *ottava rima*, it has three main plot lines and numerous subsidiary episodes which are often linked as Scott describes. See *CLA*, 42, 55, 185, 250.

143.25   knitter . . . stocking-looms   a frame for weaving stockings is supposed to have been invented by William Lee in 1589 (*OED*); this form of production superseded hand-knitting in the early 18th century. By 1811 'there were perhaps 29,000 stocking-looms in the country, and 50,000 workers employed in and about the hosiery trade' (E. P. Thomson, *The Making of the English Working Class* (London, 1963), 530–31).

144.4   religious professors   people who make an open profession of religious belief.

144.8–9   clout ower the croun   blow on the head.

144.12–13   a wee-bit skulduddery for the benefit of the kirk-treasurer   pre-marital fornication, or adultery, which, if detected, was reported to the kirk session and led to a fine. See note to 93.25–26.

144.20–21   abune stairs   *literally* above stairs, i.e. among our rulers.

144.35   run their letters   be released again after the legal period for detention without trial has elapsed.

145.1   time has been   i.e. in the period of the Scottish Reformation around 1560, and in the Covenanting period 1660–85.

145.4   silenced ministers   ministers of religion forbidden after 1662 to preach or to hold services on account of their refusal to take the oath of allegiance to the crown. See Historical Note to *The Tale of Old Mortality*, ed. Douglas Mack, EEWN 4b, 432–33.

145.5   the Bow-head and the Covenant-close   the first, at the intersection of the Bow and the Lawnmarket, was famous for its covenanting sympathies; the second (on S side of High St below St Giles) was where the Solemn League and Covenant (see note to 30.30) was signed in 1643. David Deans's pamphlet, 'Cry of an Howl in the Desart,' was supposedly printed at the Bowhead (text, 103.6–7).

145.5 tents of Kedar Psalm 120.5; Song of Solomon 1.5. *Kedar* was a place of sorrow.

145.7–8 the Laigh-Calton and the back o' the Canongate these ran at the bottom of the valley to the N of the Canongate and below the Calton Hill. As this was the edge of town no doubt it was an area where thieves and vagabonds might hide.

145.8 an' it bide and let it stay that way.

145.37 on that lay in that business.

145.39 Jock Dalgleish the Edinburgh hangman, appointed in 1722.

145.39 the finisher of the law the hangman.

146.4 wan off escaped.

146.6 play was played out events had come to a conclusion.

146.18 come on develop.

146.19–20 naebody ... but what he'll come to nobody will live as he has lived without becoming accustomed to it.

146.25 for as young as he is even though he's young.

146.25 sae that so long as.

146.33 naething for naething proverbial: *ODEP*, 579.

146.36 an ye can gi'e us a lift if you can give us a helping hand.

146.39 a wink's as gude as a nod to a blind horse proverbial: see *ODEP*, 575.

146.43 time about's fair play proverbial: see *ODEP*, 846.

147.4 gif-gaf makes gude friends *proverbial* give and take makes for good friends: see Ray, 112; *ODEP*, 301.

147.16 De'il haet o' me kens I'm damned if I know.

147.39 it's waiting for dead folks' shoon proverbial: see *ODEP*, 171.

147.41 gay and heavy very heavy, considerable.

147.41 show cause give reasons.

147.42 right and reason obsolete English phrase meaning here 'reasonable'.

148.2 de'il ma care *emphatic* what the devil, no matter.

148.4 The de'il ye did *emphatic* you didn't!

148.4 this is finding a mare's nest wi' a witness to find a mare's nest is to make an illusory discovery (*ODEP*, 512), but the sense here is that this is a real (although amazing) discovery as there is a witness to it.

148.10 drawing up wi' becoming friendly with, beginning a courtship with.

148.11 about the Pleasaunts i.e. near the Pleasance, an area then just outside the city, to the SE.

148.20 Highland bonnet kind of large beret with a broad head-band (but no brim) worn down to one side.

148.26 birth-night introduction introduction to the monarch on the evening of a royal birthday celebration.

148.27 Touchstone's directions to Audrey see *As You Like It*, 5.4.65–66.

148.30 Daddie Ratton i.e. Father Rat. 'Ratton', as well as 'daddie', can be a term of endearment in Scots.

148.31–32 half-hangit Maggie Dickson on 2 September 1724 Margaret Dickson was hanged in Edinburgh for the same crime as Effie Deans; her body was returned to her relatives for burial in Musselburgh, but on the way there she regained consciousness. She lived for several more years. See Hume, *Trial*, 2.351–52; Robert Chambers, *Traditions of Edinburgh*, 2 vols (Edinburgh, 1825), 2.188.

148.34 Madge   in the Magnum (13.36–39), there is a long note after Madge's death later in the novel suggesting that the character of Madge was based on 'Feckless Fannie'. This suggestion came from Joseph Train, who in the Magnum is frequently mentioned as providing Scott with materials. However, there is no mention of Feckless Fannie in the Scott-Train correspondence for 1817–18; Feckless Fannie as described in the note has no connection with Madge in the novel; and even Scott was unlikely to remember a personage who wandered 'over all Scotland and England' between 1767 and 1775.

148.42 De'il be in my fingers, then   *literally* let the devil be in my fingers if that's not true; i.e. *emphatic* yes indeed!

149.2 gude auld cause   the Puritan or Covenanting cause. The phrase was used by opponents of the Stewart monarchy that replaced the Commonwealth (see note to 65.42) in 1660. See John Milton, *The Ready and Easy Way to Establish a Free Commonwealth* (1660), final paragraph: 'What I have spoken is the language of that which is not called amiss "The good old Cause"'. See also John Dryden, *Absalom and Achitophel* (1681), line 82, and note to 383.25.

149.2 it's be   it will be.

149.4–7 Hey for cavaliers … for fear   see the chorus of 'The Cavaliers Song', in *Wit and Mirth, or Pills to Purge Melancholy*, ed. Thomas d'Urfey, 6 vols (1719–20), 3.131.

149.6 old Beelzebub   the devil.

149.7 Oliver   Oliver Cromwell (1599–1658). Leader of the Independents in the English Parliament, he became leader of the Parliamentary army and defeated Charles I at Naseby in 1645. After the execution of the King in 1649 Cromwell conquered the whole of the British Isles and established for the first time a single British state, under himself as Protector.

149.19 lang syne   a long time ago.

149.19 I'll ne'er fash my thumb   *proverbial* I'll never trouble myself. See *ODEP*, 246.

149.21–24 I glance like the wildfire … bonny as me   part of the song written by George Robertson (see text, 278.1) for Madge: see also 259.6–7 and 278.7–14.

149.34–36 the single carritch … calling   the Shorter and the Larger Catechism, drawn up 1643–48, and approved 1647–48. In the Shorter Catechism, justification is defined as 'an act of God's free grace, in which He pardons all our sins, and accepts us as righteous in His sight, for the sake of the righteousness of Christ alone, which is imputed to us, and received by faith alone'. Effectual calling 'is the work of God's Spirit, whereby, convincing us of our sin and misery, enlightening our minds in the knowledge of Christ, and renewing our wills, He persuades and enables us to embrace Jesus Christ, freely offered to us in the Gospel' (*The School of Faith: the Catechisms of the Reformed Church*, ed. Thomas F. Torrance (London, 1959), 267). The Shorter Catechism, a list of questions and answers which teach the doctrines of Christianity as interpreted by John Calvin, was the standard religious teaching text in 18th-century Scotland.

149.36 assembly of divines at Westminster   convened in 1643 the assembly originally met to reform the thirty nine articles of the Church of England, but after the signing of the Solemn League and Covenant in 1643 (see note to 30.30) it was joined by a Scottish delegation, and together they produced the Westminster Confession of Faith, and the Longer and the Shorter Catechisms, all approved by the General Assembly of the Church of Scotland in 1647–48, and by the English Parliament in 1648.

150.5 ilka day's claiths everyday clothes.

150.9 win ower wi' recover from, overcome.

150.15 wark-house in Leith-Wynd prison for minor offenders who, with the object of being reformed (or 'corrected', hence the alternative name correction-house), were subject to forced labour. Leith Wynd led from the Netherbow Port north towards the Calton Hill, and round its western side.

150.25 An onybody ask ye, say ye dinna ken this sounds like a line from a song, but is unidentified.

150.27 de'il ane *emphatic* not one.

150.29 Rob the Ranter i.e. Rob is a singer or bagpipe player. The term *ranter* also suggests noise and rough living.

150.35 ilka day rags see note to 150.5.

150.37 ilka day's claiths see note to 150.5.

151.5 threshie-coat coat of rushes; i.e. a good coat of extraordinary materials. Compare the Scottish folk-tale 'Rashiecoat', a version of the Cinderella story, in Robert Chambers, *The Popular Rhymes of Scotland*, 4th edn (Edinrgh, 1870), 66–68 (it does not appear in earlier edns); *A Forgotten Heritage*, ed. Hannah Aitken (Edinburgh and London, 1973), 73–76.

151.7 blessing on his bonnie face prayer for prosperity and grace, offered in response to something done for the speaker.

151.30–33 What did ye wi' the bridal ring ... an auld true love o' mine, O see 'The Wren, or, Lennox's Love to Blantyre', in Herd, 2.209–10; *SMM*, no. 483.

151.35 if Ophelia be the most affecting see *Hamlet*, 4.5.

152.11 must hame must go home.

152 motto 'Little Musgrave and Lady Barnard' (Child, 81), in Percy, 3.67–73, lines 53–56.

153.3 ill winning at difficult to get at.

153.41–42 I wish I had the skelping o' him I wish I could beat him.

154.5 It wad hae been dearly telling him that he had ne'er seen it would have been richly to his advantage if he had never seen (*OED, tell*, verb 22d).

155.39–40 as like to each other as the collier to the de'il proverbial: see *ODEP*, 465.

155.40–41 moonshine in water proverbial: see *ODEP*, 542.

156.6 Do you think me as mad as she is, to trust you must think I am as mad as her if you think I can trust her guidance.

156.16 de'il a bit he can be honest *emphatic* he can't possibly be honest.

157.17–18 bat-fleeing time dusk, when bats begin to fly.

157.32 come o't what likes whatever happens.

158.2–3 byganes suld be byganes proverbial: see *ODEP*, 96.

158.7–8 Deacon Sanders's new cleansing draps presumably a proprietary cleansing agent, but not identified.

158.35–38 Good even ... true lover of mine shall be see John Aubrey, *Miscellanies*, ed. John Buchanan-Brown (Fontwell, Sussex, 1972), 84. Scott owned the 2nd edn of 1721: *CLA*, 149.

159.11–12 like to like ... ye are baith a pair o' the deevil's peats proverbial: see *ODEP*, 465. See also note to 155.39–40 for the conventional form of the proverb. A 'peat' is vegetable matter, cut from a peat bog in a brick shape, dried, and used as fuel.

159.17–19 Folk kill ... gulley although proverbial in form these are not recognised proverbs.

159.20–23 It is the bonny butcher lad ... he slew not identified; probably by Scott.

159.25 wyte of blame for.

159.30–33   When the gledd's . . . the hill   probably by Scott. See text, 142.32–35.

159.34   if   i.e. even if.

159.36   Poinder   i.e. one who, authorised by a warrant, seizes goods to sell in settlement of unpaid debts.

159.42   done up   had it, ruined (*OED, do*, verb 52e).

160.1   get his neck raxed   get his neck stretched, i.e. get hanged.

160.2   cracking like a pen-gun   talking in a lively manner, chattering loudly.

160.7–8   gleg as Mackeachan's elshin, that ran through sax plies of bend-leather and half an inch into the king's heel   a popular story about King Robert the Bruce who needed shoe repairs, but was betrayed by the shoemaker. It was told by Burns, repeated by John Ramsay of Ochtertyre, and reported by James Currie in his edition of *The Works of Robert Burns*, 2nd edn, 4 vols (London, 1801), 1.195 (Inglis).

160.14–17   There's a bloodhound . . . between   probably by Scott.

160.19   setting off at score   breaking out suddenly and impetuously.

160.20–23   O sleep ye sound . . . where ye hide   see note to 142.41–44.

160.38   Duke's Walk   now obliterated, it lay in the King's Park just SE of Holyrood. It was said to be the favourite walk of the Duke of York (later James VII and II).

161   motto   *Measure for Measure*, 3.2.233–34.

162.8   green hill   in ballads phrases like the 'green hill' or the 'green wood' tend to imply a place where sexual violence may take place.

162.11   to crack nuts   i.e. to engage in something of no significance.

162.24   Pleasance   see note to 148.11. The Pleasance is very close to where Jeanie is supposed to live.

162.28–29   whistle on his thumb   twiddle his thumbs, be busy in a futile task.

163.3   "life and mettle" in her heels   Robert Burns, 'Tam o' Shanter' (1791), line 118 (Kinsley, no. 321).

163.21–23   may her days be long . . . honour father and mother   see the fourth commandment, Exodus 20.12.

163.23   purchased and promised blessings   see notes to 133.23–24 and 133.40.

163.24   watches of the night   the four periods into which night was conventionally divided (see *OED, watch*, noun 4), used rhetorically for night-time. The phrase is biblical: e.g. see Psalm 63.6; Matthew 14.25.

163.25   uprising of the morning   see Nehemiah 4.21.

163.26   hid thy face from them   see 2 Chronicles 6.42, 30.9; Psalm 132.10.

163.26   in truth and in sincerity   see Joshua 24.14; 1 Corinthians 5.8.

163.30–31   her head had been covered by the prayers of the just as by an helmet   not a quotation, but the terminology is biblical: compare 1 Corinthians 11.4–5; Ephesians 6.17–18.

163.31   confidence   in addition to its normal meaning of 'assurance', the term implies a strong trust in God: compare Hebrews 10.35.

163.33   its countenance   compare Psalms 42.5, 44.3, 89.15; Acts 2.28.

163.37   sun-blink on a stormy sea   see 'Life and Death of Alexander Peden', in Walker, 1.157; 'Life and Death of Richard Cameron', in Walker, 1.218; and 'Postscript', in Walker, 2.112.

164.1–2   started, like a greyhound from the slips   see *Henry V*, 3.1.31–32.

164.25   Both made their heels serve them   both ran away.

164.27–28 Then hey play up … the gee 'The Runaway Bride', lines 7–8, in Herd, 2.87; *SMM*, no. 474.

164.28 has ta'en the gee has taken the sulks.

165.4 Middleburgh the name suggests a middling social status, but may be derived from Middelburg, in Zeeland in the SW of the Netherlands, near Campvere (see note to 167.27).

165.11 content to worship God, though the devil bid you see *Othello*, 1.1.109.

165.18–19 my hint to speak *Othello*, 1.3.142.

165.20 hung by the wall, like unscoured armour see *Measure for Measure*, 1.2.160.

165.26–27 Would put in every honest hand … the world see *Othello*, 4.2.143–44. *Would scourge me* means 'would scourge for me'.

165.35 poisoned chalice *Macbeth*, 1.7.11.

166.9 under the statute see note to 140.41.

166.12 speak to speak about.

166.17 true-blue see note to 68.4.

166.18 disgrace his testimony i.e. discredit his witness to the gospel of Christ, as well as evidence given in court. To take an oath in court would have involved Deans in recognising the civil authority, which he repudiates because it did not maintain the Covenants. See note to 71.17.

166.19 defections of the times see notes to 71.17–18, and 90.16–18.

166.22 affirmation, as in the case of Quakers Quakers were permitted in civil cases to give a solemn affirmation instead of taking an oath by the act 22 George II, c. 46 (1749); the permission was not extended to criminal cases in Scotland until the act 9 George IV, c. 29 (1828). For objections to taking oaths see note to 75.35–36.

166.32 rest upon put trust in.

167.3 on a suddenty suddenly, at once. In *Letters*, 12.349, Scott ascribes this phrase to Robert Lindsay of Pitscottie (*c.* 1532–80), *The Historie and Chronicles of Scotland* (1728): see *CLA*, 8, 259.

167.4 zeal religious enthusiasm, often considered a characteristic of Protestant sects.

167.6 be fair gud-day and fair gud-e'en wi' ilka man be on civil terms with everyone.

167.8 abjuration-oath an oath repudiating the Apologetical Declaration (drawn up in 1684 by James Renwick: see note to 102.35), which argued that it was legitimate to take revenge upon the persecutors of the Covenanters (see Wodrow, 4.148–49). In December 1684 the Privy Council approved an oath (requiring repudiation of the Declaration) which could be administered on whole parishes; those who refused to make it were subject to instant execution (see Wodrow, 4.160–62).

167.8 patronage the right of a landowner to choose the minister of a parish. This was fiercely repudiated by many in the Church of Scotland in the Restoration period, and abolished after the Revolution of 1688–89; it was restored by the Patronage Act of 1712, led to the first major secession from the Church of Scotland in 1733, and ultimately split the Church in 1843. Although a landowner invested with rights of patronage could choose the minister, the presentee still had to have the qualifications demanded by the Church of Scotland, and the induction to a charge was a function of the local presbytery. In the course of the 18th century presbyteries failed on many occasions to induct a minister who had been properly presented by a landowner with rights of patronage, resulting in disciplinary measures by the General Assembly, in expulsion from the Church of Scotland of ministers who refused to induct a presentee to a charge, and thus in schism.

167.21 **naething frae nane o' ye** nothing from any of you.

167.21 **for as grand's ye are** great (or rich) though you are.

167.27 **Campvere** Veere, port in SW Netherlands, near Middelburg (see note to 165.4). In the 14th century the Scots burghs experimented with establishing a staple, i.e. a named port through which all Scottish exports would be directed; Middelburg and Bruges were tried, but Veere became the permanent outlet in 1444 and a Scots presence was maintained there until 1795. See Rosalind Mitchison, *A History of Scotland*, 2nd edn (London, 1982), 66.

167.38 **Correction-house in Leith Wynd** see note to 150.15.

167.42 **Other than a good ane** not a good person, i.e. a disreputable person.

168.2 **Frigate-Whins** Figgate Whins, an area of desolate land near Portobello in Edinburgh, formerly the haunt of footpads. See Grant, 3.143–45.

168.2–3 **set my ten commandments in your wizend face** see *2 Henry VI*, 1.3.140. The 'ten commandments' are a woman's ten fingernails (or 'claws').

168.26 **twal-pennies Scots** a Scots shilling, worth 1*d*. sterling (0.42p). In 1707 the Scottish pound was worth one-twelfth of an English pound.

168.30 **fitted for the meridian** suited to the tastes.

168.32 **the grim feature** John Milton, *Paradise Lost* (1667), 10.279. The phrase describes Death.

169.1 **Elector of Hanover's birth-day** George II's birthday (10 November), celebrated with a holiday. In Edinburgh it was frequently marked by disorder; see Robert Fergusson, on the birthday of George III, 'The King's Birth-Day in Edinburgh' (1772). Hanover was a northern German principality and its ruler was called 'Elector' because he was one of those who elected the Emperor. The Elector of Hanover was specified as the heir to the British throne by Acts of the English and Scottish parliaments and succeeded in 1714. In calling George II by his German title 'Elector of Hanover' Meg implicitly denies the legitimacy of his rule in Britain: i.e. she is a Jacobite.

169.17 **Duddingstone** village now within Edinburgh, then about 4 km SE.

169.38 **Gude Town** sobriquet for Edinburgh.

169.42 **deevil's buckie** perverse, obstinate person.

170.10 **Bess o' Bedlam** madwoman.

170.16 **after her ordinar** in her usual way.

170.20 **pay the piper** *proverbial* meet the cost: *ODEP*, 615.

170.27 **Jean Japp** not identified.

170.28 **Pettycur** near Kinghorn, in Fife, where the ferry from Leith, the port of Edinburgh, used to land.

170.29 **Inchkeith** island in the middle of the Firth of Forth between Leith and Pettycur.

170.36–38 **Up in the air ... see her yet** see 'Up in the Air', refrain and stanza 1, lines 5–7, in *TTM*, 1.73: 'Now the sun's gane out o' sight / Beet in the ingle, and snuff the light: / In glens the fairies skip and dance, / And witches wallop o'er to France. / Up in the air / On my bonny grey mare, / And I see her yet, and I see her yet.'

170.39–41 **witches in Macbeth ... fly upwards from the stage** the production in which this happened has not been identified.

171.8–9 **occupied the attention of all concerned with the administration of justice** see Roughead, 116–44, 243–333.

171.22–23 **council of regency** see note to 63.40.

171.27 **act of parliament** the offer of a £200 reward was made by proclamation (not legislation) on 23 September 1736: see Roughead, 247–48.

171.27–28 **two hundred pounds reward** for each arrest and conviction for participation in the riot, resulting from information lodged by 20 November 1736.

171.29–30 unusual and severe enactment 10 George II, c. 35; reproduced in Roughead, 332–33. In addition to making outlaws of participants in the riot, the act made them liable to 'Pains of Death, and Confiscations of Moveables' if they did not surrender within twelve months of being outlawed. It also made those who 'shall conceal, aid, abet, or succour' rioters liable to death if convicted. Scott here combines the proclamation of 23 September 1736 and the legislation enacted in June 1737, and implies one act passed in autumn 1736.

171.31 what was chiefly accounted exceptionable the objection was to the state's interference in church affairs rather than the punishments with which the clergy were threatened for non-compliance: as explained in the text at 172.4–7 it was the general view that the General Assembly of the Church of Scotland was the sole authority in religious matters.

171.33 for a certain period one year from 1 August 1737.

171.33–34 immediately before the sermon the act specifies immediately after the sermon.

171.34–37 should refuse to comply … Scotland see 10 George II, c. 35. Apparently there was no sermon in many country parishes on the Sunday after the Act came into force, 7 August 1737 (see Roughead, 138).

172.1 Lords Spiritual bishops of the Church of England with seats in the House of Lords. The Church of Scotland, being Presbyterian in government, did not recognise the 'Lords Spiritual'. The offending passage reads: 'be it therefore enacted by the King's most Excellent Majesty, by and with the Consent of the Lords, Spiritual and Temporal, and Commons…' (10 George II, c. 35).

172.2 quodammodo *Latin* in some degree.

172.4 jus divinum *Latin* divine right.

172.5 invisible Head of the Kirk i.e. Christ. The Church of Scotland recognises no earthly Head.

172.11 upon the rights and independence of Scotland after the Union in 1707 many Scots continued to think of Scotland as an independent country but one which shared a legislature with England.

172.12 steps adopted for punishing the city of Edinburgh a bill introduced in the House of Lords 1 February 1737 would have removed Alexander Wilson, the Lord Provost, from his position, disqualified him from holding office, imprisoned him for a year, abolished the Town Guard, and required that the Netherbow Port, the city gate dividing Edinburgh from the Canongate, be kept permanently open. Speakers in the debate advocated the forfeiture of the city's charter and the removal of the Courts of Justice from Edinburgh. The act that was eventually passed (10 George II, c. 34) disqualified the Lord Provost from holding public office anywhere in Great Britain and imposed a fine of £2000 sterling on the city to be applied to paying a pension to Porteous's widow.

172.21 Mr Middleburgh as there was no recognised police force evidence was often gathered by magistrates in burghs (or justices of the peace in country areas), and forwarded to the sheriff or the Lord Advocate, which one depending on the gravity of the crime.

172.26 suburban villas the first detached houses in Edinburgh were built in Newington (S of St Leonard's) which was developed from 1806: see A. J. Youngson, *The Making of Classical Edinburgh* (Edinburgh, 1966), 272.

172.34 well to pass well off, comfortably off.

173.8–9 enquiries at *Scots* enquiries of.

173.9 bounden duty bound by the duties of the office. The phrase comes from the Communion Service, in the Anglican *Book of Common Prayer* (1559; revised 1662), and the Scottish *Book of Common Order* (1564).

173.11 the tae way or the t'other the one way or the other.

173.12–13   **that did not bear the sword in vain**   see Romans 13.4.

173.13   **terror to evil doers**   see Romans 13.3.

173.15   **Provost Dick**   Sir William Dick of Baird (1580–1655), Provost of Edinburgh 1638–39. He developed a huge trade with the Baltic countries, the Netherlands and the Mediterranean, and was so rich that he could lend huge sums of money to support the Covenanting cause. He also lent money to Charles II to fight the Commonwealth (see note to 65.42), and was ruined by the fines exacted by the Commonwealth after its conquest of Scotland. His office was in the Luckenbooths (see note to 28.12). For Scott's note see Magnum, 12.90–91.

173.15–17   **General Assembly of the Kirk, walking hand in hand with the real noble Scottish-hearted barons, and with the magistrates**   the General Assembly which ruled in matters spiritual, is here represented as working in harmony with the Scottish Parliament, a single-chamber parliament in which the nobility, barons (landowners representing the counties), and magistrates (representing the Royal Burghs) sat together.

173.19   **the ark**   Presbyterian rule in Scotland in the 1640s following the National Covenant (1638): see note to 30.30. The ark of the covenant (a phrase used 9 times in the Authorised Version: see e.g. 1 Samuel 4.3) represented the presence of God among his people.

173.20   **states' use**   i.e. the use of the Estates, the Scottish Parliament.

173.21   **sclate stanes**   pieces of slate, or stone resembling slate.

173.23   **the army at Dunselaw**   in 1639 the Scottish army assembled on Duns Law, 22 km W of Berwick upon Tweed, to prevent Charles I from overturning the revolution effected by the National Covenant (see note to 30.30) and the meeting of the General Assembly of the Church in Glasgow in 1638. No engagement took place but at the Pacification of Berwick (18 June) Charles agreed to nearly all the Scottish demands, including a meeting of the General Assembly and the calling of the Estates (Parliament). At the Assembly Episcopacy was abolished and the Presbyterian system of church government adopted, acts subsequently ratified by the Privy Council and the Estates; in addition the Privy Council required the whole nation to subscribe to the National Covenant.

173.23–24   **winna believe ... the window itsell still standing**   compare 2 *Henry VI*, 4.2.143–45.

173.26   **Gossford's Close**   formerly to the S of the Lawnmarket, on the line of the modern George IV Bridge. It is possible that Deans is mistaken in specifying Gossford's Close, for the description suggests that the office in question is in the Luckenbooths, and five doors above the entry to a close.

173.28–29   **the blessing ... Peniel and Mahanaim**   at Peniel, Jacob (the Patriarch) wrestled with an angel who blessed him, and at Mahanaim met 'the angels of God': see Genesis 32.30, 2. The *covenant* is God's promise of life to all living things, including Noah and his family: see Genesis 9.9–11.

173.30   **national vows**   see note to 72.2.

173.30   **pund Scots**   1s. 8d. (8p) sterling: the Scots pound was worth one-twelfth of an English pound in 1707 when the Scots currency was abolished. Many continued to refer to pounds Scots well into the 18th century.

173.30–31   **an unguent to clear our auld rannell-trees and our beds o' the English bugs**   i.e. some kind of cleanser to clean the irons from which pots were hung over the fire and another to get rid of bed bugs. It is not known what preparations had come on the market, nor why bed bugs should be called 'English bugs'.

173.33   **Arminian caterpillars, Socinian pismires, and deistical Miss Katies**   for *Arminian* see note to 112.5. *Socinian pismires* (ants) refers to the followers of Lelio (1525–62) and Fausto (1539–1604) Sozini (Lælius and

Faustus Socinus), two Italian theologians (uncle and nephew) who rejected Trinitarian beliefs, and thus the divinity of Christ. *Miss Katies* reflects the uncertain spelling of 'mosquitoes' in the 17th and 18th centuries (e.g. musketoe, muscato, moskito, moskeitoe), but also criticises the kind of shallow person Deans thinks would be deist. Deism was a form of religious thought common in the early 18th century which rejected revelation and argued that God could be perceived through the study of the created universe.

173.34 **bottomless pit** hell: Revelation 9.1, 2, 11; 11.7; 17.8; 20.1, 3.

173.34–35 **perverse, insidious, and lukewarm generation** see Deuteronomy 32.5; Matthew 17.17; Luke 9.41; Revelation 3.16.

174.10 **After the world** according to the way the world thinks.

174.11 **according to the flesh** i.e. physically; the phrase is very common in the Authorised Version.

174.12 **child of Belial** see note to 103.36.

174.12 **company-keeper** see 1 Corinthians 5.11: 'I have written unto you not to keep company, if any man that is called brother be a fornicator'. See also note to 75.33–34, and compare Job 34.8; Proverbs 24.19 (marginal version), 29.3; 1 Corinthians 5.9.

174.18 **common portion of corruption** original sin, i.e. humanity's common inheritance of sin from Adam: 'original sin is conveyed from our first parents to their posterity by natural generation' ('The Larger Catechism', in *The School of Faith: the Catechisms of the Reformed Church*, ed. Thomas F. Torrance (London, 1959), 189).

174.19 **cast . . . off** phrase used many times in the Old Testament describing God's rejection of his people Israel or of a single person: see e.g. Psalm 74.1, 'O God, why hast thou cast us off for ever?'.

174.26–27 **Porteous Act has come doun frae London** see notes to 171.29–30, and 171.31.

174.28–29 **foul and fatal Test** the Test Act of 1681. The Act required all those in public office (including the clergy) to swear their profession of the protestant religion. This involved affirming among other things 'that the king's majesty is the only supreme governor of this realm, over all persons, and in all causes, as well ecclesiastical as civil' (Wodrow, 3.297), and repudiating the National Covenant and the Solemn League and Covenant. Both were unacceptable to Presbyterians: see notes to 30.30 and 75.35–36.

174.35–37 **Sanders Peden . . . on the back** i.e. Alexander Peden: see note to 78.34. Peden preached on Psalm 129.3 ('the plowers plowed upon my back; they made long their furrows') in Kyle in Ayrshire in 1682: see 'Life and Death of Alexander Peden', in Walker, 1.59.

174.36 **killing time** strictly 1684–85 when the legal and the summary execution of Covenanters in Scotland was at its height, but often extended to the period 1681–85.

174.38–175.1 **greet mair . . . decay** for Peden's criticism of the worldly affections of his flock see 'Life and Death of Alexander Peden', in Walker, 1.124.

174.39 **defections** see notes to 71.17–18, and 90.16–18.

174.41 **Lady Hundelslope** possibly a territorial name from a real place, Hundleshope Heights, 5 km S of Peebles.

175.2 **gude cause** see note to 149.2.

175.11 **time to amend** see the marginal version of Matthew 3.8, 'amendment of life', a phrase also used in the Communion Service in *The Book of Common Prayer* (1559, revised 1662).

175.12 **breath of their nosthrils** see The Wisdom of Solomon in the Apocrypha, 2.2. The chapter comprises a dramatic monologue in which the wicked expose their hatred of honesty and justice.

175.32   savoury sufferer   see 'Life and Death of Richard Cameron',
in Walker, 1.285. A *savoury sufferer* is someone who has the savour of holiness.

175.32   regimented band of souldiers   the Cameronian Regiment, or
26th of Foot, which took its name from the followers of Richard Cameron (see
note to 30.29). The regiment was raised when the Convention of the Scottish
Parliament in March 1689 needed an armed force to protect it as it carried
through the revolution, and 'the work of reformation in Scotland'.

175.36   name vain and contemptible, by pipes, drums   see 'Life and
Death of Richard Cameron', in Walker, 1.237.

175.37   vain carnal spring   see 'Life and Death of Richard Cameron', in
Walker, 1.239, 241. For the tune called the Cameronian Rant or Reel see *SMM*,
no. 282, and Kinsley, no. 308.

176.1–2   Cameronian or MacMillanite, one of the society people   before the Revolution of 1688–89 the Cameronians (see note to 30.29) were
already split into various groupings and factions, usually known by the names
of their leaders (see note to 176.6). According to Walker all agreed in disowning
the state as then constituted and in refusing to pay taxes (Walker, 1.142).
'Society people' were groups of Cameronians who worshipped in conventicles
in the Covenanting period and who united in a General Correspondence to
form the United Societies in 1681 (Wodrow, 3.357). The Revolution Settlement of 1689–90 created the modern Church of Scotland, and only the
Episcopalians and the Cameronians remained outside it. In 1701 John Macmillan
(1669–1753) was ordained a minister of the Church of Scotland, but was
deposed by the Presbytery of Kirkcudbright in 1703 following his refusal to
take the oath of allegiance on the accession of Queen Anne as instructed by the
Presbytery. In 1706 Macmillan received a call from 'the United Societies and
General Correspondences of the Suffering Remnant of the true Presbyterian
Church of Christ in Scotland, England and Ireland' (H. M. B. Reid, *A
Cameronian Apostle* (Paisley and London, 1896), 144) to become their minister.
He was their only minister until 1743 when, being joined by another, they were
able to constitute the first Presbytery of the Reformed Presbyterian Church. For
much of the 18th century the followers were nicknamed Macmillanites or
Cameronians.

176.6–7   MacMillanite, or a Russelite, or a Hamiltonian, or a Harleyite, or a Howdenite   for the phrase see 'Life and Death of Walter Smith',
in Walker, 2.69. Deans objects to them all as sectaries and dissenters: he
maintains his own freedom of conscience on matters that do not pertain to the
substance of the faith (and so rejects the Church's compromises with the state),
but he remains inside, as an elder in the Church of Scotland (text, 103.32).
The Russelites and the Hamiltonians were pre-Revolution factions: James
Russel, one of those who had murdered Archbishop Sharp in 1679, withdrew
from the United Societies in 1682 because they would not make a refusal to
pay customs duties a condition of fellowship (see text, 177.30–178.1, and
Wodrow, 3.376); Sir Robert Hamilton of Preston led the Covenanters at
Drumclog and at Bothwell Brig in 1679 but prevented his own followers from
uniting with the Church of Scotland following the Revolution Settlement in
1690 (Wodrow, 4.392–93) on the grounds that every difference of opinion
formed a basis for separation (Walker, 2.69). The Macmillanites (see note to
176.1) and the Harleyites were post-Revolution dissenters. John and Andrew
Harley led the 'cotmuir folk'; they too rejected taxes and other state impositions,
but also rejected the Presbyterian organisation of the church, relying on revelation to guide them, and so were accused by Walker of usurping 'the office of
the ministry, taking upon them at their own hand, not being orderly called, to
preach, marry and baptize, which all sound Presbyterians abhore' (Walker,

1.242). Andrew Lang in the Border Edition of the novel (1895; 1.xiii–iv), and Walker's editor, D. Hay Fleming (Walker, 2.214), identify the Howdenites as followers of John Howden, or Haldane, but this identification lacks conviction as Walker's list of sects predates the years of Haldane's known activity. For instance Haldane's *Active Testimony of the True Blue Presbyterians*, a denunciation of all political persons and parties for having reneged on the Covenant, was published in 1749.

176.8   vessel of clay   see Jeremiah 18.4–6.

176.10   gude auld cause   see note to 149.2.

176.17   middle and strait path   see note to 71.17.

176.17–18   where wind and water shears   watershed on the highest ground between two valleys, commonly defining a boundary on a hill-ridge.

176.18–19   right-hand snares ... way-slidings   see note to 71.18.

177.6   the Revolution   i.e. the Revolution of 1689–90.

177.8   Solemn League and Covenant   see note to 30.30.

177.10–11   anti-popish, anti-prelatic, anti-erastian, anti-sectarian, true presbyterian remnant   i.e. the remaining body of real Presbyterians defined by being opposed to the Pope and the Roman Catholic Church, to prelacy (i.e. government by bishops), to a system which subordinated church to state as in Scotland after the Revolution of 1688–89 (see notes to 90.16–18 and 90.17), and to Independency (see note to 65.31). The whole quotation comes from Robert Hamilton (see note to 176.6–7), 'Letter of Self-vindication to the Anti-popish, Anti-prelatick, Anti-erastian, Anti-sectarian, true Presbyterian Remnant of the Church of Scotland' (1684), cited in James Kirkton, *The Secret and True History of the Church in Scotland* and James Russell, *An Account of the Murder of Archbishop Sharp*, ed. in one vol. Charles Kirkpatrick Sharpe (Edinrgh, 1817), 444.

177.14   stormy and tumultuous meeting   of the United Societies (see note to 176.1).

177.22   Talla-Linns   23 km SW of Peebles.

177.30–178.8   It was the fixed judgment ... idolaters of old   the whole passage is part quotation from and part paraphrase of an editorial note in James Kirkton, *The Secret and True History of the Church in Scotland* and James Russell, *An Account of the Murder of Archbishop Sharp*, ed. in one vol. Charles Kirkpatrick Sharpe (Edinburgh, 1817), 399–401. The editorial note is in turn derived from Michael Shields, *Faithful Contendings Displayed, Being an Historical Relation of the State and Actings of the Suffering Remnant in the Church of Scotland* (1780), 114.

178.2   followers   'three men and a boy, and about seven or eight women': James Kirkton, *The Secret and True History of the Church in Scotland* and James Russell, *An Account of the Murder of Archbishop Sharp*, ed. in one vol. Charles Kirkpatrick Sharpe (Edinburgh, 1817), 401.

178.9–10   Deans ... too young to be a speaker   Deans is imagined as being about 9 on this occasion: see Historical Note, 594, 596.

178.20   act of oblivion   probably the Act of Indemnity protecting privy councillors, judges, and other officers acting on the king's commission 'against all pursuits or complaints that can be raised against them' (1685, c. 31) and the act rescinding fines and restoring property forfeited since 1665 (1690, c. 18).

178.21–22   bestowed ... titles, favours, and employments   e.g. John Dalrymple (1648–1707) was Lord Advocate under James VII, and became Lord Advocate again under William; he was made first Earl of Stair in 1703.

178.22–23   first General Assembly   in the 5th Act of the General Assembly meeting in Edinburgh in October 1690 it was decided that a return to the situation of the 1640s was 'tending rather to kindle Contentions, than to compose Divisions': *Acts of the General Assembly at Edinburgh, 1690*.

178.25 carnal wit and policy see 'Life and Death of Richard Cameron', in Walker, 1.221–22.

178.27–28 reign of Queen Anne 1702–14.

178.34–35 compelled to tolerate the co-existence of episcopacy from the Toleration Act of 1712.

178.36–37 glory of the second temple ... inferior see 'Mr John Dickson', in John Howie (1735–93), *Biographica Scoticana; or ... Scots Worthies*, 4th edn (Glasgow, 1813; originally published 1775), 496 (*CLA*, 71). The underlying analogy is with the temple of Jerusalem. Solomon's Temple was destroyed by Nebuchadnezzar in 586 BC; a second temple was begun when the Jews returned from exile in 538 BC, but it never equalled the glory of Solomon's, although constructed to a similar plan.

178.38 1639 till the battle of Dunbar from the Pacification of Berwick (see note to 173.23) which established the Presbyterian theocracy until defeat by Cromwell at Dunbar in 1650 ended Presbyterian rule and effected Scotland's absorption into the Cromwellian union.

178.40 insurrection in 1715 see note to 26.36.

178.42 King George George I (reigned 1714–27). The succession of George, Elector of Hanover, following the death of Queen Anne without surviving issue, had been determined by the Parliaments of England and Scotland prior to the Parliamentary Union of 1707.

179.1 Erastianism see note to 90.17.

179.19 mint, cummin or ... lesser tithes see Matthew 23.23. Deans means that it is easy to concern oneself with paying minor church taxes (the herbs mint and cumin), but one might in doing so neglect the 'weightier matters of the law, judgment, mercy, and faith'. In Biblical times a *tithe* or *teind* was one-tenth of one's income or produce, but by the 18th century was just a word used for a church tax upon land and its produce (see note to 69.31–32).

179 motto not identified.

180.14 citation, or sub-pœna terms in Scots and English law respectively for the document requiring a witness to appear in court.

181.4 the ninth command 'Thou shalt not bear false witness against thy neighbour': Exodus 20.16. The ninth commandment was interpreted in the Larger and Shorter Catechisms (1647–48) as requiring the preserving and promoting of truth, and of speaking the truth, and only the truth, in matters of justice: see *The School of Faith: the Catechisms of the Reformed Church*, ed. Thomas F. Torrance (London, 1959), 219, 273. For the *Catechisms* see notes to 149.34–36 and 149.36.

181.9 testifying period i.e. the Covenanting period, 1662–88.

181.22 matters of compliance Covenanting term used of conforming to the state in civil or religious matters. For Presbyterians of Deans's persuasion *compliance* was always problematic: compare 'foul compliance', in 'The Life and Death of Daniel Cargill', in Walker, 2.47.

181.25 defections see notes to 71.17–18, and 90.16–18.

181.25 haena felt freedom to separate mysell Deans did not and does not separate himself from those ministers and their parishioners who remained in or returned to their parishes through accepting the indulgence of 1669 (when ministers were allowed to return to vacant parishes), of 1672 (when specified ministers were given license to preach), of 1679 (when those who had been attending conventicles were allowed to return), or of 1687 (when James VII offered general toleration).

181.33 vile affections Romans 1.26.

181.34 will of our Father see Matthew 7.21, 18.14, 21.31; John 5.30, 6.39.

181.42 let God's will be done see Matthew 6.10; Luke 11.2.

182.28 one sure cable and anchor compare Hebrews 6.19.

183.6 ancient proverb set a thief to catch a thief: *ODEP*, 810; see Ray, 161.

183.9 the sapient Saddletree see *King Lear*, 3.6.22.

183.27 delayed for many weeks for the time-scheme see Historical Note, 595.

183.35–36 next door neighbour this probably refers not to Sharpitlaw's dwelling but his place of work (the Council Chamber) which was in the SW corner of Parliament Square and backed on to Bess-Wynd (see note to 37.41).

184 motto *Measure for Measure*, 3.1.134–37.

184.28 mair by token moreover.

184.35 tell ower repeat.

185.13 lifted up their voice and wept see Genesis 29.11; Judges 2.4, 21.2; Ruth 1.9, 14; 1 Samuel 11.4, 24.16; Job 2.12.

185.30 Newbattle by Dalkeith, 11 km SE of 18th-century Edinburgh.

185.35 bill of suspension *Scots law* warrant for a stay of execution of a decree or sentence of Court until the matter can be reviewed.

185.37 busk up your cockernonie *literally* gather up your hair with a fillet or snood, i.e. improve your appearance.

185.40 flea's hide and tallow proverbial: see *ODEP*, 267. Ratcliffe is arguing that a good-looking girl will move a jury when an ugly fellow like himself would be hanged for stealing absolutely nothing ('the very fifteenth part of a flea's hide and tallow').

186.7 faulded down the leaf of my Bible see note to 89.15.

186.11–14 He hath stripped . . . like a tree Job 19.9–10.

186.41 heart was as hard as the nether millstane see Job 41.15 in the Geneva Bible of 1560.

187.3 forgi'e our enemies see Matthew 5.43–44.

187.12 hew down the tree Daniel 4.14. Compare the variants of the proverb 'Best to bend while it is a twig' (*ODEP*, 46).

187.26–27 better sit and rue, than flit and rue proverbial: see *ODEP*, 55.

187.32 bone of my bone, and flesh of my flesh see Genesis 2.23.

187.39 wi' a witness *proverbial* with a vengeance: *ODEP*, 905.

188.21 come weal or woe whether it makes for happiness or unhappiness.

189.25–28 deeper offence . . . in the questions see 'The Larger Catechism', question 151: 'Sins are aggravated . . . when they are done deliberately, wilfully, presumptuously' (*The School of Faith: the Catechisms of the Reformed Church*, ed. Thomas F. Torrance (London, 1959), 221–22). The *questions* are the questions of the Larger and Shorter Catechisms (see notes to 149.34–36, 149.36).

189.29 save your breath to say your carritch Effie's variation of the proverb 'Save your breath to cool your porridge' (*ODEP*, 418).

189.33 Moll Blood the gallows. The phrase does not appear in Grose, *A Classical Dictionary*; 'the gallows' is given as the meaning in the *OED*, and the sole citation is from *The Heart of Mid-Lothian*.

189.33 rapping taking a false oath: see *Rap* in Grose, *A Classical Dicitonary*.

189.34–35 Whadyecallum's fables Aesop's Fables. Aesop (said to have lived 6th century BC) was the traditional composer of fables among the Greeks.

189.35 b—t me blast me, i.e. strike me with the wrath or curse of heaven. It is not clear why Scott felt this word could not be spelled out; it is also represented as 'b—t' in *Guy Mannering*, ed. P. D. Garside, EEWN 2, 293.4.

189.36 smacked calf-skin the note 'Kissed the book' provides a literal translation; Ratcliffe is talking about taking an oath on the Bible in court. See *Calf-skin Fiddle* in Grose, *A Classical Dictionary*.

190.4 what for why.

190.9–10 let life gang ... gane before it see note to 59.22.

190.11 whiles sair left to mysell at times sorely misguided, at times quite unable to 'think straight'.

190.12 Indian mines i.e. the sources of Spanish wealth in S America.

190.42 was on the pad *literally* was robbing on the path, i.e. was a footpad.

191.12 sleepit as sound as a tap *proverbial* slept as sound as a top: see *ODEP*, 741. According to the *OED* a top is said to sleep when it is spinning so quickly that its motion is imperceptible.

191.13–14 the warst may be tholed when it is kenn'd *proverbial* the worst can be borne when it is known: see *ODEP*, 435.

191.14 Better a finger aff as aye wagging *proverbial* better to cut a finger off than keep it wagging, i.e. it is better to end something troublesome than always be vexed by it: see Ray, 283; *ODEP*, 49.

191 motto see William Shenstone (1714–63), 'Jemmy Dawson', stanza 11. Shenstone's song, about a young woman's loyalty to a Manchester Jacobite put to death in 1746, was written close to the event and published in the poet's posthumous works. A version was also included in Percy, 1.306–09, where Scott is likely to have first seen it.

192.35–36 In the strength of my God ... I will go forth see Psalm 71.16.

193.1 blue Scottish bonnet flat-topped round cap worn by the peasantry of lowland Scotland. The colour was indicative of Presbyterian and Covenanting loyalties, and was adopted because of the injunction to the children of Israel that they wear 'a ribband of blue': see Numbers 15.38.

193.6–9 courts of justice ... Scottish Estates see note to 21.41.

193.9–10 imperfect and corrupted style of architecture in the early 19th century Jacobean and Caroline architecture was considered to be eclectic and lacking its own integrity, but Old Parliament House, built 1632–39 (see note to 21.41) was in any case somewhat irregular and undistinguished: for an illustration see Grant, 1.161. Parliament House was reconstructed 1804–11, and the present Georgian front added in 1807–10 (see A. J. Youngson, *The Making of Classical Edinburgh* (Edinburgh, 1966), 133–35).

193.17 Trip to the Jubilee George Farquhar (1677?–1707), *The Constant Couple; or a Trip to the Jubilee* (1699), 3.3 and 4.1, in *The Works of George Farquhar*, ed. Shirley Strum Kenny, 2 vols (Oxford, 1988), 1.188–02.

193.18 Sed transeat cum cæteris erroribus *Latin* but let it pass with other mistakes.

194.3–4 Ye're welcome ... briggs see James Hogg, *The Jacobite Relics of Scotland*, 2 vols (Edinburgh, 1819–21), 1.18. *Whigs* was originally a derogatory term for Scottish Presbyterians; *Bothwell briggs* is the name of the battle on 22 June 1679 when the insurgent Covenanters were defeated and suppressed by Charles II's army under the Duke of Monmouth. The song is highly abusive.

194.5–6 jacobitically disposed disposed towards the cause of James VII and II (who lost the throne in 1688–89), and of his descendants.

194.7 existing authority both the London government and those who held power in Scotland were strongly Whig in 1737.

194.8–11 Mess David ... Killiecrankie see Hans Hecht, *Songs from David Herd's Manuscripts* (Edinburgh, 1904), 207. 'Mess' (master) is a title often used of a minister in popular speech. Rev. David Williamson (1636–1706) became minister of St Cuthbert's Church in Edinburgh in 1661, was ejected in 1665 for being a Covenanter, was intercommuned in 1675 (i.e. he was named in a proclamation which forbade anyone from helping anyone on the list on pain of their too being classed as a rebel: see Wodrow, 2.286–88), fought at Bothwell Brig in 1679, and was eventually restored to St Cuthbert's in 1689 following the Revolution. He was married seven times. Scurrilous songs and tales about his sexual prowess, playing on his nickname 'Dainty Davie' and used satirically against Covenanters, were long in circulation, particularly the tale about his hiding from a troop of dragoons in the bed of Lady Cherrytree's daughter whom he made pregnant, but whom he also chose as his third wife: see *Scotch Presbyterian Eloquence Display'd* (1692), 5; 'Memoirs of Captain John Creighton', in *The Works of Jonathan Swift*, ed. Walter Scott, 19 vols (Edinrgh, 1814), 10.117–18; 'Dainty Davie', in Herd, 2.215 (the traditional song); 'Dainty David', in Robert Burns, *The Merry Muses of Caledonia*, ed. James Barke and Sidney Goodsir Smith (Edinburgh, 1959), 74 (Burns's reworking of the traditional song). *Chosen of twenty* probably implies that he was chosen by 20 women. *Killiecrankie* was the battle won by the Jacobites led by Viscount Dundee in 1689; for words and tune see James Hogg, *The Jacobite Relics of Scotland*, 2 vols (Edinburgh, 1819–21), 1.32–33.

194.15 in a strong north-country tone i.e. in a strong Highland accent.

194.15–16 Ta de'il ... gentlemans about *Highland English* the devil knock out his Cameronian eyes—what gives him a right to push gentlemen about? For the representation of Highland speech in writing see Graham Tulloch, *The Language of Walter Scott* (London, 1980), 254–56.

194.17 ruling elder see note to 90.33.

194.18 precious sister *literally* woman of spiritual and moral worth, but *precious* may also be used ironically of something bad or worthless.

194.18 glorify God in the Grassmarket a saying ascribed to the Duke of Lauderdale, in Gilbert Burnet, *History of His Own Time*, 2 vols (London, 1724–34), 1.416. See also notes to 30.29–30 and 30.30.

194.26–27 hear with your ears, and see with your eyes a common biblical rhetorical structure: e.g. see Mark 8.18.

194.28 defections see notes to 71.17–18, and 90.16–18.

194.30 blessed and invisible Head Jesus Christ.

194.33 prophet's ass Balaam's ass: see Numbers 22.28.

195.1–3 others apart sat on a bench retired ... statute see John Milton, *Paradise Lost* (1667), 2.557–61.

195.2 constructive crime see text, 45.1–3.

195.8–9 more liberal than that of her sister country from 1587 (1587, c. 91) accused persons in Scotland had to be legally represented at their trial, whereas until 1837 in England counsel for the defence could only raise points of law and were not permitted to cross-examine witnesses or address the jury. See Hume, *Crimes*, xliv–xlvi; Hume, *Trial*, 2.40.

195.29 to have a friend at court proverbial: see *ODEP*, 289.

195.31 sorted ye out chosen for you, selected for you.

195.32–34 They winna fence the court ... aye fenced the High Court of Justiciary sits in Edinburgh, but also goes on circuit: in this period it visited Dumfries and Jedburgh on the south circuit, Ayr, Glasgow and Stirling on the west circuit, and Aberdeen, Inverness and Perth, on the north circuit. When on circuit the court was 'fenced', i.e. proceedings were initiated with a formula forbidding disorderly interruption or obstructive behaviour; such a prohibition was permanently in force at the High Court in Edinburgh.

196.8 sequestering a witness keeping a witness secluded in an ante-room before giving evidence in court to prevent him or her hearing the evidence of others and from being interfered with.

197 motto see *Measure for Measure*, 1.3.19–23.

198.2 ocular witness eye witness; this is a common phrase both in legal testimonies, and in discussion of those who witnessed Jesus and the resurrection in the gospels.

198.4 Ichabod! ... Ichabod! my glory is departed see 1 Samuel 4.21: 'And she named the child Ichabod, saying, The glory is departed from Israel: because the ark of God was taken'. See also 'Life and Death of Richard Cameron', in Walker, 1.288.

198.12 plead to the relevancy see note to 31.40–41.

198.15–16 sending the case to the cognizance of the jury or assize *Scots law, literally* sending the case to the knowledge of a jury, i.e. sending the case to be tried before a jury. *Assize* is the Scots term for 'jury'.

198.17 counsel for the crown this phrase implies that the prosecution is not being led by the Lord Advocate in person but by a deputy (see note to 42.12).

198.17–18 frequency of the crime of infanticide see Hume, *Crimes*, 1.463. If judged by outcomes rather than charges the crime of infanticide was not common in the 1730s: see Historical Note, 590.

198.18 special statute see note to 44.33–34. The preamble to the bill talks of 'the frequent Murthers that have or may be committed upon innocent Infants'.

198.21 King's Advocate Lord Advocate (see note to 42.12).

198.22–24 strictly enforcing the Act of Parliament... their occurrence might be prevented this was not argued at the trial of Isobel Walker, and the evidence from the Books of Adjournal (the records of the High Court of Justiciary) suggests that far from there being a policy of strict enforcement in 1737–38 the Lord Advocate normally agreed to petitions from the accused that they should be banished and transported rather than hanged. See Historical Note, 590.

199.6 interlocutor of relevancy see note to 31.40–41.

199.19 put up their lip sneered.

200.18 felo de se *Anglo-Latin* self-killer.

201.7 Mr Jem i.e. Mr James. Fairbrother's Christian name is not given elsewhere, but, as both the counsel defending Isobel Walker were called James (see Historical Note, 589), 'Mr Jem' may be a slight indication that Scott was aware of the papers relating to her trial.

201.28 the confession of Euphemia Deans it was an established principle of Scots criminal law that a confession did not in itself give grounds for conviction (Hume, *Trial*, 2.119). See also text, 204.9–12.

202.10–11 dulcis Amaryllidis irae *Latin* the angers of sweet Amaryllis. See Virgil (70–19 BC), *Eclogues* (37 BC), 2.14: 'tristis Amaryllidis iras'. As this is normally translated 'the sad angers of Amaryllis' or 'Amaryllis's unhappy outbursts of anger' it would be a truer echo of Virgil to translate Scott's Latin as 'the sweet angers of Amaryllis' or 'Amaryllis's sweet outburts of anger'.

202.15 bills will be answered a financial metaphor meaning that cheques will be honoured.

203.5 Rahel weeping for her children Jeremiah 31.15; see Matthew 2.18.

203.10 spin a muckle pirn out of a wee tait of tow *proverbial* spin a hank of yarn out of a wee bundle of hemp [or flax]: see Kelly, 119; *ODEP*, 765.

203.10 De'il haet he kens *emphatic* he knows a damn lot more.

203.15 sae clever as he clinked it intill so clever as to stick it smartly into. John Jamieson writes: 'TO CLINK Used in different senses, with different prepositions; but conveying the general idea of alertness in manual operation' (*An Etymological Dictionary of the Scottish Language*, 2 vols (Edinburgh, 1808)).

203.17 Utrecht in the Netherlands. See note to 42.31.

203.18 interlocutor of relevancy see note to 31.40–41.

203 motto see *The Merchant of Venice*, 4.1.299.

203.30–31 gentlemen of the long robe members of the legal profession.

204.4 judicial examination before a magistrate Isobel Walker made her declaration to magistrates in Kirkcudbright on 28 October 1736 (SRO, JC.26/127, 2049).

204.11–12 **legal and proper evidence** circumstantial evidence and the evidence of witnesses. The point is that under Scots law a confession is not in itself evidence of guilt but could be seen as corroboration of independent evidence.

204.32 **Books of Adjournal** see note to 15.42.

206.2 **sair on** harsh with.

206.18 **drawn with wild horses** proverbial: see *ODEP*, 889. Tying the limbs of a person to four horses and then using the horses to tear the body apart was formerly used as a method of execution.

207.15 **thought is free** proverbial: *ODEP*, 814.

207.21 **deep and dangerous** *1 Henry IV*, 1.3.190.

208.11 **ultroneous evidence** *Scots Law* evidence given spontaneously, without the witness having been formally cited. Such evidence was normally rejected on the grounds that it indicated undue zeal either for or against the accused, or merely 'too forward and busy a temper' (Hume, *Trial*, 2.151), and could be considered contempt of court.

208.12 **debito tempore** *Latin* at the appropriate time.

208.43 **win ower** overcome, get over.

209.12 **heart of stone** proverbial: see *ODEP* 352. The contrast between a heart of stone and a heart of flesh and blood is traditional: see Ezekiel 36.26.

209.39 **whose word is truth** see John 17.17.

210.10 **widow of Tekoah** see 2 Samuel 14. The widow is set up by Joab to plead for Absalom before David.

210.10–11 **putten words into her mouth** see 2 Samuel 14.3, 19.

210.26 **valeat quantum** so much as to let it prevail.

211.2 **leading question** question which suggests which answer is expected.

212.19 **The bitterness of it is now passed** see 1 Samuel 15.32. The words are also used by Porteous prior to his death (see text, 56.18–19 and note), but in a different sense. The difference is due in part to a link with the words of Sir John Russel prior to his execution in 1683: see Sir John Dalrymple, *Memoirs of Great Britain and Ireland*, 3rd edn, 3 vols (London, 1790), 1.46: *CLA*, 5. This connection was noticed by James Anderson, *Sir Walter Scott and History* (Edinburgh, 1981), 65; it is discussed by Claire Lamont, '"The Bitterness of Death" in *The Heart of Mid-Lothian*', *The Scott Newsletter*, 3 (1983), 3–5.

212.21 **the weariest day will hae its end** proverbial: see Ray, 95; *ODEP*, 482.

213.13 **interlocutor of relevancy** see note to 31.40–41.

213.17 **proof which he expected to lead** evidence which he expected to produce to prove his case.

213.22 **corpus delicti** *Latin literally* body of the crime.

213.36 **in confitentem nullæ sunt partes judicis** *Latin, literally* in relation to a person who makes a confession there are no roles for a judge. See Justinian, *Digest* (compiled 530–33), 9.2.25.2: 'nullæ partes sunt iudicandi in confitentes' (there is no place for judgment when dealing with people who make a confession). The context explains that when a person confesses the judge's role is not to judge but simply to determine a penalty.

213.39–40 **Farinaceus, and Mattheus** Prospero Farinacci (1544–1618), an Italian jurist, who specialised in criminal law, and was author of *Praxis et Theorica Criminalis* (1616), which strongly influenced penal theory; Antonius Matthaeus (1601–54), a Dutch jurist from Utrecht, author of *De Criminibus* (1644), which was widely disseminated. The latter's son and grandson both bore the same name, but were professors in Leiden.

213.40–41   confessio extrajudicialis in se nulla est, et quod nullum est, non potest adminiculari   *Latin* a confession made outside the court itself is nothing, and being nothing cannot support [the case].

215   motto   not traced; probably by Scott.

216.14–15   John Kirk ... Thomas Moore   apparently fictional.

216.16   Guilty   the jury would normally have pronounced the libel proven, and the judge would have pronounced the accused guilty. But in his review of the first three volumes of Robert Pitcairn, *Ancient Criminal Trials in Scotland*, 3 vols (Edinburgh, 1829–30), Scott records that from 1728 when a Scottish jury first came to a 'not guilty' verdict, juries were increasingly liable to make this judgment 'where the judgment of relevancy was esteemed too severe'; and he adds 'nor is this valuable privilege now questioned' (*Prose Works*, 21.239). The judgment on Effie must therefore be seen to be more than a simple decision that the prosecution had proved its case. See also Hume, *Trial*, 2.290.

216.25   I have not the least hope of a pardon   this is contrary to the way in which the judicial authorities of 1736–38 normally treated this crime: see Historical Note, 590–91.

216.26   the crime has been increasing in this land   there is no evidence of this in the 1730s: see Historical Note, 591.

216.27–28   the lenity in which the laws have been exercised   in the Books of Adjournal there is no evidence of this view being taken on this particular law in the 1730s: see note to 198.22–24 and Historical Note, 591.

216.38–39   arrest of judgment   order to suspend the proceedings following a verdict for reason of manifest error.

217.5–6   Mandrin   Louis Mandrin (1724–55). He became the leader of a large band of men engaged in smuggling and extortion in eastern France. He was captured in 1755, and condemned to death on the wheel.

217.6   punishment of the wheel   form of punishment in which criminals were executed by being tied to a wheel and having their limbs broken with an iron bar.

217.20   dealt upon   worked upon, dealt with.

217.32–33   Doomster, read the sentence   the practice of having the hangman read the sentence of death was abolished in 1773 (Hume, *Trial*, 2.344).

218.7–9   Wednesday ... betwixt the hours of two and four o'clock afternoon   the normal day and time of execution.

219.1   Set him up, indeed   *contemptuous exclamation* 'he gives himself airs', 'the impudence'.

219.12   live and let live   proverbial: Ray, 131; *ODEP*, 473.

219.21   last riding of the Scots Parliament   see note to 40.7. The last session of the Scottish Parliament began on 3 October 1706.

219.23   squire of the body   officer charged with personal attendance upon a sovereign, nobleman, or other high dignitary.

219.28–29   there is aye a wimple in a lawyer's clew   *proverbial* there is always a twist in a lawyer's ball of thread: *ODEP*, 891–92, where this is the sole example.

219.39–41   auld enemies of Ingland ... printed Statute-book   see Sir Thomas Murray of Glendook, *The Laws and Acts of Parliament made by King James the First ... Kings and Queen of Scotland* (Edinburgh, 1681). The sentiments attributed to him have not been located.

219.41–42   skin and birn   completely, totally. The phrase is usually used of cattle: a *birn* was a mark branded on the hide of an animal to indicate ownership.

219.42   horse and foot   everyone. Horse and foot comprise both divisions of an army.

219.42   all and sindry   all and sundry, i.e. all and one, taken together and as individuals. The phrase is a translation of the Latin tag of the next note which was once in Scots legal use.

219.42–43 omnes et singulos *Latin* all and severally.

220.6 De'il that *emphatic* would that.

220.6 German kale-yard *literally* German cabbage-yard, i.e. Hanover.

220.10 flang his periwig in the fire compare 'When Geordie maun fling by the crown, / And hat, and wig, and a' that? / The flames will get baith hat and wig, / As often as they've done a' that', from stanza 4 of 'Though Geordie reigns in Jamie's Stead', in James Hogg, *The Jacobite Relics of Scotland*, 2 vols (1819–21), 2.56. See also Magnum, 12.175.

220.12 he might keep mair wit in his anger *proverbial* he ought to think more and be less angry: see Ramsay, 109.

220.14 tore her biggonets ripped her cap or headgear.

220.15–16 Sir Robert Walpole 1676–1745, Prime Minister 1721–42. Walpole managed the national finances with great skill, but his ways of retaining power not only infuriated those deprived of power but allowed him to be represented as wholly venal and corrupt, particularly in the 1730s.

220.18 he was for kickin he wanted to kick.

220.19 Duke of Argyle see note to 64.6.

220.22 Maccallanmore *Gaelic* MacCailein Mór, son of Colin the Great, the title of the chiefs of the clan Campbell, who claim descent from Colin Campbell of Lochow who died in 1294, and who became earls and dukes of Argyle.

220.23 Andro Ferrara in her edition of *Waverley* (Oxford, 1981), Claire Lamont writes: 'Andrea Ferrara was a North Italian swordsmith of the late sixteenth century. His name became a mark of quality for Scotsmen in the 17th and 18th centuries, and many Scots swords bear his name, but it is doubted whether any of them are in fact his work' (452). A *thirdsman* is a third person called in as a mediator or arbiter, and thus the meaning here is that kicking the Duke of Argyle was likely to result in a duel.

220.24 real Scotsman—a true friend to the country see note to 64.6.

220.28 inter parietes *Latin* indoors.

220.34 Ian Roy Cean *Gaelic* John Red Head. The 2nd Duke of Argyle was famously red-headed, and was often called 'Red John of the Battles'.

220.35 Palace-yard the open space S of Westminster Hall, in London.

220.36 he claws up their mittans he kills them, gives them the finishing stroke (*OED*, *claw*, verb 8).

220.37 bill of exchange note promising to pay a stated sum on a stated date.

221.6–23 I am no minister ... last drop of my blood see Robert Campbell, *The Life of the Most Illustrious Prince John, Duke of Argyle and Greenwich* (London, 1745), 319: *CLA*, 15. The paragraph comes from Argyle's second speech on 3 April 1737 during the third reading of the bill intended to punish Edinburgh for the Porteous riots. See Magnum, 12.174–75.

221.26 Martingale name derived from the straps or apparatus used to prevent a horse from throwing back its head or rearing.

221.29 thousand punds Scots £83 sterling.

221.29–30 Roystoun the estate of Royston, in the Granton area of Edinburgh, renamed Caroline Park on its purchase by the 2nd Duke of Argyle in 1739. The house, in Caroline Park Avenue, was built 1683–96 for Sir George Mackenzie of Tarbat.

221.31–32 deukes and drakes the Scots pronunciation of *duke* and of *duck* is 'dook'. Mrs Saddletree's pun comes from a contemporary report of the examination of the Provost of Edinburgh before the House of Lords on 10 March 1737. On being asked what kind of shot was used by the City Guard at

Wilson's execution, he replied 'Ou, juist sic as ane shutes dukes and sic-like fules [fowls] wi''. This answer was considered contempt of the House until explained by the Duke of Argyle. See Magnum, 12.76; Roughead, 121–22.

221.38 doing as they would be done by proverbial: see Luke 6.31; *ODEP*, 191.

221.43 hour of cause hour appointed for trying a case: i.e. Saddletree is proposing a return to the criminal court after the mid-afternoon recess for dinner.

222.1 for a' the gudewife's din in spite of all the fuss being made by my wife.

222 motto *Measure for Measure*, 1.4.75–76.

222.31–32 keepit his breath to hae blawn on his porridge proverbial: see Ray, 179; Ramsay, 95; *ODEP*, 418–19.

222.37–38 Singlesword ... Hackum fictitious examples.

222.39 Master of St Clair John Sinclair (1683–1750), eldest son of the 10th Lord Sinclair. While serving under Marlborough in the Netherlands, he killed brother officers Hugh and Alexander Schaw. He was court-martialled on 17 October 1708, found not guilty of challenging Hugh to a duel but guilty of killing Alexander. The Court recommended a pardon, but, on the advice of the Solicitor General, Marlborough confirmed the sentence on 17 April 1709—and ordered Sinclair to escape. Sinclair returned to Scotland to support the Jacobite cause in the 1715 rebellion. In 1726 he was pardoned for his part in the rebellion but not for the murder of Alexander Schaw, although no further action was taken. Scott edited *Proceedings in the Court-Martial, held upon John, Master of Sinclair* (Edinburgh, 1828). See William Roughead, 'The Master of Sinclair and the Fifteen', in *The Riddle of the Ruthvens and other Studies* (Edinburgh, 1919), 337–61.

223.26 purchased and promised blessings see notes to 133.23–24 and 133.40.

223.29 it is borne in upon my mind that my mind is strongly impressed with the idea that (*OED*, *bear*, verb 34).

223.32 I wish she binna roving I hope her mind is not wandering.

223.36 tak tent to take care of, treat kindly.

223.38 busk up your cockernonie see note to 185.37.

223.40 cockups a hair-style where a false pad was used to add height. It was denounced in pamphlets and Kirkton preached against them: see *The Secret and True History of the Church in Scotland* and James Russell, *An Account of the Murder of Archbishop Sharp*, ed. in one vol. Charles Kirkpatrick Sharpe (Edinburgh, 1817), xix (text and note).

224.41 in the face of the sun openly (*OED*, *face*, 5d). The phrase is a gloss upon such biblical texts as Psalm 90.8, and means that Effie will appear innocent before God and man.

225.6–7 a thousand miles from this—far ayont the saut sea Effie uses the language of ballad and folk tale: London is under 400 miles (640 km) from Edinburgh, and the normal mode of travel was overland.

225.15 if the present space be redeemed if the present space of time be put to good use: see Ephesians 5.16; Colossians 4.5.

225.16 see the King's face that gies grace proverbial: see Ramsay, 127; *Minstrelsy*, 1.356; *ODEP*, 427.

225.17–18 stranger's kindness compare Matthew 25.33–46.

225.23 fule thing foolish person.

225.32 that Argyle that suffered in my father's time Archibald Campbell (1629–85), 9th Earl of Argyle, who refused the Test Act (see note to 174.28–29) in 1681, who was tried for treason (but escaped), and who in 1685 raised a rebellion against the succession of James VII and II, but was captured and executed, nominally for having refused the Test. He was grandfather to the 2nd Duke who features in this novel.

225.43 on the lay in the business.

226.1 gybe the term appears in the *OED* as 'thieves' slang' for a 'counterfeit pass'; it does not appear in Grose.

226.1 the jark the seal; see *Jark* in Grose, *A Classical Dictionary*.

226.1 queer cuffin magistrate, justice of the peace; see *Queer Cuffin* in Grose, *A Classical Dictionary*.

226.6–7 if it does nae gude, it can do nae ill proverbial: compare Ramsay, 90.

226.8 Saint Nicholas's clerks highwaymen, as in *1 Henry IV*, 2.1.59–60; so called either because St Nicholas came to be regarded as the patron saint of thieves or, as Scott believed, because of the aural connection with 'Old Nick', the devil, often jocularly referred to as a saint (see Scott's footnote to *Ivanhoe*, ed. Graham Tulloch, EEWN 8, 357).

226.10 if ye fall amang thieves see Luke 10.30, the parable of the good Samaritan.

227.3 watches of the night see note to 163.24.

227.14–16 Barefooted, as Sancho says ... pilgrimage see Cervantes (Miguel de Cervantes Saavedra), *The History of the Renowned Don Quixote de la Mancha*, trans. Peter Motteux and John Ozell, 4 vols (Glasgow, 1757; originally published 1700–03), 1.218; Part 1 (1605), Ch. 25: 'naked came I into the world, and naked must I go out'. Compare Job 1.21.

227.22 Mahometan scrupulosity Moslems wash the face, hands and feet before prayers.

227.34 patriarchs of old i.e. like Abram who was 'very rich in cattle' (Genesis 13.2), Isaac and Jacob.

227.39 annual rent annual interest.

228.26 gall and wormwood i.e. very bitter and painful: see Lamentations 3.19.

229 motto see Isaac Watts (1674–1748), 'The Sluggard', stanza 1, in *Divine Songs Attempted in Easy Language for the Use of Children* (London, 1715), 46.

229.12–13 no matter for the exact topography Dumbiedikes House has, however, been identified with Peffermill House, in Peffermill Road, Edinburgh. For an illustration see Grant, 3.61.

229.18 Somerville of Drum the 10th Lord Somerville. Somerville participated in the suppression of the Covenanters; his *Memorie of the Somervilles* was edited by Scott (2 vols, Edinburgh, 1815). The Drum, formerly Somerville House, in Gilmerton in Edinburgh, was originally built by John Mylne 1584–85; parts of that house were incorporated in the west pavilion which was built in the late 17th century. The present house was built 1726–34 by William Adam. The 14th Lord Somerville lived near Abbotsford and was a friend of Scott's.

229.18 Lord Ross 12th Lord Ross (*c.* 1656–1738), who owned the estate of Melville Castle, W of Dalkeith, and who served as an officer under Claverhouse. His town house and estate, Ross Park, occupied the area of what is now George Square in Edinburgh.

229.19 point device in every point or respect. See *Twelfth Night*, 2.5.145.

229.20 vailed its splendour probably a quotation in that the same phrase is used in 'The Surgeons Daughter' (in *Chronicles of the Canongate*, ed. Claire Lamont, EEWN 20, 201.8), but unidentified.

229.26 cross lights *probably* windows on two opposing sides of a room.

230.15 umquhile late, deceased, a term used in legal documents as here without the definite article.

230.16 Newbattle kirk-yard 2 km SW of Dalkeith.

230.16 palace of pleasure name of a collection of translations into English by William Painter (*c.* 1525–95) from Greek, Latin, French and Italian, published in 1566, 1567, and 1575.

230.18 ploughed, but uninclosed i.e. there was as yet no division of land into fields with walls and hedges which separated different land uses and provided wind breaks. This was the norm under the older forms of agriculture that were largely replaced in the course of the 18th century.

230.25 in a fine spring morning see Historical Note, 595.

230.32 Holyroodhouse the royal palace of Edinburgh, begun around 1500, and substantially remodelled in 1671, which was just down the hill from St Leonard's.

230.32 palace at Dalkeith an old castle rebuilt 1702–11 in the Palladian manner by James Smith (d. 1731) for Anne, the first Duchess of Buccleuch (1651–1732). See also note to 65.41.

231.12–13 second Calender wanting an eye see 'The Story of the Three Calenders', in *Tales of the East*, ed. Henry Weber, 3 vols (Edinburgh, 1812), 1.32–68. In fact it is the third Calender who in his story (52–61) opens doors in the castle of 40 damsels, and who on opening the forbidden door finds himself in a stable and sets off on a winged black horse that later blinds him in one eye with a flick of its tail.

231.14 Pegasus *Greek mythology* mythical winged horse sprung from the blood of Medusa when Perseus cut off her head.

231.25 milky mother see Edmund Spenser, *The Faerie Queene*, 1.8.11 (*CLA*, 42, 187); John Dryden, 'Pastoral 6, or Silenus', line 84, in 'The Works of Virgil', in *The Works of John Dryden*, ed. Walter Scott, 18 vols (London, 1808), 13.400.

231.29 brownie benevolent spirit thought to live in farmhouses and perform housework while the inhabitants are sleeping. Scott describes the brownie in *Minstrelsy*, 1.146–50.

231.35 Whirl the long mop, and ply the airy flail see William Erskine, 'Supplementary Stanzas to Collins's Ode on the Superstitions of the Highlands' (1788), in *Minstrelsy*, 1.198.

232.30 inimicitiam contra omnes mortales *Latin* hostility towards all mortal beings.

233.5 spot o' wark piece of work (*OED*, *spot*, noun 7b).

233.14–15 bundle your pipes *proverbial* shut up: see Ray, 248; *ODEP*, 657.

233.37–38 as Don Quixote did in his helmet see Cervantes, *Don Quixote*, Part 1 (1605), Ch. 2.

233.42 Billingsgate oaths violent abuse. Billingsgate, in Lower Thames Street, was the London fish market and was notorious for its foul and abusive language.

234.4 caught in the manner in the act of doing something unlawful: see *OED*, *mainour*, 2; Numbers 5.13; *1 Henry IV*, 2.4.305.

234.8–9 something dangerous, which her wisdom taught her to fear see *Hamlet*, 5.1.256–57.

234.22 my bark's waur than my bite proverbial: see *ODEP*, 30.

234.24 gang your ways in bye make your way indoors.

234.41–42 twenty mile o' gate *literally* twenty miles of way, i.e. twenty miles on my way.

234.43 Guide and deliver us may God direct us and deliver us from evil.

235.9 I can seldom be at the plague I seldom cause trouble, I am not often a nuisance (*OED*, *plague*, noun 2b).

235.9 an' it binna *literally* and it be not, i.e. unless when.

235.21 sink or swim proverbial: *ODEP*, 737.

235.30 ye are no for you are not inclined to.

236.3 goldsmith's bills i.e. paper money. Banking services were formerly provided by goldsmiths.

236.10–11 ae wise body's aneugh in the married state although proverbial in form this is not a recognised saying. Dumbiedikes means that it is enough if one of the partners in a marriage is able to think of what is beneficial for both.

236.12–13 as gude syne as sune *proverbial* as good later as sooner, i.e. as good at another time as now: see *ODEP*, 753. The normal form is 'as gude soon as syne'.

236.30 chamber of deas best room in the house.

236.36 barony of Dalkeith, and Lugton a barony was an estate granted directly by the crown, and brought with it both criminal and civil jurisdiction (see note to 248.8). Dalkeith is 10 km SE of Edinburgh, and Lugton is an enclave of Dalkeith immediately to the N.

236.41 making fashion making a show, pretending.

237.4 wilfu' woman will hae her way proverbial: see *ODEP*, 890, which gives *Rob Roy* as the first recorded example.

237.7–8 A fair offer . . . is nae cause of feud proverbial: *ODEP*, 239.

237.8–9 Ae man may bring a horse to the water, but twenty winna gar him drink proverbial: see *ODEP*, 449, which cites James Boswell, *Life of Samuel Johnson, LLD*, 14 July 1763, where the proverb appears in this form.

237.9 wasting my substance see Luke 15.13.

237.13 on sic a score as ye pit it on for such a purpose as you suggest.

239 motto see William Wordsworth, 'Strange fits of passion have I known' (1800), lines 25–28.

239.24 Nabal and a churl see 1 Samuel 25. Nabal, who was 'churlish' (1 Samuel 25.3), refused to provide David and his men with provisions.

239.26 Meribah Exodus 17.7. The children of Israel were 'almost ready to stone' Moses (Exodus 17.4) because of the lack of water, when God told Moses to go on to the rock of Horeb, 'and thou shalt smite the rock, and there shall come water out of it, that the people may drink' (Exodus 17.6).

239.30 change of market-days with us change in her matrimonial prospects: see *SND, mercat*, 3.

239.33–34 old-fashioned church and steeple the old church in Kirkgate, Liberton, was demolished after a fire in 1815.

239.36 clumsy square tower Liberton Tower in Liberton Drive: see Grant, 3.329.

240.24 wild and wayward thoughts see motto 239, and note.

241.41 disputed high see John Milton, *Paradise Lost* (1667), 8.55.

241.41 drank deep see *Hamlet*, 1.2.175.

241.42–43 progress of writts series of title deeds sufficient to constitute a valid legal title. When conveying lands the seller had to give not only a disposition but also a history of the transmission of the title (a *progress of writs*) to show that the seller had an unimpeachable title and the right to sell. A 'confused progress of writs' would be one where the record of the transmission of the title was muddled.

242.10–11 I'm sprighted . . . angered worse see *Cymbeline*, 2.3.139–40.

242.12 gall to bitterness see Acts 8.23.

242.19–20 Brandy cannot save her while the import is clear (Effie cannot be saved by any means at all), the basis and history of this saying have not been found. Brandy was widely used as a restorative after fainting etc.

242.20 the Bow see note to 22.3.

242.20–21 lad in the pioted coat at her heels see 'Vindication of

Cameron's Name', in Walker, 1.321. In the Magnum Scott notes that the 'lad in the pioted coat' is 'The executioner, in livery of black or dark grey and silver, likened by low wit to a magpie' (Magnum, 12.212).

242.23–24 Vivat Rex, Currat Lex *Latin* may the king live; may the law run its course: *The History of Sir John Oldcastle* (first published 1600), scene 11 (line 1672). The play was attributed to Shakespeare, and included in the third folio (1664), but is now considered a collaborative work to which Anthony Munday (1560–1633) and Michael Drayton (1563–1631) contributed. *Vivat Rex*, the equivalent of 'God save the king', has its origins in the Vulgate (1 Samuel 10.24; 1 Kings 1.25). *Currat lex* was a widely current tag. Neither phrase is to be found in Horace.

242.32 Utrecht see note to 42.31.

242.33–243.1 clarissimus...ictus...peritissimus i.e. juris-consultus clarissimus et peritissimus: *Latin* very celebrated and most expert lawyer. *Clarissimus* might also mean 'very loud'. Saddletree's abbreviation *ictus* is a genuine Latin word meaning 'blow, stroke, thrust', which must add to Butler's bewilderment.

242.33–34 Grunwiggin Simon Groenewegen (1613–52), author of a treatise, *Tractatus de legibus abrogates et inusitatis in Hollandia* (1649), on those parts of the Corpus Iuris Civilis (i.e. Roman Law as codified under Justinian, *c.* 482–565, Emperor from 527) which were not received into Dutch law. He also annotated Hugo de Groot (Grotius), *Ineidinge* or *Introduction to Dutch Law* (1644).

243.1–2 Italian types italic types, called Italian because originally designed by Francesco Griffo for the great Venetian printer-publisher Aldus Manutius (Aldo Manuzzi, 1450–1515). Aldus used italic types for printing Roman literature, beginning with the works of Virgil in 1501, and as a result it became customary to print Latin in italic, as in this novel.

243.6–7 servitude of stillicide a *servitude* is an obligation over a piece of land which prevents a proprietor's full unrestricted use by allowing another some use of the land in question. The servitude here requires the proprietor to accept water from the eaves of an adjoining house.

243.8 Mary King's Close now below the W end of the current City Chambers of Edinburgh in the High Street.

243.18 win out come out.

243.18 win she or lose she whether she wins or loses.

243.27–28 made the gardy-loo threw out liquid waste. *Gardy-loo* (from the French, prenez garde à l'eau: beware of the water) was the cry used to warn passers-by that waste was about to be tipped out of an upper window. This was the standard mode of discharging liquid waste including sewage in the Old Town of Edinburgh; the streets were swept and washed down overnight.

243.32 Ten-Mark Court a municipal court in Edinburgh dealing with small debts up to the value of ten merks. A *merk* (worth 6p) was Scottish money (or coin) worth 2/3 of a pound Scots (13s. 4d.), and in 1707 (when Scottish currency ceased) the pound Scots was worth 1/12 of a pound sterling.

243.33 swear hersell free the precise meaning is not clear; the general sense is that the Highland servant wanted to escape the consequences of emptying the chamber pot out of the wrong window by apologising, but that Saddletree prevented her.

243.37–38 pitcher from the well compare Genesis 24.43, 45.

244.3 Gang in bye go inside.

244.13 hectic of a moment momentary blush: Laurence Sterne, *A Sentimental Journey through France and Italy by Mr. Yorick* (London, 1768), ed. Ian Jack (London, 1968), 7 ('The Monk: Calais', episode 2).

244.34 in initialibus *Latin* in the initial stages, in the beginning.

245.13 And what for no and why not?

245.15–17 hearts ... flesh ... stane see note to 209.12.

245.23 King Ahasuerus probably Xerxes, king of Persia (reigned 486–65 BC); see the Book of Esther in which the heroine marries Ahasuerus and saves the Jews from genocide.

245.24 sate upon his royal throne foranent the gate of his house see Esther 5.1.

245.39 duchess has at Dalkeith Jeanie probably refers to Anna, 1st Duchess of Buccleuch (1651–1732) who rebuilt the old castle and made Dalkeith House her home (see note to 230.32). It is not known whether the 2nd Duchess lived at Dalkeith.

245.40 be decently put on be decently turned out, or dressed.

246.10 Lord of Lorn title used by the heir to the dukedom of Argyle.

246.41–42 Ichabod ... house see note to 198.4.

247.6–7 no time to marry or be given in marriage see Ecclesiastes 3.1, and Matthew 24.38.

247.28 kylevine pen lead pencil.

248.8 Baron Court the court of a barony. A *barony* was an estate created by direct grant from the Crown, a grant which carried with it both civil and criminal jurisdiction in all matters except murder, rape, fire-raising (arson), and robbery which were reserved for the Justiciary court.

248.17–20 A little ... begging bread Psalm 37.16, 25.

248 motto Lord Byron (1788–1824), *Childe Harold's Pilgrimage*, Canto 1 (1812), line 125.

250.18–19 to indite two letters ... operation of some little difficulty for the spelling of Jeanie's letters see 'Essay on the Text', 499–500, 515.

250.26–27 the vow of the daughter should not be binding without consent of the father see Numbers 30.4–5.

250.28–29 borne in upon my minde see note to 223.29.

250.31 hail lands of Da'keith and Lugton see note to 236.36.

250.36 we maun forgie others, as we pray to be forgi'en see the Lord's Prayer, Matthew 6.12, Luke 11.4.

250.39 forgi'en her trespass see Matthew 6.14–15, 18.35; Mark 11.25–26.

250.40–41 like the barbarians unto the holy Apostle see Acts 28.2. The 'Holy Apostle' is Paul, for whom people in Malta kindled a fire.

250.42 chosen people the people of Israel were known as 'the chosen people', i.e. the people chosen by God to fulfil his purpose. Many Covenanters considered themselves the successors to the Jews as the people chosen by God to reveal his will. In England Jeanie finds dissenters (i.e. those who dissented from the Church of England, especially Presbyterians and Independents) who held similar views about worship as the Presbyterians of Scotland, and calls them 'a sort of chosen people'.

251.1 kirks without orguns there were no organs in Presbyterian and Independent places of worship until the late 19th century. In the Church of England almost all church organs were destroyed in the 1640s, but were gradually reintroduced after the Restoration of the Monarchy in 1660.

251.2 the minister preaches without a gown customary in dissenting churches; in Scotland ministers wore the black Genevan gown.

251.4 Roslin or Driden not identified, but landowners were often known by the names of their estate. Roslin is 10 km S of Edinburgh; Driden has not been identified.

251.13 Scots pint 3 imperial pints (1.7 litres).

251.15–16 An it does nae gude, it can do nae ill proverbial: compare Ramsay, 90.

251.29 muckle Kirk York Minster.

251.30–31 milns ... gang by the wind Jeanie contrasts the use of wind to power corn mills round York with the customary use of water in Scotland. For such mills in Yorkshire see Alan Whitworth, *Yorkshire Windmills* (Leeds, 1991).

251.33 I keep the straight road compare Mark 1.3; Luke 3.4; John 1.23.

252.6–8 bairns' rime ... poor hog-lams see *The Complaynt of Scotland*, ed. John Leyden (Edinburgh, 1801), 314: 'March said to Aperill,/ I see three hogs upon a hill;/ But lend your three first days to me,/ And I'll be bound to gar them die./ The first, it sall be wind and weet;/ The next, it sall be snaw and sleet;/ The third, it sall be sic a freeze,/ Sall gar the birds stick to the trees.—/ But when the *borrowed* days were gane,/ The three silly hogs came hirplin [limping] hame.' A *bairns' rime* is a nursery rhyme; a *hog-lam* is a lamb before its first shearing.

252.7 borrowing days the last three days of March (Old Style): see preceding note.

252.9 this hither side of Gordan on this side of Jordan, i.e. in life.

252.20 ilk land has its ain laugh *proverbial* every country has its own customs etc. See Kelly, 92; *ODEP*, 441. *Laugh* is a form of 'laich', meaning an area of low-lying, or undrained ground.

252.23 middell aisle the central area of a church (*OED*, *aisle*, 4).

252.30 The orthography see 'Essay on the Text', 499–500, 515.

253.20–21 that more impartial and wider principle of general bene-volence in the 18th century philosophers tended to argue that human beings are naturally benevolent, and that virtue is the acting out of general feelings for the good of others.

253.23 Bickerton probably from the name of a village 10 km W of York, but also recalling the Scots word *bicker*, meaning a 'drinking vessel'.

253.23 lady of the ascendant see John Webster, *The Duchess of Malfi* (written 1612–13; published 1623), ed. John Russell Brown (London, 1964), 2.1.96.

253.26–27 a Merse woman, marched with Mid-Lothian a woman from the Merse (the cultivated area of Berwickshire between the Lammermoor Hills and the River Tweed) which shared a boundary (marched) with Mid-Lothian.

254.2 Swan and two Necks Swan with two Necks, in the 18th century a busy inn and coaching and wagon office in Lad Lane (now Gresham St) in London. For an illustration see *The London Encyclopædia*, ed. Ben Weinreb and Christopher Hibbert (London, 1983), 851.

254.5 o' the gate on the road.

254.12–13 thou must pickle in thine ain poke-nook you must eat from your own bag, i.e. rely on your own resources. Although apparently proverbial this is first recorded in *Rob Roy* (1817), Vol. 2, Ch. 10.

254.13 belt thine girdle thine ain gate *proverbial* wear your belt in your own way: see Kelly, 92; *ODEP*, 89.

254.16 Braes of Doun Doune, 12 km NW of Stirling. The area around Doune was held by Drummonds and Stewarts, to whom the Macgregors were allied. The Macgregors, treated in Scott's previous novel, *Rob Roy*, may be the 'wud lads' referred to here.

255.16 Cock o' the North the name specifically refers to the Marquis of Huntly, but is here used without specific reference to indicate someone who was at the top of his profession in the north.

255.36 the flesh-pots of Egypt see Exodus 16.3. The phrase was often used by Scots to refer to English plenty.

255.37 fair water pure water.

256.2 summum bonum *Latin* highest good, a common philosophical term.

256 motto George Crabbe (1754–1832), *The Borough* (1810), Letter 18, 'The Poor and their Dwellings', lines 352–53, in Crabbe, *Poetical Works*, 1.531.

256.12 Gumoorsbury Hill Gonerby Hill, just N of Grantham, Lincolnshire. As Scott uses the form 'Gunnersbury' three times in the next two pages it must be assumed that the spelling here is intended to represent the speaker's dialect.

256.12 Robin Hood legendary outlaw of Sherwood Forest. The best scholarly opinion of Scott's time considered Robin Hood a historical figure of the 12th century: see Joseph Ritson, *Robin Hood: A Collection of All the Ancient Poems, Songs, and Ballads*, 2 vols (London, 1795): *CLA*, 174.

256.13 vale of Bever Vale of Belvoir, between Grantham and Nottingham.

256.15 Emery John Emery (1777–1822), comic actor famed for his performance in rustic and low-life parts. William Erskine considered his performance as Dandie Dinmont in the play *Guy Mannering* at Covent Garden, London, in 1816 to be 'inimitable' (*Letters*, 4.238), and Scott could have seen him in the same role at the Theatre Royal, Edinburgh, in July 1817.

256.18–21 Robin Hood ... we say so too not identified, but the final line suggests that this is a Scott pastiche written for this specific context.

256.24 Ferrybridge W Yorkshire, about 30 km SSW of York, on the Great North Road.

256.27 the Swan the White Swan Inn, Ferrybridge.

256.29 Tuxford in Nottinghamshire, about 60 km S of Ferrybridge, on the Great North Road.

256.34–35 hundred-armed Trent ... Newark Castle the town of Newark in Nottinghamshire stands on the Trent, a river which flows N into the Humber estuary, draining the whole Midlands: *hundred-armed* is indicative of the extent of its basin. Newark Castle was besieged three times during the Civil War of 1642–46; the 3rd siege ended in 1646 with Charles I surrendering. The Parliamentarians ordered the people of the town to destroy the Castle (it was in fact merely rendered ineffective as a place of defence), but it was not burnt although Scott's *blackened* may seem to imply as much.

257.6 Maritornes a loose and rather ugly maid in Cervantes, *Don Quixote*, Part 1 (1605), Ch. 16.

257.6 Saracen's Head coaching inn of 1721 in the Market Place in Newark. It is now a bookshop and a bank, but there is still a Saracen's head on the facade.

257.20 run upon the road extensive and sustained demand for post horses (*OED, run¹*, noun 15b).

257.26 Gunnersbury Hill, about three miles from Grantham Gonerby Hill, just N of Grantham, Lincolnshire. Grantham is about 22 km S of Newark.

257.32 Ingleboro' Ingleborough Hill, 723m high, and 28 km NE of Lancaster. As it is on the W side of the Pennines it is not visible from Jeanie's route along the Great North Road and the Vale of York. Scott may have made his mistake because of the saying 'Ingleborough, Pendle, and Penigent, / Are the highest hills between Scotland and Trent', a Yorkshire proverb, in Grose, *A Provincial Glossary*, where Grose states that these 'three hills are in sight of each other' and 'are indeed the highest hills in England'.

257.42–43 I'll thatch Groby pool wi' pancakes 'spoken when something improbable is promised or foretold': a Leicestershire proverb, in Grose, *A Provincial Glossary*. See also Ray, 248; *ODEP*, 809. Groby Pool is near Leicester. This and the following proverbial sayings come from the same part of Grose, *A Provincial Glossary*, and parts of Lincolnshire, Nottinghamshire, Leicestershire and Norfolk could be seen as constituting a single geographic area through which Jeanie is passing.

258.1–2   they hold together no better than the men of Marsham when they lost their common 'probably spoken ironically, and means, that by being divided into different factions, these men ruined their cause and lost their common': a Lincolnshire proverb, in Grose, *A Provincial Glossary*. See also Ray, 250; *ODEP*, 366. With the spelling *Marsham* Scott follows Grose; Ray and *ODEP* read 'Marham'. Both Marsham and Marham are in Norfolk.

258.3–4   Grantham gruel, nine grots, and a gallon of water 'Poor gruel indeed': a Lincolnshire proverb, in Grose, *A Provincial Glossary*. See also Ray, 250; *ODEP*, 331.

258.12–13   The same again, quoth Mark of Bellgrave 'This story, said to be an allusion to an ancient militia-officer, … who, exercising his company before the lord lieutenant, was so abashed, that, after giving the first word of command, he could recollect no more, but repeatedly ordered them to do the same again': a Leicestershire proverb, in Grose, *A Provincial Glossary*. See also Ray, 248.

258.20   Gaius Paul's companion and in Romans 16.23 'mine host, and of the whole church'. Gaius, whose 'House is for none but Pilgrims', is Christiana's inn-keeper in *The Pilgrim's Progress*, Part 2, 258–70.

258.38   driegh in the upgang slow on the uptake.

259.4   hist awa *OED* defines *hist* as a noise made to urge on a dog or other animal. But *hist* may be a form of the Scottish word 'heest', and so the phrase may mean 'haste away'.

259.6–7   With my curtch … and through part of the song written by George Robertson (see text, 278.1) for Madge: see also 149.21–24, and 278.7–14.

259.16–24   The airy tongues … Conscience see John Milton, *A Mask Presented at Ludlow Castle* [*Comus*] (performed 1634; published 1637), lines 208–12.

259.31–32   stand and deliver the traditional challenge of the highwayman, meaning 'stop and hand over your money and valuables'.

259.34–35   The woman … the words of action Ben Jonson (1573–1637), *Every Man in His Humour* (first performed 1598; published 1606), 1.5.109–10, in *The Complete Plays of Ben Jonson*, ed. G. A. Wilkes, 4 vols (Oxford, 1981–82), 1.200.

260.3   precious sisters see note to 194.18.

260.16–17   if it were for the benefit of my clergy even if I were trying to plead benefit of clergy. In England in the late 12th century the church succeeded in compelling Henry II and the royal courts to grant priests and clerks (members of the clergy below the priests) immunity from trial and punishment in the secular courts when charged with capital offences, thus allowing them to escape the death penalty which ecclesiastical courts never imposed. Later, anyone with any connection with the church could claim benefit of clergy if he could show that he could read Psalm 51. From the 16th century the privilege was gradually eroded and was abolished in 1827.

260.20   left the lay left the business.

260.26   beggarly country indicates a common English attitude to Scotland in the 18th century: see e.g. Charles Churchill, *The Prophecy of Famine* (1763).

260.38–39   shake by the collar shall make the Leicester beans rattle in thy guts from 'Bean-belly Leicestershire. So called from the great plenty of that grain growing therein, whence it has also been a common saying in the neighbouring counties, shake a Leicestershire yeoman by the collar, and you shall hear the beans rattle in his belly': a Leicestershire proverb in Grose, *A Provincial Glossary*. See also Ray, 247; *ODEP*, 718–19.

260.43   was of milder mood see 'The Children in the Wood', stanza 13, in Percy, 3.170–77, line 101, and compare *The Taming of the Shrew*, 1.1.60.

261.25 putting her through the mill making her suffer by putting her through a predetermined procedure.

261.33 price of oatmeal must be up in the north Levitt accounts for bad temper by an aggressive reference to a staple item in the Scottish diet, with underlying suggestions of Scottish poverty and Scottish meanness.

261.35–36 with the vengeful dexterity of a wild Indian American Indians were considered 'vengeful', and it may be the notion that 'they fight not to conquer, but to destroy' which lies behind Scott's description: see William Robertson, *The History of America*, 2 vols (London, 1777), 1.350–53 (351): see *CLA*, 204.

261.43–262.1 the menacing posture by which a maniac is intimidated by his keeper from the early 17th century Bedlam (*properly* the Bethlehem Royal Hospital) was one of the sights of London, and visitors could see inmates in cages as in a menagerie.

262.7 a hair of her head biblical phrase 'recurring', as Inglis suggests, 'in escapes (Daniel 3.27) and assurances (Luke 21.18)'.

262.7 if it were but for your insolence if for no other reason than to punish you for your insolence.

262.16 reading your prayers backward a recognised way of raising the devil: see 'Prayers said backwards', in *A Dictionary of Superstitions*, ed. Iona Opie and Moira Tatem (Oxford, 1989).

262.28 Bess of Bedlam generic name for a madwoman, *Bedlam* being the asylum for the mad in London (see note to 261.43–262.1), and *Bess* a general name for a woman of the lower orders.

262.39 sight for sair een *proverbial* sight for sore eyes: see *ODEP*, 732.

263.1 who may be his dam *proverbial* the devil and his dam: see *ODEP*, 179.

263.30 the devil to pay proverbial: *ODEP*, 184.

263.38–39 chamber of deas see note to 236.30.

263.40–41 for as braw a place as it is on the outside even although it is a fine looking place on the outside. In 1675–76 the Bethlehem Royal Hospital (Bedlam) moved into a building designed by Robert Hooke in Moorfields in London. The sculptures *Melancholy* and *Raving Madness* by Caius Gabriel Cibber (1630–1700), now in the Guildhall Museum, were formerly over the gate of Bedlam.

264.11–12 cross patch ill-tempered person. The *OED* notes that this is usually applied to a woman but that Scott uses it for men.

264.20 de'il an *emphatic* would that.

264.37 Leap, Laurence, you're long enough not found as a proverbial utterance, but as Laurence is a proverbial name for a lazy person (see *ODEP*, 448) the sense is 'Get on your feet, you lazy person; you're big enough for the job'.

264.43 There's mair shifts bye stealing there are more ways of earning a living than by stealing.

265.6–8 Cu'ross hammermen... Cu'ross girdle the hammermen (ironworkers) of Culross, a royal burgh on the N side of the Forth estuary, were given a monopoly in the manufacture of girdles (flat pans for baking oatcakes, scones, pancakes etc.) by James VI in 1599. The monopoly lasted until the 18th century.

265.9 nae fair way in no right way.

265.13 the tae gate or the tother the one way or the other.

265.16–20 In the bonnie... fasting plenty see 'Tom of Bedlam', lines 17–20, in *Ancient Songs*, ed. Joseph Ritson (London, 1790), 262: see *CLA*, 158, 174. The lines in Ritson constitute a parallel version rather than a source.

265.32 mair by token especially.

265.39–42 My banes ... now to thee see 'Sweet William's Ghost' (Child, 77A), stanza 9, in *TTM*, 325; Percy, 3.128–31; Herd, 1.77; and *SMM*, no. 363.

266.7 Waes me *literally* woe is me, i.e. oh dear, alas.

266 motto see Francis Beaumont and John Fletcher, *The Coxcomb* (first performed 1612; published 1647), 2.2.77–78. The motto means: 'Tie her up quickly or I shall turn informer, even if I hang for it'.

266.36 James Renwick see notes to 102.35 and 102.36–37.

266.36 fallen standard 'Life and Death of Richard Cameron', in Walker, 1.224, 226.

266.37–38 Daniel Cameron i.e. Richard Cameron: see note to 4.38. The name conflates that of Richard Cameron and Donald or Daniel Cargill, a mistake previously made by David Deans at 102.32.

267.5 blessed Psalmist King David. Of the 150 psalms 73 are attributed to David, but he cannot be shown to have been the author of any.

267.6–8 Why are thou cast down ... my God Psalm 43.5; see also Psalm 42.5, 11.

267.19 planked a chury the source of this phrase has not been found; it is not in Grose, *A Classical Dictionary*.

267.21–22 one good turn deserves another proverbial: *OED*, *turn*, noun 23. See also *ODEP*, 325.

267.22 loud as Tom of Lincoln 'This Tom of Lin[c]oln is an extraordinary great bell, hanging in one of the towers of Lincoln Minster': a Lincolnshire proverb, in Grose, *A Provincial Glossary*. See also Ray, 249; *ODEP*, 487–88. Tom of Lincoln is one of the Cathedral bells, and weighs 5486 kilos (5 tons 8 cwt).

267.23 Tyburn the place of public execution in London. See notes to 21.11 and 267.29.

267.23 Neddie i.e. Donkey, or Edward.

267.29 gang up Holbourn Hill backward 'come to be hanged': a London proverb, in Grose, *A Provincial Glossary*. Grose continues: 'Criminals condemned for offences committed in London and Middlesex, were, till about the year 1784, executed at Tyburn, the way to which from Newgate was up Holburn-hill. They were generally conveyed in carts ... [and] were always placed with their backs towards the horses'.

267.34 flats and sharps recourse to weapons: see *OED*, *flat*, noun³ 14d.

267.35 live out his two years no source has been found for the idea that the career of a highwayman lasted two years.

267.41 mend your hands refill your glasses, take another drink.

268.2 Dutch courage bravery induced by drinking: *OED*, *courage*, 4d. The *OED* cites Scott's *Woodstock* (1826) as the first use of the phrase.

268.20 along of on account of, because of.

269.37 the Nor'-Loch the loch or lake N of the Old Town of Edinburgh, where Princes Street Gardens now are. It was drained in the late 18th century.

270.25–26 as fast as if she were in Bedfordshire the term *fast* is a now an obsolete usage meaning 'fast asleep' (*OED*, *fast*, adjective 1d), but as a proverbial saying the phrase has not been found.

270.30 Surfleet about 30 km E of Grantham. In 1737 before the surrounding fenland had been fully drained Surfleet Seas End was accessible to sea-going vessels.

270.31 Moonshine cant word for smuggled or illicit spirit: see Grose, *A Classical Dictionary*.

270.33 blue plums lead bullets: Grose, *A Classical Dictionary*.

270.39–40 couch a hogshead lie down to sleep: Grose, *A Classical Dictionary*.

271.9–10 land of Nod asleep: Genesis 4.16.

271.15 an unco wark a great fuss.

271.19–20 havena a word to cast at a dog proverbial: see *ODEP*, 915.

272.14–15 making your heels save your hands probably a variant of the proverb 'One pair of heels is worth two pairs of hands' (Kelly, 270; *ODEP*, 607), meaning that Jeanie thinks that running away will save her trouble and effort. Ed1 changed 'hands' to 'head', but Scott intended 'hands' because he restored it in the Interleaved Set.

272.25 infirm of purpose *Macbeth*, 2.2.52.

272.30 warld's wonder someone or something notorious, or to be laughed at and scorned.

272.33 waes me alas.

272.38 what for why.

273.1–2 hillock of moss, such as the poet of Grasmere has described see William Wordsworth, 'The Thorn' (1798), line 36, where 'a hill of moss' covers a baby's grave.

273.43 narrow way, and the strait path see Matthew 7.13–14.

274.1 burning bricks in Egypt symptomatic of the slavery of the Israelites in Egypt: see Exodus 1.13–14.

274.1–2 the weary wilderness of Sinai having escaped from Egypt the Israelites were condemned to wander 40 years in the Sinai desert, prevented by God from entering the Promised Land.

274.3 to cover my lip for shame see Micah, 3.7.

274.7–8 the Devil ... lays his broad black loof on my mouth compare Isaiah 6.6–7.

274.12–13 make your breast clean an 18th-century variation of the biblical 'clean heart', for which see Psalm 51.10, 73.1; Proverbs 20.9.

274.13–14 resist the devil, and he will flee from you James 4.7. This verse is cited in the marginal note to *The Pilgrim's Progress*, Part 1, 60.

274.19–20 Apollyon ... Pilgrim's Progress see *The Pilgrim's Progress*, Part 1, 59. Apollyon is a manifestation of the devil.

274.32 Christiana wife of Christian, and heroine of the second part of *The Pilgrim's Progress*.

274.32 Mercy a neighbour of Christiana's who accompanies her on her pilgrimage.

274.33 of the fairer countenance, and the more alluring see *The Pilgrim's Progress*, Part 2, 226.

274.34–35 Great-heart Christiana's guide in *The Pilgrim's Progress*, Part 2.

274.37 Corporal MacAlpine not identified.

274.38 the guard-house i.e. the guard-house in the High Street, Edinburgh.

274.39 Lochaber axe see note to 27.32.

274.39–40 de'il pike the Highland banes o' him may the devil pick his Highland bones.

275.18–21 Feeblemind ... rifling him, and about to pick his bones ... flesh-eaters see *The Pilgrim's Progress*, Part 2, 266.

275.18 Ready-to-halt *The Pilgrim's Progress*, Part 2, 271.

275.21 Greatheart killed Giant Despair *The Pilgrim's Progress*, Part 2, 282.

276.18–20 I'll bless God ... shadow of his wing see Psalm 63. 4–7.

276.31 Drottle possibly from Scots *trottle* meaning 'toddle'.

276.31–32 turned up his nose became scornful or contemptuous.

276.36–37 gie me as muckle as sixpence ... for my weel-fa'ard face compare Robert Henryson (15th century), *The Testament of Cresseid*, lines 498–525.

277 motto Samuel Taylor Coleridge, 'Christabel' (Part 1 written 1798;

published 1816), lines 135–36, repeated 143–44.

277.12 embosomed in a tuft of trees see John Milton, 'L'Allegro' (written *c.* 1631; published 1645), line 78.

277.19–20 disjointed chat see *I Henry IV*, 1.3.65.

277.38–39 maidens' bairns are weel guided proverbial: see Ramsay, 98; *ODEP*, 24.

278.2 Lockington in N Leicestershire. The phrase 'Lockington wake' is suggested by the proverbial saying 'Put up your pipes, and go to Lockington wake', a Leicestershire proverb, in Grose, *A Provincial Glossary*; Ray, 248; and *ODEP*, 658.

278.4 better wed over the mixen as over the moor *proverbial* better marry over the midden (i.e. a neighbour) than someone from far away: *ODEP*, 57.

278.5 he may gang farther and fare waur proverbial: *ODEP*, 306.

278.7–14 I'm Madge ... bonnie as me part of the song written by George Robertson (see text, 278.1) for Madge: see also 149.21–24, and 259.6–7.

278.9 Lady of Beever Duchess of Rutland, whose seat was Belvoir Castle, near Grantham.

278.11 Queen of the Wake, and I'm Lady of May i.e. the girl chosen to lead the festivities of the wake (an annual festival in an English rural parish) and Mayday celebrations which included dancing round a maypole.

278.27–28 as they went on their way they sang see *The Pilgrim's Progress*, Part 2, 208.

278.30–38 He that is down ... age to age *The Pilgrim's Progress*, Part 2, 238.

278.40–41 feeding his father's sheep ... valley of humiliation *The Pilgrim's Progress*, Part 2, 237.

278.42–279.1 lived a merrier life ... silk and velvet see *The Pilgrim's Progress*, Part 2, 238.

279.11 City of Destruction see *The Pilgrim's Progress*, Part 1, 11, 67; Part 2, 175.

279.11 Mrs Bat's-eyes inhabitant of the City of Destruction: see *The Pilgrim's Progress*, Part 2, 184.

279.13 Mistrust and Guilt two of the robbers who despoil Little-faith: see *The Pilgrim's Progress*, Part 1, 125–26.

279.16–17 Interpreter's house Christiana and Mercy go to the Interpreter's House in *The Pilgrim's Progress*, Part 2, 197–208.

279.18–19 eyes lifted up ... pleaded wi' men see *The Pilgrim's Progress*, Part 1, 29, part of the description of a picture of the Evangelist.

279.21–28 knock at the gate ... bottle of spirits see *The Pilgrim's Progress*, Part 2, 188–90.

280.21 squires of the pad footpads. See the motto on p. 21, note to 21, motto, and Matthew Prior (1664–1721), 'The Thief and the Cordelier', line 7.

281.6 Abigail lady's maid; from *Abigail*, the name of the 'waiting Gentlewoman' in Francis Beaumont and John Fletcher's play *The Scornful Lady* (performed 1610; published 1616) who may have been called *Abigail* in allusion to the Abigail of 1 Samuel 25.24, 31 who calls herself 'thine handmaid' (*OED*).

281.15 wand as the Treasurer or High Steward bears on public occasions rod of white wood carried as a sign of office on ceremonial occasions by senior members of the royal household. In Scots a piece of stripped willow used for basket-making is also called a *wand* and so in this passage there is a certain slippage between senses.

281.19 Interpreter's house here the church, but also with a reference to *The Pilgrim's Progress*: see note to 279.16–17.

281.22 necessity had no law see Kelly, 266; *ODEP*, 557–58.

281.29–30 high-gravel blind i.e. completely blind (a comic intensification of 'stone-blind'): *The Merchant of Venice*, 2.2.31.

282.25–26 Cameronian Regiment see note to 175.32.

282.37–38 directory of the Presbyterian Kirk *A Directory for the Public Worship of God*, until 1929 the standard of worship in the Church of Scotland. It was produced by the Westminster Assembly (see note to 149.36) and approved by the General Assembly in 1645.

282.41–283.1 Cease…words of knowledge see Proverbs 19.27.

283.6 organ…flutes see note to 251.1. Inglis observes that flutes in church are not documented until the 1790s.

283.7 chancel *properly* the area reserved for the clergy in the E of a church. However, architectural terms relating to churches were more loosely used in the early 19th century and as Scott has Madge walk 'the whole length of the church' (283.19) he must mean by *chancel* the area used for worship.

283.37–38 this posture of mental devotion was entirely new in Scotland it was normal to stand during prayers during public worship if only because most churches did not have pews or other seating. (Kneeling or bowing the head was normal in family worship and private devotion.) In the course of the 18th and 19th centuries changing attitudes to worship, as well as changes in church furnishings, involved the gradual adoption of sitting and bowing the head as the normal attitude during prayer in most Scottish churches.

284.1–2 the lesson of the day the readings from the Bible appropriate to each Sunday of the year are given in *The Book of Common Prayer* (1559, revised 1662). Madge then follows the Order for Morning Prayer.

284.18 shocked at his surplice many ministers of the Church of Scotland did not wear any vestments, but might wear the black Genevan gown (the wearing of vestments had been rejected in Scotland at the Reformation); the wearing of a surplice (a short, white linen vestment worn over other gowns) was required in the Church of England (except when preaching) from 1604.

284.28 Naaman the Syrian see 2 Kings 5. Naaman, 'captain of the host of the king of Syria' (2 Kings 5.1), has leprosy, is told by Elisha to wash in the Jordan seven times, and is cured. He then professes that there is 'no God in all the earth, but in Israel' (2 Kings 5.15) but as he serves the king of Syria will still have to worship in the house of Rimmon (2 Kings 5.18).

284.29 God of my fathers Daniel 2.23; Acts 24.14.

284.29–30 in mine own language see Acts 2.6.

284.30–31 the Lord will pardon me in this thing see 2 Kings 5.18, the words of Naaman asking forgiveness for having to worship in the house of Rimmon (see note to 284.28).

284.40–41 practical doctrines of Christianity i.e. he preached on the Christian life rather than on theology, especially sin and grace, which would have been normal in the church attended by David Deans.

284.42 every word written down and read Scottish preachers were expected to preach extempore.

284.43–285.1 Boanerges sons of thunder: see Mark 3.17.

285 motto George Crabbe (1754–1832), *The Borough* (1810), Letter 19, 'The Poor of the Borough—the Parish-Clerk', lines 229–30, in Crabbe, *Poetical Works*, 1.540.

285.33–34 I will gar ye, as good I will retaliate, I'll give you as good [as I got].

286.10 rates poor rates, a local property tax levied to support the poor of the parish. As parishes supported only those born in the parish the beadle's remark provides another small hint about Madge's background.

286.11 Barkston village 6 km N of Grantham.

286.17–18 I'll be upsides wi' you I'll be even or quits with you, I'll be revenged on you.

286.34–35 gie thee lodging at the parish charge i.e. put you in a workhouse. Workhouses provided the poor with shelter and a meagre diet in return for forced labour.

287.1–2 snog and snod 'Neat, handsome', under 'snod and snog', in Grose, *A Provincial Glossary*.

287.11 the root of the matter Job 19.28.

287.16 clerical mansion was large and commodious compare the description of Donwell Abbey in Jane Austen, *Emma*, ed. R. W. Chapman, 3rd edn (London, 1933), 358, and of Mr Dennison's house in Tobias Smollett, *The Expedition of Humphry Clinker* (1771), J. Melford to Sir Watkin Phillips, [6 Oct.]; ed. Thomas R. Preston (Athens and London, 1990), 306. This passage is discussed by Alistair M. Duckworth, 'Scott's Fiction and the Migration of Settings', *Scottish Literary Journal*, 7 (May 1980), 104.

287.20 Willingham although there are real places of this name, none is in the vicinity of Grantham (one is 16 km NE of Lincoln and the other 13 km N of Cambridge), but the name 'Staunton' led to the early identification of Willingham with Staunton in the Vale, 13 km NW of Grantham, and of Willingham-hall with Staunton Hall near that village.

287.36 Romish times i.e. before the revolution of 1533–40 which severed the ties of the Church of England with the papacy.

288.3 Mr Price … picturesque Uvedale Price (1747–1829), whose *An Essay on the Picturesque*, 2 vols (London, 1794–98: see *CLA*, 202) proposed roughness and irregularity as aesthetic principles.

288.4–5 bookish man Joseph Addison (1672–1719) and Sir Richard Steele (1672–1729), *The Spectator*, no. 482 (1712), in *The Spectator*, ed. Donald F. Bond, 5 vols (1965), 4, 209.

288.9 Mony men would ha scrupled such expence because as the living is in the gift of Sir Edmund Staunton the improvements to the Rectory cannot be inherited by Mr Staunton's son.

288.15 heritors the landowners in a Scottish parish who had responsibility for maintaining the church, manse and school buildings, and for paying the minister's stipend and the schoolmaster's salary.

288.20 stone masonry while brick was the usual building material in England stone was commonly used in Scotland.

288.32–33 there was nought to be done wi' fly-fishing i.e. up here the water is clear, but further downstream it becomes muddy and unsuitable for fishing with flies.

289.4 as flat as the fens of Holland not found as an established saying. *Flat* in this context means 'slow-witted', or 'innocent' (*OED*, *flat*, adjective A8 and C13). Holland Fen (which is very flat) is in Lincolnshire, near Boston, on the Wash.

289.12 Sir William Monson (1569–1643) born at South Carlton, Lincolnshire, fought against the Spaniards under Queen Elizabeth and became an admiral under James VI and I.

289.13 James York the blacksmith of Lincoln James Yorke (dates unknown), author of *The Union of Honour* (London, 1640), described on the title page as 'Black-Smith'. Yorke describes the coats of arms of kings, dukes, marquesses, and earls, and 'of Lincolnshire gentry'.

289.13–14 Peregrine, Lord Willoughby Peregrine Bertie, 11th Lord Willoughby de Eresby (1555–1601), soldier. His valour as commander-in-chief in the Netherlands 1587–89 excited great admiration.

289.16–23 Stand to it … Willoughbee see 'Brave Lord Willoughby', stanza 3, in Percy, 2.217–21, lines 17–24.

289.27 black pot beer mug.

289.27–28 double ale ale of twice the ordinary strength.

289.28 seriously inclined see *Othello*, 1.3.146.

290.38 was not born at Witt-ham 'A punning insinuation that the person spoken of wants understanding', both a Lincolnshire and an Essex proverb, in Grose, *A Provincial Glossary*. See also Ray, 249; *ODEP*, 473.

290.42–43 footnote see note to 290.38.

291.2 put on turned out.

291.32 pith and marrow *Hamlet*, 1.4.22.

291.32–33 marrow ... of modern divinity see E. F. [Edward Fisher], *The Marrow of Modern Divinity* (London, 1645). When the book was republished in Scotland in 1718 it was considered highly controversial: for an exposition of the issues see James Hogg, *The Private Memoirs and Confessions of a Justified Sinner*, ed. P. D. Garside (Edinburgh, 2001), xxiv–vi. Deans's use of the phrase 'marrow of modern divinity' indicates his inclination towards the evangelical party in the Church of Scotland.

292.16–17 evil communication see 1 Corinthians 15.33.

292.29 bound over to prosecute be put under a legal obligation to prosecute. Until the 19th century the victim had to bring criminal prosecutions in England, unlike Scotland where prosecutions have always been brought by public prosecutors (for the crown). See Hume, *Crimes*, 1.xlvii–viii.

292.40 if her father was a Quaker the only group in England who refused to swear to tell the truth, etc.

292. 42 black commodities the phrase sounds as though it is a euphemism for illicit or smuggled goods, used here metaphorically, but no support for this interpretation has been found.

293 motto Samuel Taylor Coleridge, 'The Pains of Sleep' (written 1803; published 1816), lines 25–32.

293.35 Court of the Gentiles the outermost of the courts of the Temple in Jerusalem, which non-Jews wishing to worship could enter. Gentiles could not enter the three inner courts, which were reserved for Jewish women, men of Israel (i.e. circumcised Jews), and priests.

293.36 Common Prayer *The Book of Common Prayer* (1559, revised 1662), the service book of the Church of England.

293.38 pith and marrow see notes to 291.32 and 291.32–33.

293.38–39 Boanerges see note to 284.43–285.1.

293.40 Curate Kiltstoup see text at 69.34–35 and note.

294.36–37 well to pass well-off, prosperous.

294.37–38 would not want their share of a Leicestershire plover, and that's a bag-pudding *proverbial* would not give up eating: a Leicestershire proverb, in Grose, *A Provincial Glossary*; see also Ray, 248. A *Leicestershire plover* is a pudding boiled in a bag.

294.40–41 read where thou listest compare John 3.8: 'The wind bloweth where it listeth'.

294.42–43 parable of the good Samaritan Luke 10.30–36.

295.25 what is your business to put in your oar what business is it of yours to interfere?

295.32 an Dame Dalton curries it thus *either* if Dame Dalton beats one about like this (where *curries* is a figurative use of *OED*, *curry*, verb 3, beat one's hide for him, give a drubbing to), *or* if Dame Dalton carries on like this (where *curries* is read as a dialectal form of 'carries').

296.33–34 turn from their transgressions see Ezekiel 18.30–31.

296.34 Physician of souls i.e. Jesus Christ. The phrase is common in the 17th and 18th centuries, and although not biblical is derived from Matthew 9.12; Mark 2.17; Luke 5.31.

296.42 redeem my sister's captivity *literally* buy my sister out of prison; *metaphorically* save her soul (compare Job 42.10; Psalms 14.7, 53.6, 126.1, 4; Jeremiah 29.14; Hosea 6.11).

297.13 churning upon the bit produce froth by chewing hard on the bit. Scott may have in mind Dryden's phrase 'churning bloody foam', *Aeneid*, Bk 7, line 634, in *The Works of John Dryden*, ed. Walter Scott, 18 vols (Edinburgh, 1808), 14.447. The passage describes the Fury Alecto urging Turnus to avenge himself on the invading Trojans.

297.24–25 like the Mexican monarch on his bed of live coals Guatemozin; he was tortured by Cortés in 1521 and when placed on a bed of live coals is reputed to have said 'Am I now reposing on a bed of flowers?': William Robertson, *The History of America*, 2 vols (London, 1777), 2.127 (see *CLA*, 204).

297.36–38 the source from which I derived food ... propensity to vices it was widely believed that wet nurses communicated physical, mental and emotional qualities to the infant: see Valerie Fildes, *Breasts, Bottles and Babies* (Edinburgh, 1986), 188–91.

298.3 I will tell you more of my story Fiona Robertson suggests that elements in Staunton's story 'directly recall the plot' of Friedrich Schiller, *Die Räuber* (1780), which Scott read in the translation of Alexander Fraser Tytler in 1792: *Legitimate Histories* (Oxford, 1994), 208.

298.10–11 listen to the doctrine which causeth to err see Proverbs 19.27.

298.17 seventh heaven Jews and Moslems believed there were 7 heavens, the seventh being the place of supreme bliss, or the abode of God.

299.33–34 As dissolute ... a better hope see *Richard II*, 5.3.20–21.

301.22–23 Macheath under condemnation see John Gay, *The Beggar's Opera* (1728), Scene 13, Airs 58–67. Macheath is a highwayman in Newgate waiting for his execution; he is finally reprieved.

302.18–19 They anticipated, by half an hour, the ordinary period for execution part of the fiction and not of the historical record.

302.24 cut the rope with my own hands according to the evidence given by Bailie Hamilton to the House of Lords Wilson was 'not cut down by the Executioner but by a person from the Street, who called himself his Brother-in-Law. The same Person that cut him down had applied the day before for his body to have him buried.' (Roughead, 284).

302.30 Vengeance is mine, saith the Lord, and I will repay see Romans 12.19.

303.39 North Loch see note to 269.37.

303.39 Quarry-Holes between Lochend Road and Easter Road in Edinburgh, extending S to the Calton Hill.

305.8 well-spring of life Proverbs 16.22: 'Understanding is a wellspring of life'.

305.27–28 Sir Robert Walpole see note to 220.15–16.

305.30 Tolbooth prison in this phrase Staunton shows that in Scotland he was a foreigner; *tolbooth* is a Scots word for 'prison', but Staunton has understood it as a proper name.

306 motto George Crabbe (1754–1832), *The Borough* (1810), Letter 12, 'Players', lines 257–58, in Crabbe, *Poetical Works*, 1.478.

306.28 There goes the purple coat over my ears i.e. I shall lose my job, the purple coat being, presumably, his livery or 'uniform'.

307.30 meal of meat food; the term does not necessarily include flesh.

309.2–3 Remember ... Charles I. upon the scaffold see *Tales of a Grandfather*, 2nd Series (1829), in *Prose Works*, 24.68–69. Charles I was executed on 30 January 1649.

309.22 avenger of blood Joshua 20.3, 5, 9. The phrase also appears in the Old Testament as the 'revenger of blood': Numbers, 35.19.

311.8 suffering remnant see note to 109.28.

311.21 Naaman see note to 284.28.

312.21 in attendance ready and waiting.

313.15 like the hare, I shall be worried in the seat I started from proverbial: see *ODEP*, 354.

314.21 independence of Scotland in the 18th century Scots thought of Scotland as an independent country sharing a legislature with England.

314.24–25 fause Monteith Sir John Menteith (d. *c.* 1329) who in 1305 captured the Scottish patriot William Wallace (see note to 42.15–16) and handed him over to Edward I of England.

315.34 taken orders i.e. was ordained as a minister of the church.

315.43 pressing to death, whipping, or hanging see *Measure for Measure*, 5.1.520–21. *Pressing* . . . *to death* is the punishment of *peine forte et dure*, 'severe and hard punishment', in which the body of a felon who refused to plead was in former times crushed under heavy weights until he either entered a plea or died.

316.11–16 Headstrong . . . I'll be free George Crabbe (1754–1832), *The Borough* (1810), Letter 12, 'Players', lines 261–66, in Crabbe, *Poetical Works*, 1.478.

316 motto see 'Bannocks of Barley-meal', in Herd, 2.130, and 'Argyll is My Name', in *SMM*, no. 560.

316.36–37 John, Duke of Argyle and Greenwich see note to 64.6.

316.38–39 not without ambition, but "without the illness that attends it" see *Macbeth*, 1.5.16–17.

317.2–3 Argyle . . . the field Alexander Pope (1688–1744), *Epilogue to the Satires* (1738), 2.86–87.

317.19 rise from the earth in the whirlwind, and direct its fury see Joseph Addison (1672–1719), on the Duke of Marlborough, in *The Campaign* (1705), 291–92. In the Bible the whirlwind is the anger of God: see Isaiah 66.15; Jeremiah 23.19, 25.32, 30.23; Nahum 1.3. For a discussion of this reference see Tony Inglis, 'And an Intertextual Heart: Rewriting Origins in *The Heart of Mid-Lothian*', in *Scott and Carnival*, ed. J. H. Alexander and David Hewitt (Aberdeen, 1993), 217–18.

317.24 memorable year see note to 26.36.

317.25 acknowledged or repaid compare Samuel Johnson, 'The Vanity of Human Wishes' (1749), line 134: 'And pow'r too great to keep, or to resign'.

317.43 animated and eloquent opposition see text and note to 221.6–23.

318.8 reply to Queen Caroline see text and note to 64.6–7.

318.8–9 fragments of his speeches the single statement presented here is indeed a compendium of phrases and summary of several speeches. See Robert Campbell, *The Life of the Most Illustrious Prince John, Duke of Argyle and Greenwich* (London, 1745).

318.10 Chancellor, Lord Hardwicke Philip Yorke (1690–1764). Yorke was appointed Lord Chief Justice in 1733, with the title Lord Hardwicke, and then on 16 February 1737 Lord Chancellor, a post he held until 1754. He was created 1st Earl of Hardwicke in 1754.

318.36 somebody attributed to the Jacobite Member of Parliament, William Shippen (1673–1743), in Roughead, 130.

319.8 South-Sea funds in 1720 the South Sea Company offered to take over £31 million of the national debt; enormous speculation followed and the price of stock rose from 130 in February to 1050 in June, but a crash followed and the stock returned to 135 in November. Many people suffered heavy losses.

319.12 **in attendance** waiting.

319.16 **splendid library** see note to 349.1.

320.11 **Scots high-dried** a variety of snuff.

320.12 **time and tide ... wait for no one** proverbial: see Ray, 162; *ODEP*, 822.

320.23 **plain tale** *1 Henry IV*, 2.4.247.

320.24 **shew you have a Scots tongue in your head** proverbial: see Kelly, 388.

320.29–30 **Duncan Forbes** see note to 42.12.

320.39–40 **crime has been but too common ... example** see note to 198.22–24, and Historical Note, 590.

321.3 **None, excepting God and your Grace** see Thomas Carte, *A History of the Life of James, Duke of Ormonde*, 3 vols (1735), 2.443 (*CLA*, 27): 'he told him he had no friend at Court, but God and his Grace. "Alas! poor Cary (replied the Duke) I pity thee; thou couldst not have two friends that have less interest at court, or less respect shown them there"'. (Inglis).

321.5 **Ormond** James Butler, 1st Duke of Ormonde (1610–88).

321.15–16 **our father's transgression** Adam's sin.

321.21–22 **alike the law of God ... surely die** see Numbers 35.16–21. See also text and notes to 94.36–37 and 94.37.

321.38–39 **the country's friend** see note to 64.6.

321.42 **refuge under your shadow** see Psalm 57.1.

322.5 **gudesire and his father** i.e. the Duke's grandfather and great-grandfather. Archibald Campbell, 8th Earl and 1st Marquis of Argyle (1607–61), led the more radical Covenanters against Charles I, but came to terms with Charles II whom he crowned King of Scots in 1651. However, his collaboration with Cromwell's rule in Scotland led to his execution after the restoration of the monarchy in 1660. For his son, also Archibald Campbell, 9th Earl (1629–85), see note to 225.32.

322.7 **the cage** prison, but possibly a literal cage into which prisoners were put for public exhibition: see 388.8 and note, and also 'Walter Smith's Life', in Walker, 2.97, 98.

322.8 **Peter Walker the packman** see note to 88.35–36.

322.16–18 **Salathiel ... Thwack-away** while the list is satiric, the names reflect the strong 17th-century predilection to the biblical and, in literature, the allegorical. For Salathiel see 1 Chronicles 3.17; Matthew 1.12; and Luke 3.27. Obadiah was a minor prophet for whom see 1 Kings 18.3, 4, 7, 16, and the one-chapter book of Obadiah. Muggleton is from Lodowicke Muggleton (1609–98); he and his cousin John Reeve (1608–58) claimed to be the two witnesses of Revelation 11.3–6 and in *c.* 1651 founded the sect known as the Muggletonians. Gipps is possibly from *gip*, an expression of derision.

322.19 **Barebone's Parliament** the Little Parliament of 1653 called after Praise-God Barebones (*c.* 1596–1679), an Anabaptist and Member of Parliament for the City of London.

322.19–20 **old Noll's evangelical army** the army known as the 'new model army' organised by Cromwell in 1645 during the civil war. It was largely composed of cavalry, and combined strict discipline with religious zeal.

322.37 **Lorne** see note to 246.10.

324.15–16 **ilka man buckles his belt his ain gate** *proverbial* each man wears his belt in his own way: see Kelly, 92; *ODEP*, 89.

324.41 **hearts of kings** see Proverbs 25.3: 'the heart of kings is unsearchable'.

325 motto James Thomson (1700–48), 'Summer', lines 1406–09, in *The Seasons*, final edn (1744). Thomson describes Richmond Hill, now in SE London.

325.6 Shene or Sheen, the original name for what is now Richmond. The manor of Shene became Shene Palace in the 14th century, but the building was destroyed by fire in 1499. The palace was rebuilt by Henry VII who renamed it Richmond.

325.12 Nemo me impune *Latin* short for *nemo me impune lacessit*, no one attacks me and escapes unpunished: this is the motto of the Order of the Thistle, the Scottish order of knighthood, and of all Scottish regiments.

325.25 landward bred brought up in the country.

326.13 real Havannah tobacco. Havana, capital of Cuba, gives its name to the highest quality of tobacco.

326.26–27 hope ... the heart sick see Proverbs 13.12.

327.25–26 drove of Highland cattle from the Restoration in 1660 cattle bred in the Highlands were exported to England for fattening and slaughter. They were driven south on established routes (drove roads) by drovers, who were often Highlanders, in herds of between 100 and 300 animals.

328.5 turnpike road road sanctioned by Act of Parliament and built by trustees representing neighbouring landed interests. The roads were made of small stones covered with gravel which provided a smooth surface for coaches. The trustees were entitled to charge tolls, and the name is derived from the wooden or iron barrier that prevented free access to the road. There were many turnpike roads round London.

329.5 reading a sermon Scottish preachers were expected to preach extempore.

329.18 a pleasant village East Sheen.

329.18–30 a commanding eminence ... the whole Scott's description of the view from Richmond Hill is of a *locus classicus* in literature and art: compare James Thomson (1700–48), 'Summer', lines 1408–45, in *The Seasons*, final edn (1744). The scene was frequently painted in the 18th century, by Sir Joshua Reynolds, among others: see David Mannings, *Sir Joshua Reynolds: a Complete Catalogue of his Paintings*, 2 vols (New Haven and London, 2000), no. 2189, plate 1724. The picture, of the view from Reynolds's own villa on Richmond Hill which is exactly that described in the novel, is now in the Tate Gallery, London.

329.27 mighty monarch see John Milton, *Paradise Regained* (1671), 3.262.

330.3 a postern-door in a high brick wall presumably the wall of Richmond Lodge which lay within Richmond Palace Park, now part of the Royal Botanic Gardens at Kew. In 1722 the Lodge was given by George I to the future George II and Queen Caroline, who did much for the gardens. It became their favourite residence. The gardens were remodelled by Lancelot ('Capability') Brown *c*. 1770, and the Lodge demolished.

330 motto see John Fletcher and Philip Massinger, *Rollo, Duke of Normandy, or the Bloody Brother* (written 1617–20; published 1639), 3.1.279–83.

331.7–8 star and garter the insignia of the Order of the Garter, the highest order of chivalry in England instituted in 1378, into which Argyle was invested in 1710.

331.15 open opposition Argyle was so frequently out of favour, and so frequently resigned offices because of his opposition to both ministers and measures that it is difficult to determine exactly when he moved definitively into opposition to the Walpole government. However, his opposition to the Edinburgh bill greatly offended the government and the court, and he was certainly thought to be in opposition.

331.22 Margaret of Anjou (1430–82), the younger daughter of René, afterwards Duke of Anjou. She became the wife of Henry VI of England in 1445. Henry was deposed by the Yorkists in 1461, restored in 1470 but murdered in the following year. Margaret fought the Yorkists for the right of her son Edward (born 1453) to succeed to the throne. Edward was killed while she was defeated and taken prisoner at the battle of Tewkesbury (4 May 1471). In January 1476 she was released as part of a truce between England and France, retired to the Continent, and took no further part in politics.

331.27–29 Queen Anne . . . Hanover family Queen Anne (1665–1714; queen 1702), daughter of James VII and II, was the last Stewart monarch. When she died in 1714 she was succeeded, in accordance with acts of the parliaments of both Scotland and England, by George, Elector of Hanover (1660–1727). However many considered the son of James VII and II (Anne's half-brother James Francis (1688–1766), who was given the title Chevalier de Saint George by the King of France), as the rightful heir to the British throne, and the 1715 Rising was aimed at placing him on it. In England most supporters did not rise against George, but did maintain contacts with the Stewart court in France and, after its expulsion from France in 1717, in Rome, until the failure of the Jacobite Rising of 1745–46.

331.30 courage in the field of battle George II (acting as Elector of Hanover) was the last British monarch to lead an army in battle, at Dettingen (about 30 km SE of Frankfurt am Main) in 1743.

331.34 he jealously affected to do every thing according to his own will see Walpole, 4.305.

332.2–3 She loved the real possession of power see Walpole, 4.305.

332.4–5 the king should have the full credit see Walpole, 4.305.

332.9 cold bath with cold and sea-bathing a recognised way of alleviating the swelling that is one of the symptoms of gout, a painful condition of the joints of the foot and lower leg: see Walpole, 4.307.

332.22 Sir Robert Walpole see note to 220.15–16.

332.24 Pulteney, afterwards Earl of Bath William Pulteney (1684–1764), created Earl of Bath in 1742 on becoming a minister after the fall of Walpole, found common cause with a Tory, Henry St John, 1st Viscount Bolingbroke (1678–1751), in opposing the government of Sir Robert Walpole (see note to 220.15–16) in parliament and through the medium of *The Craftsman*, a periodical founded in 1726.

332.31 House of Brunswick the electors of Hanover were also dukes of Brunswick-Lüneburg, and the dynasty was known as the House of Brunswick.

332.37–38 court at Saint Germains Louis XIV placed the palace of St Germain outside Paris at the disposal of James VII and II after his exile in 1689. Although the Stewarts were expelled from France in 1717 the phrase 'court at St Germain' continued in use.

333.4 Lady Suffolk Henrietta Hobart (1681–1767). In the last years of Anne's reign she and her new husband, Hon. Charles Howard, went to Hanover to ingratiate themselves with the future monarchs of Britain. In 1714, after the accession of George I, she was appointed a Woman of the Bedchamber to the Princess Caroline, and became mistress to Caroline's husband, the future George II. The resulting stormy relations with her husband were reputedly resolved by a pension which brought Howard £1200 per year. Howard became 9th Earl of Suffolk in 1731 but died in 1733. Lady Suffolk retired from the court in 1734.

333.13 her good Howard Walpole, 4.304.

333.14–15 Lady Suffolk lay under strong obligations to the Duke of Argyle see Walpole, 4.302. After becoming mistress to Prince George, the future George II (see note to 333.4), Mrs Howard was fearful of being abducted by her husband, but Argyle and his brother, the Earl of Islay, conducted her to safety.

333.16 Horace Walpole's Reminiscences 'Reminiscences', in *The Works* *of Horatio Walpole, Earl of Orford*, 5 vols (London, 1798), 271–318: *CLA*, 234.

333.36–37 somewhat injured by the small-pox Queen Caroline contracted small-pox shortly after her marriage in 1705: see Walpole, 4.304.

333.37 Esculapius Aesculapius, the Latin form of the Greek Asclepius, was in Greek mythology son of Apollo. He learned the art of medicine from the Centaur Chiron and he came to be worshipped as the god of healing, particularly at Epidaurus. As such he becomes the type of all doctors.

333.38 Jenner Edward Jenner (1749–1823), an English doctor who in a crowning experiment in 1796 established that cow-pox prevented the contraction of small-pox. He published his results in *An Inquiry into the Causes and Effects of the Variolæ Vaccinæ, a Disease . . . Known by the Name of the Cow Pox* (London, 1798). Thereafter vaccination was rapidly and widely used as a means of preventing disease.

333.38–39 their tutelary deity subdued the Python in Greek mythology Apollo, god of medicine (and thus the *tutelary deity* of doctors), killed the python, the dragon or serpent which guarded the shrine at Delphi and represented the forces of the underworld, and established his own oracle.

333.40–41 countenance formed to express at will either majesty or courtesy see Walpole, 4.304–05.

334.1 disorder the most unfavourable to pedestrian exercise gout: see note to 332.9.

334.3–5 light-brown hair . . . handsome see Walpole, 4.303.

334.6 melancholy, or at least a pensive expression see Walpole, 4.303.

334.21–22 the Levee and Drawing-room the *levee* was a reception held in the early afternoon by the sovereign at which only men were received; the *drawing-room* was a reception held by the king or queen at which women were presented.

335.9–10 making his peace with the administration see note to 331.15.

335.10–11 recovering the employments of which he had been deprived Argyle was in and out of favour so frequently that the specific offices he lost on this occasion have not been recorded. Although commentators frequently assert that Argyle was deprived of official positions as a consequence of his opposition to the government's proposed legislative response to the Porteous riot, some offices were relinquished some time after the debates of 1736–37, and their loss may not have been a direct consequence.

335.40 an austere regard of controul *Twelfth Night*, 2.5.62.

336.28 a little deaf see Walpole, 4.303.

336.41 d'une grande-dame *French* of a great lady.

337.6 Inverara Inveraray Castle, the seat of the Duke of Argyle, is in Inveraray village on Loch Fyne on the W coast of Scotland. Scott's spelling *Inverara* reflects the pronunciation.

337.16 Which squires call potter, and which men call prose W. S. Rose (1775–1843), *The Court and Parliament of Beasts, freely translated from The Animali Parlanti of Giambattista Casti* (London, 1816), Canto 2, stanza 5: *CLA*, 250. *Potter* means 'inconsequential talk'.

338.5–6 voice low . . . an admirable thing in woman see *King Lear*, 5.3.272–73.

338.17–19 disputes between George the Second, and Frederick, Prince of Wales Hanoverian sons were always at war with their fathers; the origins of the estrangement of George II and his son are not known.

338.24–25 shot dead, by a kind of chance-medley see 'Memoirs of Jonathan Swift', in *Prose Works*, 2.276. In English law *chance-medley* is the casual killing of someone which although not without fault is yet without evil intent, hence haphazard or random action into which chance largely enters.

338.29–30   kirk-session ... cutty-stool   in each parish the kirk session acted as a moral court and was often particularly zealous in cases of fornication and adultery. Those found guilty either paid a fine or were required to sit on the cutty-stool, the three-legged stool of repentance, in front of the congregation on three or more Sundays. Jeanie suggests that the moral pressure put upon girls by the kirk session was a reason for their concealing their pregnancy.

338.35   light life and conversation   *either* a frivolous way of living and speaking, *or* a way of living that involves dealing with the devil: compare Ephesians 2.3.

338.36   the seventh command   'thou shalt not commit adultery': Exodus 20.14.

340.32   avenger of his blood   see note to 309.22.

340.33   gane to his place   like Judas: see Acts 1.25.

340.39–40   throne ... established in righteousness   see Proverbs 25.5.

341.26   upon thorns   proverbial: see *ODEP*, 814.

341.30   Saint James's   the palace of St James in London, then the residence of the sovereign.

343   motto   *Cymbeline*, 1.1.75–76.

343.10   Richmond Park   i.e. Richmond Palace Park: see note to 330.3.

343.15   dazzled and sunk with colloquy sublime   see John Milton, *Paradise Lost*, 8.455–57.

344.7   kings are kittle cattle to shoe behind   *proverbial* kings are difficult to manage, are not to be depended upon: see *OED*, *kittle*, adjective; and *ODEP*, 428.

344.21   bank-bill   probably a Bank of England bank-note but possibly a banker's draft, i.e. a bill drawn by one bank payable by another at a future date.

345.18   the proper channel   the pardon (with its conditions) would be prepared in the Secretary of State's office in London for the king to sign, and would then be sent by the Secretary of State to the Lord Justice Clerk in Edinburgh; the Lords of Justiciary would then instruct the magistrates of Edinburgh to release Effie.

345.22   take my tap in my lap   pack up quickly and leave. The phrase is apparently derived from *tap*, the quantity of flax put on a distaff at one time, and the practice among spinning women of carrying their work to the house of a neighbour, and of putting the distaff in their apron for transportation.

345.22   slip my ways hame   go home in a quick and quiet manner: see *OED*, *slip*, verb 15c.

345.22–23   on my ain errand   carrying my own message, *or* carrying out the business on which I have come: see *OED*, *errand*, noun 1 or 3.

346.3   Buckholmside   Scott's Magnum note reads: 'The hilly pastures of Buckholm, which the author now surveys, "Not in the frenzy of a dreamer's eye," are famed for producing the best ewe-milk cheese in the south of Scotland' (Magnum, 12.402). Buckholm Hill (323m) is immediately N of Galashiels, and visible from Abbotsford. The quotation is from Lord Byron, *Childe Harold's Pilgrimage*, Canto 1 (1812), line 613.

346.5   Lockermaikus in Lammermoor   Longformacus in the Lammermuir Hills, in the north-east of the Scottish Borders.

346.9   Caroline-Park   see note to 221.29–30.

346.17–18   distinguished agriculturalist   see Eric Cregeen, 'The Changing Role of the House of Argyll in the Scottish Highlands', in *Scotland in the Age of Improvement*, ed. N. T. Phillipson and Rosalind Mitchison (Edinburgh, 1970), 5–23. This article is relevant not just to the Argyle interest in agriculture but to the social and economic revolution carried through by the 2nd Duke, of which the resettlement of David Deans and Reuben Butler is a literary representation.

346.37–40 At the sight of Dumbarton ... barley meal see 'Bannocks of Barley-meal', in Herd, 2.131; and 'Argyll is My Name', in *SMM*, no. 560.

348.1 Mrs mistress, formerly the common form of address for an adult woman, regardless of marital status.

348.10 Rosa Solis cordial or liqueur originally made from, or flavoured with, the plant sundew, but later made from brandy with spices and sugar.

348.11 the great man's great man 'the great man' is a recurrent satiric phrase in Henry Fielding, *The History of the Life of the late Mr. Jonathan Wild the Great* (London, 1743). As 'the great man' was easily identified with the prime minister Sir Robert Walpole *the great man's great man* may appear in literature relating to Walpole; if not then Scott is the originator of a phrase later popularised by Dickens in *The Pickwick Papers*.

349.1 Argyle-house in Argyll St, built 1735–50 for the Earl of Islay, who became the 3rd Duke of Argyle on the death of his brother in 1743. One of its features was the library (Islay was a notable book-collector). The house was demolished in 1864, and the site is now occupied by the London Palladium. It is not known where the 2nd Duke lived at the time of Jeanie's supposed visit; he lived in Bruton St from 1738.

349.3 Lady Caroline Campbell (1717–1794), eldest daughter of the Duke of Argyle who married the Earl of Dalkeith (1721–50), eldest son of the 2nd Duke of Buccleuch.

349.15–16 there is ill talking between a full body and a fasting proverbial: see *ODEP*, 293.

349 motto see Alexander Pope, 'Eloisa to Abelard' (1717), lines 50–51.

349.35 fisicyian see note to 296.34.

349.38–39 turned from your iniquity ... die see Ezekiel 18.30–32, 33.8, 11.

350.4 pleased God see 1 Corinthians 1.21; Galatians 1.15; Hebrews 11.5. While Jeanie's language in this letter sounds biblical, it is, for the most part, not precisely so.

350.5 redeem that captivitie see Psalm 14.7.

350.7 redeemed her soul from the slayer see Psalm 49.15.

350.8–9 I spoke with the Queen face to face, and yet live see Genesis 32.30; Judges 6.22–23.

350.13 instriments see Romans 6.13.

350.13 wrought forth worked out, fashioned out.

350.15 skeely enow in bestial pretty knowledgeable about cattle and sheep.

350.17 Airshire breed the Ayrshire breed, a small, tan and white breed of dairy cattle.

350.26 Board of Agriculture government body founded in 1793 with a view to disseminating knowledge about agricultural improvement. It published many reports on the state of agriculture of which the series 'A General View of the Agriculture of the County of ...' is the best known. Its president was Sir John Sinclair (1754–1835), a man whom Scott thought was obsessed with minutiae.

350.33 talent Hebrew unit of weight (of uncertain size) for precious metals, but implying gold or silver of considerable value. See Matthew 18.24, part of a parable on forgiveness (Matthew 18.21–35), and the parable of the talents, Matthew 25.14–30.

350.34 to the fore in hand.

351.5 Auchtermuggitie fictitious name (burlesquing the real name of Auchtermuchty in Fife), from *auchter* meaning 'upland' (the first element in several Scottish place-names), and (possibly) *muggie*, meaning 'drizzling, wet, misty', or, as Inglis suggests, *mugitus*, Latin meaning 'lowing, bellowing'.

351.9 **the Giver of all good things** see Deuteronomy 6.10–11; Joshua 23.15; Matthew 7.11; Luke 1.53; Galatians 6.6.

351.10 **outgangings and incomings** see Psalm 121.8; Ezekiel 43.11.

351.18 **kylevine pen** lead pencil.

351.19 **he will do for you either wi' a scule or a kirk** he will do something for you by presenting you [by using his rights of patronage] to either a school or a church. As one of Scotland's largest landowners Argyle had rights of patronage to many parish churches and schools.

351.23 **a tour** the Tower of London, which had a moat until it was drained in the 1840s.

351.23–24 **tour of Libberton** see note to 239.36.

351.24 **Craigmiller** now known as Craigmillar Castle, it consists of an L-shaped tower surrounded by a curtain wall on a small hill commanding good views in all directions. It is about 3 km SE of Jeanie's supposed residence at St Leonard's.

351.25 **Nor'-Loch** see note to 269.37.

351.34 **difficulties anent aiths and patronages** see note to 90.16–18.

351.36 **harmonious call** an undisputed invitation from a congregation to undertake the office and duties of minister of their church: see *OED, call,* noun 6g.

351.38 **the root of the matter** Job 19.28.

351.38–39 **hafted in that wee murland parish than in the Canno'gate of Edinburgh** Deans implies that Covenanting commitments were much more likely to be found in country parishes (especially upland ones in Lanarkshire and Galloway) than in sophisticated urban places of worship such as the Cannongate Kirk in Edinburgh. *Hafted* is used of flocks of sheep which learn 'their' area and stay there without being confined by walls or fences.

352.8 **great deliverance** Genesis 45.7; Judges 15.18; 1 Chronicles 11.14; Psalm 18.50.

352.9 **father's house** phrase used 69 times in the Authorised Version of the Bible.

352.10–11 **rejoice and be exceedingly glad** see Matthew 5.12.

352.21–23 **like a pea ... upon one of her own tobacco-pipes** toy in which a pea or berry is put into a pipe and the aim is to keep it elevated by blowing through the pipe.

352.26 **star and garter** see note to 331.7–8.

352.26 **all, as the story-book says, very grand** unidentified.

352.36–37 **king's advocate** Lord Advocate: see note to 42.12.

352.38–39 **within the course of only seven years, twenty-one instances of child murther** see Hugo Arnot, *A Collection and Abridgement of Celebrated Trials in Scotland, From* AD *1536, to 1784* (Edinburgh, 1785), 311. Arnot is talking of the period 1700–06.

352.41 **Weary on him** expression of exasperation, meaning 'damn him', or 'may the devil take him'.

353.1 **the advocate a douce decent man** probably referring to Duncan Forbes of Culloden (see note to 42.12), Lord Advocate since 1725, but who became Lord President of the Court of Session in 1737.

353.1 **it is an ill bird** the first part of a proverb that concludes 'that fyles [fouls] its own nest': see Ray, 79; Ramsay 92; *ODEP*, 397.

353.24–25 **the worse for those who meddle with us** see note to 325.12.

353.42 **uplifted in countenance** elevated in spirit, made happy: see Numbers 6.26.

354.18–19 **Mr Deputy Dabby, of Farringdon Without** a member of the Common Council of the City of London for the ward of Farringdon Without [i.e. outside the walls] who deputises for the alderman. *Dabby* may be derived from the noun 'dab', a small flat fish, or the adjective 'dabby', used of clothes that are damp and clingy.

354.41 savoury for this use of the adjective compare the notes to 72.13–14 and 175.32.

354.42–43 do not let your heart be disquieted within you see Psalms 42.5, 11; 43.5.

354.43–355.1 horns of the altar see note to 58.12–13.

355.3 ordinances the decrees and commands of God. The term is frequently used in the Bible.

355.5–6 John Livingstone … Patrick Walker reporteth see 'Life and Death of Richard Cameron', in Walker, 1.290–91. Walker attributes the idea to Livingstone, but the actual words are those of Alexander Shiels (see note to 355.9–10). Borrowstounness is the modern Bo'ness, on the S shore of the Firth of Forth, W of Edinburgh.

355.7 Gehennah the Hebrew name for the valley of Hinnom, SW of Jerusalem. The name is used as an alternate to Topheth, a site in the valley where, according to Jeremiah (7.31, 19.6), worshippers burned their sons and daughters as offerings. By extension Gehenna came to be regarded as hell, the place of ultimate punishment by fire, and it is used in this sense in the Greek versions of Matthew, Mark and Luke (although translated as 'hell' in the Authorised Version), the Koran and in the Latin translation of 2 Esdras 7.36 in the Apocrypha.

355.9–10 the evils of Scotland … no where see 'Life and Death of Daniel Cargill', in Walker, 2.36–37.

355.12 Goshen area in Egypt, described by Pharaoh as 'the best of the land' (Genesis 47.6), where Joseph settled the children of Israel during the famine: see Genesis 45.10. Later, during the plagues sent to make Pharaoh let the Israelites depart, Goshen is kept apart from the rest of Egypt (Exodus Chs 8–11), and while there was 'thick darkness in all the land of Egypt … all the children of Israel had light in their dwellings' (Exodus 10.22–23).

355.15–16 cauld waff of wind see 'Vindication of Cameron's Name', in Walker, 1.336.

355.16–17 where never plant of grace took root or grew compare the parable of the sower, Mark 4.11–20.

355.18 ower muckle a grip of the gear of the warld in mine arms see 'Vindication of Cameron's Name', in Walker, 1.336–37; and compare Mark 4.19.

355.19 Haran in Genesis 12.1–5 Abram is commanded by God to leave Haran for a 'land that I will shew thee'.

355.20–21 leave … house see Genesis 12.1.

355.26 defections see notes to 71.17–18; 90.16–18.

355.26 lukewarm Revelation 3.16.

355.32 Wooler town in NE Northumbria.

355.32 keeping aye a shouther to the hills always keeping in the shelter of the hills.

355.38 law licks up a' proverbial: see *ODEP*, 446.

355.38–39 I have had the siller to borrow out of sax purses to assist or release [her] I have had to take money from six purses, i.e. from six different sources.

355.40 charge on his band for a thousand merks legal injunction requiring the debtor to redeem a mortgage for £667 Scots, i.e. £55.58 sterling. A merk was worth two-thirds of a pound, and a pound Scots was worth one-twelfth of a pound sterling. Scots currency was abolished in 1707, but the merk remained as a unit of account for some time.

355.41–43 a tout of a horn … out of their pulpits see 'Life and Death of Richard Cameron', in Walker, 1.299, 361, where the words are ascribed to

Alexander Shiels. In 1662 the Privy Council required ministers to take the oath of allegiance or supremacy, to accept presentation to their charges by lay patrons, to submit themselves to their bishops, and to recognise holy days, especially the anniversary of the King Charles II's birthday and restoration on 29 May. About 270 ministers, mainly in the West, refused to conform on conscientious grounds. As a result they were removed from their charges, and banished to north of the Tay: the 'tout of a horn' at the cross in the High St of Edinburgh was the technical announcement of their banishment.

355.43–356.1 adjudication … apprisings in the new process (introduced 1672 c. 19) instead of all the lands of a debtor being sold to cover the debt, part could be conveyed to the creditor (see note to 355.40) once the court had adjudicated on the outstanding debt.

356.2 weel-won gear Robert Burns, 'The Auld Farmer's New-year-morning Salutation to his Auld Mare, Maggie' (1786), line 23 (Kinsley, no. 75).

356.5–6 the establishment … kingdoms see 2 Samuel 7.12–13, 7.16; 1 Kings 9.5; 1 Chronicles 17.11–12, 22.10, 28.6–7.

356.8–9 noited thegither the heads of twa false prophets see 'Vindication of Cameron's Name', in Walker 1.253. The bishops were expelled from the Scottish Convention in 1689 after one of the bishops apparently prayed for the exiled King James. 'All the fourteen gathered together with pale faces', writes Walker, 'and stood in a cloud in the Parliament-closs' with various men including Walker close by. 'Francis Hislop with force thrust Robert Neilson upon them; their heads went hard upon one another'. For *false prophets* see Matthew 7.15: 'Beware of false prophets, which come to you in sheep's clothing, but inwardly they are ravening wolves'; see also Matthew 24.11.

356.9 ungracious Graces see 'Vindication of Cameron's Name', in Walker, 1.254.

356.10–11 Convention-parliament the meeting of the Scottish Estates in 1689, which called William and Mary to the Scottish throne. A *convention-parliament* is one assembled without the formal summons of the sovereign.

356.13 verily his reward shall not be lacking compare Matthew 6.2, 5, 16, and 10.42; Mark 9.41.

356.16 enacted caution *Scots law* having given assurance.

356.17 casting her eye backward on Egypt the Israelites having escaped Egypt frequently 'murmured' against Moses and Aaron because of the hardships of their journey to the promised land, and longed to return to Egypt; e.g. see Exodus 16.1–15, 17.1–7.

356.19 flesh-pots Exodus 16.3.

356.22 Vanity-fair see *The Pilgrim's Progress*, Part 1, 88–97: 'at this Fair are all such Merchandize sold, as Houses, Lands, Trades, Places, Honours, Preferments, Titles, Countreys, Kingdoms, Lusts, Pleasures, and Delights of all sorts, as Whores, Bawds, Wives, Husbands, Children, Masters, Servants, Lives, Blood, Bodies, Souls, Silver, Gold, Pearls, Precious Stones, and what not' (88).

356.23–24 ill mumbled mass see 'Life and Death of Alexander Peden', in Walker, 1.154. Walker's editor, D. Hay Fleming, suggests that the phrase is derived from David Calderwood, *The True History of the Church of Scotland*, ([Edinburgh], 1678), 256, where Calderwood says that at the General Assembly in 1590 James VI described the Anglican service as 'an evil said Masse in English'.

356.25–26 ower back and belly *probably* against all opposition, over all obstacles.

356.26–27 cut off as foam upon the water Hosea 10.7.

356.27–28 wanderers among the nations Hosea 9.17. After the flight of

James VII and II in 1688 the Stewarts lived in Paris and Rome.

356.30–31 **Let us return . . . bind us up** Hosea 6.1.

356.41–357.1 **bean in the nursery tale . . . "curtal axe"** see 'Jack and the Beanstalk'. Whether 'curtal axe' (a short, broad sword) identifies a written version of the tale has not been determined, but it did feature in the tale as told to Scott's children: see *Letters*, 2.156.

357.6 **harmonious call** see note to 351.35.

357.8–9 **spectacles on his nose** see *As You Like It*, 2.7.159.

357.15 **Argyle-house** see note to 349.1.

357 **motto** George Crabbe (1754–1832), *The Borough* (1810), Letter 23, 'Prisons', lines 209–10, 213–14, in Crabbe, *Poetical Works*, 1.581.

357.32–33 **daughters** Lady Mary Campbell (1726–1811) was Argyle's 5th and youngest daughter; the other daughters were older and the only one whom Jeanie could reasonably be thought to have met was Elizabeth (1722–99).

357.36 **two to one** i.e. I would not fear an opposing army twice as large as my own.

357.38 **one to two at Sheriff-moor** at the outset of the battle on 13 November 1715 Argyle commanded about 3500 troops against 8000 in the Jacobite army.

357.40–358.2 **Some say . . . man** see Herd, 1.104, stanza 1; *Scotish Songs*, ed. Joseph Ritson, 2 vols (London, 1794), 2.56: *CLA*, 174. Argyle, commanding his right wing, drove the opposing left wing off the field, while the Jacobite right wing defeated the Hanoverian left. While the battle was undetermined, Argyle had the strategic success of preventing the Jacobite army from going south.

358.3 **turned Tory** i.e. become a supporter of the Jacobite cause, by representing the battle not as a victory for her father but a draw.

358.5–6 **for the thanks we have gotten for remaining whigs** in 1716 Argyle was removed from his position of commander-in-chief in Scotland, in spite of his success.

358.8 **Bob of Dumblain** the name of a dance. *Bob* means 'dance', and Dunblane is a small town 8 km N of Stirling, and below Sheriffmuir (see note to 357.40–358.2) where the battle was fought.

358.9–10 **If it wasna weel bobbit . . . again** see 'Bob o' Dumblane', in *TTM*, 34, where a young man asks a woman to dance with him, as a prelude to marriage and sex. This is probably a 'cleaned-up' version of a traditional song for a version of which see Kinsley, no. 513. Robert Burns records: 'In the evening of the day of the battle of Dumblane (Sheriffmoor), after the action was over, a Scots officer in Argyle's army observed to His Grace that he was afraid the rebels would give out to the world that *they* had gotten the victory. "Weel, weel," returned His Grace . . . "if they think it be na weel bobbit, we'll bob it again."' (Davidson Cook, *Burns Chronicle*, No. 31 (1922), 5–6).

358.17 **for a' the ill they hae done me yet** 'Jocky's grey breeks', in *Scotish Songs*, ed. Joseph Ritson, 2 vols (London, 1794), 1.212 (*CLA*, 174); see also *Songs from David Herd's Manuscripts*, ed. Hans Hecht (London, 1904), 184.

358.33 **doch an' dorroch** stirrup-cup, parting drink. The phrase is an anglicised form of the Gaelic original.

358.40–41 **wine maketh glad the heart** see Psalm 104.15.

358.42–43 **Jonadab the son of Rechab . . . drink no wine** see Jeremiah 35.6.

359.6–7 **Saint Mungo's steeple** the 15th-century steeple of Glasgow Cathedral, traditionally believed to have been founded by the patron saint of Glasgow, St Mungo or Kentigern, around 600.

359.8 **Auld Reekie** Old Smokey, a standard nickname for Edinburgh.

359.31 ta'en the rue repented, changed his mind.

359.32 needna be at muckle fash about it needn't be much troubled about it.

360.11 half of her due i.e. she was to be hanged for persistent theft and vagrancy, but would not be burned as a witch, as the laws against witchcraft were repealed in both England and Scotland in 1736. Although the normal punishment for witchcraft in Scotland was burning, it was hanging in England.

360.11 Haribee broo' Harraby brow or Hill, the traditional place of execution in Carlisle.

360.12–13 an' cheap on't 'and that wasn't the half of what she should have got'.

360.18–19 the terrible behests of law William Shenstone (1714–63), 'Jemmy Dawson', stanza 13.

360.29 Eden the river flowing west through Carlisle.

360.31–32 Upon Harrabee, in later days, other executions had taken place the traditional place for executions in Carlisle became, after the border settled, a place where common criminals were executed, and it was here that many of the Jacobites condemned in 1746 were hanged.

360.36 Penrith town about 28 km SSE of Carlisle.

361.14–15 drops . . . burned feathers . . . assafœtida, fair water, and hartshorn all used to recover someone who is feeling faint or has fainted.

361.40 hang and drown throwing into water was a traditional test for witchcraft; this speaker first hangs the malefactor then tests her.

361.41 take awa' yealdon, take awa' low *proverbial* take away fuel (espeally peats, turf and sticks), take away flame: see *ODEP*, 293.

361.43 reckan the meaning of this term is not certain, but it is probably a present participle and a form of *rack* (see *SND*, *rack*, verb 1.3). It would here mean 'limping' or 'hobbling'.

362.6 Hinchup as *hinch* is a rhyming synonym for *pinch* the name suggests that she is wrinkled.

362.6–7 civil tone . . . stepping out of his place 'On meeting a supposed Witch, it is advisable to take the wall of her in a town or street, and the right hand of her in a lane or field': 'Superstitions', 29, in Grose, *A Provincial Glossary*.

362.8–9 we hae tint but a Scot of her *proverbial* we have only lost a Scot with her, i.e. something of no value: see Ray, 257; *ODEP*, 485.

362.9 better lost than found proverbial: *ODEP*, 54.

362.14–15 Sark-foot wife . . . Allonby i.e. the witches of Scotland and England will get together: see note to 362.17–18. A *Sark-foot wife* is a woman from Gretna in Scotland, 14 km NW of Carlisle, where the river Sark enters the Solway Firth, while *Allonby* is a village on the NW coast of Cumbria, 34 km WSW of Carlisle.

362.15 bye word proverb or proverbial saying.

362.17–18 If Skiddaw . . . weel of that 'These are two very high hills, one in this country, the other in Anan-dale, in Scotland; if the former be capped with clouds or foggy mists, it will not be long before rain falls on the other. It is spoken of such who may expect to sympathize in their sufferings, by reason of the vicinity of their situation.' This is a Cumberland proverb, in Grose, *A Provincial Glossary*. See also Ray, 238; *ODEP*, 739. Skiddaw (931m) is in the Lake District in Cumbria, and Criffel (569m) is on the opposite side of the Solway Firth, near Dumfries.

362.22 swumming her i' th' Eden testing whether she is a witch or not by throwing her in the River Eden to see if she sinks (proof of being a witch) or swims.

362.39 half-hangit Maggie Dickson see note to 148.31–32.

362.39 that cried saut that hawked salt in the street: see *OED*, *cry*, verb 5b.

362.41 kend nae odds on her known no difference in her.

363.17 Interpreter's house see note to 279.16–17.

363.26 gang thou thy gate go thy way, a common Biblical phrase, especially in the Gospels.

364.12 Longtown village 15 km N of Carlisle.

365.10–17 Our work is over ... harvest-home probably by Scott, in part imitation of the opening stanza of Thomas Gray's *An Elegy Written in a Country Churchyard* (first published London, 1751).

365.22 turn my face to the wa' said by a person on her deathbed conscious of the approach of the end (after 2 Kings 20.2; Isaiah 38.2): see *OED*, *wall*, noun 19.

365.30 Methodist hymns Methodist hymns emphasise the responsiveness of the Christian to God, and were written to facilitate community praise. The Methodist movement led by John and Charles Wesley began in Oxford in 1729; the phrase as used here is not appropriate to 1737, but is appropriate to Peter Pattieson as narrator in 1809.

365.32–39 When the fight ... come away by Scott.

366.13–20 Cauld is my bed ... to-morrow by Scott. While there is no single model, the motif of the wronged maiden is common in popular song, and while this is clearly not a traditional song various phrases can be found in ballads such as 'Proud Lady Margaret' (see note below), and ballad imitations such as David Mallet, 'William and Margaret', in Herd, 1.78–80.

366.24–42 Proud Maisie ... proud lady by Scott. C. M. Jackson-Houlston comments: 'the dramatic structure of question and answer and the common-core vocabulary of the first two and a half verses' produce a 'dynamic approximation to the feeling of an "old ballad" like "Proud Lady Margaret" in the *Minstrelsy*' (*Ballads, Songs and Snatches* (Aldershot, 1999), 40). For 'Proud Lady Margaret' see *Minstrelsy*, 3.38–42.

367 motto see Robert Southey, *Thalaba the Destroyer*, 2 vols (London, 1801), 2.293: Bk 11, stanza 37.

367.13 Longtown see note to 364.12.

367.18 Mangelman from the English term *mangle*, to mutilate, ruin by ineptitude or ignorance, or, possibly, the Scots term *mang*, to break in pieces, mutilate, injure.

368.10 two shillings and ninepence 13.75p.

368.21 to do fuss, bother; see *OED*, *do*, verb 33b.

368.25 would not be doomed to observing any one's health or temper would not be obliged to put up with her.

369.7 never hunted deer langed for its resting-place compare Psalm 42.

369.38 left hand side of the river Clyde i.e. they follow the south bank of the Clyde, Glasgow in the 18th century being on the north.

370.3 ancient bridge an eight-arched humped bridge built in 1339, on the line of what is now the Victoria Bridge. It was the only bridge over the Clyde until the 'new bridge' was built in 1768, on the line of what is now Glasgow Bridge.

370.4 Saint Mungo patron saint of Glasgow: compare note to 359.6–7.

370.8–9 captain of Carrick ... 1725 Scott's Magnum note reads: 'In 1725, there was a great riot in Glasgow on account of the malt-tax. Among the troops brought in to restore order, was one of the independent companies of Highlanders levied in Argyleshire, and distinguished, in a lampoon of the period, as "Campbell of Carrick and his Highland thieves." It was called Shawfield's Mob, because much of the popular violence was directed against Daniel Campbell, Esq. of Shawfield, M. P., Provost of the town' (Magnum, 13.45). See also notes to 22.27 and 37.27. Daniel Campbell (*c.* 1671–1753) was no longer Provost of Glasgow when the mob ransacked his town house on the Trongate, but was member of Parliament for the Glasgow burghs, and a supporter of Sir Robert Walpole. The burgh was fined to compensate Campbell for his losses: see Historical Note, 581–82. Carrick Castle is on the W shore of Loch Goil at the head of the Firth of Clyde.

370.12   the Gorbals   then Glasgow's southern suburb, on the S bank of the Clyde at the southern side of the old bridge (see note to 370.3).

370.21   him of the laurel wreath   the Poet Laureate, Robert Southey (1774–1843).

370.23–27   A broader... to the wind   Robert Southey, *Thalaba the Destroyer*, 2 vols (London, 1801), 2.292: Bk 11, stanza 36.

370.28   Inverary   see note to 337.6.

370.33   Castle of Dumbarton   on the N side of the Firth of Clyde, where the river Leven joins the Clyde. Dumbarton rock had been an important fortress since the Roman occupation and was repaired and garrisoned in the 18th century against the Jacobite threat. Compare Tobias Smollett, *The Expedition of Humphry Clinker* (1771), J. Melford to Sir Watkin Phillips, 3 Septr; ed. Thomas R. Preston (Athens and London, 1990), 231.

370.33–34   be the other what it may   in comparison with whatever other castle you care to mention.

370.34   Sir William Wallace   see note to 42.15–16.

371.4   Elfinfoot   Elvanfoot, about 60 km SE of Glasgow, where Elvan Water joins the River Clyde.

371.11–12   island called Roseneath   Roseneath is on the W side of the Gare Loch on a peninsula between the Gare Loch and Loch Long. It was frequently described as an island in charters and title deeds: see *Scottish Historical Review*, 12 (1914–15), 108, and *The Athenaeum*, 25 Jan. 1908, 95 (Corson). The words 'island' or 'isle' applied to a peninsula are frequently found in British place-names such as the Black Isle, and Canvey Island.

371.16   terra firma   *Latin* firm ground.

371.33–34   fixed his master's mandates to perform   see Joseph Addison (1672–1719), *The Campaign* (1705), line 291; see also note to 317.19.

371.37–38   a boar's-head, crested with a ducal coronet   the arms of the Duke of Argyle.

372.3   horses and carriage... be embarked there for Inverara   compare Tobias Smollett, *The Expedition of Humphry Clinker* (1771), Matt. Bramble to Dr. Lewis, 6 Sept.; ed. Thomas R. Preston (Athens and London, 1990), 248.

372.10   painted egg-shell   compare Helena described by Hermia as a 'painted maypole': *A Midsummer Night's Dream*, 3.2.296.

372.12   pillion mail   piece of luggage carried pillion, i.e. on a light saddle behind the rider on a horse.

373.11   something of the latest   somewhat late in the day, rather too late.

373.23   opposite shore   i.e. from Helensburgh or thereabouts on the northern side of the Clyde estuary.

373.30   skimming dish   dish used in skimming milk and in cheese-making.

373.34   deep waters   Psalm 69.2, 14.

374   motto   John Fletcher and Philip Massinger, *The Sea-Voyage* (first performed 1622; published 1647), 2.2.200–02.

374.9   islands in the Firth of Clyde   compare the following description with Tobias Smollett, *The Expedition of Humphry Clinker* (1771), Matt. Bramble to Dr. Lewis, 28 Aug.; ed. Thomas R. Preston (Athens and London, 1990), 240–41.

374.20–21 Loch-Seant, or the Haly-Loch *Gaelic* An Loch Seanta, the Holy Loch.

374.35–36 fishing or hunting-lodge . . . palace the hunting lodge was burned down in 1802; a new house designed by Joseph Bonomi (1739–1808) in the Italian style was built for the Duke of Argyle in 1803–05, and demolished in 1961.

375.19 Wilkie or Allan Sir David Wilkie (1785–1841) and Sir William Allan (1782–1850) were both friends of Scott. Wilkie and Scott shared (in their different media) an understanding of the interplay of moral and social forces, while Allan (whom Scott first met in 1818) painted Scott's portrait on many occasions and based many of his works on historical scenes suggested by Scott's works.

375.23 redeemed our captivity i.e. saved us; compare Job 42.10; Psalms 14.7, 53.6, 126.1, 4; Jeremiah 29.14; Hosea 6.11.

375.24 mercies promised and purchased see notes to 133.23–24 and 133.40.

375.28 melting mood *Othello*, 5.2.349.

375.37–38 lions that were in the path see Proverbs 26.13.

376.10 lives in the flesh see Galations 2.20. The import of the passage from which this phrase comes is that life which is secured by the law is worthless, and that real life comes from faith in Christ the Saviour.

376.10–11 if she were as I wish she were equally.

376.17 ower the march over the border (into England). The phrase was frequently used of an elopement, but in this case Effie was banished 'furth of Scotland': see the text at 378.39.

376.18 son of Belial 1 Samuel 25.17. More commonly found as *sons of Belial*, the phrase denotes an evil man who worships false gods, particularly sensuality. See note to 103.36.

376.18 made a moonlight flitting *proverbial* removed by stealth, usually without paying moral or monetary debts. See *ODEP*, 542.

376.23 deliverance common Biblical word denoting an escape from evil.

376.24 She went out from us . . . because she was not of us see 1 John 2.19.

376.25 withered branch will never bear fruit of grace drawn from the story of the fig-tree, Matthew 21.18–22, or the parable of the vine, John 15.1–8.

376.26–27 scape-goat . . . into the wilderness . . . sins of our little congregation see Leviticus 16.10–11. The *scape-goat* is the offering made to God as exculpation for the general sins of the community.

376.28 better peace i.e. that of Philippians 4.7: 'And the peace of God, which passeth all understanding, shall keep your hearts and minds through Christ Jesus'.

376.31 sweet savour phrase used on some 40 occasions in the Bible about sacrifices that are pleasing to God: e.g. see Genesis 8.20–21; Ephesians 5.2.

376.32 frankincense in the Bible an aromatic resin burned with sacrifices and producing a 'sweet savour'.

376.32 Lugton see note to 236.36.

376.33 let her bite on her ain bridle *proverbial* let her suffer what she has imposed on herself: see Ray, 178; *ODEP*, 62.

376.36–37 like the brook . . . patient Job see Job 6.15–17.

377.10–11 earthly tabernacle see 2 Corinthians 5.1.

377.18 for as drouthy as the weather had been even although it had been very dry.

377.30 son of Jesse King David.

377.31 This is David's spoil 1 Samuel 30.20.

377.34 experimental farm from the mid-18th century many progressive landlords experimented with different agricultural methods to establish what best effected improvements in husbandry and stock-raising, and landowners in Highland regions often 'imported' farmers from the south of Scotland to do this. Argyle was one such improving landlord, although there is no evidence that he ran an experimental farm: see Eric Cregeen, 'The Changing Role of the House of Argyll in the Scottish Highlands', in N. T. Phillipson and Rosalind Mitchison, *Scotland in the Age of Improvement* (Edinburgh, 1970), 5–23.

378.18–19 trafficking ... in Highland cattle in the Highlands and west of Scotland the raising of black cattle which were sold and driven south to be fattened for the English market was one of the big industries of 18th-century Scotland, especially after 1740.

378.19–21 "her'ship" ... black mail by the early 18th century cattle raiding and protection rackets were confined to the frontier lands of the Highlands. Farmers who refused to pay 'black mail', or protection money, were liable to have their cattle stolen.

378.34–35 heritable jurisdictions the right of landowners and chiefs holding lands from the crown to act as judges for offences (except murder, fire-raising, rape, and robbery) committed within their own areas. Heritable jurisdictions were ended by act of Parliament in 1747.

379.17 Knocktarlitie Knocktarlitie is imagined as being in or near Rhu or Helensburgh: see text, 399.43–400.3. The name is an invention. Gaelic *Cnoc* means 'hillock'; there are many 'Knock' names in Dumfries and Galloway, Ayrshire and the Highlands. The second element may come from 'Kiltarlity', 15 km W of Inverness.

379.17 baillie of the lordship deputy in legal matters to the owner of a heritable jurisdiction (see note to 378.34–35). The Laird of Knocktarlitie would have exercised his legal function for the Duke in his particular barony, not for the whole ducal estate.

379.18 tarr'd wi' the same stick proverbial: *ODEP*, 805.

379.25–27 candidate ... presentee Deans had fought for the right of the congregation and Presbytery to call and appoint the minister of a parish, a right which was secured by legislation in 1690, whereas the Patronage Act of 1712 restored to certain landowners the right to choose the parish minister. Deans's words circumvent the problem and allow him to represent the new minister not as an appointee presented by the landowner for ratification by Presbytery but as a candidate to be chosen by the people of the parish.

379.30 MacDonought i.e. son of Do-nothing.

380 motto John Dryden (1631–1700), 'To the Pious memory of Mrs Anne Killigrew' (1686), lines 172–73: *The Works of John Dryden*, ed. Walter Scott, 18 vols (Edinburgh, 1808), 11.112.

380.14–15 qualifying condition ... proper for the charge it was the Presbytery's function to determine if the learning and character of a presentee was suitable, but the Duke would not wish there to be a cause of conflict and so makes sure that Butler is qualified.

381.18 redemption of the captivity of Judah see Jeremiah 33.7; Joel 3.1.

381.19 guineas looked rather light guineas were gold coins first issued in 1663 'in the name of and for the use of the Company of Royal Adventurers of England trading with Africa'. They were distinguished by a little elephant on the obverse face and as they were made with gold from Guinea in W Africa they were immediately nicknamed 'guineas'. As they were initially not legal tender their value tended to fluctuate (which explains Dumbiedikes's fear that some look 'light'), but in 1717 their value was fixed at £1 1s. (£1.05). The last issue of guinea coins was in 1813; they were replaced by the sovereign (£1) in 1817.

381.32 meat and mault food and drink; the drink is alcoholic.

381.37 honourable state phrase from the Anglican marriage service in *The Book of Common Prayer* (1559, revised 1662), derived from Hebrews 13.4: 'Marriage is honourable in all'.

381.39 Lickpelf i.e. someone who takes in money and possessions.

381.42 cup of his liquor probably a glass of brandy: see the text at 358.42–359.2.

382.27 few ministers will be so comfortable ministers' stipends were paid by the heritors, who were for the most part the landowners in a parish. The Duke of Argyle appears to be the dominant landowner in the fictional parish of Knocktarlitie, and could therefore decide what Butler should be paid provided it was above the minimum as calculated by the formula laid down in law.

382.30 placed minister minister appointed by a presbytery to a parish ministry.

382.42 polished shaft in the temple see note to 74.27.

382.43 carnal learning see Romans 8.6–7.

383.1 root of the matter Job 19.28.

383.11 Erastian encroachments of the civil power see notes to 71.17; 90.16–18; 90.17.

383.13 shorn of its beams see John Milton, *Paradise Lost* (1667), 1.596. The phrase is also used in Tobias Smollett, *The Expedition of Humphry Clinker* (1771), J. Melford to Sir Watkin Phillips, 2 June; ed. Thomas R. Preston (Athens and London, 1990), 95.

383.15–16 spots and blemishes see 2 Peter 2.13.

383.19–20 dissenters . . . seceded from the national church see note to 176.6–7.

383.22–23 old presbyterian model and principles of 1640 i.e. Scotland in the 1640s when it was closest to being a Presbyterian theocracy governed by the covenants of 1638 and 1643, which were seen as the mutual commitments of God and his people.

383.25 humble pleader for the good old cause in a legal way see [Gavin Mitchell], *Humble Pleadings for the Good Old Way* (1713); 'Life and Death of Alexander Peden', in Walker, 1.29; 'Vindication of Cameron's Name', in Walker, 1.260. See also note to 149.2.

383.26 right-hand excesses see note to 71.18.

383.27–28 right-hand of fellowship see Galations 2.9. The right-hand of fellowship is offered by ministers and elders of Presbyterian churches to all who join the church by confession of faith, and to ministers and elders on their ordination.

383.30 Q. E. D. *Latin abbreviation* quod erat demonstrandum, that which was to be proved.

383.31 lay-patronage see note to 167.8.

383.32 coming in by the window, and over the wall see John 10.1; and compare John Milton, 'Lycidas' (1738), lines 114–18.

383.33–34 cheating and starving . . . belly of the incumbent see 'Vindication of Cameron's Name', in Walker, 1.273, and compare John Milton, 'Lycidas' (1738), lines 114–15.

383.36–37 limb of the brazen image, a portion of the evil thing compare the 'graven image', Exodus 20.4; the 'golden image', Daniel 3.5, 12. For 'limb of Satan' (a mischievous or wicked person) see *OED*, *limb*, 3b; for 'evil thing' as the devil see John Milton, *Paradise Lost* (1667), 4.563.

384.5 great virtue of IF see *As You Like It*, 5.4.97.

384.7 stumbling-block see note to 94.26.

384.7 oaths to government the oaths of allegiance and abjuration imposed on the clergy by the Toleration Act of 1712. See also note to 90.16–18.

384.9 Erastian see note to 90.17.

384.11–12 one wherein prelacy...mitre i.e. England in which the Anglican Church is ruled by bishops (prelacy). Bishops wear mitres, the peaks of which were equated with the horns of the beast in Revelation Ch. 17 by opponents of prelacy.

384.13 symptoms of defection see notes to 71.17–18, and 90.16–18.

384.14 My bowels—my bowels!—I am pained at the very heart see Jeremiah 4.19.

384.15 Bow-head see note to 145.5.

384.16 Tolbooth Church see note to 24.31.

384.16–17 brandy and burned feathers used to assist recovery from fainting.

384.18 Lords spiritual see note to 172.1.

384.20 deep compliance i.e. sinful compliance. Compare 'foul compliance', in 'The Life and Death of Daniel Cargill', in Walker, 2.47.

384.20–21 abomination...snare in the Old Testament 'abomination' is used repeatedly about things forbidden by God, or hateful to God, and a 'snare' is a trap set by the devil. The terms are also regularly used in covenanting literature.

384.21 Shibboleth formula adopted by a party or sect by which followers may be identified: see Judges 12.5–6.

384.23 the brethren word used in the New Testament of the members of the early church, and here used of those lay members of the church who supported the Covenanting cause.

384.24 reins were taken up tight opposition to patronage (see note to 167.8) in the Church of Scotland was so strong that ministers often flouted decisions of the General Assembly requiring them to accede to the patronage system. However, in 1752 the General Assembly deposed Rev. Thomas Gillespie for his refusal to participate in the induction of a presentee, and over the next 30 years the growing power of the Moderate party within the Church enforced the acceptance of patronage. See Richard B. Sher, *Church and University in the Scottish Enlightenment* (Edinburgh, 1985), 49–56, 121–35.

384.25 peace-making particle see *As You Like It*, 5.4.96–97.

385.3–4 eight hundred punds Scots £66.67 sterling.

385.4 four chalder of victual 13,546 litres of barley, oats, or malt (about 4 tons); the minister could sell the grain he did not himself need.

385.15–16 sinful compliance...defection see 'Steps of Defection', in Walker, 2.82, and notes to 71.17–18, and 90.16–18.

386.15–16 Doeg the Edomite Saul's chief herdsman who betrayed and killed the priests who had helped David: see 1 Samuel 21.1–22.18.

386.16–17 not a cloot o' them but sall be as weel cared for *literally* not a hoof of them but shall be as well cared for; i.e. every beast will be as well cared for.

386.17–18 fatted kine of Pharaoh i.e. Pharaoh's fat cattle: see Genesis 41.2; and compare Luke 15.23, 27, 30.

386.18 remove our tent see Genesis 13.18.

386.21 slippery and backsliding times terms used in Jeremiah about the Israelites falling away from obedience to God's law. For the nature of the backslidings see notes to 71.17–18, and 90.16–18.

386.23–24 mire...wallow see 2 Peter 2.22.

387.15–16 lucre of foul earthly preferment compare 1 Timothy 3.3, 8; Titus 1.7, 11; 1 Peter 5.2.

387.17 makes his kirk a stalking-horse proverbial: see *ODEP*, 670; *The Pilgrim's Progress*, Part 1, 105.

387.18 better things of you Hebrews 6.9.

387.20   backslidings, and defections   see notes to 71.17–18; 90.16–18; 386.21.

387.21   on the left and on the right   see note to 50.15–16.

387.21   day of trial   day on which the faithful are tested by temptation: compare 1 Peter 1.7.

387.24   scarlet abomination   see Revelation 17.3–4.

387.24–25   Greeks ... foolishness   see 1 Corinthians 1.23.

387.36–37   root o' the matter   see Job 19.28.

387.38   crying aloud and sparing not   see Isaiah 58.1.

387.41   Culdees   or Céli Dé, members of an ancient Scoto-Irish religious order found in the 8th–11th centuries. They were treated by George Buchanan (1506–82) in his history of Scotland, *Rerum Scoticarum Historia* (1582), as defenders of the Celtic Church against Rome, and thus Presbyterians before their time.

387.41   John Knox   (*c.* 1513–72), the greatest of the Scottish reformers. He worked in England and with Calvin in Geneva in the 1550s, and on his return to Scotland in 1559 became the moral and spiritual leader of the reformers and the reformation movement. The first *Book of Discipline* (1561) for which he was largely responsible proposed a national education system for Scotland, and his *History of the Reformation of Religion within the Realm of Scotland* is a key document in understanding both Knox and the Protestant revolution.

387.42–43   Bruce, Black, Blair, and Livingstone   Robert Bruce (*c.* 1554–1631), minister in Edinburgh from 1587, resisted James VI and his policy of promoting episcopacy and was involved in the riot of 1596 (see note to 16.5–6); David Black (d. 1603), minister of St Andrews, argued that he was not subject to civil authority and was brought to account and banished north of the Tay by James in 1596; Robert Blair (1593–1666) refused to accept the Articles of Perth (1618) which re-established episcopacy in Scotland and in 1620 felt it necessary to demit his position in Glasgow University; William Livingstone (dates unknown) was deposed in 1613 for opposing the restoration of episcopacy. Bruce, Black and Blair all feature in John Howie (1735–93), *Biographica Scoticana; or ... Scots Worthies*, originally published 1775, a 'hagiography' of Scotland's protestant martyrs, and the champions of Presbyterianism.

387.43–388.2   brief ... English independents   from 1638 when the National Covenant was signed (see note to 30.30) to 1650 when Cromwell's victory at Dunbar led to the subjugation of Scotland by the Commonwealth in which Independents (see note to 65.31) were dominant.

388.2   times of prelacy   i.e. the period in which the Scottish church was governed by bishops, from 1662 to 1690.

388.3   indulgences   see note to 181.25. There were only three indulgences in the reign of Charles II, four if the English indulgence of 1672 is included. Deans is probably exaggerating, or including in his list royal proclamations which historians do not normally consider indulgences. Presbyterians like Deans objected to the indulgences because they consistently maintained episcopacy.

388.5–6   neither an obscure actor ... sufferer   see text 102.33–40.

388.8   iron cage   the lock-up in the Canongate tolbooth, but perhaps a cage for the public exhibition of malefactors: see 322.7 and note, and also 'Walter Smith's Life', in Walker, 2.97, 98.

388.8   Canongate tolbooth   prison for the burgh of the Canongate on the north side of the Canongate.

388.12–13   Francis Gordon   see 'Life and Death of Richard Cameron', in Walker, 1.352–55. Walker was tried, probably tortured, and sent to 'the plantations' on 22 July 1682 for being present at the killing of Gordon: see Wodrow, 4.47. Scott quotes the story from Walker in a Magnum note, 13.83–84.

388.30   an inch was as good as an ell   proverbial: see *ODEP*, 403. An *ell* is 37 inches (0.94m).

388.30–33   He got a shot . . . killed him dead   'Life and Death of Richard Cameron', in Walker, 1.354.

390.3   oaths   see note to 384.7.

390   motto   see John Logan (1748–88), 'The Lovers', lines 33–34, 129–30, in *Poems* (London, 1781), 45 and 51 (see *CLA*, 190).

390.4   Shibboleth   see note to 384.21.

390.25   marriage, though honourable   see note to 381.37.

390.27–28   kirks, stipends, and wives   'Vindication of Cameron's Name', in Walker, 1.260.

390.29   defections   see notes to 71.18, and 90.16–18.

390.30   savoury professor   see note to 72.13–14.

390.31   unbelieving wife . . . revenged the text   see 1 Corinthians 7.14: 'the unbelieving wife is sanctified by the husband'. Thus David Deans feels that too often the wife has taken revenge upon the text by achieving the reverse of what is there proposed.

390.32   Donald Cargill   see note to 102.32.

390.33–34   killing-time   see note to 174.36.

390.34–91.6   Robert Marshal . . . grievous things of the day   this passage draws heavily on 'Life and Death of Daniel Cargill', in Walker, 2.47–48.

391.35–39   landing-place . . . unfrequented   see note to 168.2.

392.21–22   the angels in Heaven, that rather weep for sinners, as reckon their transgressions   compare Psalm 51.13, 'Then will I teach transgressors thy ways; and sinners shall be converted unto thee'; Matthew 9.13, Mark 2.17, Luke 5.32, 'I am not come to call the righteous, but sinners to repentance'; Luke 15.7, 'joy shall be in heaven over one sinner that repenteth, more than over ninety and nine just persons, which need no repentance'; Luke 15.10, ' there is joy in the presence of the angels of God over one sinner that repenteth'.

393.36   Knockdunder   an invented name which can be read as English or Gaelic. At 397.9 Duncan says 'I knock under to no man', i.e. I do not yield to anyone, but the medial 'd' suggests that he is 'knocked under'. *Dunder* (as in 'dunderhead') implies someone who is stupid. In Gaelic the *Knock* element represents 'Cnoc', a hillock, while *dùn* is Gaelic for a fort; both elements are common in Scottish place-names.

393.37   youthful exploits   *knock* suggests both to strike forcibly and to copulate with: see *OED*, 2nd edn, *knock*, verb 2a and d. See also text at 404.19–20.

393.40   continental parishes   i.e. mainland parishes.

393.41   Kilmun   on the Holy Loch, W of Roseneath.

393.42   Cowal   large area W of the Holy Loch, between Loch Long and Loch Fyne.

394.7   hereditary jurisdiction   see notes to 17.20 and 378.34–35.

394.17   impartiality to Trojan or Tyrian   see Virgil (70–19 BC), *Aeneid*, 1.574, where Dido offers to make no distinction between her own Tyrians and the Trojans should the latter wish to settle in her realm.

394.35   they seldom make dry wark in this kintra   in this area of the country they seldom work without having a drink.

395.2   gift of tongues   see Acts 2.7–11, where what happens is known as 'the gift of tongues'.

395.10   Never fash your peard about it   *proverbial* don't bother about it: compare *ODEP*, 246.

395.11   de'il o' them   *emphatic* not one of them.

395.41   Hout tout   tut tut, come come.

395.41 put for the English representation of Gaelic speech see Graham Tulloch, *The Language of Walter Scott* (London, 1980), 254–56.

395.42 Teil a ane *emphatic* i.e. de'il a one, not a single one.

396.2 Gallio see note to 74.22.

396 motto see Robert Burns, 'The Ordination' (1786), lines 19–22 (Kinsley, no. 85). The phrase *skirl up the Bangor* means 'sing very loudly'. 'Bangor' is a psalm-tune by William Tans'ur, published in *The Harmony of Zion* (1734).

396.11 turn...ower open.

396.13 double verse stanza of two quatrains (8 lines) in which most of the Scottish Metrical Psalms are printed, although sung to four-line tunes.

396.14 skirl up the Bangor see 396 motto.

397.2–3 Mayor...breeches are amending a Cheshire proverb, in Grose, *A Provincial Glossary*. See also Ray, 236; *ODEP*, 519.

397.9 knock under yield, submit, acknowledge oneself beaten.

397.36 coach and six 'Raarsay accompanied us in his six oar'd boat, which he said was his coach and six': Samuel Johnson to Hester Thrale, 30 Sept. 1773, in *The Letters of Samuel Johnson*, ed. Bruce Redford, 5 vols (Oxford, 1992–94), 2.89 (Inglis).

398.1 forgotten Scottish poet Alexander Ross (1699–1784), schoolmaster of Lochlee, Angus. He was the author of some Scots songs, of works in Latin, and most importantly of *The Fortunate Shepherdess* (Aberdeen, 1768), a pastoral epic in 3 cantos, and over 4000 lines in length, with both narrative and dialogue written in the dialect of NE Scotland. It was revised and republished as *Helenore or the Fortunate Shepherdess* in 1778.

398.2–11 The water...swarm did go see Alexander Ross, *Helenore or the Fortunate Shepherdess*, 2nd edn (Aberdeen, 1778), p. 23; or *The Fortunate Shepherdess*, in *The Scottish Works of Alexander Ross, M. A.*, ed. Margaret Wattie, Scottish Text Society (Edinburgh and London, 1938), lines 410–19.

398.12 Highland Arcadia see Tobias Smollett, *The Expedition of Humphry Clinker* (1771), Matt. Bramble to Dr. Lewis, 28 Aug. and 6 Sept.; ed. Thomas R. Preston (Athens and London, 1990), 241, 249. In addition to these particular references, Knocktarlitie has some general similarities to Cameron on Loch Lomond in *Humphry Clinker*.

398.16–17 men...heart see 1 Samuel 13.14.

398.18 the Lennox area N of Glasgow, taking in the east of Dumbartonshire, and the southern part of Loch Lomond.

398.20 suffered for joining his father see note to 225.32.

398.21 ill-fated attempt in 1685 the attempt of the 9th Earl of Argyle to overthrow James VII and II in 1685: see note to 225.32.

398.21 cakes of the right leaven men of the proper kind. According to the Bible unleavened bread, cakes and wafers are to be eaten at the Passover: see Exodus 29.2, etc.

399.33 an improved cottage rural housing greatly improved in the course of the 18th century. In the early years farm cottages had normally two chambers, a beaten-earth floor, a roof of turf, and a hole in the roof to let smoke escape. The byre was adjacent and separated from human living quarters only by a partition. By the end of the century people and animals were separated, and there were commonly stone floors, straw thatch or tiles, windows and chimneys. See James E. Handley, *Scottish Farming in the Eighteenth Century* (London, 1953), 76–77, 273–74; for an illustration see T. C. Smout, *A History of the Scottish People 1560–1830* (London, 1969), facing page 233.

399.42–43 hills of Dumbartonshire to the E.

399.43 fierce clan of MacFarlanes like the Macgregors the clan was considered lawless; an Act of 1594 denounces them for committing acts of robbery and violence, and in 1624 many were convicted of theft and robbery and the clan was dispersed over many parts of Scotland. MacFarlane territory was towards the N end of Loch Lomond, going W to Loch Long.

400.1 far to the right the viewer is looking W; the high hills of Argyleshire are to the N, and the Isle of Arran to the S.

400.41 come ower and ower again say over and over again.

401.1–2 prodigal . . . fatted calf see Luke 15.11–32, the parable of the prodigal son.

401.15 built and furnished by the Duke the provision and upkeep of the manse in each parish was the responsibility of the heritors (those who owned heritable property). The dominant landowner in the fictional parish of Knock-tarlitie appears to be the Duke of Argyle, and so he provides the manse. That the house was built 'for a favourite domestic' is indicative of the paternalism of clan society.

401.20 Auchingower possibly a representation of the Gaelic *Achadh na gobhair*, field of the goat; but whether Scott had a particular Gaelic meaning in mind is doubtful as in his day many names had been levelled to an Anglicised 'Auchin—'.

401.21 Semple a name implying ordinary rather than gentle rank.

401.32 things unattempted yet in prose or rhyme John Milton, *Paradise Lost* (1667), 1.16.

401.36 Miss Martha Buskbody 'a young lady who has carried on the profession of mantua-making at Gandercleugh, and in the neighbourhood, with great success, for about forty years', and who asks Peter Pattieson for 'a glimpse' of the 'future felicity' of the characters: *The Tale of Old Mortality*, ed. Douglas Mack, EEWN 4b, 349.23–25, 350.17–18.

402.20 fat ta teil what the devil.

402.26 Hesper the evening star.

402.30–31 teil ony sport wad be till he came devil any sport [i.e. nothing at all] would happen till he came. As *sport* is used of entertainment or diversion, Knockdunder refers slightingly to a church service.

402.33 rung in the tempo of strokes increased before ceasing to ring as an indication that the service was about to begin.

403.5 victual stipend the 'four chalder of victual' (385.4 and note) which will form part of Butler's stipend (salary).

403.27 Micklehose i.e. big socks.

403.34 that crosses the maggot that goes against one's prejudices.

403.34–35 to set the kiln a-low *proverbial* start trouble, raise a commotion: see *ODEP*, 424.

403.35 high hand imperiously, with an arbitrary exercise of power.

403.36–37 a' the keys o' the kintra hings at his belt proverbial: see Kelly, 11; *ODEP*, 421. But the usual form of the proverb is that all keys do not hang from one man's belt.

403.38 maistry . . . maws the meadows doun *proverbial* mastery mows the meadows down, i.e. vigour overcomes everything: see Kelly, 251; *ODEP*, 518.

403.42 Fair and softly gangs far proverbial: *ODEP*, 238; see Ray, 104.

403.42–43 if a fule may gie a wise man a counsel proverbial: see Kelly, 25; *ODEP*, 274.

404.1–2 He suld hae a lang-shankit spune that wad sup kail wi' the de'il *proverbial* he who wants to take soup with the devil should have a long-handled spoon: see *ODEP*, 480–81, and 'Life and Death of Richard Cameron', in Walker, 1.329.

404.3 come short miss out, get short provisions.

404.10 oaths to government the oaths of allegiance and abjuration imposed on the clergy by the Toleration Act of 1712.

404.14 formula the specific words in which the oaths of allegiance and abjuration were cast.

404.17 1746 i.e. in the aftermath of the Jacobite Rising of 1745–46.

404.18 Donacha Dhu na Dunaigh *Gaelic* Donnchadh Dubh na Dunaich, *literally* Black Duncan of the Misfortune or Mischief, i.e. Black Duncan the Mischievous.

404.20 the records of the foibles kirk sessions enquired about and punished those in the parish guilty of fornication and adultery. Kate Finlayson would have been easier to punish than Knockdunder, but his name must also have been recorded in the kirk-session minutes.

404 motto Robert Burns, 'The Holy Fair' (1785), lines 154–162 (Kinsley, no. 70).

404.22 butt an' ben front and back rooms.

404.23 yill-caup commentator one who discusses public affairs over his ale.

404.26 Wi' thick and thrang with crowds of people.

404.32 plentiful entertainment compare Tobias Smollett, *The Expedition of Humphry Clinker* (1771), J. Melford to Sir Watkin Phillips, 3 Septr; ed. Thomas R. Preston (Athens and London, 1990), 236.

404.36 rough and round plain but plentiful. The phrase is in inverted commas because it is Scots rather than English.

405.2 rights of admiralty as the text indicates, the right to all goods brought ashore by the sea when the owner could not be identified. Ultimately this right was reserved by the crown, but in various parts of Scotland it was held by others.

405.8 bona fide *Latin, literally* in good faith, i.e. genuine.

405.13 The Campbells are coming traditional march of the Campbells; for words and tune see *SMM*, no. 299.

405.33–34 invasion of the Highland Host the government sent Highland regiments (the 'Highland Host') to Ayrshire in February 1678, authorising them to take free quarters and horses as needed, and indemnifying them against 'all pursuits civil and criminal' (Wodrow, 2.379). Wodrow comments that the 'particular relation of the oppressions, depredations, exactions, and cruelties committed by them, would fill a volume' (2.421).

405.39 the mirth and fun grew fast and furious Robert Burns, 'Tam o' Shanter' (1791), line 144 (Kinsley, no. 321).

406.5 tam carum caput *Latin* so esteemed a person (*or* chief): see Horace (65–8 BC), *Odes*, 1.24.2.

406.10 Sir Donald Gorme of Sleat whether this is a specific person cannot be determined. The Gormes of Sleat on the Isle of Skye were a branch of the Macdonalds. There was a traditional enmity between Macdonalds and Campbells; the first *Sir* Donald Gorme of Sleat (a baronet of Nova Scotia, created in 1625) supported Charles I, and his son fought with Montrose, whereas the Argyles supported the Presbyterian cause in the 1640s; Sir Donald Macdonald, 4th baronet of Sleat, fought on the Jacobite side in the 1715 Rising, and was directly opposed to the 2nd Duke of Argyle at Sheriffmuir (see note to 26.36). It is clear that a comparison of the Duke of Argyle with any Donald Gorme of Sleat was liable to provoke anger.

406.11 comparison was odious proverbial: see *ODEP*, 138.

406.19 bull of Phalaris huge copper bull in which Phalaris, a Sicilian tyrant of the 6th century BC, burned people alive.

407.28 along shore on a course in sight of the shore and parallel to it: see *OED, alongshore.*

408.1 jorram *Gaelic* iorram, boat-song. In a note to *The Lady of the Lake*

Scott comments that they are adapted to 'keep time with the sweep of the oars': *The Poetical Works of Sir Walter Scott, Bart.*, ed. J. G. Lockhart, 12 vols (Edinrgh, 1833–34), 8.89.

409.9 if there was even if there was.

409.21–22 it's better sheltering under an auld hedge than under a new planted wood proverbial: see Ray, 274; *ODEP*, 722.

409.23 I maun drink as I hae browed proverbial: see Ray, 3; *ODEP*, 85.

410.9 that which is done and cannot be undone proverbial: see *ODEP*, 199.

410.18–19 sown the wind, and maun reap the whirlwind see Hosea 8.7.

410.24 better off than she has wrought for *literally* better off than she has worked for; i.e. better off than the fate she was fashioning for herself.

411.2 effectual conversion a version of effectual calling: see note to 149.34–36.

411.25 sit down with put up with.

411 motto see *2 Henry VI*, 4.10.16–17.

412.3–4 proclamation of banns the public announcement from the pulpit that two people intend to marry. This was required by law, and was intended to ensure that the proposed marriage would be lawful.

412.9 peyont the cairn beyond the cairn, i.e. off the estate, the cairn being the marker of the dividing line between properties.

412.21 plack cattle black cattle, i.e. ministers.

413.1 scholarly and wisely *The Merry Wives of Windsor*, 1.3.2.

413.30 babes of grace children on whom the grace of God has been shed. The phrase, probably modelled on its antithesis 'children of wrath', suggests that Jeanie and Reuben's chidren are servants of God.

414.16 division and separation see 'Life and Death of Richard Cameron', in Walker, 1.263. Comparatively minor differences in theological opinion often generated schism: see note to 176.6–7.

414.26–28 persecuting old women for witches... scandal among the young ones just as the investigation of witchcraft was a preoccupation of the 17th century, so the investigation of sexual irregularities was a preoccupation of kirk sessions in the 18th.

414.32 fama clamosa *Latin* noisy report; i.e. the activity was generally known or flagrantly undertaken.

415.5–6 Peden, and Lundie, and Cameron, and Renwick, and John Caird the tinkler for Peden, Cameron and Renwick see notes to 78.34, 102.32, and 102.35. Thomas Lundie, minister in Rattray in Perthshire, had visions of a French invasion to impose Catholicism (see 'Life and Death of Alexander Peden', in Walker, 1.92–93, and note 2.138). Caird has not been identified.

415.6–9 Elizabeth Mevill, Lady Culross... assistance see editorial note in James Kirkton, *The Secret and True History of the Church in Scotland* and James Russell, *An Account of the Murder of Archbishop Sharp*, ed. in one vol. Charles Kirkpatrick Sharpe (Edinburgh, 1817), 17. Sharpe is in turn quoting from the manuscript of the Rev. John Livingstone of Ancrum.

415.9–10 Lady Robertland see editorial note in James Kirkton, *The Secret and True History of the Church in Scotland* and James Russell, *An Account of the Murder of Archbishop Sharp*, ed. in one vol. Charles Kirkpatrick Sharpe (Edinrgh, 1817), 19. Sharpe is in turn quoting from Robert Blair, *Memoirs of the Life of Mr Robert Blair* (Edinburgh, 1754).

415.11 John Scrimgeour *c.* 1580–1635, minister of Kinghorn in Fife, who was deprived of his charge in 1620 for opposing the Articles of Perth (1618) which restored episcopacy to Scotland.

415.12–18 free to expostulate . . . time of death see John Howie
(1735–93), *Biographica Scoticana; or . . . Scots Worthies*, 4th edn (Glasgow,
1813; originally published 1775), 90 (*CLA*, 71).

415.17 heal and fere in perfect health (whole and healthy).

415.24 sundry wise in different directions.

415.29 most part of books were burned except the Bible John Howie
(1735–93), *Biographica Scoticana; or . . . Scots Worthies*, 4th edn (Glasgow,
1813; originally published 1775), 89 (*CLA*, 71).

415.31 Kittledoop *literally* ticklish, or readily aroused, bottom.

415.33 Aily diminutive of Alison.

415.34 Deepheugh *literally* deep glen or ravine.

415.34–36 abominations . . . divinations see Deuteronomy 18.10–12.

415.35 egg-shells and mutton-banes egg whites and mutton bones were
used to tell fortunes: see *eggs (whites of)* and *blade-bone* in Iona Opie and Moira
Tatem, *A Dictionary of Superstitions* (Oxford, 1996). Egg-shells were used by
witches for various purposes, but not fortune-telling.

415.36–37 suffer a witch to live Exodus 22.18.

415.40 bits o' bairns in English this would be rendered as 'children', but
bits o' indicates smallness and expresses endearment.

416.1 cast out disagree, quarrel.

416.13–14 peace-makers . . . inherit the earth see Matthew 5.5, 9. It is
the meek who 'inherit the earth', while the peacemakers 'shall be called the
children of God'.

416.15 second crook in Mrs Butler's lot see note to 103.29.

416.37 tooble or quitts *gambling* double or quits: the stake already due is
either to be doubled, or to be cancelled, according to the issue of another
chance.

416.41 strictly canonical i.e. not clearly forbidden by ecclesiastical law.
Among the sins forbidden by the eighth commandment in the *Larger Catechism*
(1647–48) is 'wasteful gaming': *The School of Faith: the Catechisms of the
Reformed Church*, ed. Thomas F. Torrance (London, 1959), 219. For the
Catechisms see notes to 149.34–36 and 149.36.

417.10 Nil conscire sibi *Latin* have nothing to feel guilty about: Horace
(65–8 BC), *Epistles*, 1.1.61.

417 motto [Lady Charlotte Campbell or Bury (1775–1861)], 'To the
Shepherd of Glen', final stanza, in *Poems upon Several Occasions* (Edinburgh,
1797), 32.

417.38 Italian hand italic handwriting (as opposed to Gothic or cursive).

418.26–27 Dundee's wars . . . Clavers John Graham of Claverhouse
(1648–89), created Viscount Dundee 1688. He was one of the most ardent
persecutors of the Covenanters; after the Revolution of 1688–89 he raised a
Jacobite army against the new regime but was killed at Killiecrankie.

418.36 how long—O how long compare Psalm 94.3: 'Lord, how long shall
the wicked, how long shall the wicked triumph?'.

419.5–6 like an Indian at the stake see William Robertson, *The History
of America*, 2 vols (London, 1777), 1.358–60 (see *CLA*, 204), for an extended
description of the torture that an American Indian is prepared to undergo when
tied to the stake after capture by an enemy. Compare also Tobias Smollett, *The
Expedition of Humphry Clinker* (1771), J. Melford to Sir Watkin Phillips, 13 July;
ed. Thomas R. Preston (Athens and London, 1990), 187–89.

419.21–22 pricking . . . with needles and pins used to detect witches; it
was believed that the devil claimed his followers with a mark which did not bleed
when pricked. By extension the phrase implies cruel, extended, but subtle
torture.

419.23 shooting-season Knockdunder refers at 421.11 to 'moor-powts and plack-cock', i.e. red and black grouse, for which the season opened on 21 June (Act 1707, c. 91).

419.28 borrowed plumes derived from Aesop's fable of the jackdaw that assumes the peacock's feathers: see *Aesopica*, ed. B. E. Parry (Urbana, 1952), Vol. 1, no. 472.

419.35 Whiterose the white rose was a Jacobite emblem.

419.37 high-church properly speaking, pertaining to opinions which give a high place to the claims of Episcopacy and the priesthood, and the saving grace of the sacraments, but in fact often describing those who in their practice emphasise the importance of church ritual.

419.39 Seton ... Winton George Seton, 5th Earl of Winton, took part in the 1715 Jacobite Rising, was sentenced to death in 1716, but escaped from the Tower of London before his execution, and lived abroad until his death in 1749. See also note to 424.20.

419.42–43 idle crackling of fire among thorns see Ecclesiastes 7.6; also 'Life and Death of Daniel Cargill', in Walker, 2.8.

419.43 thorns ... unconsumed see Exodus 3.2. The burning bush with the motto *Nec tamen consumebatur* (*Latin*: and yet it was not consumed) is an emblem of the Church of Scotland; it first appears as an emblem of the Church in 1691 when the Edinburgh printer George Mossman put the emblem and motto on the cover of that year's Acts of Assembly.

421.6 amour propre *French* self-love.

421.15 Teil ane better i.e. devil a better, not a better.

421.22–23 soft answer ... turneth away wrath Proverbs 15.1.

421.28 the proverb 'give losers leave to speak': *ODEP*, 485.

421.31 Ailie MacClure of Deepheugh see notes to 415.33 and 415.34.

421.36 no witch, but a cheat the act of 1736 which abolished the crime of witchcraft (9 George II, c. 5) made pretending to be a witch or to tell fortunes an imposture punishable by up to a year's imprisonment. In comparison being summoned before the kirk session is mild.

421.42 duck her traditional test of whether someone was a witch.

422.10 Athole brose honey and oatmeal mixed with whisky. For a traditional derivation see *SND*.

423.24 the birth-day 4 June, the day on which the birthday of the monarch was officially celebrated.

423.31 pledge me drink a toast to my health.

424.3–4 Scotch accent ... quite Doric see Tobias Smollett, *The Expedition of Humphry Clinker* (1771), J. Melford to Sir Watkin Phillips, 8 Aug.; ed. Thomas R. Preston (Athens and London, 1990), 213. In this context *Doric* means 'rustic', and in the mid-18th century had approbative overtones.

424.8 broad coarse Scotch refers not to the speech of the lower classes (for in the mid-18th century neither the Cowgate nor the Gorbals had degenerated as they did in the 19th century), but to a fully functioning Scots spoken by the majority, in contrast to the 'polite' language spoken by the educated classes. In Scott's novels the word 'Scotch' is usually part of the vocabulary of English speakers, rather than Scots.

424.9 the Gorbals see note to 370.12.

424.10–11 pure court-Scottish the language spoken by the educated and the governing classes of the period when Scotland lost its Parliament in 1707. Scott discusses this upper-class language in a letter to Archibald Constable, 25 February 1822 (*Letters*, 7.82–83), and in a famous passage in *Chronicles of the Canongate*, ed. Claire Lamont, EEWN 20, 63–64: 'It was Scottish, decidedly Scottish, often containing phrases and words little used in the present day. But then her tone and mode of pronunciation were as different from the usual accent of the ordinary Scotch *patois*, as the accent of St James's is from that of Billingsgate. The vowels were not pronounced much broader than in the Italian language, and there was none of the disagreeable drawl which is so offensive to southern ears. In short, it seemed to be the Scottish as spoken by the ancient court of Scotland, to which no idea of vulgarity could be attached.'

424.20 Setons of Windygoul a note, quoting a decision of Lord Fountainhall on 25 June 1672 in James Kirkton, *The Secret and True History of the Church in Scotland* and James Russell, *An Account of the Murder of Archbishop Sharp*, ed. in one vol. Charles Kirkpatrick Sharpe (Edinburgh, 1817), 166, explains that 'Sir Robert Seaton of Windygoule' was brother to 'the Earl of Wintoun' (see note to 419.39).

424.27 Ut flos in septis secretus nascitur hortis *Latin* as grows a flower secluded within a walled garden: Gaius Valerius Catullus (*c.* 84–*c.* 54 BC), *Carmina*, 62.39.

424.31 reversed the whole passage the passage argues that just as no one wants a flower which fades after being plucked so a girl who loses her chastity is attractive to neither boys nor girls.

424.41–42 Lord High Commissioner the representative of the monarch sent to observe the sittings of the General Assembly of the Church of Scotland.

425.20 Marrucinus Asinius addressee in Catullus's 12th poem (see note below). He is assumed to have been the brother of the orator, critic, and historian Gaius Asinius Pollio (76 BC–AD 4), who was a friend of Virgil and Horace, but nothing further is known of him.

425.21–22 Manu . . . vino *Latin* you make poor use of your hand during our merriment and drinking: see Gaius Valerius Catullus (*c.* 84–*c.* 54 BC), *Carmina*, 12.1–2. Scott selects from Catullus in a clever misappropriation of his words.

425 motto *Macbeth*, 3.1.59–63.

426.12 Duke Archibald Archibald Campbell, 3rd Duke of Argyle (1682–1761). As Earl of Islay (created 1706) he played an important part in the government of Scotland throughout the period.

426.34–35 joined Argyle's banner in the war the house of Argyle were Protestants and supporters of the Hanoverian monarchy. In 1746 the Argyle Militia formed part of Cumberland's army which defeated the Jacobites at Culloden.

427.5–7 David . . . Ziklag from the Amalekites see 1 Samuel 30.1–20. The *Amalekites* were a nomadic people of the Old Testament considered to be enemies of Israel.

427.16–17 lived upwards of ninety years see Historical Note, 596.

427.18–19 Bothwell-Bridge battle in 1679 in which the Covenanters were defeated by a royal army under the Duke of Monmouth.

427.26–27 valley of strife and trial compare Psalm 23.4.

427.32 length of days Job 12.12; Psalm 21.4; Proverbs 3.2, 16.

427.35–37 Shepherd of souls . . . wolf compare John 10.11–16.

427.37–38 Jerusalem . . . palaces see Psalm 122.6–7. Jerusalem is both the actual city and the city of God.

427.42 defections see notes to 71.17–18; 90.16–18.

427.42–43 right-hand extremes, and left-hand fallings off see note to 71.18.

428.9–10 disposable capital money, or possessions readily sold.

428.14 band ower Lounsbeck's land see text 355.39–356.2, and notes to 355.40 and 355.43–356.1.

428.16 South-sea scheme see note to 319.8.

428.17 Craigsture *literally* big rock.

428.26–27 look up a text in Scripture see text 248.13–15.

429.24 Femie to get a gude share o't a daughter had no right in law to inherit real property and so Jeanie asks that Butler specifies in his will that Femie will inherit a good share of the property.

430.3–5   the enchanted princess in the bairns' fairy tale, that kamed gold nobles out o' the tae side of her haffit locks, and Dutch dollars out o' the tother   while there are many stories in which a girl combs gold out of her hair (see e.g. 'White-toes and Bushy-Bride', in *Scandinavian Legends and Folk-tales, retold by Gwyn Jones* (Oxford, 1956)), this story in which a girl's hair produces both gold and silver has not been traced, but it is a recognised folk motif: see Stith Thompson, *Motif-Index of Folk Literature*, 6 vols (Indiana, 1955), D1454.1.1.

430.4   haffit locks   locks of hair growing on the temples.

430.8   black cast   stroke of ill-luck.

430   motto   John Milton, *Samson Agonistes* (1670), 710–13.

430.40–41   Whitsunday (15th May)   by the act of 1690 the term day Whitsunday was fixed as 15 May (see note to 68.22).

432.3   Haltwhistle   village in Northumbria, 20 km W of Hexham.

434.24   brigadier wig   wig tied back in two curls.

435.12   en bon point   *French* buxom.

435.39   turned of thirty   Effie would now be 32. At 188.42 in March 1737 she was not yet 18; it is now May 1751.

436.20   lang syne   long ago, past.

436.34   recommended to drink goats' whey by the physicians   see Tobias Smollett, *The Expedition of Humphry Clinker* (1771), Matt. Bramble to Dr. Lewis, 8 Aug.; ed. Thomas R. Preston (Athens and London, 1990), 229.

438.34–36   speaking of garrisons... unhappy for   compare Oliver Goldsmith, *She Stoops to Conquer* (1773), Act 2, in *Collected Works of Oliver Goldsmith*, ed. Arthur Friedman, 5 vols (Oxford, 1966), 5.132–33.

438.35   house of Inver-Garry   on the W side of Loch Oich, S of Fort Augustus. Soldiers were often billeted upon those who, like Macdonald or Macdonnell of Glengarry, supported the Jacobites (although Glengarry did not participate, 350 of his clansmen, led by his sons, fought in all the battles of 1745–46). Glengarry gave brief shelter to Prince Charles after Culloden in 1746; in response Cumberland's soldiers burned the house and laid waste the grounds: see *Tales of a Grandfather*, third series, in *Prose Works*, 26.361–62.

440.7   Bedreddin Hassan   see 'The Story of Noureddin Ali and Bedreddin Hassan', in *Tales of the East*, ed. Henry Weber, 3 vols (1812), 1.91–109 (*CLA*, 43).

440.24–25   Scream'd... worrie-cow   Alexander Ross, *Helenore or the Fortunate Shepherdess*, 2nd edn (Aberdeen, 1778), p. 81; or see *The Fortunate Shepherdess*, in *The Scottish Works of Alexander Ross, M. A.*, ed. Margaret Wattie, Scottish Text Society (Edinburgh and London, 1938), lines 2170–71.

440.32–34   whether... Ennerdale   William Wordsworth, 'The Brothers' (1800), lines 215–17.

441.7   five long miles   i.e. five Scots miles: 5.6 miles or 9 km. A Scots mile was 1977 yds, i.e. 217 yds longer than an English mile.

441.39   fourteen years old   i.e. in his fourteenth year: see Historical Note, 598.

442.19   elf locks   tangled mass of hair.

444.23   very short to be sae lang   see Alexander Ross, *Helenore or the Fortunate Shepherdess*, 2nd edn (Aberdeen, 1778), p. 63; or *The Fortunate Shepherdess*, in *The Scottish Works of Alexander Ross, M.A.*, ed. Margaret Wattie, Scottish Text Society (Edinburgh and London, 1938), line 1632 (Inglis).

445.10   Donald   a generic name for a Highlander.

445.23   stand of colours   set of military standards.

445.25   muckle o' a bargain   much of a fight.

445.26–27 **tyne heart tyne a'** *proverbial* lose heart lose everything: Kelly, 142; *ODEP*, 825.

445 **motto** see *Henry V*, 2.2.74–76.

446.14–15 **span commonly allotted to evil doers** see Psalm 55.23: 'bloody and deceitful men shall not live out half their days'. See also Psalm 37.9, 'For evildoers shall be cut off' (*cut off* implies a sudden or premature death: see *OED*, 2nd edn, *cut*, verb 56d).

446.19–20 **made money abroad ... undisturbed by the law** 'Within these four or five years, a person returned to this country with an affluent fortune and respectable character, who, in an early period of life, absconded on account of his being concerned in the mob which hanged Porteous, A. D. 1736.' (Hugo Arnot, *A Collection and Abridgement of Celebrated Criminal Trials in Scotland from AD 1536, to 1784* (Edinburgh, 1785), 235). It is thought that the individual in question had been in the Netherlands.

447.12–13 **Annaple Bailzou** a form of Annabel Baillie. Why Scott used this form has not been determined but perhaps the answer may be found in the gypsy literature with which he was familiar: see 'Historical Note', in *Guy Mannering*, ed. P. D. Garside, EEWN 2, 505–06.

447.22–23 **nothing for nothing** proverbial: *ODEP*, 579.

449.29 **Krames** see note to 48.18.

449.30 **poor prisoners** i.e. the begging bowl was outside the tolbooth.

450.27 **prescribed job** legal action lapsed through the passage of time. Prescription was not part of the law of Scotland, but it is argued in the 1844 edition of Hume's *Commentaries* that where an accused person has not been brought to trial because the accused fled the country, for example, there can be no prescription, but when the prosecution has delayed bringing a case then 'that equitable rule of the Roman law ... gives the accused his *quietus* at the end of twenty years' (*Commentaries on the Law of Scotland respecting Crimes*, ed. Benjamin Robert Bell, 2 vols (Edinburgh, 1844), 2.136).

450.33–34 **ganging pleas** ongoing or permanent processes in a court of law.

450.37 **negative prescription** see note to 450.27.

451.4 **Captain of the Tolbooth** that Ratcliffe became Captain of the Tolbooth seems to be a fiction: see note to 59.3.

451.34 **tied to the stake** see *Macbeth*, 5.7.1.

451 **footnote** see note to 59.3.

452.19 **for as high** however high.

454.1 **take orders** become ordained as a minister.

454.17 **in orders** in holy orders, i.e. ordained and working under the authority of the church.

455.43–456.2 **acts of generosity ... of savage tribes** see Adam Ferguson, *An Essay on the History of Civil Society*, ed. Duncan Forbes (Edinburgh, 1966; originally published 1767), Part II, Section II, 81–96, esp. 87.

456.26–27 **Use every man ... whipping** see *Hamlet*, 2.2.523–24.

457.2 **electric fluid** Franklin's term for a (supposed) subtle, imponderable, all-pervading fluid, the cause of electrical phenomena: *OED*, *electric*, 2b.

457.12 **death is to us change** see 1 Corinthians 15.51–55.

458.4–5 **nose has been on the Grindstane** proverbial: see *ODEP*, 578. The phrase is used here literally, meaning that Staunton has nearly been on the rock before, and metaphorically, meaning that he has been 'up against it' in the past.

458.25–26 **mischief shall hunt the violent man** Psalm 140.11 in the Scottish Metrical version.

458.26 **the blood-thirsty man shall not live half his days** see Psalm 55.23.

458.33 intonuit lævum *Latin* it thunders on the left, i.e. propitiously: Publius Vergilius Maro (Virgil: 70–19 BC), *Aeneid*, 2.693.

460.26 act of parliament against wearing the Highland dress by the Disarming Act of 1746 (19 George II, c. 39) wearing Highland dress (except by soldiers in the army) was forbidden.

460.27 ne'er fash your thumb *proverbial* don't worry, don't bother: see *ODEP*, 246.

460.31 gay and weel very well.

460.38 Cowal see note to 393.42.

461.2–3 pest to sit next the chimley when the lum reeks *proverbial, literally* best to stay close to the fire when the chimney is smoking, i.e. safest to stay close to the source of the trouble: see *ODEP* 738.

461 motto *1 Henry VI*, 4.5.1, 3–6.

462.43 receive the dogmata of a religion i.e. he had become a Roman Catholic.

463.42–464.2 Like a wild cub ... little man see Joanna Baillie (1762–1851), *Ethwald* (1802), Part 1, Act 2, scene 5, in *A Series of Plays; in which it is attempted to delineate the Stronger Passions of the Mind*, 5th edn, 3 vols (London, 1806), 2.154.

465.7–8 fell ... by the hand of a son in the lost epic *Telegonia* which continues the story of *The Odyssey*, Odysseus's son by Circe, Telegonus, goes in search of his father, but kills him while plundering Ithaca (Inglis).

465.15–16 heritable jurisdictions see note to 378.34–35. Even before 1747 when heritable jurisdictions were abolished Knockdunder had no right to try prisoners for murder or theft.

465.17 the Circuit the High Court of Justiciary sits in Edinburgh, but also goes on circuit: in 1736–37 it visited Dumfries, Jedburgh (the south circuit), Stirling, Glasgow, Ayr (the west circuit), and Perth, Inverness and Aberdeen (the north circuit), but in the Heritable Jurisdictions Act (20 George II, c. 43) Inveraray was assumed into the west circuit, and became the place where the High Court sat to try offences committed in Argyle and Bute.

465.43 sheep designed for slaughter see Psalm 44.22; Isaiah 53.7; Jeremiah 12.3; Acts 8.32; Romans 8.36.

466.22 Rob Roy the celebrated Scottish outlaw, and hero of Scott's novel of the same name; however Rob Roy had died in 1734.

466.22 Serjeant More Cameron freebooter who served in the French army, and then with the Jacobites in 1745–46. After a period of cattle-thieving and banditry he was executed in 1753.

466.30 destroy baith body and saul see note to 58.20.

467.35 quiet low content see *As You Like It*, 2.3.68.

467.36–37 divert her sorrow, or enhance her joy see Alexander Pope, *Homer's Odyssey* (London, 1725–26), Bk 24, line 282 (Inglis).

468.24–25 care for none of these things see note to 74.22.

469.4–5 The Heart of Mid-Lothian is now no more the tolbooth was demolished in 1817, but the doorway was rebuilt at Abbotsford.

469.5 extreme side of the city the new prison was built on the southern slope of the Calton Hill 1815–17.

469.9 Cela étoit autrefois ainsi, mais nous avons changé tout cela *French* it was thus once but we have changed all that: Molière (Jean Baptiste Poquelin), 1622–73, *Le Médecin Malgré Lui* (1666), Act 2, scene 4.

GLOSSARY

This selective glossary defines single words; phrases are treated in the Explanatory Notes. It covers Scottish and English dialectal words, archaic and technical terms, and occurrences of familiar words in senses that may be strange to the modern reader, but which are unlikely to be in commonly-used one-volume dictionaries. Irregularly spelt words from Jeanie's letters are included but labelled *Jeanie's letter* or *Jeanie's letters*; English dialectal words are labelled *dialect*; and English words as pronounced by a native Gaelic speaker are labelled *Gaelic English*. Orthographical variants of single words are listed together, usually with the most common use first. Up to four occurrences of each word (or clearly distinguishable sense) are normally noted; when a word occurs four or more times in the novel, only the first instance is normally given, followed by 'etc.'. Often the most economical and effective way of defining a word is to refer the reader to the appropriate explanatory note.

a' all 1.9 etc., every 44.4 etc.
Abaddon the angel of the bottomless pit 98.36 (see note)
abbreviate *Law* abstract, abridgement; used particularly in relation to adjudication and sequestration 243.6
abigail waiting-woman, lady's maid 281.6 (see note)
abjuration, abjuration-oath for 90.35 and 167.8 see note to 90.16–18
a'body everybody 79.4, 153.3
aboot about 394.38
abroad out of doors 14.30 etc.
abune, aboon above 106.5 etc.; for 144.20 see note to 144.20–21
accessory something contributing to a subordinate extent 108.42; something or someone aiding in a crime 198.34
acquent acquainted 143.32
acre unit of land measurement; used loosely to mean a wide expanse of land 3.26, 221.22, 425.41
actuate stir into activity, excite 8.33, 64.12
adamantine incapable of being broken, immovable, impregnable 49.39
address[1] readiness for an event; skill,

dexterity 299.20 etc.
address[2] manner of speaking, bearing in conversation 336.40, 435.31
adjudication *Scots Law* process used to take a debtor's land to satisfy a creditor's claim for debt 243.6, 355.43 (see note to 355.43–356.1)
adjuration earnest appeal 181.43; solemn charging or appealing to upon oath 209.21
adjure charge, entreat 217.24
adminicle *Law* supporting or corroborating evidence 204.10
adminiculate *Scots Law* support with corroborating evidence 213.43, 215.7
admission *Law* concession, acknowledgement 43.18
advocate member of the Scottish bar 12.6 etc. (see note to 18.35)
Advocatus *Latin* advocate, barrister 111.1
advowson right of presentation to a post of clergyman 287.17
ae one 44.9 etc.
aerial ethereal, imaginary 231.39; lofty, elevated 360.42
afeard frightened, afraid 373.26, 373.28
afenge *Gaelic English* avenge 462.11,

465.22
aff off 41.34 etc.
affirmation *Law* formal and solemn declaration having the same weight and responsibilities as an oath by persons who refuse to take an oath for conscientious reasons 166.22
afore before 102.34 etc.
aften often 88.32 etc.
after-harvest secondary, following after the main occurrence 350.27
again, against[1] in readiness for 41.22, 295.21
again[2] against 79.11 etc.
agee to one side 362.41
agen *Jeanie's letter* again 351.27
agent *Scots Law, noun* solicitor 12.5 etc.
agent *verb* act as a law agent 118.15
aggravate make worse, exacerbate 102.15 etc.
ahint behind 87.3, 259.3
ain own 27.28 etc.
ainsell self 155.17
air early 244.20
airn iron 173.25
airt direct, point out 181.35
aith oath 75.36, 89.15, 351.34
aits oats 72.5
a-kimbo in a position in which the hands rest on the hips and the elbows are turned outwards 233.41
alack exclamation of regret and pity 211.38
alane alone 115.12, 273.19, 273.20
alderman magistrate in English and Irish cities next in authority to the mayor 164.39–40
alive lively, brisk 260.28
allenarly alone, solely 355.13
alleviation mitigation, lightening 183.22
allwaies *Jeanie's letter* always 349.36
aloife *dialect* alive 360.12
along for 268.20 see note
a-low ablaze, on fire 403.35
amain with full force, violently 346.38
amaist almost 44.17 etc.
Amalekite nomadic people of the Old Testament described as the enemies of Israel 427.6–7 (see note)
amang among 1.11 etc.

Amazon tall, strong or masculine woman 51.3, 52.8
amenable answerable 16.36, 314.1
amna am not 185.28, 219.16, 352.3
an' and 1.12 etc.; if 42.2 etc.
anabaptism system of belief which rejects infant baptism 79.15 (see note)
ance once 37.26 etc.
ane one 40.27 etc.; a person 46.18 etc.; a, an 110.32 etc.
aneath beneath, below 69.23
anent concerning, about 109.40 etc.
anes once 44.8 etc.
aneugh enough 70.17 etc.
Anglice in English 164.39, 248.41
anither another 174.41, 219.41
anker cask or keg holding a measure of wine or spirits of varying quantity 37.29, 70.10
Ansar for 136.1 see note
anti-christ enemy or opponent of Christ, especially the Pope or Roman Catholic church 109.42
anticipate cause to happen earlier, bring forward 7.21, 302.18
anti-erastian opposed to erastian beliefs which maintain subordination of ecclesiastical to secular power 177.10
anti-national opposed to a national church 71.34 (see note)
anti-prelatic opposed to prelacy, the system of church government by bishops etc. 177.10
anti-sectarian opposed to the Independents 177.10 (see note)
Apollyon the devil 98.36, 274.19
apostacy abandonment or renunciation of religious faith 468.22
apostate having entirely renounced God and Chritianity 139.8
apout *Gaelic English* about 421.19, 461.10
appanage possession specifically intended for the use or benefit of younger children in a family 287.21
apparent evident, obvious, one who will certainly inherit 300.29
apprising *Scots Law* sentence of a sheriff by which the heritable property of a debtor was sold for payment of a debt to an appriser or creditor 356.1 (see note to 355.43–356.1)

approbation expression of satisfaction 74.2 etc.

aprupt *Gaelic English* abrupt 461.4

aquals for 69.15 see note

aqua-vitæ whisky, brandy 26.20

aquiline curved like an eagle's beak 148.23

Arcadia ideal and imaginary region of rural contentment 398.12

archangel *figurative* the fallen archangel, Satan 100.18

arch-deacon in the Anglican church a clergyman appointed by the bishop to give him assistance particularly as regards the oversight of rural clergy 368.4, 431.29, 433.11

arena are not 144.32 etc.

ark Ark of the Covenant; *figuratively* the holy principles of the Christian church 173.19 (see note)

armfu' armful 83.18

Arminian one who follows the doctrines of Jacobus Arminius 112.5, 112.40, 173.33 (see note to 112.5)

arraign interrogate, accuse of some fault 213.18

arrest for 216.38 see note

arriage services by horse, or carriage by horse, due by a tenant to his landlord 68.8

arrogate lay claim without reason 427.5

artificial brought about by skill, made by or resulting from art 143.24

ashler-wark ashler-work, masonry constructed of square hewn stones 60.18

assafœtida resinous gum produced in plants from Central Asia and used in medicines against spasms 361.15

assay put to the test, try 222.10

assembly for General Assembly 90.34 etc. see note to 90.34; for assembly of divines 149.36 see note

assize *Scots Law* jury 198.16, 203.24, 214.6; *English Law* session held periodically in the counties of England for administering civil and criminal justice 432.4

assizer *Scots Law* juryman 215.32

a'thegither altogether 271.33, 409.12

athwart across in various directions

54.22

attendance for 312.21, 319.12, 346.25 ssee note to 312.21

atween between 46.6

aught[1] all, anything 71.43 etc.

aught[2] eighth 122.36

aught[3] possession 149.34

aughteen eighteen 188.42

aughty-nine eighty-nine (i.e. 1689) 69.9, 69.32

auld old 37.15 etc.

auld-fashioned old-fashioned 429.28

ava at all 46.34, 144.5, 160.5

avocation ordinary work or employment 82.2–3; diversion, distraction 440.10

awa', **awa** away 37.21 etc.

awe owe 350.22

awee a little while 176.41

aweel, a-weel well, oh well 40.31 etc.

awfu' awful 37.32 etc.

awl sharp, pointed tool used for piercing holes in leather 222.4

awmous alms, food or money given in charity to the poor 94.32

awmrie wooden cupboard or dresser used for storing kitchen utensils and food 82.16

ay yes 40.12 etc.

aye always 37.18 etc.

ayont beyond 225.7, 265.40, 329.41; on the far side, behind 400.39

Baal chief deity of the Phoenician and Canaanite peoples, *figuratively* a false god 90.15

baby doll, puppet 48.26

Babylonian pertaining to the city of Babylon 43.15 (see note)

back-bane back-bone, spine 265.2

back-cast unexpected blow 450.20

back-friend supporter 105.40

back-sliding, backsliding falling away from the law of God 103.36 (see note) etc.

badly in ill health 359.30

bag-pudding pudding boiled in a bag 294.38

baillie senior member of a Scottish town council appointed to act as a magistrate 18.13 etc.; for 379.17 see **baron-baillie**

bairn child 27.30 etc.

baith both 45.39 etc.

baldrick leather belt or girdle worn hanging from one shoulder, across the breast, and under the opposite arm 281.10

band money bond 69.14 etc.

bandalier belt worn by soldiers for supporting a musket or carrying ammunition 112.32

band-box box for collars, caps, hats and millinery 372.12

banditti lawless, desperate marauders 26.24, 143.33, 455.36, 461.40

bane bone 46.14 etc.

Bangor for 396.14 see note

bank-bill for 344.21 see note

bannerman standard-bearer 266.38

bannock round, flat cake baked on a girdle 71.10, 346.40

banns proclamation in church of a forthcoming marriage 412.4

bar barrier separating the immediate precinct of the judge from the rest of the court 15.36 (see note) etc.

bargain fight, struggle 445.25

bark small ship or rowing boat 329.29, 374.6, 374.37

bar-keeper one who prevents unauthorised persons from going within the bar in a court 195.26

barkened tanned 44.3, 90.6, 115.16

barn-door reared at the barn-door 423.14

baron landowner holding his land directly as a fief from the crown 173.17 (see note); for 68.13 and 248.8 see note to 68.13

baron-baillie deputy appointed by a baron to exercise civil and criminal jurisdiction in baron courts (see note to 68.13) 248.11

barony estate created by direct grant from the crown 236.36

bartizan'd having a small battlemented area 230.1

bastard corrupt, unauthorized 126.26

bat-fleeing bat-flying 157.17–18 (see note)

bather bother, annoy 208.4

Batie generic name for a dog given contemptuously to a human being 167.30

bating excepting 191.4, 253.38

battle-axe halberd carried by guards 61.13

battlemented furnished with an indented parapet at the top of a wall 229.31

bauld bold, courageous 106.33 etc.

baulk unploughed ridge or piece of land in a cultivated field 230.19, 231.16

bauson-faced having a white spot or streak on the face 251.15

bawbee copper coin worth 6*d.* Scots (halfpenny sterling) 88.31, 353.40

beadle parish officer appointed to keep order in the church and punish petty offenders 280.7 etc.

bean-hool bean pod 164.16

bear hardy form of barley with four rows of grain on the head 74.12

beaver made of the fur of the beaver 435.15

beck curtsey 251.33

bedizen dress up in a vulgar and gaudy fashion 193.17, 280.38

Bedlam lunatic asylum, mad-house 151.38 etc.

bedral beadle, church-officer with the duty of bell-ringer 402.22

Beelzebub the devil 149.6

behounched *dialect* tricked up, smartened, finely dressed 291.3

behove have need to, to be necessary 44.26 etc.

belang belong 155.18, 208.11, 275.35, 451.38

beldame loathsome old woman, virago 168.9, 168.16, 170.32, 207.22

Belial spirit of evil personified, the devil 103.36, 174.12, 376.18

belive before long, hastily 223.16

belle handsome woman, fair lady 423.22

ben inside, within 113.19

bench seat where the judges sit in court 15.37 etc.

bend inclination, direction 187.13

bend-leather, bend leather leather shaped from half the hide, the thickest, stoutest kind used for soles of boots and shoes 42.11, 42.19, 160.8

benefit for 260.17 see note to 260.16–17

benighted surrounded by moral darkness 293.35

beseem become, befit, be suitable for 3.7 etc.

beset set about, surround 136.22, 236.32, 305.15, 427.30

Bess romping, light-headed girl 151.38, 170.10, 262.28, 286.2

be'st *dialect* are 254.15, 285.38

bestial domestic animals, particularly cattle kept for food or tillage 75.23, 350.15, 386.10

bible-aith bible-oath, solemn promise 44.17

bibliopolist bookseller 368.7

bicker small wooden bowl 46.16, 79.26

bid request, command 395.12

bide stay, remain 27.15 etc.; await, stay for 144.24 etc.; remain so 145.9; live 251.21

bien cosy, comfortable 109.28, 350.40

biggonet linen cap 220.14

bike *literally* wasps' nest, i.e. swarm, 'crew' 109.34

bilk cheat 267.32

billet note 130.7, 130.19, 313.28

Billingsgate scurrilous, abusive 233.42 (see note)

bink wooden frame fixed to the wall for holding plates, bowls etc. 131.39

binna would not be 223.32, 235.9

birkie young, lively fellow 115.9, 155.22

birn burnt mark or brand on the skin of an animal signifying ownership 219.42 (see note)

birth-day 4 June, the official birthday of the sovereign 423.24, 423.25

birth-night relating to the court-festival held on the evening of a royal birthday 148.26 (see note)

bit small 37.29 etc.

bittock small bit or portion 339.19

black-coat clergyman 444.20

blackguard idle criminal 144.28 etc.

blackit blackened, burnt 155.16

blade gallant, free and easy fellow 11.20

blandishment gentle, flattering speech, cajolery 393.32

blaw blow 355.16

blithsome happy, cheerful 265.41

blown for 56.39 see note

bludgeon short stick or club 51.36

bluff blunt, frank, plain-spoken 394.24

bluid, blude blood 27.33 etc.

bluidy bloody 113.11, 362.5

blythe happy, pleased 346.1, 352.5

board-wage wage given to a servant to cover the cost of food 372.28

boat-cloak large cloak worn at sea 456.37

bobb dance 358.9, 358.10 (see note to 358.9–10)

boddle, bodle Scottish copper coin of very small value, equivalent to a sixth of an old English penny 94.34, 155.7, 219.41, 292.21

bodie *Jeanie's letter* body 349.35

body person 44.28 etc.

boggle hesitate, raise scruples 378.23

boll measure of capacity for grain of varying amounts 124.38

bond binding engagement 75.36

bon-grace, bongrace broad-brimmed hat shaped to shade the face 249.35, 249.38, 252.22

bonnet head covering for men including all forms of cap 76.17 etc.

bonnie fair, pretty, handsome 86.38 etc.

bonorum for 18.23 etc. see note to 18.23

booby[1] pertaining to the dunce of a school class 39.12

booby[2] dull, stupid fellow 82.17

boorn *dialect* burn 360.12

boot[1] instrument of torture consisting of a case which enclosed the lower leg and foot of the victim, and between which and the leg wedges were driven to crush the bones 88.38

boot[2] for 112.26, 282.12, 402.8 see note to 112.26

boot-hose coarse hose fixed by a flap under the buckle of the shoe and covering the breeches at the knee, used in place of boots 83.41, 122.12

border-rider mounted freebooter living on the border of Scotland and England 360.29

borrow release 355.39 (see note to 355.38–39), 366.18

borrowing for 252.7 see note

bouking-washing annual washing of the family linen 158.13

bound required 111.7, 111.12

bounden for 173.9 see note
bountith something given as a reward for services 70.1; what is given to servants in addition to their wages 90.11
bourock mound, small knoll 276.28
bow for 78.30 see note
Bow-head, Bowhead for 103.7, 145.6, 384.15 see note to 103.7
bowie broad, shallow dish for holding milk, porridge, broth etc. at meal times 131.38, 131.41
brae hill, hillside 86.37 etc.
brae-side hillside 103.39, 109.30
braid broad, plain 167.31
brain-fever inflammation of the brain 206.21
brake broke, entered by force 147.12
brave fine, splendid 106.30
bravely splendidly 115.7
braw handsome, active 162.27; fine, pleasant 83.40 etc.; splendid 272.32 etc.
brawlies, brawly very well 265.10, 275.12
braws fine clothes, best apparel 148.40, 150.34
break become bankrupt 221.26
brecham collar for a horse or ox 46.9
breekens trousers 460.30
brief curt, abrupt 394.24
brief summary of the facts of a case drawn up for the information of the counsel who is to conduct the case in court 18.20, 18.38, 20.21, 195.5
brig a vessel with two masts 398.43
brigadier for 434.24, 459.32 see note to 434.24
brigg bridge 194.4
brimstane brimstone, sulphur 264.21
brisk sprightly, lively 388.32
brither brother 1.7
broadside sheet of paper printed on one side only forming one large page, used to distribute news 431.25, 433.12, 433.21, 434.1
broadside-sheet sheet of paper printed on one side only forming one large page, used to distribute news 367.41
brockit coloured like a badger with black and white stripes or spots 350.18, 377.25
brog prick, pierce 42.11

brogue rough, heavy shoe 263.18, 361.36
broider embroider, adorn 79.27
broidered embroidered 40.9, 41.21
broiled for 20.11 see note
broken ruined, bankrupt 144.4
broken-winded short-winded, breathing out with effort 69.21
broo[1] favourable opinion 222.27, 355.4
broo[2] *dialect* brow 360.11
broom shrub with yellow flowers 86.38, 86.40
broom-shank broom handle 170.27
brow brew 409.23
brownie benevolent spirit thought to live in farmhouses and perform housework while the inhabitants are sleeping 231.29 (see note), 231.30, 231.33, 231.42
brugh burgh, borough 259.7
bruilzie skirmish, commotion 145.2
brunstane brimstone 167.5
brute animal 235.7; wanting in reason or understanding 400.22
Bucephalus Alexander the Great's charger, used as a humorous name for any horse 117.27
buckie for 169.42 see note
buffet blow 263.19
buller bellow, roar like a bull 136.19
bull-headed *figurative* blindly impetuous 166.21
bull-segg bull that has been castrated at full age, thick-necked ox that has the appearance of a bull 190.14–15
bulwark powerful defence or safeguard 109.17, 422.26
bumper cup or glass of wine or spirits filled to the brim 70.43 etc.
bumper-dram drink from a cup or glass of wine or spirits filled to the brim 40.43
bunker chest used as a seat, bench, window-seat 82.38
burgess citizen or freeman of a burgh 18.14 etc.
burgh borough 124.21
burgher citizen of a burgh 36.2
burgher-magistrate magistrate who is also a citizen of a burgh 167.11
burthen restriction affecting the free use of property 236.26
busk adorn, deck, dress up 185.37,

223.38 (see note to 185.37)

butt outer room of a two-room building 404.22 (see note)

butter-milk milk which remains after the butter has been churned 71.9, 248.41, 385.17

bye[1] past, finished 145.3 etc.

bye[2] besides 264.43

bye-path side-path, unfrequented path 261.8

bye-word proverb, proverbial saying 353.2

bygane bygone, thing in the past 158.2, 158.3

by-past in the past, long ago 350.38

byre cow-house 86.12 etc.

ca', caa' call 41.20 etc.

cabinet private room in which the advisers of a sovereign meet, council chamber 34.18 (see note to 34.18–19)

cadet gentleman who enters the army without a commission to learn the profession and earn a career for himself 468.4

cadger travelling hawker or pedlar 421.33

cadie one who earned a living in Edinburgh as a porter, running errands, lighting the way in the dark etc. 194.13

cag small cask 396.25, 435.1

cage prison 322.7 (see note), 388.8 (see note)

caird tinker, gypsy 426.26 etc.

cairn pile of stones built in memory of the dead 99.23 etc.; stony hill 412.9

caitiff wretched, miserable 217.43

cake oat-cake, thin, flat cake made with oatmeal and baked on a girdle 1.7, 345.39

calash light carriage with low wheels having a removable folding hood 345.29, 362.33

Calender one of a mendicant order of dervishes in Turkey and Persia 231.12 (see note to 231.12–13)

calf-skin superior kind of leather used for the binding of books; here *figuratively*, the Bible on which oaths were taken 189.36

call call from God, obligation to follow the dictates of conscience 66.6; invitation to undertake the office and duties of a minister of a church 351.36 etc.

callant young man, fellow 74.19 etc.

callar, caller fresh, cool, refreshing 158.16, 263.39

calling for 149.35–36 see note to 149.34–36

calliver soldier armed with a light kind of musket or harquebus 289.20

calumniator slanderer 164.30

Calvinist follower of the doctrines of John Calvin (1509–1564) the Protestant reformer 279.4

cam came 44.43, 120.6, 408.40

Cameronian follower of Richard Cameron, a noted Scottish Covenanter and field preacher 4.38 etc. (see note)

camlet light cloth, in the past much used for women's clothes 148.21

camp body of troops encamping and marching together, soldiers on a campaign 300.35, 432.13

cann earthenware vessel for holding liquids 428.37

canna cannot 37.28 etc.

canny lucky, of good omen 247.41; shrewd, skilful 257.38, 358.19, 416.35; steady 271.21; pleasant 288.11

canon rule or law of the church 112.16

canonical in conformity with ecclesiastical edict or the laws of the church 293.41, 405.31, 416.41

cant peculiar language or jargon of a profession 140.41, 267.14

canty lively, cheerful 84.4

capernoity giddy, frolicsome 26.22

capper-cailzie wood-grouse 110.30

caption *Scots Law* warrant for the arrest of a debtor for failing to pay a debt after being required to do so by the courts 39.31

carcake small cake made with eggs and eaten on Shrove Tuesday in Scotland 265.6, 265.8

career run at full speed 8.3, 8.12. 18.9; course or progress through life 316.11

carena don't care 257.35, 270.37

carle man, fellow 40.33 etc.

carline woman, crone 40.33, 190.22

carnal worldly, not spiritual 66.18 etc.

carnal-witted carnal-minded, too apt to think of worldly matters 102.13

carriage service of carrying, or money in lieu, due by a tenant to his landlord or feudal superior 68.8

carried delirious 205.40

carrier one who is hired for the conveyance of goods and parcels 41.13

carritch catechism 149.35 (see note to 149.34–36), 189.29

cashier dismiss from service 66.12

cassock cloak or long coat worn by horsemen 7.27

cast *verb* toss, throw 85.14, 109.12, 131.28, 271.20; for 416.1 see note

cast *noun* turn, lot 109.14 etc.; assistance 339.29 etc.

cast-a-way, cast-away reprobate 94.19 etc.

cast-bye person cast aside and neglected 186.34

castell *Jeanie's letter* castle 351.24

casuistical relating to resolving of conflicts of duty 182.4, 388.40

casuistry moral reasoning designed to solve conflicts of duty 179.40, 180.27

catch-word rime word in verse, here also the word serving as a guide for the next speaker, a cue 160.18

catechism interrogation 325.10

ca'-throw disturbance 147.26

cattle horses 346.2; contemptuous term for persons implying lice, vermin etc. 412.21

cauld cold 43.42 etc.

cauldrife cold, indifferent 109.27

cause for 147.41 see note; for 221.43 see note

causeway street or pavement laid with cobblestones 52.10, 149.22

cautelous cautious, wary, circumspect 4.28

cavalier *noun* supporter of Charles I in the war between king and parliament, 17th century Royalist 4.41, 149.4; horseman 237.35

cavalier *adjective* off-hand, free and easy 438.25

cavalierism see note to 67.1

caviller quibbling disputant 4.25

ceet cite, summon officially to appear

in a court of law 208.5, 208.12

ceevil civil, polite 251.19

ceevilly civilly 251.34

censor magistrate in ancient Rome who had the supervision of public morals 74.15; one who supervises morals or conduct 315.14

certes assuredly, certainly 3.10, 231.36

certiorate inform authoritatively 248.39

cess tax, levy, particularly a land tax or local levy 177.31, 177.35

cessio *Scots Law* shortened form of *cessio bonorum*; for 18.23, 18.33, 18.38, 19.2 see note to 18.23

chaft jaw, cheek 87.13

chainge change 187.13

chaise carriage for travelling 13.2, 17.30, 17.31

chalder dry measure of capacity for grain, corn etc. used in the calculation of payment for parish ministers 385.4

chamber to be wanton, indulge in lewdness 90.40–41 (see note)

champaign open, unenclosed 64.31

chancel eastern part of a church reserved for the clergy 283.7 (see note)

chancellor foreman of a jury 215.28, 215.31, 216.14; before the union of 1707 highest officer of the crown in Scotland 37.17

chance-medley killing by misadventure, *figuratively* haphazard or random action 338.25 (see note)

change-house small inn or alehouse 403.31, 404.2, 404.22

chaperone person, especially an elder woman, who, for propriety's sake, accompanies a young, unmarried lady in public 89.34, 281.35

chap strike, knock 87.2, 324.37

charge requirement to pay money 355.40 (see note), 355.41

chase unenclosed park land reserved for breeding and hunting wild animals 135.17, 156.31

chase drive forcibly and precipitately away 445.30

chatellain master of a castle 394.6

cheat-the-gallows one who has escaped the gallows 409.15–16

cheveron glove 70.2

chiefest highest, head 386.15 (see note to 386.15–16)

chield, chiel, cheel man, fellow 1.11 etc.

chimerical fantastically conceived 180.28

chimley grate, hearth, fireplace 461.3

choler bile, anger, heat of temper 233.43

choleric hot-tempered, passionate 379.19

chop shop 43.43

chucky chicken 423.14

churl, churle niggard, miser 239.24 etc.; man, rustic fellow 271.12; man 285.21, 298.32; low-bred man 362.3

churn produce froth by chewing hard 297.13

chury knife 267.19

circuit *Scots Law* the circuit court, the High Court of Justiciary which deals with major crimes and which sits in various Scottish towns 195.33 (see note to 195.32–34), 465.17, 465.

citation summons to a court of law 68.12 etc.

city-clerk chief official of a city 124.17, 166.12, 166.28–29

civility-money money given in anticipation of good-will or good offices, a tip 194.37

clachan hamlet, village 403.13

claes, claise clothes 155.14, 158.13, 245.22, 351.22

claik-goose barnacle goose 395.1

claith cloth 158.7

claith-merchant cloth-merchant 173.25

claiths clothes 148.40, 150.5, 150.37, 272.32

clamant urgent, crying out 88.19

clangor loud, resonant ringing 396.12

clannish attached to one's own clan or people 353.23

clap imprison with little formality or delay 144.28

clarissimus *Latin* celebrated, famous, also loud, sonorous 242.33, 242.35. 242.43–243.1 and see note to 242.33–243

clat lump 275.17

clave adhered, clung to 75.36

claver *verb* talk idly or foolishly 157.15, 191.5, 221.25, 394.43

claver *noun* foolish talk 60.12, 160.3

claymore large two-edged sword used by the Highlanders of Scotland 346.39, 358.13–14, 358.16; the name of the sword used as a Highland battle cry or shout of command 461.38

clean completely, absolutely 39.29 etc.

clean-ganging clean-going 457.41

cleck hatch, bring forth young 168.25, 203.14

cleek seize, catch 164.14

clenched made secure, with nails 54.21

clergy for 260.17 see note to 260.16–17.

clerk clergyman 87.27; for 226.8 see note

cleuch, cleugh narrow gorge with high rocky sides 440.24, 460.35

clew ball of thread or yarn 219.29 (see note)

clift crevice 114.14

clink quickly seize upon and add in 203.15 (see note)

cloke-bag bag in which to carry a cloak or other clothes, valise 2.7

cloot division in the hoof of cloven-footed animals 386.16

close entry to a tenement house, the open passageway giving access to the common stairs and floors above 173.26 etc.; courtyard, area in front of a house or building 193.19, 193.39; enclosed field 287.29

close-head entrance of a passageway or alley off a main street 42.13, 42.21–22

closet small side room or inner room 306.8; private council-chamber of a monarch 335.43; cabinet or cupboard 417.3, 428.32

cloth clerical profession, clergy 77.43, 97.17, 97.20, 421.20

clout bang, blow 144.8

clown rustic, boorish person 248.30, 362.24

club join together, combine 17.35

clubbed drawn into a club-shape knot or tail 148.19

Cocceian for 112.42 see note

cock *verb* put a loaded firearm in readiness for firing 139.25

cock *noun* turned-up part of the brim of a hat 381.11

cockad ribbon, knot of ribbons or rosette worn in the hat to indicate office or support of a party 27.17

cock-crow early dawn 157.18

cocked with the brim permanently turned up, applied to the three-cornered hat in fashion at the end of the 18th century 118.18, 380.37, 434.25

cocked-hat three cornered hat with the brim turned up, popular at the end of the 18th century 28.3, 237.34, 286.4, 394.13

cockernonie, cockernony gathering of a young woman's hair when tied up in a fillet or snood 185.37 (see note), 223.38

cockit set up assertively, in a saucy or defiant way 168.11

cock-pit pit or enclosed area in which game-cocks fight 316.6

cockups hair-style where a false pad was used to add height 223.40

cod pillow, cushion 69.23

cognizance *Scots Law* knowledge, understanding 198.16 (see note)

cognosced pronounced to be an idiot or lunatic 41.29, 92.16

coif close-fitting night-cap 125.38

coign position, often a projecting corner, affording means for observation or action 48.22

coinage fabrication, invention 15.45

colde *Old Scots* could 41.10

collaterally indirectly 366.10–11

collector officer appointed to receive taxes, duties etc. 23.13 etc.

collegeaner student at the university 69.9

colours ensign's commission 439.7, 445.23

com *Jeanie's letter* come 251.32

comena doesn't come 400.42

comfit sweetmeat usually made with some fruit or root preserved with sugar 40.12

comfort state of physical and material well-being implying the satisfaction of bodily needs 227.18

command overlook 443.1

commandment *slang* fingernail or claw 168.3

commission instruction 19.12; appointment as military officer or similar 26.37, 468.2; written authority 46.22; direction 103.24

commons common people as opposed to those of rank or dignity 173.18

Commonwealth republican government between, in England, 1649 and 1660 65.42 (see note)

communing meeting to talk on any particular subject 243.31

commutation *Law* substitution of a lesser punishment for a greater 183.22, 347.22

commute substitute a payment in money for one in kind 124.39

company-keeper frequenter of bad company, reveller 75.33–34 (see note), 174.12 (see note)

company-keeping revelling, keeping bad company 90.41 (see notes to 75.33–34, 174.12)

compass grasp (physically or in the mind) 65.36 etc.; consider 351.35

compeer one of equal rank or standing 468.13

complaint statement of injury or grievance laid before a court or judicial authority for purposes of prosecution or redress, a formal accusation or charge 18.10, 307.10

complaisance deference, courtesy 438.24

compliance action of conforming in political or religious matters 181.22 etc. (see note)

composition settling of debt by a mutual arrangement 19.8 (see note to 19.6–8)

compound settle a dispute by compromise or mutual concession 71.38, 305.27

comprehendeth include 3.6

comprehension comprehensiveness 65.31

con study, learn 73.28, 241.15

concatenation linking together 456.8

conceitedly whimsically, eccentrically 72.6

conclusion *Scots Law* the concluding clause or paragraph of a summons, which sets forth the purpose of an action or suit 110.36

concourse crowd, throng 33.16, 61.12, 360.10

concur agree, coincide 31.8, 114.13, 212.32

condescendence *Scots Law* written statement of the facts of a case 18.40–41, 43.32, 43.34

condescending consenting, agreeing 334.14, 336.10, 347.36, 348.17

condign worthily deserved, fitting 304.20, 313.9

confeise confuse 221.31

conform in accordance with, conformably to 41.26, 460.3

conglomerated stupefied with a mixture of confusing thoughts 406.7

conjure entreat, beseech, implore 186.33, 188.15, 246.13, 322.31

Conscript see note to 13.41

consequential self-important 287.14, 367.15, 394.24

conservator preserver, guardian 27.11

consort spouse 66.31; the wife of the king 317.37, 331.36, 340.6

constable officer of the peace 143.31 etc.

constructive deduced by construction or interpretation, inferred 195.2

consumption wasting disease 73.7

continental mainland 393.40

contrair contrary 173.5–6

conveniency vehicle 10.3

Convention-parliament see note to 356.10–11

conventual characteristic of a convent 424.22

conversation manner of behaving 89.42, 311.35; for 338.35 see note

convocating calling, gathering together 108.40

coorse coarse 353.2

coot *Gaelic English* good 462.5, 462.7, 465.20, 465.22

cope-stone top, head stone of a building, *figuratively* the finishing touch 241.26

cordial comforting or exhilarating drink believed to be good for the heart 296.28, 296.33, 450.12

Corinthian brazen, showy 42.43 (see note to 42.43–43.1)

cork-jacket jacket made, or partly lined, with cork, to support a person in the water 15.7

coronet *heraldry* figure of a coronet or small crown denoting various ranks of nobility 41.26

corpse-sheet winding sheet, shroud 158.4

correction-house building for the confinement and punishment of offenders with a view to their reformation 167.38, 463.13

cot small house, little cottage 417.29

Cot *Gaelic English* God 395.15 etc.

cottar peasant who occupies a cottage, and sometimes land, belonging to a farm who has to provide labour when required 226.24, 237.4

couch for 270.39 see note

couchant *heraldry* lying down with the body resting on the legs and the head lifted up 156.22

couldna couldn't 115.24 etc.

coulter iron blade fixed in the front of a plough 54.19

counsel legal adviser 12.5 etc.

countenance *verb* encourage, favour 110.7, 125.29, 126.28

countenance *noun* favour 34.32, 73.32; moral support 163.33; for 90.9 see note; for 353.42 see note

coup upset, overturn 421.33

course hunt 141.42

court farmyard 186.20

court-beauty beautiful woman belonging to the royal court 423.34

court-Scottish court-language of Scotland 424.10–11 (see note)

couthy comfortable, agreeable 398.3

covenant the National Covenant (1638) or the Solemn League and Covenant (1643) 30.30 etc. (see note)

covenanted secured by the principles of those who have entered into a covenant with God 72.2 (see note)

Covenanter subscriber or adherent of the National Covenant (1638) and / or the Solemn League and Covenant (1643) 68.15 (see note to 30.30)

covering serving as a defence or protection 338.40

coward *verb* render cowardly, daunt 445.30

cow-feeder, cowfeeder dairy-farmer 81.21 etc.

cowslip dairy-maid 372.8, 396.20, 402.4, 407.37

cowt colt, young horse 224.33

coxswain helmsman of a boat 411.29

crack *noun* talk, gossip, free and easy conversation 157.18, 159.11, 391.15

crack *verb* for 160.2 see note

crack-rope one likely to die by the gallows 268.17

craft croft, small-holding, small farm 72.5

crag steep, rugged rock 64.25 etc.

cravat *figurative* halter for hanging 145.42

crave *Scots Law* ask (as of right) from a legal tribunal 115.23, 116.24

crazed broken, cracked, infirm 355.22

creagh booty obtained on a foray 427.2

creat *Gaelic English* great 462.4, 465.21

creature-comfort material comfort 76.8, 132.20

credential letter of recommendation 207.7, 255.39

credit believe 189.23, 242.19

creditable respectable, decent 234.14

Creole person born or naturalized in a foreign country but of European race 315.42

crewels scrofula, a disease with glandular swellings possibly related to tuberculosis 415.12

criminate incriminate 201.41, 204.38

crine *dialect* shrink, shrivel 362.1

cristian *Jeanie's letter* Christian 252.11

croft, craft small agricultural holding worked by a peasant tenant 67.14, 67.23, 72.5, 74.13

crook for 103.29 and 416.15 see note to 103.29

crook *verb* bend, curve 88.34

cross for 229.26 see note

cross-grained queer-tempered, intractable 162.21

croun crown, head 144.9; crown piece, a coin worth 5s. (25p) 151.6

crown-counsel advocate for the prosecution in a criminal case 195.4

crown-lawyer lawyer acting for the crown 320.39–40

cruppin crept 40.24

cry offer for sale in the street 362.39

cuddie donkey, ass 74.7, 164.31

cudgel short, thick stick used as a club 237.42

cuffin *slang* justice 226.1 (see note)

cuisine manner of cooking 459.21

cuivis *Latin* for 39.2 and 43.5 see note to 39.2–3

Culdee see note to 387.41

cull dupe, silly fellow 268.10

cum come 46.12, 352.4

cummer gossip, friend 158.15; female friend, married woman, midwife 277.37

cummin see note to 179.19

cupidity greed, covetousness 464.17

curate parish priest of the Scottish Episcopal Church (especially in the period 1662–88) 69.34, 293.40, 390.40

curb chain or strap passed below the jaw of a horse used particularly for checking unruly behaviour 197.3

curch, curtch square piece of linen used by women as a covering for the head in place of a cap 125.38, 259.6, 357.10

cure spiritual charge 384.2

curfew-note signal denoting the hour for dampening fires thus intimating night 241.31

curpel crupper, a leather strap buckled to the back of a horse's saddle and passing under the tail 39.37, 221.33

curry rub or brush down a horse 256.16; for 295.32 see note

curtal for 357.1 see note to 356.41–357.1

curule pertaining to high civic dignity 104.6

cushion for 60.28 see note

cutter bully, bravo, highway-robber 260.19; small boat 396.27

cutty disparaging term for a woman, often implying a little, squat female 151.31, 285.32

cutty-stool the stool of repentance on which offenders against chastity were forced to sit during the time of church services 338.29–30 (see

note)
dae do 232.39
daffing, daffin' sport, frolic, foolish behaviour 146.25, 269.37
daft foolish, stupid, crazy 26.26 etc.
daidling idle, doddering, sauntering 83.42
daiker walk slowly, saunter 83.43
dainty pleasant, agreeable 159.28, 263.38, 272.28
Dalilah *figurative* anything which seduces or entices 15.33 (see note)
dam mother 262.29, 263.1
darg, dargue day's work, task 234.41, 252.6
dark *figurative* cloud, spoil 164.30
dashing spirited, lively 8.3, 11.20
dative for 39.10, 43.21, 43.23, 43.27 see note to 43.21; for 43.22 see note to 43.22
daughty daughter, darling 132.37
daur dare 88.22, 88.33
daurna dare not 86.40, 274.18
dauter *Jeanie's letter* daughter 351.11
daw jackdaw, small, easily-tamed bird of the crow family 41.11
dazed dazzled with excess of light 294.40
deacon president of one of the Incorporated Trades in a town, and formerly an *ex officio* member of the town council 3.15 etc.
dead-room room reserved for the laying out of a body, the best room 68.41
dear for 70.11 see note
dearie dear 162.7
deas stone or turf seat on the outer side of a cottage 172.30; for 236.30, and 263.39 see note to 236.30.
death-bell bell tolled at the death of a person 242.15
deave deafen, bother, annoy 41.38, 276.27
deceitfu' deceitful 274.15
declarant *Scots Law* prisoner whose account of him or herself has been or is being taken down in writing 122.33 etc.
declaration *Scots Law* in criminal proceedings the account which a prisoner gives of him or herself on examination, and which is taken down in writing 125.26 etc.

decreet *Scots Law* judgment of a court of law 68.13 (see note to 68.13–14)
dee die 265.9
deer *Jeanie's letter* dear 250.32
deevil devil 43.27 etc.
defection falling away from faith, religion and duty 71.18 (see note) etc.
de'il devil 46.10 etc.; for 147.16, 148.2, 148.4, 148.42, 203.10, 220.6, 264.20, 395.11 see respective notes
de'il a *emphatic* not a single 156.16 etc.
de'il ane *emphatic* not one 150.27 etc.
deistical tending towards an acknowledgement of God upon the evidence of reason, but denying revealed religion or revelation 173.33
delict violation of the law 47.8
demesne estate attached to a mansion, often owned by the crown 343.13
demipique, demi-pique half-peaked, of about half the height of the older war-saddle 43.36, 231.17
dependant hanging down 361.1
depone *Scots Law* declare upon oath, testify 116.9
deponent *Scots Law* one who gives testimony under oath 206.3
depose testify, bear witness 31.43; examine on oath, cite as a witness 191.4
deserted *Scots Law* abandoned, legally inoperative 11.13 (see note), 102.40
design point out by name or descriptive phrase 43.12
desperado desperate or reckless man, always ready for violence 127.15
detachment portion of troops taken from the main body and employed on some separate service or expedition 118.7, 160.36
deuce expression of surprise, devil 322.18, 338.43
deuke *Jeanie's letter* duck, *punningly* duke 221.31; duke 252.25
dial-plate face of a watch 104.20
didna didn't 84.4 etc.
dignity person holding high office or rank 75.25

dilly public stage-coach 7.7

din loud noise, fuss, to-do 111.19 etc.

ding knock, beat, push suddenly or forcibly 105.6, 186.21, 194.15

dingle deep dell or hollow 17.6

dinna don't 37.16 etc.

dinnle thrill, knock causing a trembling sensation 224.28

dirk Highlander's dagger 443.30

dirl blow, knock 153.5

discuss settle, decide 95.37

dismission release from confinement, liberation 200.35–36

disna does not 170.20 etc.

dispensation what Providence or nature has meted out 14.31 etc.

dispone *Scots Law* make over, convey, assign, grant officially or in legal form 70.29, 70.39

disposition *Scots Law* deed of conveyance, assignation of property 70.33

dissipation frivolous amusement 467.36, 468.24

dit stop, close up 274.9

dittay *Scots Law* the charge, or grounds of indictment against a person accused of a crime 110.24, 111.20

ditty composition in verse, simple song 278.28 – 29, 463.43

diurnal daily 83.19

divers diverse 40.13, 339.30

divot-cast bit (of land) measured by the distance one divot (turf, sod) can be thrown 111.1

dock coarse, weedy herb 230.9

doer agent, factor 175.20

doggie little dog 274.43, 275.3

doited crazed, enfeebled, confused in mind 262.37, 276.31, 450.18

dolefu' doleful 109.14, 386.19

dollar large silver coin of varying value 94.33, 173.22, 430.5

dominie schoolmaster 4.9, 87.16, 237.3

dominie-depute deputy schoolmaster 237.3

domned *dialect* damned 360.10

donnard stupid, dull 59.7, 155.20, 268.12

donnot *dialect* good-for-nothing, idler 286.7, 291.1

doo dove, dear one 184.28

dook duck 233.18

dooms extremely, very 185.32; absolute 220.18

doomster the official, generally the hangman, who pronounced sentence of death in a Scottish court 217.32, 217.34, 218.22, 224.31

door-cheek door-post, door-way 88.23

door-keeper one who keeps guard at a door 194.36

Doric broad, rustic 424.4

dot-and-go-one expression representing the limp of a person lame in one leg, or with a wooden leg 275.34

double for 289.27 and 396.13 see notes

doubt fear, be afraid, expect 79.23 etc.

douce sedate, sober, quiet, respectable, cautious 68.16 etc.

doug-fish dog-fish 421.35

dought was able to, had the strength for 206.5

doun down 40.1 etc.

dour sullen, gloomy, obstinate 361.35; obstinate, unyielding 409.19

dout *Jeanie's letters* doubt 250.40, 251.20, 349.33, 352.10

doutless *Jeanie's letter* doubtless, no doubt 352.1

down, downs open expanse of high land 149.22, 271.42

downa will not 144.24, 247.34

dragoon cavalry, horse-soldier 65.28, 71.33, 293.42, 322.26

dram small draft, drink usually of spirits 4.8, 45.10, 255.8

drap *noun* drop 78.35 etc.

drap *verb* drop, fall 429.31

draught used for pulling a cart or plough 43.36

draw *Law* frame a document in proper form 110.37, 185.35

Drawing-room formal reception by a king or queen 334.22 (see note to 334.21–22)

dray-horse large and powerful horse used for pulling a cart 361.37

dress-gown formal dresses or gowns 339.7

drible *Jeanie's letter* dribble, drip 251.12

driegh slow, wearisome 258.38

drift falling snow driven by the wind 70.16

drive throw with force or speed 168.43

drolling jesting, facetious 419.19

drouthy dry 377.18

drover one who drives sheep or cattle to market 83.1

drow spasm, stupor 174.43

dud article of clothing 150.41, 167.37, 223.40, 282.10

duddie ragged, tattered 272.29

dudgeon resentment, ill-humour 42.24

duk *Jeanie's letters* duke 350.13, 351.1, 351.17

dunch knock, bump, push 194.16

dune done 111.38 etc.

Dunlop, Dunlap sweet-milk cheese made in Ayrshire, Lanarkshire and Renfrewshire 345.43 etc.

duply *Scots Law* make a second reply 111.2

durk *Jeanie's letter* dirk, Highlander's dagger 350.11

durst dared 284.7, 408.39

durstna dared not 155.18

Dutch for 268.2 see note

dyester dyer 62.22, 105.6

e'er ever 37.20 etc.

earnest intense, ardent 400.40

easement relief from physical discomfort, particularly from inconvenience when travelling 339.30

eat for 71.10 and 224.24 see note to 71.10

ebullition sudden outburst or boiling over 333.21, 440.38

eclaircissement explanation 121.8

ecod a mild oath 268.16

Edomite see note to 386.15–16

e'en evening 86.43 etc.

ee, een eye, eyes 78.41 etc.

effectual for 149.35 and 411.2 see note to 149.34–36

effeir appearance, show 108.32

efficacious effective, producing the appropriate effect 311.17

eik *Scots Law* make an addition to some formal statement or document such as a will 116.24 (see note to 116.23–24)

elder one who has been chosen and ordained for service in the ecclesiastical courts of the Presbyterian church 90.33 etc. (see note to 90.33)

eldership the body of elders, the kirk session 103.5

elected those chosen by God for salvation 376.29

ele'en *Jeanie's letter* eleven 352.3

elector one of the princes of Germany formerly entitled to take part in the election of the Emperor 169.1 (see note)

elf for 442.19 see note

elide *Scots Law* squash, annul, render ineffective 110.35, 199.8

ell unit of measurement equivalent in Scotland to 37 inches (94cm) 388.30

elshin shoemaker's awl 42.11, 160.7

elude evade the force of an argument 178.25, 211.11

embodied formed into a military body, marshalled 27.5

eme uncle 113.11

emergence unforeseen event, situation 162.30, 218.19, 259.38

emolument profit 38.3–4, 426.31

enacted made into an act; decreed, ordained by legislative authority 111.27, 384.17; for 356.16 see note

en-bon-point plump around the breasts 333.41

end-long lengthwise, as opposed to crosswise 54.21

endue put on a garment 3.17

Enemy *figuratively* the devil 135.32 etc.

eneugh enough 45.23 etc.

engine contrivance for catching game such as a snare or trap 110.29

engross write in a character appropriate to legal documents 215.38

enlevement kidnapping of a woman or child, an abduction 15.3

enow enough 273.26 etc.

ensure guarantee against 46.13 (see note); guarantee a sum of money 59.31

enthusiast one who holds extravagant or especially devout religious feelings 4.39 etc.

epidermis outer layer of skin 17.29

episcopacy government of the church by bishops 178.35

equals for 69.15 see note

equipage carriage and horses with the attendant servants 9.13, 329.18, 455.16

Erastian, Yerastian pertaining to Erastus or his doctrines 90.17 etc. (see note)

eremite recluse, hermit 137.10

ergo *Latin* therefore 383.28

errant travelling, itinerant, often in search of adventures 231.14

Esculapius Roman god of medicine, *figuratively* any doctor 333.37

Estates the Scottish Parliament 193.9 (see note to 21.41)

event outcome 59.40, 192.24, 228.10, 305.21

evince establish, prove by argument 99.39 etc.

ewe-milk made of milk from ewes 346.2

examinant one who conducts a judicial examination 121.35, 122.29, 122.43

exauctorate relieved of authority 39.30

exciseman officer employed to collect duties and prevent the breaking of the excise laws 37.27, 326.14

execrable deserving to be cursed, abominable 347.10–11

execration uttering of curses 31.16; utter detestation, abhorrence 137.20, 314.27

exercise *noun* family worship, prayers 86.18 etc.; sermon or discourse delivered to a Presbytery by one of its members 395.38

exercise *verb* expound the Scriptures 88.27

exoner free from a responsibility 39.22

express message or letter sent by special messenger(s) 63.38 etc.

extenuated shrunken, emaciated 247.15

extenuation impoverishment 5.22–23

extrajudicial, extra-judicial lying outside the proceedings in court, forming no part of the case before the court 213.38, 214.2, 214.42

eye, ey *dialect* yes 254.39 etc.

eyrie the nests of birds of prey, often situated in lofty positions 443.7

fa' fall 114.39, 243.21, 246.39, 450.37

face *military* turn the face in a particular direction 289.17

faced trimmed, adorned 196.17

facetious witty, humorous 3.11

facility easiness to be led or persuaded to good or bad, compliance 202.10

fact crime 23.43, 37.33

factor person appointed by the court to manage the property of a minor 46.22 (see notes to 46.21 and 46.22); agent or steward who has management of an estate for its owner 368.35

faculty Faculty of Advocates, the collective title of the members of the Scottish bar 18.35; department of learning such as law and medicine 68.26

fag hard work, drudgery 264.35

fain gladly, willingly 126.21 etc.; glad 258.37, 346.1

fair *of water* clear, pure 255.37, 361.15, 362.25

faithfu' faithful 173.14, 173.15, 274.39, 355.42

fal-lal showy, affected, foppish 223.40

fallow fellow 78.20, 144.13, 154.1

fame reputation 59.22 etc.

fan *Gaelic English* when 421.18

fancy-farm experimental farm 378.6

fand found 69.18, 123.26

far-awa distant 114.35, 354.16

farder *Jeanie's letter* further 349.31

fareweel farewell 225.18

farthing quarter of an old penny, coin of very small value 75.7, 259.42

fascinate cast a spell over a person or animal with a look, especially said of serpents 84.20

fascination casting a spell, especially that attributed to serpents 84.24, 145.23

fash *noun* fuss, bother 278.18, 325.18, 359.27, 359.32

fash *verb* trouble, bother, inconvenience 39.35 etc.; meddle, disturb 445.16

fasherie trouble, annoyance 226.7

fashion form, pretence, show
112.11, 112.12; for 236.41 see note
fashious troublesome, annoying,
irksome 276.10
fast fast asleep 270.25 (see note)
fastness place not easily forced,
stronghold 426.18
fat *Gaelic English* what 395.5, 402.19
fathom length covered by the outstretched arms 299.16
fatted fattened up ready for killing
386.17, 401.2
fauld fold 186.7
fause false 112.32, 314.24, 366.16
faut fault 47.13, 189.11, 350.23
feared afraid 144.5 etc.
fearfu' fearful, terrifying, frightening 182.14, 186.9, 376.21
fearna don't fear 223.10
feature creature 168.32
febrile indicative of fever, feverish
367.20
feckless weak, paltry 369.5–6
feint pretence, stratagem 270.20
fence *Scots Law* open the proceedings of a court with a formula forbidding disorderly interruption or
obstructive behaviour 195.33,
195.34 (see note to 195.32–34)
fermentation agitation, excitement
304.24
fery *Gaelic English* very 461.1
festivous festive 3.11
fetter-bolt kind of spring padlock
265.5
fey behaving as if bewitched and with
a peculiar, elated behaviour often
thought to portend death 29.35
fickle puzzle, perplex 176.5
field-meeting religious meeting
held in the open air during Covenanting times 136.4
fiftie *Jeanie's letter* fifty 351.26
fifty-ane fifty-one, the year 1751
450.31
file¹ for 69.19 see note
file² small body of men, often two
soldiers walking together 119.15
finisher for 124.39 and 145.39 see
notes
firelock musket furnished with a
lock which produced sparks 27.32
firth arm of the sea 22.39 etc.;
wooded country 459.30
fiscal for 144.27 and 164.11 see

procurator-fiscal
fisicyian *Jeanie's letter* physician
349.35
fit¹ foot 168.27
fit² *dialect* conflict, struggle 286.2
flag flag-stone 230.8
flambeau torch, especially one made
of several thick wicks dipped in wax
53.33
flang flung 220.10
flash send a rush of water down
243.24
flat¹ for 267.34 see note
flat² stupid, slow-witted 289.4
flax fibres of the flax plant 124.42,
466.1, 467.3
flee fly 235.5, 395.34
flesh-eater see note to 275.20–21
flesh-pot luxuries regarded with regret 255.36 (see note), 356.19
flight mounting or soaring of the intellect or imagination 112.15
fling dance 88.32, 88.34, 88.42
flint fragment of hard stone used to
kindle the powder in some kinds of
musket or gun 439.3
fliskmahoy woman who gives herself airs 438.1
flit remove from one place to another, to change one's dwelling
place, depart 70.11, 187.26
flitting removal 303.37, 376.18
flock-bed bed with a mattress
stuffed with coarse tufts and scraps
of wool or cotton 153.10, 439.19
flounder small flat-fish 203.16
flow-moss wet peat-bog, morass
109.30
fly-coach carriage, stagecoach 8.7
flying for 103.7 see note
fodder *verb* feed 86.12
foive *dialect* five 360.15
fo'k folk, people 145.38, 363.14,
445.26
foot-board small board at the back of
a carriage on which the footman
stands 352.24
foot-mantle garment worn by
women when riding to protect their
clothes 40.9
foot-pad highwayman on foot
261.15
foranent right opposite to, facing
245.24
forbear ancestor 246.9, 350.38,

351.16, 429.23

forbye besides, in addition to 40.9 etc.; except 235.4

fore for 350.34 see note

fore-bar in the old Court of Session, the bar at which advocates pleaded causes of first instance 43.6

forehammer heavy hammer with which a blacksmith first strikes, sledge-hammer 54.31

foreman principal juror who presides at the deliberations of the jury and gives their verdict to the court 215.31

forgather gather together, assemble 219.14

forgi'e, forgie forgive 187.3, 250.36, 250.39

forlorn-hope picked body of men chosen to begin an attack, storming-party 65.28

formalist one over-concerned about legal forms 90.38, 110.7

formula set of words in which something is defined, stated and declared 404.14 (see note)

forpit *dry measure* the fourth part of a peck, ½ gall. or 2.27 litres, equivalent to 3½ or 1¾ lbs (1.5 or 0.75 kilos) depending on the commodity 37.26, 78.29

fou drunk 26.22, 345.2

found¹ for 110.29 see note

found² establish one's argument upon 111.8

frae from 1.8 etc.

frankincense for 376.32 see note

fraught furnished, filled 104.26

free-booter one who goes about in search of plunder 124.16, 466.22–23

freeholder *Scots Law* person who before 1832 could elect or be elected as a member of parliament by virtue of holding lands direct from the crown over a certain value 344.37

free-living self-indulgent, following one's own appetites 144.17

fretted chafed, worn 29.29

friend *noun* relative, blood-relation 114.35, 147.18, 353.22

friend *verb* befriend 190.9

frizz curl 434.24

front confront 224.30

fry crowd of young or unimportant persons 286.3

fu' full 184.28 etc.

fuff smoke, emit puffs of smoke 403.40

fule¹ foul, dirty 87.35, 274.10, 362.3

fule² silly, half-witted 157.17 etc.

fund found 169.38; find 196.9

funds public funds, stock of the national debt considered as an investment 428.15

furbelow flounce, showy trimming 281.4

furlong measurement roughly equivalent to an eighth of a mile (200m) 395.14

fury ferocious or malignant woman 261.35

furze spikey evergreen plant with yellow flowers often found on wasteland, whins 391.39

fusee light musket 31.28

fusileer man armed with a light musket 29.18

fustle *Gaelic English* whistle 465.25

fustler *Gaelic English* whistler 465.25

fyke move about restlessly, fidget 88.34

gab being able to talk well 116.6 (see note)

gabble talk rapidly and unintelligibly 147.29, 218.5

gae¹ go 40.8 etc.

gae² give 151.6

gaffer elderly rustic, below the rank of 'master' 264.26 etc.

gain be victorious in 72.29

gait goat 437.22

gaitt brat 280.6

gala belonging to festive occasions, characterised by finery 459.20

gall harass or annoy, render sore in spirit 174.4, 391.29

gall *figuratively* bitterness 228.26

gallant man of fashion or pleasure 95.36 etc.

gallipot small earthen glazed pot often used for ointments and medicines 428.35

gallon English measure of liquid capacity, 4.55 litres 258.4

gallows-heels heels which have escaped, or are destined for, the gallows 267.23–24

game spirited 301.23, 361.32

game-arm lame arm 254.34

gaming-table table used for the purposes of playing at games of chance, gambling 316.6

gammon bottom piece of a flitch of bacon including the hind leg 289.26–27

gane gone 78.39 etc.

gang go 41.29 etc.

ganging for 450.33 see note

gar make 115.8 etc.; order 150.15; for 285.33 see note to 285.33–34

gardy-loo, gardyloo for 243.28 see note; the cry which servants make as they throw dirty water etc. from the windows, the water etc. itself 347.17

gare-brained crazy, hare-brained 286.10

garter badge of the highest order of English knighthood 331.8 (see note), 352.26

gate way, manner, method 87.4 etc.

gauger exciseman 37.27, 146.13, 300.30

gaunt yawn 87.13, 403.3

gawky awkward, clumsy 68.43

gawsie handsome, imposing looking 150.38; large, ample 251.13

gay very 110.2; for 112.31, 147.41, and 460.31 see respective notes

gazing for 112.13 see note

gear possessions, wealth, moveable property, effects 70.38 etc.

gee for 164.28 see note

Gehennah for 355.7 see note

generaliter Latin in general, in general terms 111.4

genius spirit, prevailing character 323.43; natural ability or capacity, intellectual power of a superior kind 329.32

gentile heathen, pagan 293.35

gentles people of good birth, families of rank and distinction 37.22, 75.31, 173.17

ghaist ghost, spirit 265.41, 408.36

ghostly spiritual 70.19

gie, gee give 27.30 etc.

gif Gaelic English give 465.31

gif-gaf give and take 147.4

gig light, two-wheeled, one horsed carriage 19.5; light, narrow boat adapted for rowing or sailing 397.37, 406.36, 407.3, 411.11, 435.1

gill measure for liquids equivalent to about a fourth of a pint (0.14 litres) 258.10, 404.24

gillie male attendant of a Highland chief 444.25

gilpie lively young girl 39.43

gin if 69.19, 70.17, 238.20

girdle circular iron plate usually with a hooped handle and suspended over the fire to bake scones, oatcakes, pancakes etc. 265.6, 265.8

girn grimace 190.19

glad gladden 78.41, 344.34

glaik for 112.14 see note

glancing-glass piece of glass or mirror used by children to reflect the sun's rays, figuratively vain person, show-off 112.13 (see note)

glebe piece of land allowed to a parish minister in addition to his salary 384.31, 454.30

gled, gledd for 46.16 see note; common kite 142.32, 159.30

gleg for 46.16 see note; lively, sprightly 84.4; keen 87.12; quickwitted, sharp in perception 118.15, 160.7

gleg-tongued quick- or smoothtongued 110.3

glibbe thick mass of hair worn on the forehead and over the eyes formerly worn by the Irish 443.12

gliff moment, instant 43.5, 170.25

glim gleam, faint streak of light 270.26

glorify advance the glory of God by faithful action or suffering 194.18

glower stare, gaze intently 87.11

godly pious, devoutly religious 145.7, 262.39, 322.16, 384.15

goldsmith worker in gold; as banker 236.3 (see note)

goodman see gudeman

goot Gaelic English good 459.28, 460.19

goot-morrow Gaelic English goodmorrow, good-morning 459.27, 459.28

Goshen see note to 355.12

goss-hawk large, short-winged hawk 168.5, 354.24

gossip friend 222.28

gothic style of architecture used in western Europe from the 12th to the 16th century 48.8 etc.

gotten got 37.11 etc.

gousty dreary, desolate, bare, cheerless 123.34

goutte drop, especially of medicine 113.38

gowan general name for several wild flowers, either yellow or white with yellow centres, such as buttercups and daisies 377.20

gowany full of wild flowers, especially daisies 398.7

gowd gold 236.24, 326.19, 420.25

gowden golden 170.30

gown-tail tail or hem of a gown or dress 154.40

gowpen *Scots Law* gratuity or additional payment allowed to a miller's servant 68.8, 124.43

grace for 413.30 see note

graie *Jeanie's letter* grey 350.31

grain little bit 158.27

graith harness, tackle, gear, especially for ploughing 40.8, 41.14, 42.27

gramash type of leggings worn to protect the legs from mud and wet 375.10

grand-dame grandmother 74.16, 75.1

grande-dame *French* great lady, lady of rank and dignified bearing 336.41

grandsire grandfather 323.2

grass for 110.42, 110.43 see note to 110.42

grass-holm low-lying level grassland on the banks of a river or stream 429.7

grat cried, wept 141.4, 188.19

grated with a grating 55.34, 57.21, 226.15

grazier one who grazes or feeds cattle for market 251.10, 363.10

great-coat large, heavy over-coat 10.18, 10.23, 50.39

Grecian-shaped see note to 84.36–37

gree¹ agree, live in harmony 170.20, 243.26, 430.9

gree² supremacy, first place 265.7

green-wood wood or forest when in leaf 142.34, 159.32

greeshoch glowing fire of red-hot embers without flame 460.34

greet cry, weep 44.25 etc.

grenadier soldier who threw grenades, usually one of the tallest and finest men in the regiment 119.15

grewsome ugly, repulsive 185.39

grey-beard large jug or pitcher for holding alcohol made of stone or earthen-ware, and with a handle and a spout 436.7, 461.14

grey-fowl female of the black grouse 110.31

grey-peard *Gaelic English* for 436.27 see **grey-beard**

grey-stone type of sandstone used as a kind of flagged roofing stone 229.30

griffin fabulous animal usually represented as having the head and wings of an eagle and the body and hind quarters of a lion 83.39

grindstane grindstone, millstone 458.4–5 (see note)

grip seize, catch, arrest 154.28

gripe grip, grasp 425.27

grips bonds, fetters 155.26

grit great 37.6, 83.18, 118.8

grot groat, fragment, particle 258.4 (see note)

ground-officer employee who supervises the practical administration of the land and farming of an estate 68.12

ground-swell deep or heavy rolling of the sea caused by a distant storm or disturbance 35.6

gruel light, liquid porridge-like food 258.4

grund ground 106.5

gruntler young pig 262.15

guard-soldier soldier who acts as a guard 167.35

gud-day good-day 167.6 (see note)

gude good 27.14 etc.

Gude God 82.24

gud-e'en, gudeen good-evening 167.6 (see note), 263.7

gudeman, goodman master or head of a household, a husband 76.15 etc.

gudeness goodness 188.26

gudes goods, wares, property 37.30, 44.4, 239.24

gudesire goodsire, grandfather 322.5, 322.11, 322.12

gudewife, gude-wife, goodwife female head of a household, mistress, wife 41.28 etc.

guide take care, protect, treat 79.9 etc.

guinea English gold coin worth £1 1s. (£1.05) 61.30 etc.

gulley large knife 159.19, 261.30

guse goose 110.42, 110.43, 226.12

gutter-blood base-born or low-bred person 167.23–24

gwone *dialect* gone 256.12

gybe pass, license 226.1

gyte mad, insane 221.37

ha' have 286.32

habiliment outfit, dress 255.12, 372.29

hack horse let out for hire, a worn out horse 249.14

hackney horse of middle size and quality used for ordinary riding 242.2

hackney-coach four-wheeled coach kept for hire, drawn by two horses 324.43 etc.

hadden held 160.3

hae have 37.12 etc.

haena haven't 150.28 etc.

haet *literally* have it; for 147.16, 203.10 see notes

haffet, haffit part of the head above and in front of the ear, temple, cheek 375.13; for 430.4 see note

hafflin half-grown, young 102.42

haft *noun* place of abode 168.38

haft *verb* establish, locate 351.38 (see note to 351.38–39)

hagbut early kind of portable firearm 110.29 (see note)

haill, hale whole, entire 45.4 etc.; well, whole 353.14

halbert military weapon consisting of a combination of a spear and a battle-axe 52.26

half-bound *of a book* having the spine and corners in leather 17.12

half-crown silver coin worth around an eighth of a pound sterling 150.12

half-hangit half-hung 148.31–32, 362.39

half-play-day half-holiday 245.40–41

halk hawk 111.16

hallan inner wall, partition or screen in a cottage between the door and the fireplace to act as a shield from the draught of the door 400.39

hall-Bible large bible used in domestic worship 294.32–33

halloo exclamation to incite dogs to the chase, call attention at a distance etc. 161.37, 164.2, 445.1

halt limp 78.39

hame home 41.27 etc.

Hamiltonian for 176.6 see note to 176.6–7

hammer see note to 85.14

hammerman smith or worker in metal 265.4, 265.6–7

hand-waled chosen or selected by hand, hand-picked 94.22

hangit hung 46.12 etc.

ha'nt *dialect* haven't 269.26

hap happen, chance 4.30; chance, fate 140.28

hapnyworth half-penny-worth (0.21p), a small amount 325.20

hard-drinker one who drinks much and often 18.4

hard-set determined, obstinate 117.21

harken listen, give attention 140.20, 140.24

Harleyite for 176.7 see note to 176.6–7

harns brains 158.15

harst harvest 117.36

hartshorn, harteshorn *Jeanie's letters* drops made from slicing the horn of a hart, formerly the main source of ammonia 251.13–14, 307.14, 361.15

hasna hasn't 44.17 etc.

hatchet-face narrow and very sharp face 254.34

hatchment square or lozenge-shaped tablet exhibiting the armorial bearings of a dead person affixed to the front of a dwelling-place 230.14

haud hold 89.10 etc.; keep to 160.35

Havannah cigar of a kind made in Havana or the tobacco from which these are made 326.13

havings manners 170.21

hawker man who goes from place to place selling his goods or selling them in the street 14.21, 220.34

hawkit *of cattle* having a white face or one spotted or streaked with white

350.17. 377.25

hay-band rope of twisted hay used to bind up bundle of hay 415.25

hazing frightening 137.41

head-band band around the top of trousers 255.10

heads chief points of a discourse or argument 463.29

heal spiritual wealth, well-being, health 376.6; recovered, in good health 415.17 (see note)

healsomeness wholesomeness 79.26

hearer *Scots* one who listens to a sermon or a particular preacher 110.23

heart-burning unexpressed discontent, embittered state of mind not openly expressed 172.16

heart-plague heart-ache 386.25

hearts-ease name applied to a number of plants, such as the pansy, *figuratively* peace of mind, tranquillity 278.43–79.1

heathen applied to people or races whose religion is neither Christian nor Jewish 45.33

heave raise, lift up 330.21

Hebe goddess of youth and spring, *figuratively* youthful 84.38

Hecate Persephone, the goddess of the underworld 263.13

heels for 79.24 see note

hegh exclamation akin to a sigh 82.18, 169.42

height high or lofty rising ground 159.36

heir *Jeanie's letter* here 350.35

hellebore plant used for medicinal purposes, especially for the treatment of mental disease 5.2

hellicat light-headed, rompish 170.10, 269.42

hell-raker scoundrel or rascal 280.7

hempen made of hemp 265.18

hempie mischievous boy or girl 431.15

hereditary for 17.20, 394.6 see notes to 17.20 and 378.34–35

heritable capable of being inherited, connected with heritable property 236.26, 428.13; for 378.34, 465.15 see notes to 17.20 and 378.34–35

heritor for 288.15 and 344.39 see note to 288.15

hermitage habitation of a hermit

137.9, 162.40

herse hoarse 265.21

hersell, hersel herself 44.17 etc.

her'ship plundering, especially the carrying off of cattle 378.19 (see note to 378.19–21)

Hesper the evening star 402.26 (see note)

hest bidding, command 139.4

het hot 70.17 etc.

hey-day flush, full-bloom 11.20

hieland Highland 243.32 etc.

Hielander Highlander 112.33

hielandman Highland man, Highlander 373.33, 379.24, 386.14, 403.36

high superior, elevated 423.15

high-church for 419.37 see note

high-dried, hie-dried *Jeanie's letters* highly dried snuff 320.11, 350.41

high-flyer fast stage-coach 7.25

high-gravel see note to 281.29–30

himsell himself 41.20 etc.

hind female deer 142.35, 159.33

hing hang 45.18 etc.

hinny, hinnie honey, a term of endearment 89.1 etc.

hint occasion, opportunity 165.19

hire reward 210.3

hist sound made to urge on an animal 259.4

hither on this side 252.9

hitt to 'take up' a man in the game of backgammon 416.37

hizzy, hussey, huzzy young woman, servant girl 153.7, 187.40, 219.7, 413.19

ho *dialect* her 361.38, 362.20; his 361.38

hobby-horse stick with a horse's head used as a child's toy 48.26

hog-lam hog-lamb, a lamb before the first shearing 252.8

hogshead large cask of varying capacity 191.5; for 270.40 see note

Hollands grain spirit manufactured in Holland, usually gin 255.8, 255.22, 267.38–39

hollow cry out loud, shout 160.36, 164.19

homologate ratify or approve a preceding event or action 384.9

honour credit, reputation, good name 95.36

hoose house 370.31

horn projection like a horn at each corner of the altar in the Jewish temple 58.13, 354.43 and see note to 58.12–13

horse for 68.17 and 219.42 see respective notes

horse-jockey one hired to ride a horse in a race 122.7

horse-match race between two horses 229.17–18

horse-milliner one who supplies ornamental trappings for horses 115.15

hose stockings 252.19

hou *dialect* how 362.11

hough hollow behind the knee-joint, the thigh 88.34

hould *dialect* hold 421.41, 462.9

house-end end or gable of a house 116.16

househald household 250.33–34

housewife pocket-case for needles, pins, thread etc. 341.20

housewifery domestic economy, housekeeping 389.37

housing trappings, ornamental cloth to cover a horse 41.26

hout *exclamation* och, come, tut 155.17 etc.; in the phrase *hout tout* come come, tut tut 112.7

houts *exclamation* used to express annoyance or in remonstrance at another's opinion 41.37

how hollow, valley 440.24

Howdenite for 176.7 see note to 176.6–7

howdie midwife 45.7

howff *noun* favourite abode, meeting place 147.17

howff *verb* frequent, lodge, loiter 154.8

howl owl 103.6

howsomever nevertheless 285.38

humourist humorous talker 42.29, 164.42

hund *Jeanie's letter* hound 251.4

hunder hundred 236.25, 266.4

hundred-weight measure of weight equal to 112 lbs (51 kgm) 59.34, 67.29

huntin' *Jeanie's letter* hunting 350.11

hunting-field field or ground on which a hunt is taking place 64.7

hurle convey in a wheeled vehicle 167.38

hush-money money paid to prevent exposure 420.24

hussy, huzzy housewife, a case for needles, thread etc. 344.26, 351.20

huzza cheer, shout of exaltation 57.37, 405.9

ice frozen confection 449.42

ictus for 242.33 etc. see note to 242.33–243.1

ideal imaginary 359.23

idolater worshipper of idols or images 178.8

ilk, ilka each, every 114.37, 114.38 etc.; for 150.5, 150.35, 150.37 see note to 150.5; for 110.27 see note

ill-starred unfortunate, unlucky 112.17

impannel *Scots Law* choose the members of a jury from an official list 203.31

impeach challenge, call into question 4.26

importunity repeated request 46.1, 390.34

imposition tax, levy 177.32

impost tax, duty, levy 22.36, 177.39

imposthume cyst, swelling 387.37

imposture fraud 14.39; deception 192.4, 421.38

imprecation curse, oath 28.35, 398.25

improve take advantage of, avail oneself of 73.43

impute reckon against, charge as a sin [by God] 310.34

inartificial not constructed with art, clumsy, plain 229.29

incarcerate imprison 19.9, 120.20–21, 166.28

inchoat just begun, in an early stage 39.28

inclose *Scots Law* shut up a witness in a room apart to prevent unauthorised communication with others and hearing earlier evidence 195.36, 195.37, 196.4

incontinent straightaway, without delay 195.32

incumbent *adjective* resting as a duty on a person 80.32, 227.38

incumbent *noun* person holding an ecclesiastical living 287.36 etc.

indented bound or engaged 467.18

independency system of ecclesiastical organisation in which each congregation is independent of any other authority 79.14 (see note to 65.31)

independent *church government* one supporting the system of independency 65.31 (see note), 71.19, 71.31, 388.2

index hand of a clock or watch 82.29

indicium *Latin* sign, token 47.2

indict charge, accuse 44.33, 198.19

inditer writer, composer 4.13

inductive inducing, cajoling 210.42

indulgence permission given to Presbyterian ministers in Scotland to return to their parishes or to preach lawfully 181.27 (see note to 181.25), 388.3 (see note)

inferior lower in position, situated below 243.19

infidel non-Christian 174.31–32

ingan onion 110.6

ingenuous innocent, guileless 201.13

ingine genius, ingenuity 112.14

Ingland England 71.43, 219.39–40

ingle-side fireside 159.13

iniquity sin and wickedness in general 174.13, 270.41, 349.38, 412.6

inside *noun* passenger sitting in the inside of coach 7.7, 8.5, 9.43

insight household goods and furniture 68.14

insnaring something which entangles a person in difficulties 386.25

instanter *Law* immediately, forthwith 195.32

institutes for 42.35 see note to 42.34; for 42.37 see note

instriment *Jeanie's letter* instrument 350.13

instruct *Scots Law* prove clearly 201.7, 201.9

in't in it 108.39

interlocutor *Scots Law* interim decision by the Court of Session 115.35, 199.6, 203.18, 213.13; see also note to 31.40–41

interposition intervention 318.3

interpreter expounder, interpreter of religious texts 279.16 etc. (see note to 279.16)

interrogatory *Law* question, put to an accused person or witness 116.10 etc.; examination 210.27

intestine civil, domestic 317.15

intill into 170.28, 173.22, 203.15, 370.1

in-town see note to 124.44

intromit intermeddle, interfere 42.10

intrusion presentation of a minister to a parish in the Church of Scotland against the wishes of the congregation 384.27

iron-crow crow-bar made of iron often with one end bent or sharpened 54.18–19

iron-staunchel iron bar used as the grating for a door or window 60.18

I'se I shall 45.2 etc.

isna isn't 169.41 etc.

Italian italic 243.1; type of handwriting which is similar to italic printing 417.38

ither other 124.2 etc.

itsell itself 173.24, 186.8, 189.9, 344.26

jabber talk rapidly and indistinctly, prattle 260.40

jack-sauce saucy or impudent fellow 295.25

Jacobite supporter of the Stewart dynasty after 1688 28.22 etc.

jacobitical, jacobitically having Jacobite principles 194.5–6, 419.37

jagg prick 79.31

jaud, jade contemptuous name for a woman, perverse woman 123.26, 148.33, 234.16, 413.21

jail-bird one who has been long or often in jail 123.31, 268.29

jark seal 226.1, 260.18, 261.24

jee move 158.28

jess *falconry* small strap fastened round each of the legs of a hawk 231.4

jilt contemptuous term for a woman or young girl, often one who has lost her chastity 264.27

jink trick, frolic, particularly one involving eluding someone 271.14

jo, joe dear 120.21, 151.25, 169.39, 184.17; lover, sweetheart 162.9, 276.23

jobber one who improperly uses public office for private or party advantage 318.13

jockey-coat great-coat formerly worn by horse dealers 122.10

jorram Gaelic boat-song 408.1

journeyman one who is qualified in a trade 19.4, 54.6

jow ring, toll 402.24

judge-carle judge-chap 222.24–25

judgment-day day of God's final judgment, doomsday 197.16

judicature church court 171.36; court of justice 175.26, 181.41, 415.37

junketting merry-making, banqueting 397.32

jurisconsult, juris-consultus one learned and expert in law 15.32, 243.3

jurisdiction for 17.20, 378.34–35, 394.7, 465.16 see note to 17.20

jurisprudence system of law and justice 16.29 etc.

just righteous in the sight of God, justified 25.8, 88.43, 114.2, 163.31

Justiciary *Scots Law* for 31.41 etc. see note to 31.41

justification see note to 149.35

kail, kale broth, soup made with vegetables 45.41, 404.1

kail-blade leaf of kail, a green leafy vegetable 158.16–17

kail-worm caterpillar 103.41

kain payment in kind made by a tenant as part of his rent 68.7

kale-yard kitchen-garden, plot where kale and other vegetables are grown, 220.6

kame comb 430.4

keep hold 176.16

keepit, keppit kept 124.12 etc.

kelpie water demon who lured people to their death by drowning 32.28

ken¹ know 37.16 etc.

ken² house, especially one where thieves and disreputable characters lodge 262.29

kend well-known, familiar 352.6

kennel mean dwelling 263.2

kenspeckle conspicuous 249.39–40, 362.38

kepp guard, keep watch 160.38

kickin kicking 220.18, 220.20

kickit kicked 220.15

kidnapper one who stole children to

provide servants or labourers for American plantations 464.33

kidnapping act of stealing children to provide servants and labourers for American plantations 463.17, 464.15

killing-time for 390.33–34 see note to 174.36

kindly native-born 40.16, 220.3

kine cows 386.17

king's-evil scrofula, a disease with glandular swellings possibly related to tuberculosis, formerly believed to be curable by the king's touch 415.43

king-cup buttercup 377.20

kintra country 394.35, 403.37, 421.15

kirk; Kirk *noun* church 90.13 etc.; the established Church of Scotland 45.20 etc.

kirkit churched, i.e. to attend church for the first time after a wedding 381.33

kirk-session lowest court in a Presbyterian church consisting of the minister and elders of a parish, exercising the duties of church government within that parish 338.29 etc.

kirk-time time of church service 281.21

kirk-treasurer treasurer of a church 144.13

kirkward towards the church, grave-yard 366.31

kirk-wark matters relating to the church 79.20

kirk-yard church-yard, grave-yard 87.23, 230.16, 254.7, 265.39

kirn-milk buttermilk 248.41

kissing-string woman's bonnet or hat string tied beneath the chin with the ends hanging loose 401.33

kittle changeable, unreliable 108.29; capricious, fickle 184.33, 344.7

knaveship quantity of corn payable as a levy to a miller's servant 68.8

knowe-head hill-top 402.23

knowing shrewd, cunning, acute 43.31 etc.

koind *dialect* kind 289.2

krames merchant's booth or stall; for 48.18, 449.29 (see note to 48.18)

kye cows, cattle 223.34, 350.16,

355.30, 398.10

kylevine lead [of a pencil] 247.28, 351.18

kythe appear, seem 103.39

laced ornamented or trimmed with braids of lace 75.19 etc.

lading load 235.6

læse-majesty, lese-majesty treason, offence against sovereign authority 108.43, 116.33

laigh lying below the rest of the building, lower 243.23

laigh-house apartment lying below the rest of the house, frequently used as a shop 243.19

laik play, sport 295.9

laird landed proprietor, the owner of an estate or farm 41.19 etc.

lamour amber 116.28

landward country, rustic 325.25

lane self 40.10, 90.7, 236.28, 265.34

lang long 45.25 etc.

lang-gown judge, advocate 109.12

lang-head shrewd, sagacious person 109.12

lang-shankit long-handled 404.1

langsyne long ago 246.9, 352.3

lass young woman, girl 43.2 etc.

lassie little girl, young lass 75.21 etc.

lassitude weariness 271.3

lathy thin, long 443.10

latitudinarian one tolerant of free-thought on religious questions, particularly one in the 17th century who, while attached to the forms of the Episcopal church, regarded them with little interest 94.21

laugh for 252.20 see note

lavrock skylark 142.33, 159.31

lawing bill for food and drink supplied in a public house 258.6, 258.7

Lawlands Lowlands 123.1

law-latin Latin used by lawyers 42.1

law-work theology based on Mosaic law implying formal morality rather than evangelical religion 103.42

lay business, pursuit 145.37, 225.43, 260.20 (see respective notes)

lay for 89.15 see note

lay-patronage right of a landowner to appoint the parish minister 383.31 (see note to 167.8)

lead *noun* action of playing the first card in a round or game of cards 14.15

lead *Scots Law* call or produce evidence etc. in court proceedings 207.35, 213.17 (see note)

leading *adjective* for 17.39 and 211.2 see notes

leading *noun* carting, specifically the carrying of harvested grain or hay from the field to the stackyard 79.20

leal true, veracious 142.15; honest, faithful, adhering to duty 276.18, 358.19

lea-land fallow land, grassy land 256.20

learn teach 186.37

leasure leisure 244.1

leaven any tempering or modifying element, particularly an agency which produces inward change 133.3; sort, character 398.21

leddy lady 246.18 etc.

leddyship ladyship 328.35 etc.

lee lie 87.10, 150.36

leech physician 68.28

leet list of candidates 18.14

legalist one who adheres to the law rather than the gospel, and who tends towards belief in salvation by works and deeds 110.7

legalized imbued with the legal spirit 90.38

leggins leggings, strong overgarment used as protection for the legs in bad weather 375.10

legislature law-making body 166.21 etc.

L'Envoy author's parting words, postscript 468.1

lese-majesty, læse-majesty treason, offence against sovereign authority 108.43, 116.33

lesson reading from the Bible at a church service 284.1, 290.40

let leave 273.19, 273.20

letters for 144.35 see note

Levee assembly held in the early afternoon by a sovereign at which only men attend 334.21; morning assembly held by a person of distinction 445.40

leveret young hare 404.39

Levite subordinate official of the Temple in Jerusalem 23.36 (see note)

libel *Scots Law* formal statement of

the grounds of prosecution 110.36 etc.

licence printed or written permission to preach 74.26, 77.32

license grant a licence to preach 45.21

liege loyal subject, those owing allegiance to a superior 108.41, 134.33

lift[1] helping hand, boost 146.36

lift[2] sky, heavens 170.27

light *noun* enlightenment 93.16

light *adjective* wanton, unchaste 233.6

light-headed frivolous 103.33, 166.32; in a delirium, fever 205.42; giddy, disordered in the head 292.12

lights lighted up portion of a picture 102.8; doctrine 218.26, 454.36; knowledge, insight 334.39, 386.33

lightsome light-hearted, cheerful 159.29, 278.10

lilt sing sweetly and in a low clear voice 86.39; sing cheerfully 396.12

limmer wild undisciplined girl 88.23; undisciplined, impudent female 149.25 etc.; woman of disreputable, loose character 233.6; rogue, scoundrel 460.32

link torch made of tow and pitch used for lighting people along the street 54.40, 61.7

linn waterfall, precipice 444.21

lip for 94.23 and 199.19 see notes

liperty *Gaelic English* liberty 465.12

lippen trust 439.2

litigant person engaged in a law-suit or dispute 12.10

livery uniform worn by servants of a particular house 288.37, 328.8, 352.25, 435.16

living ecclesiastical position as parish minister and the income pertaining to it 287.16 etc.

loaded weighted with lead 122.13

loan part of the farm ground which leads to or adjoins the house 232.40

Lochaber-axe kind of pole-axe with a hook on the other side of the head to grasp an opponent or aid in climbing walls etc. 28.5–6, 55.3, 443.30

lock lockman's position, jailer 191.1

lock small quantity or handful of meal taken by the miller's assistant as a levy for grinding 68.8, 124.37, 124.41, 124.43

lock-man public executioner, jailer 124.1

lock-up jail-keeping 124.22

loe, loo love 189.16, 189.17,

loife *dialect* life 360.15

long for 85.14 see note

loof upturned palm of the hand 39.11; paw or foot of an animal 274.8, 274.9

lookit looked 150.39, 236.23, 236.26

loose unyoke a horse from 82.21

loose-bodied loose-fitting 50.39

loot let 381.32

lordship land belonging to a lord, territory under his jurisdiction 379.17

loss lose 110.1

lounder[1] thrash, whack 168.42

lounder[2] quieter, more restrained 206.27

low flame 361.41

low-browed having a low and dark entrance 40.43, 221.42

Lowden Lothian 350.23, 353.22

lown scoundrel 112.32; rogue, fellow 267.30

Luckenbooths locked booths, the area in Edinburgh where the merchants had their shops 28.12 etc. (see note to 28.12)

luckie familiar term of address to an elderly woman 45.7, 243.26

luckie-dad grandfather 415.41–42

lucre advantage 142.7; profit 387.15, 454.32

lud lord 370.32

lug ear 108.42, 427.21

lugger small vessel with two or three masts and square sails 270.31, 391.40, 457.41

lum smoke-vent, chimney 461.3

lum-head chimney-top 239.29

lure device used by falconers to recall hawks 231.4

lusty stout, fat 24.12; hearty, abundant 40.12

lute *Jeanie's letter* let 251.38

lying-dog setter 110.28, 111.17

lying-in childbed, maternity 44.42

ma may 148.2; my 254.41, 360.15

macer *Scots Law* official who keeps order in a court of law, usher in the High Court 41.40 etc.

macerate cause the flesh to waste

away by fasting 74.42

maceration mortification, process of wearing or wasting away the body 463.1

MacMillanite follower of John Macmillan; for 176.1 and 176.6 see notes to 176.1 and 176.6–7

magg pilfer coal so that the carters can sell it on their own account 381.32

maggot for 403.34 see note

magistracy body of magistrates 33.33, 104.6, 173.12, 183.29

magnum bottle containing two quarts (2.3 litres) of wine 18.8

mahometan follower of Islam 227.22 (see note)

maiden-fame virtue 197.21

mail[1] stain, discolour 158.9

mail[2] travelling bag 372.12

mail[3] rent, payment in money or kind for a lease 68.7, 355.28

mail-coach stage-coach used primarily for carrying mail 7.24 etc.

mailing rent paid for a tenancy of land 70.40

main for 67.1 see note

main-spring principal coiled spring of a watch 82.29

mair more 37.32 etc.

maist most 108.40 etc.

maister master 351.14, 351.27, 451.31

maistry mastery, having the upper hand 403.38

mak make 152.39 etc.

maksna for 115.25 see note

malignant term applied by English parliamentarians to royalists 1641–60, and by Covenanters to their ecclesiastical opponents 71.36

mammie mummy, mother 263.15

mammon love of money 70.23 (see note)

manner for 234.4 see note.

manor-house mansion, dwelling of a landed proprietor 68.29

manse in Scotland, the house provided for a minister of a parish 288.14 etc.

man-sworn, mansworn perjured, false 141.29, 188.40

manteau loose upper-garment for a woman 401.33

mantle, mantell cloak-like garment

46.31, 129.8

manty loose flowing gown usually made of silken material 326.19

march *verb* border on, have a common boundary 253.26

march *noun* border, particularly that between Scotland and England 376.17 (see note)

marcy *dialect* mercy 373.9

mark notice 197.39, 302.40

market-day see note to 239.30

marriage-garment for 79.27 see note

marrow *literally* bone-marrow, i.e. essence, best part of something 291.32, 293.38 (see notes to 291.32 and 291.32–33)

mart market-place 8.34

martlett swift 48.23

martyr one who suffered death in the 17th century in support of the Covenants 78.35 etc.

mashacker mangle, slash, hack 158.3

Mass, Mess master, particularly when applied to a minister holding the degree of Master of Arts from a university 69.23, 69.40, 194.8

mastery *Scots Law* theft committed with the use or threat of force 292.18

matam *Gaelic English* madam 434.42, 435.23, 438.31

maukin hare 271.13

mault alcoholic drink 381.32 (see note)

maun must 42.13 etc.

maunder grumble, mutter 46.14; ramble incoherently 262.10

maunna musn't 107.27 etc.

maw mow, reap 79.19, 403.38

mayna may not 79.18

mazed bewildered, amazed 187.27

meal-ark chest for storing oatmeal 78.30

measter *dialect* master 288.40 etc.

meat food 191.8, 258.11, 307.30 (see note), 381.32 (see note)

meet suitable, proper 3.21 etc.

meeting-house nonconformist or dissenting place of worship 251.1, 357.5, 357.10

meke meek 41.11

mell meddle, interfere 403.43

memorial *Scots Law* instructions and

information given by a litigant to counsel, a brief 15.35 etc.

mend for 267.41 see note

mensefu' polite, well-behaved, respectable 264.15

mercer dealer in fabrics, especially silk, velvet etc. 48.30

mercifu' merciful 218.29

mere downright, nothing short of 266.5

meridian social mid-day drink, particularly that taken by business or professional men 40.42, 42.9; for 168.30 see note

merk for 355.40 see note

Merse area of Berwickshire which lies between the Lammermuir Hills and the Tweed 253.26

Mess for 194.8 see **Mass**

messan pet or house dog 274.34

mete deal out, measure out 58.22

mettle vigour, spirit, courage 163.3

middell *Jeanie's letter* middle 252.23

midden-cock cock on a dunghill, barnyard cock 385.23

middle meddle, interfere 369.5

midge small, gnat-like insect 133.42

mill rob, steal 269.13

miln *Jeanie's letter* mill 251.30

miln-dam mill-dam, a dam constructed across a stream so that it can turn a mill-wheel 251.30

mind remember, recollect 38.35 etc.

minde *Jeanie's letter* mind 250.29

minion darling, favourite child 72.35

ministry clergy, church 74.20 etc.

minnie affectionate term for a mother 170.15, 271.10

minny female horse 258.38

minster-close cathedral close, i.e. houses close to the cathedral occupied by the clergy 419.35–36

mint see note to 179.19

misca' slander, speak ill of 154.29

misdoubt doubt, disbelieve 108.22, 343.24–

mishguggle, misguggle spoil by rough handling 72.3; hack, slash 158.3

mis-set displease, offend, put out of humour 170.15

mista'en mistaken 44.31, 225.9

mistak mistake 220.2

mister *noun* want, need 392.32

mite small amount, the best one can offer in a situation 80.29, 103.15

mither mother 169.42, 170.1, 259.2, 362.35

mittan any glove with or without separate fingers 192.30, 220.36 (see note), 280.37

mixen dunghill 278.4, 278.43

mixture snuff of various sorts mixed together 327.14

moe *dialect* more 295.31

moggie *dialect* untidily dressed woman 256.11

moiety part, half 13.29

mon *dialect* man 362.1

monitor one who gives a warning to another regarding his conduct 98.13

monitory conveying a warning 209.33, 309.2

mony many 40.8 etc.

mooch much 437.21

moon-calf unstable person 268.15

moon-raised under the influence of the moon, i.e. mad, crazy 258.43

moonshine smuggled or illicit spirit 270.31 (see note)

moor-fowl red grouse 110.31

moor-powt, muir-poot young red grouse 271.13–14, 421.11

morass wet, swampy tract, bog 135.30

morn *in the phrase the morn* tomorrow 88.1 etc.

mortar *figurative* pharmacist's shop 367.17

moss marsh, bog 387.28, 404.41, 460.13

moss-hagg marshy hollow or pit on a moor where peat has been cut 102.31

motty with lit-up specks of dust in the atmosphere 101.41

mountaineer mountain-dweller 372.33, 398.27–28, 455.40

moveables moveable property 77.12

muchkin, mutchkin unit of capacity for liquids, equivalent to ¼ Scots pint (3 imperial gills, 0.4 litres) 251.13, 379.32

muckle, muckell much 37.16 etc.; a great many 173.21; big, great 203.10 etc.

muckle-wheel large wheel, mill-wheel 251.30

muffin light spongy cake usually eaten toasted 295.20

muffler kerchief or scarf worn by women in the 16th and 17th centuries to cover part of the face and neck 134.18

mulct *noun* fine, penalty 49.20

mulct *verb* punish by a fine 399.4

mull snuff-box 4.7, 327.18

multure payment in grain or flour to the miller or mill-owner for grinding one's corn 68.8, 124.44

mun *dialect* must 288.10

munna *dialect* musn't 287.7

mur moor 460.13

murdragium for 46.37 see note

murdrum *Latin* murder 46.37 (see note)

mur-ill *Jeanie's letter* disease of cattle which have grazed on rough, heathery pastures 251.11

murland *Jeanie's letter* moor land, rustic 351.38

murmur *Scots Law* cast reflection upon the character or integrity of a judge 109.40, 110.1

murthrum murder 46.39, 46.39 (see notes)

muster-roll official list of the officers and men in an army 247.24, 322.15

mutch woman's head-dress, particularly a close-fitting cap of linen or muslin 147.25, 151.5, 151.42

mutchkin see **muchkin**

muther mother 290.25

mutton-bane mutton-bone 415.35 (see note)

myne *dialect* my 361.42

myrmidon warlike attendant (orinally follower of Achilles) 461.32–33

mysell myself 39.35 etc.

na¹ no 94.36 etc.; not 37.18 etc.

na² now 46.32

nab catch, apprehend 260.29

Nabal churlish or miserly person 239.24 (see note)

nae no 27.16 etc.

naebody nobody 37.19 etc.

nae-the-less none-the-less 387.25

naething nothing 37.13 etc.

nag small riding horse or pony 37.41 etc.

naggie small pony 259.4

nane none 44.9 etc.

napkin neckerchief, *figuratively* halter, noose 224.32

natheless nevertheless 5.3

natural illegitimate 45.20

naut *Jeanie's letter* naught 349.33

nay-say contrary, opposite 40.33

necessitous necessary 399.16

neck-handkerchief neckerchief 280.36

neddie fool, simpleton 267.23, 268.12

needcessity necessity 196.3; need 250.30

needfu' needful, necessary 351.30

ne'er never 40.15 etc.

nefarious wicked, villainous 202.25

neger hard-natured person 168.43

negleck neglect 399.13

negus mixture of wine and hot water sweetened and flavoured 20.11 (see note), 255.30

neibour, neibor neighbour 69.8 etc.

neist next 144.31, 411.32

nerve-shaken nervous, frightened 119.10

nether lower, under 74.22 (see note to 74.22–23), 186.41 (see note)

nettle irritate, vex 41.31, 237.11

net-work open fabric made of mesh-work 444.34

nevoy nephew 439.12

new-model re-model, re-design 66.2 (see note)

nice precise, discriminative 92.29, 388.40, 388.41; reluctant, unwilling 153.6; precise, close, minute 204.12, 216.36; smart, modest agreeable 250.13; delicate, fastidious 368.20

nick deny, cheat 189.32

niffer *verb* bargain, haggle 146.31

niffer *noun* exchange 175.8; hazard 189.18

night-wind wind that blows during the night 158.16

nittle *dialect* neat, handsome 287.1

noble former English gold coin 430.4

Nod sleep 271.10 (see note)

noit knock 356.8

nominate call, designate 43.12; for 46.23 see note

nominative in grammar, that case of nouns, adjectives and pronouns which stands as, or is connected

with, the subject of a verb 39.10,
43.11, 43.27

non-chalance indifference, unconcern 439.32

non-conformist one who does not conform to the doctrines of the established church 4.37

non-conformity refusal to conform to the established church 67.8

nook corner 82.16, 159.13, 428.36

noon-day the middle of the day 137.1

noop knob 153.5

nor-east north-east 102.38–39

nosthril nostril 175.12 (see note)

notable capable, clever, particularly in matters of household management 91.6

notice acknowledge 172.35

noviciate apprenticeship 450.4

nowt cattle 412.22

nursling baby or child, particularly in relation to one who has nursed it 408.19

o' of 1.7 etc.; for 234.42 and 254.5 see notes

o't of it 37.20 etc.

objurgation rebuke, scolding 89.6, 233.25

obtrude thrust, force 10.6

ocular visual 198.2 (see note)

oe grandchild 40.19 etc.

offices buildings attached to a house often including stables, out-houses, barns etc. 230.41, 399.35, 400.13, 401.7

ominous of good omen, auspicious 458.33

onding heavy fall, continuous downpour 70.14

ony any 37.35 etc.

onybody anybody 150.25

open become accessible 418.25

opine think, suppose 176.6, 469.4

opliging *Gaelic English* obliging 421.18

or before 87.38, 88.28, 155.26, 169.38

orders for 50.2, 315.34, 454.1, 454.17 see respective notes

ordinance decree or command of God 355.3 (see note)

ordinar one's accustomed manner 70.16

orgun *Jeanie's letter* organ 251.1

orison prayer 137.14

orrery clockwork mechanism depicting the movement of the planets around the sun 291.33

osier pliant branch of the willow 442.30

oursell ourself, ourselves 155.25 etc.

outbreak insurrection 429.29

outbye outside, without 235.13, 235.14

outcast quarrel, falling out 415.42

Outer-house *Scots Law* that part of the Court of Session in which cases of first instance are heard 111.19–20

outganging *Jeanie's letter* outgoing 351.10

outgate *figurative* way of deliverance from a moral or spiritual problem, answer to a dilemma 415.10

outpost post at which a detachment of troops is placed at a distance to warn against surprise 54.11, 54.41, 118.7, 126.38

outside *noun* passenger sitting on the outside of a carriage or conveyance 8.5, 10.8

outsight moveable goods used out of doors, stock of implements and animals 68.13

outwork outer defence, detached or advanced work forming part of a defence 422.26

over-mastering conquering, overpowering 172.13–14

overmatch person or thing that proves more than a match for the other 10.28

over-weening beyond what is reasonable or just, over-confident 280.32

ow oh 263.4

ower too 44.8 etc.

owerlay neck cloth, cravat, *or* specific type of hem 37.24

owsen oxen 361.42

pack-cammon, packgammon *Gaelic English* back-gammon 416.37, 461.8

packet regular boat carrying mail 249.2

pack-saddle saddle adapted for supporting packs 263.36

pad highway, path 21.8, 190.42, 280.21 (and see respective notes)

pad *Gaelic English* bad 422.1

padder highwayman, robber 225.43, 268.17

paik blow, thump 27.30

Paip Pope 79.5, 79.10, 79.11

pairn *Gaelic English* bairn, child 439.13

paith *Gaelic English* both 439.12

paitrick partridge 110.31

palace-yard for 220.35 see note

palfrey saddle-horse for ordinary riding 230.20, 237.37, 242.7

pall *Gaelic English* ball, bullet 460.14

pallet straw bed, poor or mean bed 185.7

Pandex see note to 42.34

pannel *Scots Law* the accused person in a criminal trial 22.2 etc.

pantaloon enfeebled old man 48.28; name applied to various types of trousers 443.24

papist member of the Roman Catholic Church 69.10, 69.11, 71.36

pardun *Jeanie's letter* pardon 349.32

park area of enclosed farm-ground, a field 44.22

parochial parish 81.36, 241.9, 288.9–10

parochine parish 167.7

paroxysm violent fit of emotion 273.20, 408.22, 462.26

parritch porridge, dish of oatmeal boiled in salted water 415.18

parsonage for 69.31 see note to 69.31–32

particular remarkable, noteworthy 22.11, 262.18; distinguished, worthy of notice 345.42

partisan[1] long-handled spear used by foot-soldiers 52.26

partisan[2] blind or prejudiced supporter of a particular party 318.13

parts personal qualities and attributes, particularly of an intellectual kind 42.13, 42.21

parturition that which is brought forth 405.18

passement, passment *verb* adorn, trim, usually with gold or silver lace 148.35, 217.35

passment *noun* strip of gold or silver lace or silk braid 79.28

pat put 187.21, 239.29, 249.37, 276.28

patch for 264.11 see note to 264.11–12

pate head 150.23

patois dialect 249.41, 424.13

Patriarch father and ruler of a family or tribe, venerable old man particularly in Biblical times 227.34, 427.13; for 173.28–29 see note

patriarchal characteristic of Biblical patriarchs and their times 245.29

patronage right of certain landowners in Scotland of choosing the minister of a parish 90.17 etc. and see note to 167.8

patten overshoe or sandal with a wooden sole and leather strap worn over the ordinary shoe to protect it against mud or wet 385.23

pavé paved street, road or path 11.24

pawky wily, cunning, crafty 112.14

pe *Gaelic English* be 394.41 etc.

peace-officer constable, officer appointed to keep the public peace 168.19

peach inform against, give incriminating evidence against 269.12

pea-hen female of the peacock 160.2

peard *Gaelic English* beard 395.10

pearlin-lace lace used as a trimming for garments 236.28

pease pea 71.10, 72.5, 74.8

peat[1] term of reproach or scorn 159.12, 452.16

peat[2] dried vegetable matter cut from the ground and used as fuel 280.9

peat-hagg hole or pit left where peat has previously been cut 109.30

peculation appropriation of public money or property by someone in an official position, embezzlement 8.19

ped *Gaelic English* bed 421.13, 421.15

pedagogue school master, teacher 241.12

pedevil *Gaelic English* bedevil, subject to a spell 421.33

peeble pelt with pebbles, stones 37.18

peel strip of bark 281.14

peevish perverse, self-willed, harmful 165.28

pefore *Gaelic English* before 395.36, 421.13, 460.4, 460.23

peg *Gaelic English* beg 434.35, 459.29, 461.4

pegan *Gaelic English* began 439.3

pehove *Gaelic English* behove 397.15

pelf wealth, riches 118.29

pelieve *Gaelic English* believe 394.42 etc.

pell-rope *Gaelic English* bell-rope 465.12

penal severe 214.8

pendicle small piece of ground forming a dependant part of an estate 3.24–25

pendulous drooping, overhanging 374.28

pen-gun toy air-gun made from a quill, pop-gun 160.2

penny-stane-cast stone's throw, distance which a penny-stane (flat, round stone used as a quoit) can be thrown 37.11

penny-wedding wedding at which the guests contributed a small sum of money towards their own entertainment 69.22

penurious grudging, stingy 288.15

perch measure of length for land varying locally 3.26

perduellion *Scots Law* hostility against the state or government, treason 108.34, 108.39, 116.33

peregrination journey 11.38

perfect pure, complete 220.14

peritissimus *Latin* most expert, particularly in the law 243.1 (see note to 242.33–243.1)

periwig wig such as that worn by judges, barristers etc. 19.3, 37.37, 220.10

peroration concluding part of a speech in which the speaker reiterates the argument forcefully 214.10

perplexed intricate, intertwined 288.3

perquisite gratuity or casual fee claimed by some workers in addition to their pay 124.41

perquisition thorough or diligent search, careful inquiry 171.7

persecution worst period of the persecution of the Covenanters in the 17th century 225.33

pesides *Gaelic English* besides 460.29

pest *Gaelic English* best 412.20, 460.14, 461.2, 462.4

pestial *Gaelic English* bestial, concerning domestic animals 421.19

petition *noun* humble and earnest prayer to God 131.16, 132.9, 163.27, 427.33; application to a court 18.10 (see note)

petition *verb* make a solemn and humble prayer to God 400.37

petted sulky, vexed 420.33

petter *Gaelic English* better 416.32, 421.16, 437.21

pettle treat with special favour, make much of 167.38

peyont *Gaelic English* beyond 412.9

pharmacopeia collection of drugs 361.21

philabeg kilt 394.14, 395.36, 443.11

philosophy knowledge, wisdom 455.4, 455.6

physic medical knowledge, medicine 113.38

physics natural science 74.34

physiognomy facial expression 405.19–20

Pible *Gaelic English* Bible 421.19

pibroch classical or 'big' music of the Scottish bagpipe 439.3

pickle nibble, eat sparingly or delicately 254.12 (see note)

picqueering skirmishing, wrangling, petty quarrelling 412.12

picquet card game played by two people with a pack of 32 cards in which points are scored by various combinations of cards 20.12

pid *Gaelic English* bid 439.3

pig *Gaelic English* big 439.12, 465.24

pigg earthenware vessel, pot, jar 429.8

pigtail tobacco twisted into a thin rope or roll 191.5

pike *noun* pickaxe, pitchfork 55.2

pike *verb* pick 274.39 (see note)

pillion woman's light saddle 256.28 etc.; suitable for transportation on a light saddle 372.12

pillory stocks, device for punishing offenders consisting of a wooden frame and bars with holes for the head and hands 102.38, 322.7

pinch time of difficulty 69.42 etc.; crucial difficulty, hardship 220.1, 351.8

pinnace small light sailing vessel 371.22

pint Scottish pint equivalent to 3 imperial pints (1.7 litres) 17.14, 251.13; imperial pint 251.12

pint-stoup large pint-pot or drinking vessel 404.25

pioted resembling a magpie in colouring, multi-coloured 242.20 (see note)

pipe for 233.15 see note

pipkin small earthenware pot or pan used in cookery 131.41

pirn amount of yarn that can be wound on a weaver's shuttle, hank of yarn 203.10

pismire ant, used as a contemptuous name for a person 173.33

pistol-flint flint used to create the spark in a small fire-arm 403.17

pit *Gaelic English* bit 460.34

pit, pitt *verb* put 37.31 etc.

pit *noun* deep hole or chamber for confining prisoners 109.33

pitch tar-like substance 114.9 (see note)

pith inner core 104.37; importance, weight 291.32, 293.38

placed see note to 50.2, 382.30

plack small Scottish coin valued at around ⅓ of an old English penny 94.33, 173.32, 329.8, 405.6

plack *Gaelic English* black 412.21

plack-cock *Gaelic English* blackcock, male of the black grouse 421.11

plague nuisance, trouble 235.9 (see note)

plaid rectangular length of woollen cloth either self-coloured or tartan, used as a mantle or outer garment in rural areas of Scotland 73.19 etc.

plaid-nuik fold of a plaid, *figuratively* one's pocket 70.29 (see note)

plaister plaster 48.20

planet moon 137.30

plank hide, place 267.19

plash splash 170.30

platoon-fire volley of shot 456.35

play-actor actor 146.24, 166.38

play-book book of plays or dramatic compositions 165.40

plea *Scots Law* lawsuit 110.2 etc.

plea-house court of law 44.2

pledge see note to 423.31

pleese *Jeanie's letter* please 350.29

plenishing furniture, household equipment 398.42, 405.36

pleugh plough 82.21

pliability flexible in character, easily

influenced 202.10

plind *Gaelic English* blind 421.33

plood *Gaelic English* blood 462.12

plough-gate amount of land which a plough, pulled by 8 oxen, could till in a year, calculated to be 104 Scots acres (131 acres; 67 hectares) but varying considerably 110.33 etc.

plover see note to 294.38

plower ploughman 174.36

plum ball of lead used for various purposes 270.33

ply layer or thickness of any material 160.7

poat *Gaelic English* boat 421.34

pock simple type of bag or pouch 108.39

poco-curante indifferent person, one showing little interest or concern 365.43–44

pody *Gaelic English* body 416.35, 421.16, 438.32

pofle small parcel of land 3.25, 3.29

poinding *Scots Law* impounding of goods to be sold for debt 68.13 (see note to 68.13–14)

poke-nook corner of a bag, especially one for holding money 254.13 (see note)

pole tradesman's sign 62.22

policy ornamental grounds in which a country house is situated, the park of an estate 331.9

polititious political 112.28

polonie loose-fitting gown or coat worn by young boys 46.30

polrumptious unruly, foolish 286.43

poniard dagger 301.5

pontage toll paid for the use of the bridge 177.39

poonish *Gaelic English* punish 421.31

poorfu' powerful 74.21

poot[1] *Gaelic English* put 438.34

poot[2] *Gaelic English* boot 460.20

popple bubble up, flow in a tumbling manner 170.29

porn *Gaelic English* born 435.26

porringer small bowl or similar vessel for various kinds of food including porridge 234.36

porrow *Gaelic English* borrow 397.16

port[1] gateway, entrance, particularly one in the wall of a city 49.16 etc.

port[2] bearing, manners 100.18,

208.14

portal door 54.31, 288.35

portion moral or spiritual inheritance, that which Providence allots to a person 99.37, 174.17, 174.18, 194.31; lot 109.12, 120.37; inheritance 187.33, 376.6, 422.38

positive obstinate, pig-headed 89.25

post for 21.8 see note

post-chaise carriage either hired from stage to stage or drawn by horses so hired 11.25

post-coach coach used for carrying mail, stagecoach 7.26

postern, postern-door private door, side door 230.10, 330.3, 343.9

post-horse horse kept at an inn for hire from stage to stage 249.9, 256.28–29, 257.18, 257.36

pot for 74.30 see note

potter trifling talk 337.16

pouch pocket containing one's money 168.26, 237.5; pocket in a garment 359.6

pound *Gaelic English* bound 397.14, 397.19

pounds *Gaelic English* bounds, boundaries 460.19

pounden *Gaelic English* bounden, entered into a binding contract of service 437.41

pourtraicture portraits 4.1

pouther powder, gunpowder 462.6

pow head 386.29

powney pony 116.15, 235.9, 238.39

poy *Gaelic English* boy 421.41

practique *Scots Law* customary usage, usual practice 110.23; *plural* name formerly given to the recorded decisions of the Court of Session 113.7 (see note)

prae *Gaelic English* brae, hillside 460.29

prain *Gaelic English* brain 460.14

prandy *Gaelic English* brandy 435.1, 459.29, 461.1

prayer-book book of prayers and orders of service, specifically the Book of Common Prayer of the Church of England 69.35, 284.1

preceese precise 445.17

preceesely precisely 122.23, 395.2

precept command, instruction, especially for moral conduct 89.31,

132.16, 132.23

preceptor teacher, tutor 299.42

precessor predecessor 258.17

precious of great moral and spiritual worth 102.31 etc.; for 194.18 and 260.3 see note to 194.18

precognition *Scots Law* preliminary examination of possible witnesses or other informants 196.12

predication sermon, discourse 66.11

preferment ecclesiastical appointment 77.34 etc.; advancement in life 148.34, 268.13, 268.14, 387.16; appointment or post which gives pecuniary reward 182.42

prelacy system of church government by prelates or bishops 172.2, 384.11, 388.2

prelate ecclesiastical dignitary such as a bishop or archbishop 88.12, 356.9

prelatical, prelatic pertaining to a bishop, or to the system of church government by bishops etc. 90.17 etc.

prelatist supporter or adherent of the system of church government by bishops 4.33, 5.19, 94.21, 251.3

prent print 1.12

prentice apprentice 46.10, 220.29

prentice-lad apprentice boy 219.8

presbyterian member of a church organised on the Presbyterian system (whereby the church is governed by a system of courts, kirk session, presbytery, synod, and General Assembly) 5.20 etc.; pertaining to the Presbyterian system 78.5 etc.

presbytery the second court in the Presbyterian system composed of the minister and one ruling elder from each parish within a designated area 45.21 etc.

prescribed *Scots Law* become invalid through the passage of time 450.27 (see note), 450.28

prescription for 450.37 see note to 450.27

presentee clergyman presented to a vacant position with a view to becoming the minister 379.26–27

President senior judge of the Court of Session 42.14

press crowd 62.25; cupboard 227.24
pressed forced to enlist in the Royal Navy 319.7
pressing execution by pressing to death 315.43
prestation payment due in recognition of feudal superiority 67.35
presumption for 189.27–28 see note to 189.25–28; *Law* inference of a fact not certainly known from known facts 214.5
presumptive based on inference, presumed 45.6.1, 47.1, 213.10, 214.1
pretend claim 463.1
pretermit pass over without notice 388.11
pretty fine, good-looking 460.22
prevarication deviation from duty, especially in a court of law 211.21
prey seize and kill as prey 197.6
pridefu' *Jeanie's letter* haughty, arrogant, snobbish 350.14
priest-ridden held in subjection by priestly authority 97.19
prigg plead 219.3
pring *Gaelic English* bring 460.4, 461.5
prithee pray thee 158.36
probation *Scots Law* proof and the procedure for demonstrating it 213.11, 215.1
process *Scots Law* the legal papers in an action lodged in court by both parties 108.39
procurator solicitor entitled to represent someone in the lower courts 68.34, 175.19; but usually a shortened form of **procurator-fiscal** 147.32, 150.41, 151.10, 151.18
procurator-fiscal, prokitor *Scots Law* the public prosecutor in a sheriffdom who formerly investigated crimes and still initiates the prosecution of crimes in sheriff courts 68.34 etc.
prodigal for 401.1 see note to 401.1–2
produce evidence, document or article produced as evidence 198.33
proem preface, preamble 384.19
professor acknowledged adherent of some religious doctrine 72.14 etc.
proficiency improvement in skill or knowledge, adeptness 420.13

profligate dissipated person, abandoned to vice and debauched 94.19, 184.19, 276.41
progress *Scots Law* series or progression 241.42 (see note to 241.42–43)
prokitor procurator fiscal, responsible for investigating crimes and for prosecuting in criminal trials in sheriff courts 148.37, 162.25
prolegomen learned preface, preamble prefixed to a literary work 3.8
prolix lengthy, protracted 243.39
prolixity length of discourse 386.5
promise divine assurance of future good or blessing conceived as given to mankind through Christ 94.16, 133.24
promulgate proclaim, make known by public declaration 220.34, 314.16
proof evidence which determines the judgment of a court 207.35, 213.17 (see note)
property ownership 4.16, 379.22
propine gift, present 350.42
propitiation appeasement, conciliation 268.5
propone *Scots Law* advance or state in a court of law 110.34, 110.38
proser one who talks in a tiresome way 242.28
prosper cause to flourish, promote the prosperity or success of 223.24
protestation *Scots Law* for 116.23 see note
prought *Gaelic English* brought 437.43
providence divine direction, guidance 182.29, 373.35, 427.26
providense *Jeanie's letter* providence, divine direction, guidance 350.27
provost chairman of a town council, equivalent to the mayor elsewhere 18.13 etc.
pruh call word to a cow or calf 400.18
prute *Gaelic English* brute, animal 421.19
psalmody psalm-singing as part of public worship 283.7
pshaw make an exclamation of contempt, impatience 76.16
pu' pull 359.35, 415.24
puir poor 43.41 etc.
punctilious strictly observant of de-

tails of action or behaviour 29.16, 177.41, 240.13, 438.24

pund *money* pound, either the pound sterling or the pound Scots which was worth 1/12th of an English pound by the 17th century 114.43 etc.; *weight* unit of weight (0.454 kilos) 354.26

pupillarity *Scots Law* the period between a child's birth and the legal age of puberty, for a boy at 14 years complete 46.21 (see note)

pu'pit pulpit 109.32, 191.5, 194.10, 246.33

purchased *figurative* acquisition through suffering, sacrifice etc. 163.23

purlieu outlying district of a town, squalid, disreputable area 202.26

purn *Gaelic English* burn 460.34

purse-proud proud of one's wealth, arrogant because of wealth 315.41

pursuer *Scots Law* party who raises a civil action in court 19.8, 111.2. 111.7, 243.15

pusillanimity want of courage, timidity 257.23

put *Gaelic English* but 395.41 etc.

put-on dressed, turned-out 272.31

putt thrust forcibly from the shoulder 85.14 (see note)

putten put 170.28 etc.

py *Gaelic English* by 416.34 etc.

pye *Gaelic English* bye 416.34

pyke pick, pilfer, filch 168.26

python serpent 333.39 (see note to 333.38–39)

quadrille card game played by four persons 53.30

quadruped four-footed animal 118.20–21

Quaker member of the Religious Society of Friends, founded by George Fox 1648–50 5.22 (see note) etc.

quaker-like similar to that of a member of the Religious Society of Friends, renowned for their honesty 241.25

quarter divide the body of a condemned criminal into four quarters 102.35

quarter fourth part of a year, especially as divided by quarter-days, the fixed dates for marking off the quarters of the year 403.41; school term or similar period of instruction 469.12

quean, queen for 88.40 see note; young woman 148.11, 150.39 etc.

queen-consort wife of the king 331.22

queer *verb* cheat 207.16, 268.9; trick, cheat 236.40

queer for 226.1 see note

questions series of questions and answers of the Shorter Catechism (see notes to 149.34–36 and 149.36), used to instruct Presbyterians in Christian beliefs and doctrine 189.28

quey heifer, young cow 251.15, 350.18

quid piece of tobacco cut so that it can be held in the mouth 148.9, 394.31

quillet sharp, nice distinction 92.29

quivis *Latin* for 39.3, 43.5 see note to 39.2–3

quo' say, speak 122.35, 187.39

quodammodo *Latin* in a way, to a certain extent 172.2, 214.42

quotha indeed!, forsooth! 221.27

rabble *verb* assault by the mob 69.9, 120.9

racking torturing, causing intense pain 16.19

rackon *dialect* reckon 255.18

raillery good-humoured ridicule 423.20

raise rose 47.20

rak wander, roam 46.11

range set in order, arrange 44.4; roam, wander 160.14

rannell-tree bar of wood or iron fixed across the chimney and used for suspending cooking pots etc. 173.31

rant lively tune or song 175.37

rap swear 189.33 etc.

rape rope 136.13, 136.14, 136.18

rapine violent robbery, plunder 426.42

rapparee bandit, robber, freebooter 399.15

rappee coarse kind of inferior snuff 325.19, 348.42

rapscallion rascal, rogue 411.33, 460.12

rat drat 269.13, 270.28

rates for 286.10 see note

rat-rhyme piece of tedious, repetitive nonsense 69.27

rattan stick used for beating a person 286.12

rattle *noun* lively talk 12.35

rattle *verb* talk rapidly in a thoughtless way 69.24

rattling lively, rousing 16.28

ravish delight, enrapture 159.11

raw inexperienced 208.2

raw-boned barely covered in flesh, very lean 256.15

rax stretch 42.7 (see note), 160.1 (see note)

read advise, instruct 285.38

rear push from behind 218.30

rear-guard body of troops put at the back to protect the rear of the main force 160.36

receipt recipe 307.15, 440.6

receive understand 65.31

receptacle place to which people retire for security 58.38–39

reckan for 361.43 see note

rector incumbent of an English parish entitled to the tithe income of the parish 287.2 etc.

recusant someone who refuses to submit to authority 155.43, 372.35, 387.42, 395.18

redargue refute, disprove 115.26

redd sort, clear 184.16–17, 234.19

rede, read advise, warn 1.10, 285.38

reed *Jeanie's letter* read 251.39

reek smoke 101.41, 239.29, 403.31, 461.3

refinement improvement in thought and discourse 112.15

regency for 63.40 and 171.23 see note to 63.40

regent one assigned to rule in a country during the absence of the sovereign 35.11 (see note)

regular deliberate, following a settled line of conduct 88.14

relevancy *Scots Law* for 115.35, 198.12, 199.6, 203.18, and 213.13 see note to 31.40–41

remnant Covenanters 109.28 (see note), 114.14; those who refused to accept the Revolutionary Settlement of 1688–89 177.11

rencontre skirmish, hostile meeting 27.10, 134.38, 164.21

rent interest 69.14, 227.39

repining *adjective* grumbling, discontented 116.15

repining *noun* discontent, grumbling 426.8–9

reproach for 102.29 see note

respeck *Jeanie's letter* respect 351.2

respectit respected 460.19

respondent defendant in a legal case 122.21

response part of the service said in reply by a congregation during worship 284.5

Restoration re-establishment of the monarchy in 1660 by the return of Charles II 65.43

retain engage, hire 112.1, 196.6

retainer persons employed to support someone or something, followers 141.41, 156.19

retrograde move backwards to a less flourishing condition 19.24

revelation for 45.34 see note

revenge take revenge on 390.31

revenue annual income of a government or state 23.19, 299.11

reversion right of succeeding to a position after the death or retirement of the holder 147.36

Revolution expulsion in 1688 of the Stewart dynasty and the arrival of a Protestant succession with William and Mary 90.18 etc.

riding opening with a ceremonial procession 40.7, 219.21

riding-habit dress used by ladies for riding 227.13, 281.3

rifle plunder, rob 275.19

rigg hill-crest, ridge 176.17

rigour severity 382.34

rime *Jeanie's letter* rhyme 252.6

rin run 59.3 etc.

ring-bolt bolt with an eye at one end to which a ring is attached 265.5

rin-there-out vagabond 46.10

riot-act for 54.40 see note

ripe search, thoroughly examine 460.12

ritual form of religious worship as set down in the Book of Common Prayer 284.2

rive tear, rip 167.36, 282.10; pull or tug roughly or vigorously 415.25

roadstead place where ships may conveniently lie at anchor near the

shore 182.27
robbit robbed 37.30
rod wand 380.6
rokelay short cloak with a long cape worn by women in the 18th century 129.22, 151.6, 151.43
romps lively, boisterous play 145.32
rood measure of land, 1525 sq. yds (1275 sq. metres) 3.26
room piece of land for which rent was paid, a farm, croft etc. 398.19
root essential part 287.11 etc.
rough for 404.36 see note
round for 404.36 see note
round-spun genuine 112.25
roup turn out a bankrupt and sell his belongings 70.11
rouping sale of household and farming equipment by public auction 377.23
rouping-wife woman who buys and resells second-hand furniture 37.5
roupit hoarse, husky 362.40
rout assail with blows 68.17
roving delirious, wandering in one's thoughts 190.13, 223.32
row roll, particularly of the action of a wheeled vehicle 265.33
rue for 359.31 see note
ruffler type of vagabond 225.43, 270.35
ruling reigning, predominating 423.22
ruling-elder ordained elder in a Presbyterian church 112.26 (see note to 90.33))
run *verb* for 41.19, 144.35 and 402.33 see respective notes
run *adjective* smuggled, illegally imported 146.13
run *noun* continuous and well-sustained demand 257.20
Russelite for 176.6 see note to 176.6–7
russet-gown dress made of coarse, woollen cloth of a reddish-brown colour 400.7
rusted of the colour of rust 466.3
saam same 405.23, 415.27
Sabbath-breaker one who fails to keep the Lord's day sacred 75.35
sackless innocent 44.15, 187.16
sacque, sack kind of dress worn by ladies, and from the 18th century also a name for a piece of silk

attached to the shoulders of such dresses, 396.38, 401.33
sad-coloured sombre 37.37 (see note)
saddle-cloth cloth put on a horse's back beneath the saddle 41.21
sae so 27.31 etc.
saft soft, involving little hardship or discomfort 102.30; soft 249.33
sain bless 258.38
saint, saunt one of the elect, or chosen saved in a Calvinistic sense, used particularly in relation to the Covenanters 113.9, 181.39, 187.19, 415.24
sair sore, sorely 44.16 etc.
sall shall 105.41 etc.
sally flash of wit 168.34
sang song 87.35 etc.
sanguinary bloodthirsty 4.36; involving bloodshed 134.39
sape *Jeanie's letter* soap 251.13
sark shirt 37.23
sarvice *dialect* church-service 289.1, 290.39; service, command 397.11
sashed with a glazed frame in the upper part 291.6
Sassenach *Gaelic English* English language 394.43
satellite attendant upon a person of importance, often implying subservience 35.41
saul *Jeanie's letter* soul 349.35
sauld sold 159.17, 351.41, 355.33
saut salt 225.7, 362.39 (see note)
saut-wife female salt seller 362.41–42
saving in the habit of saving and economising 229.21
savour *verb* have the characteristic of 178.4
savoury having the savour of holiness, of saintly memory 72.13 (see note to 72.13–14), 175.32, 354.41, 390.30
saw sow 72.4, 79.19
sax six 160.7 etc.
sax-pund six-pound (in weight) 415.28
saxteen sixteen 45.8
scant scarce 69.21
scape-goat one punished for the sins of others 376.26
scape escape 224.39
scarce-tracked seldom traversed,

lonely 134.42

scart scratch, mark or score made by a pen 78.36, 226.11

scathe harm, mischief 361.42

scauding scalding 264.21

schismatic causing a breach in the unity of the church 71.34, 112.38, 375.36; one who is guilty of promoting such a breach 292.41

schule see **scule**

schule-master school-master, teacher 236.42

schuling education 294.35

sclate slate 173.21

scomfish suffocate, choke 352.7

score¹ twenty 114.43, 460.22

score² for 160.19 see note

score³ account, reckoning 237.13

scornfu' *Jeanie's letter* scornful, scoffing 350.20

Scottice in Scots, in the Scots language 124.37

scoup scurry, dart, run here and there 232.32

scour thrust 276.2

scourge beat severely, flog, whip 39.12, 40.23, 102.34, 165.27

scraughin shriek, shout 168.12

screech-owl barn owl, owl with a sharp discordant cry 242.16

screed long discourse, harangue 208.6

screen shawl, head-cover 134.18 etc.

scroll draft, write out in legal form 70.33

scruple *noun* hesitation, doubt, particularly of a moral nature 22.37 etc.

scruple *verb* hesitate to do something on moral or religious grounds 166.23 etc.

scrupulous reluctant, cautious, particularly because of moral doubts 144.6 etc.; minutely exact and careful 195.39, 211.5, 295.2–3, 319.24

scud driving shower of rain 461.10

scule, schule school 45.15 etc.

sea-fire phosphorescence at sea 407.17

sea-maw sea gull 395.1

searcher customs-officer 144.2

seat Session (i.e. Court of Session) 39.33, 39.35

secretaire cabinet for keeping private papers 428.39

sect class, kind 251.35

sectarian during the Civil War an adherent of the 'sectarian' or 'Independent' party 113.29, 113.30

sectary Protestant dissenter 292.42

sedan see note to 53.30–31

seil strain, sieve, filter 131.38

seip seep, leak 158.5

sell self 78.24, 150.38, 287.5, 408.41

seminary place of education 315.25

senator for 121.18 see note

seneschal steward, one to whom the administration of a great house was entrusted 452.33

sensible aware 51.43 etc.; evident 400.20

sententious full of wisdom, given to maxims 66.33–34

separatist Independent (for which see note to 65.31) 179.18

sequester *Scots Law* seclude 196.8, 196.11 (see note to 196.8–9)

sequestered secluded, sheltered 93.39 etc.

sequestrate *Scots Law* remove all the property of a bankrupt entrusting it to a trustee for its equitable division among creditors 19.7, 196.10, 196.13

sequestration the process by which a bankrupt's land or heritable property is placed in the care of a trustee for distribution among creditors 68.13

ser serve 167.26

servants-hall eating and meeting area for domestic servants in a large house 281.6

service-time time of church service 169.15

servitude *Scots Law* obligation attached to a piece of property giving others specified rights over it 243.6 (see note)

session Court of Session, the highest civil judicature in Scotland 39.35 etc.

set for 18.13 see note to 18.13–14; for 219.1 see note

settle sitting place, often a wooden bench 114.26

settle-bed settle adapted for alternative use as a seat or bed, a day-bed 181.12

sext sixth 356.24

sexton grave-digger 366.35

shade *verb* part the hair 197.25, 212.10

shade *noun* shed used as shelter or store-house 231.42

shaft for 74.27, 103.31, 382.42 see note to 74.27

shallop type of boat 371.36

shamefu' shameful 104.40

shanna shall not 270.36

sharge *Gaelic English* charge 438.32

sharp for 267.34 see note

shear divide, separate, go in different directions 176.18

sheen bright, glistening 160.15

sheepfauld sheepfold 400.43

sheering reaping of corn 79.19

shentleman *Gaelic English* gentleman 394.38 etc.

sheriff for 120.19 see note

sheriff-court court presided over by the sheriff or sheriff-substitute, county court 68.35

Shibboleth formula adopted by a party or sect by which followers may be identified 384.21 (see note), 390.4

shift measure, stratagem, way of making a living 264.4

shilling 12*d.* (5p) coin 194.37, 368.10, 469.12

shingle loose roundish stones or pebbles 444.12

shirt gown, shirt-gown bodice 151.5, 151.42

shoe for 344.7 see note

shoon shoes 45.24 etc.

shop-woman female shop assistant 90.3

short-gown dress with a short skirt worn by women when engaged in housework 84.40

shoudna, shouldna shouldn't 69.30, 162.21

shouther shoulder 106.16, 355.32

sic such 27.16 etc.

sicklike similar 167.39

sieur courtesy title derived from French Monsieur, Master 469.6

signet for 20.29 see note

silenced forbidden to preach or hold services because of a refusal to comply with certain conditions 145.5

siller silver, money 70.28 etc.

sillerless without silver, money 238.8

silly delicate, frail 153.27

silver-call silver whistle used to summon someone or gain attention 254.29

simmer summer 44.41, 45.18, 156.10, 444.30

simulated pretended, feigned 469.7

sin' since 64.20, 69.32, 403.36

sinder separate one from another 252.8

sindry see note to 219.42; separate 275.35

sine *Jeanie's letter* sign 252.27

sinfu' sinful 44.15, 104.40, 174.27

single of one single room in depth 229.24

sister female member of the Christian church or some part of it 194.18

sitten sat 40.1 (see note)

skaith *noun* harm, injury 60.14, 206.11

skaith *verb* harm, injure 396.40

skaithless free from harm, injury 141.37

skeel skill, knowledge 43.40, 115.8, 346.4; knowledge, experience 156.5

skeely skilful, knowledgeable 251.16, 350.15

skelping hitting, beating 153.42

skeptre *Jeanie's letter* sceptre 351.21

skiff small sea-going boat, light boat 329.29, 409.35, 410.33

skimming for 373.30 see note

skirl scream 146.41 etc.

skirling screaming 158.9, 206.26, 276.27; screech, shrill talk 264.14, 280.8

skirt lower part of a man's gown or the tail of a coat 75.31

skrimp *Jeanie's letter* scrimp, be sparing 351.29

skulduddery fornication and adultery 144.12

slake lick, smear 155.17

sledge-hammer large, heavy hammer of the sort used by blacksmiths 54.18, 55.18

sleepit slept 191.11, 191.12, 400.39

slip leash for a dog made so that it can be quickly and easily released 164.2

slip-shod shabby 17.12 (see note); slovenly 231.26

slouched see notes to 50.39, 122.13

slough piece of muddy or miry ground 19.25 (see note)

sluggard lazy, idle person 229.6, 231.24

sma' small, little 120.8 etc.

smack kiss 189.36 (see note)

smock-frock loose-fitting garment often of coarse linen, worn by farmers, farm-workers etc. over or instead of a coat 259.32

snack light meal 152.11, 349.13

snap mouthful 267.38

snapper slip in conduct, blunder, predicament 185.34

snare trap set by the devil 78.4 etc.

snaw snow 70.14

snivel weep and sniff 208.4

snod tidy, put in order 287.2

snog neaten, tidy 287.1

snood *noun* ribbon tied round the forehead and under the hair at the back, worn by young women and regarded as a sign of maidenhood 84.38, 197.21, 324.28, 357.9

snood *verb* bind the hair with a band or ribbon 134.16

snotter weep noisily 208.4

soa *dialect* so 290.19, 290.24

society for 176.1 see note

Socinian pertaining to Lælius and Faustus Socinus 173.33 (see note)

sodger soldier 151.32, 151.33

somegate, some-gate somewhere 154.9, 310.5

Somerset for 8.42–9.1, 9.37, 11.10 see note to 8.42–9.1

sonsy comely, attractive, plump 353.19

soothfast truthful 142.15

sophistry specious, intentionally deceptive reasoning 141.29

sorrel chestnut colour, reddish brown 41.21

sorrowfu' *Jeanie's letter* sorrowful 251.5

sort feed and litter 400.33

sough for 71.1 see note

soup for 70.40 see note

souther patch up 415.32

southron people belonging to or living in England 71.14, 252.30

south-sea for 319.8 and 428.16 see note to 319.8

sovereign supreme 116.34, 263.29; having superlative effect 450.12

sowens dish made with seeds or husks of oats and some fine meal steeped in water for around a week until it turns sour, then strained and separated 379.30

spae prophesy, predict, tell 415.34, 421.32

spae-wife female fortune-teller 448.30

spake spoke 222.31, 399.9

speer ask 41.13 etc.

spiel climb, clamber 190.15

spleuchan tobacco-pouch 191.6, 403.13, 403.21

spleuhan-fu tobacco pouch-full 251.19

spoliation pillaging, plundering 318.32

sponsible responsible, respectable 254.20

sporran purse or pouch worn by a Highlander in front of the kilt 403.20, 405.6

spright haunt 242.10, 242.11

spring quick, lively tune to accompany a dance 88.42, 175.37; explode 10.9

spring-saw fine saw with a folding blade 301.15

spune spoon 404.1

spunk spirit, courage 225.25

squab having thick and clumsy form 395.43

squire for 21.8 and 219.23 see respective notes

'st hush 17.29

stack stuck 235.35

stage interval of about 12 miles (19 km) over which a single set of horses pull a coach before being changed at the next post 10.42 etc.

stage-coach public coach running to a specified timetable for the conveyance of passengers, parcels etc. 7.18, 9.20, 309.33

staig bullock, young ox 132.30

stalking-horse underhand means of gaining some purpose 387.17

stamach stomach 69.19

stanchell grating for a gate, window etc. 173.25

stancheon grating for a window, or iron bar fitted behind a door to prevent it from opening 265.5

stand for 259.31 and 445.23 see respective notes

stane stone 37.18 etc.; measure of weight for cheese etc. equivalent to 17½ lbs avoirdupois (8 kilos) 346.1

star badge of rank 331.7, 352.26

stark stiff in death 144.13

start move suddenly 345.8

starve perish by a variety of means, including cold and hunger 70.12, 70.13

states for 173.20 see note

stave wooden stick 51.36

stay corset 254.14

sted situated, placed 180.20

steel weapon of various sorts 98.5, 266.12

steel-spring spring made of steel 49.3

stentorian loud and far-reaching 233.21

step-dame step-mother 77.1

sterling denoting English money 114.43, 224.33, 236.25

stern star 158.43

steward official who controls the domestic affairs of a household 289.10

stick do away with, stab 71.2, 222.37

stifler *slang* the gallows 207.16

stillicide *Scots Law* a right of servitude permitting rain-water from one person's roof to drain on a neighbour's premises 243.7, 243.15, 243.20 (see note to 243.6–7)

stipend salary paid to a clergyman 69.31 etc.

stirk bovine animal after it has been weaned being kept for slaughter at the age of 2 or 3 174.39

stock-farm farm where livestock are kept 386.6

stocking-loom knitting-machine 143.25

stoit stagger, blunder 275.33

stone for 85.14 see note

store-farm farm on which cattle are reared 355.28, 377.13

stoup drinking-vessel 70.35

stow crop 427.21

strae straw 252.22, 263.39

strait narrow 157.29 etc.

straught stretch 191.13

street-raking roaming the streets 170.7

streight, strait time of hardship, crisis 207.12, 267.2284.29, 356.21

strickly strictly 144.31

strict close, intimate 72.9

stroller vagrant, wandering beggar or pedlar 292.7, 292.8, 432.41

strolling low-class, one who travels about the country performing plays in irregular places 166.37–38

stude stood 40.10 etc.

stumbling-block scandal, offence, obstacle to belief 94.26 (see note)

sture *dialect* rough in manner, ill-tempered 361.35

sub-factor subordinate agent appointed to manage an estate 368.41

sub-poena *English Law* writ issued by a court of justice commanding the presence of a witness and with a penalty for failure to attend 180.14

subscribe sign 204.7, 313.24; sign by way of accepting 404.10

substitute *Scots Law* one nominated in place of another as a deputy etc.; for 42.34 and 42.37 see note to 42.37

suddenty for 167.3 see note

sugar-plumb something pleasant or agreeable given by way of bribe or flattery 347.38

suld should 40.6 etc.

suldna shouldn't 170.22, 195.36, 238.7, 243.31

sultana mistress 232.4

sum bring to completion 315.19

sume *Jeanie's letter* some 351.41

summary *Law* carried out rapidly by dispensing with full formalities, performed with brevity 9.43, 20.15, 100.42

summat *dialect* something, 255.7, 289.26

summerset somersault 9.37

sun-blink gleam of sunshine 133.43, 163.37 (see note)

sundry for 415.24 see note

sune soon 41.34, 63.2, 236.13 (see note)

sunket provision, tit-bit, delicacy 167.39

supercilious haughty, contemptuously superior 96.29, 317.11

superior upper, higher in position 243.21, 243.25

supersede delay, take the place of 344.16

surmise *verb* imagine, form the notion 203.11

surmise *noun* conjecture, idea 203.13

surplice loose gown of white linen with wide sleeves worn as an overgarment by clerics and others taking part in a church service 284.18, 287.9, 293.35

suspension *Scots Law* warrant for a stay of execution of a decree or sentence of Court until the matter can be reviewed 185.35

swam glide with a smooth or waving motion 283.12

sward stretch of grass 134.26

swart dusky, swarthy 442.18

sweet-meat sweet food such as cakes, pastries, confectionery etc. 40.12

swither state of nervous agitation or uncertainty, fluster 186.37

swum swim, to subject a supposed witch to trial by immersion in water, the proof of innocence being their failure to sink 362.22

synagogue place of worship 283.16

synd swill down with drink 394.34

syne ago, since 43.5 etc.; for 236.13 see note

syren one who sings sweetly with the purpose to deceive 194.12

ta *Gaelic English* the 194.15, 402.20

tabernacle tent, curtained area 9.30 (see note); the human body as the earthly abode of the soul 377.10–11

tae one 153.14 etc.

ta'en, taen, tane taken 37.21 etc.

tailzie *Scots Law* entail, settlement of heritable property upon a specified line of heirs 42.38, 109.9, 244.19

tait tuft, bundle 203.10

tak take 1.9 etc.

taker thief, robber 256.13

talent money 350.33 (see note)

tallow animal fat used for candles 185.40 (see note)

tamn *Gaelic English* damn 395.16 etc.

tane one 109.27, 115.24

tangs tongs 150.34

tap spinning top 191.12 (see note); for 345.22 see note

tape measure out exactly, use economically and sparingly 115.8

tart sharp, cutting 8.36

tassell buffeting or knocking about, rough handling, severe tussle 459.36

tauld, tell'd told 69.17 etc.

tawpie giddy, scatter-brained, awkward young woman 152.32, 170.12, 223.37

tawse leather strap with several tails used for punishment 150.15

teem pour, empty 251.14

tefil *Gaelic English* devil 465.31, 465.32

teil *Gaelic English* devil 395.42 etc.

teind for 69.31 see note to 69.31–32

tell for 94.30 see note

temper temperament, character 4.43 etc.

templar barrister occupying chambers in the Inner or Middle Temple in London 12.22 (see note); for 32.36 see note

temple the temple in Jerusalem 112.20 (see note to 112.19–20), 178.37 (see note)

Temple-bar name of the barrier or gateway formerly between the City of London and the Strand 51.22 (see note), 51.25

temporal relating to earthly, physical life as opposed to spiritual existence 69.5 etc.

tenantable habitable 75.6

tender in delicate health, ailing 44.41

tenement large building, usually of three or more storeys, divided into flats for separate householders 32.32 etc.

Ten-Mark see note to 243.32

tent take notice of, pay attention to 1.10; for 223.36 see note

tentation temptation 386.25

termagant overbearing, quarrelsome, brawling woman 167.31, 168.1, 232.36, 233.1

term-day *Scots law* for 68.22 see note

tesire *Gaelic English* desire 460.12

test for 174.29 see note

tether halter 152.24

thae those 42.19 etc.

than then 42.19, 188.20, 190.9, 221.33

thankfu' thankful 219.19

theft-boot taking a bribe from a thief to secure him from prosecution 420.23

thegither together 70.38–39 etc.

thick for 404.26 see note

thickset something densely and closely arranged 443.13

thirdsman third person called in as a mediator or arbiter 220.23 (see note), 421.43

thirlage *Scots Law* condition of servitude whereby tenants are compelled to have their corn ground at a particular mill 124.44

thistell *Jeanie's letter* thistle 252.27

thole endure 91.14

thrang for 404.26 see note

thraw throw, fling 114.20

thrawart perverse, contrary 123.25

thrawn obstinate, cross-grained, not amenable 157.42

thread made of linen or cotton thread 227.16

threshie-coat old working coat 151.5

thretty thirty 115.5, 116.19, 116.20, 116.24

thretty-seven thirty-seven (i.e. 1737) 450.32

thrist thirst 305.7

throe spasm or convulsion of the face 405.19

thumbikin thumb-screw, used as a means of torture 88.38

tidy organised, well-ordered 295.8, 345.34

tie-wig wig where the hair is pulled behind and tied with a knot of ribbon 394.12–13

tight competent, neat 254.30

till to 112.37 etc.

tinker gypsy, itinerant tradesman, beggar 444.7, 455.38

tinkler travelling tinsmith and pedlar 415.6, 426.26

tinsel material interwoven with gold or silver thread to make a sparkling effect 281.7

tint lost 59.22 (see note), 362.8 (see note to 362.8–9)

tippling given to drinking 420.28

'tis it is 15.22 etc.

tithe, tythe originally tax of a tenth of the annual produce for the support of the church, later just a church tax 179.19 (see note), 299.17

tither, t'ither other 115.25, 399.7

tittie, titty sister 184.32 etc.

tobaka *Jeanie's letter* tobacco 350.42

tocher marriage portion, dowry 76.43

tod fox 185.33

tolbooth prison 13.38 etc. (and see note to 13.16)

toleration for 90.16–17, 103.3, 110.9 see note to 90.16–18

tong *Jeanie's letter* tongue 251.34

tooble *Gaelic English* double 416.37

took, touk beating, banging 108.41, 386.26

toom *adjective* empty 123.34

toom *verb* empty out, pour out 173.21

tory for 68.14 etc. see note to 68.14

to-tay *Gaelic English* to-day 434.42

tour *Jeanie's letter* tower 351.23

tout toot 355.41

tow flax, hemp 203.10; rope 220.5 etc.

town-clerk clerk to a burgh in charge of records, legal business, correspondence etc. 18.14 etc.

toy close cap or head-dress with flaps coming down to the shoulders worn by women of the lower classes 400.7

track tract, extent of land 257.29

tract route, path 79.24

trade the 'trade' of being a thief 59.6

traffic *verb* have dealings with 175.22; trade 378.18

traffic *noun* trade 300.36, 464.15

traik roam about, prowl 219.9

traitor *Scots* dealer 174.12

tramper tramp 232.40

transverse lying across 443.39

travail *noun* labour and pain of child-birth 142.14, 202.23

travail *verb* toil, work hard, labour 376.16

trench cut with trenches for the purposes of drainage 257.30

trenchant sharp-pointed 88.38

treviss wooden partition separating two stalls in a stable 231.19

trews trousers, often close-fitting and of a tartan pattern 397.16, 443.24

tribute tax paid for security and protection 177.31

trim character, nature 344.8

trink *Gaelic English* drink 460.43

trinquet have underhand dealings with 175.22

Trojan see note to 394.17

trooper horse soldier 65.27 etc.

troth in truth 44.4 etc.; promise of marriage 101.11, 105.33

troublesum *Jeanie's letter* troublesome 350.38

trow believe 110.42 etc.

trowl descend by rolling, spin 435.25

truant vagabond, beggar, idle person 27.22

true-blue *as applied to Covenanters and Presbyterians* staunch, devoted, derived from the choice of blue as their colour 68.4 (see note), 166.17

truss hang 207.25, 266.13 (see note)

tuilzie skirmish, scuffle 146.13

tumble throw or cast down 44.3

turbid cloudy, perplexed, troubled 100.13

turf practice of horse-racing 316.5

turf-seat seat made of turfs 172.30

turnkey one who has charge of the keys of a prison, jailer 48.33 etc.

turnpike spiral or winding 119.31; barrier across a road to deny access until is paid 177.39, 328.5

turnpike-stair spiral or winding staircase 230.1

tutelary guardian, patron 333.38 (see note)

tutor *Scots Law* guardian of a child under the age of minority 46.23 (see note)

tutor-at-law *Scots Law* nearest male relative on the father's side to a child under the age of minority who becomes tutor (guardian) in default of one appointed by the father 46.23 (see note)

twa two 39.43 etc.

twal twelve 37.13, 44.42

twal-pennies Scots shilling, equivalent to an English penny 168.26

twa-three two or three, a few 460.28

twelmonth twelve months, a year 255.17

twenty-ane twenty-one 110.33

twist piece of tobacco made into a thick cord 403.14

two-mont two months 361.43

twopenny sold at two pence per Scots pint 47.38

twopenny-hit gambling at the rate of two pennies per man taken 417.15

tympanum drum 79.8, 233.30

tyne lose 59.22 (see note), 445.26, 445.27

Tyrian see note to 394.17

ultroneous see note to 208.11

umph ejaculation expressing doubt or hesitation 114.32, 118.12, 146.15

umquhile late, deceased 230.15 (see note)

unalloyed pure, not mixed 56.37

uncanny malicious, mischievous, not to be trusted 438.41

unceevil *Jeanie's letter* uncivil 252.24

unchancy threatening, treacherous, not to be meddled with 439.2

unco unseemly, rude 37.4; extremely, strangely 84.4; very 109.4, 209.1, 371.22, 420.23; strange, uncommon 111.19; great 122.41 etc.

uncock take the match out of the cock of a matchlock gun, lower the hammer of a firearm so that it cannot be accidentally fired 139.29

unconscionable unreasonably excessive 115.15–16

uncovenanted not having subscribed to the National Covenant or Solemn League and Covenant 179.5

unction spiritual feeling, religious earnestness 329.6

uncustomed on which no custom or duty has been paid 144.3, 302.5

under-turnkey deputy jailer 123.43, 147.35

ungalled not oppressed or sore in spirit 459.15

ungenteel with little good breeding or courteousness 220.17

ungratefu' ungrateful 282.7, 285.32

unguent ointment, salve 173.30

uninclosed not enclosed, common 73.16, 230.19

Union, union Union in 1707 of the Scottish and English parliaments 40.8 etc.

unjust faithless, not free from wrong-doing, not righteous or justified in the eyes of God 25.8, 114.2

unlawfu' unlawful 139.23
unlettered uneducated 414.19
unlineal not a blood descendant 425.28
unscoured not polished or scrubbed 165.20 (see note)
unscythed not having chariot-like scythes attached to the wheels 8.26 (see note)
unshaped imperfectly formed 143.16
unsophisticated uncorrupted, genuine 176.23
unwordy unworthy 78.27
unwullin unwilling 265.11
upgang act of ascending a slope 258.38
uphaud maintain, vouch, affirm 186.37, 415.37
upo' *dialect* upon 360.11
upsides see note to 286.17
use habituate, accustom 245.1
usefu' useful 43.43, 74.24, 146.32, 246.32
usher assistant to a schoolmaster 241.15 etc.
usquebaugh whisky 379.32, 394.26, 394.34, 404.42
vail humble, lower 229.20
vain-glorious proud, boastful, ostentatious 176.25
vale for 72.31 see note
valedictory *adjective* farewell 393.30
veil hide, conceal 187.7, 200.21, 440.11
venture danger, risk 40.28, 187.21; enterprise, undertaking 77.1
vest garment 365.33
vestry room in a church in which clergymen robe etc. 285.24
vicarage for 69.32 see note to 69.31–32
vicinage neighbourhood 55.37
vidette sentry, particularly one placed in advance to observe the actions of the enemy 53.35, 54.41
visitation for 111.41 see note
vizier high state official in a Muslim country 440.8
vociferation outcry, loud speaking 108.12
voluntary freely engaged in 88.14
wa'¹ wall 168.40, 365.22
wa'² away 233.10
wa'-stane stone forming part of a wall

154.37
wad¹ would 39.24 etc.
wad² wager, bet 329.8
wadna wouldn't 37.14 etc.
wadset *Scots Law* mortgage on a property 236.26
wae dismal, sad 186.22; for 44.40 see note; for 266.7 see note; for 272.33, 302.33, 353.3–4, and 359.29 see note to 272.33
waefu' woeful 109.27
waesome sorrowful, melancholy 392.35
waff blast 355.15; flap, flutter 460.36
wag habitual joker 38.13
waggoner carter, type of farm-servant 259.33
wain wagon, cart 36.9, 365.12
wainscot oak panelling used to line a room 235.40
wait for 110.23 see note
waiter under-porter or watchman at one of the city gates of Edinburgh in the 18th century 50.23 etc.
wake local annual festival of an English parish 278.2, 278.11, 295.10
wald *Jeanie's letters* would 250.30, 251.32
waled carefully chosen, select 174.38
wall well 64.19
wallet bag for holding provisions, clothing etc. when on a journey 263.37
wally-draggle thin, ill-grown animal 173.27
wame belly, hollow 429.8
wampish flap, wave 430.6
wan won 357.40, 357.41; for 124.13 and 146.4 see respective notes
wand for 281.15 see note
wanter *dialect* one who seeks a husband or wife 254.5
wan-thriven stunted, in a state of decline 186.16–17
wantin wanting, seeking 168.8
ward ridge projecting from the inside plate of a lock preventing the use of the wrong key to open it 49.1; division or compartment of a prison 119.32, 184.29
wardrope wardrobe 236.27
ware expend, employ 141.37, 189.23, 224.16
wark work 42.26 etc.

warld world 70.36 etc.; for 271.15 see note to 271.15

warld-hunting seeking after things of the world 112.5

warldly worldly 131.39, 226.36

warldly-wise worldly-wise, wise in worldly affairs 110.5, 112.28

warse worse 108.43

warst worst 108.39 etc.

warstle *verb* wrestle, struggle 70.36, 94.38, 109.29

wrastle *noun* mental and moral struggle 400.36

wasna wasn't 37.31 etc.

waster squanderer, spendthrift 252.18

wastrife wastefulness, extravagance 249.31

wat wet 115.22

watch periods into which the night was anciently divided, the night-time 163.24

water-cart barrel or tank on wheels, often punctured with holes to lay street dust 12.2

water-dog dog bred to retrieve wild-fowl from water 10.24

water-drap drip from the eaves 243.7, 243.21

water-gruel thin gruel made with water instead of milk 367.2

watna know not 146.24

wauken waken 263.8

waur worse 46.18 etc.

waurna were not 233.16

way-faring travelling by road 307.29

way-sliding literally sliding from the path, i.e. moral or spiritual deviation 176.19

weal well-being, prosperity 80.33, 105.37, 188.21, 429.39

wean child 40.19 etc.

wearie *Jeanie's letter* weary 250.28

weary for 37.20, 109.13, 352.41 see respective notes

weasand gullet 262.15, 267.31

wee little, small 44.7 etc.

weel well 37.31 etc.

weel-being well-being 356.5

weel-fa'ard handsome, good-looking 276.36

weel-wisher well-wisher 114.35, 387.26

weel-won well-won, gained by hard and honourable effort 356.2

Weigh-house see note to 40.39

weird fate, destiny 107.34

well-dowered left well-off on the death of a husband 467.43

Wellington type of trousers named after the Duke of Wellington 10.19 (see note)

well-scented with a keen sense of tracking by smell, *figuratively* keen, sharp 303.17

we'se we shall 286.32, 286.34, 363.25

west-land the west of Scotland 322.9

wha, whae who 26.21 etc.

whadyecallum what-do-you-call-him 189.34–35

whan when 38.34 etc.

whang cut in chunks, slice 346.40

whare where 70.41 etc.

whaten *Jeanie's letter* what 351.39

whatfor why 242.34, 275.8

whaup doubling, kink 136.13

wheat-close enclosed field where wheat is growing 264.26, 264.27

wheeling the movement of troops like that of the spokes of a wheel 322.20

where-anent concerning which 103.5–6

whet sharpen, get ready for an attack 165.21

whey watery part of the milk which remains after the curds have been separated in cheese-making 436.34

whig adherent to the Presbyterian and Covenanting cause in Scotland from 1648 onwards 68.12 etc.

whiggery whig principles and beliefs 69.34, 278.25

whiles times, sometimes 45.39 etc.

whin gorse, furze 73.18, 272.10

whin, wheen a number of, a few 39.36, 39.38, 272.29, 274.10

whipping-post, whuppin-post post set up in a public place to which offenders were tied to be whipped 123.37, 123.39

whirligig mechanical contrivance that turns rapidly, used disparagingly for a coach 363.28

whirry move rapidly, hurry 170.27

whisht hush! be quiet! 86.41 etc.

whiskin shallow type of drinking vessel 289.27

whister-poop blow on the side of the head 285.39

whistle for 162.28 see note to 162.28–29

Whitsunday 15 May, a Scottish term day when interest, rent, etc. were paid, and property entered or quitted 430.23, 430.40

whittle large knife carried as a weapon 269.28

whorn *Jeanie's letter* horn 251.14

whoy interjection indicating surprise 46.35, 46.36

whully cheat, especially by means of flattery, cajole 115.12

whup whip 123.41

wi' with 27.32 etc.

wicket small door or gate inside a large one to allow access when the larger gate is locked 49.18, 50.26, 50.31, 63.3

wifie woman, married or otherwise 162.25

wight strong and courageous, bold 42.15, 42.17

wildfire, wild-fire lightning, especially sheet lightning without thunder 149.21, 259.7, 278.13

wile coax, lure, entice 203.16

wilfu' wilful, stubborn 144.24 etc.

willyard undisciplined, obstinate, unmanageable 117.22, 238.39

wimple twist, turn 219.29

win succeed in arriving at a destination 225.7, 252.25, 258.37, 351.8; get 120.7, 120.8, 247.31, 247.33, 257.37; make one's way 271.32; reach, get to 343.6

win at get at, reach 153.3 (see note), 223.2

win out escape 120.8, 124.11, 170.25; get off 243.18

win owre overcome 150.9 (see note), 208.43

windfa' windfall 430.11

winna won't 37.31 etc.

wise ways, directions 415.24 (see note)

wiselike sensible, reasonable 222.29

wish recommend 205.14, 205.24

witchering witchcraft 363.15

withal moreover 254.15; along with 266.40

witty-pated clever, ingenious, skilful, but also crafty, cunning 109.13

wizend thin, shrivelled 168.3

woife *dialect* woman 361.35

woman-body female person, woman 90.6

woodie gallows 152.35

work-house house established to provide work for the unemployed poor of a parish 364.4, 364.28, 447.37

worldly-wise wise in worldly affairs 90.29

wormwood *figuratively* bitterness to the soul 228.26

worry choke, strangle 313.15

worrycow, worrie-cow scarecrow, hobgoblin 252.24, 440.25

worset-lace lace made of long-fibred, well-twisted woollen yarn 148.36

worsted made of long-fibred, well-twisted woollen yarn with the wool combed to make the fibres lie parallel 192.30

worthy worthy man 88.35

wot know 98.22 etc.

wotna don't know 174.35

wrang wrong 111.13 etc.

wrap-rascal loose overcoat or great-coat 122.10–11

wrastling involving moral and mental struggle and also physical struggle and hardship 415.1

wreath snow drift 71.9

writer lawyer, solicitor, attorney 14.14, 20.29 (see note), 47.35

writer-lad young lawyer 219.8

writt for 241.43 see note to 241.42–43

wrought made (with implied effort) 29.24 etc.; agitated 31.2; worked 240.27, 268.42, 350.13 (see note), 410.24 (see note)

wud fierce, violent, wild in behaviour 254.15

wull-cat wild-cat 87.11

wuss wish 108.22 etc.

wynd narrow street or lane leading off a main roadway 222.3

wyte blame, responsibility 159.23, 286.17

yard cottage- or kitchen-garden 83.25, 186.19

ye you 1.10 etc.

yealdon fuel 361.41

year-auld year-old 251.15

yearn curdle milk for the purposes of cheese-making by adding rennet and applying heat 350.23

yer your 149.25

Yerastian Erastian; for 110.9, 112.5, and 112.27 see note to 112.5

yerk bind tightly, fasten 466.32

yerl earl 69.14

yesternight last night, the night of yesterday 120.29

yestreen last night, yesterday 119.24, 123.18, 150.38, 460.32

yield not giving milk because they are in calf or because of old age 357.4

yill ale 251.12

yill-caup drinking-bowl of wood or horn 401.23 (see note)

yon that, yonder 173.12 etc.

yont at a distance, apart 27.15

yoursell, yersell yourself 45.14 etc.

Zion for 109.16 see note to 109.16–17

Zipporah wife of Moses 94.19 (see note to 94.19–20)

zone girdle 66.22 (see note)

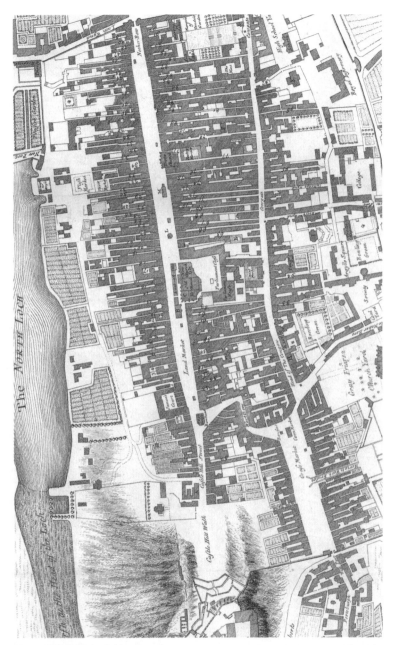

Central Edinburgh in 1742

from William Edgar's Plan of the City and Castle of Edinburgh as reproduced in William Maitland, *The History of Edinburgh from its Foundation to the Present Time* (1753), courtesy of Aberdeen University Library

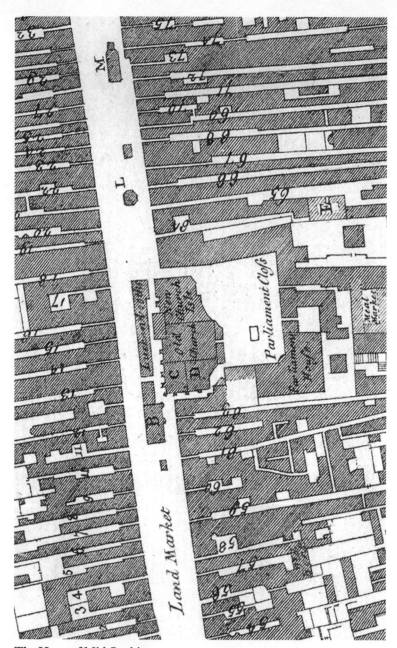

The Heart of Mid-Lothian

detail from William Edgar's Plan of the City and Castle of Edinburgh

B tolbooth; C Little Kirk (Haddo's Hole); D Tolbooth Kirk; M guard house; 63 Bess Wynd;
Land Market = Lawn-market